MONROE COLLEGE LIBRARY
32468000009036

D0948646

THE NEW OXFORD BOOK OF ENGLISH PROSE

THE NEW OXFORD BOOK OF ENGLISH PROSE

Edited by

JOHN GROSS

Oxford New York
OXFORD UNIVERSITY PRESS
1998

Oxford University Press, Great Clarendon Street, Oxford OX2 6DP

Oxford New York
Athens Auckland Bangkok Bogota Bombay Buenos Aires
Calcutta Cape Town Dar es Salaam Delhi Florence Hong Kong Istanbul
Karachi Kuala Lumpur Madras Madrid Melbourne Mexico City
Nairobi Paris Singapore Taipei Tokyo Toronto Warsaw
and associated companies in
Berlin Ibadan

Oxford is a registered trade mark of Oxford University Press

First published 1998

British Library Cataloguing in Publication Data
Data available

Library of Congress Cataloging in Publication Data
The new Oxford book of English prose / edited by John Gross.
Includes index.
1. English prose literature. 2. American prose literature. 3. English-speaking countries—Literary collections. I. Gross, John J.
PR1285.N48 1998 828'.08—dc21 97-49397
ISBN 0–19–214246–1

1 3 5 7 9 10 8 6 4 2

Typeset by Best-set Typesetter Ltd., Hong Kong
Printed in the United States of America

Contents

Introduction

This anthology has three principal aims. First, it attempts to provide a representative selection from the work of the major prose-writers in the English language, and as many of the more interesting lesser ones as space will allow. Secondly, it is meant to illustrate the resources and achievements of English prose as an artistic medium and an instrument of expression; to that extent it is an anthology not simply of prose, but of prose-styles. Finally, nothing it contains has been included merely on the grounds of historical interest: each extract has been chosen on its own account—because I find it moving, enlightening, or entertaining, and in the hope that readers will feel the same.

It would have been possible, in pursuit of the book's second aim, to have ranged much more widely. Monsieur Jourdain, in *Le Bourgeois Gentilhomme*, was famously surprised to discover that he had been speaking prose for the previous forty years—but then so had everyone else. Prose is the ordinary form of spoken or written language: it fulfils innumerable functions, and it can attain many different kinds of excellence. A well-argued legal judgment, a lucid scientific paper, a readily grasped set of technical instructions all represent triumphs of prose after their fashion. And quantity tells. Inspired prose may be as rare as great poetry—though I am inclined to doubt even that; but good prose is unquestionably far more common than good poetry. It is something you can come across every day: in a letter, in a newspaper, almost anywhere.

When I began work on this book, I considered devoting a substantial amount of it to non-literary prose—to writing by authors whose names, for whatever reason, you wouldn't normally expect to find in a history of literature. Such an approach had its undoubted attractions; but on reflection, the case against it seemed much stronger. An anthology which strayed too far from literature as commonly conceived would not, I think, be what most people were looking for in a *New Oxford Book of English Prose*. It would be too arbitrary, too personal, too much of a miscellany.

For the most part, then, the material I have selected is unashamedly literary. But it also demonstrates, I hope, that 'literary' is not the narrow term which it is sometimes made to sound—that it embraces an enormous range of experience and response.

The authors chosen appear in chronological order, and anyone who works through the book systematically (not necessarily a course I recommend) is bound to come away with some general sense of the evolution of English prose. 'Evolution', needless to say, doesn't mean a simple progression from one point to the next. It is a highly elaborate process, throwing up many different species. Yet a chronological reading leaves one with renewed respect, however qualified, for the familiar 'phases' and labels of the literary historians—Augustan, Romantic, and the rest. They are imperfect terms, but on the whole they are the best we have.

Of all the evolutionary changes which the textbooks record, the most celebrated is the transformation said to have taken place in the latter part of the seventeenth century. Before the Restoration, or so the story runs at its simplest, prose was eloquent, ornate, and cumbersome. After the Restoration it became plain, colloquial, serviceable, and (largely thanks to the Royal Society) scientific.

This is a parody of what actually occurred. Plain writing didn't spring up overnight, any more than magniloquence died at a stroke. The grand style, designed to elevate or persuade, was never more than part of the picture: from the beginning, whenever prose had a businesslike function, it tended to assume a businesslike form. Even David Hume, who took about as dim an eighteenth-century view of pre-Restoration prose as anyone could, conceded that when he condemned Jacobean and Caroline authors as pedantic and uncouth, it was 'authors by profession' he had in mind. The practical men of that age—the example he cited was Sir John Davis the navigator—had been capable of expressing themselves perfectly decently.

Yet *something* happened in the late seventeenth century—less dramatically than the textbooks suggest, perhaps, but no less decisively. Plain prose gained in confidence, perfected its means, and extended its range. By the eighteenth century it was recognizably modern prose, equipped to perform most of the tasks we have come to expect of it. And meanwhile the 'large utterance' of the earlier masters had faded away. Donne, Jeremy Taylor, Milton, Sir Thomas Browne became figures from an irrecoverable past.

New forms of eloquence arose in time, however, some of them soaring almost as high—the political eloquence of a Burke; the eloquence of a Carlyle or a Ruskin, at once pictorial and prophetic; the tremendous rhetoric of a Melville; many others. And the pendulum has gone on swinging: there have always been other writers ready to react against the rhetoricians and bring prose back to earth—figures as various as Hemingway, whose pared-down style was once seen as having put paid to a great mass of nineteenth-century verbiage; Orwell, proclaiming that good prose should be as transparent as a window-pane, or Joyce, perfecting the 'scrupulous meanness' of *Dubliners* (though he was soon to move on towards an idiom even more exotic than anything the seventeenth century dreamed up).

In the past, most prose-anthologists assumed that eloquence was their main concern (tempered by humour and quaintness—but the eloquence came first). Their prize exhibits were the finely wrought declamation and the elaborate set-piece. The spirit they worked in was essentially one of connoisseurship; and today it looks sadly out of date. A contemporary literary historian (Roger Pooley, in *English Prose of the Seventeenth Century*, 1992) has spoken dismissively in this connection of 'delicious extracts'—and from the point of view of rugged scholarship, an old-fashioned bedside anthology such as Logan Pearsall Smith's *A Little Treasury of English Prose* can hardly help looking superficial. But the modern aversion to 'fine writing' goes far beyond academia. We live in a world where the exhortation to 'take eloquence and wring its neck' has found a ready audience. We have all learned to mistrust the lush description and the purple patch—especially when they are singled out for our benefit.

We should be equally on guard, however, against a provincialism which estranges us from some of the great achievements of the past. If we don't distinguish between true eloquence and fake eloquence, if we allow our fear of pretentious or precious 'fine writing' to frighten us off the real thing, the loss will be ours; and it will be a large one.

One should add that the contrast between plainness and eloquence is seldom clear-cut. An exalted style can often be concise and direct. A plain style often turns out to be more exuberant than its reputation suggests. (Orwell's, for example, owes a great deal to his gift for pungent imagery.) And if the writers in this book were divided between plain and adorned, say, or natural and elevated, it would be hard to say to which category many of them should be assigned. Where would Bunyan fit in? Where would Dickens? Once again, labels are inadequate: the expressive powers of prose are too varied for them to be neatly grouped and stacked.

The original *Oxford Book of English Prose*, edited by Sir Arthur Quiller-Couch, was published in November 1925, twenty-five years to the day after the appearance of Quiller-Couch's celebrated *Oxford Book of English Verse*. The present book is a new compilation, not a revision; many of the same authors are represented, but few of the same pieces reappear.

In his preface, Quiller-Couch explained that he had decided to end with 'writers who had already solidified their work by 1914': the most recent figures included were Lytton Strachey, Compton Mackenzie, and Rupert Brooke. A younger editor might have found room for D. H. Lawrence or Virginia Woolf, or even Joyce; but most of Quiller-Couch's original readers probably felt that he was as up to date as they could reasonably have expected, or would have wanted.

The most immediate task of a *New Oxford Book of English Prose* is plainly to admit the twentieth century—or rather, in the currently fashionable phrase, 'the short twentieth century'. Like Quiller-Couch, I have not attempted to keep up with the very latest generation of writers: it may be that the new Lawrence or Joyce I could have included is staring me in the face. But that still leaves seventy additional years to be covered, which in turn modifies the proportions of the book as a whole.

The new book differs from the old in one other major respect, which is closely related, and no less apparent. It attaches a great deal more weight to the assumption that English prose means prose written in the English language. Its scope is multinational; and this has had an inescapable effect on its general drift, certainly in comparison with that of its predecessor.

Quiller-Couch believed that an anthologist ought to have a 'notion' of his own, 'a pattern in the carpet'. The pattern in his book of prose, as he made clear, was an emphasis on Englishness (and more particularly rural Englishness); the notion behind it, no less powerful for being vague, was that of continuity, of an English spirit transmitted from one generation to the next. He was not, it should be stressed, compiling an anthology of patriotism. His editorial policy was far more catholic and inconsistent than that. But an underlying love of country undoubtedly colours his selection, and it is pointed up at various strategic points. The first extract in the book, by the fourteenth-century writer John Trevisa, is headed 'This Realm, this England'. (It can hardly be a chance that Trevisa was a Cornishman: Quiller-Couch was a great local patriot, too.) The last extract is an evocation of England by Rupert Brooke. Written shortly before his death, it carries the epigraph, 'Her foundations are upon the holy hills'.

The emotions which Quiller-Couch brought to his editorial role were deep rather than fierce. He was no jingo; and his mood, after the First World War, was relatively subdued. (He never really recovered from the loss of his only son, who survived active service throughout the war, in which he was twice wounded, only to fall ill and die shortly afterwards.) As a statement of faith, the preface to *The Oxford Book of English Prose* commands respect; like most of Quiller-Couch's work, it is marked by warmth and generosity of spirit. But it speaks to us from another age. It would be absurd, even in an anthology confined to British writers, to try to replicate its spirit today. In an anthology which ranges over the English language at large, it would be impossible.

Although the preface doesn't raise the question of writers from outside Britain, Quiller-Couch took it for granted that they were eligible for inclusion. In practice, at the time, that meant American writers; and he found space for fifteen of them, ranging from Washington Irving to William James. In spite of some notable absentees (nothing from the Colonial or Revolutionary periods; no Mark Twain), they make a decent showing; but among 320 British authors their presence is too slight to have much effect on the impression created by the book as a whole.

In the *New Oxford Book* America naturally looms very much larger. Extending the transatlantic horizons of what is meant by 'English prose' has in fact been a twofold operation. It has partly involved an attempt to improve on Quiller-Couch's coverage of American literature before 1900, and partly an attempt to give some idea of what has been accomplished since. A great deal, it need hardly be said. Few critics would deny that the achievements of twentieth-century American authors, since the 1920s or 1930s at least, have measured up to those of their British contemporaries. Many would claim that they have surpassed them.

At the same time America has become only one strand in the story. The broadest strand; but the time has long since gone by when a British reader could suppose that, as far as literature went, Americans effectively monopolized 'the rest of the world' (except for Ireland, that is—always a special case). In the past forty or fifty years an increasing number of English-language authors from Commonwealth or former Commonwealth countries, and in one or two cases even beyond, have acquired international standing. And there is no question of their owing their success—the best of them, at least—to extra-literary considerations. In Britain, as elsewhere, they compete on equal terms with the local product.

All this is reflected, within the limits of space, in the book which follows. It includes work by writers from places as far apart as Australia and Nigeria, India and Canada, South Africa and New Zealand, Trinidad and Egypt. Many of them are international figures by residence (often in Britain) as well as reputation. The final extract is by a writer who grew up in England, but who was born to Japanese parents in Nagasaki.

It would be tempting to conclude that multinationalism is the new 'figure in the carpet'—that an anglocentric story has been replaced by one of English literature slowly evolving into a worldwide 'literature in English'. This has not been my intention, however. Indeed, I don't believe it would really be possible. The growth of 'literature in English', with all its subdivisions, seems to me far too complex and many-sided to be reduced to a single story—certainly not a story as compact as Quiller-Couch's.

Meanwhile literature continues to draw half its flavour from national traditions and circumstances. It is an excellent thing that a Nigerian novel, because it is written in English, should be more accessible than it would otherwise be to an Indian or a Canadian; but there would be no virtue in the author trying to make it even more accessible by making it less Nigerian. The imagination feeds on local material. And an anthology, too, would be a dull, synthetic affair if it aimed at some perfect international balance—if, for example, it excluded those authors who don't travel particularly well. (The pleasures they afford are often, in cultural terms, the most intimate.) I hope that the present anthology is reasonably international in outlook; but I would be disappointed if it wasn't also regarded as unmistakably British in origin.

Sooner rather than later the editor of an anthology of verse finds himself facing the problem of the longer poem. How can he adequately represent *Paradise Lost* or *The Prelude*? Should he even try? He can at least console himself with the thought that there are innumerable short poems, and that many anthologies, including some of the most famous, have consisted solely of lyrics.

For the prose-anthologist, the corresponding problem is far more acute. If we set aside a few special categories, such as letters and diary-entries, very few works of prose are as short as lyrics; most are long—'book-length', in fact, and only properly appreciated when they are read in full.

Of the limitations which follow, from an anthologist's point of view, the worst are probably those affecting fiction. An extract from a novel can illustrate the writer's descriptive powers, his ability to establish a character or a setting, and, on a small scale, his mastery of incident and dialogue. But *no* extract, and hence no anthology, can convey the dynamic qualities of a novel—the multiplication of interests, the building up of emotional power. It would be futile to try.

It is almost as hard for an anthology to do justice to a critical exposition or a sustained argument. A point in an argument, yes, or its conclusion; but the stages by which that conclusion is reached usually require far more space than the most generous anthologist can spare.

Even when he adjusts to his limitations, an anthologist is liable to find himself confronting a recurrent practical problem. He needs material which makes its impact quickly, and which can stand up by itself—the scene where it is immediately clear what is going on, the passage which doesn't call for further explanation. It isn't surprising if he tends to become excessively attached to a quality which can only be called excerptability.

Pondering these various constraints, I decided to follow Quiller-Couch in one fundamental respect. The extracts I have chosen, like his, are fairly short—on average, somewhat shorter than his (and in a few cases, a good deal so, since I have occasionally tried to demonstrate what can be achieved by a brief self-contained paragraph or a single sentence).

The chief reason for my decision was that it enabled me to do more—to print more extracts from more books by more authors; to give a more rounded account of major figures; to provide a more detailed map of the territory. But I was also influenced by the realization that even if the extracts were longer, they would still be very short in comparison to the works from which they were taken, and that the same essential objections would apply: they would still fail to convey the dynamics of a novel, and so on. Of course, I don't doubt that there would have been some gains if they were, say, twice as long as they are at present—gains in scope and depth. But the price to be paid was that half the authors in the book would have had to go, and I judged that to be the greater evil.

One editorial principle was originally suggested by the publishers. They asked me not to include dramatic literature—prose from plays. I agreed, with some reluctance; but after a short while, as I began to be haunted by all the authors whom I wasn't going to be able to find room for, I became convinced of their wisdom. Trying to cram in the dramatists would have stretched an already overcrowded book to bursting-point. I have, however, been inconsistent (forgivably, perhaps) and included some passages from Shakespeare.

To my great regret, the anthology contains nothing by Ernest Hemingway or F. Scott Fitzgerald. I had planned to include work by both of them, but unfortunately it proved impossible on account of North American copyright problems.

Spelling and punctuation have been modernized throughout, except in a few very minor instances where to have done so would have been to create unnecessary problems. Idiosyncrasies of spelling and punctuation have been preserved in letters, diaries, journals, and other material not originally intended for publication. In the one case where these two editorial principles came into conflict—the letters of Dorothy Osborne—it seemed to me that there was more to lose by modernizing, and I have followed the original text.

JOHN GROSS

THE NEW
OXFORD BOOK OF
ENGLISH
PROSE

SIR THOMAS MALORY
d. 1471?

The Sword in the Stone

Then stood the realm in great jeopardy long while, for every lord that was mighty of men made him strong, and many weened to have been king. Then Merlin went to the Archbishop of Canterbury, and counselled him for to send for all the lords of the realm, and all the gentlemen of arms, that they should to London come by Christmas, upon pain of cursing; and for this cause, that Jesus, that was born on that night, that he would of his great mercy show some miracle, as he was come to be king of mankind, for to show some miracle who should be rightwise king of this realm. So the Archbishop, by the advice of Merlin, sent for all the lords and gentlemen of arms that they should come by Christmas even unto London. And many of them made them clean of their life, that their prayer might be the more acceptable unto God. So in the greatest church of London, whether it were Paul's or not the French book maketh no mention, all the estates were long ere day in the church for to pray. And when matins and the first mass was done, there was seen in the churchyard, against the high altar, a great stone four square, like unto a marble stone, and in midst thereof was like an anvil of steel a foot on high, and therein stuck a fair sword naked by the point, and letters there were written in gold about the sword that said thus:—Whoso pulleth out this sword of this stone and anvil, is rightwise king born of all England. Then the people marvelled, and told it to the Archbishop. I command, said the Archbishop, that ye keep you within your church, and pray unto God still; that no man touch the sword till the high mass be all done. So when all masses were done all the lords went to behold the stone and the sword. And when they saw the scripture, some assayed; such as would have been king. But none might stir the sword nor move it. He is not here, said the Archbishop, that shall achieve the sword, but doubt not God will make him known.

Morte Darthur, completed *c.*1469; first printed 1485

The Queen and the Knight

'Of the sorrow that Sir Bors had for the hurt of Launcelot; and of the anger that the Queen had because Launcelot bare the sleeve'

And when Sir Bors heard that, wit ye well he was an heavy man, and so were all his kinsmen. But when Queen Guenever wist that Sir Launcelot bare the red sleeve of the Fair Maiden of Astolat she was nigh out of her mind for wrath. And then she sent for Sir Bors de Ganis in all the haste that might be. So when Sir Bors was come tofore the queen, then she said: Ah Sir Bors, have ye heard say how falsely Sir Launcelot hath betrayed me? Alas madam, said Sir Bors, I am afeared he hath betrayed himself and us all. No force, said the queen, though he be destroyed, for he is a false traitor-knight. Madam, said Sir Bors, I pray you say ye not so, for wit you well I may not hear such language of him. Why Sir Bors, said she, should I not call him traitor when he bare the red sleeve upon his head at Winchester, at the great jousts? Madam, said Sir Bors, that sleeve-bearing repenteth me sore, but I dare say he did it to none evil intent, but for this cause he bare the red sleeve that none of his blood should know him. For ere then we nor none of us all never knew that ever he bare token or sign of maid, lady, ne gentlewoman. Fie on him, said the queen, yet for all his pride and bobaunce there ye proved yourself his better. Nay madam, say ye never more so, for he beat me and my fellows, and might have slain us an he had would. Fie on him, said the queen, for I heard Sir Gawaine say before my lord Arthur that it were marvel to tell the great love that is between the Fair Maiden of Astolat and him. Madam, said Sir Bors, I may not warn Sir Gawaine to say what it pleased him; but I dare say, as for my lord, Sir Launcelot, that he loveth no lady, gentlewoman, nor maid, but all he loveth in like much. And therefore madam, said Sir Bors, ye may say what ye will, but wit ye well I will haste me to seek him, and find him wheresomever he be, and God send me good tidings of him.

Morte Darthur

The Passing of Arthur

Therefore, said Arthur unto Sir Bedivere, take thou Excalibur, my good sword, and go with it to yonder water side, and when thou comest there I charge thee throw my sword in that water, and come again and tell me what thou there seest. My lord, said Bedivere, your commandment shall be done, and lightly bring you word again. So Sir Bedivere departed, and by the way he beheld that noble sword, that the pommel and the haft was all of precious stones; and then he said to himself: If I throw this rich sword in the water, thereof shall never come good, but harm and loss. And then Sir Bedivere hid Excalibur under a tree. And so, as soon as he might, he came again unto the king, and said he had been at the water, and had thrown the sword in the water. What saw thou there? said the king. Sir, he said, I saw nothing but waves and winds. That is untruly said of thee, said the king, therefore go thou lightly again, and do my com-

no force] no matter   bobaunce] bombast

mandment; as thou art to me lief and dear, spare not, but throw it in. Then Sir Bedivere returned again, and took the sword in his hand; and then him thought sin and shame to throw away that noble sword, and so eft he hid the sword, and returned again, and told to the king that he had been at the water, and done his commandment. What saw thou there? said the king. Sir, he said, I saw nothing but the waters wappe and waves wanne. Ah, traitor untrue, said King Arthur, now hast thou betrayed me twice. Who would have weened that, thou that hast been to me so lief and dear? and thou art named a noble knight, and would betray me for the richness of the sword. But now go again lightly, for thy long tarrying putteth me in great jeopardy of my life, for I have taken cold. And but if thou do now as I bid thee, if ever I may see thee, I shall slay thee with mine own hands; for thou wouldst for my rich sword see me dead. Then Sir Bedivere departed, and went to the sword, and lightly took it up, and went to the water side; and there he bound the girdle about the hilts, and then he threw the sword as far into the water as he might; and there came an arm and an hand above the water and met it, and caught it, and so shook it thrice and brandished, and then vanished away the hand with the sword in the water. So Sir Bedivere came again to the king, and told him what he saw. Alas, said the king, help me hence, for I dread me I have tarried over long.

Then Sir Bedivere took the king upon his back, and so went with him to that water side. And when they were at the water side, even fast by the bank hoved a little barge with many fair ladies in it, and among them all was a queen, and all they had black hoods, and all they wept and shrieked when they saw King Arthur. Now put me into the barge, said the king. And so he did softly; and there received him three queens with great mourning; and so they set them down, and in one of their laps King Arthur laid his head. And then that queen said: Ah, dear brother, why have ye tarried so long from me? alas, this wound on your head hath caught over-much cold. And so then they rowed from the land, and Sir Bedivere beheld all those ladies go from him. Then Sir Bedivere cried: Ah my lord Arthur, what shall become of me, now ye go from me and leave me here alone among mine enemies? Comfort thyself, said the king, and do as well as thou mayest, for in me is no trust for to trust in; for I will into the vale of Avilion to heal me of my grievous wound: and if thou hear never more of me, pray for my soul. But ever the queens and ladies wept and shrieked, that it was pity to hear. And as soon as Sir Bedivere had lost the sight of the barge, he wept and wailed, and so took the forest; and so he went all that night, and in the morning he was ware betwixt two holts hoar, of a chapel and an hermitage.

Morte Darthur

wappe] lap   wanne] ebb   ware] aware   holts hoar] bare woods

WILLIAM CAXTON

*c.*1422–1491

The Character of a King

The king must be thus made. For he must sit in a chair clothed in purple, crowned on his head, in his right hand a sceptre and in the left hand an apple of gold. For he is the most greatest and highest in dignity above all other and most worthy. And that is signified by the crown. For the glory of the people is the dignity of the king. And above all other the king ought to be replenished with virtues and of grace, and this signifieth the purple. For in like wise as robes of purple maketh fair and embellisheth the body, the same wise virtues maketh the soul. He ought alway think on the government of the Royaume and who hath the administration of justice. And this should be by himself principally. This signifieth the apple of gold that he holdeth in his left hand. And for as much as it appertaineth unto him to punish the rebels hath he the sceptre in his right hand. And for as much as misericord and truth conserve and keep the king in his throne therefore ought a king to be merciful and debonair.

The Game and Play of the Chess, 1475, translated from the Latin of Jacobus de Cessolis, *Liber de ludo scacchorum*, thirteenth century, and from French versions of de Cessolis

The Proem to the Canterbury Tales

Great thanks, laud, and honour ought to be given unto the clerks, poets, and historiographs that have written many noble books of wisdom of the lives, passions, and miracles of holy saints, of histories of noble and famous acts and faites, and of the chronicles since the beginning of the creation of the world unto this present time, by which we be daily informed and have knowledge of many things of whom we should not have known if they had not left to us their monuments written. Among whom and in especial before all others, we ought to give a singular laud unto that noble and great philosopher Geoffrey Chaucer, the which for his ornate writing in our tongue may well have the name of a laureate poet. For to-fore that he by labour embellished, ornated, and made fair our English, in this realm was had rude speech and incongruous, as yet it appeareth by old books, which at this day ought not to have place nor be compared among, nor to, his beauteous volumes and ornate writings, of whom he made many books and treatises of many a noble history, as well in metre as in rhyme and prose; and them so craftily made that he comprehended his matters in short, quick, and high sentences, eschewing prolixity, casting away the chaff of superfluity, and shewing the picked grain of sentence uttered by crafty and sugared eloquence; of whom among all others of his books I purpose to print, by the grace of God, the book of the tales of Canterbury, in which I find many a noble history of every state and degree; first rehearsing the conditions and the array of each of them as properly as possible is to be said; and after their tales which be of noblesse, wisdom, gentilesse, mirth, and also of very holiness and virtue, wherein he finisheth this said book; which book I have diligently overseen and duly examined, to the end that it be made according unto his own making.

The Canterbury Tales (Caxton's edition, 1484)

JOHN BOURCHIER, LORD BERNERS
1467–1533

[from the French of Froissart]

The Scots Go to War

These Scottish men are right hardy and sore travailing in harness and in wars. For when they will enter into England, within a day and a night they will drive their whole host twenty-four mile, for they are all a-horseback, without it be the trandals and laggers of the host, who follow after afoot. The knights and squires are well horsed, and the common people and others on little hackneys and geldings; and they carry with them no carts nor chariots, for the diversities of the mountains that they must pass through in the country of Northumberland. They take with them no purveyance of bread nor wine, for their usage and soberness is such in time of war, that they will pass in the journey a great long time with flesh half sodden, without bread, and drink of the river water without wine, and they neither care for pots nor pans, for they seethe beasts in their own skins. They are ever sure to find plenty of beasts in the country that they will pass through: therefore they carry with them none other purveyance, but on their horse between the saddle and the panel they truss a broad plate of metal, and behind the saddle they will have a little sack full of oatmeal, to the intent that when they have eaten of the sodden flesh, then they lay this plate on the fire and temper a little of the oatmeal; and when the plate is hot, they cast of the thin paste thereon, and so make a little cake in manner of a cracknell or biscuit, and that they eat to comfort withal their stomachs. Wherefore it is no great marvel though they make greater journeys than other people do.

Froissart's *Chronicles* (Berners' translation, 1523–5)

trandals] camp-followers

The Madness of King Charles VI of France

A great influence fro heaven fell the said day upon the French king, and as divers said, it was his own fault, for according to the disposition of his body, and the state that he was in, and the warning that his physicians did give him, he should not have ridden in such a hot day, at that hour, but rather in the morning and in the evening in the fresh air: wherefore it was a shame to them that were near about him, to suffer or to counsel him to do as he did. Thus as the French king rode upon a fair plain in the heat of the sun, which was as then of a marvellous height, and the king had on a jack covered with black velvet, which sore chafed him, and on his head a single bonnet of scarlet, and a chaplet of great pearls, which the queen had given him at his departure, and he had a page that rode behind him, bearing on his head a chapew of Montauban, bright and clear shining against the sun, and behind that page rode another bearing the king's spear, painted red, and fringed with silk, with a sharp head of steel: the lord de la Riviere had brought a dozen of them with him fro Toulouse, and that was one of them: he had given the whole dozen to the king, and the king had given three of them to his brother the duke of Orleans, and three to the duke of Bourbon. And as they rode thus forth, the page that bare the spear, whether it were by negligence, or that he fell asleep, he let the spear fall on the other page's head that rode before him, and the head of the spear made a great clash on the bright chapew of steel. The king, who rode but afore them, with the noise suddenly started, and his heart trembled, and into his imagination ran the impression of the words of the man that stopped his horse in the forest of Mans, and it ran into his thought that his enemies ran after him to slay and destroy him; and with that abusion he fell out of his wit by feebleness of his head, and dashed his spurs to his horse, and drew out the sword, and turned to his pages, having no knowledge of any man, weening in himself to be in a battle enclosed with his enemies, and lift up his sword to strike, he cared not where, and cried and said: 'On, on, upon these traitors!' When the pages saw the king so inflamed with ire, they took good heed to themself, as it was time; they thought the king had been displeased because the spear fell down: then they stepped away fro the king.

The duke of Orleans was not as then far off fro the king. The king came to him with his naked sword in his hand: the king was as then in such a frenzy, and his heart so feeble, that he neither knew brother nor uncle. When the duke of Orleans saw the king coming on him with his sword naked in his hand, he was abashed, and would not abide him: he wist not what he meant: he dashed his spurs to his horse and rode away, and the king after him. The duke of Burgoyne, who rode a little way off fro the king, when he heard the rushing of the horses, and heard the pages cry,

chapew] cap   abusion] delusion

he regarded that way, and saw how the king with his naked sword chased his brother the duke of Orleans. He was sore abashed and said: 'Out, harrow! what mischief is this? The king is not in his right mind, God help him: fly away, nephew, fly away, for the king would slay you.' The duke of Orleans was not well assured of himself, and fled away as fast as his horse might bear him, and knights and squires followed after, every man began to draw thither. Such as were far off thought they had chased an hare or a wolf, till at last they heard that the king was not well in his mind. The duke of Orleans saved himself. Then men of arms came all about the king, and suffered him to weary himself, and the more that he travailed the feebler he was, and when he strake at any man, they would fall down before the stroke: at this matter there was no hurt, but many overthrown, for there was none that made any defence. Finally, when the king was well wearied, and his horse sore chafed with sweat and great heat, a knight of Normandy, one of the king's chamberlains, whom the king loved very well, called Guilliam Martel, he came behind the king suddenly and took him in his arms, and held him still. Then all other approached, and took the sword out of his hands, and took him down fro his horse, and did off his jack to refresh him: then came his brother, and his three uncles, but he had clean lost the knowledge of them, and rolled his eyen in his head marvellously, and spake to no man. The lords of his blood were sore abashed, and wist not what to say or do. Then the dukes of Berry and of Burgoyne said: 'It behoveth us to return to Mans: this voyage is done for this time.' They said not as much as they thought . . .

Froissart's *Chronicles*

JOHN FISHER, BISHOP OF ROCHESTER
1469–1535

Labours of Love

What life is more painful and laborious of itself than is the life of hunters which, most early in the morning, break their sleep and rise when others do take their rest and ease, and in his labour he may use no plain highways and the soft grass, but he must tread upon the fallows, run over the hedges, and creep through the thick bushes, and cry all the long day upon his dogs, and so continue without meat or drink until the very night drive him home; these labours be unto him pleasant and joyous, for the desire and love that he hath to see the poor hare chased with dogs. Verily, verily, if he were compelled to take upon him such labours, and not for this cause, he would soon be weary of them, thinking them full tedious unto him; neither would he rise out of his bed so soon, nor fast so long, nor endure these other labours unless he had a very love therein. For the earnest desire of his mind is so fixed upon his game, that all these pains be thought to him but very pleasures. And therefore I may well say that love is the principal thing that maketh any work easy, though the work be right painful of itself, and that without love no labour can be comfortable to the doer. The love of his game delighteth him so much that he careth for no worldly honour, but is content with full simple and homely array. Also the goods of the world he seeketh not, nor studieth how to attain them. For the love and desire of his game so greatly occupieth his mind and heart. The pleasures also of his flesh he forgetteth by weariness and wasting of his body in earnest labour. All his mind, all his soul, is busied to know where the poor hare may be found. Of that is his thought, of that is his communication, and all his delight is to hear and speak of that matter, every other matter but this is tedious for him to give ear unto; in all other things he is dull and unlusty, in this only quick and stirring. For this also to be done, there is no office so humble, nor so vile, that he refuseth not to serve his own dogs himself, to bathe their feet, and anoint them where they be sore, yea, and to cleanse their kennel where they shall lie and rest them. Surely if religious persons had so earnest a mind and desire to the service of Christ, as have these hunters to see a course at a hare, their life should be unto them a very joy and pleasure. For what other be the pains of religion but these that I have spoken of? That is to say, much fasting, crying, and coming to the choir, forsaking of worldly honours, worldly riches and fleshly pleasures, and communication of the world, humble service and obedience to his sovereign, and charitable dealing to his sister, which pains, in every point, the hunter taketh and sustaineth more largely for the love that he hath to his game, than do many religious persons for the love of Christ.

The Ways to Perfect Religion, 1534

SIR THOMAS MORE

1478–1535

The Law in Utopia

They do not only fear their people from doing evil by punishments, but also allure them to virtue with rewards of honour. Therefore they set up in the market-place the images of notable men, and of such as have been great and bountiful benefactors to the commonwealth, for the perpetual memory of their good acts, and also that the glory and renown of the ancestors may stir and provoke their posterity to virtue. He that inordi-

fear] frighten

nately and ambitiously desireth promotions is left all hopeless for ever attaining any promotion as long as he liveth. They live together lovingly. For no magistrate is either haughty or fearful. Fathers they be called, and like fathers they use themselves. The citizens (as it is their duty) do willingly exhibit unto them due honour, without any compulsion. Nor the prince himself is not known from the other by his apparel, nor by a crown or diadem or cap of maintenance, but by a little sheaf of corn carried before him. And so a taper of wax is borne before the bishop, whereby only he is known.

They have but few laws. For to people so instruct and institute very few do suffice. Yea, this thing they chiefly reprove among other nations, that innumerable books of laws and expositions upon the same be not sufficient. But they think it against all right and justice that men should be bound to those laws, which either be in number more than they be able to read, or else blinder and darker than that any man can well understand them. Furthermore they utterly exclude and banish all proctors and sergeants at the law, which craftily handle matters and subtly dispute of the laws. For they think it most meet, that every man should plead his own matter, and tell the same tale before the judge that he would tell to his man of law. So shall there be less circumstance of words, and the truth shall sooner come to light; whiles the judge with a discreet judgment doth weigh the words of him whom no lawyer hath instruct with deceit, and whiles he helpeth and beareth out simple wits against the false and malicious circumversions of crafty children. This is hard to be observed in other countries, in so infinite a number of blind and intricate laws. But in Utopia every man is a cunning lawyer. For, as I said, they have very few laws; and the plainer and grosser that any interpretation is, that they allow as most just. For all laws (say they) be made and published only to the intent that by them every man should be put in remembrance of his duty. But the crafty and subtle interpretation of them can put very few in that remembrance (for they be but few that do perceive them), whereas the simple, the plain and gross meaning of the laws is open to every man.

Utopia, published in Latin, 1516; English translation by Ralph Robynson, published 1551

The Execution of Lord Hastings

Whereupon soon after, that is to wit, on the Friday the 13th day of June many Lords assembled in the Tower, and there sat in council, devising the honourable solemnity of the King's coronation, of which the time appointed then so near approached, that the pageants and subtleties were in making day and night at Westminster, and much victual killed therefore,

fearful] frightening   instruct and institute] instructed and trained
whiles] sometimes   children] people   cunning] competent

that afterwards was cast away. These Lords so sitting together commoning of this matter, the Protector came in among them, first about nine of the clock, saluting them courteously, and excusing himself that he had been from them so long, saying merely that he had been asleep that day. And after a little talking with them, he said unto the Bishop of Ely: 'My lord, you have very good strawberries at your garden in Holborn, I require you let us have a mess of them.' 'Gladly, my lord,' quoth he, 'would God I had some better thing as ready to your pleasure as that.' And therewith in all the haste he sent his servant for a mess of strawberries. The Protector set the Lords fast in commoning, and thereupon praying them to spare him for a little while, departed thence. And soon, after one hour, between ten and eleven he returned into the chamber among them, all changed, with a wonderful sour angry countenance, knitting the brows, frowning and frothing and gnawing on his lips, and so sat him down in his place; all the Lords much dismayed and sore marvelling of this manner of sudden change, and what thing should him ail. Then when he had sitten still a while, thus he began: 'What were they worthy to have, that compass and imagine the destruction of me, being so near of blood unto the King and Protector of his royal person and his realm?' At this question, all the Lords sat sore astonished, musing much by whom this question should be meant, of which every man wist himself clear. Then the Lord Chamberlain, as he that for the love between them thought be might be boldest with him, answered and said, that they were worthy to be punished as heinous traitors, whatsoever they were. And all the other affirmed the same. 'That is' (quoth he) 'yonder sorceress, my brother's wife and other with her,' meaning the Queen. At these words many of the other Lords were greatly abashed that favoured her. But the Lord Hastings was in his mind better content, that it was moved by her, than by any other whom he loved better. Albeit his heart somewhat grudged, that he was not afore made of counsel in this matter, as he was of the taking of her kindred, and of their putting to death, which were by his assent before devised to be beheaded at Pomfret, this self same day, in which he was not ware that it was by other devised, that himself should the same day be beheaded at London. Then said the Protector: 'Ye shall all see in what wise that sorceress and that other witch of her counsel, Shore's wife, with their affinity, have by their sorcery and witchcraft wasted my body.' And therewith he plucked up his doublet sleeve to his elbow upon his left arm, where he shewed a werish withered arm and small, as it was never other. And thereupon every man's mind sore misgave them, well perceiving that this matter was but a quarrel. For well they wist, that the Queen was too wise to go about any such folly. And also if she would, yet would she of all folk least make Shore's wife of counsel, whom of all women she most

werish] misshapen

hated, as that concubine whom the King her husband had most loved. And also no man was there present, but well knew that his arm was ever such since his birth. Natheles the Lord Chamberlain answered and said: 'Certainly, my Lord, if they have so heinously done, they be worthy heinous punishment.' 'What,' quoth the Protector, 'thou servest me, I wene, with ifs and with ands, I tell thee they have so done, and that I will make good on thy body, traitor.' And, therewith, as in great anger, he clapped his fist upon the board a great rap. At which token given, one cried treason without the chamber. Therewith a door clapped, and in come there rushing men in harness, as many as the chamber might hold. And anon the Protector said to the Lord Hastings: 'I arrest thee, traitor.' 'What, me, my Lord?' quoth he. 'Yea thee, traitor,' quoth the Protector. And another let fly at the Lord Stanley, which shrank at the stroke and fell under the table, or else his head had been cleft to the teeth: for as shortly as he shrank, yet ran the blood about his ears. Then were they all quickly bestowed in diverse chambers, except the Lord Chamberlain, whom the Protector bade speed and shrive him apace, 'for by Saint Paul' (quoth he) 'I will not to dinner till I see thy head off.' It boded him not to ask why, but heavily he took a priest at adventure, and made a short shrift, for a longer would not be suffered, the Protector made so much haste to dinner; which he might not go to till this were done for saving of his oath. So was he brought forth into the green beside the chapel within the Tower, and his head laid down upon a long log of timber; and there stricken off, and afterward his body with the head interred at Windsor beside the body of King Edward, whose both souls our Lord pardon.

The History of King Richard III, written *c.*1518; first published 1557

THOMAS CRANMER, ARCHBISHOP OF CANTERBURY 1489–1556

Sects and Superstitions

Thus have you heard how much the world, from the beginning until Christ's time, was ever ready to fall from the commandments of God, and to seek other means to honour and serve him, after a devotion imagined of their own heads; and how they extolled their own traditions as high or above God's commandments; which hath happened also in our times (the more it is to be lamented) no less than it did among the Jews, and that by the corruption, or at the least by the negligence of them that chiefly ought to have preferred God's commandments, and to have preserved the sincere and heavenly doctrine left by Christ. What man, having any judgment or learning, joined with a true zeal unto God, doth not see and lament to have entered into Christ's religion, such false doctrine, superstition, idolatry, hypocrisy, and other enormities and abuses, so as by little and little, through the sour leaven thereof, the sweet bread of God's holy word hath been much hindered and laid apart? Never had the Jews in their most blindness so many pilgrimages unto images, nor used so much kneeling, kissing, and censing of them, as hath been used in our time. Sects and feigned religions were neither the forty part so many among the Jews, nor more superstitiously and ungodly abused, than of late days they have been among us: which sects and religions had so many hypocritical works in their state of religion, as they arrogantly named it, that their lamps, as they said, ran always over, able to satisfy not only for their own sins, but also for all other their benefactors, brothers, and sisters of their religion, as most ungodly and craftily they had persuaded the multitude of ignorant people; keeping in divers places, as it were, marts or markets of merits, being full of their holy relics, images, shrines, and works of supererogation ready to be sold. And all things which they had were called holy, holy cowls, holy girdles, holy pardoned beads, holy shoes, holy rules, and all full of holiness. And what thing can be more foolish, more superstitious, or ungodly, than that men, women, and children, should wear a friar's coat to deliver them from agues or pestilence? or when they die, or when they be buried, cause it to be cast upon them, in hope thereby to be saved? Which superstition, although (thanks be to God) it hath been little used in this realm, yet in divers other realms it hath been and yet is used among many, both learned and unlearned.

An Homily of Good Works Annexed unto Faith, 1547

SIR THOMAS ELYOT
1490?–1546

A Dearth of Good Teachers

Lord God, how many good and clean wits of children be nowadays perished by ignorant schoolmasters. How little substantial doctrine is apprehended by the fewness of good grammarians. Notwithstanding I know there be some well learned, which have taught, and also do teach, but God knoweth a few; and they with small effect, having thereto no comfort, their aptest and most proper scholars, after they be well instructed in speaking Latin, and understanding some poets, being taken from their school by their parents, and either be brought to the court, and made lackeys or pages, or else are bounden prentices; whereby the worship that the master, above any reward, coveteth to have by the praise of his scholar, is utterly drowned; whereof I have heard schoolmasters, very well learned, of good right complain. But yet (as I said) the fewness of good grammarians is a great impediment to doctrine . . .

Undoubtedly there be in this realm many well learned, which if the name of a schoolmaster were not so much had in contempt, and also if their labours with abundant salaries might be requited, were right sufficient and able to induce their hearers to excellent learning, so they be not plucked away green, and ere they be in doctrine sufficiently rooted. But nowadays, if to a bachelor or master of art the study of philosophy waxeth tedious, if he have a spoonful of Latin, he will show forth a hogshead without any learning, and offer to teach grammar and expound noble writers, and to be in the room of a master; he will, for a small salary, set a false colour of learning on proper wits, which will be washed away with one shower of rain. For if the children be absent from school by the space of one month, the best learned of them will scarcelly tell whether *Fato*, whereby Aeneas was brought in to Italy, were either a man, a horse, a ship or a wild goose. Although their master will perchance avaunt himself to be a good philosopher.

The Book named the Governor, 1531

Man and Woman Dancing

In every dance, of a most ancient custom, there danceth together a man and a woman, holding each other by the hand or the arm, which betokeneth concord. Now it behoveth the dancers and also the beholders of them to know all qualities incident to a man, and also all qualities to a woman likewise pertaining.

A man in his natural perfection is fierce, hardy, strong in opinion, covetous of glory, desirous of knowledge, appetiting by generation to bring forth his semblable. The good nature of a woman is to be mild, timorous, tractable, benign, of sure remembrance, and shamefast. Divers other qualities of each of them might be found out, but these be most apparent, and for this time sufficient.

Wherefore, when we behold a man and a woman dancing together, let us suppose there to be a concord of all the said qualities, being joined together as I have set them in order. And the moving of the man would be more vehement, of the woman more delicate, and with less advancing of the body, signifying the courage and strength that ought to be in a man, and the pleasant soberness that should be in a woman. And in this wise fierceness joined with mildness maketh severity; audacity with timorosity maketh magnanimity; wilful opinion and tractability (which is to be shortly persuaded and moved) maketh constancy a virtue; covetousness of glory adorned with benignity causeth honour; desire of knowledge with sure remembrance procureth sapience; shamefastness joined to appetite of generation maketh continence, which is a mean between chastity and inordinate lust. These qualities, in this wise being knit together and signified in the personages of man and woman dancing, do express or set out the figure of very nobility; which in the higher estate it is contained, the more excellent is the virtue in estimation.

The Book named the Governor

HUGH LATIMER

1491–1555

Oh, London, London!

Now what shall we say of these rich citizens of London? What shall I say of them? Shall I call them proud men of London, malicious men of London, merciless men of London? No, no, I may not say so; they will be offended with me then. Yet must I speak. For is there not reigning in London as much pride, as much covetousness, as much cruelty, as much oppression, as much superstition, as was in Nebo? Yes, I think, and much more too. Therefore I say, repent, O London; repent, repent. Thou hearest thy faults told thee, amend them, amend them. I think, if Nebo had had the preaching that thou hast, they would have converted. And, you rulers and officers, be wise and circumspect, look to your charge, and see you do your duties; and rather be glad to amend your ill living than to be angry when you are warned or told of your fault. What ado was there made in London at a certain man, because he said (and indeed at that time on a just cause), 'Burgesses!' quoth he, 'nay, butterflies.' Lord, what ado there was for that word! And yet would God they were no worse than butterflies! Butterflies do but their nature: the butterfly is not covetous, is not greedy of other men's goods; is not full of envy and hatred, is not malicious, is not cruel, is not merciless. The butterfly glorieth not in her own deeds, nor preferreth the traditions of men before God's word; it committeth not idolatry, nor worshippeth false gods. But London cannot abide to be rebuked; such is the nature of man. If they be pricked, they will kick; if they be rubbed on the gall, they will wince; but yet they will not amend their faults, they will not be ill spoken of. But how shall I speak well of them? If you could be content to receive and follow the word of God, and favour good preachers, if you could bear to be told of your faults, if you could amend when you hear of them, if you would be glad to reform that is amiss; if I might see any such inclination in you, that you would leave to be merciless, and begin to be charitable, I would then hope well of you, I would then speak well of you. But London was never so ill as it is now. In times past men were full of pity and compassion, but now there is no pity; for in London their brother shall die in the streets for cold, he shall lie sick at their door between stock and stock, I cannot tell what to call it, and perish there for hunger: was there ever more unmercifulness in Nebo? I think not. In times past, when any rich man died in London, they were wont to help the poor scholars of the Universities with exhibition. When any man died, they would bequeath great sums of money toward the relief of the poor. When I was a scholar in Cambridge myself, I heard very good report of London, and knew many that had relief of the rich men of London: but now I can hear no such good report, and yet I inquire of it, and hearken for it; but now charity is waxen cold, none helpeth the scholar, nor yet the poor. And in those days, what did they when they helped the scholars? Marry, they maintained and gave them livings that were very papists, and professed the pope's doctrine: and now that the knowledge of God's word is brought to light, and many earnestly study and labour to set it forth, now almost no man helpeth to maintain them.

Oh London, London! repent; repent; for I think God is more displeased with London than ever he was with the city of Nebo. Repent therefore, repent, London, and remember that the same God liveth now that punished Nebo, even the same God, and none other; and he will punish sin as well now as he did then: and he will punish the iniquity of London, as well as he did them of Nebo. Amend therefore. And ye that be prelates, look well to your office; for right prelating is busy labouring, and not lording. Therefore preach and teach, and let your plough be doing. Ye lords, I say, that live like loiterers, look well to your office; the plough is your office and charge. If you live idle and loiter, you do not your duty, you follow not your vocation: let your plough therefore be going, and not cease, that the ground may bring forth fruit.

'The Sermon of the Plough', 1548

WILLIAM TYNDALE

*c.*1495–1536

The Book of Leviticus

The ceremonies which are described in the book following were chiefly ordained of God to occupy the minds of that people the Israelites, and to keep them from serving of God after the imagination of their blind zeal and good intent: that their consciences might be stablished and they sure that they pleased God therein, which were impossible, if a man did of his own head that which was not commanded of God, nor depended of any appointment made between him and God. Such ceremonies were unto them as an ABC to learn to spell and read, and as a nurse to feed them with milk and pap, and to speak unto them after their own capacity and to lisp the words unto them according as the babes and children of that age might sound them again. For all that were before Christ were in the infancy and childhood of the world and saw that sun which we see openly but through a cloud, and had but weak and feeble imaginations of Christ, as children have of men's deeds, a few prophets except, which yet described him unto others in sacrifices and ceremonies, likenesses, riddles, proverbs, and dark and strange speaking, until the full age were come that God would shew him openly unto the whole world and deliver them from their shadows and cloudlight and the heathen out of their dead sleep of stark blind ignorance. And as the shadow vanisheth away at the coming of the light, even so do the sacrifices and ceremonies at the coming of Christ, and are henceforth no more necessary than a token left in remembrance of a bargain is necessary when the bargain is fulfilled. And though they seem plain childish, yet they be not altogether fruitless: as the puppets and twenty manner of trifles which mothers permit unto their young children be not all in vain. For albeit that such fantasies be permitted to satisfy the children's lusts, yet in that they are the mother's gift and be done in place and time and her commandment, they keep the children in awe and make them know the mother and also make them more apt against a more stronger age to obey in things of greater earnest.

Prologue to Leviticus, translation of the Pentateuch, 1530

THE ENGLISH BIBLE: I

From William Tyndale's translation of the Pentateuch (1530)

The Fall

But the serpent was subtler than all the beasts of the field which the Lord God had made, and said unto the woman, Ah sure, that God hath said ye shall not eat of all manner trees in the garden. And the woman said unto the serpent, Of the fruit of the trees in the garden we may eat, but of the fruit of the tree that is in the midst of the garden, said God, see that ye eat not, and see that ye touch it not, lest ye die.

Then said the serpent unto the woman, Tush, ye shall not die. But God doth know that whensoever ye should eat of it, your eyes should be opened and ye should be as God, and know both good and evil. And the woman saw that it was a good tree to eat of, and lusty unto the eyes, and a pleasant tree for to make wise. And took of the fruit of it and ate, and gave unto her husband also with her, and he ate. And the eyes of both of them were opened, that they understood how that they were naked. Then they sowed fig leaves together and made them aprons.

And they heard the voice of the Lord God as he walked in the garden in the cool of the day. And Adam hid himself, and his wife also, from the face of the Lord God, among the trees of the garden. And the Lord called Adam, and said unto him, Where art thou? And he answered, Thy voice I heard in the garden, but I was afraid because I was naked, and therefore hid myself. And he said, Who told thee that thou wast naked? Hast thou eaten of the tree, of which I bade thee that thou shouldst not eat? And Adam answered, The woman which thou gavest to bear me company, she took me of the tree, and I ate. And the Lord God said unto the woman, Wherefore didst thou so? And the woman answered, The serpent deceived me, and I ate.

And the Lord God said unto the serpent, Because thou hast so done, most cursed be thou of all cattle and of all beasts of the field. Upon thy belly shalt thou go, and earth shalt thou eat all days of thy life. Moreover, I will put hatred between thee and the woman, and between thy seed and her seed. And that seed shall tread thee on the head, and thou shalt tread it on the heel.

And unto the woman he said, I will surely increase thy sorrow, and make thee oft with child, and with pain shalt thou be delivered. And thy lusts shall pertain unto thy husband, and he shall rule thee.

And unto Adam he said, For as much as thou hast obeyed the voice of thy wife, and hast eaten of the tree of which I commanded thee, saying, See thou eat not thereof, cursed be the earth for thy sake. In sorrow shalt thou eat thereof all days of thy life. And it shall bear thorns and thistles unto thee. And thou shalt eat the herbs of the field. In the sweat of thy face shalt thou eat bread, until thou return unto the earth whence thou wast taken, for earth thou art, and unto earth shalt thou return.

Genesis 3: 1–19

THE ENGLISH BIBLE: II

1 Corinthians 13: 4–13

WILLIAM TYNDALE'S TRANSLATION (1525)

Love suffereth long and is courteous. Love envieth not. Love doth not frowardly, swelleth not, dealeth not dishonestly, seeketh not her own, is not provoked to anger, thinketh not evil, rejoiceth not in iniquity: but rejoiceth in the truth, suffereth all things, believeth all things, hopeth all things, endureth in all things. Though that prophesying fail, other tongues shall cease, or knowledge vanish away, yet love falleth never away.

For our knowledge is unperfect and our prophesying is unperfect. But when that which is perfect is come, then that which is unperfect shall be done away. When I was a child, I spake as a child, I understood as a child, I imagined as a child. But as soon as I was a man, I put away childishness. Now we see in a glass, even in a dark speaking, but then shall we see face to face. Now I know unperfectly: but then shall I know even as I am known. Now abideth faith, hope, and love, even these three: but the chief of these is love.

THE AUTHORIZED VERSION (1611)

Charity suffereth long, and is kind; charity envieth not; charity vaunteth not itself, is not puffed up, doth not behave itself unseemly, seeketh not her own, is not easily provoked, thinketh no evil; rejoiceth not in iniquity, but rejoiceth in the truth; beareth all things, believeth all things, hopeth all things, endureth all things. Charity never faileth: but whether there be prophecies, they shall fail; whether there be tongues, they shall cease; whether there be knowledge, it shall vanish away. For we know in part, and we prophesy in part. But when that which is perfect is come, then that which is in part shall be done away. When I was a child, I spake as a child, I understood as a child, I thought as a child: but when I became a man, I put away childish things. For now we see through a glass, darkly; but then face to face: now I know in part; but then shall I know even as also I am known. And now abideth faith, hope, charity, these three; but the greatest of these is charity.

THE NEW ENGLISH BIBLE (1970)

Love is patient; love is kind and envies no one. Love is never boastful, nor conceited, nor rude; never selfish, not quick to take offence. Love keeps no score of wrongs; does not gloat over other men's sins, but delights in the truth. There is nothing love cannot face; there is no limit to its faith, its hope, and its endurance.

Love will never come to an end. Are there prophets? their work will be over. Are there tongues of ecstasy? they will cease. Is there knowledge? it will vanish away; for our knowledge and our prophecy alike are partial, and the partial vanishes when wholeness comes. When I was a child, my speech, my outlook, and my thoughts were all childish. When I grew up, I had finished with childish things. Now we see only puzzling reflections in a mirror, but then we shall see face to face. My knowledge now is partial; then it will be whole, like God's knowledge of me. In a word, there are three things that last for ever: faith, hope, and love; but the greatest of them all is love.

WILLIAM ROPER
1498–1578

Thomas More's Wife Visits Him in the Tower

When Sir Thomas More had continued a good while in the Tower, my lady his wife obtained licence to see him, who at her first coming like a simple woman, and somewhat worldly too, with this manner of salutations bluntly saluted him, 'What the good year, Mr More,' quoth she, 'I marvel that you, that have been always hitherunto taken for so wise a man, will now so play the fool to lie here in this close filthy prison, and be content to be shut up among mice and rats, when you might be abroad at your liberty, and with the favour and good will both of the King and his Council, if you would but do as all the bishops and best learned of this Realm have done. And seeing you have at Chelsea a right fair house, your library, your books, your gallery, your garden, your orchards, and all other necessaries so handsomely about you, where you might, in the company of me your wife, your children, and household be merry, I muse what a God's name you mean here still thus fondly to tarry.' After he had a while quietly heard her, with a cheerful countenance he said unto her, 'I pray thee good Mrs Alice, tell me, tell me one thing.' 'What is that?' (quoth she). 'Is not this house as nigh heaven as mine own?' To whom she, after her accustomed fashion, not liking such talk, answered, '*Tille valle, tille valle.*' 'How say you, Mrs Alice, is it not so?' quoth he. '*Bone Deus, bone Deus*, man, will this gear never be left?' quoth she. 'Well then, Mrs Alice, if it be so, it is very well. For I see no great cause why I should much joy of my gay house, or of anything belonging thereunto, when, if I should but seven years lie buried under the ground, and then arise and come thither again, I should not fail to find some therein that would bid me get me out of the doors, and tell me that were none of mine. What cause have I then to like such an house as would so soon forget his master?' So her persuasions moved him but a little.

The Life of Sir Thomas More, written *c.*1555; first printed in Paris, 1626

GEORGE CAVENDISH
1500–1561

Cardinal Wolsey Nears Death

After that he was in his confession the space of an hour. And then Master Kingston came to him and bid him good morrow, and asked him how he did. 'Sir,' quoth he, 'I watch but God's pleasure to render up my poor soul to him. I pray you have me heartily commended unto his Royal Majesty, and beseech him on my behalf to call to his princely remembrance all matters that have been between us from the beginning and the progress; and especially between good Queen Katherine and him, and then shall his Grace's conscience know whether I have offended him or not.

'He is a prince of a most royal carriage, and hath a princely heart, and rather than he will miss or want any part of his will, he will endanger the one half of his kingdom.

'I do assure you I have often kneeled before him, sometimes three hours together, to persuade him from his will and appetite, but could not prevail. And, Master Kingston, had I but served God as diligently as I have served the King, he would not have given me over in my grey hairs. But this is the just reward that I must receive for my diligent pains and study, not regarding my service to God, but only to my prince. Therefore let me advise you, if you be one of the Privy Council, as by your wisdom you are fit, take heed what you put in the King's head, for you can never put it out again.

'Master Kingston, farewell; I wish all things may have good success. My time draws on; I may not tarry with you. I pray you remember my words.'

Thomas Wolsey, late Cardinal, his Life and Death, written *c.*1555; first printed 1641

SIMON FISH
d. 1531

The Cormorants of the Commonwealth

To the King our Sovereign lord:

Most lamentably complaineth their woeful misery unto your Highness, your poor daily beadmen, the wretched hideous monsters (on whom scarcely for horror any eye dare look), the foul unhappy sort of lepers and other sore people—needy, impotent, blind, lame, and sick—that live only by alms: how that their number is daily so sore increased that all the alms of all the well-disposed people of this your realm is not half enough for to sustain them, but that for very constraint they die for hunger.

And this most pestilent mischief is come upon your said poor beadmen by the reason that there is in the times of your noble predecessors passed, craftily crept into this your realm another sort, not of impotent but of strong, puissant, counterfeit, holy, and idle beggars and vagabonds which since the time of their first entrance by all the craft and wiliness of Satan are now increased under your sight, not only into a great number but also into a kingdom.

These are (not the herds but the ravenous wolves, going in herds-clothing, devouring the flock) the bishops, abbots, priors, deacons, archdeacons, suffragans, priests, monks, canons, friars, pardoners, and summoners. And who is able to number this idle ravenous sort which (setting all labour aside) have begged so importunately that they have gotten into their hands more than the third part of all your realm. The goodliest lordships, manors, lands, and territories are theirs. Besides this they have the tenth part of all the corn, meadows, pasture, grass, wool, colts, calves, lambs, pigs, geese, and chickens; over and besides the tenth part of every servant's wages; the tenth part of the wool, milk, honey, wax, cheese, and butter . . .

Is it any marvel that your people so complain of poverty? Is it any marvel that the taxes, fifteens, and subsidies that your Grace, most tenderly of great compassion, hath taken among your people to defend them from the threatened ruin of their commonwealth have been so slothfully, yea, painfully levied, seeing that almost the utmost penny that might have been levied, hath been gathered before yearly by this ravenous, cruel, and insatiable generation.

The Danes neither the Saxons, in the time of the ancient Britons, should never have been able to have brought their armies from so far hither into your land to have conquered it if they had had at that time such a sort of idle gluttons to find at home. The noble King Arthur had never been able to have carried his army to the foot of the mountains to resist the coming down of Lucius, the Emperor, if such yearly exaction had been taken of his people.

The Greeks had never been able to have so long continued at the siege of Troy if they had had at home such an idle sort of cormorants to find. The ancient Romans had never been able to have put all the whole world under their obeisance if their people had been thus yearly oppressed. The Turk now in your time should never be able to get so much ground of Christendom if he had in his empire such a sort of locusts to devour his substance . . .

A Supplication for the Beggars, 1529

THE BOOK OF COMMON PRAYER

Psalm 126

When the Lord turned again the captivity of Sion, then were we like unto them that dream. Then was our mouth filled with laughter, and our tongue with joy. Then said they among the heathen, the Lord hath done great

fifteens] units of taxation

things for them. Yea, the Lord hath done great things for us already, whereof we rejoice. Turn our captivity, O Lord, as the rivers in the South. They that sow in tears, shall reap in joy. He that now goeth his way weeping and beareth forth good seed, shall come again with joy and bring his sheaves with him.

The First Prayer Book of Edward VI, 1549

From the Form of Solemnization of Matrimony

Dearly beloved friends, we are gathered together here in the sight of God, and in the face of his congregation, to join together this man and this woman in holy matrimony; which is an honourable estate, instituted of God in Paradise, in the time of man's innocency, signifying unto us the mystical union that is betwixt Christ and his church; which holy estate Christ adorned and beautified with his presence, and first miracle that he wrought, in Cana of Galilee; and is commended of Saint Paul to be honourable among all men: and is therefore not to be enterprised, nor taken in hand unadvisedly, lightly, or wantonly, to satisfy man's carnal lusts and appetites, like brute beasts that have no understanding; but reverently, discreetly, advisedly, soberly, and in the fear of God; duly considering the causes for the which matrimony was ordained. One cause was the procreation of children, to be brought up in the fear and nurture of the Lord, and praise of God. Secondly, it was ordained for a remedy against sin, and to avoid fornication; that such persons as be married might live chastely in matrimony, and keep themselves undefiled members of Christ's body. Thirdly, for the mutual society, help, and comfort, that the one ought to have of the other, both in prosperity and adversity. Into the which holy estate these two persons present come now to be joined. Therefore if any man can shew any just cause why they may not lawfully be joined so together, let him now speak, or else hereafter for ever hold his peace.

The First Prayer Book of Edward VI

ROGER ASCHAM

1515–1568

The Wind Made Visible

To see the wind, with a man his eyes, it is unpossible, the nature of it is so fine, and subtile; yet this experience of the wind had I once myself, and that was in the great snow that fell four years ago: I rode in the highway betwixt Topcliff-upon-Swale, and Borowe Bridge, the way being somewhat trodden afore, by wayfaring men. The fields on both sides were plain and lay almost yard deep with snow, the night afore had been a little frost, so that the snow was hard and crusted above. That morning the sun shone bright and clear, the wind was whistling aloft, and sharp according to the time of the year. The snow in the highway lay loose and trodden with horse feet: so as the wind blew, it took the loose snow with it, and made it so slide upon the snow in the field which was hard and crusted by reason of the frost overnight, that thereby I might see very well the whole nature of the wind as it blew that day. And I had a great delight and pleasure to mark it, which maketh me now far better to remember it. Sometime the wind would be not past two yards broad, and so it would carry the snow as far as I could see. Another time the snow would blow over half the field at once. Sometime the snow would tumble softly, by and by it would fly wonderful fast. And this I perceived also, that the wind goeth by streams and not whole together. For I should see one stream within a score on me, then the space of two score no snow would stir, but after so much quantity of ground, another stream of snow at the same very time should be carried likewise, but not equally. For the one would stand still when the other flew apace, and so continue sometime swiftlier, sometime slowlier, sometime broader, sometime narrower, as far as I could see. Nor it flew not straight, but sometime it crooked this way, sometime that way, and sometime it ran round about in a compass. And sometime the snow would be lift clean from the ground up into the air, and by and by it would be all clapped to the ground as though there had been no wind at all, straightway it would rise and fly again.

And that which was the most marvel of all, at one time two drifts of snow flew, the one out of the West into the East, the other out of the North into the East: and I saw two winds by reason of the snow the one cross over the other, as it had been two highways. And again I should hear the wind blow in the air, when nothing was stirred at the ground. And when all was still where I rode, not very far from me the snow should be lifted wonderfully. This experience made me more marvel at the nature of the wind, than it made me cunning in the knowledge of the wind: but yet thereby I learned perfectly that it is no marvel at all though men in a wind lose their length in shooting, seeing so many ways the wind is so variable in blowing.

Toxophilus, 1545

Quick Wits

Quick wits commonly be apt to take, unapt to keep; soon hot, and desirous of this and that; as cold, and soon weary of the same again; more quick to enter speedily, than able to pierce far; even like over-sharp tools, whose edges be very soon turned. Such wits delight themselves in easy and pleasant studies, and never pass far forward in high and hard sciences. And therefore the quickest wits commonly may prove the best poets, but not the wisest orators; ready of tongue to speak boldly, not deep of judgment, either for good council or wise writing. Also for manners and life, quick wits commonly be, in desire, newfangled; in purpose, unconstant; light to promise anything, ready to forget every thing, both benefit and injury; and thereby neither fast to friend, nor fearful to foe: inquisitive of every trifle, not secret in the greatest affairs; bold with any person; busy in every matter; soothing such as be present, nipping any that is absent: of nature also, always flattering their betters, envying their equals, despising their inferiors; and by quickness of wit, very quick and ready to like none so well as themselves.

Moreover, commonly, men very quick of wit be also very light of conditions; and thereby very ready of disposition to be carried over quickly, by any light company, to any riot and unthriftiness when they be young; and therefore seldom either honest of life, or rich in living when they be old. For quick in wit, and light in manners, be either seldom troubled, or very soon weary, in carrying a very heavy purse. Quick wits also be, in most part of all their doings, over quick, hasty, rash, heady, and brain-sick. These two last words, Heady and Brain-sick, be fit and proper words, rising naturally of the matter, and termed aptly by the condition of over-much quickness of wit. In youth also they be ready scoffers, privy mockers, and ever over-light and merry: in age, soon testy, very waspish, and always over-miserable. And yet few of them come to any great age, by reason of their misordered life when they were young; but a great deal fewer of them come to show any great countenance, or bear any great authority abroad in the world, but either live obscurely, men know not how, or die obscurely, men mark not when.

The Schoolmaster, 1570

The Light Reading of Our Ancestors

In our forefathers' time, when papistry, as a standing pool, covered and overflowed all England, few books were read in our tongue, saving certain books of chivalry, as they said for pastime and pleasure; which, as some say, were made in monasteries by idle monks or wanton canons. As one for example, *Morte Arthur*; the whole pleasure of which book standeth in two special points, in open manslaughter and bold bawdry. In which book those be counted the noblest knights, that do kill most men without any quarrel, and commit foulest adulteries by subtlest shifts: as Sir Launcelot, with the wife of King Arthur his master; Sir Tristram, with the wife of King Mark his uncle; Sir Lamerock, with the wife of King Lote, that was his own aunt. This is good stuff for wise men to laugh at, or honest men to take pleasure at: yet I know, when God's Bible was banished the court, and *Morte Arthur* received into the prince's chamber.

The Schoolmaster

RAPHAEL HOLINSHED
d. 1580?

The Weird Sisters

It fortuned as Makbeth and Banquho journeyed towards Fores, where the king then lay, they went sporting by the way together without other company save only themselves, passing through the woods and fields, when suddenly in the middest of a laund, there met them three women in strange and wild apparel, resembling creatures of the elder world, whom when they attentively beheld, wondering much at the sight, the first of them spake and said: 'All hail Makbeth, thane of Glammis!' (for he had lately entered into that office by the death of his father Sinell). The second of them said: 'Hail Makbeth, thane of Cawdor!' But the third said: 'All hail Makbeth, that hereafter shall be king of Scotland!'

Then Banquho: 'What manner of women (saith he) are you that seem so little favourable unto me, whereas to my fellow here, besides high offices, ye assign also the kingdom, appointing forth nothing for me at all?' 'Yes,' (saith the first of them,) 'we promise greater benefits unto thee than unto him; for he shall reign indeed, but with an unlucky end; neither shall he leave any issue behind him to succeed in his place, when certainly thou shalt not reign at all, but of thee those shall be born which shall govern the Scottish kingdom by long order of continual descent.' Herewith the foresaid women vanished immediately out of their sight. This was reputed at the first but some vain fantastical illusion by Makbeth and Banquho, insomuch that Banquho would call Makbeth in jest, King of Scotland; and Makbeth again would call him in sport likewise, father of many kings. But afterwards the common opinion was, that these women were either the weird sisters, that is (as ye would say) the goddesses of destiny, or else some nymphs or fairies, indued with knowledge of prophecie by their necromantical science, because everything came to pass as they had spoken.

Chronicles, 1577

SIR THOMAS CHALONER

1521–1565

[from the Latin of Erasmus]

The Social Ineptitude of Wise Men

Now though these wise men be as unapt for all public offices and affairs 'as an ass is to finger a harp', yet might it so be abidden if they were not also as untoward in any private duty pertaining to this life. For bid once one of these sages to dinner, and either with his silent glooming or his dark and elvish problems he will trouble all the board. Desire him to take hands in a ball—ye will say a camel danceth. Bring him to a midsummer watch, or a stage play, and even with his very look he will seem to disdain the people's pastime so that wise Don Cato must be fain to avoid the place because he cannot forbear it frowning.

Let him light on a knot of good company talking merrily, and by and by every wight holds his peace. If he must buy anything, make a bargain, or, briefly, do ought of those things without which this common life cannot be led, then sooner will ye take him for a block than a reasonable creature. So much lacketh, lo, that he may stand his country or his friends in profitable stead, who neither is skilled in things daily inured and much differeth from the common opinion and manners of the other people. Perconsequent whereof he must needs deserve their hatred and displeasure through great diversity of livings and dispositions atwixt them.

For, and if ye list to judge indifferently, is there ought done here among mortal men not full of folly, both by fools and afore fools? So that if one only wight would take upon him to kick against all the rest, him would I advise that, as Timon [of Athens] did, he should shrink into some desert, there to enjoy his wisdom to himself.

The Praise of Folly, Chaloner's translation, 1549

JOHN STOW

1525–1605

The Traffic Problem

Then the number of cars, drays, carts, and coaches, more than hath been accustomed, the streets and lanes being straitened, must needs be dangerous, as daily experience proveth.

The coachman rides behind the horse tails, lasheth them, and looketh not behind him; the drayman sitteth and sleepeth on his dray, and letteth his horse lead him home. I know that, by the good laws and customs of this city, shodde carts are forbidden to enter the same, except upon reasonable cause, as service of the prince, or such like, they be tolerated. Also that the fore horse of every carriage should be led by hand; but these good orders are not observed. Of old time coaches were not known in this island, but chariots or whirlicotes, then so called, and they only used of princes or great estates, such as had their footmen about them; and for example to note, I read that Richard II, being threatened by the rebels of Kent, rode from the Tower of London to the Myles end, and with him his mother, because she was sick and weak, in a whirlicote, the Earls of Buckingham, Kent, Warwicke, and Oxford, Sir Thomas Percie, Sir Robert Knowles, the Mayor of London, Sir Aubery de Vere, that bare the king's sword, with other knights and esquires attending on horseback. But in the next year, the said King Richard took to wife Anne, daughter to the King of Bohemia, that first brought hither the riding upon side-saddles; and so was the riding in wherlicoates and chariots forsaken, except at coronations and such like spectacles; but now of late years the use of coaches, brought out of Germany, is taken up, and made so common, as there is neither distinction of time nor difference of persons observed; for the world runs on wheels with many whose parents were glad to go on foot.

A Survey of London, 1598; revised 1603

A High-Handed Neighbour

On the south side, and at the west end of this church, many fair houses are built; namely, in Throgmorton street, one very large and spacious; built in the place of old and small tenements by Thomas Cromwell, master of the king's jewel-house, after that master of the rolls, then Lord Cromwell, knight, lord privy seal, vicar-general, Earl of Essex, high chamberlain of England, etc. This house being finished, and having some reasonable plot of ground left for a garden, he caused the pales of the gardens adjoining to the north part thereof on a sudden to be taken down; twenty-two feet to be measured forth right into the north of every man's ground; a line there to be drawn, a trench to be cast, a foundation laid, and a high brick wall to be built. My father had a garden there, and a house standing close to his south pale; this house they loosed from the ground, and bare upon rollers into my father's garden twenty-two feet, ere my father heard thereof; no warning was given him, nor other answer, when he spake to the

shodde carts] carts shod or bound with iron

this church] Austin Friars

surveyors of that work, but that their master Sir Thomas commanded them so to do; no man durst go to argue the matter, but each man lost his land, and my father paid his whole rent, which was 6*s.* 6*d.* the year, for that half which was left. Thus much of mine own knowledge have I thought good to note, that the sudden rising of some men causeth them to forget themselves.

A Survey of London

QUEEN ELIZABETH I

1533–1603

Speech to the Troops at Tilbury

My loving people,

We have been persuaded by some that are careful of our safety, to take heed how we commit our selves to armed multitudes, for fear of treachery; but I assure you I do not desire to live to distrust my faithful and loving people. Let tyrants fear, I have always so behaved myself that, under God, I have placed my chiefest strength and safeguard in the loyal hearts and good-will of my subjects; and therefore I am come amongst you, as you see, at this time, not for my recreation and disport, but being resolved, in the midst and heat of the battle, to live or die amongst you all; to lay down for my God, and for my kingdom, and my people, my honour and my blood, even in the dust. I know I have the body but of a weak and feeble woman; but I have the heart and stomach of a king, and of a king of England too, and think foul scorn that Parma or Spain, or any prince of Europe, should dare to invade the borders of my realm; to which rather than any dishonour shall grow by me, I myself will take up arms, I myself will be your general, judge, and rewarder of every one of your virtues in the field. I know already, for your forwardness you have deserved rewards and crowns; and We do assure you in the word of a prince, they shall be duly paid you. In the mean time, my lieutenant general shall be in my stead, than whom never prince commanded a more noble or worthy subject; not doubting but by your obedience to my general, by your concord in the camp, and your valour in the field, we shall shortly have a famous victory over those enemies of my God, of my kingdom, and of my people.

1588

SIR THOMAS NORTH
1535?–1601?

[translated from the French version of Plutarch by Jacques Amyot]

Timon

This Timon was a citizen of Athens, that lived about the war of the Peloponnesus, as appeareth by Plato and Aristophanes' comedies: in the which they mocked him, calling him a viper and malicious man unto mankind, to shun all other men's companies, but the company of young Alcibiades, a bold and insolent youth, whom he would greatly feast and make much of, and kissed him very gladly. Apemantus wondering at it, asked him the cause what he meant to make so much of that young man alone, and to hate all others; Timon answered him, 'I do it,' said he, 'because I know that one day he shall do great mischief unto the Athenians.' This Timon would sometimes have Apemantus in his company, because he was much like of his nature and his conditions, and also followed him in manner and life. On a time when they solemnly celebrated the festival called Choae at Athens (to wit, the feasts of the dead where they make sprinklings and sacrifices for the dead) and that they two then feasted together by themselves, Apemantus said unto the other, 'O here is a trim banquet, Timon.' Timon answered again: 'Yea,' said he, 'so thou wert not here.' It is reported of him also, that this Timon on a time (the people being assembled in the market place about dispatch of some affairs) got up into the pulpit for orations, where the orators commonly use to speak unto the people; and silence being made, every man listening to hear what he would say, because it was a wonder to see him in that place, at length began to speak in this manner: 'My lords of Athens, I have a little yard at my house where there groweth a fig-tree, on the which many citizens hanged themselves; and because I mean to make some building on the place, I thought good to let you all understand it, that before the fig-tree be cut down, if any of you be desperate, you may there in time go hang yourselves.' He died in the city of Hales, and was buried upon the sea side.

Plutarch's *Lives of the Noble Grecians and Romans*, North's translation, 1579

The Banishment of Caius Martius Coriolanus

After declaration of the sentence, the people made such joy, as they never rejoiced more for any battle they had won upon their enemies, they were so brave and lively, and went home so jocundly from the assembly, for triumph of this sentence. The Senate again in contrary manner were as sad and heavy, repenting themselves beyond measure, that they had not rather determined to have done and suffered anything whatsoever, before the common people should so arrogantly and outrageously have abused their authority. There needed no difference of garments, I warrant you, nor outward shows to know a plebeian from a patrician, for they were easily discerned by their looks. For he that was on the people's side looked cheerily on the matter: but he that was sad, and hung down his head, he was sure of the nobleman's side. Saving Martius alone, who neither in his countenance nor in his gait did ever show himself abashed, or once let fall his great courage: but he only of all other gentlemen that were angry at his fortune did outwardly show no manner of passion, nor care at all of himself. Not that he did patiently bear and temper his good-hap, in respect of any reason he had, or by his quiet condition: but because he was so carried away with the vehemency of anger, and desire of revenge, that he had no sense nor feeling of the hard state he was in, which the common people judge not to be sorrow, although indeed it be the very same. For when sorrow (as you would say) is set afire, then it is converted into spite and malice, and driveth away for that time all faintness of heart and natural fear. And this is the cause why the choleric man is so altered and mad in his actions, as a man set on fire with a burning ague: for, when a man's heart is troubled within, his pulse will beat marvellous strongly. Now, that Martius was even in that taking, it appeared true soon after by his doings. For when he was come home to his house again, and had taken his leave of his mother and wife, finding them weeping and shrieking out for sorrow, and had also comforted and persuaded them to be content with his chance: he went immediately to the gate of the city, accompanied with a great number of patricians that brought him thither, from whence he went on his way with three or four of his friends only, taking nothing with him, nor requesting anything of any man. So he remained a few days in the country at his houses, turmoiled with sundry sorts and kinds of thoughts, such as the fire of his choler did stir up. In the end, seeing he could resolve no way to take a profitable or honourable course, but only was pricked forward still to be revenged of the Romans: he thought to raise up some great wars against them, by their nearest neighbours.

Lives of the Noble Grecians and Romans

A Lean and Hungry Look

Caesar also had Cassius in great jealousy, and suspected him much: whereupon he said on a time to his friends, 'what will Cassius do, think ye? I like not his pale looks.' Another time when Caesar's friends complained unto him of Antonius and Dolabella, that they pretended some mischief towards him, he answered them again, 'As for those fat men and smooth-combed heads,' quoth he, 'I never reckon of them; but these pale-visaged and carrion-lean people, I fear them most,' meaning Brutus and Cassius.

Lives of the Noble Grecians and Romans

Cleopatra Sets Out to Meet Antony

Guessing by the former access and credit she had with Julius Caesar and Cneus Pompey (the son of Pompey the Great) only for her beauty, she began to have good hope that she might more easily win Antonius. For Caesar and Pompey knew her when she was but a young thing, and knew not then what the world meant; but now she went to Antonius at the age when a woman's beauty is at the prime, and she also of best judgment. So she furnished herself with a world of gifts, store of gold and silver, and of riches and other sumptuous ornaments, as is credible enough she might from so great a house, and from so wealthy and rich a realm as Egypt was. But yet she carried nothing with her wherein she trusted more than in herself, and in the charms and enchantment of her passing beauty and grace.

Therefore when she was sent unto by divers letters, both from Antonius himself, and also from his friends, she made so light of it, and mocked Antonius so much, that she disdained to set forward otherwise, but to take her barge in the river of Cydnus, the poop whereof was of gold, the sails of purple, and the oars of silver, which kept stroke in rowing after the sound of the musick of flutes, hautboys, citherns, viols, and such other instruments as they played upon in the barge. And now for the person of herself: she was laid under a pavilion of cloth of gold, apparelled and attired like the goddess Venus, commonly drawn in picture, and hard by her, on either side of her, pretty fair boys apparelled as painters do set forth god Cupid, with little fans in their hands, with the which they fanned wind upon her. Her ladies and gentlewomen also, the fairest of them, were apparelled like the nymphs Nereides (which are the mermaids of the waters) and like the Graces, some steering the helm, others tending the tackle and ropes of the barge, out of which there came a wonderful passing sweet savour of perfumes, that perfumed the wharf's side, pestered with innumerable multitudes of people. Some of them followed the barge all alongst the river's side; others also ran out of the city to see her coming in. So that in the end, there ran such multitudes of people one after another to see her, that Antonius was left post alone in the market place in his imperial seat to give audience; and there went a rumour in the people's mouths that the goddess Venus was come to play with the god Bacchus, for the general good of all Asia.

Lives of the Noble Grecians and Romans

ROBERT PARSONS
1546–1610

The Earth is the Lord's

If we cast down our eyes from Heaven to earth, we behold the same of an immense bigness, distinguished with hills and dales, woods and pasture, covered with all variety of grass, herbs, flowers and leaves; moistened with rivers, as a body with veins; inhabited by creatures of innumerable kinds and qualities; enriched with inestimable and endless treasures: and yet itself standing, or hanging rather, with all this weight and poise, as a little ball without prop or pillar.

At which surprising and most wonderful miracle of nature, God Himself, as it were glorying, said unto Job: 'Where wast thou when I laid the foundations of the earth? tell me, if thou hast understanding. Who set the measures thereof, if thou know? or who stretched out the line upon it? upon what are the foundations thereof grounded? or who let down the cornerstone thereof, when the morning stars praised me together, and all the sons of God made jubilation?'

The Christian Directory, 1582

RICHARD KNOLLES
1550?–1610

The Death of Sultan Murad I

Who had fought greater battles? who had gained greater victories or obtained more glorious triumphs than had Amurath? Who by the spoils of so many mighty kings and princes, and by the conquest of so many proud and warlike nations, again restored and established the Turk's kingdom, before by Tamerlane and the Tartars in a manner clean defaced. He it was that burst the heart of the proud Grecians, establishing his empire at Adrianople, even in the centre of their bowels: from whence have proceeded so many miseries and calamities into the greatest part of Christendom, as no tongue is able to express. He it was that first brake down the Hexamile or wall of separation on the Strait of Corinth, and conquered the greater part of Peloponesus. He it was that subdued unto the Turks so many great countries and provinces in Asia; that in plain field and set battle overthrew many puissant kings and princes, and brought them under his subjection; who having slain Vladislaus the King of Polonia and Hungary, and more than once chased out of the field Huniades, that famous and redoubted warrior, had in his proud and ambitious heart promised unto himself the conquest of a great part of Christendom. But O how far was he now changed from the man he then was! How far did these his last speeches differ from the course of his forepassed life! full of such base passionate complaints and lamentations, as beseemed not a man of his place and spirit; but some vile wretch overtaken with despair, and yet afraid to die. Where were now those haughty looks, those thundering and commanding speeches, whereat so many great commanders, so many troops and legions, so many thousands of armed soldiers were wont to tremble and quake? Where is that head, before adorned with so many trophies and triumphs? Where is that victorious hand that swayed so many sceptres? Where is the majesty of his power and strength, that commanded over so many nations and kingdoms? O how is the case now altered!

The General History of the Turks, 1603

EDMUND SPENSER
1552?–1599

Ireland: A Most Beautiful and Sweet Country

And sure it is yet a most beautiful and sweet country as any is under Heaven, seamed throughout with many goodly rivers, replenished with all sorts of fish, most abundantly sprinkled with many sweet islands and goodly lakes, like little inland seas, that will carry even ships upon their waters, adorned with goodly woods fit for building of houses and ships, so commodiously, that if some princes in the world had them, they would soon hope to be lords of all the seas, and ere long of all the world; also full of good ports and havens opening upon England and Scotland, as inviting us to come to them, to see what excellent commodities that country can afford, besides the soil itself most fertile, fit to yield all kind of fruit that shall be committed thereunto. And lastly, the heavens most mild and temperate, though somewhat more moist than the part toward the West.

A View of the Present State of Ireland, 1596; first published 1633

Ireland: The Aftermath of the Munster Rising

Out of every corner of the woods and glens they came creeping forth upon their hands, for their legs could not bear them; they looked like anatomies of death, they spake like ghosts crying out of their graves; they did eat of the dead carrions, happy were they if they could find them, yea, and one another soon after, insomuch as the very carcasses they spared not to scrape out of their graves; and if they found a plot of water-cresses or shamrocks, there they flocked as to a feast for the time, yet not able long to continue therewithall; that in short space there were none almost left, and a most populous and plentiful country suddenly made void of man or beast: yet sure in all that war, there perished not many by the sword, but all by the extremity of famine which they themselves had wrought.

A View of the Present State of Ireland

SIR WALTER RALEIGH
1552?–1618

The End of the Revenge

All the powder of the *Revenge* to the last barrel was now spent, all her pikes broken, forty of her best men slain, and the most part of the rest hurt. In the beginning of the fight she had but one hundred free from sickness, and fourscore and ten sick, laid in hold upon the ballast. A small troop to man such a ship, and a weak garrison to resist so mighty an army. By those hundred all was sustained, the volleys, boardings, and enterings of fifteen ships of war, besides those which beat her at large. On the contrary, the Spanish were always supplied with soldiers brought from every squadron: all manner of arms and powder at will. Unto ours there remained no comfort at all, no hope, no supply either of ships, men, or weapons; the masts all beaten overboard, all her tackle cut asunder, her upper work altogether rased, and in effect evened she was with the water, but the very foundation or bottom of a ship, nothing being left overhead either for flight or defence. Sir Richard finding himself in this distress, and unable any longer to make resistance, having endured in this fifteen hours' fight the assault of fifteen several Armadoes, all by turns aboard him, and by estimation eight hundred shot of great artillery, besides many assaults and entries; and that himself and the ship must needs be possessed by the enemy, who were now all cast in a ring round about him; the *Revenge* not able to move one way or other, but as she was moved with the waves and billow of the sea: commanded the Master-Gunner, whom he knew to be a most resolute man, to split and sink the ship; that thereby nothing might remain of glory or victory to the Spaniards, seeing in so many hours' fight, and with so great a navy they were not able to take her, having had fifteen hours' time, fifteen thousand men, and fifty and three sail of men-of-war to perform it withal: and persuaded the company, or as many as he could induce, to yield themselves unto God, and to the mercy of none else; but as they had like valiant resolute men repulsed so many enemies, they should not now shorten the honour of their nation, by prolonging their own lives for a few hours, or a few days. The Master-Gunner readily condescended, and divers others; but the Captain and the Master were of another opinion, and besought Sir Richard to have care of them: alleging that the Spaniard would be as ready to entertain a composition as they were willing to offer the same: and that there being divers sufficient and valiant men yet living, and whose wounds were not mortal, they might do their country and prince acceptable service hereafter. And (that where Sir Richard had alleged that the Spaniards should never glory to have taken one ship of Her Majesty's, seeing that they had so long and so notably defended themselves) they answered, that the ship had six foot water in hold, three shot under water, which were so weakly stopped as with the first working of the sea she must need sink, and was besides so crushed and bruised as she could never be removed out of the place.

A Report of the Truth of the Fight about the Isles of Azores, 1591

Drawing Near to El Dorado

When we ran to the tops of the first hills of the plains adjoining to the river, we beheld that wonderful breach of waters, which ran down Caroli: and might from that mountain see the river how it ran in three parts, above twenty miles off, and there appeared some ten or twelve overfalls in sight, every one as high over the other as a church-tower, which fell with that fury that the rebound of waters made it seem as if it had been all covered over with a great shower of rain: and in some places we took it at the first for a smoke that had risen over some great town. For mine own part, I was well persuaded from thence to have returned, being a very ill footman, but the rest were all so desirous to go near the said strange thunder of waters, as they drew me on by little and little, till we came into the next valley, where we might better discern the same. I never saw a more beautiful country, nor more lively prospects, hills so raised here and there over the valleys, the river winding into divers branches, the plains adjoining without bush or stubble, all fair green grass, the ground of hard sand easy to march on, either for horse or foot, the deer crossing in every path, the birds towards the evening singing on every tree with a thousand several tunes, cranes and herons of white, crimson, and carnation perching on the river's side, the air fresh with a gentle easterly wind, and every stone that we stooped to take up, promised either gold or silver by his complexion.

The Discovery of the Large, Rich and Beautiful Empire of Guiana, 1596

The Dangers of Writing Contemporary History

I know that it will be said by many, that I might have been more pleasing to the reader, if I had written the history of mine own times; having been permitted to draw water as near the well-head as another. To this I answer, that whosoever in writing a modern history shall follow truth too near the heels, it may haply strike out his teeth. There is no mistress or guide that hath led her followers and servants into greater miseries. He that goes after her too far off loseth her sight, and loseth himself; and he that walks after her at a middle distance, I know not whether I should call that kind of course Temper or Baseness. It is true that I never travailed after men's opinions, when I might have made the best use of them; and I have now too few days remaining to imitate those that either out of extreme ambition, or extreme cowardice, or both, do yet (when death hath them on his shoulders) flatter the world, between the bed and the grave. It is enough for me (being in that state I am) to write of the eldest times; wherein also why may not it be said, that in speaking of the past, I point at the present, and tax the vices of those that are yet living, in their persons that are long since dead; and have it laid to my charge? But this I cannot help, though innocent. And certainly if there be any, that finding themselves spotted like the tigers of old time, shall find fault with me for painting them over anew, they shall therein accuse themselves justly, and me falsely.

The History of the World, 1614

Death

It is therefore Death alone that can suddenly make man to know himself. He tells the proud and insolent that they are but abjects, and humbles them at the instant; makes them cry, complain, and repent, yea, even to hate their forepassed happiness. He takes the account of the rich, and proves him a beggar; a naked beggar, which hath interest in nothing, but in the gravel that fills his mouth. He holds a glass before the eyes of the most beautiful, and makes them see therein their deformity and rottenness; and they acknowledge it.

O eloquent, just, and mighty Death! whom none could advise, thou hast persuaded; what none hath dared thou hast done; and whom all the world hath flattered, thou only hast cast out of the world and despised: thou hast drawn together all the far-stretched greatness, all the pride, cruelty, and ambition of man, and covered it all over with these two narrow words, *Hic jacet.*

The History of the World

RICHARD HAKLUYT
1552?–1616

English Explorers in the North-East Seas

But besides the aforesaid uncertainty, into what dangers and difficulties they plunged themselves, *Animus meminisse horret*, I tremble to recount. For first they were to expose themselves unto the rigour of the stern and uncouth northern seas, and to make trial of the swelling waves and boisterous winds which there commonly do surge and blow; then were they to sail by the ragged and perilous coast of Norway, to frequent the unhaunted shores of Finmark, to double the dreadful and misty North cape, to bear with Willoughbie's land, to run along within kenning of the countries of Lapland and Corelia, and as it were to open and unlock the sevenfold mouth of the Duina. Moreover, in their north-easterly navigations, upon the seas and by the coasts of Condora, Colgoieve, Petzora, Joughoria, Samoedia, Nova Zembla, etc., and their passing and return through the straits of Vaigatz, unto what drifts of snow and mountains of ice even in June, July and August, unto what hideous overfalls, uncertain currents, dark mists and fogs, and divers other fearful inconveniences they were subject and in danger of, I wish you rather to learn out of the voyages of Sir Hugh Willoughbie, Stephen Burrough, Arthur Pet and the rest, than to expect in this place an endless catalogue thereof. And here by the way I cannot but highly commend the great industry and magnanimity of the Hollanders, who within these few years have discovered to 78, yea (as they themselves affirm) to 81 degrees of northerly latitude; yet with this proviso, that our English nation led them the dance, brake the ice before them, and gave them good leave to light their candle at our torch.

Principal Navigations, Voyages, Traffics and Discoveries of the English Nation, Preface to the second edition, 1598

JOHN FLORIO
1553?–1625

[from the French of Montaigne]

The Power of Imagination

I am one of those who feel a very great conflict and power of imagination. All men are shocked therewith, and some overthrown by it. The impression of it pierceth me, and for want of strength to resist her, my endeavour is to avoid it. I could live with the only assistance of holy and merry-hearted men. The sight of others' anguish doth sensibly drive me into anguish: and my sense hath often usurped the sense of a third man. If one cough continually, he provokes my lungs and throat. I am more unwilling to visit the sick whom duty doth engage me to, than those to whom I am little beholding, and regard least. I apprehend the evil which I study, and place it in me. I deem it not strange that she brings both agues and death to such as give her scope to work her will, and applaud her.

Simon Thomas was a great physician in his days. I remember upon a time coming by chance to visit a rich old man that dwelt in Toulouse, and who was troubled with the cough of the lungs, who discoursing with the said Simon Thomas of the means of his recovery, he told him, that one of the best was, to give me occasion to be delighted in his company, and that fixing his eyes upon the liveliness and freshness of my face, and acting his thoughts upon the jollity and vigour, wherewith my youthful age did then flourish, and filling all his senses with my flourishing estate, his habitude might thereby be amended, and his health recovered. But he forgot to say, that mine might also be impaired and infected. Gallus Vibius did so well inure his mind to comprehend the essence and motions of folly, that he so transported his judgment from out his seat, as he could never afterward bring it to his right place again: and might rightly boast, to have become a fool through wisdom.

Some there be, that through fear anticipate the hangman's hand; as he did, whose friends having obtained his pardon, and putting away the cloth wherewith he was hood-winked, that he might hear it read, was found stark dead upon the scaffold, wounded only by the stroke of imagination. We sweat, we shake, we grow pale, and we blush at the motions of our imaginations; and wallowing in our beds we feel our bodies agitated and turmoiled at their apprehensions, yea in such manner, as sometimes we are ready to yield up the spirit. And burning youth (although asleep) is often therewith so possessed and enfolded, that dreaming it doth satisfy and enjoy her amorous desires.

'Of the force of Imagination', *The Essays of Michael Lord of Montaigne* (Florio's translation, 1603)

JOHN LYLY
1554?–1606

Advice to a Foreigner Visiting England

At thy coming into England be not too inquisitive of news, neither curious in matters of State, in assemblies ask no questions, either concerning manners or men. Be not lavish of thy tongue, either in causes of weight, lest thou shew thyself an espiall, or in wanton talk, lest thou prove thyself a fool. It is the nature of that country to sift strangers: everyone that shaketh thee by the hand, is not joined to thee in heart. They think Italians wanton, and Grecians subtle, they will trust neither, they are so incredulous, but undermine both, they are so wise. Be not quarrellous for every light occasion: they are impatient in their anger of any equal, ready to revenge an injury, but never wont to proffer any: they never fight without provoking, and once provoked they never cease. Beware thou fall not into the snares of love, the women there are wise, the men crafty: they will gather love by thy looks, and pick thy mind out of thy hands. It shall be there better to hear what they say, than to speak what thou thinkest. They have long ears and short tongues, quick to hear, and slow to utter, broad eyes and light fingers, ready to espy and apt to strike. Every stranger is a mark for them to shoot at: yet this must I say which in no country I can tell the like, that it is as seldom to see a stranger abused there, as it is rare to see any well used elsewhere. Yet presume not too much of the courtesies of those, for they differ in natures, some are hot, some cold, one simple, another wily; yet if thou use few words and fair speeches, thou shalt command anything thou standest in need of.

Euphues and His England, 1580

STEPHEN GOSSON
1554–1624

Theatre Audiences

In our assemblies at plays in London, you shall see such heaving, and shoving, such itching and shouldering to sit by women: such care for their garments, that they be not trod on: such eyes to their laps, that no chips light in them: such pillows to their backs, that they take no hurt: such masking in their ears, I know not what: such giving them pippins to pass the time: such playing at foot-saunt without cards: such tickling, such toying, such smiling, such winking, and such manning them home, when the sports are ended, that it is a right comedy to mark their behaviour, to watch their conceits, as the cat for the mouse, and as good as a course at the game itself, to dog them a little, or follow aloof by the print of their feet, and so discover by slot where the deer taketh soil. If this were as well noted as ill seen, or as openly punished as secretly practised, I have no doubt but the cause would be seared to dry up the effect, and these pretty rabbits very cunningly ferreted from their burrows. For they that lack customers all the week, either because their haunt is unknown or the constables and officers of their parish watch them so narrowly that they dare not quetch, to celebrate the sabbath flock to theatres, and there keep a general market of bawdry. Not that any filthiness in deed is committed within the compass of that ground, as was done in Rome, but that every wanton and his paramour, every man and his mistress, every John and his Joan, every knave and his quean, are there first acquainted and cheapen the merchandize in that place, which they pay for elsewhere as they can agree.

The School of Abuse, 1579

SIR PHILIP SIDNEY
1554–1586

An Ill-Natured King

This country whereon he fell was Phrygia, and it was to the king thereof to whom he was sent, a prince of a melancholy constitution both of body and mind; wickedly sad, ever musing of horrible matters, suspecting, or rather condemning all men of evil, because his mind had no eye to spy goodness: and therefore accusing Sycophants, of all men, did best sort to his nature . . . fearful, and never secure, while the fear he had figured in his own mind had any possibility of event. A toadlike retiredness, and closeness of mind; nature teaching the odiousness of poison, and the danger of odiousness. Yet while youth lasted in him, the exercises of that age, and his humour, not yet fully discovered, made him something the more frequentable, and less dangerous. But after that years began to come on with some, though more seldom, shows of a bloody nature, and that the prophecy of Musidorus's destiny came to his ears (delivered unto him, and received of him with the hardest interpretation, as though his subjects did delight in the hearing thereof). Then gave he himself indeed to the full current of his disposition, especially after the war of Thessalia, wherein, though in truth wrongly, he deemed his unsuccess proceeded of their unwillingness to have him prosper: and then thinking himself contemned (knowing no countermine against contempt, but terror) began to let nothing pass which might bear the colour of a fault without sharp punishment: and when he wanted faults, excellency grew a fault! and it was sufficient to make one guilty, that he had power to be guilty. And as there is no humour, to which impudent poverty cannot make itself serviceable, so were there enough of those of desperate ambition, who would build their houses upon other's ruins, which after should fall by like practices. So as a servitude came mainly upon that poor people, whose deeds were not only punished, but words corrected, and even thoughts by some mean or other pulled out of them; while suspicion bred the mind of cruelty, and the effects of cruelty stirred up a new cause of suspicion.

Arcadia, 1590

quetch] stir

A Wise Queen

This day it happened that divers famous knights came thither from the court of Helen Queen of Corinth; a lady whom fame at that time was so desirous to honour that she borrowed all men's mouths to join with the sound of her trumpet. For as her beauty hath won the prize from all women that stand in degree of comparison, for as for the two sisters of Arcadia, they are far beyond all conceit of comparison, so hath her government been such as hath been no less beautiful to men's judgments than her beauty to the eyesight. For being brought by right of birth, a woman, a young woman, a fair woman, to govern a people in nature mutinously proud, and always before so used to hard governors, that they knew not how to obey without the sword were drawn, could she for some years so carry herself among them, that they found cause in the delicacy of her sex, of admiration, not of contempt: and which was not able, even in the time that many countries about her were full of wars, which for old grudges to Corinth were thought still would conclude there, yet so handled she the matter, that the threatened ever smarted in the threateners; she using so strange, and yet so well succeeding a temper that she made her people by peace warlike; her courtiers by sports, learned; her ladies by love, chaste. For by continual martial exercises without blood, she made them perfect in that bloody art. Her sports were such as carried riches of knowledge upon the stream of delight: and such the behaviour both of herself and her ladies, as builded their chastity not upon waywardness, but choice of worthiness: so as it seemed that court to have been the marriage-place of love and virtue, and that herself was a Diana apparelled in the garments of Venus.

Arcadia

The Supreme Form of Teaching

The philosopher therefore and the historian are they which would win the goal, the one by precept, the other by example. But both, not having both, do both halt. For the philosopher, setting down with thorny argument the bare rule, is so hard of utterance and so misty to be conceived, that one that hath no other guide but him shall wade in him till he be old before he shall find sufficient cause to be honest. For his knowledge standeth so upon the abstract and general, that happy is that man who may understand him, and more happy that can apply what he doth understand. On the other side the historian, wanting the precept, is so tied, not to what should be but to what is, to the particular truth of things and not to the general reason of things, that his example draweth no necessary consequence, and therefore a less fruitful doctrine.

Now doth the peerless poet perform both: for whatsoever the

philosopher saith should be done, he giveth a perfect picture of it in someone by whom he presupposeth it was done; so as he coupleth the general notion with the particular example. A perfect picture I say, for he yieldeth to the powers of the mind an image of that whereof the philosopher bestoweth but a wordish description: which doth neither strike, pierce, nor possess the sight of the soul so much as that other doth.

For as in outward things, to a man that had never seen an elephant or a rhinoceros, who should tell him most exquisitely all their shapes, colour, bigness, and particular marks, or of a gorgeous palace the architecture, with declaring the full beauties might well make the hearer able to repeat, as it were by rote, all he had heard, yet should never satisfy his inward conceits with being witness to itself of a true lively knowledge: but the same man, as soon as he might see those beasts well painted, or the house well in model, should straightways grow, without need of any description, to a judicial comprehending of them: so no doubt the philosopher with his learned definition—be it of virtue, vices, matters of public policy or private government—replenisheth the memory with many infallible grounds of wisdom, which, notwitstanding, lie dark before the imaginative and judging power, if they be not illuminated or figured forth by the speaking picture of poesy.

The Defence of Poesy, first published 1595

Poetry and the Praise of Valour

Is it the Lyric that most displeaseth, who with his tuned lyre and well-accorded voice, giveth praise, the reward of virtue, to virtuous acts; who gives moral precepts, and natural problems; who sometimes raiseth up his voice to the height of the heavens, in singing the lauds of the immortal God? Certainly, I must confess my own barbarousness, I never heard the old song of Percy and Douglas that I found not my heart moved more than with a trumpet; and yet is it sung but by some blind crowder, with no rougher voice than rude style; which, being so evil apparelled in the dust and cobwebs of that uncivil age, what would it work trimmed in the gorgeous eloquence of Pindar? In Hungary I have seen it the manner at all feasts, and other such meetings, to have songs of their ancestors' valour, which that right soldierlike nation think one of the chiefest kindlers of brave courage. The incomparable Lacedemonians did not only carry that kind of music ever with them to the field, but even at home, as such songs were made, so were they all content to be singers of them—when the lusty men were to tell what they did, the old men what they had done, and the young what they would do.

The Defence of Poesy

crowder] fiddler

RICHARD HOOKER
1554–1600

Defending the Social Order

He that goeth about to persuade a multitude, that they are not so well governed as they ought to be, shall never want attentive and favourable hearers; because they know the manifold defects whereunto every kind of regiment is subject; but the secret lets and difficulties, which in public proceedings are innumerable and inevitable, they have not ordinarily the judgment to consider. And because such as openly reprove supposed disorders of State, are taken for principal friends to the common benefit of all, and for men that carry singular freedom of mind; under this fair and plausible colour, whatsoever they utter, passeth for good and current. That which wanteth in the weight of their speech, is supplied by the aptness of men's minds to accept and believe it. Whereas on the other side, if we maintain things that are established, we have not only to strive with a number of heavy prejudices, deeply rooted in the hearts of men, who think that herein we serve the time, and speak in favour of the present State, because thereby we either hold or seek preferment; but also to bear such exceptions as minds, so averted beforehand, usually take against that which they are loath should be poured into them.

Of the Laws of Ecclesiastical Polity, 1594

The Laws of Nature

Now if Nature should intermit her course, and leave altogether, though it were but for a while, the observation of her own laws; if those principal and mother elements of the world, whereof all things in this lower world are made, should lose the qualities which now they have; if the frame of that heavenly arch erected over our heads should loosen and dissolve itself; if celestial spheres should forget their wonted motions, and by irregular volubility turn themselves any way as it might happen; if the prince of the lights of Heaven, which now as a giant doth run his unwearied course, should as it were through a languishing faintness begin to stand and to rest himself; if the moon should wander from her beaten way, the times and seasons of the year blend themselves by disordered and confused mixture, the winds breathe out their last gasp, the clouds yield no rain, the earth be defeated of heavenly influence, the fruits of the earth pine away as children at the withered breasts of their mother no longer able to yield them relief; what would become of man himself, whom these things now do all serve? See we not plainly, that obedience of creatures unto the law of nature is the stay of the whole world?

Of the Laws of Ecclesiastical Polity

The Pursuit of Happiness

Now if men had not naturally this desire to be happy how were it possible that all men should have it? All men have. Therefore this desire in man is natural. It is not in our power not to do the same; how should it then be in our power to do it coldly or remissly? So that our desire being natural is also in that degree of earnestness whereunto nothing can be added. And is it probable that God should frame the hearts of all men so desirous of that which no man may obtain? It is an axiom of Nature that natural desire cannot utterly be frustrate. This desire of ours being natural should be frustrate, if that which may satisfy the same were a thing impossible for man to aspire unto. Man doth seek a triple perfection: first a sensual, consisting in those things which very life itself requireth either as necessary supplements, or as beauties and ornaments thereof; then an intellectual, consisting in those things which none underneath man is either capable of or acquainted with; lastly a spiritual and divine, consisting in those things whereunto we tend by supernatural means here, but cannot here attain unto them. They who make the first of these three the scope of their whole life, are said by the Apostle to have no god but only their belly, to be earthly-minded men. Unto the second they bend themselves, who seek especially to excel in all such knowledge and virtue as doth most commend men. To this branch belongeth the law of moral and civil perfection. That there is somewhat higher than either of these two, no other proof doth need than the very process of man's desire, which being natural should be frustrate, if there were not some farther thing wherein it might rest at the length contented, which in the former it cannot do. For man doth not seem to rest satisfied, either with fruition of that wherewith his life is preserved, or with performance of such actions as advance him most deservedly in estimation; but doth further covet, yea oftentimes manifestly pursue with great sedulity and earnestness, that which cannot stand him in any stead for vital use; that which exceedeth the reach of sense; yea somewhat above capacity of reason, somewhat divine and heavenly, which with hidden exultation it rather surmiseth than conceiveth; somewhat it seeketh, and what that is directly it knoweth not, yet very intentive desire thereof doth so incite it, that all other known delights and pleasures are laid aside, they give place to the search of this but only suspected desire. If the soul of man did serve only to give him being in this life, then things appertaining unto this life would content him, as we see they do other creatures; which creatures enjoying what they live by seek no further, but in this contentation do show a kind of acknowledgement that there is no higher good which doth any way belong unto them. With us it is otherwise. For although the beauties, riches, honours, sciences, virtues, and perfections of all men living, were in the present possession of one; yet somewhat beyond and above all this there would still be sought and earnestly thirsted for. So that Nature even in this life doth plainly claim and call for a more divine perfection than either of these two that have been mentioned.

Of the Laws of Ecclesiastical Polity

FULKE GREVILLE, LORD BROOKE
1554–1628

Sir Philip Sidney's Fatal Wound

When that unfortunate stand was to be made before Zutphen to stop the issuing out of the Spanish army from a straight, with what alacrity soever he went to actions of honour, yet remembering that upon just grounds the ancient sages describe the worthiest persons to be ever best armed, he had completely put on his; but meeting the marshal of the camp lightly armed (whose honour in that art would not suffer this unenvious Themistocles to sleep) the unspotted emulation of his heart, to venture without any inequality, made him cast off his cuisses; and so, by the secret influence of destiny, to disarm that part where God, it seems, had resolved to strike him. Thus they go on, every man in the head of his own troop; and, the weather being misty, fell unawares upon the enemy who had made a strong stand to receive them near to the very walls of Zutphen; by reason of which accident their troops fell not only unexpectedly to be engaged within the level of the great shot that played from the rampiers, but more fatally within shot of their muskets which were laid in ambush within their own trenches.

Now whether this were a desperate cure in our leaders for a desperate disease; or whether misprision, neglect, audacity or what else induced it, it is no part of my office to determine, but only to make the narration clear and deliver rumour, as it passed then, without any stain or enamel.

However, by this stand, an unfortunate hand out of those fore-spoken trenches, brake the bone of Sir Philip's thigh with a musket-shot. The horse he rode upon was rather furiously choleric than bravely proud and so forced him to forsake the field, but not his back, as the noblest and fittest bier to carry a martial commander to his grave. In which sad progress, passing along by the rest of the army where his uncle the General was and being thirsty with excess of bleeding, he called for drink, which was presently brought him; but as he was putting the bottle to his mouth, he saw a poor soldier carried along, who had eaten his last at the same feast, ghastly casting up his eyes at the bottle. Which Sir Philip perceiving, took it from his head before he drank and delivered it to the poor man with these words, 'Thy necessity is yet greater than mine.' And when he had pledged this poor soldier, he was presently carried to Arnheim.

The Life of Sir Philip Sidney, first published 1652

NICHOLAS BRETON
1555?–1626

December

It is now December, and he that walks the streets shall find dirt on his shoes, except he go all in boots. Now doth the lawyer make an end of his harvest, and the client of his purse. Now capons and hens, beside turkeys, geese and ducks, besides beef and mutton, must all die for the great feast, for in twelve days a multitude of people will not be fed with a little. Now plums and spice, sugar and honey, square it among pies and broth, and Gossip I drink to you, and you are welcome, and I thank you, and how do you, and I pray you be merry. Now are the tailors and the tiremakers full of work against the holidays, and musick now must be in tune, or else never; the youth must dance and sing, and the aged sit by the fire. It is the law of nature, and no contradiction in reason. The ass that hath borne all the year must now take a little rest, and the lean ox must feed till he be fat; the footman now shall have many a foul step, and the ostler shall have work enough about the heels of the horses, while the tapster, if he take not heed, will be drunk in the cellar. The price of meat will rise apace, and the apparel of the proud will make the tailor rich; dice and cards will benefit the butler; and if the cook do not lack wit, he will sweetly lick his fingers. Starchers and launderers will have their hands full of work, and periwigs and painting will not be a little set by, strange stuffs will be well sold, strange tales well told, strange sights much sought, strange things much bought; and what else as falls out.

Fantasticks, 1604(?)

ROBERT GREENE
1558–1592

The Improvident Poet

I espied afar off a certain kind of an overworn gentleman attired in velvet and satin, but it was somewhat dropped and greasy, and boots on his legs, whose soles waxed thin and seemed to complain of their master, which treading thrift under his feet had brought them unto that consumption. He walked not as other men in the common beaten way, but came compassing *circumcirca*, as if we had been devils, and he would draw a circle about us, and at every third step he looked back as if he were afraid of a bailey or a sergeant . . .

A poet is a waste-good and an unthrift, that he is born to make the taverns rich and himself a beggar. If he have forty pound in his purse together, he puts it not to usury, neither buys land nor merchandise with it, but a month's commodity of wenches and capons. Ten pound a supper, why 'tis nothing, if his plough goes and his ink-horn be clear. Take one of them with twenty thousand pounds and hang him. He is a king of his pleasure, and counts all other boors and peasants that, though they have money at command, yet know not like him how to domineer with it to any purpose as they should. But to speak plainly, I think him an honest man, if he would but live within his compass, and generally no man's foe but his own.

A Quip for an Upstart Courtier, 1592

A Warning to Fellow-Writers against Shakespeare and the Actors

Base-minded men all three of you, if by my misery ye be not warned; for unto none of you (like me) sought those burs to cleave,—those antics garnished in our colours. Is it not strange that I, to whom they all have been beholden,—is it not like that you, to whom they all have been beholden,—shall (were ye in that case that I am now) be both at once of them forsaken? Yes, trust them not: for there is an upstart crow, beautified with our feathers, that with his *tiger's heart wrapt in a player's hide*, supposes he is as well able to bombast out a blank-verse as the best of you: and being an absolute *Johannes factotum*, is in his own conceit the only *Shakescene* in a country. Oh, that I might entreat your rare wits to be employed in more profitable courses, and let those apes imitate your past excellence, and never more acquaint them with your admired inventions! I know the best husband of you all will never prove an usurer, and the kindest of them all will never prove a kind nurse: yet, whilst you may, seek you better masters; for it is pity men of such rare wits should be subject to the pleasures of such rude grooms.

Greene's Groats-worth of Wit bought with a Million of Repentance, 1592

THOMAS LODGE
1558?–1625

A Lover's Sonnet Called in Question

[Ganymede is Rosalynde in disguise]

Now surely, forester (quoth *Aliena*), when thou madest this sonnet thou wert in some amorous quandary, neither too fearful, as despairing of thy mistress' favours, nor too gleesome, as hoping in thy fortunes.

I can smile (quoth *Ganymede*) at the sonettoes, canzones, madrigals, rounds and roundelays, that these pensive patients pour out, when their eyes are more full of wantonness than their hearts of passions. Then, as the fishers put the sweetest bait to the fairest fish, so these Ovidians (holding *Amo* in their tongues, when their thoughts are hap-hazard) write that they be wrapt in an endless labyrinth of sorrow, when walking in the large lease of liberty they only have their humours in their inkpot. If they find women so fond, that they will with such painted lures come to their lust, then they triumph till they be full gorged with pleasures; and then they fly away (like ramage kites) to their own content, leaving the tame fool their mistress full of fancy, yet without ever a feather. If they miss (as dealing with some wary wanton, that wants not such a one as themselves, but spies their subtlety), they end their amours with a few feigned sighs: amd so their excuse is, their mistress is cruel, and they smother passions with patience. Such, gentle forester, we may deem you to be, that rather pass away the time here in these woods with writing amorets than to be deeply enamoured (as you say) of your Rosalynde. If you be such a one, then I pray God, when you think your fortunes at the highest, and your desires to be most excellent, then that you may with Ixion embrace Juno in a cloud, and have nothing but a marble mistress to release your martyrdom: but if you be true and trusty, eye-pained and heart-sick, then accursed be Rosalynde if she prove cruel: for forester (I flatter not), thou art worthy of as fair as she.

Aliena, spying the storm by the wind, smiled to see how Ganymede flew to the fist without any call . . .

Rosalynde, Euphues' Golden Legacy, 1590

ramage] untamed

SIR RANULPHE CREWE
1558–1646

Ubi Sunt

And yet time hath his revolutions; there must be a period and an end to all temporal things, *finis rerum*, an end of whatsoever is terrene; and why not of De Vere? Where is Bohun, where's Mowbray, where's Mortimer? Nay, which is more and most of all, where is Plantagenet? They are entombed in the urns and sepulchres of mortality. And yet let the name and dignity of De Vere stand so long as it pleaseth God.

Oxford peerage case, 1625

THOMAS HARIOT
1560–1621

The Religion of the Natives of Virginia

Some religion they have already, which although it be far from the truth, yet being as it is, there is hope it may be the easier and sooner reformed.

They believe that there are many gods, which they call *Mantóac*, but of different sorts and degrees, one only chief and great god, which hath been from all eternity. Who, as they affirm, when he purposed to make the world, made first other gods of a principal order to be as means and instruments to be used in the creation and government to follow, and after the sun, moon, and stars as petty gods, and the instruments of the other order more principal. First, they say, were made waters, out of which by the gods was made all diversity of creatures that are visible or invisible.

For mankind, they say a woman was made first which, by the working of one of the gods, conceived and brought forth children. And in such sort, they say, they had their beginning. But how many years or ages have passed since, they say they can make no relation, having no letters nor other such means as we to keep records of the particularities of times past, but only tradition from father to son.

They think that all the gods are of human shape, and therefore, they represent them by images in the forms of men, which they call *Kewasówok*, one alone is called *Kewás*. These they place in houses appropriate or temples, which they call *Machicómuck*, where they worship, pray, sing, and make many times offering unto them. In some Machicómuck, we have seen but one Kewas, in some two, and in other some three. The common sort think them to be also gods.

They believe also the immortality of the soul that, after this life as soon as the soul is departed from the body, according to the works it hath done, it is either carried to heaven, the habitacle of gods, there to enjoy perpetual bliss and happiness, or else to a great pit or hole, which they think to be in the furthest parts of their part of the world toward the sunset, there to burn continually. The place they call *Popogusso.*

A Brief and True Report of the New-found Land of Virginia, 1588; published in Hakluyt, *Principal Navigations*, 1600

FRANCIS BACON, VISCOUNT ST ALBANS
1561–1626

The Student's Prayer

To God the Father, God the Word, God the Spirit, we pour forth most humble and hearty supplications; that He, remembering the calamities of mankind and the pilgrimage of this our life, in which we wear out days few and evil, would please to open to us new refreshments out of the fountains of his goodness, for the alleviating of our miseries. This also we humbly and earnestly beg, that Human things may not prejudice such as are Divine; neither that from the unlocking of the gates of sense, and the kindling of a greater natural light, anything of incredulity or intellectual night may arise in our minds towards the Divine Mysteries. But rather that by our mind throughly cleansed and purged from fancy and vanities, and yet subject and perfectly given up to the Divine Oracles, there may be given unto Faith the things that are Faith's. Amen.

n.d.; first published 1679

Cobwebs of Speculation

Surely, like as many substances in nature which are solid do putrefy and corrupt into worms, so it is the property of good and sound knowledge to putrefy and dissolve into a number of subtile, idle, unwholesome, and (as I may term them) vermiculate questions, which have indeed a kind of quickness and life of spirit, but no soundness of matter or goodness of quality. This kind of degenerate learning did chiefly reign amongst the schoolmen; who having sharp and strong wits, and abundance of leisure, and small variety of reading; but their wits being shut up in the cells of a few authors (chiefly Aristotle their dictator) as their persons were shut up in the cells of monasteries and colleges; and knowing little history, either of nature or time; did out of no great quantity of matter, and infinite agitation of wit, spin out unto us those laborious webs of learning which are extant in their books. For the wit and mind of man, if it work upon matter, which is the contemplation of the creatures of God, worketh according to the stuff, and is limited thereby; but if it work upon itself, as the spider worketh his web, then it is endless, and brings forth indeed cobwebs of learning, admirable for the fineness of thread and work, but of no substance or profit.

The Advancement of Learning, 1605

The Furthest End of Knowledge

But the greatest error of all the rest is the mistaking or misplacing of the last or furthest end of knowledge. For men have entered into a desire of learning and knowledge, sometimes upon a natural curiosity and inquisitive appetite; sometimes to entertain their minds with variety and delight; sometimes for ornament and reputation; and sometimes to enable them to victory of wit and contradiction; and most times for lucre and profession; and seldom sincerely to give a true account of their gift of reason, to the benefit and use of men: as if there were sought in knowledge a couch, whereupon to rest a searching and restless spirit; or a terrace, for a wandering and variable mind to walk up and down with a fair prospect; or a tower of state, for a proud mind to raise itself upon; or a fort or commanding ground, for strife and contention; or a shop, for profit or sale; and not a rich storehouse, for the glory of the Creator and the relief of man's estate.

The Advancement of Learning

Across Seas of Time

We see then how far the monuments of wit and learning are more durable than the monuments of power or of the hands. For have not the verses of Homer continued twenty-five hundred years or more, without the loss of a syllable or letter; during which time infinite palaces, temples, castles, cities, have been decayed and demolished? It is not possible to have the true pictures or statuaes of Cyrus, Alexander, Caesar, no nor of the kings or great personages of much later years; for the originals cannot last, and the copies cannot but leese of the life and truth. But the images of men's wits and knowledges remain in books, exempted from the wrong of time and capable of perpetual renovation. Neither are they fitly to be called images, because they generate still, and cast their seeds in the minds of others, provoking and causing infinite actions and opinions in succeeding ages. So that if the invention of the ship was thought so noble, which carrieth riches and commodities from place to place, and consociateth the most remote regions in participation of their fruits, how much more are letters to be magnified, which as ships pass through the vast seas of time, and make ages so distant to participate of the wisdom, illuminations, and inventions, the one of the other?

The Advancement of Learning

What Is Truth?

'What is truth?' said jesting Pilate; and would not stay for an answer. Certainly there be that delight in giddiness, and count it a bondage to fix a belief; affecting free will in thinking, as well as in acting. And though the sects of philosophers of that kind be gone, yet there remain certain discoursing wits, which are of the same veins, though there be not so much blood in them as was in those of the ancients. But it is not only the difficulty and labour which men take in finding out of truth; nor again, that when it is found, it imposeth upon men's thoughts, that doth bring lies in favour; but a natural though corrupt love of the lie itself. One of the later school of the Grecians examineth the matter, and is at a stand to think what should be in it, that men should love lies, where neither they make for pleasure, as with poets, nor for advantage, as with the merchant, but for the lie's sake. But I cannot tell: this same truth is a naked and open daylight, that doth not show the masks and mummeries and triumphs of the world half so stately and daintily as candlelights. Truth may perhaps come to the price of a pearl, that showeth best by day, but it will not rise to the price of a diamond or carbuncle, that showeth best in varied lights. A mixture of a lie doth ever add pleasure. Doth any man doubt that if there were taken out of men's minds vain opinions, flattering hopes, false valuations, imaginations as one would, and the like, but it would leave the minds of a number of men poor shrunken things, full of melancholy and indisposition, and unpleasing to themselves?

'Of Truth', *Essays*, 1625

Parents and Children

The joys of parents are secret, and so are their griefs and fears. They cannot utter the one, nor they will not utter the other. Children sweeten labours, but they make misfortunes more bitter. They increase the cares of life, but they mitigate the remembrance of death. The perpetuity by generation is common to beasts, but memory, merit and noble works are proper to men; and surely a man shall see the noblest works and foundations have proceeded from childless men, which have sought to express the images of their minds, when those of their body have failed. So the care of posterity is most in them that have no posterity. They that are the first raisers of their houses are most indulgent towards their children; beholding them as the continuance, not only of their kind but of their work; and so both children and creatures.

'Of Parents and Children', *Essays*, 1625

The Optical Triumphs of New Atlantis

'We have also perspective-houses, where we make demonstrations of all lights and radiations; and of all colours; and out of things uncoloured and transparent, we can represent unto you all several colours; not in rainbows, as it is in gems and prisms, but of themselves single. We represent also all multiplications of light, which we carry to great distance, and make so sharp as to discern small points and lines; also all colorations of light: all delusions and deceits of the sight, in figures, magnitudes, motions, colours: all demonstrations of shadows. We find also divers means, yet unknown to you, of producing of light originally from divers bodies. We procure means of seeing objects afar off; as in the heaven and remote places; and represent things near as afar off, and things afar off as near; making feigned distances. We have also helps for the sight, far above spectacles and glasses in use. We have also glasses and means to see small and minute bodies perfectly and distinctly; as the shapes and colours of small flies and worms, grains and flaws in gems, which cannot otherwise be seen; observations in urine and blood, not otherwise to be seen. We make artificial rain-bows, halos, and circles about light. We represent also all manner of reflexions, refractions, and multiplications of visual beams of objects.'

New Atlantis, 1627

SAMUEL DANIEL
1562–1619

This Manifold Creature Man

It is not books, but only that great book of the world, and the all overspreading grace of Heaven that makes men truly judicial. Nor can it but touch of arrogant ignorance, to hold this or that nation barbarous, these or those times gross, considering how this manifold creature man, wheresoever he stand in the world, hath always some disposition of worth, entertains the order of society, affects that which is most in use, and is eminent in some one thing or other that fits his humour and the times. The Grecians held all other nations barbarous but themselves; yet Pyrrhus, when he saw the well-ordered marching of the Romans, which made them see their presumptuous error, could say it was no barbarous manner of proceeding. The Goths, Vandals and Longobards, whose coming down like an inundation overwhelmed, as they say, all the glory of learning in Europe, have yet left us still their laws and customs, as the originals of most of the provincial constitutions of Christendom; which well considered with their other courses of government, may serve to clear them from this imputation of ignorance. And though the vanquished never speak well of the conqueror, yet even through the unsound coverings of malediction appear those monuments of truth, as argue well their worth, and prove them not without judgment, though without Greek and Latin.

A Defence of Rhyme, 1603

WILLIAM SHAKESPEARE
1564–1616

Bottom's Dream

Heigh-ho! Peter Quince? Flute, the bellows-mender? Snout, the tinker? Starveling? God's my life! Stolen hence, and left me asleep! I have had a most rare vision. I have had a dream, past the wit of man to say what dream it was. Man is but an ass if he go about to expound this dream. Methought I was—there is no man can tell what. Methought I was—and methought I had—but man is but a patched fool if he will offer to say what methought I had. The eye of man hath not heard, the ear of man hath not seen, man's hand is not able to taste, his tongue to conceive, nor his heart to report, what my dream was. I will get Peter Quince to write a ballad of this dream: it shall be called 'Bottom's Dream', because it hath no bottom; and I will sing it in the latter end of a play, before the Duke. Peradventure, to make it the more gracious, I shall sing it at her death.

A Midsummer Night's Dream, c.1594–5

Harry Hotspur

I am not yet of Percy's mind, the Hotspur of the north; he that kills me some six or seven dozen of Scots at a breakfast, washes his hands, and says to his wife, 'Fie upon this quiet life! I want work.' 'O my sweet Harry,' says she, 'how many hast thou kill'd to-day?' 'Give my roan horse a drench,' says he; and answers, 'Some fourteen,' an hour after,—'a trifle, a trifle.'

1 Henry IV, c.1596

Falstaff Plays the King

—Harry, I do not only marvel where thou spendest thy time, but also how thou art accompanied; for though the camomile, the more it is trodden on, the faster it grows, yet youth, the more it is wasted, the sooner it wears. That thou art my son I have partly thy mother's word, partly my own opinion, but chiefly a villainous trick of thine eye and a foolish hanging of thy nether lip that doth warrant me. If then thou be son to me, here lies the point: why, being son to me, art thou so pointed at? Shall the blessed sun of heaven prove a micher and eat blackberries? A question not to be asked. Shall the son of England prove a thief and take purses? A question to be asked. There is a thing, Harry, which thou hast often heard of, and it is known to many in our land by the name of pitch. This pitch, as ancient writers do report, doth defile; so doth the company thou keepest. For, Harry, now I do not speak to thee in drink, but in tears; not in pleasure, but in passion; not in words only, but in woes also. And yet there is a virtuous man whom I have often noted in thy company, but I know not his name.

Prince Henry. What manner of man, an it like your majesty?

Falstaff. A goodly portly man, i'faith, and a corpulent; of a cheerful look, a pleasing eye, and a most noble carriage; and, as I think, his age some fifty, or, by'r lady, inclining to threescore; and now I remember me, his name is Falstaff. If that man should be lewdly given, he deceiveth me; for, Harry, I see virtue in his looks. If then the tree may be known by the fruit, as the fruit by the tree, then, peremptorily I speak it, there is virtue in that Falstaff. Him keep with, the rest banish . . .

1 Henry IV

The Death of Falstaff

Bardolph. Would I were with him, wheresome'er he is, either in heaven or in hell!

Hostess. Nay sure, he's not in hell: he's in Arthur's bosom, if ever man went to Arthur's bosom: a' made a finer end, and went away an it had been any christom child: a' parted e'en just between twelve and one, e'en at the turning o'th'tide: for after I saw him fumble with the sheets, and play with flowers, and smile upon his finger's end, I knew there was but one way: for his nose was as sharp as a pen, and a' babbled of green fields. 'How now, Sir John?' quoth I. 'What, man! be o' good cheer': so a' cried out, 'God, God, God!' three or four times: now I, to comfort him, bid him a' should not think of God; I hoped there was no need to trouble himself with any such thoughts yet: so a' bad me lay more clothes on his feet: I put my hand into the bed, and felt them, and they were as cold as any stone: then I felt to his knees, and so up'ard and up'ard, and all was as cold as any stone.

Henry V, c.1599

Monmouth and Macedon

Gower. I think Alexander the Great was born in Macedon: his father was call'd Philip of Macedon, as I take it.

Fluellen. I think it is in Macedon where Alexander is porn. I tell you, captain, if you look in the maps of the 'orld, I warrant you sall find, in the comparisons between Macedon and Monmouth, that the situations, look you, is both alike. There is a river in Macedon; and there is also moreover a river at Monmouth: it is called Wye at Monmouth; but it is out of my prains what is the name of the other river; but 'tis all one, 'tis alike as my fingers is to my fingers, and there is salmons in both.

Henry V

The Marks of Love

Rosalind. There is none of my uncle's marks upon you: he taught me how to know a man in love; in which cage of rushes I am sure you are not prisoner.

Orlando. What were his marks?

Rosalind. A lean cheek,—which you have not; a blue eye and sunken,—which you have not; an unquestionable spirit,—which you have not; a beard neglected,—which you have not;—but I pardon you for that; for simply your having in beard is a younger brother's revenue:—then your hose should be ungarter'd, your bonnet unbanded, your sleeve unbutton'd, your shoe untied, and every thing about you demonstrating a careless desolation;—but you are no such a man,—you are rather point-devise in your accoutrements, as loving yourself than seeming the lover of any other.

*As You Like It, c.*1599–1600

Fathom Deep

O coz, coz, coz, my pretty little coz, that thou didst know how many fathom deep I am in love! But it cannot be sounded: my affection hath an unknown bottom, like the bay of Portugal.

As You Like It

Man Delights Not Me

I have of late—but wherefore I know not—lost all my mirth, forgone all custom of exercises; and indeed it goes so heavily with my disposition that this good frame, the earth, seems to me a sterile promontory; this most excellent canopy, the air, look you, this brave o'er-hanging firmament, this majestical roof fretted with golden fire, why, it appears no other thing to me than a foul and pestilent congregation of vapours. What a piece of work is man! How noble in reason! how infinite in faculty! in form, in moving, how express and admirable! in action how like an angel! in apprehension how like a god! the beauty of the world! the paragon of animals! And yet, to me, what is this quintessence of dust? Man delights not me; no, nor woman neither, though, by your smiling you seem to say so.

Hamlet, c.1601–2

Yorick

Alas, poor Yorick!—I knew him, Horatio: a fellow of infinite jest, of most excellent fancy: he hath borne me on his back a thousand times; and now, how abhorred in my imagination it is! my gorge rises at it. Here hung those lips that I have kist I know not how oft. Where be your gibes now? your gambols? your songs? your flashes of merriment, that were wont to set the table on a roar? Not one now, to mock your own grinning? quite chop-faln? Now get you to my lady's chamber, and tell her, let her paint an inch thick, to this favour she must come; make her laugh at that.

Hamlet

Good and Ill Together

The web of our life is of a mingled yarn, good and ill together: our virtues would be proud, if our faults whipt them not: and our crimes would despair, if they were not cherisht by our virtues.

All's Well That Ends Well, c.1602

Handy-Dandy

King Lear. See how yond justice rails upon yond simple thief. Hark, in thine ear: change places; and, handy-dandy, which is the justice, which is the thief?—Thou hast seen a farmer's dog bark at a beggar?

Earl of Gloucester. Ay, sir.

King Lear. And the creature run from the cur? There thou mightst behold the great image of authority: a dog's obey'd in office.

King Lear, c.1605–6

A Soldier's Son

Valeria. How does your little son?

Virgilia. I thank your ladyship; well, good madam.

Volumnia. He had rather see the swords, and hear a drum, than look upon his schoolmaster.

Valeria. O'my word, the father's son: I'll swear, 'tis a very pretty boy. O'my troth, I lookt upon him o'Wednesday half an hour together: has such a confirm'd countenance. I saw him run after a gilded butterfly; and when he caught it, he let it go again; and after it again; and over and over he comes, and up again; catcht it again: or whether his fall enraged him, or how 'twas, he did so set his teeth, and tear it: O, I warrant, how he mammockt it!

Volumnia. One on's father's moods.

Coriolanus, c.1608

THOMAS CAMPION
1567–1620

The Procrustes Bed of Rhyme

But there is yet another fault in Rhyme altogether intolerable, which is, that it enforceth a man oftentimes to abjure his matter and extend a short conceit beyond all bounds of art; for in quatorzains, methinks, the poet handles his subject as tyrannically as Procrustes the thief his prisoners, whom, when he had taken, he used to cast upon a bed which if they were too short to fill, he would stretch them longer, if too long, he would cut them shorter. Bring before me now any the most self-loved rhymer, and let me see if without blushing he be able to read his lame halting rhymes. Is there not a curse of nature laid upon such rude Poesy, when the writer is himself ashamed of it, and the hearers in contempt call it rhyming and ballading? What divine in his sermon, or grave counsellor in his oration, will allege the testimony of a rhyme? But the divinity of the Romans and Grecians was all written in verse; and Aristotle, Galen, and the books of all the excellent philosophers are full of the testimonies of the old poets. By them was laid the foundation of all human wisdom, and from them the knowledge of all antiquity is derived. I will propound but one question, and so conclude this point. If the Italians, Frenchmen, and Spaniards, that with commendation have written in rhyme, were demanded whether they had rather the books they have published (if their tongue would bear it) should remain as they are in rhyme or be translated into the ancient numbers of the Greeks and Romans, would they not answer, Into numbers? What honour were it then for our English language to be the first that after so many years of barbarism could second the perfection of the industrious Greeks and Romans?

Observations in the Art of English Poesy, 1602

THOMAS NASHE
1567–1601

Mistress Minx

In another corner Mistress Minx, a merchant's wife, that will eat no cherries, forsooth, but when they are at twenty shillings a pound; that looks as simperingly as if she were besmeared, and jets it as gingerly as if she were dancing the Canaries. She is so finical in her speech as though she spake nothing but what she had first sewed over before in her samplers, and the puling accent of her voice is like a feigned treble, or one's voice that interprets to the puppets. What should I tell how squeamish she is in her diet, what toil she puts her poor servants unto to make her looking-glasses in the pavement—how she will not go into the fields to cower on the green grass but she must have a coach for her convoy, and spends half a day in pranking herself if she be invited to any strange place? Is not this the excess of pride, Signor Satan? Go to, you are unwise if you make her not a chief saint in your calendar.

Pierce Penniless his Supplication to the Devil, 1592

An Exhortation to Drunkards

Gentlemen—all you that will not have your brains twice sodden, your flesh rotten with the dropsy, that love not to go in greasy doublets, stockings out at the heels, and wear alehouse daggers at your backs—, forswear this slavering bravery that will make you have stinking breaths and your bodies smell like brewers' aprons. Rather keep a snuff in the bottom of the glass to light you to bed withal than leave never an eye in your head to lead you over the threshold. It will bring you in your old age to be companions with none but porters and car-men, to talk out of a cage railing as drunken men are wont, a hundred boys wondering about them, and to die suddenly, as Fol Long the fencer did, drinking aqua vitae. From which, as all the rest, good Lord deliver Pierce Penniless.

Pierce Penniless

Dreams and Anxieties

A dream is nothing else but a bubbling scum or froth of the fancy, which the day hath left undigested; or an after-feast made of the fragments of idle imaginations. How many sorts there be of them, no man can rightly set down, since it scarce hath been heard there were ever two men that dreamed alike. Divers have written diversely of their causes, but the best reason among them all that I could ever pick out was this: that, as an arrow which is shot out of a bow is sent forth many times with such force that it flyeth far beyond the mark whereat it was aimed, so our thoughts, intentively fixed all the day-time upon a mark we are to hit, are now and then overdrawn with such force that they fly beyond the mark of the day into the confines of the night. There is no man put to any torment but quaketh and trembleth a great while after the executioner hath withdrawn his hand from him. In the day-time we torment our thoughts and imaginations with sundry cares and devices; all the night-time they quake and tremble after the terror of their late suffering, and still continue thinking of the perplexities they have endured. To nothing more aptly can I compare the working of our brains after we have unyoked and gone to bed than to the glimmering and dazzling of a man's eyes when he comes newly out of the bright sun into the dark shadow. Even as one's eyes glimmer and dazzle when they are withdrawn out of the light into darkness, so are our thoughts troubled and vexed when they are retired from labour to ease, and from skirmishing to surgery. You must give a wounded man leave to groan while he is in dressing: dreaming is no other than groaning while sleep, our surgeon, hath us in cure.

The Terrors of the Night, 1593

City of Disdain

In London, the rich disdain the poor. The courtier the citizen. The citizen the country man. One occupation disdaineth another. The merchant the retailer. The retailer the craftsman. The better sort of craftsmen the baser. The shoemaker the cobbler. The cobbler the carman. One nice dame disdains her next neighbour should have that furniture to her house, or dainty dish or device, which she wants. She will not go to church, because she disdains to mix herself with base company, and cannot have her close pew by herself. She disdains to wear that everyone wears, or hear that preacher which everyone hears. So did Jerusalem disdain God's prophets, because they came in the likeness of poor men. She disdained Amos, because he was a keeper of oxen, as also the rest, for they were of the dregs of the people. But their disdain prospered not with them. Their house, for their disdain, was left desolate unto them.

Christ's Tears over Jerusalem, 1593

Ambitious Dust

The dust in the streets—being come of the same house that we are of, and seeing us so proud and ambitious—thinks with herself why should not she, that is descended as well as we, raise up her plumes as we do? And that's the reason she borrows the wings of the wind so oft to mount into the air; and many times she dasheth herself in our eyes as who should say 'Are you my kinsmen and will not know me?' O, what is it to be ambitious when the dust of the street, when it pleaseth her, can be ambitious?

Christ's Tears over Jerusalem

An Exhortation against Puritans

In the days of Nero there was an odd fellow that had found out an exquisite way to make glass as hammerproof as gold; shall I say that the like experiment he made upon glass, we have practised on the Gospel? Ay, confidently will I. We have found out a sleight to hammer it to any heresy whatsoever. But those furnaces of falsehood and hammerheads of heresy must be dissolved and broken as his was, or else I fear me the false glittering glass of innovation will be better esteemed of than the ancient gold of the Gospel.

The Unfortunate Traveller, 1594

Robbery, Murder, and Rape

Therewith he flew upon her and threatened her with his sword—but it was not that he meant to wound her with. He grasped her by the ivory throat and shook her as a mastiff would shake a young bear, swearing and staring he would tear out her weasand if she refused. Not content with that savage constraint, he slipped his sacrilegious hand from her lily lawn-skinned neck and enscarfed it in her long silver locks, which with struggling were unrolled. Backward he dragged her even as a man backward would pluck a tree down by the twigs; and then—like a traitor that is drawn to execution on a hurdle—he traileth her up and down the chamber by those tender untwisted braids, and, setting his barbarous foot on her bare, snowy breast, bade her yield or have her wind stamped out. She cried 'Stamp, stifle me in my hair, hang me up by it on a beam and so let me die, rather than I should go to heaven with a beam in my eye.'

'No,' quoth he, 'nor stamped, nor stifled, nor hanged, nor to heaven shalt thou go till I have had my will of thee. Thy busy arms in these silken fetters I'll enfold.'

Dismissing her hair from his fingers, and pinioning her elbows therewithal, she struggled, she wrested; but all was in vain. So struggling, and so resisting, her jewels did sweat, signifying there was poison coming towards her. On the hard boards he threw her, and used his knee as an iron ram to beat ope the two-leaved gate of her chastity. Her husband's dead body he made a pillow to his abomination. Conjecture the rest. My words stick fast in the mire and are clean tired. Would I had never undertook this tragical tale. Whatsoever is born is born to have an end. Thus ends my tale: his whorish lust was glutted; his beastly desire satisfied. What in the house of any worth was carriageable he put up, and went his way.

The Unfortunate Traveller

Hero and the Drowning of Leander

Down she ran in her loose nightgown, and her hair about her ears (even as Semiramis ran out with her lye-pot in her hand, and her black dangling tresses about her shoulders, with her ivory comb ensnarled in them, when she heard that Babylon was taken) and thought to have kissed his dead corpse alive again. But, as on his blue-jellied-sturgeon lips she was about to clap one of those warm plasters, boisterous wool-packs of ridged tides came rolling in and raught him from her, with a mind, belike, to carry him back to Abydos. At that she became a frantic bacchanal outright, and made no more bones but sprang after him, and so resigned up her priesthood, and left work for Musaeus and Kit Marlowe.

Nashe's Lenten Stuff, 1599

THOMAS DEKKER
1570?–1632

The Streets of London

In every street, carts and coaches make such a thundering as if the world ran upon wheels: at every corner, men, women and children meet in such shoals, that posts are set up of purpose to strengthen the houses, lest with jostling one another they should shoulder them down. Besides, hammers are beating in one place, tubs hooping in another, pots clinking in a third, water-tankards running at tilt in a fourth. Here are porters sweating under burdens, their merchant's men bearing bags of money. Chapmen (as if they were at leap frog) skip out of one shop into another. Tradesmen (as if they were dancing galliards) are lusty at legs and never stand still. All are as busy as country attorneys at an assizes.

The Seven Deadly Sins of London, 1606

In Praise of Sleep

For do but consider what an excellent thing sleep is: it is so inestimable a jewel, that, if a tyrant would give his crown for an hour's slumber, it cannot be bought: of so beautiful a shape is it, that, though a man lie with an empress, his heart cannot be at quiet till he leaves her embracements to be at rest with the other: yea, so greatly indebted are we to this kinsman of death, that we owe the better tributary half of our life to him; and there's good cause why we should do so, for sleep is that golden chain that ties health and our bodies together. Who complains of want, of wounds, of cares, of great men's oppressions, of captivity, whilst he sleepeth? Beggars in their beds take as much pleasure as kings. Can we therefore surfeit on this delicate ambrosia? Can we drink too much of that, whereof to taste too little tumbles us into a churchyard; and to use it but indifferently throws us into Bedlam? No, no! Look upon Endymion, the Moon's minion, who slept threescore and fifteen years; and was not a hair the worse for it.

The Gull's Hornbook, 1609

THE ENGLISH BIBLE: III
From the Authorized Version (1611)

Wrestling Jacob

And he rose up that night, and took his two wives, and his two women servants, and his eleven sons, and passed over the ford Jabbok. And he took them, and sent them over the brook, and sent over that he had.

And Jacob was left alone; and there wrestled a man with him, until the breaking of the day. And when he saw that he prevailed not against him, he touched the hollow of his thigh: and the hollow of his thigh was out of joint, as he wrestled with him. And he said, Let me go, for the day breaketh: and he said, I will not let thee go, except thou bless me.

And he said unto him, What is thy name? and he said, Jacob. And he said, Thy name shall be called no more Jacob, but Israel: for as a prince hast thou power with God, and with men, and hast prevailed. And Jacob asked him, and said, Tell me, I pray thee, thy name; and he said, Wherefore is it, that thou dost ask after my name? and he blessed him there.

And Jacob called the name of the place Peniel: for I have seen God face to face, and my life is preserved.

Genesis 32: 22–30

David's Lament for Saul and Jonathan

Saul and Jonathan were lovely and pleasant in their lives, and in their death they were not divided: they were swifter than eagles, they were stronger than lions. Ye daughters of Israel, weep over Saul, who clothed you in scarlet, with other delights, who put on ornaments of gold upon your apparel.

How are the mighty fallen in the midst of the battle! O Jonathan, thou wast slain in thine high places. I am distressed for thee, my brother Jonathan: very pleasant hast thou been unto me: thy love to me was wonderful, passing the love of women.

How are the mighty fallen, and the weapons of war perished!

2 Samuel 1: 23–7

The Horse

Hast thou given the horse strength? hast thou clothed his neck with thunder? Canst thou make him afraid as a grasshopper? the glory of his nostrils is terrible.

He paweth in the valley, and rejoiceth in his strength: he goeth on to meet the armed men. He mocketh at fear, and is not affrighted; neither turneth he back from the sword. The quiver rattleth against him, the glittering spear and the shield.

He swalloweth the ground with fierceness and rage: neither believeth he that it is the sound of the trumpet. He saith among the trumpets, Ha, ha; and he smelleth the battle afar off, the thunder of the captains, and the shouting.

Job 39: 19–25

The Young Man and the Harlot

For at the window of my house I looked through my casement, and beheld among the simple ones, I discerned among the youths, a young man void of understanding, passing through the street near her corner; and he went the way to her house, in the twilight, in the evening, in the black and dark night.

And, behold, there met him a woman with the attire of an harlot, and subtle of heart. (She is loud and stubborn; her feet abide not in her house. Now she is without, now in the streets, and lieth in wait at every corner.) So she caught him and kissed him, and with an impudent face said unto him, I have peace offerings with me; this day have I payed my vows. Therefore came I forth to meet thee, diligently to seek thy face, and I have found thee. I have decked my bed with coverings of tapestry, with carved works, with fine linen of Egypt. I have perfumed my bed with myrrh, aloes and cinnamon. Come, let us take our fill of love until the morning; let us solace ourselves with loves.

Proverbs 7: 6–18

Youth and Age

Rejoice, O young man, in thy youth; and let thy heart cheer thee in the days of thy youth, and walk in the ways of thine heart, and in the sight of thine eyes: but know thou, that for all these things God will bring thee into judgment. Therefore remove sorrow from thy heart, and put away evil from thy flesh: for childhood and youth are vanity. Remember now thy Creator in the days of thy youth, while the evil days come not, nor the years draw nigh, when thou shalt say, I have no pleasure in them; while the sun, or the light, or the moon, or the stars, be not darkened, nor the clouds return after the rain: in the day when the keepers of the house shall tremble, and the strong men shall bow themselves, and the grinders cease, because they are few, and those that look out of the windows be darkened, and the doors shall be shut in the streets, when the sound of the grinding is low, and he shall rise up at the voice of the bird, and all the daughters of music shall be brought low; also when they shall be afraid of that which is high, and fears shall be in the way, and the almond tree shall flourish, and the grasshopper shall be a burden, and desire shall fail: because man goeth to his long home, and the mourners go about the streets: or ever the silver cord be loosed, or the golden bowl be broken, or the pitcher be broken at the fountain, or the wheel broken at the cistern. Then shall the dust return to the earth as it was: and the spirit shall return unto God who gave it.

Ecclesiastes 11: 9–10, 12: 1–7

Love

Set me as a seal upon thine heart, as a seal upon thine arm: for love is strong as death; jealousy is cruel as the grave: the coals thereof are coals of fire, which hath a most vehement flame. Many waters cannot quench love, neither can the floods drown it: if a man would give all the substance of his house for love, it would be utterly contemned.

Song of Solomon 8: 6–7

Words of Comfort

Comfort ye, comfort ye my people, saith your God, speak ye comfortably to Jerusalem, and cry unto her that her warfare is accomplished, that her iniquity is pardoned: for she hath received of the Lord's hand double for all her sins.

The voice of him that crieth in the wilderness, Prepare ye the way of the Lord, make straight in the desert a highway for our God. Every valley shall be exalted, and every mountain and hill shall be made low: and the crooked shall be made straight, and the rough places plain; and the glory of the Lord shall be revealed, and all flesh shall see it together: for the mouth of the Lord hath spoken it.

The voice said, Cry. And he said, What shall I cry? All flesh is grass, and all the goodliness thereof as the flower of the field: the grass withereth, the flower fadeth, because the spirit of the Lord bloweth upon it: surely the people is grass. The grass withereth and the flower fadeth, but the word of our God shall stand for ever. . . .

Isaiah 40: 1–8

How Beautiful upon the Mountains

How beautiful upon the mountains are the feet of him that bringeth good tidings, that publisheth peace; that bringeth good tidings of good, that publisheth salvation; that saith unto Zion, Thy God reigneth! Thy watchmen shall lift up the voice; with the voice together shall they sing: for they shall see eye to eye, when the Lord shall bring again Zion.

Isaiah 52: 7–8

Consider the Lilies

Therefore I say unto you, Take no thought for your life, what ye shall eat, or what ye shall drink; nor yet for your body, what ye shall put on. Is not the life more than meat, and the body than raiment?

Behold the fowls of the air; for they sow not, neither do they reap, nor gather into barns; yet your heavenly Father feedeth them. Are ye not much better than they? Which of you by taking thought can add one cubit unto his stature? And why take ye thought for raiment? Consider the lilies of the field, how they grow; they toil not, neither do they spin: and yet I say unto you, That even Solomon in all his glory was not arrayed like one of these.

Matthew 6: 25–9

Nunc Dimittis

And, behold, there was a man in Jerusalem, whose name was Simeon; and the same man was just and devout, waiting for the consolation of Israel: and the Holy Ghost was upon him. And it was revealed unto him by the Holy Ghost, that he should not see death, before he had seen the Lord's Christ. And he came by the Spirit into the temple: and when the parents brought in the child Jesus, to do for him after the

custom of the law, then took he him up in his arms, and blessed God, and said,
Lord, now lettest thou thy servant depart in peace,
According to thy word:
For mine eyes have seen thy salvation,
Which thou hast prepared before the face of all people;
A light to lighten the Gentiles,
And the glory of thy people Israel.

Luke 2: 25–32

St Paul in Athens

Then Paul stood in the midst of Mars' hill, and said, Ye men of Athens, I perceive that in all things ye are too superstitious. For as I passed by, and beheld your devotions, I found an altar with this inscription, TO THE UNKNOWN GOD. Whom therefore ye ignorantly worship, him declare I unto you. God that made the world and all things therein, seeing that he is Lord of heaven and earth, dwelleth not in temples made with hands; neither is worshipped with men's hands, as though he needed any thing, seeing he giveth to all life, and breath, and all things; and hath made of one blood all nations of men for to dwell on all the face of the earth, and hath determined the times before appointed, and the bounds of their habitation; that they should seek the Lord, if haply they might feel after him, and find him, though he be not far from every one of us: for in him we live, and move, and have our being; as certain also of your own poets have said, For we are also his offspring. Forasmuch then as we are the offspring of God, we ought not to think that the Godhead is like unto gold, or silver, or stone, graven by art and man's device. And the times of this ignorance God winked at; but now commandeth all men every where to repent: because he hath appointed a day, in the which he will judge the world in righteousness by that man whom he hath ordained; whereof he hath given assurance unto all men, in that he hath raised him from the dead.

And when they heard of the resurrection of the dead, some mocked: and others said, We will hear thee again of this matter. So Paul departed from among them. Howbeit certain men clave unto him, and believed: among the which was Dionysius the Areopagite, and a woman named Damaris, and others with them.

Acts 17: 22–34

JOHN DONNE
1572–1631

A Weary Round

The covetous man lies still, and attends his quarter days, and studies the endorsements of his bonds, and he wonders that the ambitious man can endure the shufflings and thrustings of courts, and can measure his happiness by the smile of a greater man; and he that does so wonders as much, that this covetous man can date his happiness by the almanack, and such revolutions, and though he have quick returns of receipt, yet scarce affords himself bread to live till that day come, and though all his joy be in his bonds, yet denies himself a candle's end to look upon them. Hilly ways are wearisome ways, and tire the ambitious man; carnal pleasures are dirty ways, and tire the licentious man; desires of gain are thorny ways, and tire the covetous man; emulations of higher men, are dark and blind ways, and tire the envious man; every way, that is out of the way, wearies us. But, *lassati sumus, sed lassis non datur requies*; we labour, and have no rest when we are done; we are wearied with our sins, and have no satisfaction in them; we go to bed tonight, weary of our sinful labours, and we will rise freshly tomorrow, to the same sinful labours again; and when a sinner does so little remember yesterday, how little does he consider tomorrow? He that forgets what he hath done, foresees not what he shall suffer; so sin is a burden; it crookens us, it wearies us.

Fifty Sermons (1649), Sermon 23, preached after 1616

Unceasing Arrows

Every temptation, every tribulation is not deadly. But their multiplicity disorders us, discomposes us, unsettles us, and so hazards us. Not only every periodical variation of our years, youth and age, but every day hath a divers arrow, every hour of the day a divers temptation. An old man wonders then, how an arrow from an eye could wound him, when he was young, and how love could make him do those things which he did then; and an arrow from the tongue of inferior people, that which we make shift to call honour, wounds him deeper now; and ambition makes him do as strange things now, as love did then. A fair day shoots arrows of visits, and comedies, and conversation, and so we go abroad; and a foul day shoots arrows of gaming, or chambering, and wantonness, and so we stay at home.

Fifty Sermons, Sermon 19, preached after 1616

The Pervasiveness of Pride

O the earliness! O the lateness! how early a Spring, and no Autumn! how fast a growth, and no declination, of this branch of this sin Pride, against which this first word of ours, *Sequere*, Follow, come after, is opposed! This love of place, and precedency, it rocks us in our cradle, it lies down with us in our graves. There are diseases proper to certain things, rots to sheep, murrain to cattle. There are diseases proper to certain places, as the sweat was to us. There are diseases proper to certain times, as the plague is in divers parts of the Eastern countries, where they know assuredly, when it will begin and end. But for this infectious disease of precedency, and love of place, it is run over all places, as well cloisters as courts, and over all men, as well spiritual as temporal, and over all times, as well the Apostles' as ours.

LXXX Sermons (1640), Sermon 72, preached 1619

Ex Nihilo

The drowning of the first world, and the repairing that again; the burning of this world, and establishing another in heaven, do not so much strain a man's reason, as the Creation, a Creation of all out of nothing. For, for the repairing of the world after the Flood, compared to the Creation, it was eight to nothing; eight persons to begin a world upon, then; but in the Creation, none. And for the glory which we receive in the next world, it is (in some sort) as the stamping of a print upon a coin; the metal is there already, a body and a soul to receive glory; but at the Creation, there was no soul to receive glory, no body to receive a soul, no stuff, no matter, to make a body of. The less anything is, the less we know it; how invisible, how unintelligible a thing then, is this Nothing! We say in the School, *Deus cognoscibilior Angelis*, We have better means to know the nature of God, than of angels, because God hath appeared and manifested himself more in actions, than angels have done; we know what they are, by knowing that they have done, and it is very little related to us, what angels have done. What then is there that can bring this Nothing to our understanding? What hath that done? A Leviathan, a whale, from a grain of spawn; an oak, from a buried acorn, is a great; but a great world from nothing, is a strange improvement. We wonder to see a man rise from nothing to a great estate, but that nothing is but nothing in comparison; but absolutely nothing, merely nothing, is more incomprehensible than anything, than all things together.

XXVI Sermons (1660), Sermon 25, preached 1622

Impotent Assistances

How barren a thing is arithmetic! (and yet arithmetic will tell you how many single grains of sand will fill this hollow vault to the firmament). How empty a thing is rhetoric! (and yet rhetoric will make absent and remote things present to your understanding). How weak a thing is poetry! (and yet poetry is a counterfeit creation, and makes things that are not, as though they were). How infirm, how impotent are all assistances, if they be put to express this Eternity!

LXXX Sermons, Sermon 26, preached 1622

When the Body Fails

The heavens are not the less constant, because they move continually, because they move continually one and the same way. The earth is not the more constant, because it lies still continually, because continually it changes and melts in all the parts thereof. Man, who is the noblest part of the earth, melts so away, as if he were a statue, not of earth, but of snow. We see his own envy melts him, he grows lean with that; he will say, another's beauty melts him; but he feels that a fever doth not melt him like snow, but pour him out like lead, like iron, like brass melted in a furnace; it doth not only melt him, but calcine him, reduce him to atoms, and to ashes; not to water, but to lime. And how quickly? Sooner than thou canst receive an answer, sooner than thou canst conceive the question; earth is the centre of my body, heaven is the centre of my soul; these two are the natural places of these two; but those go not to these two in an equal pace: my body falls down without pushing; my soul does not go up without pulling; ascension is my soul's pace and measure, but precipitation my body's. And even angels, whose home is heaven, and who are winged too, yet had a ladder to go to heaven by steps. The sun which goes so many miles in a minute, the stars of the firmament which go so very many more, go not so fast as my body to the earth. In the same instant that I feel the first attempt of the disease, I feel the victory; in the twinkling of an eye I can scarce see; instantly the taste is insipid and fatuous; instantly the appetite is dull and desireless; instantly the knees are sinking and strengthless; and in an instant, sleep, which is the picture, the copy of death, is taken away, that the original, death itself, may succeed, and that so I might have death to the life. It was part of Adam's punishment, *In the sweat of thy brows thou shalt eat thy bread*: it is multiplied to me, I have earned bread in the sweat of my brows, in the labour of my calling, and I have it; and I sweat again and again, from the brow to the sole of the foot, but I eat no bread, I taste no sustenance: miserable distribution of mankind, where one half lacks meat, and the other stomach!

Devotions upon Emergent Occasions, 1624

A Tolling Bell

Perchance he for whom this bell tolls may be so ill, as that he knows not it tolls for him; and perchance I may think myself so much better than I am, as that they who are about me, and see my state, may have caused it to toll for me, and I know not that. The church is Catholic, universal, so are all her actions; all that she does belongs to all. When she baptizes a child, that action concerns me; for that child is thereby connected to that body which is my head too, and ingrafted into that body whereof I am a member. And when she buries a man, that action concerns me: all mankind is of one author, and is one volume; when one man dies, one chapter is not torn out of the book, but translated into a better language; and every chapter must be so translated; God employs several translators; some pieces are translated by age, some by sickness, some by war, some by justice; but God's hand is in every translation, and his hand shall bind up all our scattered leaves again for that library where every book shall lie open to one another. As therefore the bell that rings to a sermon calls not upon the preacher only, but upon the congregation to come, so this bell calls us all; but how much more me, who am brought so near the door by this sickness. There was a contention as far as a suit (in which both piety and dignity, religion and estimation, were mingled), which of the religious orders should ring to prayers first in the morning; and it was determined, that they should ring first that rose earliest. If we understand aright the dignity of this bell that tolls for our evening prayer, we would be glad to make it ours by rising early, in that application, that it might be ours as well as his, whose indeed it is. The bell doth toll for him that thinks it doth; and though it intermit again, yet from that minute that that occasion wrought upon him, he is united to God. Who casts not up his eye to the sun when it rises? but who takes off his eye from a comet when that breaks out? Who bends not his ear to any bell which upon any occasion rings? but who can remove it from that bell which is passing a piece of himself out of this world? No man is an island, entire of itself; every man is a piece of the continent, a part of the main. If a clod be washed away by the sea, Europe is the less, as well as if a promontory were, as well as if a manor of thy friend's or of thine own were: any man's death diminishes me, because I am involved in mankind, and therefore never send to know for whom the bells tolls; it tolls for thee. Neither can we call this a begging of misery, or a borrowing of misery, as though we were not miserable enough of ourselves, but must fetch in more from the next house, in taking upon us the misery of our neighbours. Truly it were an excusable covetousness if we did, for affliction is a treasure, and scarce any man hath enough of it. No man hath affliction enough that is not matured and ripened by it, and made fit for God by that affliction. If a man carry treasure in bullion, or in a wedge of gold, and have none coined into current money, his treasure will not defray him as he travels. Tribulation is treasure in the nature of it, but it is not current money in the use of it, except we get nearer and nearer our home, heaven, by it. Another man may be sick too, and sick to death, and this affliction may lie in his bowels, as gold in a mine, and be of no use to him; but this bell, that tells me of his affliction, digs out and applies that gold to me: if by this consideration of another's danger I take mine own into contemplation, and so secure myself, by making my recourse to my God, who is our only security.

Devotions upon Emergent Occasions

BEN JONSON

1573–1637

A Chronicle of Lost Time

What a deal of cold business doth a man misspend the better part of life in! In scattering compliments, tendering visits, gathering and venting news, following feasts and plays, making a little winter-love in a dark corner.

Timber, or Discoveries, 1641

An Age of Slander

The time was, when men would learn, and study good things; not envy those that had them. Then men were had in price for learning: now letters only make men vile. He is upbraidingly called a poet, as if it were a most contemptible nickname. But the professors (indeed) have made the learning cheap. Railing, and tinkling rhymers, whose writings the vulgar more greedily read; as being taken with the scurrility, and petulancy of such wits. He shall not have a reader now, unless he jeer and lie. It is the food of men's natures: the diet of the times! Gallants cannot sleep else. The writer must lie, and the gentle reader rests happy, to hear the worthiest works misinterpreted; the clearest actions obscured; the innocentest life traduced; and in such a licence of lying, a field so fruitful of slanders, how can there be matter wanting to his laughter? Hence comes the epidemical infection. For how can they escape the contagion of the writings, whom the virulency of the calumnies hath not staved off from reading?

Nothing doth more invite a greedy reader, than an unlooked-for subject. And what more unlooked-for, than to see a person of an unblamed life, made ridiculous, or odious by the artifice of lying? But it is the disease of the age: and no wonder if the world, growing old, begin to be infirm: old age itself is a disease. It is long since the sick world began to dote, and talk idly: would she had but doted still; but her dotage is now broke forth into a madness, and become a mere frenzy.

Timber, or Discoveries

Shakespeare

I remember, the players have often mentioned it as an honour to Shakespeare, that in his writing (whatsoever he penned) he never blotted out line. My answer hath been, would he had blotted a thousand. Which they thought a malevolent speech. I had not told posterity this, but for their ignorance, who choose that circumstance to commend their friend by, wherein he most faulted. And to justify mine own candour (for I loved the man, and do honour his memory—on this side idolatry—as much as any). He was (indeed) honest, and of an open, and free nature: had an excellent fancy; brave notions, and gentle expressions: wherein he flowed with that facility, that sometime it was necessary he should be stopped: *sufflaminandus erat*; as Augustus said of Haterius. His wit was in his own power; would the rule of it had been so too. Many times he fell into those things, could not escape laughter: as when he said in the person of Caesar, one speaking to him; 'Caesar, thou dost me wrong'. He replied: 'Caesar did never wrong, but with just cause': and such like; which were ridiculous. But he redeemed his vices, with his virtues. There was ever more in him to be praised, than to be pardoned.

Timber, or Discoveries

An Index of the Mind

There cannot be one colour of the mind; another of the wit. If the mind be staid, grave, and composed, the wit is so; that vitiated, the other is blown, and deflowered. Do we not see, if the mind languish, the members are dull? Look upon an effeminate person: his very gait confesseth him. If a man be fiery, his motion is so: if angry, 'tis troubled, and violent. So that we may conclude: wheresoever manners, and fashions are corrupted, language is. It imitates the public riot. The excess of feasts, and apparel, are the notes of a sick state; and the wantonness of language, of a sick mind.

Timber, or Discoveries

SAMUEL PURCHAS
1575?–1626

Xanadu

In Xamdu did Cublai Can build a stately palace, encompassing sixteen miles of plain ground with a wall, wherein are fertile meadows, pleasant springs, delightful streams, and all sorts of beasts of chase and game, and in the midst thereof a sumptuous house of pleasure, which may be removed from place to place. Here he doth abide in the months of June, July and August, on the eight and twentieth day whereof, he departeth thence to another place to do sacrifice in this manner. He hath a herd or drove of horses and mares, about ten thousand, as white as snow; of the milk whereof none may taste except he be of the blood of Cingis Can. Yea, the Tartars do these beasts great reverence, nor dare any cross their way, or go before them. According to the directions of his astrologers or magicians, he on the eight and twentieth day of August aforesaid spendeth and poureth forth the milk of these mares in the air, and on the earth, to give drink to the spirits and idols which they worship, that they may preserve the men, women, beasts, birds, corn and other things growing on the earth.

Purchas His Pilgrimage, 1617

ROBERT BURTON
1577–1640

A Wicked World

What's the market? A place, according to Anacharsis, wherein they cozen one another, a trap; nay, what's the world itself? A vast chaos, a confusion of manners, as fickle as the air, *domicilium insanorum*, a turbulent troop full of impurities, a mart of walking spirits, goblins, the theatre of hypocrisy, a shop of knavery, flattery, a nursery of villainy, the scene of babbling, the school of giddiness, the academy of vice; a warfare, *ubi velis nolis pugnandum, aut vincas aut succumbas*, in which kill or be killed; wherein every man is for himself, his private ends, and stands upon his own guard. No charity, love, friendship, fear of God, alliance, affinity,

domicilium insanorum] a madhouse   *ubi velis . . . aut succumbas*] where you have to fight whether you will or no, and either conquer or go under

consanguinity, Christianity, can contain them, but if they be anyways offended, or that string of commodity be touched, they fall foul. Old friends become bitter enemies on a sudden for toys and small offences, and they that erst were willing to do all mutual offices of love and kindness, now revile and persecute one another to death, with more than Vatinian hatred, and will not be reconciled. So long as they are behoveful, they love, or may bestead each other, but when there is no more good to be expected, as they do by an old dog, hang him up or cashier him: which Cato counts a great indecorum, to use men like old shoes or broken glasses, which are flung to the dunghill; he could not find in his heart to sell an old ox, much less to turn away an old servant: but they, instead of recompense, revile him, and when they have made him an instrument of their villainy, as Bajazet the Second, Emperor of the Turks, did by Acomethes Bassa, make him away, or instead of reward, hate him to death, as Silius was served by Tiberius. In a word, every man for his own ends. Our *summum bonum* is commodity, and the goddess we adore *Dea Moneta*, Queen Money, to whom we daily offer sacrifice, which steers our hearts, hands, affections, all: that most powerful goddess, by whom we are reared, depressed, elevated, esteemed the sole commandress of our actions, for which we pray, run, ride, go, come, labour, and contend as fishes do for a crumb that falleth into the water. It is not worth, virtue (that's *bonum theatrale*), wisdom, valour, learning, honesty, religion, or any sufficiency for which we are respected, but money, greatness, office, honour, authority; honesty is accounted folly; knavery, policy; men admired out of opinion, not as they are, but as they seem to be: such shifting, lying, cogging, plotting, counterplotting, temporizing, flattering, cozening, dissembling, 'that of necessity one must highly offend God if he be conformable to the world,' *Cretizare cum Crete*, 'or else live in contempt, disgrace, and misery.'

The Anatomy of Melancholy, 1621; successive editions until 1651

A Bitter Jest

Tiberius the emperor withheld a legacy from the people of Rome, which his predecessor Augustus had lately given, and perceiving a fellow round a dead corse in the ear, would needs know wherefore he did so; the fellow replied, that he wished the departed soul to signify to Augustus, the commons of Rome were yet unpaid: for this bitter jest the emperor caused him forthwith to be slain, and carry the news himself.

The Anatomy of Melancholy

bonum theatrale] a theatrical good *Cretizare cum Crete*] to do at Crete as the Cretans do

Melancholy Men: Some Classic Symptoms

Suspicion and jealousy are general symptoms: they are commonly distrustful, apt to mistake, and amplify, *facile irascibiles*, testy, pettish, peevish, and ready to snarl upon every small occasion, *cum amicissimis*, and without a cause, *datum vel non datum*, it will be *scandalum acceptum*. If they speak in jest, he takes it in good earnest. If they be not saluted, invited, consulted with, called to counsel, etc., or that any respect, small compliment, or ceremony be omitted, they think themselves neglected and contemned; for a time that tortures them. If two talk together, discourse, whisper, jest, or tell a tale in general, he thinks presently they mean him, applies all to himself, *de se putat omnia dici*. Or if they talk with him, he is ready to misconster every word they speak, and interpret it to the worst; he cannot endure any man to look steadily on him, speak to him almost, laugh, jest, or be familiar, or hem, or point, cough, or spit, or make a noise sometimes, etc. He thinks they laugh or point at him, or do it in disgrace of him, circumvent him, contemn him; every man looks at him, he is pale, red, sweats for fear and anger, lest somebody should observe him. He works upon it, and long after this false conceit of an abuse troubles him.

The Anatomy of Melancholy

A Stubborn Delusion

Felix Platerus, *Observat. lib.* 1, hath a most memorable example of a countryman of his, that by chance falling into a pit where frogs and frogs' spawn was, and a little of that water swallowed, began to suspect that he had likewise swallowed frogs' spawn, and with that conceit and fear his phantasy wrought so far, that he verily thought he had young live frogs in his belly *qui vivebant ex alimento suo*, that lived by his nourishment, and was so certainly persuaded of it, that for many years following he could not be rectified in his conceit. He studied physic seven years together to cure himself, travelled into Italy, France and Germany to confer with the best physicians about it, and *anno* 1609, asked his counsel amongst the rest; he told him it was wind, his conceit, etc., but *mordicus contradicere et ore et scriptis probare nitebatur*: no saying would serve; it was no wind, but real frogs: 'and do you not hear them croak?'

The Anatomy of Melancholy

cum amicissimis] with their dearest friends *datum vel non datum . . . scandalum acceptum*] they will take offence, whether it is given or not

'O Cupid'

At Abdera in Thrace (*Andromeda*, one of Euripides' tragedies, being played), the spectators were so much moved with the object, and those pathetical love-speeches of Perseus (amongst the rest, 'O Cupid, prince of gods and men,' etc.), that every man almost, a good while after, spake pure iambics, and raved still on Perseus' speech, 'O Cupid, prince of gods and men.' As carmen, boys, and prentices, when a new song is published with us, go singing that new tune still in the streets, they continually acted that tragical part of Perseus, and in every man's mouth was 'O Cupid,' in every street, 'O Cupid,' in every house almost, 'O Cupid prince of gods and men,' pronouncing still like stage-players, 'O Cupid'; they were so possessed all with that rapture, and thought of that pathetical love-speech, they could not a long time after forget, or drive it out of their minds, but 'O Cupid, prince of gods and men,' was ever in their mouths.

The Anatomy of Melancholy

The Cause of All Good Conceits

This love is the cause of all good conceits, neatness, exornations, plays, elegancies, delights, pleasant expressions, sweet motions and gestures, joys, comforts, exultancies, and all the sweetness of our life; *Qualis jam vita foret, aut quid jucundi sine aurea Venere? Emoriar cum ista non amplius mihi cura fuerit*, let me live no longer than I may love, saith a mad merry fellow in Mimnermus. This love is that salt that seasoneth our harsh and dull labours, and gives a pleasant relish to our other unsavoury proceedings; *Absit amor, surgunt tenebræ, torpedo, veternum, pestis, etc.* All our feasts almost, masques, mummings, banquets, merry meetings, weddings, pleasing songs, fine tunes, poems, love stories, plays, comedies, Atellanes, jigs, Fescennines, elegies, odes, etc., proceed hence. Danaus, the son of Belus, at his daughter's wedding at Argos, instituted the first plays (some say) that ever were heard of. Symbols, emblems, impresses, devices, if we shall believe Jovius, Contiles, Paradine, Camillus de Camillis, may be ascribed to it. Most of our arts and sciences; painting amongst the rest was first invented, saith Patricius, *ex amoris beneficio*, for love's sake. For when the daughter of Dibutades the Sicyonian was to take leave of her sweetheart now going to wars, *ut desiderio ejus minus tabesceret*, to comfort herself in his absence, she took his picture with coal upon a wall, as the candle gave the shadow, which her father admiring perfected afterwards, and it was the first picture by report that ever was made. And long after, Sicyon for

Qualis . . . aurea Venere] what would life be, what joy would there be, without golden Aphrodite? *Absit amor . . . pestis, etc.*] when love departs, there enter darkness, sluggishness, senility, disease, etc.

painting, carving, statuary, music, and philosophy, was preferred before all the cities in Greece. Apollo was the first inventor of physic, divination, oracles; Minerva found out weaving, Vulcan curious ironwork, Mercury letters; but who prompted all this into their heads? Love. *Nunquam talia invenissent, nisi talia adamassent*, they loved such things, or some party, for whose sake they were undertaken at first.

The Anatomy of Melancholy

Religion's Ape

A lamentable thing it is to consider, how many myriads of men this idolatry and superstition (for that comprehends all) hath infatuated in all ages, besotted by this blind zeal, which is religion's ape, religion's bastard, religion's shadow, false glass. For where God hath a temple, the devil will have a chapel: where God hath sacrifices, the devil will have his oblations: where God hath ceremonies, the devil will have his traditions: where there is any religion, the devil will plant superstition; and 'tis a pitiful sight to behold and read what tortures, miseries it hath procured, what slaughter of souls it hath made, how it raged amongst those old Persians, Syrians, Egyptians, Greeks, Romans, Tuscans, Gauls, Germans, Britons, etc.

The Anatomy of Melancholy

THOMAS CORYATE
1577?–1617

A Domestic Novelty

Here I will mention a thing that might have been spoken of before, in discourse of the first Italian town. I observed a custom in all those Italian cities and towns through the which I passed, that is not used in any other country that I saw in my travels, neither do I think that any other nation of Christendom doth use it, but only Italy. The Italians, and also most strangers that are commorant in Italy, do always at their meals use a little fork when they cut their meat. For while with their knife, which they hold in one hand, they cut the meat out of the dish, they fasten their fork which they hold in their other hand upon the same dish, so that whatsoever he be that, sitting in the company of any others at meal, should unadvisedly touch the dish of meat with his fingers from which all at the table do cut, he will give occasion of offence unto the company, as having transgressed the laws of good manners, in so much that for his

commorant] resident

error he shall be at the least brow-beaten if not reprehended in words. This form of feeding I understand is generally used in all places of Italy, their forks being for the most part made of iron or steel, and some of silver, but those are used only by gentlemen. The reason of this their curiosity is, because the Italian cannot by any means endure to have his dish touched with fingers, seeing all men's fingers are not alike clean. Hereupon I myself thought good to imitate the Italian fashion by this forked cutting of meat, not only while I was in Italy, but also in Germany, and oftentimes in England since I came home: being once equipped for that frequent using of my fork by a certain learned gentleman, a familiar friend of mine, one Mr Laurence Whitaker, who in his merry humour doubted not to call me at table *furcifer*, only for using a fork at feeding, but for no other cause.

Coryats Crudities, 1611

JOHN SMITH
1580–1631

A Captive of the Indians

Not long after, early in a morning, a great fire was made in a long-house and a mat spread on the one side as on the other; on the one they caused him to sit, and all the guard went out of the house, and presently came skipping in a great grim fellow all painted over with coal mingled with oil, and many snakes' and weasels' skins stuffed with moss, and all their tails tied together so as they met on the crown of his head in a tassel, and round about the tassel was as a coronet of feathers, the skins hanging round about his head, back, and shoulders and in a manner covered his face, with a hellish voice, and a rattle in his hand. With most strange gestures and passions be began his invocation and environed the fire with a circle of meal; which done, three more such like devils came rushing in with the like antic tricks, painted half black, half red, but all their eyes were painted white and some red strokes like mustaches along their cheeks. Round about him those fiends danced a pretty while, and then came in three more as ugly as the rest, with red eyes and white strokes over their black faces. At last they all sat down right against him, three of them on the one hand of the chief priest and three on the other. Then all with their rattles began a song; which ended, the chief priest laid down five wheat corns; then straining his arms and hands with such violence that he sweat and his veins swelled, he began a short oration; at the conclusion they all gave a short groan and

coal] charcoal   an oration] a prayer

then laid down three grains more. After that, began their song again, and then another oration, ever laying down so many corns as before till they had twice encircled the fire; that done, they took a bunch of little sticks prepared for that purpose, continuing still their devotion, and at the end of every song and oration they laid down a stick betwixt the divisions of corn. Till night, neither he nor they did either eat or drink, and then they feasted merrily with the best provisions they could make. Three days they used this ceremony; the meaning whereof, they told him, was to know if he intended them well or no. The circle of meal signified their country, the circles of corn the bounds of the sea, and the sticks his country. They imagined the world to be flat and round, like a trencher, and they in the midst.

The General History of Virginia, 1624

SIR THOMAS OVERBURY
1581–1613

An Amorist

Is a man blasted or planet-strooken, and is the dog that leads blind Cupid; when he is at the best his fashion exceeds the worth of his weight. He is never without verses and musk confects, and sighs to the hazard of his buttons. His eyes are all white, either to wear the livery of his mistress' complexion or to keep Cupid from hitting the black. He fights with passion, and loseth much of his blood by his weapon; dreams, thence his paleness. His arms are carelessly used, as if their best use was nothing but embracements. He is untrussed, unbuttoned, and ungartered, not out of carelessness, but care; his farthest end being but going to bed. Sometimes he wraps his petition in neatness, but he goeth not alone; for then he makes some other quality moralize his affection, and his trimness is the grace of that grace. Her favour lifts him up as the sun moisture; when he disfavours, unable to hold that happiness, it falls down in tears. His fingers are his orators, and he expresseth much of himself upon some instrument. He answers not, or not to the purpose, and no marvel, for he is not at home. He scotcheth time with dancing with his mistress, taking up of her glove, and wearing her feather, he is confined to her colour, and dares not pass out of the circuit of her memory. His imagination is a fool, and it goeth in a pied coat of red and white. Shortly he is translated out of a man into folly; his imagination is the glass of lust, and himself the traitor to his own discretion.

Characters, 1614

JOHN SELDEN
1584–1654

Preaching Damnation

To preach long, loud, and damnation, is the way to be cried up. We love a man that damns us, and we run after him again to save us. If a man had a sore leg, and he should go to an honest judicious surgeon, and he should only bid him keep it warm, and anoint with such an oil (an oil well known), that would do the cure, haply he would not much regard him, because he knew the medicine beforehand an ordinary medicine. But if he should go to a surgeon that should tell him, your leg will gangrene within three days, and it must be cut off, and you will die, unless you do something that I could tell you; what listening there would be to this man! Oh, for the lord's sake, tell me what this is, I will give you any content for your pains.

Table-Talk, first published 1689

The Measure of Things

We measure from ourselves, and as things are for our use and purpose, so we approve them. Bring a pear to the table that is rotten, we cry it down, 'tis naught; but bring a medlar that is rotten, and 'tis a fine thing; and yet I warrant you, the pear thinks as well of itself as the medlar does.

We measure the excellency of other men, by some excellency we conceive to be in ourselves. Nash, a poet poor enough (as poets use to be), seeing an alderman with his gold chain, upon his great horse, said by way of scorn to one of his companions, Do you see yon fellow, how goodly, how big he looks? why that fellow cannot make a blank verse.

Nay, we measure the excellency of God from ourselves. We measure his goodness, his justice, his wisdom, by something we call just, good, or wise in ourselves; and in so doing, we judge proportionably to the country-fellow in the play, who said, If he were a king, he would live like a lord, and have peas and bacon every day, and a whip that cried slash.

Table-Talk

WILLIAM DRUMMOND OF HAWTHORNDEN
1585–1649

To Every Thing There is a Season

If thou dost complain that there shall be a time in the which thou shalt not be, why dost thou not too grieve that there was a time in the which thou wast not, and so that thou art not as old as that enlivening planet of time? For not to have been a thousand years before this moment is as much to be deplored as not to be a thousand after it, the effect of them both being one: that will be after us which long long ere we were was. Our children's children have that same reason to murmur that they were not young men in our days, which we now to complain that we shall not be old in theirs. The violets have their time, though they empurple not the winter, and the roses keep their season, though they discover not their beauty in the spring.

Empires, states, kingdoms have, by the doom of the supreme Providence, their fatal periods; great cities lie sadly buried in their dust; arts and sciences have not only their eclipses, but their wanings and deaths; the ghastly wonders of the world, raised by the ambition of ages, are overthrown and trampled; some lights above (deserving to be entitled stars) are loosed and never more seen of us; the excellent fabric of this universe itself shall one day suffer ruin, or a change like a ruin, and poor earthlings thus to be handled complain!

The Cypress Grove, 1623

THOMAS HOBBES
1588–1679

Laughter

There is a passion that hath no name; but the sign of it is that distortion of the countenance which we call *laughter*, which is always joy: but what joy, what we think, and wherein we triumph when we laugh, is not hitherto declared by any. That it consisteth in wit, or, as they call it, in the jest, experience confuteth: for men laugh at mischances and indecencies, wherein there lieth no wit nor jest at all. And forasmuch as the same thing is no more ridiculous when it groweth stale or usual, whatsoever it be that moveth laughter, it must be new and unexpected. Men laugh often, especially such as are greedy of applause from every thing they do well, at their own actions performed never so little beyond their own expectations; as also at their own jests: and in this case it is manifest, that the passion of laughter proceedeth from a sudden conception of some ability in himself that laugheth. Also men laugh at the infirmities of others, by comparison wherewith their own abilities are set off and illustrated. Also men laugh at jests, the wit whereof always consisteth in the elegant discovering and conveying to our minds some absurdity of another: and in this case also the passion of laughter proceedeth from the sudden imagination of our own odds and eminency: for what is else the recommending of ourselves to our own good opinion, by comparison with another man's infirmity or absurdity? For when a jest is broken upon ourselves, or friends of whose dishonour we participate, we never laugh thereat. I may therefore conclude, that the passion of laughter is nothing else but sudden glory arising from some sudden conception of some eminency in ourselves, by comparison with the infirmity of others, or with our own formerly: for men laugh at the follies of themselves past, when they come suddenly to remembrance, except they bring with them any present dishonour. It is no wonder therefore that men take heinously to be laughed at or derided, that is, triumphed over. Laughter without offence, must be at absurdities and infirmities abstracted from persons, and when all the company may laugh together: for laughing to one's-self putteth all the rest into jealousy and examination of themselves.

Human Nature, 1650

A State of War

So that in the nature of man, we find three principal causes of quarrel. First, competition; secondly, diffidence; thirdly, glory.

The first maketh men invade for gain; the second, for safety; and the third, for reputation. The first use violence to make themselves masters of other men's persons, wives, children, and cattle; the second, to defend them; the third, for trifles, as a word, a smile, a different opinion, and any other sign of undervalue, either direct in their persons, or by reflection in their kindred, their friends, their nation, their profession, or their name.

Hereby it is manifest that during the time men live without a common power to keep them all in awe, they are in that condition which is called war; and such a war as is of every man against every man. For war consisteth not in battle only, or the act of fighting, but in a tract of time wherein the will to contend by battle is sufficiently known; and therefore the notion of time is to be considered in the nature of war, as it is in the nature of weather. For as the nature of foul weather lieth not in a shower or two of rain, but in an inclination thereto of many days together; so the nature of war consisteth not in actual fighting, but in the known disposition thereto, during all the time there is no assurance to the contrary. All other time is peace.

Whatsoever therefore is consequent to a time of war, where every man is enemy to every man, the same is consequent to the time wherein men live without other security than what their own strength and their own invention shall furnish them withal. In such condition there is no place for industry, because the fruit thereof is uncertain, and consequently no culture of the earth; no navigation, nor use of the commodities that may be imported by sea; no commodious building; no instruments of moving, and removing, such things as require much force; no knowledge of the face of the earth; no account of time; no arts; no letters; no society; and, which is worst of all, continual fear, and danger of violent death; and the life of man, solitary, poor nasty, brutish, and short.

It may seem strange to some man that has not well weighed these things, that nature should thus dissociate and render men apt to invade and destroy one another; and he may therefore, not trusting to this inference, made from the passions, desire perhaps to have the same confirmed by experience. Let him therefore consider with himself, when taking a journey, he arms himself and seeks to go well accompanied; when going to sleep, he locks his doors; when even in his house he locks his chests; and this when he knows there be laws, and public officers, armed, to revenge all injuries shall be done him; what opinion he has of his fellow subjects, when he rides armed; of his fellow citizens, when he locks his doors; and of his children and servants, when he locks his chests. Does he not there as much accuse mankind by his actions, as I do by my words? But neither of us accuse man's nature in it. The desires and other passions of man are in themselves no sin. No more are the actions that proceed from those passions, till they know a law that forbids them, which, till laws be made, they cannot know; nor can any law be made, till they have agreed upon the person that shall make it.

It may peradventure be thought there was never such a time nor condition of war as this; and I believe it was never generally so, over all the world; but there are many places where they live so now. For the savage people in many places of America, except the government of small families, the concord whereof dependeth on natural lust, have no government at all and live at this day in that brutish manner as I said before. Howsoever, it may be perceived what manner of life there would be, where there were no common power to fear, by the manner of life which men that have formerly lived under a peaceful government use to degenerate into in a civil war.

But though there had never been any time wherein particular men were in a condition of war one against another, yet in all times, kings and persons of sovereign authority, because of their independency, are in continual jealousies, and in the state and posture of gladiators; having their weapons pointing, and their eyes fixed on one another; that is, their forts, garrisons, and guns upon the frontiers of their kingdoms, and continual spies upon their neighbours, which is a posture of war. But because they uphold thereby the industry of their subjects, there does not follow from it that misery which accompanies the liberty of particular men.

To this war of every man against every man, this also is consequent: that nothing can be unjust. The notions of right and wrong, justice and injustice, have there no place. Where there is no common power, there is no law; where no law, no injustice. Force and fraud are in war the two cardinal virtues. Justice and injustice are none of the faculties neither of the body nor mind. If they were, they might be in a man that were alone in the world, as well as his senses and passions. They are qualities that relate to men in society, not in solitude.

Leviathan, 1651

JOHN WINTHROP
1588–1649

A City upon a Hill

Thus stands the cause between God and us. We are entered into covenant with him for this work. We have taken out a commission, the Lord hath given us leave to draw our own articles. We have professed to enterprise these actions, upon these and those ends, we have hereupon besought him of favor and blessing. Now if the Lord shall please to hear us, and bring us in peace to the place we desire, then hath he ratified this covenant and sealed our commission, [and] will expect a strict performance of the articles contained in it. But if we shall neglect the observation of these articles which are the ends we have propounded and, dissembling with our God, shall fall to embrace this present world and prosecute our carnal intentions, seeking great things for ourselves and our posterity, the Lord will surely break out in wrath against us, be revenged of such a perjured people, and make us know the price of the breach of such a covenant.

Now the only way to avoid this shipwrack, and to provide for our posterity, is to follow the counsel of Micah, to do justly, to love mercy, to walk humbly with our God. For this end, we must be knit together in this work as one man. We must entertain each other in brotherly affection, we must be willing to abridge ourselves of our superfluities, for the supply of others' necessities. We must uphold a familiar commerce together in all meekness, gentleness, patience, and liberality. We must delight in each other, make others' conditions our own, rejoice together, mourn together, labor and suffer together, always having before our eyes our commission and community in the work, our community as members of the same body. So shall we keep the unity of the spirit in the bond of peace. The Lord will be our God, and delight to dwell among us as his own people, and will command a blessing upon us in all our ways, so that we shall see much more of his wisdom, power, goodness, and truth, than formerly we have been acquainted with. We shall find that the God of Israel is among us, when ten of us shall be able to resist a thousand of our enemies; when he shall make us a praise and glory that men shall say of succeeding plantations, 'the Lord make it like that of New England.' For we must consider that we shall be as a city upon a hill. The eyes of all people are upon us, so that if we shall deal falsely with our God in this work we have undertaken, and so cause him to withdraw his present help from us, we shall be made a story and a by-word through the world. We shall open the mouths of enemies to speak evil of the ways of God, and all professors for God's sake. We shall shame the faces of many of God's worthy servants, and cause their prayers to be turned into curses upon us till we be consumed out of the good land whither we are agoing.

'A Model of Christian Charity', sermon delivered on board the *Arbella*, 1630

WILLIAM BRADFORD
1590–1657

The Pilgrim Fathers Arrive at Cape Cod

But here I cannot but stay and make a pause, and stand half amazed at this poor people's present condition; and so I think will the reader, too, when he well considers the same. Being thus passed the vast ocean, and a sea of troubles before in their preparation (as may be remembered by that which went before), they had now no friends to welcome them nor inns to entertain or refresh their weatherbeaten bodies; no houses or much less towns to repair to, to seek for succour. It is recorded in Scripture as a mercy to the Apostle and his shipwrecked company, that the barbarians showed them no small kindness in refreshing them, but these savage barbarians, when they met with them (as after will appear) were readier to fill their sides full of arrows than otherwise. And for the season it was winter, and they that know the winters of that country know them to be sharp and violent, and subject to cruel and fierce storms, dangerous to travel to known places, much more to search an unknown coast. Besides, what could they see but a hideous and desolate wilderness, full of wild beasts and wild men—and what multitudes there might be of them they knew not. Neither could they, as it were, go up to the top of Pisgah to view from this wilderness a more goodly country to feed their hopes; for which way soever they turned their eyes (save upward to the heavens) they could have little solace or content in respect of any outward objects. For summer being done, all things stand upon them with a weather-beaten face, and the whole country, full of woods and thickets, represented a wild and savage hue. If they looked behind them, there was the mighty ocean which they had passed and was now as a main bar and gulf to separate them from all the civil parts of the world. If it be said they had a ship to succour them, it is true; but what heard they daily from the master and company? But that with speed they should look out a place (with their shallop) where they would be, at some near distance; for the season was such as he would not stir from thence till a safe harbor was discovered by them, where they would be, and he might go without danger; and that victuals consumed apace but he must and would keep sufficient for themselves and their return. Yea, it was muttered by some that if they got not a place in time, they would turn them and their goods ashore and leave them. Let it also be considered what weak hopes of supply and succour they left behind them, that might bear up their minds in this sad condition and trials they were under; and they could not but be very small. It is true, indeed, the affections and love of their brethren at Leyden was cordial and entire towards them, but they had little power to help them or themselves; and how the case stood between them and the merchants at their coming away hath already been declared.

What could now sustain them but the Spirit of God and His grace? May not and ought not the children of these fathers rightly say: 'Our fathers were Englishmen which came over this great ocean, and were ready to perish in this wilderness; but they cried unto the Lord, and He heard their voice and looked on their adversity,' etc. 'Let them therefore praise the Lord, because He is good: and His mercies endure forever.' 'Yea, let them which have been redeemed of the Lord, shew how He hath delivered them from the hand of the oppressor. When they wandered in the desert wilderness out of the way, and found no city to dwell in, both hungry and thirsty, their soul was overwhelmed in them. Let them confess before the Lord His loving kindness and His wonderful works before the sons of men.'

Of Plymouth Plantation, 1630–50

IZAAK WALTON
1593–1683

John Donne

He was of stature moderately tall; of a straight and equally proportioned body, to which all his words and actions gave an unexpressible addition of comeliness.

The melancholy and pleasant humor were in him so contempered that each gave advantage to the other, and made his company one of the delights of mankind.

His fancy was unimitably high, equalled only by his great wit; both being made useful by a commanding judgment.

His aspect was cheerful, and such as gave a silent testimony of a clear knowing soul, and of a conscience at peace with itself.

His melting eye showed that he had a soft heart, full of noble compassion; of too brave a soul to offer injuries and too much a Christian not to pardon them in others.

He did much contemplate (especially after he entered into his sacred calling) the mercies of Almighty God, the immortality of the soul, and the joys of heaven; and would often say, in a kind of sacred ecstasy, 'Blessed be God that he is God, only and divinely like himself.'

He was by nature highly passionate, but more apt to reluct at the excesses of it. A great lover of the offices of humanity, and of so merciful a spirit that he never beheld the miseries of mankind without pity and relief.

He was earnest and unwearied in the search of knowledge, with which his vigorous soul is now satisfied, and employed in a continual praise of that God that first breathed it into his active body: that body, which once was a temple of the Holy Ghost and is now become a small quantity of Christian dust:

But I shall see it reanimated.

The Life of Dr John Donne, 1640

An Undoubted Art

[Piscator addresses Venator]

O sir, doubt not but that angling is an art. Is it not an art to deceive a trout with an artificial fly? a trout that is more sharp-sighted than any hawk you have named, and more watchful and timorous than your high-mettled merlin is bold! and yet I doubt not to catch a brace or two to-morrow for a friend's breakfast. Doubt not, therefore, sir, but that angling is an art, and an art worth your learning; the question is rather, whether you be capable of learning it? for angling is somewhat like poetry, men are to be born so—I mean with inclinations to it, though both may be heightened by discourse and practice; but he that hopes to be a good angler must not only bring an inquiring, searching, observing wit, but he must bring a large measure of hope and patience, and a love and propensity to the art itself; but having once got and practised it, then doubt not but angling will prove to be so pleasant that it will prove to be like virtue, a reward to itself.

The Compleat Angler, 1653

Sweet Content

[Venator addresses Piscator]

But, master, first let me tell you that, that very hour which you were absent from me, I sat down under a willow-tree by the water-side, and considered what you had told me of the owner of that pleasant meadow in which you then left me; that he had a plentiful estate, and not a heart to think so; that he had at this time many lawsuits depending, and that they both damped his mirth, and took up so much of his time and thoughts, that he himself had not leisure to take the sweet content that I, who pretended no title to them, took in his fields; for I could there sit quietly, and, looking on the water, see some fishes sport themselves in the silver streams, others leaping at flies of several shapes and colours; looking on the hills I could behold them spotted with woods and groves; looking down the meadows, could see here a boy gathering lilies and lady-smocks, and there a girl cropping culverkeyes and cowslips, all to make garlands suitable to this present month of May. These, and many other field-flowers, so perfumed the air, that I thought that very meadow like that field in Sicily, of which Diodorous speaks, where the perfumes arising from the place make all dogs that hunt in it to fall off, and to lose their hottest scent. I say, as I thus sat, joying in my own happy condition, and pitying this poor rich man that owned this and many other pleasant groves and meadows about me, I did thankfully remember what my Saviour said, that the meek possess the earth—or rather, they enjoy what the other possess and enjoy not; for anglers, and meek, quiet-spirited men, are free from those high, those restless thoughts which corrode the sweets of life.

The Compleat Angler

George Herbert

His chiefest recreation was music, in which heavenly art he was a most excellent master, and did himself compose many divine hymns and anthems, which he set and sung to his lute or viol: and though he was a lover of retiredness, yet his love to music was such, that he went usually twice every week, on certain appointed days, to the Cathedral Church in Salisbury; and at his return would say 'That his time spent in prayer, and Cathedral-music, elevated his soul, and was his Heaven upon earth.' But before his return thence to Bemerton, he would usually sing and play his part at an appointed private Music-meeting; and, to justify this practice, he would often say, 'Religion does not banish mirth, but only moderates and sets rules to it.'

And as his desire to enjoy his Heaven upon earth drew him twice every week to Salisbury, so his walks thither were the occasion of many happy accidents to others; of which I will mention some few.

In one of his walks to Salisbury, he overtook a gentleman, that is still living in that City; and in their walk together, Mr Herbert took a fair occasion to talk with him, and humbly begged to be excused, if he asked some account of his faith; and said, 'I do this the rather, because though you are not of my parish, yet I receive tithe from you by the hand of your tenant; and, Sir, I am the bolder to do it, because I know there be some sermon-hearers that be like those fishes, that always live in salt water, and yet are always fresh.'

After which expression, Mr Herbert asked him some needful questions, and having received his answer, gave him such rules for the trial of his sincerity, and for a practical piety, and in so loving and meek a manner, that the gentleman did so fall in love with him, and his discourse, that he would often contrive to meet him in his walk to Salisbury, or to attend him back to Bemerton; and still mentions the name of Mr George Herbert with veneration, and still praiseth God for the occasion of knowing him . . .

In another walk to Salisbury, he saw a poor man with a poorer horse, that was fallen under his load: they were both in distress, and needed present help; which Mr Herbert perceiving, put off his canonical coat, and helped the poor man to unload, and after to load his horse. The poor man blessed him for it, and he blessed the poor man; and was so like the Good Samaritan, that he gave him money to refresh both himself and his horse; and told him, 'That if he loved himself he should be merciful to his beast.' Thus he left the poor man: and at his coming to his musical friends at Salisbury, they began to wonder that Mr George Herbert, which used to be so trim and clean, came into that company so soiled and discomposed: but he told them the occasion. And when one of the company told him 'He had disparaged himself by so dirty an employment,' his answer was, 'That the thought of what he had done would prove music to him at midnight; and that the omission of it would have upbraided and made discord in his conscience, whensoever he should pass by that place: for if I be found to pray for all that be in distress, I am sure that I am bound, so far as it is in my power, to practise what I pray for. And though I do not wish for the like occasion every day, yet let me tell you, I would not willingly pass one day of my life without comforting a sad soul, or shewing mercy; and I praise God for this occasion. And now let's tune our instruments.'

The Life of Mr George Herbert, 1670

JOHN EARLE
1601?–1665

The World's Wise Man

Is an able and sufficient wicked man. It is a proof of his sufficiency that he is not called wicked, but wise. A man wholly determined in himself and his own ends, and his instruments herein anything that will do it. His friends are a part of his engines, and as they serve to his works, used or laid by. Indeed he knows not this thing of friend, but if he give you the name it is a sign he has a plot on you. Never more active in his businesses than when they are mixed with some harm to others; and 'tis his best play in this game to strike off and lie in the place. Successful commonly in these undertakings because he passes smoothly those rubs which others stumble at, as conscience and the like; and gratulates himself much in this advantage. Oaths and falsehood he counts the nearest way, and loves not by any means to go about. He has many fine quips at this folly of plain dealing, but his 'tush' is greatest at religion; yet he uses this too, and virtue and good words, but is less dangerously a Devil than a Saint. He ascribes all honesty to an unpractisedness in the world, and conscience a thing merely for children. He scorns all that are so silly to trust him, and only not scorns his enemy, especially if as bad as himself. He fears him as a man well armed and provided, but sets boldly on good natures, as the most vanquishable. One that seriously admires those worst Princes, as Sforza, Borgia, and Richard the Third; and calls matters of deep villainy 'things of difficulty.' To whom murders are but 'resolute acts,' and treason 'a business of great consequence.' One whom two or three countries make up to this completeness, and he has travelled for the purpose. His deepest endearment is a communication of mischief, and then only you have him fast. His conclusion is commonly one of these two, either a great man, or hanged.

Microcosmography, 1628

An Ordinary Honest Man

Is one whom it concerns to be called honest, for if he were not this he were nothing: and yet he is not this neither, but a good dull vicious fellow, that complies well with the deboshments of the time, and is fit for it. One that has no good part in him to offend his company, or make him to be suspected a proud fellow; but is sociably a dunce, and sociably a drinker. That does it fair and above-board without legerdemain, and neither sharks for a cup or a reckoning. That is kind o'er his beer, and protests he loves you, and begins to you again, and loves you again. One that quarrels with no man but for not pledging him, but takes all absurdities and commits as many, and is no tell-tale next morning, though he remember it. One that will fight for his friend if he hear him abused, and his friend commonly is he that is most likely, and he lifts up many a jug in his defence. He rails against none but censurers, against whom he thinks he rails lawfully, and censurers are all those that are better than himself. These good properties qualify him for honesty enough, and raise him high in the Ale-house commendation, who, if he had any other good quality, would be named by that. But now for refuge he is an honest man, and hereafter a sot. Only those that commend him think not so, and those that commend him are honest fellows.

Microcosmography

OWEN FELLTHAM
1602?–1668

A Glimpse of Perfection

Whatsoever is rare and passionate carries the soul to the thought of eternity; and, by contemplation, gives it some glimpses of more absolute perfection, than here it is capable of. When I see the royalty of a state show, at some unwonted solemnity, my thoughts present me something more royal than this. When I see the most enchanting beauties that earth can show me, I yet think, there is something far more glorious: methinks I see a kind of higher perfection peeping through the frailty of a face. When I hear the ravishing strains of a sweet tuned voice, married to the warbles of the artful instrument, I apprehend, by this, a higher diapason; and do almost believe, I hear a little deity whispering through the pory substance of the tongue. But this I can but grope after. I can neither find nor say what it is.

Resolves: Divine, Moral and Political, 1631 edition

Poverty

The poverty of the poor man is the least part of his misery. In all the storms of fortune he is the first that must stand the shock of extremity. Poor men are perpetual sentinels, watching in the depth of night against the incessant assaults of want; while the rich lie stowed in secure reposes, and compassed with a large abundance. If the land be russeted with a bloodless famine, are not the poor the first that sacrifice their lives to hunger? If war thunders in the trembling country's lap, are not the poor those that are exposed to the enemy's sword and outrage? If the plague, like a loaded spunge, flies, sprinkling poison through a populous kingdom, the poor are the fruit that are shaken from the burthened tree: while the rich, furnished with the helps of fortune, have means to wind out themselves, and turn these sad endurances on the poor, that cannot avoid them. Like salt marshes, that lie low, they are sure, whensoever the sea of this world rages, to be the first under, and imbarrened with a fretting care. Who, like the poor, are harrowed with oppression, ever subject to the imperious taxes and the gripes of mightiness? Continual care checks the spirit; continual labour checks the body; and continual insultation both. He is like one rolled in a vessel full of pikes: which way soever he turns, he something finds that pricks him.

Resolves

A Dutch Interior

When you are entered the house the first thing you encounter is a looking-glass. No question but a true emblem of politic hospitality; for though it reflects yourself in your own figure, 'tis yet no longer than while you are there before it. When you are gone once, it flatters the next comer, without the least remembrance that you ere were there.

The next are the vessels of the house marshalled about the room like watchmen. All as neat as if you were in a citizens' wives' cabinet: for unless it be themselves, they let none of God's creatures lose anything of their native beauty.

Their houses, especially in their cities, are the best eye beauties of their country. For cost and sight they far exceed our English, but they want their magnificence. Their lining is yet more rich than their outside; not in hangings, but in pictures, which even the poorest are there furnisht with. Not a cobbler but has his toys for ornament. Were the knacks of all their houses set together, there would not be such another Bartholomew Fair in Europe.

Whatsoever their estates be, their house must be fair. Therefore from Amsterdam they have banished sea-coal, lest it soil their buildings, of which the statelier sort are sometimes sententious, and in the front carry some conceit of the owner.

Every door seems studded with diamonds. The nails and hinges hold a constant brightness, as if rust there were not a quality incident to iron. Their houses they keep cleaner than their bodies; their bodies than their souls. Go to one you shall find the andirons shut up in net-work. At a second, the warming-pan muffled in Italian cut-work. At a third the sconce clad in cambric.

A Brief Character of the Low Countries, 1652

SIR THOMAS BROWNE
1605–1682

The Man Within

I were unjust unto mine own conscience, if I should say I am at variance with anything like myself. I find there are many pieces in this one fabric of man; this frame is raised upon a mass of antipathies. I am one, methinks, but as the world, wherein there are a swarm of distinct essences, and in them another world of contrarieties; we carry private and domestic enemies within, public and more hostile adversaries without. The Devil that did but buffet *Saint Paul* plays methinks at sharp with me. Let me be nothing if within the compass of myself I do not find the battle of *Lepanto*, passion against reason, reason against faith, faith against the Devil, and my conscience against all. There is another man within me that's angry with me, rebukes, commands and dastards me . . .

Religio Medici, 1642

The Music of the Spheres

It is my temper, and I like it the better, to affect all harmony; and sure there is music even in the beauty, and the silent note which Cupid strikes, far sweeter than the sound of an instrument. For there is a Music where ever there is a Harmony, order or proportion; and thus far we may maintain the Musick of the Spheres: for those well ordered motions and regular paces, though they give no sound unto the ear, yet to the understanding they strike a note most full of harmony. Whatsoever is harmonically composed delights in harmony; which makes me much distrust the symmetry of those heads which declaim against all Church-Music. For myself, not only from my obedience, but my particular genius, I do embrace it: for even that vulgar and tavern-music, which makes one man merry, another mad, strikes in me a deep fit of Devotion, and a profound contemplation of the first Composer; there is something in it of divinity more than the ear discovers: it is an hieroglyphical and shadowed lesson of the whole world, and creatures of God—such a melody to the ear, as the whole world well understood, would afford the understanding. In brief, it is a sensible fit of that harmony, which intellectually sounds in the ears of God.

Religio Medici

The Death-Watch Beetle

Few ears have escaped the noise of the death-watch, that is, the little clickling sound heard often in many rooms, somewhat resembling that of a watch; and this is conceived to be of an evil omen or prediction of some person's death: wherein notwithstanding there is nothing of rational presage or just cause of terror unto melancholy and meticulous heads. For this noise is made by a little sheathwinged grey insect, found often in wainscot benches and wood-work in the summer. We have taken many thereof, and kept them in thin boxes, wherein I have heard and seen them work and knock with a little proboscis or trunk against the side of the box, like a *picus martius*, or woodpecker against a tree. It worketh best in warm weather, and for the most part giveth not over under nine or eleven strokes at a time. He that could extinguish the terrifying apprehensions hereof, might prevent the passions of the heart, and many cold sweats in grandmothers and nurses, who, in the sickness of children, are so startled with these noises.

Pseudodoxia Epidemica, or *Vulgar Errors*, 1646

Unidentified Bones

What song the Sirens sang, or what name Achilles assumed when he hid himself among women, though puzzling questions, are not beyond all conjecture. What time the persons of these ossuaries entered the famous nations of the dead, and slept with princes and counselors, might admit a wide solution. But who were the proprietaries of these bones, or what bodies these ashes made up, were a question above antiquarism; not to be resolved by man, nor easily perhaps by spirits, except we consult the provincial guardians, or tutelary observators. Had they made as good provision for their names, as they have done for their relics, they had not so grossly erred in the art of perpetuation. But to subsist in bones, and be but pyramidally extant, is a fallacy in duration. Vain ashes which in the oblivion of names, persons, times, and sexes, have found unto themselves a fruitless continuation, and only arise unto late posterity, as emblems of mortal vanities, antidotes against pride, vainglory, and madding vices.

Urn-Burial, 1658

The Poppy of Oblivion

But the iniquity of oblivion blindly scattereth her poppy, and deals with the memory of men without distinction to merit of perpetuity. Who can but pity the founder of the pyramids? Herostratus lives that burnt the temple of Diana, he is almost lost that built it. Time hath spared the epitaph of Adrian's horse, confounded that of himself. In vain we compute our felicities by the advantage of our good names, since bad have equal durations, and Thersites is like to live as long as Agamemnon. Who knows whether the best of men be known, or whether there be not more remarkable persons forgot, than any that stand remembered in the known account of time? Without the favour of the everlasting register, the first man had been as unknown as the last, and Methuselah's long life had been his only chronicle.

Oblivion is not to be hired. The greater part must be content to be as though they had not been, to be found in the register of God, not in the record of man. Twenty-seven names make up the first story, and the recorded names ever since contain not one living century. The number of the dead long exceedeth all that shall live. The night of time far surpasseth the day, and who knows when was the equinox? Every hour adds unto that current arithmetic, which scarce stands one moment. And since death must be the Lucina of life, and even Pagans could doubt, whether thus to live were to die; since our longest sun sets at right descensions, and makes but winter arches, and therefore it cannot be long before we lie down in darkness, and have our light in ashes; since the brother of death daily haunts us with dying mementos, and time that grows old in itself, bids us hope no long duration; diuturnity is a dream and folly of expectation.

Darkness and light divide the course of time, and oblivion shares with memory a great part even of our living beings; we slightly remember our felicities, and the smartest strokes of affliction leave but short smart upon us. Sense endureth no extremities, and sorrows destroy us or themselves. To weep into stones are fables. Afflictions induce callosities; miseries are slippery, or fall like snow upon us, which notwithstanding is no unhappy stupidity. To be ignorant of evils to come, and forgetful of evils past, is a merciful provision in nature, whereby we digest the mixture of our few and evil days, and, our delivered senses not relapsing into cutting remembrances, our sorrows are not kept raw by the edge of repetitions.

Urn-Burial

A Pure Flame

Life is a pure flame, and we live by an invisible sun within us. A small fire sufficeth for life, great flames seemed too little after death, while men vainly affected precious pyres, and to burn like Sardanapalus; but the wisdom of funeral laws found the folly of prodigal blazes, and reduced undoing fires unto the rule of sober obsequies, wherein few could be so mean as not to provide wood, pitch, a mourner, and an urn.

Urn-Burial

The Realm of Sleep

But the quincunx of heaven runs low, and 'tis time to close the five ports of knowledge. We are unwilling to spin out our awaking thoughts into the phantasms of sleep, which often continueth precogitations; making cables of cobwebs, and wildernesses of handsome groves. Beside Hippocrates hath spoke so little, and the oneirocritical masters have left such frigid interpretations from plants, that there is little encouragement to dream of paradise itself. Nor will the sweetest delight of gardens afford much comfort in sleep; wherein the dulness of that sense shakes hands with delectable odours; and though in the bed of Cleopatra, can hardly with any delight raise up the ghost of a rose.

Night, which Pagan theology could make the daughter of Chaos, affords no advantage to the description of order; although no lower than that mass can we derive its genealogy. All things began in order, so shall they end, and so shall they begin again; according to the ordainer of order and mystical mathematicks of the city of heaven.

Though Somnus in Homer be sent to rouse up Agamemnon, I find no such effects in these drowsy approaches of sleep. To keep our eyes open longer were but to act our antipodes. The huntsmen are up in America, and they are already past their first sleep in Persia. But who can be drowsy at that hour which freed us from everlasting sleep? or have slumbering thoughts at that time, when sleep itself must end, and as some conjecture all shall awake again.

The Garden of Cyrus, 1658

Noble Patterns

'Tis hard to find a whole age to imitate, or what century to propose for example. Some have been far more approvable than others, but virtue and vice, panegyricks and satires, scatteringly to be found in all. History sets down not only things laudable, but abominable; things which should never have been or never have been known. So that noble patterns must be fetched here and there from single persons, rather than whole nations, and from all nations, rather than one.

Christian Morals, first published 1716

Inward Opticks

Behold thyself by inward opticks and the crystalline of thy soul. Strange it is that in the most perfect sense there should be so many fallacies, that we are fain to make a doctrine, and often to see by art. But the greatest imperfection is in our inward sight, that is, to be ghosts unto our own eyes; and while we are so sharp-sighted as to look through others, to be invisible unto ourselves; for the inward eyes are more fallacious than the outward. The vices we scoff at in others, laugh at us within ourselves. Avarice, pride, falsehood lie undiscerned and blindly in us, even to the age of blindness; and, therefore, to see ourselves interiorly, we are fain to borrow other men's eyes; wherein true friends are good informers, and censurers no bad friends. Conscience only, that can see without light, sits in the areopagy and dark tribunal of our hearts, surveying our thoughts and condemning their obliquities.

Christian Morals

BULSTRODE WHITELOCKE
1605–1675

An Audience with Queen Christina

Whitelocke had a private audience with the Queen above two hours together. She was pleased first to discourse of private matters.

Queen. Hath your General a wife and children?

Whitelocke. He hath a wife and five children.

Qu. What family were he and his wife of?

Wh. He was of the family of a baron, and his wife the like from Bourchiers.

Qu. Of what parts are his children?

Wh. His two sons and three daughters are all of good parts and liberal education.

Qu. Some unworthy mention and mistakes have been made to me of them.

Wh. Your Majesty knows that to be frequent; but from me you shall have nothing but truth.

Qu. Much of the story of your General hath some parallel with that of my ancestor Gustavus the First, who, from a private gentleman of a noble family, was advanced to the title of Marshal of Sweden, because he had risen up and rescued his country from the bondage and oppression which the King of Denmark had put upon them, and expelled that king; and for

Your General] Cromwell

his reward he was at last elected King of Sweden, and I believe that your General will be King of England in conclusion.

Wh. Pardon me, Madam, that cannot be, because England is resolved into a Commonwealth; and my General hath already sufficient power and greatness as General of all their forces both by sea and land, which may content him.

Qu. Resolve what you will, I believe he resolves to be king; and hardly can any power or greatness be called sufficient, when the nature of man is so prone, as in these days, to all ambition.

Wh. I find no such nature in my General.

Qu. It may easily be concealed till an opportunity serve, and then it will show itself.

Wh. All are mortal men, subject to affections.

Qu. How many wives have you had?

Wh. I have had three wives.

Qu. Have you had children by all of them?

Wh. Yes, by every one of them.

Qu. Pardieu, vous êtes incorrigible!

Wh. Madam, I have been a true servant to your sex; and as it was my duty to be kind to my wives, so I count it my happiness and riches and strength to have many children.

Qu. You have done well; and if children do prove well, it is no small nor usual blessing.

A Journal of the Swedish Embassy in the Years 1653 and 1654

A Visit from Chancellor Oxenstierna

Presently after dinner, the Chancellor's secretary came to Whitelocke with a message from his lord, to know if he would be within at two o'clock; the Chancellor would come to visit him. Whitelocke said he should take his visit for a great honour, and should be within. About three o'clock the Chancellor came. Whitelocke met him at the door of his house; he was in his coach with six horses, though his lodging was not far off; ten or twelve gentlemen, well habited, walking on foot, and four lacqueys attended him.

Whitelocke offered to conduct him into a lower chamber, because he understood it was troublesome to the old man to go up so many stairs as to his rooms of entertainment; and he was willing to accept of this ease, and was brought by Whitelocke into his steward's chamber, which he had caused to be hung with his own rich hangings full of silk and gold. He desired to sit with his back or one side to the fire, saying that the light of the fire was hurtful to his eyes.

He was a tall, proper, straight, handsome old man, of the age of seventy-one years; his habit was black cloth, a close coat lined with fur, a velvet cap on his head furred, and no hat, a cloak, his hair grey, his beard broad and long, his countenance sober and fixed, and his carriage grave and civil.

He spake Latin, plain and fluent and significant; and though he could, yet would not speak French, saying he knew no reason why that nation should be so much honoured more than others as to have their language used by strangers; but he thought the Latin more honourable and more copious, and fitter to be used, because the Romans had been masters of so great a part of the world, and yet at present that language was not peculiar to any people.

In his conferences he would often mix pleasant stories with his serious discourses, and took delight in recounting former passages of his life, and actions of his King, and would be very large excusing his *senilis garrulitas*, as he termed it, the talkativeness of old-age; but there was great pleasure to hear his discourses, and much wisdom and knowledge to be gathered from them.

Journal of the Swedish Embassy

JOHN MILTON
1608–1674

The Hour of Final Deliverance

O how much more glorious will those former deliverances appear, when we shall know them not only to have saved us from greatest miseries past, but to have reserved us for greatest happiness to come! Hitherto thou hast but freed us, and that not fully, from the unjust and tyrannous claim of thy foes; now unite us entirely, and appropriate us to thyself, tie us everlastingly in willing homage to the prerogative of thy eternal throne . . .

Then, amidst the hymns and hallelujahs of saints, some one may perhaps be heard offering at high strains in new and lofty measure to sing and celebrate thy divine mercies and marvellous judgments in this land throughout all ages; whereby this great and warlike nation, instructed and inured to the fervent and continual practice of truth and righteousness, and casting far from her the rags of her whole vices, may press on hard to that high and happy emulation to be found the soberest, wisest, and most Christian people at that day, when thou, the eternal and shortly expected King, shalt open the clouds to judge the several kingdoms of the world, and distributing national honours and rewards to religious and just commonwealths, shalt put an end to all earthly tyrannies, proclaiming thy universal and mild monarchy through heaven and earth; where they undoubtedly, that by their labours, counsels, and prayers, have been earnest for the common good of religion and their country, shall receive above the inferior orders of the blessed, the regal addition of principalities, legions, and thrones into their glorious titles, and in supereminence of beatific vision, progressing the dateless and irrevoluble circle of eternity, shall clasp inseparable hands with joy and bliss, in overmeasure for ever.

Of Reformation in England, 1641

An Exchange of Views

Remonstrant. No one clergy in the whole Christian world yields so many eminent scholars, learned preachers, grave, holy and accomplished divines as this Church of England doth at this day.

Answer. Ha, ha, ha!

Animadversions upon the Remonstrant's Defence, 1641

A Lofty Ambition

For although a poet, soaring in the high reason of his fancies, with his garland and singing robes about him, might, without apology, speak more of himself than I mean to do; yet for me sitting here below in the cool element of prose, a mortal thing among many readers of no empyreal conceit, to venture and divulge unusual things of myself, I shall petition to the gentler sort, it may not be envy to me. I must say, therefore, that after I had for my first years, by the ceaseless diligence and care of my father, (whom God recompense!) been exercised to the tongues, and some sciences, as my age would suffer, by sundry masters and teachers both at home and at the schools, it was found, that whether aught was imposed me by them that had the overlooking, or betaken to of mine own choice in English, or other tongue, prosing or versing, but chiefly this latter, the style, by certain vital signs it had, was likely to live. But much latelier in the private academies of Italy, whither I was favoured to resort, perceiving that some trifles which I had in memory, composed at under twenty or thereabout, (for the manner is, that every one must give some proof of his wit and reading there) met with acceptance above what was looked for; and other things, which I had shifted in scarcity of books and convenience to patch up amongst them, were received with written encomiums, which the Italian is not forward to bestow on men of this side the Alps; I began thus far to assent both to them and divers of my friends here at home, and not less to an inward prompting which now grew daily upon me, that by labour and intense study, (which I take to be my portion in this life) joined with the strong propensity of nature, I might perhaps leave something so written to aftertimes, as they should not willingly let it die. These thoughts at once possessed me, and these other; that if I were certain to write as men buy leases, for three lives and downward, there ought no regard be sooner had than to God's glory, by the honour and instruction of my country. For which cause, and not only for that I knew it would be hard to arrive at the second rank among the Latins, I applied myself to that resolution, which Ariosto followed against the persuasions of Bembo, to fix all the industry and art I could unite to the adorning of my native tongue; not to make verbal curiosities the end, (that were a toilsome vanity,) but to be an interpreter and relater of the best and sagest things, among mine own citizens, throughout this island in the mother dialect. That what the greatest and choicest wits of Athens, Rome, or modern Italy, and those Hebrews of old did for their country, I, in my proportion, with this over and above, of being a Christian, might do for mine; not caring to be once named abroad, though perhaps I could attain to that, but content with these British islands as my world; whose fortune hath hitherto been, that if the Athenians, as some say, made their small deeds great and renowned by their eloquent writers, England hath had her noble achievements made small by the unskilful handling of monks and mechanics.

The Reason of Church Government, 1642

From Censorship to Cultural Tyranny

If we think to regulate printing, thereby to rectify manners, we must regulate all recreations and pastimes, all that is delightful to man. No music must be heard, no song be set or sung, but what is grave and doric. There must be licensing dancers, that no gesture, motion, or deportment be taught our youth, but what by their allowance shall be thought honest; for such Plato was provided of. It will ask more than the work of twenty licensers to examine all the lutes, the violins, and the guitars in every house; they must not be suffered to prattle as they do, but must be licensed what they may say. And who shall silence all the airs and madrigals that whisper softness in chambers? The windows also, and the balconies, must be thought on; these are shrewd books, with dangerous frontispieces, set to sale: who shall prohibit them, shall twenty licensers? The villages also must have their visitors to inquire what lectures the bagpipe and the rebec reads, even to the ballatry and the gamut of every municipal fiddler; for these are the countryman's Arcadias, and his Monte Mayors.

Areopagitica, 1644

Putting Virtue to the Test

Good and evil we know in the field of this world grow up together almost inseparably; and the knowledge of good is so involved and interwoven with the knowledge of evil, and in so many cunning resemblances hardly to be discerned, that those confused seeds which were imposed on Psyche as an incessant labor to cull out and sort asunder were not more intermixed. It was from out the rind of one apple tasted, that the knowledge of good and evil, as two twins cleaving together, leaped forth into the world. And perhaps this is that doom which Adam fell into of knowing good and evil, that is to say of knowing good by evil.

As therefore the state of man now is, what wisdom can there be to choose, what continence to forbear, without the knowledge of evil? He that can apprehend and consider vice with all her baits and seeming pleasures, and yet abstain, and yet distinguish, and yet prefer that which is truly better, he is the true wayfaring Christian. I cannot praise a fugitive and cloistered virtue, unexercised and unbreathed, that never sallies out and sees her adversary, but slinks out of the race where that immortal garland is to be run for, not without dust and heat. Assuredly we bring not innocence into the world, we bring impurity much rather; that which purifies us is trial, and trial is by what is contrary.

Areopagitica

A Vision of England

Now once again by all concurrence of signs, and by the general instinct of holy and devout men, as they daily and solemnly express their thoughts, God is decreeing to begin some new and great period in His Church, even to the reforming of reformation itself; what does He then but reveal Himself to His servants, and as His manner is, first to His Englishmen? I say, as His manner is, first to us, though we mark not the method of His counsels, and are unworthy. Behold now this vast city, a city of refuge, the mansion-house of liberty, encompassed and surrounded with His protection; the shop of war hath not there more anvils and hammers working, to fashion out the plates and instruments of armed justice in defence of beleaguered truth, than there be pens and heads there, sitting by their studious lamps, musing, searching, revolving new notions and ideas wherewith to present, as with their homage and their fealty, the approaching reformation: others as fast reading, trying all things, assenting to the force of reason and convincement.

What could a man require more from a nation so pliant and so prone to seek after knowledge? What wants there to such a towardly and pregnant soil, but wise and faithful labourers, to make a knowing people, a nation of prophets, of sages, and of worthies? We reckon more than five months yet to harvest; there need not be five weeks, had we but eyes to lift up, the fields are white already. Where there is much desire to learn, there of necessity will be much arguing, much writing, many opinions; for opinion in good men is but knowledge in the making. Under these fantastic terrors of sect and schism, we wrong the earnest and zealous thirst after knowledge and understanding, which God hath stirred up in this city. What some lament of, we rather should rejoice at, should rather praise this pious forwardness among men, to reassume the ill-deputed care of their religion into their own hands again. A little generous prudence, a little forbearance of one another, and some grain of charity might win all these diligences to join and unite into one general and brotherly search after truth; could we but forego this prelatical tradition of crowding free consciences and Christian liberties into canons and precepts of men.

Areopagitica

God's Englishmen and Their Limitations

For Britain, to speak a truth not often spoken, as it is a land fruitful enough of men stout and courageous in war, so it is naturally not over-fertile of men able to govern justly and prudently in peace, trusting only in their mother-wit; who consider not justly, that civility, prudence, love of the public good, more than of money or vain honour, are to this soil in a manner outlandish; grow not here, but in minds well implanted with solid and elaborate breeding, too impolitic else and rude, if not headstrong and intractable to the industry and virtue of executing or understanding true civil government. Valiant indeed, and prosperous to win a field; but to know the end and reason of winning: unjudicious and unwise: in good or bad success, alike unteachable. For the sun, which we want, ripens wits as well as fruits; and as wine and oil are imported to us from abroad, so must ripe understanding, and many civil virtues, be imported into our minds from foreign writings, and examples of best ages: we shall else miscarry still, and come short in the attempts of any great enterprise.

The History of Britain, written *c.*1645–6

On the Eve of the Restoration

Certainly then that people must needs be mad or strangely infatuated, that build the chief hope of their common happiness or safety on a single person; who, if he happen to be good, can do no more than another man; if to be bad, hath in his hands to do more evil without check, than millions of other men. The happiness of a nation must needs be firmest and certainest in full and free council of their own electing, where no single person, but reason only, sways. And what madness is it for them who might manage nobly their own affairs themselves, sluggishly and weakly to devolve all on a single person; and, more like boys under age than men, to commit all to his patronage and disposal, who neither can perform what he undertakes; and yet for undertaking it, though royally paid, will not be their servant, but their lord! How unmanly must it needs be, to count such a one the breath of our nostrils, to hang all our felicity on him, all our safety, our well-being, for which if we were aught else but sluggards or babies, we need depend on none but God and our own counsels, our own active virtue and industry!

The Ready and Easy Way to Establish a Free Commonwealth, 1660

THOMAS FULLER
1608–1661

Geoffrey Chaucer

His father was a vintner in London; and I have heard his arms quarrelled at, being argent and gules strangely contrived, and hard to be blazoned. Some more wits have made it the dashing of white and red wine (the parents of our ordinary claret), as nicking his father's profession. But were Chaucer alive, he would justify his own arms in the face of all his opposers, being not so devoted to the Muses, but he was also a son of Mars. He was the prince of English poets; married the daughter of Pain Roëc, king of arms in France, and sister to the wife of John of Gaunt, king of Castile.

He was a great refiner and illuminer of our English tongue; and, if he left it so bad, how much worse did he find it!

Indeed, Verstegan, a learned antiquary, condemns him for spoiling the purity of the English tongue by the mixture of so many French and Latin words. But he who mingles wine with water, though he destroys the nature of water, improves the quality thereof.

I find this Chaucer fined in the Temple two shillings for striking a Franciscan friar in Fleet Street; and it seems his hands ever after itched to be revenged, and have his pennyworth's out of them, so tickling religious orders with his tales, and yet so pinching them with his truths, that friars, in reading his books, know not how to dispose their faces betwixt crying and laughing. He lies buried in the south aisle of St. Peter's, Westminster; and since hath got the company of Spenser and Drayton, a pair royal of poets, enough almost to make passengers' feet to move metrically, who go over the place where so much poetical dust is interred.

The Church History of Britain, 1655

Sir John Fastolfe

John Fastolf, knight [b. 1378] was a native of this county [Norfolk], as I have just cause to believe, though some have made him a Frenchman, merely because he was baron of Silly-Guillem in France, on which account they may rob England of many other worthies. He was a ward (and that the last) to John duke of Bedford, a sufficient evidence, to such who understand time and place, to prove him of English extraction. To avouch him by many arguments valiant is to maintain that the sun is bright, though since the stage hath been over-bold with his memory, making him a thrasonical puff, and emblem of mock valour.

True it is, Sir John Oldcastle did first bear the brunt of the one, being made the make-sport in all plays for a coward. It is easily known out of what purse this black penny came: the papists railing on him for a heretic, and therefore he must also be a coward, though indeed he was a man of arms, every inch of him, and as valiant as any in his age.

Now as I am glad that Sir John Oldcastle is put out, so I am sorry that Sir John Fastolf is put in, to relieve his memory in this base service, to be the anvil for every dull wit to strike upon. Nor is our comedian excusable, by some alteration of his name, writing him Sir John Falstaff, and making him the property of pleasure of King Henry the Fifth to abuse, seeing the vicinity of sounds entrench on the memory of that worthy knight, and few do heed the inconsiderable difference in spelling of their name. He was made knight of the Garter by King Henry the Sixth; and died [1459].

The Worthies of England, 1662

An Incident in the Life of Sir Walter Raleigh

This captain Ralegh, coming out of Ireland to the English court in good habit (his clothes being then a considerable part of his estate) found the queen walking, till meeting with a plashy place, she seemed to scruple going thereon. Presently Ralegh cast and spread his new plush cloak on the ground, whereon the queen trod gently, rewarding him afterwards with many suits, for his so free and seasonable tender of so fair a footcloth. Thus an advantageous admission into the first notice of a prince is more than half a degree to preferment.

The Worthies of England

Rutland

Rutland is, by a double diminutive, called by Mr Camden *Angliae provinciola minima*. Indeed it is but the pestle of a lark, which is better than a quarter of some bigger bird, having the most cleanly profit in it; no place, so fair for the *rider*, being more fruitful for the *abider* therein.

Banishing the fable of King Rott, and their fond conceit who will have Rutland so called from *rouet*, the French word for a wheel, from the rotundity thereof (being in form almost exactly orbicular); it is so termed *quasi Red-land*, for as if Nature kept a *dye-vat* herein, a reddish tincture discoloureth the earth, stones, yea the very fleeces of the sheep feeding therein. If the Rabbins' observation be true, who distinguish betwixt *Arets*, the general element of the earth, and *Adamah*, red ground, from which Adam was taken and named (making the latter the former refined) Rutland's soil, on the same reason, may lay claim to more than ordinary purity and perfection.

The Worthies of England

A Lancashire Wonder

About Wigan and elsewhere in this county men go a-fishing with spades and mattocks; more likely, one would think, to catch moles than fishes with such instruments. First, they pierce the turfy ground, and under it meet with a black and deadish water, and in it small fishes do swim. Surely these *pisces fossiles*, or subterranean fishes, must needs be unwholesome, the rather because an unctuous matter is found about them. Let them be thankful to God, in the first place, who need not such meat to feed upon. And next them, let those be thankful which have such meat to feed upon when they need it.

The Worthies of England

A Flood in Somerset

May He who bindeth the sea in a girdle of sand, confine it within the proper limits thereof, that Somersetshire may never see that sad accident return, which happened here 1607, when by the irruption of the Severn sea, much mischief was, more had been done, if the west wind had continued longer with the like violence. The country was overflowed, almost twenty miles in length, and four in breadth, and yet but eighty persons drowned therein. It was then observable that creatures of contrary natures, dogs, hares, foxes, conies, cats, mice, getting up to the tops of some hills, dispensed at that time with their antipathies, remaining peaceably together, without sign of fear or violence one towards another: to lesson men in public dangers, to depose private differences, and prefer their safety before their revenge.

The Worthies of England

EDWARD HYDE, EARL OF CLARENDON 1609–1674

John Selden

Mr Selden was a person whom no character can flatter, or transmit in any expressions equal to his merit and virtue. He was of so stupendous learning in all kinds and in all languages, (as may appear in his excellent and transcendent writings,) that a man would have thought he had been entirely conversant amongst books, and had never spent an hour but in reading and writing; yet his humanity, courtesy, and affability was such, that he would have been thought to have been bred in the best courts, but that his good nature, charity, and delight in doing good, and in communicating all he knew, exceeded that breeding. His style in all his writings seems harsh and sometimes obscure; which is not wholly to be imputed to the abstruse subjects of which he commonly treated, out of the paths trod by other men; but to a little undervaluing the beauty of a style, and too much propensity to the language of antiquity: but in his conversation he was the most clear discourser, and had the best faculty of making hard things easy, and presenting them to the understanding, of any man that hath been known.

The Life of Edward, Earl of Clarendon, by Himself, first published 1759

Dr Morley and the Arminians

From some academic contests he had been engaged in, during his living in Christ Church in Oxford, where he was always of the first eminency, he had by the natural faction and animosity of those disputes, fallen under the reproach of holding some opinions, which were not then grateful to those churchmen who had the greatest power in ecclesiastical promotions; and some sharp answers and replies he used to make in accidental discourses, and which in truth were made for mirth and pleasantness sake, (as he was of the highest facetiousness,) were reported, and spread abroad to his prejudice: as being once asked by a grave country gentleman, (who was desirous to be instructed what their tenets and opinions were,) 'what the Arminians held', he pleasantly answered, that *they held all the best bishoprics and deaneries in England*; which was quickly reported abroad, as Dr Morley's definition of the Arminian tenets.

The Life

Lord Falkland

When there was any overture or hope of peace, he would be more erect and vigorous, and exceedingly solicitous to press any thing which he thought might promote it; and sitting among his friends, often, after a deep silence and frequent sighs, would, with a shrill and sad accent, ingeminate the word *Peace, Peace*; and would passionately profess, 'that the very agony of the war, and the view of the calamities and desolation the kingdom did and must endure, took his sleep from him, and would shortly break his heart'. This made some think, or pretend to think, 'that he was so much enamoured on peace, that he would have been glad the king should have bought it at any price'; which was a most unreasonable calumny. As if a man, that was himself the most punctual and precise in every circumstance that might reflect upon conscience or honour, could have wished the king to have committed a trespass against either. And yet this senseless scandal made some impression upon him, or at least he used it for an excuse of the daringness of his spirit; for at the leaguer before Gloucester, when his friends passionately reprehended him for exposing his person unnecessarily to danger, (as he delighted to visit the trenches and nearest approaches, and to discover what the enemy did,) as being so much beside the duty of his place, that it might be understood against it, he would say merrily, 'that his office could not take away the privileges of his age; and that a secretary in war might be present at the greatest secret of danger;' but withal alleged seriously, 'that it concerned him to be more active in enterprises of hazard, than other men; that all might see, that his impatiency for peace proceeded not from pusillanimity, or fear to adventure his own person'.

In the morning before the battle, as always upon action, he was very cheerful, and put himself into the first rank of the lord Byron's regiment, who was then advancing upon the enemy, who had lined the hedges on both sides with musketeers; from whence he was shot with a musket in the lower part of the belly, and in the instant falling from his horse, his body was not found till the next morning; till when, there was some hope he might have been a prisoner; though his nearest friends, who knew his temper, received small comfort from that imagination. Thus fell that incomparable young man, in the four and thirtieth year of his age, having so much despatched the business of life, that the oldest rarely attain to that immense knowledge, and the youngest enter not into the world with more innocence: whosoever leads such a life, needs not care upon how short warning it be taken from him.

The History of the Rebellion, first published 1702–4

Oliver Cromwell

He was one of those men, *quos vituperare ne inimici quidem possunt, nisi ut simul laudent*; for he could never have done half that mischief without great parts of courage, industry, and judgment. He must have had a wonderful understanding in the natures and humours of men, and as great a dexterity in applying them; who, from a private and obscure birth, (though of a good family,) without interest or estate, alliance or friendship, could raise himself to such a height, and compound and knead such opposite and contradictory tempers, humours, and interests into a consistence, that contributed to his designs, and to their own destruction; whilst himself grew insensibly powerful enough to cut off those by whom he had climbed, in the instant that they projected to demolish their own building. What Velleius Paterculus said of Cinna may very justly be said of him, *ausum eum, quae nemo auderet bonus; perfecisse, quae a nullo, nisi fortissimo, perfici possent.* Without doubt, no man with more wickedness ever attempted any thing, or brought to pass what he desired more wickedly, more in the face and contempt of religion, and moral honesty; yet wickedness as great as his could never have accomplished those trophies, without the assistance of a great spirit, an admirable circumspection and sagacity, and a most magnanimous resolution.

When he appeared first in the parliament, he seemed to have a person in no degree gracious, no ornament of discourse, none of those talents which use to reconcile the affections of the stander by: yet as he grew into place and authority, his parts seemed to be raised, as if he had had concealed faculties, till he had occasion to use them; and when he was to act the part of a great man, he did it without any indecency, notwithstanding the want of custom . . .

To reduce three nations, which perfectly hated him, to an entire obedience, to all his dictates; to awe and govern those nations by an army that was indevoted to him, and wished his ruin, was an instance of a very prodigious address. But his greatness at home was but a shadow of the glory he had abroad. It was hard to discover, which feared him most, France, Spain, or the Low Countries, where his friendship was current at the value he put upon it. As they did all sacrifice their honour and their interest to his pleasure, so there is nothing he could have demanded, that either of them would have denied him.

He was not a man of blood, and totally declined Machiavel's method; which prescribes, upon any alteration of government, as a thing absolutely necessary, to cut off all the heads of those, and extirpate their families, who

quos vituperare . . . laudent] whom even their enemies cannot condemn without praising them at the same time *ausum eum . . . possent*] he attempted those things which no good man would have dared venture on, and achieved those in which only a great man could have succeeded

are friends to the old one. It was confidently reported, that, in the council of officers, it was more than once proposed, 'that there might be a general massacre of all the royal party, as the only expedient to secure the government', but that Cromwell would never consent to it; it may be, out of too much contempt of his enemies. In a word, as he had all the wickedness against which damnation is denounced, and for which hell-fire is prepared, so he had some virtues which have caused the memory of some men in all ages to be celebrated; and he will be looked upon by posterity as a brave bad man.

History of the Rebellion

The Stuarts

The truth is, it was the unhappy fate and constitution of that family, that they trusted naturally the judgments of those, who were as much inferior to them in understanding as they were in quality, before their own, which was very good; and suffered even their natures, which disposed them to virtue and justice, to be prevailed upon and altered and corrupted by those, who knew how to make use of some one infirmity that they discovered in them; and by complying with that, and cherishing and serving it, they by degrees wrought upon the mass, and sacrificed all the other good inclinations to that single vice. They were too much inclined to like men at first sight, and did not love the conversation of men of many more years than themselves, and thought age not only troublesome but impertinent. They did not love to deny, and less to strangers than to their friends; not out of bounty or generosity, which was a flower that did never grow naturally in the heart of either of the families, that of Stuart or the other of Bourbon, but out of an unskilfulness and defect in the countenance: and when they prevailed with themselves to make some pause rather [than] to deny, importunity removed all resolution, which they knew neither how to shut out nor to defend themselves against, even when it was evident enough that they had much rather not consent; which often made that which would have looked like bounty lose all its grace and lustre.

The Life

GERRARD WINSTANLEY
1609?–1676?

A Common Treasury

In the beginning of time, the great creator Reason made the earth to be a common treasury to preserve beasts, birds, fishes, and man, the lord that was to govern this creation; for man had domination given to him over the beasts, birds, and fishes; but not one word was spoken in the beginning that one branch of mankind should rule over another.

And the reason is this: Every single man, male and female, is a perfect creature of himself; and the same spirit that made the globe dwells in man to govern the globe; so that the flesh of man, being subject to Reason his maker, hath him to be his teacher and ruler within himself, therefore needs not run abroad after any teacher or ruler without him; for he needs not that any man should teach him, for the same anointing that ruled in the Son of Man teacheth him all things.

But since human flesh (that king of beasts) began to delight himself in the objects of the creation more than in the Spirit Reason and Righteousness, who manifests himself to be the indweller in the five senses of hearing, seeing, tasting, smelling, feeling, then he fell into blindness of mind and weakness of heart, and runs abroad for a teacher and ruler. And so selfish Imagination taking possession of the five senses, and ruling as king in the room of Reason therein, and working with Covetousness, did set up one man to teach and rule over another; and thereby the Spirit was killed, and man was brought into bondage and became a greater slave to such of his own kind than the beasts of the field were to him.

And hereupon the earth (which was made to be a common treasury of relief for all, both beasts and men) was hedged into enclosures by the teachers and rulers, and the others were made servants and slaves; and that earth, that is within this creation made a common storehouse for all, is bought and sold and kept in the hands of a few, whereby the great Creator is mightily dishonoured, as if he were a respecter of persons, delighting in the comfortable livelihood of some and rejoicing in the miserable poverty and straits of others. From the beginning it was not so.

The True Levellers' Standard Advanced, 1649

ANNE BRADSTREET
1612–1672

Spiritual Advantages

There is no object that we see, no action that we do, no good that we enjoy, no evil that we feel or fear, but we may make some spiritual advantage of all; and he that makes such improvement is wise as well as pious.

*

It is reported of the peacock that, priding himself in his gay feathers, he ruffles them up, but spying his black feet, he soon lets fall his plumes; so he that glories in his gifts and adornings should look upon his corruptions, and that will damp his high thoughts.

*

We often see stones hang with drops not from any innate moisture, but from a thick air about them; so may we sometime see marble-hearted sinners seem full of contrition, but it is not from any dew of grace within but from some black clouds that impends them, which produces these sweating effects.

*

All men are truly said to be tenants at will, and it may as truly be said that all have a lease of their lives, some longer, some shorter, as it pleases our great Landlord to let. All have their bounds set, over which they cannot pass, and till the expiration of that time, no dangers, no sickness, no pains, nor troubles shall put a period to our days. The certainty that that time will come, together with the uncertainty, how, where, and when, should make us so to number our days as to apply our hearts to wisdom, that when we are put out of these houses of clay we may be sure of an everlasting habitation that fades not away.

Meditations Divine and Moral, c.1660

JEREMY TAYLOR
1613–1667

Daydreaming

Entertain no fancies of vanity and private whispers of this devil of pride, such as was that of Nebuchadnezzar, *Is not this great Babylon which I have built for the honour of my name, and the might of my majesty, and the power of my kingdom?* Some phantastick spirits will walk alone, and dream waking, of greatnesses, of palaces, of excellent orations, full theatres, loud applauses, sudden advancement, great fortunes; and so will spend an hour with imaginative pleasure, all their employment being nothing but fumes of pride, and secret, indefinite desires, and significations of what their heart wishes. In this, although there is nothing of its own nature directly vicious, yet it is either an ill mother, or an ill daughter, an ill sign or an ill effect; and therefore at no hand consisting with the safety and interests of humility.

Holy Living, 1650

The Deceits of the Heart

A man's heart is infinitely deceitful, unknown to itself, not certain in its own acts, praying one way and desiring another, wandering and imperfect, loose and various, worshipping God and entertaining sin, following what it hates and running from what it flatters, loving to be tempted and betrayed, petulant like a wanton girl, running from, that it might invite the fondness and enrage the appetite of the foolish young man or the evil temptation that follows it; cold and indifferent one while, and presently zealous and passionate, furious and indiscreet; not understood of itself or anyone else, and deceitful beyond all the arts and numbers of observation.

Holy Dying, 1651

Death and Its Trappings

It is a thing that everyone suffers, even persons of the lowest resolution, of the meanest virtue, of no breeding, of no discourse. Take away but the pomps of death, the disguises and solemn bugbears, the tinsel, and the actings by candlelight, and proper and phantastic ceremonies, the minstrels and the noise-makers, the women and the weepers, the swoonings and the shriekings, the nurses and the physicians, the dark room and the ministers, the kindred and the watchers, and then to die is easy, ready and quitted from its troublesome circumstances. It is the same harmless thing, that a poor shepherd suffered yesterday, or a maidservant today; and at the same time in which you die, in that very night, a thousand creatures die with you, some wise men and many fools; and the wisdom of the first will not quit him, and the folly of the latter does not make him unable to die.

Holy Dying

Show Mercy While You Can

Let us take heed: for mercy is like a rainbow, which God set in the clouds to remember mankind; it shines here as long as it is not hindered; but we must never look for it after it is night, and it shines not in the other world; if we refuse mercy here, we shall have justice to eternity.

XXVIII Sermons, 1651

Cheerfulness

Cheerfulness and a festival spirit fills the soul full of harmony, it composes musick for churches and hearts, it makes and publishes glorifications of God, it produces thankfulness and serves the ends of charity, and when the oil of gladness runs over, it makes bright and tall emissions of light and holy fires, reaching up to a cloud, and making joy round about. And therefore since it is so innocent, and may be so pious and full of holy advantage, whatsoever can minister to this holy joy does set forward the work of religion and charity. And indeed charity itself, which is the vertical top of all religion, is nothing else but an union of joys, concentred in the heart, and reflected from all the angles of our life and intercourse. It is a rejoicing in God, a gladness in our neighbour's good, a pleasure in doing good, a rejoicing with him; and without love we cannot have any joy at all. It is this that makes children to be a pleasure, and friendship to be so noble and divine a thing; and upon this account it is certain that all that which can innocently make a man cheerful does also make him charitable; for grief, and age, and sickness, and weariness, these are peevish and troublesome; but mirth and cheerfulness is content, and civil, and compliant, and communicative, and loves to do good, and swells up to felicity only upon the wings of charity.

XXV Sermons, 1653

The Death of a Child

Dear Sir, I am in some little disorder by reason of the death of a little child of mine, a boy that lately made us very glad; but now he rejoices in his little orb, while we think, and sigh, and long to be as safe as he is . . .

letter to John Evelyn, July 1656

A Box of Quicksilver

Reason is such a box of quicksilver that it abides nowhere; it dwells in no settled mansion; it is like a dove's neck, or a changeable taffeta, it looks to me otherwise than to you who do not stand in the same light as I do; and if we inquire after the law of nature by the rules of our reason, we shall be as uncertain as the discourses of the people, or the dreams of disturbed fancies. For some having (as Lucian calls it) weighed reasons in a pair of scales thought them so even, that they concluded no truth to be in the reasonings of men; or if there be, they knew not on which side it stood, and then it is, and if it were not at all: these were the *Scepticks*; and when Varro reckoned two hundred and eighty eight opinions concerning the chiefest good or end of mankind, it is not likely that these wise men should any more agree about the intricate ways and turnings that lead thither, when they so little could agree about the journey's end, which all agreed could have in it no variety, but must be one, and ought to stand fair in the eyes of all men, and to invite the industry of all mankind to the pursuit of it.

Ductor Dubitantium, 1660

A Thin Divide

Virtues and vices have not in all their instances a great landmark set between them, like warlike nations separate by prodigious walls, vast seas and portentous hills; but they are oftentimes like the bounds of a parish; men are fain to cut a cross upon the turf, and make little marks and annual perambulations for memorials. So it is in lawful and unlawful: by a little mistake a man may be greatly ruined.

Righteousness Evangelical, 1663

SIR CHRISTOPHER GUISE
1618–1670

The Circes of Oxford

The vice of Oxford scholars is their frequenting tippling houses, and commonly that liberty most taken by the most ingenious. I was inclined to poetry and all ingenious studies, the scraps of which dropped in at our compotations. There we censured and extolled whom we pleased, and the title of ingenious was a sugared sop that gave a good relish to all concomitant qualities and made us swallow licentiousness and, by consequence, idleness. For whoso begins to think well of himself from that time neglects to improve his stock.

Post vinum Venus is the old saying, and so it was with us; for we being in the blooming time of our youth, our bloods heated with wine and prompted by the spur of our own lazy thoughts and desires, no wonder if we followed and courted any whom we found to be indued with the least beauty, and those tippling houses that make it their business to draw custom by any means are seldom without such sirens, who are taught by all allurements to draw on expenses and yet avoid the last act, well knowing that fruition cloys; so that the youth of Oxford are like to leopards, to whom Bacchus shows the face of Venus in a glass and thereby ensnares them. I cannot forget how many willing glasses I have drunk without any advantage from those women; and so do most young men, their complexions naturally disposing them to hope till they grow into an unhealthy, evil and debauched habit, and so are cozened out of their health and hopeful youths by such Circes; and this perhaps deserves the care of publick authority.

Memoirs of the Family of Guise, written *c.*1665

ABRAHAM COWLEY
1618–1667

Madmen Abroad

Lucretius, by his favour, though a good poet, was but an ill-natured man, when he said, 'it was delightful to see other men in a great storm.' And no less ill-natured should I think Democritus, who laughs at all the world, but that he retired himself so much out of it, that we may perceive he took no great pleasure in that kind of mirth. I have been drawn twice or thrice by company to go to Bedlam, and have seen others very much delighted with the fantastical extravagancy of so many various madnesses, which upon me wrought so contrary an effect, that I always returned, not only melancholy, but even sick with the sight. My compassion there was perhaps too tender, for I meet a thousand madmen abroad, without any perturbation; though to weigh the matter justly, the total loss of reason is less deplorable than the total depravation of it. An exact judge of human blessings, of riches, honours, beauty, even of wit itself, should pity the abuse of them more than the want.

'The Dangers of an Honest Man in Much Company', *Works*, 1668

JOHN EVELYN
1620–1706

Trees, Tears and Precious Balms

Can we look on the prodigious quantity of liquor, which one poor wounded birch will produce in a few hours, and not be astonished? Is it not wonderful that some trees should, in a short space of time, weep more than they weigh? And that so dry, so feeble, and wretched a branch, as that which bears the grape, should yield a juice that cheers the heart of man? That the Pine, Fir, Larch, and other resinous trees, planted in such rude and uncultivated places, amongst rocks and dry pumices, should transude into turpentine, and pearl out into gums and precious balms?

Sylva, or a Discourse of Forest Trees, 1664

The Execution of the Duke of Monmouth

Thus ended this quondam Duke, darling of his father and the ladies, being extremely handsome and adroit; an excellent soldier and dancer, a favourite of the people, of an easy nature, debauched by lust; seduced by crafty knaves, who would have set him up only to make a property, and taken the opportunity of the King being of another religion, to gather a party of discontented men. He failed, and perished.

He was a lovely person, had a virtuous and excellent lady that brought him great riches, and a second dukedom in Scotland. He was Master of the Horse, General of the King his father's army, Gentleman of the Bedchamber, Knight of the Garter, Chancellor of Cambridge; in a word, had accumulations without end. See what ambition and want of principles brought him to! He was beheaded on Tuesday, 14th July.

Diary, 1685

The Death of Samuel Pepys

26*th May* 1703.—This day died Mr Sam. Pepys, a very worthy, industrious, and curious person, none in England exceeding him in knowledge of the Navy, in which he had passed through all the most considerable offices (clerk of the Acts, and secretary of the Admiralty), all which he performed with great integrity. When King James II went out of England, he laid down his office, and would serve no more, but withdrawing himself from all public affairs, he lived at Clapham with his partner Mr Hewer, formerly his clerk, in a very noble house and sweet place, where he enjoyed the fruit of his labours in great prosperity. He was universally beloved, hospitable, generous, learned in many things, skilled in music, a very great cherisher of learned men of whom he had the conversation. His library and collection of other curiosities were of the most considerable, the models of ships especially. Besides what he published of an account of the Navy, as he found and left it, he had for divers years under his hand the *History of the Navy*, or *Navalia* as he called it; but how far advanced, and what will follow of his, is left, I suppose, to his sister's son Mr Jackson, a young gentleman whom Mr Pepys had educated in all sorts of useful learning, sending him to travel abroad, from whence he returned with extraordinary accomplishments, and worthy to be heir. Mr Pepys had been for near forty years so much my particular friend, that Mr Jackson sent me complete mourning, desiring me to be one to hold up the pall at his magnificent obsequies, but my indisposition hindered me from doing him this last office.

Diary

LUCY HUTCHINSON
1620–c.1675

Colonel John Hutchinson

He was of a middle stature, of a slender and exactly well-proportioned shape in all parts, his complexion fair, his hair of a light brown, very thick set in his youth, softer than the finest silk, curling into loose great rings at the ends, his eyes of a lively grey, well shaped and full of life and vigour, graced with many becoming motions, his visage thin, his mouth well made, and his lips very ruddy and graceful, although the nether chap shut over the upper, yet it was in such a manner as was not unbecoming, his teeth were even and white as the purest ivory, his chin was something long, and the mould of his face, his forehead was not very high, his nose was raised and sharp, but withal he had a most amiable countenance, which carried in it something of magnanimity and majesty mixed with sweetness, that at the same time bespoke love and awe in all that saw him; his skin was smooth and white, his legs and feet excellently well made, he was quick in his pace and turns, nimble and active and graceful in all his motions, he was apt for any bodily exercise, and any that he did became him, he could dance admirably well, but neither in youth nor riper years made any practice of it, he had skill in fencing such as became a gentleman, he had a great love of music, and often diverted himself with a viol, on which he played masterly, he had an exact ear and judgment in other music, he shot excellently in bows and guns, and much used them for his exercise, he had great judgment in paintings, graving, sculpture, and all liberal arts, and had many curiosities of value in all kinds, he took great delight in perspective glasses, and for his other rarities was not so much affected with the antiquity as the merit of the work—he took much pleasure in improvement of grounds, in planting groves and walks, and fruit-trees, in opening springs and making fish ponds; of country recreations he loved none but hawking, and in that was very eager and much delighted for the time he used it, but soon left it off; he was wonderfully neat, cleanly and gentle in his habit, and had a very good fancy in it, but he left off very early the wearing of anything that was costly, yet in his plainest negligent habit appeared very much a gentleman; he had more address than force of body, yet the courage of his soul so supplied his members that he never wanted strength when he found occasion to employ it; his conversation was very pleasant, for he was naturally cheerful, had a ready wit and apprehension; he was eager in every thing he did, earnest in dispute, but withal very rational, so that he was seldom overcome, every thing that it was necessary for him to do he did with delight, free and unconstrained, he hated ceremonious compliment, but yet had a natural civility and complaisance to all people, he was of a tender constitution, but through the vivacity of his spirit could undergo labours, watchings and journeys, as well as any of stronger compositions; he was rheumatic, and had a long sickness and distemper occasioned thereby two or three years after the war ended, but else for the latter half of his life was healthy though tender, in his youth and childhood he was sickly, much troubled with weakness and tooth aches, but then his spirit carried him through them; he was very patient under sickness or pain or any common accidents, but yet upon occasions, though never without just ones, he would be very angry, and had even in that such a grace as made him to be feared, yet he was never outrageous in passion; he had a very good faculty in persuading, and would speak very well pertinently and effectually without premeditation upon the greatest occasions that could be offered, for indeed his judgment was so nice, that he could never frame any speech beforehand to please himself, but his invention was so ready and wisdom so habitual in all his speeches, that he never had reason to repent himself of speaking at any time without ranking the words beforehand, he was not talkative yet free of discourse, of a very spare diet, not much given to sleep, an early riser when in health, he never was at any time idle, and hated to see any one else so, in all his natural and ordinary inclinations and composure, there was something extraordinary and tending to virtue, beyond what I can describe, or can be gathered from a bare dead description; there was a life of spirit and power in him that is not to be found in any copy drawn from him: to sum up therefore all that can be said of his outward frame and disposition we must truly conclude, that it was a very handsome and well furnished lodging prepared for the reception of that prince, who in the administration of all excellent virtues reigned there awhile, till he was called back to the palace of the universal emperor.

Memoirs of Colonel Hutchinson, written after 1664; first published 1806

JOHN TILLOTSON, ARCHBISHOP OF CANTERBURY

1624–1690

A Glittering Ignorance

If a man, by a vast and imperious mind, and a heart large as the sand upon the sea-shore (as it is said of Solomon), could command all knowledge of nature and art, of words and things—could attain to a mastery of all languages, and sound the depths of all arts and sciences, their order and motions—could discourse of the interests of all states, the intrigues of all courts, the reason of all civil laws and constitutions, and give an account of the history of all ages—could speak of trees, 'from the cedar-tree that is in Lebanon, even unto the hyssop that springs out of the wall; and of beasts, also, and of fowls, and of creeping things, and of fishes'—and yet should, in the mean time, be destitute of the knowledge of God and Christ, and his duty: all this would be but an impertinent vanity, and a more glittering kind of ignorance; and such a man (like the philosopher, who, whilst he was gazing upon the stars, fell into the ditch) would but *sapienter descendere in infernum*, be undone with all this knowledge, and with a great deal of wisdom go down to hell.

Sermons, 1695–1704

Survival and Insecurity

And when we are grown up, we are liable to a great many mischiefs and dangers, every moment of our lives; and, without the providence of God, continually insecure, not only of the good things of this life, but even of life itself: so that when we come to be men, we cannot but wonder how ever we arrived at that state, and how we have continued in it so long, considering the infinite difficulties and dangers which have continually attended us: that in running the gantlet of a long life, when so many hands have been lifted up against us, and so many strokes levelled at us, we have escaped so free, and with so few marks and scars upon us: that when we are besieged with so many dangers, and so many arrows of death are perpetually flying about us, to which we do so many ways lie open, we should yet hold our twenty, forty, sixty years, and some of us perhaps longer, and do still stand at the mark untouched, at least not dangerously wounded, by any of them: and, considering likewise this fearful and wonderful frame of a human body, this infinitely complicated engine; in which, to the due performance of the several functions and offices of life, so many strings and springs, so many receptacles and channels, are necessary, and all in their right form and order; and in which, besides the infinite imperceptible and secret ways of mortality, there are so many sluices and flood-gates to let death in, and life out, that it is next to a miracle, though we take but little notice of it, that every one of us did not die every day since we were born.

Sermons

GEORGE FOX
1624–1690

A Great Cloud

One morning, as I was sitting by the fire, a great cloud came over me, and a temptation beset me, and I sate still. And it was said, All things come by nature; and the Elements and Stars came over me, so that I was in a moment quite clouded with it; but, inasmuch as I sate still and said nothing, the people of the house perceived nothing. And as I sate still under it and let it alone, a living hope rose in me, and a true voice arose in me which cried: There is a living God who made all things. And immediately the cloud and temptation vanished away, and the life rose over it all, and my heart was glad, and I praised the living God.

The Journal of George Fox, first published 1894

Judicial Proceedings

Judge. Sirrah, will you take the oath?

G.F. I am none of thy sirrahs, I am no sirrah, I am a Christian. Art thou a judge and sits there and gives names to prisoners? It does not become either thy gray hairs or thy office. Thou ought not to give names to prisoners.

Judge. I am a Christian too.

G.F. Then do Christian works.

Journal

MARGARET CAVENDISH, DUCHESS OF NEWCASTLE
1625–1674

A Modest Self-Tribute

My serious study could not be much, by reason I took great delight in attiring, fine dressing, and fashions, especially such fashions as I did invent myself, not taking that pleasure in such fashions as was invented by others. Also I did dislike any should follow my fashions, for I always took delight in a singularity, even in accoutrements of habits. But whatsoever I was addicted to, either in fashion of clothes, contemplation of thoughts, actions of life, they were lawful, honest, honourable, and modest, of which I can avouch to the world with a great confidence, because it is a pure truth. As for my disposition, it is more inclining to be melancholy than merry, but not crabbed or peevishly melancholy, but soft, melting, solitary, and contemplating melancholy. And I am apt to weep rather than laugh, not that I do often either of them. Also I am tender-natured, for it troubles my conscience to kill a fly, and the groans of a dying beast strike my soul. Also where I place a particular affection, I love extraordinarily and constantly, yet not fondly, but soberly and observingly, not to hang about them as a trouble, but to wait upon them as a servant; but this affection will take no root, but where I think or find merit, and have leave both from divine and moral laws. Yet I find this passion so troublesome, as it is the only torment to my life, for fear any evil misfortune or accident, or sickness, or death, should come unto them, insomuch as I am never freely at rest. Likewise I am grateful, for I never received a courtesy—but I am impatient and troubled until I can return it. Also I am chaste, both by nature and education, insomuch as I do abhor an unchaste thought. Likewise I am seldom angry, as my servants may witness for me, for I rather choose to suffer some inconveniences than disturb my thoughts, which makes me wink many times at their faults; but when I am angry, I am very angry, but yet it is soon over, and I am easily pacified, if it be not such an injury as may create a hate. Neither am I apt to be exceptious or jealous, but if I have the least symptom of this passion, I declare it to those it concerns, for I never let it lie smothering in my breast to breed a malignant disease in the mind, which might break out into extravagant passions, or railing speeches, or indiscreet actions; but I examine moderately, reason soberly, and plead gently in my own behalf, through a desire to keep those affections I had, or at least thought to have. And truly I am so vain, as to be so self-conceited, or so naturally partial, to think my friends have as much reason to love me as another, since none can love more sincerely than I, and it were an injustice to prefer a fainter affection, or to esteem the body more than the mind. Likewise I am neither spiteful, envious, nor malicious. I repine not at the gifts that Nature or Fortune bestows upon others, yet I am a great emulator; for, though I wish none worse than they are, yet it is lawful for me to wish myself the best, and to do my honest endeavour thereunto. For I think it no crime to wish myself the exactest of Nature's works, my thread of life the longest, my chain of destiny the strongest, my mind the peaceablest, my life the pleasantest, my death the easiest, and the greatest saint in heaven; also to do my endeavour, so far as honour and honesty doth allow of, to be the highest on Fortune's wheel, and to hold the wheel from turning, if I can. And if it be commendable to wish another's good, it were a sin not to wish my own; for as envy is a vice, so emulation is a virtue, but emulation is in the way to ambition, or indeed it is a noble ambition. But I fear my ambition inclines to vainglory, for

Thomas Hobbes

The wits at court were wont to bait him. But he feared none of them, and would make his part good. The King would call him *the bear*: 'Here comes the bear to be baited.'

He was marvellous happy and ready in his replies, and that without rancour (except provoked), but now I speak of his readiness in replies as to wit and drollery. He would say that he did not care to give, neither was he adroit at, a present answer to a serious *quaere*: he had as lief they should have expected an extemporary solution to an arithmetical problem, for he turned and winded and compounded in philosophy, politics, etc, as if he had been at analytical work. He always avoided, as much as he could, to conclude hastily . . .

In his youth he was unhealthy, of an ill complexion (yellowish): he took colds, being wet in his feet (there were no hackney coaches to stand in the streets) and trod both his shoes aside the same way. Notwithstanding he was well beloved: they loved his company for his pleasant facetiousness and good nature.

From forty, or better, he grew healthier, and then he had a fresh, ruddy complexion . . .

In his old age he was very bald (which claimed a veneration) yet within door he used to study, and sit bare-headed, and said he never took cold in his head, but that the greatest trouble was to keep off the flies from pitching on the baldness.

Face not very great; ample forehead; whiskers yellowish-reddish, which naturally turned up—which is a sign of a brisk wit. Below he was shaved close, except a little tip under his lip. Not but that nature could have afforded a venerable beard, but being naturally of a cheerful and pleasant humour, he affected not at all austerity and gravity to look severe. He desired not the reputation of his wisdom to be taken from the cut of his beard, but from his reason.

He had a good eye, and that of a hazel colour, which was full of life and spirit, even to the last. When he was earnest in discourse, there shone (as it were) a bright live-coal within it. He had two kinds of looks: when he laugh't, was witty, and in a merry humour, one could scarce see his eyes; by and by, when he was serious and positive, he open'd his eyes round (i.e. his eye-lids). He had middling eyes, not very big, not very little . . .

He had read much, if one considers his long life; but his contemplation was much more than his reading. He was wont to say that if he had read as much as other men, he should have known no more than other men.

Brief Lives

facetiousness] amiability

Thomas Goffe

Thomas Goffe the poet was rector here; he was buried in the middle of the chancel, but there is nothing in remembrance of him: his wife, it seems, was not so kind. I find by the register-book that he was buried July 27, 1629. His wife pretended to fall in love with him, by hearing him preach; upon which, said one Thomas Thimble (one of the Squire Bedell's in Oxford, and his confidant) to him, Do not marry her; if thou dost, she will break thy heart. He was not obsequious to his friend's sober advice, but for her sake altered his condition, and cast anchor here.

One time some of his Oxford friends made a visit to him. She look'd upon them with an ill eye, as if they had come to eat her out of her house and home (as they say). She provided a dish of milk, and some eggs for supper, and no more. They perceived her niggardliness, and that her husband was inwardly troubled with it (she wearing the breeches), so they resolv'd to be merry at supper, and talk all in Latin, and laugh'd exceedingly. She was so vex'd at their speaking Latin, that she could not hold, but fell out a-weeping, and rose from the table. The next day, Mr Goffe ordered a better dinner for them, and sent for some wine: they were merry, and his friends took their final leave of him.

'Twas no long time before this Xanthippe made Mr Thimble's prediction good; and when he died, the last words he spake were, *Oracle, Oracle, Tom Thimble*, and so he gave up the ghost.

Brief Lives

John Milton

His harmonical and ingenious soul did lodge in a beautiful and well-proportioned body. He was a spare man. He was scarce so tall as I am (*quaere*, quot feet I am tall: *resp.*, of middle stature).

He had brown hair. His complexion exceeding fair—he was so fair that they call'd him *the Lady of Christ's College*. Oval face. His eye a dark grey.

He was very healthy and free from all diseases; seldom took any physic (only sometimes he took manna); only towards his latter end he was visited with the gout, Spring and Fall.

He had a delicate tunable voice, and good skill. His father instructed him. He had an organ in his house; he played on that most. Of a very cheerful humour. He would be cheerful even in his gout-fits, and sing . . .

Temperate man, rarely drank between meals. Extreme pleasant in his conversation, and at dinner, supper, etc; but satirical. (He pronounced the letter R, *littera canina*, very hard—a certain sign of a satirical wit—*from John Dryden*) . . .

His widow assures me that Mr T. Hobbes was not one of his acquaintance, that her husband did not like him at all, but he would acknowledge him to be a man of great parts, and a learned man. Their interests and tenets did run counter to each other.

Brief Lives

Carlo Fantom

Captain Carlo Fantom, a Croatian, spake 13 languages, was a captain under the Earl of Essex. He was very quarrelsome, and a great ravisher. He left the Parliament party and went to King Ch. the first at Oxford, where he was hanged for ravishing.

Sd. he, I care not for your cause: I come to fight for your half-crown, and your handsome women. My father was a R. Catholiq, and so was my grandfather. I have fought for the Christians against the Turks; and for the Turks against the Christians.

Sir Robert Pye was his colonel, who shot at him for not returning a horse that he took away before the regiment. This was done in a field near Bedford, where the army then was, as they were marching to the relief of Gainsborough. Many are yet living that saw it. Capt. Hamden was by: the bullets went through his buff-coat, and Capt. H saw his shirt on fire. Capt. Carl. Fantom took the bullets, and said he, Sir Rob., here, take your bullets again. None of the soldiers would dare to fight with him; they said, they would not fight with the Devil.

Brief Lives

Eleanor Radcliffe, Countess of Sussex

Countess of Sussex, a great and sad example of the power of lust and slavery of it. She was as great a beauty as any in England, and had a good wit. After her lord's death (he was jealous) she sends for one (formerly her footman) and makes him groom of the chamber. He had the pox and she knew it; a damnable sot. He was not very handsome, but his body of an exquisite shape (*hinc sagittae*). His nostrils were stuff'd and borne out with corks in which were quills to breathe through. About 1666 this Countess died of the pox.

Brief Lives

hinc sagittae] hence the arrows (of love)

ROBERT BOYLE
1627–1691

Seeing the World with New Eyes

The bare prospect of this magnificent fabric of the universe, furnished and adorned with such strange variety of curious and useful creatures, would suffice to transport us both with wonder and joy if their commonness did not hinder their operations. Of which truth Mr Stepkins, the famous oculist, did not long since supply us with a memorable instance; for (as both himself and an illustrious person that was present at the cure, informed me) a maid of about eighteen years of age, having by a couple of cataracts that she brought with her into the world, lived absolutely blind from the moment of her birth, being brought to the free use of her eyes, was so ravished at the surprising spectacle of so many and various objects as presented themselves to her unacquainted sight, that almost everything she saw transported her with such admiration and delight that she was in danger to lose the eyes of her mind by those of her body, and expound that mystical Arabian proverb which advises to shut the windows that the house may be light.

The Usefulness of Experimental Natural Philosophy, 1663

Good Hypotheses and Excellent Hypotheses

The requisites of a *good* hypothesis are:

1. That it be intelligible.
2. That it neither assume nor suppose anything impossible, unintelligible, absurd, or demonstrably false.
3. That it be constant with itself.
4. That it be fit and sufficient to explicate the phaenomena, especially the chief.
5. That it be at least consistent, with the rest of the phaenomena it particularly relate to, and do not contradict any other known phaenomena of nature, or manifest physical truth.

The qualities and conditions of an *excellent* hypothesis are:

1. That it be not precarious, but have sufficient grounds in the nature of the thing itself, or at least be well recommended by some auxiliary grounds.
2. That it be the *simplest* of all the good ones we are able to frame, at least containing nothing that is superfluous or impertinent.
3. That it be the *only* hypothesis that can explicate the phaenomena; or at least, that does explicate them so well.

4. That it enable a skilful naturalist to foretell future phaenomena by their congruity or incongruity to it; and especially the events of such experiments as are aptly devis'd to examine it, as things that ought or ought not to be consequent to it.

manuscript notes

The Moon Demystified

The moon which was anciently a principal deity, is so rude and mountainous a body, that 'tis a wonder speculative men, who consider'd how many, how various, and how noble functions belong to a sensitive soul, could think a mass of matter, so very remote from being fitly organiz'd, should be animated and govern'd by a true, living and sensitive soul.

A Free Inquiry into the Vulgarly Received Notions of Nature, 1685

DOROTHY OSBORNE
1627–1695

What Marriage Can and Can't Do

It was nothing that I expected made me refuse these, but something that I feared, and seriously I finde I want Courage to marry where I doe not like. If we should once come to disputes, I know who would have the worst on't, and I have not faith enough to beleeve a doctrine that is often preached, which is, that though at first one has noe kindenesse for them yet it will grow strangly after marriage. Let them truste to it that think good, for my Parte I am cleerly of opinion (and shall dye int) that as the more one sees, and know's, a person that one likes, one has still the more kindenesse for them, soe on the other side one is but the more weary of and the more averse to an unpleasant humor for haveing it perpetualy by one, and though I easily beleeve that to marry one for whome wee have already some affection, will infinitely Encrease that kindenesse yet I shall never bee perswaded that Marriage has a Charme to raise love out of nothing, much lesse out of dislike.

letter to William Temple, January 1653

Stately Looks

O mee whilest I think ont let mee aske you one question seriously, and pray resolve mee truely, doe I look soe Stately as People aprehende. I vowe to you I made nothing on't when Sir Emperour sayed soe, because I had noe great opinion of his Judgment, but Mr Freeman makes mee mistruste my self Extreamly (not that I am sorry I did apeare soe to him since it kept mee from the displeasure of refuseing an offer, which I doe not perhaps deserve), but that is a scurvy quality in it self, and I am affrayde I have it in great measure if I showed any of it to him, for whome I have soe much of respect and Esteem. If it bee soe you must need's know it, for though my kindnesse will not let mee look soe upon you, you can see what I doe to other People, and besydes there was a time when wee our selves were indifferent to one another, did I doe soe then or have I learn't it since. for god sake tell mee that I may try to mend it. I could wish too, that you would lay your commands on mee to forbeare fruite, heer is Enough to kill a 1000 such as I am, and soe Exelently good, that nothing but your power can secure mee, therfor forbid it mee that I may live to bee Your

letter to William Temple, June 1653

Melancholy Looks

Would you could make your words good, that my Ey's can dispell all mellancholy Clouded humors, I would looke in the glasse all day longe but I would cleare up my owne. Alasse, they are soe farr from that, they would teach one to bee sad, that knew nothing on't, for in other peoples opinions as well as my owne they have the most of it in them that Ey's can have. My Mother (I remember) used to say I needed noe tear's to perswade my trouble, and that I had lookes soe farr beyonde them, that were all the friends I had in the world, dead, more could not bee Expected then such a sadnesse in my Ey's, this indeed I think is naturall to them, or at least long custome has made it soe. 'Tis most true that our friendship has bin brought up hardly enough, and posibly it thrives the better for't, tis observed that surfeits kill more then fasting do's, but ours is in noe danger of that . . .

Last night, I was in the Garden till Eleven a clock, it was the Sweetest night that ere I saw, the Garden looked soe well, and the Jessomin smelt beyond all perfumes, and yet I was not pleased. The place had all the Charmes it used to have when I was most sattisfied with it and had you bin there I should have liked it much more than Ever I did, but that not being it was noe more to mee then the next feilde . . .

letter to William Temple, July 1653

Free and Easy

In my Opinion these great Schollers are not the best writer's, (of Letters I mean, of books perhaps they are) I never had I think but one letter from Sir Jus: but twas worth twenty of any body's else to make mee sport, it was the most sublime nonsence that in my life I ever read and yet I beleeve hee decended as low as hee could to come neer my weak understanding. Twill bee noe Complement after this to say I like your letters in themselv's, not as they come from one that is not indifferent to mee. But seriously I doe. All Letters mee thinks should bee free and Easy as ones discourse, not studdyed, as an Oration, nor made up of hard words like a Charme. Tis an admirable thing to see how some People will labour to finde out term's that may Obscure a plaine sence, like a gentleman I knew, whoe would never say the weather grew cold, but that Winter began to salute us.

letter to William Temple, September 1653

Like a Wasted Country

Alasse were I in my owne disposall you should come to my Grave to bee resolved, but Greif alone will not kill. All that I can say then is, that I resolve on nothing but to Arme my self with patience, to resist nothing that is layd upon mee, not struggle for what I have noe hope to gett. I have noe End's nor noe designes nor will my heart ever bee capable of any, but like a Country wasted by a Civill warr, where two opposeing Party's have disputed theire right soe long till they have made it worth neither of theire conquest's, tis Ruin'd and desolated by the long striffe within it to that degree as twill bee usefull to none, nobody that know's the condition tis in will think it worth the gaineing, and I shall not cousen any body with it.

letter to William Temple, December 1653

JOHN BUNYAN
1628–1688

The Desperateness of Man's Heart

But to be brief, one morning, as I did lie in my bed, I was, as at other times, most fiercely assaulted with this temptation, to sell and part with Christ; the wicked suggestion still running in my mind. Sell him, sell him, sell him, sell him, sell him, as fast as a man could speak; against which also, in my mind, as at other times, I answered, No, no, not for thousands, thousands, thousands, at least twenty times together. But at last, after much striving, even until I was almost out of breath, I felt this thought pass through my heart, Let him go, if he will! and I thought also, that I felt my heart freely consent thereto. Oh, the diligence of Satan! Oh, the desperateness of man's heart!

Now was the battle won, and down fell I, as a bird that is shot from the top of a tree, into great guilt, and fearful despair. Thus getting out of my bed, I went moping into the field; but God knows, with as heavy a heart as mortal man, I think, could bear; where, for the space of two hours, I was like a man bereft of life, and as now past all recovery, and bound over to eternal punishment.

Grace Abounding, 1666

A Man Clothed in Rags

As I walked through the wilderness of this world, I lighted on a certain place, where was a den; and I laid me down in that place to sleep: and as I slept I dreamed a dream. I dreamed, and behold I saw a man clothed with rags, standing in a certain place, with his face from his own house, a book in his hand, and a great burden upon his back. I looked, and saw him open the book, and read therein; and as he read, he wept and trembled: and not being able longer to contain, he brake out with a lamentable cry; saying, 'What shall I do?'

The Pilgrim's Progress, 1678

The Slough of Despond

Now I saw in my dream, that just as they had ended this talk they drew near to a very miry slough, that was in the midst of the plain; and they, being heedless, did both fall suddenly into the bog. The name of the slough was Despond. Here, therefore, they wallowed for a time, being grievously bedaubed with dirt; and Christian, because of the burden that was on his back, began to sink in the mire.

Pliable. Then said Pliable, Ah, neighbor Christian, where are you now?

Christian. Truly, said Christian, I do not know.

Pliable. At that Pliable began to be offended, and angrily said to his fellow, Is this the happiness you have told me all this while of? If we have such ill speed at our first setting out, what may we expect 'twixt this and our journey's end? May I get out again with my life, you shall possess the brave country alone for me. And, with that, he gave a desperate struggle or two, and got out of the mire on that side of the slough which was next to his own house: so away he went, and Christian saw him no more.

Wherefore Christian was left to tumble in the Slough of Despond alone: but still he endeavored to struggle to that side of the slough that was further from his own house, and next to the wicket-gate; the which he did, but could not get out, because of the burden that was upon his back: but I beheld in my dream, that a man came to him, whose name was Help, and asked him what he did there?

Christian. Sir, said Christian, I was bid go this way by a man called Evangelist, who directed me also to yonder gate, that I might escape the wrath to come; and as I was going thither I fell in here.

Help. But why did not you look for the steps?

Christian. Fear followed me so hard that I fled the next way, and fell in.

Help. Then said he, Give me thy hand; so he gave him his hand, and he drew him out, and set him upon sound ground, and bid him go on his way.

Then I stepped to him that plucked him out, and said, Sir, wherefore, since over this place is the way from the City of Destruction to yonder gate, is it that this plat is not mended, that poor travelers might go thither with more security? And he said unto me, This miry slough is such a place as cannot be mended; it is the descent whither the scum and filth that attends conviction for sin doth continually run, and therefore it was called the Slough of Despond; for still, as the sinner is awakened about his lost condition, there ariseth in his soul many fears, and doubts, and discouraging apprehensions, which all of them get together, and settle in his place. And this is the reason of the badness of this ground.

The Pilgrim's Progress

The Trial of Faithful

Then went the jury out, whose names were Mr Blind-man, Mr No-good, Mr Malice, Mr Love-lust, Mr Live-loose, Mr Heady, Mr High-mind, Mr Enmity, Mr Liar, Mr Cruelty, Mr Hate-light, and Mr Implacable; who every one gave in his private verdict against him among themselves, and afterwards unanimously concluded to bring him in guilty before the Judge. And first, among themselves, Mr Blind-man, the foreman, said, I see clearly that this man is a heretic. Then said Mr No-good, Away with such a fellow from the earth. Ay, said Mr Malice, for I hate the very looks of him. Then said Mr Love-lust, I could never endure him. Nor I, said Mr Live-loose, for he would always be condemning my way. Hang him, hang him, said Mr Heady. A sorry scrub, said Mr High-mind. My heart riseth against him, said Mr Enmity. He is a rogue, said Mr Liar. Hanging is too good for him, said Mr Cruelty. Let's despatch him out of the way, said Mr Hate-light. Then said Mr Implacable, Might I have all the world given me, I could not be reconciled to him; therefore, let us forthwith bring him in guilty of death. And so they did; therefore he was presently condemned to be had from the place where he was, to the place from whence he came, and there to be put to the most cruel death that could be invented.

They therefore brought him out to do with him according to their law; and, first, they scourged him, then they buffeted him, then they lanced his flesh with knives; after that, they stoned him with stones, then pricked him with their swords; and, last of all, they burned him to ashes at the stake. Thus came Faithful to his end.

Now I saw that there stood behind the multitude a chariot and a couple of horses, waiting for Faithful, who (so soon as his adversaries had despatched him) was taken up into it, and straightway was carried up through the clouds, with sound of trumpet, the nearest way to the celestial gate.

The Pilgrim's Progress

Mr By-ends

Christian. Pray sir, what may I call you? said Christian.

By-ends. I am a stranger to you, and you to me; if you be going this way, I shall be glad of your company; if not, I must be content.

Christian. This town of Fair-speech, said Christian, I have heard of it, and, as I remember, they say it's a wealthy place.

By-ends. Yes, I will assure you that it is, and I have very many rich kindred there.

Christian. Pray who are your kindred there, if a man may be so bold?

By-ends. Almost the whole town; and in particular, my Lord Turn-about, my Lord Time-server, my Lord Fair-speech (from whose ancestors that town first took its name), also Mr Smooth-man, Mr Facing-bothways, Mr Any-thing, and the parson of our parish, Mr Two-tongues, was my mother's own brother by father's side: and to tell you the truth, I am become a gentleman of good quality; yet my great-grandfather was but a waterman, looking one way and rowing another: and I got most of my estate by the same occupation.

Christian. Are you a married man?

By-ends. Yes, and my wife is a very virtuous woman, the daughter of a virtuous woman. She was my Lady Faining's daughter, therefore she came of a very honourable family, and is arrived to such a pitch of breeding that she knows how to carry it to all, even to prince and peasant. 'Tis true, we somewhat differ in religion from those of the stricter sort, yet but in two small points: first, we never strive against wind and tide; secondly, we are always most zealous when religion goes in his silver slippers; we love much to walk with him in the street if the sun shines and the people applaud it.

The Pilgrim's Progress

The Doubters Infest Mansoul

Now a man might have walked for days together in Mansoul, and scarce have seen one in town that looked like a religious man. O the fearful state of Mansoul now! Now every corner swarmed with outlandish Doubters; red-coats and black-coats walked the town by clusters, and filled up all the houses with hideous noises, vain songs, lying stories, and blasphemous language against Shaddai and his Son. Now, also, those Diabolonians that lurked in the walls and dens and holes that were in the town of Mansoul, came forth and showed themselves, yea, walked with open face in company with the Doubters that were in Mansoul. Yea, they had more boldness now to walk the streets, to haunt the houses, and to show themselves abroad, than had any of the honest inhabitants of the now woful town of Mansoul.

The Holy War, 1682

A Summons

After this it was noised abroad that Mr Valiant-for-Truth was taken with a summons, by the same Post as the other; and had this for a token that the summons was true, *That his pitcher was broken at the fountain.* When he understood it, he called for his friends, and told them of it. Then said he, 'I am going to my fathers, and though with great difficulty I am got hither, yet now I do not repent me of all the trouble I have been at to arrive where I am. My sword, I give to him that shall succeed me in my pilgrimage, and my courage and skill, to him that can get it. My marks and scars I carry with me, to be a witness for me that I have fought his battles who now will be my rewarder.' When the day that he must go hence was come many accompanied him to the River side, into which, as he went, he said, '*Death, where is thy sting?*' And as he went down deeper, he said, '*Grave where is thy victory?*' So he passed over, and the trumpets sounded for him on the other side.

The Pilgrim's Progress, Part II, 1684.

SIR WILLIAM TEMPLE
1628–1699

Poetry, Music and a Froward Child

I know very well that many, who pretend to be wise by the forms of being grave, are apt to despise both poetry and music as toys and trifles too light for the use or entertainment of serious men: but whoever find themselves wholly insensible to these charms, would, I think, do well to keep their own counsel, for fear of reproaching their own temper, and bringing the goodness of their natures, if not of their understandings, into question: it may be thought at least an ill sign, if not an ill constitution, since some of the fathers went so far, as to esteem the love of music a sign of predestination, as a thing divine, and reserved for the felicities of heaven itself. While this world lasts, I doubt not but the pleasure and requests of these two entertainments will do so too: and happy those that content themselves with these, or any other so easy and so innocent and do not trouble the world, or other men, because they cannot be quiet themselves though no body hurts them!

When all is done, human life is, at the greatest and the best, but like a froward child, that must be played with and humoured a little to keep it quiet till it falls asleep, and then the care is over.

'Of Poetry', *Miscellanies*, 1680–1701

JOHN DRYDEN
1631–1700

The Spread of True Science

Is it not evident, in these last hundred years, when the study of philosophy has been the business of all the virtuosi in Christendom, that almost a new nature has been revealed to us? that more errors of the School have been detected, more useful experiments in philosophy have been made, more noble secrets in optics, medicine, anatomy, astronomy discovered, than in all those credulous and doting ages from Aristotle to us?—so true it is, that nothing spreads more fast than science, when rightly and generally cultivated.

An Essay of Dramatic Poesy, 1668

On-Stage and Off-Stage

But there is another sort of relations, that is, of things happening in the action of the play, and supposed to be done behind the scenes; and this is many times both convenient and beautiful; for by it the French avoid the tumult to which we are subject in England by representing duels, battles, and the like; which renders our stage too like the theatres where they fight prizes. For what is more ridiculous than to represent an army with a drum and five men behind it; all which the hero of the other side is to drive in before him; or to see a duel fought, and one slain with two or three thrusts of the foils, which we know are so blunted, that we might give a man an hour to kill another in good earnest with them.

I have observed that in all our tragedies the audience cannot forbear laughing when the actors are to die; it is the most comic part of the whole play. All *passions* may be lively represented on the stage, if to the well-writing of them the actor supplies a good commanded voice, and limbs that move easily, and without stiffness; but there are many *actions* which can never be imitated to a just height: dying especially is a thing which none but a Roman gladiator could naturally perform on the stage, when he did not imitate or represent, but do it; and therefore it is better to omit the representation of it.

The words of a good writer, which describe it lively, will make a deeper impression of belief in us than all the actor can insinuate into us, when he seems to fall dead before us; as a poet in the description of a beautiful garden, or a meadow, will please our imagination more than the place itself can please our sight. When we see death represented, we are convinced it is but fiction; but when we hear it related, our eyes, the strongest witnesses, are wanting, which might have undeceived us; and we are all willing to favour the sleight, when the poet does not too grossly impose on us.

An Essay of Dramatic Poesy

The Satirist's Art

How easy is it to call rogue and villain, and that wittily! But how hard to make a man appear a fool, a blockhead, or a knave without using any of those opprobrious terms! To spare the grossness of the names, and to do the thing yet more severely, is to draw a full face, and to make the nose and cheeks stand out, and yet not to employ any depth of shadowing. This is the mystery of that noble trade, which yet no master can teach to his apprentice; he may give the rules, but the scholar is never the nearer in his practice. Neither is it true that this fineness of raillery is offensive. A witty man is tickled while he is hurt in this manner, and a fool feels it not. The occasion of an offense may possibly be given, but he cannot take it. If it be granted that in effect this way does more mischief; that a man is secretly wounded, and though he be not sensible himself, yet the malicious world will find it out for him; yet there is still a vast difference betwixt the slovenly butchering of a man, and the fineness of a stroke that separates the head from the body, and leaves it standing in its place. A man may be capable, as Jack Ketch's wife said of his servant, of a plain piece of work, a bare hanging; but to make a malefactor die sweetly was only belonging to her husband. I wish I could apply it to myself, if the reader would be kind enough to think it belongs to me. The character of Zimri in my *Absalom* is, in my opinion, worth the whole poem: it is not bloody, but it is ridiculous enough; and he, for whom it was intended, was too witty to resent it as an injury. If I had railed, I might have suffered for it justly; but I managed my own work more happily, perhaps more dexterously. I avoided the mention of great crimes, and applied myself to the representing of blindsides, and little extravagancies; to which, the wittier a man is, he is generally the more obnoxious. It succeeded as I wished; the jest went round, and he was laughed at in his turn who began the frolic.

A Discourse Concerning the Original and Progress of Satire, 1693

In His Seventieth Year

I have added some original papers of my own, which whether they are equal or inferior to my other poems, an author is the most improper judge; and therefore I leave them wholly to the mercy of the reader. I will hope the best, that they will not be condemned; but if they should, I have the excuse of an old gentleman, who, mounting on horseback before some ladies, when I was present, got up somewhat heavily, but desired of the fair spectators, that they would count fourscore and eight before they judged him. By the mercy of God, I am already come within twenty years of his number; a cripple in my limbs, but what decays are in my mind, the reader must determine. I think myself as vigorous as ever in the faculties of my soul, excepting only my memory, which is not impaired to any great degree; and if I lose not more of it, I have no great reason to complain. What judgement I had, increases rather than diminishes; and thoughts, such as they are, come crowding in so fast upon me, that my only difficulty is to choose or to reject, to run them into verse, or to give them the other harmony of prose: I have so long studied and practised both, that they are grown into a habit, and become familiar to me. In short, though I may lawfully plead some part of the old gentleman's excuse, yet I will reserve it till I think I have greater need, and ask no grains of allowance for the faults of this my present work, but those which are given of course to human frailty.

Preface to the Fables, 1700

JOHN LOCKE
1632–1704

A Sort of Hawking and Hunting

He that hawks at larks and sparrows, has no less sport, though a much less considerable quarry, than he that flies at nobler game: and he is little acquainted with the subject of this treatise, the UNDERSTANDING, who does not know, that as it is the most elevated faculty of the soul, so it is employed with a greater and more constant delight than any of the other. Its searches after truth, are a sort of hawking and hunting, wherein the very pursuit makes a great part of the pleasure. Every step the mind takes in its progress towards knowledge, makes some discovery, which is not only new, but the best too, for the time at least.

An Essay concerning Human Understanding, 1690

Working Within Our Limits

We shall not have much reason to complain of the narrowness of our minds, if we will but employ them about what may be of use to us; for of that they are very capable: and it will be an unpardonable, as well as childish peevishness, if we undervalue the advantages of our knowledge, and neglect to improve it to the ends for which it was given us, because there are some things that are set out of the reach of it. It will be no excuse to an idle and untoward servant, who would not attend his business by candle-light, to plead that he had not broad sunshine. The candle, that is set up in us, shines bright enough for all our purposes. The discoveries we can make with this, ought to satisfy us; and we shall then use our understandings right, when we entertain all objects in that way and proportion that they are suited to our faculties, and upon those grounds they are capable of being proposed to us, and not peremptorily, or intemperately require demonstration, and demand certainty, where probability only is to be had, and which is sufficient to govern all our concernments. If we will disbelieve every thing, because we certainly cannot know all things; we shall do much-what as wisely as he, who would not use his legs, but sit still and perish, because he had no wings to fly.

An Essay Concerning Human Understanding

Passionate Chiding

As children should very seldom be corrected by blows; so, I think, frequent, and especially, passionate chiding, of almost as ill consequence. It lessens the authority of the parents, and the respect of the child: for I bid you still remember, they distinguish early betwixt passion and reason: and as they cannot but have a reverence for what comes from the latter, so they quickly grow into a contempt of the former; or if it causes a present terrour, yet it soon wears off; and natural inclination will easily learn to slight such scarecrows, which make a noise, but are not animated by reason.

Some Thoughts Concerning Education, 1693

Keeping Guard against Cruelty

One thing I have frequently observed in children, that, when they have got possession of any poor creature, they are apt to use it ill; they often torment and treat very roughly young birds, butterflies, and such other poor animals, which fall into their hands, and that with a seeming kind of pleasure. This, I think, should be watched in them; and if they incline to any such cruelty, they should be taught the contrary usage; for the custom of tormenting and killing of beasts will, by degrees, harden their minds even towards men; and they who delight in the suffering and destruction of inferior creatures, will not be apt to be very compassionate or benign to those of their own kind. Children should from the beginning be bred up in an abhorrence of killing or tormenting any living creature, and be taught not to spoil or destroy any thing unless it be for the preservation or advantage of some other that is nobler. And truly, if the preservation of all mankind, as much as in him lies, were every one's persuasion, as indeed it is every one's duty, and the true principle to regulate our religion, politics, and morality by, the world would be much quieter, and better natured, than it is.

Some Thoughts Concerning Education

A Test for Prejudice

Every one is forward to complain of the prejudices that mislead other men or parties, as if he were free, and had none of his own. This being objected on all sides, it is agreed, that it is a fault and an hindrance to knowledge. What now is the cure? No other but this, that every man should let alone other prejudices, and examine his own. Nobody is convinced of his by the accusation of another; he recriminates by the same rule, and is clear. The only way to remove this great cause of ignorance and errour out of the world, is, for every one impartially to examine himself . . .

To those who are willing to get rid of this great hindrance of knowledge (for to such only I write) to those who would shake off this great and dangerous impostor, prejudice, who dresses up falsehood in the likeness of truth, and so dexterously hoodwinks men's minds, as to keep them in the dark, with a belief that they are more in the light than any that do not see with their eyes; I shall offer this one mark whereby prejudice may be known. He that is strongly of any opinion, must suppose (unless he be self-condemned) that his persuasion is built upon good grounds; and that his assent is no greater than what the evidence of the truth he holds forces him to; and that they are arguments, and not inclination, or fancy, that make him so confident and positive in his tenets. Now, if after all his profession, he cannot bear any opposition to his opinion, if he cannot so much as give a patient hearing, much less examine and weigh the arguments on the other side, does he not plainly confess it is prejudice governs him? and is it not the evidence of truth, but some lazy anticipation, some beloved presumption, that he desires to rest undisturbed in. For, if what he holds be, as he gives out, well fenced with evidence, and he sees it to be true, what need he fear to put it to the proof? If his opinion be settled upon a firm foundation, if the arguments that support it, and have obtained his assent, be clear, good, and convincing, why should he be shy to have it tried whether they be proof or not?

Of the Conduct of the Understanding, 1706

The Ruminating Kind

This is that which I think great readers are apt to be mistaken in. Those who have read of every thing, are thought to understand every thing too; but it is not always so. Reading furnishes the mind only with materials of knowledge, it is thinking makes what we read ours. We are of the ruminating kind, and it is not enough to cram ourselves with a great load of collections; unless we chew them over again, they will not give us strength and nourishment.

Of the Conduct of the Understanding

SAMUEL PEPYS
1633–1703

The Book of Common Prayer and a Black Patch

Lords day. In the morn to our own church, where Mr Mills did begin to nibble at the Common Prayer by saying 'Glory be to the Father,' &c after he had read the two psalms. But the people have beene so little used to it that they could not tell what to answer. After dinner to Westminster, where I went to my Lord; and having spoke with him, I went to the abby, where the first time that ever I heard the organs in a Cathedrall. My wife seemed very pretty today, it being the first time that I have given her leave to weare a black patch.

Diary, November 1660

A Warm Winter's Day

It is strange what weather we have had all this winter; no cold at all, but the ways are dusty and the flyes fly up and down, and the rosebushes are full of leaves; such a time of the year as never was known in this world before here. This day, many more of the fith monarchy men were hanged.

Diary, January 1661

Incident at the Theatre

At the office all the morning. Dined at home. And after dinner to Mr Crews and thence to the Theatre, where I saw again *The Lost Lady*, which doth now please me better then before. And here, I sitting behind in a dark place, a lady spat backward upon me by a mistake, not seeing me. But after seeing her to be a very pretty lady, I was not troubled at it at all.

Diary, January 1661

A Liberal Genius

Lords day. This day I stirred not out, but took physique and it did work very well; and all the day, as I was at leisure, I did read in Fuller's *Holy Warr* (which I have of late bought) and did try to make a Song in the prayse of a Liberall genius (as I take my own to be) to all studies and pleasures; but it not proving to my mind, I did reject it and so proceeded not in it. At night my wife and I had a good supper by ourselfs, of a pullet hashed; which pleased me much to see my condition come to allow ourselfs a dish like that. And so at night to bed.

Diary, November 1661

What Dreams May Come . . .

Up by 4 a-clock and walked to Greenwich, where called at Capt. Cockes and to his chamber, he being in bed—where something put my last night's dream into my head, which I think is the best that ever was dreamed—which was, that I had my Lady Castlemayne in my armes and was admitted to use all the dalliance I desired with her, and then dreamed that this could not be awake but that it was only a dream. But that since it was a dream and that I took so much real pleasure in it, what a happy thing it would be, if when we are in our graves (as Shakespeere resembles it), we could dream, and dream but such dreams as this—that then we should not need to be so fearful of death as we are this plague-time.

Diary, August 1665

The Great Fire

Lords day. Some of our maids sitting up late last night to get things ready against our feast today, Jane called us up, about 3 in the morning, to tell us of a great fire they saw in the City. So I rose, and slipped on my night-gown and went to her window, and thought it to be on the back side of Markelane at the furthest; but being unused to such fires as fallowed, I thought it far enough off, and so went to bed again and to sleep. About 7 rose again to dress myself, and there looked out at the window and saw the fire not so much as it was, and further off. So to my closet to set things to rights after yesterday's cleaning. By and by Jane comes and tells me that she hears that above 300 houses have been burned down tonight by the fire we saw, and that it was now burning down all Fishstreet by London Bridge. So I made myself ready presently, and walked to the Tower and there got up upon one of the high places, Sir J. Robinsons little son going up with me; and there I did see the houses at that end of the bridge all on fire, and an infinite great fire on this and the other side the end of the bridge—which, among other people, did trouble me for poor little Michell and our Sarah on the Bridge. So down, with my heart full of trouble, to the Lieutenant of the Tower, who tells me that it begun this morning in the King's bakers house in Pudding lane, and that it hath burned down St. Magnes Church and most part of Fishstreete already. So I down to the waterside and there got a boat and through the bridge, and there saw a lamentable fire. Poor Michells house, as far as the Old Swan, already burned that way and the fire running further, that in a very little time it got as far as the Stillyard while I was there. Everybody endeavouring to remove their goods, and flinging into the River or bringing them into lighters that lay off. Poor people staying in their houses as long as till the very fire touched them, and then running into boats or clambering from one pair of stair by the waterside to another. And among other things, the poor pigeons I perceive were loath to leave their houses, but hovered about the windows and balconies till they were some of them burned, their wings, and fell down . . .

Diary, September 1666

On Epsom Downs

The women and W. Hewer and I walked upon the Downes, where a flock of sheep was, and the most pleasant and innocent sight that ever I saw in my life; we find a shepheard and his little boy reading, far from any houses or sight of people, the Bible to him. So I made the boy read to me, which he did with the forced Tone that children do usually read, that was mighty pretty; and then I did give him something and went to the father and talked with him; and I find he had been a servant in my Cosen Pepys's house, and told me what was become of their old servants. He did content himself mightily in my liking his boy's reading and did bless God for him, the most like one of the old Patriarchs that ever I saw in my life, and it brought those thoughts of the old age of the world in my mind for two or three days after. We took notice of his woolen knit stockings of two colours mixed, and of his shoes shod with Iron shoes, both at the toe and heels, and with great nails in the soles of his feet, which was mighty pretty; and taking notice of them, 'Why,' says the poor man, 'the Downes, you see, are full of stones, and we are fain to shoe ourselfs thus; and these,' says he, 'will make the stones fly till they sing before me.' I did give the poor man something, for which he was mighty thankful, and I tried to cast stones with his Horne Crooke. He values his dog mightily, that would turn a sheep any way which he would have him when he goes to fold them. Told me there was about 18 Scoare sheep in his flock, and that he hath 4*s*. a week the year round for keeping of them. So we parted thence, with mighty pleasure in the discourse we had with this poor man; and Mrs Turner, in the common fields here, did gather one of the prettiest nosegays that ever I saw in my life.

Diary, July 1667

A Bawdy Book

Homeward by coach and stopped at Martins my bookseller, where I saw the French book which I did think to have had for my wife to translate, called *L'escholle de Filles*, but when I came to look into it, it is the most bawdy, lewd book that ever I saw, rather worse then *putana errante*—so that I was ashamed of reading in it; and so away home . . .

Diary, 13 January 1668

Away to the Strand to my bookseller's, and there stayed an hour and bought that idle, roguish book, *L'escholle des Filles*; which I have bought in plain binding (avoiding the buying of it better bound) because I resolve, as soon as I have read it, to burn it, that it may not stand in the list of books, nor among them, to disgrace them if it should be found. Thence home, and busy late at the office; and then home to supper and to bed.

8 February

Lords day. Up, and at my chamber all the morning and the office, doing business and also reading a little of *L'escolle des Filles*, which is a mighty lewd book, but yet not amiss for a sober man once to read over to inform himself in the villainy of the world. At noon home to dinner, where by appointment Mr Pelling came, and with him three friends: Wallington that sings the good bass, and one Rogers, and a gentleman, a young man, his name Tempest, who sings very well endeed and understands anything in the world at first sight . . . We sang till almost night, and drank my good store of wine; and then they parted and I to my chamber, where I did read through *L'escholle des Filles*; and after I had done it, I burned it, that it might not be among my books to my shame; and so at night to supper and then to bed.

9 February

In Flagrante

Lords day. Up, and discoursing with my wife about our house and many new things we are doing of; and so to church I, and there find Jack Fen come, and his wife, a pretty black woman; I never saw her before, nor took notice of her now. So home and to dinner; and after dinner, all the afternoon got my wife and boy to read to me. And at night W. Batelier comes and sups with us; and after supper, to have my head combed by Deb, which occasioned the greatest sorrow to me that ever I knew in this world; for my wife, coming up suddenly, did find me imbracing the girl con my hand sub su coats; and endeed, I was with my main in her cunny. I was at a wonderful loss upon it, and the girl also; and I endeavoured to put it off, but my wife was struck mute and grew angry, and as her voice came to her, grew quite out of order; and I do say little, but to bed; and my wife said little also, but could not sleep all night; but about 2 in the morning waked me and cried, and fell to tell me as a great secret that she was a Roman Catholique and had received the Holy Sacrament; which troubled me but I took no notice of it, but she went on from one thing to another, till at last it appeared plainly her trouble was at what she saw; but yet I did not know how much she saw and therefore said nothing to her. But after her much crying and reproaching me with inconstancy and preferring a sorry girl before her, I did give her no provocations but did promise all fair usage to her, and love, and foreswore any hurt that I did with her—till at last she seemed to be at ease again; and so toward morning, a little sleep; and so I, with some little repose and rest, rose, and up and by water to White-hall, but with my mind mightily troubled for the poor girl, whom I fear I have undone by this, my [wife] telling me that she would turn her out of door.

Diary, October 1668

GEORGE SAVILE, MARQUESS OF HALIFAX 1633–1695

In Praise of Parliamentary Government

Our Government is like our climate. There are winds which are sometimes loud and unquiet, and yet with all the trouble they give us, we owe great part of our health unto them; they clear the air, which else would be like a standing pool, and instead of refreshment would be a disease unto us. There may be fresh gales of asserting liberty, without turning into such storms or hurricanes, as that the state should run any hazard of being cast away by them. These strugglings, which are natural to all mixed governments, while they are kept from growing into convulsions do by a mutual agitation from the several parts rather support and strengthen than weaken or maim the constitution; and the whole frame, instead of being torn or disjointed, cometh to be the better and closer knit by being thus exercised. But whatever faults our Government may have, or a discerning critic may find in it when he looketh upon it alone, let any other be set against it, and then it showeth its comparative beauty. Let us look upon the most glittering outside of unbounded authority, and upon a nearer enquiry we shall find nothing but poor and miserable deformity within.

The Character of a Trimmer, 1688

Charles the Second

It may be said that his inclinations to love were the effects of health and a good constitution, with as little mixture of the seraphic part as ever man had; and though from that foundation men often raise their passions I am apt to think his stayed as much as any man's ever did in the lower region. This made him like easy mistresses.

*

He was so good at finding out other men's weak sides that it made him less intent to cure his own; that generally happeneth. It may be called a treacherous talent, for it betrayeth a man to forget to judge himself, by being so eager to censure others; this doth so misguide men the first part of their lives, that the habit of it is not easily recovered when the greater ripeness of their judgment inclineth them to look more into themselves than into other men.

Men love to see themselves in the false looking-glass of other men's failings. It maketh a man think well of himself at the time, and by sending his thoughts abroad to get food for laughing they are less at leisure to see faults at home. Men choose rather to make the war in another country than to keep all well at home.

*

He had a mechanical head, which appeared in his inclination to shipping and fortification, &c. This would make one conclude that his thoughts would naturally have been more fixed to business, if his pleasures had not drawn them away from it.

He had a very good memory, though he would not always make equal good use of it. So that if he had accustomed himself to direct his faculties to his business I see no reason why he might not have been a good deal master of it. His chain of memory was longer than his chain of thought;

the first could bear any burden, the other was tired by being carried on too long; it was fit to ride a heat, but it had not wind enough for a long course.

A very great memory often forgetteth how much time is lost by repeating things of no use. It was one reason of his talking so much; since a great memory will always have something to say, and will be discharging itself, whether in or out of season, if a good judgment doth not go along with it, to make it stop and turn. One might say of his memory, that it was a *beauté journalière*; sometimes he would make shrewd application, &c., at others he would bring things out of it that never deserved to be laid in it.

A Character of Charles the Second, written *c.*1690

Look to Your Moat

I will make no other introduction to the following discourse, than that as the importance of our being strong at sea was ever very great, so in our present circumstances it is grown to be much greater; because, as formerly our force of shipping contributed greatly to our trade and safety, so now it is become indispensably necessary to our very being.

It may be said now to England, Martha, Martha, thou art busy about many things, but one thing is necessary. To the question, What shall we do to be saved in this world? there is no other answer but this, Look to your moat.

The first article of an Englishman's political creed must be, that he believeth in the sea, &c.; without that there needeth no General Council to pronounce him incapable of salvation here.

A Rough Draft of a New Model at Sea, 1694

Politics and Hard Drink

Great drinkers are less fit to serve in Parliament than is apprehended. Men's virtue as well as their understanding is apt to be tainted by it. The appearance of it is sociable and well-natured, but it is by no means to be relied upon. Nothing is more frail than a man too far engaged in wet popularity. The habit of it maketh men careless of their business, and that naturally leadeth them into circumstances that make them liable to temptation. It is seldom seen that any principles have such a root as that they can be proof against the continual droppings of a bottle.

As to the faculties of the mind, there is not less objection; the vapours of wine may sometimes throw out sparks of wit, but they are like scattered pieces of ore, there is no vein to work upon . . .

beauté journalière] an inconstant beauty

I will suppose this fault was less frequent when Solon made it one of his laws that it was lawful to kill a magistrate if he was found drunk. Such a liberty taken in this age, either in the Parliament or out of it, would do terrible execution.

Some Cautions Offered, 1695

ROBERT SOUTH
1634–1716

The World Before the Fall

All those arts, rarities, and inventions, which vulgar minds gaze at, the ingenious pursue, and all admire, are but the relics of an intellect defaced with sin and time. We admire it now, only as antiquaries do a piece of old coin, for the stamp it once bore, and not for those vanishing lineaments and disappearing draughts that remain upon it at present. And certainly that must needs have been very glorious, the decays of which are so admirable. He that is comely when old and decrepid, surely was very beautiful when he was young. An Aristotle was but the rubbish of an Adam, and Athens but the rudiments of Paradise.

Sermons, 1679–1715

Words of Soberness

'I speak the words of soberness,' said Saint Paul (Acts xxvi. 25), and I preach the gospel not with the 'enticing words of man's wisdom' (1 Cor. ii. 4). This was the way of the apostles' discoursing of things sacred. Nothing here 'of the fringes of the north star'; nothing of 'nature's becoming unnatural'; nothing of the 'down of angels' wings', or 'the beautiful locks of cherubims': no starched similitudes introduced with a 'Thus have I seen a cloud rolling in its airy mansion', and the like. No, these were sublimities above the rise of the apostolic spirit. For the apostles, poor mortals, were content to take lower steps, and to tell the world in plain terms, 'that he who believed should be saved, and that he who believed not should be damned.' And this was the dialect which pierced the conscience, and made the hearers cry out, 'Men and brethren, what shall we do?' It tickled not the ear, but sunk into the heart: and when men came from such sermons, they never commended the preacher for his taking voice or gesture; for the fineness of such a simile, or the quaintness of such a sentence; but they spoke like men conquered with the overpowering force and evidence of the most concerning truths; much in the words of the two disciples going to

Emmaus: 'Did not our hearts burn within us, while he opened to us the Scriptures?'

In a word, the apostles' preaching was therefore mighty, and successful, because plain, natural, and familiar, and by no means above the capacity of their hearers; nothing being more preposterous, than for those who were professedly aiming at men's hearts to miss the mark, by shooting over their heads.

Sermons

THOMAS BURNET
1635?–1715

Caves and Dens and Hollow Passages

That the inside of the Earth is hollow and broken in many places, and is not one firm and united mass, we have both the testimony of sense and of easy observations to prove: how many caves and dens and hollow passages into the ground do we see in many countries, especially amongst mountains and rocks; and some of them endless and bottomless so far as can be discovered? We have many of these in our own island, in *Derbyshire*, *Somersetshire*, *Wales*, and other counties, and in every continent or island they abound more or less. These hollownesses of the Earth the Ancients made prisons, or store houses for the winds, and set a god over them to confine them, or let them loose at his pleasure. For some ages after the Flood, as all antiquity tells us, there were the first houses men had, at least in some parts of the Earth; here rude mortals sheltered themselves, as well as they could, from the injuries of the air, till they were beaten out by wild beasts that took possession of them. The ancient Oracles also us'd to be given out of these vaults and recesses under ground, the *Sibyls* had their caves, and the *Delphick* Oracle, and their temples sometimes were built upon an hollow rock. Places that are strange and solemn strike an awe into us, and incline us to a kind of superstitious timidity and veneration, and therefore they thought them fit for the seats and residences of their deities. They fancied also that steams rise sometimes, or a sort of vapour in those hollow places, that gave a kind of a divine fury or inspiration. But all these uses and employments are now in a great measure worn out, we know no use of them but to make the places talk'd of where they are, to be the wonders of the country, to please our curiosity to gaze upon and admire; but we know not how they came, nor to what purpose they were made at first.

A Sacred Theory of the Earth, 1684–90

THOMAS SPRAT,
BISHOP OF ROCHESTER
1635–1713

Fine Language and Plain Words

There is one thing more about which the Society has been most solicitous; and that is, the manner of their discourse: which unless they had been very watchful to keep in due temper, the whole spirit and vigour of their design had been soon eaten out by the luxury and redundance of speech. The ill effects of this superfluity of talking have already overwhelmed most other arts and professions; inasmuch, that when I consider the means of happy living, and the causes of their corruption, I can hardly forbear recanting what I said before, and concluding that eloquence ought to be banished out of all civil societies, as a thing fatal to peace and good manners. To this opinion I should wholly incline; if I did not find that it is a weapon which may be as easily procured by bad men as good: and that, if these should only cast it away, and those retain it; the naked innocence of virtue would be upon all occasions exposed to the armed malice of the wicked. This is the chief reason that should now keep up the ornaments of speaking in any request; since they are so much degenerated from their original usefulness. They were at first, no doubt, an admirable instrument in the hands of wise men; when they were only employed to describe goodness, honesty, obedience, in larger, fairer, and more moving images: to represent truth, clothed with bodies; and to bring knowledge back again to our very senses, from whence it was at first derived to our understandings. But now they are generally changed to worse uses: they make the fancy disgust the best things, if they come sound and unadorned; they are in open defiance against reason, professing not to hold much correspondence with that; but with its slaves, the passions: they give the mind a motion too changeable and bewitching to consist with right practice. Who can behold without indignation how many mists and uncertainties these specious tropes and figures have brought on our knowledge? How many rewards, which are due to more profitable and difficult arts, have been still snatched away by the easy vanity of fine speaking? For, now I am warmed with this just anger, I cannot withhold myself from betraying the shallowness of all these seeming mysteries, upon which we writers, and speakers, look so big. And, in few words, I dare say that of all the studies of men, nothing may be sooner obtained than this vicious abundance of phrase, this trick of metaphors, this volubility of tongue, which makes so great a noise in the world. But I spend words in vain; for the evil is now so inveterate, that it is hard to know whom to blame, or where to begin to reform. We all value one another so much upon this beautiful deceit, and labour so long after it in the years of our education, that we cannot but ever after think kinder of it than it deserves. And indeed, in most other parts of learning, I look upon it as a thing almost utterly desperate in its cure: and I think it may be placed among those general mischiefs, such as the dissension of Christian princes, the want of practice in religion, and the like, which have been so long spoken against that men are become insensible about them; every one shifting off the fault from himself to others; and so they are only made bare common-places of complaint. It will suffice my present purpose to point out what has been done by the Royal Society towards the correcting of its excesses in natural philosophy; to which it is, of all others, a most professed enemy.

They have therefore been most rigorous in putting in execution the only remedy that can be found for this extravagance, and that has been, a constant resolution to reject all the amplifications, digressions, and swellings of style; to return back to the primitive purity, and shortness, when men delivered so many things, almost in an equal number of words. They have exacted from all their members a close, naked, natural way of speaking; positive expressions; clear senses; a native easiness: bringing all things as near the mathematical plainness as they can; and preferring the language of artizans, countrymen, and merchants, before that of wits or scholars.

The History of the Royal Society, 1667

THOMAS TRAHERNE
1637–1674

Childhood

The corn was orient and immortal wheat, which never should be reaped, nor was ever sown. I thought it had stood from everlasting to everlasting. The dust and stones of the street were as precious as gold: the gates were at first the end of the world. The green trees when I saw them first through one of the gates transported and ravished me, their sweetness and unusual beauty made my heart to leap, and almost mad with ecstasy, they were such strange and wonderful things. The men! Oh what venerable and reverend creatures did the aged seem! Immortal cherubims! And young men glittering and sparkling angels, and maids strange seraphic pieces of life and beauty! Boys and girls tumbling in the street, and playing, were moving jewels. I knew not that they were born or should die; but all things abided eternally as they were in their proper places. Eternity was manifest in the light of the day, and something infinite behind everything appeared, which talked with my expectation and moved my desire. The city seemed to stand in Eden, or to be built in heaven. The streets were mine, the temple was mine, the people were mine, their clothes and gold and silver were mine, as much as their sparkling eyes, fair skins and ruddy faces. The skies were mine, and so were the sun and moon and stars, and all the world was mine; and I the only spectator and enjoyer of it. I knew no churlish proprieties, nor bounds, nor divisions: but all proprieties and divisions were mine: all treasures and the possessors of them. So that with much ado I was corrupted, and made to learn the dirty devices of this world. Which now I unlearn, and become, as it were, a little child again that I may enter into the Kingdom of God.

Centuries of Meditation, first published 1908

Shades of the Prison-House

The first light which shined in my infancy in its primitive and innocent clarity was totally eclipsed: insomuch that I was fain to learn all again. If you ask me how it was eclipsed? Truly by the customs and manners of men, which like contrary winds blew it out: by an innumerable company of other objects, rude, vulgar and worthless things, that like so many loads of earth and dung did overwhelm and bury it; by the impetuous torrent of wrong desires in all others whom I saw or knew that carried me away and alienated me from it: by a whole sea of other matters and concernments that covered and drowned it: finally by the evil influence of a bad education that did not foster and cherish it. All men's thoughts and words were about other matters. They all prized new things which I did not dream of. I was a stranger and unacquainted with them; I was little and reverenced their authority; I was weak, and easily guided by their example; ambitious also, and desirous to approve myself unto them. And finding no one syllable in any man's mouth of those things, by degrees they vanished, my thoughts (as indeed what is more fleeting than a thought?) were blotted out; and at last all the celestial, great, and stable treasures to which I was born, as wholly forgotten as if they had never been.

Centuries of Meditation

A Palace of Glory

You never enjoy the world aright, till the Sea itself floweth in your veins, till you are clothed with the heavens, and crowned with the stars: and perceive yourself to be the sole heir of the whole world, and more than so, because men are in it who are every one sole heirs as well as you. Till you can sing and rejoice and delight in God, as misers do in gold, and Kings in sceptres, you never enjoy the world.

Till your spirit filleth the whole world, and the stars are your jewels; till you are as familiar with the ways of God in all Ages as with your walk and table: till you are intimately acquainted with that shady nothing out of which the world was made: till you love men so as to desire their happiness, with a thirst equal to the zeal of your own; till you delight in God for being good to all: you never enjoy the world. Till you more feel it than your private estate, and are more present in the hemisphere, considering the glories and the beauties there, than in your own house: Till you remember how lately you were made, and how wonderful it was when you came into it: and more rejoice in the palace of your glory, than if it had been made but to-day morning.

Centuries of Meditation

APHRA BEHN
1640–1689

A Woman Playwright Defends Herself

Indeed that day 'twas acted first, there comes into the pit a long, lither, phlegmatic, white, ill-favour'd wretched fop, an officer in masquerade newly transported with a scarf and feather out of France, a sorry animal that has naught else to shield it from the uttermost contempt of mankind but that respect which we afford to rats and toads, which though we do not well allow to live, yet when considered as a part of God's creation, we make honourable mention of them. This thing, I tell ye, opening that which serves it for a mouth, out issued such a noise as this to those that sat about it, that they were to expect a woeful play, God damn him, for it was a woman's. Now how this came about I am not sure, but I suppose he brought it piping hot from some who had with him the reputation of a villainous wit: for creatures of his size of sense talk without all imagination, such scraps as they pick up from other folks.

I would not for a world be taken arguing with such a property as this; but if I thought there were a man of any tolerable parts, who could upon mature deliberation distinguish well his right hand from his left, and justly state the difference between the number of sixteen and two, yet had this prejudice upon him, I would take a little pains to make him know how much he errs. For waiving the examination why women, having equal education with men, were not as capable of knowledge of whatsoever sort as well as they, I'll only say as I have touch'd before, that plays have no great room for that which is men's great advantage over women, that is Learning. We all well know that the immortal Shakespeare's plays (who was not guilty of much more of this than often falls to women's share) have better pleas'd the world than Jonson's works, though by the way 'tis said that Benjamin was no such Rabbi either, for I am informed that his learning was but grammar-high (sufficient indeed to rob poor Sallust of his best orations), and it hath been observ'd that they are apt to admire him most confoundedly, who have just such a scantling of it as he had . . . And as for our modern ones, except our most unimitable Laureate [Dryden], I dare to say I know of none that write at such a formidable rate, but that a woman may well hope to reach their greatest heights.

Preface to *The Dutch Lover*, 1673

The Power of Love

As love is the most noble and divine passion of the soul, so it is that to which we may justly attribute all the real satisfactions of life; and without it man is unfinished and unhappy. There are a thousand things to be said of the advantages this generous passion brings to those whose hearts are capable of receiving its soft impressions; for 'tis not everyone that can be sensible of its tender touches. How many examples from history and observation could I give of its wondrous power; nay, even to a degree of transmigration! How many idiots has it made wise! How many fools eloquent! How many home-bred squires accomplished! How many cowards brave!

The Fair Jilt, 1688

The Fate of a Rebellious Slave

The governor was no sooner recovered, and had heard of the menaces of Caesar, but he called his council; who (not to disgrace them, or burlesque the government there) consisted of such notorious villains as Newgate never transported; and possibly originally were such who understood neither the laws of God or man, and had no sort of principles to make 'em worthy the name of men; but at the very council table would contradict and fight with one another, and swear so bloodily that 'twas terrible to hear and see 'em. (Some of 'em were afterwards hanged when the Dutch took possession of the place, others sent off in chains.) But calling these special rulers of the nation together, and requiring their counsel in this weighty affair, they all concluded that (Damn 'em) it might be their own cases; and that Caesar ought to be made an example to all the Negroes, to fright 'em from daring to threaten their betters, their lords and masters; and at this rate no man was safe from his own slaves; and concluded, *nemine contradicente*, that Caesar should be hanged.

Oroonoko, 1688

WILLIAM PENN
1644–1718

A Free Solitude

The inward, steady righteousness of Jesus is another thing, than all the contrived devotion of poor superstitious man; and to stand approved in the sight of God, excels that bodily exercise in religion, resulting from the invention of men. And the soul that is awakened and preserved by His holy power and spirit, lives to Him in the way of His own institution, and worships Him in His own spirit—that is, in the holy sense, life, and leadings of it: which indeed is the evangelical worship.

Not that I would be thought to slight a true retirement: for I do not only acknowledge but admire solitude. Christ Himself was an example of it: He loved and chose to frequent mountains, gardens, sea-sides. It is requisite to the growth of piety, and I reverence the virtue that seeks and used it; wishing there were more of it in the world; but then it should be free, not constrained. . . .

Nay, I have long thought it an error among all sorts, that use not monastick lives, that they have no retreats for the afflicted, the tempted, the solitary, and the devout; where they might undisturbedly wait upon God, pass through their religious exercises, and being thereby strengthened, may with more power over their own spirits enter into the business of the world again: though the less the better to be sure. For divine pleasures are found in a free solitude.

No Cross, No Crown, 1669

ROGER NORTH
1653–1734

Lord Chief Justice Saunders

He raised himself from a very low estate, being a poor boy in the Inns of Chancery who by service to clerks there was allowed a hole upon an upper stairs, where he sat and taught himself to write, and by that means got hackney employment, and so lived; but, passing on in the same way of industry, he went from writing to drawing of pleadings, and mixed reading with his work, which at length made him an exquisite pleader, and that was his intromission to the King's Bench practice, until he was one of the prime. He was born but not bred a gentleman, for his mind had an extraordinary candour, but his low and precarious beginnings led him into a sordid way of living; for he fell into the conversation of a tradesman's wife, which was great scandal upon him, and it was believed he had children by her. But notwithstanding all he might be innocent and she only his nurse. For either by constitution, or using a sedentary life, drinking much ale, without exercise, he was extremely corpulent and diseased. It is certain he lived in the family, maintained them out of his plenty, and all in peace and friendship with husband as well as wife, so that if the horns were in the case they were well gilded. He addicted himself to little ingenuities, as playing on the virginals, plantings, and knick-knacks in his chamber. He took a house at Parson's Green, where he bestowed much on the gardens and fruits. He would stamp the name of every plant in lead and make it fast to the stem. And in short he had as active a soul in as unactive a body as ever met. He would cover his infirmities with jesting, and never expostulate with those he offended in anger, but always droll. And how touchy soever we were that stood in the very great stench of his carcase at the bar, we could not be heartily angry, because he would so ply the jests and droll upon us and himself that reconciled us to patience. His first employment from the court was the drawing pleadings upon *quo warrantos* against corporations, which was his original study and practice. This he performed with so much zeal (for he was ever very earnest for his client) and slight of reward, that King Charles II. was much pleased with him, and often sent him good round fees out of his own cabinet. And these he accepted with so much modest gratitude in the manner as obliged as much as was possible. At length, upon the dismissal of Sir Francis Pemberton he was made Chief Justice of the King's Bench. But the preferment was an honour fatal to him; for from great labour, sweat, toil, and vulgar diet, he came to ease, plenty, and of the best, which he could not forbear, being luxurious in eating and drinking. So in a short time, for want of his ordinary exercises and evacuations, he fell into a sort of apoplexy, which ceased with an hemiplegia, and in a short time after he died.

Autobiography, published 1887

DANIEL DEFOE
1661–1731

A Footprint

It happened one day, about noon, going towards my boat, I was exceedingly surprised with the print of a man's naked foot on the shore, which was very plain to be seen in the sand. I stood like one thunderstruck, or as if I had seen an apparition. I listened, I looked round me, I could hear nothing, nor see anything. I went up to a rising ground, to look farther. I went up the shore, and down the shore, but it was all one; I could see no other impression but that one. I went to it again to see if there were any more, and to observe if it might not be my fancy; but there was no room for that, for there was exactly the very print of a foot—toes, heel, and every part of a foot. How it came thither I knew not, nor could in the least imagine. But after innumerable fluttering thoughts, like a man perfectly confused and out of myself, I came home to my fortification, not feeling, as we say, the ground I went on, but terrified to the last degree, looking behind me at every two or three steps, mistaking every bush and tree, and fancying every stump at a distance to be a man; nor is it possible to describe how many various shapes affrighted imagination represented things to me in, how many wild ideas were found every moment in my fancy, and what strange unaccountable whimsies came into my thoughts by the way.

When I came to my castle, for so I think I called it ever after this, I fled into it like one pursued. Whether I went over by the ladder, as first contrived, or went in at the hole in the rock, which I called a door, I cannot remember; no, nor could I remember the next morning, for never frighted hare fled to cover, or fox to earth, with more terror of mind than I to this retreat.

Robinson Crusoe, 1719

Our Dear Self

The world, I say, is nothing to us but as it is more or less to our relish. All reflection is carried home, and our dear self is, in one respect, the end of living. Hence man may be properly said to be alone in the midst of the crowds and hurry of men and business. All the reflections which he makes are to himself; all that is pleasant he embraces for himself; all that is irksome and grievous is tasted but by his own palate.

What are the sorrows of other men to us, and what their joy? Something we may be touched indeed with by the power of sympathy, and a secret turn of the affections; but all the solid reflection is directed to ourselves. Our meditations are all solitude in perfection; our passions are all exercised in retirement; we love, we hate, we covet, we enjoy, all in privacy and solitude. All that we communicate of those things to any other is but for their assistance in the pursuit of our desires; the end is at home; the enjoyment, the contemplation, is all solitude and retirement; it is for ourselves we enjoy, and for ourselves we suffer.

Serious Reflections During the Life of Robinson Crusoe, 1720

Victims and Survivors

It is true that shutting up of houses had one effect, which I am sensible was of moment, namely, it confined the distempered people, who would otherwise have been both very troublesome and very dangerous in their running about streets with the distemper upon them—which, when they were delirious, they would have done in a most frightful manner, and as indeed they began to do at first very much, till they were thus restrained; nay, so very open they were that the poor would go about and beg at people's doors, and say they had the plague upon them, and beg rags for their sores, or both, or anything that delirious nature happened to think of.

A poor, unhappy gentlewoman, a substantial citizen's wife, was (if the story be true) murdered by one of these creatures in Aldersgate Street, or that way. He was going along the street, raving mad to be sure, and singing; the people only said he was drunk, but he himself said he had the plague upon him, which it seems was true; and meeting this gentlewoman, he would kiss her. She was terribly frighted, as he was only a rude fellow, and she ran from him, but the street being very thin of people, there was nobody near enough to help her. When she saw he would overtake her, she turned and gave him a thrust so forcibly, he being but weak, and pushed him down backward. But very unhappily, she being so near, he caught hold of her and pulled her down also, and getting up first, mastered her and kissed her; and which was worst of all, when he had done, told her he had the plague, and why should not she have it as well as he? She was frighted enough before, being also young with child; but when she heard him say he had the plague, she screamed out and fell down into a swoon, or in a fit, which, though she recovered a little, yet killed her in a very few days; and I never heard whether she had the plague or no.

Another infected person came and knocked at the door of a citizen's house where they knew him very well; the servant let him in, and being told the master of the house was above, he ran up and came into the room to them as the whole family was at supper. They began to rise up, a little surprised, not knowing what the matter was; but he bid them sit still, he only came to take his leave of them. They asked him, 'Why, Mr——, where are you going?' 'Going,' says he; 'I have got the sickness, and shall die tomorrow night.' 'Tis easy to believe, though not to describe, the consternation they were all in. The women and the man's daughters, which were but little girls, were frighted almost to death and got up, one running out at one door and one at another, some downstairs and some upstairs, and getting together as well as they could, locked themselves into their chambers and screamed out at the window for help, as if they had been frighted out of their wits. The master, more composed than they, though both frighted and provoked, was going to lay hands on him and throw him downstairs, being in a passion; but then, considering a little the condition of the man and the danger of touching him, horror seized his mind, and he stood still like one astonished. The poor distempered man all this while, being as well diseased in his brain as in his body, stood still like one amazed. At length he turns round: 'Ay!' says he, with all the seeming calmness imaginable, 'is it so with you all? Are you all disturbed at me? Why, then I'll e'en go home and die there.' And so he goes immediately downstairs. The servant that had let him in goes down after him with a candle, but was afraid to go past him and open the door, so he stood on the stairs to see what he would do. The man went and opened the door, and went out and flung the door after him. It was some while before the family recovered the fright, but as no ill consequence attended, they have had occasion since to speak of it (you may be sure) with great satisfaction. Though the man was gone, it was some time—nay, as I heard, some days—before they recovered themselves of the hurry they were in; nor did they go up and down the house with any assurance till they had burnt a great variety of fumes and perfumes in all the rooms, and made a great many smokes of pitch, of gunpowder, and of sulphur, all separately shifted, and washed their clothes, and the like. As to the poor man, whether he lived or died I don't remember.

A Journal of the Plague Year, 1722

A Trick of the Trade

I knew a woman that was so dexterous with a fellow, who indeed deserved no better usage, that while he was busy with her another way, conveyed his purse with twenty guineas in it out of his fobpocket, where he had put it for fear of her, and put another purse with gilded counters in it into the room of it. After he had done he says to her, 'Now han't you picked my pocket?' She jested with him, and told him she supposed he had not much to lose; he put his hand to his fob, and with his fingers felt that his purse was there, which fully satisfied him, and so she brought off his money. And this was a trade with her; she kept a sham gold watch and a purse of counters in her pocket to be ready on all such occasions, and I doubt not practised it with success.

Moll Flanders, 1722

Moll in Newgate

I got no sleep for several nights or days after I came into that wretched place, and glad I would have been for some time to have died there, though I did not consider dying as it ought to be considered neither; indeed, nothing could be filled with more horror to my imagination than the very place, nothing was more odious to me than the company that was there. Oh! if I had but been sent to any place in the world, and not to Newgate, I should have thought myself happy.

In the next place, how did the hardened wretches that were there before me triumph over me! What! Mrs Flanders come to Newgate at last? What! Mrs Mary, Mrs Molly, and after that plain Moll Flanders! They thought the devil had helped me, they said, that I had reigned so long; they expected me there many years ago, they said, and was I come at last? Then they flouted me with dejections, welcomed me to the place, wished me joy, bid me have a good heart, not be cast down, things might not be so bad as I feared, and the like; then called for brandy, and drank to me, but put it all up to my score, for they told me I was but just come to the college, as they called it, and sure I had money in my pocket, though they had none.

I asked one of this crew how long she had been there. She said four months. I asked her how the place looked to her when she first came into it. 'Just as it did now to me,' says she, 'dreadful and frightful;' that she thought she was in hell; 'and I believe so still,' adds she, 'but it is natural to me now, I don't disturb myself about it.' 'I suppose,' says I, 'you are in no danger of what is to follow?' 'Nay,' says she, 'you are mistaken there, I am sure, for I am under sentence, only I pleaded my belly, but am no more with child than the judge that tried me, and I expect to be called down next session.' This 'calling down' is calling down to their former judgment, when a woman has been respited for her belly, but proves not to be with child, or if she has been with child, and has been brought to bed. 'Well,' says I, 'and are you thus easy?' 'Ay,' says she, 'I can't help myself; what signifies being sad? if I am hanged, there's an end of me.' And away she turned dancing, and sings as she goes, the following piece of Newgate wit:—

> 'If I swing by the string,
> I shall hear the bell ring,
> And then there's an end of poor Jenny.'

I mention this because it would be worth the observation of any prisoner, who shall hereafter fall into the same misfortune, and come to that dreadful place of Newgate, how time, necessity, and conversing with the wretches that are there familiarises the place to them; how at last they become reconciled to that which at first was the greatest dread upon their spirits in the world, and are as impudently cheerful and merry in their misery as they were when out of it.

I cannot say, as some do, this devil is not so black as he is painted; for indeed no colours can represent that place to the life, nor any soul conceive aright of it but those who have been sufferers there. But how hell should become by degrees so natural, and not only tolerable, but even agreeable, is a thing unintelligible but by those who have experienced it, as I have.

Moll Flanders

A Lead-Miner

For his person, he was lean as a skeleton, pale as a dead corpse, his hair and beard a deep black, his flesh lank, and, as we thought, something of the colour of the lead itself, and being very tall and very lean he looked, or we that saw him ascend *ab inferis*, fancied he looked like an inhabitant of the dark regions below, and who was just ascended into the world of light.

Besides his basket of tools, he brought up with him about three quarters of a hundred weight of ore, which we wondered at, for the man had no small load to bring, considering the manner of his coming up; and this indeed make him come heaving and struggling up, as I said at first, as if he had great difficulty to get out; whereas it was indeed the weight that he brought with him.

A Tour through the Whole Island of Great Britain, 1724–6

COTTON MATHER
1663–1728

Wonders Flying Westwards

I write the wonders of the Christian religion, flying from the depravations of Europe to the American strand; and, assisted by the holy author of that religion, I do, with all conscience of truth, required therein by Him who is the truth itself, report the wonderful displays of His infinite power, wisdom, goodness, and faithfulness, wherewith His divine providence hath irradiated an Indian wilderness.

Magnalia Christi Americana, 1702

The Allusive Style and its Critics

There has been a deal of ado about a style, so much that I must offer you my sentiments upon it. There is a way of writing wherein the author endeavors that the reader may have something to the purpose in every paragraph. There is not only a vigor sensible in every sentence, but the paragraph is embellished with profitable references even to something beyond what is directly spoken. Formal and painful quotations are not studied; yet all that could be learnt from them is insinuated. The writer pretends not unto reading, yet he could not have writ as he does if he had not read very much in his time; and his composures are not only a cloth of gold, but also stuck with as many jewels, as the gown of a Russian ambassador. This way of writing has been decried by many, and is at this day more than ever so, for the same reason that in the old story the grapes were decried, that they were not ripe. A lazy, ignorant, conceited set of authors would persuade the whole tribe to lay aside that way of writing, for the same reason that one would have persuaded his brethren to part with the encumbrance of their bushy tails. But however fashion and humor may prevail, they must not think that the club at their coffee-house is all the world; but there will always be those who will in this case be governed by indisputable reason, and who will think that the real excellency of a book will never lie in saying of little; that the less one has for his money in a book, 'tis really the more valuable for it; and that the less one is instructed in a book, and the more of superfluous margin and superficial harangue, and the less of substantial matter one has in it, the more 'tis to be accounted of.

Manuductio ad Ministerium, 1726

MARY ASTELL
1666–1731

If All Men Are Born Free . . .

If absolute sovereignty be not necessary in a state, how comes it to be so in a family? or if in a family why not in a state; since no reason can be alledg'd for the one that will not hold more strongly for the other? If the authority of the husband so far as it extends, is sacred and inalienable, why not of the Prince? The domestic sovereign is without dispute elected, and the stipulations and contract are mutual, is it not then partial in men to the last degree, to contend for, and practice that arbitrary dominion in their own families, which they abhor and exclaim against in the state? For if arbitrary power is evil in itself, and an improper method of governing rational and free agents, it ought not to be practis'd anywhere; Nor is it less, but rather more mischievous in families than in kingdoms, by how much 100,000 tyrants are worse than one. What tho' a husband can't deprive a wife of life without being responsible to the law, he may however do what is much more grievous to a generous mind, render life miserable, for which she has no redress, scarce pity which is afforded to every other complainant, it being thought a wife's duty to suffer everything without complaint. If all men are born free, how is it that all women are born slaves?

Some Reflections upon Marriage, 1700

SARAH KEMBLE KNIGHT
1666–1727

A New England Lodging-House

Being come to Mr Havens', I was very civilly received, and courteously entertained, in a clean comfortable house; and the good woman was very active in helping off my riding clothes, and then asked what I would eat. I told her I had some chocolate, if she would prepare it; which with the help of some milk, and a little clean brass kettle, she soon effected to my satisfaction. I then betook me to my apartment, which was a little room parted from the kitchen by a single board partition; where, after I had noted the occurrences of the past day, I went to bed, which, though pretty hard, yet neat and handsome. But I could get no sleep, because of the clamor of some of the town topers in next room, who were entered into strong debate concerning the signification of the name of their country (*viz.*), *Narragansett.* One said it was named so by the Indians, because there grew a brier there, of a prodigious height and bigness, the like hardly ever known, called by the Indians narragansett; and quotes an Indian of so barbarous a name for his author, that I could not write it. His antagonist replied no—it was from a spring it had its name, which he well knew where it was, which was extreme cold in summer, and as hot as could be imagined in the winter, which was much resorted to by the natives, and by them called Narragansett (hot and cold), and that was the original of their place's name—with a thousand impertinances not worth notice, which he uttered with such a roaring voice and thundering blows with the fist of wickedness on the table, that it pierced my very head. I heartily fretted, and wished 'um tonguetied; but with as little success as a friend of mine once, who was (as she said) kept a whole night awake, on a journey, by a country left, and a sergeant, insigne and a deacon, contriving how to bring a triangle into a square. They kept calling for t'other gill, which while they were swallowing, was some intermission; but presently, like oil to fire, increased the flame. I set my candle on a chest by the bedside, and setting up, fell to my old way of composing my resentments, in the following manner:

> I ask thy aid, O potent rum!
> To charm these wrangling topers dumb.

Thou hast their giddy brains possessed—
The man confounded with the beast—
And I, poor I, can get no rest.
Intoxicate them with thy fumes:
O still their tongues 'til morning comes!

And I know not but my wishes took effect; for the dispute soon ended with t'other dram; and so good night!

The Private Journal of a Journey from Boston to New York, 1704; first published 1825

JONATHAN SWIFT
1667–1745

Preserving Peace of Mind

In the proportion that credulity is a more peaceful possession of the mind than curiosity; so far preferable is that wisdom which converses about the surface, to that pretended philosophy which enters into the depth of things, and then comes gravely back with the informations and discoveries that in the inside they are good for nothing. The two senses to which all objects first address themselves are the sight and the touch. These never examine further than the colour, the shape, the size, and whatever other qualities dwell, or are drawn by art, upon the outward of bodies; and then comes reason officiously, with tools for cutting, and opening, and mangling, and piercing, offering to demonstrate that they are not of the same consistence quite through. Now I take all this to be the last degree of perverting Nature, one of whose eternal laws it is, to put her best furniture forward. And therefore, in order to save the charges of all such expensive anatomy for the time to come, I do here think fit to inform the reader that in such conclusions as these, reason is certainly in the right, and that in most corporeal beings which have fallen under my cognizance, the *outside* hath been infinitely preferable to the *in*; whereof I have been further convinced from some late experiments. Last week I saw a woman *flayed*, and you will hardly believe how much it altered her person for the worse. Yesterday I ordered the carcass of a *beau* to be stripped in my presence, when we were all amazed to find so many unsuspected faults under one suit of clothes. Then I laid open his *brain*, his *heart*, and his *spleen*; but I plainly perceived at every operation that the farther we proceeded, we found the defects increase upon us in number and bulk; from all which, I justly formed this conclusion to myself. That whatever philosopher or projector can find out an art to solder and patch up the flaws and imperfections of nature will deserve much better of mankind, and teach us a more useful science than that so much in present esteem, of widening and exposing them (like him who held *anatomy* to be the ultimate end of *physic*). And he whose fortunes and dispositions have placed him in a convenient station to enjoy the fruits of this noble art; he that can with Epicurus content his ideas with the *films* and *images* that fly off upon his senses from the *superficies* of things; such a man, truly wise, creams off Nature, leaving the sour and the dregs for philosophy and reason to lap up. This is the sublime and refined point of felicity, called *the possession of being well deceived*; the serene peaceful state, of being a fool among knaves.

'Digression Concerning the Use of Madness', *A Tale of a Tub*, 1704

A Defence of Preaching

'Tis again objected as a very absurd ridiculous custom, that a set of men should be suffered, much less employed and hired, to bawl one day in seven against the lawfulness of those methods most in use towards the pursuit of greatness, riches and pleasure, which are the constant practice of all men alive on the other six. But this objection is, I think, a little unworthy so refined an age as ours. Let us argue this matter calmly. I appeal to the breast of any polite free-thinker whether in the pursuit of gratifying a predominant passion, he hath not always felt a wonderful incitement by reflecting it was a thing forbidden; and therefore we see, in order to cultivate this taste, the wisdom of the nation hath taken special care that the ladies should be furnished with prohibited silks, and the men with prohibited wine. And indeed it were to be wished that some other prohibitions were promoted, in order to improve the pleasures of the town; which for want of such expedients begin already, as I am told, to flag and grow languid, giving way daily to cruel inroads from the spleen.

An Argument Against Abolishing Christianity, 1708

The Lord Lieutenant

T[homas] E[arl] of W[harton], L[ord] L[ieutenant] of I[reland], by the force of a wonderful constitution hath passed some years his grand climacteric, without any visible effects of old age either on his body or his mind, and in spite of a continual prostitution to those vices which usually wear out both. His behaviour is in all the forms of a young man at five-and-twenty. Whether he walks, or whistles, or swears, or talks bawdy, or calls names, he acquits himself in each beyond a Templar of three years standing. With the same grace and in the same style, he will rattle his coachman in the midst of the street, where he is governor of the kingdom: and all this is without consequence, because it is in his character and what every body expects. He seems to be but an ill dissembler and an ill liar, though they are the two talents he most practises and most values himself upon. The ends he has gained by lying appear to be more owing to the frequency than the art of them, his lies being sometimes detected in an hour, often in a day, and always in a week. He tells them freely in mixed companies, though he knows half of those that hear him to be his enemies and is sure they will discover them the moment they leave him. He swears solemnly he loves and will serve you, and your back is no sooner turned but he tells those about him, you are a dog and a rascal. He goes constantly to prayers in the forms of his place and will talk bawdy and blasphemy at the chapel door. He is a Presbyterian in politics, and an atheist in religion, but he chooses at present to whore with a *Papist.*

A Short Character of His Excellency, Thomas Earl of Wharton, 1710

From Journal to Stella

Oct. 14. [1710]

Is that tobacco at the top of the paper, or what? I don't remember I slobbered. Lord, I dreamt of *Stella*, &c. so confusedly last night, and that we saw dean *Bolton* and *Sterne* go into a shop; and she bid me call them to her, and they proved to be two parsons I know not; and I walked without till she was shifting, and such stuff, mixt with much melancholy and uneasiness, and things not as they should be, and I know not how: and it is now an ugly gloomy morning.

London, Dec. 24. 1710

... LADY MOUNTJOY carried me home to dinner, where I staid not long after, and came home early, and now am got into bed, for you must always write to your *MD's* in bed, that's a maxim. Mr *White* and Mr *Red*, Write to *MD* when abed; Mr *Black* and Mr *Brown*, Write to *MD* when you're down; Mr *Oak* and Mr *Willow*, Write to *MD* on your pillow.—What's this? faith I smell fire; what can it be; this house has a thousand s——ks in it. I think to leave it on *Thursday*, and lodge over the way. Faith I must rise, and look at my chimney, for the smell grows stronger, stay—I have been up, and in my room, and found all safe, only a mouse within the fender to warm himself, which I could not catch. I smelt nothing there, but now in my bedchamber I smell it again; I believe I have singed the woolen curtain, and that's all, though I cannot smoak it. *Presto's* plaguy silly tonight, an't he? Yes, and so he be. Aye, but if I should wake and see fire. Well; I'll venture; so good night, &c.

London, Feb. 5. 1710–11

MORNING. I am going this morning to see *Prior*, who dines with me at Mr *Harley's*; so I can't stay fiddling and talking with dear little brats in a morning, and 'tis still terribly cold.—I wish my cold hand was in the warmest place about you, young women, I'd give ten guineas upon that account with all my heart, faith; oh, it starves my thigh; so I'll rise, and bid you good morrow, my ladies both, good morrow. Come stand away, let me rise: *Patrick*, take away the candle. Is there a good fire?—So—up a-dazy.

April 1. [1711]

The duke of *Buckingham's* house fell down last night with an earth-quake, and is half swallowed up;—Won't you go and see it?—An *April* fool, an *April* fool, oh ho, young women. Well, don't be angry, I'll make you an *April* fool no more till the next time: we had no sport here, because it is *Sunday*, and *Easter-Sunday*. I dined with the secretary, who seemed terribly down and melancholy, which Mr *Prior* and *Lewis* observed as well as I: perhaps something is gone wrong; perhaps there is nothing in it. God bless my own dearest *MD*, and all is well.

Outwitting the Law

I have been often considering how it comes to pass that the dexterity of mankind in evil should always outgrow, not only the prudence and caution of private persons, but the continual expedients of the wisest laws contrived to prevent it. I cannot imagine a knave to possess a greater share of natural wit or genius than an honest man. I have known very notable sharpers at play, who upon all other occasions were as great dunces as human shape can well allow, and I believe the same might be observed among the other knots of thieves and pickpockets about this town. The proposition however is certainly true and to be confirmed by an hundred instances. A scrivener, an attorney, a stockjobber, and many other *retailers of fraud*, shall not only be able to overreach others much wiser than themselves, but find out new inventions to elude the force of any law made against them. I suppose the reason of this may be that as the *aggressor* is said to have generally the advantage of the *defender*, so the makers of the law, which is to defend our rights, have usually not so much industry or vigour as those whose interest leads them to attack it. Besides, it rarely happens that men are rewarded by the public for their justice and virtue; neither do those who act upon such principles expect any recompense till the next world; whereas fraud, where it succeeds, gives present pay, and this is allowed the greatest spur imaginable both to labour and invention. When a law is made to stop some growing evil, the wits of those whose interest it is to break it with secrecy or impunity, are immediately at work;

and even among those who pretend to fairer characters, many would gladly find means to avoid what they would not be thought to violate. They desire to reap the advantage, if possible, without the shame, or at least without the danger.

The Examiner, no. 39 (1711)

The Capital of Lilliput

The first request I made after I had obtained my liberty, was, that I might have licence to see Mildendo, the metropolis; which the Emperor easily granted me, but with a special charge to do no hurt, either to the inhabitants, or their houses. The people had notice by proclamation of my design to visit the town. The wall which encompassed it is two foot and an half high, and at least eleven inches broad, so that a coach and horses may be driven very safely round it; and it is flanked with strong towers at ten foot distance. I stepped over the great western gate, and passed very gently, and sideling through the two principal streets, only in my short waistcoat, for fear of damaging the roofs and eaves of the houses with the skirts of my coat. I walked with the utmost circumspection, to avoid treading on any stragglers, who might remain in the streets, although the orders were very strict, that all people should keep in their houses, at their own peril. The garret windows and tops of houses were so crowded with spectators, that I thought in all my travels I had not seen a more populous place. The city is an exact square, each side of the wall being five hundred foot long. The two great streets, which run cross and divide it into four quarters, are five foot wide. The lanes and alleys, which I could not enter, but only viewed them as I passed, are from twelve to eighteen inches. The town is capable of holding five hundred thousand souls. The houses are from three to five stories. The shops and markets well provided.

Gulliver's Travels, 1726

An Execution in Brobdingnag

One day a young gentleman, who was nephew to my nurse's governess, came and pressed them both to see an execution. It was of a man who had murdered one of that gentleman's intimate acquaintance. Glumdalclitch was prevailed on to be of the company, very much against her inclination, for she was naturally tender-hearted: and as for my self, although I abhorred such kind of spectacles, yet my curiosity tempted me to see something that I thought must be extraordinary. The malefactor was fixed in a chair upon a scaffold erected for the purpose, and his head cut off at one blow with a sword of about forty foot long. The veins and arteries spouted up such a prodigious quantity of blood, and so high in the air, that the great *jet d'eau* at Versailles was not equal for the time it lasted; and the head, when it fell on the scaffold floor, gave such a bounce as made me start, although I was at least an English mile distant.

Gulliver's Travels

The Yahoos

At last I beheld several animals in a field, and one or two of the same kind sitting in trees. Their shape was very singular, and deformed, which a little discomposed me, so that I lay down behind a thicket to observe them better. Some of them coming forward near the place where I lay, gave me an opportunity of distinctly marking their form. Their heads and breasts were covered with a thick hair, some frizzled and others lank; they had beards like goats, and a long ridge of hair down their backs, and the foreparts of their legs and feet, but the rest of their bodies were bare, so that I might see their skins, which were of a brown buff colour. They had no tails, nor any hair at all on their buttocks, except about the anus; which, I presume, nature had placed there to defend them as they sat on the ground; for this posture they used, as well as lying down, and often stood on their hind feet. They climbed high trees, as nimbly as a squirrel, for they had strong extended claws before and behind, terminating in sharp points, and hooked. They would often spring, and bound, and leap with prodigious agility. The females were not so large as the males; they had long lank hair on their heads, and only a sort of down on the rest of their bodies, except about the anus, and pudenda. Their dugs hung between their fore-feet, and often reached almost to the ground as they walked. The hair of both sexes was of several colours, brown, red, black, and yellow. Upon the whole, I never beheld in all my travels so disagreeable an animal, or one against which I naturally conceived so strong antipathy.

Gulliver's Travels

A Substitute for Venison

A very worthy person, *a true lover of his country*, and whose virtues I highly esteem, was lately pleased in discoursing on this matter, to offer a refinement upon my scheme. He said that many gentlemen of this kingdom, having of late destroyed their deer, he conceived that the want of venison might be well supplied by the bodies of young lads and maidens not exceeding fourteen years of age, nor under twelve, so great a number of both sexes in every country being now ready to starve for want of work and service: and these to be disposed of by their parents if alive, or otherwise by their nearest relations. But with due deference to so excellent a friend and so deserving a patriot, I cannot be altogether in his sentiments; for as to the males, my American acquaintance assured me from frequent experience that their flesh was generally tough and lean, like that of our schoolboys, by continual exercise, and their taste disagreeable, and to fatten them would not answer the charge. Then as to the females, it would I think with humble submission, *be a loss to the public*, because they soon would become breeders themselves. And besides, it is not improbable that some scrupulous people might be apt to censure such a practice (although indeed very unjustly) as a little bordering upon cruelty, which, I confess, hath always been with me the strongest objection against any project, however so well intended.

A Modest Proposal, 1729

The Ladies at Tea

Lady Smart. Well, ladies; now let us have a cup of discourse to ourselves.

Lady Answerall. What do you think of your friend, Sir John Spendall?

Lady Smart. Why, madam, 'tis happy for him that his father was born before him.

Miss Notable. They say he makes a very ill husband to my lady.

Lady Answ. But he must be allow'd to be the fondest father in the world.

Lady Smart. Ay madam, that's true; for they say the Devil is kind to his own.

Miss. I am told my lady manages him to admiration.

Lady Smart. That I believe, for she's as cunning as a dead pig; but not half so honest.

Lady Answ. They say she's quite a stranger to all his gallantries.

Lady Smart. Not at all; but you know, there's none so blind as they that won't see.

Miss. Oh madam, I'm told she watches him as a cat watches a mouse.

Lady Answ. Well, if she ben't foully belied, she pays him in his own coin.

Lady Smart. Madam, I fancy I know your thoughts as well as if I were within you.

Lady Answ. Madam, I was t'other day in company with Mrs Clatter; I find she gives herself airs of being acquainted with your ladyship.

Miss. Oh, the hideous creature! Did you observe her nails? They were long enough to scratch her granum out of her grave.

Lady Smart. Well, she and Tom Gosling were banging compliments backwards and forwards; it look'd like two asses scrubbing one another.

Miss. Ay, claw me, and I'll claw thou . . .

Polite Conversation, 1738

WILLIAM CONGREVE
1670–1729

At a Masquerade

Well, what followed? Why, she pulled off her mask, and appeared to him at once in the glory of beauty. But who can tell the astonishment Aurelian felt? He was for a time senseless; admiration had suppressed his speech, and his eyes were entangled in light. In short, to be made sensible of his condition, we must conceive some idea of what he beheld, which is not to be imagined till seen, nor then to be expressed. Now see the impertinence and conceitedness of an author, who will have a fling at a description, which he has prefaced with an impossibility. One might have seen something in her composition resembling the formation of Epicurus his world, as if every atom of beauty had concurred to unite an excellency. Had that curious painter lived in her days, he might have avoided his painful search, when he collected from the choicest pieces the most choice features, and by a due disposition and judicious symmetry of those exquisite parts, made one whole and perfect Venus. Nature seemed here to have played the plagiary, and to have moulded into substance the most refined thoughts of inspired poets. Her eyes diffused rays comfortable as warmth, and piercing as the light; they would have worked a passage through the straitest pores, and with a delicious heat have played about the most obdurate frozen heart, until 'twere melted down to love. Such majesty and affability were in her looks; so alluring, yet commanding was her presence, that it mingled awe with love, kindling a flame which trembled to aspire. She had danced much, which together with her being close masked gave her a tincture of carnation more than ordinary. But Aurelian (from whom I had every tittle of her description) fancied he saw a little nest of cupids break from the tresses of her hair, and every one officiously betake himself to his task. Some fanned with their downy wings her glowing cheeks; while others brushed the balmy dew from off her face, leaving alone a heavenly moisture blubbing on her lips, on which they drank and revelled for their pains; nay, so particular were their allotments in her service, that Aurelian was very positive a young cupid who was but just pen-feathered, employed his naked quills to pick her teeth. And a thousand other things his transport represented to him, which none but lovers who have experience of such visions will believe.

Incognita, 1691

BERNARD MANDEVILLE
1670–1733

Some Social Benefits of Highway Robbery

A highwayman having met with a considerable booty, gives a poor common harlot he fancies ten pounds to new-rig her from top to toe; is there a spruce mercer so conscientious that he will refuse to sell her a thread satin though he knew who she was? She must have shoes and stockings, gloves; the stay and mantua-maker, the sempstress, the linen-draper, all must get something by her, and a hundred different tradesmen dependent on those she laid her money out with may touch part of it before a month is at an end.

The Fable of the Bees, 1714

The Contempt of Wealth

I could swagger about fortitude and the contempt of riches as much as Seneca himself and would undertake to write twice as much in behalf of poverty as ever he did; for the tenth part of his estate, I could teach the way to his *summum bonum* as exactly as I know my way home. I could tell people to extricate themselves from all worldly engagements; and to purify the mind they must divest themselves of their passions, as men take out the furniture when they would clean a room thoroughly; and I am clearly of the opinion that the malice and most severe strokes of fortune can do no more injury to a mind thus stripped of all fears, wishes, and inclinations, than a blind horse can do in an empty barn. In the theory of all this I am very perfect, but the practice is very difficult; and if you went about picking my pocket, offered to take the victuals from before me when I am hungry, or made but the least motion of spitting in my face, I dare not promise how philosophically I should behave myself. But that I am forced to submit to every caprice of my unruly nature, you will say, is no argument that others are as little masters of theirs, and therefore I am willing to pay adoration to virtue whenever I can meet with it, with a proviso that I shall not be obliged to admit any as such where I can see no self-denial, or to judge of men's sentiments from their words where I have their lives before me.

The Fable of the Bees

ANTHONY ASHLEY COOPER, EARL OF SHAFTESBURY
1671–1713

Popular Fury

We read in history that Pan, when he accompanied Bacchus in an expedition to the Indies, found means to strike a terror through a host of enemies by the help of a small company, whose clamours he managed to good advantage among the echoing rocks and caverns of a woody vale. The hoarse bellowing of the caves, joined to the hideous aspect of such dark and desert places, raised such a horror in the enemy, that in this state their imagination helped them to hear voices, and doubtless to see forms too, which were more than human: whilst the uncertainty of what they feared made their fear yet greater, and spread it faster by implicit looks than any narration could convey it. And this was what in after-times men called a *panic.* The story indeed gives a good hint of the nature of this passion, which can hardly be without some mixture of enthusiasm and horrors of a superstitious kind.

One may with good reason call every passion panic which is raised in a multitude and conveyed by aspect or, as it were, by contact of sympathy. Thus popular fury may be called panic when the rage of the people, as we have sometimes known, has put them beyond themselves; especially where religion has had to do. And in this state their very looks are infectious. The fury flies from face to face; and the disease is no sooner seen than caught. They who in a better situation of mind have beheld a multitude under the power of this passion, have owned that they saw in the countenances of men something more ghastly and terrible than at other times is expressed on the most passionate occasion. Such force has society in ill as well as in good passions: and so much stronger any affection is for being social and communicative.

Characteristics of Men, Manners, Opinions and Times, 1711

COLLEY CIBBER
1671–1757

Thomas Betterton—an Actor Without Equal

Betterton was an actor, as Shakespear was an author, both without competitors! form'd for the mutual assistance and illustration of each other's genius! How Shakespear wrote, all men who have a taste for nature may read, and know—but with what higher rapture would he still be *read*, could they conceive how Betterton *play'd* him! Then might they know, the one was born alone to speak what the other only knew to write! Pity it is, that the momentary beauties flowing from an harmonious elocution, cannot like those of poetry be their own record! That the animated graces of the player can live no longer than the instant breath and motion that presents them; or at best can but faintly glimmer through the memory, or imperfect attestation of a few surviving spectators. Could *how* Betterton spoke be as easily known as *what* he spoke; then might you see the muse of Shakespear in her triumph, with all her beauties in their best array, rising into real life, and charming her beholders. But alas! since all this is so far out of the reach of description, how shall I shew you Betterton? Should I therefore tell you, that all the Othellos, Hamlets, Hotspurs, Mackbeths, and Brutus's whom you may have seen since his time, have fallen far short of him; this still should give you no idea of his particular excellence. Let us see then what a particular comparison may do! whether that may yet draw him nearer to you?

You have seen a Hamlet perhaps, who, on the first appearance of his father's spirit, has thrown himself into all the straining vociferation requisite to express rage and fury, and the house has thunder'd with applause; tho' the mis-guided actor was all the while (as Shakespear terms it) tearing a passion into rags.—I am the more bold to offer you this particular instance, because the late Mr Addison, while I sate by him, to see this scene acted, made the same observation, asking me with some surprise, if I thought Hamlet should be in so violent a passion with the Ghost, which tho' it might have astonish'd, it had not provok'd him? for you may observe that in this beautiful speech, the passion never rises beyond an almost breathless astonishment, or an impatience, limited by filial reverence, to enquire into the suspected wrongs that may have rais'd him from his peaceful tomb! and a desire to know what a spirit so seemingly distrest, might wish or enjoin a sorrowful son to execute towards his future quiet in the grave? This was the light into which Betterton threw this scene; which he open'd with a pause of mute amazement! then rising slowly to a solemn, trembling voice, he made the ghost equally terrible to the spectator as to himself! and in the descriptive part of the natural emotions which the ghastly vision gave him, the boldness of his expostulation was still govern'd by decency, manly, but not braving; his voice never rising into that seeming outrage, or wild defiance of what he naturally rever'd. But alas! to preserve this medium, between mouthing, and meaning too little, to keep the attention more pleasingly awake, by a temper'd spirit, than by mere vehemence of voice, is of all the master-strokes of an actor the most difficult to reach. In this none yet have equall'd Betterton.

An Apology for the Life of Colley Cibber, 1739

SIR RICHARD STEELE
1672–1729

Early Sorrow

The first sense of sorrow I ever knew was upon the death of my father, at which time I was not quite five years of age; but was rather amazed at what all the house meant, than possessed with a real understanding why nobody was willing to play with me. I remember I went into the room where his body lay, and my mother sat weeping alone by it. I had my battledore in my hand, and fell a beating the coffin, and calling Papa; for, I know not how, I had some slight idea that he was locked up there. My mother catched me in her arms, and, transported beyond all patience of the silent grief she was before in, she almost smothered me in her embraces; and told me in a flood of tears, 'Papa could not hear me, and would play with me no more, for they were going to put him under ground, whence he could never come to us again.' She was a very beautiful woman, of a noble spirit, and there was a dignity in her grief amidst all the wildness of her transport; which, methought, struck me with an instinct of sorrow, that, before I was sensible of what it was to grieve, seized my very soul, and has made pity the weakness of my heart ever since. The mind in infancy is, methinks, like the body in embryo; and receives impressions so forcible, that they are as hard to be removed by reason, as any mark with which a child is born is to be taken away by any future application. Hence it is, that good-nature in me is no merit; but having been so frequently overwhelmed with her tears before I knew the cause of any affliction, or could draw defences from my own judgment, I imbibed commiseration, remorse, and an unmanly gentleness of mind, which has since insnared me into ten thousand calamities; and from whence I can reap no advantage, except it be, that, in such a humour as I am now in, I can the better indulge myself in the softnesses of humanity, and enjoy that sweet anxiety which arises from the memory of past afflictions.

'On Recollections of Childhood', *The Tatler*, no. 181 (1710)

A Wealth of Detail

As the choosing of pertinent circumstances is the life of a story, and that wherein humour principally consists; so the collectors of impertinent particulars are the very bane and opiates of conversation. Old men are great transgressors this way. Poor Ned Poppy,—he's gone—was a very honest man, but was so excessively tedious over his pipe, that he was not to be endured. He knew so exactly what they had for dinner, when such a thing happened; in what ditch his bay stone-horse had his sprain at that time, and how his man John,—no! it was William, started a hare in the common-field; that he never got to the end of his tale. Then he was extremely particular in marriages and inter-marriages, and cousins twice or thrice removed; and whether such a thing happened at the latter end of July, or the beginning of August. He had a marvellous tendency likewise to digressions; insomuch that if a considerable person was mentioned in his story, he would straightway launch out into an episode on him; and again, if in that person's story he had occasion to remember a third man, he broke off, and gave us his history, and so on. He always put me in mind of what Sir William Temple informs us of the tale-tellers in the north of Ireland, who are hired to tell stories of giants and enchanters to lull people asleep. These historians are obliged, by their bargain, to go on without stopping; so that after the patient hath by this benefit enjoyed a long nap, he is sure to find the operator proceeding in his work. Ned procured the like effect in me the last time I was with him. As he was in the third hour of his story, and very thankful that his memory did not fail him, I fairly nodded in the elbow chair. He was much affronted at this, till I told him, 'Old friend, you have your infirmity, and I have mine.'

'On Story-Telling', *The Guardian*, 1713

JOSEPH ADDISON

1672–1719

A Critic Pays Court

About a week ago I was engaged at a friend's house of mine in an agreeable conversation with his wife and daughters, when, in the height of our mirth, Sir Timothy, who makes love to my friend's eldest daughter, came in amongst us puffing and blowing, as if he had been very much out of breath. He immediately called for a chair, and desired leave to sit down, without any further ceremony. I asked him, 'Where he had been? Whether he was out of order?' He only replied, that he was quite spent, and fell a cursing in soliloquy. I could hear him cry, 'A wicked rogue!—An execrable wretch!—Was there ever such a monster!'—The young ladies upon this began to be affrighted, and asked, 'Whether any one had hurt him?' He answered nothing, but still talked to himself. 'To lay the first scene (says he) in St. James's Park, and the last in Northamptonshire!' 'Is that all? (says I:) Then I suppose you have been at the rehearsal of the play this morning.' 'Been! (says he;) I have been at Northampton, in the Park, in a lady's bed-chamber, in a dining-room, everywhere; the rogue has led me such a dance!'—Though I could scarce forbear laughing at his discourse, I told him I was glad it was no worse, and that he was only metaphorically weary. 'In short, sir, (says he,) the author has not observed a single unity in his whole play; the scene shifts in every dialogue; the villain has hurried me up and down at such a rate, that I am tired off my legs.' I could not but observe with some pleasure, that the young lady whom he made love to, conceived a very just aversion towards him, upon seeing him so very passionate in trifles. And as she had that natural sense which makes her a better judge than a thousand critics, she began to rally him upon this foolish humour. 'For my part, (says she,) I never knew a play take that was written up to your rules, as you call them.' 'How, Madam! (says he,) is that your opinion? I am sure you have a better taste.' 'It is a pretty kind of magic (says she) the poets have to transport an audience from place to place without the help of a coach and horses. I could travel round the world at such a rate. 'Tis such an entertainment as an enchantress finds when she fancies herself in a wood, or upon a mountain, at a feast, or a solemnity; though at the same time she has never stirred out of her cottage.' 'Your simile, madam, (says Sir Timothy,) is by no means just.' 'Pray, (says she,) let my similes pass without a criticism. I must confess, (continued she, for I found she was resolved to exasperate him,) I laughed very heartily at the last new comedy which you found so much fault with.' 'But, madam, (says he,) you ought not to have laughed; and I defy any one to show me a single rule that you could laugh by.' 'Ought not to laugh! (says she:) Pray who should hinder me?' 'Madam, (says he,) there are such people in the world as Rapin, Dacier, and several others, that ought to have spoiled your mirth.' 'I have heard, (says the young lady,) that your great critics are very bad poets: I fancy there is as much difference between the works of one and the other, as there is between the carriage of a dancing-master and a gentleman. I must confess, (continued she,) I would not be troubled with so fine a judgment as yours is; for I find you feel more vexation in a bad comedy, than I do in a deep tragedy.' 'Madam, (says Sir Timothy,) that is not my fault; they should learn the art of writing.' 'For my part, (says the young lady,) I should think the greatest art in your writers of comedies is to please.' 'To please!' (says Sir Timothy;) and immediately fell a laughing. 'Truly, (says she,) that is my opinion.' Upon this, he composed his countenance, looked upon his watch, and took his leave.

The Tatler, no. 165 (1710)

The Receiving End

It must indeed be confessed, that a lampoon or a satire do not carry in them robbery or murder; but at the same time, how many are there that would not rather lose a considerable sum of money, or even life itself, than be set up as a mark of infamy and derision? And in this case a man should consider, that an injury is not to be measured by the notions of him that gives, but of him that receives it.

Those who can put the best countenance upon the outrages of this nature which are offered them, are not without their secret anguish. I have often observed a passage in Socrates's behaviour at his death, in a light wherein none of the critics have considered it. That excellent man, entertaining his friends, a little before he drank the bowl of poison, with a discourse on the immortality of the soul, at his entering upon it says, that he does not believe any the most comic genius can censure him for talking upon such a subject at such a time. This passage, I think, evidently glances upon Aristophanes, who writ a comedy on purpose to ridicule the discourses of that divine philosopher. It has been observed by many writers, that Socrates was so little moved at this piece of buffoonery, that he was several times present at its being acted upon the stage, and never expressed the least resentment of it. But, with submission, I think the remark I have here made shows us, that this unworthy treatment made an impression upon his mind, though he had been too wise to discover it.

The Spectator, no. 23 (1711)

On Taking Too Much Care of One's Health

I do not mean, by what I have here said, that I think any one to blame for taking due care of their health. On the contrary, as cheerfulness of mind and capacity for business are in a great measure the effects of a well-tempered constitution, a man cannot be at too much pains to cultivate and preserve it. But this care, which we are prompted to not only by common sense but by duty and instinct, should never engage us in groundless fears, melancholy apprehensions, and imaginary distempers, which are natural to every man who is more anxious to live than how to live. In short, the preservation of life should be only a secondary concern, and the direction of it our principal.

The Spectator, no. 25 (1711)

The Royal Exchange

There is no place in the town which I so much love to frequent as the Royal Exchange. It gives me a secret satisfaction, and, in some measure, gratifies my vanity, as I am an Englishman, to see so rich an assembly of countrymen and foreigners consulting together upon the private business of mankind, and making this metropolis a kind of emporium for the whole earth. I must confess I look upon high-change to be a great council, in which all considerable nations have their representatives. Factors in the trading world are what ambassadors are in the politic world; they negotiate affairs, conclude treaties, and maintain a good correspondence between those wealthy societies of men that are divided from one another by seas and oceans, or live on the different extremities of a continent. I have often been pleased to hear disputes adjusted between an inhabitant of Japan and an alderman of London, or to see a subject of the Great Mogul entering into a league with one of the Czar of Muscovy. I am infinitely delighted in mixing with these several ministers of commerce, as they are distinguished by their different walks and different languages: sometimes I am justled among a body of Armenians; sometimes I am lost in a crowd of Jews; and sometimes make one in a group of Dutchmen. I am a Dane, Swede, or Frenchman at different times; or rather fancy myself like the old philosopher, who upon being asked what countryman he was, replied, that he was a citizen of the world.

The Spectator, no. 69 (1711)

Sir Roger de Coverley at Church

As Sir Roger is landlord to the whole congregation, he keeps them in very good order, and will suffer nobody to sleep in it besides himself; for if by chance he has been surprised into a short nap at sermon, upon recovering out of it he stands up and looks about him, and if he sees anybody else nodding, either wakes them himself, or sends his servant to them. Several other of the old knight's particularities break out upon these occasions: sometimes he will be lengthening out a verse in the singing-psalms, half a minute after the rest of the congregation have done with it; sometimes, when he is pleased with the matter of his devotion, he pronounces Amen three or four times to the same prayer; and sometimes stands up when everybody else is upon their knees, to count the congregation, or see if any of his tenants are missing.

The Spectator, no. 112 (1711)

WILLIAM BYRD
1674–1744

A Ball in Virginia

It was night before we went to supper, which was very fine and in good order. It rained so that several did not come that were expected. About 7 o'clock the company went in coaches from the Governor's house to the capitol where the Governor opened the ball with a French dance with my wife. Then I danced with Mrs Russell and then several others and among the rest Colonel Smith's son, who made a sad freak. Then we danced country dances for an hour and the company was carried into another room where was a very fine collation of sweetmeats. The Governor was very gallant to the ladies and very courteous to the gentlemen. About 2 o'clock the company returned in the coaches and because the drive was dirty the Governor carried the ladies into their coaches. My wife and I lay at my lodgings. Colonel Carter's family and Mr Blair were stopped by the unruliness of the horses and Daniel Wilkinson was so gallant as to lead the horses himself through all the dirt and rain to Mr Blair's house. My cold continued bad. I neglected to say my prayers and had good thoughts, good humor, but indifferent health, thank God Almighty. It rained all day and all night. The President had the worst clothes of anybody there . . .

I rose at 8 o'clock and found my cold continued. I said my prayers and ate boiled milk for breakfast. I went to see Mr Clayton who lay sick of the gout. About 11 o'clock my wife and I went to wait on the Governor in the President's coach. We went there to take our leave but were forced to stay all day. The Governor had made a bargain with his servants that if they would forbear to drink upon the Queen's birthday, they might be drunk this day. They observed their contract and did their business very well and got very drunk today, in such a manner that Mrs Russell's maid was forced to lay the cloth, but the cook in that condition made a shift to send in a pretty little dinner. I ate some mutton cutlets. In the afternoon I persuaded my wife to stay all night in town and so it was resolved to spend the evening in cards. My cold was very bad and I lost my money. About 10 o'clock the Governor's coach carried us home to our lodgings where my wife was out of humor and I out of order. I said a short prayer and had good thoughts and good humor, thank God Almighty.

The Secret Diary of William Byrd of Westover, first published 1941; entries for 6–7 February 1711

HENRY ST JOHN, VISCOUNT BOLINGBROKE
1678–1751

Political Wisdom and Political Cunning

My Lord Bacon says, that cunning is left-handed or crooked wisdom. I would rather say, that it is a part, but the lowest part, of wisdom; employed alone by some, because they have not the other parts to employ; and by some, because it is as much as they want, within those bounds of action which they prescribe to themselves and sufficient to the ends that they propose. The difference seems to consist in degree, and application, rather than in kind. Wisdom is neither left-handed, nor crooked: but the heads of some men contain little, and the hearts of others employ it wrong. To use my Lord Bacon's own comparison, the cunning man knows how to pack the cards, the wise man how to play the game better: but it would be of no use to the first to pack the cards, if his knowledge stopped here, and he had no skill in the game; nor to the second to play the game better, if he did not know how to pack the cards, that he might unpack them by new shuffling. Inferior wisdom or cunning may get the better of folly: but superior wisdom will get the better of cunning. Wisdom and cunning have often the same objects; but a wise man will have more and greater in his view. The least will not fill his soul, nor ever become the principal there; but will be pursued in subserviency, in subordination at least, to the other. Wisdom and cunning may employ sometimes the same means too: but the wise man stoops to these means, and the other cannot rise above them. Simulation and dissimulation, for instance, are the chief arts of cunning: the first will be esteemed always by a wise man unworthy of him and will be therefore avoided by him, in every possible case; for, to resume my Lord Bacon's comparison, simulation is put on that we may look into the cards of another, whereas dissimulation intends nothing more than to hide our own. Simulation is a stiletto, not only an offensive, but an unlawful weapon; and the use of it may be rarely, very rarely, excused, but never justified. Dissimulation is a shield, as secrecy is armour: and it is no more possible to preserve secrecy in the administration of public affairs without some degree of dissimulation, than it is to succeed in it without secrecy. Those two arts of cunning are like the alloy mingled with pure ore. A little is necessary, and will not debase the coin below its proper standard; but if more than that little be employed, the coin loses its currency, and the coiner his credit.

The Idea of a Patriot King, 1749

GEORGE BERKELEY, BISHOP OF CLOYNE 1685–1753

Philosophy and Its Discontents

Philosophy being nothing else but the study of wisdom and truth, it may with reason be expected that those who have spent most time and pains in it should enjoy a greater calm and serenity of mind, a greater clearness and evidence of knowledge, and be less disturbed with doubts and difficulties than other men. Yet so it is, we see the illiterate bulk of mankind, that walk the high-road of plain common sense, and are governed by the dictates of nature, for the most part easy and undisturbed. To them nothing that is familiar appears unaccountable or difficult to comprehend. They complain not of any want of evidence in their senses, and are out of all danger of becoming Sceptics. But no sooner do we depart from Sense and Instinct to follow the light of a superior Principle—to reason, meditate, and reflect on the nature of things, but a thousand scruples spring up in our minds concerning those things which before we seemed fully to comprehend. Prejudices and errors of sense do from all parts discover themselves to our view; and, endeavouring to correct these by reason, we are insensibly drawn into uncouth paradoxes, difficulties, and inconsistencies, which multiply and grow upon us as we advance in speculation, till at length, having wandered through many intricate mazes, we find ourselves just where we were, or, which is worse, sit down in a forlorn Scepticism.

The Principles of Human Knowledge, 1710

A Dusky Region

Human souls in this low situation, bordering on mere animal life, bear the weight and see through the dusk of a gross atmosphere, gathered from wrong judgements daily passed, false opinions daily learned, and early habits of an older date than either judgment or opinion. Through such a medium the sharpest eye cannot see clearly. And if by some extraordinary effort the mind should surmount this dusky region and snatch a glimpse of pure light, she is soon drawn backwards, and depressed by the heaviness of the animal nature to which she is chained. And if again she chanceth, amidst the agitation of wild fancies and strong affections, to spring upwards, a second relapse speedily succeeds into this region of darkness and dreams.

Nevertheless, as the mind gathers strength by repeated acts, we should not despond, but continue to exert the prime and flower of our faculties, still recovering, and reaching on, and struggling, into the upper region, whereby our natural weakness and blindness may be in some degree remedied, and a taste obtained of truth and intellectual life.

Siris, 1744

WILLIAM LAW
1686–1761

A City Merchant

Calidus has traded above thirty years in the greatest city of the kingdom; he has been so many years constantly increasing his trade and his fortune. Every hour of the day is with him an hour of business; and though he eats and drinks very heartily, yet every meal seems to be in a hurry, and he would say grace if he had time. Calidus ends every day at the tavern, but has not leisure to be there till near nine o'clock. He is always forced to drink a good hearty glass, to drive thoughts of business out of his head, and make his spirits drowsy enough for sleep. He does business all the time that he is rising, and has settled several matters before he can get to his counting-room. His prayers are a short ejaculation or two, which he never misses in stormy, tempestuous weather, because he has always something or other at sea. Calidus will tell you, with great pleasure, that he has been in this hurry for so many years, and that it must have killed him long ago, but that it has been a rule with him to get out of the town every Saturday, and make the Sunday a day of quiet, and good refreshment in the country.

He is now so rich, that he would leave off his business, and amuse his old age with building, and furnishing a fine house in the country, but that he is afraid he should grow melancholy if he was to quit his business. He will tell you, with great gravity, that it is a dangerous thing for a man that has been used to get money, ever to leave it off. If thoughts of religion happen at any time to steal into his head, Calidus contents himself with thinking, that he never was a friend to heretics, and infidels, that he has always been civil to the minister of his parish, and very often given something to the charity schools.

A Serious Call to a Devout and Holy Life, 1728

A Fashionable Lady

But turn your eyes now another way, and let the trifling joys, the gewgaw happiness of Feliciana, teach you how wise they are, what delusion they escape, whose hearts and hopes are fixed upon a happiness in God.

If you were to live with Feliciana but one half year, you would see all the happiness that she is to have as long as she lives. She has no more to come, but the poor repetition of that which could never have pleased once, but through a littleness of mind, and want of thought.

She is to be again dressed fine, and keep her visiting day. She is again to change the colour of her clothes, again to have a new head-dress, and again put patches on her face. She is again to see who acts best at the playhouse, and who sings finest at the opera. She is again to make ten visits in a day, and be ten times in a day trying to talk artfully, easily, and politely, about nothing.

She is to be again delighted with some new fashion; and again angry at the change of some old one. She is to be again at cards, and gaming at midnight, and again in bed at noon. She is to be again pleased with hypocritical compliments, and again disturbed at imaginary affronts. She is to be again pleased with her good luck at gaming, and again tormented with the loss of her money. She is again to prepare herself for a birthnight, and again to see the town full of good company. She is again to hear the cabals and intrigues of the town; again to have a secret intelligence of private amours, and early notices of marriages, quarrels, and partings.

If you see her come out of her chariot more briskly than usual, converse with more spirit, and seem fuller of joy than she was last week, it is because there is some surprising new dress or new diversion just come to town.

These are all the substantial and regular parts of Feliciana's happiness; and she never knew a pleasant day in her life, but it was owing to some one, or more, of these things.

It is for this happiness that she has always been deaf to the reasonings of religion, that her heart has been too gay and cheerful to consider what is right or wrong in regard to eternity; or to listen to the sound of such dull words, as wisdom, piety, and devotion.

A Serious Call

All Men Are Singers

Our blessed Saviour and His Apostles sang a hymn: but it may reasonably be supposed, that they rather rejoiced in God, than made fine music.

Do but so live, that your heart may truly rejoice in God, that it may feel itself affected with the praises of God; and then you will find that this state of your heart will neither want a voice nor ear to find a tune for a psalm. Every one, at some time or other, finds himself able to sing in some degree; there are some times and occasions of joy, that make all people ready to express their sense of it in some sort of harmony. The joy that they feel forces them to let their voice have a part in it.

He therefore that saith he wants a voice, or an ear, to sing a psalm, mistakes the case: he wants that spirit that really rejoices in God; the dulness is in his heart, and not in his ear: and when his heart feels a true joy in God, when it has a full relish of what is expressed in the Psalms, he will find it very pleasant to make the motions of his voice express the motions of his heart.

Singing, indeed, as it is improved into an art,—as it signifies the running of the voice through such and such a compass of notes, and keeping time with a studied variety of changes, is not natural, nor the effect of any natural state of the mind; so in this sense, it is not common to all people, any more than those antic and invented motions which make fine dancing are common to all people.

But singing, as it signifies a motion of the voice suitable to the motions of the heart, and the changing of its tone according to the meaning of the words which we utter, is as natural and common to all men, as it is to speak high when they threaten in anger, or to speak low when they are dejected and ask for a pardon.

All men therefore are singers, in the same manner as all men think, speak, laugh, and lament. For singing is no more an invention, than grief or joy are inventions.

A Serious Call

ALEXANDER POPE
1688–1744

The Same Religion

Your lordship has formerly advised me to read the best controversies between the churches. Shall I tell you a secret? I did so at fourteen years old, for I loved reading, and my father had no other books; there was a collection of all that had been written on both sides in the reign of King James the Second. I wormed my head with them, and the consequence was, that I found myself a Papist and a Protestant by turns, according to the last book I read. I am afraid most seekers are in the same case, and when they stop, they are not so properly converted as outwitted. You see how little glory you would gain by my conversion. And, after all, I verily believe your lordship and I are both of the same religion, if we were thoroughly understood by one another; and that all honest and reasonable Christians would be so, if they did but talk enough together every day, and had nothing to do together, but to serve God, and live in peace with their neighbour.

letter to Francis Atterbury, Bishop of Rochester, 1717

Counter-Attack

Were it the mere excess of your Lordship's wit, that carried you thus triumphantly over all the bounds of decency, I might consider your Lordship on your Pegasus, as a sprightly hunter on a mettled horse; and while you were trampling down all our works, patiently suffer the injury, in pure admiration of the noble sport. But should the case be quite otherwise, should your Lordship be only like a boy that is run away with; and run away with by a very foal; really common charity, as well as respect for a noble family, would oblige me to stop your career, and to help you down from this Pegasus.

Surely the little praise of a *writer* should be a thing below your ambition: you, who were no sooner born, but in the lap of the Graces; no sooner at school, but in the arms of the Muses; no sooner in the world, but you practised all the skill of it; no sooner in the court, but you possessed all the art of it! Unrivalled as you are, in making a figure, and in making a speech, methinks, my Lord, you may well give up the poor talent of turning a distich. And why this fondness for poetry? Prose admits of the two excellences you most admire, diction and fiction; it admits of the talents you chiefly possess, a most fertile invention, and a most florid expression; it is with prose, nay the plainest prose, that you best could teach our nobility to vote, which you justly observe, is half at least of their business: and give me leave to prophesy, it is to your talent in prose, and not in verse, to your speaking, not your writing, to your art at court, not your art of poetry, that your lordship must owe your future figure in the world.

A Letter to a Noble Lord (Lord Hervey), 1733

LADY MARY WORTLEY MONTAGU
1689–1762

Adrianople (Edirne): The Sultan Visits the Mosque

I went yesterday with the French Embassadress to see the Grand Signior in his passage to the mosque. He was preceded by a numerous guard of janissaries, with vast white feathers on their heads, *spahis* and *bostangees* (these are foot and horse guard), and the royal gardeners, which are a very considerable body of men, dressed in different habits of fine lively colours, that, at a distance, they appeared like a parterre of tulips. After them the aga of the janissaries, in a robe of purple velvet, lined with silver tissue, his horse led by two slaves richly dressed. Next him the *kyzlár-aga* (your ladyship knows this is the chief guardian of the seraglio ladies) in a deep yellow cloth (which suited very well to his black face) lined with sables, and last his Sublimity himself, in green lined with the fur of a black Muscovite fox, which is supposed worth a thousand pounds sterling, mounted on a fine horse, with furniture embroidered with jewels. Six more horses richly furnished were led after him; and two of his principal courtiers bore, one his gold, and the other his silver coffee-pot, on a staff; another carried a silver stool on his head for him to sit on.

letter to Lady Bristol, 1717

Disenchantment

This is a vile world, dear sister, and I can easily comprehend, that whether one is at Paris or London, one is stifled with a certain mixture of fool and knave, that most people are composed of. I would have patience with a parcel of polite rogues, or your downright honest fools; but father Adam shines through his whole progeny. So much for our inside,—then our outward is so liable to ugliness and distempers, that we are perpetually plagued with feeling our own decays and seeing those of other people. Yet, sixpennyworth of common-sense, divided among a whole nation, would make our lives roll away glibly enough; but then we make laws, and we follow customs. By the first we cut off our own pleasures, and by the second we are answerable for the faults and extravagances of others. All these things, and five hundred more, convince me (as I have the most profound veneration for the Author of Nature) that we are here in an actual state of punishment; I am satisfied I have been one of *the condemned* ever since I was born; and, in submission to the Divine justice, I don't at all doubt but I deserved it in some pre-existent state. I will still hope that I am only in purgatory; and that after whining and grunting a certain number of years, I shall be translated to some more happy sphere, where virtue will be natural, and custom reasonable; that is, in short, where common-sense will reign. I grow very devout, as you see, and place all my hopes in the next life, being totally persuaded of the nothingness of this. Don't you remember how miserable we were in the little parlour at Thoresby? We then thought marrying would put us at once into possession of all we wanted. Then came being with child, etc., and you see what comes of being with child. Though, after all, I am still of opinion that it is extremely silly to submit to ill-fortune. One should pluck up a spirit, and live upon cordials when one can have no other nourishment. These are my present endeavours, and I run about, though I have five thousand pins and needles running into my heart. I try to console myself with a small damsel, who is at present everything I like—but, alas! she is yet in a white frock. At fourteen, she may run away with the butler:—there's one of the blessed consequences of great disappointments; you are not only hurt by the thing present, but it cuts off all future hopes, and makes your future expectations melancholy. *Quelle vie!!!*

letter to her sister, Lady Mar, 1727

'The Same Characters Are Formed by the Same Lessons'

I could give many examples of ladies whose ill conduct has been very notorious, which has been owing to that ignorance which has exposed them to idleness, which is justly called the mother of mischief. There is nothing so like the education of a woman of quality as that of a prince: they are taught to dance, and the exterior part of what is called good breeding, which, if they attain, they are extraordinary creatures in their kind, and have all the accomplishments required by their directors. The same characters are formed by the same lessons, which inclines me to think (if I dare say it) that nature has not placed us in an inferior rank to men, no more than the females of other animals, where we see no distinction of capacity; though, I am persuaded, if there was a commonwealth of rational horses (as Doctor Swift has supposed), it would be an established maxim among them, that a mare could not be taught to pace.

letter to her daughter, Lady Bute, 1753

On the Death of Fielding

I am sorry for H. Fielding's death, not only as I shall read no more of his writings, but I believe he lost more than others, as no man enjoyed life more than he did, though few had less reason to do so, the highest of his preferment being raking in the lowest sinks of vice and misery. . . . His happy constitution (even when he had, with great pains, half demolished it) made him forget everything when he was before a venison pasty, or over a flask of champagne; and I am persuaded he has known more happy moments than any prince upon earth. His natural spirits gave him rapture with his cook-maid, and cheerfulness in a garret. There was a great similitude between his character and that of Sir Richard Steele. He had the advantage both in learning and, in my opinion, genius: they both agreed in wanting money in spite of all their friends, and would have wanted it, if their hereditary lands had been as extensive as their imagination; yet each of them [was] so formed for happiness, it is pity he was not immortal.

letter to Lady Bute, 1755

Tenderness Revives

I am so highly delighted with this, dated August 4, giving an account of your little colony, I cannot help setting pen to paper, to tell you the melancholy joy I had in reading it. You would have laughed to see the old fool weep over it. I now find that age, when it does not harden the heart and sour the temper, naturally returns to the milky disposition of infancy. Time has the same effect on the mind as on the face. The predominant passion, the strongest feature, become more conspicuous from the others retiring; the various views of life are abandoned, from want of ability to pursue them, as the fine complexion is lost in wrinkles; but, as surely as a large nose grows larger, and a wide mouth wider, the tender child in your nursery will be a tender old woman, though, perhaps, reason may have restrained the appearance of it, till the mind, relaxed, is no longer capable of concealing its weakness; for weakness it is to indulge any attachment at a period of life when we are sure to part with life itself, at a very short warning. According to the good English proverb, young people may die, but old must. You see I am very industrious in finding comfort to myself in my exile, and to guard, as long as I can, against the peevishness which makes age miserable in itself and contemptible to others.

letter to Lady Bute, 1758

SAMUEL RICHARDSON
1689–1761

A Faint Sketch of Clarissa

[Lovelace writes to Belford]

Expect therefore a faint sketch of her admirable person with her dress.

Her wax-like flesh (for, after all, flesh and blood I think she is), by its delicacy and firmness, answers for the soundness of her health. Thou hast often heard me launch out in praise of her complexion. I never in my life beheld a skin so *illustriously* fair. The lily and the driven snow it is nonsense to talk of: her lawn and her laces one might indeed compare to those: but what a whited wall would a woman appear to be who had a complexion which would justify such unnatural comparisons? But this lady is all glowing, all charming flesh and blood; yet so clear that every meandering vein is to be seen in all the lovely parts of her which custom permits to be visible.

Thou hast heard me also describe the wavy ringlets of her shining hair, needing neither art nor powder; of itself an ornament defying all other ornaments; wantoning in and about a neck that is beautiful beyond description.

Her head-dress was a Brussels lace mob, peculiarly adapted to the charming air and turn of her features. A sky-blue ribbon illustrated that. But although the weather was somewhat sharp, she had not on either hat or hood; for, besides that she loves to use herself hardily (by which means, and by a temperance truly exemplary, she is allowed to have given high health and vigour to an originally tender constitution), she seems to have intended to show me that she was determined not to stand to her appointment. O Jack! that such a sweet girl should be a rogue!

Her morning gown was a pale primrose-coloured paduasoy: the cuffs and robings curiously embroidered by the fingers of this ever-charming Arachne, in a running pattern of violets and their leaves; the light in the flowers silver; gold in the leaves. A pair of diamond snaps in her ears. A white handkerchief, wrought by the same inimitable fingers, concealed—O Belford! what still more inimitable beauties did it not conceal! And I saw, all the way we rode, the bounding heart (by its throbbing motions I saw it!) dancing beneath the charming umbrage.

Her ruffles were the same as her mob. Her apron a flowered lawn. Her coat white satin, quilted: blue satin her shoes, braided with the same colour, without lace; for what need has the prettiest foot in the world of ornament? Neat buckles in them: and on her charming arms a pair of black velvet glovelike muffs of her own invention; for she makes and gives fashions as she pleases. Her hands, velvet of themselves, thus uncovered the freer to be grasped by those of her adorer.

Clarissa, 1748

Rusty Hinges

But now I hear the rusty hinges of my beloved's door give me creaking invitation. My heart creaks and throbs with respondent trepidations. Whimsical enough though! for what relation has a lover's heart to a rusty pair of hinges? But they are the hinges that open and shut the door of my beloved's bed-chamber. Relation enough in that.

Clarissa

A Sharp Exchange

Miss Howe to Miss Arabella Harlowe
Thursday, July 20

Miss Harlowe,—I cannot help acquainting you (however it may be received, coming from *me*) that your poor sister is dangerously ill, at the house of one Smith, who keeps a glover's and perfume shop in King Street, Covent Garden. She knows not that I write. Some violent words, in the nature of an imprecation, from her father, afflict her greatly in her weak state. I presume not to direct you what to do in this case. You are her sister. I therefore could not help writing to you, not only for her sake, but for your own. I am, madam,

Your humble servant,
Anna Howe

Miss Arabella Harlowe. [In answer]
Thursday, July 20

Miss Howe,—I have yours of this morning. All that has happened to the unhappy body you mention is what we foretold and expected. Let *him*, for whose sake she abandoned us, be her comfort. We are told he has remorse, and would marry her. We don't believe it, indeed. She *may* be very ill. Her disappointment may make her so, or ought. Yet is she the only one I know who is disappointed.

I cannot say, miss, that the notification from you is the *more* welcome for the liberties you have been pleased to take with our whole family, for resenting a conduct that it is a shame any young lady should justify. Excuse this freedom, occasioned by greater. I am, miss,

Your humble servant,

ARABELLA HARLOWE

Miss Howe. [*In reply*]
Friday, July 21

MISS ARABELLA HARLOWE,—If you had half as much sense as you have ill-nature, you would (notwithstanding the exuberance of the latter) have been able to distinguish between a kind intention to you all (that you might have the less to reproach yourselves with, if a deplorable case should happen), and an officiousness I owed you not, by reason of freedoms at least reciprocal. I will not, for the *unhappy body's* sake, as you call a sister you have helped to make so, say all that I *could* say. If what I fear happen, you shall hear (whether desired or not) all the mind of

ANNA HOWE

Miss Arabella Harlowe to Miss Howe
Friday, July 21

MISS ANN HOWE,—Your pert letter I have received. You, that spare nobody, I cannot expect should spare me. You are very happy in a prudent and watchful mother—but else mine cannot be exceeded in prudence: but we had all too good an opinion of somebody, to think watchfulness needful. There may possibly be some reason why *you* are so much attached to her in an error of this flagrant nature.

I help to make a sister unhappy! It is false, miss! It is all her own doings!—except, indeed, what she may owe to somebody's advice—you know who can best answer for that.

Let us *know your mind* as soon as you please: as we shall know it to be *your* mind, we shall judge what attention to give it. That's all, from, etc.

AR. H.

Clarissa

A Limited Wish

[Clarissa writes to Anna Howe]

May you, my dear Miss Howe, have no discomforts but what you make to yourself! As it will be in your own power to lessen such as these, they ought to be your punishment if you do not. There is no such thing as *perfect happiness* here, since the busy mind will *make* to itself evils, were it to *find* none. You will therefore pardon this limited wish, strange as it may appear till you consider it: for to wish you no infelicities, either within or without you, were to wish you what can never happen in this world; and what perhaps ought not to be wished for, if *by a wish* one could give one's friend such an exemption; since we are not to live here always.

We must not, in short, expect that our roses will grow without thorns: but then they are useful and instructive thorns; which, by pricking the fingers of the too hasty plucker, teach future caution. And who knows not that difficulty gives poignancy to our enjoyments; which are apt to lose their relish with us when they are over-easily obtained?

Clarissa

At the Deathbed of a Bawd

There were no less than eight of her cursed daughters surrounding her bed when I entered; one of her partners, Polly Horton, at their head; and now Sally, her other partner, and *Madam* Carter, as they called her (for they are all *madams* with one another), made the number ten: all in shocking dishabille, and without stays, except Sally, Carter, and Polly; who, not daring to leave her, had not been in bed all night.

The other seven seemed to have been but just up, risen perhaps from their customers in the fore house, and their nocturnal orgies, with faces, three or four of them, that had run, the paint lying in streaky seams not half blowzed off, discovering coarse wrinkled skins: the hair of some of them of divers colours, obliged to the blacklead comb where black was affected; the artificial jet, however, yielding apace to the natural brindle: that of others plastered with oil and powder; the oil predominating: but every one's hanging about her ears and neck in broken curls or ragged ends; and each at my entrance taken with one motion, stroking their matted locks with both hands under their coifs, mobs, or pinners, every one of which was awry. They were all slip-shoed; stockingless some; only under-petticoated all; their gowns, made to cover straddling hoops, hanging trollopy, and tangling about their heels; but hastily wrapped round them as soon as I came upstairs. And half of them (unpadded, shoulder-bent, pallid-lipped, limber-jointed wretches) appearing, from a blooming nineteen or twenty perhaps over night, haggard well-worn strumpets of thirty-eight or forty . . .

But these were the veterans, the chosen band; for now and then flitted in, to the number of half a dozen or more, by turns, subordinate sinners, undergraduates, younger then some of the chosen phalanx, but not less obscene in their appearance, though indeed not so much beholden to the plastering fucus; yet unpropped by stays, squalid, loose in attire, sluggish-haired, under-petticoated only as the former, eyes half opened, winking and pinking, mispatched, yawning, stretching, as if from the unworn-off effects of the midnight revel; all armed in succession with supplies of cordials (of which every one present was either taster or partaker), under the direction of the busier Dorcas, who frequently popped in, to see her slops duly given and taken.

Clarissa

JOSEPH BUTLER, BISHOP OF DURHAM
1692–1752

Choices and Consequences

How much soever men differ in the course of life they prefer, and in their ways of palliating and excusing their vices to themselves; yet all agree in the one thing, desiring to 'die the death of the righteous.' This is surely remarkable. The observation may be extended further, and put thus: Even without determining what that is which we call guilt or innocence, there is no man but would choose, after having had the pleasure or advantage of a vicious action, to be free of the guilt of it, to be in the state of an innocent man. This shows at least the disturbance, and implicit dissatisfaction in vice. If we inquire into the grounds of it, we shall find it proceeds partly from an immediate sense of having done evil; and partly from an apprehension that this inward sense shall, one time or another, be seconded by an higher judgment, upon which our whole being depends. Now, to suspend and drown this sense, and these apprehensions, be it by the hurry of business or of pleasure, or by superstition, or moral equivocations, this is in a manner one and the same, and makes no alteration at all in the nature of our case. Things and actions are what they are, and the consequences of them will be what they will be: Why then should we desire to be deceived? As we are reasonable creatures, and have any regard to ourselves, we ought to lay these things plainly and honestly before our mind, and upon this, act as you please, as you think most fit; make that choice, and prefer that course of life, which you can justify to yourselves, and which sits most easy upon your own mind. It will immediately appear, that vice cannot be the happiness, but must, upon the whole, be the misery of such a creature as man; a moral, and accountable agent. Superstitious observances, self-deceit, though of a more refined sort, will not, in reality, at all amend matters with us. And the result of the whole can be nothing else, but that with simplicity and fairness we 'keep innocency, and take heed unto the thing that is right; for this alone shall bring a man peace at the last.'

Fifteen Sermons, 1726

PHILIP DORMER STANHOPE, EARL OF CHESTERFIELD

1694–1773

An Awkward Fellow

When an awkward fellow first comes into a room it is highly probable that his sword gets between his legs, and throws him down, or makes him stumble at least; when he has recovered this accident, he goes and places himself in the very place of the whole room where he should not; there he soon lets his hat fall down, and, in taking it up again, throws down his cane; in recovering his cane, his hat falls a second time: so that he is a quarter of an hour before he is in order again. If he drinks tea or coffee, he certainly scalds his mouth, and lets either the cup or the saucer fall, and spills the the tea or coffee in his breeches. At dinner his awkwardness distinguishes itself particularly, as he has more to do; there he holds his knife, fork, and spoon differently from other people; eats with his knife to the great danger of his mouth, picks his teeth with his fork, and puts his spoon, which has been in his throat twenty times, into the dishes again. If he is to carve, he can never hit the joint; but, in his vain efforts to cut through the bone, scatters the sauce in everybody's face. He generally daubs himself with soup and grease, though his napkin is commonly stuck through a buttonhole, and tickles his chin. When he drinks, he infallibly coughs in his glass and besprinkles the company. Besides all this, he has strange tricks and gestures; such as snuffing up his nose, making faces, putting his fingers in his nose, or blowing it and looking afterwards in his handkerchief, so as to make the company sick. His hands are troublesome to him when he has not something in them, and he does not know where to put them; but they are in perpetual motion between his bosom and his breeches; he does not wear his clothes, and, in short, does nothing like other people. All this, I own, is not in any degree criminal; but it is highly disagreeable and ridiculous in company, and ought most carefully to be avoided by whoever desires to please.

letter to his son, 1741

Contempt

Every man is not ambitious, or covetous, or passionate; but every man has pride enough in his composition to feel and resent the least slight and contempt. Remember, therefore, most carefully to conceal your contempt, however just, wherever you would not make an implacable enemy. Men are much more unwilling to have their weaknesses and their imperfections known, than their crimes; and, if you hint to a man that you think him silly, ignorant, or even ill bred, or awkward, he will hate you more and longer than if you tell him, plainly, that you think him a rogue. Never yield to that temptation, which, to most young men, is very strong, of exposing other people's weaknesses and infirmities, for the sake either of diverting the company, or of showing your own superiority. You may get the laugh on your side by it, for the present; but you will make enemies by it for ever; and even those who laugh with you then, will, upon reflection, fear, and consequently hate you: besides that, it is ill-natured; and a good heart desires rather to conceal, than expose, other people's weaknesses or misfortunes. If you have wit, use it to please, and not to hurt: you may shine, like the sun in the temperate zones, without scorching. Here it is wished for; under the line it is dreaded.

letter to his son, 1748

Putting a Wit in His Place

I always put these pert jackanapeses out of countenance, by looking extremely grave, when they expect that I should laugh at their pleasantries; and by saying *Well, and so*; as if they had not done, and that the sting were still to come. This disconcerts them, as they have no resources in themselves, and have but one set of jokes to live upon.

letter to his son, 1748

Complicated Machines

I have often told you (and it is most true) that, with regard to mankind, we must not draw general conclusions from certain particular principles, though, in the main, true ones. We must not suppose that, because a man is a rational animal, he will, therefore, always act rationally; or, because he has such or such a predominant passion, that he will act invariably and consequentially in the pursuit of it. No, we are complicated machines; and though we have one main spring that gives motion to the whole, we have an infinity of little wheels, which, in their turns, retard, precipitate, and sometimes stop that motion.

letter to his son, 1749

Small Talk

I am far from meaning by this, that you should always be talking wisely, in company, of books, history, and matters of knowledge. There are many companies which you will and ought to keep, where such conversations would be misplaced and ill-timed; your own good-sense must distinguish the company, and the time. You must trifle with triflers, and be serious only with the serious, but dance to those who pipe. *Cur in theatrum Cato severe venisti?* was justly said to an old man; how much more so would it be to one of your age? From the moment that you are dressed, and go out, pocket all your knowledge with your watch, and never pull it out in company unless desired: the producing of the one unasked implies that you are weary of the company; and the producing of the other unrequired will make the company weary of you. Company is a republic too jealous of its liberties to suffer a dictator even for a quarter of an hour; and yet in that, as in all republics, there are some few who really govern, but then it is by seeming to disclaim, instead of attempting to usurp, the power; that is the occasion in which manners, dexterity, address, and the undefinable *je ne sais quoi* triumph; if properly exerted, their conquest is sure, and the more lasting for not being perceived.

letter to his son, 1750

JOHN, LORD HERVEY
1696–1743

A Royal Mistress Discarded

That the King went no more in an evening to Lady Suffolk was whispered about the Court by all that belonged to it, and was one of those secrets that everybody knows, and everybody avoids publicly to seem to know.

Various were the sentiments of people on this occasion. The Queen was both glad and sorry. Her pride was glad to have even this ghost of a rival removed; and she was sorry to have so much more of her husband's time thrown upon her hands, when she had already enough to make her often heartily weary of his company, and to deprive her of other company which she gladly would have enjoyed.

I am sensible, when I say the Queen was pleased with the removal of Lady Suffolk as a rival, that I seem to contradict what I have formerly said in these papers of her being rather desirous (for fear of a successor) to keep Lady Suffolk about the King, than solicitous to banish her; but, in describing the sentiments of the same people at different times, human creatures are so inconsistent with themselves, that the inconsistency of such descriptions often arises, not from the mistakes or forgetfulness of the describer, but from the instability and changeableness of the person described.

The Prince, I believe, wished Lady Suffolk removed, as he would have wished anybody detached from the King's interest; and, added to this, Lady Suffolk having many friends, it was a step that he hoped would make his father many enemies. Neither was he sorry, perhaps, to have so eminent a precedent for a prince's discarding a mistress he was tired of.

The Princess Emily wished Lady Suffolk's disgrace because she wished misfortune to most people; the Princess Caroline, because she thought it would please her mother; the Princess Royal was violently for having her crushed, and when Lord Hervey said he wondered she was so desirous to have this lady's disgrace pushed to such extremity, she replied: 'Lady Suffolk's conduct with regard to politics has been so impertinent that she cannot be too ill-used;' and when Lord Hervey intimated the danger there might be, from the King's coquetry, of some more troublesome and powerful successor, she said (not very judiciously with regard to her mother, nor very respectfully with regard to her father): 'I wish, with all my heart, he would take somebody else, then Mamma might be a little relieved from the ennui of seeing him for ever in her room.' At the same time the King was always bragging how dearly his daughter Anne loved him.

Sir Robert Walpole hated Lady Suffolk, and was hated by her, but did not wish her driven out of St James's, imagining somebody would come in her place who, from his attachment to the Queen, must hate him as strongly, and might hate him more dangerously.

The true reasons of her disgrace were the King's being thoroughly tired of her; her constant opposition to all his measures; her wearying him with her perpetual contradiction; her intimacy with Mr Pope, who had published several satires, with his name to them, in which the King and all his family were rather more than obliquely sneered at; the acquaintance she was known to have with many of the opposing party, and the correspondence she was suspected to have with many more of them; and, in short, her being no longer pleasing to the King in her private capacity, and every day more disagreeable to him in her public conduct.

Memoirs of the Reign of George the Second, first published 1848; first complete edition 1931

JOHN WESLEY
1703–1791

Fear and Faith on an Atlantic Crossing

At noon, our third storm began. At four it was more violent than before. Now indeed we could say, 'The waves of the sea were mighty and raged horribly. They rose up to the heavens above and clave down to the hell beneath.' The winds roared round about us, and (what I never heard before) whistled as distinctly as if it had been a human voice. The ship not only rocked to and fro with the utmost violence, but shook and jarred with so unequal, grating a motion, that one could not but with great difficulty keep one's hold of any thing, nor stand a moment without it. Every ten minutes came a shock against the stern or side of the ship which one would think should dash the planks in pieces.

At seven I went to the Germans. I had long before observed the great seriousness of their behaviour. Of their humility they had given a continual proof by performing those servile offices for the other passengers which none of the English would undertake; for which they desired and would receive no pay, saying, 'It was good for their proud hearts,' and 'their loving Saviour had done more for them,' and every day had given them an occasion of showing a meekness which no injury could move. If they were pushed, struck or thrown down, they rose again and went away; but no complaint was found in their mouth. There was now an opportunity of trying whether they were delivered from the spirit of fear as well as from that of pride, anger and revenge.

In the midst of the psalm wherewith their service began, the sea broke over, split the main-sail in pieces, covered the ship and poured in between the decks as if the great deep had already swallowed us up. A terrible screaming began among the English. The Germans calmly sung on. I asked one of them afterwards, 'Was you not afraid?' He answered, 'I thank God, no.' I asked, 'But were not your women and children afraid?' He replied mildly, 'No; our women and children are not afraid to die.' From them I went to their crying, trembling neighbours and pointed out to them the difference, in the hour of trial, between him that feareth God and him that feareth him not. At twelve the wind fell. This was the most glorious day which I have hitherto seen.

Journal, 1736

The Rabble Frustrated

I rode once more to Pensford, at the earnest request of several serious people. The place where they desired me to preach was a little green spot near the town. But I had no sooner begun, than a great company of rabble, hired (as we afterwards found) for that purpose, came furiously upon us, bringing a bull which they had been baiting and now drove in among the people. But the beast was wiser than his drivers, and continually ran either on one side of us or the other, while we quietly sang praise to God and prayed for about an hour. The poor wretches finding themselves disappointed, at length seized upon the bull, now weak and tired after being so long torn and beaten both by dogs and men, and by main strength partly dragged and partly thrust him in among the people. When they had forced their way to the little table on which I stood, they strove several times to throw it down by thrusting the helpless beast against it, who of himself stirred no more than a log of wood. I once or twice put aside his head with my hand, that the blood might not drop upon my clothes, intending to go on as soon as the hurry should be a little over. But the table falling down, some of our friends caught me in their arms and carried me right away on their shoulders, while the rabble wreaked their vengeance on the table which they tore bit from bit. We went a little way off, where I finished my discourse without any noise or interruption.

Journal, 1742

Off Limits

Having been sent for several times, I went to see a young woman in Bedlam. But I had not talked with her long before one gave me to know that 'None of these Preachers were to come there.' So we are forbid to go to Newgate, for fear of making them wicked; and to Bedlam, for fear of driving them mad.

Journal, 1750

Sterne

I casually took a volume of what is called *A Sentimental Journal through France and Italy*. Sentimental! What is that? It is not English; he might as well say Continental. It is not sense. It conveys no determinate idea; yet one fool makes many. And this nonsensical word (who would believe it?) is become a fashionable one! However, the book agrees full well with the title; for one is as queer as the other. For oddity, uncouthness and unlikeness to all the world beside, I suppose the writer is without a rival!

Journal, 1772

The Crowned Heads of Europe

I was desired to see the celebrated wax-work at the museum in Spring Gardens. It exhibits most of the crowned heads in Europe, shows their characters in their countenance. Sense and majesty appear in the King of Spain; dullness and sottishness in the King of France; infernal subtlety in the late King of Prussia, as well as in the skeleton of Voltaire; calmness and humanity in the Emperor, and King of Portugal; exquisite stupidity in the Prince of Orange; and amazing coarseness, with everything that is unamiable, in the Czarina.

Journal, 1787

JONATHAN EDWARDS
1703–1758

Two Types of Knowledge

Thus there is a difference between having an opinion, that God is holy and gracious, and having a sense of the loveliness and beauty of that holiness and grace. There is a difference between having a rational judgment that honey is sweet, and having a sense of its sweetness. A man may have the former, that knows not how honey tastes; but a man cannot have the latter unless he has an idea of the taste of honey in his mind. So there is a difference between believing that a person is beautiful, and having a sense of his beauty. The former may be obtained by hearsay, but the latter only by seeing the countenance. When the heart is sensible of the beauty and amiableness of a thing, it necessarily feels pleasure in the apprehension. It is implied in a person's being heartily sensible of the loveliness of a thing, that the idea of it is pleasant to his soul; which is a far different thing from having a rational opinion that it is excellent.

A Divine and Supernatural Light: sermon, 1733

An Inward Sweetness

After this my sense of divine things gradually increased, and became more and more lively, and had more of that inward sweetness. The appearance of everything was altered: there seemed to be, as it were, a calm, sweet cast, or appearance of divine glory, in almost everything. God's excellency, His wisdom, His purity and love, seemed to appear in everything: in the sun, moon and stars; in the clouds, and blue sky; in the grass, flowers, trees; in the water, and all nature; which used greatly to fix my mind. I often used to sit and view the moon for a long time, and so in the daytime spent much time in viewing the clouds and sky to behold the sweet glory of God in these things, in the meantime, singing forth with a low voice my contemplations of the Creator and Redeemer. And scarce anything, among all the works of nature, was so sweet to me as thunder and lightning. Formerly, nothing had been so terrible to me. I used to be a person uncommonly terrified with thunder, and it used to strike me with terror when I saw a thunderstorm rising. But now, on the contrary, it rejoiced me. I felt God at the first appearance of a thunderstorm. And used to take the opportunity at such times to fix myself to view the clouds, and see the lightnings play, and hear the majestic and awful voice of God's thunder, which often times was exceeding entertaining, leading me to sweet contemplations of my great and glorious God. And while I viewed, used to spend my time, as it always seemed natural to me, to sing or chant forth my meditations, to speak my thoughts in soliloquies, and speak with a singing voice.

Personal Narrative, c.1740

A Spider Held over a Fire

The God that holds you over the pit of hell, much as one holds a spider or some loathsome insect over the fire, abhors you, and is dreadfully provoked: His wrath towards you burns like fire; He looks upon you as worthy of nothing else but to be cast into the fire; He is of purer eyes than to bear to have you in His sight; you are ten thousand times more abominable in His eyes than the most hateful venomous serpent is in ours. You have offended Him infinitely more than ever a stubborn rebel did his prince; and yet it is nothing but His hand that holds you from falling into the fire every moment. It is to be ascribed to nothing else, that you did not go to hell the last night; that you was suffered to awake again in this world, after you closed your eyes to sleep. And there is no other reason to be given, why you have not dropped into hell since you arose in the morning, but that God's hand has held you up. There is no other reason to be given why you have not gone to hell, since you have sat here in the house of God, provoking His pure eyes by your sinful wicked manner of attending His solemn worship. Yea, there is nothing else that is to be given as a reason why you do not this very moment drop down into hell.

Sinners in the Hands of an Angry God: sermon, 1741

WILLIAM MURRAY, EARL OF MANSFIELD 1705–1793

The Gordon Riots

Upon the whole, my Lords, while I deeply lament the cause which rendered it indispensably necessary to call out the military, and to order them to act in suppression of the late disturbances, I am clearly of opinion that no steps have been taken for that purpose which were not strictly legal, as well as fully justifiable in point of policy. Certainly, the civil power, whether through native imbecility, through neglect, or the very formidable force they would have had to contend with, were unequal to the task of putting an end to the insurrection. When the rabble had augmented their numbers by breaking open the prisons and setting the felons at liberty, they had become too formidable to be opposed only by the staff of a constable. If the military had not acted at last, none of your Lordships can hesitate to agree with me that the conflagrations would have spread over the whole capital; and, in a few hours, it would have been a heap of rubbish. The King's extraordinary prerogative to proclaim martial law (whatever that may be) is clearly out of the question. His Majesty, and those who have advised him (I repeat it), have acted in strict conformity to the common law. The military have been called in—and very wisely called in—not as *soldiers*, but as *citizens*. No matter whether their coats be red or brown, they were employed, not to subvert, but to preserve, the laws and constitution which we all prize so highly.

Speech in the House of Lords, 1780

BENJAMIN FRANKLIN
1706–1790

Some Lessons in the Art of Writing

About this time I met with an odd volume of the *Spectator*. It was the third. I had never before seen any of them. I bought it, read it over and over, and was much delighted with it. I thought the writing excellent, and wished, if possible, to imitate it. With this view I took some of the papers, and, making short hints of the sentiment in each sentence, laid them by a few days, and then, without looking at the book, tried to complete the papers again, by expressing each hinted sentiment at length, and as fully as it had been expressed before, in any suitable words that should come to hand. Then I compared my *Spectator* with the original, discovered some of my faults, and corrected them. But I found I wanted a stock of words, or a readiness in recollecting and using them, which I thought I should have acquired if I had gone on making verses; since the continual occasion for words of the same import, but of different length, to suit the measure, or of different sound for the rhyme, would have laid me under a constant necessity of searching for variety, and also have tended to fix that variety in my mind, and make me master of it. Therefore I took some of the tales and turned them into verse; and, after a time, when I had pretty well forgotten the prose, turned them back again. I also sometimes jumbled my collection of hints into confusion, and after some weeks endeavoured to reduce them into the best order, before I began to form the full sentences and complete the paper. This was to teach me method in the arrangement of thoughts. By comparing my work afterwards with the original, I discovered many faults and amended them; but I sometimes had the pleasure of fancying that, in certain particulars of small import, I had been lucky enough to improve the method or the language, and this encouraged me to think I might possibly in time come to be a tolerable English writer, of which I was extremely ambitious.

Autobiography, 1771; first published 1791

Poor Mungo

To Miss Georgiana Shipley, on the loss of her American squirrel, who, escaping from his cage, was killed by a shepherd's dog

London, 26 September, 1772.

DEAR MISS,

I lament with you most sincerely the unfortunate end of poor MUNGO. Few squirrels were better accomplished; for he had had a good education, had travelled far, and seen much of the world. As he had the honor of being, for his virtues, your favorite, he should not go, like common skuggs, without an elegy or an epitaph. Let us give him one in the monumental style and measure, which, being neither prose nor verse, is perhaps the properest for grief; since to use common language would look as if we were not affected, and to make rhymes would seem trifling in sorrow.

EPITAPH.

Alas! poor MUNGO!
Happy wert thou, hadst thou known
Thy own felicity.
Remote from the fierce bald eagle,
Tyrant of thy native woods,
Thou hadst nought to fear from his piercing talons,
Nor from the murdering gun
Of the thoughtless sportsman.
Safe in thy wired castle,
GRIMALKIN never could annoy thee.
Daily wert thou fed with the choicest viands,
By the fair hand of an indulgent mistress;
But, discontented,
Thou wouldst have more freedom.
Too soon, alas! didst thou obtain it;
And wandering,
Thou art fallen by the fangs of wanton, cruel RANGER!
Learn hence,
Ye who blindly seek more liberty,
Whether subjects, sons, squirrels, or daughters,
That apparent restraint may be real protection,
Yielding peace and plenty
With security.

skugg] dialect word for a squirrel

You see, my dear Miss, how much more decent and proper this broken style is, than if we were to say, by way of epitaph,—

Here Skugg
Lies snug,
As a bug
In a rug.

And yet, perhaps, there are people in the world of so little feeling as to think that this would be a good-enough epitaph for poor Mungo . . .

Proposed New Version of the Bible

To the Printer of * * * *

Sir,

It is now more than one hundred and seventy years since the translation of our common English Bible. The language in that time is much changed, and the style, being obsolete, and thence less agreeable, is perhaps one reason why the reading of that excellent book is of late so much neglected. I have therefore thought it would be well to procure a new version, in which, preserving the sense, the turn of phrase and manner of expression should be modern. I do not pretend to have the necessary abilities for such a work myself; I throw out the hint for the consideration of the learned; and only venture to send you a few verses of the first chapter of Job, which may serve as a sample of the kind of version I would recommend.

A. B.

PART OF THE FIRST CHAPTER OF JOB MODERNIZED.

Old Text.	New Version.
Verse 6. Now there was a day when the sons of God came to present themselves before the Lord, and Satan came also amongst them.	Verse 6. And it being *levee* day in heaven, all God's nobility came to court, to present themselves before him; and Satan also appeared in the circle, as one of the ministry.
7. And the Lord said unto Satan, Whence comest thou? Then Satan answered the Lord, and said, From going to and fro in the earth, and from walking up and down in it.	7. And God said to Satan, You have been some time absent; where were you? And Satan answered, I have been at my country-seat, and in different places visiting my friends.
8. And the Lord said unto Satan, Hast thou considered my servant Job, that there is none like him in the earth, a perfect	8. And God said, Well, what think you of Lord Job? You see he is my best friend, a perfectly honest man, full of respect for

and an upright man, one that feareth God, and escheweth evil?

9. Then Satan answered the Lord, and said, Doth Job fear God for naught?

10. Hast thou not made an hedge about his house, and about all that he hath on every side? Thou hast blessed the work of his hands, and his substance is increased in the land.

11. But put forth thine hand now, and touch all that he hath, and he will curse thee to thy face.

me, and avoiding every thing that might offend me.

9. And Satan answered, Does your Majesty imagine that his good conduct is the effect of mere personal attachment and affection?

10. Have you not protected him, and heaped your benefits upon him, till he is grown enormously rich?

11. Try him;—only withdraw your favor, turn him out of his places, and withhold his pensions, and you will soon find him in the opposition.

An Imperfect Constitution

I confess, that I do not entirely approve of this Constitution at present; but, Sir, I am not sure I shall never approve it; for, having lived long, I have experienced many instances of being obliged, by better information or fuller consideration, to change my opinions even on important subjects, which I once thought right, but found to be otherwise. It is therefore that, the older I grow, the more apt I am to doubt my own judgment of others. Most men, indeed, as well as most sects in religion, think themselves in possession of all truth, and that wherever others differ from them, it is so far error. Steele, a Protestant, in a dedication, tells the Pope, that the only difference between our two churches in their opinions of the certainty of their doctrine, is, the Romish Church is *infallible*, and the Church of England is *never in the wrong*. But, though many private Persons think almost as highly of their own infallibility as of that of their Sect, few express it so naturally as a certain French Lady, who, in a little dispute with her sister, said, 'But I meet with nobody but myself that is *always* in the right.' '*Je ne trouve que moi qui aie toujours raison.*'

In these sentiments, Sir, I agree to this Constitution, with all its faults,—if they are such; because I think a general Government necessary for us, and there is no *form* of government but what may be a blessing to the people, if well administered; and I believe, farther, that this is likely to be well administered for a course of years, and can only end in despotism, as other forms have done before it, when the people shall become so corrupted as to need despotic government, being incapable of any other. I doubt, too, whether any other Convention we can obtain, may be able to make a better constitution; for, when you assemble a number of men, to have the advantage of their joint wisdom, you inevitably assemble with those men all their prejudices, their passions, their errors of opinion, their local interests, and their selfish views. From such an assembly can a *perfect* production be expected? It therefore astonishes me, Sir, to find this system approaching so near to perfection as it does; and I think it will astonish our enemies, who are waiting with confidence to hear, that our councils are confounded like those of the builders of Babel, and that our States are on the point of separation, only to meet hereafter for the purpose of cutting one another's throats. Thus I consent, Sir, to this Constitution, because I expect no better, and because I am not sure that it is not the best.

Speech at the Constitutional Convention, 1787

HENRY FIELDING
1707–1754

Parson Adams and a Man of Means

The chariot had not proceeded far before Mr Adams observed it was a very fine day. 'Ay, and a very fine country too,' answered Pounce.—'I should think so more,' returned Adams, 'if I had not lately travelled over the Downs, which I take to exceed this and all other prospects in the universe.'—'A fig for prospects!' answered Pounce; 'one acre here is worth ten there; and for my own part, I have no delight in the prospect of any land but my own.'—'Sir,' said Adams, 'you can indulge yourself with many fine prospects of that kind.'—'I thank God I have a little,' replied the other, 'with which I am content, and envy no man: I have a little, Mr Adams, with which I do as much good as I can.' Adams answered, 'That riches without charity were nothing worth; for that they were a blessing only to him who made them a blessing to others.'—'You and I,' said Peter, 'have different notions of charity. I own, as it is generally used, I do not like the word, nor do I think it becomes one of us gentlemen; it is a mean parson-like quality; though I would not infer many parsons have it neither.'—'Sir,' said Adams, 'my definition of charity is, a generous disposition to relieve the distressed.'—'There is something in that definition,' answered Peter, 'which I like well enough; it is, as you say, a disposition, and does not so much consist in the act as in the disposition to do it. But, alas! Mr Adams, who are meant by the distressed? Believe me, the distresses of mankind are mostly imaginary, and it would be rather folly than goodness to relieve them.'—'Sure, sir,' replied Adams, 'hunger and thirst, cold and nakedness, and other distresses which attend the poor, can never be said to be imaginary evils.'—'How can any man complain of hunger,' said Peter, 'in a country where such excellent salads are to be gathered in almost every field? or of thirst, where every river and stream produces such delicious potations? And as for cold and nakedness, they are evils introduced by luxury and custom. A man naturally wants clothes no more than a horse or any other animal; and there are whole nations who go without them; but these are things perhaps which you, who do not know the world'—'You will pardon me, sir,' returned Adams; 'I have read of the Gymnosophists.'—'A plague of your Jehosaphats!' cried Peter; 'the greatest fault in our constitution is the provision made for the poor, except that perhaps made for some others. Sir, I have not an estate which doth not contribute almost as much again to the poor as to the land-tax; and I do assure you I expect to come myself to the parish in the end.' To which Adams giving a dissenting smile, Peter thus proceeded: 'I fancy, Mr Adams, you are one of those who imagine I am a lump of money; for there are many who, I fancy, believe that not only my pockets, but my whole clothes, are lined with bank-bills; but I assure you, you are all mistaken; I am not the man the world esteems me. If I can hold my head above water it is all I can. I have injured myself by purchasing. I have been too liberal of my money. Indeed, I fear my heir will find my affairs in a worse situation than they are reputed to be. Ah! he will have reason to wish I had loved money more and land less. Pray, my good neighbour, where should I have that quantity of riches the world is so liberal to bestow on me? Where could I possibly, without I had stole it, acquire such a treasure?' 'Why, truly,' says Adams, 'I have been always of your opinion; I have wondered as well as yourself with what confidence they could report such things of you, which have to me appeared as mere impossibilities; for you know, sir, and I have often heard you say it, that your wealth is of your own acquisition; and can it be credible that in your short time you should have amassed such a heap of treasure as these people will have you worth? Indeed, had you inherited an estate like Sir Thomas Booby, which had descended in your family for many generations, they might have had a colour for their assertions.' 'Why, what do they say I am worth?' cries Peter, with a malicious sneer. 'Sir,' answered Adams, 'I have heard some aver you are not worth less than twenty thousand pounds.' At which Peter frowned. 'Nay, sir,' said Adams, 'you ask me only the opinion of others; for my own part, I have always denied it, nor did I ever believe you could possibly be worth half that sum.' 'However, Mr Adams,' said he, squeezing him by the hand, 'I would not sell them all I am worth for double that sum; and as to what you believe, or they believe, I care not a fig, no not a fart. I am not poor because you think me so, nor because you attempt to undervalue me in the country. I know the envy of mankind very well; but I thank Heaven I am above them. It is true, my wealth is of my own acquisition. I have not an estate, like Sir Thomas Booby, that has descended in my family through many generations; but I know heirs of such estates who are forced to travel about the country like some people in torn cassocks, and might be glad to accept of a pitiful curacy for what I know. Yes, sir, as shabby fellows as yourself, whom no man of my figure, without that vice of good-nature about him, would suffer to ride in a chariot with him.' 'Sir,' said Adams, 'I value not your chariot of a rush; and if I had known you had intended to affront me, I would have walked to the world's end on foot ere I would have accepted a place in it. However, sir, I will soon rid you of that inconvenience;' and, so saying, he opened the chariot door, without calling to the coachman, and leapt out into the highway, forgetting to take his hat along with him; which, however, Mr Pounce threw after him with great violence.

Joseph Andrews, 1742

A Mark of Greatness

Wild no sooner parted from the chaste Laetitia than, recollecting that his friend the count was returned to his lodgings in the same house, he resolved to visit him; for he was none of those half-bred fellows who are ashamed to see their friends when they have plundered and betrayed them; from which base and pitiful temper many monstrous cruelties have been transacted by men, who have sometimes carried their modesty so far as to the murder or utter ruin of those against whom their consciences have suggested to them that they have committed some small trespass, either by the debauching a friend's wife or daughter, belying or betraying the friend himself, or some other such trifling instance. In our hero there was nothing not truly great: he could, without the least abashment, drink a bottle with the man who knew he had the moment before picked his pocket; and, when he had stripped him of everything he had, never desired to do him any further mischief; for he carried good-nature to that wonderful and uncommon height that he never did a single injury to man or woman by which he himself did not expect to reap some advantage.

Jonathan Wild, 1743

The Pleasures of Marriage

One situation only of the married state is excluded from pleasure: and that is, a state of indifference: but as many of my readers, I hope, know what an exquisite delight there is in conveying pleasure to a beloved object, so some few, I am afraid, may have experienced the satisfaction of tormenting one we hate. It is, I apprehend, to come at this latter pleasure, that we see both sexes often give up that ease in marriage which they might otherwise possess, though their mate was never so disagreeable to them. Hence the wife often puts on fits of love and jealousy, nay, even denies herself any pleasure, to disturb and prevent those of her husband; and he again, in return, puts frequent restraints on himself, and stays at home in company which he dislikes, in order to confine his wife to what she equally detests. Hence, too, must flow those tears which a widow sometimes so plentifully sheds over the ashes of a husband with whom she led a life of constant disquiet and turbulency, and whom now she can never hope to torment any more.

Tom Jones, 1749

Taking Friends as They Are

It is possible, however, that Mr Allworthy saw enough to render him a little uneasy; for we are not always to conclude, that a wise man is not hurt, because he doth not cry out and lament himself, like those of a childish or effeminate temper. But indeed it is possible he might see some faults in the captain without any uneasiness at all; for men of true wisdom and goodness are contented to take persons and things as they are, without complaining of their imperfections, or attempting to amend them. They can see a fault in a friend, a relation, or an acquaintance, without ever mentioning it to the parties themselves, or to any others; and this often without lessening their affection. Indeed, unless great discernment be tempered with this overlooking disposition, we ought never to contract friendship but with a degree of folly which we can deceive; for I hope my friends will pardon me when I declare, I know none of them without a fault; and I should be sorry if I could imagine I had any friend who could not see mine. Forgiveness of this kind we give and demand in turn. It is an exercise of friendship, and perhaps none of the least pleasant. And this forgiveness we must bestow, without desire of amendment. There is, perhaps, no surer mark of folly, than an attempt to correct the natural infirmities of those we love. The finest composition of human nature, as well as the finest china, may have a flaw in it; and this, I am afraid, in either case, is equally incurable; though, nevertheless, the pattern may remain of the highest value.

Tom Jones

Tastes in Music

It was Mr Western's custom every afternoon, as soon as he was drunk, to hear his daughter play on the harpsichord; for he was a great lover of music, and perhaps, had he lived in town, might have passed for a connoisseur; for he always excepted against the finest compositions of Mr Handel. He never relished any music but what was light and airy; and indeed his most favourite tunes were Old Sir Simon the King, St George he was for England, Bobbing Joan, and some others.

His daughter, though she was a perfect mistress of music, and would never willingly have played any but Handel's, was so devoted to her father's pleasure, that she learnt all those tunes to oblige him. However, she would now and then endeavour to lead him into her own taste; and when he required the repetition of his ballads, would answer with a 'Nay, dear sir;' and would often beg him to suffer her to play something else.

This evening, however, when the gentleman was retired from his bottle, she played all his favourites three times over without any solicitation. This so pleased the good squire, that he started from his couch, gave his daughter a kiss, and swore her hand was greatly improved.

Tom Jones

Mr Partridge's Opinion of Garrick

Little more worth remembering occurred during the play, at the end of which Jones asked him, 'Which of the players he had liked best?' To this he answered, with some appearance of indignation at the question, 'The king, without doubt.' 'Indeed, Mr Partridge,' says Mrs Miller, 'you are not of the same opinion with the town; for they are all agreed, that Hamlet is acted by the best player who ever was on the stage.' 'He the best player!' cries Partridge, with a contemptuous sneer, 'why, I could act as well as he myself. I am sure, if I had seen a ghost, I should have looked in the very same manner, and done just as he did. And then, to be sure, in that scene, as you called it, between him and his mother, where you told me he acted so fine, why, Lord help me, any man, that is, any good man, that had such a mother, would have done exactly the same. I know you are only joking with me; but indeed, madam, though I was never at a play in London, yet I have seen acting before in the country; and the king for my money; he speaks all his words distinctly, half as loud again as the other.—Anybody may see he is an actor.'

Tom Jones

A Sick Man Goes on Board Ship

To go on board the ship it was necessary first to go into a boat; a matter of no small difficulty, as I had no use of my limbs, and was to be carried by men who, though sufficiently strong for their burthen, were, like

Archimedes, puzzled to find a steady footing. Of this, as few of my readers have not gone into wherries on the Thames, they will easily be able to form to themselves an idea. However, by the assistance of my friend Mr Welch, whom I never think or speak of but with love and esteem, I conquered this difficulty, as I did afterwards that of ascending the ship, into which I was hoisted with more ease by a chair lifted with pulleys. I was soon seated in a great chair in the cabin, to refresh myself after a fatigue which had been more intolerable, in a quarter of a mile's passage from my coach to the ship, that I had before undergone in a land-journey of twelve miles, which I had travelled with the utmost expedition.

This latter fatigue was, perhaps, somewhat heightened by an indignation which I could not prevent arising in my mind. I think, upon my entrance into the boat, I presented a spectacle of the highest horror. The total loss of limbs was apparent to all who saw me, and my face contained marks of a most diseased state, if not of death itself. Indeed, so ghastly was my countenance, that timorous women with child had abstained from my house, for fear of the ill consequences of looking at me. In this condition I ran the gauntlope (so I think I may justly call it) through rows of sailors and watermen, few of whom failed of paying their compliments to me by all manner of insults and jests on my misery. No man who knew me will think I conceived any personal resentment at this behaviour; but it was a lively picture of that cruelty and inhumanity in the nature of men which I have often contemplated with concern, and which leads the mind into a train of very uncomfortable and melancholy thoughts.

The Journal of a Voyage to Lisbon, 1755

SAMUEL JOHNSON
1709–1784

Richard Savage and His Benefactors

Whoever was acquainted with him was certain to be solicited for small sums, which the frequency of the request made in time considerable, and he was therefore quickly shunned by those who were become familiar enough to be trusted with his necessities; but his rambling manner of life, and constant appearance at houses of public resort, always procured him a new succession of friends, whose kindness had not been exhausted by repeated requests, so that he was seldom absolutely without resources, but had in his utmost exigences this comfort, that he always imagined himself sure of speedy relief.

It was observed that he always asked favours of this kind without the least submission or apparent consciousness of dependence, and that he did not seem to look upon a compliance with his request as an obligation that deserved any extraordinary acknowledgements, but a refusal was resented by him as an affront, or complained of as an injury; nor did he readily reconcile himself to those who either denied to lend, or gave him afterwards any intimation that they expected to be repaid.

He was sometimes so far compassionated by those who knew both his merit and his distresses that they received him into their families, but they soon discovered him to be a very incommodious inmate; for being always accustomed to an irregular manner of life, he could not confine himself to any stated hours, or pay any regard to the rules of a family, but would prolong his conversation till midnight, without considering that business might require his friend's application in the morning; nor, when he had persuaded himself to retire to bed, was he, without equal difficulty, called up to dinner; it was therefore impossible to pay him any distinction without the entire subversion of all economy, a kind of establishment which, wherever he went, he always appeared ambitious to overthrow.

The Life of Richard Savage, 1744

On a Common Form of Disenchantment

Among the many inconsistencies which folly produces, or infirmity suffers, in the human mind, there has often been observed a manifest and striking contrariety between the life of an author and his writings; and Milton, in a letter to a learned stranger, by whom he had been visited, with great reason congratulates himself upon the consciousness of being found equal to his own character, and having preserved, in a private and familiar interview, that reputation which his works had procured him.

Those whom the appearance of virtue, or the evidence of genius, has tempted to a nearer knowledge of the writer in whose performances these may be found, have indeed had frequent reason to repent their curiosity: the bubble that sparkled before them has become common water at the touch; the phantom of perfection has vanished when they wished to press it to their bosom. They have lost the pleasure of imagining how far humanity may be exalted, and, perhaps, felt themselves less inclined to toil up the steeps of virtue, when they observe those who seem best able to point the way, loitering below, as either afraid of the labour, or doubtful of the reward.

The Rambler, no. 14 (1750)

Small Incidents and Petty Occurrences

The main of life is, indeed, composed of small incidents and petty occurrences: of wishes for objects not remote and grief for disappointments of no fatal consequence, of insect vexations which sting us and fly away, impertinences which buzz awhile about us and are heard no more, of meteorous pleasures which dance before us and are dissipated, of compliments which glide off the soul like other music and are forgotten by him that gave and him that received them.

Such is the general heap out of which every man is to cull his own condition; for, as the chemists tell us that all bodies are resolvable into the same elements and that the boundless variety of things arises from the different proportions of a very few ingredients, so a few pains and a few pleasures are all the materials of human life, and of these the proportions are partly allotted by Providence and partly left to the arrangement of reason and of choice.

The Rambler, no. 68 (1750)

The Madness of William Collins

How little can we venture to exult in any intellectual powers or literary attainments, when we consider the condition of poor Collins. I knew him a few years ago full of hopes and full of projects, versed in many languages, high in fancy, and strong in retention. This busy and forcible mind is now under the government of those who lately would not have been able to comprehend the least and most narrow of its designs.

letter to the Revd Joseph Warton, 1754

Letter to Lord Chesterfield

My Lord

I have been lately informed by the proprietor of *The World* that two papers in which my Dictionary is recommended to the public were written by your Lordship. To be so distinguished is an honour which, being very little accustomed to favours from the great, I know not well how to receive, or in what terms to acknowledge.

When upon some slight encouragement I first visited your Lordship, I was overpowered like the rest of mankind by the enchantment of your address, and could not forbear to wish that I might boast myself *le vainqueur du vainqueur de la terre*, that I might obtain that regard for which I saw the world contending, but I found my attendance so little encouraged that neither pride nor modesty would suffer me to continue it. When I had once addressed your Lordship in public, I had exhausted all the art of pleasing which a retired and uncourtly scholar can possess. I had done all that I could, and no man is well pleased to have his all neglected, be it ever so little.

Seven years, My Lord, have now passed since I waited in your outward rooms or was repulsed from your door, during which time I have been pushing on my work through difficulties of which it is useless to complain, and have brought it at last to the verge of publication without one act of assistance, one word of encouragement, or one smile of favour. Such treatment I did not expect, for I never had a patron before.

The shepherd in Virgil grew at last acquainted with Love, and found him a native of the rocks. Is not a patron, My Lord, one who looks with unconcern on a man struggling for life in the water and when he has reached ground encumbers him with help? The notice which you have been pleased to take of my labours, had it been early, had been kind; but it has been delayed till I am indifferent and cannot enjoy it, till I am solitary and cannot impart it, till I am known and do not want it.

I hope it is no very cynical asperity not to confess obligation where no benefit has been received, or to be unwilling that the public should consider me as owing to a patron which Providence has enabled me to do for myself.

Having carried on my work thus far with so little obligation to any favourer of learning, I shall not be disappointed though I should conclude it, if less be possible, with less, for I have been long wakened from that dream of hope in which I once boasted myself with so much exultation, My Lord,

Your Lordship's most humble, most obedient servant,

Sam: Johnson

1755

Some Definitions from the Dictionary

anfra′ctuose, anfra′ctuous. Winding; mazy; full of turnings and winding passages.

co′medy. A dramatick representation of the lighter faults of mankind.

da′rkling. (A participle, as it seems, from *darkle*, which yet I have never found.) Being in the dark; being without light: a word merely poetical.

heigh-ho. (1) An expression of slight languour and uneasiness. (2) It is used by Dryden, contrarily to custom, as a voice of exultation.

We'll toss off our ale 'till we cannot stand,
And *heigh-ho* for the honour of old England.
Dryden.

lu′bber. A sturdy drone; an idle, fat, bulky losel; a booby.

to pump. (2) To examine artfully by sly interrogatories, so as to draw out any secrets or concealments.

revi′val. Recall from a state of languour, oblivion, or obscurity.

to sni′cker. To laugh slily, wantonly, or contemptuously; to laugh in one's sleeve.

strut. An affectation of stateliness in the walk.

to′uchy. Peevish; irritable; irascible; apt to take fire. A low word.

A Dictionary of the English Language, 1755

On the Dangers of Educating the Poor

I am always afraid of determining on the side of envy or cruelty. The privileges of education may sometimes be improperly bestowed, but I shall always fear to withhold them, lest I should be yielding to the suggestions of pride, while I persuade myself that I am following the maxims of policy; and under the appearance of salutary restraints, should be indulging the lust of dominion, and that malevolence which delights in seeing others depressed.

Review of Soame Jenyns, *A Free Inquiry into the Nature and Origins of Evil*, 1757

Playthings of the Gods

How the origin of evil is brought nearer to human conception by any *inconceivable* means, I am not able to discover. We believed that the present system of creation was right, though we could not explain the adaptation of one part to the other, or for the whole succession of causes and consequences. Where has the enquirer added to the little knowledge that we had before? He has told us of the benefits of evil which no man feels, and relations between distant parts of the universe which he cannot himself conceive. There was enough in this question inconceivable before, and we have little advantage from a new inconceivable solution.

I do not mean to reproach this author for not knowing what is equally hidden from learning and from ignorance. The shame is to impose words for ideas upon ourselves or others. To imagine that we are going forward when we are only turning round. To think that there is any difference between him that gives no reason, and him that gives a reason which by his own confession cannot be conceived.

But that he may not be thought to conceive nothing but things inconceivable, he has at last thought on a way by which human sufferings may produce good effects. He imagines that as we have not only animals for food, but choose some for our diversion, the same privilege may be allowed to some beings above us, *who may deceive, torment, or destroy us for the ends only of their own pleasure or utility.* This he again finds impossible to be conceived, *but that impossibility lessens not the probability of the conjecture, which by analogy is so strongly confirmed.*

I cannot resist the temptation of contemplating this analogy, which I think he might have carried further very much to the advantage of his argument. He might have shown that these *hunters, whose game is man* have many sports analogous to our own. As we drown whelps and kittens, they amuse themselves now and then with sinking a ship, and stand round the fields of Blenheim, or the walls of Prague, as we encircle a cockpit. As we shoot a bird flying, they take a man in the midst of his business or pleasure, and knock him down with an apoplexy. Some of them, perhaps, are virtuosi, and delight in the operations of an asthma, as a human philosopher in the effects of the air pump. To swell a man with a tympany is as good sport as to blow a frog. Many a merry bout have these frolic beings at the vicissitudes of an ague, and good sport it is to see a man tumble with an epilepsy, and revive and tumble again, and all this he knows not why. As they are wiser and more powerful than we, they have more exquisite diversions; for we have no way of procuring any sport so brisk and so lasting as the paroxysms of the gout and stone, which undoubtedly must make high mirth, especially if the play be a little diversified with the blunders and puzzles of the blind and deaf. We know not how far their sphere of observation may extend. Perhaps now and then a merry being may place himself in such a situation as to enjoy at once all the varieties of an epidemical disease, or amuse his leisure with the tossings and contortions of every possible pain exhibited together.

Review of Soame Jenyns, *A Free Inquiry into the Nature and Origins of Evil*

On What Can They Be Thinking?

When man sees one of the inferior creatures perched upon a tree, or basking in the sunshine, without any apparent endeavour or pursuit, he often asks himself, or his companion, *On what that animal can be supposed to be thinking?*

Of this question, since neither bird nor beast can answer it, we must be content to live without the resolution. We know not how much the brutes recollect of the past, or anticipate of the future; what power they have of comparing and preferring; or whether their faculties may not rest in motionless indifference, till they are moved by the presence of their proper object, or stimulated to act by corporal sensations.

I am the less inclined to these superfluous inquiries, because I have always been able to find sufficient matter for curiosity in my own species. It is useless to go far in quest of that which may be found at home; a very narrow circle of observation will supply a sufficient number of men and women, who might be asked, with equal propriety, *On what they can be thinking?*...

To every act a subject is required. He that thinks, must think upon something. But tell me, ye that pierce deepest into nature, ye that take the widest surveys of life, inform me, kind shades of Malebranche and of Locke, what that something can be, which excites and continues thought in maiden aunts with small fortunes; in younger brothers that live upon annuities; in traders retired from business; in soldiers absent from their regiments; or in widows that have no children?

Life is commonly considered as either active or contemplative; but surely this division, how long soever it has been received, is inadequate and fallacious. There are mortals whose life is certainly not active, for they do neither good nor evil; and whose life cannot be properly called contemplative, for they never attend either to the conduct of men, or the works of nature, but rise in the morning, look round them till night in careless stupidity, go to bed and sleep, and rise again in the morning.

The Idler, no. 24 (1758)

An Appeal for Enemy Prisoners

The Committee entrusted with the money contributed to the relief of the subjects of France, now prisoners in the British Dominions, here lay before the public an exact account of all the sums received and expended; that the donors may judge how properly their benefactions have been applied.

Charity would lose its name, were it influenced by so mean a motive as human praise: it is, therefore, not intended to celebrate, by any particular memorial, the liberality of single persons, or distinct societies; it is sufficient that their works praise them.

Yet he who is far from seeking honour may very justly obviate censure. If a good example has been set, it may lose its influence by misrepresentation; and to free charity from reproach is itself a charitable action.

Against the relief of the French, only one argument has been brought; but that one is so popular and specious that if it were to remain unexamined, it would by many be thought irrefragable. It has been urged that charity, like other virtues, may be improperly and unseasonably exerted; that while we are relieving Frenchmen, there remain many Englishmen unrelieved; that while we lavish pity on our enemies, we forget the misery of our friends.

Grant this argument all it can prove, and what is the conclusion?—that to relieve the French is a good action, but that a better may be conceived.

This is all the result, and this all is very little. To do the best can seldom be the lot of man; it is sufficient if, when opportunities are presented, he is ready to do good. How little virtue could be practised, if beneficence were to wait always for the most proper objects, and the noblest occasions; occasions that may never happen, and objects that never may be found?

It is far from certain that a single Englishman will suffer by the charity to the French. New scenes of misery make new impressions; and much of the charity which produced these donations may be supposed to have been generated by a species of calamity never known among us before. Some imagine that the laws have provided all necessary relief in common cases, and remit the poor to the care of the public; some have been deceived by fictitious misery, and are afraid of encouraging imposture; many have observed want to be the effect of vice, and consider casual almsgivers as patrons of idleness. But all these difficulties vanish in the present case: we know that for the prisoners of war there is no legal provision; we see their distress, and are certain of its cause; we know that they are poor and naked, and poor and naked without a crime.

But it is not necessary to make any concessions. The opponents of this charity must allow it to be good, and will not easily prove it not to be the best. That charity is best of which the consequences are most extensive: the relief of enemies has a tendency to unite mankind in fraternal affection; to soften the acrimony of adverse nations, and dispose them to peace and amity: in the mean time, it alleviates captivity, and takes away something from the miseries of war. The rage of war, however mitigated, will always fill the world with calamity and horror: let it not then be unnecessarily extended; let animosity and hostility cease together; and no man be longer deemed an enemy than while his sword is drawn against us.

The effects of these contributions may, perhaps, reach still further. Truth is best supported by virtue: we may hope from those who feel or who see our charity that they shall no longer detest as heresy that religion which makes its professors the followers of Him who has commanded us to *do good to them that hate us.*

Proceedings of the Committee for Clothing French Prisoners of War, 1759

A Visit to the Pyramids

Pekuah descended to the tents, and the rest entered the pyramid: they passed through the galleries, surveyed the vaults of marble, and examined the chest in which the body of the founder is supposed to have been reposited. They then sat down in one of the most spacious chambers to rest a while before they attempted to return.

'We have now,' said Imlac, 'gratified our minds with an exact view of the greatest work of man, except the wall of China.

'Of the wall it is very easy to assign the motives. It secured a wealthy and timorous nation from the incursions of barbarians, whose unskilfulness in arts made it easier for them to supply their wants by rapine than by industry, and who from time to time poured in upon the habitations of peaceful commerce, as vultures descend upon domestic fowl. Their celerity and fierceness made the wall necessary, and their ignorance made it efficacious.

'But for the pyramids no reason has ever been given adequate to the cost and labour of the work. The narrowness of the chambers proves that it could afford no retreat from enemies, and treasures might have been reposited at far less expense with equal security. It seems to have been erected only in compliance with that hunger of imagination which preys incessantly upon life, and must be always appeased by some employment. Those who have already all that they can enjoy must enlarge their desires. He that has built for use, till use is supplied, must begin to build for vanity, and extend his plan to the utmost power of human performance, that he may not be soon reduced to form another wish.

'I consider this mighty structure as a monument of the insufficiency of human enjoyments. A king whose power is unlimited, and whose treasures surmount all real and imaginary wants, is compelled to solace, by the erection of a pyramid, the satiety of dominion and tastelessness of pleasures, and to amuse the tediousness of declining life, by seeing thousands labouring without end, and one stone, for no purpose, laid upon another. Whoever thou art that, not content with a moderate condition, imaginest happiness in royal magnificence, and dreamest that command or riches can feed the appetite of novelty with perpetual gratifications, survey the pyramids, and confess thy folly!'

Rasselas, 1759

Shakespeare's World

Shakespeare's plays are not in the rigorous and critical sense either tragedies or comedies, but compositions of a distinct kind; exhibiting the real state of sublunary nature, which partakes of good and evil, joy and sorrow, mingled with endless variety of proportion and innumerable modes of combination; and expressing the course of the world, in which the loss of one is the gain of another; in which, at the same time, the reveller is hasting to his wine, and the mourner burying his friend; in which the malignity of one is sometimes defeated by the frolic of another; and many mischiefs and many benefits are done and hindered without design.

Preface to *The Plays of William Shakespeare*, 1765

Shakespeare's Wordplay

A quibble is to Shakespeare what luminous vapours are to the traveller; he follows it at all adventures, it is sure to lead him out of his way, and sure to engulf him in the mire. It has some malignant power over his mind, and its fascinations are irresistible. Whatever be the dignity or profundity of his disquisition, whether he be enlarging knowledge or exalting affection, whether he be amusing attention with incidents, or enchaining it in suspense, let but a quibble spring up before him, and he leaves his work unfinished. A quibble is the golden apple for which he will always turn aside from his career, or stoop from his elevation. A quibble, poor and barren as it is, gave him such delight that he was content to purchase it by the sacrifice of reason, propriety and truth. A quibble was to him the fatal Cleopatra for which he lost the world, and was content to lose it.

Preface to *Shakespeare*

Iona

We were now treading that illustrious island which was once the luminary of the Caledonian regions, whence savage clans and roving barbarians derived the benefits of knowledge, and the blessings of religion. To abstract the mind from all local emotion would be impossible, if it were endeavoured, and would be foolish, if it were possible. Whatever withdraws us from the power of our senses; whatever makes the past, the distant, or the future predominate over the present advances us in the dignity of thinking beings. Far from me and from my friends be such frigid philosophy as may conduct us indifferent and unmoved over any ground which has been dignified by wisdom, bravery, or virtue. That man is little to be envied whose patriotism would not gain force upon the plain of Marathon, or whose piety would not grow warmer among the ruins of Iona!

A Journey to the Western Isles of Scotland, 1775

The Author of Ossian

Mr James Macpherson—I received your foolish and impudent note. Whatever insult is offered me I will do my best to repel, and what I cannot do for myself the law will do for me. I will not desist from detecting what I think a cheat from any fear of the menaces of a ruffian.

You want me to retract. What shall I retract? I thought your book an imposture from the beginning, I think it upon yet surer reasons an imposture still. For this opinion I give the public my reasons, which I here dare you to refute.

But however I may despise you, I reverence truth and if you can prove the genuineness of the work I will confess it. Your rage I defy, your abilities since your Homer are not so formidable, and what I have heard of your morals disposes me to pay regard not to what you shall say, but to what you can prove.

You may print this if you will.

letter, 1775

Satirizing the Puritans

Much of that humour which transported the last century with merriment is lost to us, who do not know the sour solemnity, the sullen superstition, the gloomy moroseness, and the stubborn scruples of the ancient puritans; or, if we know them, derive our information only from books, or from tradition, have never had them before our eyes, and cannot but by recollection and study understand the lines in which they are satirized. Our grandfathers knew the picture from the life; we judge of the life by contemplating the picture.

'Butler', *Lives of the Poets*, 1779–81

Addison's Prose

His prose is the model of the middle style; on grave subjects not formal, on light occasions not groveling; pure without scrupulosity, and exact without apparent elaboration; always equable, and always easy, without glowing words or pointed sentences. Addison never deviates from his track to snatch a grace; he seeks no ambitious ornaments, and tries no hazardous innovations. His page is always luminous, but never blazes in unexpected splendour.

It was apparently his principal endeavour to avoid all harshness and severity of diction; he is therefore sometimes verbose in his transitions and connections, and sometimes descends too much to the language of conversation: yet if his language had been less idiomatical it might have lost somewhat of its genuine Anglicism. What he attempted, he performed; he is never feeble, and he did not wish to be energetic; he is never rapid, and he never stagnates. His sentences have neither studied amplitude, nor affected brevity; his periods, though not diligently rounded, are voluble and easy. Whoever wishes to attain an English style familiar but not coarse, and elegant but not ostentatious, must give his days and nights to the volumes of Addison.

Lives of the Poets

Alexander Pope

Of his intellectual character, the constituent and fundamental principle was Good Sense, a prompt and intuitive perception of consonance and propriety. He saw immediately, of his own conceptions, what was to be chosen, and what to be rejected; and, in the works of others, what was to be shunned, and what was to be copied.

But good sense alone is a sedate and quiescent quality, which manages its possessions well, but does not increase them; it collects few materials for its own operations, and preserves safety, but never gains supremacy. Pope had likewise genius; a mind active, ambitious, and adventurous, always investigating, always aspiring; in its widest searches still longing to go forward, in its highest flights still wishing to be higher; always imagining something greater than it knows, always endeavouring more than it can do.

Lives of the Poets

The Poet David Mallet

His stature was diminutive, but he was regularly formed; his appearance, till he grew corpulent, was agreeable, and he suffered it to want no recommendation that dress could give it. His conversation was elegant and easy. The rest of his character may, without injury to his memory, sink into silence.

Lives of the Poets

Gray's Elegy

In the character of his Elegy I rejoice to concur with the common reader; for by the common sense of readers, uncorrupted with literary prejudices, after all the refinements of subtilty and the dogmatism of learning, must be finally decided all claim to poetical honours. The *Church-yard* abounds with images which find a mirror in every mind, and with sentiments to which every bosom returns an echo. The four stanzas, beginning 'Yet even these bones,' are to me original: I have never seen the notions in any other place; yet he that reads them here persuades himself that he has always felt them. Had Gray written often thus, it had been vain to blame, and useless to praise him.

Lives of the Poets

Remembering His Wife

This is the day on which in 1752 dear Tetty died. On what we did amiss, and our faults were great, I have thought of late with more regret than at any former time. She was I think very penitent. May God have accepted her repentance: may he accept mine. I have now uttered a prayer of repentance and c[ontritio]n, perhaps Tetty knows that I prayed for her. Thou, God, art merciful, hear my prayers, and enable me to trust in Thee.

Perhaps Tetty is now praying for me. God, help me.

Diary, 29 March 1782

DAVID HUME
1711–1776

The Measure of Man

In forming our notions of human nature, we are apt to make a comparison between men and animals, the only creatures endowed with thought that fall under our senses. Certainly this comparison is favourable to mankind. On the one hand, we see a creature whose thoughts are not limited by any narrow bounds, either of place or time; who carries his researches into the most distant regions of this globe, and beyond this globe, to the planets and heavenly bodies; looks backward to consider the first origin, at least the history of the human race; casts his eye forward to see the influence of his actions upon posterity, and the judgments which will be formed of his character a thousand years hence; a creature, who traces causes and effects to a great length and intricacy; extracts general principles from particular appearances; improves upon his discoveries; corrects his mistakes; and makes his very errors profitable. On the other hand, we are presented with a creature the very reverse of this; limited in its observations and reasonings to a few sensible objects which surround it; without curiosity, without foresight; blindly conducted by instinct, and attaining, in a short time, its utmost perfection, beyond which it is never able to advance a single step. What a wide difference is there between these creatures! And how exalted a notion must we entertain of the former, in comparison of the latter!

There are two means commonly employed to destroy this conclusion: *First*, by making an unfair representation of the case, and insisting only upon the weakness of human nature. And, *secondly*, by forming a new and secret comparison between man and beings of the most perfect wisdom. Among the other excellences of man, this is one, that he can form an idea of perfections much beyond what he has experience of in himself; and is not limited in his conception of wisdom and virtue. He can easily exalt his notions, and conceive a degree of knowledge, which, when compared to his own, will make the latter appear very contemptible, and will cause the difference between that and the sagacity of animals, in a manner, to disappear and vanish. Now this being a point in which all the world is agreed, that human understanding falls infinitely short of perfect wisdom, it is proper we should know when this comparison takes place, that we may not dispute where there is no real difference in our sentiments. Man falls much more short of perfect wisdom, and even of his own ideas of perfect wisdom, than animals do of man; yet the latter difference is so considerable, that nothing but a comparison with the former can make it appear of little moment.

'On the Dignity or Meanness of Human Nature', *Essays, Moral and Political*, 1741

Artificial Happiness

But of all the fruitless attempts of art, no one is so ridiculous as that which the severe philosophers have undertaken, the producing of an *artificial happiness*, and making us be pleased by rules of reason and by reflection. Why did none of them claim the reward which XERXES promised to him who should invent a new pleasure? Unless, perhaps, they invented so many pleasures for their own use, that they despised riches, and stood in no need of any enjoyments which the rewards of that monarch could produce them. I am apt, indeed, to think, that they were not willing to furnish the PERSIAN court with a new pleasure, by presenting it with so new and unusual an object of ridicule. Their speculations, when confined to theory, and gravely delivered in the schools of GREECE, might excite admiration in their ignorant pupils; but the attempting to reduce such principles to practice would soon have betrayed their absurdity.

'The Epicurean', *Essays*, 1742 edition

Religion and Reason

I am the better pleased with the method of reasoning here delivered, as I think it may serve to confound those dangerous friends or disguised enemies to the Christian religion, who have undertaken to defend it by the principles of human reason. Our most holy religion is founded on faith, not on reason; and it is a sure method of exposing it to put it to such a trial as it is by no means fitted to endure. To make this more evident, let us examine those miracles related in Scripture; and not to lose ourselves in too wide a field, let us confine ourselves to such as we find in the *Pentateuch*, which we shall examine according to the principles of those pretended Christians, not as the word or testimony of God himself, but as the production of a mere human writer and historian. Here then we are first to consider a book, presented to us by a barbarous and ignorant people, written in an age when they are still more barbarous, and in all probability long after the facts which it relates, corroborated by no concurring testimony, and resembling those fabulous accounts which every nation gives of its origin. Upon reading this book we find it full of prodigies and miracles. It gives an account of a state of the world and of human nature entirely different from the present; of our fall from that state; of the age of man, extended to near a thousand years; of the destruction of the world by a deluge; of the arbitrary choice of one people as the favourites of heaven, and that people the countrymen of the author; of their deliverance from bondage by prodigies the most astonishing imaginable. I desire any one to lay his hand upon his heart, and after a serious consideration declare whether he thinks that the falsehood of such a book, supported by such a testimony, would be more extraordinary and miraculous than all the miracles it relates; which is, however, necessary to make it be received, according to the measures of probability above established.

What we have said of miracles may be applied, without any variation, to prophecies; and, indeed, all prophecies are real miracles, and as such only can be admitted as proofs of any revelation. If it did not exceed the capacity of human nature to foretell future events, it would be absurd to employ any prophecy as an argument for a divine mission or authority from heaven. So that, upon the whole, we may conclude that the Christian religion not only was at first attended with miracles, but even at this day cannot be believed by any reasonable person without one. Mere reason is insufficient to convince us of its veracity. And whoever is moved by faith to assent to it, is conscious of a continued miracle in his own person, which subverts all the principles of his understanding, and gives him a determination to believe what is most contrary to custom and experience.

An Enquiry concerning Human Understanding, 1748

Jacobean Prose

If the poetry of the English was so rude and imperfect during that age, we may reasonably expect, that their prose would be liable to still greater objections. Tho' the latter appears the more easy, as it is the more natural method of composition; it has ever in practice been found the more rare and difficult; and there scarce is an instance, in any language, that it has reached a degree of perfection, before the refinement of poetical numbers and expression. English prose, during the reign of James, was wrote with little regard to the rules of grammar, and with a total disregard of the elegance and harmony of the period. Stuffed with Latin sentences and citations, it likeways imitated those inversions, which, however forcible and graceful in the ancient languages, are entirely contrary to the idiom of the English. I shall indeed venture to affirm, that, whatever uncouth phrases and expressions occur in old books, they were owing chiefly to the unformed taste of the author; and that the language, spoke in the courts of Elizabeth and James, was very little different from that which, in good company, we meet with at present. Of this opinion, the little scraps of speeches, which are found in the parliamentary journals, and which carry an air so opposite to the labored orations, seem to be a sufficient proof; and there want not productions of that age, which, being wrote by men, who were not authors by profession, retain a very natural manner, and may give us some idea of the language, which prevailed in polite conversation.

The History of Great Britain, vol. i, 1754

Archbishop Laud

Whatever ridicule, to a philosophic mind, may be thrown on pious ceremonies, it must be confessed, that, during a very religious age, no institutions can be more advantageous to the rude multitude, and tend more to mollify that fierce and gloomy spirit of devotion, to which they are so subject. Even the English church, tho' it had retained a share of popish superstition, may justly be thought too naked and unadorned, and still to approach too near the abstract and spiritual religion of the puritans. Laud and his associates, by reviving a few primitive institutions of this nature, corrected the error of the first reformers, and presented, to the affrightened and astonished mind, some sensible, exterior observances, which might occupy it during its religious exercises, and abate the violence of its disappointed efforts. The thought, no longer bent on that divine and mysterious Essence, so superior to the narrow capacities of mankind, was able, by means of the new model of devotion, to relax itself in the contemplation of pictures, postures, vestments, buildings; and all the fine arts, which ministered to religion, thereby received additional encouragement. The primate, 'tis true, conducted this scheme, not with the enlarged sentiments and cool disposition of a legislator, but with the intemperate zeal of a sectary; and by overlooking the circumstances of the times, served rather to inflame that religious fury, which he meant to repress. But this blemish is rather to be regarded as a general imputation on the whole age, than any particular failing of Laud; and 'tis sufficient for his vindication to observe, that his errors were the most excusable of all those which prevailed during that zealous period.

The History of Great Britain, vol. i, 1754

Heaven and Hell and the Common Run of Mankind

Punishment, according to *our* conception, should bear some proportion to the offence. Why then eternal punishment for the temporary offences of so frail a creature as man? Can any one approve of *Alexander's* rage, who intended to exterminate a whole nation because they had seized his favourite horse *Bucephalus*?

Heaven and hell suppose two distinct species of men, the good and the bad; but the greatest part of mankind float betwixt vice and virtue.

Were one to go round the world with an intention of giving a good supper to the righteous and a sound drubbing to the wicked, he would frequently be embarrassed in his choice, and would find the merits and demerits of most men and women scarcely amount to the value of either.

'On the Immortality of the Soul', 1777; written *c.*1755

An Inveterate Prejudice

Nay, if we should suppose, what never happens, that a popular religion were found, in which it was expressly declared, that nothing but morality could gain the divine favour; if an order of priests were instituted to inculcate this opinion, in daily sermons, and with all the arts of persuasion; yet so inveterate are the people's prejudices, that, for want of some other superstition, they would make the very attendance on these sermons the essentials of religion, rather than place them in virtue and good morals.

'The Natural History of Religion', 1757

Predilections

One person is more pleased with the sublime, another with the tender, a third with raillery. One has a strong sensibility to blemishes, and is extremely studious of correctness; another has a more lively feeling of beauties, and pardons twenty absurdities and defects for one elevated or pathetic stroke. The ear of this man is entirely turned towards conciseness and energy; that man is delighted with a copious, rich, and harmonious expression. Simplicity is affected by one; ornament by another. Comedy, tragedy, satire, odes, have each its partisans, who prefer that particular species of writing to all others. It is plainly an error in a critic, to confine his approbation to one species or style of writing, and condemn all the rest. But it is almost impossible not to feel a predilection for that which suits our particular turn and disposition. Such performances are innocent and unavoidable, and can never reasonably be the object of dispute, because there is no standard by which they can be decided.

'Of the Standard of Taste', *Four Dissertations*, 1757

Summing Up His Own Character

In spring 1775, I was struck with a disorder in my bowels, which at first gave me no alarm, but has since, as I apprehend it, become mortal and incurable. I now reckon upon a speedy dissolution. I have suffered very little pain from my disorder; and what is more strange, have, notwithstanding the great decline of my person, never suffered a moment's abatement of my spirits; insomuch, that were I to name the period of my life, which I should most choose to pass over again, I might be tempted to point to this latter period. I possess the same ardour as ever in study, and the same gaiety in company. I consider, besides, that a man of sixty-five, by dying, cuts off only a few years of infirmities; and though I see many symptoms of my literary reputation's breaking out at last with additional lustre, I know that I could have but few years to enjoy it. It is difficult to be more detached from life than I am at present.

To conclude historically with my own character. I am, or rather was,—for that is the style I must now use in speaking of myself, which emboldens me the more to speak my sentiments;—I was, I say, a man of mild dispositions, of command of temper, of an open, social, and cheerful humour, capable of attachment, but little susceptible of enmity, and of great moderation in all my passions. Even my love of literary fame, my ruling passion, never soured my temper, notwithstanding my frequent disappointments. My company was not unacceptable to the young and careless, as well as to the studious and literary; and as I took a particular pleasure in the company of modest women, I had no reason to be displeased with the reception I met with from them. In a word, though most men anywise eminent, have found reason to complain of calumny, I never was touched, or even attacked by her baleful tooth: and though I wantonly exposed myself to the rage of both civil and religious factions, they seemed to be disarmed in my behalf of their wonted fury. My friends never had occasion to vindicate any one circumstance of my character and conduct: not but that the zealots, we may well suppose, would have been glad to invent and propagate any story to my disadvantage, but they could never find any which they thought would wear the face of probability. I cannot say there is no vanity in making this funeral oration of myself, but I hope it is not a misplaced one; and this is a matter of fact which is easily cleared and ascertained.

'My Own Life', *Essays*, 1777 edition

LAURENCE STERNE
1713–1768

A Chain of Discoveries

—Pray what was that man's name,—for I write in such a hurry, I have no time to recollect or look for it,——who first made the observation, 'That there was great inconstancy in our air and climate?' Whoever he was, 'twas a just and good observation in him.—But the corollary drawn from it, namely, 'That it is this which has furnished us with such a variety of odd and whimsical characters;'—that was not his;—it was found out by another man, at least a century and a half after him:—Then again,—that this copious store-house of original materials, is the true and natural cause that our Comedies are so much better than those of *France*, or any others that either have, or can be wrote upon the Continent;——that discovery was not fully made till about the middle of king *William*'s reign,—when the great *Dryden*, in writing one of his long prefaces, (if I mistake not) most fortunately hit upon it. Indeed towards the latter end of queen *Anne*, the great *Addison* began to patronize the notion, and more fully explained it to the world in one or two of his Spectators;—but the discovery was not his.—Then, fourthly and lastly, that this strange irregularity in our climate, producing so strange an irregularity in our characters,——doth thereby, in some sort, make us amends, by giving us somewhat to make us merry with when the weather will not suffer us to go out of doors,—that observation is my own;—and was struck out by me this very rainy day, *March* 26, 1759, and betwixt the hours of nine and ten in the morning.

Tristram Shandy, 1760–7

The Soul Stark Naked

If the fixture of *Momus*'s glass, in the human breast, according to the proposed emendation of that arch-critick, had taken place,——first, This foolish consequence would certainly have followed,—That the very wisest and the very gravest of us all, in one coin or other, must have paid window-money every day of our lives.

And, secondly, That had the said glass been there set up, nothing more would have been wanting, in order to have taken a man's character, but to have taken a chair and gone softly, as you would to a dioptrical bee-hive, and look'd in,—view'd the soul stark naked;—observ'd all her motions,—her machinations;—traced all her maggots from their first engendering to their crawling forth;—watched her loose in her frisks, her gambols, her capricios; and after some notice of her more solemn deportment, consequent upon such frisks, *&c.*——then taken your pen and ink and set down nothing but what you had seen, and could have sworn to:—But this is an advantage not to be had by the biographer in this planet . . .

Tristram Shandy

A History-Book

Pray, Sir, in all the reading which you have ever read, did you ever read such a book as *Locke*'s Essay upon the Human Understanding?——— Don't answer me rashly,—because many, I know, quote the book, who have not read it,—and many have read it who understand it not:—If either of these is your case, as I write to instruct, I will tell you in three words what the book is.—It is a history.—A history! of who? what? where? when? Don't hurry yourself.——It is a history-book, Sir, (which may possibly recommend it to the world) of what passes in a man's own mind; and if you will say so much of the book, and no more, believe me, you will cut no contemptible figure in a metaphysic circle.

But this by the way.

Tristram Shandy

Writing and Talking

Writing, when properly managed, (as you may be sure I think mine is) is but a different name for conversation: As no one, who knows what he is about in good company, would venture to talk all;—so no author, who understands the just boundaries of decorum and good breeding, would presume to think all: The truest respect which you can pay to the reader's understanding, is to halve this matter amicably, and leave him something to imagine, in his turn, as well as yourself.

For my own part, I am eternally paying him compliments of this kind, and do all that lies in my power to keep his imagination as busy as my own.

Tristram Shandy

Uncle Toby and the Fly

My uncle *Toby* was a man patient of injuries;—not from want of courage,—I have told you in the fifth chapter of this second book, 'That he was a man of courage:'—And will add here, that where just occasions presented, or called it forth,—I know no man under whose arm I would sooner have taken shelter; nor did this arise from any insensibility or obtuseness of his intellectual parts;—for he felt this insult of my father's as feelingly as a man could do;—but he was of a peaceful, placid nature,—no jarring element in it—all was mix'd up so kindly within him; my uncle *Toby* had scarce a heart to retaliate upon a fly.

—Go—says he, one day at dinner, to an over-grown one which had buzz'd about his nose, and tormented him cruelly all dinner-time, —and which, after infinite attempts, he had caught at last, as it flew by him;——I'll not hurt thee, says my uncle *Toby*, rising from his chair, and going across the room, with the fly in his hand,——I'll not hurt a hair of thy head:—Go, says he, lifting up the sash, and opening his hand as he spoke, to let it escape;—go, poor Devil, get thee gone, why should I hurt thee?—This world surely is wide enough to hold both thee and me.

I was but ten years old when this happened;——but whether it was, that the action itself was more in unison to my nerves at that age of pity, which instantly set my whole frame into one vibration of most pleasureable sensation;—or how far the manner and expression of it might go towards it;——or in what degree, or by what secret magick,——a tone of voice and harmony of movement, attuned by mercy, might find a passage to my heart, I know not;—this I know, that the lesson of universal good-will then taught and imprinted by my uncle *Toby*, has never since been worn out of my mind: And tho' I would not depreciate what the study of the *Literae humaniores*, at the university, have done for me in that respect, or discredit the other helps of an expensive education bestowed upon me, both at home and abroad since;—yet I often think that I owe one half of my philanthropy to that one accidental impression.

Tristram Shandy

Soldiers and Men of Letters

It was a thousand pities——though I believe, an' please your honour, I am going to say but a foolish kind of a thing for a soldier——

A soldier, cried my uncle *Toby*, interrupting the corporal, is no more exempt from saying a foolish thing, *Trim*, than a man of letters——But not so often; an' please your honour, replied the corporal——My uncle *Toby* gave a nod.

Tristram Shandy

An Argument for Celibacy

Nothing, continued the Corporal, can be so sad as confinement for life—or so sweet, an' please your honour, as liberty.

Nothing, *Trim*——said my uncle *Toby*, musing——

Whilst a man is free—cried the corporal, giving a flourish with his stick thus——

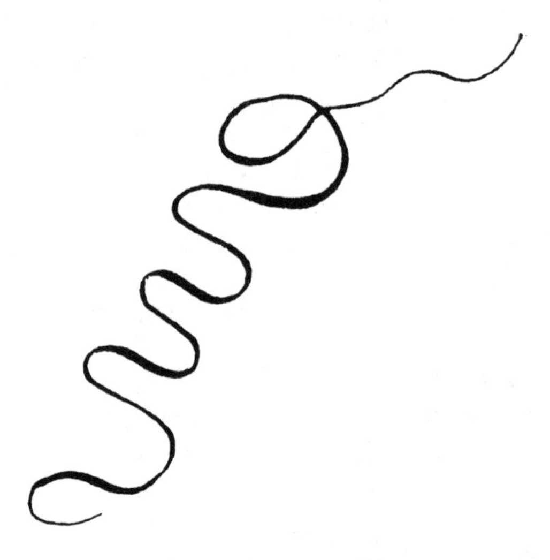

A thousand of my father's most subtle syllogisms could not have said more for celibacy.

Tristram Shandy

'I Can't Get Out'

In my return back through the passage, I heard the same words repeated twice over; and looking up, I saw it was a starling hung in a little cage.— 'I can't get out—I can't get out,' said the starling.

I stood looking at the bird: and to every person who came through the passage it ran fluttering to the side towards which they approach'd it, with the same lamentation of its captivity.—'I can't get out,' said the starling— God help thee! said I, but I'll let thee out, cost what it will; so I turn'd about the cage to get to the door; it was twisted and double twisted so fast with wire, there was no getting it open without pulling the cage to pieces—I took both hands to it.

The bird flew to the place where I was attempting his deliverance, and thrusting his head through the trellis, press'd his breast against it, as if impatient—I fear, poor creature! said I, I cannot set thee at liberty—'No,' said the starling—'I can't get out—I can't get out,' said the starling.

A Sentimental Journey through France and Italy, 1768

THOMAS GRAY
1716–1771

The Elegy Written in a Country Churchyard

Dear Sir,

As I live in a place, where even the ordinary tattle of the town arrives not till it is stale, and which produces no events of its own, you will not desire any excuse from me for writing so seldom, especially as of all people living I know you are the least a friend to letters spun out of one's own brains, with all the toil and constraint that accompanies sentimental productions. I have been here at Stoke a few days (where I shall continue good part of the summer); and having put an end to a thing, whose beginning you have seen long ago, I immediately send it you. You will, I hope, look upon it in the light of a thing with an end to it: a merit that most of my writings have wanted, and are like to want, but which this epistle I am determined shall not want, when it tells you that I am ever

Yours,
T. Gray

letter to Horace Walpole, 1750

Low Spirits in Stoke Poges

But you know I am at Stoke, hearing, seeing, doing absolutely nothing. Not such a nothing as you do at Tunbridge, chequered and diversified with a succession of fleeting colours; but heavy, lifeless, without form and void; sometimes almost as black as the moral of Voltaire's 'Lisbon,' which angers you so. I have had no more muscular inflations, and am only troubled with this depression of mind. You will not expect therefore I should give you any account of my *verve*, which is at best (you know) of so delicate a constitution, and has such weak nerves, as not to stir out of its chamber above three days in a year.

letter to William Mason, 1756

Sunrise on the South Coast

I must not close my letter without giving you one principal event of my history; which was, that (in the course of my late tour) I set out one morning before five o'clock, the moon shining through a dark and misty autumnal air, and got to the seacoast time enough to be at the sun's levee. I saw the clouds and dark vapours open gradually to right and left, rolling over one another in great smoky wreaths, and the tide (as it flowed gently in upon the sands) first whitening, then slightly tinged with gold and blue;

and all at once a little line of insufferable brightness that (before I can write these five words) was grown to half an orb, and now to a whole one, too glorious to be distinctly seen. It is very odd it makes no figure on paper; yet I shall remember it as long as the sun, or at least as long as I endure. I wonder whether anybody ever saw it before? I hardly believe it.

letter to the Revd Norton Nicholls, 1764

HORACE WALPOLE
1717–1797

The Drunken Constables

There has lately been the most shocking scene of murder imaginable; a parcel of *drunken* constables took it into their heads to put the laws in execution against *disorderly* persons, and so took up every woman they met, till they had collected five or six-and-twenty, all of whom they thrust into St Martin's round-house, where they kept them all night, with doors and windows closed. The poor creatures, who could not stir or breathe, screamed as long as they had any breath left, begging at least for water: one poor wretch said she was worth eighteen pence, and would gladly give it for a draught of water, but in vain! So well did they keep them there, that in the morning four were found stifled to death, two died soon after, and a dozen more are in a shocking way. In short, it is horrid to think what the poor creatures suffered: several of them were beggars, who, from having no lodging, were necessarily found in the street, and others honest labouring women. One of the dead was a poor washerwoman, big with child, who was returning home late from washing. One of the constables is taken, and others absconded; but I question if any of them will suffer death, though the greatest criminals in this town are the officers of justice; there is no tyranny they do not exercise, no villany of which they do not partake. These same men, the same night, broke into a bagnio in Covent-Garden and took up Jack Spencer, Mr Stewart, and Lord George Graham, and would have thrust them into the round-house with the poor women, if they had not been worth more than eighteen-pence!

letter to Sir Horace Mann, 1742

'The Learned Gentleman'

Pray, my dear child, don't compliment me any more upon my learning; there is nobody so superficial. Except a little history, a little poetry, a little painting, and some divinity, I know nothing. How should I? I, who have always lived in the big busy world; who lie a-bed all the morning, calling it morning as long as you please; who sup in company; who have played at pharaoh half my life, and now at loo till two or three in the morning; who have always loved pleasure; haunted auctions—in short, who don't know so much astronomy as would carry me to Knightsbridge, nor more physic than a physician, nor in short anything that is called science. If it were not that I lay up a little provision in summer, like the ant, I should be as ignorant as all the people I live with. How I have laughed, when some of the Magazines have called me *the learned gentleman!* Pray don't be like the Magazines.

letter to Sir Horace Mann, 1760

Strawberry Hill by Night

I am just come out of the garden in the most oriental of all evenings, and from breathing odours beyond those of Araby. The acacias, which the Arabians have the sense to worship, are covered with blossoms, the honeysuckles dangle from every tree in festoons, the seringas are thickets of sweets, and the new-cut hay in the field tempers the balmy gales with simple freshness; while a thousand sky-rockets launched into the air at Ranelagh or Marybone illuminate the scene, and give it an air of Haroun Alraschid's paradise. I was not quite so content by daylight; some foreigners dined here, and, though they admired our verdure, it mortified me by its brownness—we have not had a drop of rain this month to cool the tip of our daisies.

letter to George Montagu, 1765

The East India Company

The East-India Company is all faction and gaming. Such fortunes are made and lost every day as are past belief. Our history will appear a gigantic lie hereafter, when we are shrunk again to our own little island. People trudge to the other end of the town to vote who shall govern empires at the other end of the world. Panchaud, a banker from Paris, broke yesterday for seventy thousand pounds, by buying and selling stock; and Sir Laurence Dundas *paid in* an hundred and forty thousand pounds for what he had bought. The Company have more and greater places to give away than the First Lord of the Treasury. Riches, abuse, cabals, are so enormously overgrown, that one wants conception and words to comprehend or describe them. Even Jewish prophets would have found Eastern hyperboles deficient, if Nineveh had been half so extravagant, luxurious, and rapacious as this wicked good town of London. I expect it will set itself on fire at last, and light the match with India bonds and bank-bills. As I pass by it and look at it, I cannot help talking to it, as Ezekiel would do, and saying, 'with all those combustibles in thy bowels, with neither government, police, or prudence, how is it that thou still existeth?

letter to Sir Horace Mann, 1769

Adjusting to Old Age

You commend me too for not complaining of my chronical evil; but, my dear Madam, I should be blameable for the reverse. If I would live to seventy-two, ought I not to compound for the encumbrances of old age? And who has fewer? And who has more cause to be thankful to Providence for his lot? The gout, it is true, comes frequently, but the fits are short, and very tolerable; the intervals are full health. My eyes are perfect, my hearing but little impaired, chiefly to whispers, for which I certainly have little occasion; my spirits never fail; and though my hands and feet are crippled, I can use both, and do not wish to box, wrestle, or dance a hornpipe. In short, I am just infirm enough to enjoy all the prerogatives of old age, and to plead them against anything that I have not a mind to do. Young men must conform to every folly in fashion: drink when they had rather be sober; fight a duel if somebody else is wrong headed; marry to please their fathers, not themselves; and shiver in a white waistcoat, because ancient almanacs, copying the Arabian, placed the month of June after May; though, when the style was reformed, it ought to have been intercalated between December and January. Indeed, I have been so childish as to cut my hay for the same reason, and am now weeping over it by the fireside.

letter to Hannah More, July 1789

Dr Johnson and Thomas Gray

Johnson's blind Toryism and known brutality kept me aloof; nor did I ever exchange a syllable with him: nay, I do not think I ever was in a room with him six times in my days. Boswell came to me, said Dr Johnson was writing the 'Lives of the Poets,' and wished I would give him anecdotes of Mr Gray. I said, very coldly, I had given what I knew to Mr Mason. Boswell hummed and hawed, and then dropped, 'I suppose you know Dr Johnson does not admire Mr Gray.' Putting as much contempt as I could into my look and tone, I said, 'Dr Johnson don't!—humph!'—and with that monosyllable ended our interview. After the Doctor's death, Burke, Sir Joshua Reynolds, and Boswell sent an ambling circular-letter to me, begging subscriptions for a Monument for him—the two last, I think, impertinently; as they could not but know my opinion, and could not suppose I would contribute to a Monument for one who had endeavoured, poor soul! to degrade my friend's superlative poetry. I would not deign to write an answer; but sent down word by my footman, as I would have done to parish officers with a brief, that I would not subscribe. In the two new volumes Johnson says, and very probably did, or is made to say, that Gray's poetry is *dull*, and that he was a *dull* man! The same oracle dislikes Prior, Swift, and Fielding. If an elephant could write a book perhaps one that had read a great deal would say, that an Arabian horse is a very clumsy ungraceful animal. Pass to a better chapter!

letter to Mary Berry, 1791

GILBERT WHITE
1720–1793

A Propensity to Bees

We had in this village more than twenty years ago an idiot-boy, whom I well remember, who, from a child, showed a strong propensity to bees; they were his food, his amusement, his sole object. And as people of this cast have seldom more than one point in view, so this lad exerted all his few faculties on this one pursuit. In the winter he dosed away his time, within his father's house, by the fire-side, in a kind of torpid state, seldom departing from the chimney-corner; but in the summer he was all alert, and in quest of his game in the fields, and on sunny banks. Honey-bees, humble-bees, and wasps, were his prey wherever he found them: he had no apprehensions from their stings, but would seize them *nudis manibus*, and at once disarm them of their weapons, and suck their bodies for the sake of their honey-bags. Sometimes he would fill his bosom between his shirt and his skin with a number of these captives; and sometimes would confine them in bottles. He was a very *merops apiaster*, or bee-bird; and very injurious to men that kept bees; for he would slide into their bee-gardens, and, sitting down before the stools, would rap with his finger on the hives, and so take the bees as they came out. He has been known to overturn hives for the sake of honey, of which he was passionately fond. Where metheglin was making he would linger round the tubs and vessels, begging a draught of what he called bee-wine. As he ran about he used to make a humming noise with his lips, resembling the buzzing of bees. This lad was lean and sallow, and of a cadaverous complexion; and, except in his favourite pursuit, in which he was wonderfully adroit, discovered no manner of understanding.

The Natural History of Selborne, 1789

A Superstitious Remedy

It is the hardest thing in the world to shake off superstitious prejudices: they are sucked in as it were with our mother's milk; and growing up with us at a time when they take the fastest hold and make the most lasting impressions, become so interwoven into our very constitutions, that the strongest good sense is required to disengage ourselves from them. No wonder therefore that the lower people retain them their whole lives through, since their minds are not invigorated by a liberal education, and therefore not enabled to make any efforts adequate to the occasion.

Such a preamble seems to be necessary before we enter on the superstitions of this district, lest we should be suspected of exaggeration in a recital of practices too gross for this enlightened age.

But the people of Tring, in Hertfordshire, would do well to remember, that no longer ago than the year 1751, and within twenty miles of the capital, they seized on two superannuated wretches, crazed with age, and overwhelmed with infirmities, on a suspicion of witchcraft; and, by trying experiments, drowned them in a horse-pond.

In a farm-yard near the middle of this village stands, at this day, a row of pollard-ashes, which, by the seams and long cicatrices down their sides, manifestly show that, in former times, they have been cleft asunder. These trees, when young and flexible, were severed and held open by wedges, while ruptured children, stripped naked, were pushed through the apertures, under a persuasion that, by such a process, the poor babes would be cured of their infirmity. As soon as the operation was over, the tree, in the suffering part, was plastered with loam, and carefully swathed up. If the parts coalesced and soldered together, as usually fell out, where the feat was performed with any adroitness at all, the party was cured; but, where the cleft continued to gape, the operation, it was supposed, would prove ineffectual. Having occasion to enlarge my garden not long since, I cut down two or three such trees, one of which did not grow together.

We have several persons now living in the village, who, in their childhood, were supposed to be healed by this superstitious ceremony, derived down perhaps from our Saxon ancestors, who practised it before their conversion to Christianity.

The Natural History of Selborne

Baby Vipers

On August the 4th, 1775, we surprised a large viper, which seemed very heavy and bloated, as it lay in the grass basking in the sun. When we came to cut it up, we found that the abdomen was crowded with young, fifteen in number; the shortest of which measured full seven inches, and were about the size of full-grown earth-worms. This little fry issued into the world with true viper-spirit about them, showing great alertness as soon as disengaged from the belly of the dam: they twisted and wriggled about, and set themselves up, and gaped very wide when touched with a stick, showing manifest tokens of menace and defiance, though as yet they had no manner of fangs that we could find, even with the help of our glasses.

To a thinking mind nothing is more wonderful than that early instinct which impresses young animals with the notion of the situation of their natural weapons, and of using them properly in their own defence, even before those weapons subsist or are formed. Thus a young cock will spar at his adversary before his spurs are grown; and a calf or a lamb will push with their heads before their horns are sprouted. In the same manner did these young adders attempt to bite before their fangs were in being. The dam however was furnished with very formidable ones, which we lifted up (for they fold down when not used) and cut them off with the point of our scissors.

The Natural History of Selborne

In the Season of Love

Some birds have movements peculiar to the season of love: thus ring-doves, though strong and rapid at other times, yet in the spring hang about on the wing in a toying and playful manner; thus the cock-snipe, while breeding, forgetting his former flight, fans the air like the wind-hover; and the green-finch in particular exhibits such languishing and faltering gestures as to appear like a wounded and dying bird; the king-fisher darts along like an arrow; fern-owls, or goat-suckers, glance in the dusk over the tops of trees like a meteor: starlings as it were swim along, while missel-thrushes use a wild and desultory flight; swallows sweep over the surface of the ground and water, and distinguish themselves by rapid turns and quick evolutions; swifts dash round in circles; and the bank-martin moves with frequent vacillations like a butterfly.

The Natural History of Selborne

A Goldfish Bowl

Nothing can be more amusing than a glass bowl containing such fishes: the double refractions of the glass and water represent them, when moving, in a shifting and changeable variety of dimensions, shades, and colours; while the two mediums, assisted by the concavo-convex shape of the vessel, magnify and distort them vastly; not to mention that the introduction of another element and its inhabitants into our parlours engages the fancy in a very agreeable manner.

The Natural History of Selborne

JOHN WOOLMAN
1720–1772

A Strange Dream and a Guilty Deed

I had a dream about the ninth year of my age as follows: I saw the moon rise near the west and run a regular course eastward, so swift that in about a quarter of an hour she reached our meridian, when there descended from her a small cloud on a direct line to the earth, which lighted on a pleasant green about twenty yards from the door of my father's house (in which I thought I stood) and was immediately turned into a beautiful green tree. The moon appeared to run on with equal swiftness and soon set in the east, at which time the sun arose at the place where it commonly does in the summer, and shining with full radiance in a serene air, it appeared as pleasant a morning as ever I saw.

All this time I stood still in the door in an awful frame of mind, and I observed that as heat increased by the rising sun, it wrought so powerfully on the little green tree that the leaves gradually withered; and before noon it appeared dry and dead. There then appeared a being, small of size, full of strength and resolution, moving swift from the north, southward, called a sun worm.

Another thing remarkable in my childhood was that once, going to a neighbor's house, I saw on the way a robin sitting on her nest; and as I came near she went off, but having young ones, flew about and with many cries expressed her concern for them. I stood and threw stones at her, till one striking her, she fell down dead. At first I was pleased with the exploit, but after a few minutes was seized with horror, as having in a sportive way killed an innocent creature while she was careful for her young. I beheld her lying dead and thought those young ones for which she was so careful must now perish for want of their dam to nourish them; and after some painful considerations on the subject, I climbed up the tree, took all the young birds and killed them, supposing that better than to leave them to pine away and die miserably, and believed in this case that Scripture proverb was fulfilled, 'The tender mercies of the wicked are cruel.' I then went on my errand, but for some hours could think of little else but the cruelties I had committed, and was much troubled.

Thus He whose tender mercies are over all His works hath placed a principle in the human mind which incites to exercise goodness toward every living creature; and this being singly attended to, people become tender-hearted and sympathizing, but being frequently and totally rejected, the mind shuts itself up in a contrary disposition.

Journal, 1774

TOBIAS SMOLLETT

1721–1771

An Examination at Surgeons' Hall

At length the beadle called my name, with a voice that made me tremble as much as if it had been the sound of the last trumpet: however, there was no remedy: I was conducted into a large hall, where I saw about a dozen of grim faces sitting at a long table; one of whom bade me come forward, in such an imperious tone that I was actually for a minute or two bereft of my senses. The first question he put to me was, 'Where was you born?' To which I answered, 'In Scotland.'—'In Scotland,' said he; 'I know that very well; we have scarce any other countrymen to examine here; you Scotchmen have overspread us of late as the locusts did Egypt: I ask you in what part of Scotland was you born?' I named the place of my nativity, which he had never before heard of: he then proceeded to interrogate me about my age, the town where I served my time, with the term of my apprenticeship; and when I informed him that I served three years only, he fell into a violent passion; swore it was a shame and a scandal to send such raw boys into the world as surgeons; that it was a great presumption in me, and an affront upon the English, to pretend to sufficient skill in my business, having served so short a time, when every apprentice in England was bound seven years at least; that my friends would have done better if they had made me a weaver or shoemaker, but their pride would have me a gentleman, he supposed, at any rate, and their poverty could not afford the necessary education.

This exordium did not at all contribute to the recovery of my spirits, but, on the contrary, reduced me to such a situation that I was scarce able to stand; which being perceived by a plump gentleman who sat opposite to me, with a skull before him, he said, Mr Snarler was too severe upon the young man; and, turning towards me, told me, I need not to be afraid, for nobody would do me any harm; then bidding me take time to recollect myself, he examined me touching the operation of the trepan, and was very well satisfied with my answers. The next person who questioned me was a wag, who began by asking if I had ever seen amputation performed; and I replying in the affirmative, he shook his head, and said, 'What! upon a dead subject, I suppose?' 'If,' continued he, 'during an engagement at sea, a man should be brought to you with his head shot off, how would you behave?' After some hesitation, I owned such a case had never come under my observation, neither did I remember to have seen any method of cure proposed for such an accident, in any of the systems of surgery I had perused. Whether it was owing to the simplicity of my answer, or the archness of the question, I know not, but every member of the board deigned to smile, except Mr Snarler, who seemed to have very little of the *animal risibile* in his constitution. The facetious member, encouraged by the success of his last joke, went on thus: 'Suppose you was called to a patient of a plethoric habit, who had been bruised by a fall, what would you do?' I answered, I would bleed him immediately. 'What,' said he, 'before you had tied up his arm?' But this stroke of wit not answering his expectation, he desired me to advance to the gentleman who sat next him; and who, with a pert air, asked what method of cure I would follow in wounds of the intestines. I repeated the method of cure as it is prescribed by the best chirurgical writers; which he heard to an end, and then said, with a supercilious smile, 'So you think by such treatment the patient might recover?'—I told him I saw nothing to make me think otherwise. 'That may be,' resumed he, 'I won't answer for your foresight; but did you ever know a case of this kind succeed'; I answered I did not; and was about to tell him I had never seen a wounded intestine; but he stopped me, by saying, with some precipitation, 'Nor never will. I affirm, that all wounds of the intestines, whether great or small, are mortal.'—'Pardon me, brother,' says the fat gentleman, 'there is very good authority.'—Here he was interrupted by the other, with 'Sir, excuse me, I despise all authority. *Nullius in verba.* I stand upon my own bottom.'—'But, sir, sir,' replied his antagonist, 'the reason of the thing shows.'—'A fig for reason,' cried this sufficient member, 'I laugh at reason; give me ocular demonstration.' The corpulent gentleman began to wax warm, and observed, that no man acquainted with the anatomy of the parts would advance such an extravagant assertion. This innuendo enraged the other so much, that he started up, and in a furious tone, exclaimed, 'What, sir! do you question my knowledge in anatomy?' By this time, all the examiners had espoused the opinion of one or other of the disputants, and raised their voices all together, when the chairman commanded silence, and ordered me to withdraw. In less than a quarter of an hour I was called in again, received my qualification sealed up, and was ordered to pay five shillings.

I laid down my half-guinea upon the table, and stood some time, until one of them bade me begone; to this I replied, 'I will, when I have got my change'; upon which another threw me five shillings and sixpence, saying, I should not be a true Scotchman if I went away without my change. I was afterwards obliged to give three shillings and sixpence to the beadles, and a shilling to an old woman who swept the hall.

Roderick Random, 1748

Veterans in Bath

[Matthew Bramble writes to Dr Lewis]

The spirits and good humour of the company seemed to triumph over the wreck of their constitutions. They had even philosophy enough to joke upon their own calamities; such is the power of friendship, the sovereign cordial of life—I afterwards found, however, that they were not without their moments, and even hours of disquiet. Each of them apart, in succeeding conferences, expatiated upon his own particular grievances; and they were all malecontents at bottom—Over and above their personal disasters, they thought themselves unfortunate in the lottery of life. Balderick complained, that all the recompence he had received for his long and hard service, was the half-pay of a rear-admiral. The colonel was mortified to see himself over-topped by upstart generals, some of whom he had once commanded; and, being a man of a liberal turn, could ill put up with a moderate annuity, for which he had sold his commission. As for the baronet, having run himself considerably in debt, on a contested election, he has been obliged to relinquish his seat in parliament, and his seat in the country at the same time, and put his estate to nurse; but his chagrin, which is the effect of his own misconduct, does not affect me half so much as that of the other two, who have acted honourable and distinguished parts on the great theatre, and are now reduced to lead a weary life in this stew-pan of idleness and insignificance. They have long left off using the waters, after having experienced their inefficacy. The diversions of the place they are not in a condition to enjoy. How then do they make shift to pass their time? In the forenoon, they crawl out to the Rooms or the coffeehouse, where they take a hand at whist, or descant upon the General Advertiser; and their evenings they murder in private parties, among peevish invalids, and insipid old women—This is the case with a good number of individuals, whom nature seems to have intended for better purposes.

Humphry Clinker, 1771

Ranelagh Gardens: 1

[Matthew Bramble to Dr Lewis]

The diversions of the times are not ill suited to the genius of this incongruous monster, called *the public*. Give it noise, confusion, glare, and glitter; it has no idea of elegance and propriety—What are the amusements of Ranelagh? One half of the company are following at the other's tails, in an eternal circle; like so many blind asses in an olive-mill, where they can neither discourse, distinguish, nor be distinguished; while the other half are drinking hot water, under the denomination of tea, till nine or ten o'clock at night, to keep them awake for the rest of the evening. As for the orchestra, the vocal music especially, it is well for the performers that they cannot be heard distinctly.

Humphry Clinker

Ranelagh Gardens: 2

[Lydia Melford to Laetitia Willis]

Ranelagh looks like the inchanted palace of a genie, adorned with the most exquisite performances of painting, carving, and gilding, enlightened with a thousand golden lamps, that emulate the noon-day sun; crowded with the great, the rich, the gay, the happy, and the fair; glittering with cloth of gold and silver, lace, embroidery, and precious stones. While these exulting sons and daughters of felicity tread this round of pleasure, or regale in different parties, and separate lodges, with fine imperial tea and other delicious refreshments, their ears are entertained with the most ravishing delights of music, both instrumental and vocal. There I heard the famous Tenducci, a thing from Italy——It looks for all the world like a man, though they say it is not. The voice, to be sure, is neither man's nor woman's; but it is more melodious than either; and it warbled so divinely, that, while I listened, I really thought myself in paradise.

Humphry Clinker

Miss Jenkins in Love

[Winifred Jenkins to Mary Jones]

Mr Clinker (Loyd I would say) had best look to his tackle—There be other chaps in the market, as the saying is—What would he say if I should except the soot and sarvice of the young 'squire's valley? Mr Machappy is a gentleman born, and has been abroad in the wars—He has a world of buck larning, and speaks French, and Ditch, and Scotch, and all manner of outlandish lingos; to be sure he's a little the worse for the ware, and is much given to drink; but then he's good-tempered in his liquor, and a prudent woman mought wind him about her finger—But I have no thoughts of him, I'll assure you—I scorn for to do, or to say, or to think any thing that mought give unbreech to Mr Loyd, without furder occasion—But then I have such vapours, Molly—I sit and cry by myself, and take ass of etida, and smill to burnt fathers, and kindal-snuffs; and I pray constantly for grease, that I may have a glimpse of the new-light, to shew me the way through this wretched veil of tares—And yet, I want for nothing in this family of love, where every sole is so kind and so courteous, that wan would think they are so many saints in haven.

Humphry Clinker

WILLIAM ROBERTSON

1721–1793

The Rise of the Legal Profession in the Middle Ages

These various improvements in the system of jurisprudence, and administration of justice, occasioned a change in manners, of great importance, and of extensive effect. They gave rise to a distinction of professions; they obliged men to cultivate different talents, and to aim at different accomplishments, in order to qualify themselves for the various departments and functions which became necessary in society. Among uncivilized nations, there is but one profession honourable,—that of arms. All the ingenuity and vigour of the human mind are exerted in acquiring military skill or address. The functions of peace are few and simple; and require no particular course of education or of study as a preparation for discharging them. This was the state of Europe during several centuries. Every gentleman, born a soldier, scorned any other occupation; he was taught no science but that of war; even his exercises and pastimes were feats of martial prowess. Nor did the judicial character, which persons of noble birth were alone entitled to assume, demand any degree of knowledge beyond that which such untutored soldiers possessed. To recollect a few traditionary customs which time had confirmed, and rendered respectable; to mark out the lists of battle with due formality; to observe the issue of the combat; and to pronounce whether it had been conducted according to the laws of arms, included everything that a baron, who acted as a judge, found it necessary to understand.

But when the forms of legal proceedings were fixed, when the rules of decision were committed to writing, and collected into a body, law became a science, the knowledge of which required a regular course of study, together with long attention to the practice of courts. Martial and illiterate nobles had neither leisure nor inclination to undertake a task so laborious, as well as so foreign from all the occupations which they deemed entertaining, or suitable to their rank. They gradually relinquished their places in courts of justice, where their ignorance exposed them to contempt. They became weary of attending to the discussion of cases, which grew too intricate for them to comprehend. Not only the judicial determination of points which were the subject of controversy, but the conduct of all legal business and transactions was committed to persons trained by previous study and application to the knowledge of law. An order of men, to whom their fellow-citizens had daily recourse for advice, and to whom they looked up for decision in their most important concerns, naturally acquired consideration and influence in society. They were advanced to honours which had been considered hitherto as the peculiar rewards of military virtue. They were intrusted with offices of the highest dignity and most extensive power. Thus, another profession than that of arms came to be introduced among the laity, and was reputed honourable. The functions of civil life were attended to. The talents requisite for discharging them were cultivated. A new road was opened to wealth and eminence. The arts and virtues of peace were placed in their proper rank, and received their due recompense.

The History of the Reign of Charles the Fifth, 1769

SIR JOSHUA REYNOLDS

1723–1792

Art and the Language of Common Sense

It has been the fate of arts to be enveloped in mysterious and incomprehensible language, as if it was thought necessary that even the terms should correspond to the idea entertained of the instability and uncertainty of the rules which they expressed.

To speak of genius and taste, as in any way connected with reason or common sense, would be, in the opinion of some towering talkers, to speak like a man who possessed neither; who had never felt that enthusiasm, or, to use their own inflated language, was never warmed by that Promethean fire, which animates the canvas and vivifies the marble.

If, in order to be intelligible, I appear to degrade art by bringing her down from her visionary situation in the clouds, it is only to give her a more solid mansion upon the earth. It is necessary that at some time or other we should see things as they really are, and not impose on ourselves by that false magnitude with which objects appear when viewed indistinctly as through a mist.

Discourses on Art, Discourse VII, 1776

Fullness of Effect

What I just now mentioned of the supposed reason why Ariadne has part of her drapery red, gives me occasion here to observe, that this favourite quality of giving objects relief, and which Du Piles and all the critics have considered as a requisite of the utmost importance, was not one of those objects which much engaged the attention of Titian; painters of an inferior rank have far exceeded him in producing this effect. This was a great object of attention when art was in its infant state; as it is at present with the vulgar and ignorant, who feel the highest satisfaction in seeing a figure which, as they say, looks as if they could walk round it. But however low I may rate this pleasure of deception, I should not oppose it, did it not oppose itself to a quality of a much higher kind, by counteracting entirely that fulness of manner which is so difficult to express in words, but which is found in perfection in the best works of Correggio, and, we may add, of Rembrandt. This effect is produced by melting and losing the shadows in a ground still darker than those shadows; whereas that relief is produced by opposing and separating the ground from the figure, either by light, or shadow, or colour. This conduct of in-laying (as it may be called) figures on their ground, in order to produce relief, was the practice of the old painters, such as Andrea Mantegna, Pietro Perugino, and Albert Dürer; and to these we may add the first manner of Leonardo da Vinci, Giorgione, and even Correggio; but these three were among the first who began to correct themselves in dryness of style, by no longer considering relief as a principal object. As those two qualities, relief, and fulness of effect, can hardly exist together, it is not very difficult to determine to which we ought to give the preference. An artist is obliged for ever to hold a balance in his hand, by which he must determine the value of different qualities; that, when *some* fault must be committed, he may choose the least. Those painters who have best understood the art of producing a good effect, have adopted one principle that seems perfectly conformable to reason; that a part may be sacrificed for the good of the whole. Thus, whether the masses consist of light or shadow, it is necessary that they should be compact and of a pleasing shape: to this end some parts may be made darker and some lighter, and reflections stronger than nature would warrant. Paul Veronese took great liberties of this kind. It is said, that, being once asked why certain figures were painted in shade, as no cause was seen in the picture itself, he turned off the inquiry by answering, '*una nuevola che passa*,' a cloud is passing, which has overshadowed them.

But I cannot give a better instance of this practice than a picture which I have of Rubens; it is a representation of a Moonlight. Rubens has not only diffused more light over the picture than is in nature, but has bestowed on it those warm glowing colours by which his works are so much distinguished. It is so unlike what any other painters have given us of Moonlight, that it might be easily mistaken, if he had not likewise added stars, for a fainter Setting Sun. Rubens thought the eye ought to be satisfied in this case above all other considerations: he might, indeed, have made it more natural, but it would have been at the expense of what he thought of much greater consequence—the harmony proceeding from the contrast and variety of colours.

Discourses on Art, Discourse VIII, 1778

ADAM SMITH

1723–1790

The Invention of Money

When the division of labour has been once thoroughly established, it is but a very small part of a man's wants which the produce of his own labour can supply. He supplies the far greater part of them by exchanging that surplus part of the produce of his own labour, which is over and above his own consumption, for such parts of the produce of other men's labour as he has occasion for. Every man thus lives by exchanging, or becomes in some measure a merchant, and the society itself grows to be what is properly a commercial society.

But when the division of labour first began to take place, this power of exchanging must frequently have been very much clogged and embarrassed in its operations. One man, we shall suppose, has more of a certain commodity than he himself has occasion for, while another has less. The former consequently would be glad to dispose of, and the latter to purchase, a part of this superfluity. But if this latter should chance to have nothing that the former stands in need of, no exchange can be made between them. The butcher has more meat in his shop than he himself can consume, and the brewer and the baker would each of them be willing to purchase a part of it. But they have nothing to offer in exchange, except the different productions of their respective trades, and the butcher is already provided with all the bread and beer which he has immediate occasion for. No exchange can, in this case, be made between them. He cannot be their merchant, nor they his customers; and they are all of them thus mutually less serviceable to one another. In order to avoid the inconveniency of such situations, every prudent man in every period of society, after the first establishment of the division of labour, must naturally have endeavoured to manage his affairs in such a manner, as to have at all times by him, besides the peculiar produce of his own industry, a certain quantity of some one commodity or other, such as he imagined few people would be likely to refuse in exchange for the produce of their industry.

Many different commodities, it is probable, were successively both thought of and employed for this purpose. In the rude ages of society, cattle are said to have been the common instrument of commerce; and, though they must have been a most inconvenient one, yet in old times we find things were frequently valued according to the number of cattle which had been given in exchange for them. The armour of Diomede, says Homer, cost only nine oxen; but that of Glaucus cost an hundred oxen. Salt is said to be the common instrument of commerce and exchanges in Abyssinia; a species of shells in some parts of the coast of India; dried cod at Newfoundland; tobacco in Virginia; sugar in some of our West India colonies; hides or dressed leather in some other countries; and there is at this day a village in Scotland where it is not uncommon, I am told, for a workman to carry nails instead of money to the baker's shop or the ale-house.

In all countries, however, men seem at last to have been determined by irresistible reasons to give the preference, for this employment, to metals above every other commodity. Metals can not only be kept with as little loss as any other commodity, scarce any thing being less perishable than they are, but they can likewise, without any loss, be divided into any number of parts, as by fusion those parts can easily be reunited again; a quality which no other equally durable commodities possess, and which more than any other quality renders them fit to be the instruments of commerce and circulation. The man who wanted to buy salt, for example, and had nothing but cattle to give in exchange for it, must have been obliged to buy salt to the value of a whole ox, or a whole sheep, at a time. He could seldom buy less than this, because what he was to give for it could seldom be divided without loss; and if he had a mind to buy more, he must, for the same reasons, have been obliged to buy double or triple the quantity, the value, to wit, of two or three oxen, or of two or three sheep. If, on the contrary, instead of sheep or oxen, he had metals to give in exchange for it, he could easily proportion the quantity of the metal to the precise quantity of the commodity which he had immediate occasion for.

Different metals have been made use of by different nations for this purpose. Iron was the common instrument of commerce among the antient Spartans; copper among the antient Romans; and gold and silver among all rich and commercial nations.

Those metals seem originally to have been made use of for this purpose in rude bars, without any stamp or coinage. Thus we are told by Pliny, upon the authority of Timæus, an antient historian, that, till the time of Servius Tullius, the Romans had no coined money, but made use of unstamped bars of copper, to purchase whatever they had occasion for. These rude bars, therefore, performed at this time the function of money.

The use of metals in this rude state was attended with two very considerable inconveniencies; first with the trouble of weighing; and, secondly, with that of assaying them. In the precious metals, where a small difference in the quantity makes a great difference in the value, even the business of weighing, with proper exactness, requires at least very accurate weights and scales. The weighing of gold in particular is an operation of some nicety. In the coarser metals, indeed, where a small error would be of little consequence, less accuracy would, no doubt, be necessary. Yet we should find it excessively troublesome, if every time a poor man had occasion either to buy or sell a farthing's worth of goods, he was obliged to weigh the farthing. The operation of assaying is still more difficult, still more tedious, and, unless a part of the metal is fairly melted in the crucible, with proper dissolvents, any conclusion that can be drawn from it, is extremely uncertain. Before the institution of coined money, however, unless they went through this tedious and difficult operation, people must always have been liable to the grossest frauds and impositions, and instead of a pound weight of pure silver, or pure copper, might receive in exchange for their goods, an adulterated composition of the coarsest and cheapest materials, which had, however, in their outward appearance, been made to resemble those metals. To prevent such abuses, to facilitate exchanges, and thereby to encourage all sorts of industry and commerce, it has been found necessary, in all countries that have made any considerable advances towards improvement, to affix a public stamp upon certain quantities of such particular metals, as were in those countries commonly made use of to purchase goods. Hence the origin of coined money, and of those public offices called mints; institutions exactly of the same nature with those of the aulnagers and stampmasters of woollen and linen cloth. All of them are equally meant to ascertain, by means of a public stamp, the quantity and uniform goodness of those different commodities when brought to market.

The Wealth of Nations, 1776

SIR WILLIAM BLACKSTONE
1723–1780

Proof and Presumption

Positive proof is always required, where from the nature of the case it appears it might possibly have been had. But, next to *positive* proof, *circumstantial* evidence or the doctrine of *presumptions* must take place: for when the fact itself cannot be demonstratively evinced, that which comes nearest to the proof of the fact is the proof of such circumstances which either *necessarily*, or *usually*, attend such facts; and these are called presumptions, which are only to be relied upon till the contrary be actually proved. *Stabitur praesumptioni donec probetur in contrarium. Violent* presumption is many times equal to full proof; for there those circumstances appear, which *necessarily* attend the fact. As if a landlord sues for rent due at Michaelmas 1754, and the tenant cannot prove the payment, but produces an acquittance for rent due at a subsequent time, in full of all demands, this is a violent presumption of his having paid the former rent, and is equivalent to full proof; for though the actual payment is not proved, yet the acquittance in full of all demands is proved, which could not be without such payment; and it therefore induces so forcible a presumption, that no proof shall be admitted to the contrary. *Probable* presumption, arising from such circumstances as *usually* hath also its due weight: as if, in a suit for rent due 1754, the tenant proves the payment of rent due in 1755; this will prevail to exonerate the tenant, unless it be clearly shown that the rent of 1754 was retained for some special reason, or that there was some fraud or mistake: for otherwise it will be presumed to have been paid before that in 1755, as it is most usual to receive first the rents of longest standing. *Light*, or rash, presumptions have no weight or validity at all.

Commentaries on the Laws of England, 1765–9

OLIVER GOLDSMITH
1728–1774

Large Heaps and Little Heaps

When we reflect on the manner in which mankind generally confer their favours, we shall find that they who seem to want them least, are the very persons who most liberally share them. There is something so attractive in riches, that the large heap generally collects from the smaller; and the poor find as much pleasure in encreasing the enormous mass, as the miser, who owns it, sees happiness in its encrease. Nor is there in this any thing repugnant to the laws of true morality. Seneca himself allows, that in conferring benefits, the present should always be suited to the dignity of the receiver. Thus the rich receive large presents, and are thanked for accepting them. Men of middling stations are obliged to be content with presents something less, while the beggar, who may be truly said to want indeed, is well paid if a farthing rewards his warmest solicitations.

Every man who has seen the world, and has had his *ups and downs in life*, as the expression is, must have frequently experienced the truth of this doctrine, and must know that to have much, or to seem to have it, is the only way to have more. Ovid finely compares a man of broken fortune to a falling column; the lower it sinks, the greater weight it is obliged to sustain. Thus, when a man has no occasion to borrow, he finds numbers willing to lend him. Should he ask his friend to lend him an hundred pounds, it is possible, from the largeness of the demand, he may find credit for twenty; but should he humbly only sue for a trifle, it is two to one whether he might be trusted for two pence.

'On the Use of Language', *The Bee*, 1759

An Innocent Abroad

From Lien Chi Altangi, to Fum Hoam, first president of the Ceremonial Academy at Pekin, in China

In spite of taste, in spite of prejudice, I now begin to think their women tolerable; I can now look on a languishing blue eye without disgust, and pardon a set of teeth, even though whiter than ivory. I now begin to fancy there is no universal standard for beauty. The truth is, the manners of the ladies in this city are so very open, and so vastly engaging, that I am inclined to pass over the more glaring defects of their persons, since compensated by the more solid, yet latent beauties of the mind; what tho' they want black teeth, or are deprived of the allurements of feet no bigger than their thumbs, yet still they have souls, my friend, such souls, so free, so pressing, so hospitable, and so engaging—I have received more invitations in the streets of London from the sex in one night, than I have met with at Pekin in twelve revolutions of the moon.

Every evening as I return home from my usual solitary excursions, I am met by several of those well disposed daughters of hospitality, at different times and in different streets, richly dressed, and with minds not less noble than their appearance. You know that nature has indulged me with a person by no means agreeable; yet are they too generous to object to my homely appearance; they feel no repugnance at my broad face and flat nose; they perceive me to be a stranger, and that alone is a sufficient recommendation. They even seem to think it their duty to do the honours of the country by every act of complaisance in their power. One takes me under the arm, and in a manner forces me along; another catches me round the neck, and desires to partake in this office of hospitality; while a third kinder still, invites me to refresh my spirits with wine. Wine is in England reserved only for the rich, yet here even wine is given away to the stranger!

A few nights ago, one of those generous creatures, dressed all in white, and flaunting like a meteor by my side, forcibly attended me home to my own apartment. She seemed charmed with the elegance of the furniture, and the convenience of my situation. And well indeed she might, for I have hired an apartment for not less than two shillings of their money every week. But her civility did not rest here; for at parting, being desirous to know the hour, and perceiving my watch out of order, she kindly took it to be repaired by a relation of her own, which you may imagine will save some expence, and she assures me that it will cost her nothing.

The Citizen of the World, 1760–1

Beau Nash in Old Age

He found poverty now denied him the indulgence not only of his favourite follies, but of his favourite virtues. The poor now solicited him in vain; he was himself a more pitiable object than they. The child of the public seldom has a friend, and he who once exercised his wit at the expence of others, must naturally have enemies. Exasperated at last to the highest degree, an unaccountable whim struck him; poor *Nash* was resolved to become an author; he who, in the vigour of manhood, was incapable of the task, now at the impotent age of eighty-six, was determined to write his own history! From the many specimens already given of his style, the reader will not much regret that the historian was interrupted in his design. Yet as *Montaigne* observes, as the adventures of an infant, if an infant could inform us of them, would be pleasing; so the life of a Beau, if a beau could write, would certainly serve to regale curiosity.

The Life of Richard Nash of Bath, Esq., 1762

Dr Primrose and His Wife

I was ever of opinion, that the honest man who married and brought up a large family, did more service than he who continued single, and only talked of population. From this motive, I had scarce taken orders a year before I began to think seriously of matrimony, and chose my wife as she did her wedding gown, not for a fine glossy surface, but such qualities as would wear well. To do her justice, she was a good-natured notable woman; and as for breeding, there were few country ladies who could shew more. She could read any English book without much spelling; but for pickling, preserving, and cookery, none could excel her. She prided herself also upon being an excellent contriver in house-keeping; tho' I could never find that we grew richer with all her contrivances.

However, we loved each other tenderly, and our fondness encreased as we grew old. There was in fact nothing that could make us angry with the world or each other. We had an elegant house, situated in a fine country, and a good neighbourhood. The year was spent in moral or rural amusements; in visiting our rich neighbours, and relieving such as were poor. We had no revolutions to fear, nor fatigues to undergo; all our adventures were by the fire-side, and all our migrations from the blue bed to the brown.

As we lived near the road, we often had the traveller or stranger visit us to taste our gooseberry wine, for which we had great reputation; and I profess with the veracity of an historian, that I never knew one of them find fault with it. Our cousins too, even to the fortieth remove, all remembered their affinity, without any help from the herald's office, and came very frequently to see us. Some of them did us no great honour by these claims of kindred; as we had the blind, the maimed, and the halt amongst the number. However, my wife always insisted that as they were the same *flesh and blood*, they should sit with us at the same table. So that if we had not very rich, we generally had very happy friends about us; for this remark will hold good thro' life, that the poorer the guest, the better pleased he ever is with being treated: and as some men gaze with admiration at the colours of a tulip, or the wing of a butterfly, so I was by nature an admirer of happy human faces. However, when any one of our relations was found to be a person of very bad character, a troublesome guest, or one we desired to get rid of, upon his leaving my house, I ever took care to lend him a riding coat, or a pair of boots, or sometimes an horse of small value, and I always had the satisfaction of finding he never came back to return them. By this the house was cleared of such as we did not like; but never was the family of Wakefield known to turn the traveller or the poor dependant out of doors.

Thus we lived several years in a state of much happiness, not but that we sometimes had those little rubs which Providence sends to enhance the value of its favours. My orchard was often robbed by school-boys, and my wife's custards plundered by the cats or the children. The 'Squire would sometimes fall asleep in the most pathetic parts of my sermon, or his lady return my wife's civilities at church with a mutilated curtesy. But we soon got over the uneasiness caused by such accidents, and usually in three or four days began to wonder how they vext us.

The Vicar of Wakefield, 1766

The Mole

The smallness of its eyes, which induced the ancients to think it was blind, is, to this animal, a peculiar advantage. A small degree of vision is sufficient for a creature that is ever destined to live in darkness. A more extensive sight would only have served to shew the horrors of its prison, while Nature had denied it the means of an escape. Had this organ been larger, it would have been perpetually liable to injuries, by the falling of the earth into it; but Nature, to prevent the inconvenience, has not only made them very small, but very closely covered them with hair. Anatomists mention, beside these advantages, another, that contributes to their security; namely, a certain muscle, by which the animal can draw back the eye whenever it is necessary or in danger.

As the eye is thus perfectly fitted to the animal's situation, so also are the senses of hearing and smelling. The first gives it notice of the most distant appearance of danger; the other directs it, in the midst of darkness, to its food. The wants of a subterraneous animal can be but few; and these are sufficient to supply them: to eat, and to produce its kind, are the whole employments of such a life; and for both these purposes it is wonderfully adapted by Nature.

An History of the Earth, 1774

EDMUND BURKE

1729–1797

May Better Counsels Guide You!

Let us, Sir, embrace some system or other before we end this session. Do you mean to tax America, and to draw a productive revenue from thence? If you do, speak out; name, fix, ascertain this revenue; settle its quantity; define its objects; provide for its collection; and then fight when you have something to fight for. If you murder, rob; if you kill, take possession: and do not appear in the character of madmen, as well as assassins, violent, vindictive, bloody, and tyrannical, without an object. But may better counsels guide you!

Again, and again, revert to your own principles—seek peace and ensue it—leave America, if she has taxable matter in her, to tax herself. I am not here going into the distinctions of rights, not attempting to mark their boundaries. I do not enter into these metaphysical distinctions; I hate the very sound of them. Leave the Americans as they anciently stood, and these distinctions, born of our unhappy contest, will die along with it. They and we, and their and our ancestors, have been happy under that system. Let the memory of all actions, in contradiction to that good old mode, on both sides, be extinguished for ever. Be content to bind America by laws of trade; you have always done it. Let this be your reason for binding their trade. Do not burthen them by taxes; you were not used to do so from the beginning. Let this be your reason for not taxing. These are the arguments of states and kingdoms. Leave the rest to the schools; for there only they may be discussed with safety. But if, intemperately, unwisely, fatally, you sophisticate and poison the very source of government, by urging subtle deductions, and consequences odious to those you govern, from the unlimited and illimitable nature of supreme sovereignty, you will teach them by these means to call that sovereignty itself in question. When you drive him hard, the boar will surely turn upon the hunters. If that sovereignty and their freedom cannot be reconciled, which will they take? They will cast your sovereignty in your face. Nobody will be argued into slavery.

Speech on American Taxation, 1774

Compromise and Barter

All government, indeed every human benefit and enjoyment, every virtue, and every prudent act, is founded on compromise and barter. We balance inconveniences; we give and take; we remit some rights that we may enjoy others; and we choose rather to be happy citizens than subtle disputants.

Speech on Conciliation with America, 1775

The British in India

The several irruptions of Arabs, Tartars, and Persians, into India were, for the greater part, ferocious, bloody, and wasteful in the extreme: our entrance into the dominion of that country was, as generally, with small comparative effusion of blood; being introduced by various frauds and delusions, and by taking advantage of the incurable, blind, and senseless animosity, which the several country powers bear towards each other, rather than by open force. But the difference in favour of the first conquerors is this; the Asiatic conquerors very soon abated of their ferocity, because they made the conquered country their own. They rose or fell with the rise or fall of the territory they lived in. Fathers there deposited the hopes of their posterity; and children there beheld the monuments of their fathers. Here their lot was finally cast; and it is the natural wish of all, that their lot should not be cast in a bad land. Poverty, sterility, and desolation, are not a recreating prospect to the eye of man; and there are very few who can bear to grow old among the curses of a whole people. If their passion or their avarice drove the Tartar lords to acts of rapacity or tyranny, there was time enough, even in the short life of man, to bring round the ill effects of an abuse of power upon the power itself. If hoards were made by violence and tyranny, they were still domestic hoards; and domestic profusion, or the rapine of a more powerful and prodigal hand, restored them to the people. With many disorders, and with few political checks upon power, Nature had still fair play; the sources of acquisition were not dried up; and therefore the trade, the manufactures, and the commerce of the country flourished. Even avarice and usury itself operated, both for the preservation and the employment of national wealth. The husbandman and manufacturer paid heavy interest, but then they augmented the fund from whence they were again to borrow. Their resources were dearly bought, but they were sure; and the general stock of the community grew by the general effort.

But under the English government all this order is reversed. The Tartar invasion was mischievous; but it is our protection that destroys India. It was their enmity, but it is our friendship. Our conquest there, after twenty years, is as crude as it was the first day. The natives scarcely know what it is to see the grey head of an Englishman. Young men (boys almost) govern there, without society, and without sympathy with the natives. They have no more social habits with the people, than if they still resided in England; nor indeed any species of intercourse but that which is necessary to making a sudden fortune, with a view to a remote settlement. Animated with all the avarice of age, and all the impetuosity of youth, they roll in one after another; wave after wave; and there is nothing before the eyes of the natives but an endless, hopeless prospect of new flights of birds of prey and passage, with appetites continually renewing for a food that is continually wasting. Every rupee of profit made by an Englishman is lost for ever to India. With us are no retributory superstitions, by which a foundation of charity compensates, through ages, to the poor, for the rapine and injustice of a day. With us no pride erects stately monuments which repair the mischiefs which pride had produced, and which adorn a country, out of its own spoils. England has erected no churches, no hospitals, no palaces, no schools; England has built no bridges, made no high roads, cut no navigations, dug out no reservoirs. Every other conqueror of every other description has left some monument, either of state or beneficence, behind him. Were we to be driven out of India this day, nothing would remain, to tell that it had been possessed, during the inglorious period of our dominion, by any thing better than the ouran-outang or the tiger.

Speech on the East India Bill, 1783

The Rights of Man

Far am I from denying in theory; full as far is my heart from withholding in practice (if I were of power to give or to withhold) the *real* rights of men. In denying their false claims of right, I do not mean to injure those which are real, and are such as their pretended rights would totally destroy. If civil society be made for the advantage of man, all the advantages for which it is made become his right. It is an institution of beneficence; and law itself is only beneficence acting by a rule. Men have a right to live by that rule; they have a right to justice; as between their fellows, whether their fellows are in politic function or in ordinary occupation. They have a right to the fruits of their industry; and to the means of making their industry fruitful. They have a right to the acquisitions of their parents; to the nourishment and improvement of their offspring; to instruction in life, and to consolation in death. Whatever each man can separately do, without trespassing upon others, he has a right to do for himself; and he has a right to a fair portion of all which society, with all its combinations of skill and force, can do in his favour. In this partnership all men have equal rights; but not to equal things. He that has but five shillings in the partnership, has as good a right to it, as he that has five hundred pounds has to his larger proportion. But he has not a right to an equal dividend in the product of the joint stock; and as to the share of power, authority, and direction which each individual ought to have in the management of the state, that I must deny to be amongst the direct original rights of man in civil society; for I have in my contemplation the civil social man, and no other. It is a thing to be settled by convention.

If civil society be the offspring of convention, that convention must be its law. That convention must limit and modify all the descriptions of constitution which are formed under it. Every sort of legislative judicial, or executory power are its creatures. They can have no being in any other state of things; and how can any man claim, under the conventions of civil society, rights which do not so much as suppose its existence? Rights which are absolutely repugnant to it? One of the first motives to civil society, and which becomes one of its fundamental rules, is, *that no man should be judge in his own cause.* By this each person has at once divested himself of the first fundamental right of uncovenanted man, that is, to judge for himself, and to assert his own cause. He abdicates all right to be his own governor. He inclusively, in a great measure, abandons the right of self-defence, the first law of nature. Men cannot enjoy the rights of an uncivil and of a civil state together. That he may obtain justice he gives up his right of determining what it is in points the most essential to him. That he may secure some liberty, he makes a surrender in trust of the whole of it.

Government is not made in virtue of natural rights, which may and do exist in total independence of it; and exist in much greater clearness, and in a much greater degree of abstract perfection: but their abstract perfection is their practical defect. By having a right to every thing they want every thing. Government is a contrivance of human wisdom to provide for human *wants.* Men have a right that these wants should be provided for by this wisdom. Among these wants is to be reckoned the want, out of civil society, of a sufficient restraint upon their passions. Society requires not only that the passions of individuals should be subjected, but that even in the mass and body as well as in the individuals, the inclinations of men should frequently be thwarted, their will controlled, and their passions brought into subjection. This can only be done *by a power out of themselves*; and not, in the exercise of its function, subject to that will and to those passions which it is its office to bridle and subdue. In this sense the restraints on men, as well as their liberties, are to be reckoned among their rights. But as the liberties and the restrictions vary with times and circumstances, and admit of infinite modifications, they cannot be settled upon any abstract rule; and nothing is so foolish as to discuss them upon that principle.

Reflections on the Revolution in France, 1790

Causes and Pretexts

We do not draw the moral lessons we might from history. On the contrary, without care it may be used to vitiate our minds and to destroy our happiness. In history a great volume is unrolled for our instruction, drawing the materials of future wisdom from the past errors and infirmities of mankind. It may, in the perversion, serve for a magazine, furnishing offensive and defensive weapons for parties in church and state, and supplying the means of keeping alive, or reviving dissensions and animosities, and adding fuel to civil fury. History consists, for the greater part, of the miseries brought upon the world by pride, ambition, avarice, revenge, lust, sedition, hypocrisy, ungoverned zeal, and all the train of disorderly appetites, which strike the public with the same

troublous storms that toss
The private state, and render life unsweet.

These vices are the *causes* of those storms. Religion, morals, laws, prerogatives, privileges, liberties, rights of men, are the *pretexts*. The pretexts are always found in some specious appearance of a real good. You would not secure men from tyranny and sedition, by rooting out of the mind the principles to which these fraudulent pretexts apply? If you did, you would root out every thing that is valuable in the human breast. As these are the pretexts, so the ordinary actors and instruments in great public evils are kings, priests, magistrates, senates, parliaments, national assemblies, judges, and captains. You would not cure the evil by resolving, that there should be no more monarchs, nor ministers of state, nor of the gospel; no interpreters of law; no general officers; no public councils. You might change the names. The things in some shape must remain. A certain *quantum* of power must always exist in the community, in some hands, and under some appellation. Wise men will apply their remedies to vices, not to names; to the causes of evil which are permanent, not to the occasional organs by which they act, and the transitory modes in which they appear. Otherwise you will be wise historically, a fool in practice. Seldom have two ages the same fashion in their pretexts and the same modes of mischief. Wickedness is a little more inventive. Whilst you are discussing fashion, the fashion is gone by. The very same vice assumes a new body. The spirit transmigrates; and, far from losing its principle of life by the change of its appearance, it is renovated in its new organs with the fresh vigour of a juvenile activity. It walks abroad; it continues its ravages; whilst you are gibbeting the carcass, or demolishing the tomb. You are terrifying yourself with ghosts and apparitions, whilst your house is the haunt of robbers. It is thus with all those, who attending only to the shell and husk of history, think they are waging war with intolerance, pride, and cruelty, whilst, under colour of abhorring the ill principles of antiquated parties, they are authorizing and feeding the same odious vices in different factions, and perhaps in worse.

Reflections on the Revolution in France

A Commodious Bugbear

As little shall I detain you with matters that can as little obtain admission into a mind like yours; such as the fear, or pretence of fear, that, in spite of your own power, and the trifling power of Great Britain, you may be conquered by the pope; or that this commodious bugbear (who is of infinitely more use to those who pretend to fear, than to those who love him) will absolve his Majesty's subjects from their allegiance, and send over the Cardinal of York to rule you as his viceroy; or that, by the plenitude of his power, he will take that fierce tyrant, the king of the French, out of his jail, and arm that nation (which on all occasions treats his Holiness so very politely) with his bulls and pardons, to invade poor old Ireland, to reduce you to Popery and slavery, and to force the free-born, naked feet of your people into the wooden shoes of that arbitrary monarch. I do not believe that discourses of this kind are held, or that anything like them will be held, by any who walk about without a keeper. Yet, I confess, that on occasions of this nature, I am the most afraid of the weakest reasonings; because they discover the strongest passions. These things will never be brought out in indefinite propositions. They would not prevent pity towards any persons; they would only cause it for those who were capable of talking in such a strain. But I know, and am sure, that such ideas as no man will distinctly produce to another, or hardly venture to bring in any plain shape to his own mind—he will utter in obscure, ill-explained doubts, jealousies, surmises, fears, and apprehensions; and that, in such a fog, they will appear to have a good deal of size, and will make an impression; when, if they were clearly brought forth and defined, they would meet with nothing but scorn and derision.

A Letter to Sir Hercules Langrishe, 1792

Old Friends in a New Guise

I am afraid you will find me, my Lord, again falling into my usual vanity, in valuing myself on the eminent men whose society I once enjoyed. I remember, in a conversation I once had with my ever dear friend Garrick, who was the first of actors, because he was the most acute observer of Nature I ever knew, I asked him how it happened, that, whenever a senate appeared on the stage, the audience seemed always disposed to laughter. He said, the reason was plain: the audience was well acquainted with the faces of most of the senators. They knew that they were no other than candle-snuffers, revolutionary scene-shifters, second and third mob, prompter, clerks, executioners, who stand with their axe on their shoulders by the wheel, grinners in the pantomime, murderers in tragedies, who make ugly faces under black wigs,—in short, the very scum and refuse of the theatre; and it was of course that the contrast of the vileness of the actors with the pomp of their habits naturally excited ideas of contempt and ridicule.

So it was at Paris on the inaugural day of the Constitution for the present year. The foreign ministers were ordered to attend at this investitute of the Directory;—for so they call the managers of their burlesque government. The diplomacy, who were a sort of strangers, were quite awe-struck with the 'pride, pomp, and circumstance' of this majestic senate; whilst the *sans-culotte* gallery instantly recognized their own insurrectionary acquaintance, burst out into a horse-laugh at their absurd finery, and held them in infinitely greater contempt than whilst they prowled about the streets in the pantaloon of the last year's Constitution, when their legislators appeared honestly, with their daggers in their belts, and their pistols peeping out of their side-pocket-holes, like a bold, brave banditti, as they are.

Letters on a Regicide Peace, 1796

An Attack on Burke's Pension

The Duke of Bedford conceives, that he is obliged to call the attention of the House of Peers to his Majesty's grant to me, which he considers as excessive, and out of all bounds.

I know not how it has happened, but it really seems, that, whilst his Grace was meditating his well-considered censure upon me, he fell into a sort of sleep. Homer nods; and the Duke of Bedford may dream; and as dreams (even his golden dreams) are apt to be ill-pieced and incongruously put together, his Grace preserved his idea of reproach to *me*, but took the subject-matter from the Crown grants *to his own family*. This is 'the stuff of which his dreams are made.' In that way of putting things together his Grace is perfectly in the right. The grants to the house of Russell were so enormous, as not only to outrage economy, but even to stagger credibility. The Duke of Bedford is the leviathan among all the creatures of the Crown. He tumbles about his unwieldy bulk; he plays and frolics in the ocean of the royal bounty. Huge as he is, and whilst 'he lies floating many a rood,' he is still a creature. His ribs, his fins, his whalebone, his blubber, the very spiracles through which he spouts a torrent of brine against his origin, and covers me all over with the spray,—everything of him and about him is from the throne. Is it for *him* to question the dispensation of the royal favour?

A Letter to a Noble Lord, 1797

JAMES BRUCE
1730–1794

African Heat

I call it *hot*, when a man sweats at rest, and excessively on moderate motion. I call it *very hot*, when a man, with thin or little clothing, sweats much, though at rest. I call it *excessive hot*, when a man in his shirt, at rest, sweats excessively, when all motion is painful, and the knees feel feeble, as if after a fever. I call it *extreme hot*, when the strength fails, a disposition to faint comes on, a straitness is found round the temples, as if a small cord were drawn round the head, the voice impaired, the skin dry, and the head seems more than ordinary large and light. This, I apprehend, denotes death at hand.

Travels to Discover the Source of the Nile, 1790

WILLIAM COWPER
1731–1800

How to Write a Letter

A letter is written as a conversation is maintained, or a journey performed; not by preconcerted or premeditated means, a new contrivance, or an invention never heard of before,—but merely by maintaining a progress, and resolving as a postilion does, having once set out, never to stop till we reach the appointed end. If a man may talk without thinking, why may he not write upon the same terms? A grave gentleman of the last century, a tie-wig, square-toe, Steinkirk figure, would say—'My good sir, a man has no right to do either.' But it is to be hoped that the present century has nothing to do with the mouldy opinions of the last; and so good Sir Launcelot, or Sir Paul, or whatever be your name, step into your picture-frame again, and look as if you thought for another century, and leave us moderns in the meantime to think when we can, and to write whether we can or not, else we might as well be dead as you are.

letter to the Revd William Unwin, 1780

A Kind-Hearted Candidate

As when the sea is uncommonly agitated, the water finds its way into creeks and holes of rocks, which in its calmer state it never reaches, in like manner the effect of these turbulent times is felt even at Orchard side, where in general we live as undisturbed by the political element, as shrimps or cockles that have been accidentally deposited in some hollow beyond the water mark, by the usual dashing of the waves. We were sitting yesterday after dinner, the two ladies and myself, very composedly, and without the least apprehension of any such intrusion in our snug parlour, one lady knitting, the other netting, and the gentleman winding worsted, when to our unspeakable surprise a mob appeared before the window; a smart rap was heard at the door, the boys halloo'd, and the maid announced Mr Grenville. Puss [his tame hare] was unfortunately let out of her box, so that the candidate, with all his good friends at his heels, was refused admittance at the grand entry, and referred to the back door, as the only possible way of approach.

Candidates are creatures not very susceptible of affronts, and would rather, I suppose, climb in at a window, than be absolutely excluded. In a minute, the yard, the kitchen, and the parlour, were filled. Mr Grenville, advancing toward me, shook me by the hand with a degree of cordiality that was extremely seducing. As soon as he and as many more as could find chairs were seated, he began to open the intent of his visit. I told him I had no vote, for which he readily gave me credit. I assured him I had no influence, which he was not equally inclined to believe, and the less, no doubt, because Mr Ashburner, the draper, addressing himself to me at this moment, informed me that I had a great deal. Supposing that I could not be possessed of such a treasure without knowing it, I ventured to confirm my first assertion, by saying, that if I had any I was utterly at a loss to imagine where it could be, or wherein it consisted. Thus ended the conference. Mr Grenville squeezed me by the hand again, kissed the ladies, and withdrew. He kissed likewise the maid in the kitchen, and seemed upon the whole a most loving, kissing, kind-hearted gentleman. He is very young, genteel, and handsome. He has a pair of very good eyes in his head, which not being sufficient as it should seem for the many nice and difficult purposes of a senator, he has a third also, which he wore suspended by a riband from his buttonhole. The boys halloo'd, the dogs barked, Puss scampered, the hero, with his long train of obsequious followers, withdrew. We made ourselves very merry with the adventure, and in a short time settled into our former tranquillity, never probably to be thus interrupted more. I thought myself, however, happy in being able to affirm truly that I had not that influence for which he sued; and which, had I been possessed of it, with my present views of the dispute between the Crown and the Commons, I must have refused him, for he is on the side of the former. It is comfortable to be of no consequence in a world where one cannot exercise any without disobliging somebody. The town, however, seems to be much at his service, and if he be equally successful throughout the county, he will undoubtedly gain his election. Mr Ashburner perhaps was a little mortified, because it was evident that I owed the honour of this visit to his misrepresentation of my importance. But had he thought proper to assure Mr Grenville that I had three heads, I should not I suppose have been bound to produce them.

letter to the Revd John Newton, 1784

A Winter Walk

Wintry as the weather is, do not suspect that it confines me. I ramble daily, and everyday change my ramble. Wherever I go, I find short grass under my feet, and when I have travelled perhaps five miles, come home with shoes not at all too dirty for a drawing-room. I was pacing yesterday under the elms, that surround the field in which stands the great alcove, when lifting my eyes I saw two black genteel figures bolt through a hedge into the path where I was walking. You guess already who they were, and that they could be nobody but our neighbours. They had seen me from a hill at a distance, and had traversed a great turnip-field to get at me. You see therefore, my dear, that I am in some request.

letter to Lady Hesketh, 1786

Beau and the Water-Lily

I must tell you a feat of my dog Beau. Walking by the river side, I observed some water-lilies floating at a little distance from the bank. They are a large white flower, with an orange-coloured eye, very beautiful. I had a desire to gather one, and, having your long cane in my hand, by the help of it endeavoured to bring one of them within my reach. But the attempt proved vain, and I walked forward. Beau had all the while observed me attentively. Returning soon after toward the same place, I observed him plunge into the river, while I was about forty yards distance from him; and, when I had nearly reached the spot, he swam to land with a lily in his mouth, which he came and laid at my foot.

letter to Lady Hesketh, 1788

A Dream about Milton

Oh! you rogue! what would you give to have such a dream about Milton, as I had about a week since? I dreamed that being in a house in the city, and with much company, looking towards the lower end of the room from the upper end of it, I descried a figure which I immediately knew to be Milton's. He was very gravely, but very neatly attired in the fashion of his day, and had a countenance which filled me with those feelings that an affectionate child has for a beloved father, such, for instance, as Tom has for you. My first thought was wonder, where he could have been concealed so many years; my second, a transport of joy to find him still alive; my third, another transport to find myself in his company; and my fourth, a resolution to accost him. I did so, and he received me with a complacence, in which I saw equal sweetness and dignity. I spoke of his *Paradise Lost*, as every man must, who is worthy to speak of it at all, and told him a long story of the manner in which it affected me, when I first discovered it, being at that time a schoolboy. He answered me by a smile and a gentle inclination of his head. He then grasped my hand affectionately, and with a smile that charmed me, said, 'Well, you for your part will do well also'; at last recollecting his great age (for I understood him to be two hundred years old), I feared that I might fatigue him by much talking, I took my leave, and he took his, with an air of the most perfect good breeding. His person, his features, his manner, were all so perfectly characteristic, that I am persuaded an apparition of him could not represent him more completely.

letter to William Hayley, 1793

HECTOR ST JEAN DE CREVECŒUR
1735–1813

What Then is the American?

What attachment can a poor European emigrant have for a country where he had nothing? The knowledge of the language, the love of a few kindred as poor as himself, were the only cords that tied him: his country is now that which gives him land, bread, protection, and consequence: *Ubi panis ibi patria* is the motto of all emigrants. What then is the American, this new man? He is either a European, or the descendant of a European, hence that strange mixture of blood, which you will find in no other country. I could point out to you a family whose grandfather was an Englishman, whose wife was Dutch, whose son married a French woman, and whose present four sons have now four wives of different nations. *He* is an

American, who, leaving behind him all his ancient prejudices and manners, receives new ones from the new mode of life he has embraced, the new government he obeys, and the new rank he holds. He becomes an American by being received in the broad lap of our great *Alma Mater*. Here individuals of all nations are melted into a new race of men, whose labors and posterity will one day cause great changes in the world. Americans are the western pilgrims, who are carrying along with them that great mass of arts, sciences, vigor, and industry which began long since in the east; they will finish the great circle. The Americans were once scattered all over Europe; here they are incorporated into one of the finest systems of population which has ever appeared, and which will hereafter become distinct by the power of the different climates they inhabit. The American ought therefore to love this country much better than that wherein either he or his forefathers were born. Here the rewards of his industry follow with equal steps the progress of his labor; his labor is founded on the basis of nature, *self-interest*; can it want a stronger allurement? Wives and children, who before in vain demanded of him a morsel of bread, now, fat and frolicsome, gladly help their father to clear those fields whence exuberant crops are to arise to feed and to clothe them all; without any part being claimed, either by a despotic prince, a rich abbot, or a mighty lord. Here religion demands but little of him; a small voluntary salary to the minister, and gratitude to God; can he refuse these? The American is a new man, who acts upon new principles; he must therefore entertain new ideas, and form new opinions. From involuntary idleness, servile dependence, penury, and useless labor, he has passed to toils of a very different nature, rewarded by ample subsistence.—This is an American.

Letters from an American Farmer, 1782

EDWARD GIBBON

1737–1794

Marcus Aurelius

The virtue of Marcus Aurelius Antoninus was of a severer and more laborious kind. It was the well-earned harvest of many a learned conference, of many a patient lecture, and many a midnight lucubration. At the age of twelve years he embraced the rigid system of the Stoics, which taught him to submit his body to his mind, his passions to his reason; to consider virtue as the only good, vice as the only evil, all things external as things indifferent. His Meditations, composed in the tumult of a camp, are still extant; and he even condescended to give lessons of philosophy, in a more public manner than was perhaps consistent with the modesty of a sage or the dignity of an emperor. But his life was the noblest commentary on the precepts of Zeno. He was severe to himself, indulgent to the imperfection of others, just and beneficent to all mankind. He regretted that Avidius Cassius, who excited a rebellion in Syria, had disappointed him, by a voluntary death, of the pleasure of converting an enemy into a friend; and he justified the sincerity of that sentiment, by moderating the zeal of the senate against the adherents of the traitor. War he detested, as the disgrace and calamity of human nature, but when the necessity of a just defence called upon him to take up arms, he readily exposed his person to eight winter campaigns on the frozen banks of the Danube, the severity of which was at last fatal to the weakness of his constitution. His memory was revered by a grateful posterity, and, above a century after his death, many persons preserved the image of Marcus Antoninus among those of their household gods.

The Decline and Fall of the Roman Empire, 1776–88

The Early Church

The scanty and suspicious materials of ecclesiastical history seldom enable us to dispel the dark cloud that hangs over the first age of the church. The great law of impartiality too often obliges us to reveal the imperfections of the uninspired teachers and believers of the Gospel; and, to a careless observer, *their* faults may seem to cast a shade on the faith which they professed. But the scandal of the pious Christian, and the fallacious triumph of the Infidel, should cease as soon as they recollect not only *by whom*, but likewise *to whom*, the Divine Revelation was given. The theologian may indulge the pleasing task of describing Religion as she descended from Heaven, arrayed in her native purity. A more melancholy duty is imposed on the historian. He must discover the inevitable mixture of error and corruption which she contracted in a long residence upon earth, among a weak and degenerate race of beings.

The Decline and Fall of the Roman Empire

Virtuous Pagans and Their Fate

The condemnation of the wisest and most virtuous of the Pagans, on account of their ignorance or disbelief of the divine truth, seems to offend the reason and the humanity of the present age. But the primitive church, whose faith was of a much firmer consistence, delivered over, without hesitation, to eternal torture, the far greater part of the human species. A charitable hope might perhaps be indulged in favour of Socrates, or some other sages of antiquity, who had consulted the light of reason before that of the Gospel had arisen. But it was unanimously affirmed that those who, since the birth or the death of Christ, had obstinately persisted in the worship of the daemons, neither deserved nor could expect a pardon from the irritated justice of the Deity. These rigid sentiments, which had been unknown to the ancient world, appear to have infused a spirit of bitterness into a system of love and harmony. The ties of blood and friendship were frequently torn asunder by the difference of religious faith; and the Christians, who, in this world, found themselves oppressed by the power of the Pagans, were sometimes seduced by resentment and spiritual pride to delight in the prospect of their future triumph. 'You are fond of spectacles,' exclaims the stern Tertullian, 'expect the greatest of all spectacles, the last and eternal judgment of the universe. How shall I admire, how laugh, how rejoice, how exult, when I behold so many proud monarchs, and fancied gods, groaning in the lowest abyss of darkness; so many magistrates, who persecuted the name of the Lord, liquefying in fiercer fires than they ever kindled against the Christians; so many sage philosophers blushing in red-hot flames with their deluded scholars; so many celebrated poets trembling before the tribunal, not of Minos, but of Christ; so many tragedians, more tuneful in the expression of their own sufferings; so many dancers——' But the humanity of the reader will permit me to draw a veil over the rest of this infernal description, which the zealous African pursues in a long variety of affected and unfeeling witticisms.

The Decline and Fall of the Roman Empire

St Athanasius

We have seldom an opportunity of observing, either in active or speculative life, what effect may be produced, or what obstacles may be surmounted, by the force of a single mind, when it is inflexibly applied to the pursuit of a single object. The immortal name of Athanasius will never be separated from the catholic doctrine of the Trinity, to whose defence he consecrated every moment and every faculty of his being. Educated in the family of Alexander, he had vigorously opposed the early progress of the Arian heresy: he exercised the important functions of secretary under the aged prelate; and the fathers of the Nicene council beheld with surprise and respect the rising virtues of the young deacon. In a time of public danger the dull claims of age and of rank are sometimes superseded; and within five months after his return from Nice the deacon Athanasius was seated on the archiepiscopal throne of Egypt. He filled that eminent station above forty-six years, and his long administration was spent in a perpetual combat against the powers of Arianism. Five times was Athanasius expelled from his throne; twenty years he passed as an exile or a fugitive; and almost every province of the Roman empire was successively witness to his merit, and his sufferings in the cause of the Homoousion, which he considered as the sole pleasure and business, as the duty, and as the glory of his life. Amidst the storms of persecution, the archbishop of Alexandria was patient of labour, jealous of fame, careless of safety; and although his mind was tainted by the contagion of fanaticism, Athanasius displayed a superiority of character and abilities which would have qualified him, far better than the degenerate sons of Constantine, for the government of a great monarchy. His learning was much less profound and extensive than that of Eusebius of Caesarea, and his rude eloquence could not be compared with the polished oratory of Gregory or Basil; but whenever the primate of Egypt was called upon to justify his sentiments or his conduct, his unpremeditated style, either of speaking or writing, was clear, forcible, and persuasive. He has always been revered in the orthodox school as one of the most accurate masters of the Christian theology; and he was supposed to possess two profane sciences, less adapted to the episcopal character—the knowledge of jurisprudence, and that of divination. Some fortunate conjectures of future events, which impartial reasoners might ascribe to the experience and judgment of Athanasius, were attributed by his friends to heavenly inspiration, and imputed by his enemies to infernal magic.

The Decline and Fall of the Roman Empire

Julian the Apostate

The remains of Julian were interred at Tarsus in Cilicia; but his stately tomb, which arose in that city on the banks of the cold and limpid Cydnus, was displeasing to the faithful friends who loved and revered the memory of that extraordinary man. The philosopher expressed a very reasonable wish that the disciple of Plato might have reposed amidst the groves of the Academy, while the soldier exclaimed, in bolder accents, that the ashes of Julian should have been mingled with those of Caesar, in the field of Mars, and among the ancient monuments of Roman virtue. The history of princes does not very frequently renew the example of a similar competition.

The Decline and Fall of the Roman Empire

A Source of Instruction

The attentive study of the military operations of Xenophon, or Caesar, or Frederic, when they are described by the same genius which conceived and executed them, may tend to improve (if such improvement can be wished) the art of destroying the human species.

The Decline and Fall of the Roman Empire

The Thuringians

The Thuringians served in the army of Attila: they traversed, both in their march and in their return, the territories of the Franks; and it was perhaps in this war that they exercised the cruelties which, about fourscore years afterwards, were revenged by the son of Clovis. They massacred their hostages, as well as their captives: two hundred young maidens were tortured with exquisite and unrelenting rage; their bodies were torn asunder by wild horses, or their bones were crushed under the weight of rolling waggons; and their unburied limbs were abandoned on the public roads as a prey to dogs and vultures. Such were those savage ancestors whose imaginary virtues have sometimes excited the praise and envy of civilised ages!

The Decline and Fall of the Roman Empire

St Simeon Stylites

Among these heroes of the monastic life, the name and genius of Simeon Stylites have been immortalised by the singular invention of an aërial penance. At the age of thirteen the young Syrian deserted the profession of a shepherd, and threw himself into an austere monastery. After a long and painful noviciate, in which Simeon was repeatedly saved from pious suicide, he established his residence on a mountain, about thirty or forty miles to the east of Antioch. Within the space of a *mandra*, or circle of stones, to which he had attached himself by a ponderous chain, he ascended a column, which was successively raised from the height of nine, to that of sixty, feet from the ground. In this last and lofty station, the Syrian Anachoret resisted the heat of thirty summers, and the cold of as many winters. Habit and exercise instructed him to maintain his dangerous situation without fear or giddiness, and successively to assume the different postures of devotion. He sometimes prayed in an erect attitude, with his outstretched arms in the figure of a cross; but his most familiar practice was that of bending his meagre skeleton from the forehead to the feet; and a curious spectator, after numbering twelve hundred and forty-four repetitions, at length desisted from the endless account.

The Decline and Fall of the Roman Empire

The Influence of Mahomet

It is not the propagation, but the permanency of his religion, that deserves our wonder: the same pure and perfect impression which he engraved at Mecca and Medina is preserved, after the revolutions of twelve centuries, by the Indian, the African, and the Turkish proselytes of the Koran. If the

Christian apostles, St Peter or St Paul, could return to the Vatican, they might possibly inquire the name of the Deity who is worshipped with such mysterious rites in that magnificent temple: at Oxford or Geneva they would experience less surprise; but it might still be incumbent on them to peruse the catechism of the church, and to study the orthodox commentators on their own writings and the words of their Master. But the Turkish dome of St Sophia, with an increase of splendour and size, represents the humble tabernacle erected at Medina by the hands of Mahomet. The Mahometans have uniformly withstood the temptation of reducing the object of their faith and devotion to a level with the senses and imagination of man. 'I believe in one God, and Mahomet the apostle of God,' is the simple and invariable profession of Islam. The intellectual image of the Deity has never been degraded by any visible idol; the honours of the prophet have never transgressed the measure of human virtue; and his living precepts have restrained the gratitude of his disciples within the bounds of reason and religion.

The Decline and Fall of the Roman Empire

St Bernard of Clairvaux

In speech, in writing, in action, Bernard stood high above his rivals and contemporaries; his compositions are not devoid of wit and eloquence; and he seems to have preserved as much reason and humanity as may be reconciled with the character of a saint.

The Decline and Fall of the Roman Empire

Bajazet Threatens Rome

In the pride of victory, Bajazet threatened that he would besiege Buda; that he would subdue the adjacent countries of Germany and Italy; and that he would feed his horse with a bushel of oats on the altar of St Peter at Rome. His progress was checked, not by the miraculous interposition of the apostle, not by a crusade of the Christian powers, but by a long and painful fit of the gout. The disorders of the moral, are sometimes corrected by those of the physical, world; and an acrimonious humour falling on a single fibre of one man may prevent or suspend the misery of nations.

The Decline and Fall of the Roman Empire

Petrarch

In the apprehension of modern times Petrarch is the Italian songster of Laura and love. In the harmony of his Tuscan rhymes Italy applauds, or rather adores, the father of her lyric poetry; and his verse, or at least his name, is repeated by the enthusiasm or affection of amorous sensibility. Whatever may be the private taste of a stranger, his slight and superficial knowledge should humbly acquiesce in the taste of a learned nation; yet I may hope or presume that the Italians do not compare the tedious uniformity of sonnets and elegies with the sublime compositions of their epic muse, the original wildness of Dante, the regular beauties of Tasso, and the boundless variety of the incomparable Ariosto. The merits of the lover I am still less qualified to appreciate: nor am I deeply interested in a metaphysical passion for a nymph so shadowy, that her existence has been questioned; for a matron so prolific, that she was delivered of eleven legitimate children, while her amorous swain sighed and sung at the fountain of Vaucluse. But in the eyes of Petrarch and those of his graver contemporaries his love was a sin, and Italian verse a frivolous amusement. His Latin works of philosophy, poetry, and eloquence established his serious reputation which was soon diffused from Avignon over France and Italy: his friends and disciples were multiplied in every city; and if the ponderous volume of his writings be now abandoned to a long repose, our gratitude must applaud the man who, by precept and example, revived the spirit and study of the Augustan age.

The Decline and Fall of the Roman Empire

Burke and the French Revolution

Burke's book is a most admirable medicine against the French disease, which has made too much progress even in this happy country [Switzerland]. I admire his eloquence. I approve his politics. I adore his chivalry, and I can forgive even his superstition. The primitive church, which I have treated with some freedom, was itself at that time an innovation, and I was attached to the old Pagan establishment. The French spread so many lies about the sentiments of the English nation, that I wish the most considerable men of all parties and descriptions would join in some public act, declaring themselves satisfied with, and resolved to support our present constitution. Such a declaration would have a wonderful effect in Europe; and, were I thought worthy, I myself would be proud to subscribe it.

letter to Lord Sheffield, 1790

Henry Fielding and the Habsburgs

Our immortal Fielding was of the younger branch of the Earls of Denbigh, who draw their origin from the Counts of Habsburg, the lineal descendants of Eltrico, in the seventh century, Duke of Alsace. Far different have been the fortunes of the English and German divisions of the family of Habsburg: the former, the knights and sheriffs of Leicestershire, have slowly risen to the dignity of a peerage; the latter, the Emperors of Germany, and Kings of Spain, have threatened the liberty of the old, and invaded the treasures of the new world. The successors of Charles the Fifth may disdain their brethren of England; but the romance of *Tom Jones*, that exquisite picture of human manners, will outlive the palace of the Escurial, and the imperial eagle of the house of Austria.

Autobiography, 1796

Closing Years

The present is a fleeting moment, the past is no more; and our prospect of futurity is dark and doubtful. This day may *possibly* be my last: but the laws of probability, so true in general, so fallacious in particular, still allow about fifteen years. I shall soon enter into the period which, as the most agreeable of his long life, was selected by the judgement and experience of the sage Fontenelle. His choice is approved by the eloquent historian of nature, who fixes our moral happiness to the mature season in which our passions are supposed to be calmed, our duties fulfilled, our ambition satisfied, our fame and fortune established on a solid basis. In private conversation, that great and amiable man added the weight of his own experience; and this autumnal felicity might be exemplified in the lives of Voltaire, Hume, and many other men of letters. I am far more inclined to embrace than to dispute this comfortable doctrine. I will not suppose any premature decay of the mind or body; but I must reluctantly observe that two causes, the abbreviation of time, and the failure of hope, will always tinge with a browner shade the evening of life.

Autobiography

THOMAS PAINE
1737–1809

A Necessary Evil

Some writers have so confounded society with government, as to leave little or no distinction between them; whereas they are not only different, but have different origins. Society is produced by our wants, and government by our wickedness; the former promotes our happiness *positively* by uniting our affections, the latter *negatively* by restraining our vices. The one encourages intercourse, the other creates distinctions. The first is a patron, the last a punisher.

Society in every state is a blessing, but Government, even in its best state, is but a necessary evil; in its worst state an intolerable one: for when we suffer, or are exposed to the same miseries *by a Government*, which we might expect in a country *without Government*, our calamity is heightened by reflecting that we furnish the means by which we suffer. Government, like dress, is the badge of lost innocence; the palaces of kings are built upon the ruins of the bowers of paradise. For were the impulses of conscience clear, uniform and irresistibly obeyed, man would need no other lawgiver; but that not being the case, he finds it necessary to surrender up a part of his property to furnish means for the protection of the rest; and this he is induced to do by the same prudence which in every other case advises him, out of two evils to choose the least. Wherefore, security being the true design and end of government, it unanswerably follows that whatever form thereof appears most likely to ensure it to us, with the least expense and greatest benefit, is preferable to all others.

Common Sense, 1776

A Rallying-Cry

These are the times that try men's souls. The summer soldier and the sunshine patriot will, in this crisis, shrink from the service of their country; but he that stands it now, deserves the love and thanks of man and woman. Tyranny, like hell, is not easily conquered; yet we have this consolation with us, that the harder the conflict, the more glorious the triumph. What we obtain too cheap, we esteem too lightly: it is dearness only that gives everything its value. Heaven knows how to put a proper price upon its goods; and it would be strange indeed if so celestial an article as freedom should not be highly rated. Britain, with an army to enforce her tyranny, has declared that she has a right (not only to tax) but 'to bind us in all cases whatsoever,' and if being bound in that manner is not slavery, then is there not such a thing as slavery upon earth. Even the expression is impious; for so unlimited a power can belong only to God.

The American Crisis: I (December 1776)

Welcoming a British General to America

[addressed to General Sir William Howe]

The usual honors of the dead, to be sure, are not sufficiently sublime to escort a character like you to the republic of dust and ashes; for however men may differ in their ideas of grandeur or of government here, the grave is nevertheless a perfect republic. Death is not the monarch of the dead, but of the dying. The moment he obtains a conquest he loses a subject, and, like the foolish king you serve, will, in the end, war himself out of all his dominions.

As a proper preliminary towards the arrangement of your funeral honors, we readily admit of your new rank of *knighthood.* The title is perfectly in character, and is your own, more by merit than creation. There are knights of various orders, from the knight of the windmill to the knight of the post. The former is your patron for exploits, and the latter will assist you in settling your accounts. No honorary title could be more happily applied! The ingenuity is sublime! And your royal master has discovered more genius in fitting you therewith, than in generating the most finished figure for a button, or descanting on the properties of a button mould.

The American Crisis: V (March 1778)

A New Era

If systems of government can be introduced, less expensive, and more productive of general happiness, than those which have existed, all attempts to oppose their progress will in the end be fruitless. Reason, like time, will make its own way, and prejudice will fall in a combat with interest. If universal peace, civilization, and commerce, are ever to be the happy lot of man, it cannot be accomplished but by a revolution in the system of governments. All the monarchical governments are military. War is their trade, plunder and revenue their objects. While such governments continue, peace has not the absolute security of a day. What is the history of all monarchical governments, but a disgustful picture of human wretchedness, and the accidental respite of a few years' repose? Wearied with war, and tired with human butchery, they sat down to rest, and called it peace. This certainly is not the condition that Heaven intended for man; and if *this be monarchy*, well might monarchy be reckoned among the sins of the Jews.

The revolutions which formerly took place in the world, had nothing in them that interested the bulk of mankind. They extended only to a change of persons and measures, but not of principles, and rose or fell among the common transactions of the moment. What we now behold, may not improperly be called a '*counter-revolution.*' Conquest and tyranny, at some early period, dispossessed man of his rights, and he is now recovering them. And as the tide of all human affairs has its ebb and flow in directions contrary to each other, so also is it in this. Government founded on a *moral theory, on a system of universal peace, on the indefeasible hereditary Rights of Man*, is now revolving from west to east, by a stronger impulse than the government of the sword revolved from east to west. It interests not particular individuals, but nations, in its progress, and promises a new era to the human race.

The Rights of Man, 1791–2

The Doctrine of Redemption

If I owe a person money and cannot pay him, and he threatens to put me in prison, another person can take the debt upon himself and pay it for me; but if I have committed a crime, every circumstance of the case is changed; moral justice cannot take the innocent for the guilty, even if the innocent would offer itself. To suppose justice to do this is to destroy the principle of its existence, which is the thing itself; it is then no longer justice, it is indiscriminate revenge. This single reflection will show that the doctrine of redemption is founded on a mere pecuniary idea corresponding to that of a debt which another person might pay; and as this pecuniary idea corresponds again with the system of second redemption, obtained through the means of money given to the church for pardons, the probability is that the same persons fabricated both the one and the other of those theories: and that in truth there is no such thing as redemption—that it is fabulous, and that man stands in the same relative condition with his Maker as he ever did stand since man existed, and that it is his greatest consolation to think so.

The Age of Reason, 1794

WILLIAM BARTRAM

1739–1823

The Alligators of Florida

The alligator when full grown is a very large and terrible creature, and of prodigious strength, activity and swiftness in the water. I have seen them twenty feet in length, and some are supposed to be twenty-two or twenty-three feet. Their body is as large as that of a horse; their shape exactly resembles that of a lizard, except their tail, which is flat or cuneiform, being compressed on each side, and gradually diminishing from the abdomen to the extremity, which, with the whole body is covered with horny plates or squamae, impenetrable when on the body of the live animal, even to a rifle ball, except about their head and just behind their fore-legs or arms, where it is said they are only vulnerable. The head of a full grown one is about three feet, and the mouth opens nearly the same length; their eyes are small in proportion, and seem sunk deep in the head, by means of the prominency of the brows; the nostrils are large, inflated and prominent on the top, so that the head in the water resembles, at a distance, a great chunk of wood floating about. Only the upper jaw moves, which they raise almost perpendicular, so as to form a right angle with the lower one. In the fore-part of the upper jaw, on each side, just under the nostrils, are two very large, thick, strong teeth or tusks, not very sharp, but rather the shape of a cone: these are as white as the finest polished ivory, and are not covered by any skin or lips, and always in sight, which gives the creature a frightful appearance: in the lower jaw are holes opposite to these teeth, to receive them: when they clap their jaws together it causes a surprising noise, like that which is made by forcing a heavy plank with violence upon the ground, and may be heard at a great distance.

But what is yet more surprising to a stranger, is the incredible loud and terrifying roar, which they are capable of making, especially in the spring season, their breeding time. It most resembles very heavy distant thunder, not only shaking the air and waters, but causing the earth to tremble; and when hundreds and thousands are roaring at the same time, you can scarcely be persuaded, but that the whole globe is violently and dangerously agitated.

Travels Through North and South Carolina, 1791

JAMES BOSWELL

1740–1795

Thoughts During a Sermon

I went to St. James's Church and heard service and a good sermon on 'By what means shall a young man learn to order his ways,' in which the advantages of early piety were well displayed. What a curious, inconsistent thing is the mind of man! In the midst of divine service I was laying plans for having women, and yet I had the most sincere feelings of religion. I imagine that my want of belief is the occasion of this, so that I can have all the feelings. I would try to make out a little consistency this way. I have a warm heart and a vivacious fancy. I am therefore given to love, and also to piety or gratitude to God, and to the most brilliant and showy method of public worship.

Journals, November 1762

Like Lambs upon Moffat Hill

How easily and cleverly do I write just now! I am really pleased with myself; words come skipping to me like lambs upon Moffat Hill; and I turn my periods smoothly and imperceptibly like a skilful wheelwright turning tops in a turning-loom. There's fancy! There's simile! In short, I am at present a genius: in that does my opulence consist, and not in base metal.

Journals, February 1763

The Great Mr Samuel Johnson

I drank tea at Davies's in Russell Street, and about seven came in the great Mr Samuel Johnson, whom I have so long wished to see. Mr Davies introduced me to him. As I knew his mortal antipathy at the Scotch, I cried to Davies, 'Don't tell where I come from.' However, he said, 'From Scotland.' 'Mr Johnson,' said I, 'indeed I come from Scotland, but I cannot help it.' 'Sir,' replied he, 'that, I find, is what a very great many of your countrymen cannot help.' Mr Johnson is a man of a most dreadful appearance. He is a very big man, is troubled with sore eyes, the palsy, and the king's evil. He is very slovenly in his dress and speaks with a most uncouth voice. Yet his great knowledge and strength of expression command vast respect and render him very excellent company. He has great humour and is a worthy man. But his dogmatical roughness of manners is disagreeable. I shall mark what I remember of his conversation.

Journals, May 1763

Recovering His Spirits

At night Temple, Claxton, Bob, and I went to Vauxhall by water. Somehow or another, I was very low-spirited and melancholy, and could not relish that gay entertainment, and was very discontent. I left my company, and mounting on the back of a hackney-coach, rattled away to town in the attitude of a footman. The whimsical oddity of this, the jolting of the machine, and the soft breeze of the evening made me very well again.

Journals, June 1763

A First Interview with Voltaire

At last Monsieur de Voltaire opened the door of his apartment, and stepped forth. I surveyed him with eager attention, and found him just as his print had made me conceive him. He received me with dignity, and that air of the world which a Frenchman acquires in such perfection. He had a slate-blue, fine frieze greatcoat night-gown, and a three-knotted wig. He sat erect upon his chair, and simpered when he spoke. He was not in spirits, nor I neither. All I presented was the 'foolish face of wondering praise.'

We talked of Scotland. He said the Glasgow editions were 'très belles.' I said, 'An Academy of Painting was also established there, but it did not succeed. Our Scotland is no country for that.' He replied with a keen archness, 'No; to paint well it is necessary to have warm feet. It's hard to paint when your feet are cold.' Another would have given a long dissertation on the coldness of our climate. Monsieur de Voltaire gave the very essence of raillery in half a dozen words.

I mentioned the severe criticism which the *Gazette littéraire* has given upon Lord Kames's *Elements.* I imagined it to be done by Voltaire, but would not ask him. He repeated me several of the *bons mots* in it, with an air that confirmed me in my idea of his having written this criticism. He called my Lord always 'ce Monsieur Kames'.

I told him that Mr Johnson and I intended to make a tour through the Hebrides, the Northern Isles of Scotland. He smiled, and cried, 'Very well; but I shall remain here. You will allow me to stay here?' 'Certainly.' 'Well then, go. I have no objections at all.'

I asked him if he still spoke English. He replied, 'No. To speak English one must place the tongue between the teeth, and I have lost my teeth.'

Journals, 1764

In the Highlands

A redcoat of the 15th regiment, whether officer or only sergeant I could not be sure, came to the house in his way to the mountains to shoot deer, which it seems the Laird of Glenmorison does not hinder anybody to do. Few, indeed, can do them harm. We had him to breakfast with us. We got away about eight. M'Queen walked some miles to give us a convoy. He had, in 1745, joined the Highland army at Fort Augustus, and continued in it till after battle of Culloden. As he narrated the particulars of that ill-advised but brave attempt, I could not refrain from tears. There is a certain association of ideas in my mind upon that subject, by which I am strongly affected. The very Highland names, or the sound of a bagpipe, will stir my blood, and fill me with a mixture of melancholy and respect for courage; with pity for the unfortunate, and superstitious regard for antiquity, and thoughtless inclination for war; in short, with a crowd of sensations with which sober rationality has nothing to do.

Journal of a Tour of the Hebrides, 1785

Some Johnsonian Singularities

That the most minute singularities which belonged to him, and made very observable parts of his appearance and manner, may not be omitted, it is requisite to mention, that while talking or even musing as he sat in his chair, he commonly held his head to one side towards his right shoulder, and shook it in a tremulous manner, moving his body backwards and forwards, and rubbing his left knee in the same direction, with the palm of his hand. In the intervals of articulating he made various sounds with his mouth, sometimes as if ruminating, or what is called chewing the cud, sometimes giving a half whistle, sometimes making his tongue play backwards from the roof of his mouth, as if clucking like a hen, and sometimes protruding it against his upper gums in front, as if pronouncing quickly under his breath, *too, too, too*: all this accompanied sometimes with a thoughtful look, but more frequently with a smile. Generally when he had concluded a period, in the course of a dispute, by which time he was a good deal exhausted by violence and vociferation, he used to blow out his breath like a Whale. This I suppose was a relief to his lungs; and seemed in him to be a contemptuous mode of expression, as if he had made the arguments of his opponent fly like chaff before the wind.

The Life of Samuel Johnson, 1791

Good Talk

When I called upon Dr Johnson next morning, I found him highly satisfied with his colloquial prowess the preceding evening. 'Well (said he) we had good talk.'
BOSWELL: 'Yes, Sir; you tossed and gored several persons.'

1769; *Life of Johnson*

Putting His Books in Order

On Wednesday, April 3, in the morning I found him very busy putting his books in order, and as they were generally very old ones, clouds of dust were flying around him. He had on a pair of large gloves such as hedgers use. His present appearance put me in mind of my uncle, Dr Boswell's description of him, 'A robust genius, born to grapple with whole libraries.'

1776; *Life of Johnson*

At Dinner with John Wilkes

When we entered Mr Dilly's drawing room, he found himself in the midst of a company he did not know. I kept myself snug and silent, watching how he would conduct himself. I observed him whispering to Mr Dilly, 'Who is that gentleman, Sir?'—'Mr Arthur Lee.'—JOHNSON. 'Too, too, too,' (under his breath,) which was one of his habitual mutterings. Mr Arthur Lee could not but be very obnoxious to Johnson, for he was not only a *patriot* but an *American*. He was afterwards minister from the United States at the court of Madrid. 'And who is the gentleman in lace?'—'Mr Wilkes, Sir.' This information confounded him still more: he had some difficulty to restrain himself, and taking up a book, sat down upon a window-seat and read, or at least kept his eye upon it intently for some time, till he composed himself. His feelings, I dare say, were aukward enough. But he no doubt recollected his having rated me for supposing that he could be at all disconcerted by any company, and he, therefore, resolutely set himself to behave quite as an easy man of the world, who could adapt himself at once to the disposition and manners of those whom he might chance to meet.

The cheering sound of 'Dinner is upon the table,' dissolved his reverie, and we *all* sat down without any symptom of ill humour. There were present, beside Mr Wilkes, and Mr Arthur Lee, who was an old companion of mine when he studied physick at Edinburgh, Mr (now Sir John) Miller, Dr Lettsom, and Mr Slater the druggist. Mr Wilkes placed himself next to Dr Johnson, and behaved to him with so much attention and politeness, that he gained upon him insensibly. No man eat more heartily than Johnson, or loved better what was nice and delicate. Mr Wilkes was very assiduous in helping him to some fine veal. 'Pray give me leave, Sir:—It is better here—A little of the brown—Some fat, Sir—A little of the stuffing—Some gravy—Let me have the pleasure of giving you some butter—Allow me to recommend a squeeze of this orange;—or the lemon, perhaps, may have more zest.'—'Sir, Sir, I am obliged to you, Sir,' cried Johnson, bowing, and turning his head to him with a look for some time of 'surly virtue,' but, in a short while, of complacency.

1776; *Life of Johnson*

Defending His Style

I read to him a letter which Lord Monboddo had written to me, containing some critical remarks upon the style of his *Journey to the Western Islands of Scotland*. His Lordship praised the very fine passage upon landing at Icolmkill; but his own style being exceedingly dry and hard, he disapproved of the richness of Johnson's language, and of his frequent use of metaphorical expressions. JOHNSON. 'Why, Sir, this criticism would be just, if in my style, superfluous words, or words too big for the thoughts, could be pointed out; but this I do not believe can be done. For instance; in the passage which Lord Monboddo admires, 'We were now treading that illustrious region,' the word *illustrious*, contributes nothing to the mere narration; for the fact might be told without it: but it is not, therefore, superfluous; for it wakes the mind to peculiar attention, where something of more than usual importance is to be presented. 'Illustrious!'—for what? and then the sentence proceeds to expand the circumstances connected with Iona. And, Sir, as to metaphorical expression, that is a great excellence in style, when it is used with propriety, for it gives you two ideas for one;—conveys the meaning more luminously, and generally with a perception of delight.'

1777; *Life of Johnson*

Voracity

Every thing about his character and manners was forcible and violent; there never was any moderation; many a day did he fast, many a year did he refrain from wine; but when he did eat, it was voraciously; when he did drink wine, it was copiously. He could practise abstinence, but not temperance.

Life of Johnson

A Very Fine Cat

Nor would it be just, under this head, to omit the fondness which he shewed for animals which he had taken under his protection. I never shall forget the indulgence with which he treated Hodge, his cat: for whom he himself used to go out and buy oysters, lest the servants having that trouble should take a dislike to the poor creature. I am, unluckily, one of those who have an antipathy to a cat, so that I am uneasy when in the room with one; and I own, I frequently suffered a good deal from the presence of this same Hodge. I recollect him one day scrambling up Dr Johnson's breast, apparently with much satisfaction, while my friend smiling and half-whistling, rubbed down his back, and pulled him by the tail; and when I observed he was a fine cat, saying, 'Why yes, Sir, but I have had cats whom I liked better than this;' and then as if perceiving Hodge to be out of countenance, adding, 'but he is a very fine cat, a very fine cat indeed.'

Life of Johnson

Johnson's and Boswell's Last Meeting

I accompanied him in Sir Joshua Reynolds's coach, to the entry of Bolt-court. He asked me whether I would not go with him to his house; I declined it, from an apprehension that my spirits would sink. We bade adieu to each other affectionately in the carriage. When he had got down upon the foot-pavement, he called out, 'Fare you well;' and without looking back, sprung away with a kind of pathetick briskness, if I may use that expression, which seemed to indicate a struggle to conceal uneasiness, and impressed me with a foreboding of our long, long separation.

1784; *Life of Johnson*

'JUNIUS',
generally supposed to be
SIR PHILIP FRANCIS
1740–1818

A Prime Minister Castigated

What then, my Lord, is this the event of all the sacrifices you have made to Lord Bute's patronage, and to your own unfortunate ambition? Was it for this you abandoned your earliest friendships,—the warmest connexions of your youth, and all those honourable engagements, by which you once solicited, and might have acquired the esteem of your country? Have you secured no recompense for such a waste of honour?—Unhappy man! What party will receive the common deserter of all parties? Without a client to flatter, without a friend to console you, and with only one companion from the honest house of Bloomsbury, you must now retire into a dreadful solitude. At the most active period of life, you must quit the busy scene, and conceal yourself from the world, if you would hope to save the wretched remains of a ruined reputation. The vices operate like age,—bring on disease before its time, and in the prime of youth leave the character broken and exhausted.

Yet your conduct has been mysterious, as well as contemptible. Where is now that firmness, or obstinacy so long boasted of by your friends, and acknowledged by your enemies? We were taught to expect, that you would not leave the ruin of this country to be completed by other hands, but were determined either to gain a decisive victory over the constitution, or to perish bravely at least behind the last dyke of the prerogative. You knew the danger, and might have been provided for it. You took sufficient time to prepare for a meeting with your parliament, to confirm the mercenary fidelity of your dependants, and to suggest to your Sovereign a language suited to his dignity at least, if not to his benevolence and wisdom. Yet, while the whole kingdom was agitated with anxious expectation upon one great point, you meanly evaded the question, and, instead of the explicit firmness and decision of a King, gave us nothing but the misery of a ruined grazier, and the whining piety of a Methodist. We had reason to expect, that notice would have been taken of the petitions which the King has received from the English nation; and although I can conceive some personal motives for not yielding to them, I can find none, in common prudence or decency, for treating them with contempt. Be assured, my Lord, the English people will not tamely submit to this unworthy treatment;—they had a right to be heard, and their petitions, if not granted, deserved to be considered. Whatever be the real views and doctrine of a court, the Sovereign should be taught to preserve some forms of attention to his subjects, and if he will not redress their grievances, not to make them a topic of jest and mockery among lords and ladies of the bedchamber. Injuries may be atoned for and forgiven; but insults admit of no compensation. They degrade the mind in its own esteem, and force it to recover its level by revenge.

To the Duke of Grafton, *Public Advertiser*, 1770

HENRY FUSELI
1741–1825

Some Thoughts on Art and Artists

Some enter the gates of art with golden keys, and take their seats with dignity among the demi-gods of fame; some burst the doors and leap into a niche with savage power; thousands consume their time in chinking useless keys, and aiming feeble pushes against the inexorable doors.

*

If you mean to reign dictator over the arts of your own times, assail not your rivals with the blustering tone of condemnation and rigid censure;—sap with conditional or lamenting praise—confine them to unfashionable excellence—exclude them from the avenues of fame.

*

The lessons of disappointment, humiliation and blunder, impress more than those of a thousand masters.

*

The male forms of Rubens are the brawny pulp of slaughtermen, his females are hillocks of roses: overwhelmed muscles, dislocated bones, and distorted joints are swept along in a gulph of colours, as herbage, trees and shrubs are whirled, tossed, or absorbed by vernal inundation.

*

The veiled eyes of Guercino's females dart insidious fire.

John Knowles, *Life and Writings of Henry Fuseli*, 1831

ARTHUR YOUNG
1741–1820

Cleanliness, French and English

In table-linen, they are, I think, cleaner and wiser than the English: that the change may be incessant, it is every where coarse. The idea of dining without a napkin seems ridiculous to a Frenchman, but in England we dine at the tables of people of tolerable fortune, without them. A journeyman carpenter in France has his napkin as regularly as his fork; and at an inn, the *fille* always lays a clean one to every cover that is spread in the kitchen, for the lowest order of pedestrian travellers. The expence of linen in England is enormous, from its fineness; surely a great change of that which is coarse, would be much more rational. In point of cleanliness, I think the merit of the two nations is divided; the French are cleaner in their persons, and the English in their houses; I speak of the mass of the people, and not of individuals of considerable fortune. A *bidet* in France is as universally in every apartment, as a bason to wash your hands, which is a trait of personal cleanliness I wish more common in England; on the other hand their necessary houses are temples of abomination; and the practice of spitting about a room, which is amongst the highest as well as the lowest ranks, is detestable: I have seen a gentleman spit so near the cloaths of a dutchess, that I have stared at his unconcern.

Travels in France, 1792

SIR JOSEPH BANKS
1743–1820

The Bell-Birds of New Zealand

17th Jan. 1770. This morn I was awaked by the singing of the birds ashore from whence we were distant not a quarter of a mile; the numbers of them were certainly very great, who seem'd to strain their throats with emulation; perhaps their voices were certainly the most melodious wild music I have ever heard, almost imitating small bells, but with the most tunable silver sound imaginable to which may be the distance was no small addition; on inquiring of our people I was told that they had observed them ever since we have been here and that they begin to sing at about one or two in the morn and continue till sunrise, after which they are silent all day like our nightingales.

Journal during Captain Cook's First Voyage in HMS Endeavour

THOMAS JEFFERSON
1743–1826

From The Declaration of Independence

When, in the course of human events, it becomes necessary for one people to dissolve the political bonds which have connected them with another, and to assume among the powers of the earth the separate and equal station to which the laws of Nature and of Nature's God entitle them, a decent respect to the opinions of mankind requires that they should declare the causes which impel them to the separation.

We hold these truths to be self evident: that all men are created equal; that they are endowed by their Creator with [*inherent and*] inalienable rights; that among these are life, liberty and the pursuit of happiness; that to secure these rights, governments are instituted among men, deriving their just powers from the consent of the governed; that whenever any form of government becomes destructive of these ends, it is the right of the people to alter or to abolish it, and to institute new government, laying its foundation on such principles, and organizing its powers in such form, as to them shall seem most likely to effect their safety and happiness.

A Declaration by the Representatives of the United States of America, in General Congress Assembled, 1776

Moral Science and the Moral Sense

Moral Philosophy. I think it lost time to attend lectures on this branch. He who made us would have been a pitiful bungler if he had made the rules of our moral conduct a matter of science. For one man of science there are thousands who are not. What would have become of them?

inherent and] in the version approved by Congress, this was changed to 'certain'

Man was destined for society. His morality, therefore, was to be formed to this object. He was endowed with a sense of right and wrong, merely relative to this. This sense is as much a part of his nature as the sense of hearing, seeing, feeling; it is the true foundation of morality, and not Tὸ Καλόν, truth, etc., as fanciful writers have imagined. The moral sense, or conscience, is as much a part of man as his leg or arm. It is given to all human beings in a stronger or weaker degree, as force of members is given them in a greater or less degree. It may be strengthened by exercise, as may any particular limb of the body. This sense is submitted, indeed, in some degree, to the guidance of reason; but it is a small stock which is required for this: even a less one than what we call common sense. State a moral case to a ploughman and a professor. The former will decide it as well, and often better than, the latter, because he has not been led astray by artificial rules. In this branch, therefore, read good books, because they will encourage, as well as direct your feelings. The writings of Sterne, particularly, form the best course of morality that ever was written. Besides these, read the books mentioned in the enclosed paper; and, above all things, lose no occasion of exercising your dispositions to be grateful, to be generous, to be charitable, to be humane, to be true, just, firm, orderly, courageous, etc. Consider every act of this kind as an exercise which will strengthen your moral faculties and increase your worth.

letter to Peter Carr, 1787

Puzzling over Plato

I amused myself with reading seriously Plato's *Republic.* I am wrong, however, in calling it amusement, for it was the heaviest taskwork I ever went through. I had occasionally before taken up some of his other works, but scarcely ever had patience to go through a whole dialogue. While reading through the whimsies, the puerilities and unintelligible jargon of this work, I laid it down often to ask myself how it could have been, that the world should have consented to give reputation to such nonsense as this? How the *soi-disant* Christian world, indeed, should have done it, is a piece of historical curiosity. But how could the Roman good sense do it? And particularly, how could Cicero bestow such eulogies on Plato? Although Cicero did not wield the dense logic of Demosthenes yet he was able, learned, laborious, practiced in the business of the world and honest. He could not be the dupe of mere style, of which he was himself the first master in the world.

letter to John Adams, 1814

Tὸ Καλόν] the beautiful

OLAUDAH EQUIANO

c.1745–1797

Aboard a Slave Ship

At last, when the ship we were in, had got in all her cargo, they made ready with many fearful noises, and we were all put under deck, so that we could not see how they managed the vessel. But this disappointment was the least of my sorrow. The stench of the hold while we were on the coast was so intolerably loathsome, that it was dangerous to remain there for any time, and some of us had been permitted to stay on the deck for the fresh air; but now that the whole ship's cargo were confined together, it became absolutely pestilential. The closeness of the place, and the heat of the climate, added to the number in the ship, which was so crowded that each had scarcely room to turn himself, almost suffocated us. This produced copious perspirations, so that the air soon became unfit for respiration, from a variety of loathsome smells, and brought on a sickness among the slaves, of which many died—thus falling victims to the improvident avarice, as I may call it, of their purchasers. This wretched situation was again aggravated by the galling of the chains, now become insupportable, and the filth of the necessary tubs, into which the children often fell, and were almost suffocated. The shrieks of the women, and the groans of the dying, rendered the whole a scene of horror almost inconceivable. Happily perhaps, for myself, I was soon reduced so low here that it was thought necessary to keep me almost always on deck; and from my extreme youth I was not put in fetters. In this situation I expected every hour to share the fate of my companions, some of whom were almost daily brought upon deck at the point of death, which I began to hope would soon put an end to my miseries. Often did I think many of the inhabitants of the deep much more happy than myself. I envied them the freedom they enjoyed, and as often wished I could change my condition for theirs. Every circumstance I met with, served only to render my state more painful, and heightened my apprehensions, and my opinion of the cruelty of the whites.

One day they had taken a number of fishes; and when they had killed and satisfied themselves with as many as they thought fit, to our astonishment who were on deck, rather than give any of them to us to eat, as we expected, they tossed the remaining fish into the sea again, although we begged and prayed for some as well as we could, but in vain; and some of my countrymen, being pressed by hunger, took an opportunity, when they thought no one saw them, of trying to get a little privately; but they were discovered, and the attempt procured them some very severe floggings. One day, when we had a smooth sea and moderate wind, two of my wearied countrymen who were chained together, (I was near them at the time,) preferring death to such a life of misery, somehow made through the nettings and jumped into the sea: immediately, another quite dejected fellow, who, on account of his illness, was suffered to be out of irons, also followed their example; and I believe many more would very soon have done the same, if they had not been prevented by the ship's crew, who were instantly alarmed. Those of us that were the most active, were in a moment put down under the deck, and there was such a noise and confusion amongst the people of the ship as I never heard before, to stop her, and get the boat out to go after the slaves. However, two of the wretches were drowned, but they got the other, and afterwards flogged him unmercifully, for thus attempting to prefer death to slavery.

The Interesting Narrative of the Life of Olaudah Equiano, 1789

WILLIAM HICKEY

1749–1830

A Disturbance in Calcutta

A day being appointed for the argument of the demurrer, the court by eight o'clock in the morning was crowded by the British inhabitants of Calcutta, both civil and military; but the Chief Justice, being indisposed, could not attend. The discussion was therefore postponed. This happened in the middle of the Mahomedan festival of the Mohurrem, during which the lowest orders of Mussulman, by swallowing large quantities of an intoxicating drug called bang, work themselves up to a state of absolute madness and commit great excess. Their zeal was increased that year by the Nabob Sydaat Ali being in Calcutta. Soon after Sir Robert Chambers and Mr Justice Hyde had taken their seats upon the bench and the common routine of business was entered upon, a prodigious mob assembled directly under the windows, when the beating of tom-toms (a small sort of drum in use all over Hindustan), and the shrill squeaking of their trumpets, made such a horrible din the counsellors could not possibly make themselves heard by the judges. Sir Robert therefore directed the constables in attendance to go down and disperse the people. In a few minutes, one of these constables, whose name was Roop, an old German, ran into court in great agitation, without his wig, crying out that he had been violently assailed by the mob who had severely beat him, carried off his hat and wig; and, upon his showing his staff of office, requiring peace in His Majesty's name, two English sailors, who were amongst the crowd, seized his said staff, swearing if that was the b——r's authority they would ram it up his a——e, and actually carried it off in triumph. Sir Robert Chambers, upon hearing this account, observed, 'Mr Constable, you need not be so very particular in your description.'

written 1778; *Memoirs*, first published 1913–25; first unexpurgated selection 1960

A Rejected Suitor

Upon my return to Bengal, I found my Margate acquaintance, Metcalfe, with the rank of major in the army, and filling the post of military storekeeper, a situation in those days the most lucrative in the Company's service, which he had attained by most perseveringly courting the heads of the Government. Shortly after his last arrival in Calcutta, he married Mrs Smith, widow of Major Smith of the Company's Infantry . . .

This fair dame (who is now Lady Metcalfe, her husband having purchased the title of baronet) had no one merit to recommend her, at least that I could discover, unless it was a great similarity in figure, in masculine vulgarity of manners, to his ci-devant favourite, that notorious jack whore, Mrs Cuyler. But, having expressed these unfavourable sentiments of the lady, it is only common candour to admit that everyone did not see with my eyes; for Mr William Pawson, an old civil servant of the Company's upon the Bengal establishment, was so deeply enamoured with her charms that, although she had not a single guinea in the world, he proposed marrying and settling a handsome sum upon her, an offer she spurned at with the utmost scorn. Notwithstanding which, the unhappy lover persevered in his endeavours to make her relent, renewing his attack three different times, all equally unsuccessful.

He was as worthy a creature as ever breathed, but clearly not the brightest genius. In proof of which I must state that I was once present with him in a large company, where matrimony was the topic under discussion. After much had been said pro and con upon the subject, Mrs Smith, looking full in Mr Pawson's face, with a marked and peculiar manner, and in a sharp, angry voice, said, 'I certainly cannot tell who is destined to be my future husband; but this I can confidently affirm, that I never will become the wife of *a fool*!' Poor Mr Pawson, who was on the next chair to the one I sat in, thereupon turned to me and, with the utmost simplicity, accompanied by a long-drawn sigh, said, '*That's me!*'

written 1783; *Memoirs*

THOMAS ERSKINE, FIRST BARON ERSKINE
1750–1823

The Natural Parent of Resistance

Engage the people by their affections, convince their reason, and they will be loyal from the only principle that can make loyalty sincere, vigorous, or rational—a conviction that it is their truest interest and that their government is for their good. Constraint is the natural parent of resistance, and a frequent proof that reason is not on the side of those who use it. You must all remember Lucian's pleasant story: Jupiter and a countryman were walking together, conversing with great freedom and familiarity upon the subject of heaven and earth. The countryman listened with attention and acquiescence while Jupiter strove only to convince him; but happening to hint a doubt, Jupiter turned hastily round and threatened him with his thunder. 'Ah Ah!' says the countryman, 'now, Jupiter, I know that you are wrong: you are always wrong when you appeal to your thunder.'

Speech as defence counsel for Thomas Paine, 1792

JAMES MADISON
1751–1836

Checks and Balances

In order to lay a due foundation for that separate and distinct exercise of the different powers of government, which to a certain extent is admitted on all hands to be essential to the preservation of liberty, it is evident that each department should have a will of its own; and consequently should be so constituted that the members of each should have as little agency as possible in the appointment of the members of the others . . .

It is equally evident, that the members of each department should be as little dependent as possible on those of the others, for the emoluments annexed to their offices. Were the executive magistrate, or the judges, not independent of the legislature in this particular, their independence in every other would be merely nominal.

But the great security against a gradual concentration of the several powers in the same department, consists in giving to those who administer each department the necessary constitutional means and personal motives to resist encroachments of the others. The provision for defence must in this, as in all other cases, be made commensurate to the danger of attack. Ambition must be made to counteract ambition. The interest of the man must be connected with the constitutional rights of the place. It may be a reflection on human nature that such devices should be necessary to control the abuses of government. But what is government itself but the greatest of all reflections on human nature? If men were angels, no government would be necessary. If angels were to govern men, neither external nor internal controls on government would be necessary. In framing a government which is to be administered by men over men, the great difficulty lies in this: you must first enable the government to control the governed; and in the next place oblige it to control itself. A dependence on the people is, no doubt, the primary control on the government; but experience has taught mankind the necessity of auxiliary precautions.

The Federalist, no. 51 (1788)

FANNY BURNEY

1752–1840

A Man of Gallantry

Such was the conversation till tea-time, when the appearance of Mr Smith gave a new turn to the discourse.

Miss Branghton desired me to remark with what a *smart air* he entered the room, and asked me if he had not very much a *quality look*?

'Come,' cried he, advancing to us, 'you ladies must not sit together; wherever I go I always make it a rule to part the ladies.'

And then, handing Miss Branghton to the next chair, he seated himself between us.

'Well, now, ladies, I think we sit very well. What say you? for my part I think it was a very good motion.'

'If my cousin likes it,' said Miss Branghton, 'I'm sure I've no objection.'

'O,' cried he, 'I always study what the ladies like,—that's my first thought. And, indeed, it is but natural that you should like best to sit by the gentlemen, for what can you find to say to one another?'

'Say!' cried young Branghton; 'O, never you think of that, they'll find enough to say, I'll be sworn. You know the women are never tired of talking.'

'Come, come, Tom,' said Mr Smith, 'don't be severe upon the ladies; when I'm by, you know I always take their part.'

Soon after, when Miss Branghton offered me some cake, this man of gallantry said, 'Well, if I was that lady, I'd never take any thing from a woman.'

'Why not, Sir?'

'Because I should be afraid of being poisoned for being so handsome.'

'Who is severe upon the ladies *now*?' said I.

'Why, really, Ma'am, it was a slip of the tongue; I did not intend to say such a thing, but one can't always be on one's guard.'

Evelina, 1778

Polite Company

The party was Mr and Mrs Vanbrugh—the former a good sort of man—the latter, Captain Bouchier says, reckons herself a woman of humour, but she kept it prodigious snug; Lord Huntingdon, a very deaf old lord; Sir Robert Pigot, a very thin old baronet; Mr Tyson, a very civil master of the ceremonies; Mr and Mrs White, a very insignificant couple; Sir James C——, a bawling old man; two Misses C——, a pair of tonish misses; Mrs and Miss Byron; Miss W——, and certain others I knew nothing of.

Diary and Letters, 1780

A Royal Equerry

One evening, when he had been out very late hunting with the King, he assumed so doleful an air of weariness, that had not Miss P——exerted her utmost powers to revive him, he would not have uttered a word the whole night; but when once brought forward, he gave us more entertainment than ever, by relating his hardships.

'After all the labours,' cried he, 'of the chase, all the riding, the trotting, the galloping, the leaping, the—with your favour, ladies, I beg pardon, I was going to say a strange word, but the—the perspiration,—and—and all that—after being wet through over head, and soused through under feet, and popped into ditches, and jerked over gates, what lives we do lead! Well, it's all honour! that's my only comfort! Well, after all this, fagging away like mad from eight in the morning to five or six in the afternoon, home we come, looking like so many drowned rats, with not a dry thread about us, nor a morsel within us—sore to the very bone, and forced to smile all the time! and then, after all this, what do you think follows?—"Here, Goldsworthy," cried his Majesty: so up I comes to him, bowing profoundly, and my hair dripping down to my shoes; "Goldsworthy," cries his Majesty. "Sir," says I, smiling agreeably, with the rheumatism just creeping all over me! but still, expecting something a little comfortable, I wait patiently to know his gracious pleasure, and then, "Here, Goldsworthy, I say!" he cries, "will you have a little barley water!" Barley water in such a plight as that! Fine compensation for a wet jacket, truly!—barley water! I never heard of such a thing in my life! Barley water after a whole day's hard hunting!'

'And pray did you drink it?'

'I drink it?—drink barley water? No, no; not come to that neither! But there it was, sure enough! in a jug fit for a sick room; just such a thing as you put upon a hob in a chimney, for some poor miserable soul that keeps his bed! just such a thing as that!—And, "Here, Goldsworthy," says his Majesty, "here's the barley water"!'

'And did the King drink it himself?'

'Yes, God bless his Majesty! but I was too humble a subject to do the same!—barley water, quoth I!—ha! ha!—a fine treat truly!—Heaven defend me! I'm not come to that, neither! bad enough too, but not so bad as that.'

Diary and Letters, 1786

Burke at a Dinner-Party

At dinner Mr Burke sat next Mrs Crewe, and I had the happiness to be seated next Mr Burke; and my other neighbour was his amiable son.

The dinner, and the dessert when the servants were removed, were delightful. How I wish my dear Susanna and Fredy could meet this wonderful man when he is easy, happy, and with people he cordially likes! But politics, even on his own side, must always be excluded; his irritability is so terrible on that theme that it gives immediately to his face the expression of a man who is going to defend himself from murderers.

Diary and Letters, 1792

Brussels During the Battle of Waterloo

At the same time the 'hurrah!' came nearer. I flew to the window; my host and hostess came also, crying, '*Bonaparte est pris! le voilà! le voilà!*'

I then saw on a noble war-horse in full equipment, a general in the splendid uniform of France; but visibly disarmed, and, to all appearance, tied to his horse, or, at least, held on, so as to disable him from making any effort to gallop off, and surrounded, preceded, and followed by a crew of roaring wretches, who seemed eager for the moment when he should be lodged where they had orders to conduct him, that they might unhorse, strip, pillage him, and divide the spoil.

His high, feathered, glittering helmet he had pressed down as low as he could on his forehead, and I could not discern his face; but I was instantly certain he was not Bonaparte, on finding the whole commotion produced by the rifling crew above-mentioned, which, though it might be guided, probably, by some subaltern officer, who might have the captive in charge, had left the field of battle at a moment when none other could be spared, as all the attendant throng were evidently amongst the refuse of the army followers.

I was afterwards informed that this unfortunate general was the Count Lobau.

Diary and Letters, 1815

THOMAS BEWICK
1753–1828

A Self-Taught Artist

I was for some time kept at reading, writing, and figures—how long, I know not, but I know that as soon as my question was done upon my slate, I spent as much time as I could find in filling with my pencil all the unoccupied spaces, with representations of such objects as struck my fancy; and these were rubbed out, for fear of a beating, before my question was given in. As soon as I reached fractions, decimals, etc., I was put to learn Latin, and in this I was for some time complimented by my master for the great progress I was making; but, as I never knew for what purpose I had to learn it, and was wearied out with getting off long tasks, I rather flagged in this department of my education, and the margins of my books, and every space of spare and blank paper, became filled with various kinds of devices or scenes I had met with; and these were often accompanied with wretched rhymes explanatory of them. As soon as I filled all the blank spaces in my books, I had recourse, at all spare times, to the gravestones and the floor of the church porch, with a bit of chalk, to give vent to this propensity of mind of figuring whatever I had seen. At that time I had never heard of the word 'drawing'; nor did I know of any other paintings beside the king's arms in the church, and the signs in Ovingham of the Black Bull, the White Horse, the Salmon, and the Hounds and Hare. I always thought I could make a far better hunting scene than the latter: the others were beyond my hand. I remember once of my master overlooking me while I was very busy with my chalk in the porch, and of his putting me very greatly to the blush by ridiculing and calling me a conjuror. My father, also, found a deal of fault for 'mis-spending my time in such idle pursuits'; but my propensity for drawing was so rooted that nothing could deter me from persevering in it; and many of my evenings at home were spent in filling the flags of the floor and the hearthstone with my chalky designs.

After I had long scorched my face in this way, a friend, in compassion, furnished me with some paper upon which to execute my designs. Here I had more scope. Pen and ink, and the juice of the brambleberry, made a grand change. These were succeeded by a camel-hair pencil and shells of colours; and, thus supplied, I become completely set up; but of patterns, or drawings, I had none. The beasts and birds which enlivened the beautiful scenery of woods and wilds surrounding my native hamlet, furnished me with an endless supply of subjects. I now, in the estimation of my rustic neighbours, became an eminent painter, and the walls of their houses were ornamented with an abundance of my rude productions, at a very cheap rate. These chiefly consisted of particular hunting scenes, in which the portraits of the hunters, the horses, and of every dog in the pack, were, in their opinion, *as well as my own*, faithfully delineated.

A Memoir, first published 1862

WILLIAM GODWIN
1756–1836

Party Politics and Individual Judgment

Party has a more powerful tendency, than perhaps any other circumstance in human affairs, to render the mind quiescent and stationary. Instead of making each man an individual, which the interest of the whole requires, it resolves all understandings into one common mass, and subtracts from each the varieties, that could alone distinguish him from a brute machine. Having learned the creed of our party, we have no longer any employment for those faculties, which might lead us to detect its errors. We have arrived, in our own opinion, at the last page of the volume of truth; and all that remains, is by some means to effect the adoption of our sentiments, as the standard of right to the whole race of mankind. . . . In fine, from these considerations it appears, that associations, instead of promoting the growth and diffusion of truth, tend only to check its accumulation, and render its operation, as far as possible, unnatural and mischievous.

There is another circumstance to be mentioned, strongly calculated to confirm this position. A necessary attendant upon political associations, is harangue and declamation. A majority of the members of any numerous popular society, will look to these harangues, as the school in which they are to study, in order to become the reservoirs of practical truth to the rest of mankind. But harangues and declamation, lead to passion, and not to knowledge. The memory of the hearer is crowded with pompous nothings, with images and not arguments. He is never permitted to be sober enough, to weigh things with an unshaken hand. It would be inconsistent with the art of eloquence, to strip the subject of every meretricious ornament. Instead of informing the understanding of the hearer by a slow and regular progression, the orator must beware of detail, must render every thing rapid, and from time to time work up the passions of his hearers to a tempest of applause. Truth can scarcely be acquired in crowded halls and amidst noisy debates. Where hope and fear, triumph and resentment, are perpetually afloat, the severer faculties of investigation are compelled to quit the field. Truth dwells with contemplation. We can seldom make much progress in the business of disentangling error and delusion, but in sequestered privacy, or in the tranquil interchange of sentiments that takes place between two persons.

An Enquiry Concerning Political Justice, 1793

WILLIAM BLAKE
1757–1827

Fun, Mirth, Happiness, and Imagination

I percieve that your Eye is perverted by Caricature Prints, which ought not to abound so much as they do. Fun I love, but too much Fun is of all things the most loathsom. Mirth is better than Fun, & Happiness is better than Mirth. I feel that a Man may be happy in This World. And I know that This World Is a World of imagination & Vision. I see Every thing I paint In This World, but Every body does not see alike. To the Eyes of a Miser a Guinea is more beautiful than the Sun, & a bag worn with the use of Money has more beautiful proportions than a Vine filled with Grapes. The tree which moves some to tears of joy is in the Eyes of others only a Green thing that stands in the way. Some See Nature all Ridicule & Deformity, & by these I shall not regulate my proportions; & Some Scarce see Nature at all. But to the Eyes of the Man of Imagination, Nature is Imagination itself. As a man is, So he Sees. As the Eye is formed, such are its Powers. You certainly Mistake, when you say that the Visions of Fancy are not to be found in This World. To Me This World is all One continued Vision of Fancy or Imagination & I feel Flatter'd when I am told so. What is it sets Homer, Virgil & Milton in so high a rank of Art? Why is the Bible more Entertaining & Instructive than any other book? Is it not because they are addressed to the Imagination, which is Spiritual Sensation, & but mediately to the Understanding or Reason? Such is True Painting, and such was alone valued by the Greeks & the best modern Artists.

letter to John Trusler, 1799

The Canterbury Pilgrims

The characters of Chaucer's Pilgrims are the characters which compose all ages and nations. As one age falls, another rises, different to mortal sight, but to immortals only the same; for we see the same characters repeated again and again, in animals, vegetables, minerals, and in men. Nothing new occurs in identical existence; accident ever varies, substance can never suffer change nor decay.

Of Chaucer's characters, as described in his *Canterbury Tales*, some of the names or titles are altered by time, but the characters themselves for ever remain unaltered; and consequently they are the physiognomies or lineaments of universal human life, beyond which Nature never steps. Names alter, things never alter. I have known multitudes of those who would have been monks in the age of monkery, who in this deistical age are deists. As Newton numbered the stars, and as Linnaeus numbered the plants, so Chaucer numbered the classes of men.

A Descriptive Catalogue of Pictures, 1809

MARY WOLLSTONECRAFT

1759–1797

A Wanton Solace

Women then must be considered as only the wanton solace of men, when they become so weak in mind and body that they cannot exert themselves unless to pursue some frothy pleasure, or to invent some frivolous fashion. What can be a more melancholy sight to a thinking mind, than to look into the numerous carriages that drive helter-skelter about this metropolis in a morning full of pale-faced creatures who are flying from themselves! I have often wished, with Dr Johnson, to place some of them in a little shop with half a dozen children looking up to their languid countenances for support. I am much mistaken, if some latent vigor would not soon give health and spirit to their eyes, and some lines drawn by the exercise of reason on the blank cheeks, which before were only undulated by dimples, might restore lost dignity to the character, or rather enable it to attain the true dignity of its nature. Virtue is not to be acquired even by speculation, much less by the negative supineness that wealth naturally generates.

A Vindication of the Rights of Woman, 1792

WILLIAM BECKFORD
1760–1844

A Mausoleum in Portugal

And now the Prior, with his wonted solemn and courteous demeanour, offering to be himself my guide to the mausoleum of Don Emanuel, we traversed a wilderness of weeds,—this part of the conventual precincts being much neglected,—and entered a dreary area, surrounded by the roofless, unfinished cluster of chapels, on which the most elaborately sculptured profusion of ornaments had been lavished, as often happens in similar cases, to no very happy result. I cannot in conscience persuade myself to admire such deplorable waste of time and ingenuity—'the quips, and cranks, and wanton wiles' of a corrupt, meretricious architecture; and when the good Prior lamented pathetically the unfinished state of this august mausoleum, and almost dropped a tear for the death of Emanuel its founder, as if it had only occurred a week ago, I did not pretend to share his affliction; for had the building been completed according to the design we are favoured with by that dull draughtsman Murphy, most preciously ugly would it have been;—ponderous and lumpish in the general effect, exuberantly light and fantastic in the detail, it was quite a mercy that it was never finished. Saxon crinklings and cranklings are bad enough; the preposterous long and lanky marrow-spoon-shaped arches of the early Norman, still worse; and the Moorish horse-shoe-like deviations from beautiful curves, little better.

I have often wondered how persons of correct taste could ever have tolerated them, and batten on garbage when they might enjoy the lovely Ionic so prevalent in Greece, the Doric grandeur of the Parthenon, and the Corinthian magnificence of Balbec and Palmyra. If, however, you wish to lead a quiet life, beware how you thwart established prejudices. I began to perceive, that to entertain any doubts of the supreme excellence of Don Emanuel's scollops and twistifications amounted to heresy. Withdrawing, therefore, my horns of defiance, I reserved my criticisms for some future display to a more intelligent auditor, and chimed in at length with the Prior's high-flown admiration of all this filigree, and despair for its non-completion; so we parted good friends. My Arabian was brought out, looking bright and happy: I bade a most grateful adieu to the Prior and his attendant swarm of friars and novices, and before they had ceased staring and wondering at the velocity with which I was carried away from them, I had reached a sandy desert above a mile from Batalha.

Night was already drawing on—the moon had not yet risen—a dying glow, reflected from the horizon above the hills, behind which the sun had just retired, was thrown over the whole landscape. 'Era già l' hora'—it *was* that soothing, solemn hour, when by some occult, inexplicable sympathy, the interior spirit, folded up within itself, inclines to repel every grovelling doubt of its divine essence, and feels, even without seeking to feel it, the consciousness of immortality.

The dying glow had expired; a sullen twilight, approaching to blackness, prevailed: I kept wandering on, however, not without some risk of being soon acquainted with the mysteries of a future world; for had not my horse been not only the fleetest, but the surest of foot of his high-born tribe, he must have stumbled, and in dangerous places, for such abounded at every step. As good fortune would have it, all the perils of the way were got over; the grand outline of the colossal monastery and its huge church emerged from the surrounding gloom; innumerable lights, streaming from the innumerable casements, cast a broad gleam over the great platform, where my Lord Almoner and his guests were walking to and fro, enjoying the fresh evening air, and waiting my return, they were pleased to say, with trembling anxiety.

Excursion to the Monasteries of Alcobaca and Batalha, 1835

WILLIAM COBBETT

1762–1835

Selborne

As I was coming into this village, I observed to a farmer who was standing at his gateway, that people ought to be happy here, for that God had done everything for them. His answer was, that he did not believe there was a more unhappy place in England: for that there were always quarrels of some sort or other going on.

Rural Rides, written 1823

Salisbury

For my part, I could not look up at the spire and the whole of the church at Salisbury without feeling that I lived in degenerate times. Such a thing never could be made *now*. We *feel* that, as we look at the building. It really does appear that if our forefathers had not made these buildings we should have forgotten, before now, what the Christian religion was!

Rural Rides, written 1826

Frome

This appears to be a sort of little Manchester. A very small Manchester, indeed; for it does not contain above ten to twelve thousand people, but it has all the *flash* of a Manchester, and the innkeepers and their people look and behave like the Manchester fellows. I was, I must confess, glad to find proofs of the irretrievable decay of the place. I remembered how ready the bluff manufacturers had been to *call in the troops* of various descriptions. 'Let them,' said I to myself, 'call the troops in now, to make their trade revive.'

Rural Rides, written 1826

Understanding the Poor

Before we got this supply of bread and cheese, we, though in ordinary times a couple of singularly jovial companions, and seldom going a hundred yards (except going very fast) without one or the other speaking, began to grow *dull*, or rather *glum*. The way seemed long; and, when I had to speak in answer to Richard, the speaking was as brief as might be. Unfortunately, just at this critical period, one of the loops that held the straps of Richard's little portmanteau broke; and it became necessary (just before we overtook Mr Bailey) for me to fasten the portmanteau on before me, upon my saddle. This, which was not the work of more than five minutes, would, had I had *a breakfast*, have been nothing at all, and, indeed, matter of laughter. But, *now*, it was *something*. It was his '*fault*' for capering and jerking about '*so*.' I jumped off, saying, '*Here!* I'll carry it *myself*.' And then I began to take off the remaining strap, pulling with great violence and in great haste. Just at this time my eyes met his, in which I saw *great surprise*; and, feeling the just rebuke, feeling heartily ashamed of myself, I instantly changed my tone and manner, cast the blame upon the saddler, and talked of the effectual means which we would take to prevent the like in future.

Now, if such was the effect produced upon me by the want of food for only two or three hours; me, who had dined well the day before and eaten toast and butter the over night; if the missing of only one breakfast, and that, too, from my own whim, while I had money in my pocket, to get one at any public-house, and while I could get one only for asking for at any farm-house; if the not having breakfasted could, and under such circumstances, make me what you may call '*cross*' to a child like this, whom I must necessarily love so much, and to whom I never speak but in the very kindest manner; if this mere absence of a breakfast could thus put me *out of temper*, how great are the allowances that we ought to make for the poor creatures who, in this once happy and now miserable country, are doomed to lead a life of constant labour and of half starvation.

Rural Rides, written 1825

JOHN NYREN
1764–1837

The Beau Ideal of Cricketers

William Beldham was a close-set, active man, standing about 5 ft. 8½ in. He had light-coloured hair, a fair complexion, and handsome as well as intelligent features. We used to call him 'Silver Billy.' No one within my recollection could stop a ball better, or make more brilliant hits all over the ground. Wherever the ball was bowled, there she was hit away, and in the most severe, venomous style. Besides this, he was so remarkably safe a player; he was safer than the Bank, for no mortal ever thought of doubting Beldham's stability. He received his instructions from a ginger-bread baker, at Farnham, of the name of Harry Hall . . .

He would get in at the balls and hit them away in gallant style; yet in this single feat, I think I have known him excelled: but when he could cut them at the point of the bat, he was in his glory: and upon my life their speed was as the speed of thought. One of the most beautiful sights that can be imagined, was to see him make himself up to hit a ball. It was the beau ideal of grace, animation and concentrated energy. In this particular exhibition of grace and vigour, the nearest approach to him I think was Lord Frederick Beauclerk. Upon one occasion at Marylebone, I remember these two admirable batters being in together, and though Beldham was then verging towards his climacteric, yet both were excited to a competition, and the display of talent that was exhibited between them that day was the most interesting sight of its kind I ever witnessed. I should not forget, among his other excellencies, that Beldham was one of the best judges of a short run I ever knew. . . . As a general fieldsman there were few better: he could take any post in the field: latterly he chose slip. He was a good change bowler too.

The Young Cricketer's Tutor, 1833

ISAAC D'ISRAELI
1766–1848

A Collector's Rage

The personal dislike which Pope Innocent X bore to the French had originated in his youth, when a cardinal, from having been detected in the library of an eminent French collector of having purloined a most rare volume. The delirium of a collector's rage overcame even French politesse; the Frenchman not only openly accused his illustrious culprit, but was resolved that he should not quit the library without replacing the precious volume—from accusation and denial both resolved to try their strength: but in this literary wrestling-match the book dropped out of the cardinal's robes—and from that day he hated the French.

Curiosities of Literature, 1791–3

A Critic to the last

An anecdote little known, relative to Dennis, will close his character. It appears, that the *Provoked Husband* was acted for his benefit, which procured him about a hundred pounds. Thomson and Pope generously supported the old critic, and Savage, who had nothing but a verse to give, returned them poetical thanks in the name of Dennis. When Dennis heard these lines repeated (for he was then blind) his critical severity, and this natural brutality, overcame that grateful sense he should have expressed, of their kindness and their elegance. He swore 'by G——they could be no one's but that fool Savage's.' This, perhaps, was the last peevish snuff from the dismal torch of criticism, for two days after was the redoubted Dennis numbered with the mighty dead.

Literary Miscellanies, 1796–1801

MARIA EDGEWORTH
1767–1849

The Passing of Sir Patrick Rackrent

Sir Patrick died that night: just as the company rose to drink his health with three cheers, he fell down in a sort of fit, and was carried off; they sat it out, and were surprised, on inquiry in the morning, to find that it was all over with poor Sir Patrick. Never did any gentleman live and die more beloved in the country by rich and poor. His funeral was such a one as was never known before or since in the county! All the gentlemen in the three counties were at it; far and near, how they flocked! my great-grandfather said, that to see all the women, even in their red cloaks, you would have taken them for the army drawn out. Then such a fine whillaluh! you might have heard it to the farthest end of the county, and happy the man who could get but a sight of the hearse! But who'd have thought it! Just as all was going on right, through his own town they were passing, when the body was seized for debt—a rescue was apprehended from the mob; but the heir, who attended the funeral, was against that, for fear of consequences, seeing that those villains who came to serve acted under the disguise of the law: so, to be sure, the law must take its course, and little gain had the creditors for their pains. First and foremost, they had the curses of the country: and Sir Murtagh Rackrent, the new heir, in the next place, on account of this affront to the body, refused to pay a shilling of the debts, in which he was countenanced by all the best gentlemen of property, and others of his acquaintance; Sir Murtagh alleging in all companies that he all along meant to pay his father's debts of honour, but the moment the law was taken of him, there was an end of honour to be sure. It was whispered (but none but the enemies of the family believe it) that this was all a sham seizure to get quit of the debts which he had bound himself to pay in honour.

Castle Rackrent, 1800

An Irishwoman in London

'Lady Langdale's carriage stops the way!' Lord Colambre made no offer of his services, notwithstanding a look from his mother. Incapable of the meanness of voluntarily listening to a conversation not intended for him to hear, he had, however, been compelled, by the pressure of the crowd, to remain a few minutes stationary, where he could not avoid hearing the remarks of the fashionable friends. Disdaining dissimulation, he made no attempt to conceal his displeasure. Perhaps his vexation was increased by his consciousness that there was some mixture of truth in their sarcasms. He was sensible that his mother, in some points—her manners, for instance—was obvious to ridicule and satire. In Lady Clonbrony's address there was a mixture of constraint, affectation, and indecision, unusual in a person of her birth, rank, and knowledge of the world. A natural and unnatural manner seemed struggling in all her gestures, and in every syllable that she articulated—a naturally free, familiar, good-natured, precipitate, Irish manner, had been schooled, and schooled late in life, into a sober, cold, still, stiff deportment, which she mistook for English. A strong, Hibernian accent, she had, with infinite difficulty, changed into an English tone. Mistaking reverse of wrong for right, she caricatured the English pronunciation; and the extraordinary precision of her London phraseology betrayed her not to be a Londoner, as the man, who strove to pass for an Athenian, was detected by his Attic dialect. Not aware of her real danger, Lady Clonbrony was, on the opposite side, in continual apprehension, every time she opened her lips, lest some treacherous *a* or *e*, some strong *r*, some puzzling aspirate, or non-aspirate, some unguarded note, interrogative or expostulatory, should betray her to be an Irishwoman. Mrs Dareville had, in her mimickry, perhaps a little exaggerated as to the *teebles* and *cheers*, but still the general likeness of the representation of Lady Clonbrony was strong enough to strike and vex her son. He had now, for the first time, an opportunity of judging of the estimation in which his mother and his family were held by certain leaders of the ton, of whom, in her letters, she had spoken so much, and into whose society, or rather into whose parties, she had been admitted. He saw that the renegado cowardice, with which she denied, abjured, and reviled her own country, gained nothing but ridicule and contempt. He loved his mother; and, whilst he endeavoured to conceal her faults and foibles as much as possible from his own heart, he could not endure those who dragged them to light and ridicule.

The Absentee, 1812

WILLIAM WORDSWORTH
1770–1850

A Narrow View of Human Nature

People in our rank in life are perpetually falling into one sad mistake, namely, that of supposing that human nature and the persons they associate with are one and the same thing. Whom do we generally associate with? Gentlemen, persons of fortune, professional men, ladies, persons who can afford to buy, or can easily procure, books of half-a-guinea price, hot-pressed, and printed upon superfine paper. These persons are, it is true, a part of human nature, but we err lamentably if we suppose them to be fair representatives of the vast mass of human existence. And yet few ever consider books but with reference to their power of pleasing these persons and men of a higher rank; few descend lower, among cottages and fields, and among children. A man must have done this habitually before his judgment upon *The Idiot Boy* would be in any way decisive with me. I *know* I have done this myself habitually; I wrote the poem with exceeding delight and pleasure, and whenever I read it I read it with pleasure. You have given me praise for having reflected faithfully in my Poems the feelings of human nature. I would fain hope that I have done so. But a great Poet ought to do more than this; he ought, to a certain degree, to rectify men's feelings, to give them new compositions of feeling, to render their feelings more sane, pure, and permanent, in short, more consonant to nature, that is, to eternal nature, and the great moving spirit of things. He ought to travel before men occasionally as well as at their sides.

letter to John Wilson, 1802

Freedom and the Arts of Peace

The works of peace cannot flourish in a country governed by an intoxicated Despot; the motions of whose distorted benevolence must be still more pernicious than those of his cruelty. '*I have bestowed: I have created: I have regenerated; I have been pleased to organise*':—this is the language perpetually upon his lips, when his ill-fated activities turn that way. Now commerce, manufactures, agriculture, and all the peaceful arts, are of the nature of virtues or intellectual powers; they cannot be given; they cannot be stuck in here and there; they must spring up; they must grow of themselves: they may be encouraged; they thrive better with encouragement, and delight in it; but the obligation must have bounds nicely defined; for they are delicate, proud, and independent. But a Tyrant has no joy in anything which is endued with such excellence: he sickens at the sight of it: he turns away from it, as an insult to his own attributes.

The Convention of Cintra, 1809

Tarns

Having spoken of Lakes I must not omit to mention, as a kindred feature of this country, those bodies of still water called TARNS. These are found in some of the valleys, and are very numerous upon the mountains. A Tarn, in a *Vale*, implies, for the most part, that the bed of the vale is not happily formed; that the water of the brooks can neither wholly escape, nor diffuse itself over a large area. Accordingly, in such situations, Tarns are often surrounded by a tract of boggy ground which has an unsightly appearance; but this is not always the case, and in the cultivated parts of the country, when the shores of the Tarn are determined, it differs only from the Lake in being smaller, and in belonging mostly to a smaller valley or circular recess. Of this class of miniature lakes Loughrigg Tarn, near Grasmere, is the most beautiful example. It has a margin of green firm meadows, of rocks, and rocky woods, a few reeds here, a little company of water-lilies there, with beds of gravel or stone beyond; a tiny stream issuing neither briskly nor sluggishly out of it; but its feeding rills, from the shortness of their course, so small as to be scarcely visible. Five or six cottages are reflected in its peaceful bosom; rocky and barren steeps rise up above the hanging enclosures; and the solemn pikes of Langdale overlook, from a distance, the low cultivated ridge of land that forms the northern boundary of this small, quiet, and fertile domain. The *mountain* Tarns can only be recommended to the notice of the inquisitive traveller who has time to spare. They are difficult of access and naked; yet some of them are, in their permanent forms, very grand; and there are accidents of things which would make the meanest of them interesting. At all events, one of these pools is an acceptable sight to the mountain wanderer, not merely as an incident that diversifies the prospect, but as forming in his mind a centre or conspicuous point to which objects, otherwise disconnected or unsubordinated, may be referred. Some few have a varied outline, with bold heath-clad promontories; and, as they mostly lie at the foot of a steep precipice, the water, where the sun is not shining upon it, appears black and sullen; and round the margin huge stones and masses of rock are scattered; some defying conjecture as to the means by which they came there, and others obviously fallen from on high—the contribution of ages! The sense, also, of some repulsive power strongly put forth—excited by the prospect of a body of pure water unattended with groves and other cheerful rural images by which fresh water is usually accompanied, and unable to give any furtherance to the meagre vegetation around it—heightens the melancholy natural to such scenes. Nor is the feeling of solitude often more forcibly or more solemnly impressed than by the side of one of these mountain pools: though desolate and forbidding, it seems a distinct place to repair to; yet where the visitants must be rare, and there can be no disturbance. Water-fowl flock hither; and the lonely Angler may oftentimes here be seen: but the imagination, not content with this scanty allowance of society, is tempted to attribute a voluntary power to every change which takes place in such a spot, whether it be the breeze that wanders over the surface of the water, or the splendid lights of evening resting upon it in the midst of awful precipices.

Description of the Country of the Lakes, 1822

JAMES HOGG

1770–1835

An Intrusive Young Man

The very next time that George was engaged at tennis, he had not struck the ball above twice till the same intrusive being was again in his way. The party played for considerable stakes that day, namely, a dinner and wine at the Black Bull tavern; and George, as the hero and head of his party, was much interested in its honour; consequently, the sight of this moody and hellish-looking student affected him in no very pleasant manner. 'Pray, Sir, be so good as keep without the range of the ball,' said he.

'Is there any law or enactment that can compel me to do so?' said the other, biting his lip with scorn.

'If there is not, they are here that shall compel you,' returned George: 'so, friend, I rede you to be on your guard.'

As he said this, a flush of anger glowed in his handsome face, and flashed from his sparkling blue eye; but it was a stranger to both, and momently took its departure. The black-coated youth set up his cap before, brought his heavy brows over his deep dark eyes, put his hands in the pockets of his black plush breeches, and stepped a little farther into the semi-circle, immediately on his brother's right hand, than he had ever ventured to do before. There he set himself firm on his legs, and, with a face as demure as death, seemed determined to keep his ground. He pretended to be following the ball with his eyes; but every moment they were glancing aside at George. One of the competitors chanced to say rashly, in the moment of exultation. 'That's a d——d fine blow, George!' On which the intruder took up the word, as characteristic of the competitors, and repeated it every stroke that was given, making such a ludicrous use of it, that several of the on-lookers were compelled to laugh immoderately; but the players were terribly nettled at it, as he really contrived, by dint of sliding in some canonical terms, to render the competitors and their game ridiculous.

But matters at length came to a crisis that put them beyond sport. George, in flying backward to gain the point at which the ball was going to light, came inadvertently so rudely in contact with this obstreperous interloper, that he not only overthrew him, but also got a grievous fall over his legs; and, as he arose, the other made a spurn at him with his foot, which, if it had hit to its aim, would undoubtedly have finished the course of the young laird of Dalcastle and Balgrennan. George, being irritated beyond measure, as may well be conceived, especially at the deadly stroke aimed at him, struck the assailant with his racket, rather slightly, but so that his mouth and nose gushed out blood; and, at the same time, he said, turning to his cronies, —'Does any of you know who the infernal puppy is?'

'Do you not know, Sir?' said one of the onlookers, a stranger: 'The gentleman is your own brother, Sir—Mr Robert Wringhim Colwan!'

The Private Memoirs and Confessions of a Justified Sinner, 1824

SIR WALTER SCOTT

1771–1832

Two Views of the Act of Union

While we paced easily forward, by a road which conducted us north-eastward from the town, I had an opportunity to estimate and admire the good qualities of my new friend. Although, like my father, he considered commercial transactions the most important objects of human life, he was not wedded to them so as to undervalue more general knowledge. On the contrary, with much oddity and vulgarity of manner, with a vanity which he made much more ridiculous by disguising it now and then under a thin veil of humility, and devoid as he was of all the advantages of a learned education, Mr Jarvie's conversation showed tokens of a shrewd, observing, liberal, and, to the extent of its opportunities, a well-improved mind. He was a good local antiquary, and entertained me, as we passed along, with an account of remarkable events which had formerly taken place in the scenes through which we passed. And as he was well acquainted with the ancient history of his district, he saw, with the prospective eye of an enlightened patriot, the buds of many of those future advantages which have only blossomed and ripened within these few years. I remarked also, and with great pleasure, that although a keen Scotchman, and abundantly zealous for the honour of his country, he was disposed to think liberally of the sister kingdom. When Andrew Fairservice (whom, by the way, the Bailie could not abide) chose to impute the accident of one of the horses casting his shoe to the deteriorating influence of the Union, he incurred a severe rebuke from Mr Jarvie.

'Whisht, sir! whisht! it's ill-scraped tongues like yours that make mischief atween neighbourhoods and nations. There's naething sae gude on this side o' time but it might hae been better, and that may be said o' the Union. Nane were keener against it than the Glasgow folk, wi' their rablings and their risings and their mobs, as they ca' them nowadays. But it's an ill wind blaws naebody gude. Let ilka ane roose the ford as they find it. I say, Let Glasgow flourish! whilk is judiciously and elegantly putten round the town's arms, by way of by-word. Now, since Saint Mungo catched herrings in the Clyde, what was ever like to gar us flourish like the sugar and tobacco trade? Will onybody tell me that, and grumble at the treaty that opened us a road west-awa' yonder?'

Andrew Fairservice was far from acquiescing in these arguments of expedience, and even ventured to enter a grumbling protest 'That it was an unco change to hae Scotland's laws made in England; and that, for his share, he wadna for a' the herring-barrels in Glasgow, and a' the tobacco-casks to boot, hae gien up the riding o' the Scots Parliament, or sent awa' our crown and our sword and our sceptre and Mons Meg, to be keepit by thae English pock-puddings in the Tower o' Lunnon. What wad Sir William Wallace or auld Davie Lindsay hae said to the Union, or them that made it?'

Rob Roy, 1817

A Gathering of Ghosts

But, Lord take us in keeping! what a set of ghastly revellers they were that sat round that table!—My gudesire kend mony that had long before gane to their place, for often had he piped to the most part in the hall of Redgauntlet. There was the fierce Middleton, and the dissolute Rothes; and the crafty Lauderdale; and Dalyell, with his bald head and a beard to his girdle; and Earlshall, with Cameron's blude on his hand; and wild Bonshaw, that tied blessed Mr Cargill's limbs till the blude sprung; and Dumbarton Douglas, the twice-turned traitor baith to country and king. There was the Bluidy Advocate MacKenyie, who, for his worldly wit and wisdom, had been to the rest as a god. And there was Claverhouse, as beautiful as when he lived, with his long, dark, curled locks, streaming down over his laced buff-coat, and his left hand always on his right spule-blade, to hide the wound that the silver bullet had made. He sat apart from them all, and looked at them with a melancholy, haughty countenance; while the rest hallooed, and sung, and laughed, that the room rang. But their smiles were fearfully contorted from time to time; and their laughter passed into such wild sounds as made my gudesire's very nails grow blue, and chilled the marrow in his banes.

They that waited at the table were just the wicked serving-men and troopers that had done their work and cruel bidding on earth. There was the Lang Lad of the Nethertown, that helped to take Argyle; and the Bishop's summoner, that they called the Deil's Rattle-bag; and the wicked guardsmen, in their laced coats; and the savage Highland Amorites, that shed blood like water; and many a proud serving-man, haughty of heart and bloody of hand, cringing to the rich, and making them wickeder than they would be; grinding the poor to powder, when the rich had broken them to fragments. And mony, mony mair were coming and ganging, a' as busy in their vocation as if they had been alive.

'Wandering Willie's Tale', *Redgauntlet*, 1824

In the Shadow of Bankruptcy

What a life mine has been!—half educated, almost wholly neglected or left to myself, stuffing my head with most nonsensical trash, and undervalued in society for a time by most of my companions—getting forward and held a bold and clever fellow contrary to the opinion of all who thought me a mere dreamer—Broken-hearted for two years—my heart handsomely pieced again—but the crack will remain till my dying day. Rich and poor four or five times, once at the verge of ruin, yet opend new sources of wealth almost overflowing—now taken in my pitch of pride, and nearly winged (unless the good news hold), because London chuses to be in an uproar, and in the tumult of bulls and bears, a poor inoffensive lion like myself is pushd to the wall. And what is to be the end of it? God knows. And so ends the chatechism.

Journal, December 1825

What a detestable feeling this fluttering of the heart is! I know it is nothing organic, and that it is entirely nervous, but the sickening effects of it are dispiriting to a degree. Is it the body brings it on the mind, or the mind inflicts it upon the body? I cannot tell; but it is a severe price to pay for the *Fata Morgana* with which Fancy sometimes amuses men of warm imagination. As to body and mind, I fancy I might as well inquire whether the fiddle or fiddle-stick makes the tune. In youth this complaint used to throw [me] into involuntary passions of causeless tears. But I will drive it away in the country by exercise. I wish I had been a mechanic—a turning-lathe or a chest of tools would have been a God-send; for thought makes the access of melancholy rather worse than better. I have it seldom, thank God, and, I believe, lightly, in comparaison of others.

It was the fiddle after all was out of order, not the fiddlestick; the body, not the mind. I walkd out; met Mrs Skene, who took a turn with me in Princes Street—Bade Constable and Cadell farewell—and had a brisk walk home, which enables me to face the desolation here with more spirit.

Journal, March 1826

Here is a disagreeable morning, snowing and hailing, with gleams of bright sunshine between, and all the ground white, and all the air frozen. I don't like this jumbling of weather. It is ungenial, and gives chilblains. Besides with its whiteness and its coldness and its glister, and its discomfort it resembles that most disagreeable of all things, a vain, cold, empty, beautiful woman, who has neither head nor heart, but only features like a doll. I do not know but it is like this disagreeable day, when the sun is so bright, and yet so uninfluential, that

'One may gaze upon its beams
Till he is starved with cold.'

No matter, it will serve as well as another day to finish *Woodstock*. Walked out to the lake, and coquetted with this disagreeable weather, whereby I catch chilblains on my fingers and cold in my head. Fed the swans.

Journal, March 1826

We have now been in solitude for some time—myself nearly totally so, excepting at meals, or on a call as yesterday from Henry and William Scott of Harden. One is tempted to ask himself, knocking at the door of his own heart, Do you love this extreme loneliness? I can answer conscientiously, *I do*. The love of solitude was with me a passion of early youth when in my teens I used to fly from company to indulge visions and airy castles of my own—the disposal of ideal wealth, and the exercize of imaginary power. This feeling prevaild even till I was eighteen, when love and ambition awaking with other passions threw me more into society, from which I have, however, at times withdrawn myself, and have been always glad to do so. I have risen from a feast satiated, and unless it be one or two persons of very strong intellect, or whose spirits and good-humour amuse me, I wish neither to see the high the low nor the middling class of society. This is a feeling without the least tinge of misanthropy, which I always consider as a kind of blasphemy of a shocking description. If God bears with the very worst of us, we may surely endure each other. If thrown into society, I always have, and always will endeavour to bring pleasure with me, at least to shew willingness to please. But for all this 'I had rather live alone,' and I wish my appointment so convenient otherwise did not require my going to Edinburgh. But this must be, and in my little lodging I will be lonely enough.

Journal, March 1826

SYDNEY SMITH
1771–1845

Connections

By what curious links, and fantastical relations, are mankind connected together! At the distance of half the globe, a Hindoo gains his support by groping at the bottom of the sea, for the morbid concretion of a shell-fish, to decorate the throat of a London alderman's wife.

'The Island of Ceylon', *Edinburgh Review*, 1803

Ridicule

Give up to the world, and to the ridicule with which the world enforces its dominion, every trifling question of manner and appearance: it is to toss courage and firmness to the winds, to combat with the mass upon such subjects as these. But learn from the earliest days to inure your principles against the perils of ridicule: you can no more exercise your reason, if you live in the constant dread of laughter, than you can enjoy your life, if you are in the constant terror of death.

Sketches of Moral Philosophy, 1804–6

The Three Ruling Passions

Look at the bustle of Bond Street; drive from thence to the Royal Exchange; observe the infinite variety of occupations, movements, and agitations, as you go along: nothing can appear more intricate,—more impossible to be reduced to anything like rule or system; and yet, a very few elements put all this mass of human beings into action. If a messenger from heaven were on a sudden to annihilate the love of power, the love of wealth, and the love of esteem, in the human heart; in half an hour's time the streets would be as empty, and as silent, as they are in the middle of the night.

Sketches of Moral Philosophy

A Noble Bore

Lord Chesterton we have often met with; and suffered a good deal from his Lordship: a heavy, pompous, meddling peer, occupying a great share of the conversation—saying things in ten words which required only two, and evidently convinced that he is making a great impression; a large man, with a large head, and very landed manner; knowing enough to torment his fellow creatures, not to instruct them—the ridicule of young ladies, and the natural butt and target of wit. It is easy to talk of carnivorous animals and beasts of prey; but does such a man, who lays waste a whole party of civilized beings by prosing, reflect upon the joy he spoils, and the misery he creates, in the course of his life? and that any one who listens to him through politeness, would prefer toothache or earache to his conversation? Does he consider the extreme uneasiness which ensues, when the company have discovered a man to be an extremely absurd person, at the same time that it is absolutely impossible to convey, by words or manner, the most distant suspicion of the discovery? And then, who punishes this bore? What sessions and what assizes for him? What bill is found against him? Who indicts him? When the judges have gone their vernal and autumnal rounds—the sheep-stealer disappears—the swindler gets ready for the Bay—the solid parts of the murderer are preserved in anatomical collections. But, after twenty years of crime, the bore is discovered in the same house, in the same attitude, eating the same soup,—unpunished, untried, undissected—no scaffold, no skeleton—no mob of gentlemen and ladies to gape over his last dying speech and confession.

Review of Thomas Lister's novel *Granby*, *Edinburgh Review*, 1826

Tropical Insects

Insects are the curse of tropical climates. The bête rouge lays the foundation of a tremendous ulcer. In a moment you are covered with ticks. Chigoes bury themselves in your flesh, and hatch a large colony of young chigoes in a few hours. They will not live together, but every chigoe sets up a separate ulcer, and has his own private portion of pus. Flies get entry into your mouth, into your eyes, into your nose; you eat flies, drink flies, and breathe flies. Lizards, cockroaches, and snakes, get into the bed; ants eat up the books; scorpions sting you on the foot. Every thing bites, stings, or bruises; every second of your existence you are wounded by some piece of animal life that nobody has ever seen before, except Swammerdam and Meriam. An insect with eleven legs is swimming in your teacup, a non-descript with nine wings is struggling in the small beer, or a caterpillar with several dozen eyes in his belly is hastening over the bread and butter! All nature is alive, and seems to be gathering all her entomological hosts to eat you up, as you are standing, out of your coat, waistcoat, and breeches. Such are the tropics. All this reconciles us to our dews, fogs, vapours, and drizzle—to our apothecaries rushing about with gargles and tinctures—to our old, British, constitutional coughs, sore throats, and swelled faces.

'Waterton's Wanderings in South America', *Edinburgh Review*, 1826

The Metaphysics of the Toucan

The toucan has an enormous bill, makes a noise like a puppy dog, and lays his eggs in hollow trees. How astonishing are the freaks and fancies of nature! To what purpose, we say, is a bird placed in the woods of Cayenne, with a bill a yard long, making a noise like a puppy dog, and laying eggs in hollow trees? The toucans, to be sure, might retort, to what purpose were gentlemen in Bond Street created? To what purpose were certain foolish prating Members of Parliament created?—pestering the House of Commons with their ignorance and folly, and impeding the business of the country? There is no end of such questions. So we will not enter into the metaphysics of the toucan.

'Waterton's Wanderings in South America'

Distractions

The cry of a child, the fall of a book, the most trifling occurrence, is sufficient to dissipate religious thought, and to introduce a more willing train of ideas; a sparrow fluttering about the church is an antagonist which the most profound theologian in Europe is wholly unable to overcome.

Memoir by Lady Holland, 1855

The Definition of a Nice Person

A nice person is neither too tall nor too short, looks clean and cheerful, has no prominent feature, makes no difficulties, is never misplaced, sits bodkin, is never foolishly affronted, and is void of affectations.

A nice person helps you well at dinner, understands you, is always gratefully received by young and old, Whig and Tory, grave and gay.

There is something in the very air of a nice person which inspires you with confidence, makes you talk, and talk without fear of malicious misrepresentation; you feel that you are reposing upon a nature which God has made kind, and created for the benefit and happiness of society. It has the effect upon the mind which soft air and a fine climate has upon the body.

A nice person is clear of little, trumpery passions, acknowledges superiority, delights in talent, shelters humility, pardons adversity, forgives deficiency, respects all men's rights, never stops the bottle, is never long and never wrong, always knows the day of the month, the name of every body at table, and never gives pain to any human being.

If any body is wanted for a party, a nice person is the first thought of; when the child is christened, when the daughter is married—all the joys of life are communicated to nice people; the hand of the dying man is always held out to a nice person.

A nice person never knocks over wine or melted butter, does not tread upon the dog's foot, or molest the family cat, eats soup without noise, laughs in the right place, and has a watchful and attentive eye.

Memoir by Lady Holland

DOROTHY WORDSWORTH
1771–1855

The Call of a Raven

[*July*] *27th, Sunday.* Very warm. Molly ill. John bathed in the lake. I wrote out *Ruth* in the afternoon. In the morning, I read Mr Knight's *Landscape.* After tea we rowed down to Loughrigg Fell, visited the white foxglove, gathered wild strawberries, and walked up to view Rydale. We lay a long time looking at the lake; the shores all embrowned with the scorching sun. The ferns were turning yellow, that is, here and there one was quite turned. We walked round by Benson's wood home. The lake was now most still, and reflected the beautiful yellow and blue and purple and grey colours of the sky. We heard a strange sound in the Bainriggs wood, as we were floating on the water; it *seemed* in the wood, but it must have been above it, for presently we saw a raven very high above us. It called out, and the dome of the sky seemed to echo the sound. It called again and again as it flew onwards, and the mountains gave back the sound, seeming as if from their center; a musical bell-like answering to the bird's hoarse voice. We heard both the call of the bird, and the echo, after we could see him no longer. We walked up to the top of the hill again in view of Rydale—met Mr and Miss Simpson on horseback. The crescent moon which had shone upon the water was now gone down. Returned to supper at 10 o'clock.

Grasmere Journal, 1800

A More Splendid World

[*April*] *29th, Thursday*. A beautiful morning—the sun shone and all was pleasant. We sent off our parcel to Coleridge by the waggon. Mr Simpson heard the Cuckow to-day. Before we went out, after I had written down *The Tinker*, which William finished this morning, Luff called—he was very lame, limped into the kitchen. He came on a little pony. We then went to John's Grove, sate a while at first. Afterwards William lay, and I lay, in the trench under the fence—he with his eyes shut, and listening to the waterfalls and the birds. There was no one waterfall above another—it was a sound of waters in the air—the voice of the air. William heard me breathing and rustling now and then, but we both lay still, and unseen by one another; he thought that it would be as sweet thus to lie so in the grave, to hear the *peaceful* sounds of the earth, and just to know that our dear friends were near. The lake was still; there was a boat out. Silver How reflected with delicate purple and yellowish hues, as I have seen spar; lambs on the island, and running races together by the half-dozen, in the round field near us. The copses greenish, hawthorns green. Came home to dinner, then went to Mr Simpson—we rested a long time under a wall, sheep and lambs were in the field—cottages smoking. As I lay down on the grass, I observed the glittering silver line on the ridge of the backs of the sheep, owing to their situation respecting the sun, which made them look beautiful, but with something of strangeness, like animals of another kind, as if belonging to a more splendid world.

Grasmere Journal, 1802

A Fine Woman

June 2nd, Wednesday. In the morning we observed that the scarlet beans were drooping in the leaves in great numbers, owing, we guess, to an insect. We sate awhile in the orchard—then we went to the old carpenter's about the hurdles. Yesterday an old man called, a grey-headed man, above 70 years of age. He said he had been a soldier, that his wife and children had died in Jamaica. He had a beggar's wallet over his shoulders; a coat of shreds and patches, altogether of a drab colour; he was tall, and though his body was bent, he had the look of one used to have been upright.

I talked a while, and then gave him a piece of cold bacon and a penny. Said he, 'You're a fine woman!' I could not help smiling; I suppose he meant, 'You're a kind woman'.

Grasmere Journal, 1802

SAMUEL TAYLOR COLERIDGE
1772–1834

Genius and Novelty

But how shall I avert the scorn of those critics who laugh at the oldness of my topics, Evil and Good, Necessity and Arbitrement, Immortality and the Ultimate Aim? By what shall I regain *their* favour? My themes must be *new*, a French constitution; a balloon; a change of ministry; a fresh batch of kings on the Continent, or of peers in our happier island; or who had the best of it of two parliamentary gladiators, and whose speech, on the subject of Europe bleeding at a thousand wounds, or our own country struggling for herself and all human nature, was cheered by the greatest number of *laughs, loud laughs, and very loud laughs*: (which, carefully marked by italics, form most conspicuous and strange parentheses in the newspaper reports.) Or if I must be philosophical, the last chemical discoveries, provided I do not trouble my reader with the principle which gives them their highest interest, and the character of intellectual grandeur to the discoverer; or the last shower of stones, and that they were supposed, by certain philosophers, to have been projected from some volcano in the moon, taking care, however, not to add any of the *cramp* reasons for this opinion! Something new, however, it must be, quite new and quite out of themselves! for whatever is within them, whatever is deep within them, must be as old as the first dawn of human reason. But to find no contradiction in the union of old and new, to contemplate the ANCIENT OF DAYS with feelings as fresh, as if they then sprang forth at his own fiat, this characterizes the minds that feel the riddle of the world, and may help to unravel it! To carry on the feelings of childhood into the powers of manhood, to combine the child's sense of wonder and novelty with the appearances which every day for perhaps forty years had rendered familiar,

> With Sun and Moon and Stars throughout the year,
> And Man and Woman—

this is the character and privilege of genius, and one of the marks which distinguish genius from talents. And so to represent familiar objects as to awaken the minds of others to a like freshness of sensation concerning them (that constant accompaniment of mental, no less than of bodily, convalescence)—this is the prime merit of genius, and its most unequivocal mode of manifestation. Who has not, a thousand times, seen it snow upon water? who has not seen it with a new feeling, since he has read Burns's comparison of sensual pleasure,

> To snow that falls upon a river,
> A moment white—then gone for ever!

In philosophy equally, as in poetry, genius produces the strongest impressions of novelty, while it rescues the stalest and most admitted truths from the impotence caused by the very circumstance of their universal admission. Extremes meet—a proverb, by the bye, to collect and explain all the instances and exemplifications of which, would constitute and exhaust all philosophy. Truths, of all others the most awful and mysterious, yet being at the same time of universal interest, are too often considered as so true that they lose all the powers of truth, and lie bed-ridden in the dormitory of the soul, side by side with the most despised and exploded errors.

The Friend, 1809

Popular Reading

For as to the devotees of the circulating libraries, I dare not compliment their pass-time, or rather kill-time, with the name of reading. Call it rather a sort of beggarly day-dreaming during which the mind of the dreamer furnishes for itself nothing but laziness and a little mawkish sensibility; while the whole *materiel* and imagery of the doze is supplied *ab extra* by a sort of mental *camera obscura* manufactured at the printing office, which *pro tempore* fixes, reflects and transmits the moving phantasms of one man's delirium, so as to people the barrenness of an hundred other brains afflicted with the same trance or suspension of all common sense and all definite purpose. We should therefore transfer this species of amusement (if indeed those can be said to retire *a musis*, who were never in their company, or relaxation be attributable to those whose bows are never bent) from the genus, reading, to that comprehensive class characterized by the power of reconciling the two contrary yet co-existing propensities of human nature, namely indulgence of sloth and hatred of vacancy. In addition to novels and tales of chivalry in prose or rhyme, (by which last I mean neither rhythm nor metre) this genus comprises as its species, gaming, swinging or swaying on a chair or gate; spitting over a bridge; smoking; snuff-taking: tête-à-tête quarrels after dinner between husband and wife; conning word by word all the advertisements of the *Daily Advertizer* in a public house on a rainy day, etc. etc. etc.

Biographia Literaria, 1817

From the Notebooks

The reader of Milton must be always on his duty: he is surrounded with sense; it rises in every line; every word is to the purpose. There are no lazy intervals; all has been considered, and demands and merits observation. If this be called obscurity, let it be remembered that it is such an obscurity as is a compliment to the reader; not that vicious obscurity, which proceeds from a muddled head.

*c.*1796

The immovableness of all things through which so many men were moving,—a harsh contrast compared with the universal motion, the harmonious system of motions in the country, and everywhere in Nature. In the dim light London appeared to be a huge place of sepulchres through which hosts of spirits were gliding.

1799

The sunny mist, the luminous gloom of Plato.

1799

Never to lose an opportunity of reasoning against the head-dimming, heart-damping principle of judging a work by its defects, not its beauties. Every work must have the former—we know it *a priori*—but every work has not the latter, and he, therefore, who discovers them, tells you something that you could not with certainty, or even with probability, have anticipated.

1803

The old stump of the tree, with briar-roses and bramble leaves wreathed round and round—a bramble arch—a foxglove in the centre.

*c.*1803

Tremendous as a Mexican god is a strong sense of duty—separate from an enlarged and discriminating mind, and gigantically disproportionate to the size of the understanding; and, if combined with obstinacy of self-opinion and indocility, it is the parent of tyranny, a promoter of inquisitorial persecution in public life, and of inconceivable misery in private families. Nay, the very virtue of the person, and the consciousness that *it* is sacrificing its own happiness, increases the obduracy, and selects those whom it best loves for its objects.

1808

If one thought leads to another, so often does it blot out another—This I find, when having lain musing on my Sopha, a number of interesting

Thoughts having suggested themselves, I conquer my bodily indolence & rise to record them in these books, alas! my only Confidants.—The first Thought leads me on indeed to new ones; but nothing but the faint memory of having had them remains of the others, which had been even more interesting to me.—I do not know, whether this be an idiosyncracy, a peculiar disease, of *my* particular memory—but so it is with *me*—My Thoughts crowd each other to death.

1808

The giant shadows sleeping amid the wan yellow light of the December morning, looked like wrecks and scattered ruins of the long, long night.

1812

We all look up to the blue sky for comfort, but nothing appears there, nothing comforts, nothing answers us, and so we die.

1817

If a man could pass through Paradise in a dream, and have a flower presented to him as a pledge that his soul had really been there, and if he found that flower in his hand when he awoke—Aye! and what then?

1818

ROBERT SOUTHEY
1774–1843

Nelson (aged 12) Joins the Navy

Early on a cold and dark spring morning Mr Nelson's servant arrived at this school at North Walsham with the expected summons for Horatio to join his ship. The parting from his brother William, who had been for so many years his playmate and bed-fellow, was a painful effort, and was the beginning of those privations which are the sailor's lot through life. He accompanied his father to London. The *Raisonnable* was lying in the Medway. He was put into the Chatham stage, and on its arrival was set down with the rest of the passengers, and left to find his way on board as he could. After wandering about in the cold, without being able to reach the ship, an officer observed the forlorn appearance of the boy, questioned him, and happening to be acquainted with his uncle, took him home, and gave him some refreshments. When he got on board, Captain Suckling was not in the ship, nor had any person been apprised of the boy's coming. He paced the deck the whole remainder of the day, without being noticed by any one; and it was not till the second day that somebody, as he expressed it, 'took compassion on him.' The pain which is felt when we are first transplanted from our native soil—when the living branch is cut from the parent tree—is one of the most poignant which we have to endure through life. There are after-griefs which wound more deeply, which leave behind them scars never to be effaced, which bruise the spirit, and sometimes break the heart: but never, never do we feel so keenly the want of love, the necessity of being loved, and the sense of utter desertion, as when we first leave the haven of home, and are, as it were, pushed off upon the stream of life. Added to these feelings, the sea-boy has to endure physical hardships, and the privation of every comfort, even of sleep. Nelson had a feeble body and an affectionate heart, and he remembered through life his first days of wretchedness in the service.

Life of Nelson, 1813

JANE AUSTEN
1775–1817

An Unfailing Theme

Conversation however was not wanted, for Sir John was very chatty, and Lady Middleton had taken the wise precaution of bringing with her their eldest child, a fine little boy about six years old, by which means there was one subject always to be recurred to by the ladies in case of extremity, for they had to inquire his name and age, admire his beauty, and ask him questions which his mother answered for him, while he hung about her and held down his head, to the great surprise of her ladyship, who wondered at his being so shy before company as he could make noise enough at home. On every formal visit a child ought to be of the party, by way of provision for discourse. In the present case it took up ten minutes to determine whether the boy were most like his father or mother, and in what particular he resembled either, for of course every body differed, and every body was astonished at the opinion of the others.

Sense and Sensibility, 1811

Invited to Play

In the evening, as Marianne was discovered to be musical, she was invited to play. The instrument was unlocked, every body prepared to be charmed, and Marianne, who sang very well, at their request went through the chief of the songs which Lady Middleton had brought into the family on her marriage, and which perhaps had lain ever since in the same position on the pianoforté, for her ladyship had celebrated that event by giving up music, although by her mother's account she had played extremely well, and by her own was very fond of it.

Marianne's performance was highly applauded. Sir John was loud in his admiration at the end of every song, and as loud in his conversation with the others while every song lasted. Lady Middleton frequently called him to order, wondered how any one's attention could be diverted from music for a moment, and asked Marianne to sing a particular song which Marianne had just finished. Colonel Brandon alone, of all the party, heard her without being in raptures. He paid her only the compliment of attention; and she felt a respect for him on the occasion, which the others had reasonably forfeited by their shameless want of taste. His pleasure in music, though it amounted not to that extatic delight which alone could sympathize with her own, was estimable when contrasted against the horrible insensibility of the others; and she was reasonable enough to allow that a man of five and thirty might well have outlived all acuteness of feeling and every exquisite power of enjoyment. She was perfectly disposed to make every allowance for the colonel's advanced state of life which humanity required.

Sense and Sensibility

A Man of Fashion

On ascending the stairs, the Miss Dashwoods found so many people before them in the room, that there was not a person at liberty to attend to their orders; and they were obliged to wait. All that could be done was, to sit down at that end of the counter which seemed to promise the quickest succession; one gentleman only was standing there, and it is probable that Elinor was not without hopes of exciting his politeness to a quicker dispatch. But the correctness of his eye, and the delicacy of his taste, proved to be beyond his politeness. He was giving orders for a toothpick-case for himself, and till its size, shape, and ornaments were determined, all of which, after examining and debating for a quarter of an hour over every toothpick-case in the shop, were finally arranged by his own inventive fancy, he had no leisure to bestow any other attention on the two ladies, than what was comprised in three or four very broad stares; a kind of notice which served to imprint on Elinor the remembrance of a person and face, of strong, natural, sterling insignificance, though adorned in the first style of fashion.

Sense and Sensibility

Gothic Romance and English Reality

Charming as were all Mrs Radcliffe's works, and charming even as were the works of all her imitators, it was not in them perhaps that human nature, at least in the midland counties of England, was to be looked for. Of the Alps and Pyrenees, with their pine forests and their vices, they might give a faithful delineation; and Italy, Switzerland, and the South of France, might be as fruitful in horrors as they were there represented. Catherine dared not doubt beyond her own country, and even of that, if hard pressed, would have yielded the northern and western extremities. But in the central part of England there was surely some security for the existence even of a wife not beloved, in the laws of the land, and the manners of the age. Murder was not tolerated, servants were not slaves, and neither poison nor sleeping potions to be procured, like rhubarb, from every druggist. Among the Alps and Pyrenees, perhaps, there were no mixed characters. There, such as were not as spotless as an angel, might have the dispositions of a fiend. But in England it was not so; among the English, she believed, in their hearts and habits, there was a general though unequal mixture of good and bad.

Northanger Abbey, 1818; written 1798–9

Elizabeth at the Ball

She danced next with an officer, and had the refreshment of talking of Wickham, and of hearing that he was universally liked. When those dances were over she returned to Charlotte Lucas, and was in conversation with her, when she found herself suddenly addressed by Mr Darcy, who took her so much by surprise in his application for her hand, that, without knowing what she did, she accepted him. He walked away again immediately, and she was left to fret over her own want of presence of mind; Charlotte tried to console her.

'I dare say you will find him very agreeable.'

'Heaven forbid!—*That* would be the greatest misfortune of all!—To find a man agreeable whom one is determined to hate!—Do not wish me such an evil.'

When the dancing recommenced, however, and Darcy approached to claim her hand, Charlotte could not help cautioning her in a whisper not to be a simpleton and allow her fancy for Wickham to make her appear unpleasant in the eyes of a man of ten times his consequence. Elizabeth made no answer, and took her place in the set, amazed at the dignity to which she was arrived in being allowed to stand opposite to Mr Darcy, and reading in her neighbours' looks their equal amazement in beholding it. They stood for some time without speaking a word; and she began to imagine that their silence was to last through the two dances, and at first was resolved not to break it; till suddenly fancying that it would be the greater punishment to her partner to oblige him to talk, she made some slight observation on the dance. He replied, and was again silent. After a pause of some minutes she addressed him a second time with

'It is *your* turn to say something now, Mr Darcy.—*I* talked about the dance, and *you* ought to make some kind of remark on the size of the room, or the number of couples.'

He smiled, and assured her that whatever she wished him to say should be said.

'Very well.—That reply will do for the present.—Perhaps by and bye I may observe that private balls are much pleasanter than public ones.—But *now* we may be silent.'

'Do you talk by rule then, while you are dancing?'

'Sometimes. One must speak a little, you know. It would look odd to be entirely silent for half an hour together, and yet for the advantage of *some*, conversation ought to be so arranged as that they may have the trouble of saying as little as possible.'

'Are you consulting your own feelings in the present case, or do you imagine that you are gratifying mine?'

'Both,' replied Elizabeth archly; 'for I have always seen a great similarity in the turn of our minds.—We are each of an unsocial, taciturn disposition, unwilling to speak, unless we expect to say something that will amaze the whole room, and be handed down to posterity with all the eclat of a proverb.'

'This is no very striking resemblance of your own character, I am sure,' said he. 'How near it may be to *mine*, I cannot pretend to say.—*You* think it a faithful portrait undoubtedly.'

'I must not decide on my own performance.'

He made no answer, and they were again silent till they had gone down the dance, when he asked her if she and her sisters did not very often walk to Meryton. She answered in the affirmative, and, unable to resist the temptation, added, 'When you met us there the other day, we had just been forming a new acquaintance.'

The effect was immediate. A deeper shade of hauteur overspread his features, but he said not a word, and Elizabeth, though blaming herself for her own weakness, could not go on. At length Darcy spoke, and in a constrained manner said,

'Mr Wickham is blessed with such happy manners as may ensure his *making* friends—whether he may be equally capable of *retaining* them, is less certain.'

'He has been so unlucky as to lose *your* friendship,' replied Elizabeth with emphasis, 'and in a manner which he is likely to suffer from all his life.'

Darcy made no answer, and seemed desirous of changing the subject. At that moment Sir William Lucas appeared close to them, meaning to pass through the set to the other side of the room; but on perceiving Mr Darcy he stopt with a bow of superior courtesy to compliment him on his dancing and his partner.

'I have been most highly gratified indeed, my dear Sir. Such very superior dancing is not often seen. It is evident that you belong to the first circles. Allow me to say, however, that your fair partner does not disgrace you, and that I must hope to have this pleasure often repeated, especially when a certain desirable event, my dear Miss Eliza, (glancing at her sister and Bingley,) shall take place. What congratulations will then flow in! I appeal to Mr Darcy:—but let me not interrupt you, Sir.—You will not thank me for detaining you from the bewitching converse of that young lady, whose bright eyes are also upbraiding me.'

The latter part of this address was scarcely heard by Darcy; but Sir William's allusion to his friend seemed to strike him forcibly, and his eyes were directed with a very serious expression towards Bingley and Jane, who were dancing together. Recovering himself, however, shortly, he turned to his partner, and said,

'Sir William's interruption has made me forget what we were talking of.'

'I do not think we were speaking at all. Sir William could not have interrupted any two people in the room who had less to say for themselves.—We have tried two or three subjects already without success, and what we are to talk of next I cannot imagine.'

'What think you of books?' said he, smiling.

'Books—Oh! no.—I am sure we never read the same, or not with the same feelings.'

'I am sorry you think so; but if that be the case, there can at least be no want of subject.—We may compare our different opinions.'

'No—I cannot talk of books in a ball-room; my head is always full of something else.'

'The *present* always occupies you in such scenes—does it?' said he, with a look of doubt.

'Yes, always,' she replied, without knowing what she said, for her thoughts had wandered far from the subject, as soon afterwards appeared by her suddenly exclaiming, 'I remember hearing you once say, Mr Darcy, that you hardly ever forgave, that your resentment once created was unappeasable. You are very cautious, I suppose, as to its *being created*.'

'I am,' said he, with a firm voice.

'And never allow yourself to be blinded by prejudice?'

'I hope not.'

'It is particularly incumbent on those who never change their opinion, to be secure of judging properly at first.'

'May I ask to what these questions tend?'

'Merely to the illustration of *your* character,' said she, endeavouring to shake off her gravity. 'I am trying to make it out.'

'And what is your success?'

She shook her head. 'I do not get on at all. I hear such different accounts of you as puzzle me exceedingly.'

'I can readily believe,' answered he gravely, 'that report may vary greatly with respect to me; and I could wish, Miss Bennet, that you were not to sketch my character at the present moment, as there is reason to fear that the performance would reflect no credit on either.'

'But if I do not take your likeness now, I may never have another opportunity.'

'I would by no means suspend any pleasure of yours,' he coldly replied. She said no more, and they went down the other dance and parted in silence; on each side dissatisfied, though not to an equal degree, for in Darcy's breast there was a tolerable powerful feeling towards her, which soon procured her pardon, and directed all his anger against another.

Pride and Prejudice, 1813

Fanny Price Returns Home

The living in incessant noise was to a frame and temper, delicate and nervous like Fanny's, an evil which no superadded elegance or harmony could have entirely atoned for. It was the greatest misery of all. At Mansfield, no sounds of contention, no raised voice, no abrupt bursts, no tread of violence was ever heard; all proceeded in a regular course of cheerful orderliness; every body had their due importance; every body's feelings were consulted. If tenderness could be ever supposed wanting, good sense and good breeding supplied its place; and as to the little irritations, sometimes introduced by aunt Norris, they were short, they were trifling, they were as a drop of water to the ocean, compared with the ceaseless tumult of her present abode. Here, every body was noisy, every voice was loud, (excepting, perhaps, her mother's, which resembled the soft monotony of Lady Bertram's, only worn into fretfulness.)—Whatever was wanted, was halloo'd for, and the servants halloo'd out their excuses from the kitchen. The doors were in constant banging, the stairs were never at rest, nothing was done without a clatter, nobody sat still, and nobody could command attention when they spoke.

Mansfield Park, 1814

Mrs Elton's Morning Scheme

'It is to be a morning scheme, you know, Knightley; quite a simple thing. I shall wear a large bonnet, and bring one of my little baskets hanging on my arm. Here,—probably this basket with pink ribbon. Nothing can be more simple, you see. And Jane will have such another. There is to be no form or parade—a sort of gipsy party. We are to walk about your gardens, and gather the strawberries ourselves, and sit under trees; and whatever else you may like to provide, it is to be all out of doors—a table spread in the shade, you know. Every thing as natural and simple as possible. Is not that your idea?'

'Not quite. My idea of the simple and the natural will be to have the table spread in the dining-room. The nature and the simplicity of gentlemen and ladies, with their servants and furniture, I think is best observed by meals within doors. When you are tired of eating strawberries in the garden, there shall be cold meat in the house.'

'Well—as you please; only don't have a great set out. And, by the bye, can I or my housekeeper be of any use to you with our opinion? Pray be sincere, Knightley. If you wish me to talk to Mrs Hodges, or to inspect anything——'

'I have not the least wish for it, I thank you.'

'Well—but if any difficulties should arise, my housekeeper is extremely clever.'

'I will answer for it, that mine thinks herself full as clever, and would spurn anybody's assistance.'

'I wish we had a donkey. The thing would be for us all to come on donkies, Jane, Miss Bates, and me—and my caro sposo walking by. I really must talk to him about purchasing a donkey. In a country life I conceive it to be a sort of necessary; for, let a woman have ever so many resources, it is not possible for her to be always shut up at home;—and very long walks, you know—in summer there is dust, and in winter there is dirt.'

'You will not find either, between Donwell and Highbury. Donwell-lane is never dusty, and now it is perfectly dry. Come on a donkey, however, if you prefer it. You can borrow Mrs Cole's. I would wish every thing to be as much to your taste as possible.'

'That I am sure you would. Indeed I do you justice, my good friend. Under that peculiar sort of dry, blunt manner, I know you have the warmest heart. As I tell Mr E., you are a thorough humourist. Yes, believe me, Knightley, I am fully sensible of your attention to me in the whole of this scheme. You have hit upon the very thing to please me.'

Emma, 1816

A Rebuke

While waiting for the carriage, she found Mr Knightley by her side. He looked around, as if to see that no one were near, and then said,

'Emma, I must once more speak to you as I have been used to do: a privilege rather endured than allowed, perhaps, but I must still use it. I cannot see you acting wrong, without a remonstrance. How could you be so unfeeling to Miss Bates? How could you be so insolent in your wit to a woman of her character, age, and situation? Emma, I had not thought it possible.'

Emma recollected, blushed, was sorry, but tried to laugh it off.

'Nay, how could I help saying what I did? Nobody could have helped it. It was not so very bad. I dare say she did not understand me.'

'I assure you she did. She felt your full meaning. She has talked of it since. I wish you could have heard how she talked of it—with what candour and generosity. I wish you could have heard her honouring your forbearance, in being able to pay her such attentions, as she was for ever receiving from yourself and your father, when her society must be so irksome.'

'Oh!' cried Emma, 'I know there is not a better creature in the world: but you must allow, that what is good and what is ridiculous are most unfortunately blended in her.'

'They are blended,' said he, 'I acknowledge; and, were she prosperous, I could allow much for the occasional prevalence of the ridiculous over the good. Were she a woman of fortune, I could leave every harmless absurdity to take its chance, I would not quarrel with you for any liberties of manner. Were she your equal in situation—but, Emma, consider how far this is from being the case. She is poor; she has sunk from the comforts she was born to; and, if she live to old age, must probably sink more. Her situation should secure your compassion. It was badly done, indeed!—You, whom she had known from an infant, whom she had seen grow up from a period when her notice was an honour, to have you now, in thoughtless spirits, and the pride of the moment, laugh at her, humble her—and before her niece, too—and before others, many of whom (certainly *some*,) would be entirely guided by *your* treatment of her.—This is not pleasant to you, Emma—and it is very far from pleasant to me; but I must, I will,—I will tell you truths while I can, satisfied with proving myself your friend by very faithful counsel, and trusting that you will some time or other do me greater justice than you can do now.'

While they talked, they were advancing towards the carriage; it was ready; and, before she could speak again, he had handed her in. He had misinterpreted the feelings which had kept her face averted, and her tongue motionless. They were combined only of anger against herself, mortification, and deep concern. She had not been able to speak; and, on entering the carriage, sunk back for a moment overcome—then reproaching herself for having taken no leave, making no acknowledgement, parting in apparent sullenness, she looked out with voice and hand eager to show a difference; but it was just too late. He had turned away, and the horses were in motion. She continued to look back, but in vain; and soon, with what appeared unusual speed, they were half way down the hill, and every thing left far behind. She was vexed beyond what could have been expressed—almost beyond what she could conceal. Never had she felt so agitated, mortified, grieved, at any circumstance in her life. She was most forcibly struck. The truth of his representation there was no denying. She felt it at her heart. How could she have been so brutal, so cruel to Miss Bates! How could she have exposed herself to such ill opinion in any one she valued! And how suffer him to leave her without saying one word of gratitude, of concurrence, of common kindness!

Time did not compose her. As she reflected more, she seemed but to feel it more. She never had been so depressed. Happily it was not necessary to speak. There was only Harriet, who seemed not in spirits herself, fagged, and very willing to be silent; and Emma felt the tears running down her cheeks almost all the way home, without being at any trouble to check them, extraordinary as they were.

Emma

A Degree of Gravity

The following day brought news from Richmond to throw every thing else into the background. An express arrived at Randalls to announce the death of Mrs Churchill! Though her nephew had had no particular reason to hasten back on her account, she had not lived above six-and-thirty hours after his return. A sudden seizure of a different nature from any thing foreboded by her general state, had carried her off after a short struggle. The great Mrs Churchill was no more.

It was felt as such things must be felt. Every body had a degree of gravity and sorrow; tenderness towards the departed, solicitude for the surviving friends; and, in a reasonable time, curiosity to know where she would be buried. Goldsmith tells us, that when lovely woman stoops to folly, she has nothing to do but to die; and when she stoops to be disagreeable, it is equally to be recommended as a clearer of ill-fame. Mrs Churchill, after being disliked at least twenty-five years, was now spoken of with compassionate allowances. In one point she was fully justified. She had never been admitted before to be seriously ill. The event acquitted her of all the fancifulness, and all the selfishness of imaginary complaints.

Emma

Once More in the Same Room!

The morning hours of the Cottage were always later than those of the other house; and on the morrow the difference was so great, that Mary and Anne were not more than beginning breakfast when Charles came in to say that they were just setting off, that he was come for his dogs, that his sisters were following with Captain Wentworth, his sisters meaning to visit Mary and the child, and Captain Wentworth proposing also to wait on her for a few minutes, if not inconvenient; and though Charles had answered for the child's being in no such state as could make it inconvenient, Captain Wentworth would not be satisfied without his running on to give notice.

Mary, very much gratified by this attention, was delighted to receive him; while a thousand feelings rushed on Anne, of which this was the most consoling, that it would soon be over. And it was soon over. In two minutes after Charles's preparation, the others appeared; they were in the drawing-room. Her eye half met Captain Wentworth's; a bow, a curtsey passed; she heard his voice—he talked to Mary, said all that was right; said something to the Miss Musgroves, enough to mark an easy footing: the room seemed full—full of persons and voices—but a few minutes ended it. Charles shewed himself at the window, all was ready, their visitor had bowed and was gone; the Miss Musgroves were gone too, suddenly resolving to walk to the end of the village with the sportsmen: the room was cleared, and Anne might finish her breakfast as she could.

'It is over! it is over!' she repeated to herself again, and again, in nervous gratitude. 'The worst is over!'

Mary talked, but she could not attend. She had seen him. They had met. They had been once more in the same room!

Persuasion, 1818

The Eye of the Beholder

Every body has their tastes in noises as well as in other matters; and sounds are quite innoxious, or most distressing, by their sort rather than their quantity. When Lady Russell, not long afterwards, was entering Bath on a wet afternoon, and driving through the long course of streets from the Old Bridge to Camden-place, amidst the dash of other carriages, the heavy rumble of carts and drays, the bawling of newsmen, muffin-men and milk-men, and the ceaseless clink of pattens, she made no complaint. No, these were noises which belonged to the winter pleasures; her spirits rose under their influence; and, like Mrs Musgrove, she was feeling, though not saying, that, after being long in the country, nothing could be so good for her as a little quiet cheerfulness.

Anne did not share these feelings. She persisted in a very determined, though very silent, disinclination for Bath; caught the first dim view of the extensive buildings, smoking in rain, without any wish of seeing them better; felt their progress through the streets to be, however disagreeable, yet too rapid; for who would be glad to see her when she arrived?

Persuasion

Streets Full of Scarecrows

Sir Walter thought much of Mrs Wallis; she was said to be an excessively pretty woman, beautiful. 'He longed to see her. He hoped she might make some amends for the many very plain faces he was continually passing in the streets. The worst of Bath was, the number of its plain women. He did not mean to say that there were no pretty women, but the number of the plain was out of all proportion. He had frequently observed, as he walked, that one handsome face would be followed by thirty, or five and thirty frights; and once, as he had stood in a shop in Bond-street, he had counted eighty-seven women go by, one after another, without there being a tolerable face among them. It had been a frosty morning, to be sure, a sharp frost, which hardly one woman in a thousand could stand the test of. But still, there certainly were a dreadful multitude of ugly women in Bath; and as for the men! they were infinitely worse. Such scare-crows as the streets were full of! It was evident how little the women were used to the sight of any thing tolerable, by the effect which a man of decent appearance produced. He had never walked any where arm in arm with Colonel Wallis, (who was a fine military figure, though sandy-haired) without observing that every woman's eye was upon him; every woman's eye was sure to be upon Colonel Wallis.' Modest Sir Walter! He was not allowed to escape, however. His daughter and Mrs Clay united in hinting that Colonel Wallis's companion might have as good a figure as Colonel Wallis, and certainly was not sandy-haired.

Persuasion

CHARLES LAMB

1775–1834

The Pleasures of London

Streets, streets, streets, markets, theatres, churches, Covent Gardens, shops sparkling with pretty faces of industrious milliners, neat sempstresses, ladies cheapening, gentlemen behind counters lying, authors in the street with spectacles, George Dyers (you may know them by their gait), lamps lit at night, pastrycooks' and silversmiths' shops, beautiful Quakers of Pentonville, noise of coaches, drowsy cry of watchmen at night, with bucks reeling home drunk; if you happen to wake at midnight, cries of 'Fire!' and 'Stop thief!' inns of court, with their learned air, and halls, and butteries, just like Cambridge colleges; old book-stalls, 'Jeremy Taylors,' 'Burtons on

Melancholy,' and 'Religio Medicis' on every stall. These are thy pleasures, O London, with thy many sins. O City, abounding in w . . ., for these may Keswick and her giant brood go hang!

letter to Thomas Manning, 1800

Fading Fears and Strange Cities

My night-fancies have long ceased to be afflictive. I confess an occasional night-mare: but I do not, as in early youth, keep a stud of them. Fiendish faces, with the extinguished taper, will come and look at me; but I know them for mockeries, even while I cannot elude their presence, and I fight and grapple with them. For the credit of my imagination, I am almost ashamed to say how tame and prosaic my dreams are grown. They are never romantic, seldom even rural. They are of architecture and of buildings—cities abroad, which I have never seen, and hardly have hope to see. I have traversed, for the seeming length of a natural day, Rome, Amsterdam, Paris, Lisbon—their churches, palaces, squares, market-places, shops, suburbs, ruins, with an inexpressible sense of delight—a map-like distinctness of trace—and a day-light vividness of vision, that was all but being awake. . . .

'Witches and other Night Fears', 1821

Bensley's Iago

Bensley's Iago was the only endurable one which I remember to have seen. No spectator from his action could divine more of his artifice than Othello was supposed to do. His confessions in soliloquy alone put you in possession of the mystery. There were no by-intimations to make the audience fancy their own discernment so much greater than that of the Moor—who commonly stands like a great helpless mark set up for mine Ancient, and a quantity of barren spectators, to shoot their bolts at. The Iago of Bensley did not go to work so grossly. There was a triumphant tone about the character, natural to a general consciousness of power; but none of that petty vanity which chuckles and cannot contain itself upon any little successful stroke of its knavery—as is common with your small villains, and green probationers in mischief. It did not clap or crow before its time. It was not a man setting his wits at a child, and winking all the while at other children who are mightily pleased at being let into the secret; but a consummate villain entrapping a noble nature into toils, against which no discernment was available, where the manner was as fathomless as the purpose seemed dark, and without motive.

'On Some of the Old Actors', 1822

An Imperfect Intellect

There is an order of imperfect intellects (under which mine must be content to rank) which in its constitution is essentially anti-Caledonian. The owners of the sort of faculties I allude to, have minds rather suggestive than comprehensive. They have no pretences to much clearness or precision in their ideas, or in their manner of expressing them. Their intellectual wardrobe (to confess fairly) has few whole pieces in it. They are content with fragments and scattered pieces of Truth. She presents no full front to them—a feature or side-face at the most. Hints and glimpses, germs and crude essays at a system, is the utmost they pretend to. They beat up a little game peradventure—and leave it to knottier heads, more robust constitutions, to run it down. The light that lights them is not steady and polar, but mutable and shifting: waxing, and again waning. Their conversation is accordingly. They will throw out a random word in or out of season, and be content to let it pass for what it is worth. They cannot speak always as if they were upon their oath—but must be understood, speaking or writing, with some abatement. They seldom wait to mature a proposition, but e'en bring it to market in the green ear. They delight to impart their defective discoveries as they arise, without waiting for their full developement. They are no systematizers, and would but err more by attempting it. Their minds, as I said before, are suggestive merely.

'Imperfect Sympathies', 1821

Byron

I never can make out his great *power*, which his admirers talk of. Why, a line of Wordsworth's is a lever to lift the immortal spirit! Byrons can only move the Spleen. He was at best a Satyrist—in any other way he was mean enough.

letter to Bernard Barton, 1824

WALTER SAVAGE LANDOR
1775–1864

Dark and Damaging

Barrow. We must not indulge in unfavourable views of mankind, since by doing it we make bad men believe that they are no worse than others, and we teach the good that they are good in vain.

Imaginary Conversations: 'Barrow and Newton', 1829

A Barbarous Practice

Lucullus. To dine in company with more than two is a Gaulish and a German thing. I can hardly bring myself to believe that I have eaten in concert with twenty; so barbarous and herdlike a practice does it now appear to me: such an incentive to drink much and talk loosely; not to add, such a necessity to speak loud, which is clownish and odious in the extreme.

Imaginary Conversations: 'Lucullus and Caesar', 1829

A Note in Music

Aesop. Laodameia died; Helen died; Leda, the beloved of Jupiter, went before. It is better to repose in the earth betimes than to sit up late; better, than to cling pertinaciously to what we feel crumbling under us, and to protract an inevitable fall. We may enjoy the present while we are insensible of infirmity and decay: but the present, like a note in music, is nothing but as it appertains to what is past and what is to come. There are no fields of amaranth on this side of the grave: there are no voices, O Rhodopè, that are not soon mute, however tuneful: there is no name, with whatever emphasis of passionate love repeated, of which the echo is not faint at last.

Imaginary Conversations: 'Aesop and Rhodope', 1844

WILLIAM HAZLITT
1778–1830

Common Sense

The thing is plain. All that men really understand is confined to a very small compass; to their daily affairs and experience; to what they have an opportunity to know, and motives to study or practise. The rest is affectation and imposture. The common people have the use of their limbs; for they live by their labour or skill. They understand their own business and the characters of those they have to deal with; for it is necessary that they should. They have eloquence to express their passions, and wit at will to express their contempt and provoke laughter. Their natural use of speech is not hung up in monumental mockery, in an obsolete language; nor is their sense of what is ludicrous, or readiness at finding out allusions to express it, buried in collections of *Anas*. You will hear more good things on the outside of a stage-coach from London to Oxford than if you were to pass a twelvemonth with the undergraduates, or heads of colleges, of that famous university; and more *home* truths are to be learnt from listening to a noisy debate in an alehouse than from attending to a formal one in the House of Commons. An elderly country gentlewoman will often know more of character, and be able to illustrate it by more amusing anecdotes taken from the history of what has been said, done, and gossiped in a country town for the last fifty years, than the best blue-stocking of the age will be able to glean from that sort of learning which consists in an acquaintance with all the novels and satirical poems published in the same period. People in towns, indeed, are woefully deficient in a knowledge of character, which they see only *in the bust*, not as a whole-length. People in the country not only know all that has happened to a man, but trace his virtues or vices, as they do his features, in their descent through several generations, and solve some contradiction in his behaviour by a cross in the breed half a century ago. The learned know nothing of the matter, either in town or country. Above all, the mass of society have common sense, which the learned in all ages want. The vulgar are in the right when they judge for themselves; they are wrong when they trust to their blind guides. The celebrated nonconformist divine, Baxter, was almost stoned to death by the good women of Kidderminster, for asserting from the pulpit that 'hell was paved with infants' skulls'; but, by the force of argument, and of learned quotations from the Fathers, the reverend preacher at length prevailed over the scruples of his congregation, and over reason and humanity.

'On the Ignorance of the Learned', 1818

The Late John Cavanagh

Died at his house in Burbage-street, St Giles's, John Cavanagh, the famous hand fives-player. When a person dies, who does any one thing better than any one else in the world, which so many others are trying to do well, it leaves a gap in society. It is not likely that any one will now see the game of fives played in its perfection for many years to come—for Cavanagh is dead, and has not left his peer behind him. It may be said that there are things of more importance than striking a ball against a wall—there are things indeed which make more noise and do as little good, such as making war and peace, making speeches and answering them, making verses and blotting them; making money and throwing it away. But the game of fives is what no one despises who has ever played at it. It is the finest exercise for the body, and the best relaxation for the mind. The Roman poet said that 'Care mounted behind the horseman and stuck to his skirts.' But this remark would not have applied to the fives-player. He who takes to playing at fives is twice young. He feels neither the past nor future 'in the instant.' Debts, taxes, 'domestic reason, foreign levy, nothing can touch him further.'

He has no other wish, no other thought, from the moment the game begins, but that of striking the ball, of placing it, of *making* it! This Cavanagh was sure to do. Whenever he touched the ball, there was an end of the chase. His eye was certain, his hand fatal, his presence of mind complete. He could do what he pleased, and he always knew exactly what to do. He saw the whole game, and played it; took instant advantage of his adversary's weakness, and recovered balls, as if by a miracle and from sudden thought, that every one gave for lost. He had equal power and skill, quickness, and judgment. He could either out-wit his antagonist by finesse, or beat him by main strength. Sometimes, when he seemed preparing to send the ball with the full swing of his arm, he would by a slight turn of his wrist drop it within an inch of the line. In general, the ball came from his hand, as if from a racket, in a straight horizontal line; so that it was in vain to attempt to overtake or stop it. As it was said of a great orator that he never was at a loss for a word, and for the properest word, so Cavanagh always could tell the degree of force necessary to be given to a ball, and the precise direction in which it should be sent. He did his work with the greatest ease; never took more pains than was necessary; and while others were fagging themselves to death, was as cool and collected as if he had just entered the court.

Death notice, 1819; later incorporated in 'The Indian Jugglers'

Enmity and Actuality

We can scarcely hate any one that we know. An acute observer complained, that if there was any one to whom he had a particular spite, and a wish to let him see it, the moment he came to sit down with him his enmity was disarmed by some unforeseen circumstance. If it was a Quarterly Reviewer, he was in other respects like any other man. Suppose, again, your adversary turns out a very ugly man, or wants an eye, you are baulked in that way: he is not what you expected, the object of your abstract hatred and implacable disgust. He may be a very disagreeable person, but he is no longer the same. If you come into a room where a man is, you find, in general, that he has a nose upon his face. 'There's sympathy!' This alone is a diversion to your unqualified contempt. He is stupid, and says nothing, but he seems to have something in him when he laughs. You had conceived of him as a rank Whig or Tory—yet he talks upon other subjects. You knew that he was a virulent party-writer; but you find that the man himself is a tame sort of animal enough. He does not bite. That's something. In short, you can make nothing of it. Even opposite vices balance one another. A man may be pert in company, but he is also dull; so that you cannot, though you try, hate him cordially, merely for the wish to be offensive. He is a knave. Granted. You learn, on a nearer acquaintance, what you did not know before—that he is a fool as well; so you forgive him. On the other hand, he may be a profligate public character, and may make no secret of it; but he gives you a hearty shake by the hand, speaks kindly to servants, and supports an aged father and mother. Politics apart, he is a very honest fellow. You are told that a person has carbuncles on his face; but you have ocular proofs that he is sallow, and pale as a ghost. This does not much mend the matter; but it blunts the edge of the ridicule, and turns your indignation against the inventor of the lie; but he is ——, the editor of a Scotch magazine; so you are just where you were. I am not very fond of anonymous criticism; I want to know who the author can be: but the moment I learn this, I am satisfied. Even —— would do well to come out of his disguise. It is the mask only that we dread and hate: the man may have something human about him!

'Why Distant Objects Please', 1822

A Lonely Pleasure

How fine it is to enter some old town, walled and turreted, just at the approach of night-fall, or to come to some straggling village, with the lights streaming through the surrounding gloom; and then after inquiring for the best entertainment that the place affords, to 'take one's ease at one's inn!' These eventful moments in our lives are in fact too precious, too full of solid, heart-felt happiness to be frittered and dribbled away in imperfect sympathy. I would have them all to myself, and drain them to the last drop: they will do to talk of or to write about afterwards.

'On Going a Journey', 1822

Coleridge, Southey, and Lamb

I saw no more of him [Coleridge] for a year or two, during which period he had been wandering in the Hartz Forest, in Germany; and his return was cometary, meteorous, unlike his setting out. It was not till some time after that I knew his friends Lamb and Southey. The last always appears to me (as I first saw him) with a common-place book under his arm, and the first with a *bon-mot* in his mouth. It was at Godwin's that I met him with Holcroft and Coleridge, where they were disputing fiercely which was the best—*Man as he was, or man as he is to be.* 'Give me,' says Lamb, 'man as he is *not* to be.' This saying was the beginning of a friendship between us, which I believe still continues.

'My First Acquaintance with the Poets', 1823

Social Priorities

In estimating the value of an acquaintance or even a friend, we give a preference to intellectual or convivial over moral qualities. The truth is, that in our habitual intercourse with others, we much oftener require to be amused than assisted. We consider less, therefore, what a person with whom we are intimate is ready to do for us in critical emergencies, than what he has to say on ordinary occasions. We dispense with his services, if he only saves us from *ennui.* In civilized society, words are of as much importance as things.

Characteristics, 1823

Bentham's Style

Our author's page presents a very nicely dove-tailed mosaic pavement of legal common-places. We slip and slide over its even surface without being arrested anywhere. Or his view of the human mind resembles a map, rather than a picture: the outline, the disposition is correct, but it wants colouring and relief. There is a technicality of manner, which renders his writings of more value to the professional inquirer than to the general reader. Again, his style is unpopular, not to say unintelligible. He writes a language of his own that *darkens knowledge.* His works have been translated into French—they ought to be translated into English. People wonder that Mr Bentham has not been prosecuted for the boldness and severity of some of his invectives. He might wrap up high treason in one of his inextricable periods, and it would never find its way into Westminster Hall. He is a kind of Manuscript author—he writes a cypher-hand, which the vulgar have no key to. The construction of his sentences is a curious frame-work with pegs and hooks to hang his thoughts upon, for his own use and guidance, but almost out of the reach of everybody else. It is a barbarous philosophical jargon, with all the repetitions, parentheses, formalities, uncouth nomenclature and verbiage of law-Latin; and what makes it worse, it is not mere verbiage, but has a great deal of acuteness and meaning in it, which you would be glad to pick out if you could.

In short, Mr Bentham writes as if he was allowed but a single sentence to express his whole view of a subject in, and as if, should he omit a single circumstance or step of the argument, it would be lost to the world for ever, like an estate by a flaw in the title-deeds. This is over-rating the importance of our own discoveries, and mistaking the nature and object of language altogether. Mr Bentham has *acquired* this disability: it is not natural to him. His admirable little work *On Usury,* published forty years ago, is clear, easy, and vigorous. But Mr Bentham has shut himself up since then 'in nook monastic,' conversing only with followers of his own or with 'men of Ind,' and has endeavoured to overlay his natural humour, sense, spirit, and style with the dust and cobwebs of an obscure solitude. The best of it is, he thinks his present mode of expressing himself perfect, and that whatever may be objected to his law or logic, no one can find the least fault with the purity, simplicity, and perspicuity of his style.

The Spirit of the Age, 1825

William Gifford

Mr Gifford was originally bred to some handicraft. He afterwards contrived to learn Latin, and was for some time an usher in a school, till he became a tutor in a nobleman's family. The low-bred, self-taught man, the pedant, and the dependent on the great, contribute to form the Editor of the *Quarterly Review*. He is admirably qualified for this situation, which he has held for some years, by a happy combination of defects, natural and acquired; and in the event of his death it will be difficult to provide him a suitable successor.

The Spirit of the Age

Going without Breakfast

It is hard to go without one's dinner through sheer distress, but harder still to go without one's breakfast. Upon the strength of that first and aboriginal meal, one may muster courage to face the difficulties before one, and to dare the worst: but to be roused out of one's warm bed, and perhaps a profound oblivion of care, with golden dreams (for poverty does not prevent golden dreams), and told there is nothing for breakfast, is cold comfort for which one's half-strung nerves are not prepared, and throws a damp upon the prospects of the day. It is a bad beginning. A man without a breakfast is a poor creature, unfit to go in search of one, to meet the frown of the world, or to borrow a shilling of a friend. He may beg at the corner of a street—nothing is too mean for the tone of his feelings—robbing on the highway is out of the question, as requiring too much courage, and some opinion of a man's self. It is, indeed, as old Fuller, or some worthy of that age, expresses it, 'the heaviest stone which melancholy can throw at a man,' to learn, the first thing after he rises in the morning, or even to be dunned with it in bed, that there is no loaf, tea, or butter in the house, and that the baker, the grocer, and butter-man have refused to give any farther credit. This is taking one sadly at a disadvantage. It is striking at one's spirit and resolution in their very source,—the stomach—it is attacking one on the side of hunger and mortification at once; it is casting one into the very mire of humility and Slough of Despond. The worst is, to know what face to put upon the matter, what excuse to make to the servants, what answer to send to the tradespeople; whether to laugh it off, or be grave, or angry, or indifferent; in short, to know how to parry off an evil which you cannot help. What a luxury, what a God's-send in such a dilemma, to find a half-crown which had slipped through a hole in the lining of your waistcoat, a crumpled bank-note in your breeches-pocket, or a guinea clinking in the bottom of your trunk, which had been thoughtlessly left there out of a former heap! Vain hope! Unfounded illusion! The experienced in such matters know better, and laugh in their sleeves at so improbable a suggestion. Not a corner, not a cranny, not a pocket, not a drawer has been left unrummaged, or has not been subjected over and over again to more than the strictness of a custom-house scrutiny. Not the slightest rustle of a piece of bank-paper, not the gentlest pressure of a piece of hard metal, but would have given notice of its hiding-place with electrical rapidity, long before, in such circumstances.

'On the Want of Money', 1827

As We Grow Old

As we grow old, our sense of the value of time becomes vivid. Nothing else, indeed, seems of any consequence. We can never cease wondering that that which has ever been should cease to be. We find many things remain the same: why then should there be change in us. This adds a convulsive grasp of whatever is, a sense of fallacious hollowness in all we see. Instead of the full, pulpy feeling of youth tasting existence and every object in it, all is flat and vapid,—a whited sepulchre, fair without but full of ravening and all uncleanness within. The world is a witch that puts us off with false shows and appearances. The simplicity of youth, the confiding expectation, the boundless raptures, are gone: we only think of getting out of it as well as we can, and without any great mischance or annoyance.

'On the Feeling of Immortality in Youth', 1827

LORD COCKBURN
1779–1854

A Scottish Judge: George Fergusson, Lord Hermand

Hermand's external appearance was as striking as everything else about him. Tall and thin, with grey lively eyes, and a long face, strongly expressive of whatever emotion he was under, his air and manner were distinctly those of a well-born and well-bred gentleman. His dress for society, the style of which he stuck to almost as firmly as he did to his principles, reminded us of the olden time, when trousers would have insulted any company, and braces were deemed an impeachment of nature. Neither the disclosure of the long neck by the narrow bit of muslin stock, nor the outbreak of the linen between the upper and nether garments, nor the short coat sleeves, with the consequent length of bare wrist, could hide his being one of the aristocracy. And if they had, the thin and powdered grey hair, flowing down into a long thin gentleman-like pig-tail, would have attested it. His morning raiment in the country was delightful. The articles, rough and strange, would of themselves have attracted notice in a museum. But set upon George Fergusson, at his paradise of Hermand, during vacation, on going forth for a long day's work—often manual—at his farm with his grey felt hat and tall weeding hoe—what could be more agrestic or picturesque?

What was it that made Hermand such an established wonder and delight? It seems to me to have been the supremacy in his composition of a single quality—intensity of temperament, which was so conspicuous that it prevented many people from perceiving anything else in him. He could not be indifferent. Repose, except in bed, where however he slept zealously, was unnatural and contemptible to him. His constitutional animation never failed to carry him a flight beyond ordinary mortals. Those who only saw the operation of this ardour in public conflict, were apt to set him down as a phrenzied man. But to those who knew Hermand personally, the lamb was the truer type. When removed from contests which provoke impatience, and placed in the private scene, where innocent excesses are only amusing, what a heart! what conversational wildness! There never was a more pleasing example of the superiority of right affections over intellectual endowments in the creation of happiness. Had he depended on his understanding alone, or chiefly, he would have been wrecked every week. But honesty, humanity, social habits, and diverting public explosions, always kept him popular.

With very simple tastes, and rather a contempt of epicurism, but very gregarious, he was fond of the pleasures of the table. He had acted in more of the severest scenes of old Scotch drinking than any man at last living. Commonplace topers think drinking a pleasure; but with Hermand it was a virtue.

Hermand combined strong Tory principles with stronger Whig friendships, and a taste for Calvinism, under the creed of which he deemed himself extremely pious, with the indulgence of every social propensity.

Two young gentlemen, great friends, went together to the theatre in Glasgow, supped at the lodgings of one of them, and passed a whole summer night over their punch. In the morning a kindly wrangle broke out, one of them was stabbed and died on the spot. The survivor was tried at Edinburgh, and was convicted of culpable homicide. It was one of the sad cases where the legal guilt was greater than the moral; and, very properly, he was sentenced to only a short imprisonment. Hermand, who felt that discredit had been brought on the cause of drinking, had no sympathy with the tenderness of his temperate brethren, and was vehement for transportation. 'We are told that there was no malice, and that the prisoner must have been in liquor. In liquor! Why, he was drunk! And yet he murdered the very man who had been drinking with him! They had been carousing the whole night; and yet he stabbed him after drinking a whole bottle of rum with him. Good God, my Laards, if he will do this when he's drunk, what will he not do when he's sober?'

Memorials of His Own Time, 1856

WASHINGTON IRVING
1783–1859

A Portrait of William the Testy (and a Partial Portrait of Thomas Jefferson)

Wilhelmus Kieft, who, in 1634, ascended the gubernatorial chair (to borrow a favorite though clumsy appellation of modern phraseologists), was of a lofty descent, his father being inspector of wind-mills in the ancient town of Saardam; and our hero, we are told, when a boy, made very curious investigations into the nature and operation of these machines, which was one reason why he afterwards came to be so ingenious a governor. His name, according to the most authentic etymologists, was a corruption of Kyver; that is to say, a *wrangler* or *scolder*; and expressed the characteristic of his family, which, for nearly two centuries, had kept the windy town of Saardam in hot water, and produced more tartars and brimstones than any ten families in the place; and so truly did he inherit this family peculiarity, that he had not been a year in the government of the province, before he was universally denominated William the Testy. His appearance answered to his name. He was a brisk, wiry, waspish little old gentleman; such a one as may now and then be seen stumping about our city in a broad-skirted coat with huge buttons, a cocked hat stuck on the back of his head, and a cane as high as his chin. His face was broad, but his features were sharp; his cheeks were scorched into a dusky red, by two fiery little gray eyes; his nose turned up, and the corners of his month turned down, pretty much like the muzzle of an irritable pugdog.

I have heard it observed by a profound adept in human physiology, that if a woman waxes fat with the progress of years, her tenure of life is somewhat precarious, but if haply she withers as she grows old, she lives forever. Such promised to be the case with William the Testy, who grew tough in proportion as he dried. He had withered, in fact, not through the process of years, but through the tropical fervor of his soul, which burnt like a vehement rush-light in his bosom; inciting him to incessant broils and bickerings. Ancient traditions speak much of his learning, and of the gallant inroads he had made into the dead languages, in which he had made captive a host of Greek nouns and Latin verbs; and brought off rich booty in ancient saws and apothegms; which he was wont to parade in his public harangues, as a triumphant general of yore, his *spolia opima*. Of metaphysics he knew enough to confound all hearers and himself into the bargain. In logic, he knew the whole family of syllogisms and dilemmas, and was so proud of his skill that he never suffered even a self-evident fact to pass unargued. It was observed, however, that he seldom got into an argument without getting into a perplexity, and then into a passion with his adversary for not being convinced gratis.

He had, moreover, skirmished smartly on the frontiers of several of the sciences, was fond of experimental philosophy, and prided himself upon inventions of all kinds. His abode, which he had fixed at a Bowerie or country-seat at a short distance from the city, just at what is now called Dutch-street, soon abounded with proofs of his ingenuity: patent smoke-jacks that required a horse to work them; Dutch ovens that roasted meat without fire; carts that went before the horses; weather-cocks that turned against the wind; and other wrong-headed contrivances that astonished and confounded all beholders. The house, too, was beset with paralytic cats and dogs, the subjects of his experimental philosophy; and the yelling and yelping of the latter unhappy victims of science, while aiding in the pursuit of knowledge, soon gained for the place the name of 'Dog's Misery,' by which it continues to be known even at the present day.

It is in knowledge as in swimming; he who flounders and splashes on the surface, makes more noise, and attracts more attention, than the pearl-diver who quietly dives in quest of treasures to the bottom. The vast acquirements of the new governor were the theme of marvel among the simple burghers of New Amsterdam; he figured about the place as learned a man as a Bonze at Pekin, who has mastered one half of the Chinese alphabet: and was unanimously pronounced a 'universal genius!'

I have known in my time many a genius of this stamp; but, to speak my mind freely, I never knew one who, for the ordinary purposes of life, was worth his weight in straw. In this respect, a little sound judgment and plain common sense is worth all the sparkling genius that ever wrote poetry or invented theories.

A History of New York by Diedrich Knickerbocker, 1809

LEIGH HUNT
1784–1859

The Irresistible Theatre

That is a pleasant time of life, the playgoing time in youth, when the coach is packed full to go to the theatre, and brothers and sisters, parents and lovers (none of whom, perhaps, go very often) are all wafted together in a flurry of expectation; when the only wish as they go (except with the lovers) is to go as fast as possible, and no sound is so delightful as the cry of 'Bill of the Play'; when the smell of links in the darkest and muddiest winter's night is charming; and the steps of the coach are let down; and a roar of hoarse voices round the door, and *mud-shine* on the pavement, are accompanied with the sight of the warm-looking lobby which is about to be entered; and then enter, and pay, and ascend the pleasant stairs, and begin to hear the *silence* of the house, perhaps the first jingle of the music; and the box is entered amidst some little awkwardness in descending to their places, and being looked at; and at length they sit, and are become used to by their neighbours, and shawls and smiles are adjusted, and the play-bill is handed round or pinned to the cushion, and the gods are a little noisy, and the music veritably commences, and at length the curtain is drawn up, and the first delightful syllables are heard:

'Ah! my dear Charles, when did you see the lovely Olivia?'

'Oh, my dear Sir George, talk not to me of Olivia. The cruel guardian,' etc.

Autobiography, 1850

Shelley in Hampstead

To return to Hampstead.—Shelley often came there to see me, sometimes to stop for several days. He delighted in the natural broken ground, and in the fresh air of the place, especially when the wind set in from the north-west, which used to give him an intoxication of animal spirits. Here also he swam his paper boats on the ponds, and delighted to play with my children, particularly with my eldest boy, the seriousness of whose imagination, and his susceptibility of a 'grim' impression (a favourite epithet of Shelley's), highly interested him. He would play at 'frightful creatures' with him, from which the other would snatch 'a fearful joy', only begging him occasionally 'not to do the horn', which was a way that Shelley had of screwing up his hair in front, to imitate a weapon of that sort.

Autobiography

Lord Castlereagh

He should have led a private life, and been counted one of the models of the aristocracy; for though a ridiculous speaker, and a cruel politician (out of impatience of seeing constant trouble, and not knowing otherwise how to end it), he was an intelligent and kindly man in private life, and could be superior to his position as a statesman. He delighted in the political satire of the *Beggar's Opera*; has been seen applauding it from a stage box; and Lady Morgan tells us, would ask her in company to play him the songs on the pianoforte, and good-humouredly accompany them with a bad voice. How pleasant it is thus to find oneself reconciled to men whom we have ignorantly undervalued! and how fortunate to have lived long enough to say so!

Autobiography

THOMAS DE QUINCEY
1785–1859

Opium Visions

I

And now came a tremendous change, which, unfolding itself slowly like a scroll, through many months, promised an abiding torment; and, in fact, it never left me, though recurring more or less intermittingly. Hitherto the human face had often mixed in my dreams, but not despotically, nor with any special power of tormenting. But now that affection which I have called the tyranny of the human face began to unfold itself. Perhaps some part of my London life (the searching for Ann amongst fluctuating crowds) might be answerable for this. Be that as it may, now it was that upon the rocking waters of the ocean the human face began to reveal itself; the sea appeared paved with innumerable faces, upturned to the heavens; faces, imploring, wrathful, despairing; faces that surged upwards by thousands, by myriads, by generations: infinite was my agitation; my mind tossed, as it seemed, upon the billowy ocean, and weltered upon the weltering waves.

II

Under the connecting feeling of tropical heat and vertical sunlights, I brought together all creatures, birds, beasts, reptiles, all trees and plants, usages and appearances, that are found in all tropical regions, and assembled them together in China or Hindostan. From kindred feelings, I soon brought Egypt and her gods under the same law. I was stared at, hooted at, grinned at, chattered at, by monkeys, by paroquets, by cockatoos. I ran into pagodas, and was fixed for centuries at the summit, or in secret rooms; I was the idol; I was the priest; I was worshipped; I was sacrificed. I fled from the wrath of Brama through all the forests of Asia; Vishnu hated me; Seeva lay in wait for me. I came suddenly upon Isis and Osiris: I had done a deed, they said, which the ibis and the crocodile trembled at. Thousands of years I lived and was buried in stone coffins, with mummies and sphinxes, in narrow chambers at the heart of eternal pyramids. I was kissed, with cancerous kisses, by crocodiles, and was laid, confounded with all unutterable abortions, amongst reeds and Nilotic mud.

Confessions of an English Opium-Eater, 1822

A Glorious Blaze

If you are summoned to the spectacle of a great fire, undoubtedly the first impulse is—to assist in putting it out. But that field of exertion is very limited, and is soon filled by regular professional people, trained and equipped for the service. In the case of a fire which is operating upon *private* property, pity for a neighbour's calamity checks us at first in treating the affair as a scenic spectacle. But perhaps the fire may be confined to public buildings. And in any case, after we have paid our tribute of regret to the affair, considered as a calamity, inevitably, and without restraint, we go on to consider it as a stage spectacle. Exclamations of—How grand! how magnificent! arise in a sort of rapture from the crowd. For instance, when Drury Lane was burned down in the first decennium of this century, the falling in of the roof was signalised by a mimic suicide of the protecting Apollo that surmounted and crested the centre of this roof. The god was stationary with his lyre, and seemed looking down upon the fiery ruins that were so rapidly approaching him. Suddenly the supporting timbers below him gave way; a convulsive heave of the billowing flames seemed for a moment to raise the statue; and then, as if on some impulse of despair, the presiding deity appeared not to fall, but to throw himself into the fiery deluge, for he went down head foremost; and in all respects, the descent had the air of a voluntary act. What followed? From every one of the bridges over the river, and from other open areas which commanded the spectacle, there arose a sustained uproar of admiration and sympathy.

'On Murder Considered as One of the Fine Arts', 1827

Wordsworth's Legs

He was, upon the whole, not a well-made man. His legs were pointedly condemned by all female connoisseurs in legs; not that they were bad in any way which *would* force itself upon your notice—there was no absolute deformity about them; and undoubtedly they had been serviceable legs beyond the average standard of human requisition; for I calculate, upon good data, that with these identical legs Wordsworth must have traversed a distance of 175,000 to 180,000 English miles—a mode of exertion which, to him, stood in the stead of alcohol and all other stimulants whatsoever to the animal spirits; to which, indeed, he was indebted for a life of unclouded happiness, and we for much of what is most excellent in his writings. But, useful as they have proved themselves, the Wordsworthian legs were certainly not ornamental; and it was really a pity, as I agreed with a lady in thinking, that he had not another pair for evening dress parties—when no boots lend their friendly aid to mask our imperfections from the eyes of female rigorists—those *elegantes formarum spectatrices.* A sculptor would certainly have disapproved of their contour.

'Recollections of the Lake Poets', 1839

A Lost Girl

Sweet funeral bells from some incalculable distance, wailing over the dead that die before the dawn, awakened me as I slept in a boat moored to some familiar shore. The morning twilight even then was breaking; and, by the dusky revelations which it spread, I saw a girl, adorned with a garland of white roses about her head for some great festival, running along the solitary strand in extremity of haste. Her running was the running of panic; and often she looked back as to some dreadful enemy in the rear. But when I leaped ashore, and followed on her steps to warn her of a peril in front, alas! from me she fled as from another peril, and vainly I shouted to her of quick-sands that lay ahead. Faster and faster she ran; round a promontory of rocks she wheeled out of sight; in an instant I also wheeled round it, but only to see the treacherous sands gathering above her head. Already her person was buried; only the fair young head and the diadem of white roses around it were still visible to the pitying heavens; and, last of all, was visible, one white marble arm. I saw by the early twilight this fair young head, as it was sinking down to darkness—saw this marble arm, as it rose above her head and her treacherous grave, tossing, faltering, rising, clutching, as at some false deceiving hand stretched out from the clouds—saw this marble arm uttering her dying hope, and then uttering her dying despair. The head, the diadem, the arm—these all had sunk; at last over these also the cruel quicksand had closed; and no memorial of the fair young girl remained on earth, except my own solitary tears, and the funeral bells from the desert seas, that, rising again more softly, sang a requiem over the grave of the buried child, and over her blighted dawn.

'The English Mail Coach: Dream Fugue', 1849

THOMAS LOVE PEACOCK
1785–1866

Clarinda and the Captain

The Captain took his portfolio under his right arm, his camp stool in his right hand, offered his left arm to Lady Clarinda, and followed at a reasonable distance behind Miss Crotchet and Lord Bossnowl, contriving, in the most natural manner possible, to drop more and more into the rear.

Lady Clarinda. I am glad to see you can make yourself so happy with drawing old trees and mounds of grass.

Captain Fitzchrome. Happy, Lady Clarinda! oh, no! How can I be happy when I see the idol of my heart about to be sacrificed on the shrine of Mammon?

Lady Clarinda. Do you know, though Mammon has a sort of ill name, I really think he is a very popular character; there must be at the bottom something amiable about him. He is certainly one of those pleasant creatures whom every body abuses, but without whom no evening party is endurable. I dare say, love in a cottage is very pleasant; but then it positively must be a cottage ornée: but would not the same love be a great deal safer in a castle, even if Mammon furnished the fortification?

Captain Fitzchrome. Oh, Lady Clarinda! there is a heartlessness in that language that chills me to the soul.

Lady Clarinda. Heartlessness! No: my heart is on my lips. I speak just what I think. You used to like it, and say it was as delightful as it was rare.

Captain Fitzchrome. True, but you did not then talk as you do now, of love in a castle.

Lady Clarinda. Well, but only consider: a dun is a horridly vulgar creature; it is a creature I cannot endure the thought of: and a cottage lets him in so easily. Now a castle keeps him at bay. You are a half-pay officer, and are at leisure to command the garrison: but where is the castle? and who is to furnish the commissariat?

Captain Fitzchrome. Is it come to this, that you make a jest of my poverty? Yet is my poverty only comparative. Many decent families are maintained on smaller means.

Lady Clarinda. Decent families: aye, decent is the distinction from respectable. Respectable means rich, and decent means poor. I should die if I heard my family called decent. And then your decent family always lives in a snug little place: I hate a little place; I like large rooms and large looking-glasses, and large parties, and a fine large butler, with a tinge of smooth red in his face; an outward and visible sign that the family he serves is respectable; if not noble, highly respectable.

Captain Fitzchrome. I cannot believe that you say all this in earnest. No man is less disposed than I am to deny the importance of the substantial comforts of life. I once flattered myself that in our estimate of these things we were nearly of a mind.

Lady Clarinda. Do you know, I think an opera-box a very substantial comfort, and a carriage. You will tell me that many decent people walk arm in arm through the snow, and sit in clogs and bonnets in the pit at the English theatre. No doubt it is very pleasant to those who are used to it; but it is not to my taste.

Captain Fitzchrome. You always delighted in trying to provoke me; but I cannot believe that you have not a heart.

Lady Clarinda. You do not like to believe that I have a heart, you mean. You wish to think I have lost it, and you know to whom; and when I tell you that it is still safe in my own keeping, and that I do not mean to give it away, the unreasonable creature grows angry.

Captain Fitzchrome. Angry! far from it: I am perfectly cool.

Lady Clarinda. Why, you are pursing your brows, biting your lips, and lifting up your foot as if you would stamp it into the earth. I must say anger becomes you; you would make a charming Hotspur. Your every-day-dining-out face is rather insipid: but I assure you my heart is in danger when you are in the heroics. It is so rare, too, in these days of smooth manners, to see any thing like natural expression in a man's face. There is one set form for every man's face in female society; a sort of serious comedy, walking gentleman's face; but the moment the creature falls in love, he begins to give himself airs, and plays off all the varieties of his physiognomy, from the Master Slender to the Petruchio; and then he is actually very amusing.

Captain Fitzchrome. Well, Lady Clarinda, I will not be angry, amusing as it may be to you: I listen more in sorrow than in anger. I half believe you in earnest, and mourn as over a fallen angel.

Crotchet Castle, 1831

Newspapers

Mrs Opimian. Perhaps, Doctor, the world is too good to see any novelty except in something wrong.

The Reverend Doctor Opimian. Perhaps it is only wrong that arrests attention, because right is common, and wrong is rare. Of the many thousand persons who walk daily through a street you only hear of one who has been robbed or knocked down. If ever Hamlet's news—'that the world has grown honest'—should prove true, there would be an end of our newspaper. For, let us see, what is the epitome of a newspaper? In the first place, specimens of all the deadly sins, and infinite varieties of violence and fraud; a great quantity of talk, called by courtesy legislative wisdom, of which the result is 'an incoherent and undigested mass of law, shot down, as from a rubbish-cart, on the heads of the people;' lawyers barking at each other in that peculiar style of hylactic delivery which is called forensic eloquence, and of which the first and most distinguished practitioner was Cerberus; bear-garden meetings of mismanaged companies, in which directors and shareholders abuse each other in choice terms, not all to be found even in Rabelais; burstings of bank bubbles, which, like a touch of harlequin's wand, strip off their masks and dominoes from 'highly respectable' gentlemen, and leave them in their true figures of cheats and pickpockets; societies of all sorts, for teaching everybody everything, meddling with everybody's business, and mending everybody's morals; mountebank advertisements promising the beauty of Helen in a bottle of cosmetic, and the age of Old Parr in a box of pills; folly all alive in things called reunions; announcements that some exceedingly stupid fellow has been 'entertaining' a select company; matters, however multiform, multifarious, and multitudinous, all brought into family likeness by the varnish of false pretension with which they are all overlaid.

Gryll Grange, 1860

BENJAMIN ROBERT HAYDON
1786–1846

The Smoke of London

So far from the smoke of London being offensive to me, it has always been to my imagination the sublime canopy that shrouds the City of the World. Drifted by the wind or hanging in gloomy grandeur over the vastness of our Babylon, the sight of it always filled my mind with feelings of energy such as no other spectacle could inspire.

'Be Gode,' said Fuseli to me one day, 'it's like de smoke of de Israelites making bricks.' 'It is grander,' said I, 'for it is the smoke of a people who would have made the Egyptians make bricks for them.' 'Well done, John Bull,' replied Fuseli.

Often have I studied its peculiarities from the hills near London, whence in the midst of its drifted clouds you catch a glimpse of the great dome of St Paul's, announcing at once civilisation and power.

Autobiography and Journals, 1853

Macbeth *and Toast*

Haydon spent an evening with Mrs Siddons to hear her read *Macbeth*. 'She acts Macbeth herself,' he writes, 'better than either Kemble or Kean. It is extraordinary the awe this wonderful woman inspires. After her first reading the men retired to tea. While we were all eating toast and tingling cups and saucers, she began again. It was like the effect of a mass bell at Madrid. All noise ceased; we slunk to our seats like boors, two or three of the most distinguished men of the day, with the very toast in their mouths, afraid to bite. It was curious to see Lawrence in this predicament, to hear him bite by degrees, and then stop for fear of making too much crackle, his eyes full of water from the constraint; and at the same time to hear Mrs Siddons' "eye of newt and toe of frog!" and then to see Lawrence give a sly bite, and then look awed and pretend to be listening. I went away highly gratified, and as I stood on the landing-place to get cool I overheard my own servant in the hall say: "What! is that the old lady making such a noise?" "Yes." "Why, she makes as much noise as ever!" "Yes," was the answer; "she tunes her pipes as well as ever she did."'

written 1821; *Autobiography and Journals*

The Coronation of George IV

Every movement, as the time approached for the King's appearance, was pregnant with interest. The appearance of a monarch has something in it like the rising of a sun. There are indications which announce the luminary's approach; a streak of light—the tipping of a cloud—the singing of the lark—the brilliance of the sky, till the cloud edges get brighter and brighter, and he rises majestically into the heavens. So with a king's advance. A whisper of mystery turns all eyes to the throne. Suddenly two or three rise; others fall back; some talk, direct, hurry, stand still, or disappear. Then three or four of high rank appear from behind the throne; an interval is left; the crowds scarce breathe. Something rustles, and a being buried in satin, feathers, and diamonds rolls gracefully into his seat. The room rises with a sort of feathered, silken thunder. Plumes wave, eyes sparkle, glasses are out, mouths smile, and one man becomes the prime object of attraction to thousands.

written 1821; *Autobiography and Journals*

GEORGE GORDON, LORD BYRON
1788–1824

'Actions—actions'

[Rogers] thinks the *Quarterly* will attack me next. Let them. I have been 'peppered so highly' in my time, *both* ways, that it must be cayenne or aloes to make me taste. I can sincerely say that I am not very much alive *now* to criticism. But—in tracing this—I rather believe that it proceeds from my not attaching that importance to authorship which many do, and which, when young, I did also. 'One gets tired of every thing, my angel,' says Valmont. The 'angels' are the only things of which I am not a little sick—but I do think the preference of *writers* to *agents*—the mighty stir made about scribbling and scribes, by themselves and others—a sign of effeminacy, degeneracy, and weakness. Who would write, who had any thing better to do? 'Action—action—action'—said Demosthenes: 'Actions—actions,' I say, and not writing,—least of all, rhyme. Look at the querulous and monotonous lives of the 'genus;'—except Cervantes, Tasso, Dante, Ariosto, Kleist (who were brave and active citizens), Æschylus, Sophocles, and some other of the antiques also—what a worthless, idle brood it is!

Journal, 1813

Downright Existence

When one subtracts from life infancy (which is vegetation),—sleep, eating, and swilling—buttoning and unbuttoning—how much remains of downright existence? The summer of a dormouse.

Journal, 1813

A Great Scholar

I remember to have seen Porson at Cambridge in the Hall of our College—and in private parties—but not frequently—and I never can recollect him except as drunk or brutal and generally both—I mean in an Evening for in the hall he dined at the Dean's table—& I at the Vice-Master's so that I was not near him, and he then & there appeared sober in his demeanour—nor did I ever hear of excess or outrage—on his part in public—Commons—college—or Chapel—but I have seen him in a private party of under-Graduates—many of them freshmen & strangers—take up a poker to one of them—& heard him use language as blackguard as his action; I have seen Sheridan drunk too with all the world, but his intoxication was that of Bacchus—& Porson's that of Silenus—of all the disgusting brutes—sulky—abusive—and intolerable—Porson was the most bestial as far as the few times that I saw him went—which were only at Wm. Bankes's (the Nubian Discoverer's) rooms—I saw him once go away in a rage—because nobody knew the name of the 'Cobbler of Messina' insulting their ignorance with the most vulgar terms of reprobation.—He was tolerated in this state amongst the young men—for his talents—as the Turks think a Madman—inspired—& bear with him;—he used to recite—or rather vomit pages of all languages—& could hiccup Greek like a

Helot—& certainly Sparta never shocked her children with a grosser exhibition than this Man's intoxication.

letter to John Murray, 1818

Teresa Guiccioli

I have fallen in love within the last month with a Romagnuola Countess from Ravenna—the Spouse of a year of Count Guiccioli—who is sixty—the Girl twenty—he has eighty thousand ducats of rent—and has had two wives before—but he is Sixty—he is the first of Ravenna Nobles—but he is sixty—She is fair as Sunrise—and warm as Noon—we had but ten days—to manage all our little matters in beginning middle and end. & we managed them;—and I have done my duty—with the proper consummation.—But She is young—and was not content with what she had done—unless it was to be turned to the advantage of the public—and so She made an eclat which rather astonished even the Venetians—and electrified the Conversazioni of the Benzone—the Albrizzi—& the Michelli—and made her husband look embarrassed.—They have been gone back to Ravenna—some time—but they return in the Winter.—She is the queerest woman I ever met with—for in general they cost one something in one way or other—whereas by an odd combination of circumstances—I have proved an expence to HER—which is not my custom,—but an accident—however it don't matter.—She is a sort of an Italian Caroline Lamb, except that She is much prettier, and not so savage.—But She has the same red-hot head—the same noble dis*dain* of public opinion—with the superstructure of all that Italy can add to such natural dispositions.—To be sure they may go much further here with impunity—as her husband's rank ensured their reception at all societies including the Court—and as it was her first outbreak since Marriage—the Sympathizing world was liberal.—She is also of the Ravenna noblesse—educated in a convent—sacrifice to Wealth—filial duty and all that.—I am damnably in love—but they are gone—gone—for many months—and nothing but Hope—keeps me alive seriously.

letter to Douglas Kinnaird, 1818

An Unlucky Rascal

The lapse of ages *changes* all things—time—language—the earth—the bounds of the sea—the stars of the sky, and every thing 'about, around, and underneath' man, *except man himself*, who has always been, and always will be, an unlucky rascal. The infinite variety of lives conduct but to death, and the infinity of wishes lead but to disappointment. All the discoveries which have yet been made have multiplied little but existence.

Journal, 1821

A First Dash

My first dash into poetry, was as early as 1800.——It was the ebullition of a passion for my first Cousin Margaret Parker (daughter and grand-daughter of the two Admirals Parker) one of the most beautiful of Evanescent beings.—I have long forgotten the verses—but it would be difficult for me to forget her——Her dark eyes!—her long eyelashes! her completely Greek cast of face and figure!—I was then about twelve—She rather older—perhaps a year.——She died about a year or two afterwards—in consequence of a fall which injured her spine and induced consumption.

Journal, 1822

SAMUEL BAMFORD
1788–1872

Peterloo

On the cavalry drawing up they were received with a shout, of good will, as I understood it. They shouted again, waving their sabres over their heads; and then, slackening rein, and striking spur into their steeds, they dashed forward, and began cutting the people.

'Stand fast,' I said, 'they are riding upon us, stand fast.' And there was a general cry in our quarter of 'Stand fast.' The cavalry were in confusion: they evidently could not, with all the weight of man and horse, penetrate that compact mass of human beings; and their sabres were plied to hew a way through naked held-up hands, and defenceless heads; and then chopped limbs, and wound-gaping skulls were seen; and groans and cries were mingled with the din of that horrid confusion. 'Ah! ah!' 'for shame! for shame!' was shouted. Then, 'Break! break! they are killing them in front, and they cannot get away'; and there was a general cry of 'break! break.' For a moment the crowd held back as in a pause; then was a rush, heavy and resistless as a headlong sea; and a sound like low thunder, with screams, prayers, and imprecations from the crowd-moiled, and sabre-doomed, who could not escape.

In ten minutes from the commencement of the havock, the field was an open and almost deserted space. The sun looked down through a sultry and motionless air. The curtains and blinds of the windows within view were all closed. A gentleman or two might occasionally be seen looking out from one of the new houses before-mentioned, near the door of which, a group of persons, (special constables) were collected, and apparently in conversation; others were assisting the wounded, or carrying off the dead.

The hustings remained, with a few broken and hewed flag-staves erect, and a torn and gashed banner or two dropping; whilst over the whole field, were strewed caps, bonnets, hats, shawls, and shoes, and other parts of male and female dress; trampled, torn, and bloody. The yeomanry had dismounted,—some were easing their horses' girths, others adjusting their accoutrements; and some were wiping their sabres. Several mounds of human beings still remained where they had fallen, crushed down, and smothered. Some of these still groaning,—others with staring eyes, were gasping for breath, and others would never breathe more. All was silent save those low sounds, and the occasional snorting and pawing of steeds. Persons might sometimes be noticed peeping from attics and over the tall ridgings of houses, but they quickly withdrew, as if fearful of being observed, or unable to sustain the full gaze, of a scene so hideous and abhorrent.

Passages in the Life of a Radical, 1844

JAMES FENIMORE COOPER
1789–1851

Enter Natty Bumppo

The sun had fallen below the crest of the nearest wave of the prairie, leaving the usual rich and glowing train on its track. In the centre of this flood of fiery light, a human form appeared, drawn against the gilded background, as distinctly, and, seemingly as palpable, as though it would come within the grasp of any extended hand. The figure was colossal; the attitude musing and melancholy, and the situation directly in the route of the travellers. But imbedded, as it was, in its setting of garish light, it was impossible to distinguish its just proportions or true character.

The effect of such a spectacle was instantaneous and powerful. The man in front of the emigrants came to a stand, and remained gazing at the mysterious object, with a dull interest, that soon quickened into superstitious awe. His sons, so soon as the first emotions of surprise had a little abated, drew slowly around him, and, as they who governed the teams gradually followed their example, the whole party was soon condensed in one, silent, and wondering group. Notwithstanding the impression of a supernatural agency was very general among the travellers, the ticking of gun-locks was heard, and one or two of the bolder youths cast their rifles forward, in readiness for service.

The Prairie, 1827

Natty Bumppo and Hurry Harry

'I look upon the red-men to be quite as human as we are ourselves, Hurry. They have their gifts, and their religion, it's true; but that makes no difference in the end, when each will be judged according to his deeds, and not according to his skin.'

'That's downright missionary, and will find little favour up in this part of the country, where the Moravians don't congregate. Now, skin makes the man. This is reason; else how are people to judge of each other. The skin is put on, over all, in order that when a creatur', or a mortal, is fairly seen, you may know at once what to make of him. You know a bear from a hog, by his skin, and a grey squirrel from a black.'

'True, Hurry,' said the other looking back and smiling; 'nevertheless, they are both squirrels.'

'Who denies it? But you'll not say that a red man and a white man are both Injins?'

'No; but I *do* say they are both men. Men of different races and colours, and having different gifts and traditions, but, in the main, with the same natur'. Both have souls; and both will be held accountable for their deeds in this life.'

Hurry was one of those theorists who believed in the inferiority of all the human race who were not white. His notions on the subject were not very clear, nor were his definitions at all well settled; but his opinions were none the less dogmatical or fierce. His conscience accused him of sundry lawless acts against the Indians, and he had found it an exceedingly easy mode of quieting it, by putting the whole family of red men, incontinently, without the category of human rights. Nothing angered him sooner than to deny his proposition, more especially if the denial were accompanied by a show of plausible argument; and he did not listen to his companion's remarks with much composure of either manner or feeling.

The Deerslayer, 1841

FREDERICK MARRYAT
1792–1848

The Author's First Day at Sea

The *Impérieuse* sailed; the Admiral of the port was one who *would* be obeyed, but *would not* listen always to reason or common sense. The signal for sailing was enforced by gun after gun; the anchor was hove up, and, with all her stores on deck, her guns not even mounted, in a state of confusion unparalleled from her being obliged to hoist in faster than it was possible she could stow away, she was driven out of harbour to encounter a heavy gale. A few hours more would have enabled her to proceed to sea with security, but they were denied; the consequences were appalling, they might have been fatal. In the general confusion some iron too near the binnacles had attracted the needle of the compasses; the ship was steered out of her course. At midnight, in a heavy gale at the close of November, so dark that you could not distinguish any object, however close, the *Impérieuse* dashed upon the rocks between Ushant and the Main. The cry of terror which ran through the lower decks; the grating of the keel as she was forced in; the violence of the shocks which convulsed the frame of the vessel; the hurrying up of the ship's company without their clothes; and then the enormous wave which again bore her up, and carried her clean over the reef, will never be effaced from my memory.

private log; Florence Marryat, *Life of Marryat*, 1872

An Under Usher

'My father was a gentleman, and, until I was fourteen years old, I was a gentleman, or the son of one; then he died, and that profession was over, for he left me nothing; my mother married again, and left me; she left me at school, and the master kept me there for a year, in hopes of being paid; but, hearing nothing of my mother, and not knowing what to do with me, he at last (for he was a kind man) installed me as under usher of the school; for, you see, my education had been good, and I was well qualified for the situation, as far as capability went; it was rather a bathos, though, to sink from a gentleman's son to an under usher; but I was not a philosopher at that time. I handed the toast to the master and mistress, the head ushers and parlour boarders, but was not allowed any myself; I taught Latin and Greek, and English Grammar, to the little boys, who made faces at me, and put crooked pins on the bottom of my chair; I walked at the head of the string when they went out for an airing, and walked upstairs the last when it was time to go to bed. I had all the drudgery, and none of the comforts; I was up first, and held answerable for all deficiencies; I had to examine all their nasty little trousers, and hold weekly conversation with the botcher, as to the possibility of repairs; to run out if a hen cackled, that the boys should not get the egg; to wipe the noses of my mistress's children, and carry them if they roared, to pay for all broken glass, if I could not discover the culprit, to account for all bad smells, for all noise, and for all ink spilled; to make all the pens and to keep one hundred boys silent and attentive at church: for all which, with deductions, I received £40 a-year, and found my own washing. I stayed two years, during which time I contrived to save about £6; and with that, one fine morning, I set off on my travels, fully satisfied that, come what would, I could not change for the worse.'

Joseph Rushbrook, or The Poacher, 1841

PERCY BYSSHE SHELLEY

1792–1822

The Mind in Creation

Poetry is not like reasoning, a power to be exerted according to the determination of the will. A man cannot say, 'I will compose poetry.' The greatest poet even cannot say it; for the mind in creation is as a fading coal, which some invisible influence, like an inconstant wind, awakens to transitory brightness; this power arises from within, like the colour of a flower which fades and changes as it is developed, and the conscious portions of our natures are unprophetic either of its approach or its departure. Could this influence be durable in its original purity and force, it is impossible to predict the greatness of the results; but when composition begins, inspiration is already on the decline, and the most glorious poetry that has ever been communicated to the world is probably a feeble shadow of the original conceptions of the poet.

A Defence of Poetry, 1821

A Statue of Venus

She seems to have just issued from the bath, and yet to be animated with the enjoyment of it. She seems all soft and mild enjoyment, and the curved lines of her fine limbs flow into each other with never-ending continuity of sweetness. Her face expresses a breathless yet passive and innocent voluptuousness without affectation, without doubt; it is at once desire and enjoyment and the pleasure arising from both. Her lips which are without the sublimity of lofty and impetuous passion like [. . .] or the grandeur of enthusiastic imagination like the Apollo of the Capitol, or an union of both like the Apollo Belvedere, have the tenderness of arch yet pure and affectionate desire, and the mode in which the ends are drawn in yet opened by the smile which forever circles round them, and the tremulous curve into which they are wrought by inextinguishable desire, and the tongue lying against the lower lip as in the listlessness of passive joy, express love, still love.

Her eyes seem heavy and swimming with pleasure, and her small forehead fades on both sides into that sweet swelling and then declension of the bone over the eye and prolongs itself to the cheek in that mode which expresses simple and tender feelings.

The neck is full and swollen as with the respiration of delight and flows with gentle curves into her perfect form.

Her form is indeed perfect. She is half sitting on and half rising from a shell, and the fulness of her limbs, and their complete roundness and perfection, do not diminish the vital energy with which they seem to be embued. The mode in which the lines of the curved back flow into and around the thighs, and the wrinkled muscles of the belly, wrinkled by the attitude, is truly astonishing. The attitude of her arms which are lovely beyond imagination is natural, unaffected, and unforced. This perhaps is the finest personification of Venus, the Deity of superficial desire, in all antique statuary. Her pointed and pear-like bosom ever virgin—the virgin Mary might have this beauty, but alas! . . .

'Notes on Sculptures in Rome and Florence', 1819–20

JOHN CLARE
1793–1864

The Robin and the Wren

It is not commonly known that the robin is a very quarrelsome bird it is not only at frequent warfare with its own species but attacks boldly every other small bird that comes in its way & is generally the conqueror I have seen it chase the house sparrow which tho a very pert bird never ventures to fight it hedgesparrows linnets & finches that crowd the barn doors in winter never stand against its authority but flye from its interferances & acknowledge it the cock of the walk & he always seems to consider the right of the yard is his own.

The Wren is another of these domestic birds that has found favour in the affections of man the hardiest gunner will rarely attempt to shoot either of them & tho it loves to haunt the same places as the Robin it is not so tame & never ventures to seek the protection of man in the hardest winter blasts it finds its food in stackyards & builds its nest mostly in the roof of hovels & under the eaves of sheds about the habitations of man tho it is often found in the cowshed in closes & sometimes aside the roots of underwood in the woods its nest is made of green moss & lind with feathers the entrance is a little hole in the side like a corkhole in a barrel it lays as many as 15 or 16 white eggs very small & faintly spotted with pink spots it is a pert bird among its fellows & always seems in a conceited sort of happiness with its tail strunted up oer its back & its wings dropping down—its song is more loud than the Robins & very pleasant tho it is utterd in broken raptures by sudden starts & sudden endings it begins to sing in March & continues till the end of Spring when it becomes moping & silent.

Letters on Natural History, 1825

Snail-Shells

A person had been digging a dyke in the old roman bank by the side of a fence & in some places it was 6 feet deep & in the deepest places I found the most shells most of them of the large garden kind which had been clarsified as it were in the sandy soil in which they were bedded I suppose them to have lain ever since the road was made & if that is so what a pigmy it makes of the pride of man Those centurions of their thousands & 10 thousands that commanded those soldiers to make these roads little thought that the house of a poor simple snail horn woud outlive them & their proudest temples by centurys it is almost a laughable gravity to reflect so profoundly over a snail horn but every trifle owns the triumph of a lesson to humble the pride of man—every trifle also has a lesson to bespeak the wisdom & forethought of the Deity.

Letters on Natural History

CHARLES GREVILLE
1794–1865

The Duchess of Cannizzaro

The other day died the Duchess of Cannizzaro, a woman of rather amusing notoriety, whom the world laughed with and laughed at, while she was alive, and will regret a little because she contributed in some degree to their entertainment. She was a Miss Johnstone, and got from her brother a large fortune; she was very short and fat, with rather a handsome face, totally uneducated, but full of humour, vivacity, and natural drollery, at the same time passionate and capricious. Her all-absorbing interest and taste was music, to which all her faculties and time were devoted. She was eternally surrounded with musical artists, was their great patroness, and at her house the world was regaled with the best music that art could supply. Soon after her brother's death, she married the Count St Antonio (who was afterwards made Duke of Cannizzaro), a good-looking, intelligent, but penniless Sicilian of high birth, who was pretty successful in all ways in society here. He became disgusted with her, however, and went off to Italy, on a separate allowance which she made him. After a few years he returned to England, and they lived together again; he not only became more disgusted than before, but he had in the meantime formed a *liaison* at Milan with a very distinguished woman there, once a magnificent beauty, but now as old and as large as his own wife, and to her he was very anxious to return. This was Madame Visconti (mother of the notorious Princess Belgioso), who, though no longer young, had fine remains of good looks, and was eminently pleasing and attractive. Accordingly, St Antonio took occasion to elope (by himself) from some party of pleasure at which he was present with his spouse, and when she found that he had gone off without notice or warning, she first fell into violent fits of grief, which were rather ludicrous than affecting, and then set off in pursuit of her faithless lord. She got to Dover, where the sight of the rolling billows terrified her so much, that she resolved to return, and weep away her vexation in London. Not long afterwards, however, she plucked up courage, and taking advantage of a smooth sea she ventured over the Straits, and set off for Milan, if not to recover her fugitive better half, at all events to terrify her rival and disturb their joys. The advent of the Cannizzaro woman was to the Visconti like the irruption of the Huns of old. She fled to a villa near Milan, which she proceeded to garrison and fortify, but finding that the other was not provided with any implements for a siege, and did not stir from Milan, she ventured to return to the city, and for some time these ancient heroines drove about the town glaring defiance and hate at each other, which was the whole amount of the hostilities that took place between them. Finding her husband was irrecoverable, she at length got tired of the hopeless pursuit, and resolved to return home, and console herself with her music and whatever other gratifications she could command. Not long after, she fell in love with a fiddler at a second-rate theatre in Milan, and carried him off to England, which he found, if not the most agreeable, the most profitable business he could engage in. The affair was singular and curious, as showing what society may be induced to put up with. There was not the slightest attempt to conceal this connexion: on the contrary it was most ostentatiously exhibited to the world, but the world agreed to treat it as a joke, and do nothing but laugh at it. The only difference 'the Duchesse' ever found was, that her Sunday parties were less well attended; but this was because the world (which often grows religious, but never grows moral) had begun to take it into its head that it would keep holy the Sabbath *night*. The worst part of the story was, that this profligate blackguard bullied and plundered her without mercy or shame, and she had managed very nearly to ruin herself before her death. What she had left,

my pocket, and another stuffed in my hat; being thus with great reluctance compelled to travel barefoot: yet I soon turned even this to account, when I reflected that it would enhance the merit of my pilgrimage, and that every fresh blister would bring down a fresh blessing. 'Tis true I was nettled to the soul, on perceiving the face of a labourer on the way-side, or of a traveller who met me, gradually expanding into a broad sarcastic grin, as such an unaccountable figure passed him. But these I soon began to suspect were Protestant grins; for none but heretics would presume by any means to give me a sneer. The Romans taking me for a priest, were sure to doff their hats to me, or if they wore none, as is not unfrequent when at labour, they would catch their forelocks with their finger and thumb, and bob down their heads in act of veneration. This attention of my brethren more than compensated for the mirth of all other sects; in fact their mistaking me for a priest began to give me a good opinion of myself, and perfectly reconciled me to the fatiguing severity of the journey.

The Lough Dearg Pilgrim, 1829

On a Hill-Farm in Ulster

The day was bitter and wintry, the men were thinly clad, and as the keen blast swept across the hill with considerable violence, the sleetlike rain which it bore along, pelted into their garments with pitiless severity. The father had advanced into more than middle-age; and having held, at a rack-rent, the miserable waste of farm which he occupied, he was compelled to exert himself in its cultivation, despite either obduracy of soil, or inclemency of weather. This day, however, was so unusually severe, that the old man began to feel incapable of continuing his toil. The son bore it better; but whenever a cold rush of stormy rain came over them, both were compelled to stand with their sides against it, and their heads turned, so as that the ear almost rested back upon the shoulder, in order to throw the rain off their faces. Of each, however, that cheek which was exposed to the rain and storm was beaten into a red hue; whilst the other part of their faces was both pale and hunger-pinched.

The father paused to take breath, and supported by his spade, looked down upon the sheltered inland which, inhabited chiefly by Protestants and Presbyterians, lay rich and warm-looking under him.

'Why thin', he exclaimed to his son—a lad about fifteen,—'sure I know well I oughtn't to curse yees, anyway, you black set! an'yit, the Lord forgive me my sins, I'm almost timpted to give yez a volley, an' that from my heart out! Look at thim, Jimmy agra—only look at the black thieves!

how warm and wealthy they sit there in our own ould possessions, an' here we must toil till our fingers are worn to the stumps, upon this thievin' bent.'

'The Poor Scholar', *Traits and Stories of the Irish Peasantry*, 1830–3

The Sign of the Cross

'God save the house!' exclaimed Darby, on entering—'God save the house, an' all that's in it! God save it to the North!' and he formed the sign of the cross in *that* direction; God save it to the South! ✠ to the Aiste! ✠ and to the Waiste! ✠ Save it upwards! ✠ and save it downwards! ✠ Save it backwards! ✠ and save it forwards! ✠ Save it right! ✠ and save it left! ✠ Save it by night! ✠ save it by day! ✠ Save it here! ✠ save it there! ✠ Save it this way! ✠ an' save it that way! ✠ Save it atin! ✠✠✠ an' save it drinkin'! ✠✠✠✠✠✠✠. Oxis Doxis Glorioxis—Amin. An' now that I've blessed the place, in the name of the nine Patriarchs, how are yees all, man, woman, an' child? An' a merry Christmas to yees, says Darby More!'

'The Midnight Mass', *Traits and Stories of the Irish Peasantry*

JOHN KEATS
1795–1821

Preface to Endymion

Knowing within myself the manner in which this Poem has been produced, it is not without a feeling of regret that I make it public.

What manner I mean, will be quite clear to the reader, who must soon perceive great inexperience, immaturity, and every error denoting a feverish attempt, rather than a deed accomplished. The two first books, and indeed the two last, I feel sensible are not of such completion as to warrant their passing the press; nor should they if I thought a year's castigation would do them any good;—it will not: the foundations are too sandy. It is just that this youngster should die away: a sad thought for me, if I had not some hope that while it is dwindling I may be plotting, and fitting myself for verses fit to live.

This may be speaking too presumptuously, and may deserve a punishment: but no feeling man will be forward to inflict it: he will leave me alone, with the conviction that there is not a fiercer hell than the failure in a great object. This is not written with the least atom of purpose to forestall criticisms of course, but from the desire I have to conciliate men who are competent to look, and who do look with a zealous eye, to the honour of English literature.

The imagination of a boy is healthy, and the mature imagination of a man is healthy; but there is a space of life between, in which the soul is in a ferment, the character undecided, the way of life uncertain, the ambition thick-sighted: thence proceeds mawkishness, and all the thousand bitters which those men I speak of must necessarily taste in going over the following pages.

I hope I have not in too late a day touched the beautiful mythology of Greece, and dulled its brightness: for I wish to try once more, before I bid it farewell.

1818

Country Dancing

After Skiddaw, we walked to Ireby, the oldest Market town in Cumberland—where we were greatly amused by a Country Dancing School holden at the Inn, it was indeed 'no new cotillon fresh from France'. No, they kickit and jumpit with mettle extraordinary, and whiskit, and friskit, and toed it, and go'd it, and twirld it, and whirl'd it, and stamp't it, and sweated it, tattooing the floor like mad; The difference between our Country Dances and these Scottish figures is about the same as leisurely stirring a cup o' Tea and beating up a batter pudding. I was extremely gratified to think, that if I had pleasures they knew nothing of, they had also some into which I could not possibly enter.

letter to Thomas Keats, 1818

The Poetical Character

As to the poetical Character itself (I mean that sort of which, if I am any thing, I am a Member; that sort distinguished from the wordsworthian or egotistical sublime; which is a thing per se and stands alone) it is not itself—it has no self—it is every thing and nothing—It has no character—it enjoys light and shade; it lives in gusto, be it foul or fair, high or low, rich or poor, mean or elevated—It has as much delight in conceiving an Iago as an Imogen. What shocks the virtuous philosopher, delights the camelion Poet. It does no harm from its relish of the dark side of things any more than from its taste for the bright one; because they both end in speculation. A Poet is the most unpoetical of any thing in existence; because he has no Identity—he is continually informing and filling some other Body—The Sun, the Moon, the Sea and Men and Women who are creatures of impulse are poetical and have about them an unchangeable attribute—the poet has none; no identity—he is certainly the most unpoetical of all God's Creatures.

letter to Richard Woodhouse, 1818

Parsons

Every body is in his own mess. Here is the parson at Hampstead quarrelling with all the world, he is in the wrong by this same token; when the black Cloth was put up in the Church for the Queen's mourning, he asked the workmen to hang it the wrong side outwards, that it might be better when taken down, it being his perquisite—Parsons will always keep up their Character, but as it is said there are some animals, the ancients knew, which we do not, let us hope our posterity will miss the black badger with tri-cornered hat; Who knows but some Revisor of Buffon or Pliny, may put an account of the parson in the Appendix; No one will then believe it any more than we believe in the Phoenix.

letter to George and Georgiana Keats, 1819

Imaginary Woes

Do not suffer me to disturb you unpleasantly: I do not mean that you should not suffer me to occupy your thoughts, but to occupy them pleasantly; for, I assure you, I am as far from being unhappy as possible. Imaginary grievances have always been more my torment than real ones. You know this well. Real ones will never have any other effect upon me than to stimulate me to get out of or avoid them. This is easily accounted for. Our imaginary woes are conjured up by our passions, and are fostered by passionate feeling: our real ones come of themselves, and are opposed by an abstract exertion of mind. Real grievances are displacers of passion. The imaginary nail a man down for a sufferer, as on a cross; the real spur him up into an agent.

letter to Charles Brown, 1819

THOMAS CARLYLE

1795–1881

A Receding Star

But, on the whole, as time adds much to the sacredness of Symbols, so likewise in his progress he at length defaces or even desecrates them; and Symbols, like all terrestrial Garments, wax old. Homer's Epos has not ceased to be true; yet it is no longer *our* Epos, but shines in the distance, if clearer and clearer, yet also smaller and smaller, like a receding Star. It needs a scientific telescope, it needs to be reinterpreted and artificially brought near us, before we can so much as know that it *was* a Sun. So likewise a day comes when the Runic Thor, with his Eddas, must withdraw into dimness; and many an African Mumbo-Jumbo and Indian Pawaw be utterly abolished. For all things, even Celestial Luminaries, much more atmospheric meteors, have their rise, their culmination, their decline.

Sartor Resartus, 1833

Cobwebs

The world looks often quite spectral to me; sometimes, as in Regent Street the other night (my nerves being all shattered), quite hideous, discordant, almost infernal. I had been at Mrs Austin's, heard Sidney Smith for the first time guffawing, other persons prating, jargoning. To me through these thin cobwebs Death and Eternity sate glaring.

1835; quoted in Froude, *Carlyle's Life in London*, 1884

New Styles for Old

But finally do you reckon this really a time for purism of style, or that style (mere dictionary style) has much to do with the worth or unworth of a book? I do not. With whole ragged battalions of Scott's novel Scotch, with Irish, German, French, and even newspaper Cockney (where literature is little other than a newspaper) storming in on us, and the whole structure of our Johnsonian English breaking up from its foundations, revolution *there* is visible as everywhere else.

letter to John Sterling, 1835

The Death of Marat

It is yellow July evening, we say, the thirteenth of the month; eve of the Bastille day,—when 'M. Marat,' four years ago, in the crowd of the Pont Neuf, shrewdly required of that Besenval Hussar-party, which had such friendly dispositions, 'to dismount, and give up their arms, then;' and became notable among Patriot men. Four years: what a road he has travelled;—and sits now about half-past seven of the clock, stewing in slipper-bath; sore afflicted; ill of Revolution Fever,—of what other malady this History had rather not name. Excessively sick and worn, poor man: with precisely eleven-pence-halfpenny of ready-money in paper; with slipper-bath; strong three-footed stool for writing on, the while; and a squalid—Washer-woman, one may call her: that is his civic establishment in Medical-School Street; thither and not elsewhither has his road led him. Not to the reign of Brotherhood and Perfect Felicity; yet surely on the way towards that?—Hark, a rap again! A musical woman's voice, refusing to be rejected: it is the Citoyenne who would do France a service.

Marat, recognising from within, cries, Admit her. Charlotte Corday is admitted.

Citoyen Marat, I am from Caen the seat of rebellion, and wished to speak with you.—Be seated, *mon enfant*. Now what are the Traitors doing at Caen? What Deputies are at Caen?—Charlotte names some Deputies. 'Their heads shall fall within a fortnight,' croaks the eager People's-friend, clutching his tablets to write: *Barbaroux, Pétion*, writes he with bare shrunk arm, turning aside in the bath: *Pétion*, and *Louvet*, and—Charlotte has drawn her knife from the sheath; plunges it, with one sure stroke, into the writer's heart. '*À moi, chère amie*, Help, dear!' no more could the Death-choked say or shriek. The helpful Washerwoman running in, there is no Friend of the People, or Friend of the Washerwoman left; but his life with a groan gushes out, indignant, to the shades below.

And so Marat People's-friend is ended; the lone Stylites has got hurled down suddenly from his Pillar—*whitherward* He that made him knows. Patriot Paris may sound triple and tenfold, in dole and wail; re-echoed by Patriot France; and the Convention, 'Chabot pale with terror, declaring that they are to be all assassinated,' may decree him Pantheon Honours, Public Funeral, Mirabeau's dust making way for him; and Jacobin Societies, in lamentable oratory, summing up his character, parallel him to One, whom they think it honour to call 'the good Sansculotte,'—whom we name not here; also a Chapel may be made, for the urn that holds his Heart, in the Place du Carrousel; and new-born children be named Marat; and Lago-di-Como Hawkers bake mountains of stucco into unbeautiful Busts; and David paint his Picture, or Death-Scene; and such other Apotheosis take place as the human genius, in these circumstances, can devise: but Marat returns no more to the light of this Sun. One sole circumstance we have read with clear sympathy, in the old *Moniteur* Newspaper: how Marat's Brother comes from Neuchâtel to ask of the Convention, 'that the deceased Jean-Paul Marat's musket be given him.' For Marat too had a brother, and natural affections; and was wrapt once in swaddling-clothes, and slept safe in a cradle like the rest of us. Ye children of men!—A sister of his, they say, lives still to this day in Paris.

The French Revolution, 1837

The Death of the Dauphin

The Royal Family is now reduced to two: a girl and a little boy. The boy, once named Dauphin, was taken from his Mother while she yet lived; and given to one Simon, by trade a Cordwainer, on service then about the Temple-Prison, to bring him up in principles of Sansculottism. Simon taught him to drink, to swear, to sing the *carmagnole*. Simon is now gone to the Municipality: and the poor boy, hidden in a tower of the Temple, from which in his fright and bewilderment and early decrepitude he wishes not to stir out, lies perishing, 'his shirt not changed for six months;' amid squalor and darkness, lamentably,—so as none but poor Factory Children and the like are wont to perish, and *not* be lamented!

The French Revolution

Through the London Twilight

The tea was up before I could stir from the spot. It was towards sunset when I first got into the air, with the feeling of a *finished* man—finished in more than one sense. Avoiding crowds and highways, I went along Battersea Bridge, and thence by a wondrous path across cow fields, mud ditches, river embankments, over a waste expanse of what attempted to pass for country, wondrous enough in the darkening dusk, especially as I had never been there before, and the very road was uncertain. I had left my watch and my purse. I had a good stick in my hand. Boat people sate drinking about the Red House; steamers snorting about the river, each with a lantern at its nose. Old women sate in strange old cottages trimming their evening fire. Bewildered-looking mysterious coke furnaces (with a very bad smell) glowed at one place, I know not why. Windmills stood silent. Blackguards, improper females, and miscellanii sauntered, harmless all. Chelsea lights burnt many-hued, bright over the water in the distance—under the great sky of silver, under the great still twilight. So I wandered full of thoughts, or of things I could not think.

letter to John Carlyle, 1840

Peterloo

Who shall compute the waste and loss, the obstruction of every sort, that was produced in the Manchester region by Peterloo alone! Some thirteen unarmed men and women cut down,—the number of the slain and maimed is very countable: but the treasury of rage, burning hidden or visible in all hearts ever since, more or less perverting the effort and aim of all hearts ever since, is of unknown extent. 'How ye came among us, in your cruel armed blindness, ye unspeakable County Yeomanry, sabres flourishing, hoofs prancing, and slashed us down at your brute pleasure; deaf, blind to all *our* claims and woes and wrongs; of quick sight and sense to your own claims only! There lie poor sallow workworn weavers, and complain no more now; women themselves are slashed and sabred, howling terror fills the air; and ye ride prosperous, very victorious,—ye unspeakable: give *us* sabres too, and then come on a little!' Such are Peterloos. In all hearts that witnessed Peterloo, stands written, as in fire-characters, or smoke-characters prompt to become fire again, a legible balance-account of grim vengeance; very unjustly balanced, much exaggerated, as is the way with such accounts: but payable readily at sight, in full with compound interest!

Past and Present, 1843

The Twelfth Century—and the Nineteenth

How much is still alive in England; how much has not yet come into life! A Feudal Aristocracy is still alive, in the prime of life; superintending the cultivation of the land, and less consciously the distribution of the produce of the land, the adjustment of the quarrels of the land; judging, soldiering, adjusting; everywhere governing the people,—so that even a Gurth, born thrall of Cedric lacks not his due parings of the pigs he tends. Governing;—and, alas, also game-preserving, so that a Robin Hood, a William Scarlet and others have, in these days, put on Lincoln coats, and taken to living, in some universal-suffrage manner, under the greenwood-tree!

How silent, on the other hand, lie all Cotton-trades and such like; not a steeple-chimney yet got on end from sea to sea! North of the Humber, a stern Willelmus Conquestor burnt the Country, finding it unruly, into very stern repose. Wild fowl scream in those ancient silences, wild cattle roam in those ancient solitudes; the scanty sulky Norse-bred population all coerced into silence,—feeling that, under these new Norman Governors, their history has probably as good as *ended*. Men and Northumbrian Norse populations know little what has ended, what is but beginning! The Ribble and the Aire roll down, as yet unpolluted by dyers' chemistry; tenanted by merry trouts and piscatory otters; the sunbeam and the vacant wind's-blast alone traversing those moors. Side by side sleep the coal-strata and the iron-strata for so many ages; no Steam-Demon has yet risen smoking into being. Saint Mungo rules in Glasgow; James Watt still slumbering in the deep of Time. *Mancunium*, Manceaster, what we now call Manchester, spins no cotton,—if it be not *wool* 'cottons', clipped from the backs of mountain sheep. The Creek of the Mersey gurgles, twice in the four-and-twenty hours, with eddying brine, clangorous with sea-fowl; and is a *Lither*-Pool, a *lazy* or sullen Pool, no monstrous pitchy City, and Seahaven of the world! The Centuries are big; and the birth-hour is coming, not yet come.

Past and Present

Coleridge in old Age

The good man, he was now getting old, towards sixty perhaps; and gave you the idea of a life that had been full of sufferings; a life heavy-laden, half-vanquished, still swimming painfully in seas of manifold physical and other bewilderment. Brow and head were round, and of massive weight, but the face was flabby and irresolute. The deep eyes, of a light hazel, were as full of sorrow as of inspiration; confused pain looked mildly from them, as in a kind of mild astonishment. The whole figure and air, good and amiable otherwise, might be called flabby and irresolute; expressive of weakness under possibility of strength. He hung loosely on his limbs, with knees bent, and stooping attitude; in walking, he rather shuffled than decisively stept; and a lady once remarked, he never could fix which side of the garden walk would suit him best, but continually shifted, in corkscrew fashion, and kept trying both. A heavy-laden, high-aspiring and surely much suffering man. His voice, naturally soft and good, had contracted itself into a plaintive snuffle and sing-song; he spoke as if preaching,—you would have said, preaching earnestly and also hopelessly the weightiest things. I still recollect his 'object' and 'subject', terms of continual recurrence in the Kantean province; and how he sang and snuffled them into 'om-m-mject' and 'sum-m-mject,' with a kind of solemn shake or quaver, as he rolled along . . .

Nothing could be more copious than his talk; and furthermore it was always, virtually or literally, of the nature of a monologue; suffering no interruption, however reverent; hastily putting aside all foreign additions, annotations, or most ingenuous desires for elucidation, as well-meant superfluities which would never do. Besides, it was talk not flowing anywhither like a river, but spreading everywhither in inextricable currents and regurgitations like a lake or sea; terribly deficient in definite goal or aim, nay often in logical intelligibility; *what* you were to believe or do, on any earthly or heavenly thing, obstinately refusing to appear from it. So that, most times, you felt logically lost; swamped near to drowning in this tide of ingenious vocables, spreading out boundless as if to submerge the world.

To sit as a passive bucket and be pumped into, whether you consent or not, can in the long-run be exhilarating to no creature; how eloquent soever the flood of utterance that is descending. But if it be withal a confused unintelligible flood of utterance, threatening to submerge all known landmarks of thought, and drown the world and you!—I have heard Coleridge talk, with eager musical energy, two stricken hours, his face radiant and moist, and communicate no meaning whatsoever to any individual of his hearers,—certain of whom, I for one, still kept eagerly listening in hope; the most had long before given up, and formed (if the room were large enough) secondary humming groups of their own . . .

The truth is, I now see, Coleridge's talk and speculation was the emblem of himself: in it as in him, a ray of heavenly inspiration struggled, in a tragically ineffectual degree, with the weakness of flesh and blood. He says once, he 'had skirted the howling deserts of Infidelity;' this was evident enough: but he had not had the courage, in defiance of pain and terror, to press resolutely across said deserts to the new firm lands of Faith beyond; he preferred to create logical fatamorganas for himself on this hither side, and laboriously solace himself with these.

To the man himself Nature had given, in high measure, the seeds of a noble endowment; and to unfold it had been forbidden him. A subtle lynx-eyed intellect, tremulous pious sensibility to all good and all beautiful; truly a ray of empyrean light;—but imbedded in such weak laxity of character, in such indolences and esuriences as had made strange work with it. Once more, the tragic story of a high endowment with an insufficient will.

Life of John Sterling, 1851

A Great Scottish Preacher (Thomas Chalmers)

Chalmers was himself very beautiful to us during that hour, grave—not too grave—earnest, cordial face and figure very little altered, only the head had grown white, and in the eyes and features you could read something of a serene sadness, as if evening and starcrowned night were coming on, and the hot noises of the day growing unexpectedly insignificant to one. We had little thought this would be the last of Chalmers; but in a few weeks after he suddenly died . . . He was a man of much natural dignity, ingenuity, honesty, and kind affection, as well as sound intellect and imagination. A very eminent vivacity lay in him, which could rise to complete impetuosity (growing conviction, passionate eloquence, fiery play of heart and head) all in a kind of *rustic* type, one might say, though wonderfully true and tender. He had a burst of genuine fun too, I have heard, of the same honest but most plebeian broadly natural character; his laugh was a hearty low guffaw; and his tones in preaching would rise to the piercingly pathetic—no preacher ever went so into one's heart. He was a man essentially of little culture, of narrow sphere, all his life; such an intellect professing to be educated, and yet so ill *read*, so ignorant in all that lay beyond the horizon in place or in time, I have almost nowhere met with. A man capable of much soaking indolence, lazy brooding and do-nothingism, as the first stage of his life well indicated; a man thought to be timid almost to the verge of cowardice, yet capable of impetuous activity and blazing audacity, as his latter years showed.

I suppose there will never again be such a preacher in any Christian church.

Reminiscences, 1881; written 1866–7

A Failed Scottish Preacher

Macbeth was a Scotch preacher, or licentiate, who had failed of a kirk, as he had deserved to do, though his talents were good, and was now hanging very miscellaneously on London, with no outlooks that were not bog meteors, and a steadily increasing tendency to strong drink. He knew town well, and its babble and bits of temporary cynosures, and frequented haunts good and perhaps bad; took me one evening to the poet Campbell's, whom I had already seen, but not successfully.

Macbeth had a sharp sarcastic, clever kind of tongue; not much real knowledge, but was amusing to talk with on a chance walk through the streets; older than myself by a dozen years or more. Like him I did not; there was nothing of wisdom, generosity, or worth in him, but in secret, evidently discernible, a great deal of bankrupt vanity which had taken quite the malignant shape. Undeniable envy, spite, and bitterness looked through every part of him. A tallish, slouching, lean figure, face sorrowful malignant, black, not unlike the picture of a devil. To me he had privately much the reverse of liking. I have seen him in Irving's and elsewhere (perhaps with a little drink on his stomach, poor soul!) break out into oblique little spurts of positive spite, which I understood to mean merely, 'Young Jackanapes, getting yourself noticed and honoured while a mature man of genius is etc. etc.!' and took no notice of, to the silent comfort of self and neighbours.

Reminiscences

Francis Jeffrey

I used to find in him a finer talent than any he has evidenced in writing: this was chiefly when he got to speak Scotch, and gave me anecdotes of old Scotch *Braxfields*, and vernacular (often enough, but not always, *cynical*) curiosities of that type. Which he did with a greatness of *gusto* quite peculiar to the topic; with a fine and deep sense of humour, of real comic mirth, much beyond what was noticeable in him otherwise; not to speak of the perfection of the mimicry, which itself was something. I used to think to myself, 'Here is a man whom they have kneaded into the shape of an *Edinburgh Reviewer*, and clothed the soul of in Whig formulas, and blue-and-yellow; but he might have been a beautiful Goldoni, too, or something better in that kind, and have given us beautiful *Comedies*, and aerial pictures, true and poetic, of Human Life in a far other way!'

Reminiscences

WILLIAM HICKLING PRESCOTT
1796–1859

Cortes and the Massacre of Cholula

He had entered Cholula as a friend, at the invitation of the Indian emperor, who had a real, if not avowed, control over the state. He had been received as a friend, with every demonstration of goodwill; when, without any offence of his own or his followers, he found they were to be the victims of an insidious plot,—that they were standing on a mine which might be sprung at any moment and bury them all in its ruins. His safety, as he truly considered, left no alternative but to anticipate the blow of his enemies. Yet who can doubt that the punishment thus inflicted was excessive,—that the same end might have been attained by directing the blow against the guilty chiefs, instead of letting it fall on the ignorant rabble who but obeyed the commands of their masters? But when was it ever seen that fear, armed with power, was scrupulous in the exercise of it? or that the passions of a fierce soldiery, inflamed by conscious injuries, could be regulated in the moment of explosion?

We shall, perhaps, pronounce more impartially on the conduct of the Conquerors if we compare it with that of our own contemporaries under somewhat similar circumstances. The atrocities at Cholula were not so bad as those inflicted on the descendants of these very Spaniards, in the later war of the Peninsula, by the most polished nations of our time; by the British at Badajoz, for example,—at Tarragona, and a hundred other places, by the French. The wanton butchery, the ruin of property, and, above all, those outrages worse than death, from which the female part of the population were protected at Cholula, show a catalogue of enormities quite as black as those imputed to the Spaniards, and without the same apology for resentment,—with no apology, indeed, but that afforded by a brave and patriotic resistance. The consideration of these events, which, from their familiarity, make little impression on our senses, should render us more lenient in our judgments of the past, showing, as they do, that man in a state of excitement, savage or civilized, is much the same in every age. It may teach us—it is one of the best lessons of history—that, since such are the *inevitable* evils of war, even among the most polished people, those who hold the destinies of nations in their hands, whether rulers or legislators, should submit to every sacrifice, save that of honour, before authorizing an appeal to arms. The extreme solicitude to avoid these calamities, by the aid of peaceful congresses and impartial mediation, is, on the whole, the strongest evidence, stronger than that afforded by the progress of science and art, of our boasted advance in civilization.

It is far from my intention to vindicate the cruel deeds of the old Conquerors. Let them lie heavy on their heads. They were an iron race, who perilled life and fortune in the cause; and, as they made little account of danger and suffering for themselves, they had little sympathy to spare for their unfortunate enemies. But, to judge them fairly, we must not do it by the lights of our own age. We must carry ourselves back to theirs, and take the point of view afforded by the civilization of their time. Thus only can we arrive at impartial criticism in reviewing the generations that are past. We must extend to them the same justice which we shall have occasion to ask from posterity, when, by the light of a higher civilization, it surveys the dark or doubtful passages in our own history, which hardly arrest the eye of the contemporary.

The Conquest of Mexico, 1843

MARY SHELLEY
1797–1851

Frankenstein and His Creature

It was on a dreary night of November, that I beheld the accomplishment of my toils. With an anxiety that almost amounted to agony, I collected the instruments of life around me, that I might infuse a spark of being into the lifeless thing that lay at my feet. It was already one in the morning; the rain pattered dismally against the panes, and my candle was nearly burnt out, when, by the glimmer of the half-extinguished light, I saw the dull yellow eye of the creature open: it breathed hard, and a convulsive motion agitated its limbs.

How can I describe my emotions at this catastrophe, or how delineate the wretch whom with such infinite pains and care I had endeavoured to form? His limbs were in proportion, and I had selected his features as beautiful. Beautiful!—Great God! His yellow skin scarcely covered the work of muscles and arteries beneath; his hair was of a lustrous black, and flowing; his teeth of pearly whiteness; but these luxuriances only formed a more horrid contrast with his watery eyes, that seemed almost of the same colour as the dun-white sockets in which they were set, his shrivelled complexion and straight black lips.

The different accidents of life are not so changeable as the feelings of human nature. I had worked hard for nearly two years, for the sole purpose of infusing life into an inanimate body. For this I had deprived myself of rest and health. I had desired it with an ardour that far exceeded moderation: but now that I had finished, the beauty of the dream vanished, and breathless horror and disgust filled my heart. Unable to endure the aspect of the being I had created, I rushed out of the room, and continued a long time traversing my bedchamber, unable to compose my mind to sleep. At length lassitude succeeded to the tumult I had before endured: and I threw myself on the bed in my clothes, endeavouring to seek a few moments of forgetfulness. But it was in vain: I slept, indeed, but I was disturbed by the wildest dreams. I thought I saw Elizabeth, in the bloom of health, walking in the streets of Ingolstadt. Delighted and surprised, I embraced her, but as I imprinted the first kiss on her lips, they became livid with the hue of death; her features appeared to change, and I thought that I held the corpse of my dead mother in my arms; a shroud enveloped her form, and I saw the grave-worms crawling in the folds of flannel. I started from my sleep with horror; a cold dew covered my forehead, my teeth chattered, and every limb became convulsed: when, by the dim and yellow light of the moon, as it forced its way through the window shutters, I beheld the wretch—the miserable monster whom I had created. He held up the curtain of the bed: and his eyes, if eyes they may be called, were fixed on me. His jaws opened, and he muttered some inarticulate sounds, while a grin wrinkled his cheeks. He might have spoken, but I did not hear: one hand was stretched out, seemingly to detain me, but I escaped, and rushed downstairs. I took refuge in the courtyard belonging to the house which I inhabited; where I remained during the rest of the night, walking up and down in the greatest agitation, listening attentively, catching and fearing each sound as if it were to announce the approach of the demoniacal corpse to which I had so miserably given life.

Frankenstein, or The Modern Prometheus, 1818

The Creature Reads Milton

But *Paradise Lost* excited different and far deeper emotions. I read it, as I had read the other volumes which had fallen into my hands, as a true history. It moved every feeling of wonder and awe, that the picture of an omnipotent God warring with his creatures was capable of exciting. I often referred the several situations, as their similarity struck me, to my own. Like Adam, I was apparently united by no link to any other being in existence: but his state was far different from mine in every other respect. He had come forth from the hands of God a perfect creature, happy and prosperous, guarded by the especial care of his Creator: he was allowed to converse with and acquire knowledge from beings of a superior nature: but I was wretched, helpless, and alone. Many times I considered Satan as the fitter emblem of my condition: for often, like him, when I viewed the bliss of my protectors, the bitter gall of envy rose within me.

Frankenstein, or The Modern Prometheus

EMILY EDEN
1797–1869

On the Road to Simla

Futtygunge, Jan. 17, 1838

We have had a Sunday halt, and some bad roads, and one desperate long march. A great many of the men here have lived in the jungles for years, and their poor dear manners are utterly gone—jungled out of them.

Luckily the band plays all through dinner, and drowns the conversation. The thing they all like best is the band, and it was an excellent idea, that of making it play from five to six. There was a lady yesterday in perfect ecstasies with the music. I believe she was the wife of an indigo planter in the neighbourhood, and I was rather longing to go and speak to her, as she probably had not met a countrywoman for many months; but then, you know, she might not have been his wife, or anybody's wife, or he might not be an indigo planter. In short, my dear Mrs D., you know what a world it is—impossible to be too careful, &c.

We never stir out now from the camp; there is nothing to see, and the dust is a little laid just in front of our tents. We have had a beautiful subject for drawing the last two days. A troop of irregular horse joined us at Futtehghur. The officer, a Russaldar—a sort of sergeant, I believe—wears a most picturesque dress, and has an air of Timour the Tartar, with a touch of Alexander the Great—and he comes and sits for his picture with great patience. All these irregular troops are like parts of a melodrama. They go about curvetting and spearing, and dress themselves fancifully, and they are most courteous-mannered natives. G. and I walked up to their encampment on Sunday.

They had no particular costume when first we came in sight, being occupied in cleaning their horses—and the natives think nature never intended that they should work with clothes on; but they heard G. was coming, and by the time we arrived they were all scarlet and silver and feathers—such odd, fanciful dresses; and the Russaldar and his officers brought theirswords that we might touch them, and we walked through their lines. My jemadar interpreted that the Lord Sahib and Lady Sahib never saw such fine men, or such fine horses, and they all salaamed down to the ground. An hour after, this man and his attendant rode up to W.'s tent (they are under him in his military secretary capacity) to report that they certainly *were* the finest troops in the world—the Lord Sahib had said so;

jemadar] chief servant

and they begged also to mention that they should be very glad to have their pictures drawn. So the chief man has come for his, and is quite satisfied with it.

Up the Country, 1866

THOMAS BABINGTON MACAULAY, LORD MACAULAY
1800–1859

Britain and India

It may be that the public mind of India may expand under our system till it has outgrown that system; that by good government we may educate our subjects into a capacity for better government; that, having become instructed in European knowledge, they may, in some future age, demand European institutions. Whether such a day will ever come I know not. But never will I attempt to avert or retard it. Whenever it comes, it will be the proudest day in English history. To have found a great people sunk in the lowest depths of slavery and superstitition, to have so ruled them as to have made them desirous and capable of all the privileges of citizens, would indeed be a title to glory all our own. The sceptre may pass away from us. Unforeseen accidents may derange our most profound schemes of policy. Victory may be inconstant to our arms. But there are triumphs which are followed by no reverse. There is an empire exempt from all natural causes of decay. Those triumphs are the pacific triumphs of reason over barbarism; that empire is the imperishable empire of our arts and our morals, our literature and our laws.

Speech on the India Bill, 1833

Horace Walpole

He was, unless we have formed a very erroneous judgment of his character, the most eccentric, the most artificial, the most fastidious, the most capricious of men. His mind was a bundle of inconsistent whims and affectations. His features were covered by mask within mask. When the outer disguise of obvious affectation was removed, you were still as far as ever from seeing the real man. He played innumerable parts, and over-acted them all. When he talked misanthropy, he out-Timoned Timon. When he talked philanthropy, he left Howard at an immeasurable distance. He scoffed at courts, and kept a chronicle of their most trifling scandal; at society, and was blown about by its slightest veerings of opinion; at literary fame, and left fair copies of his private letters, with copious notes, to be published after his decease; at rank, and never for a moment forgot that he was an Honourable; at the practice of entail, and tasked the ingenuity of conveyancers to tie up his villa in the strictest settlement.

The conformation of his mind was such that whatever was little seemed to him great, and whatever was great seemed to him little. Serious business was a trifle to him, and trifles were his serious business. To chat with blue stockings, to write little copies of complimentary verses on little occasions, to superintend a private press, to preserve from natural decay the perishable topics of Ranelagh and White's, to record divorces and bets, Miss Chudleigh's absurdities and George Selwyn's good sayings, to decorate a grotesque house with pie-crust battlements, to procure rare engravings and antique chimney-boards, to match odd gauntlets, to lay out a maze of walks within five acres of ground, these were the grave employments of his long life. From these he turned to politics as to an amusement. After the labours of the print-shop and the auction-room, he unbent his mind in the House of Commons. And, having indulged in the recreation of making laws and voting millions, he returned to more important pursuits, to researches after Queen Mary's comb, Wolsey's red hat, the pipe which Van Tromp smoked during his last sea-fight, and the spur which King William struck into the flank of Sorrel.

'Horace Walpole', 1833

England in 1685: The Country Gentlemen

We should be much mistaken if we pictured to ourselves the squires of the seventeenth century as men bearing a close resemblance to their descendants, the county members and chairmen of quarter sessions with whom we are familiar. The modern country gentleman generally receives a liberal education, passes from a distinguished school to a distinguished college, and has ample opportunity to become an excellent scholar. He has generally seen something of foreign countries. A considerable part of his life has generally been passed in the capital; and the refinements of the capital follow him into the country. There is perhaps no class of dwellings so pleasing as the rural seats of the English gentry. In the parks and pleasure grounds, nature, dressed yet not disguised by art, wears her most alluring form. In the buildings good sense and good taste combine to produce a happy union of the comfortable and the graceful. The pictures, the musical instruments, the library, would in any other country be considered as proving the owner to be an eminently polished and accomplished man. A country gentleman who witnessed the revolution was probably in receipt of about a fourth part of the rent which his acres now yield to his posterity. He was, therefore, as compared with his posterity, a poor man, and was generally under the necessity of residing, with little interruption, on his estate. To travel on the Continent, to maintain an establishment in London, or even to visit London frequently, were pleasures in which only the great proprietors could indulge. It may be confidently affirmed that of the squires whose names were then in the Commissions of Peace and Lieutenancy not one in twenty went to town once in five years, or had ever in his life wandered so far as Paris. Many lords of manors had received an education differing little from that of their menial servants. The heir of an estate often passed his boyhood and youth at the seat of his family with no better tutors than grooms and gamekeepers, and scarce attained learning enough to sign his name to a Mittimus. If he went to school and to college, he generally returned before he was twenty to the seclusion of the old hall, and there, unless his mind were very happily constituted by nature, soon forgot his academical pursuits in rural business and pleasures. His chief serious employment was the care of his property. He examined samples of grain, handled pigs, and, on market days, made bargains over a tankard with drovers and hop merchants. His chief pleasures were commonly derived from field sports and from an unrefined sensuality. His language and pronunciation were such as we should now expect to hear only from the most ignorant clowns. His oaths, coarse jests, and scurrilous terms of abuse, were uttered with the broadest accent of his province. It was easy to discern, from the first words which he spoke, whether he came from Somersetshire or Yorkshire. He troubled himself little about decorating his abode, and, if he attempted decoration, seldom produced anything but deformity. The litter of a farmyard gathered under the windows of his bedchamber, and the cabbages and gooseberry bushes grew close to his hall door. His table was loaded with coarse plenty; and guests were cordially welcomed to it. But, as the habit of drinking to excess was general in the class to which he belonged, and as his fortune did not enable him to intoxicate large assemblies daily with claret or canary, strong beer was the ordinary beverage. The quantity of beer consumed in those days was indeed enormous. For beer then was to the middle and lower classes, not only all that beer now is, but all that wine, tea, and ardent spirits now are. It was only at great houses, or on great occasions, that foreign drink was placed on the board. The ladies of the house, whose business it had commonly been to cook the repast, retired as soon as the dishes had been devoured, and left the gentlemen to their ale and tobacco. The coarse jollity of the afternoon was often prolonged till the revellers were laid under the table.

It was very seldom that the country gentleman caught glimpses of the great world; and what he saw of it tended rather to confuse than to enlighten his understanding. His opinions respecting religion, government, foreign countries and former times, having been derived, not from study, from observation, or from conversation with enlightened companions, but from such traditions as were current in his own small circle, were the opinions of a child. He adhered to them, however, with the obstinacy which is generally found in ignorant men accustomed to be fed with flattery. His animosities were numerous and bitter. He hated Frenchmen and Italians, Scotchmen and Irishmen, Papists and Presbyterians, Independents and Baptists, Quakers and Jews. Towards London and Londoners he felt an aversion which more than once produced important political effects. His wife and daughter were in tastes and acquirements below a housekeeper or a stillroom maid of the present day. They stitched and spun, brewed gooseberry wine, cured marigolds, and made the crust for the venison pasty.

From this description it might be supposed that the English esquire of the seventeenth century did not materially differ from a rustic miller or alehouse keeper of our time. There are, however, some important parts of his character still to be noted, which will greatly modify this estimate. Unlettered as he was and unpolished, he was still in some most important points a gentleman. He was a member of a proud and powerful aristocracy, and was distinguished by many both of the good and of the bad qualities which belong to aristocrats. His family pride was beyond that of a Talbot or a Howard. He knew the genealogies and coats of arms of all his neighbours, and could tell which of them had assumed supporters without any right, and which of them were so unfortunate as to be greatgrandsons of aldermen. He was a magistrate, and, as such, administered gratuitously to those who dwelt around him a rude patriarchal justice, which, in spite of innumerable blunders and of occasional acts of tyranny, was yet better than no justice at all. He was an officer of the trainbands; and his military dignity, though it might move the mirth of gallants who had served a campaign in Flanders, raised his character in his own eyes and in the eyes of his neighbours. Nor indeed was his soldiership justly a subject of derision. In every county there were elderly gentlemen who had seen service which was no child's play. One had been knighted by Charles the First, after the battle of Edgehill. Another still wore a patch over the scar which he had received at Naseby. A third had defended his old house till Fairfax had blown in the door with a petard. The presence of these old Cavaliers, with their old swords and holsters, and with their old stories about Goring and Lunsford, gave to the musters of militia an earnest and warlike aspect which would otherwise have been wanting. Even those country gentlemen who were too young to have themselves exchanged blows with the cuirassiers of the Parliament had, from childhood, been surrounded by the traces of recent war, and fed with stories of the martial exploits of their fathers and uncles. Thus the character of the English esquire of the seventeenth century was compounded of two elements which we seldom or never find united. His ignorance and uncouthness, his low tastes and gross phrases, would, in our time, be considered as indicating a nature and a breeding thoroughly plebeian. Yet he was essentially a patrician, and had, in large measure, both the virtues and the vices which flourish among men set from their birth in high place, and used to respect themselves and to be respected by others. It is not easy for a generation accustomed to find chivalrous sentiments only in company with liberal studies and polished manners to image to itself a man with the deportment, the vocabulary, and the accent of a carter, yet punctilious on matters of genealogy and precedence, and ready to risk his life rather than see a stain cast on the honour of his house. It is, however, only by thus joining together things seldom or never found together in our own experience, that we can form a just idea of that rustic aristocracy which constituted the main strength of the armies of Charles the First, and which long supported, with strange fidelity, the interests of his descendants.

History of England, vol. i, 1849

Pitt the Younger in Parliament

At his first appearance in Parliament he showed himself superior to all his contemporaries in command of language. He could pour forth a long succession of round and stately periods, without premeditation, without ever pausing for a word, without ever repeating a word, in a voice of silver clearness, and with a pronunciation so articulate that not a letter was slurred over. He had less amplitude of mind and less richness of imagination than Burke, less ingenuity than Windham, less wit than Sheridan, less perfect mastery of dialectical fence, and less of that highest sort of eloquence which consists of reason and passion fused together, than Fox. Yet the almost unanimous judgment of those who were in the habit of listening to that remarkable race of men placed Pitt, as a speaker, above Burke, above Windham, above Sheridan, and not below Fox. His declamation was copious, polished, and splendid. In power of sarcasm he was probably not surpassed by any speaker, ancient or modern; and of this formidable weapon he made merciless use. In two parts of the oratorical art which are of the highest value to a minister of state he was singularly expert. No man knew better how to be luminous or how to be obscure. When he wished to be understood, he never failed to make himself understood. He could with ease present to his audience, not perhaps an exact or profound, but a clear, popular, and plausible view of the most extensive and complicated subject. Nothing was out of place; nothing was forgotten; minute details, dates, sums of money, were all faithfully preserved in his memory. Even intricate questions of finance, when explained by him, seemed clear to the plainest man among his hearers. On the other hand, when he did not wish to be explicit,—and no man who is at the head of affairs always wishes to be explicit,—he had a marvellous power of saying nothing in language which left on his audience the impression that he had said a great deal. He was at once the only man who could open a budget without notes, and the only man who, as Windham said, could speak that most elaborately evasive and unmeaning of human compositions, a King's speech, without premeditation.

'William Pitt', 1859

An Age of Diversity

I went to the Athenaeum, and stayed there two hours to read John Mill on Liberty and on Reform. Much that is good in both. What he says about individuality in the treatise on Liberty is open, I think, to some criticism. What is meant by the complaint that there is no individuality now? Genius takes its own course, as it always did. Bolder invention was never known in science than in our time. The steam-ship, the steam-carriage, the electric telegraph, the gas lights, the new military engines, are instances. Geology is quite a new true science. Phrenology is quite a new false one. Whatever may be thought of the theology, the metaphysics, the political theories of our time, boldness and novelty is not what they want. Comtism, St Simonianism, Fourierism, are absurd enough, but surely they are not indications of a servile respect for usage and authority. Then the clairvoyance, the spirit-rapping, the table-turning, and all those other dotages and knaveries indicate rather a restless impatience of the beaten paths than a stupid determination to plod on in those paths. Our lighter literature, as far as I know it, is spasmodic and eccentric. Every writer seems to aim at doing something odd,—at defying all rules and canons of criticism. The metre must be queer; the diction queer. So great is the taste for oddity that men who have no recommendation but oddity hold a high place in vulgar estimation. I therefore do not like to see a man of Mill's excellent abilities recommending eccentricity as a thing almost good in itself—as tending to prevent us from sinking into that Chinese, that Byzantine, state which I should agree with him in considering as a great calamity. He is really crying 'Fire!' in Noah's flood.

Journal, 1859

JOHN HENRY NEWMAN
1801–1890

Producing Opinions to Order

An intellectual man, as the world now conceives of him, is one who is full of 'views', on all subjects of philosophy, on all matters of the day. It is almost thought a disgrace not to have a view at a moment's notice on any question from the Personal Advent to the Cholera or Mesmerism. This is owing in great measure to the necessities of periodical literature, now so much in request. Every quarter of a year, every month, every day, there must be a supply, for the gratification of the public, of new and luminous theories on the subjects of religion, foreign politics, home politics, civil economy, finance, trade, agriculture, emigration, and the colonies. Slavery, the gold-fields, German philosophy, the French Empire, Wellington, Peel, Ireland, must all be practised on, day after day, by what are called original thinkers. As the great man's guest must produce his good stories or songs at the evening banquet, as the platform orator exhibits his telling facts at mid-day, so the journalist lies under the stern obligation of extemporising his lucid views, leading ideas, and nutshell truths for the breakfast table.

Discourses on University Education, 1852

An Aboriginal Calamity

Starting then with the being of a God, (which, as I have said, is as certain to me as the certainty of my own existence, though when I try to put the grounds of that certainty into logical shape I find a difficulty in doing so in mood and figure to my satisfaction,) I look out of myself into the world of men, and there I see a sight which fills me with unspeakable distress. The world seems simply to give the lie to that great truth, of which my whole being is so full; and the effect upon me is, in consequence, as a matter of necessity, as confusing as if it denied that I am in existence myself. If I looked into a mirror, and did not see my face, I should have the sort of feeling which actually comes upon me, when I look into this living busy world, and see no reflexion of its Creator. This is, to me, one of those great difficulties of this absolute primary truth, to which I referred just now. Were it not for this voice, speaking so clearly in my conscience and my heart, I should be an atheist, or a pantheist, or a polytheist when I looked into the world. I am speaking for myself only; and I am far from denying the real force of the arguments in proof of a God, drawn from the general facts of human society and the course of history, but these do not warm me or enlighten me; they do not take away the winter of my desolation, or make the buds unfold and the leaves grow within me, and my moral being rejoice. The sight of the world is nothing else than the prophet's scroll, full of 'lamentations, and mourning, and woe.'

To consider the world in its length and breadth, its various history, the many races of man, their starts, their fortunes, their mutual alienation, their conflicts; and then their ways, habits, governments, forms of worship; their enterprises, their aimless courses, their random achievements and acquirements, the impotent conclusion of long-standing facts, the tokens so faint and broken of a superintending design, the blind evolution of what turn out to be great powers or truths, the progress of things, as if from unreasoning elements, not towards final causes, the greatness and littleness of man, his far-reaching aims, his short duration, the curtain hung over his futurity, the disappointments of life, the defeat of good, the success of evil, physical pain, mental anguish, the prevalence and intensity of sin, the pervading idolatries, the corruptions, the dreary hopeless irreligion, that condition of the whole race, so fearfully yet exactly described in the Apostle's words, 'having no hope and without God in the world,'—all this is a vision to dizzy and appal; and inflicts upon the mind the sense of a profound mystery, which is absolutely beyond human solution.

What shall be said to this heart-piercing, reason-bewildering fact? I can only answer, that either there is no Creator, or this living society of men is in a true sense discarded from His presence. Did I see a boy of good make and mind, with the tokens on him of a refined nature, cast upon the world without provision, unable to say whence he came, his birth-place or his family connexions, I should conclude that there was some mystery connected with his history, and that he was one, of whom, from one cause or other, his parents were ashamed. Thus only should I be able to account for the contrast between the promise and the condition of his being. And so I argue about the world;—*if* there be a God, *since* there is a God, the human race is implicated in some terrible aboriginal calamity. It is out of joint with the purposes of its Creator. This is a fact, a fact as true as the fact of its existence; and thus the doctrine of what is theologically called original sin becomes to me almost as certain as that the world exists, and as the existence of God.

Apologia pro Vita Sua, 1864

An Invitation Declined

The Oratory, Birmingham: July 25, 1864

DEAR MONSIGNORE TALBOT,—I have received your letter, inviting me to preach next Lent in your Church at Rome to 'an audience of Protestants more educated than could ever be the case in England.'

However, Birmingham people have souls; and I have neither taste nor talent for the sort of work which you cut out for me. And I beg to decline your offer.

I am, yours truly,
John H. Newman

WILLIAM BARNES
1801–1886

The Rwose o'Sharon

I be the rwose o'Sharon, an' the lily o' the valleys.

Lik' a lily wi' thorns, is my love among maïdens.

Lik' an apple-tree in wi' the trees o' the wood, is my love among sons. I long'd vor his sheäde, an' zot down, an' his fruit wer vull sweet to my teäste.

He brought me into the feäst, an' his flag up above me wer love.

Refresh me wi' ceäkes, uphold me wi' apples: vor I be a-pinèn vor love.

His left hand wer under my head, an' his right a-cast round me.

I do warn ye, Jerusalem's da'ters, by the roes an' the hinds o' the vield, not to stir, not to weäke up my love, till he'd like.

The vaïce o' my true-love! behold, he's a-comèn; a-leäpèn up on the mountains, a-skippèn awver the hills.

My true-love is lik' a young roe or a hart: he's a-standèn behind our wall, a-lookèn vwo'th vrom the windors, a-showèn out droo the lattice.

My true-love he spoke, an' he call'd me, O rise up, my love, my feäir maïd, come away.

Vor, lo, the winter is awver, the raïn's a-gone by.

The flowers do show on the ground; the zong o' the birds is a-come, an' the coo o' the culver's a-heärd in our land.

The fig-tree do show his green figs, an' the vines out in blooth do smell sweet. O rise up, my true-love, feäir-maïd, come away.

from *The Zong o'Solomon* (1859), a version of the Song of Solomon in Dorset dialect

JANE WELSH CARLYLE
1801–1866

From Liverpool Home to London

I got into that Mail the other night, with as much repugnance and trepidation as if it had been a Phalaris's brazen bull, instead of a Christian vehicle, invented for purposes of mercy not of cruelty. There were three besides myself when we started, but two dropt off at the end of the first stage, and the rest of the way I had, as usual, half the coach to myself. My fellow-passenger had that highest of all terrestrial qualities which, for me, a fellow-passenger can possess, *he was silent.* I think his name was Roscoe, and he read sundry long papers to himself, with the pondering air of a lawyer.

We breakfasted at Litchfield, at five in the morning, on muddy coffee and scorched toast, which made me once more lyrically recognise in my heart (not without a sigh of regret) the very different coffee and toast with which you helped me out of my headache. At *two*, there was another stop of ten minutes, that might be employed in lunching or otherwise—feeling myself more fevered than hungry, I determined on spending the time in combing my hair and washing my face and hands *with vinegar.* In the midst of this solacing operation I heard what seemed to be the Mail resuming its rapid course, and quick as lightning it flashed on me, 'There it goes!—and my luggage is on the top of it!—and *my purse* is in the pocket of it!—and here am I stranded on an unknown beach, without so much as a sixpence in my pocket to pay for the vinegar I have already consumed!' Without my bonnet, my hair hanging down my back, my face half dried, and the towel with which I was drying it firm grasped in my hand, I dashed out—along—down, opening wrong doors, stumbling over steps, cursing the day I was born, still more the day on which I took a notion to travel, and arrived finally, at the bar of the Inn in a state of excitement bordering on lunacy. The bar-maids looked at me 'with weender and amazement'. 'Is the coach gone?' I gasped out. 'The coach? Yes!' 'O! and you have let it away without *me*! O! stop it—cannot you stop it?' and out I rushed into the street, with streaming hair and streaming towel, and almost brained myself against—the *Mail*! which was standing there in all stillness, without so much as horses in it! What I had heard was a heavy coach! And now, having descended like a maniac, I ascended again like a fool, and dried the other half of my face, and put on my bonnet, and came back 'a sadder and a wiser' woman.

I did not find my Husband at the *Swan with Two Necks*; for we were *in*, a quarter of an hour before the appointed time. So I had my luggage put on the backs of two porters, and walked on to Cheapside, where I presently found a Chelsea omnibus. By and by, however, the omnibus stopt, and amid cries of '*No room, Sir*', '*Can't get in*', Carlyle's face, beautifully set off by a broad-brimmed white hat, gazed in at the door, like the Peri, who '*at the Gate of Heaven, stood disconsolate*'. In hurrying along the Strand, pretty sure of being too late, amidst all the imaginable and unimaginable Phenomena which that immense thorough-fare of a street presents, his *eye* (Heaven bless the mark) had lighted on *my trunk* perched on the top of the omnibus, and had recognised it. This seems to me one of the most indubitable proofs of *genius* which he ever manifested. Happily, a passenger went out a little further on, and then he got in.

letter to Jeannie Welsh, 1836

Mr and Mrs George Henry Lewes

Little Lewes came the other night with his little wife—speaking gratefully of you all—but it is Julia Paulet who has taken his soul captive!! he raves about her 'dark luxurious eyes' and 'smooth firm flesh'—! his wife asked 'how did he know? had he been feeling it?' In fact his wife seems rather *contemptuous* of his raptures about all the women he has fallen in love with on this journey, which is the best way of taking the thing—when one *can*.

I used to think these Lewes a perfect pair of love-birds always cuddling together on the same perch—to speak figuratively—but the female love-bird appears to have hopped off to some distance and to be now taking a somewhat critical view of her little shaggy mate!

In the most honey-marriages one has only to *wait*—it is all a question of time—sooner or later 'reason resumes its empire', as the phrase is . . .

letter to Jeannie Welsh, 1849

Domestic Storms

A stormy day within doors, so I walked out early, and walked, walked, walked. If peace and quietness be not in one's own power, one can always give oneself at least bodily fatigue—no such bad succedaneum after all. Life gets to look for me like a sort of kaleidoscope—a few things of different colours—black predominating, which fate shakes into new and ever new combinations, but always the same things over again. To-day has been so like a day I still remember out of ten years ago; the same still dreamy October weather, the same tumult of mind contrasting with the outer stillness; the same causes for that tumult. Then, as now, I had walked, walked, walked with no aim but to tire myself.

Journal, 1855

A Rasping Day

To-day, it has blown knives and files; a cold, rasping, savage day; excruciating for sick nerves. Dear Geraldine, as if she would contend with the very elements on my behalf, brought me a bunch of violets and a bouquet of the loveliest most fragrant flowers. Talking with her all I have done or could do.

Journal, 1856

RALPH WALDO EMERSON
1803–1882

The Missing Man

Yes! it is true there are no men. Men hang upon things. They are overcrowed by their own creation. A man is not able to subdue the world. He is a Greek grammar. He is a money machine. He is an appendage to a great fortune, or to a legislative majority, or to the Massachusetts Revised Statutes, or to some barking and bellowing institution, association or church. But the deep and high and entire man, not parasitic upon time and space, upon traditions, upon his senses, or his organs, but who utters out of a central hope an eternal voice of sovereignty, we are not, and when he comes, we hoot at him: Behold this dreamer cometh!

Journal, 1837

The Confines of Character

I suppose no man can violate his nature. All the sallies of his will are rounded in by the law of his being, as the inequalities of Andes and Himmaleh are insignificant in the curve of the sphere. Nor does it matter how you gauge and try him.

A character is like an acrostic or Alexandrian stanza;—read it forward, backward, or across, it still spells the same thing. In this pleasing, contrite wood-life which God allows me, let me record day by day my honest thought without prospect or retrospect, and, I cannot doubt, it will be found symmetrical, though I mean it not, and see it not. My book should smell of pines and resound with the hum of insects. The swallow over my window should interweave that thread or straw he carries in his bill into my web also. We pass for what we are. Character teaches above our wills. Men imagine that they communicate their virtue or vice only by overt actions, and do not see that virtue or vice emit a breath every moment.

Self-Reliance—Essays: First Series, 1841

Facing the Camera

Were you ever daguerrotyped, O immortal man? And did you look with all vigor at the lens of the camera, or rather, by the direction of the operator, at the brass peg a little below it, to give the picture the full benefit of your expanded and flashing eye? and in your zeal not to blur the image, did you keep every finger in its place with such energy that your hands became clenched as for fight or despair, and in your resolution to keep your face still, did you feel every muscle becoming every moment more rigid; the brows contracted into a Tartarean frown, and the eyes fixed as they are fixed in a fit, in madness, or in death? And when, at last you are relieved of your dismal duties, did you find the curtain drawn perfectly, and the coat perfectly, and the hands true, clenched for combat, and the shape of the face and head?—but, unhappily, the total expression escaped from the face and the portrait of a mask instead of a man? Could you not by grasping it very tight hold the stream of a river, or of a small brook, and prevent it from flowing?

Journal, 1841

Unmaskers and Conservers

Society ought to be forgiven if it do not love its rude unmaskers. The Council of Trent did not love Father Paul Sarpi. 'But I show you,' says the philosopher, 'the leprosy which is covered by these gay coats.' 'Well, I had rather see the handsome mask than the unhandsome skin,' replies Beacon Street. Do you not know that this is a masquerade? Did you suppose I took these harlequins for the kings and queens, the gods and goddesses they represent? I am not such a child. There is a terrific skepticism at the bottom of the determined conservers.

Journal, 1841

A Lost Child

January 28, 1842

Yesterday night, at fifteen minutes after eight, my little Waldo ended his life.

January 30

What he looked upon is better; what he looked not upon is insignificant. The morning of Friday, I woke at three o'clock, and every cock in every barnyard was shrilling with the most unnecessary noise. The sun went up the morning sky with all his light, but the landscape was dishonored by this loss. For this boy, in whose remembrance I have both slept and awaked so oft, decorated for me the morning star, the evening cloud, how much more all the particulars of daily economy; for he had touched with his lively curiosity every trivial fact and circumstance in the household, the hard coal and the soft coal which I put into my stove; the wood, of which he brought his little quota for grandmother's fire; the hammer, the pincers and file he was so eager to use; the microscope, the magnet, the little globe, and every trinket and instrument in the study; the loads of gravel on the meadow, the nests in the hen-house, and many and many a little visit to the dog-house and to the barn.—For everything he had his own name and way of thinking, his own pronunciation and manner. And every word came mended from that tongue. A boy of early wisdom, of a grave and even majestic deportment, of a perfect gentleness.

Every tramper that ever tramped is abroad, but the little feet are still.

He gave up his little innocent breath like a bird.

He dictated a letter to his Cousin Willie on Monday night, to thank him for the magic lantern which he had sent him, and said, 'I wish you would tell Cousin Willie that I have so many presents that I do not need that he should send me any more unless he wishes to very much.'

The boy had his full swing in this world; never, I think, did a child enjoy more; he had been thoroughly respected by his parents and those around him, and not interfered with . . .

Sorrow makes us all children again,—destroys all differences of intellect. The wisest knows nothing.

It seems as if I ought to call upon the winds to describe my boy, my fast receding boy, a child of so large and generous a nature that I cannot paint him by specialties, as I might another.

'Are there any other countries?' 'Yes. I wish you to name the other countries'; so I went on to name London, Paris, Amsterdam, Cairo, etc. But Henry Thoreau well said, in allusion to his large way of speech, that 'his questions did not admit of an answer; they were the same which you would ask yourself.'

He named the parts of the toy house he was always building by fancy names which had a good sound, as 'the interspeglium' and 'the coridaga,' which names, he told Margaret, 'the children could not understand.'

If I go down to the bottom of the garden it seems as if some one had fallen into the brook.

Journal

A Visit to Coleridge

From London, on the 5th August, I went to Highgate, and wrote a note to Mr Coleridge, requesting leave to pay my respects to him. It was near noon. Mr Coleridge sent a verbal message, that he was in bed, but if I would call after one o'clock, he would see me. I returned at one, and he appeared, a short, thick old man, with bright blue eyes and fine clear complexion, leaning on his cane. He took snuff freely, which presently soiled his cravat and neat black suit. He asked whether I knew Allston, and spoke warmly of his merits and doings when he knew him in Rome; what a master of the Titianesque he was, &c., &c. He spoke of Dr Channing. It was an unspeakable misfortune that he should have turned out a Unitarian after all. On this, he burst into a declamation on the folly and ignorance of Unitarianism,—its high unreasonableness; and taking up Bishop Waterland's book, which lay on the table, he read with vehemence two or three pages written by himself in the fly-leaves,—passages, too, which, I believe, are printed in the 'Aids to Reflection.' When he stopped to take breath, I interposed, that, 'whilst I highly valued all his explanations, I was bound to tell him that I was born and bred a Unitarian.' 'Yes,' he said, 'I supposed so;' and continued as before.

English Traits, 1856

The Times

Was never such arrogancy as the tone of this paper. Every slip of an Oxonian or Cantabrigian who writes his first leader, assumes that we subdued the earth before we sat down to write this particular 'Times.' One would think, the world was on its knees to the 'Times' Office, for its daily breakfast. But this arrogance is calculated. Who would care for it, if it 'surmised,' or 'dared to confess,' or 'ventured to predict,' &c. No; *it is so*, and so it shall be.

English Traits

Thoreau

His interest in the flower or the bird lay very deep in his mind, was connected with Nature,—and the meaning of Nature was never attempted to be defined by him. He would not offer a memoir of his observations to the Natural History Society. 'Why should I? To detach the description from its connections in my mind would make it no longer true or valuable to me: and they do not wish what belongs to it.' His power of observation seemed to indicate additional senses. He saw as with microscope, heard as with ear-trumpet, and his memory was a photographic register of all he saw and heard. And yet none knew better than he that it is not the fact that imports, but the impression or effect of the fact on your mind. Every fact lay in glory in his mind, a type of the order and beauty of the whole.

His determination on Natural History was organic. He confessed that he sometimes felt like a hound or a panther, and, if born among Indians, would have been a fell hunter. But, restrained by his Massachusetts culture, he played out the game in this mild form of botany and ichthyology. His intimacy with animals suggested what Thomas Fuller records of Butler the apiologist, that 'either he had told the bees things or the bees had told him.' Snakes coiled round his leg; the fishes swam into his hand, and he took them out of the water; he pulled the woodchuck out of its hole by the tail and took the foxes under his protection from the hunters. Our naturalist had perfect magnanimity; he had no secrets: he would carry you to the heron's haunt, or even to his most prized botanical swamp,—possibly knowing that you could never find it again, yet willing to take his risks.

No college ever offered him a diploma, or a professor's chair; no academy made him its corresponding secretary, its discoverer, or even its member. Perhaps these learned bodies feared the satire of his presence. Yet so much knowledge of Nature's secret and genius few others possessed, none in a more large and religious synthesis. For not a particle of respect had he to the opinions of any man or body of men, but homage solely to the truth itself; and as he discovered everywhere among doctors some leaning of courtesy, it discredited them. He grew to be revered and admired by his townsmen, who had at first known him only as an oddity. The farmers who employed him as a surveyor soon discovered his rare accuracy and skill, his knowledge of their lands, of trees, of birds, of Indian remains, and the like, which enabled him to tell every farmer more than he knew before of his own farm; so that he began to feel a little as if Mr Thoreau had better rights in his land than he. They felt, too, the superiority of character which addressed all men with a native authority.

Thoreau, 1863

BENJAMIN DISRAELI
1804–1881

Rigby

Mr Rigby was member for one of Lord Monmouth's boroughs. He was the manager of Lord Monmouth's parliamentary influence, and the auditor of his vast estates. He was more; he was Lord Monmouth's companion when in England, his correspondent when abroad; hardly his counsellor, for Lord Monmouth never required advice; but Mr Rigby could instruct him in matters of detail, which Mr Rigby made amusing. Rigby was not a professional man; indeed, his origin, education, early pursuits, and studies, were equally obscure; but he had contrived in good time to squeeze himself into parliament, by means which no one could ever comprehend, and then set up to be a perfect man of business. The world took him at his word, for he was bold, acute, and voluble; with no thought, but a good deal of desultory information; and though destitute of all imagination and noble sentiment, was blessed with a vigorous, mendacious fancy, fruitful in small expedients, and never happier than when devising shifts for great men's scrapes.

They say that all of us have one chance in this life, and so it was with Rigby. After a struggle of many years, after a long series of the usual alternatives of small successes and small failures, after a few cleverish speeches and a good many cleverish pamphlets, with a considerable reputation, indeed, for pasquinades, most of which he never wrote, and articles in reviews to which it was whispered he had contributed, Rigby, who had already intrigued himself into a subordinate office, met with Lord Monmouth.

He was just the animal that Lord Monmouth wanted, for Lord Monmouth always looked upon human nature with the callous eye of a jockey. He surveyed Rigby, and he determined to buy him. He bought him; with his clear head, his indefatigable industry, his audacious tongue, and his ready and unscrupulous pen; with all his dates, all his lampoons; all his private memoirs, and all his political intrigues. It was a good purchase. Rigby became a great personage, and Lord Monmouth's man.

Coningsby, 1844

Exit Lord Monmouth

Lord Monmouth had died suddenly at his Richmond villa, which latterly he never quitted, at a little supper, with no persons near him but those who were amusing. He suddenly found he could not lift his glass to his lips, and being extremely polite, waited a few minutes before he asked Clotilde, who was singing a sparkling drinking-song, to do him that service. When, in accordance with his request, she reached him, it was too late. The ladies shrieked, being frightened: at first they were in despair, but, after reflection, they evinced some intention of plundering the house. Villebecque, who was absent at the moment, arrived in time; and everybody became orderly and broken-hearted.

Coningsby

A Times *Leader*

I read this morning an awful, though monotonous, manifesto in the great organ of public opinion, which always makes me tremble: Olympian bolts; and yet I could not help fancying amid their rumbling terrors I heard the plaintive treble of the Treasury Bench.

Speech in the House of Commons, 1851

A Comely Presence

Sir Robert Peel was a very good-looking man. He was tall, and, though of latter years he had become portly, had to the last a comely presence. Thirty years ago, when he was young and lithe, with curling brown hair, he had a radiant expression of countenance. His brow was distinguished, not so much for its intellectual development, although that was of a high order, as for its remarkably frank expression, so different from his character in life. The expression of the brow might even be said to amount to beauty. The rest of the features did not, however, sustain this impression. The eye was not good; it was sly, and he had an awkward habit of looking askance. He had the fatal defect, also, of a long upper lip, and his mouth was compressed.

Life of Lord George Bentinck, 1852

An Oxford Professor

The Oxford Professor, who was the guest of the American Colonel, was quite a young man, of advanced opinions on all subjects, religious, social, and political. He was clever, extremely well-informed, so far as books can make a man knowing, but unable to profit even by that limited experience of life from a restless vanity and overflowing conceit, which prevented him from ever observing or thinking of anything but himself. He was gifted with a great command of words, which took the form of endless exposition, varied by sarcasm and passages of ornate jargon. He was the last person one would have expected to recognise in an Oxford professor; but we live in times of transition.

Lothair, 1870

Gentlemen of the Stock Exchange

She was diverted by the gentlemen of the Stock Exchange, so acute, so audacious, and differing so much from the merchants in the style even of their dress, and in the ease, perhaps too great facility, of their bearing. They called each other by their Christian names, and there were allusions to practical jokes, which intimated a life something between a public school and a garrison.

Endymion, 1880

NATHANIEL HAWTHORNE
1804–1864

A Witches' Sabbath

'Bring forth the converts!' cried a voice that echoed through the field and rolled into the forest.

At the word, Goodman Brown stepped forth from the shadow of the trees and approached the congregation, with whom he felt a loathful brotherhood by the sympathy of all that was wicked in his heart. He could have well-nigh sworn that the shape of his own dead father beckoned him to advance, looking downward from a smoke wreath, while a woman, with dim features of despair, threw out her hand to warn him back. Was it his mother? But he had no power to retreat one step, nor to resist, even in thought, when the minister and good old Deacon Gookin seized his arms and led him to the blazing rock. Thither came also the slender form of a veiled female, led between Goody Cloyse, that pious teacher of the catechism, and Martha Carrier, who had received the devil's promise to be queen of hell. A rampant hag was she. And there stood the proselytes beneath the canopy of fire.

'Welcome, my children,' said the dark figure, 'to the communion of your race. Ye have found thus young your nature and your destiny. My children, look behind you!'

They turned; and flashing forth, as it were, in a sheet of flame, the fiend worshippers were seen; the smile of welcome gleamed darkly on every visage.

'There,' resumed the sable form, 'are all whom ye have reverenced from youth. Ye deemed them holier than yourselves, and shrank from your own sin, contrasting it with their lives of righteousness and prayerful aspirations heavenward. Yet here are they all in my worshipping assembly. This night it shall be granted you to know their secret deeds: how hoary-bearded elders of the church have whispered wanton words to the young maids of their households; how many a woman, eager for widows' weeds, has given her husband a drink at bedtime and let him sleep his last sleep in her bosom; how beardless youths have made haste to inherit their fathers' wealth; and how fair damsels—blush not, sweet ones—have dug little graves in the garden, and bidden me, the sole guest, to an infant's funeral. By the sympathy of your human hearts for sin ye shall scent out all the places—whether in church, bed-chamber, street, field, or forest—where crime has been committed, and shall exult to behold the whole earth one stain of guilt, one mighty blood spot. Far more than this. It shall be yours to penetrate, in every bosom, the deep mystery of sin, the fountain of all wicked arts, and which inexhaustibly supplies more evil impulses than human power—than my power at its utmost—can make manifest in deeds. And now, my children, look upon each other.'

They did so; and, by the blaze of the hell-kindled torches, the wretched man beheld his Faith, and the wife her husband, trembling before that unhallowed altar.

'Lo, there ye stand, my children,' said the figure, in a deep and solemn tone, almost sad with its despairing awfulness, as if his once angelic nature could yet mourn for our miserable race. 'Depending upon one another's hearts, ye had still hoped that virtue were not all a dream. Now are ye undeceived. Evil is the nature of mankind. Evil must be your only happiness. Welcome again, my children, to the communion of your race.'

'Welcome,' repeated the fiend worshippers, in one cry of despair and triumph.

And there they stood, the only pair, as it seemed, who were yet hesitating on the verge of wickedness in this dark world.

Young Goodman Brown, 1835

A Suit of Armour

At about the centre of the oaken panels, that lined the hall, was suspended a suit of mail, not, like the pictures, an ancestral relic, but of the most modern date; for it had been manufactured by a skilful armorer in London, the same year in which Governor Bellingham came over to New England. There was a steel headpiece, a cuirass, a gorget, and greaves, with a pair of gauntlets and a sword hanging beneath; all, and especially the helmet and breastplate, so highly burnished as to glow with white radiance, and scatter an illumination everywhere about upon the floor. This bright panoply was not meant for mere idle show, but had been worn by the Governor on many a solemn muster and training field, and had glittered, moreover, at the head of a regiment in the Pequod war. For, though bred a lawyer, and accustomed to speak of Bacon, Coke, Noye, and Finch as his professional associates, the exigencies of this new country had transformed Governor Bellingham into a soldier as well as a statesman and ruler.

Little Pearl—who was as greatly pleased with the gleaming armor as she had been with the glittering frontispiece of the house—spent some time looking into the polished mirror of the breastplate.

'Mother,' cried she, 'I see you here. Look! Look!'

Hester looked, by way of humoring the child; and she saw that, owing to the peculiar effect of this convex mirror, the scarlet letter was represented in exaggerated and gigantic proportions, so as to be greatly the most prominent feature of her appearance. In truth, she seemed absolutely hidden behind it. Pearl pointed upward, also, at a similar picture in the headpiece; smiling at her mother, with the elfish intelligence that was so familiar an expression on her small physiognomy. That look of naughty merriment was likewise reflected in the mirror, with so much breadth and intensity of effect, that it made Hester Prynne feel as if it could not be the image of her own child, but of an imp who was seeking to mould itself into Pearl's shape.

The Scarlet Letter, 1850

Speculations

Much of the marble coldness of Hester's impression was to be attributed to the circumstance, that her life had turned, in a great measure, from passion and feeling, to thought. Standing alone in the world,—alone, as to any dependence on society, and with little Pearl to be guided and protected,—alone, and hopeless of retrieving her position, even had she not scorned to consider it desirable,—she cast away the fragments of a broken chain. The world's law was no law for her mind. It was an age in which the human intellect, newly emancipated, had taken a more active and a wider range than for many centuries before. Men of the sword had overthrown nobles and kings. Men bolder than these had overthrown and rearranged—not actually, but within the sphere of theory, which was their most real abode—the whole system of ancient prejudice, wherewith was linked much of ancient principle. Hester Prynne imbibed this spirit. She assumed a freedom of speculation, then common enough on the other side of the Atlantic, but which our forefathers, had they known it, would have held to be a deadlier crime than that stigmatized by the scarlet letter. In her lonesome cottage, by the sea-shore, thoughts visited her, such as dared to enter no other dwelling in New England; shadowy guests, that would have been as perilous as demons to their entertainer, could they have been seen so much as knocking at her door.

It is remarkable that persons who speculate the most boldly often conform with the most perfect quietude to the external regulations of society. The thought suffices them, without investing itself in the flesh and blood of action. So it seemed to be with Hester. Yet, had little Pearl never come to her from the spiritual world, it might have been far otherwise. Then, she might have come down to us in history, hand in hand with Anne Hutchinson, as the foundress of a religious sect. She might, in one of her phases, have been a prophetess. She might, and not improbably would, have suffered death from the stern tribunals of the period, for attempting to undermine the foundations of the Puritan establishment. But, in the education of her child, the mother's enthusiasm of thought had something to wreak itself upon. Providence, in the person of this little girl, had assigned to Hester's charge the germ and blossom of womanhood, to be cherished and developed amid a host of difficulties. Everything was against her. The world was hostile. The child's own nature had something wrong in it, which continually betokened that she had been born amiss,—the effluence of her mother's lawless passion,—and often impelled Hester to ask, in bitterness of heart, whether it were for ill or good that the poor little creature had been born at all.

Indeed, the same dark question often rose into her mind, with reference to the whole race of womanhood. Was existence worth accepting, even to the happiest among them? As concerned her own individual existence, she had long ago decided in the negative, and dismissed the point as settled. A tendency to speculation, though it may keep woman quiet, as it does man, yet makes her sad. She discerns, it may be, such a hopeless task before her. As a first step, the whole system of society is to be torn down, and built up anew. Then, the very nature of the opposite sex, or its long hereditary habit, which has become like nature, is to be essentially modified, before woman can be allowed to assume what seems a fair and suitable position. Finally, all other difficulties being obviated, woman cannot take advantage of these preliminary reforms, until she herself shall have undergone a still mightier change; in which, perhaps, the ethereal essence, wherein she has her truest life, will be found to have evaporated. A woman never overcomes these problems by any exercise of thought. They are not to be solved, or only in one way. If her heart chance to come uppermost, they vanish. Thus, Hester Prynne, whose heart had lost its regular and healthy throb, wandered without a clew in the dark labyrinth of mind: now turned aside by an insurmountable precipice; now starting back from a deep chasm. There was wild and ghastly scenery all around her, and a home and comfort nowhere. At times, a fearful doubt strove to possess her soul, whether it were not better to send Pearl at once to heaven, and go herself to such futurity as Eternal Justice should provide.

The scarlet letter had not done its office.

The Scarlet Letter

A Tide of Benevolence

I began to discern that he had come among us actuated by no real sympathy with our feelings and our hopes, but chiefly because we were estranging ourselves from the world, with which his lonely and exclusive object in life had already put him at odds. Hollingsworth must have been originally endowed with a great spirit of benevolence, deep enough and warm enough to be the source of as much disinterested good as Providence often allows a human being the privilege of conferring upon his fellows. This native instinct yet lived within him. I myself had profited by it, in my necessity. It was seen, too, in his treatment of Priscilla. Such casual circumstances as were here involved would quicken his divine power of sympathy, and make him seem, while their influence lasted, the tenderest man and the truest friend on earth. But, by and by, you missed the tenderness of yesterday, and grew drearily conscious that Hollingsworth had a closer friend than ever you could be; and this friend was the cold, spectral monster which he had himself conjured up, and on which he was wasting all the warmth of his heart, and of which, at last,—as these men of a mighty purpose so invariably do,—he had grown to be the bond-slave. It was his philanthropic theory.

This was a result exceedingly sad to contemplate, considering that it had been mainly brought about by the very ardour and exuberance of his philanthropy. Sad, indeed, but by no means unusual: he had taught his benevolence to pour its warm tide exclusively through one channel; so that there was nothing to spare for other great manifestations of love to man, nor scarcely for the nutriment of individual attachments, unless they would minister, in some way, to the terrible egotism which he mistook for an angel of God.

The Blithedale Romance, 1852

Englishwomen

I have heard a good deal of the tenacity with which English ladies retain their personal beauty to a late period of life; but (not to suggest that an American eye needs use and cultivation before it can quite appreciate the charm of English beauty at any age) it strikes me that an English lady of fifty is apt to become a creature less refined and delicate, so far as her physique goes, than anything that we western people class under the name of woman. She has an awful ponderosity of frame, not pulpy, like the looser development of our few fat women, but massive with solid beef and streaky tallow; so that (though struggling manfully against the idea) you inevitably think of her as made up of steaks and sirloins. When she walks, her advance is elephantine. When she sits down, it is on a great round space of her Maker's footstool, where she looks as if nothing could ever move her. She imposes awe and respect by the muchness of her personality, to such a degree that you probably credit her with far greater moral and intellectual force than she can fairly claim. Her visage is usually grim and stern, seldom positively forbidding, yet calmly terrible, not merely by its breadth and weight of feature, but because it seems to express so much well-founded self-reliance, such acquaintance with the world, its toils, troubles, and dangers, and such sturdy capacity for trampling down a foe. Without anything positively salient, or actively offensive, or, indeed, unjustly formidable to her neighbours, she has the effect of a seventy-four gun-ship in time of peace; for, while you assure yourself that there is no real danger, you cannot help thinking how tremendous would be her onset, if pugnaciously inclined, and how futile the effort to inflict any counter-injury. She certainly looks tenfold—nay, a hundred-fold—better able to take care of herself than our slender-framed and haggard womankind; but I have not found reason to suppose that the English dowager of fifty has actually greater courage, fortitude, and strength of character than our women of similar age, or even a tougher physical endurance than they. Morally, she is strong, I suspect, only in society, and in the common routine of social affairs, and would be found powerless and timid in any exceptional strait that might call for energy outside of the conventionalities amid which she has grown up.

You can meet this figure in the street, and live, and even smile at the recollection. But conceive of her in a ball-room, with the bare, brawny arms that she invariably displays there, and all the other corresponding development, such as is beautiful in the maiden blossom, but a spectacle to howl at in such an overblown cabbage-rose as this.

Yet, somewhere in this enormous bulk there must be hidden the modest, slender, violet-nature of a girl, whom an alien mass of earthliness has unkindly overgrown; for an English maiden in her teens, though very seldom so pretty as our own damsels, possesses, to say the truth, a certain charm of half-blossom, and delicately folded leaves, and tender womanhood shielded by maidenly reserves, with which, somehow or other, our American girls often fail to adorn themselves during an appreciable moment. It is a pity that the English violet should grow into such an outrageously developed peony as I have attempted to describe.

Our Old Home, 1863

R. S. SURTEES
1805–1864

Mr Sponge and Lucy Glitters

'WHO-HOOP!' screamed Mr Sponge, throwing himself off his horse and rushing in amongst them. 'WHO-HOOP!' repeated he, still louder, holding the fox up in grim death above the baying pack.

'*Who-hoop!*' exclaimed Miss Glitters, reining up in delight alongside the chestnut. '*Who-hoop!*' repeated she, diving into the saddle-pocket for her lace-fringed handkerchief.

'Throw me my whip!' cried Mr Sponge, repelling the attacks of the hounds from behind his heels. Having got it, he threw the fox on the ground, and, clearing a circle, whipped off his brush in an instant. 'Tear him and eat him!' cried he, as the pack broke in on the carcase. 'Tear him and eat him!' repeated he, as he made his way up to Miss Glitters with the brush. 'We'll put this in your hat, alongside the cock's feathers,' said he.

The fair lady leant towards him, and as he adjusted it becomingly in her hat, looking at her bewitching eyes, her lovely face, and feeling the sweet fragrance of her breath, a something shot through Mr Sponge's pull-devil, pull-baker coat, his corduroy waistcoat, his Eureka shirt and Angola vest, and penetrated the very cockles of his heart. He gave her such a series of smacking kisses as startled her horse and astonished a poacher who happened to be hid in the adjoining hedge.

Mr Sponge's Sporting Tour, 1853

SAMUEL PALMER
1805–1881

Stars, Elms and Loop Holes

So exquisite is the glistering of the stars through loop holes in the thick woven canopy of ancient elm trees—of stars differing in glory, and one of prime lustre piercing the gloom—and all dancing with instant change as the leaves play in the wind that I cannot help thinking that Milton intended his 'Shady roof Of branching elm *star proof*' as a double stroke—as he tells of the impervious leafy gloom—glancing at its beautiful opposite—'Loop holes cut through thickest shade' and in them socketed the gems which sparkle on the Ethiopic forehead of the night.

Sketchbook, 1824

A World of Vision—and of Waddling Aldermen

Note. That when you go to Dulwich it is not enough on coming home to make recollections in which shall be united the scattered parts about those sweet fields into a sentimental and Dulwich looking whole. No. But considering Dulwich as the gate into the world of vision one must try behind the hills to bring up a mystic glimmer like that which lights our dreams. And those same hills, (hard task) should give us promise that the country beyond them is Paradise—for to the wise and prudent of this world what are Raffaelle's backgrounds but visionary nonsense, what the background of the Last Supper but empty wind—and its figures but a party of old fashioned Guys at supper? What to a waddling alderman is Raffaelle's heavenly colour? The body and mind both in sweet union nourished, with solid facts and still more solid pudding, forming their notions of loveliness from their ladies, straddling, scrofulous and oily, with faces richly imbrowned with youthful servitude and blazing kitchen fires, whence did their charms advance them to grease their masters' sofas which once they dusted. What wonder that the Alderman surrounded with nymphs like these, fair city Naiads swimming in greasy grandeur like sops in dripping—should worship the immortal Rubens? should laud him king of nature, should trace in his St Elizabeths their wives, in his Madonnas their daughters, should hail his colour as the tone of nature and his luscious handling as the outline of a melting oil man's widow?

Solid facts solid beef and solid gold needs must kill the visions of —— and M. Angelo—what would the *prudent* Ass dining *substantially* on thistles, care for a peach or nectrine dropped into his mouth? Why he scarce would feel them at all, or would, insulted with such a mockery of hope bray out his anger.

But God reveals not the beauties of ancient art to the wise and prudent but to babes; to the self abased, to the mourners in Zion. 'Even so Blessed Father, for so it seemeth good in thy sight.'

Sketchbook, 1824

The Domestic Circumstances of William Blake

Late as we parted last night, I awaked at dawn with the question in my ear, Squalor?—squalor?

Crush it; it is a roc's egg to your fabric.

I have met with this perverse mistake elsewhere. It gives a notion altogether false of the man, his house, and his habits.

No, certainly;—whatever was in Blake's house, there was no squalor. Himself, his wife, and his rooms, were clean and orderly; everything was in its place. His delightful working corner had its implements ready—tempting to the hand. The millionaire's upholsterer can furnish no enrichments like those of Blake's enchanted room.

letter to Alexander Gilchrist, 1860; published in Gilchrist's *Life of William Blake*

Tight Stays

One of our family (permit me to say, neither Mrs Palmer nor myself) at prayers this morning turned pale and nearly fainted through TIGHT STAYS. It is the business of the Devil to deface the works of God, and of God's loveliest work these hateful corsets cramp and impede the vitals, utterly destroy the shapeliness and grace, which we in our hopeless barbarism fancy they improve, and even twist and distort the bony structure. They impair the action of the lungs and heart, corrupt the breath, prevent ease and gracefulness of movement and sometimes any sudden movement at all but at the cost of sudden death. To call these Babylonish gyves Satanic would be to libel him against whom St Michael would not bring a railing accusation: we can not father them on Belial if with Milton we concede him somewhat of the 'graceful and humane'. Asmodeus perhaps devised them—certainly some ugly drudge and servile incubus of the Pit.

Blessed was the day in which Matthew Arnold christened us 'Philistines'.

Here is a case in which health and shapeliness and graceful movement are sacrificed to Custom our great all worshipped Dagon: physicians protest, artists are scandalized, and yet we know nothing better than to run in the rut, glide in the groove, and goose goes after goose, stooping under the gateway to a paltry and pernicious fashion worthy of the Fegee Indians who eat their aunts.

letter to John Preston Bright, 1868

JOHN STUART MILL
1806–1873

A Fixed Point

In all political societies which have had a durable existence, there has been some fixed point; something which men agreed in holding sacred; which it might or might not be lawful to contest in theory, but which no one could either fear or hope to see shaken in practice; which, in short (except perhaps during some temporary crisis), was in the common estimation placed *above* discussion. And the necessity of this may easily be made evident. A state never is, nor, until mankind are vastly improved, can hope to be, for any long time exempt from internal dissension; for there neither is nor has ever been any state of society in which collisions did not occur between the immediate interests and passions of powerful sections of the people. What, then, enables society to weather these storms, and pass through turbulent times without any permanent weakening of the ties which hold it together? Precisely this—that however important the interests about which men fall out, the conflict does not affect the fundamental principles of the system of social union which happens to exist; nor threaten large portions of the community with the subversion of that on which they have built their calculations, and with which their hopes and aims have become identified. But when the questioning of these fundamental principles is (not an occasional disease, but) the habitual condition of the body politic; and when all the violent animosities are called forth, which spring naturally from such a situation, the state is virtually in a position of civil war; and can never long remain free from it in act and fact.

'Coleridge', 1840

A Standardized World

The circumstances which surround different classes and individuals, and shape their characters, are daily becoming more assimilated. Formerly, different ranks, different neighbourhoods, different trades and professions, lived in what might be called different worlds; at present, to a great degree in the same. Comparatively speaking, they now read the same things, listen to the same things, see the same things, go to the same places, have their hopes and fears directed to the same objects, have the same rights and liberties, and the same means of asserting them. Great as are the differences of position which remain, they are nothing to those which have ceased. And the assimilation is still proceeding. All the political changes of the age promote it, since they all tend to raise the low and to lower the high. Every extension of education promotes it, because education brings people under common influences, and gives them access to the general stock of facts and sentiments. Improvements in the means of communication promote it, by bringing the inhabitants of distant places into personal contact, and keeping up a rapid flow of changes of residence between one place and another. The increase of commerce and manufactures promotes it, by diffusing more widely the advantages of easy circumstances, and opening all objects of ambition, even the highest, to general competition, whereby the desire of rising becomes no longer the character of a particular class, but of all classes. A more powerful agency than even all these, in bringing about a general similarity among mankind, is the complete establishment, in this and other free countries, of the ascendancy of public opinion in the State. As the various social eminences which enabled persons entrenched on them to disregard the opinion of the multitude, gradually become levelled; as the very idea of resisting the will of the public, when it is positively known that they have a will, disappears more and more from the minds of practical politicians; there ceases to be any social support for nonconformity—any substantive power in society, which, itself opposed to the ascendancy of numbers, is interested in taking under its protection opinions and tendencies at variance with those of the public.

On Liberty, 1859

A Grief without a Pang

It was in the autumn of 1826. I was in a dull state of nerves, such as everybody is occasionally liable to; unsusceptible to enjoyment or pleasurable excitement; one of those moods when what is pleasure at other times, becomes insipid or indifferent; the state, I should think, in which converts to Methodism usually are, when smitten by their first 'conviction of sin.' In this frame of mind it occurred to me to put the question directly to myself: 'Suppose that all your objects in life were realized; that all the changes in institutions and opinions which you are looking forward to, could be completely effected at this very instant: would this be a great joy and happiness to you?' And an irrepressible self-consciousness distinctly answered, 'No!' At this my heart sank within me: the whole foundation on which my life was constructed fell down. All my happiness was to have been found in the continual pursuit of this end. The end had ceased to charm, and how could there ever again be any interest in the means? I seemed to have nothing left to live for.

At first I hoped that the cloud would pass away of itself; but it did not. A night's sleep, the sovereign remedy for the smaller vexations of life, had no effect on it. I awoke to a renewed consciousness of the woful fact. I carried it with me into all companies, into all occupations. Hardly anything had power to cause me even a few minutes' oblivion of it. For some months the cloud seemed to grow thicker and thicker. The lines in Coleridge's 'Dejection'—I was not then acquainted with them—exactly describe my case:

> A grief without a pang, void, dark and drear,
> A drowsy, stifled, unimpassioned grief,
> Which finds no natural outlet or relief
> In word, or sigh, or tear.

In vain I sought relief from my favourite books; those memorials of past nobleness and greatness from which I had always hitherto drawn strength and animation. I read them now without feeling, or with the accustomed feeling *minus* all its charm; and I became persuaded, that my love of mankind, and of excellence for its own sake, had worn itself out. I sought no comfort by speaking to others of what I felt. If I had loved any one sufficiently to make confiding my griefs a necessity, I should not have been in the condition I was. I felt, too, that mine was not an interesting, or in any way respectable distress. There was nothing in it to attract sympathy.

Autobiography, 1873

Finding a Cure

This state of my thoughts and feelings made the fact of my reading Wordsworth for the first time (in the autumn of 1828), an important event in my life. I took up the collection of his poems from curiosity, with no expectation of mental relief from it, though I had before resorted to poetry with that hope. In the worst period of my depression, I had read through the whole of Byron (then new to me), to try whether a poet, whose peculiar department was supposed to be that of the intenser feelings, could rouse any feeling in me. As might be expected, I got no good from this reading, but the reverse. The poet's state of mind was too like my own. His was the lament of a man who had worn out all pleasures, and who seemed to think that life, to all who possess the good things of it, must necessarily be the vapid, uninteresting thing which I found it. His Harold and

Manfred had the same burden on them which I had; and I was not in a frame of mind to desire any comfort from the vehement sensual passion of his Giaours, or the sullenness of his Laras. But while Byron was exactly what did not suit my condition, Wordsworth was exactly what did. I had looked into the Excursion two or three years before, and found little in it; and I should probably have found as little, had I read it at this time. But the miscellaneous poems, in the two-volume edition of 1815 (to which little of value was added in the latter part of the author's life), proved to be the precise thing for my mental wants at that particular juncture.

In the first place, these poems addressed themselves powerfully to one of the strongest of my pleasurable susceptibilities, the love of rural objects and natural scenery; to which I had been indebted not only for much of the pleasure of my life, but quite recently for relief from one of my longest relapses into depression. In this power of rural beauty over me, there was a foundation laid for taking pleasure in Wordsworth's poetry; the more so, as his scenery lies mostly among mountains, which, owing to my early Pyrenean excursion, were my ideal of natural beauty. But Wordsworth would never have had any great effect on me, if he had merely placed before me beautiful pictures of natural scenery. Scott does this still better than Wordsworth, and a very second-rate landscape does it more effectually than any poet. What made Wordsworth's poems a medicine for my state of mind, was that they expressed, not mere outward beauty, but states of feeling, and of thought coloured by feeling, under the excitement of beauty. They seemed to be the very culture of the feelings, which I was in quest of. In them I seemed to draw from a source of inward joy, of sympathetic and imaginative pleasure, which could be shared in by all human beings; which had no connexion with struggle or imperfection, but would be made richer by every improvement in the physical or social condition of mankind. From them I seemed to learn what would be the perennial sources of happiness, when all the greater evils of life shall have been removed. And I felt myself at once better and happier as I came under their influence.

Autobiography

EDWARD FITZGERALD
1809–1883

'Derby Day'

Now, as to Frith, etc., I didn't half read the Review: but sent it to you to see what you would make of it. I quite agree with you about Hogarth, who (I always thought) made his pictures unnatural by overcrowding what was natural in Part, as also by caricature. For this reason, I always thought his Apprentices his best Series. But there are passages of Tragedy and Comedy in his Works that go very deep into Human Nature, and into one's Soul. He was also an Artist in Composition, Colour, etc., though in all respects, I think, a little over-rated of late years.

I don't say that Frith is not more natural (in the sense you use the word, I suppose) than Hogarth; but then does he take so difficult a Face of Nature to deal with, and, even on his own lower ground, does he go to the bottom of it? Is there in his Derby Day the one typical Face and Figure of the Jockey, the Gambler, etc., such as Hogarth would have painted for ever on our Imaginations? Is Frith at all better (if so good) as Leech in Punch? If as good or better, are his Pictures worth a thousandth Part of the Prices given for them? Which, I think, is the Question with the Reviewer. I don't know about his Colour; but I have never heard of it as beyond the usual.

If we take the mere representation of common Nature as the sum total of Art, we must put the modern Everyday life Novel above Shakespeare: for certainly Macbeth and Coriolanus, etc., did not spout Blank Verse, etc. But they dealt in great, deep, and terrible Passions, and Shakespeare has made them live again out of the dead Ashes of History by the force of his Imagination, and by the 'Thoughts that breathe, and Words that burn' that he has put into their Mouths. Nor can I think that Frith's veracious Portraitures of people eating Luncheons at Epsom are to be put in the Scale with Raffaelle's impossible Idealisation of the Human made Divine.

letter to Herman Biddell, 1863

'Champagne Charlie'

Are you overrun in London with 'Champagne Charlie is my Name'? A brutal Thing; nearly worthless—the Tune, I mean—but yet not quite—else it would not become so great a Bore. No: I can see, to my Sorrow, that it has some Go—which Mendelssohn had not. But Mozart, Rossini, and Handel had.

letter to W. F. Pollock, 1867

A Visit from Tennyson

Dear Mrs Kemble,

Have your American Woods begun to hang out their Purple and Gold yet? on this Day of Equinox. Some of ours begin to look rusty, after the Summer Drought; but have not turned Yellow yet . . .

Now too one's Garden begins to be haunted by that Spirit which Tennyson says is heard talking to himself among the flower-borders. Do you remember him?

And now—Who should send in his card to me last week—but the old Poet himself—he and his elder Son Hallam passing through Woodbridge from a Tour in Norfolk. 'Dear old Fitz,' ran the Card in pencil, 'We are passing thro'.' I had not seen him for twenty years—he looked much the same, except for his fallen Locks; and what really surprised me was, that we fell at once into the old Humour, as if we had only been parted twenty Days instead of so many Years. I suppose this is a Sign of Age—not altogether desirable. But so it was. He stayed two Days, and we went over the same old grounds of Debate, told some of the old Stories, and all was well. I suppose I may never see him again: and so I suppose we both thought as the Rail carried him off: and each returned to his ways as if scarcely diverted from them. Age again!—I liked Hallam much; unaffected, unpretending—no Slang—none of Young England's nonchalance—speaking of his Father as 'Papa' and tending him with great Care, Love, and Discretion.

letter to Fanny Kemble, 1876

Omar

I never see any Paper but my old Athenaeum, which, by the way, now tells me of some Lady's Edition of Omar which is to discover all my Errors and Perversions. So this will very likely turn the little Wind that blew my little Skiff on.

letter to Elizabeth Cowell, 1877

CHARLES DARWIN
1809–1882

The Plains of Patagonia

Among the scenes which are deeply impressed on my mind, none exceed in sublimity the primeval forests undefaced by the hand of man; whether those of Brazil, where the powers of Life are predominant, or those of Tierra del Fuego, where Death and Decay prevail. Both are temples filled with the varied productions of the God of Nature:—no one can stand in these solitudes unmoved, and not feel that there is more in man than the mere breath of his body. In calling up images of the past, I find that the plains of Patagonia frequently cross before my eyes; yet these plains are pronounced by all wretched and useless. They can be described only by negative characters; without habitations, without water, without trees, without mountains, they support merely a few dwarf plants. Why then, and the case is not peculiar to myself, have these arid wastes taken so firm a hold on my memory? Why have not the still more level, the greener and more fertile Pampas, which are serviceable to mankind, produced an equal impression? I can scarcely analyse these feelings: but it must be partly owing to the free scope given to the imagination. The plains of Patagonia are boundless, for they are scarcely passable, and hence unknown: they bear the stamp of having lasted, as they are now, for ages, and there appears no limit to their duration through future time. If, as the ancients supposed, the flat earth was surrounded by an impassable breadth of water or by deserts heated to an intolerable excess, who would not look at these last boundaries to man's knowledge with deep but ill-defined sensations?

The Voyage of the Beagle, 1839

The Struggle for Life

Nothing is easier than to admit in words the truth of the universal struggle for life, or more difficult—at least I have found it so—than constantly to bear this conclusion in mind. Yet unless it be thoroughly engrained in the mind, the whole economy of nature, with every fact on distribution, rarity, abundance, extinction, and variation, will be dimly seen or quite misunderstood. We behold the face of nature bright with gladness, we often see superabundance of food; we do not see or we forget, that the birds which are idly singing round us mostly live on insects or seeds, and are thus constantly destroying life; or we forget how largely these songsters, or their eggs, or their nestlings, are destroyed by birds and beasts of prey; we do not always bear in mind, that, though food may be now superabundant, it is not so at all seasons of each recurring year.

The Origin of Species, 1859

Man, Nature, and the Sense of Beauty

With respect to the belief that organic beings have been created beautiful for the delight of man,—a belief which it has been pronounced is subversive of my whole theory,—I may first remark that the sense of beauty obviously depends on the nature of the mind, irrespective of any real quality in the admired object; and that the idea of what is beautiful, is not innate or unalterable. We see this, for instance, in the men of different races admiring an entirely different standard of beauty in their women. If beautiful objects had been created solely for man's gratification, it ought to be shown that before man appeared, there was less beauty on the face of the earth than since he came on the stage. Were the beautiful volute and cone shells of the Eocene epoch, and the gracefully sculptured ammonites of the

Secondary period, created that man might ages afterwards admire them in his cabinet? Few objects are more beautiful than the minute siliceous cases of the diatomaceae: were these created that they might be examined and admired under the higher powers of the microscope? The beauty in this latter case, and in many others, is apparently wholly due to symmetry of growth. Flowers rank amongst the most beautiful productions of nature; but they have been rendered conspicuous in contrast with the green leaves, and in consequence at the same time beautiful, so that they may be easily observed by insects. I have come to this conclusion from finding it an invariable rule that when a flower is fertilised by the wind it never has a gaily-coloured corolla. Several plants habitually produce two kinds of flowers; one kind open and coloured so as to attract insects; the other closed, not coloured, destitute of nectar, and never visited by insects. Hence we may conclude that, if insects had not been developed on the face of the earth, our plants would not have been decked with beautiful flowers, but would have produced only such poor flowers as we see on our fir, oak, nut and ash trees, on grasses, spinach, docks, and nettles, which are all fertilised through the agency of the wind. A similar line of argument holds good with fruits; that a ripe strawberry or cherry is as pleasing to the eye as to the palate,—that the gaily-coloured fruit of the spindle-wood tree and the scarlet berries of the holly are beautiful objects,—will be admitted by every one. But this beauty serves merely as a guide to birds and beasts, in order that the fruit may be devoured and the matured seeds disseminated: I infer that this is the case from having as yet found no exception to the rule that seeds are always thus disseminated when embedded within a fruit of any kind (that is within a fleshy or pulpy envelope), if it be coloured of any brilliant tint, or rendered conspicuous by being white or black.

On the other hand, I willingly admit that a great number of male animals, as all our most gorgeous birds, some fishes, reptiles, and mammals, and a host of magnificently coloured butterflies, have been rendered beautiful for beauty's sake; but this has been effected through sexual selection, that is, by the more beautiful males having been continually preferred by the females, and not for the delight of man. So it is with the music of birds. We may infer from all this that a nearly similar taste for beautiful colours and for musical sounds runs through a large part of the animal kingdom. When the female is as beautifully coloured as the male, which is not rarely the case with birds and butterflies, the cause apparently lies in the colours acquired through sexual selection having been transmitted to both sexes, instead of to the males alone. How the sense of beauty in its simplest form—that is, the reception of a peculiar kind of pleasure from certain colours, forms, and sounds—was first developed in the mind of man and of the lower animals, is a very obscure subject. The same sort of difficulty is presented, if we enquire how it is that certain flavours and odours give pleasure, and others displeasure. Habit in all these cases appears to have come to a certain extent into play; but there must be some fundamental cause in the constitution of the nervous system in each species.

The Origin of Species

Is a Belief in God Instinctive?

The belief in God has often been advanced as not only the greatest, but the most complete of all the distinctions between man and the lower animals. It is however impossible, as we have seen, to maintain that this belief is innate or instinctive in man. On the other hand a belief in all-pervading spiritual agencies seems to be universal; and apparently follows from a considerable advance in man's reason, and from a still greater advance in his faculties of imagination, curiosity and wonder. I am aware that the assumed instinctive belief in God has been used by many persons as an argument for His existence. But this is a rash argument, as we should thus be compelled to believe in the existence of many cruel and malignant spirits, only a little more powerful than man; for the belief in them is far more general than in a beneficent Deity. The idea of a universal and beneficent Creator does not seem to arise in the mind of man, until he has been elevated by long-continued culture.

The Descent of Man, 1871

The Human Pedigree

Man may be excused for feeling some pride at having risen, though not through his own exertions, to the very summit of the organic scale; and the fact of his having thus risen, instead of having been aboriginally placed there, may give him hope for a still higher destiny in the distant future. But we are not here concerned with hopes or fears, only with the truth as far as our reason permits us to discover it; and I have given the evidence to the best of my ability. We must, however, acknowledge, as it seems to me, that man with all his noble qualities, with sympathy which feels for the most debased, with benevolence which extends not only to other men but to the humblest living creature, with his god-like intellect which has penetrated into the movements and constitution of the solar system—with all these exalted powers—Man still bears in his bodily frame the indelible stamp of his lowly origin.

The Descent of Man

EDGAR ALLAN POE
1809–1849

Buried Alive

We continued our route in search of the Amontillado. We passed through a range of low arches, descended, passed on, and descending again, arrived at a deep crypt, in which the foulness of the air caused our flambeaux rather to glow than flame.

At the most remote end of the crypt there appeared another less spacious. Its walls had been lined with human remains piled to the vault overhead, in the fashion of the great catacombs of Paris. Three sides of this interior crypt were still ornamented in this manner. From the fourth the bones had been thrown down, and lay promiscuously upon the earth, forming at one point a mound of some size. Within the wall thus exposed by the displacing of the bones, we perceived a still interior recess, in depth about four feet, in width three, in height six or seven. It seemed to have been constructed for no especial use within itself, but formed merely the interval between two of the colossal supports of the roof of the catacombs, and was backed by one of their circumscribing walls of solid granite.

It was in vain that Fortunato, uplifting his dull torch, endeavoured to pry into the depths of the recess. Its termination the feeble light did not enable us to see.

'Proceed,' I said; 'herein is the Amontillado. As for Luchesi'——

'He is an ignoramus,' interrupted my friend, as he stepped unsteadily forward, while I followed immediately at his heels. In an instant he had reached the extremity of the niche, and finding his progress arrested by the rock, stood stupidly bewildered. A moment more and I had fettered him to the granite. In its surface were two iron staples, distant from each other about two feet, horizontally. From one of these depended a short chain, from the other a padlock. Throwing the links about his waist, it was but the work of a few seconds to secure it. He was too much astounded to resist. Withdrawing the key I stepped back from the recess.

'Pass your hand,' I said, 'over the wall; you cannot help feeling the nitre. Indeed it is *very* damp. Once more let me *implore* you to return. No? Then I must positively leave you. But I must first render you all the little attentions in my power.'

'The Amontillado!' ejaculated my friend, not yet recovered from his astonishment.

'True,' I replied; 'the Amontillado.'

As I said these words I busied myself among the pile of bones of which I have before spoken. Throwing them aside, I soon uncovered a quantity of building stone and mortar. With these materials and with the aid of my trowel, I began vigorously to wall up the entrance of the niche.

I had scarcely laid the first tier of the masonry when I discovered that the intoxication of Fortunato had in a great measure worn off. The earliest indication I had of this was a low moaning cry from the depth of the recess. It was *not* the cry of a drunken man. There was then a long and obstinate silence. I laid the second tier, and the third, and the fourth; and then I heard the furious vibrations of the chain. The noise lasted for several minutes, during which, that I might hearken to it with the more satisfaction, I ceased my labours and sat down upon the bones. When at last the clanking subsided, I resumed the trowel, and finished without interruption the fifth, the sixth, and the seventh tier. The wall was now nearly upon a level with my breast. I again paused, and holding the flambeaux over the mason-work, threw a few feeble rays upon the figure within.

A succession of loud and shrill screams, bursting suddenly from the throat of the chained form, seemed to thrust me violently back. For a brief moment I hesitated—I trembled. Unsheathing my rapier, I began to grope with it about the recess; but the thought of an instant reassured me. I placed my hand upon the solid fabric of the catacombs, and felt satisfied. I reapproached the wall. I replied to the yells of him who clamoured. I re-echoed—I aided—I surpassed them in volume and in strength. I did this, and the clamourer grew still.

'The Cask of Amontillado', 1850

A Low, Dull, Quick Sound

As the bell sounded the hour, there came a knocking at the street door. I went down to open it with a light heart,—for what had I *now* to fear? There entered three men, who introduced themselves, with perfect suavity, as officers of the police. A shriek had been heard by a neighbour during the night; suspicion of foul play had been aroused; information had been lodged at the police office, and they (the officers) had been deputed to search the premises.

I smiled,—for *what* had I to fear? I bade the gentlemen welcome. The shriek, I said, was my own in a dream. The old man, I mentioned, was absent in the country. I took my visitors all over the house. I bade them search—search *well.* I led them, at length, to *his* chamber. I showed them his treasures, secure, undisturbed. In the enthusiasm of my confidence, I brought chairs into the room, and desired them *here* to rest from their fatigues, while I myself, in the wild audacity of my perfect triumph, placed my own seat upon the very spot beneath which reposed the corpse of the victim.

The officers were satisfied. My *manner* had convinced them. I was singularly at ease. They sat, and while I answered cheerily, they chatted of familiar things. But, ere long, I felt myself getting pale and wished them gone. My head ached, and I fancied a ringing in my ears; but still they sat, and still chatted. The ringing became more distinct;—it continued and became more distinct: I talked more freely to get rid of the feeling: but it continued and gained definitiveness—until, at length, I found that the noise was *not* within my ears.

No doubt I now grew *very* pale;—but I talked more fluently, and with a heightened voice. Yet the sound increased—and what could I do? It was *a low, dull, quick sound—much such a sound as a watch makes when enveloped in cotton.* I gasped for breath—and yet the officers heard it not. I talked more quickly—more vehemently; but the noise steadily increased. I arose and argued about trifles, in a high key and with violent gesticulations; but the noise steadily increased. Why *would* they not be gone! I paced the floor to and fro with heavy strides, as if excited to fury by the observations of the men—but the noise steadily increased. O God! what *could* I do? I foamed—I raved—I swore! I swung the chair upon which I had been sitting, and grated it upon the boards, but the noise arose over all and continually increased. It grew louder—louder—*louder!* And still the men chatted pleasantly, and smiled. Was it possible they heard not? Almighty God!—no, no! They heard!—they suspected!—they *knew!*—they were making a mockery of my horror!—this I thought, and this I think. But anything was better than this agony! Anything was more tolerable than this derision! I could bear those hypocritical smiles no longer! I felt that I must scream or die!—and now—again!—hark! louder! louder! louder! *louder!*—

'Villains!' I shrieked, 'dissemble no more! I admit the deed!—tear up the planks!—here, here!—it is the beating of his hideous heart!'

'The Tell-Tale Heart', 1850

The Literary System and How It Works

The author accustomed to seclusion, and mingling for the first time freely with the literary people about him, is invariably startled and delighted to find that the decisions of his own unbiassed judgment—decisions to which he has refrained from giving voice on account of their broad contradiction to the decision of the press—are sustained and considered quite as matters of course by almost every person with whom he converses. The fact is that when brought face to face with each other we are constrained to a certain amount of honesty by the sheer trouble it causes us to mould the countenance to a lie. We put on paper with a grave air what we could not for our lives assert personally to a friend without either blushing or laughing outright. That the opinion of the press is not an honest opinion—that necessarily it is impossible that it should be an honest opinion, is never denied by the members of the press themselves.

Individual presses, of course, are now and then honest, but I speak of the combined effect. Indeed, it would be difficult for those conversant with the *modus operandi* of public journals to deny the general falsity of impression conveyed. Let in America a book be published by an unknown, careless, or uninfluential author; if he publishes it 'on his own account' he will be confounded at finding that no notice of it is taken at all. If it has been entrusted to a publisher of *caste*, there will appear forthwith in each of the leading *business* papers a variously-phrased *critique* to the extent of three or four lines, and to the effect that 'we have received from the fertile press of So and So a volume entitled This and That, which appears to be well worthy perusal, and which is 'got up' in the customary neat style of the enterprising firm of So and So.' On the other hand, let our author have acquired influence, experience, or (what will stand him in good stead of either) effrontery, on the issue of his book he will obtain from his publisher a hundred copies (or more, as the case may be), 'for distribution among friends connected with the press.' Armed with these, he will call personally either at the office or (if he understands his game) at the private residence of every editor within his reach, enter into conversation, compliment the journalist, interest him, as if incidentally, in the subject of the book, and finally, watching an opportunity, beg leave to hand him 'a volume which, quite opportunely, is on the very matter now under discussion.' If the editor seems sufficiently interested, the rest is left to fate; but if there is any lukewarmness (usually indicated by a polite regret on the editor's part that he really has 'no time to render the work that justice which its importance demands'), then our author is prepared to understand and to sympathise; has, luckily, a friend thoroughly conversant with the topic, and who (perhaps) could be persuaded to write some account of the volume—provided that the editor would be kind enough just to glance over the *critique* and amend it in accordance with his own particular views. Glad to fill half a column or so of his editorial space, and still more glad to get rid of his visitor, the journalist assents. The author retires, consults the friend, instructs him touching the strong points of the volume, and insinuating in *some* shape a *quid pro quo* gets an elaborate *critique* written (or, what is more usual and far more simple, writes it himself), and his business in this individual quarter is accomplished. Nothing more than sheer impudence is requisite to accomplish it in all.

Now the effect of this system (for it has really grown to be such) is obvious. In ninety-nine cases out of a hundred, men of genius, too indolent and careless about worldly concerns to bestir themselves after this fashion, have also that pride of intellect which would prevent them, under any circumstances, from even insinuating, by the presentation of a book to a member of the press, a desire to have that book reviewed. They, consequently, and their works, are utterly overwhelmed and extinguished in the flood of the *apparent* public adulation upon which in gilded barges are borne triumphant the ingenious toady and the diligent quack.

'William Cullen Bryant', 1846

ABRAHAM LINCOLN
1809–1865

At a Time of Distress

Dear Fanny: It is with deep regret that I learn of the death of your kind and brave father, and especially that it is affecting your young heart beyond what is common in such cases. In this sad world of ours sorrow comes to all, and to the young it comes with bittered agony because it takes them unawares. The older have learned ever to expect it. I am anxious to afford some alleviation of your present distress. Perfect relief is not possible except with time. You cannot now realize that you will ever feel better. Is not this so? And yet it is a mistake. You are sure to be happy again. To know this, which is certainly true, will make you some less miserable now. I have had experience enough to know what I say, and you need only to believe it to feel better at once. The memory of your dear father, instead of an agony, will yet be a sad, sweet feeling in your heart, of a purer and holier sort than you have known before.

Please present my kind regards to your afflicted mother.

Your sincere friend,
A. Lincoln

letter to Fanny McCullough, December 1862

The Gettysburg Address

Four score and seven years ago our fathers brought forth on this continent, a new nation, conceived in Liberty, and dedicated to the proposition that all men are created equal.

Now we are engaged in a great civil war; testing whether that nation, or any nation so conceived and so dedicated, can long endure. We are met on a great battlefield of that war. We have come to dedicate a portion of that field as a final resting-place for those who here gave their lives that that nation might live. It is altogether fitting and proper that we should do this.

But, in a larger sense, we cannot dedicate—we cannot consecrate—we cannot hallow—this ground. The brave men, living and dead, who struggled here have consecrated it, far above our poor power to add or detract.

The world will little note, nor long remember, what we say here, but it can never forget what they did here. It is for us the living, rather, to be dedicated here to the unfinished work which they who fought here have thus far so nobly advanced. It is rather for us to be here dedicated to the great task remaining before us—that from these honored dead we take increased devotion to that cause for which they gave the last full measure of devotion; that we here highly resolve that these dead shall not have died in vain; that this nation, under God, shall have a new birth of freedom; and that government of the people, by the people, for the people, shall not perish from the earth.

1863

OLIVER WENDELL HOLMES SR.

1809–1894

The Case for Conceit

Little localised powers, and little narrow streaks of specialised knowledge, are things men are very apt to be conceited about. Nature is very wise; but for this encouraging principle how many small talents and little accomplishments would be neglected! Talk about conceit as much as you like, it is to human character what salt is to the ocean; it keeps it sweet and renders it endurable. Say rather it is like the natural unguent of the sea-fowl's plumage, which enables him to shed the rain that falls on him and the wave in which he dips. When one has had *all* his conceit taken out of him, when he has lost *all* his illusions, his feathers will soon soak through, and he will fly no more.

'So you admire conceited people, do you?' said the young lady who has come to the city to be finished off for—the duties of life.

I am afraid you do not study logic at your school, my dear. It does not follow that I wish to be pickled in brine because I like a salt-water plunge at Nahant. I say that conceit is just as natural a thing to human minds as a centre is to a circle. But littleminded people's thoughts move in such small circles that five minutes' conversation gives you an arc long enough to determine their whole curve. An arc in the movement of a large intellect does not sensibly differ from a straight line. Even if it have the third vowel as its centre, it does not soon betray it. The highest thought, that is, is the most seemingly impersonal; it does not obviously imply any individual centre.

The Autocrat of the Breakfast-Table, 1858

ELIZABETH GASKELL
1810–1865

Dr Johnson and Mr Boz

When the trays reappeared with biscuits and wine, punctually at a quarter to nine, there was conversation, comparing of cards, and talking over tricks; but by-and-by Captain Brown sported a bit of literature.

'Have you seen any numbers of "The Pickwick Papers"?' said he. (They were then publishing in parts.) 'Capital thing!'

Now Miss Jenkyns was daughter of a deceased rector of Cranford; and, on the strength of a number of manuscript sermons, and a pretty good library of divinity, considered herself literary, and looked upon any conversation about books as a challenge to her. So she answered and said, 'Yes, she had seen them; indeed, she might say she had read them.'

'And what do you think of them?' exclaimed Captain Brown. 'Aren't they famously good?'

So urged, Miss Jenkyns could not but speak.

'I must say, I don't think they are by any means equal to Dr Johnson. Still, perhaps, the author is young. Let him persevere, and who knows what he may become if he will take the great Doctor for his model?' This was evidently too much for Captain Brown to take placidly; and I saw the words on the tip of his tongue before Miss Jenkyns had finished her sentence.

'It is quite a different sort of thing, my dear madam,' he began.

'I am quite aware of that,' returned she. 'And I make allowances, Captain Brown.'

'Just allow me to read you a scene out of this month's number,' pleaded he. 'I had it only this morning, and I don't think the company can have read it yet.'

'As you please,' said she, settling herself with an air of resignation. He read the account of the 'swarry' which Sam Weller gave at Bath. Some of us laughed heartily. *I* did not dare, because I was staying in the house. Miss Jenkyns sat in patient gravity. When it was ended, she turned to me, and said with mild dignity—

'Fetch me "Rasselas," my dear, out of the book-room.'

When I brought it to her, she turned to Captain Brown—

'Now allow *me* to read you a scene, and then the present company can judge between your favourite, Mr Boz, and Dr Johnson.'

She read one of the conversations between Rasselas and Imlac, in a high-pitched majestic voice: and when she had ended, she said, 'I imagine I am now justified in my preference of Dr Johnson as a writer of fiction.'

The Captain screwed his lips up, and drummed on the table, but he did not speak. She thought she would give a finishing blow or two.

'I consider it vulgar, and below the dignity of literature, to publish in numbers.'

'How was the *Rambler* published, ma'am?' asked Captain Brown in a low voice, which I think Miss Jenkyns could not have heard.

'Dr Johnson's style is a model for young beginners. My father recommended it to me when I began to write letters—I have formed my own style upon it; I recommend it to your favourite.'

'I should be very sorry for him to exchange his style for any such pompous writing,' said Captain Brown.

Miss Jenkyns felt this as a personal affront, in a way of which the Captain had not dreamed. Epistolary writing she and her friends considered as her *forte*. Many a copy of many a letter have I seen written and corrected on the slate, before she 'seized the half-hour just previous to post-time to assure' her friends of this or of that; and Dr Johnson was, as she said, her model in these compositions. She drew herself up with dignity, and only replied to Captain Brown's last remark by saying, with marked emphasis on every syllable, 'I prefer Dr Johnson to Mr Boz.'

It is said—I won't vouch for the fact—that Captain Brown was heard to say, *sotto voce*, 'D—n Dr Johnson!' If he did, he was penitent afterwards, as he showed by going to stand near Miss Jenkyns's arm-chair, and endeavouring to beguile her into conversation on some more pleasing subject. But she was inexorable.

Cranford, 1853

The Assembly Room

We went into the cloak-room adjoining the Assembly Room; Miss Matty gave a sigh or two to her departed youth, and the remembrance of the last time she had been there, as she adjusted her pretty new cap before the strange, quaint old mirror in the cloak-room. The Assembly Room had been added to the inn, about a hundred years before, by the different county families, who met together there once a month during the winter to dance and play at cards. Many a county beauty had first swung through the minuet that she afterwards danced before Queen Charlotte in this very room. It was said that one of the Gunnings had graced the apartment with her beauty; it was certain that a rich and beautiful widow, Lady Williams, had here been smitten with the noble figure of a young artist, who was staying with some family in the neighbourhood for professional purposes, and accompanied his patrons to the Cranford Assembly. And a pretty bargain poor Lady Williams had of her handsome husband, if all tales were true. Now, no beauty blushed and dimpled along the sides of the Cranford Assembly Room; no handsome artist won hearts by his brow, *chapeau bras* in hand; the old room was dingy; the salmon-coloured paint had faded into a drab; great pieces of plaster had chipped off from the white wreaths and festoons on its walls; but still a mouldy odour of aristocracy lingered about the place, and a dusty recollection of the days that were gone made Miss Matty and Mrs Forrester bridle up as they entered, and walk mincingly up the room, as if there were a number of genteel observers, instead of two little boys with a stick of toffy between them with which to beguile the time.

Cranford

A Mill-Owner's House

The lodge-door was like a common garden-door; on one side of it were great closed gates for the ingress and egress of lurries and waggons. The lodge-keeper admitted them into a great oblong yard, on one side of which were offices for the transaction of business; on the opposite, an immense many-windowed mill, whence proceeded the continual clank of machinery and the long groaning roar of the steam-engine, enough to deafen those who lived within the enclosure. Opposite to the wall, along which the street ran, on one of the narrow sides of the oblong, was a handsome stone-coped house—blackened, to be sure, by the smoke, but with paint, windows, and steps kept scrupulously clean. It was evidently a house which had been built some fifty or sixty years. The stone facings—the long, narrow windows and the number of them—the flights of steps up to the front door, ascending from either side, and guarded by railing—all witnessed to its age. Margaret only wondered why people who could afford to live in so good a house, and keep it in such perfect order, did not prefer a much smaller dwelling in the country, or even some suburb; not in the continual whirl and din of the factory. Her unaccustomed ears could hardly catch her father's voice, as they stood on the steps awaiting the opening of the door. The yard, too, with the great doors in the dead wall as a boundary, was but a dismal look-out for the sitting-rooms of the house—as Margaret found when they had mounted the old-fashioned stairs, and been ushered into the drawing-room, the three windows of which went over the front door and the room on the right-hand side of the entrance. There was no one in the drawing-room. It seemed as though no one had been in it since the day when the furniture was bagged up with as much care as if the house was to be overwhelmed with lava, and discovered a thousand years hence. The walls were pink and gold; the pattern on the carpet represented bunches of flowers on a light ground, but it was carefully covered up in the centre by a linen drugget, glazed and colourless. The window-curtains were lace; each chair and sofa had its own particular veil of netting or knitting. Great alabaster groups occupied every flat surface, safe from dust under their glass shades. In the middle of the room, right under the bagged-up chandelier, was a large circular table, with smartly-bound books arranged at regular intervals round the circumference of its polished surface, like gaily coloured spokes of a wheel. Everything reflected light, nothing absorbed it. The whole room had a painfully spotted, spangled, speckled look about it, which impressed Margaret so unpleasantly that she was hardly conscious of the peculiar cleanliness required to keep everything so white and pure in such an atmosphere, or of the trouble that must be willingly expended to secure that effect of icy, snowy discomfort. Wherever she looked there was evidence of care and labour, but not care and labour to procure ease, to help on habits of tranquil home employment; solely to ornament and then to preserve ornament from dirt or destruction.

North and South, 1855

'Papa, I've Been Writing a Book'

The sisters had kept the knowledge of their literary ventures from their father, fearing to increase their own anxieties and disappointment by witnessing his; for he took an acute interest in all that befell his children, and his own tendency had been towards literature in the days when he was young and hopeful. It was true he did not much manifest his feelings in words; he would have thought that he was prepared for disappointment as the lot of man, and that he could have met it with stoicism; but words are poor and tardy interpreters of feelings to those who love one another, and his daughters knew how he would have borne ill-success worse for them than for himself. So they did not tell him what they were undertaking. He says now that he suspected it all along, but his suspicions could take no exact form, as all he was certain of was, that his children were perpetually writing—and not writing letters. We have seen how the communications from their publishers were received 'under cover to Miss Brontë.' Once, Charlotte told me, they overheard the postman meeting Mr Brontë, as the latter was leaving the house, and inquiring from the parson where one Currer Bell could be living, to which Mr Brontë replied that there was no such person in the parish . . .

Now, however, when the demand for the work had assured success to *Jane Eyre*, her sisters urged Charlotte to tell their father of its publication. She accordingly went into his study one afternoon after his early dinner, carrying with her a copy of the book, and one or two reviews, taking care to include a notice adverse to it.

She informed me that something like the following conversation took place between her and him. (I wrote down her words the day after I heard them; and I am pretty sure they are quite accurate.)

'Papa, I've been writing a book.'

'Have you, my dear?'

'Yes, and I want you to read it.'

'I am afraid it will try my eyes too much.'

'But it is not in manuscript: it is printed.'

'My dear! you've never thought of the expense it will be! It will be almost sure to be a loss, for how can you get a book sold? No one knows you or your name.'

'But, papa, I don't think it will be a loss; no more will you, if you will just let me read you a review or two, and tell you more about it.'

So she sat down and read some of the reviews to her father; and then, giving him the copy of *Jane Eyre* that she intended for him, she left him to read it. When he came in to tea, he said, 'Girls, do you know Charlotte has been writing a book, and it is much better than likely?'

Life of Charlotte Brontë, 1857

'I Wish I Was Good!'

The two girls were silent for some time, both gazing into the fire. Cynthia spoke first:

'I wish I could love people as you do, Molly!'

'Don't you?' said the other, in surprise.

'No. A good number of people love me, I believe, or at least they think they do; but I never seem to care much for any one. I do believe I love you, little Molly, whom I have only known for ten days, better than any one.'

'Not than your mother?' said Molly, in grave astonishment.

'Yes, than my mother!' replied Cynthia, half-smiling. 'It's very shocking, I daresay; but it is so. Now, don't go and condemn me. I don't think love for one's mother quite comes by nature; and remember how much I have been separated from mine! I love my father, if you will,' she continued, with the force of truth in her tone, and then she stopped; 'but he died when I was quite a little thing, and no one believes that I remember him. I heard mamma say to a caller, not a fortnight after his funeral, "Oh, no, Cynthia is too young; she has quite forgotten him"—and I bit my lips, to keep from crying out, "Papa! papa! have I?" But it's of no use. Well, then mamma had to go out as a governess; she couldn't help it, poor thing! but she didn't much care for parting with me. I was a trouble, I daresay. So I was sent to school at four years old; first one school, and then another; and in the holidays, mamma went to stay at grand houses, and I was generally left with the schoolmistresses. Once I went to the Towers; and mamma lectured me continually, and yet I was very naughty, I believe. And so I never went again; and I was very glad of it, for it was a horrid place.'

'That it was!' said Molly, who remembered her own day of tribulation there.

'And once I went to London, to stay with my uncle Kirkpatrick. He is a lawyer, and getting on now; but then he was poor enough, and had six or seven children. It was winter-time, and we were all shut up in a small house in Doughty Street. But, after all, that wasn't so bad.'

'But then you lived with your mother when she began school at Ashcombe. Mr Preston told me that, when I stayed that day at the Manor-house.'

'What did he tell you?' asked Cynthia, almost fiercely.

'Nothing but that. Oh, yes! He praised your beauty, and wanted me to tell you what he had said.'

'I should have hated you if you had,' said Cynthia.

'Of course I never thought of doing such a thing,' replied Molly. 'I didn't like him; and Lady Harriet spoke of him the next day, as if he wasn't a person to be liked.'

Cynthia was quite silent. At length she said:

'I wish I was good!'

'So do I,' said Molly simply. She was thinking again of Mrs Hamley:

> 'Only the actions of the just
> Smell sweet and blossom in the dust.'

and 'goodness' just then seemed to her to be the only enduring thing in the world.

'Nonsense, Molly! You are good. At least, if you're not good, what am I? There's a rule-of-three sum for you to do! But it's no use talking; I am not good, and I never shall be now. Perhaps I might be a heroine still, but I shall never be a good woman, I know.'

'Do you think it easier to be a heroine?'

'Yes, as far as one knows of heroines from history. I'm capable of a great jerk, an effort, and then a relaxation—but steady, every-day goodness is beyond me. I must be a moral kangaroo!'

Wives and Daughters, 1866

WILLIAM MAKEPEACE THACKERAY
1811–1863

A Public Execution

How cool and clean the streets look, as the carriage startles the echoes that have been asleep in the corners all night. Somebody has been sweeping the pavements clean in the night-time surely; they would not soil a lady's white satin shoes, they are so dry and neat. There is not a cloud or a breath in the air, except Z——'s cigar, which whiffs off, and soars straight upwards in volumes of white, pure smoke. The trees in the squares look bright and green—as bright as leaves in the country in June. We who keep late hours don't know the beauty of London air and verdure; in the early morning they are delightful—the most fresh and lively companions possible. But they cannot bear the crowd and the bustle of mid-day. You don't know them then—they are no longer the same things. We have come to Gray's Inn; there is actually dew upon the grass in the gardens; and the windows of the stout old red houses are all in a flame.

As we enter Holborn the town grows more animated; and there are already twice as many people in the streets as you see at midday in a German *Residenz* or an English provincial town. The gin-shop keepers have many of them taken their shutters down, and many persons are issuing from them pipe in hand. Down they go along the broad bright street, their blue shadows marching *after* them; for they are all bound the same way, and are bent like us upon seeing the hanging.

It is twenty minutes past four as we pass St Sepulchre's: by this time many hundred people are in the street, and many more are coming up Snow Hill. Before us lies Newgate Prison; but something a great deal more awful to look at, which seizes the eye at once, and makes the heart beat, is

There it stands black and ready, jutting out from a little door in the prison. As you see it, you feel a kind of dumb electric shock, which causes one to start a little, and give a sort of gasp for breath. The shock is over in a second; and presently you examine the object before you with a certain feeling of complacent curiosity. At least, such was the effect that the gallows produced upon the writer, who is trying to set down all his feelings as they occurred, and not to exaggerate them at all.

After the gallows-shock had subsided, we went down into the crowd, which was very numerous, but not dense as yet. It was evident that the day's *business* had not begun. People sauntered up, and formed groups, and talked; the new comers asking those who seemed *habitués* of the place about former executions; and did the victim hang with his face towards the clock or towards Ludgate Hill? and had he the rope round his neck when he came on the scaffold, or was it put on by Jack Ketch afterwards? and had Lord W—— taken a window, and which was he? I may mention the noble Marquis's name, as he was not at the exhibition. A pseudo W—— was pointed out in an opposite window, towards whom all the people in our neighbourhood looked eagerly, and with great respect too. The mob seemed to have no sort of ill-will against him, but sympathy and admiration. This noble lord's personal courage and strength have won the plebs over to him. Perhaps his exploits against policemen have occasioned some of this popularity; for the mob hate them, as children the schoolmaster . . .

'Going to See a Man Hanged', 1840

Castle Carabas

At the entrance of the park, there are a pair of great gaunt mildewed lodges—mouldy Doric temples with black chimney-pots, in the finest classic taste, and the gates of course are surmounted by the *chats bottés*, the well-known supporters of the Carabas family. 'Give the lodge-keeper a shilling,' says Ponto, (who drove me near to it in his four-wheeled cruelty-chaise). 'I warrant it's the first piece of ready money he has received for some time.' I don't know whether there was any foundation for this sneer, but the gratuity was received with a curtsey, and the gate opened for me to enter. 'Poor old porteress!' says I, inwardly. 'You little know that it is the Historian of Snobs whom you let in!' The gates were passed. A damp green stretch of park spread right and left immeasurably, confined by a chilly gray wall, and a damp long straight road between two huge rows of moist, dismal lime-trees, leads up to the Castle. In the midst of the park is a great black tank or lake, bristling over with rushes, and here and there covered over with patches of pea-soup. A shabby temple rises on an island in this delectable lake, which is approached by a rotten barge that lies at roost in dilapidated boat-house. Clumps of elms and oaks dot over the huge green flat. Every one of them would have been down long since, but that the Marquis is not allowed to cut the timber.

Up that long avenue the Snobographer walked in solitude. At the seventy-ninth tree on the left-hand side, the insolvent butcher hanged himself. I scarcely wondered at the dismal deed, so woful and sad were the impressions connected with the place. So, for a mile and a half I walked—alone and thinking of death.

I forgot to say the house is in full view all the way—except when intercepted by the trees on the miserable island in the lake—an enormous red-brick mansion, square, vast, and dingy. It is flanked by four stone towers with weathercocks. In the midst of the grand façade is a huge Ionic portico, approached by a vast, lonely, ghastly staircase. Rows of black windows, framed in stone, stretch on either side, right and left—three storeys and eighteen windows of a row. You may see a picture of the palace and staircase, in the 'Views of England and Wales,' with four carved and gilt carriages waiting at the gravel walk, and several parties of ladies and gentlemen in wigs and hoops, dotting the fatiguing lines of the stairs.

But these stairs are made in great houses for people *not* to ascend. The first Lady Carabas (they are but eighty years in the peerage), if she got out of her gilt coach in a shower, would be wet to the skin before she got half-way to the carved Ionic portico, where four dreary statues of Peace, Plenty, Piety and Patriotism, are the only sentinels. You enter these palaces by back-doors. 'That was the way the Carabases got their peerage,' the misanthropic Ponto said after dinner.

Well—I rang the bell at a little low side-door; it clanged and jingled and echoed for a long, long while, till at length a face, as of a housekeeper, peered through the door, and, as she saw my hand in my waistcoat pocket, opened it. Unhappy, lonely, housekeeper, I thought. Is Miss Crusoe in her island more solitary? The door clapped to, and I was in Castle Carabas.

The Book of Snobs, 1848

A Moral Sheepdog

'Rawdon,' said Becky, very late one night, as a party of gentlemen were seated round her crackling drawing-room fire (for the men came to her house to finish the night; and she had ice and coffee for them, the best in London): 'I must have a sheep-dog.'

'A what?' said Rawdon, looking up from an écarté table.

'A sheep-dog!' said young Lord Southdown. 'My dear Mrs Crawley, what a fancy! Why not have a Danish dog? I know of one as big as a camelopard, by Jove. It would almost pull your brougham. Or a Persian greyhound, eh? (I propose, if you please); or a little pug that would go into one of Lord Steyne's snuff-boxes? There's a man at Bayswater got one with such a nose that you might,—I mark the king and play,—that you might hang your hat on it.'

'I mark the trick,' Rawdon gravely said. He attended to his game commonly, and didn't much meddle with the conversation except when it was about horses and betting.

'What *can* you want with a shepherd's dog?' the lively little Southdown continued.

'I mean a *moral* shepherd's dog,' said Becky, laughing, and looking up at Lord Steyne.

'What the devil's that?' said his lordship.

'A dog to keep the wolves off me,' Rebecca continued. 'A companion.'

'Dear little innocent lamb, you want one,' said the marquis; and his jaw thrust out, and he began to grin hideously, his little eyes leering towards Rebecca.

The great Lord of Steyne was standing by the fire sipping coffee. The fire crackled and blazed pleasantly. There was a score of candles sparkling round the mantelpiece, in all sorts of quaint sconces, of gilt and bronze and porcelain. They lighted up Rebecca's figure to admiration, as she sat on a sofa covered with a pattern of gaudy flowers. She was in a pink dress, that looked as fresh as a rose; her dazzling white arms and shoulders were half covered with a thin hazy scarf through which they sparkled; her hair hung in curls round her neck; one of her little feet peeped out from the fresh crisp folds of the silk: the prettiest little foot in the prettiest little sandal in the finest silk stocking in the world.

The candles lighted up Lord Steyne's shining bald head, which was fringed with red hair. He had thick bushy eyebrows, with little twinkling bloodshot eyes, surrounded by a thousand wrinkles. His jaw was underhung, and when he laughed, two white buck-teeth protruded themselves and glistened savagely in the midst of the grin. He had been dining with royal personages, and wore his garter and ribbon. A short man was his lordship, broad-chested, and bow-legged, but proud of the fineness of his foot and ankle, and always caressing his garter-knee.

'And so the Shepherd is not enough,' said he, 'to defend his lambkin?'

'The Shepherd is too fond of playing at cards and going to his clubs,' answered Becky, laughing.

'Gad, what a debauched Corydon!' said my lord—'what a mouth for a pipe!'

'I take your three to two,' here said Rawdon, at the card-table.

'Hark at Meliboeus,' snarled the noble marquis; 'he's pastorally occupied too: he's shearing a Southdown. What an innocent mutton, hey? Damme, what a snowy fleece!'

Rebecca's eyes shot out gleams of scornful humour. 'My lord,' she said, 'you are a knight of the Order.' He had the collar round his neck, indeed—a gift of the restored princes of Spain.

Lord Steyne in early life had been notorious for his daring and his success at play. He had sat up two days and two nights with Mr Fox at hazard. He had won money of the most august personages of the realm:

he had won his marquisate, it was said, at the gaming-table; but he did not like an allusion to those bygone *fredaines*. Rebecca saw the scowl gathering over his heavy brow.

She rose up from her sofa, and went and took his coffee-cup out of his hand with a little curtsy. 'Yes,' she said, 'I must get a watch-dog. But he won't bark at *you*.' And, going into the other drawing-room, she sat down to the piano, and began to sing little French songs in such a charming, thrilling voice, that the mollified nobleman speedily followed her into that chamber, and might be seen nodding his head and bowing time over her.

Rawdon and his friend meanwhile played écarté until they had enough. The colonel won; but, say that he won ever so much and often, nights like these, which occurred many times in the week—his wife having all the talk and all the admiration, and he sitting silent without the circle, not comprehending a word of the jokes, the allusions, the mystical language within—must have been rather wearisome to the ex-dragoon.

'How is Mrs Crawley's husband?' Lord Steyne used to say to him by way of a good day when they met: and indeed that was now his avocation in life. He was Colonel Crawley no more. He was Mrs Crawley's husband.

Vanity Fair, 1848

St Adelaide Villas

It arrived that evening at a wonderful small cottage in a street leading from the Fulham Road—one of those streets which have the finest romantic names—(this was called St Adelaide Villas, Anna-Maria Road, West), where the houses look like baby houses; where the people, looking out of the first-floor windows, must infallibly, as you think, sit with their feet in the parlours; where the shrubs in the little gardens in front bloom with a perennial display of little children's pinafores, little red socks, caps, &c. (polyandria polygynia); whence you hear the sound of jingling spinets and women singing; where little porter pots hang on the railings sunning themselves; whither of evenings you see City clerks padding wearily.

Vanity Fair

We March On without Them

In this vast town one has not the time to go and seek one's friends; if they drop out of the rank they disappear, and we march on without them. Who is ever missed in Vanity Fair?

Vanity Fair

A Famous Pastrycook's

On the arm of her Fitzroy, Rosa went off to Fubsby's, that magnificent shop at the corner of Parliament Place and Alicompayne Square,—a shop into which the rogue had often cast a glance of approbation as he passed: for there are not only the most wonderful and delicious cakes and confections in the window, but at the counter there are almost sure to be three or four of the prettiest women in the whole of this world, with little darling caps of the last French make, with beautiful wavy hair, and the neatest possible waists and aprons. Yes, there they sit; and others, perhaps, besides Fitz have cast a sheep's-eye through those enormous plate-glass window-panes. I suppose it is the fact of perpetually living among such a quantity of good things that makes those young ladies so beautiful. They come into the place, let us say, like ordinary people, and gradually grow handsomer and handsomer, until they grow out into the perfect angels you see. It can't be otherwise: if you and I, my dear fellow, were to have a course of that place, we should become beautiful too. They live in an atmosphere of the most delicious pine-apples, blancmanges, creams, (some whipt, and some so good that of course they don't want whipping,) jellies, tipsy-cakes, cherry-brandy—one hundred thousand sweet and lovely things. Look at the preserved fruits, look at the golden ginger, the outspreading ananas, the darling little rogues of China oranges, ranged in the gleaming crystal cylinders. *Mon Dieu!* Look at the strawberries in the leaves. Each of them is as large nearly as a lady's reticule, and looks as if it had been brought up in a nursery to itself. One of those strawberries is a meal for those young ladies behind the counter; they nibble off a little from the side, and if they are very hungry, which can scarcely ever happen, they are allowed to go to the crystal canisters and take out a rout-cake or macaroon. In the evening they sit and tell each other little riddles out of the bonbons; and when they wish to amuse themselves, they read the most delightful remarks, in the French language, about Love, and Cupid, and Beauty, before they place them inside the crackers. They always are writing down good things into Mr Fubsby's ledgers. It must be a perfect feast to read them. Talk of the Garden of Eden! I believe it was nothing to Mr Fubsby's house; and I have no doubt that after those young ladies have been there a certain time they get to such a pitch of loveliness at last, that they become complete angels, with wings sprouting out of their lovely shoulders, when (after giving just a preparatory balance or two) they fly up to the counter and perch there for a minute, hop down again, and affectionately kiss the other young ladies, and say, 'Good-bye, dears! We shall meet again *là haut*.' And then with a whirr of their deliciously scented wings, away they fly for good, whisking over the trees of Brobdingnag Square, and up into the sky, as the policeman touches his hat. It is up there that they invent the legends for the crackers, and the wonderful riddles and remarks on the bonbons. No mortal, I am sure, could write them.

A Little Dinner at Timmins's, 1848

HENRY JAMES SR.
1811–1882

Carlyle and the Americans

It always appeared to me that Carlyle valued truth and good as a painter does his pigments,—not for what they are in themselves, but for the effects they lend themselves to in the sphere of production. Indeed, he always exhibited a contempt, so characteristic as to be comical, for every one whose zeal for truth or good led him to question existing institutions with a view to any practical reform. He himself was wont to question established institutions and dogmas with the utmost license of scepticism, but he obviously meant nothing beyond the production of a certain literary surprise, or the enjoyment of his own aesthetic power. Nothing maddened him so much as to be mistaken for a reformer, really intent upon the interests of God's righteousness upon the earth, which are the interests of universal justice. This is what made him hate Americans, and call us a nation of bores,—that we took him at his word, and reckoned upon him as a sincere well-wisher to his species. He hated us, because a secret instinct told him that our exuberant faith in him would never be justified by closer knowledge; for no one loves the man who forces him upon a premature recognition of himself. I recall the uproarious mirth with which he and Mrs Carlyle used to recount the incidents of a visit they had received from a young New England woman, and describe the earnest, devout homage her credulous soul had rendered him. It was her first visit abroad, and she supposed—poor thing!—that these famous European writers and talkers, who so dominated her fancy at a distance, really meant all they said, were as innocent and lovely in their lives as in their books; and she no sooner crossed Carlyle's threshold, accordingly, than her heart offered its fragrance to him as liberally as the flower opens to the sun. And Carlyle, the inveterate comedian, instead of being humbled to the dust by the revelation which such simplicity suddenly flashed upon his own eyes of his essentially dramatic genius and exploits, was irritated, vexed, and outraged by it as by a covert insult. His own undevout soul had never risen to the contemplation of himself as the priest of a really infinite sanctity; and when this clear-eyed barbarian, looking past him to the substance which informed him, made him feel himself for the moment the transparent mask or unconscious actor he was, his self-consciousness took the alarm.

'Some Personal Recollections of Carlyle', 1881

CHARLES DICKENS
1812–1870

Sam Weller Reads His Valentine

Sam dipped his pen into the ink to be ready for any corrections, and began with a very theatrical air:

'"Lovely——"'

'Stop,' said Mr Weller, ringing the bell. 'A double glass o' the inwariable, my dear.'

'Very well, sir,' replied the girl; who with great quickness appeared, vanished, returned, and disappeared.

'They seem to know your ways here,' observed Sam.

'Yes,' replied his father, 'I've been here before, in my time. Go on, Sammy.'

'"Lovely creetur,"' repeated Sam.

''Tain't in poetry, is it?' interposed his father.

'No, no,' replied Sam.

'Werry glad to hear it,' said Mr Weller. 'Poetry's unnat'ral; no man ever talked poetry 'cept a beadle on boxin' day, or Warren's blackin', or Rowland's oil, or some o' them low fellows; never you let yourself down to talk poetry, my boy. Begin agin, Sammy.'

Mr Weller resumed his pipe with critical solemnity, and Sam once more commenced, and read as follows:

'"Lovely creetur i feel myself a dammed"—.'

'That ain't proper,' said Mr Weller, taking his pipe from his mouth.

'No; it ain't "dammed",' observed Sam, holding the letter up to the light, 'it's "shamed," there's a blot there—"I feel myself ashamed."'

'Werry good,' said Mr Weller. 'Go on.'

'"Feel myself ashamed, and completely cir—" I forget what this here word is,' said Sam, scratching his head with the pen, in vain attempts to remember.

'Why don't you look at it, then?' inquired Mr Weller.

'So I *am* a lookin' at it,' replied Sam, 'but there's another blot. Here's a "c," and a "i," and a "d."'

'Circumwented, p'raps,' suggested Mr Weller.

'No, it ain't that,' said Sam, 'circumscribed; that's it.'

'That ain't as good a word as circumwented, Sammy,' said Mr Weller, gravely.

'Think not?' said Sam.

'Nothin' like it,' relied his father.

'But don't you think it means more?' inquired Sam.

'Vell p'raps it is a more tenderer word,' said Mr Weller, after a few moments' reflection. 'Go on, Sammy.'

'"Feel myself ashamed and completely circumscribed in a dressin' of you, for you *are* a nice gal and nothin' but it."'

'That's a werry pretty sentiment,' said the elder Mr Weller, removing his pipe to make way for the remark.

'Yes, I think it is rayther good,' observed Sam, highly flattered.

'Wot I like in that 'ere style of writin',' said the elder Mr Weller, 'is, that there ain't no callin' names in it,—no Wenuses, nor nothin' o' that kind. Wot's the good o' callin' a young 'ooman a Wenus or a angel, Sammy?'

'Ah! what, indeed?' replied Sam.

'You might jist as well call her a griffin, or a unicorn, or a king's arms at once, which is werry well known to be a col-lection o' fabulous animals,' added Mr Weller.

'Just as well,' replied Sam.

'Drive on, Sammy,' said Mr Weller.

Sam complied with the request, and proceeded as follows; his father continuing to smoke, with a mixed expression of wisdom and complacency, which was particularly edifying.

'"Afore I see you, I thought all women was alike."'

'So they are,' observed the elder Mr Weller, parenthetically.

'"But now," continued Sam, "now I find what a reg'lar soft-headed, inkred'lous turnip I must ha' been; for there ain't nobody like you, though *I* like you better than nothin' at all." I thought it best to make that rayther strong,' said Sam, looking up.

Mr Weller nodded approvingly, and Sam resumed.

'"So, I take the privilidge of the day, Mary, my dear—as the gen'l'm'n in difficulties did, ven he valked out of a Sunday,—to tell you that the first and only time I see you, your likeness was took on my hart in much quicker time and brighter colours than ever a likeness was took by the profeel macheen (wich p'raps you may have heerd on Mary my dear) altho it *does* finish a portrait and put the frame and glass on complete, with a hook at the end to hang it up by, and all in two minutes and a quarter."'

'I am afeerd that werges on the poetical, Sammy,' said Mr Weller, dubiously.

'No it don't,' replied Sam, reading on very quickly, to avoid contesting the point:

'"Except of me Mary my dear as your walentine and think over what I've said.—My dear Mary I will now conclude." That's all,' said Sam.

'That's rather a sudden pull up, ain't it, Sammy?' inquired Mr Weller.

'Not a bit on it,' said Sam; 'she'll vish there wos more, and that's the great art o' letter writin'.'

'Well,' said Mr Weller, 'there's somethin' in that; and I wish your mother-in-law 'ud only conduct her conwersation on the same gen-teel principle. Ain't you a goin' to sign it?'

'That's the difficulty,' said Sam; 'I don't know what *to* sign it.'

'Sign it, Veller,' said the oldest surviving proprietor of that name.

'Won't do,' said Sam. 'Never sign a walentine with your own name.'

'Sign it "Pickvick," then,' said Mr Weller; 'it's a werry good name, and a easy one to spell.'

'The wery thing,' said Sam. 'I *could* end with a werse; what do you think?'

'I don't like it, Sam,' rejoined Mr Weller. 'I never know'd a respectable coachman as wrote poetry, 'cept one, as made an affectin' copy o' werses the night afore he wos hung for a highway robbery; and *he* wos only a Cambervell man, so even that's no rule.'

But Sam was not to be dissuaded from the poetical idea that had occurred to him, so he signed the letter,

'Your love-sick
Pickwick.'

The Pickwick Papers, 1836–7

Wax-Work

'I never saw any wax-work, ma'am,' said Nell. 'Is it funnier than Punch?'

'Funnier!' said Mrs Jarley in a shrill voice. 'It is not funny at all.'

'Oh! said Nell, with all possible humility.

'It isn't funny at all,' repeated Mrs Jarley. 'It's calm and—what's that word again—critical?—no—classical, that's it—it is calm and classical. No low beatings and knockings about, no jokings and squeakings like your precious Punches, but always the same, with a constantly unchanging air of coldness and gentility; and so like life, that if wax-work only spoke and walked about, you'd hardly know the difference. I won't go so far as to say, that, as it is, I've seen wax-work quite like life, but I've certainly seen some life that was exactly like wax-work.'

The Old Curiosity Shop, 1840–1

Mr Pecksniff

I

He was a most exemplary man: fuller of virtuous precept than a copy-book. Some people likened him to a direction-post, which is always telling the way to a place, and never goes there: but these were his enemies; the shadows cast by his brightness; that was all. His very throat was moral. You saw a good deal of it. You looked over a very low fence of white cravat (whereof no man had ever beheld the tie, for he fastened it behind), and there it lay, a valley between two jutting heights of collar, serene and whiskerless before you. It seemed to say, on the part of Mr Pecksniff, 'There is no deception, ladies and gentlemen, all is peace, a holy calm pervades me.' So did his hair, just grizzled with an iron-grey, which was all brushed off his forehead, and stood bolt upright, or slightly drooped in kindred action with his heavy eyelids. So did his person, which was sleek though free from corpulency. So did his manner, which was soft and oily. In a word, even his plain black suit, and state of widower, and dangling double eyeglass, all tended to the same purpose, and cried aloud, 'Behold the moral Pecksniff!'

II

'Oh! let us not be for ever calculating, devising, and plotting for the future,' said Mr Pecksniff, smiling more and more, and looking at the fire as a man might, who was cracking a joke with it: 'I am weary of such arts. If our inclinations are but good and open-hearted, let us gratify them boldly, though they bring upon us Loss instead of Profit . . .'

III

'I am a man, my dear madam,' said Mr Pecksniff, shedding tears, and speaking with an imperfect articulation, 'but I am also a father. I am also a widower. My feelings, Mrs Todgers, will not consent to be entirely smothered, like the young children in the Tower. They are grown up, and the more I press the bolster on them, the more they look round the corner of it.'

IV

'My standard for the merits I would require in a son-in-law,' said Mr Pecksniff, after a short silence, 'is a high one. Forgive me, my dear Mr Jonas,' he added, greatly moved, 'if I say that you have spoiled me, and made it a fanciful one: an imaginative one; a prismatically tinged one, if I may be permitted to call it so.'

'What do you mean by that?' growled Jonas, looking at him with increased disfavour.

'Indeed, my dear friend,' said Mr Pecksniff, 'you may well inquire. The heart is not always a royal mint, with patent machinery to work its metal into current coin. Sometimes it throws it out in strange forms, not easily recognised as coin at all. But it is sterling gold. It has at least that merit. It is sterling gold.'

Martin Chuzzlewit, 1843

An American Statesman

'Our fellow-countryman is a model of a man, quite fresh from Natur's mould!' said Pogram, with enthusiasm. 'He is true-born child of this free hemisphere! Verdant as the mountains of our country; bright and flowing as our mineral Licks; unspiled by withering conventionalities as air our broad and boundless Perearers! Rough he may be. So air our Barrs. Wild he may be. So air our Buffalers. But he is a child of Natur', and a child of Freedom; and his boastful answer to the Despot and the Tyrant is, that his bright home is in the Settin Sun.'

Martin Chuzzlewit

An Earthquake in Camden Town

The first shock of a great earthquake had, just at that period, rent the whole neighbourhood to its centre. Traces of its course were visible on every side. Houses were knocked down; streets broken through and stopped; deep pits and trenches dug in the ground; enormous heaps of earth and clay thrown up; buildings that were undermined and shaking, propped by great beams of wood. Here, a chaos of carts, overthrown and jumbled together, lay topsy-turvy at the bottom of a steep unnatural hill; there, confused treasures of iron soaked and rusted in something that had accidentally become a pond. Everywhere were bridges that led nowhere; thoroughfares that were wholly impassable; Babel towers of chimneys, wanting half their height; temporary wooden houses and enclosures, in the most unlikely situations; carcases of ragged tenements, and fragments of unfinished walls and arches, and piles of scaffolding, and wildernesses of bricks, and giant forms of cranes, and tripods straddling above nothing. There were a hundred thousand shapes and substances of incompleteness, wildly mingled out of their places, upside down, burrowing in the earth, aspiring in the air, mouldering in the water, and unintelligible as any dream. Hot springs and fiery eruptions, the usual attendants upon earthquakes, lent their contributions of confusion to the scene. Boiling water hissed and heaved within dilapidated walls; whence, also, the glare and roar of flames came issuing forth; and mounds of ashes blocked up rights of way, and wholly changed the law and custom of the neighbourhood.

In short, the yet unfinished and unopened Railroad was in progress; and, from the very core of all this dire disorder, trailed smoothly away, upon its mighty course of civilisation and improvement.

Dombey and Son, 1846–8

Brooks of Sheffield

We went to an hotel by the sea, where two gentlemen were smoking cigars in a room by themselves. Each of them was lying on at least four chairs, and had a large rough jacket on. In a corner was a heap of coats and boat-cloaks, and a flag, all bundled up together.

They both rolled on to their feet, in an untidy sort of manner, when we came in, and said, 'Halloa, Murdstone! We thought you were dead!'

'Not yet,' said Mr Murdstone.

'And who's this shaver?' said one of the gentlemen, taking hold of me.

'That's Davy,' returned Mr Murdstone.

'Davy who?' said the gentleman. 'Jones?'

'Copperfield,' said Mr Murdstone.

'What! Bewitching Mrs Copperfield's incumbrance?' cried the gentleman. 'The pretty little widow?'

'Quinion,' said Mr Murdstone, 'take care, if you please. Somebody's sharp.'

'Who is?' asked the gentleman, laughing.

I looked up, quickly; being curious to know.

'Only Brooks of Sheffield,' said Mr Murdstone.

I was quite relieved to find that it was only Brooks of Sheffield; for, at first, I really thought it was I.

There seemed to be something very comical in the reputation of Mr Brooks of Sheffield, for both the gentlemen laughed heartily when he was mentioned, and Mr Murdstone was a good deal amused also. After some laughing, the gentleman whom he had called Quinion said:

'And what is the opinion of Brooks of Sheffield, in reference to the projected business?'

'Why, I don't know that Brooks understands much about it at present,' replied Mr Murdstone; 'but he is not generally favourable, I believe.'

There was more laughter at this, and Mr Quinion said he would ring the bell for some sherry in which to drink to Brooks. This he did; and when the wine came, he made me have a little, with a biscuit, and before I drank it, stand up and say, 'Confusion to Brooks of Sheffield!' The toast was received with great applause, and such hearty laughter that it made me laugh too; at which they laughed the more. In short, we quite enjoyed ourselves.

David Copperfield, 1849–50

Some Wise Advice

'My dear young friend,' said Mr Micawber, 'I am older than you; a man of some experience in life, and—and of some experience, in short, in difficulties, generally speaking. At present, and until something turns up (which I am, I may say, hourly expecting), I have nothing to bestow but advice. Still my advice is so far worth taking that—in short, that I have never taken it myself, and am the'—here Mr Micawber, who had been beaming and smiling, all over his head and face, up to the present moment, checked himself and frowned—'the miserable wretch you behold.'

'My dear Micawber!' urged his wife.

'I say,' returned Mr Micawber, quite forgetting himself, and smiling again, 'the miserable wretch you behold. My advice is, never do to-morrow what you can do to-day. Procrastination is the thief of time. Collar him!'

'My poor papa's maxim,' Mrs Micawber observed.

'My dear,' said Mr Micawber, 'your papa was very well in his way, and Heaven forbid that I should disparage him. Take him for all in all, we ne'er shall—in short, make the acquaintance, probably, of anybody else possessing, at his time of life, the same legs for gaiters, and able to read the same description of print, without spectacles. But he applied that maxim to our marriage, my dear; and that was so far prematurely entered into, in consequence, that I never recovered the expense.'

Mr Micawber looked aside at Mrs Micawber, and added: 'Not that I am sorry for it. Quite the contrary, my love.' After which he was grave for a minute or so.

'My other piece of advice, Copperfield,' said Mr Micawber, 'you know. Annual income twenty pounds, annual expenditure nineteen nineteen six, result happiness. Annual income twenty pounds, annual expenditure twenty pounds ought and six, result misery. The blossom is blighted, the leaf is withered, the God of day goes down upon the dreary scene, and—and in short you are for ever floored. As I am!'

To make his example the more impressive, Mr Micawber drank a glass of punch with an air of great enjoyment and satisfaction, and whistled the College Hornpipe.

David Copperfield

The Return of Julia Mills

What ship comes sailing home from India, and what English lady is this, married to a growling old Scotch Crœsus with great flaps of ears? Can this be Julia Mills?

Indeed it is Julia Mills, peevish and fine, with a black man to carry cards and letters to her on a golden salver, and a copper-coloured woman in linen, with a bright handkerchief round her head, to serve her Tiffin in her dressing-room. But Julia keeps no diary in these days; never sings Affection's Dirge; eternally quarrels with the old Scotch Crœsus, who is a sort of yellow bear with a tanned hide. Julia is steeped in money to the throat, and talks and thinks of nothing else.

David Copperfield

Mr Tulkinghorn

The old gentleman is rusty to look at, but is reputed to have made good thrift out of aristocratic marriage settlements and aristocratic wills, and to be very rich. He is surrounded by a mysterious halo of family confidences; of which he is known to be the silent depository. There are noble Mausoleums rooted for centuries in retired glades of parks, among the growing timber and the fern, which perhaps hold fewer noble secrets than walk abroad among men, shut up in the breast of Mr Tulkinghorn. He is of what is called the old school—a phrase generally meaning any school that seems never to have been young—and wears knee breeches tied with ribbons, and gaiters or stockings. One peculiarity of his black clothes, and of his black stockings, be they silk or worsted, is, that they never shine. Mute, close, irresponsive to any glancing light, his dress is like himself. He never converses, when not professionally consulted. He is found sometimes, speechless but quite at home, at corners of dinner-tables in great country houses, and near doors of drawing-rooms, concerning which the fashionable intelligence is eloquent; where everybody knows him, and where half the Peerage stops to say, 'How do you do, Mr Tulkinghorn?' he receives these salutations with gravity, and buries them along with the rest of his knowledge.

Bleak House, 1852–3

Gome

'Beg pardon, sir,' said a brisk waiter, rubbing the table. 'Wish see bedroom?'

'Yes. I have just made up my mind to do it.'

'Chaymaid!' cried the waiter. 'Gelen box num seven wish see room!'

'Stay!' said Clennam, rousing himself. 'I was not thinking of what I said; I answered mechanically. I am not going to sleep here. I am going home.'

'Deed, sir? Chaymaid! Gelen box num seven, not go sleep here, gome.'

Little Dorrit, 1855–7

The Last of Mr Merdle

When they came to the warm-baths, all the other people belonging to that establishment were looking out for them at the door, and running up and down the passages. 'Request everybody else to keep back, if you please,' said the physician aloud to the master; 'and do you take me straight to the place, my friend,' to the messenger.

The messenger hurried before him, along a grove of little rooms, and, turning into one at the end of the grove, looked round the door. Physician was close upon him, and looked round the door too.

There was a bath in that corner, from which the water had been hastily drained off. Lying in it, as in a grave or sarcophagus, with a hurried drapery of sheet and blanket thrown across it, was the body of a heavily-made man, with an obtuse head, and coarse, mean, common features. A sky-light had been opened to release the steam with which the room had been filled; but, it hung, condensed into water-drops, heavily upon the walls, and heavily upon the face and figure in the bath. The room was still hot, and the marble of the bath still warm; but, the face and figure were clammy to the touch. The white marble at the bottom of the bath was veined with a dreadful red. On the ledge at the side, were an empty laudanum-bottle and a tortoiseshell handled penknife—soiled, but not with ink.

'Separation of jugular vein—death rapid—been dead at least half an hour.' This echo of the physician's words ran through the passages and little rooms, and through the house while he was yet straightening himself from having bent down to reach to the bottom of the bath, and while he was yet dabbling his hands in water: redly veining it as the marble was veined, before it mingled into one tint.

Little Dorrit

At the Zoo

I have been (by mere accident) seeing the serpents fed to-day, with the live birds, rabbits, and guinea pigs—a sight so very horrible that I cannot get rid of the impression, and am, at this present, imagining serpents coming up the legs of the table, with their infernal flat heads, and their tongues like the Devil's tail (evidently taken from that model, in the magic lanterns and other such popular representations), elongated for dinner. I saw one small serpent, whose father was asleep, go up to a guinea pig (white and yellow, and with a gentle eye—every hair upon him erect with horror); corkscrew himself on the tip of his tail; open a mouth which couldn't have swallowed the guinea pig's nose; dilate a throat which wouldn't have made him a stocking; and show him what his father meant to do with him when he came out of that ill-looking Hookah into which he had resolved himself. The guinea pig backed against the side of the cage—said 'I know it, I know it!'—and his eye glared and his coat turned wiry, as he made the remark. Five small sparrows crouching together in a little trench at the back of the cage, peeped over the brim of it, all the time; and when they saw the guinea pig give it up, and the young serpent go away looking at him over about two yards and a quarter of shoulder, struggled which should get into the innermost angle and be seized last. Everyone of them hid his eyes in another's breast, and then they all shook together like dry leaves—as I daresay they may be doing now, for old Hookah was as dull as laudanum. ... Please to imagine two small serpents, one beginning on the tail of a white mouse, and one on the head, and each pulling his own way, and the mouse very much alive all the time, with the middle of him madly writhing....

letter to John Forster, 1857

In the Churchyard

Ours was the marsh country, down by the river, within, as the river wound, twenty miles of the sea. My first most vivid and broad impression of the identity of things, seems to me to have been gained on a memorable raw afternoon towards evening. At such a time I found out for certain, that this bleak place overgrown with nettles was the churchyard; and that Philip Pirrip, late of this parish, and also Georgiana wife of the above, were dead and buried; and that Alexander, Bartholomew, Abraham, Tobias, and Roger, infant children of the aforesaid, were also dead and buried; and that the dark flat wilderness beyond the churchyard, intersected with dykes and mounds and gates, with scattered cattle feeding on it, was the marshes; and that the low leaden line beyond was the river; and that the distant savage lair from which the wind was rushing, was the sea; and that the small bundle of shivers growing afraid of it all and beginning to cry, was Pip.

'Hold your noise!' cried a terrible voice, as a man started up from among the graves at the side of the church porch. 'Keep still, you little devil, or I'll cut your throat!'

Great Expectations, 1860–1

The Veneerings Receive Their Guests

Mr and Mrs Veneering were bran-new people in a bran-new house in a bran-new quarter of London. Everything about the Veneerings was spick and span new. All their furniture was new, all their friends were new, all their servants were new, their plate was new, their carriage was new, their harness was new, their horses were new, their pictures were new, they themselves were new, they were as newly married as was lawfully compatible with their having a bran-new baby, and if they had set up a great-grandfather, he would have come home in matting from the Pantechnicon, without a scratch upon him, French-polished to the crown of his head.

For, in the Veneering establishment, from the hall-chairs with the new coat of arms, to the grand pianoforte with the new action, and up-stairs again to the new fire-escape, all things were in a state of high varnish and polish. And what was observable in the furniture, was observable in the Veneerings—the surface smelt a little too much of the workshop and was a trifle sticky.

There was an innocent piece of dinner-furniture that went upon easy castors and was kept over a livery stable-yard in Duke Street, Saint James's, when not in use, to whom the Veneerings were a source of blind confusion. The name of this article was Twemlow. Being first cousin to Lord Snigsworth, he was in frequent requisition, and at many houses might be said to represent the dining-table in its normal state. Mr and Mrs Veneering, for example, arranging a dinner, habitually started with Twemlow, and then put leaves in him, or added guests to him. Sometimes, the table consisted of Twemlow and half-a-dozen leaves; sometimes, of Twemlow and a dozen leaves; sometimes, Twemlow was pulled out to his utmost extent of twenty leaves. Mr and Mrs Veneering on occasions of ceremony faced each other in the centre of the board, and thus the parallel still held; for, it always happened that the more Twemlow was pulled out, the further he found himself from the centre, and the nearer to the sideboard at one end of the room, or the window-curtains at the other . . .

This evening the Veneerings give a banquet. Eleven leaves in the Twemlow; fourteen in company all told. Four pigeon-breasted retainers in plain clothes stand in line in the hall. A fifth retainer, proceeding up the staircase with a mournful air—as who should say, 'Here is another wretched creature come to dinner; such is life!'—announces, 'Mis-ter Twemlow!'

Mrs Veneering welcomes her sweet Mr Twemlow. Mr Veneering welcomes his dear Twemlow. Mrs Veneering does not expect that Mr Twemlow can in nature care much for such insipid things as babies, but so old a friend must please look at baby. 'Ah! You will know the friend of your family better, Tootleums,' says Mr Veneering, nodding emotionally at that new article, 'when you begin to take notice.' He then begs to make his dear Twemlow known to his two friends, Mr Boots and Mr Brewer—and clearly has no distinct idea which is which.

But now a fearful circumstance occurs.

'Mis-ter and Mis-sis Podsnap!'

'My dear,' says Mr Veneering to Mrs Veneering, with an air of much friendly interest, while the door stands open, 'the Podsnaps.'

A too, too smiling large man, with a fatal freshness on him, appearing with his wife, instantly deserts his wife and darts at Twemlow with:

'How do you do? So glad to know you. Charming house you have here. I hope we are not late. So glad of this opportunity, I am sure!'

When the first shock fell upon him, Twemlow twice skipped back in his neat little shoes and his neat little silk stockings of a bygone fashion, as if impelled to leap over a sofa behind him; but the large man closed with him and proved too strong.

'Let me,' says the large man, trying to attract the attention of his wife in the distance, 'have the pleasure of presenting Mrs Podsnap to her host. She will be,' in his fatal freshness he seems to find perpetual verdure and eternal youth in the phrase, 'she will be so glad of the opportunity, I am sure!'

In the meantime, Mrs Podsnap, unable to originate a mistake on her own account, because Mrs Veneering is the only other lady there, does her best in the way of handsomely supporting her husband's, by looking towards Mr Twemlow with a plaintive countenance and remarking to Mrs Veneering in a feeling manner, firstly, that she fears he has been rather bilious of late, and, secondly, that the baby is already very like him.

It is questionable whether any man quite relishes being mistaken for any other man; but Mr Veneering having this very evening set up the shirt-front of the young Antinous (in new worked cambric just come home), is not at all complimented by being supposed to be Twemlow, who is dry and weazen and some thirty years older. Mrs Veneering equally resents the imputation of being the wife of Twemlow. As to Twemlow, he is so sensible of being a much better bred man than Veneering, that he considers the large man an offensive ass.

In this complicated dilemma, Mr Veneering approaches the large man with extended hand, and smilingly assures that incorrigible personage that he is delighted to see him: who in his fatal freshness instantly replies:

'Thank you. I am ashamed to say that I cannot at this moment recall where we met, but I am so glad of this opportunity, I am sure!'

Then pouncing upon Twemlow, who holds back with all his feeble might, he is haling him off to present him, as Veneering, to Mrs Podsnap, when the arrival of more guests unravels the mistake. Whereupon, having re-shaken hands with Veneering as Veneering, he re-shakes hands with Twemlow as Twemlow, and winds it all up to his own perfect satisfaction by saying to the last-named, 'Ridiculous opportunity—but so glad of it, I am sure!'

Now, Twemlow having undergone this terrific experience, having likewise noted the fusion of Boots in Brewer and Brewer in Boots, and having further observed that of the remaining seven guests four discreet characters enter with wandering eyes and wholly decline to commit themselves as to which is Veneering, until Veneering has them in his grasp;—Twemlow having profited by these studies, finds his brain wholesomely hardening as he approaches the conclusion that he really is Veneering's oldest friend, when his brain softens again and all is lost, through his eyes encountering Veneering and the large man linked together as twin brothers in the back drawing-room near the conservatory door, and through his ears informing him in the tones of Mrs Veneering that the same large man is to be baby's godfather.

'Dinner is on the table!'

Thus the melancholy retainer, as who should say, 'Come down and be poisoned, ye unhappy children of men!'

Our Mutual Friend, 1864–5

The Charms of Reading

'You charm me, Mortimer, with your reading of my weaknesses. (By-the-bye, that very word, Reading, in its critical use, always charms me. An actress's Reading of a chambermaid, a dancer's Reading of a hornpipe, a singer's Reading of a song, a marine painter's Reading of the sea, the kettle-drum's Reading of an instrumental passage, are phrases ever youthful and delightful.) I was mentioning your perception of my weaknesses . . .

Our Mutual Friend

A Cathedral at Nightfall

'Dear me,' said Mr Grewgious, peeping in, 'it's like looking down the throat of Old Time.'

Old Time heaved a mouldy sigh from tomb and arch and vault; and gloomy shadows began to deepen in corners; and damps began to rise from green patches of stone; and jewels, cast upon the pavement of the nave from stained glass by the declining sun, began to perish. Within the grill-gate of the chancel, up the steps surmounted loomingly by the fast-darkening organ, white robes could be dimly seen, and one feeble voice, rising and falling in a cracked monotonous mutter, could at intervals be faintly heard. In the free outer air, the river, the green pastures, and the brown arable lands, the teeming hills and dales, were reddened by the sunset: while the distant little windows in windmills and farm homesteads, shone, patches of bright beaten gold. In the Cathedral, all became grey, murky, and sepulchral, and the cracked monotonous mutter went on like a dying voice, until the organ and the choir burst forth, and drowned it in a sea of music. Then, the sea fell, and the dying voice made another feeble effort, and then the sea rose high, and beat its life out, and lashed the roof, and surged among the arches, and pierced the heights of the great tower; and then the sea was dry, and all was still.

Edwin Drood, 1870

HENRY MAYHEW
1812–1887

A Ham-Sandwich Seller

I work the theatres this side of the water, chiefly the 'Lympic and the 'Delphi. The best theatre I ever had was the Garding, when it had two galleries, and was dramatic—the operas there wasn't the least good to me. The Lyceum was good, when it was Mr Keeley's. I hardly know what sort my customers are, but they're those that go to theaytres: shopkeepers and clerks, I think. Gentlemen don't often buy of me. They *have* bought, though. Oh, no, they never give a farthing over; they're more likely to want seven for 6*d*. The women of the town buy of me, when it gets late, for themselves and their fancy men. They're liberal enough when they've money. They sometimes treat a poor fellow in a public-house. In summer I'm often out till four in the morning, and then must lie in bed half next day. The 'Delphi was better than it is. I've taken 3*s*. at the first 'turn out' (the leaving the theatre for a short time after the first piece), but the turn-outs at the Garding was better than that. A penny pie-shop has spoiled us at the 'Delphi and at Ashley's. I go out between eight and nine in the evening. People often want more in my sandwiches, though I'm starving on them. 'Oh,' they'll say, 'you've been 'prenticed to Vauxhall, you have.' 'They're 1*s*. there,' says I, 'and no bigger. I haven't Vauxhall prices.' I stand by the night-houses when it's late—not the fashionables. Their customers wouldn't look at me; but I've known women, that carried their heads very high, glad to get a sandwich afterwards. Six times I've been upset by drunken fellows, on purpose, I've no doubt, and lost all my stock. Once, a gent kicked my basket into the dirt, and he was going off—for it was late—but some people by began to make remarks about using a poor fellow that way, so he paid for all, after he had them counted. I am *so* sick of this life, sir. I *do* dread the winter so. I've stood up to the ankles in snow till after midnight, and till I've wished I was snow myself, and could melt like it and have an end. I'd do anything to get away from this, but I can't.

London Labour and the London Poor, 1861–2

The Charity of a Crossing-Sweeper

This old dame is remarkable from the fact of being the chief support of a poor deaf cripple, who is as much poorer than the crossing-sweeper as she is poorer than Mrs ——, in —— street, who allows the sweeper sixpence a week. The crossing-sweeper is a rather stout old woman, with a carneying tone, and constant curtsey. She complains, in common with most of her class, of the present hard times, and reverts longingly to the good old days when people were more liberal than they are now, and had more to give. She says:—

'I was on my crossing before the police was made, for I am not able to work, and only get helped by the people who knows me. Mr ——, in the square, gives me a shilling a-week; Mrs ——, in —— street, gives me sixpence; (she has gone in the country now, but she has left it at the oil-shop for me); that's what I depinds upon, darlin', to help pay my rent, which is half-a-crown. My rent was three shillings, till the landlord didn't wish me to go, 'cause I was so punctual with my money. I give a corner of my room to a poor cretur, who's deaf as a beadle; she works at the soldiers' coats, and is a very good hand at it, and would earn a good deal of money if she had constant work. She owed as good as twelve shillings and sixpence for rent, poor thing, where she was last, and the landlord took all her goods except her bed; she's got that, so I give her a corner of my room for charity's sake. We must look to one another; she's as poor as a church mouse. I thought she would be company for me, still a deaf person is but poor company to one. She had that heavy sickness they call the cholera about five years ago, and it fell in her side and in the side of her head too—that made her deaf. Oh! she's a poor object. She has been with me since the month of February, I've lent her money out of my own pocket. I give her a cup of tea or a slice of bread when I see she hasn't got any. Then the people up-stairs are kind to her, and give her a bite and a sup.

'My husband was a soldier; he fought at the battle of Waterloo. His pension was ninepence a-day. All my family are dead, except my grandson, what's in New Orleans. I expect him back this very month that now we have; he gave me four pounds before he went, to carry me over the last winter.

'If the Almighty God pleases to send him back, he'll be a great help to me. He's all I've got left. I never had but two children in all my life.

'I worked in noblemen's houses before I was married to my husband, who is dead; but he came to be poor, and I had to leave my houses where I used to work.

'I took twopence-halfpenny yesterday, and threepence to-day; the day before yesterday I didn't take a penny. I never come out on Sunday; I goes to Rosomon-street Chapel. Last Saturday I made one shilling and sixpence; on Friday, sixpence. I dare say I make three shillings and sixpence a week, besides the one shilling and sixpence I gets allowed me. I am forced to make a do of it somehow, but I've no more strength left in me than this ould broom.'

London Labour and the London Poor

DAVID LIVINGSTONE
1813–1873

Rural Elegance

We made a little détour to the southward, in order to get provisions in a cheaper market. This led us along the rivulet called Tamba, where we found the people, who had not been visited so frequently by the slave-traders as the rest, rather timid and very civil. It was agreeable to get again among the uncontaminated, and to see the natives look at us without that air of superciliousness, which is so unpleasant and common in the beaten track. The same olive colour prevailed. They file their teeth to a point, which makes the smile of the women frightful, as it reminds one of the grin of an alligator. The inhabitants throughout this country, exhibit as great a variety of taste, as appears on the surface of society amongst ourselves. Many of the men are dandies; their shoulders are always wet with the oil dropping from their lubricated hair, and everything about them is ornamented in one way or another. Some thrum a musical instrument the livelong day, and, when they wake at night, proceed at once to their musical performance. Others try to appear warlike by never going out of their huts, except with a load of bows and arrows, or a gun ornamented with a strip of hide for every animal they have shot; and others never go anywhere without a canary in a cage. Ladies may be seen carefully tending little lapdogs, which are intended to be eaten.

Missionary Travels, 1857

A Mantle of Happy Existence

While waiting by the elephant, I observed a great number of insects, like grains of fine sand, moving on my boxes. On examination with a glass, four species were apparent; one of green and gold preening its wings, which glanced in the sun with metallic lustre, another clear as crystal, a third of the colour of vermilion, and a fourth black. Almost every plant has its own peculiar insect, and when the rains are over, very few seeds remain untouched; even the fiery bird's-eye pepper, is itself devoured by a maggot. I observed here, what I had often seen before, that certain districts abound in centipedes. Here they have light reddish bodies and blue legs; great myriapedes are seen crawling everywhere. Although they do no harm, they excite in man a feeling of loathing. Perhaps our appearance produces a similar feeling in the elephant and other large animals. When they have been much disturbed, they certainly look upon us with great distrust. In the quietest parts of the forest there is heard a faint but distinct hum, which tells of insect joy. One may see many whisking about in the clear sunshine in patches among the green glancing leaves; but there are invisible myriads working with never-tiring mandibles on leaves, and stalks, and beneath the soil. They are all brimful of enjoyment. Indeed the universality of organic life may be called a mantle of happy existence encircling the world, and imparts the idea of its being caused by the consciousness of our benignant Father's smile on all the works of His hands.

Missionary Travels

The Theft of a Medicine-Chest

The two Waiyau, who joined us at Kandé's village, now deserted. Knowing the language well, they were extremely useful, and no one thought that they would desert, for they were free men—their masters had been killed by the Mazitu—and this circumstance, and their uniform good conduct, made us trust them more than we should have done any others who had been slaves. But they left us in the forest, and heavy rain came on, which obliterated every vestige of their footsteps. To make the loss the more galling, they took what we could least spare—the medicine-box, which they would only throw away as soon as they came to examine their booty. One of these deserters exchanged his load that morning with a boy called Baraka, who had charge of the medicine-box, because he was so careful. This was done because with the medicine-box were packed five large cloths and all Baraka's clothing and beads, of which he was very careful. The Waiyau also offered to carry this burden a stage to help Baraka, while he gave his own load, in which there was no cloth, in exchange. The forest was so dense and high, there was no chance of getting a glimpse of the fugitives, who took all the dishes, a large box of powder, the flour we had purchased dearly to help us as far as the Chambezé, the tools, two guns, and a cartridge-pouch; but the medicine-chest was the sorest loss of all!

All the other goods I had divided in case of loss or desertion, but had never dreamed of losing the precious quinine and other remedies; other losses and annoyances I felt as just parts of that undercurrent of vexation which is not wanting in even the smoothest life, and certainly not worthy of being moaned over by an explorer anxious to benefit a country and people—but this loss I feel most keenly. It is difficult to say from the heart, 'Thy will be done'; but I shall try. These men had few advantages: sold into slavery in early life, they were in the worst possible school for learning to be honest and honourable. They behaved well for a long time; but, having had hard and scanty fare in Lobisa, wet and misery in passing through dripping forests, hungry nights and fatiguing days, their patience must have been worn out, and they had no sentiments of honour, or at least none so strong as we ought to have; they gave way to the temptation which their good conduct had led us to put in their way. Some we have come across in this journey seemed born essentially mean and base—a great misfortune to them and all who have to deal with them, but they cannot be so blamable as those who have no natural tendency to meanness, and whose education has taught them to abhor it. True; yet this loss of the medicine-box gnaws at the heart terribly. I felt as if I had now received the sentence of death, like poor Bishop Mackenzie.

Last Journals, 1874

Siding with Slaveocracy

The emancipation of our West-Indian slaves was the work of but a small number of the people of England—the philanthropists and all the more advanced thinkers. Numerically they were a very small minority, and powerful only from the superior abilities of the leading men, and from having the right, the true, and just on their side. Of the rest of the population an immense number had no sympathies to spare for any beyond their own fireside circles. We must never lose sight of the fact that though the majority perhaps are on the side of freedom, large numbers of Englishmen are not slaveholders only because the law forbids the practice. In this we see a great part of the reason of the frantic sympathy with the rebels in the great Black war in America. It is true that we do sympathize with brave men, though we may not approve of the objects for which they fight. We admired Stonewall Jackson and we praised Lee, but, unquestionably, there existed besides an eager desire that slaveocracy might prosper, and the Negro go to the wall.

Last Journals

SHERIDAN LE FANU
1814–1873

A Small Black Monkey

'I had met with a man who had some odd old books, German editions in mediaeval Latin, and I was only too happy to be permitted access to them. This obliging person's books were in the City, a very out-of-the-way part of it. I had rather out-stayed my intended hour, and, on coming out, seeing no cab near, I was tempted to get into the omnibus which used to drive past this house. It was darker than this by the time the 'bus had reached an old house, you may have remarked, with four poplars at each side of the door, and there the last passenger but myself got out. We drove along rather faster. It was twilight now. I leaned back in my corner next the door ruminating pleasantly.

'The interior of the omnibus was nearly dark. I had observed in the corner opposite to me at the other side, and at the end next the horses, two small circular reflections, as it seemed to me of a reddish light. They were about two inches apart, and about the size of those small brass buttons that yachting men used to put upon their jackets. I began to speculate, as listless men will, upon this trifle, as it seemed. From what centre did that faint but deep red light come, and from what—glass beads, buttons, toy decorations—was it reflected? We were lumbering along gently, having nearly a mile still to go. I had not solved the puzzle, and it became in another minute more odd, for these two luminous points, with a sudden jerk, descended nearer the floor, keeping still their relative distance and horizontal position, and then, as suddenly, they rose to the level of the seat on which I was sitting and I saw them no more.

'My curiosity was now really excited, and, before I had time to think, I saw again these two dull lamps, again together near the floor; again they disappeared, and again in their old corner I saw them.

'So, keeping my eyes upon them, I edged quietly up my own side, towards the end at which I still saw these tiny discs of red.

'There was very little light in the 'bus. It was nearly dark. I leaned forward to aid my endeavour to discover what these little circles really were. They shifted their position a little as I did so. I began now to perceive an outline of something black, and I soon saw, with tolerable distinctness, the outline of a small black monkey, pushing its face forward in mimicry to meet mine; those were its eyes, and I now dimly saw its teeth grinning at me.

'I drew back, not knowing whether it might not meditate a spring. I fancied that one of the passengers had forgot this ugly pet, and wishing to ascertain something of its temper, though not caring to trust my fingers to it, I poked my umbrella softly towards it. It remained immovable—up to it—*through* it. For through it, and back and forward it passed, without the slightest resistance.

'I can't, in the least, convey to you the kind of horror that I felt. When I had ascertained that the thing was an illusion, as I then supposed, there came a misgiving about myself and a terror that fascinated me in impotence to remove my gaze from the eyes of the brute for some moments. As I looked, it made a little skip back, quite into the corner, and I, in a panic, found myself at the door, having put my head out, drawing deep breaths of the outer air, and staring at the lights and trees we were passing, too glad to reassure myself of reality.

'I stopped the 'bus and got out. I perceived the man look oddly at me as I paid him. I daresay there was something unusual in my looks and manner, for I had never felt so strangely before.'

'Green Tea', *In a Glass Darkly*, 1872

JOHN LOTHROP MOTLEY
1814–1877

William the Silent

He went through life bearing the load of a people's sorrows upon his shoulders with a smiling face. Their name was the last word upon his lips, save the simple affirmative with which the soldier who had been battling for the right all his lifetime commended his soul in dying 'to his great captain, Christ.' The people were grateful and affectionate, for they trusted the character of their 'Father William,' and not all the clouds which calumny could collect ever dimmed to their eyes the radiance of that lofty mind to which they were accustomed, in their darkest calamities, to look for light. As long as he lived, he was the guiding-star of a whole brave nation, and when he died the little children cried in the streets.

The Rise of the Dutch Republic, 1856

Thackeray

He has the appearance of a colossal infant, smooth, white, shiny, ringlety hair, flaxen, alas, with advancing years, a roundish face, with a little dab of a nose upon which it is a perpetual wonder how he keeps his spectacles, a sweet but rather piping voice, with something of the childish treble about it, and a very tall, slightly stooping figure—such are the characteristics of the great 'snob' of England. His manner is like that of everybody else in England,—nothing original, all planed down into perfect uniformity with that of his fellow-creatures. There was not much more distinction in his talk than in his white choker or black coat and waistcoat.

letter to his wife, 1858

RICHARD HENRY DANA JR.

1815–1882

A Flogging

'Now for you,' said the captain, making up to John and taking his irons off. As soon as he was loose, he ran forward to the forecastle. 'Bring that man aft,' shouted the captain. The second mate, who had been a shipmate of John's, stood still in the waist, and the mate walked slowly forward; but our third officer, anxious to show his zeal, sprang forward over the windlass, and laid hold of John; but he soon threw him from him. At this moment I would have given worlds for the power to help the poor fellow; but it was all in vain. The captain stood on the quarterdeck, bare-headed, his eyes flashing with rage, and his face as red as blood, swinging the rope, and calling out to his officers, 'Drag him aft!—Lay hold of him! I'll *sweeten* him!' etc. The mate now went forward and told John quietly to go aft; and he, seeing resistance in vain, threw the blackguard third mate from him; said he would go aft of himself; that they should not drag him; and went up to the gangway and held out his hands; but as soon as the captain began to make him fast, the indignity was too much, and he began to resist; but the mate and Russell holding him, he was soon seized up. When he was made fast, he turned to the captain, who stood turning up his sleeves and getting ready for the blow, and asked him what he was to be flogged for. 'Have I ever refused my duty, sir? Have you ever known me to hang back, or to be insolent, or not to know my work?'

'No,' said the captain, 'it is not that that I flog you for; I flog you for your interference—for asking questions.'

'Can't a man ask a question here without being flogged?'

'No,' shouted the captain; 'nobody shall open his mouth aboard this vessel, but myself;' and he began laying the blows upon his back, swinging half round between each blow, to give it full effect. As he went on, his passion increased, and he danced about the deck, calling out as he swung the rope,—'If you want to know what I flog you for, I'll tell you. It's because I like to do it!—because I like to do it!—It suits me! That's what I do it for!'

The man writhed under the pain, until he could endure it no longer, when he called out, with an exclamation more common among foreigners than with us—'Oh, Jesus Christ! Oh, Jesus Christ!'

'Don't call on Jesus Christ,' shouted the captain; '*he can't help you. Call on Captain T——*. He's the man! He can help you! Jesus Christ can't help you now!'

At these words, which I never shall forget, my blood ran cold. I could look on no longer. Disgusted, sick, and horror-struck, I turned away and leaned over the rail, and looked down into the water. A few rapid thoughts of my own situation, and of the prospect of future revenge, crossed my mind; but the falling of the blows and the cries of the man called me back at once. At length they ceased, and turning round, I found that the mate, at a signal from the captain, had cut him down. Almost doubled up with pain, the man walked slowly forward, and went down into the forecastle. Every one else stood still at his post, while the captain, swelling with rage and with the importance of his achievement, walked the quarter-deck, and at each turn, as he came forward, calling out to us,—'You see your condition! You see where I've got you all, and you know what to expect!'—'You've been mistaken in me—you didn't know what I was! Now you know what I am!'—'I'll make you toe the mark, every soul of you, or I'll flog you all, fore and aft, from the boy, up!'—'You've got a driver over you! Yes, a *slave-driver—a negro-driver!* I'll see who'll tell me he isn't a negro slave!' With this and the like matter, equally calculated to quiet us, and to allay any apprehensions of future trouble, he entertained us for about ten minutes, when he went below.

Two Years Before the Mast, 1840

ANTHONY TROLLOPE
1815–1882

A Decisive Defeat

The bishop was sitting listlessly in his study when the news reached him of the dean's illness. It was brought to him by Mr Slope, who of course was not the last person in Barchester to hear it. It was also not slow in finding its way to Mrs Proudie's ears. It may be presumed that there was not just then much friendly intercourse between these two rival claimants for his lordship's obedience. Indeed, though living in the same house, they had not met since the stormy interview between them in the bishop's study on the preceding day.

On that occasion Mrs Proudie had been defeated. That the prestige of continual victory should have been torn from her standards was a subject of great sorrow to that militant lady; but though defeated, she was not overcome. She felt that she might yet recover her lost ground, that she might yet hurl Mr Slope down to the dust from which she had picked him, and force her sinning lord to sue for pardon in sackcloth and ashes.

On that memorable day, memorable for his mutiny and rebellion against her high behests, he had carried his way with a high hand, and had really begun to think it possible that the days of his slavery were counted.

He had begun to hope that he was now about to enter into a free land, a land delicious with milk which he himself might quaff, and honey which would not tantalise him by being only honey to the eye. When Mrs Proudie banged the door, as she left his room, he felt himself every inch a bishop. To be sure his spirit had been a little cowed by his chaplain's subsequent lecture; but on the whole he was highly pleased with himself, and flattered himself that the worst was over. 'Ce n'est que le premier pas qui coûte,' he reflected; and now that the first step had been so magnanimously taken, all the rest would follow easily.

He met his wife as a matter of course at dinner, where little or nothing was said that could ruffle the bishop's happiness. His daughters and the servants were present and protected him.

He made one or two trifling remarks on the subject of his projected visit to the archbishop, in order to show to all concerned that he intended to have his own way; and the very servants perceiving the change transferred a little of their reverence from their mistress to their master. All which the master perceived; and so also did the mistress. But Mrs Proudie bided her time.

After dinner he returned to his study where Mr Slope soon found him, and there they had tea together and planned many things. For some few minutes the bishop was really happy; but as the clock on the chimney piece warned him that the stilly hours of night were drawing on, as he looked at his chamber candlestick and knew that he must use it, his heart sank within him again. He was as a ghost, all whose power of wandering free through these upper regions ceases at cock-crow; or rather he was the opposite of the ghost, for till cock-crow he must again be a serf. And would that be all? Could he trust himself to come down to breakfast a free man in the morning?

He was nearly an hour later than usual, when he betook himself to his rest. Rest! what rest? However, he took a couple of glasses of sherry, and mounted the stairs. Far be it from us to follow him thither. There are some things which no novelist, no historian, should attempt; some few scenes in life's drama which even no poet should dare to paint. Let that which passed between Dr Proudie and his wife on this night be understood to be among them.

He came down the following morning a sad and thoughtful man. He was attenuated in appearance; one might almost say emaciated. I doubt whether his now grizzled locks had not palpably become more grey than on the preceding evening. At any rate he had aged materially. Years do not make a man old gradually and at an even pace. Look through the world and see if this is not so always, except in those rare cases in which the human being lives and dies without joys and without sorrows, like a vegetable. A man shall be possessed of florid youthful blooming health till, it matters not what age. Thirty—forty—fifty, then comes some nipping frost, some period of agony, that robs the fibres of the body of their succulence, and the hale and hearty man is counted among the old.

He came down and breakfasted alone; Mrs Proudie being indisposed took her coffee in her bed-room, and her daughters waited upon her there. He ate his breakfast alone, and then, hardly knowing what he did, he betook himself to his usual seat in his study. He tried to solace himself with his coming visit to the archbishop. That effort of his own free will at any rate remained to him as an enduring triumph. But somehow, now that he had achieved it, he did not seem to care so much about it. It was his ambition that had prompted him to take his place at the archi-episcopal table, and his ambition was now quite dead within him.

Barchester Towers, 1857

An Heiress

She had a very high colour, very red cheeks, a large mouth, big white teeth, a broad nose, and bright, small, black eyes. Her hair also was black and bright, but very crisp and strong, and was combed close round her face in small crisp black ringlets. Since she had been brought out into the fashionable world some one of her instructors in fashion had given her to understand that curls were not the thing. 'They'll always pass muster,' Miss Dunstable had replied, 'when they are done up with bank-notes.' It may therefore be presumed that Miss Dunstable had a will of her own.

Doctor Thorne, 1858

Mrs Lupex

I should simply mislead a confiding reader if I were to tell him that Mrs Lupex was an amiable woman. Perhaps the fact that she was not amiable is the one great fault that should be laid to her charge; but that fault had spread itself so widely, and had cropped forth in so many different places of her life, like a strong rank plant that will show itself all over a garden, that it may almost be said that it made her odious in every branch of life, and detestable alike to those who knew her little and to those who knew her much. If a searcher could have got at the inside spirit of the woman, that searcher would have found that she wished to go right,—that she did make, or at any rate promise to herself that she would make, certain struggles to attain decency and propriety. But it was so natural to her to torment those whose misfortune brought them near to her, and especially that wretched man who in an evil day had taken her to his bosom as his wife, that decency fled from her, and propriety would not live in her quarters.

The Small House at Allington, 1864

At the Mirror

She moved up her hair from off her ears, knowing where she would find a few that were grey, and shaking her head, as though owning to herself that she was old; but as her fingers ran almost involuntarily across her locks, her touch told her that they were soft and silken; and she looked into her own eyes, and saw that they were bright; and her hand touched the outline of her cheek, and she knew that something of the fresh bloom of youth was still there; and her lips parted, and there were her white teeth; and there came a smile and a dimple, and a slight purpose of laughter in her eye, and then a tear. She pulled her scarf tighter across her bosom, feeling her own form, and then she leaned forward and kissed herself in the glass.

Miss Mackenzie, 1865

The Revd Josiah Crawley

He was a man who when seen could hardly be forgotten. The deep angry remonstrant eyes, the shaggy eyebrows, telling tales of frequent anger,—of anger frequent but generally silent,—the repressed indignation of the habitual frown, the long nose and large powerful mouth, the deep furrows on the cheek, and the general look of thought and suffering, all combined to make the appearance of the man remarkable, and to describe to the beholders at once his true character. No one ever on seeing Mr Crawley took him to be a happy man, or a weak man, or an ignorant man, or a wise man.

The Last Chronicle of Barset, 1867

After the Banquet

And then the people went, and when they had all gone Melmotte put his wife and daughter into his own carriage, telling them that he would follow them on foot to Bruton Street when he had given some last directions to the people who were putting out the lights, and extinguishing generally the embers of the entertainment. He had looked round for Lord Alfred, taking care to avoid the appearance of searching; but Lord Alfred had gone. Lord Alfred was one of those who knew when to leave a falling house. Melmotte at the moment thought of all that he had done for Lord Alfred, and it was something of the real venom of ingratitude that stung him at the moment rather than this additional sign of coming evil. He was more than ordinarily gracious as he put his wife into the carriage, and remarked that, considering all things, the party had gone off very well. 'I only wish it could have been done a little cheaper,' he said laughing. Then he went back into the house, and up into the drawing-rooms which were now utterly deserted. Some of the lights had been put out, but the men were busy in the rooms below, and he threw himself into the chair in which the Emperor had sat. It was wonderful that he should come to such a fate as this;—that he, the boy out of the gutter, should entertain at his own house, in London, a Chinese Emperor and English and German Royalty,—and that he should do so almost with a rope round his neck. Even if this were to be the end of it all, men would at any rate remember him. The grand dinner which he had given before he was put into prison would live in history. And it would be remembered, too, that he had been the Conservative candidate for the great borough of Westminster,—perhaps, even, the elected member. He, too, in his manner, assured himself that a great part of him would escape Oblivion. 'Non omnis moriar,' in some language of his own, was chanted by him within his own breast, as he sat there looking out on his own magnificent suite of rooms from the armchair which had been consecrated by the use of an Emperor.

No policemen had come to trouble him yet. No hint that he would be 'wanted' had been made to him. There was no tangible sign that things were not to go on as they went before. Things would be exactly as they were before, but for the absence of those guests from the dinner-table, and for the words which Miles Grendall had spoken. Had he not allowed himself to be terrified by shadows? Of course he had known that there must be such shadows. His life had been made dark by similar clouds before now, and he had lived through the storms which had followed them. He was thoroughly ashamed of the weakness which had overcome him at the dinner-table, and of that palsy of fear which he had allowed himself to exhibit. There should be no more shrinking such as that. When people talked of him they should say that he was at least a man.

The Way We Live Now, 1875

A Little Latin

'Is that all?'

'All what, sir?'

'Are there other debts?' To this Gerald made no reply. 'Other gambling debts.'

'No, sir;—not a shilling of that kind. I have never played before.'

'Does it ever occur to you that going on at that rate you may very soon lose all the fortune that will ever come to you? You were not yet of age and you lost three thousand four hundred pounds at cards to a man whom you probably knew to be a professed gambler!' The Duke seemed to wait for a reply, but poor Gerald had not a word to say. 'Can you explain to me what benefit you proposed to yourself when you played for such stakes as that?'

'I hoped to win back what I had lost.'

'Facilis descensus Averni!' said the Duke, shaking his head. 'Noctes atque dies patet atri janua Ditis.' No doubt, he thought, that as his son was at Oxford, admonitions in Latin would serve him better than in his native tongue. But Gerald, when he heard the grand hexameter rolled out in his father's grandest tone, entertained a comfortable feeling that the worst of the interview was over.

The Duke's Children, 1880

CHARLOTTE BRONTË
1816–1855

A Discord

I was a discord in Gateshead Hall; I was like nobody there; I had nothing in harmony with Mrs Reed or her children, or her chosen vassalage. If they did not love me, in fact, as little did I love them. They were not bound to regard with affection a thing that could not sympathize with one amongst them; a heterogeneous thing, opposed to them in temperament, in capacity, in propensities; a useless thing, incapable of serving their interest, or adding to their pleasure; a noxious thing, cherishing the germs of indignation at their treatment, of contempt of their judgement. I know that had I been a sanguine, brilliant, careless, exacting, handsome, romping child—though equally dependent and friendless—Mrs Reed would have endured my presence more complacently; her children would have entertained for me more of the cordiality of fellow-feeling; the servants would have been less prone to make me the scapegoat of the nursery.

Jane Eyre, 1847

The Flight across the Moors

I touched the heath: it was dry, and yet warm with the heat of the summer day. I looked at the sky; it was pure: a kindly star twinkled just above the chasm ridge. The dew fell, but with propitious softness; no breeze whispered. Nature seemed to me benign and good; I thought she loved me, outcast as I was; and I, who from man could anticipate only mistrust, rejection, insult, clung to her with filial fondness. To-night, at least, I would be her guest, as I was her child: my mother would lodge me without money and without price. I had one morsel of bread yet: the remnant of a roll I had bought in a town we had passed through at noon with a stray penny—my last coin. I saw ripe bilberries gleaming here and there, like jet beads in the heath: I gathered a handful, and ate them with the bread. My hunger, sharp before, was, if not satisfied, appeased by this hermit's meal. I said my evening prayers at its conclusion, and then chose my couch.

Beside the crag the heath was very deep: when I lay down my feet were buried in it; rising high on each side, it left only a narrow space for the night-air to invade. I folded my shawl double, and spread it over me for a coverlet; a low, mossy swell was my pillow. Thus lodged, I was not, at least at the commencement of the night, cold.

My rest might have been blissful enough, only a sad heart broke it. It plained of its gaping wounds, its inward bleeding, its riven chords. It trembled for Mr Rochester and his doom; it bemoaned him with bitter pity; it demanded him with ceaseless longing; and, impotent as a bird with both wings broken, it still quivered its shattered pinions in vain attempts to seek him.

Worn out with this torture of thought, I rose to my knees. Night was come, and her planets were risen: a safe, still night: too serene for the companionship of fear. We know that God is everywhere; but certainly we feel His presence most when His works are on the grandest scale spread before us; and it is in the unclouded night-sky, where His worlds wheel their silent course, that we read clearest His infinitude, His omnipotence, His omnipresence. I had risen to my knees to pray for Mr Rochester. Looking up, I, with tear-dimmed eyes, saw the mighty Milky Way. Remembering what it was—what countless systems there swept space like a soft trace of light—I felt the might and strength of God. Sure was I of His efficiency to save what He had made: convinced I grew that neither earth should perish, nor one of the souls it treasured. I turned my prayer to thanksgiving: the Source of Life was also the Saviour of spirits. Mr Rochester was safe: he was God's, and by God would he be guarded. I again nestled to the breast of the hill; and ere long in sleep forgot sorrow.

But next day, Want came to me, pale and bare. Long after the little birds had left their nests; long after bees had come in the sweet prime of day to gather the heath honey before the dew was dried—when the long morning shadows were curtailed, and the sun filled earth and sky—I got up, and I looked round me.

What a still, hot, perfect day! What a golden desert this spreading moor! Everywhere sunshine. I wished I could live in it and on it. I saw a lizard run over the crag; I saw a bee busy among the sweet bilberries. I would fain at the moment have become bee or lizard, that I might have found fitting nutriment, permanent shelter here. But I was a human being, and had a human being's wants: I must not linger where there was nothing to supply them. I rose; I looked back at the bed I had left. Hopeless of the future, I wished but this—that my Maker had that night thought good to require my soul of me while I slept; and that this weary frame, absolved by death from further conflict with fate, had now but to decay quietly, and mingle in peace with the soil of this wilderness. Life, however, was yet in my possession, with all its requirements, and pains, and responsibilities. The burden must be carried; the want provided for; the suffering endured; the responsibility fulfilled. I set out.

Jane Eyre

The Long Vacation

That vacation! Shall I ever forget it? I think not. Madame Beck went, the first day of the holidays, to join her children at the seaside; all the three teachers had parents or friends with whom they took refuge; every professor quitted the city; some went to Paris, some to Boue-Marine; M. Paul set forth on a pilgrimage to Rome; the house was left quite empty, but for me, a servant, and a poor deformed and imbecile pupil, a sort of crétin, whom her stepmother in a distant province would not allow to return home.

My heart almost died within me; miserable longings strained its chords. How long were the September days! How silent, how lifeless! How vast and void seemed the desolate premises! How gloomy the forsaken garden—grey now with the dust of a town summer departed. Looking forward at the commencement of those eight weeks, I hardly knew how I was to live to the end. My spirits had long been gradually sinking; now that the prop of employment was withdrawn, they went down fast. Even to look forward was not to hope: the dumb future spoke no comfort, offered no promise, gave no inducement to bear present evil in reliance on future good. A sorrowful indifference to existence often pressed on me—a despairing resignation to reach betimes the end of all things earthly. Alas! When I had full leisure to look on life as life must be looked on by such as me, I found it but a hopeless desert: tawny sands, with no green fields, no palm tree, no well in view. The hopes which are dear to youth, which bear it up and lead it on, I knew not and dared not know. If they knocked at my heart sometimes, an inhospitable bar to admission must be inwardly drawn. When they turned away thus rejected, tears sad enough sometimes flowed; but it could not be helped: I dared not give such guests lodging. So mortally did I fear the sin and weakness of presumption.

Religious reader, you will preach to me a long sermon about what I have just written, and so will you, moralist; and you, stern sage: you, stoic, will frown; you, cynic, sneer; you, epicure, laugh. Well, each and all, take it your own way. I accept the sermon, frown, sneer, and laugh; perhaps you are all right: and perhaps, circumstanced like me, you would have been, like me, wrong. The first month was, indeed, a long, black, heavy month to me.

The crétin did not seem unhappy. I did my best to feed her well and keep her warm, and she only asked food and sunshine, or when that lacked, fire. Her weak faculties approved of inertion: her brain, her eyes, her ears, her heart slept content; they could not wake to work, so lethargy was their Paradise.

Three weeks of that vacation were hot, fair, and dry, but the fourth and fifth were tempestuous and wet. I do not know why that change in the atmosphere made a cruel impression on me, why the raging storm and beating rain crushed me with a deadlier paralysis than I had experienced while the air had remained serene; but so it was, and my nervous system could hardly support what it had for many days and nights to undergo in that huge empty house. How I used to pray to Heaven for consolation and support! With what dread force the conviction would grasp me that Fate was my permanent foe, never to be conciliated. I did not, in my heart, arraign the mercy or justice of God for this; I concluded it to be a part of His great plan that some must deeply suffer while they live, and I thrilled in the certainty that of this number, I was one.

It was some relief when an aunt of the crétin, a kind old woman, came one day and took away my strange, deformed companion. The hapless creature had been at times a heavy charge; I could not take her out beyond the garden, and I could not leave her a minute alone: for her poor mind, like her body, was warped: its propensity was to evil. A vague bent to mischief, an aimless malevolence, made constant vigilance indispensable. As she very rarely spoke, and would sit for hours together moping and mowing and distorting her features with indescribable grimaces, it was more like being prisoned with some strange tameless animal, than associating with a human being. Then there were personal attentions to be rendered which required the nerve of a hospital nurse; my resolution was so tried, it sometimes fell dead sick. These duties should not have fallen on me; a servant, now absent, had rendered them hitherto, and in the hurry of holiday departure, no substitute to fill this office had been provided. This tax and trial were by no means the least I have known in life. Still, menial and distasteful as they were, my mental pain was far more wasting and wearing. Attendance on the crétin deprived me often of the power and inclination to swallow a meal, and sent me faint to the fresh air, and the well or fountain in the court; but this duty never wrung my heart, or brimmed my eyes, or scalded my cheek with tears hot as molten metal.

Villette, 1853

HENRY DAVID THOREAU
1817–1862

The Tameness of English Poetry

English literature from the days of the minstrels to the Lake Poets, Chaucer and Spenser and Shakspeare and Milton included, breathes no quite fresh and, in this sense, wild strain. It is an essentially tame and civilized literature, reflecting Greece and Rome. Her wilderness is a greenwood, her wild man a Robin Hood. There is plenty of genial love of nature in her poets, but not so much of nature herself. Her chronicles inform us when her wild animals, but not when the wild man in her, became extinct. There was need of America.

Journal, 1851

The High Cost of Kindness

Men are very generally spoiled by being so civil and well-disposed. You can have no profitable conversation with them, they are so conciliatory, determined to agree with you. They exhibit such long-suffering and kindness in a short interview. I would meet with some provoking strangeness, so that we may be guest and host and refresh one another. It is possible for a man wholly to disappear and be merged in his manners. The thousand and one gentlemen whom I meet, I meet despairingly, and but to part from them, for I am not cheered by the hope of any rudeness from them. A cross man, a coarse man, an eccentric man, a silent, a man who does not drill well—of him there is some hope. Your gentlemen, they are all alike.

Journal, 1851

The Death of a Pine Tree

This afternoon, being on Fair Haven Hill, I heard the sound of a saw, and soon after from the Cliff saw two men sawing down a noble pine beneath, about forty rods off. I resolved to watch it till it fell, the last of a dozen or more which were left when the forest was cut and for fifteen years have waved in solitary majesty over the sproutland. I saw them like beavers or insects gnawing at the trunk of this noble tree, the diminutive manikins with their cross-cut saw which could scarcely span it. It towered up a hundred feet as I afterward found by measurement, one of the tallest probably in the township and straight as an arrow, but slanting a little toward the hillside, its top seen against the frozen river and the hills of Conantum. I watch closely to see when it begins to move. Now the sawers stop, and with an axe open it a little on the side toward which it leans, that it may break the faster. And now their saw goes again. Now surely it is going; it is inclined one quarter of the quadrant, and, breathless, I expect its crashing fall. But no, I was mistaken; it has not moved an inch; it stands at the same angle as at first. It is fifteen minutes yet to its fall. Still its branches wave in the wind, as if it were destined to stand for a century, and the wind soughs through its needles as of yore; it is still a forest tree, the most majestic tree that waves over Musketaquid. The silvery sheen of the sunlight is reflected from its needles; it still affords an inaccessible crotch for the squirrel's nest; not a lichen has forsaken its mast-like stem, its raking mast—the hill is the hulk. Now, now's the moment! The manikins at its base are fleeing from their crime. They have dropped the guilty saw and axe. How slowly and majestically it starts! as if it were only swayed by a summer breeze, and would return without a sigh to its location in the air. And now it fans the hillside with its fall, and it lies down to its bed in the valley, from which it is never to rise, as softly as a feather, folding its green mantle about it like a warrior, as if, tired of standing, it embraced the earth with silent joy, returning its elements to the dust again. But hark! there you only saw, but did not hear. There now comes up a deafening crash to these rocks, advertising you that even trees do not die without a groan. It rushes to embrace the earth, and mingle its elements with the dust. And now all is still once more and forever, both to eye and ear.

Journal, 1851

Simplicity

I went to the woods because I wished to live deliberately, to front only the essential facts of life, and see if I could not learn what it had to teach, and not, when I came to die, discover that I had not lived. I did not wish to live what was not life, living is so dear; nor did I wish to practise resignation, unless it was quite necessary. I wanted to live deep and suck out all the marrow of life, to live so sturdily and Spartan-like as to put to rout all that was not life, to cut a broad swath and shave close, to drive life into a corner, and reduce it to its lowest terms, and, if it proved to be mean, why then to get the whole and genuine meanness of it, and publish its meanness to the world; or if it were sublime, to know it by experience, and be able to give a true account of it in my next excursion. For most men, it appears to me, are in a strange uncertainty about it, whether it is of the devil or of God, and have *somewhat hastily* concluded that it is the chief end of man here to 'glorify God and enjoy him forever.'

Still we live meanly, like ants: though the fable tells us that we were long ago changed into men; like pygmies we fight with cranes; it is error upon error, and clout upon clout, and our best virtue has for its occasion a superfluous and evitable wretchedness. Our life is frittered away by detail. An honest man has hardly need to count more than his ten fingers, or in extreme cases he may add his ten toes, and lump the rest. Simplicity, simplicity, simplicity! I say, let your affairs be as two or three, and not a hundred or a thousand; instead of a million count half a dozen, and keep your accounts on your thumb nail. In the midst of this chopping sea of civilized life, such are the clouds and storms and quicksands and thousand-and-one items to be allowed for, that a man has to live, if he would not founder and go to the bottom and not make his port at all, by dead reckoning, and he must be a great calculator indeed who succeeds. Simplify, simplify. Instead of three meals a day, if it be necessary eat but one; instead of a hundred dishes, five; and reduce other things in proportion. Our life is like a German Confederacy, made up of petty states, with its boundary forever fluctuating, so that even a German cannot tell you how it is bounded at any moment. The nation itself, with all its so called internal improvements, which, by the way, are all external and superficial, is just such an unwieldy and overgrown establishment, cluttered with furniture and tripped up by its own traps, ruined by luxury and heedless expense, by want of calculation and a worthy aim, as the million households in the land; and the only cure for it as for them is in a rigid economy, a stern and more than Spartan simplicity of life and elevation of purpose. It lives too fast. Men think that it is essential that the *Nation* have commerce, and export ice, and talk through a telegraph, and ride thirty miles an hour, without a doubt, whether *they* do or not; but whether we should live like baboons or like men, is a little uncertain. If we do not get out sleepers, and forge rails, and devote days and nights to the work, but go to tinkering upon our *lives* to improve *them*, who will build railroads? And if railroads are not built, how shall we get to heaven in season? But if we stay at home and mind our business, who will want railroads? We do not ride on the railroad; it rides upon us. Did you ever think what those sleepers are that underlie the railroad? Each one is a man, an Irish-man, or a Yankee man. The rails are laid on them, and they are covered with sand, and the cars run smoothly over them. They are sound sleepers, I assure you. And every few years a new lot is laid down and run over; so that, if some have the pleasure of riding on a rail, others have the misfortune to be ridden upon. And when they run over a man that is walking in his sleep, a supernumerary sleeper in the wrong position, and wake him up, they suddenly stop the cars, and make a hue and cry about it, as if this were an exception. I am glad to know that it takes a gang of men for every five miles to keep the sleepers down and level in their beds as it is, for this is a sign that they may sometime get up again.

Walden, 1854

Incident at Mrs Brooks's

On the morning of the 17th, Mrs Brooks's Irish girl Joan fell down the cellar stairs, and was found by her mistress lying at the bottom, apparently lifeless. Mrs Brooks ran to the street-door for aid to get her up, and asked a Miss Farmer, who was passing, to call the blacksmith near by. The latter lady turned instantly, and, making haste across the road on this errand, fell flat in a puddle of melted snow, and came back to Mrs Brooks's, bruised and dripping and asking for opodeldoc. Mrs Brooks again ran to the door and called to George Bigelow to complete the unfinished errand. He ran nimbly about it and fell flat in another puddle near the former, but, his joints being limber, got along without opodeldoc and raised the blacksmith. He also notified James Burke, who was passing, and he, rushing in to render aid, fell off one side of the cellar stairs in the dark. They no sooner got the girl upstairs than she came to and went raving, then had a fit.

Haste makes waste. It never rains but it pours. I have this from those who have heard Mrs Brooks's story, seen the girl, the stairs, and the puddles.

Journal, 1856

EMILY BRONTË
1818–1848

A Bad Dream

This time, I remembered I was lying in the oak closet, and I heard distinctly the gusty wind, and the driving of the snow; I heard, also, the fir-bough repeat its teasing sound, and ascribed it to the right cause: but it annoyed me so much, that I resolved to silence it, if possible; and, I thought, I rose and endeavoured to unhasp the casement. The hook was soldered into the staple: a circumstance observed by me when awake, but forgotten. 'I must stop it, nevertheless!' I muttered, knocking my knuckles through the glass, and stretching an arm out to seize the importunate branch; instead of which, my fingers closed on the fingers of a little, ice-cold hand! The intense horror of nightmare came over me: I tried to draw back my arm, but the hand clung to it, and a most melancholy voice sobbed, 'Let me in—let me in!' 'Who are you?' I asked, struggling, meanwhile, to disengage myself. 'Catherine Linton,' it replied shiveringly (why did I think of *Linton*? I had read *Earnshaw* twenty times for Linton). 'I'm come home: I'd lost my way on the moor!' As it spoke, I discerned, obscurely, a child's face looking through the window. Terror made me cruel; and, finding it useless to attempt shaking the creature off, I pulled its wrist on to the broken pane, and rubbed it to and fro till the blood ran down and soaked the bedclothes: still it wailed, 'Let me in!' and maintained its tenacious gripe, almost maddening me with fear. 'How can I!' I said at length. 'Let *me* go, if you want me to let you in!' The fingers relaxed, I snatched mine through the hole, hurriedly piled the books up in a pyramid against it, and stopped my ears to exclude the lamentable prayer. I seemed to keep them closed above a quarter of an hour; yet, the instant I listened again, there was the doleful cry moaning on! 'Begone!' I shouted, 'I'll never let you in, not if you beg for twenty years.' 'It is twenty years,' mourned the voice: 'twenty years. I've been a waif for twenty years!' Thereat began a feeble scratching outside, and the pile of books moved as if thrust forward. I tried to jump up; but could not stir a limb; and so yelled aloud, in a frenzy of fright. To my confusion, I discovered the yell was not ideal: hasty footsteps approached my chamber door; somebody pushed it open, with a vigorous hand, and a light glimmered through the squares at the top of the bed. I sat shuddering yet, and wiping the perspiration from my forehead: the intruder appeared to hesitate, and muttered to himself. At last, he said in a half-whisper, plainly not expecting an answer, 'Is any one here?' I considered it best to confess my presence; for I knew Heathcliff's accents, and feared he might search further, if I kept quiet. With this intention, I turned and opened the panels.

Wuthering Heights, 1847

Catherine and Heathcliff

'I cannot express it; but surely you and everybody have a notion that there is or should be an existence of yours beyond you. What were the use of my creation, if I were entirely contained here? My great miseries in this world have been Heathcliff's miseries, and I watched and felt each from the beginning: my great thought in living is himself. If all else perished, and *he* remained, I should still continue to be; and if all else remained, and he were annihilated, the universe would turn to a mighty stranger: I should not seem a part of it. My love for Linton is like the foliage in the woods: time will change it, I'm well aware, as winter changes the trees. My love for Heathcliff resembles the eternal rocks beneath: a source of little visible delight, but necessary. Nelly, I *am* Heathcliff! He's always, always in my mind: not as a pleasure, any more than I am always a pleasure to myself, but as my own being.'

Wuthering Heights

A Haunted Room

Tossing about, she increased her feverish bewilderment to madness, and tore the pillow with her teeth; then raising herself up all burning, desired that I would open the window. We were in the middle of winter, the wind blew strong from the north-east, and I objected. Both the expressions flitting over her face, and the changes of her moods, began to alarm me terribly; and brought to my recollection her former illness, and the doctor's injunction that she should not be crossed. A minute previously she was violent; now, supported on one arm, and not noticing my refusal to obey her, she seemed to find childish diversion in pulling the feathers from the rents she had just made, and ranging them on the sheet according to their different species: her mind had strayed to other associations.

'That's a turkey's,' she murmured to herself; 'and this is a wild duck's; and this is a pigeon's. Ah, they put pigeons' feathers in the pillows—no wonder I couldn't die! Let me take care to throw it on the floor when I lie down. And here is a moor-cock's; and this—I should know it among a thousand—it's a lapwing's. Bonny bird; wheeling over our heads in the middle of the moor. It wanted to get to its nest, for the clouds had touched the swells, and it felt rain coming. This feather was picked up from the heath, the bird was not shot: we saw its nest in the winter, full of little skeletons. Heathcliff set a trap over it, and the old ones dare not come. I made him promise he'd never shoot a lapwing after that, and he didn't. Yes, here are more! Did he shoot my lapwings, Nelly? Are they red, any of them? Let me look.'

'Give over with that baby-work!' I interrupted, dragging the pillow away, and turning the holes towards the mattress, for she was removing its contents by handfuls. 'Lie down and shut your eyes: you're wandering. There's a mess! The down is flying about like snow.'

I went here and there collecting it.

'I see in you, Nelly,' she continued, dreamily, 'an aged woman: you have grey hair and bent shoulders. This bed is the fairy cave under Peniston Crag, and you are gathering elf-bolts to hurt our heifers; pretending, while I am near, that they are only locks of wool. That's what you'll come to fifty years hence: I know you are not so now. I'm not wandering: you're mistaken, or else I should believe you really *were* that withered hag, and I should think I *was* under Penistone Crag; and I'm conscious it's night, and there are two candles on the table making the black press shine like jet.'

'The black press? where is that?' I asked. 'You are talking in your sleep!'

'It's against the wall, as it always is,' she replied. 'It *does* appear odd—I see a face in it!'

'There is no press in the room, and never was,' said I, resuming my seat, and looping up the curtain that I might watch her.

'Don't *you* see that face?' she enquired, gazing earnestly at the mirror.

And say what I could, I was incapable of making her comprehend it to be her own; so I rose and covered it with a shawl.

'It's behind there still!' she pursued, anxiously. 'And it stirred. Who is it? I hope it will not come out when you are gone! Oh! Nelly, the room is haunted! I'm afraid of being alone!'

Wuthering Heights

At Rest

My walk home was lengthened by a diversion in the direction of the kirk. When beneath its walls, I perceived decay had made progress, even in seven months: many a window showed black gaps deprived of glass; and slates jutted off, here and there, beyond the right line of the roof, to be gradually worked off in coming autumn storms.

I sought, and soon discovered, the three headstones on the slope next the moor: the middle one grey, and half buried in heath; Edgar Linton's only harmonized by the turf, and moss creeping up its foot; Heathcliff's still bare.

I lingered round them, under that benign sky: watched the moths fluttering among the heath and hare-bells; listened to the soft wind breathing through the grass; and wondered how any one could ever imagine unquiet slumbers for the sleepers in that quiet earth.

Wuthering Heights

JAMES ANTHONY FROUDE
1818–1894

The Trial of Latimer

Ridley withdrew, and Latimer was then introduced—eighty years old now—dressed in an old threadbare gown of Bristol frieze, a handkerchief on his head with a night-cap over it, and over that again another cap, with two broad flaps buttoned under the chin. A leather belt was round his waist, to which a Testament was attached; his spectacles, without a case, hung from his neck. So stood the greatest man perhaps then living in the world, a prisoner on his trial, waiting to be condemned to death by men professing to be the ministers of God. As it was in the days of the prophets, so it was in the Son of man's days; as it was in the days of the Son of man, so was it in the Reformers' days; as it was in the days of the Reformers, so will it be to the end, so long and so far as a class of men are permitted to hold power, who call themselves the commissioned and authoritative teachers of truth. Latimer's trial was the counterpart of Ridley's: the charge was the same, and the result was the same, except that the stronger intellect vexed itself less with nice distinctions. Bread was bread, said Latimer, and wine was wine; there was a change in the sacrament, it was true, but the change was not in the nature, but the dignity. He too was reprieved for the day. The following morning, the court sat in St Mary's Church, with the authorities of town and university, heads of houses, mayor, aldermen, and sheriff. The prisoners were brought to the bar. The same questions were asked, the same answers were returned, and sentence was pronounced upon them, as heretics obstinate and incurable.

History of England, vol. v, 1860

Newman at Oxford

It has been said that men of letters are either much less or much greater than their writings. Cleverness and the skilful use of other people's thoughts produce works which take us in till we see the authors, and then we are disenchanted. A man of genius, on the other hand, is a spring in which there is always more behind than flows from it. The painting or the poem is but a part of him inadequately realized, and his nature expresses itself, with equal or fuller completeness, in his life, his conversation, and personal presence. This was eminently true of Newman. Greatly as his poetry had struck me, he was himself all that the poetry was, and something far beyond. I had then never seen so impressive a person. I met him now and then in private; I attended his church and heard him preach Sunday after Sunday; he is supposed to have been insidious, to have led his disciples on to conclusions to which he designed to bring them, while his purpose was carefully veiled. He was, on the contrary, the most transparent of men. He told us what he believed to be true. No one who has ever risen to any great height in this world refuses to move till he knows where he is going. He is impelled in each step which he takes by a force within himself. He satisfies himself only that the step is a right one, and he leaves the rest to Providence. Newman's mind was world-wide. He was interested in everything which was going on in science, in politics, in literature. Nothing was too large for him, nothing too trivial, if it threw light upon the central question, what man really was, and what was his destiny. He was careless about his personal prospects. He had no ambition to make a career, or to rise to rank and power. Still less had pleasure any seductions for him. His natural temperament was bright and light; his senses, even the commonest, were exceptionally delicate. I was told that, though he rarely drank wine, he was trusted to choose the vintages for the college cellar. He could admire enthusiastically any greatness of action and character, however remote the sphere of it from his own. Gurwood's 'Dispatches of the Duke of Wellington' came out just then. Newman had been reading the book, and a friend asked him what he thought of it. 'Think?' he said, 'it makes one burn to have been a soldier.' But his own subject was the absorbing interest with him.

'The Oxford Counter-Reformation', *Short Studies on Great Subjects: Fourth Series*, 1883

False Gods

The accumulation of wealth, with its daily services at the Stock Exchange and the Bourse, with international exhibitions for its religious festivals, and political economy for its gospel, is progress, if it be progress at all, towards the wrong place. Baal, the god of the merchants of Tyre, counted four hundred and fifty prophets when there was but one Elijah. Baal was a visible reality. Baal rose in his sun-chariot in the morning, scattered the evil spirits of the night, lightened the heart, quickened the seed in the soil, clothed the hill-side with waving corn, made the gardens bright with flowers, and loaded the vineyard with its purple clusters. When Baal turned away his face the earth languished, and dressed herself in her winter mourning robe. Baal was the friend who held at bay the enemies of mankind—cold, nakedness, and hunger; who was kind alike to the evil and the good, to those who worshipped him and those who forgot their benefactor. Compared to him, what was the being that 'hid himself,' the name without a form—that was called on, but did not answer—who appeared in visions of the night, terrifying the uneasy sleeper with visions of horror? Baal was god. The other was but the creation of a frightened imagination—a phantom that had no existence outside the brain of fools and dreamers. Yet in the end Baal could not save Samaria from the Assyrians, any more than progress and 'unexampled prosperity' have rescued Paris from Von Moltke.

'On Progress', *Short Studies on Great Subjects: Fourth Series*

FREDERICK DOUGLASS
1818–1895

The Songs of the Slave

The slaves selected to go to the Great House Farm, for the monthly allowance for themselves and their fellow-slaves, were peculiarly enthusiastic. While on their way, they would make the dense old woods, for miles around, reverberate with their wild songs, revealing at once the highest joy and the deepest sadness. They would compose and sing as they went along, consulting neither time nor tune. The thought that came up, came out— if not in the word, in the sound;—and as frequently in the one as in the other. They would sometimes sing the most pathetic sentiment in the most rapturous tone, and the most rapturous sentiment in the most pathetic tone. Into all of their songs they would manage to weave something of the Great House Farm. Especially would they do this, when leaving home. They would then sing most exultingly the following words:—

> 'I am going away to the Great House Farm!
> O, yea! O, yea! O!'

This they would sing, as a chorus, to words which to many would seem unmeaning jargon, but which, nevertheless, were full of meaning to themselves. I have sometimes thought that the mere hearing of those songs would do more to impress some minds with the horrible character of slavery, than the reading of whole volumes of philosophy on the subject could do.

I did not, when a slave, understand the deep meaning of those rude and apparently incoherent songs. I was myself within the circle: so that I neither saw nor heard as those without might see and hear. They told a tale of woe which was then altogether beyond my feeble comprehension; they were tones loud, long, and deep; they breathed the prayer and complaint of souls boiling over with the bitterest anguish. Every tone was a testimony against slavery, and a prayer to God for deliverance from chains. The hearing of those wild notes always depressed my spirit, and filled me with ineffable sadness. I have frequently found myself in tears while hearing them. The mere recurrence to those songs, even now, afflicts me; and while I am writing these lines, an expression of feeling has already found its way down my cheek. To those songs I trace my first glimmering conception of the dehumanizing character of slavery. I can never get rid of that conception. Those songs still follow me, to deepen my hatred of slavery, and quicken my sympathies for my brethren in bonds. If any one wishes to be impressed with the soul-killing effects of slavery, let him go to Colonel Lloyd's plantation, and, on allowance-day, place himself in the deep pine woods, and there let him, in silence, analyze the sounds that shall pass through the chambers of his soul,—and if he is not thus impressed, it will only be because 'there is no flesh in his obdurate heart.'

I have often been utterly astonished, since I came to the north, to find persons who could speak of the singing, among slaves, as evidence of their contentment and happiness. It is impossible to conceive of a greater mistake. Slaves sing most when they are most unhappy. The songs of the slave represent the sorrows of his heart; and he is relieved by them, only as an aching heart is relieved by its tears. At least, such is my experience. I have often sung to drown my sorrow, but seldom to express my happiness. Crying for joy, and singing for joy, were alike uncommon to me while in the jaws of slavery. The singing of a man cast away upon a desolate island might be as appropriately considered as evidence of contentment and happiness, as the singing of a slave; the songs of the one and of the other are prompted by the same emotion.

Narrative of the Life of Frederick Douglass, an American Slave, 1845

JOHN RUSKIN
1819–1900

A Bird amid the Alps

I had seen also for the third time, by the Chartreuse torrent, the most wonderful of all Alpine birds—a grey, fluttering stealthy creature, about the size of a sparrow, but of colder grey, and more graceful, which haunts the side of the fiercest torrents. There is something more strange in it than in the seagull—*that* seems a powerful creature; and the power of the sea, not of a kind so adverse, so hopelessly destructive; but this small creature, silent, tender and light, almost like a moth in its low and irregular flight,—almost touching with its wings the crests of waves that would overthrow a granite wall, and haunting the hollows of the black, cold, herbless rocks that are continually shaken by their spray, has perhaps the nearest approach to the look of a spiritual existence that I know in animal life.

Diary, 1849

The Abstract Element in Art

We are to remember, in the first place, that the arrangement of colours and lines is an art analogous to the composition of music, and entirely independent of the representation of facts. Good colouring does not necessarily convey the image of anything but itself. It consists in certain proportions and arrangements of rays of light, but not in likenesses to anything. A few touches of certain greys and purples laid by a master's hand on white paper will be good colouring; as more touches are added beside them, we may find out that they were intended to represent a dove's neck, and we may praise, as the drawing advances, the perfect imitation of the dove's neck. But the good colouring does not consist in that imitation, but in the abstract qualities and relations of the grey and purple.

In like manner, as soon as a great sculptor begins to shape his work out of the block, we shall see that its lines are nobly arranged, and of noble character. We may not have the slightest idea for what the forms are intended, whether they are of man or beast, of vegetation or drapery. Their likeness to anything does not affect their nobleness. They are magnificent forms, and that is all we need care to know of them, in order to say whether the workman is a good or bad sculptor.

The Stones of Venice, vol. iii, 1853

Mountain Purples

Consider, first, the difference produced in the whole tone of landscape colour by the introduction of purple, violet, and deep ultramarine blue, which we owe to mountains. In an ordinary lowland landscape we have the blue of the sky; the green of grass, which I will suppose (and this is an unnecessary concession to the lowlands) entirely fresh and bright; the green of trees; and certain elements of purple, far more rich and beautiful than we generally should think, in their bark and shadows (bare hedges and thickets, or tops of trees, in subdued afternoon sunshine, are nearly perfect purple, and of an exquisite tone), as well as in ploughed fields, and dark ground in general. But among mountains, in *addition* to all this, large unbroken spaces of pure violet and purple are introduced in their distances; and even near, by films of cloud passing over the darkness of ravines or forests, blues are produced of the most subtle tenderness; these azures and purples passing into rose-colour of otherwise wholly unattainable delicacy among the upper summits, the blue of the sky being at the same time purer and deeper than in the plains. Nay, in some sense a person who has never seen the rose-colour of the rays of dawn crossing a blue mountain twelve or fifteen miles away, can hardly be said to know what *tenderness* in colour means at all; *bright* tenderness he may, indeed, see in the sky or in a flower, but this grave tenderness of the far-away hill-purples he cannot conceive.

Modern Painters, vol. iv, 1856

Cloud Shapes

How is a cloud outlined? Granted whatever you choose to ask, concerning its material, or its aspect, its loftiness and luminousness,—how of its limitation? What hews it into a heap, or spins it into a web? Cold is usually shapeless, I suppose, extending over large spaces equally, or with gradual diminution. You cannot have, in the open air, angles, and wedges, and coils, and cliffs of cold. Yet the vapour stops suddenly, sharp and steep as a rock, or thrusts itself across the gates of heaven in likeness of a brazen bar; or braids itself in and out, and across and across, like a tissue of tapestry; or falls into ripples like sand; or into waving shreds and tongues, as fire. On what anvils and wheels is the vapour pointed, twisted, hammered, whirled, as the potter's clay? By what hands is the incense of the sea built up into domes of marble?

Modern Painters, vol. v, 1860

The Boyhood of Turner

Now this fond companying with sailors must have divided his time, it appears to me, pretty equally between Covent Garden and Wapping (allowing for incidental excursions to Chelsea on one side, and Greenwich on the other), which time he would spend pleasantly, but not magnificently, being limited in pocket-money, and leading a kind of 'Poor Jack' life on the river.

In some respects, no life could be better for a lad. But it was not calculated to make his ear fine to the niceties of language, nor form his moralities on an entirely regular standard. Picking up his first scraps of vigorous English chiefly at Deptford and in the markets, and his first ideas of female tenderness and beauty among nymphs of the barge and the barrow,—another boy might, perhaps, have become what people usually term 'vulgar.' But the original make and frame of Turner's mind being not vulgar, but as nearly as possible a combination of the minds of Keats and Dante, joining capricious waywardness, and intense openness to every fine pleasure of sense, and hot defiance of formal precedent, with a quite infinite tenderness, generosity, and desire of justice and truth—this kind of mind did not become vulgar, but very tolerant of vulgarity, even fond of it in some forms; and on the outside, visibly infected by it, deeply enough; the curious result, in its combination of elements, being to most people wholly incomprehensible. It was as if a cable had been woven of blood-crimson silk, and then tarred on the outside. People handled it, and the tar came off on their hands; red gleams were seen through the black underneath, at the places where it had been strained. Was it ochre?—said the world—or red lead?

Modern Painters, vol. v, 1860

The Laws of History

There is no law of history any more than of a kaleidoscope. With certain bits of glass—shaken so, and so—you will get pretty figures, but what figures, heaven only knows. Add definite attractions and repulsions to the angles of the tube—your figures will have such and such modifications. But the history of the world will be for ever new.

The wards of a Chubb's lock are infinite in their chances. Is the Key of Destiny made on a less complex principle?

letter to J. A. Froude, 1864

A Locomotive

I cannot express the amazed awe, the crushed humility, with which I sometimes watch a locomotive take its breath at a railway station, and think what work there is in its bars and wheels, and what manner of men they must be who dig brown iron-stone out of the ground, and forge it into THAT! What assemblage of accurate and mighty faculties in them; more than fleshly power over melting crag and coiling fire, fettered, and finessed at last into the precision of watchmaking; Titanian hammer-strokes beating, out of lava, these glittering cylinders and timely-respondent valves, and fine ribbed rods, which touch each other as a serpent writhes, in noiseless gliding, and omnipotence of grasp; infinitely complex anatomy of active steel, compared with which the skeleton of a living creature would seem, to a careless observer, clumsy and vile—a mere morbid secretion and phosphatous prop of flesh! What would the men who thought out this—who beat it out, who touched it into its polished calm of power, who set it to its appointed task, and triumphantly saw it fulfil this task to the utmost of their will—feel or think about this weak hand of mine, timidly leading a little strain of watercolour, which I cannot manage, into an imperfect shadow of something else—mere failure in every motion, and endless disappointment; what, I repeat, would these Iron-dominant Genii think of me? and what ought I to think of them?

The Cestus of Aglaia, 1865

The Money Game

The first of all English games is making money. That is an all-absorbing game; and we knock each other down oftener in playing at that, than at football, or any other roughest sport: and it is absolutely without purpose; no one who engages heartily in that game ever knows why. Ask a great money-maker what he wants to do with his money,—he never knows. He doesn't make it to do anything with it. He gets it only that he *may* get it. 'What will you make of what you have got?' you ask. 'Well, I'll get more,' he says. Just as, at cricket, you get more runs. There's no use in the runs, but to get more of them than other people is the game. And there's no use in the money, but to have more of it than other people is the game. So all that great foul city of London there,—rattling, growling, smoking, stinking,—a ghastly heap of fermenting brickwork, pouring out poison at every pore,—you fancy it is a city of work? Not a street of it! It is a great city of play; very nasty play, and very hard play, but still play. It is only Lord's cricket-ground without the turf:—a huge billiard-table without the cloth, and with pockets as deep as the bottomless pit; but mainly a billiard-table, after all.

The Crown of Wild Olive, 1866

In Need of a Blessing

My Friends,—You would pity me, if you knew how seldom I see a newspaper, just now; but I chanced on one yesterday, and found that all the world was astir about the marriage of the Marquis of B., and that the Pope had sent him, on that occasion, a telegraphic blessing of superfine quality.

I wonder what the Marquis of B. has done to deserve to be blessed to that special extent, and whether a little mild beatitude, sent here to Pisa, might not have been better spent. For, indeed, before getting hold of the papers, I had been greatly troubled, while drawing the east end of the Duomo, by three fellows who were leaning against the Leaning Tower, and expectorating loudly and copiously, at intervals of half a minute each, over the white marble base of it, which they evidently conceived to have been constructed only to be spit upon. They were all in rags, and obviously proposed to remain in rags all their days, and pass what leisure of life they could obtain, in spitting. There was a boy with them, in rags also, and not less expectorant, but having some remains of human activity in him still (being not more than twelve years old); and he was even a little interested in my brushes and colours, but rewarded himself, after the effort of some attention to these, by revolving slowly round the iron railing in front of me like a pensive squirrel. This operation at last disturbed me so much, that I asked him if there were no other railings in Pisa he could turn upside down over, but these. 'Sono cascato, Signor—' 'I tumbled over them, please, Sir,' said he, apologetically, with infinite satisfaction in his black eyes.

Now it seemed to me that these three moist-throated men and the squirrelline boy stood much more in need of a paternal blessing than the Marquis of B.—a blessing, of course, with as much of the bloom off it as would make it consistent with the position in which Providence had placed them; but enough, in its moderate way, to bring the good out of them instead of the evil. For there was all manner of good in them, deep and pure—yet for ever to be dormant; and all manner of evil, shallow and superficial, yet for ever to be active and practical, as matters stood that day, under the Leaning Tower.

Fors Clavigera, Letter 18, 1872

The Power of a Curse

Cursing is invoking the aid of a Spirit to a harm you wish to see accomplished, but which is too great for your own immediate power: and to-day I wish to point out to you what intensity of faith in the existence and activity of a spiritual world is evinced by the curse which is characteristic of the English tongue.

For, observe, habitual as it has become, there is still so much life and sincerity in the expression, that we all feel our passion partly appeased in its use; and the more serious the occasion, the more practical and effective the cursing becomes. In Mr Kinglake's *History of the Crimean War*, you will find the —th Regiment at Alma is stated to have been materially assisted in maintaining position quite vital to the battle by the steady imprecation delivered at it by its colonel for half-an-hour on end. No quantity of benediction would have answered the purpose; the colonel might have said, 'Bless you, my children,' in the tenderest tones, as often as he pleased,—yet not have helped his men to keep their ground.

Fors Clavigera, Letter 20, 1872

The Cruellest Century

Yes, believe me, in spite of our political liberality, and poetical philanthropy; in spite of our almshouses, hospitals, and Sunday-schools; in spite of our missionary endeavours to preach abroad what we cannot get believed at home; and in spite of our wars against slavery, indemnified by the presentation of ingenious bills,—we shall be remembered in history as the most cruel, and therefore the most unwise, generation of men that ever yet troubled the earth:—the most cruel in proportion to their sensibility,—the most unwise in proportion to their science. No people, understanding pain, ever inflicted so much: no people, understanding facts, ever acted on them so little.

The Eagle's Nest, 1872

A Thick Skin and a Sad Mood

Mr Leslie Stephen rightly says how much better it is to have a thick skin and a good digestion. Yes, assuredly; but what is the use of knowing that, if one hasn't? In one of my saddest moods, only a week or two ago, because I had failed twice over in drawing the lifted hand of Giotto's 'Poverty'; utterly beaten and comfortless, at Assisi, I got some wholesome peace and refreshment by mere sympathy with a Bewickian little pig in the roundest and conceitedest burst of pig-blossom. His servant,—a grave old woman, with much sorrow and toil in the wrinkles of *her* skin, while his was only dimpled in its divine thickness,—was leading him, with magnanimous length of rope, down a grassy path behind the convent; stopping, of course, where he chose. Stray stalks and leaves of eatable things, in various stages of ambrosial rottenness, lay here and there; the convent walls made more savoury by their fumigation, as Mr Leslie Stephen says the Alpine pines are by his cigar. And the little joyful darling of Demeter shook his curly tail, and munched; and grunted the goodnaturedest of grunts, and snuffled the approvingest of snuffles, and was a balm and beatification to behold; and I would fain have changed places with him for a little while, or with Mr Leslie Stephen for a little while,—at luncheon, suppose,—anywhere but among the Alps. But it can't be.

Fors Clavigera, Letter 48, 1874

The Riviera

I don't think the reader has yet been informed that I inherited to the full my mother's love of tidiness and cleanliness; so that quite one of the most poetical charms of Switzerland to me, next to her white snows, was her white sleeves. Also I had my father's love of solidity and soundness,—of unveneered, unroughed, and well-finished things; and here on the Riviera there were lemons and palms, yes,—but the lemons pale, and mostly skin; the palms not much larger than parasols; the sea—blue, yes, but its beach nasty; the buildings, pompous, luxurious, painted like Grimaldi,—usually broken down at the ends, and in the middle, having sham architraves daubed over windows with no glass in them; the rocks shaly and ragged, the people filthy: and over everything, a coat of plaster dust.

Praeterita, 1885–9

Fireflies

Fonte Branda I last saw with Charles Norton, under the same arches where Dante saw it. We drank of it together, and walked together that evening on the hills above, where the fireflies among the scented thickets shone fitfully in the still undarkened air. *How* they shone! moving like fine-broken starlight through the purple leaves. How they shone! through the sunset that faded into thunderous night as I entered Siena three days before, the white edges of the mountainous clouds still lighted from the west, and the openly golden sky calm behind the Gate of Siena's heart, with its still golden words, 'Cor magis tibi Sena pandit,' and the fireflies everywhere in sky and cloud rising and falling, mixed with the lightning, and more intense than the stars.

Praeterita

HERMAN MELVILLE
1819–1891

Queequeg

With much interest I sat watching him. Savage though he was, and hideously marred about the face—at least to my taste—his countenance yet had a something in it which was by no means disagreeable. You cannot hide the soul. Through all his unearthly tattooings, I thought I saw the traces of a simple honest heart; and in his large, deep eyes, fiery black and bold, there seemed tokens of a spirit that would dare a thousand devils. And besides all this, there was a certain lofty bearing about the Pagan, which even his uncouthness could not altogether maim. He looked like a man who had never cringed and never had had a creditor. Whether it was, too, that his head being shaved, his forehead was drawn out in freer and brighter relief, and looked more expansive than it otherwise would, this I will not venture to decide; but certain it was his head was phrenologically an excellent one. It may seem ridiculous, but it reminded me of General Washington's head, as seen in the popular busts of him. It had the same long regularly graded retreating slope from above the brows, which were likewise very projecting, like two long promontories thickly wooded on top. Queequeg was George Washington cannibalistically developed.

Moby-Dick, 1851

Brit

Steering north-eastward from the Crozetts, we fell in with vast meadows of brit, the minute, yellow substance, upon which the Right Whale largely feeds. For leagues and leagues it undulated round us, so that we seemed to be sailing through boundless fields of ripe and golden wheat.

On the second day, numbers of Right Whales were seen, who, secure from the attack of a Sperm Whaler like the Pequod, with open jaws sluggishly swam through the brit, which, adhering to the fringing fibres of that wondrous Venetian blind in their mouths, was in that manner separated from the water that escaped at the lip.

As morning mowers, who side by side slowly and seethingly advance their scythes through the long wet grass of marshy meads; even so these monsters swam, making a strange, grassy, cutting sound; and leaving behind them endless swathes of blue upon the yellow sea.

Moby-Dick

A Slaughtered Whale

'Haul in the chains! Let the carcase go astern!'

The vast tackles have now done their duty. The peeled white body of the beheaded whale flashes like a marble sepulchre; though changed in hue, it has not perceptibly lost anything in bulk. It is still colossal. Slowly it floats more and more away, the water round it torn and splashed by the insatiate sharks, and the air above vexed with rapacious flights of screaming fowls, whose beaks are like so many insulting poniards in the whale. The vast white headless phantom floats further and further from the ship, and every rod that it so floats, what seem square roods of sharks and cubic roods of fowls, augment the murderous din. For hours and hours from the almost stationary ship that hideous sight is seen. Beneath the unclouded and mild azure sky, upon the fair face of the pleasant sea, wafted by the joyous breezes, that great mass of death floats on and on, till lost in infinite perspectives.

There's a most doleful and most mocking funeral! The sea-vultures all in pious mourning, the air-sharks all punctiliously in black or speckled. In life but few of them would have helped the whale, I ween, if peradventure he had needed it; but upon the banquet of his funeral they most piously do pounce. Oh, horrible vulturism of earth! from which not the mightiest whale is free.

Nor is this the end. Desecrated as the body is, a vengeful ghost survives and hovers over it to scare. Espied by some timid man-of-war or blundering discovery-vessel from afar, when the distance obscuring the swarming fowls, nevertheless still shows the white mass floating in the sun, and the white spray heaving high against it; straightway the whale's unharming corpse, with trembling fingers is set down in the log—*shoals, rocks, and breakers hereabouts: beware!* And for years afterwards, perhaps, ships shun the place; leaping over it as silly sheep leap over a vacuum, because their leader originally leaped there when a stick was held. There's your law of precedents; there's your utility of traditions; there's the story of your obstinate survival of old beliefs never bottomed on the earth, and now not even hovering in the air! There's orthodoxy!

Thus, while in life the great whale's body may have been a real terror to his foes, in his death his ghost becomes a powerless panic to a world.

Moby-Dick

Closing in for the Kill

And now that at the proper time and place, after so long and wide a preliminary cruise, Ahab,—all other whaling waters swept—seemed to have chased his foe into an ocean-fold, to slay him the more securely there; now, that he found himself hard by the very latitude and longitude where his tormenting wound had been inflicted; now that a vessel had been spoken which on the very day preceding had actually encountered Moby-Dick;—and now that all his successive meetings with various ships contrastingly concurred to show the demoniac indifference with which the white whale tore his hunters, whether sinning or sinned against; now it was that there lurked a something in the old man's eyes, which it was hardly sufferable for feeble souls to see. As the unsetting polar star, which through the live-long, arctic, six months' nights sustains its piercing, steady, central gaze; so Ahab's purpose now fixedly gleamed down upon the constant midnight of the gloomy crew. It domineered above them so, that all their bodings, doubts, misgivings, fears, were fain to hide beneath their souls, and not sprout forth a single spear or leaf.

In this foreshadowing interval too, all humour, forced or natural, vanished. Stubb no more strove to raise a smile; Starbuck no more strove to check one. Alike, joy and sorrow, hope and fear, seemed ground to finest dust, and powdered, for the time, in the clamped mortar of Ahab's iron soul. Like machines, they dumbly moved about the deck, ever conscious that the old man's despot eye was on them.

Moby-Dick

An Apparition at the Office

Now, one Sunday morning I happened to go to Trinity Church, to hear a celebrated preacher, and finding myself rather early on the ground I thought I would walk round to my chambers for a while. Luckily I had my key with me; but upon applying it to the lock, I found it resisted by something inserted from the inside. Quite surprised, I called out; when to my consternation a key was turned from within; and thrusting his lean visage at me, and holding the door ajar, the apparition of Bartleby appeared, in his shirt-sleeves, and otherwise in a strangely tattered deshabille, saying quietly that he was sorry, but he was deeply engaged just then, and—preferred not admitting me at present. In a brief word or two, he moreover added, that perhaps I had better walk round the block two or three times, and by that time he would probably have concluded his affairs.

Now, the utterly unsurmised appearance of Bartleby, tenanting my law-chambers of a Sunday morning, with his cadaverously gentlemanly *non-chalance*, yet withal firm and self-possessed, had such a strange effect upon me, that incontinently I slunk away from my own door, and did as desired. But not without sundry twinges of impotent rebellion against the mild effrontery of this unaccountable scrivener. Indeed, it was his wonderful mildness chiefly, which not only disarmed me, but unmanned me, as it were. For I consider that one, for the time, is a sort of unmanned when he tranquilly permits his hired clerk to dictate to him, and order him away from his own premises. Furthermore, I was full of uneasiness as to what Bartleby could possibly be doing in my office in his shirt-sleeves, and in an otherwise dismantled condition of a Sunday morning. Was anything amiss going on? Nay, that was out of the question. It was not to be thought of for a moment that Bartleby was an immoral person. But what could he be doing there?—copying? Nay again, whatever might be his eccentricities, Bartleby was an eminently decorous person. He would be the last man to sit down to his desk in any state approaching to nudity. Besides, it was Sunday; and there was something about Bartleby that forbade the supposition that he would by any secular occupation violate the proprieties of the day.

Nevertheless, my mind was not pacified; and full of a restless curiosity, at last I returned to the door. Without hindrance I inserted my key, opened it, and entered. Bartleby was not to be seen. I looked round anxiously, peeped behind his screen; but it was very plain that he was gone. Upon more closely examining the place, I surmised that for an indefinite period Bartleby must have ate, dressed, and slept in my office, and that too without plate, mirror, or bed. The cushioned seat of a rickety old sofa in one corner bore the faint impress of a lean, reclining form. Rolled away under his desk, I found a blanket; under the empty grate, a blacking box and brush; on a chair, a tin basin, with soap and a ragged towel; in a newspaper a few crumbs of ginger-nuts and a morsel of cheese. Yes, thought I, it is evident enough that Bartleby has been making his home here, keeping bachelor's hall all by himself. Immediately then the thought came sweeping across me, what miserable friendlessness and loneliness are here revealed! His poverty is great; but his solitude, how horrible! Think of it. Of a Sunday, Wall Street is deserted as Petra; and every night of every day it is an emptiness. This building, too, which of week-days hums with industry and life, at nightfall echoes with sheer vacancy, and all through Sunday is forlorn. And here Bartleby makes his home; sole spectator of a solitude which he has seen all populous—a sort of innocent and transformed Marius brooding among the ruins of Carthage!

For the first time in my life a feeling of overpowering stinging melancholy seized me. Before, I had never experienced aught but a not unpleasing sadness. The bond of a common humanity now drew me irresistibly to gloom. A fraternal melancholy! For both I and Bartleby were sons of Adam. I remembered the bright silks and sparkling faces I had seen that day, in gala trim, swan-like sailing down the Mississippi of Broadway; and I contrasted them with the pallid copyist, and thought to myself, Ah, happiness courts the light, so we deem the world is gay; but misery hides aloof, so we deem that misery there is none. These sad fancyings—chimeras, doubtless, of a sick and silly brain—led on to other and more special thoughts, concerning the eccentricities of Bartleby. Presentiments of strange discoveries hovered round me. The scrivener's pale form appeared to me laid out, among uncaring strangers, in its shivering winding-sheet.

Bartleby, 1853

Claggart and Billy Budd

In view of the greediness of hate for provocation, it hardly needed a purveyor to feed Claggart's passion. An uncommon prudence is habitual with the subtler depravity, for it has everything to hide. And in case of any merely suspected injury, its secretiveness voluntarily cuts it off from enlightenment or disillusion; and not unreluctantly, action is taken upon surmise as upon certainty. And the retaliation is apt to be in monstrous disproportion to the supposed offence; for when in anybody was revenge in its exactions aught else but an inordinate usurer? But how with Claggart's conscience? For though consciences are unlike as foreheads, every intelligence, not excluding the Scriptural devils who 'believe and tremble,' has one. But Claggart's conscience, being but the lawyer to his will, made ogres of trifles, probably arguing that the motive imputed to Billy in spilling the soup just when he did, together with the epithets alleged, these, if nothing more, made a strong case against him; nay, justified animosity into a sort of retributive righteousness. The Pharisee is the Guy Fawkes prowling in the hid chambers underlying some natures like Claggart's. And they can really form no conception of an unreciprocated malice. Probably, the master-at-arms' clandestine persecution of Billy was started to try the temper of the man; but it had not developed any quality in him that enmity could make official use of, or ever pervert into even plausible self-justification; so that the occurrence at the mess, petty if it were, was a welcome one to that peculiar conscience assigned to be the private mentor of Claggart; and for the rest, not improbably, it put him upon new experiments.

Billy Budd, Foretopman, written 1888–91

CHARLES KINGSLEY
1819–1875

Harthover House

And by this time they were come up to the great iron gates in front of the house; and Tom stared through them at the rhododendrons and azaleas, which were all in flower; and then at the house itself, and wondered how many chimneys there were in it, and how long ago it was built, and what was the man's name that built it, and whether he got much money for his job?

These last were very difficult questions to answer. For Harthover had been built at ninety different times, and in nineteen different styles, and looked as if somebody had built a whole street of houses of every imaginable shape, and then stirred them together with a spoon.

For the attics were Anglo-Saxon.

The third floor Norman.

The second Cinque-cento.

The first-floor Elizabethan.

The right wing Pure Doric.

The centre Early English, with a huge portico copied from the Parthenon.

The left wing pure Bœotian, which the country folk admired most of all, because it was just like the new barracks in the town, only three times as big.

The grand staircase was copied from the Catacombs at Rome.

The back staircase from the Tajmahal at Agra. This was built by Sir John's great-great-great-uncle, who won, in Lord Clive's Indian Wars, plenty of money, plenty of wounds, and no more taste than his betters.

The cellars were copied from the caves of Elephanta.

The offices from the Pavilion at Brighton.

And the rest from nothing in heaven, or earth, or under the earth.

So that Harthover House was a great puzzle to antiquarians, and a thorough Naboth's vineyard to critics, and architects, and all persons who like meddling with other men's business, and spending other men's money.

The Water-Babies, 1863

The Fens

A certain sadness is pardonable to one who watches the destruction of a grand natural phenomenon, even though its destruction bring blessings to the human race. Reason and conscience tell us, that it is right and good that the Great Fen should have become, instead of a waste and howling wilderness, a garden of the Lord, where

'All the land in flowery squares,
Beneath a broad and equal-blowing wind,
Smells of the coming summer.'

And yet the fancy may linger, without blame, over the shining meres, the golden reed-beds, the countless water-fowl, the strange and gaudy insects, the wild nature, the mystery, the majesty—for mystery and majesty there were—which haunted the deep fens for many a hundred years.

Little thinks the Scotsman, whirled down by the Great Northern Railway from Peterborough to Huntingdon, what a grand place, even twenty years ago, was that Holme and Whittlesea, which is now but a black, unsightly, steaming flat, from which the meres and reed-beds of the old world are gone, while the corn and roots of the new world have not as yet taken their place.

But grand enough it was, that black ugly place, when backed by Caistor Hanglands and Holme Wood, and the patches of the primaeval forest; while dark-green alders, and pale-green reeds, stretched for miles round the broad lagoon, where the coot clanked, and the bittern boomed, and the sedge-bird, not content with its own sweet song, mocked the notes of all the birds around; while high overhead hung, motionless, hawk beyond hawk, buzzard beyond buzzard, kite beyond kite, as far as eye could see. Far off, upon the silver mere, would rise a puff of smoke from a punt, invisible from its flatness and its white paint. Then down the wind came the boom of the great stanchion-gun; and after that sound another sound, louder as it neared; a cry as of all the bells of Cambridge, and all the hounds of Cottesmore; and overhead rushed and whirled the skein of terrified wild-fowl, screaming, piping, clacking, croaking, filling the air with the hoarse rattle of their wings, while clear above all sounded the wild whistle of the curlew, and the trumpet note of the great wild swan.

They are all gone now. No longer do the ruffs trample the sedge into a hard floor in their fighting-rings, while the sober reeves stand round, admiring the tournament of their lovers, gay with ears and tippets, no two of them alike. Gone are ruffs and reeves, spoonbills, bitterns, avosets; the very snipe, one hears, disdains to breed. Gone, too, not only from Whittlesea but from the whole world, is that most exquisite of English butterflies, *Lycaena dispar*—the great copper; and many a curious insect more. Ah, well, at least we shall have wheat and mutton instead, and no more typhus and ague; and, it is to be hoped, no more brandy-drinking and opium-eating; and children will live and not die. For it was a hard place to live in, the old Fen; a place wherein one heard of 'unexampled instances of longevity,' for the same reason that one hears of them in savage tribes—that few lived to old age at all, save those iron constitutions which nothing could break down.

Prose Idylls, 1873

WALT WHITMAN
1819–1892

New York Uniforms

Soldiers and militiamen are not the only people who wear uniforms. A uniform serves two purposes; first, to distinguish the wearers from others, and secondly, to assimilate them to each other. The universal uniform is more for the former of these than the latter; and is not only the style and substance of garments, but appearance and carriage. Come and walk in New York streets, or sit in a restaurant; we will detect some people for you by their uniforms.

Mild, foolish, dough-colored, simpering face; black cloth suit—shad-bellied, single-breasted coat, with low standing collar all round, vest buttoned close to throat, knees a little bent, toes turned out, and chin down. Episcopalian deacon.

Wild cataract of hair; absurd, bunged-up felt hat, with peaked crown; velvet coat, all friggled over with gimp, but worn; eyes rather staring, look upward. Third-rate artist.

Dress strictly respectable; hat well down on forehead; face thin, dry, close-shaven; mouth with a gripe like a vice; eye sharp and quick; brows bent; forehead scowling; step jerky and bustling. Wall Street broker.

Hands crossed behind him; step slow; dress well enough, but careless all over; face bent downward, and full of thought. Leading lawyer.

Rusty black costume; white choker; look oddly compounded of severity, superiority, curiosity, apprehension, and suspicion; shoulders stooping, chest flat. Country clergyman.

Half-a-dozen ill-dressed fellows together (this in the evening); dirty, unshorn faces; debauched expression; the halfshut eyes, and loose, hanging lips of the tribe; hoarse voices, incredibly tuneless; oaths and curses; laughs made up of a yell and a cackle; a peculiar quick, eager step, as they flock along close together. Short-boys; damnable dangerous villains.

Dirty finery, excessively plentiful; paint, both red and white; draggle-tailed dress, ill-fitting; coarse features, unintelligent; bold glance, questioning, shameless, perceptibly anxious; hideous croak or dry, brazen ring in voice; affected, but awkward, mincing, waggling gait. Harlot.

Heavy moustache; obtrusively expensive dress; big breast pin; heavy gold chain; rings; hat down over brows; loafing attitude on corner; eye furtive, glassy, expressionless; oaths; tobacco-spit. Gambler.

There, somewhat in that manner, you may learn even to distinguish the trades from each other. But now let us sketch individuals. We are sitting, we will suppose, in the St Nicholas front windows, or standing in front of Delmonico's, or anywhere in a thoroughfare. The crowd flows by; among it goes, now and then, one of these following:

A tall, slender man, round-shouldered, chin stuck out, deep-set eyes, sack-coat. His step is quick, and his arms swing awkwardly, as if he were trying to knock his elbows together behind him. Albert Brisbane the Socialist; the capitalist, too—an odd circumstance for a radical in New York! Somehow or other he always looks as if he were attempting to think out some problem a little too hard for him.

Old gentleman in carriage. A well-built, portly old man, full, ruddy face, abundant wavy—almost frizzly—white hair, good forehead, kindly, intelligent look. Dr Francis, the encyclopaedia of historical information, especially in local history and genealogy.

Tall, large, rough-looking man, in a journeyman carpenter's uniform. Coarse, sanguine complexion; strong, bristly, grizzled beard; singular eyes, of a semi-transparent, indistinct light blue, and with that sleepy look that comes when the lid rests half way down over the pupil; careless, lounging gait. Walt Whitman, the sturdy, self-conscious microcosmic, prose-poetical author of that incongruous hash of mud and gold—*Leaves of Grass.*

'Street Yarn' (newpaper article, 1856)

'A Glimpse of War's Hell-Scenes'

In one of the late movements of our troops in the valley, (near Upperville, I think,) a strong force of Moseby's mounted guerillas attack'd a train of wounded, and the guard of cavalry convoying them. The ambulances contain'd about 60 wounded, quite a number of them officers of rank. The rebels were in strength, and the capture of the train and its partial guard after a short snap was effectually accomplish'd. No sooner had our men surrender'd, the rebels instantly commenced robbing the train and murdering their prisoners, even the wounded. Here is the scene, or a sample of it, ten minutes after. Among the wounded officers in the ambulances were one, a lieutenant of regulars, and another of higher rank. These two were dragg'd out on the ground on their backs, and were now surrounded by the guerillas, a demoniac crowd, each member of which was stabbing them in different parts of their bodies. One of the officers had his feet pinn'd firmly to the ground by bayonets stuck through them and thrust into the ground. These two officers, as afterwards found on examination, had receiv'd about twenty such thrusts, some of them through the mouth, face, etc. The wounded had all been dragg'd (to give a better chance also for plunder,) out of their wagons; some had been effectually dispatch'd, and their bodies were lying there lifeless and bloody. Others, not yet dead, but horribly mutilated, were moaning or groaning. Of our men who surrender'd, most had been thus maim'd or slaughter'd.

At this instant a force of our cavalry, who had been following the train at some interval, charged suddenly upon the secesh captors, who proceeded at once to make the best escape they could. Most of them got away, but we gobbled two officers and seventeen men, in the very acts just described. The sight was one which admitted of little discussion, as may be imagined. The seventeen captur'd men and two officers were put under guard for the night, but it was decided there and then that they should die. The next morning the two officers were taken in the town, separate places, put in the centre of the street, and shot. The seventeen men were taken to an open ground, a little one side. They were placed in a hollow square, half-encompass'd by two of our cavalry regiments, one of which regiments had three days before found the bloody corpses of three of their men hamstrung and hung up by the heels to limbs of trees by Moseby's guerillas, and the other had not long before had twelve men, after surrendering, shot and then hung by the neck to limbs of trees, and jeering inscriptions pinn'd to the breast of one of the corpses, who had been a sergeant. Those three, and those twelve, had been found, I say, by these environing regiments. Now, with revolvers, they form'd the grim cordon of the seventeen prisoners. The latter were placed in the midst of the hollow square, unfasten'd, and the ironical remark made to them they were now to be given 'a chance for themselves'. A few ran for it. But what use? From every side the deadly pills came. In a few minutes the seventeen corpses strew'd the hollow square. I was curious to know whether some of the Union soldiers, some few, (some one or two at least of the youngsters,) did not abstain from shooting on the helpless men. Not one. There was no exultation, very little said, almost nothing, yet every man there contributed his shot.

Multiply the above by scores, aye hundreds—verify it in all the forms that different circumstances, individuals, places, could afford—light it with every lurid passion, the wolf's, the lion's lapping thirst for blood—the passionate, boiling volcanoes of human revenge for comrades, brothers slain—with the light of burning farms, and heaps of smutting, smouldering black embers—and in the human heart everywhere black, worse embers—and you have an inkling of this war.

Specimen Days, 1882; written 1864

A Contralto Voice

Visit this evening to my friends the J.'s—good supper, to which I did justice—lively chat with Mrs J. and I. and J. As I sat out front on the walk afterward, in the evening air, the church-choir and organ on the corner opposite gave Luther's hymn, *Ein feste burg*, very finely. The air was borne by a rich contralto. For nearly half an hour there in the dark (there was a good string of English stanzas,) came the music, firm and unhurried, with long pauses. The full silver star-beams of Lyra rose silently over the church's dim roof-ridge. Vari-color'd lights from the stain'd glass windows broke through the tree-shadows. And under all—under the Northern Crown up there, and in the fresh breeze below, and the *chiaroscuro* of the night, that liquid-full contralto.

Specimen Days

Darwinism

Of this old theory, evolution, as broach'd anew, trebled, with indeed all-devouring claims, by Darwin, it has so much in it, and is so needed as a counterpoise to yet widely prevailing and unspeakably tenacious, enfeebling superstitions—is fused, by the new man, into such grand, modest, truly scientific accompaniments—that the world of erudition, both moral and physical, cannot but be eventually better'd and broaden'd in its speculations, from the advent of Darwinism. Nevertheless, the problem of origins, human and other, is not the least whit nearer its solution. In due time the Evolution theory will have to abate its vehemence, cannot be allow'd to dominate every thing else, and will have to take its place as a segment of the circle, the cluster—as but one of many theories, many thoughts, of profoundest value—and readjusting and differentiating much, yet leaving the divine secrets just as inexplicable and unreachable as before—maybe more so.

Specimen Days

GEORGE ELIOT
(Marian Evans)
1819–1880

A Sunny Day

The eighteenth of August was one of these days, when the sunshine looked brighter in all eyes for the gloom that went before. Grand masses of cloud were hurried across the blue, and the great round hills behind the Chase seemed alive with their flying shadows; the sun was hidden for a moment, and then shone out warm again like a recovered joy; the leaves, still green, were tossed off the hedgerow trees by the wind; around the farmhouses there was a sound of clapping doors; the apples fell in the orchards; and the stray horses on the green sides of the lanes and on the common had their manes blown about their faces. And yet the wind seemed only part of the general gladness because the sun was shining. A merry day for the children, who ran and shouted to see if they could top the wind with their voices; and the grown-up people, too, were in good spirits, inclined to believe in yet finer days, when the wind had fallen. If only the corn were not ripe enough to be blown out of the husk and scattered as untimely seed!

And yet a day on which a blighting sorrow may fall upon a man. For if it be true that Nature at certain moments seems charged with a presentiment of one individual lot, must it not also be true that she seems unmindful, unconscious of another? For there is no hour that has not its births of gladness and despair, no morning brightness that does not bring new sickness to desolation as well as new forces to genius and love. There are so many of us, and our lots are so different: what wonder that Nature's mood is often in harsh contrast with the great crisis of our lives? We are children of a large family, and must learn, as such children do, not to expect that our hurts will be made much of—to be content with little nurture and caressing, and help each other the more.

Adam Bede, 1859

Jam Puffs

'Tom,' said Maggie, as they sat on the boughs of the elder-tree, eating their jam puffs, 'shall you run away tomorrow?'

'No,' said Tom slowly, when he had finished his puff, and was eyeing the third, which was to be divided between them—'No, I shan't.'

'Why, Tom? Because Lucy's coming?'

'No,' said Tom, opening his pocket-knife and holding it over the puff, with his head on one side in a dubitative manner. (It was a difficult problem to divide that very irregular polygon into two equal parts.) 'What do *I* care about Lucy? She's only a girl—*she* can't play at bandy.'

'Is it the tipsy-cake, then?' said Maggie, exerting her hypothetic powers, while she leaned forward towards Tom with her eyes fixed on the hovering knife.

'No, you silly, that'll be good the day after. It's the pudden. I know what the pudden's to be—apricot roll up—O my buttons!'

With this interjection, the knife descended on the puff and it was in two, but the result was not satisfactory to Tom, for he still eyed the halves doubtfully. At last he said:

'Shut your eyes, Maggie.'

'What for?'

'You never mind what for. Shut 'em, when I tell you.' Maggie obeyed.

'Now, which'll you have, Maggie—right hand or left?'

'I'll have that with the jam run out,' said Maggie, keeping her eyes shut to please Tom.

'Why, you don't like that, you silly. You may have it if it comes to you fair, but I shan't give it you without. Right or left—you choose, now. Ha-a-a!' said Tom, in a tone of exasperation, as Maggie peeped. 'You keep your eyes shut, now, else you shan't have any.'

Maggie's power of sacrifice did not extend so far; indeed, I fear she cared less that Tom should enjoy the utmost possible amount of puff, than that he should be pleased with her for giving him the best bit. So she shut her eyes quite close, till Tom told her to say which, and then she said, 'Left-hand.'

'You've got it,' said Tom, in rather a bitter tone.

'What! the bit with the jam run out?'

'No; here, take it,' said Tom firmly, handing decidedly the best piece to Maggie.

'O, please, Tom, have it: I don't mind—I like the other: please take this.'

'No, I shan't,' said Tom, almost crossly, beginning on his own inferior piece.

Maggie, thinking it was no use to contend further, began too, and ate up her half puff with considerable relish as well as rapidity. But Tom had finished first, and had to look on while Maggie ate her last morsel or two, feeling in himself a capacity for more. Maggie didn't know Tom was looking at her; she was seesawing on the elder bough, lost to almost everything but a vague sense of jam and idleness.

'O, you greedy thing!' said Tom, when she had swallowed the last morsel. He was conscious of having acted very fairly, and thought she ought to have considered this, and made up to him for it. He would have refused a bit of hers beforehand, but one is naturally at a different point of view before and after one's own share of puff is swallowed.

Maggie turned quite pale. 'O, Tom, why didn't you ask me?'

'*I* wasn't going to ask you for a bit, you greedy. You might have thought of it without, when you knew I gave you the best bit.'

'But I wanted you to have it—you know I did,' said Maggie in an injured tone.

'Yes, but I wasn't going to do what wasn't fair, like Spouncer. He always takes the best bit, if you don't punch him for it; and if you choose the best piece with your eyes shut, he changes his hands. But if I go halves, I'll go 'em fair—only I wouldn't be a greedy.'

With this cutting innuendo, Tom jumped down from his bough, and threw a stone with a 'hoigh!' as a friendly attention to Yap, who had also been looking on while the eatables vanished, with an agitation of his ears and feelings which could hardly have been without bitterness. Yet the excellent dog accepted Tom's attention with as much alacrity as if he had been treated quite generously.

But Maggie, gifted with that superior power of misery which distinguishes the human being and places him at a proud distance from the most melancholy chimpanzee, sat still on her bough, and gave herself up to the keen sense of unmerited reproach. She would have given the world not to have eaten all her puff, and to have saved some of it for Tom. Not but that the puff was very nice, for Maggie's palate was not at all obtuse, but she would have gone without it many times over, sooner than Tom should call her greedy and be cross with her. And he had said he wouldn't have it—and she ate it without thinking—how could she help it? The tears flowed so plentifully that Maggie saw nothing around her for the next ten minutes; but by that time resentment began to give way to the desire of reconciliation, and she jumped from her bough to look for Tom.

The Mill on the Floss, 1860

Dorothea's Engagement

'Is any one else coming to dine besides Mr Casaubon?'

'Not that I know of.'

'I hope there is some one else. Then I shall not hear him eat his soup so.'

'What is there remarkable about his soup-eating?'

'Really, Dodo, can't you hear how he scrapes his spoon? And he always blinks before he speaks. I don't know whether Locke blinked, but I'm sure I am sorry for those who sat opposite to him if he did.'

'Celia,' said Dorothea, with emphatic gravity, 'pray don't make any more observations of that kind.'

'Why not? They are quite true,' returned Celia, who had her reasons for persevering, though she was beginning to be a little afraid.

'Many things are true which only the commonest minds observe.'

'Then I think the commonest minds must be rather useful. I think it is a pity Mr Casaubon's mother had not a commoner mind: she might have taught him better.' Celia was inwardly frightened, and ready to run away, now she had hurled this light javelin.

Dorothea's feelings had gathered to an avalanche, and there could be no further preparation.

'It is right to tell you, Celia, that I am engaged to marry Mr Casaubon.'

Perhaps Celia had never turned so pale before. The paper man she was making would have had his leg injured, but for her habitual care of whatever she held in her hands. She laid the fragile figure down at once, and sat perfectly still for a few moments. When she spoke there was a tear gathering.

'O Dodo, I hope you will be happy.' Her sisterly tenderness could not but surmount other feelings at this moment, and her fears were the fears of affection.

Dorothea was still hurt and agitated.

'It is quite decided, then?' said Celia, in an awed undertone. 'And uncle knows?'

'I have accepted Mr Casaubon's offer. My uncle brought me the letter that contained it; he knew about it beforehand.'

'I beg your pardon, if I have said anything to hurt you, Dodo,' said Celia, with a slight sob. She never could have thought that she should feel as she did. There was something funereal in the whole affair, and Mr Casaubon seemed to be the officiating clergyman, about whom it would be indecent to make remarks.

'Never mind, Kitty, do not grieve. We should never admire the same people. I often offend in something of the same way; I am apt to speak too strongly of those who don't please me.'

In spite of this magnanimity Dorothea was still smarting: perhaps as much from Celia's subdued astonishment as from her small criticisms.

Middlemarch, 1871–2

A Honeymoon in Rome

Our moods are apt to bring with them images which succeed each other like the magic-lantern pictures of a doze; and in certain states of dull forlornness Dorothea all her life continued see the vastness of St Peter's, the huge bronze canopy, the excited intention in the attitudes and garments of the prophets and evangelists in the mosaics above, and the red drapery which was being hung for Christmas spreading itself everywhere like a disease of the retina.

Middlemarch

A Hidden Life

Sir James never ceased to regard Dorothea's second marriage as a mistake; and indeed this remained the tradition concerning it in Middlemarch, where she was spoken of to a younger generation as a fine girl who married a sickly clergyman, old enough to be her father, and in little more than a year after his death gave up her estate to marry his cousin—young enough to have been his son, with no property, and not well-born. Those who had not seen anything of Dorothea usually observed that she could not have been 'a nice woman', else she would not have married either the one or the other.

Certainly those determining acts of her life were not ideally beautiful. They were the mixed result of young and noble impulse struggling amidst the conditions of an imperfect social state, in which great feelings will often take the aspect of error, and great faith the aspect of illusion. For there is no creature whose inward being is so strong that it is not greatly determined by what lies outside it. A new Theresa will hardly have the opportunity of reforming a conventual life, any more than a new Antigone will spend her heroic piety in daring all for the sake of a brother's burial: the medium in which their ardent deeds took shape is for ever gone. But we insignificant people with our daily words and acts are preparing the lives of many Dorotheas, some of which may present a far sadder sacrifice than that of the Dorothea whose story we know.

Her finely-touched spirit had still its fine issues, though they were not widely visible. Her full nature, like that river of which Cyrus broke the strength, spent itself in channels which had no great name on the earth. But the effect of her being on those around her was incalculably diffusive: for the growing good of the world is partly dependent on unhistoric acts; and that things are not so ill with you and me as they might have been, is half owing to the number who lived faithfully a hidden life, and rest in unvisited tombs.

Middlemarch

Dancing Partners

Whatever might come, she, Gwendolen, was not going to be disappointed: the affair was a joke whichever way it turned, for she had never committed herself even by a silent confidence in anything Mr Grandcourt would do. Still, she noticed that he did sometimes quietly and gradually change his position according to hers, so that he could see her whenever she was dancing, and if he did not admire her—so much the worse for him.

This movement for the sake of being in sight of her was more direct than usual rather late in the evening, when Gwendolen had accepted Klesmer as a partner; and that wide-glancing personage, who saw everything and nothing by turns, said to her when they were walking, 'Mr Grandcourt is a man of taste. He likes to see you dancing.'

'Perhaps he likes to look at what is against his taste,' said Gwendolen, with a light laugh: she was quite courageous with Klesmer now. 'He may be so tired of admiring that he likes disgust for a variety.'

'Those words are not suitable to your lips,' said Klesmer, quickly, with one of his grand frowns, while he shook his hand as if to banish the discordant sounds.

'Are you as critical of words as of music?'

'Certainly I am. I should require your words to be what your face and form are—always among the meanings of a noble music.'

'That is a compliment as well as a correction. I am obliged for both. But do you know I am bold enough to wish to correct *you*, and require you to understand a joke?'

'One may understand jokes without liking them,' said the terrible Klesmer. 'I have had opera books sent me full of jokes; it was just because I understood them that I did not like them. The comic people are ready to challenge a man because he looks grave. "You don't see the witticism, sir?" "No, sir, but I see what you meant." Then I am what we call ticketed as a fellow without *esprit*. But, in fact,' said Klesmer, suddenly dropping from his quick narrative to a reflective tone, with an impressive frown, 'I am very sensible to wit and humour.'

'I am glad you tell me that,' said Gwendolen, not without some wickedness of intention. But Klesmer's thoughts had flown off on the wings of his own statement, as their habit was, and she had the wickedness all to herself. 'Pray, who is that standing near the card-room door?' she went on, seeing there the same stranger with whom Klesmer had been in animated talk on the archery-ground. 'He is a friend of yours, I think.'

'No, no; an amateur I have seen in town: Lush, a Mr Lush—too fond of Meyerbeer and Scribe—too fond of the mechanical-dramatic.'

'Thanks. I wanted to know whether you thought his face and form required that his words should be among the meanings of noble music?' Klesmer was conquered, and flashed at her a delightful smile which made them quite friendly until she begged to be deposited by the side of her mamma.

Three minutes afterwards her preparations for Grandcourt's indifference were all cancelled. Turning her head after some remark to her mother, she found that he had made his way up to her.

'May I ask if you are tired of dancing, Miss Harleth?' he began, looking down with his former unperturbed expression.

'Nor in the least.'

'Will you do me the honour—the next—or another quadrille?'

'I should have been very happy,' said Gwendolen, looking at her card, 'but I am engaged for the next to Mr Clintock—and indeed I perceive that I am doomed for every quadrille: I have not one to dispose of.' She was not sorry to punish Mr Grandcourt's tardiness, yet at the same time she would have liked to dance with him. She gave him a charming smile as she looked up to deliver her answer, and he stood still looking down at her with no smile at all.

'I am unfortunate in being too late,' he said, after a moment's pause.

'It seemed to me that you did not care for dancing,' said Gwendolen. 'I thought it might be one of the things you had left off.'

'Yes, but I have not begun to dance with you,' said Grandcourt. Always there was the same pause before he took up his cue. 'You make dancing a new thing, as you make archery.'

'Is novelty always agreeable?'

'No, no—not always.'

'Then I don't know whether to feel flattered or not. When you had once danced with me there would be no more novelty in it.'

'On the contrary; there would probably be much more.'

'That is deep. I don't understand.'

'Is it difficult to make Miss Harleth understand her power?' Here Grandcourt had turned to Mrs Davilow, who, smiling gently at her daughter, said—

'I think she does not generally strike people as slow to understand.'

'Mamma,' said Gwendolen, in a deprecating tone, 'I am adorably stupid, and want everything explained to me—when the meaning is pleasant.'

'If you are stupid, I admit that stupidity is adorable,' returned Grandcourt, after the usual pause, and without change of tone. But clearly he knew what to say.

Daniel Deronda, 1876

WILKIE COLLINS
1819–1880

A Flutter of Expectation

My first glance round me, as the man opened the door, disclosed a well-furnished breakfast-table, standing in the middle of a long room, with many windows in it. I looked from the table to the window farthest from me, and saw a lady standing at it, with her back turned towards me. The instant my eyes rested on her, I was struck by the rare beauty of her form, and by the unaffected grace of her attitude. Her figure was tall, yet not too tall; comely and well-developed, yet not fat; her head set on her shoulders with an easy, pliant firmness; her waist, perfection in the eyes of a man, for it occupied its natural place, it filled out its natural circle, it was visibly and delightfully undeformed by stays. She had not heard my entrance into the room; and I allowed myself the luxury of admiring her for a few moments, before I moved one of the chairs near me, as the least embarassing means of attracting her attention. She turned towards me immediately. The easy elegance of every movement of her limbs and body as soon as she began to advance from the far end of the room, set me in a flutter of expectation to see her face clearly. She left the window—and I said to myself, The lady is dark. She moved forward a few steps—and I said to myself, The lady is young. She approached nearer—and I said to myself (with a sense of surprise which words fail me to express), The lady is ugly!

The Woman in White, 1860

A Lawyer's Clerk

The figure came on, clad from head to foot in dreary black—a moving blot on the brilliant white surface of the sun-brightened road. He was a lean, elderly, miserably respectable man. He wore a poor old black dress-coat, and a cheap brown wig, which made no pretence of being his own natural hair. Short black trousers clung like attached old servants round his wizen legs; and rusty black gaiters hid all they could of his knobbed ungainly feet. Black crape added its mite to the decayed and dingy wretchedness of his old beaver hat; black mohair in the obsolete form of a stock, drearily encircled his neck and rose as high as his haggard jaws. The one morsel of colour he carried about him, was a lawyer's bag of blue serge as lean and limp as himself. The one attractive feature in his clean-shaven, weary old face, was a neat set of teeth—teeth (as honest as his wig), which said plainly to all inquiring eyes, 'We pass our nights on his looking-glass, and our days in his mouth.'

Armadale, 1866

The Sergeant and the Superintendent

Having brought his investigation to this point, Sergeant Cuff discovered that such a person as Superintendent Seegrave was still left in the room, upon which he summed up the proceedings for his brother-officer's benefit, as follows:

'This trifle of yours, Mr Superintendent,' says the Sergeant, pointing to the place on the door, 'has grown a little in importance since you noticed it last. At the present stage of the inquiry there are, as I take it, three discoveries to make, starting from that smear. Find out (first) whether there is any article of dress in this house with the smear of the paint on it. Find out (second) who that dress belongs to. Find out (third) how the person can account for having been in this room, and smeared the paint, between midnight and three in the morning. If the person can't satisfy you, you haven't far to look for the hand that has got the Diamond. I'll work this by myself, if you please, and detain you no longer from your regular business in the town. You have got one of your men here, I see. Leave him here at my disposal, in case I want him—and allow me to wish you good morning.'

Superintendent Seegrave's respect for the Sergeant was great; but his respect for himself was greater still. Hit hard by the celebrated Cuff, he hit back smartly, to the best of his ability, on leaving the room.

'I have abstained from expressing any opinion, so far,' says Mr Superintendent, with his military voice still in good working order. 'I have now only one remark to offer on leaving this case in your hands. There *is* such a thing, Sergeant, as making a mountain out of a molehill. Good morning.'

'There is also such a thing as making nothing out of a molehill, in consequence of your head being too high to see it.' Having returned his brother-officer's compliments in those terms, Sergeant Cuff wheeled about, and walked away to the window by himself.

Mr Franklin and I waited to see what was coming next. The Sergeant stood at the window with his hands in his pockets, looking out, and whistling the tune of 'The Last Rose of Summer' softly to himself. Later in the proceedings, I discovered that he only forgot his manners so far as to whistle, when his mind was hard at work, seeing its way inch by inch to its own private ends, on which occasions 'The Last Rose of Summer' evidently helped and encouraged him. I suppose it fitted in somehow with his character. It reminded him, you see, of his favourite roses, and, as *he* whistled it, it was the most melancholy tune going.

Turning from the window, after a minute or two, the Sergeant walked into the middle of the room, and stopped there, deep in thought, with his eyes on Miss Rachel's bedroom door. After a little he roused himself, nodded his head, as much as to say, 'That will do,' and, addressing me, asked for ten minutes' conversation with my mistress, at her ladyship's earliest convenience.

Leaving the room with this message, I heard Mr Franklin ask the Sergeant a question, and stopped to hear the answer also at the threshold of the door.

'Can you guess yet,' inquired Mr Franklin, 'who has stolen the Diamond?'

'*Nobody has stolen the Diamond*,' answered Sergeant Cuff.

We both started at that extraordinary view of the case, and both earnestly begged him to tell us what he meant.

'Wait a little,' said the Sergeant. 'The pieces of the puzzle are not all put together yet.'

The Moonstone, 1868

JOHN TYNDALL
1820–1893

Michael Faraday

We have heard much of Faraday's gentleness and sweetness and tenderness. It is all true, but it is very incomplete. You cannot resolve a powerful nature into these elements, and Faraday's character would have been less admirable than it was had it not embraced forces and tendencies to which the silky adjectives 'gentle' and 'tender' would by no means apply. Underneath his sweetness and gentleness was the heat of a volcano. He was a man of excitable and fiery nature; but through high self-discipline he had converted the fire into a central glow and motive power of life, instead of permitting it to waste itself in useless passion. 'He that is slow to anger,' saith the sage, 'is greater than the mighty, and he that ruleth his own spirit than he that taketh a city.' Faraday was *not* slow to anger, but he completely ruled his own spirit, and thus, though he took no cities, he captivated all hearts.

Faraday as a Discoverer, 1868

MATTHEW ARNOLD
1822–1888

Arthur Hugh Clough

In the study of art, poetry, or philosophy, he had the most undivided and disinterested love for his object in itself, the greatest aversion to mixing up with it anything accidental or personal. His interest was in literature itself; and it was this which gave so rare a stamp to his character, which kept him so free from all taint of littleness. In the saturnalia of ignoble personal passions, of which the struggle for literary success, in old and crowded communities, offers so sad a spectacle, he never mingled. He had not yet traduced his friends, nor flattered his enemies, nor disparaged what he admired, nor praised what he despised. Those who knew him well had the conviction that, even with time, these literary arts would never be his.

On Translating Homer: Last Words, 1862

Children of the Future

Children of the future, whose day has not yet dawned, you, when that day arrives, will hardly believe what obstructions were long suffered to prevent its coming! You who, with all your faults, have neither the aridity of aristocracies, nor the narrow-mindedness of middle classes, you, whose power of simple enthusiasm is your great gift, will not comprehend how progress towards man's best perfection—the adorning and ennobling of his spirit—should have been reluctantly undertaken; how it should have been for years and years retarded by barren commonplaces, by worn-out clap-traps. You will wonder at the labour of its friends in proving the self-proving; you will know nothing of the doubts, the fears, the prejudices they had to dispel; nothing of the outcry they had to encounter; of the fierce protestations of life from policies which were dead and did not know it, and the shrill querulous upbraiding from publicists in their dotage. But you, in your turn, with difficulties of your own, will then be mounting some new step in the arduous ladder whereby man climbs towards his perfection;

towards that unattainable but irresistible lode-star, gazed after with earnest longing, and invoked with bitter tears; the longing of thousands of hearts, the tears of many generations.

A French Eton, 1864

Vivacity

Mr Wright, one of the many translators of Homer, has published a letter to the Dean of Canterbury, complaining of some remarks of mine, uttered now a long while ago, on his version of the *Iliad*. One cannot be always studying one's own works, and I was really under the impression, till I saw Mr Wright's complaint, that I had spoken of him with all respect. The reader may judge of my astonishment, therefore, at finding, from Mr Wright's pamphlet, that I had 'declared with much solemnity that there is not any proper reason for his existing.' That I never said; but, on looking back at my Lectures on translating Homer, I find that I did say, not that Mr Wright, but that Mr Wright's version of the *Iliad*, repeating in the main the merits and defects of Cowper's version, as Mr Sotheby's repeated those of Pope's version, had, if I might be pardoned for saying so, no proper reason for existing. Elsewhere I expressly spoke of the merit of his version; but I confess that the phrase, qualified as I have shown, about its want of a proper reason for existing, I used. Well, the phrase had, perhaps, too much vivacity; we have all of us a right to exist, we and our works; an unpopular author should be the last person to call in question this right. So I gladly withdraw the offending phrase, and I am sorry for having used it; Mr Wright, however, would perhaps be more indulgent to my vivacity, if he considered that we are none of us likely to be lively much longer. My vivacity is but the last sparkle of flame before we are all in the dark, the last glimpse of colour before we all go into drab,—the drab of the earnest, prosaic, practical, austerely literal future. Yes, the world will soon be the Philistines'! and then, with every voice, not of thunder, silenced, and the whole earth filled and ennobled every morning by the magnificent roaring of the young lions of the *Daily Telegraph*, we shall all yawn in one another's faces with the dismallest, the most unimpeachable gravity.

Preface to *Essays in Criticism*, 1865

Oxford

No, we are all seekers still! seekers often make mistakes, and I wish mine to redound to my own discredit only, and not to touch Oxford. Beautiful city! so venerable, so lovely, so unravaged by the fierce intellectual life of our century, so serene!

'There are our young barbarians, all at play!'

And yet, steeped in sentiment as she lies, spreading her gardens to the moonlight, and whispering from her towers the last enchantments of the

Middle Age, who will deny that Oxford, by her ineffable charm, keeps ever calling us nearer to the true goal of all of us, to the ideal, to perfection,—to beauty, in a word, which is only truth seen from another side?—nearer, perhaps, than all the science of Tübingen. Adorable dreamer, whose heart has been so romantic! who hast given thyself so prodigally, given thyself to sides and to heroes not mine, only never to the Philistines! home of lost causes, and forsaken beliefs, and unpopular names, and impossible loyalties! what example could ever so inspire us to keep down the Philistine in ourselves, what teacher could ever so save us from that bondage to which we are all prone, that bondage which Goethe, in his incomparable lines on the death of Schiller, makes it his friend's highest praise (and nobly did Schiller deserve the praise) to have left miles out of sight behind him;—the bondage of '*was uns alle bändigt,* DAS GEMEINE!' She will forgive me, even if I have unwittingly drawn upon her a shot or two aimed at her unworthy son; for she is generous, and the cause in which I fight is, after all, hers. Apparitions of a day, what is our puny warfare against the Philistines, compared with the warfare which this queen of romance has been waging against them for centuries, and will wage after we are gone?

Preface to *Essays in Criticism*

Sweetness, Light, and the Social Idea

The pursuit of perfection, then, is the pursuit of sweetness and light. He who works for sweetness and light, works to make reason and the will of God prevail. He who works for machinery, he who works for hatred, works only for confusion. Culture looks beyond machinery, culture hates hatred; culture has one great passion, the passion for sweetness and light. It has one even yet greater!—the passion for making them *prevail.* It is not satisfied till we *all* come to a perfect man; it knows that the sweetness and light of the few must be imperfect until the raw and unkindled masses of humanity are touched with sweetness and light. If I have not shrunk from saying that we must work for sweetness and light, so neither have I shrunk from saying that we must have a broad basis, must have sweetness and light for as many as possible. Again and again I have insisted how those are the happy moments of humanity, how those are the marking epochs of a people's life, how those are the flowering times for literature and art and all the creative power of genius, when there is a *national* glow of life and thought, when the whole of society is in the fullest measure permeated by thought, sensible to beauty, intelligent and alive. Only it must be *real* thought and *real* beauty; *real* sweetness and *real* light. Plenty of people will try to give the masses, as they call them, an intellectual food prepared and adapted in the way they think proper for the actual condition of the masses. The ordinary popular literature is an example of this way of working on the masses. Plenty of people will try to indoctrinate the masses with the set of ideas and judgments constituting the creed of their own profession or party. Our religious and political organisations give an example of this way of working on the masses. I condemn neither way; but culture works differently. It does not try to teach down to the level of inferior classes; it does not try to win them for this or that sect of its own, with ready-made judgments and watchwords. It seeks to do away with classes; to make the best that has been thought and known in the world current everywhere; to make all men live in an atmosphere of sweetness and light, where they may use ideas, as it uses them itself, freely,—nourished, and not bound by them.

This is the *social idea*; and the men of culture are the true apostles of equality. The great men of culture are those who have had a passion for diffusing, for making prevail, for carrying from one end of society to the other, the best knowledge, the best ideas of their time; who have laboured to divest knowledge of all that was harsh, uncouth, difficult, abstract, professional, exclusive; to humanise it, to make it efficient outside the clique of the cultivated and learned, yet still remaining the *best* knowledge and thought of the time . . .

Culture and Anarchy, 1869

What to Look For in Wordsworth

Finally, the 'scientific system of thought' in Wordsworth gives us at last such poetry as this, which the devout Wordsworthian accepts—

'O for the coming of that glorious time
When, prizing knowledge as her noblest wealth
And best protection, this Imperial Realm,
While she exacts allegiance, shall admit
An obligation, on her part, to *teach*
Them who are born to serve her and obey;
Binding herself by statute to secure,
For all the children whom her soil maintains,
The rudiments of letters, and inform
The mind with moral and religious truth.'

Wordsworth calls Voltaire dull, and surely the production of these un-Voltairian lines must have been imposed on him as a judgment! One can hear them being quoted at a Social Science Congress; one can call up the whole scene. A great room in one of our dismal provincial towns; dusty air and jaded afternoon daylight; benches full of men with bald heads and women in spectacles; an orator lifting up his face from a manuscript written within and without to declaim these lines of Wordsworth; and in the soul of any poor child of nature who may have wandered in thither, an unutterable sense of lamentation, and mourning, and woe!

'But turn we,' as Wordsworth says, 'from these bold, bad men,' the haunters of Social Science Congresses. And let us be on our guard, too, against the exhibitors and extollers of a 'scientific system of thought' in Wordsworth's poetry. The poetry will never be seen aright while they thus exhibit it. The cause of its greatness is simple, and may be told quite simply. Wordsworth's poetry is great because of the extraordinary power with which Wordsworth feels the joy offered to us in nature, the joy offered to us in the simple primary affections and duties; and because of the extraordinary power with which, in case after case, he shows us this joy, and renders it so as to make us share it.

'Wordsworth', *Essays in Criticism, Second Series,* 1888

Criticism of Life

It is important, therefore, to hold fast to this: that poetry is at bottom a criticism of life; that the greatness of a poet lies in his powerful and beautiful application of ideas to life,—to the question: How to live. Morals are often treated in a narrow and false fashion; they are bound up with systems of thought and belief which have had their day; they are fallen into the hands of pedants and professional dealers; they grow tiresome to some of us. We find attraction, at times, even in a poetry of revolt against them; in a poetry which might take for its motto Omar Kheyam's words: 'Let us make up in the tavern for the time which we have wasted in the mosque.' Or we find attractions in a poetry indifferent to them; in a poetry where the contents may be what they will, but where the form is studied and exquisite. We delude ourselves in either case; and the best cure for our delusion is to let our minds rest upon that great and inexhaustible word *life*, until we learn to enter into its meaning. A poetry of revolt against moral ideas is a poetry of revolt against *life*; a poetry of indifference towards moral ideas is a poetry of indifference towards *life*.

'Wordsworth', *Essays in Criticism, Second Series*

ULYSSES S. GRANT
1822–1885

The Surrender of Robert E. Lee

I had known General Lee in the old army, and had served with him in the Mexican War; but did not suppose, owing to the difference in our age and rank, that he would remember me; while I would more naturally remember him distinctly, because he was the chief of staff of General Scott in the Mexican War.

When I had left camp that morning I had not expected so soon the result that was then taking place, and consequently was in rough garb. I was without a sword, as I usually was when on horseback on the field, and wore a soldier's blouse for a coat, with the shoulder straps of my rank to indicate to the army who I was. When I went into the house I found General Lee. We greeted each other, and after shaking hands took our seats. I had my staff with me, a good portion of whom were in the room during the whole of the interview.

What General Lee's feelings were I do not know. As he was a man of much dignity, with an impassible face, it was impossible to say whether he felt inwardly glad that the end had finally come, or felt sad over the result, and was too manly to show it. Whatever his feelings, they were entirely concealed from my observation; but my own feelings, which had been quite jubilant on the receipt of his letter, were sad and depressed. I felt like anything rather than rejoicing at the downfall of a foe who had fought so long and valiantly, and had suffered so much for a cause, though that cause was, I believe, one of the worst for which a people ever fought, and one for which there was the least excuse. I do not question, however, the sincerity of the great mass of those who were opposed to us.

General Lee was dressed in a full uniform which was entirely new, and was wearing a sword of considerable value, very likely the sword which had been presented by the State of Virginia; at all events, it was an entirely different sword from the one that would ordinarily be worn in the field. In my rough traveling suit, the uniform of a private with the straps of a lieutenant-general, I must have contrasted very strangely with a man so handsomely dressed, six feet high and of faultless form. But this was not a matter that I thought of until afterwards.

We soon fell into a conversation about old army times. He remarked that he remembered me very well in the old army; and I told him that as a matter of course I remembered him perfectly, but from the difference in our rank and years (there being about sixteen years' difference in our ages), I had thought it very likely that I had not attracted his attention sufficiently to be remembered by him after such a long interval. Our conversation grew so pleasant that I almost forgot the object of our meeting. After the conversation had run on in this style for some time, General Lee called my attention to the object of our meeting, and said that he had asked for this interview for the purpose of getting from me the terms I proposed to give his army. I said that I meant merely that his army should lay down their arms, not to take them up again during the continuance of the war unless duly and properly exchanged. He said that he had so understood my letter.

Personal Memoirs, 1885

FRANCIS PARKMAN
1823–1893

Hunting Buffalo

The danger of the chase arises not so much from the onset of the wounded animal as from the nature of the ground which the hunter must ride over. The prairie does not always present a smooth, level, and uniform surface; very often it is broken with hills and hollows, intersected by ravines, and in the remoter parts studded by the stiff wild-sage bushes. The most formidable obstructions, however, are the burrows of wild animals, wolves, badgers, and particularly prairie-dogs, with whose holes the ground for a very great extent is frequently honeycombed. In the blindness of the chase the hunter rushes over it unconscious of danger; his horse, at full career, thrusts his leg deep into one of the burrows; the bone snaps, the rider is hurled forward to the ground and probably killed. Yet accidents in buffalo running happen less frequently than one would suppose; in the recklessness of the chase, the hunter enjoys all the impunity of a drunken man, and may ride in safety over gullies and declivities where, should he attempt to pass in his sober senses, he would infallibly break his neck.

The Oregon Trail, 1849

The Character of La Salle

Here is a strange confession for a man like La Salle. Without doubt, the timidity of which he accuses himself had some of its roots in pride; but not the less was his pride vexed and humbled by it. It is surprising that, being what he was, he could have brought himself to such an avowal under any circumstances or any pressure of distress. Shyness; a morbid fear of committing himself; and incapacity to express, and much more to simulate, feeling,—a trait sometimes seen in those with whom feeling is most deep,—are strange ingredients in the character of a man who had grappled so dauntlessly with life on its harshest and rudest side. They were deplorable defects for one in his position. He lacked that sympathetic power, the inestimable gift of the true leader of men, in which lies the difference between a willing and a constrained obedience. This solitary being, hiding his shyness under a cold reserve, could rouse no enthusiasm in his followers. He lived in the purpose which he had made a part of himself, nursed his plans in secret, and seldom asked or accepted advice. He trusted himself, and learned more and more to trust no others. One may fairly infer that distrust was natural to him; but the inference may possibly be wrong. Bitter experience had schooled him to it; for he lived among snares, pitfalls, and intriguing enemies. He began to doubt even the associates who, under representations he had made them in perfect good faith, had staked their money on his enterprise, and lost it, or were likely to lose it. They pursued him with advice and complaint, and half believed that he was what his maligners called him,—a visionary or a madman. It galled him that they had suffered for their trust in him, and that they had repented their trust. His lonely and shadowed nature needed the mellowing sunshine of success, and his whole life was a fight with adversity.

All that appears to the eye is his intrepid conflict with obstacles without; but this, perhaps, was no more arduous than the invisible and silent strife of a nature at war with itself,—the pride, aspiration, and bold energy that lay at the base of his character battling against the superficial weakness that mortified and angered him. In such a man, the effect of such an infirmity is to concentrate and intensify the force within. In one form or another, discordant natures are common enough; but very rarely is the antagonism so irreconcilable as it was in him. And the greater the antagonism, the greater the pain. There are those in whom the sort of timidity from which he suffered is matched with no quality that strongly revolts against it. These gentle natures may at least have peace, but for him there was no peace.

Cavelier de La Salle stands in history like a statue cast in iron; but his own unwilling pen betrays the man, and reveals in the stern, sad figure an object of human interest and pity.

La Salle and the Discovery of the Great West, 1869

The Expedition against Louisbourg (1744–5): The Chaplain

Equally zealous, after another fashion, was the Rev. Samuel Moody, popularly known as Father Moody, or Parson Moody, minister of York and senior chaplain of the expedition. Though about seventy years old, he was amazingly tough and sturdy. He still lives in the traditions of York as the spiritual despot of the settlement and the uncompromising guardian of its manners and doctrine, predominating over it like a rough little village pope. The comparison would have kindled his burning wrath, for he abhorred the Holy Father as an embodied Antichrist. Many are the stories told of him by the descendants of those who lived under his rod, and sometimes felt its weight; for he was known to have corrected offending parishioners with his cane. When some one of his flock, nettled by his strictures from the pulpit, walked in dudgeon towards the church door, Moody would shout after him, 'Come back, you graceless sinner, come back!' or if any ventured to the alehouse of a Saturday night, the strenuous pastor would go in after them, collar them, drag them out, and send them home with rousing admonition. Few dared gainsay him, by reason both of his irritable temper and of the thick-skinned insensibility that encased him like armor of proof. And while his pachydermatous nature made him invulnerable as a rhinoceros, he had at the same time a rough and ready humor that supplied keen weapons for the warfare of words and made him a formidable antagonist. This commended him to the rude borderers, who also relished the sulphurous theology of their spiritual dictator, just as they liked the raw and fiery liquors that would have scorched more susceptible stomachs. What they did not like was the pitiless length of his prayers, which sometimes kept them afoot above two hours shivering in the polar cold of the unheated meeting-house, and which were followed by sermons of equal endurance; for the old man's lungs were of brass, and his nerves of hammered iron. Some of the sufferers ventured to remonstrate; but this only exasperated him, till one parishioner, more worldly wise than the rest, accompanied his modest petition for mercy with the gift of a barrel of cider, after which the parson's ministrations were perceptibly less exhausting than before. He had an irrepressible conscience and a highly aggressive sense of duty, which made him an intolerable meddler in the affairs of other people, and which, joined to an underlying kindness of heart, made him so indiscreet in his charities that his wife and children were often driven to vain protest against the excesses of his almsgiving. The old Puritan fanaticism was rampant in him; and when he sailed for Louisbourg, he took with him an axe, intended, as he said, to hew down the altars of Antichrist and demolish his idols.

A Half-Century of Conflict, 1892

WILLIAM ALLINGHAM
1824–1889

A Pew in Ballyshannon

Our Pew, painted like the rest a yellowish colour supposed to imitate oak, was half-way up the Church, on the right-hand side of the central aisle, and had the distinction of a tall flat Monument of wood (or it seemed tall), painted black in George the Second taste, rising on the wall behind it. Atop was a black urn with faded gold festoons; at each side a pilaster with faded gold flutings; and there was a long inscription in faded gold letters.

It seems to me very curious that, after sitting so many an hour, so many a year, in that Pew, and recollecting numberless little things around me there, I cannot find in my memory one word of that inscription, except 'SACRED' in a line by itself at the top, in Old English letters—not even the chief name, which was a lady's, (a remote and very slightly interesting relation or connection of ours, she must have been) nor the import of those Roman symbols which so ingeniously disguise a date to modern eyes. The wording no doubt was highly conventional, as nearly as possible meaningless, and felt by the child to be a sort of dull puzzle which after some attempts it was better to avoid. Had it been *verse*, of even moderate quality, it would have fixed itself in my memory; with point, it would have stuck there for ever.

A Diary, published 1907

A Reading by Tennyson

Farringford, Sunday, June 25.—Fine—at breakfast A. T. with his letters, one from D. of Argyll. Swinburne—Venables. Out and meet the Kings—Mrs Cameron. Return to Farringford. Dinner (which is at 6.30 always). Sitting at claret in the drawing-room we see the evening sunlight on the landscape. I go to the top of the house alone; have a strong sense of being in Tennyson's; green summer, ruddy light in the sky. When I came down to drawing-room found A. T. with a book in his hand; the Kings expectant. He accosted me, 'Allingham, would it disgust you if I read "Maud"? Would you expire?'

I gave a satisfactory reply and he accordingly read 'Maud' all through, with some additions recently made. His interpolated comments very amusing.

'This is what was called namby-pamby!'—'That's wonderfully fine!'—'That was very hard to read; could you have read it? I don't think so.'

1865; *A Diary*

A Conversation with Browning

March 10.—At Hyde Park Corner meet Browning. 'How odd! made sure I had just seen you in another part of town and differently dressed. I don't quite believe in *doppelgängers*.'

Browning asks me about Byron article in *Fraser*, and praises it most warmly. 'Shouldn't mind if my name were at the bottom of it. Only you did not say half a hundredth part as much as might be said of Byron's baseness and brutality.

'I might have rated Byron higher intellectually than you have done, in some respects, but what you have said of him morally is mild to what he deserves.'

He then spoke of Disraeli. 'What a humbug he is! Won't I give it him one of these days!' Royal Academy dinner, Dizzy's speech. 'What struck him most was "the *imagination* of the British School of Art, amid ugly streets and dull skies, etc. etc."'

Afterwards Disraeli came up to Browning and said, 'What do you think of this Exhibition?'

Browning wished to hear Disraeli's opinion. Disraeli said—'What strikes me is the utter and hopeless want of imagination' (as much as to say, you didn't think me such a fool as I seemed in my speech!)

Browning told this to Gladstone, who said pungently, 'It's hellish! He is like that in the House too—it's hellish!'

'And so it is,' added Browning.

1876; *A Diary*

GEORGE MACDONALD
1824–1905

The Goblins' Creatures

About this time, the gentlemen whom the king had left behind him to watch over the princess, had each occasion to doubt the testimony of his own eyes, for more than strange were the objects to which they would bear witness. They were of one sort—creatures—but so grotesque and misshapen as to be more like a child's drawings upon his slate than anything natural. They saw them only at night, while on guard about the house. The testimony of the man who first reported having seen one of them was that, as he was walking slowly round the house, while yet in the shadow, he caught sight of a creature standing on its hind legs in the moonlight, with its fore feet upon a window ledge, staring in at the window. Its body might have been that of a dog or wolf—he thought, but he declared on his honour that its head was twice the size it ought to have been for the size of its body, and as round as a ball, while the face, which it turned upon him as it fled, was more like one carved by a boy upon the turnip inside which he is going to put a candle, than anything else he could think of. It rushed into the garden. He sent an arrow after it, and thought he must have struck it; for it gave an unearthly howl, and he could not find his arrow any more than the beast, although he searched all about the place where it vanished. They laughed at him until he was driven to hold his tongue; and said he must have taken too long a pull at the ale-jug. But before two nights were over, he had one to side with him; for he too had seen something strange, only quite different from that reported by the other. The description the second man gave of the creature he had seen, was yet more grotesque and unlikely. They were both laughed at by the rest; but night after night another came over to their side, until at last there was only one left to laugh at all his companions. Two nights more passed, and he saw nothing; but on the third, he came rushing from the garden to the other two before the house, in such an agitation that they declared—for it was their turn now—that the band of his helmet was cracking under his chin with the rising of his hair inside it. Running with him into that part of the garden which I have already described, they saw a score of creatures, to not one of which they could give a name, and not one of which was like another, hideous and ludricrous at once, gambolling on the lawn in the moonlight. The supernatural or rather subnatural ugliness of their faces, the length of legs and necks in some, the apparent absence of both or either in others, made the spectators, although in one consent as to what they saw, yet doubtful, as I have said, of the evidence of their own eyes—and ears as well; for the noises they made, although not loud, were as uncouth and varied as their forms, and could be described neither as grunts nor squeaks nor roars nor howls nor barks nor yells nor screams nor croaks nor hisses nor mews nor shrieks, but only as something like all of them mingled in one horrible dissonance. Keeping in the shade, the watchers had a few moments to recover themselves before the hideous assembly suspected their presence; but all at once, as if by common consent, they scampered off in the direction of a great rock, and vanished before the men had come to themselves sufficiently to think of following them.

My readers will suspect what these were; but I will now give them full information concerning them. They were of course household animals belonging to the goblins, whose ancestors had taken their ancestors many centuries before from the upper regions of light into the lower regions of darkness. The original stocks of these horrible creatures were very much the same as the animals now seen about farms and homes in the country, with the exception of a few of them, which had been wild creatures, such as foxes, and indeed wolves and small bears, which the goblins, from their proclivity towards the animal creation, had caught when cubs and tamed. But in the course of time, all had undergone even greater changes than had passed upon their owners. They had altered—that is, their descendants had altered—into such creatures as I have not attempted to describe except in the vaguest manner—the various parts of their bodies assuming, in an apparently arbitrary and self-willed manner, the most abnormal developments. Indeed, so little did any distinct type predominate in some of the bewildering results, that you could only have guessed at any known animal as the original, and even then, what likeness remained would be more one of general expression than of definable conformation. But what increased the gruesomeness tenfold, was that, from constant domestic, or indeed rather family association with the goblins, their countenances had grown in grotesque resemblance to the human. No one understands animals who does not see that every one of them, even amongst the fishes, it may be with a dimness and vagueness infinitely remote, yet shadows the human; in the case of these the human resemblance had greatly increased: while their owners had sunk towards them, they had risen towards their owners. But the conditions of subterranean life being equally unnatural for both, while the goblins were worse, the creatures had not improved by the approximation, and its result would have appeared far more ludicrous than consoling to the warmest lover of animal nature.

The Princess and the Goblin, 1872

THOMAS HENRY HUXLEY
1825–1895

A Word for Cinderella

Thus, when Mr Lilly, like another Solomon Eagle, goes about proclaiming 'Woe to this wicked city,' and denouncing physical science as the evil genius of modern days—mother of materialism, and fatalism, and all sorts of other condemnable isms—I venture to beg him to lay the blame on the right shoulders; or, at least, to put in the dock, along with Science, those sinful sisters of hers, Philosophy and Theology, who, being so much older, should have known better than the poor Cinderella of the schools and universities over which they have so long dominated. No doubt modern society is diseased enough; but then it does not differ from older civilisations in that respect. Societies of men are fermenting masses, and, as beer has what the Germans call 'Oberhefe' and 'Unterhefe,' so every society that has existed has had its scum at the top and its dregs at the bottom; but I doubt if any of the 'ages of faith' had less scum or less dregs, or even showed a proportionally greater quantity of sound wholesome stuff in the vat. I think it would puzzle Mr Lilly, or any one else, to adduce convincing evidence that, at any period of the world's history, there was a more widespread sense of social duty, or a greater sense of justice, or of the obligation of mutual help, than in this England of ours. Ah! but, says Mr Lilly, these are all products of our Christian inheritance; when Christian dogmas vanish virtue will disappear too, and the ancestral ape and tiger will have full play. But there are a good many people who think it obvious that Christianity also inherited a good deal from Paganism and from Judaism; and that, if the Stoics and the Jews revoked their bequest, the moral property of Christianity would realise very little. And, if morality has survived the stripping off of several sets of clothes which have been found to fit badly, why should it not be able to get on very well in the light and handy garments which Science is ready to provide?

But this by the way. If the diseases of society consist in the weakness of its faith in the existence of the God of the theologians, in a future state, and in uncaused volitions, the indication, as the doctors say, is to suppress Theology and Philosophy, whose bickerings about things of which they know nothing have been the prime cause and continual sustenance of that evil scepticism which is the Nemesis of meddling with the unknowable.

Cinderella is modestly conscious of her ignorance of these high matters. She lights the fire, sweeps the house, and provides the dinner; and is rewarded by being told that she is a base creature, devoted to low and material interests. But in her garret she has fairy visions out of the ken of the pair of shrews who are quarrelling down stairs. She sees the order which pervades the seeming disorder of the world; the great drama of evolution, with its full share of pity and terror, but also with abundant goodness and beauty, unrolls itself before her eyes; and she learns, in her heart of hearts, the lesson, that the foundation of morality is to have done, once and for all, with lying; to give up pretending to believe that for which there is no evidence, and repeating unintelligible propositions about things beyond the possibilities of knowledge.

She knows that the safety of morality lies neither in the adoption of this or that philosophical speculation, or this or that theological creed, but in a real and living belief in that fixed order of nature which sends social disorganisation upon the track of immorality, as surely as it sends physical disease after physical trespasses. And of that firm and lively faith it is her high mission to be the priestess.

'Science and Morals', 1886

Kicking Down the Ladder

Man, the animal, in fact, has worked his way to the headship of the sentient world, and has become the superb animal which he is, in virtue of his success in the struggle for existence. The conditions having been of a certain order, man's organization has adjusted itself to them better than that of his competitors in the cosmic strife. In the case of mankind, the self-assertion, the unscrupulous seizing upon all that can be grasped, the tenacious holding of all that can be kept, which constitute the essence of the struggle for existence, have answered. For his successful progress, throughout the savage state, man has been largely indebted to those qualities which he shares with the ape and the tiger; his exceptional physical organization; his cunning, his sociability, his curiosity, and his imitativeness; his ruthless and ferocious destructiveness when his anger is roused by opposition.

But, in proportion as men have passed from anarchy to social organization, and in proportion as civilization has grown in worth, these deeply ingrained serviceable qualities have become defects. After the manner of successful persons, civilized man would gladly kick down the ladder by which he has climbed. He would be only too pleased to see 'the ape and tiger die.' But they decline to suit his convenience; and the unwelcome intrusion of these boon companions of his hot youth into the ranged existence of civil life adds pains and griefs, innumerable and immeasurably great, to those which the cosmic process necessarily brings on the mere animal. In fact, civilized man brands all these ape and tiger promptings with the name of sins; he punishes many of the acts which flow from them as crimes; and, in extreme cases, he does his best to put an end to the survival of the fittest of former days by axe and rope.

'Evolution and Ethics', 1893

An Incomparable Chameleon

Man is the most consummate of all mimics in the animal world; none but himself can draw or model; none comes near him in the scope, variety, and exactness of vocal imitation; none is such a master of gesture; while he seems to be impelled thus to imitate for the pure pleasure of it. And there is no such another emotional chameleon. By a purely reflex operation of the mind, we take the hue of passion of those who are about us, or, it may be, the complementary colour. It is not by any conscious 'putting one's self in the place' of a joyful or a suffering person that the state of mind we call sympathy usually arises; indeed, it is often contrary to one's sense of right, and in spite of one's will, that 'fellow-feeling makes us wondrous kind,' or the reverse. However complete may be the indifference to public opinion, in a cool, intellectual view, of the traditional sage, it has not yet been my fortune to meet with any actual sage who took its hostile manifestations with entire equanimity. Indeed, I doubt if the philosopher lives, or ever has lived, who could know himself to be heartily despised by a street boy without some irritation.

'Evolution and Ethics: Prolegomena', 1894

HENRY WALTER BATES

1825–1892

At the Mercy of the Fire-Ant

The soil of the whole village is undermined by it: the ground is perforated with the entrances to their subterranean galleries, and a little sandy dome occurs here and there, where the insects bring their young to receive warmth near the surface. The houses are over-run with them; they dispute every fragment of food with the inhabitants, and destroy clothing for the sake of the starch. All eatables are obliged to be suspended in baskets from the rafters, and the cords well soaked with copaüba balsam, which is the only means known of preventing them from climbing. They seem to attack persons out of sheer malice; if we stood for a few moments in the street, even at a distance from their nests, we were sure to be over-run and severely punished, for the moment an ant touched the flesh, he secured himself with his jaws, doubled in his tail, and stung with all his might. When we were seated on chairs in the evenings in front of the house to enjoy a chat with our neighbours, we had stools to support our feet, the legs of which as well as those of the chairs, were well anointed with balsam. The cords of hammocks are obliged to be smeared in the same way to prevent the ants from paying sleepers a visit.

The Naturalist on the River Amazons, 1863

A Jungle Chorus

The noises of animals began just as the sun sunk behind the trees after a sweltering afternoon, leaving the sky above the intensest shade of blue. Two flocks of howling monkeys, one close to our canoe, the other about a furlong distant, filled the echoing forests with their dismal roaring. Troops of parrots, including the hyacinthine macaw we were in search of, began to pass over; the different styles of cawing and screaming of the various species making a terrible discord. Added to these noises were the songs of strange Cicadas, one large kind perched high on the trees around our little haven setting up a most piercing chirp; it began with the usual harsh jarring note of its tribe, until it ended in a long and loud note resembling the steam-whistle of a locomotive engine. Half-a-dozen of these wonderful performers made a considerable item in the evening concert. . . . The uproar of beasts, birds and insects lasted but a short time; the sky quickly lost its intense hue, and the night set in. Then began the tree-frogs—quack-quack, drum-drum, hoo-hoo; these, accompanied by a melancholy nightjar, kept up their monotonous cries until very late.

The Naturalist on the River Amazons

WALTER BAGEHOT
1826–1877

Statesmanship and Public Opinion

A constitutional statesman is in general a man of common opinions and uncommon abilities. The reason is obvious. When we speak of a free government, we mean a government in which the sovereign power is divided, in which a single decision is not absolute, where argument has an office. The essence of the 'gouvernement des avocats,' as the Emperor Nicholas called it, is that you must persuade so many persons. The appeal is not to the solitary decision of a single statesman; not to Richelieu or Nesselrode alone in his closet; but to the jangled mass of men, with a thousand pursuits, a thousand interests, a thousand various habits. Public opinion, as it is said, rules; and public opinion is the opinion of the average man. Fox used to say of Burke: 'Burke is a wise man; but he is wise too soon.' The average man will not bear this. He is a cool, common person, with a considerate air, with figures in his mind, with his own business to attend to, with a set of ordinary opinions arising from and suited to ordinary life. He can't bear novelty or originalities. He says: 'Sir, I never heard such a thing *before* in my life;' and he thinks this a *reductio ad absurdum*. You may see his taste by the reading of which he approves. Is there a more splendid monument of talent and industry than *The Times*? No wonder that the average man—that any one—believes in it. As Carlyle observes: 'Let the highest intellect able to write epics try to write such a leader for the morning newspapers, it cannot do it; the highest intellect will fail.' But did you ever see any thing there you had never seen before? Out of the million articles that everybody has read, can any one person trace a single marked idea to a single article? Where are the deep theories, and the wise axioms, and the everlasting sentiments which the writers of the most influential publication in the world have been the first to communicate to an ignorant species? Such writers are far too shrewd. The two million, or whatever number of copies it may be, they publish, are not purchased because the buyers wish to know new truth. The purchaser desires an article which he can appreciate at sight; which he can lay down and say: 'An excellent article, very excellent; exactly *my own* sentiments.'

'The Character of Sir Robert Peel', 1856

Shelley

The predominant impulse in Shelley from a very early age was 'a passion for reforming mankind.' Mr Newman has told us in his *Letters from the*

East how much he and his half-missionary associates were annoyed at being called 'young people trying to convert the world.' In a strange land, ignorant of the language, beside a recognised religion, in the midst of an immemorial society, the aim, though in a sense theirs, seemed ridiculous when ascribed to them. Shelley would not have felt this at all. No society, however organised, would have been too strong for him to attack. He would not have paused. The impulse was upon him. He would have been ready to preach that mankind were to be 'free, equal, and pure, and wise,'—in favour of 'justice, and truth, and time, and the world's natural sphere,'—in the Ottoman empire, or to the Czar, or to George III. Such truths were independent of time and place and circumstance; some time or other, something, or somebody (his faith was a little vague), would most certainly intervene to establish them.

'Percy Bysshe Shelley', 1856

What Does it All Have to Do with Us?

Every one who has religious ideas must have been puzzled by what we may call the irrelevancy of creation to his religion. We find ourselves lodged in a vast theatre, in which a ceaseless action, a perpetual shifting of scenes, an unresting life, is going forward; and that life seems physical, unmoral, having no relation to what our souls tell us to be great and good, to what religion says is the design of all things. Especially when we see any new objects, or scenes, or countries, we feel this. Look at a great tropical plant, with large leaves stretching everywhere, and great stalks branching out on all sides; with a big beetle on a leaf, and a humming-bird on a branch, and an ugly lizard just below. What has such an object to do with *us*—with anything we can conceive, or hope, imagine? What *could* it be created for, if creation has a moral end and object? Or go into a gravel-pit, or stone-quarry; you see there a vast accumulation of dull matter, yellow or grey, and you ask, involuntarily and of necessity, why is all this waste and irrelevant production, as it would seem, of material? Can anything seem more stupid than a big stone *as* a big stone, than gravel for gravel's sake? What is the use of such cumbrous, inexpressive objects in a world where there are minds to be filled, and imaginations to be aroused, and souls to be saved?

'The Ignorance of Man', 1862

Alexander Pope and Lady Mary Wortley Montagu

Why Pope and Lady Mary quarrelled is a question on which much discussion has been expended, and on which a judicious German professor might even now compose an interesting and exhaustive monograph. A curt English critic will be more apt to ask, 'Why they should *not* have quarrelled?' We know that Pope quarrelled with almost every one; we know that Lady Mary quarrelled or half quarrelled with most of her acquaintances. Why, then, should they not have quarrelled with one another?

It is certain that they were very intimate at one time; for Pope wrote to her some of the most pompous letters of compliment in the language. And the more intimate they were to begin with, the more sure they were to be enemies in the end. Human nature will not endure that sort of proximity. An irritable vain poet, who always fancies that people are trying to hurt him, whom no argument could convince that every one is not perpetually thinking about him, cannot long be friendly with a witty woman of unscrupulous tongue, who spares no one, who could sacrifice a good friend for a bad *bon-mot*, who thinks of the person whom she is addressing, not of those about whom she is speaking. The natural relation of the two is that of victim and torturer, and no other will long continue. There appear also to have been some money matters (of all things in the world) between the two. Lady Mary was intrusted by Pope with some money to use in speculation during the highly fashionable panic which derives its name from the South-Sea Bubble,—and as of course it was lost, Pope was very angry. Another story goes, that Pope made serious love to Lady Mary, and that she laughed at him; upon which a very personal, and not always very correct, controversy has arisen as to the probability or improbability of Pope's exciting a lady's feelings. Lord Byron took part in it with his usual acuteness and incisiveness, and did not leave the discussion more decent than he found it. Pope doubtless was deformed, and had not the large red health that uncivilised women admire; yet a clever lady might have taken a fancy to him, for the little creature knew what he was saying. There is, however, no evidence that Lady Mary did so. We only know that there was a sudden coolness or quarrel between them, and that it was the beginning of a long and bitter hatred.

In their own times Pope's sensitive disposition probably gave Lady Mary a great advantage. Her tongue perhaps gave him more pain than his pen gave her. But in later times she has fared the worse. What between Pope's sarcasms and Horace Walpole's anecdotes, Lady Mary's reputation has suffered very considerably. As we have said, her offences are *non proven*; there is no evidence to convict her; but she is likely to be condemned upon the general doctrine that a person who is accused of much is probably guilty of something.

'Lady Mary Wortley Montagu', 1862

The Secret of English Commerce

This increasingly democratic structure of English commerce is very unpopular in many quarters, and its effects are no doubt exceedingly mixed. On the one hand, it prevents the long duration of great families of merchant princes, such as those of Venice and Genoa, who inherited nice cultivation as well as great wealth, and who, to some extent, combined the tastes of an aristocracy with the insight and verve of men of business. These are pushed out, so to say, by the dirty crowd of little men. After a generation or two they retire into idle luxury. Upon their immense capital they can only obtain low profits, and these they do not think enough to compensate them for the rough companions and rude manners they must meet in business. This constant levelling of our commercial houses is, too, unfavourable to commercial morality. Great firms, with a reputation which they have received from the past, and which they wish to transmit to the future, cannot be guilty of small frauds. They live by a *continuity* of trade, which detected fraud would spoil. When we scrutinise the reason of the impaired reputation of English goods, we find it is the fault of new men with little money of their own, created by bank 'discounts.' These men want business at once, and they produce an inferior article to get it. They rely on cheapness, and rely successfully.

But these defects and others in the democratic structure of commerce are compensated by one great excellence. No country of great hereditary trade, no European country at least, was ever so little 'sleepy,' to use the only fit word, as England; no other was ever so prompt at once to seize new advantages. A country dependent mainly on great 'merchant princes' will never be so prompt; their commerce perpetually slips more and more into a commerce of routine. A man of large wealth, however intelligent, always thinks, more or less—'I have a great income, and I want to keep it. If things go on as they are I shall certainly keep it; but if they change I *may* not keep it.' Consequently he considers every change of circumstance a 'bore,' and thinks of such changes as little as he can. But a new man, who has his way to make in the world, knows that such changes are his opportunities; he is always on the look-out for them, and always heeds them when he finds them. The rough and vulgar structure of English commerce is the secret of its life; for it contains 'the propensity to variation,' which, in the social as in the animal kingdom, is the principle of progress.

Lombard Street, 1873

Lord Brougham

Lord Brougham had the first great essential of an agitator—the faculty of easy anger. He was sure that he did well to be angry on a hundred occasions. To the end of his life—in the peaceful repose of a long old age—he kept this faculty. There was a vicious look about him always; 'if he was a horse, no one would buy him with that eye,' some one is reported to have said; and many persons who joined with him in benevolent undertakings were unpleasantly reminded by sudden outbreaks that philanthropy and conciliation are by no means always united. To the last, a sudden eruption was apt to terrify his quiet co-operators. But in his zenith, a bad temper was of singular use. He could, without any notice, state a grievance with appropriate indignation; most men require an interval to prepare their wrath, but Lord Brougham's was always boiling and only needed a vent. If others could find the occasion of complaint he could always add the vehemence.

'The Death of Lord Brougham', 1868

GEORGE MEREDITH
1828–1909

A Master and His Impact

Rosamund noticed the peculiarity of the books he selected for his private reading. They were not boys' books, books of adventure and the like. His favourite author was one writing of Heroes, in (so she esteemed it) a style resembling either early architecture or utter dilapidation, so loose and rough it seemed; a wind-in-the-orchard style, that tumbled down here and there an appreciable fruit with uncouth bluster; sentences without commencements running to abrupt endings and smoke, like waves against a sea-wall, learned dictionary words giving a hand to street-slang, and accents falling on them haphazard, like slant rays from driving clouds; all the pages in a breeze, the whole book producing a kind of electrical agitation in the mind and the joints. This was its effect on the lady. To her the incomprehensible was the abominable, for she had our country's high critical feeling; but he, while admitting that he could not quite master it, liked it. He had dug the book out of a book-seller's shop in Malta, captivated by its title, and had, since the day of his purchase, gone at it again and again, getting nibbles of golden meaning by instalments, as with a solitary pick in a very dark mine, until the illumination of an idea struck him that there was a great deal more in the book than there was in himself.

Beauchamp's Career, 1876

The Young Sir Willoughby

Willoughby's comportment while the showers of adulation drenched him might be likened to the composure of Indian Gods undergoing worship, but unlike them he reposed upon no seat of amplitude to preserve him from a betrayal of intoxication; he had to continue tripping, dancing, exactly balancing himself, head to right, head to left, addressing his idolaters in phrases of perfect choiceness. This is only to say, that it is easier to be a wooden idol than one in the flesh; yet Willoughby was equal to his task. The little prince's education teaches him that he is other than you, and by virtue of the instruction he receives, and also something, we know not what, within, he is enabled to maintain his posture where you would be tottering. Urchins upon whose curly pates grey seniors lay their hands with conventional encomium and speculation look older than they are immediately, and Willoughby looked older than his years, not for want of freshness, but because he felt that he had to stand eminently and correctly poised.

The Egoist, 1879

A Morning Drive

They drove out immediately after breakfast, on one of those high mornings of the bared bosom of June when distances are given to our eyes, and a soft air fondles leaf and grassblade, and beauty and peace are overhead, reflected, if we will. Rain had fallen in the night. Here and there hung a milkwhite cloud with folded sail. The South-west left it in its bay of blue, and breathed below. At moments the fresh scent of herb and mould swung richly in warmth. The young beech-leaves glittered, pools of rain-water made the roadways laugh, the grass-banks under hedges rolled their interwoven weeds in cascades of many-shaded green to right and left of the pair of dappled ponies, and a squirrel crossed ahead, a lark went up a little way to ease his heart, closing his wings when the burst was over, startled blackbirds, darting with a clamour like a broken cockcrow, looped the wayside woods from hazel to oak-scrub; short flights, quick spirts everywhere, steady sunshine above.

Diana held the reins . . . Through an old gravel-cutting a gateway led to the turf of the down, springy turf bordered on a long line, clear as a racecourse, by golden gorse covers, and leftward over the gorse the dark ridge of the fir and heath country ran companionably to the South-west, the valley between, with undulations of wood and meadow sunned or shaded, clumps, mounds, promontories, away to broad spaces of tillage banked by wooded hills, and dimmer beyond and farther, the faintest shadowiness of heights, as a veil to the illimitable. Yews, junipers, radiant beeches, and gleams of the service-tree or the white-beam spotted the semicircle of swelling green Down black and silver. The sun in the valley sharpened his beams on squares of buttercups, and made a pond a diamond.

Diana of the Crossways, 1885

SIR JAMES FITZJAMES STEPHEN
1829–1894

Discussion and Coercion

Men are so constructed that whatever theory as to goodness and badness we choose to adopt, there are and always will be in the world an enormous mass of bad and indifferent people—people who deliberately do all sorts of things which they ought not to do, and leave undone all sorts of things which they ought to do. Estimate the proportion of men and women who are selfish, sensual, frivolous, idle, absolutely commonplace and wrapped up in the smallest of petty routines, and consider how far the freest of free discussion is likely to improve them. The only way by which it is practically possible to act upon them at all is by compulsion or restraint. Whether it is worth while to apply to them both or either I do not now inquire; I confine myself to saying that the utmost conceivable liberty which could be bestowed upon them would not in the least degree tend to improve them. It would be as wise to say to the water of a stagnant marsh, 'Why in the world do not you run into the sea? you are perfectly free. There is not a single hydraulic work within a mile of you. There are no pumps to suck you up, no defined channel down which you are compelled to run, no harsh banks and mounds to confine you to any particular course, no dams and no floodgates; and yet there you lie, putrefying and breeding fever, frogs, and gnats, just as if you were a mere slave!' The water might probably answer, if it knew how, 'If you want me to turn mills and carry boats, you must dig proper channels and provide proper waterworks for me.'

Liberty, Equality, Fraternity, 1873

EMILY DICKINSON
1830–1886

To Thomas Wentworth Higginson, Enclosing Four Poems

Mr Higginson,

Are you too deeply occupied to say if my Verse is alive?

The Mind is so near itself—it cannot see, distinctly—and I have none to ask—

Should you think it breathed—and had you the leisure to tell me, I should feel quick gratitude—

If I make the mistake—that you dared to tell me—would give me sincerer honor—toward you—

I enclose my name—asking you, if you please—Sir—to tell me what is true?

That you will not betray me—it is needless to ask—since Honor is it's own pawn—

April 1862

To Thomas Wentworth Higginson, In Reply to a Request for a Photograph

Could you believe me—without? I had no portrait, now, but am small, like the Wren, and my Hair is bold, like the Chestnut Bur—and my eyes, like the Sherry in the Glass, that the Guest leaves—Would this do just as well?

It often alarms Father—He says Death might occur, and he has Molds of all the rest—but has no Mold of me, but I noticed the Quick wore off those things, in a few days, and forestall the dishonor—You will think no caprice of me—

You said 'Dark.' I know the Butterfly—and the Lizard—and the Orchis—

Are not those *your* Countrymen?

I am happy to be your scholar, and will deserve the kindness, I cannot repay.

If you truly consent, I recite, now—

Will you tell me my fault, frankly as to yourself, for I had rather wince, than die. Men do not call the surgeon, to commend—the Bone, but to set it, Sir, and fracture within, is more critical. And for this, Preceptor, I shall bring you—Obedience—the Blossom from my Garden, and every gratitude I know. Perhaps you smile at me. I could not stop for that—My Business is Circumference—An ignorance, not of Customs, but if caught with the Dawn—or the Sunset see me—Myself the only Kangaroo among the Beauty, Sir, if you please, it afflicts me, and I thought that instruction would take it away.

Because you have much business, beside the growth of me—you will appoint, yourself, how often I shall come—without your inconvenience. And if at any time—you regret you received me, or I prove a different fabric to that you supposed—you must banish me—

When I state myself, as the Representative of the Verse—it does not mean—me—but a supposed person.

July 1862

MARK RUTHERFORD
(William Hale White)
1831–1913

A Devouring Desire

The desire for something like sympathy and love absolutely devoured me. I dwelt on all the instances in poetry and history in which one human being had been bound to another human being, and I reflected that my existence was of no earthly importance to anybody. I could not altogether lay the blame on myself. God knows that I would have stood against a wall and have been shot for any man or woman whom I loved, as cheerfully as I would have gone to bed, but nobody seemed to wish for such a love, or to know what to do with it. Oh the humiliations under which this weakness has bent me! Often and often I have thought that I have discovered somebody who could really comprehend the value of a passion which could tell everything and venture everything. I have overstepped all bounds of etiquette in obtruding myself on him, and have opened my heart even to shame. I have then found that it was all on my side. For every dozen times I went to his house, he came to mine once, and only when pressed: I have languished in sickness for a mouth without his finding it out; and if I were to drop into the grave, he would perhaps never give me another thought. If I had been born a hundred years earlier, I should have transferred this burning longing to the unseen God and have become a devotee. But I was a hundred years too late, and I felt that it was mere cheating of myself and a mockery to think about love for the only God whom I knew, the forces which maintained the universe. I am now getting old, and have altered in many things. The hunger and thirst of those years have abated, or rather, the fire has had ashes heaped on it, so that it is well-nigh extinguished. I have been repulsed into self-reliance and reserve, having learned wisdom by experience; but still I know that the desire has not died, as so many other desires have died, by the natural evolution of age. It has been forcibly suppressed, and that is all.

The Autobiography of Mark Rutherford, 1881

'God Bless King George IV!'

The next day, Thursday, His Sacred Majesty, or Most Christian Majesty, as he was then called, was solemnly made a Knight of the Garter, the Bishops of Salisbury and Winchester assisting. On Friday he received the Corporation of London, and on Saturday the 23rd he prepared to take his departure. There was a great crowd in the street when he came out of the hotel, and immense applause; the mob crying out, 'God bless your Majesty!' as if they owed him all they had, and even their lives. It was very touching, people thought at the time, and so it was. Is there anything more touching than the waste of human loyalty and love? As we read the history of the Highlands or a story of Jacobite loyalty such as that of Cooper's Admiral Bluewater, dear to boys, we sadden that destiny should decree that in a world in which piety is not too plentiful it should run so pitifully to waste, and that men and women should weep hot tears and break their hearts over bran-stuffing and wax.

The Revolution in Tanner's Lane, 1887

The Most Real Thing in Existence

At last they reached Barnet, the last stage, and immediately afterwards they saw the line of the smoke-cloud which lay over the goal of all their aspirations, the promised land in which nothing but golden romance awaited them. Presently a waypost was passed, with the words *To the West End* upon it, so that they might now be fairly said to be at least in a suburb. Ten minutes more brought them to Highgate Archway, and there, with its dome just emerging above the fog, was St Paul's! They could hardly restrain themselves, and Miriam squeezed Andrew's hand in ecstasy. They rattled on through Islington, and made their first halt at the 'Angel,' astonished and speechless at the crowds of people, at the shops, and most of all at the infinity of streets branching off in all directions. Dingy Clerkenwell and Aldersgate Street were gilded with a plentiful and radiant deposit of that precious metal of which healthy youth has such an infinite store—actual metal, not the 'delusive ray' by any means, for it is the most real thing in existence, more real than the bullion forks and spoons which we buy later on, when we feel we can afford them, and far more real than the silver tea-service with which, still later, we are presented amidst cheers by our admiring friends in the ward which we represent in the Common Council, for our increasing efforts to uphold their interests.

Miriam's Schooling, 1890

Deceivers

It is sometimes thought that it is those who habitually speak the truth who are most easily deceived. It is not quite so. If the deceivers are not entirely deceived, they profess acquiescence, and perpetual acquiescence induces half-deception. It is, perhaps, more correct to say that the word deception has no particular meaning for them, and implies a standard which is altogether inapplicable. There is a tacit agreement through all society to say things which nobody believes, and that being the constitution under which we live, it is absurd to talk of truth or falsity in the strict sense of the terms. A thing is true when it is in accordance with the system and on a level with it, and false when it is below it. Every now and then at rarest intervals a creature is introduced to us who speaks the veritable reality and wakes in us the slumbering conviction of universal imposture. We know that he is not as other men are; we look into his eyes and see that they penetrate us through and through, but we cannot help ourselves, and we jabber to him as we jabber to the rest of the world.

Catharine Furze, 1893

LEWIS CARROLL
(Charles Lutwidge Dodgson)
1832–1898

A Great Huge Game of Chess

'She's coming!' cried the Larkspur. 'I hear her footstep, thump, thump, along the gravel-walk!'

Alice looked round eagerly and found that it was the Red Queen. 'She's grown a good deal!' was her first remark. She had indeed: when Alice first found her in the ashes, she had been only three inches high—and here she was, half a head taller than Alice herself!

'It's the fresh air that does it,' said the Rose: 'wonderfully fine air it is, out here.'

'I think I'll go and meet her,' said Alice, for, though the flowers were interesting enough, she felt that it would be far grander to have a talk with a real Queen.

'You ca'n't possibly do that,' said the Rose: '*I* should advise you to walk the other way.'

This sounded nonsense to Alice, so she said nothing, but set off at once towards the Red Queen. To her surprise she lost sight of her in a moment, and found herself walking in at the front-door again.

A little provoked, she drew back, and, after looking everywhere for the Queen (whom she spied out at last, a long way off), she thought she would try the plan, this time, of walking in the opposite direction.

It succeeded beautifully. She had not been walking a minute before she found herself face to face with the Red Queen, and full in sight of the hill she had been so long aiming at.

'Where do you come from?' said the Red Queen. 'And where are you going? Look up, speak nicely, and don't twiddle your fingers all the time.'

Alice attended to all these directions, and explained, as well as she could, that she had lost her way.

'I don't know what you mean by *your* way,' said the Queen: 'all the ways about here belong to *me*—but why did you come out here at all?' she added in a kinder tone, 'Curtsey while you're thinking what to say. It saves time.'

Alice wondered a little at this, but she was too much in awe of the Queen to disbelieve it. 'I'll try it when I go home,' she thought to herself, 'the next time I'm a little late for dinner.'

'It's time for you to answer now,' the Queen said looking at her watch: 'open your mouth a *little* wider when you speak, and always say "your Majesty." '

'I only wanted to see what the garden was like, your Majesty——'

'That's right,' said the Queen, patting her on the head, which Alice didn't like at all: 'though, when you say "garden"—*I've* seen gardens, compared with which this would be a wilderness.'

Alice didn't dare to argue the point, but went on: '—and I thought I'd try and find my way to the top of that hill——'

'When you say "hill," ' the Queen interrupted, '*I* could show you hills, in comparison with which you'd call that a valley.'

'No, I shouldn't,' said Alice, surprised into contradicting her at last: 'a hill *ca'n't* be a valley, you know. That would be nonsense——'

The Red Queen shook her head. 'You may call it "nonsense" if you like,' she said, 'but *I've* heard nonsense, compared with which that would be as sensible as a dictionary!'

Alice curtseyed again, as she was afraid from the Queen's tone that she was a *little* offended: and they walked on in silence till they got to the top of the little hill.

For some minutes Alice stood without speaking, looking out in all directions over the country—and a most curious country it was. There were a number of tiny little brooks running straight across it from side to side, and the ground between was divided up into squares by a number of little green hedges, that reached from brook to brook.

'I declare it's marked out just like a large chess-board!' Alice said at last. 'There ought to be some men moving about somewhere—and so there are!' she added in a tone of delight, and her heart began to beat quick with excitement as she went on. 'It's a great huge game of chess that's being played—all over the world—if this *is* the world at all, you know. Oh, what fun it is! How I *wish* I was one of them! I wouldn't mind being a Pawn, if only I might join—though of course I should *like* to be a Queen, best.'

Through the Looking-Glass, 1871

SIR LESLIE STEPHEN
1832–1904

William Godwin

The fullest English exposition of the creed which Burke had to oppose is to be found in the 'Political Justice' of William Godwin. Godwin, like many other prophets of revolutionary principles, began life as a dissenting minister. His mind, clear, systematic, and passionless, speedily threw off the prejudices from which Price and Priestley never emancipated themselves. More than any English thinker, he resembles in intellectual temperament those French theorists who represented the early revolutionary impulse. His doctrines are developed with a logical precision which shrinks from no consequences, and which placidly ignores all inconvenient facts. The Utopia in which his imagination delights is laid out with geometrical symmetry and simplicity. Godwin believes as firmly as any early Christian in the speedy revelation of a new Jerusalem, four-square and perfect in its plan. Three editions of his 'Political Justice' were published, in 1793, 1796, and 1798. Between those dates events had occurred calculated to upset the faith of many enthusiasts. Godwin's opinions, however, were rooted too deeply in abstract speculation to be affected by any storms raging in the region of concrete phenomena. Condorcet, whose writings show curious parallels to the speculations of Godwin, had shown a fidelity to his creed still more touching because exposed to severer trials. The colleagues of the French philosopher in the great task of regenerating the world had become sanguinary tyrants thirsting for his blood. In his precarious hiding-place, haunted by the constant dread of discovery, he composed his treatise on the progress of the human spirit, setting forth the perfectibility of man and the speedy advent of a reign of peace and reason. Godwin, safe from such dangers, persisted in his creed, in spite of discouragements almost equally trying to his intellectual balance. The dawn had become overcast; enthusiasts were dropping off as their dreams grew faint; the free republic was becoming a despotism; the obsolete British Constitution, the very embodiment of effete prejudice, was developing unexpected strength; peace, if peace was coming, was heralded by wars all over the world, and the reign of reason had been inaugurated by the mad saturnalia of anarchy. Godwin stuck to his creed; added a few corollaries, and went on his way unmoved. He remained a republican Abdiel throughout the long dark winter of reaction, though his unfitness for actual political warfare kept him somewhat aloof from his party. He was essentially a closet-philosopher, and both by principle and temperament an advocate of persuasion rather than of physical force. To a later generation he is chiefly interesting as the teacher from whom Shelley received lessons which, in the poetical imagination of the disciple, acquired a magical colouring, though their texture became still more dreamlike. In later years, the philosopher who would have abolished all human institutions became a quiet bookseller, publishing innocent books for children. He died in the enjoyment of a small pension given to him by one of those aristocrats whose corrupting influence he had striven to undermine. Had England suffered a revolution, Godwin might have been its Condorcet, as Paine might have been its Marat. As it was, Godwin remained to the last a quiet and amiable dreamer, who, whatever his errors, deserves at least the credit of maintaining throughout dark days a fervid belief in the progress of his race and in the possibility of making politics rational. Conservative politicians owe more than they know to the thinkers who keep alive a faith which renders the world tolerable, and puts arbitrary rulers under some moral stress of responsibility.

History of English Thought in the Eighteenth Century, 1876

WILLIAM MORRIS
1834–1896

A Chaos of Waste

To say ugly words again. Do we not *know* that the greater part of men in civilised societies are dirty, ignorant, brutal—or at best, anxious about the next week's subsistence—that they are in short *poor*? And we know, when we think of it, that this is unfair.

It is an old story of men who have become rich by dishonest and tyrannical means, spending in terror of the future their ill-gotten gains liberally and in charity as 'tis called: nor are such people praised; in the old tales 'tis thought that the devil gets them after all. An old story—but I say '*De te fabula*'—*of thee* is the story told: *thou* art the man!

I say that we of the rich and well-to-do classes are daily doing in likewise: unconsciously, or half consciously it may be, we gather wealth by trading on the hard necessity of our fellows, and then we give driblets of it away to those of them who in one way or other cry out loudest to us. Our poor laws, our hospitals, our charities, organised and unorganised, are but tubs thrown to the whale; blackmail paid to lame-foot justice, that she may not hobble after us too fast.

When will the time come when honest and clear-seeing men will grow sick of all this chaos of waste, this robbing of Peter to pay Paul, which is the essence of Commercial war? When shall we band together to replace the system whose motto is 'The devil take the hindmost' with a system whose motto shall be really and without qualification 'One for all and all for one.'

Who knows but the time may be at hand, but that we now living may see the beginning of that end which shall extinguish luxury and poverty? when the upper, middle, and lower classes shall have melted into one class, living contentedly a simple and happy life.

That is a long sentence to describe the state of things which I am asking you to help to bring about: the abolition of slavery is a shorter one and means the same thing.

Art and Socialism, 1884

LORD ACTON
1834–1902

'I would hang them, higher than Haman'

I cannot accept your canon that we are to judge Pope and King unlike other men, with a favourable presumption that they did no wrong. If there is any presumption it is the other way against holders of power, increasing as the power increases. Historic responsibility has to make up for the want of legal responsibility. Power tends to corrupt and absolute power corrupts absolutely. Great men are almost always bad men, even when they exercise influence and not authority: still more when you superadd the tendency or the certainty of corruption by authority. There is no worse heresy than that the office sanctifies the holder of it. That is the point at which the negation of Catholicism and the negation of Liberalism meet and keep high festival, and the end learns to justify the means. You would hang a man of no position, like Ravaillac; but if what one hears is true, then Elizabeth asked the gaoler to murder Mary, and William III ordered his Scots minister to extirpate a clan. Here are the greater names coupled with the greater crimes. You would spare these criminals, for some mysterious reason. I would hang them, higher than Haman, for reasons of quite obvious justice; still more, still higher, for the sake of historical science.

The standard having been lowered in consideration of date, is to be still further lowered out of deference to station. Whilst the heroes of history become examples of morality, the historians who praise them, Froude, Macaulay, Carlyle, become teachers of morality and honest men. Quite frankly, I think there is no greater error. The inflexible integrity of the moral code is, to me, the secret of the authority, the dignity, the utility of history. If we may debase the currency for the sake of genius, or success, or rank, or reputation, we may debase it for the sake of a man's influence, of his religion, of his party, of the good cause which prospers by his credit and suffers by his disgrace. Then history ceases to be a science, an arbiter of controversy, a guide of the wanderer, the upholder of that moral standard which the powers of earth, and religion itself, tend constantly to depress. It serves where it ought to reign; and it serves the worst cause better than the purest.

letter to Mandell Creighton, 1887

JAMES ABBOTT MCNEILL WHISTLER
1834–1903

Art and Pedantry

There are those also, sombre of mien, and wise with the wisdom of books, who frequent museums and burrow in crypts; collecting—comparing—compiling—classifying—contradicting.

Experts these—for whom a date is an accomplishment—a hall-mark, success!

Careful in scrutiny are they, and conscientious of judgment—establishing, with due weight, unimportant reputations—discovering the picture, by the stain on the back—testing the torso, by the leg that is missing—filling folios with doubts on the way of that limb—disputatious and dictatorial, concerning the birthplace of inferior persons—speculating, in much writing, upon the great worth of bad work.

True clerks of the collection, they mix memoranda with ambition, and, reducing Art to statistics, they 'file' the fifteenth century, and 'pigeon-hole' the antique!

Ten O'Clock Lecture, 1885

The Home of Taste

The other day I happened to call on Mr Blank,—Japanese Blank, you know, whose house is in far Fulham. The garden door flew open at my summons, and my eye was at once confronted with a house, the hue of whose face reminded me of a Venetian palazzo, for it was of a subdued pink. . . . If the exterior was Venetian, however, the interior was a compound of Blank and Japan. Attracted by the curiously pretty hall, I begged the artist to explain this—the newest style of house decoration.

I need not say that Blank, being a man of an *original* turn of mind, with the decorative bump strongly developed, holds what are at present peculiar views upon wall papers, room tones, and so on. The day is dark and gloomy, yet once within the halls of Blank there is sweetness and light.

You must look through the open door into a luminous little chamber covered with a soft wash of lemon yellow.

From the antechamber we passed through the open door into a large drawing-room, of the same soft lemon-yellow hue. The blinds were down, the fog reigned without, and yet you would have thought that the sun was in the room.

Here let me pause in my description, and put on record the gist of our conversation concerning the Home of Taste.

'Now, Mr Blank, would you tell me how you came to prefer tones to papers?'

'Here the walls used to be covered with a paper of sombre green, which oppressed me and made me sad,' said Blank. 'Why cannot I bring the sun into the house,' I said to myself, 'even in this land of fog and clouds?' Then I thought of my experiment and invoked the aid of the British house-painter. He brought his colours and his buckets, and I stood over him as he mixed his washes.

'One night, when the work was nearing completion, one of them caught sight of himself in the mirror, and remarked with astonishment upon the loveliness of his own features. It was the lemon-yellow beautifying the British workman's flesh tones.

'I assure you the effect of a room full of people in evening dress seen against the yellow ground is extraordinary, and,' added Blank, 'perhaps flattering.'

'Then do I understand that you would remove all wall papers?'

'A good ground for distemper,' chuckled Mr Blank.

'But you propose to inaugurate a revolution.'

'I don't go so far as that, but I am glad to be able to introduce my ideas of house furnishing and house decoration to the public,' said Blank, 'and I may tell you that when I go to America with my Paris pictures, I shall try and decorate a house according to my own ideas, and ask the Americans to think about the matter.'

The Gentle Art of Making Enemies, 1890

MARK TWAIN
(Samuel Langhorne Clemens)
1835–1910

A Mississippi Apprenticeship

Now when I had mastered the language of this water and had come to know every trifling feature that bordered the great river as familiarly as I knew the letters of the alphabet, I had made a valuable acquisition. But I had lost something, too. I had lost something which could never be restored to me while I lived. All the grace, the beauty, the poetry had gone out of the majestic river! I still keep in mind a certain wonderful sunset which I witnessed when steamboating was new to me. A broad expanse of the river was turned to blood; in the middle distance the red hue brightened into gold, through which a solitary log came floating, black and conspicuous; in one place a long, slanting mark lay sparkling upon the water; in another the surface was broken by boiling, tumbling rings, that were as many-tinted as an opal; where the ruddy flush was faintest, was a smooth spot that was covered with graceful circles and radiating lines, ever so delicately traced; the shore on our left was densely wooded, and the sombre shadow that fell from this forest was broken in one place by a long, ruffled trail that shone like silver; and high above the forest wall a clean-stemmed dead tree waved a single leafy bough that glowed like a flame in the unobstructed splendor that was flowing from the sun. There were graceful curves, reflected images, woody heights, soft distances; and over the whole scene, far and near, the dissolving lights drifted steadily, enriching it, every passing moment, with new marvels of coloring.

I stood like one bewitched. I drank it in, in a speechless rapture. The world was new to me, and I had never seen anything like this at home. But as I have said, a day came when I began to cease from noting the glories and the charms which the moon and the sun and the twilight wrought upon the river's face; another day came when I ceased altogether to note them. Then, if that sunset scene had been repeated, I should have looked upon it without rapture, and should have commented upon it, inwardly, after this fashion: This sun means that we are going to have wind tomorrow; that floating log means that the river is rising, small thanks to it; that slanting mark on the water refers to a bluff reef which is going to kill somebody's steamboat one of these nights, if it keeps on stretching out like that; those tumbling 'boils' show a dissolving bar and a changing channel there; the lines and circles in the slick water over yonder are a warning that that troublesome place is shoaling up dangerously; that silver streak in the shadow of the forest is the 'break' from a new snag, and he has located himself in the very best place he could have found to fish for steamboats; that tall dead tree, with a single living branch, is not going to last long, and then how is a body ever going to get through this blind place at night without the friendly old landmark?

Life on the Mississippi, 1883

Tricks and Trash

It was a monstrous big river here, with the tallest and the thickest kind of timber on both banks; just a solid wall, as well as I could see, by the stars.

I looked away down stream, and seen a black speck on the water. I took out after it; but when I got to it it warn't nothing but a couple of saw-logs made fast together. Then I see another speck, and chased that; then another, and this time I was right. It was the raft.

When I got to it Jim was setting there with his head down between his knees, asleep, with his right arm hanging over the steering oar. The other oar was smashed off, and the raft was littered up with leaves and branches and dirt. So she'd had a rough time.

I made fast and laid down under Jim's nose on the raft, and begun to gap, and stretch my fists out against Jim, and says:

'Hello, Jim, have I been asleep? Why didn't you stir me up?'

'Goodness gracious, is dat you, Huck? En you ain' dead—you ain' drownded—you's back agin? It's too good for true, honey, it's too good for true. Lemme look at you, chile, lemme feel o' you. No, you ain' dead! you's back agin, 'live en soun', jis de same ole Huck—de same ole Huck, thanks to goodness!'

'What's the matter with you, Jim? You been a drinking?'

'Drinkin'? Has I ben a drinkin'? Has I had a chance to be a drinkin'?'

'Well, then, what makes you talk so wild?'

'How does I talk wild?'

'*How?* why, hain't you been talking about my coming back, and all that stuff, as if I'd been gone away?'

'Huck—Huck Finn, you look me in de eye; look me in de eye. *Hain't* you ben gone away?'

'Gone away? Why, what in the nation do you mean? *I* hain't been gone anywheres. Where would I go to?'

'Well, looky here, boss, dey's sumf'n wrong, dey is. Is I *me*, or who *is* I? Is I heah, or whah *is* I? Now dat's what I wants to know?'

'Well, I think you're here, plain enough, but I think you're a tangle-headed old fool, Jim.'

'I is, is I? Well you answer me dis. Didn't you tote out de line in de canoe, fer to make fas' to de tow-head?'

'No, I didn't. What tow-head? I hain't seen no tow-head.'

'You hain't seen no tow-head? Looky here—didn't de line pull loose en de raf' go a hummin' down de river, en leave you en de canoe behine in de fog?'

'What fog?'

'Why *de* fog. De fog dat's ben aroun' all night. En didn't you whoop, en didn't I whoop, tell we got mix' up in de islands en one un us got los' en 'tother one was jis' as good as los', 'kase he didn' know whah he wuz? En didn't I bust up agin a lot er dem islands en have a turrible time en mos' git drownded? Now ain' dat so, boss—ain't it so? You answer me dat.'

'Well, this is too many for me, Jim. I hain't seen no fog, nor no islands, nor no troubles, nor nothing. I been setting here talking with you all night till you went to sleep about ten minutes ago, and I reckon I done the same. You couldn't a got drunk in that time, so of course you've been dreaming.'

'Dad fetch it, how is I gwyne to dream all dat in ten minutes?'

'Well, hang it all, you did dream it, because there didn't any of it happen.'

'But Huck, it's all jis' as plain to me as——'

'It don't make no difference how plain it is, there ain't nothing in it. I know, because I've been here all the time.'

Jim didn't say nothing for about five minutes, but set there studying over it. Then he says:

'Well, den, I reck'n I did dream it, Huck; but dog my cats ef it ain't de powerfullest dream I ever see. En I hain't ever had no dream b'fo' dat's tired me like dis one.'

'Oh, well, that's all right, because a dream does tire a body like everything, sometimes. But this one was a staving dream—tell me all about it, Jim.'

So Jim went to work and told me the whole thing right through, just as it happened, only he painted it up considerable. Then he said he must start in and ' 'terpret' it, because it was sent for a warning. He said the first tow-head stood for a man that would try to do us some good, but the current was another man that would get us away from him. The whoops was warnings that would come to us every now and then, and if we didn't try hard to make out to understand them they'd just take us into bad luck, 'stead of keeping us out of it. The lot of tow-heads was troubles we was going to get into with quarrelsome people and all kinds of mean folks, but if we minded our business and didn't talk back and aggravate them, we would pull through and get out of the fog and into the big clear river, which was the free States, and wouldn't have no more trouble.

It had clouded up pretty dark just after I got onto the raft, but it was clearing up again, now.

'Oh, well, that's all interpreted well enough, as far as it goes, Jim,' I says; 'but what does *these* things stand for?'

It was the leaves and rubbish on the raft, and the smashed oar. You could see them first rate, now.

Jim looked at the trash, and then looked at me, and back at the trash again. He had got the dream fixed so strong in his head that he couldn't seem to shake it loose and get the facts back into its place again, right away. But when he did get the thing straightened around, he looked at me steady, without ever smiling, and says:

'What do dey stan for? I's gwyne to tell you. When I got all wore out wid work, en wid de callin' for you, en went to sleep, my heart wuz mos' broke bekase you wuz los', en I didn' k'yer no mo' what become er me en de raf'. En when I wake up en fine you back agin', all safe en soun', de tears come en I could a got down on my knees en kiss' yo' foot I's so thankful. En all you wuz thinkin 'bout wuz how you could make a fool uv ole Jim wid a lie. Dat truck dah is *trash*; en trash is what people is dat puts dirt on de head er dey fren's en makes 'em ashamed.'

Then he got up slow, and walked to the wigwam, and went in there, without saying anything but that. But that was enough. It made me feel so mean I could almost kissed *his* foot to get him to take it back.

It was fifteen minutes before I could work myself up to go and humble myself to a nigger—but I done it, and I warn't ever sorry for it afterwards, neither. I didn't do him no more mean tricks, and I wouldn't done that one if I'd a knowed it would make him feel that way.

Huckleberry Finn, 1884

A Little Town

The scene of this chronicle is the town of Dawson's Landing, on the Missouri side of the Mississippi, half a day's journey, per steamboat, below St Louis.

In 1830 it was a snug little collection of modest one- and two-story frame dwellings whose whitewashed exteriors were almost concealed from sight by climbing tangles of rose vines, honeysuckles and morning-glories. Each of these pretty homes had a garden in front fenced with white palings and opulently stocked with hollyhocks, marigolds, touch-me-nots, prince's feathers and other old-fashioned flowers; while on the window-sills of the houses stood wooden boxes containing moss-rose plants and terra-cotta pots in which grew a breed of geranium whose spread of intensely red blossoms accented the prevailing pink tint of the rose-clad house-front like an explosion of flame. When there was room on the ledge outside of the pots and boxes for a cat, the cat was there—in sunny weather—stretched at full length, asleep and blissful, with her furry belly to the sun and a paw curved over her nose. Then that house was complete, and its contentment and peace were made manifest to the world by this symbol, whose testimony is infallible. A home without a cat—and a well-fed, well-petted and properly revered cat—may be a perfect home, perhaps, but how can it prove title?

All along the streets, on both sides, at the outer edge of the brick sidewalks, stood locust-trees with trunks protected by wooden boxing, and these furnished shade for summer and a sweet fragrance in spring when the clusters of buds came forth. The main street, one block back from the river, and running parallel with it, was the sole business street. It was six blocks long, and in each block two or three brick stores three stories high towered above interjected bunches of little frame shops. Swinging signs creaked in the wind, the street's whole length. The candy-striped pole which indicates nobility proud and ancient along the palace-bordered canals of Venice, indicated merely the humble barber-shop along the main street of Dawson's Landing. On a chief corner stood a lofty unpainted pole wreathed from top to bottom with tin pots and pans and cups, the chief tinmonger's noisy notice to the world (when the wind blew) that his shop was on hand for business at that corner.

The hamlet's front was washed by the clear waters of the great river; its body stretched itself rearward up a gentle incline; its most rearward border fringed itself out and scattered its houses about the base-line of the hills; the hills rose high, inclosing the town in a half-moon curve, clothed with forests from foot to summit.

Steamboats passed up and down every hour or so. Those belonging to the little Cairo line and the little Memphis line always stopped; the big Orleans liners stopped for hails only, or to land passengers or freight; and this was the case also with the great flotilla of 'transients.' These latter came out of a dozen rivers—the Illinois, the Missouri, the Upper Mississippi, the Ohio, the Monongahela, the Tennessee, the Red River, the White River, and so on; and were bound every whither and stocked with every imaginable comfort or necessity which the Mississippi's communities could want, from the frosty Falls of St Anthony down through nine climates to torrid New Orleans.

Dawson's Landing was a slaveholding town . . .

Pudd'nhead Wilson, 1894

Fullness of Days

I think it likely that people who have not been here will be interested to know what it is like. I arrived on the thirtieth of November, fresh from care-free and frivolous 69, and was disappointed.

There is nothing novel about it, nothing striking, nothing to thrill you and make your eye glitter and your tongue cry out, 'Oh, but it *is* wonderful, perfectly wonderful!' Yes, it is disappointing. You say, 'Is *this* it?—*this?* after all this talk and fuss of a thousand generations of travelers who have crossed this frontier and looked about them and told what they saw and felt? why, it looks just like 69.'

'Old Age', December, 1905

Infant Theology

Mamma, is Christ God?

Yes, my child.

Mamma, how can He be Himself and Somebody Else at the same time?

He isn't, my darling. It is like the Siamese twins—two persons, one born ahead of the other, but equal in authority, equal in power.

I understand it, now, mamma, and it is quite simple. One twin has sexual intercourse with his mother, and begets himself and his brother; and next he has sexual intercourse with his grandmother and begets his mother. I should think it would be difficult, mamma, though interesting. Oh, ever so difficult. I should think that the Corespondent—

All things are possible with God, my child.

Yes, I suppose so. But not with any other Siamese twin, I suppose. *You* don't think any ordinary Siamese twin could beget himself and his brother on his mother, do you, mamma, and then go on back while his hand is in and beget *her*, too, on his grandmother?

Certainly not, my child. None but God can do these wonderful and holy miracles.

And enjoy them. For of course He enjoys them, or He wouldn't go foraging around among the family like that, *would* He, mamma?—injuring their reputations in the village and causing talk. Mr Hollister says it was wonderful and awe-inspiring in those days, but wouldn't work now. He says that if the Virgin lived in Chicago now, and got in the family way and explained to the newspaper fellows that God was the Corespondent, she couldn't get two in ten of them to believe it. He says they are a hell of a lot!

My child!

Well, that is what he says, anyway.

Oh, I do *wish* you would keep away from that wicked, wicked man!

He doesn't *mean* to be wicked, mamma, and he doesn't blame God. No, he doesn't blame Him; he says they all do it—gods do. It's their habit, they've always been that way.

What way, dear?

Going around unvirgining the virgins. He says our God did not invent the idea—it was old and mouldy before He happened on it. Says He hasn't invented anything, but got His Bible and His Flood and His morals and all His ideas from earlier gods, and they got them from still earlier gods. He says there never was a god yet that wasn't born of a Virgin. Mr Hollister says no virgin is safe where a god is. He says he wishes he was a god; he says he would make virgins so scarce that—

Peace, peace! *Don't* run on so, my child. If you—

—and he advised me to lock my door nights, because—

Hush, *hush*, will you!

—because although I am only three and a half years old and quite safe from *men*—

Mary Ann, come and get this child! There, now, go along with you, and don't come near me again until you can interest yourself in some subject of a lower grade and less awful than theology.

Bessie, (disappearing.) Mr Hollister says there *ain't* any.

Little Bessie, 1908

A Final Revelation

'You perceive, *now*, that these things are all impossible except in a dream. You perceive that they are pure and puerile insanities, the silly creations of an imagination that is not conscious of its freaks—in a word, that they are a dream, and you the maker of it. The dream-marks are all present; you should have recognized them earlier.

'It is true, that which I have revealed to you; there is no God, no universe, no human race, no earthly life, no heaven, no hell. It is all a dream—a grotesque and foolish dream. Nothing exists but you. And you are but a *thought*—a vagrant thought, a useless thought, a homeless thought, wandering forlorn among the empty eternities!'

He vanished, and left me appalled; for I knew, and realized, that all he had said was true.

The Mysterious Stranger (published posthumously, 1916)

SAMUEL BUTLER
1835–1902

The Start of the Honeymoon

For some time the pair said nothing: what they must have felt during their first half hour, the reader must guess, for it is beyond my power to tell him; at the end of that time, however, Theobald had rummaged up a conclusion from some odd corner of his soul to the effect that now he and Christina were married the sooner they fell into their future mutual relations the better. If people who are in a difficulty will only do the first little reasonable thing which they can clearly recognise as reasonable, they will always find the next step more easy both to see and take. What, then, thought Theobald, was here at this moment the first and most obvious matter to be considered, and what would be an equitable view of his and Christina's relative positions in respect to it? Clearly their first dinner was their first joint entry into the duties and pleasures of married life. No less clearly it was Christina's duty to order it, and his own to eat it and pay for it.

The arguments leading to this conclusion, and the conclusion itself, flashed upon Theobald about three and a half miles after he had left Crampsford on the road to Newmarket. He had breakfasted early, but his usual appetite had failed him. They had left the vicarage at noon without staying for the wedding breakfast. Theobald liked an early dinner; it dawned upon him that he was beginning to be hungry; from this to the conclusion stated in the preceding paragraph the steps had been easy. After a few minutes' further reflection he broached the matter to his bride, and thus the ice was broken.

Mrs Theobald was not prepared for so sudden an assumption of importance. Her nerves, never of the strongest, had been strung to their highest tension by the event of the morning. She wanted to escape observation; she was conscious of looking a little older than she quite liked to look as a bride who had been married that morning; she feared the landlady, the chamber-maid, the waiter—everybody and everything; her heart beat so fast that she could hardly speak, much less go through the ordeal of ordering dinner in a strange hotel with a strange landlady. She begged and prayed to be let off. If Theobald would only order dinner this once, she would order it any day and every day in future,

But the inexorable Theobald was not to be put off with such absurd excuses. He was master now. Had not Christina less than two hours ago promised solemnly to honour and obey him, and was she turning restive over such a trifle as this? The loving smile departed from his face, and was succeeded by a scowl which that old Turk, his father, might have envied. 'Stuff and nonsense, my dearest Christina,' he exclaimed mildly, and stamped his foot upon the floor of the carriage. 'It is a wife's duty to order her husband's dinner; you are my wife, and I shall expect you to order mine.' For Theobald was nothing if he was not logical.

The bride began to cry, and said he was unkind; whereon he said nothing, but revolved unutterable things in his heart. Was this, then, the end of his six years of unflagging devotion? Was it for this that when Christina had offered to let him off, he had stuck to his engagement? Was this the outcome of her talks about duty and spiritual mindedness—that now upon the very day of her marriage she should fail to see that the first step in obedience to God lay in obedience to himself? He would drive back to Crampsford; he would complain to Mr and Mrs Allaby; he didn't mean to have married Christina; he hadn't married her; it was all a hideous dream; he would——But a voice kept ringing in his ears which said: 'YOU CAN'T, CAN'T, CAN'T.'

'CAN'T I?' screamed the unhappy creature to himself.

'No,' said the remorseless voice, 'YOU CAN'T. YOU ARE A MARRIED MAN.'

He rolled back in his corner of the carriage and for the first time felt how iniquitous were the marriage laws of England. But he would buy Milton's prose works and read his pamphlet on divorce. He might perhaps be able to get them at Newmarket.

So the bride sat crying in one corner of the carriage; and the bridegroom sulked in the other, and he feared her as only a bridegroom can fear.

Presently, however, a feeble voice was heard from the bride's corner saying:

'Dearest Theobald—dearest Theobald, forgive me; I have been very, very wrong. Please do not be angry with me. I will order the—the——' but the word 'dinner' was checked by rising sobs.

When Theobald heard these words a load began to be lifted from his heart, but he only looked towards her, and that not too pleasantly.

'Please tell me,' continued the voice, 'what you think you would like, and I will tell the landlady when we get to Newmar——'but another burst of sobs checked the completion of the word.

The load on Theobald's heart grew lighter and lighter. Was it possible that she might not be going to henpeck him after all? Besides, had she not diverted his attention from herself to his approaching dinner?

He swallowed down more of his apprehensions and said, but still gloomily, 'I think we might have a roast fowl with bread sauce, new potatoes and green peas, and then we will see if they could let us have a cherry tart and some cream.'

After a few minutes more he drew her towards him, kissed away her tears, and assured her that he knew she would be a good wife to him.

'Dearest Theobald,' she exclaimed in answer, 'you are an angel.'

Theobald believed her, and in ten minutes more the happy couple alighted at the inn at Newmarket.

The Way of All Flesh (published posthumously, 1903)

George Bernard Shaw

I have long been repelled by this man though at the same time attracted by his coruscating power. Emery Walker once brought him up to see me, on the score that he was a great lover of Handel. He did nothing but cry down Handel and cry up Wagner. I did not like him and am sure that neither did he like me.

Still at the Fabian Society when I had delivered my lecture—'Was the *Odyssey* written by a woman?'—(not, heaven forbid, that I belong to or have any sympathy with the Fabian Society) he got up at once and said that when he had heard of my title first he supposed it was some mere fad or fancy of mine, but that on turning to the *Odyssey* to see what had induced me to take it up, he had not read a hundred lines before he found himself saying, 'Why, of course it is a woman,' He spoke so strongly that people who had only laughed with me all through my lecture began to think there might be something in it after all. Still, there is something uncomfortable about the man which makes him uncongenial to me.

The dislike—no this is too strong a word—the dissatisfaction with which he impressed me has been increased by his articles in the *Saturday Review* since it has been under Frank Harris's management—brilliant, amusing, and often sound though many of them have been. His cult of

Ibsen disgusts me, and my displeasure has been roused to such a pitch as to have led me to this note, by his article 'Better than Shakespeare' in this morning's *Saturday Review*. Of course Bunyan is better than Shakespeare in some respects, so is Bernard Shaw himself, so am I, so is everybody. Of course also Bunyan is one of our very foremost classics—but I cannot forgive Bernard Shaw for sneering at Shakespeare as he has done this morning. If he means it, there is no trusting his judgement—if he does not mean it I have no time to waste on such trifling. If Shaw embeds his plums in such a cake as this, they must stay there. I cannot trouble to pick them out.

Note Books, 1912

ALGERNON CHARLES SWINBURNE
1837–1909

Philanthropists

In the spring of 1849, old Lord Cheyne, the noted philanthropist, was, it will be remembered by all those interested in social reform, still alive and energetic. Indeed, he had some nine years of active life before him—public baths, institutes, reading-rooms, schools, lecture-halls, all manner of improvements, were yet to bear witness to his ardour in the cause of humanity. The equable eye of philosophy has long since observed that the appetite of doing good, unlike those baser appetites which time effaces and enjoyment allays, gains in depth and vigour with advancing years—a cheering truth, attested alike by the life and death of this excellent man. Reciprocal amelioration, he was wont to say, was the aim of every acquaintance he made—of every act of benevolence he allowed himself. Religion alone was wanting to complete a character almost painfully perfect. The mutual moral friction of benefits bestowed and blessings received had, as it were, rubbed off the edge of those qualities which go to make up the religious sentiment. The spiritual cuticle of this truly good man was so hardened by the incessant titillations of charity, and of that complacency with which virtuous people look back on days well spent, that the contemplative emotions of faith and piety had no effect on it; no stimulants of doctrine or provocatives of devotion could excite his fancy or his faith—at least, no clearer reason than this has yet been assigned in explanation of a fact so lamentable.

His son Edmund, the late lord, was nineteen at the above date. Educated in the lap of philanthropy, suckled at the breasts of all the virtues in turn, he was even then the worthy associate of his father in all schemes of improvement; only, in the younger man, this inherited appetite for goodness took a somewhat singular turn. Mr Cheyne was a Socialist—a Democrat of the most advanced kind. The father was quite happy in the construction of a model cottage; the son was busied with plans for the equalization of society. The wrongs of women gave him many a sleepless night; their cause excited in him an interest all the more commendable when we consider that he never enjoyed their company in the least, and was, in fact, rather obnoxious to them than otherwise. The fact of this mutual repulsion had nothing to do with philanthropy. It was undeniable; but, on the other hand, the moral-sublime of this young man's character was something incredible. Unlike his father, he was much worried by religious speculations—certain phases of belief and disbelief he saw fit to embody in a series of sonnets, which were privately printed under the title of 'Aspirations, by a Wayfarer.' Very flabby sonnets they were, leaving in the mouth a taste of chaff and dust; but the genuine stamp of a sincere and single mind was visible throughout; which was no small comfort.

The wife of Lord Cheyne, not unnaturally, had died in giving birth to such a meritorious portent. Malignant persons, incapable of appreciating the moral-sublime, said that she died of a plethora of conjugal virtue on the part of her husband. It is certain that less sublime samples of humanity did find the society of Lord Cheyne a grievous infliction. Reform, emancipation, manure, the right of voting, the national burden, the adulteration of food, mechanics, farming, sewerage, beet-root sugar, and the loftiest morality, formed each in turn the staple of that excellent man's discourse. If an exhausted visitor sought refuge in the son's society, Mr Cheyne would hold forth by the hour on divorce, Church questions, pantheism, socialism (Christian or simple), the equilibrium of society, the duties of each class, the mission of man, the balance of ranks, education, development, the stages of faith, the meaning of the age, the relation of parties, the regeneration of the priesthood, the reformation of criminals, and the destiny of woman.

Love's Cross-Currents, 1877

WILLIAM DEAN HOWELLS
1837–1920

A Night Ride through New York

At Third Avenue they took the Elevated, for which she confessed an infatuation. She declared it the most ideal way of getting about in the world, and was not ashamed when he reminded her of how she used to say that nothing under the sun could induce her to travel on it. She now said that the night transit was even more interesting than the day, and that the fleeting intimacy you formed with people in second and third floor interiors, while all the usual street life went on underneath, had a domestic intensity mixed with a perfect repose that was the last effect of good society with all its security and exclusiveness. He said it was better than the theatre, of which it reminded him, to see those people through their windows: a family party of work-folk at a late tea, some of the men in their shirt sleeves; a woman sewing by a lamp; a mother laying her child in its cradle; a man with his head fallen on his hands upon a table; a girl and her lover leaning over the window-sill together. What suggestion! what drama! what infinite interest! At the Forth-second Street station they stopped a minute on the bridge that crosses the track to the branch road for the Central Depôt, and looked up and down the long stretch of the Elevated to north and south. The track that found and lost itself a thousand times in the flare and tremor of the innumerable lights; the moony sheen of the electrics mixing with the reddish points and blots of gas far and near; the architectural shapes of houses and churches and towers, rescued by the obscurity from all that was ignoble in them, and the coming and going of the trains marking the stations with vivider or fainter plumes of flame-shot steam—formed an incomparable perspective. They often talked afterward of the superb spectacle, which in a city full of painters nightly works its unrecorded miracles; and they were just to the Arachne roof spun in iron over the cross street on which they ran to the depôt; but for the present they were mostly inarticulate before it. They had another moment of rich silence when they paused in the gallery that leads from the elevated station to the waiting-rooms in the Central Depôt and looked down upon the great night trains lying on the tracks dim under the rain of gas-lights that starred without dispersing the vast darkness of the place. What forces, what fates, slept in these bulks which would soon be hurling themselves north and east and west through the night! Now they waited there like fabled monsters of Arab story ready for the magician's touch, tractable, reckless, will-less—organised lifelessness full of a strange semblance of life.

A Hazard of New Fortunes, 1889

A Farewell to Mark Twain

It is in vain that I try to give a notion of the intensity with which he pierced to the heart of life, and the breadth of vision with which he compassed the whole world, and tried for the reason of things, and then left trying. We had other meetings, insignificantly sad and brief; but the last time I saw him alive was made memorable to me by the kind clear judicial sense with which he explained and justified the labor unions as the sole present help of the weak against the strong.

Next I saw him dead, lying in his coffin amid those flowers with which we garland our despair in that pitiless hour. After the voice of his old friend Twichell had been lifted in the prayer which it wailed through in broken-hearted supplication, I looked a moment at the face I knew so well; and it was patient with the patience I had so often seen in it: something of puzzle, a great silent dignity, an assent to what must be from the depths of a nature whose tragical seriousness broke in the laughter which the unwise took for the whole of him. Emerson, Longfellow, Lowell, Holmes—I knew them all and all the rest of our sages, poets, seers, critics, humorists; they were like one another and like other literary men; but Clemens was sole, incomparable, the Lincoln of our literature.

My Mark Twain, 1910

JOHN BURROUGHS
1837–1921

The Concealments of the Whip-Poor-Will

One day in May, walking in the woods, I came upon the nest of a whip-poor-will, or rather its eggs, for it builds no nest,—two elliptical whitish spotted eggs lying upon the dry leaves. My foot was within a yard of the mother-bird before she flew. I wondered what a sharp eye would detect curious or characteristic in the ways of the bird, so I came to the place many times and had a look. It was always a task to separate the bird from her surroundings, though I stood within a few feet of her, and knew exactly where to look. One had to bear on with his eye, as it were, and refuse to be baffled. The sticks and leaves, and bits of black or dark-brown bark, were all exactly copied in the bird's plumage. And then she did sit so close, and simulate so well a shapeless decaying piece of wood or bark! Twice I brought a companion, and guiding his eye to the spot, noted how difficult it was for him to make out there, in full view upon the dry leaves, any semblance to a bird. When the bird returned after being disturbed, she would alight within a few inches of her eggs, and then, after a moment's pause, hobble awkwardly upon them.

After the young had appeared all the wit of the bird came into play. I was on hand the next day, I think. The mother-bird sprang up when I was within a pace of her, and in doing so fanned the leaves with her wings till they sprang up too; as the leaves started the young started, and, being of the same colour, to tell which was the leaf and which the bird was a trying task to any eye. I came the next day, when the same tactics were repeated. Once a leaf fell upon one of the young birds and nearly hid it. The young are covered with a reddish down, like a young partridge, and soon follow their mother about. When disturbed, they gave but one leap, then settled down perfectly motionless and stupid, with eyes closed. The parent bird, on these occasions, made frantic efforts to decoy me away from her young. She would fly a few paces and fall upon her breast, and a spasm, like that of death, would run through her tremulous outstretched wings and prostrate body. She kept a sharp eye out the meanwhile to see if the ruse took, and if it did not, she was quickly cured, and, moving about to some other point, tried to draw my attention as before. When followed she always alighted upon the ground, dropping down in a sudden peculiar way. The second or third day both old and young had disappeared.

The whip-poor-will walks as awkwardly as a swallow, which is as awkward as a man in a bag, and yet she manages to lead her young about the woods. The latter, I think, move by leaps and sudden spurts, their protective colouring shielding them most effectively. Wilson once came upon the mother-bird and her brood in the woods, and, though they were at his very feet, was so baffled by the concealment of the young that he was about to give up the search, much disappointed, when he perceived something 'like a slight mouldiness among the withered leaves, and, on stooping down, discovered it to be a young whip-poor-will, seemingly asleep.' Wilson's description of the young is very accurate, as its downy covering does look precisely like a 'slight mouldiness.' Returning a few moments afterward to the spot to get a pencil he had forgotten, he could find neither old nor young.

Locusts and Wild Honey, 1879

HENRY ADAMS
1838–1918

The Lady and the Senator

'I heard your speech yesterday, Mr Ratcliffe. I am glad to have a chance of telling you how much I was impressed by it. It seemed to me masterly. Do you not find that it has had a great effect?'

'I thank you, madam. I hope it will help to unite the party, but as yet we have had no time to measure its results. That will require several days more.' The Senator spoke in his senatorial manner, elaborate, condescending, and a little on his guard.

'Do you know,' said Mrs Lee, turning towards him as though he were a valued friend, and looking deep into his eyes, 'Do you know that every one told me I should be shocked by the falling off in political ability at Washington? I did not believe them, and since hearing your speech I am sure they are mistaken. Do you yourself think there is less ability in Congress than there used to be?'

'Well, madam, it is difficult to answer that question. Government is not so easy now as it was formerly. There are different customs. There are many men of fair abilities in public life; many more than there used to be; and there is sharper criticism and more of it.'

'Was I right in thinking that you have a strong resemblance to Daniel Webster in your way of speaking? You come from the same neighborhood, do you not?'

Mrs Lee here hit on Ratcliffe's weak point; the outline of his head had, in fact, a certain resemblance to that of Webster, and he prided himself upon it, and on a distant relationship to the Expounder of the Constitution; he began to think that Mrs Lee was a very intelligent person. His modest admission of the resemblance gave her the opportunity to talk of Webster's oratory, and the conversation soon spread to a discussion of the merits of Clay and Calhoun. The Senator found that his neighbor—a fashionable New York woman, exquisitely dressed, and with a voice and manner seductively soft and gentle—had read the speeches of Webster and Calhoun. She did not think it necessary to tell him that she had persuaded the honest Carrington to bring her the volumes and to mark such passages as were worth her reading; but she took care to lead the conversation, and she criticized with some skill and more humor the weak points in Websterian oratory, saying with a little laugh and a glance into his delighted eyes:

'My judgment may not be worth much, Mr Senator, but it does seem to me that our fathers thought too much of themselves, and till you teach me better I shall continue to think that the passage in your speech of yesterday which began with, 'Our strength lies in this twisted and tangled mass of isolated principles, the hair of the half-sleeping giant of Party,' is both for language and imagery quite equal to anything of Webster's.'

The Senator from Illinois rose to this gaudy fly like a huge, two-hundred-pound salmon; his white waistcoat gave out a mild silver reflection as he slowly came to the surface and gorged the hook. He made not even a plunge, not one perceptible effort to tear out the barbed weapon, but floating gently to her feet, allowed himself to be landed as though it were a pleasure. Only miserable casuists will ask whether this was fair play on Madeleine's part; whether flattery so gross cost her conscience no twinge, and whether any woman can without self-abasement be guilty of such shameless falsehood. She, however, scorned the idea of falsehood. She would have defended herself by saying that she had not so much praised Ratcliffe as depreciated Webster, and that she was honest in her opinion of the old-fashioned American oratory. But she could not deny that she had wilfully allowed the Senator to draw conclusions very different from any she actually held. She could not deny that she had intended to flatter him to the extent necessary for her purpose, and that she was pleased at her success.

Democracy, 1878

A Race of Eccentrics

Knowledge of human nature is the beginning and end of political education, but several years of arduous study in the neighborhood of Westminster led Henry Adams to think that knowledge of English human nature had little or no value outside of England. In Paris, such a habit stood in one's way; in America, it roused all the instincts of native jealousy. The English mind was one-sided, eccentric, systematically unsystematic, and logically illogical. The less one knew of it, the better.

This heresy, which scarcely would have been allowed to penetrate a Boston mind—it would, indeed, have been shut out by instinct as a rather foolish exaggeration—rested on an experience which Henry Adams gravely thought he had a right to think conclusive—for him. That it should be conclusive for any one else never occurred to him, since he had no thought of educating anybody else. For him—alone—the less English education he got, the better!

For several years, under the keenest incitement to watchfulness, he observed the English mind in contact with itself and other minds. Especially with the American the contact was interesting because the limits and defects of the American mind were one of the favorite topics of the European. From the old-world point of view, the American had no mind; he had an economic thinking-machine which could work only on a fixed line. The American mind exasperated the European as a buzz-saw might exasperate a pine forest. The English mind disliked the French mind because it was antagonistic, unreasonable, perhaps hostile, but recognized it as at least a thought. The American mind was not a thought at all; it was a convention, superficial, narrow, and ignorant; a mere cutting instrument, practical, economical, sharp, and direct.

The English themselves hardly conceived that their mind was either economical, sharp, or direct; but the defect that most struck an American was its enormous waste in eccentricity. Americans needed and used their whole energy, and applied it with close economy; but English society was eccentric by law and for sake of the eccentricity itself.

The commonest phrase overheard at an English club or dinner-table was that So-and-So 'is quite mad.' It was no offence to So-and-So; it hardly distinguished him from his fellows; and when applied to a public man, like Gladstone, it was qualified by epithets much more forcible. Eccentricity was so general as to become hereditary distinction. It made the chief charm of English society as well as its chief terror.

The American delighted in Thackeray as a satirist, but Thackeray quite justly maintained that he was not a satirist at all, and that his pictures of English society were exact and good-natured. The American, who could not believe it, fell back on Dickens, who, at all events, had the vice of exaggeration to extravagance, but Dickens's English audience thought the exaggeration rather in manner or style, than in types. Mr Gladstone himself went to see Sothern act Dundreary, and laughed till his face was distorted—not because Dundreary was exaggerated, but because he was ridiculously like the types that Gladstone had seen—or might have seen—in any club in Pall Mall. Society swarmed with exaggerated characters; it contained little else.

The Education of Henry Adams, privately printed 1907; published 1918

WALTER PATER
1839–1894

Mona Lisa

The presence that thus rose so strangely beside the waters, is expressive of what in the ways of a thousand years men had come to desire. Hers is the head upon which 'all the ends of the world are come,' and the eyelids are a little weary. It is a beauty wrought out from within upon the flesh, the deposit, little cell by cell, of strange thoughts and fantastic reveries and exquisite passions. Set it for a moment beside one of those white Greek goddesses or beautiful women of antiquity, and how would they be troubled by this beauty, into which the soul with all its maladies has passed! All the thoughts and experience of the world have etched and moulded there, in that which they have of power to refine and make expressive the outward form, the animalism of Greece, the lust of Rome, the reverie of the middle age with its spiritual ambition and imaginative loves, the return of the Pagan world, the sins of the Borgias. She is older than the rocks among which she sits; like the vampire, she has been dead many times, and learned the secrets of the grave; and has been a diver in deep seas, and keeps their fallen day about her; and trafficked for strange webs with Eastern merchants: and, as Leda, was the mother of Helen of Troy, and, as Saint Anne, the mother of Mary; and all this has been to her but as the sound of lyres and flutes, and lives only in the delicacy with which it has moulded the changing lineaments, and tinged the eye-lids and the hands.

Studies in the History of the Renaissance, 1873

The Impress of Childhood

So the child of whom I am writing lived on there quietly; things without thus ministering to him, as he sat daily at the window with the birdcage hanging below it, and his mother taught him to read, wondering at the ease with which he learned, and at the quickness of his memory. The perfume of the little flowers of the lime-tree fell through the air upon them like rain; while time seemed to move ever more slowly to the murmur of the bees in it, till it almost stood still on June afternoons. How insignificant, at the moment, seem the influences of the sensible things which are tossed and fall and lie about us, so, or so, in the environment of early childhood. How indelibly, as we afterwards discover, they affect us; with what capricious attractions and associations they figure themselves on the white paper, the smooth wax, of our ingenuous souls, as 'with lead in the rock for ever,' giving form and feature, and as it were assigned house-room in our memory, to early experiences of feeling and thought, which abide with us ever afterwards, thus, and not otherwise. The realities and passions, the rumours of the greater world without, steal in upon us, each by its own special little passage-way, through the wall of custom about us; and never afterwards quite detach themselves from this or that accident, or trick, in the mode of their first entrance to us. Our susceptibilities, the discovery of our powers, manifold experiences—our various experiences of the coming and going of bodily pain, for instance—belong to this or the other well-remembered place in the material habitation—that little white room with the window across which the heavy blossoms could beat so peevishly in the wind, with just that particular catch or throb, such a sense of teasing in it, on gusty mornings; and the early habitation thus gradually becomes a sort of material shrine or sanctuary of sentiment; a system of visible symbolism interweaves itself through all our thoughts and passions; and irresistibly, little shapes, voices, accidents—the angle at which the sun in the morning fell on the pillow—become parts of the great chain wherewith we are bound.

'The Child in the House', 1878

THOMAS HARDY

1840–1928

Swordplay

The pit was a saucer-shaped concave, naturally formed, with a top diameter of about thirty feet, and shallow enough to allow the sunshine to reach their heads. Standing in the centre, the sky overhead was met by a circular horizon of fern: this grew nearly to the bottom of the slope and then abruptly ceased. The middle within the belt of verdure was floored with a thick flossy carpet of moss and grass intermingled, so yielding that the foot was half-buried within it.

'Now,' said Troy, producing the sword, which, as he raised it into the sunlight, gleamed a sort of greeting, like a living thing, 'first, we have four right and four left cuts; four right and four left thrusts. Infantry cuts and guards are more interesting than ours, to my mind; but they are not so swashing. They have seven cuts and three thrusts. So much as a preliminary. Well, next, our cut one is as if you were sowing your corn—so.' Bathsheba saw a sort of rainbow, upside down in the air, and Troy's arm was still again. 'Cut two, as if you were hedging—so. Three, as if you were reaping—so. Four, as if you were threshing—in that way. Then the same on the left. The thrusts are these: one, two, three, four, right; one, two, three, four, left.' He repeated them. 'Have 'em again?' he said. 'One, two——'

She hurriedly interrupted: 'I'd rather not; though I don't mind your twos and fours; but your ones and threes are terrible!'

'Very well. I'll let you off the ones and threes. Next, cuts, points and guards altogether.' Troy duly exhibited them. 'Then there's pursuing practice, in this way.' He gave the movements as before. 'There, those are the stereotyped forms. The infantry have two most diabolical upward cuts, which we are too humane to use. Like this—three, four.'

'How murderous and bloodthirsty!'

'They are rather deathy. Now I'll be more interesting, and let you see some loose play—giving all the cuts and points, infantry and cavalry, quicker than lightning, and as promiscuously—with just enough rule to regulate instinct and yet not to fetter it. You are my antagonist, with this difference from real warfare, that I shall miss you every time by one hair's breadth, or perhaps two. Mind you don't flinch, whatever you do.'

'I'll be sure not to!' she said invincibly.

He pointed to about a yard in front of him.

Bathsheba's adventurous spirit was beginning to find some grains of relish in these highly novel proceedings. She took up her position as directed, facing Troy.

'Now just to learn whether you have pluck enough to let me do what I wish, I'll give you a preliminary test.'

He flourished the sword by way of introduction number two, and the next thing of which she was conscious was that the point and blade of the sword were darting with a gleam towards her left side, just above her hip; then of their reappearance on her right side, emerging as it were from between her ribs, having apparently passed through her body. The third item of consciousness was that of seeing the same sword, perfectly clean and free from blood held vertically in Troy's hand (in the position technically called 'recover swords'). All was as quick as electricity.

'Oh!' she cried out in affright, pressing her hand to her side. 'Have you run me through?—no, you have not! Whatever have you done!'

'I have not touched you,' said Troy, quietly. 'It was mere sleight of hand. The sword passed behind you. Now you are not afraid, are you? Because if you are I can't perform. I give my word that I will not only not hurt you, but not once touch you.'

'I don't think I am afraid. You are quite sure you will not hurt me?'

'Quite sure.'

'Is the sword very sharp?'

'O no—only stand as still as a statue. Now!'

In an instant the atmosphere was transformed to Bathsheba's eyes. Beams of light caught from the low sun's rays, above, around, in front of her, well-nigh shut out earth and heaven—all emitted in the marvellous evolutions of Troy's reflecting blade, which seemed everywhere at once, and yet nowhere specially. These circling gleams were accompanied by a keen rush that was almost a whistling—also springing from all sides of her at once. In short, she was enclosed in a firmament of light, and of sharp hisses, resembling a sky-full of meteors close at hand.

Never since the broadsword became the national weapon had there been more dexterity shown in its management than by the hands of Sergeant Troy, and never had he been in such splendid temper for the performance as now in the evening sunshine among the ferns with Bathsheba. It may safely be asserted with respect to the closeness of his cuts, that had it been possible for the edge of the sword to leave in the air a permanent substance wherever it flew past, the space left untouched would have been almost a mould of Bathsheba's figure.

Behind the luminous streams of this *aurora militaris*, she could see the hue of Troy's sword arm, spread in a scarlet haze over the space covered by its motions, like a twanged harpstring, and behind all Troy himself, mostly facing her; sometimes, to show the rear cuts, half turned away, his eye nevertheless always keenly measuring her breadth and outline, and his lips tightly closed in sustained effort. Next, his movements lapsed slower, and she could see them individually. The hissing of the sword had ceased, and he stopped entirely.

'That outer loose lock of hair wants tidying,' he said, before she had moved or spoken. 'Wait: I'll do it for you.'

An arc of silver shone on her right side: the sword had descended. The lock dropped to the ground.

Far from the Madding Crowd, 1874

A Country Town

Casterbridge was the complement of the rural life around; not its urban opposite. Bees and butterflies in the cornfields at the top of the town, who desired to get to the meads at the bottom, took no circuitous course, but flew straight down High Street without any apparent consciousness that they were traversing strange latitudes. And in autumn airy spheres of thistledown floated into the same street, lodged upon the shop fronts, blew into drains; and innumerable tawny and yellow leaves skimmed along the pavement, and stole through people's door-ways into their passages, with a hesitating scratch on the floor, like the skirts of timid visitors.

The Mayor of Casterbridge, 1886

The Sound of a Harp

It was a typical summer evening in June, the atmosphere being in such delicate equilibrium and so transmissive that inanimate objects seemed endowed with two or three senses, if not five. There was no distinction between the near and the far, and an auditor felt close to everything within the horizon. The soundlessness impressed her as a positive entity rather than as the mere negation of noise. It was broken by the strumming of strings.

Tess had heard those notes in the attic above her head. Dim, flattened, constrained by their confinement, they had never appealed to her as now, when they wandered in the still air with a stark quality like that of nudity. To speak absolutely, both instrument and execution were poor; but the relative is all, and as she listened Tess, like a fascinated bird, could not leave the spot. Far from leaving she drew up towards the performer, keeping behind the hedge that he might not guess her presence.

The outskirt of the garden in which Tess found herself had been left uncultivated for some years, and was now damp and rank with juicy grass which sent up mists of pollen at a touch; and with tall blooming weeds emitting offensive smells—weeds whose red and yellow and purple hues formed a polychrome as dazzling as that of cultivated flowers. She went stealthily as a cat through this profusion of growth, gathering cuckoo-spittle on her skirts, cracking snails that were underfoot, staining her hands with thistle-milk and slug-slime, and rubbing off upon her naked arms sticky blights which, though snow-white on the apple-tree trunks, made madder stains on her skin; thus she drew quite near to Clare, still unobserved of him.

Tess was conscious of neither time nor space. The exaltation which she had described as being producible at will by gazing at a star, came now without any determination of hers; she undulated upon the thin notes of the second-hand harp, and their harmonies passed like breezes through her, bringing tears into her eyes. The floating pollen seemed to be his notes made visible, and the dampness of the garden the weeping of the garden's sensibility. Though near nightfall, the rank-smelling weed-flowers glowed as if they would not close for intentness, and the waves of colour mixed with the waves of sound.

The light which still shone was derived mainly from a large hole in the western bank of cloud; it was like a piece of day left behind by accident, dusk having closed in elsewhere. He concluded his plaintive melody, a very simple performance, demanding no great skill; and she waited, thinking another might be begun. But, tired of playing, he had desultorily come round the fence, and was rambling up behind her. Tess, her cheeks on fire, moved away furtively, as if hardly moving at all.

Tess of the d'Urbervilles, 1891

The Retreat from Moscow

The winter is more merciless, and snow continues to fall upon a deserted expanse of unenclosed land in Lithuania. Some scattered birch bushes merge in a forest in the background.

It is growing dark, though nothing distinguishes where the sun sets. There is no sound except that of a shuffling of feet in the direction of a bivouac. Here are gathered tattered men like skeletons. Their noses and ears are frost-bitten, and pus is oozing from their eyes.

These stricken shades in a limbo of gloom are among the last survivors of the French army. Few of them carry arms. One squad, ploughing through snow above their knees, and with icicles dangling from their hair that clink like glass-lustres as they walk, go into the birch wood, and are heard chopping. They bring back boughs, with which they make a screen on the windward side, and contrive to light a fire. With their swords they cut rashers from a dead horse, and grill them in the flames, using gunpowder for salt to eat them with. Two others return from a search, with a dead rat and some candle-ends. Their meal shared, some try to repair their gaping shoes and to tie up their feet, that are chilblained to the bone. . . .

Exhausted, they again crouch round the fire. Officers and privates press together for warmth. Other stragglers arrive, and sit at the backs of the first. With the progress of the night the stars come out in unusual brilliancy, Sirius and those in Orion flashing like stilettos; and the frost stiffens.

The fire sinks and goes out; but the Frenchmen do not move. The day dawns, and still they sit on.

In the background enter some light horse of the Russian army, followed by KUTÚZOF himself and a few of his staff. He presents a terrible appearance now—bravely serving though slowly dying, his face puffed with the intense cold, his one eye staring out as he sits in a heap in the saddle, his head sunk into his shoulders. The whole detachment pauses at the sight of the French asleep. They shout; but the bivouackers give no sign.

Kutúzof. Go, stir them up! We slay not sleeping men.

[*The Russians advance and prod the French with their lances.*]

Russian Officer. Prince, here's a curious picture. They are dead.

The Dynasts, 1904–8

FRANCIS KILVERT

1840–1879

After the Cattle-Fair

All the evening a crowd of excited people swarming about the Swan door and steps, laughing, talking loud, swearing and quarrelling in the quiet moonlight.

Here come a fresh drove of men from the fair, half tipsy, at the quarrelsome stage judging by the noise they make, all talking at once loud fast and angry, humming and buzzing like a swarm of angry bees. Their blood is on fire. It is like a gunpowder magazine. There will be an explosion in a minute. It only wants one word, a spark. Here it is. Some one had said something. A sudden blaze of passion, a retort, a word and a blow, a rush, a scuffle, a Babel of voices, a tumult, the furious voices of the combatants rising high and furious above the din. Now the bystanders have come between them, are holding them back, soothing them, explaining that no insult was intended at first, and persuading them not to fight. Then a quick tramp of horsehoofs and a farmer dashes past on his way home from the fair. Twenty voices shout to him to stop. He pulls up with difficulty and joins the throng. Meanwhile the swarm and bustle and hum goes on, some singing, some shouting, some quarrelling and wrangling, the World and the Flesh reeling about arm in arm and Apollyon straddling the whole breadth of the way. Tonight I think many are sore, angry and desperate about their misfortunes and prospects. Nothing has sold today but fat cattle. No one would look at poor ones, because no one has keep for them during the winter. Every one wants to sell poor cattle to pay their rent and to get so many mouths off their hay. No one wants to buy them. Where are the rents to come from?

October 1870; *Diaries*, first published 1938

On the Train to Liverpool

At Wrexham two merry saucy Irish hawking girls got into our carriage. The younger had a handsome saucy daring face showing splendid white teeth when she laughed and beautiful Irish eyes of dark grey which looked sometimes black and sometimes blue, with long silky black lashes and finely pencilled black eyebrows. This girl kept her companion and the whole carriage laughing from Wrexham to Chester with her merriment, laughter and songs and her antics with a doll dressed like a boy, which she made dance in the air by pulling a string. She had a magnificent voice and sung to a comic popular air while the doll danced wildly,

> 'A-dressed in his Dolly Varden,
> A-dressed in his Dolly Varden,
> He looks so neat
> And he smells so sweet,
> A-dressed in his Dolly Varden.'

Then breaking down into merry laughter she hid her face and glanced roguishly at me from behind the doll. Suddenly she became quiet and pensive and her face grew grave and sad as she sang a love song.

The two girls left the carriage at Chester and as she passed the younger put out her hand and shook hands with me. They stood by the carriage door on the platform for a few moments and Irish Mary, the younger girl, asked me to buy some nuts. I gave her sixpence and took a dozen nuts out of a full measure she was going to pour into my hands. She seemed surprised and looked up with a smile. 'You'll come and see me,' she said coaxingly. 'You are not Welsh are you?' 'No, we are a mixture of Irish and English.' 'Born in Ireland?' 'No, I was born at Huddersfield in Yorkshire.' 'You look Irish—you have the Irish eye.' She laughed and blushed and hid her face. 'What do you think I am?' asked the elder girl, 'do you think I am Spanish?' 'No,' interrupted the other laughing, 'you have too much Irish between your eyes.' 'My eyes are blue,' said the elder girl, 'your eyes are grey, the gentleman's eyes are black.' 'Where did you get in?' I asked Irish Mary. 'At Wrexham,' she said. 'We were caught in the rain, walked a long way in it and got wet through,' said the poor girl pointing to a bundle of wet clothes they were carrying and which they had changed for dry ones. 'What do you do?' 'We go out hawking,' said the girl in a low voice. 'You have a beautiful voice.' 'Hasn't she?' interrupted the elder girl eagerly and delightedly. 'Where did you learn to sing?' She smiled and blushed and hid her face. A porter and some other people were looking wonderingly on, so I thought it best to end the conversation. But there was an attractive power about this poor Irish girl that fascinated me strangely. I felt irresistibly drawn to her. The singular beauty of her eyes, a beauty of deep sadness, a wistful sorrowful imploring look, her swift rich humour, her sudden gravity and sadnesses, her brilliant laughter, a certain intensity and power and richness of life and the extraordinary sweetness, softness and beauty of her voice in singing and talking gave her a power over me which I could not understand nor describe, but the power of a stronger over a weaker will and nature. She lingered about the carriage door. Her look grew more wistful, beautiful, imploring. Our eyes met again and again. Her eyes grew more and more beautiful. My eyes were fixed and riveted on hers. A few minutes more and I know not what might have happened. A wild reckless feeling came over me. Shall I leave all and follow her? No—Yes—No. At that moment the train moved on. She was left behind. Goodbye, sweet Irish Mary. So we parted. shall we meet again? Yes—No—Yes.

June 1872; *Diaries*

A Delirium of Joy

As I came down from the hill into the valley across the golden meadows and along the flower-scented hedges a great wave of emotion and happiness stirred and rose up within me. I know not why I was so happy, nor what I was expecting, but I was in a delirium of joy, it was one of the supreme few moments of existence, a deep delicious draft from the strong sweet cup of life.

May 1875; *Diaries*

Evensong

As I went to Church in the sultry summer afternoon the hum and murmur of the multitudinous insects sounded like the music of innumerable bells. As I sat on the terrace reading Farrar's *Life of Christ*, the evening was soft, dark and cloudy and filled with sweet scents of earth and flowers. At the gloaming a robin suddenly flew into the trees overhead and began singing his latest evensong in the sycamore.

August 1875; *Diaries*

A Fairy Web—and Etty Meredith Brown

All night the heavy drenching fog brooded over the land, clinging to the meadows long after the sun was risen, and it was not until after he had gained some height in the sky that he was able to break through and dispel the mists. Then the morning suddenly became glorious and we saw what had happened in the night. All night long millions of gossamer spiders had been spinning and the whole country was covered as if with one vast fairy web. They spread over lawn and meadow grass and gate and hawthorn hedge, and as the morning sun glinted upon their delicate threads drenched and beaded with the film of the mist the gossamer webs gleamed and twinkled into crimson and gold and green, like the most exquisite shot-silk dress in the finest texture of gauzy silver wire. I never saw anything like it or anything so exquisite as 'the Virgin's webs' glowed with changing opal lights and glanced with all the colours of the rainbow.

At 4 oclock Miss Meredith Brown and her beautiful sister Etty came over to afternoon tea with us and a game of croquet. Etty Meredith Brown is one of the most striking-looking and handsomest girls who I have seen for a long time. She was admirably dressed in light grey with a close fitting crimson body which set off her exquisite figure and suited to perfection her black hair and eyes and her dark Spanish brunette complexion with its rich glow of health which gave her cheeks the dusky bloom and flush of a ripe pomegranate. But the greatest triumph was her hat, broad and picturesque, carelessly twined with flowers and set jauntily on one side of her pretty dark head, while round her shapely slender throat she wore a rich gold chain necklace with broad gold links. And from beneath the shadow of the picturesque hat the beautiful dark face and the dark wild fine eyes looked with a true gipsy beauty.

The sun shone golden on the lawn between the lengthening shadows and the evening sunlight dappled with bright green on the front of the Rectory with rick spots of light and shade. It lighted the broad gold links of the necklace and the graceful crimson figure of the dark handsome girl, and into the midst of the game came the tabby cat carrying in her mouth her tabby kitten which she dropped on the lawn and looked round proudly for applause.

September 1875; *Diaries*

W. H. HUDSON
1841–1922

The Gaucho

That anyone should be able to think better lying, sitting, or standing, than when speeding along on horseback, is to me incomprehensible. This is doubtless due to early training and long use; for on those great pampas where I first saw the light and was taught at a tender age to ride, we come to look on man as a parasitical creature, fitted by nature to occupy the back of a horse, in which position only he has the full and free use of all his faculties. Possibly the gaucho—the horseman of the pampas—is born with this idea in his brain; if so, it would only be reasonable to suppose that its correlative exists in a modification of structure. Certain it is that an intoxicated gaucho lifted on to the back on his horse is perfectly safe in his seat. The horse may do his best to rid himself of his burden; the rider's legs—or posterior arms as they might appropriately be called—retain their iron grip notwithstanding the fuddled brain.

The gaucho is more or less bow-legged; and, of course, the more crooked his legs are, the better for him in his struggle for existence. Off his horse his motions are awkward, like those of certain tardigrade mammals of arboreal habits when removed from their tree. He waddles in his walk; his hands feel for the reins; his toes turn inwards like a duck's. And here, perhaps, we can see why foreign travellers, judging him from their own standpoint, invariably bring against him the charge of laziness. On horseback he is of all men most active. His patient endurance under privations that would drive other men to despair, his laborious days and feats of horsemanship, the long journeys he performs without rest or food, seem to simple dwellers on the surface of the earth almost like miracles. Deprive him of his horse and he can do nothing but sit on the ground cross-legged or *en cuclillas*—on his heels. You have, to use his own figurative language, cut off his feet.

The Naturalist in La Plata, 1893

A Young Girl Singing

On the other side of the hedge in which the bird sat concealed was a cottage garden, and there on a swing fastened to a pair of apple trees, a girl about eleven years old sat lazily swinging herself. Once or twice after she began singing the nightingale broke out again, and then at last he became silent altogether, his voice overpowered by hers. Girl and bird were not five yards apart.

It greatly surprised me to hear her singing, for it was eleven o'clock, when all the village children were away at the national school, a time of day when, so far as human sounds were concerned, there reigned an almost unbroken silence. But very soon I recalled the fact that this was a very lazy child, and concluded that she had coaxed her mother into sending an excuse for keeping her at home, and so had kept her liberty on this beautiful morning. About two minutes' walk from the cottage, at the side of the crooked road running through the village, there was a group of ancient pollarded elm trees with huge, hollow trunks, and behind them an open space, a pleasant green slope, where some of the village children used to go every day to play on the grass. Here I used to see this girl lying in the sun, her dark chestnut hair loosed and scattered on the sward, her arms stretched out, her eyes nearly closed, basking in the sun, as happy as some heat-loving wild animal. No, it was not strange that she had not gone to school with the others when her disposition was remembered, but most strange to hear a voice of such quality in a spot where nature was rich and lovely, and only man was, if not vile, at all events singularly wanting in the finer human qualities.

Looking out from the open window across the low hedge-top, I could see her as she alternately rose and fell with slow, indolent motion, now waist-high above the green dividing wall, then only her brown head visible resting against the rope just where her hand had grasped it. And as she swayed herself to and fro she sang that simple melody—probably some child's hymn which she had been taught at the Sunday school; but it was a very long hymn, or else she repeated the same few stanzas many times, and after each there was a brief pause, and then the voice that seemed to fall and rise with the motion went on as before. I could have stood there for an hour—nay, for hours—listening to it, so fresh and so pure was the clear young voice, which had no earthly trouble in it, and no passion, and was in this like the melody of the birds of which I had lately heard so much; and with it all that tenderness and depth which is not theirs, but is human only and of the soul.

Birds in Town and Village, 1893

The Raven

Thinking, after leaving him, of the sublime conflict he had described, and of the raven's savage nature, Blake's question in his 'Tiger, tiger, burning bright,' came to my mind:

Did He who made the lamb make thee?

We can but answer that it was no other; that when the Supreme Artist had fashioned it with bold, free lines out of the blue-black rock, He smote upon it with His mallet and bade it live and speak; and its voice when it spoke was in accord with its appearance and temper—the savage, human-like croak, and the loud, angry bark, as if a deep-chested man had barked like a bloodhound.

Birds and Man, 1901

White Ducks

In the middle of a green pasture I came on a pool of rain-water, thirty or forty feet long, collected in a depression in the ground, of that blue colour sometimes seen in a shallow pool in certain states of the atmosphere and sunlight—an indescribable and very wonderful tint, unlike the blue of a lake or of the deep sea, or of any blue flower or mineral, but you perhaps think it more beautiful than any of these; and if it must be compared with something else it perhaps comes nearest to deep sapphire blues. When an artist in search of a subject sees it he looks aside and, going on his way, tries to forget it, as when he sees the hedges hung with spiders' lace sparkling with rainbow-coloured dewdrops, knowing that these effects are beyond the reach of his art. And on this fairy lake in the midst of the pale green field, its blue surface ruffled by the light wind, floated three or four white ducks; whiter than the sea-gulls, for they were all purest white, with no colour except on their yellow beaks. The light wind ruffled their feathers too, a little, as they turned this way and that, disturbed at my approach; and just then, when I stood to gaze, the sun shone full out after the passing of a light cloud, and flushed the blue pool and floating birds, silvering the ripples and causing the plumage to shine as if with a light of its own.

Adventures among Birds, 1913

The Hover-Fly

The whole life of this fly, as a fly, is passed in a perpetual joyous game, or rather dance, with little intervals for rest and refreshment; a miraculous dance in which it suspends itself, still as a stone-fly suspended in the air, then suddenly vanishes to describe a hundred fantastic figures in its flight, like a skater figure-skating on the ice, with such velocity as to be now invisible and now seen as a faint shadowy line by the onlooker.

It has the habit, like that of the humming-bird, of darting close to your face and remaining motionless in the air for some time, and when thus suspended close to your face you are able to hear and appreciate the sounds it emits—the fine clear musical note and its changes. I cannot but believe at such times that its wing-music is as much to the insect itself as are its brilliant fantastic motions; that if the fly could be magnified to the size of, let us say, a humming-bird, and the sound it produced increased in the same degree and made audible to us, we should find the music an appropriate and an essential part of the performance.

A Hind in Richmond Park, 1922

OLIVER WENDELL HOLMES JR.

1841–1935

The Life of the Law

The life of the law has not been logic: it has been experience. The felt necessities of the time, the prevalent moral and political theories, intuitions of public policy, avowed or unconscious, even the prejudices which judges share with their fellow-men, have had a good deal more to do than the syllogism in determining the rules by which men should be governed. The law embodies the story of a nation's development through many centuries, and it cannot be dealt with as if it contained only the axioms and corollaries of a book of mathematics.

The Common Law, 1881

Certitude and Scepticism

Certitude is not the test of certainty. We have been cock-sure of many things that were not so. If I may quote myself again, property, friendship, and truth have a common root in time. One can not be wrenched from the rocky crevices into which one has grown for many years without feeling that one is attacked in one's life. What we most love and revere generally is determined by early associations. I love granite rocks and barberry bushes, no doubt because with them were my earliest joys that reach back through the past eternity of my life. But while one's experience thus makes certain preferences dogmatic for oneself, recognition of how they came to be so leaves one able to see that others, poor souls, may be equally dogmatic about something else. And this again means scepticism. Not that one's belief or love does not remain. Not that we would not fight and die for it if important—we all, whether we know it or not, are fighting to make the kind of a world that we should like—but that we have learned to recognize that others will fight and die to make a different world, with equal sincerity or belief. Deep-seated preferences can not be argued about—you can not argue a man into liking a glass of beer—and therefore, when differences are sufficiently far reaching, we try to kill the other man rather than let him have his way. But that is perfectly consistent with admitting that, so far as appears, his grounds are just as good as ours.

'Natural Law', 1918, *Collected Legal Papers*

H. M. STANLEY

1841–1904

A Quest Accomplished

We were now about three hundred yards from the village of Ujiji, and the crowds are dense about me. Suddenly I hear a voice on my right say,

'Good morning, sir!'

Startled at hearing this greeting in the midst of such a crowd of black people, I turn sharply around in search of the man, and see him at my side, with the blackest of faces, but animated and joyous—a man dressed in a long white shirt, with a turban of American sheeting around his woolly head, and I ask:

'Who the mischief are you?'

'I am Susi, the servant of Dr Livingstone,' said he, smiling, and showing a gleaming row of teeth.

'What! Is Dr Livingstone here?'

'Yes, sir.'

'In this village?'

'Yes, sir.'

'Are you sure?'

'Sure, sure, sir. Why, I leave him just now.' . . .

'Now, you Susi, run, and tell the Doctor I am coming.'

'Yes, sir,' and off he darted like a madman. . . .

Soon Susi came running back, and asked me my name; he had told the Doctor that I was coming, but the Doctor was too surprised to believe him, and, when the Doctor asked him my name, Susi was rather staggered.

But, during Susi's absence, the news had been conveyed to the Doctor that it was surely a white man that was coming, whose guns were firing and whose flag could be seen; and the great Arab magnates of Ujiji—Mohammed bin Sali, Sayd bin Majid, Abid bin Suleiman, Mohammed bin Gharib, and others—had gathered together before the Doctor's house, and the Doctor had come out from his veranda to discuss the matter and await my arrival.

In the meantime, the head of the Expedition had halted, and the *kirangozi* was out of the ranks, holding his flag aloft, and Selim said to me, 'I see the Doctor, sir. Oh, what an old man! He has got a white beard.' And I—what would I not have given for a bit of friendly wilderness, where, unseen, I might vent my joy in some mad freak, such as idiotically biting my hand, turning a somersault, or slashing at trees, in order to allay those exciting feelings that were well-nigh uncontrollable. My heart beats fast, but I must not let my face betray my emotions, lest it shall detract from the dignity of a white man appearing under such extraordinary circumstances.

So I did that which I thought was most dignified. I pushed back the crowds, and, passing from the rear, walked down a living avenue of people, until I came in front of the semicircle of Arabs, in the front of which stood the white man with the grey beard. As I advanced slowly towards him I noticed he was pale, looked wearied, had a grey beard, wore a bluish cap with a faded gold band round it, had on a red-sleeved waistcoat, and a pair of grey tweed trousers. I would have run to him, only I was a coward in the presence of such a mob—would have embraced him, only, he being an Englishman, I did not know how he would receive me; so I did what cowardice and false pride suggested was the best thing—walked deliberately to him, took off my hat, and said:

'Dr Livingstone, I presume?'

'YES,' said he, with a kind smile, lifting his cap slightly.

I replace my hat on my head, and he puts on his cap, and we both grasp hands, and I then say aloud:

'I thank God, Doctor, I have been permitted to see you.'

He answered, 'I feel thankful that I am here to welcome you.'

How I Found Livingstone, 1872

WILLIAM JAMES
1842–1910

Belief and Action

Now, I wish to show what to my knowledge has never been clearly pointed out, that belief (as measured by action) not only does and must continually outstrip scientific evidence, but that there is a certain class of truths of whose reality belief is a factor as well as a confessor; and that as regards this class of truths faith is not only licit and pertinent, but essential and indispensable. The truths cannot become true till our faith has made them so.

Suppose, for example, that I am climbing in the Alps and have had the ill-luck to work myself into a position from which the only escape is by a terrible leap. Being without similar experience, I have no evidence of my ability to perform it successfully; but hope and confidence in myself make me sure I shall not miss my aim, and nerve my feet to execute what without those subjective emotions would perhaps have been impossible. But suppose that, on the contrary, the emotions of fear and mistrust preponderate; or suppose that, having just read the *Ethics of Belief*, I feel it would be sinful to act upon an assumption unverified by previous experience—why, then I shall hesitate so long that at last, exhausted and trembling, and launching myself in a moment of despair, I miss my foothold and roll into the abyss. In this case (and it is one of an immense class) the part of wisdom clearly is to believe what one desires; for the belief is one of the indispensable preliminary conditions of the realization of its object. *There are then cases where faith creates its own verification.* Believe, and you shall be right, for you shall save yourself; doubt, and you shall again be right, for you shall perish. The only difference is that to believe is greatly to your advantage.

'The Sentiment of Rationality', 1880; reprinted in *The Will to Believe*

On Refusing to Subscribe to a Monument to Schopenhauer

As for what you propose, what could be more tempting to an obscure chicken like myself than to see his name printed in the company of the Illustrious whom you enumerate. But is there no other man than Schopenhauer on whom we can combine? I really *must* decline to stir a finger for the glory of one who studiously lived for no other purpose than to spit upon the lives of the like of me and all those I care for. Isn't there something rather immoral in *publicly* doing homage to one whose writings, if the public could but understand and heed them, would undo whatever of simple kindliness and hope keeps its life sweet? And isn't there something inwardly farcical in getting up a mundane celebration and signing an 'uproar,' and what vanity more I know not, for the personal magnification of one, the burden of whose song—however little his life may have consisted with it—was the annihilation of personal selfhood? Isn't it like offering a fur overcoat to a sweating equatorial African? And won't Schopenhauer's spirit, looking down from the Isles of the Blest, make gibes at the Committee more drastic than any of those to be found in his printed works? It seems to me that the indiscriminate newspaper optimism of our day rather overshoots the mark when it takes to hurrahing for pessimism itself. It is as if the Parisians should raise a monument to Bismarck or the Comte de Chambord to Robespierre, because 'after all, they are good fellows too.'

There *are* intellectual distinctions; why should scholars, of all men, be called on to wipe them out? If the citizens of Frankfort want to embellish their town by monuments to the celebrated men who lived there, merely because they were celebrated, for the country people to gape at, without knowing which is which—well and good, that's all included in the great popular, country-fair, animal-spirit side of life, which Schopenhauer so much loathed. But if there be any kernel of truth in Schopenhauer's system (and it seems to me there is a deep one), it ought to be celebrated in silence and in secret, by the inner lives of those to whom it speaks; taking some things seriously is incompatible with 'celebrating' them!

letter to Karl Hillebrand, 1883

Habit

Habit is thus the enormous fly-wheel of society, its most precious conservative agent. It alone is what keeps us all within the bounds of ordinance, and saves the children of fortune from the envious uprisings of the poor. It alone prevents the hardest and most repulsive walks of life from being deserted by those brought up to tread therein. It keeps the fisherman and the deck-hand at sea through the winter; it holds the miner in his darkness, and nails the countryman to his log-cabin and his lonely farm through all the months of snow; it protects us from invasion by the natives of the desert and the frozen zone. It dooms us all to fight out the battle of life upon the lines of our nurture or our early choice, and to make the best of a pursuit that disagrees, because there is no other for which we are fitted, and it is too late to begin again. It keeps different social strata from mixing. Already at the age of twenty-five you see the professional mannerism settling down on the young commercial traveller, on the young doctor, on the young minister, on the young counsellor-at-law. You see the little lines of cleavage running through the character, the tricks of thought, the prejudices, the ways of the 'shop,' in a word, from which the man can by-and-by no more escape than his coat-sleeve can suddenly fall into a new set of folds. On the whole, it is best he should not escape. It is well for the world that in most of us, by the age of thirty, the character has set like plaster, and will never soften again.

Psychology: Briefer Course, 1892

On a Frozen Lake

The lustre of the present hour is always borrowed from the background of possibilities it goes with. Let our common experiences be enveloped in an eternal moral order; let our suffering have an immortal significance; let Heaven smile upon the earth, and deities pay their visits; let faith and hope be the atmosphere which man breathes in;—and his days pass by with zest; they stir with prospects, they thrill with remoter values. Place round them on the contrary the curdling cold and gloom and absence of all permanent meaning which for pure naturalism and the popular science evolutionism of our time are all that is visible ultimately, and the thrill stops short, or turns rather to an anxious trembling.

For naturalism, fed on recent cosmological speculations, mankind is in a position similar to that of a set of people living on a frozen lake, surrounded by cliffs over which there is no escape, yet knowing that little by little the ice is melting, and the inevitable day drawing near when the last film of it will disappear, and to be drowned ignominiously will be the human creature's portion. The merrier the skating, the warmer and more sparkling the sun by day, and the ruddier the bonfires at night, the more poignant the sadness with which one must take in the meaning of the total situation.

The Varieties of Religious Experience, 1902

Bad Dreams and Hard Facts

The normal process of life contains moments as bad as any of those which insane melancholy is filled with, moments in which radical evil gets its innings and takes its solid turn. The lunatic's visions of horror are all drawn from the material of daily fact. Our civilization is founded on the shambles, and every individual existence goes out in a lonely spasm of helpless agony. If you protest, my friend, wait till you arrive there yourself! To believe in the carnivorous reptiles of geologic times is hard for our imagination—they seem too much like mere museum specimens. Yet there is no tooth in any one of those museum-skulls that did not daily through long years of the foretime hold fast to the body struggling in despair of some fated living victim. Forms of horror just as dreadful to the victims, if on a small spatial scale, fill the world about us to-day. Here on our very hearths and in our gardens the infernal cat plays with the panting mouse, or holds the hot bird fluttering in her jaws. Crocodiles and rattlesnakes and pythons are at this moment vessels of life as real as we are; their loathsome existence fills every minute of every day that drags its length along; and whenever they or other wild beasts clutch their living prey, the deadly horror which an agitated melancholiac feels is the literally right reaction on the situation.

The Varieties of Religious Experience

On the Later Style of Henry James

You know how opposed your whole 'third manner' of execution is to the literary ideals which animate my crude and Orson-like breast, mine being to say a thing in one sentence as straight and explicit as it can be made, and then to drop it forever; yours being to avoid naming it straight, but by dint of breathing and sighing all round and round it, to arouse in the reader who may have had a similar perception already (Heaven help him if he has n't!) the illusion of a solid object, made (like the 'ghost' at the Polytechnic) wholly out of impalpable materials, air, and the prismatic interferences of light, ingeniously focused by mirrors upon empty space. But you *do* it, that's the queerness! And the complication of innuendo and associative reference on the enormous scale to which you give way to it does so *build out* the matter for the reader that the result is to solidify, by the mere bulk of the process, the like perception from which *he* has to start. As air, by dint of its volume, will weight like a corporeal body; so his own poor little initial perception, swathed in this gigantic envelopment of suggestive atmosphere, grows like a germ into something vastly bigger and more substantial. But it's the rummest method for one to employ systematically as you do nowadays; and you employ it at your peril. In this crowded and hurried reading age, pages that require such close attention remain unread and neglected. You can't skip a word if you are to get the effect, and 19 out of 20 worthy readers grow intolerant. The method seems perverse: 'Say it *out*, for God's sake,' they cry, 'and have done with it.' And so I say now, give us *one* thing in your older directer manner, just to show that, in spite of your paradoxical success in this unheard-of method, you *can* still write according to accepted canons. Give us that interlude; and then continue like the 'curiosity of literature' which you have become. For gleams and innuendoes and felicitous verbal insinuations you are unapproachable, but the *core* of literature is solid. Give it to us *once* again! The bare perfume of things will not support existence, and the effect of solidity you reach is but perfume and simulacrum.

letter to Henry James, 1907

AMBROSE BIERCE
1842–1914?

An Escape from Hanging

As Peyton Farquhar fell straight downward through the bridge he lost consciousness and was as one already dead. From this state he was awakened—ages later, it seemed to him—by the pain of a sharp pressure upon his throat, followed by a sense of suffocation. Keen, poignant agonies seemed to shoot from his neck downward through every fibre of his body and limbs. These pains appeared to flash along well-defined lines of ramification and to beat with an inconceivably rapid periodicity. They seemed like streams of pulsating fire heating him to an intolerable temperature. As to his head, he was conscious of nothing but a feeling of fullness—of congestion. These sensations were unaccompanied by thought. The intellectual part of his nature was already effaced; he had power only to feel, and feeling was torment. He was conscious of motion. Encompassed in a luminous cloud, of which he was now merely the fiery heart, without material substance, he swung through unthinkable arcs of oscillation, like a vast pendulum. Then all at once, with terrible suddenness, the light about him shot upward with the noise of a loud plash; a frightful roaring was in his ears, and all was cold and dark. The power of thought was restored; he knew that the rope had broken and he had fallen into the stream. There was no additional strangulation; the noose about his neck was already suffocating him and kept the water from his lungs. To die of hanging at the bottom of a river!—the idea seemed to him ludicrous. He opened his eyes in the darkness and saw above him a gleam of light, but how distant, how inaccessible! He was still sinking, for the light became fainter and fainter until it was a mere glimmer. Then it began to grow and brighten, and he knew that he was rising toward the surface—knew it with reluctance, for he was now very comfortable. 'To be hanged and drowned,' he thought, 'that is not so bad; but I do not wish to be shot. No, I will not be shot; that is not fair.'

He was not conscious of an effort, but a sharp pain in his wrist apprised him that he was trying to free his hands. He gave the struggle his attention, as an idler might observe the feat of a juggler, without interest in the outcome. What splendid effort!—what magnificent, what superhuman strength! Ah, that was a fine endeavour! Bravo! The cord fell away; his arms parted and floated upward, the hands dimly seen on each side in the growing light. He watched them with a new interest as first one and then the other pounced upon the noose at his neck. They tore it away and thrust it fiercely aside, its undulations resembling those of a water-snake. 'Put it back, put it back!' He thought he shouted these words to his hands, for the undoing of the noose had been succeeded by the direst pang that he had yet experienced. His neck ached horribly; his brain was on fire; his heart, which had been fluttering faintly, gave a great leap, trying to force itself out at his mouth. His whole body was racked and wrenched with an insupportable anguish! But his disobedient hands gave no heed to the command. They beat the water vigorously with quick, downward strokes, forcing him to the surface. He felt his head emerge; his eyes were blinded by the sunlight; his chest expanded convulsively, and with a supreme and crowning agony his lungs engulfed a great draught of air, which instantly he expelled in a shriek!

He was now in full possession of his physical senses. They were, indeed, preternaturally keen and alert. Something in the awful disturbance of his organic system had so exalted and refined them that they made record of things never before perceived. He felt the ripples upon his face and heard their separate sounds as they struck. He looked at the forest on the bank of the stream, saw the individual trees, the leaves and the veining of each leaf—saw the very insects upon them: the locusts, the brilliant-bodied flies, the grey spiders stretching their webs from twig to twig. He noted the prismatic colours in all the dewdrops upon a million blades of grass. The humming of the gnats that danced above the eddies of the stream, the beating of the dragon-flies' wings, the strokes of the water-spiders' legs, like oars which had lifted their boat—all these made audible music. A fish slid along beneath his eyes and he heard the rush of its body parting the water.

He had come to the surface facing down the stream; in a moment the visible world seemed to wheel slowly round, himself the pivotal point, and he saw the bridge, the fort, the soldiers upon the bridge, the captain, the sergeant, the two privates, his executioners . . .

'An Occurrence at Owl Creek Bridge', *Tales of Soldiers and Civilians*, 1891

HENRY JAMES
1843–1916

A Prospective Brother-in-Law

M. de Bellegarde then presented his prospective brother-in-law to some twenty other persons of both sexes, selected apparently for their typically august character. In some cases this character was written in a good round hand upon the countenance of the wearer; in others Newman was thankful for such help as his companion's impressively brief intimations contributed to the discovery of it. There were large, majestic men, and small demonstrative men; there were ugly ladies in yellow lace and quaint jewels, and pretty ladies with white shoulders from which jewels and everything else were absent. Every one gave Newman extreme attention, every one smiled, every one was charmed to make his acquaintance, every one looked at him with that soft hardness of good society which puts out its hand but keeps its fingers closed over the coin. If the marquis was going about as a bear-leader, if the fiction of Beauty and the Beast was supposed to have found its companion-piece, the general impression appeared to be that the bear was a very fair imitation of humanity. Newman found his reception among the marquis's friends very 'pleasant'; he could not have said more for it. It was pleasant to be treated with so much explicit politeness; it was pleasant to hear neatly turned civilities, with a flavor of wit, uttered from beneath carefully-shaped mustaches; it was pleasant to see clever Frenchwomen—they all seemed clever—turn their backs to their partners to get a good look at the strange American whom Claire de Cintré was to marry, and reward the object of the exhibition with a charming smile.

The American, 1877

The Doctor Gives His Instructions

'It is congestion of the lungs,' Dr Sloper said to Catherine, 'I shall need very good nursing. It will make no difference, for I shall not recover; but I wish everything to be done, to the smallest detail, as if I should. I hate an ill-conducted sick-room; and you will be so good as to nurse me on the hypothesis that I shall get well.' But he had never been wrong in his life, and he was not wrong now. He died after three weeks' illness.

Washington Square, 1881

Isabel Archer

Altogether, with her meagre knowledge, her inflated ideals, her confidence at once innocent and dogmatic, her temper at once exacting and indulgent, her mixture of curiosity and fastidiousness, of vivacity and indifference, her desire to look very well and to be if possible even better, her determination to see, to try, to know, her combination of the delicate desultory flame-like spirit and the eager and personal creature of conditions: she would be an easy victim of scientific criticism: if she were not intended to awaken on the reader's part an impulse more tender and more purely expectant.

The Portrait of a Lady, 1881

Gilbert Osmond

It was the house of darkness, the house of dumbness, the house of suffocation. Osmond's beautiful mind gave it neither light nor air; Osmond's beautiful mind indeed seemed to peep down from a small high window and mock at her. Of course it had not been physical suffering; for physical suffering there might have been a remedy. She could come and go; she had her liberty; her husband was perfectly polite. He took himself so seriously; it was something appalling. Under all his culture, all his cleverness, his amenity, under his good-nature, his facility, his knowledge of life, his egoism lay hidden like a serpent in a bank of flowers.

The Portrait of a Lady

Trollope

His great, his inestimable merit was a complete appreciation of the usual. Trollope, therefore, with his eyes comfortably fixed on the familiar, the actual, was far from having invented a new category; his distinction is that in resting just there his vision took in so much of the field. And then he *felt* all daily and immediate things as well as saw them; felt them in a simple, direct, salubrious way, with their sadness, their gladness, their charm, their comicality, all their obvious and measureable meanings.

'Anthony Trollope', 1883

A Brilliant Young Journalist

He had small, fair features, remarkably neat, and pretty eyes, and a moustache that he caressed, and an air of juvenility much at variance with his grizzled locks, and the free familiar reference in which he was apt to indulge in his career as a journalist. His friends knew that in spite of his delicacy and his prattle he was what they called a live man; his appearance was perfectly reconcilable with a large degree of literary entertainment. It should be explained that for the most part they attached to this idea the same meaning as Selah Tarrant—a state of intimacy with the newspapers, the cultivation of the great arts of publicity. For this ingenuous son of his age all distinction between the person and the artist had ceased to exist; the writer was personal, the person food for newsboys, and everything and every one were every one's business. All things, with him, referred themselves to print, and print meant simply infinite reporting, a promptitude of announcement, abusive when necessary, or even when not, about his fellow-citizens. He poured contumely on their private life, on their personal appearance, with the best conscience in the world. His faith, again, was the faith of Selah Tarrant—that being in the newspapers is a condition of bliss, and that it would be fastidious to question the terms of the privilege. He was an *enfant de la balle*, as the French say; he had begun his career, at the age of fourteen, by going the rounds of the hotels, to cull flowers from the big, greasy registers which lie on the marble counters; and he might flatter himself that he had contributed in his measure, and on behalf of a vigilant public opinion, the pride of a democratic State, to the great end of preventing the American citizen from attempting clandestine journeys. Since then he had ascended other steps of the same ladder; he was the most brilliant young interviewer on the Boston press.

The Bostonians, 1886

Feminization

'Oh, I suppose you want to destroy us by neglect, by silence!' Verena exclaimed, with the same brightness.

'No, I don't want to destroy you, any more than I want to save you. There has been far too much talk about you, and I want to leave you alone altogether. My interest is in my own sex; yours evidently can look after itself. That's what I want to save.'

Verena saw that he was more serious now than he had been before, that he was not piling it up satirically, but saying really and a trifle wearily, as if suddenly he were tired of much talk, what he meant. 'To save it from what?' she asked.

'From the most damnable feminization! I am so far from thinking, as you set forth the other night, that there is not enough woman in our general life, that it has long been pressed home to me that there is a great deal too much. The whole generation is womanized; the masculine tone is passing out of the world; it's a feminine, a nervous, hysterical, chattering, canting age, an age of hollow phrases and false delicacy and exaggerated solicitudes and coddled sensibilities, which, if we don't soon look out, will usher in the reign of mediocrity, of the feeblest and flattest and the most pretentious that has ever been. The masculine character, the ability to dare and endure, to know and yet not fear reality, to look the world in the face and take it for what it is—a very queer and partly very base mixture—that is what I want to preserve, or rather, as I may say, to recover; and I must tell you that I don't in the least care what becomes of you ladies while I make the attempt!'

The Bostonians

The Vicar's Sister

The guest next to me, dear woman, was Miss Poyle, the vicar's sister, a robust, unmodulated person.

The Figure in the Carpet, 1896

The Diamond Jubilee

The foremost, the immense impression is of course the constant, the permanent, the ever-supreme—the impression of that greatest glory of our race, its passionate feeling for trade. I doubt if the commercial instinct be not, as London now feels it throb and glow, quite as striking as any conceivable projection of it that even our American pressure of the pump might, at the highest, produce. That is the real tent of the circus—that is the real back of the tapestry. There have long, I know, been persons ready to prove by book that the explanation of the 'historical event' has always been somebody's desire to make money; never, at all events, from the near view, will that explanation have covered so much of the ground. No result of the fact that the Queen has reigned sixty years—no sort of sentimental or other association with it—begins to have the air of coming home to the London conscience like this happy consequence of the chance in it to sell something dear. As yet that chance is the one sound that fills the air, and will probably be the only note audibly stuck till the plaudits of the day itself begin to substitute, none too soon, a more mellifluous one. When the people are all at the windows, and in the trees and on the water-spouts, house-tops, scaffolds and other ledges and coigns of vantage set as traps for them by the motive power, *then* doubtless there will be another aspect to reckon with—then we shall see, of the grand occasion, nothing but what is decently and presentably historic. All I mean is that, pending the apotheosis, London has found in this particular chapter of the career of its aged sovereign only an enormous selfish advertisement.

'London Notes', *Harper's Weekly*, 1897

Beauty in London

'What I was going to say was that she has in her expression all that's charming in her nature. But beauty, in London'—and feeling that he held his visitor's attention, he gave himself the pleasure of freely unfolding his idea—'staring, glaring, obvious, knockdown beauty, as plain as a poster on a wall, an advertisement of soap or whisky, something that speaks to the crowd and crosses the foot-lights, fetches such a price in the market that the absence of it, for a woman with a girl to marry, inspires endless terrors and constitutes for the wretched pair—to speak of mother and daughter alone—a sort of social bankruptcy. London doesn't love the latent or the lurking, has neither time, nor taste, nor sense for anything less discernible than the red flag in front of the steam-roller. It wants cash over the counter and letters ten feet high. Therefore, you see, it's all as yet rather a dark question for poor Nanda—a question that, in a way, quite occupies the foreground of her mother's earnest little life. How *will* she look, what will be thought of her and what will she be able to do for herself? She's at the age when the whole thing—speaking of her appearance, her possible share of good looks—is still, in a manner, in a fog. But everything depends on it.'

The Awkward Age, 1899

Lambs to the Slaughter

Little Aggie differed from any young person he had ever met in that she had been deliberately prepared for consumption and in that furthermore the gentleness of her spirit had immensely helped the preparation. Nanda, beside her, was a northern savage, and the reason was partly that the elements of that young lady's nature were already, were publicly, were almost indecorously active. They were practically there for good or for ill; experience was still to come and what they might work out to still a mystery; but the sum would get itself done with the figures now on the slate. On little Aggie's slate the figures were yet to be written; which sufficiently accounted for the difference of the two surfaces. Both the girls struck him as lambs with the great shambles of life in their future; but while one, with its neck in pink ribbon, had no consciousness but that of being fed from the hand with the small sweet biscuit of unobjectionable knowledge, the other struggled with instinct and forebodings, with the suspicion of its doom and the far-borne scent, in the flowery fields, of blood.

The Awkward Age

An Image in the Mirror

Man rejoices in an incomparable faculty for presently mutilating and disfiguring any plaything that has helped create for him the illusion of leisure; nevertheless, so long as life retains its power of projecting itself upon his imagination, he will find the novel work off the impression better than anything he knows. Anything better for the purpose has assuredly yet to be discovered. He will give it up only when life itself too thoroughly disagrees with him. Even then, indeed, may fiction not find a second wind, or a fiftieth, in the very portrayal of that collapse? Till the world is an unpeopled void there will be an image in the mirror. What need more immediately concern us, therefore, is the care of seeing that the image shall continue various and vivid.

'The Future of the Novel', 1899

Kate Croy

She stared into the tarnished glass too hard indeed to be staring at her beauty alone. She readjusted the poise of her black, closely-feathered hat; retouched, beneath it, the thick fall of her dusky hair; kept her eyes, aslant, no less on her beautiful averted than on her beautiful presented oval. She was dressed altogether in black, which gave an even tone, by contrast, to her clear face and made her hair more harmoniously dark. Outside, on the balcony, her eyes showed as blue; within at the mirror, they showed almost as black. She was handsome, but the degree of it was not sustained by items and aids; a circumstance moreover playing its part at almost any time in the impression she produced. The impression was one that remained, but as regards the sources of it no sum in addition would have made up the total. She had stature without height, grace without motion, presence without mass. Slender and simple, frequently soundless, she was somehow always in the line of the eye—she counted singularly for its pleasure. More 'dressed,' often, with fewer accessories, than other women, or less dressed, should occasion require, with more, she probably could not have given the key to these felicities. They were mysteries of which her friends were conscious—those friends whose general explanation was to say that she was clever, whether or no it were taken by the world as the cause or as the effect of her charm. If she saw more things than her fine face in the dull glass of her father's lodgings, she might have seen that, after all, she was not herself a fact in the collapse. She didn't judge herself cheap, she didn't make for misery. Personally, at least, she was not chalk-marked for the auction. She hadn't given up yet, and the broken sentence, if she was the last word, *would* end with a sort of meaning. There was a minute during which, though her eyes were fixed, she quite visibly lost herself in the thought of the way she might still pull things round had she only been a man. It was the name, above all, she would take in hand—the precious name she so liked and that, in spite of the harm her wretched father had done it, was not yet past praying for. She loved it in fact the more tenderly for that bleeding wound. But what could a penniless girl do with it but let it go?

The Wings of the Dove, 1902

A Venetian Palazzo

Not yet so much as this morning had she felt herself sink into possession; gratefully glad that the warmth of the southern summer was still in the high, florid rooms, palatial chambers where hard, cool pavements took reflections in their lifelong polish, and where the sun on the stirred sea-water, flickering up through open windows, played over the painted 'subjects' in the splendid ceilings—medallions of purple and brown, of brave old melancholy colour, medals as of old reddened gold, embossed and beribboned, all toned with time and all flourished and scalloped, and gilded about, set in their great moulded and figured concavity (a nest of white cherubs, friendly creatures of the air).

The Wings of the Dove

Evenings in Paris

I

The little waxed *salle-à-manger* was sallow and sociable; François dancing over it, all smiles, was a man and a brother; the high-shouldered *patronne*, with her high-held, much-rubbed hands, seemed always assenting exuberantly to something unsaid; the Paris evening in short, was, for Strether, in the very taste of the soup, in the goodness, as he was innocently pleased to think, of the wine, in the pleasant coarse texture of the napkin and the crunch of the thick-crusted bread.

II

It was the evening hour, but daylight was long now and Paris more than ever penetrating. The scent of flowers was in the streets, he had the whiff of violets perpetually in his nose; and he had attached himself to sounds and suggestions, vibrations of the air, human and dramatic, he imagined, as they were not in other places, that came out for him more and more as the mild afternoon deepened, a far-off hum, a sharp, near click on the asphalt, a voice calling, replying, somewhere, and as full of tone as an actor's in a play.

The Ambassadors, 1903

Jim

Small and fat, and constantly facetious, straw-coloured and destitute of marks, he would have been practically indistinguishable had not his constant preference for light-grey clothes, for white hats, for very big cigars and very little stories, done what it could for his identity.

The Ambassadors

Colonel Assingham

Bob Assingham was distinguished altogether by a leanness of person, a leanness quite distinct from physical laxity, which might have been determined, on the part of superior powers, by views of transport and accommodation, and which in fact verged on the abnormal. He 'did' himself well as his friends mostly knew, yet remained hungrily thin, with facial, with abdominal cavities quite grim in their effect, and with a consequent looseness of apparel that, combined with a choice of queer light shades and of strange straw-like textures, of the aspect of Chinese mats, provocative of wonder at his sources of supply, suggested the habit of tropic islands, a continual cane-bottomed chair, a governorship exercised on wide verandahs. His smooth round head, with the particular shade of its white hair, was like a silver pot reversed; his cheekbones and the bristle of his moustache were worthy of Attila the Hun. The hollows of his eyes were deep and darksome, but the eyes, within them, were like little blue flowers plucked that morning. He knew everything that could be known about life, which he regarded as for far the greater part, a matter of pecuniary arrangement. His wife accused him of a want, alike, of moral and of intellectual reaction, or rather indeed of a complete incapacity for either. He never went even so far as to understand what she meant, and it didn't at all matter, since he could be in spite of the limitation a perfectly social creature. The infirmities, the predicaments of men neither surprised nor shocked him, and indeed—which was perhaps his only real loss in a thrifty career—scarce even amused; he took them for granted without horror, classifying them after their kind and calculating results and chances.

The Golden Bowl, 1905

The Skyscrapers of New York

The 'tall buildings,' which have so promptly usurped a glory that affects you as rather surprised, as yet, at itself, the multitudinous sky-scrapers standing up to the view, from the water, like extravagant pins in a cushion already overplanted, and stuck in as in the dark, anywhere and anyhow, have at least the felicity of carrying out the fairness of tone, of taking the sun and the shade in the manner of towers of marble. They are not all of marble, I believe, by any means, even if some may be, but they are impudently new and still more impudently 'novel'—this in common with so many other terrible things in America—and they are triumphant payers of dividends; all of which uncontested and unabashed pride, with flash of innumerable windows and flicker of subordinate gilt attributions, is like the flare, up and down their long, narrow faces, of the lamps of some general permanent 'celebration.'

You see the pin-cushion in profile, so to speak, on passing between Jersey City and Twenty-third Street, but you get it broadside on, this loose nosegay of architectural flowers, if you skirt the Battery, well out, and embrace the whole plantation. Then the 'American beauty,' the rose of interminable stem, becomes the token of the cluster at large—to that degree that, positively, this is all that is wanted for emphasis of your final impression. Such growths, you feel, have confessedly arisen but to be 'picked,' in time, with a shears; nipped short off, by waiting fate, as soon as 'science,' applied to gain, has put upon the table, from far up its sleeve, some more winning card. Crowned not only with no history, but with no credible possibility of time for history, and consecrated by no uses save the commercial at any cost, they are simply the most piercing notes in that concert of the expensively provisional into which your supreme sense of New York resolves itself. They never begin to speak to you, in the manner of the builded majesties of the world as we have heretofore known such—towers or temples or fortresses or palaces—with the authority of things of permanence or even of things of long duration. One story is good only till another is told, and sky-scrapers are the last word of economic ingenuity only till another word be written.

The American Scene, 1907

The Concord Bridge

I had forgotten, in all the years, with what thrilling clearness that supreme site speaks—though anciently, while so much of the course of the century was still to run, the distinctness might have seemed even greater. But to stand there again was to take home this fore-shortened view, the gained nearness, to one's sensibility; to look straight over the heads of the 'American Weimar' company at the inestimable hour that had so handsomely set up for them their background. The Fight had been the hinge—so one saw it—on which the large revolving future was to turn; or it had been better, perhaps, the large firm nail, ringingly driven in, from which the beautiful portrait-group, as we see it to-day, was to hang. Beautiful exceedingly the local Emerson and Thoreau and Hawthorne and (in a fainter way) *tutti quanti*; but beautiful largely because the fine old incident down in the valley had so seriously prepared their effect.

The American Scene

JOSEPH FURPHY

1843–1912

Idle Hands

Unemployed at last!

Scientifically, such a contingency can never have befallen of itself. According to one *theory of the Universe*, the momentum of Original Impress has been tending toward this far-off, divine event ever since a scrap of fire-mist flew from the solar centre to form our planet. Not this event alone, of course; but every occurrence, past and present, from *the fall of captured Troy* to the fall of a captured insect. According to another theory, I hold an *independent diploma* as one of the architects of our Social System, with a *commission* to use my own judgement, and take my own risks, like any other unit of humanity. This theory, unlike the first, entails frequent hitches and cross-purposes; and to some malign operation of these I should owe my present holiday.

Orthodoxly, we are reduced to one assumption: namely, that my *indomitable old Adversary* has suddenly called to mind *Dr Watts's friendly hint* respecting the easy *enlistment* of idle hands.

Good. If either of the two first hypotheses be correct, my enforced *furlough* tacitly conveys the responsibility of extending a ray of *information*, however narrow and feeble, across the *path* of such *fellow-pilgrims* as have led lives more sedentary than my own—particularly as I have enough money, to *frank myself in a frugal way* for some weeks, as well as to purchase the few requisites of authorship.

If, on the other hand, my supposed safeguard of drudgery has been cut off at the meter by that *amusingly short-sighted old Conspirator*, it will be only fair to notify him that his age and experience, even his captivating habits and well-known hospitality, will be treated with scorn, rather than respect, in the paragraphs which he virtually forces me to write; and he is hereby invited to view his own *feather on the fatal dart*.

Such is Life, 1903

GERARD MANLEY HOPKINS

1844–1889

From the Early Diaries

Flick, fillip, flip, fleck, flake.

Flick means to touch or strike lightly as with the end of a whip, a finger etc. To *fleck* is the next tone above flick, still meaning to touch or strike lightly (and leave a mark of the touch or stroke) but in a broader less slight manner. Hence substantively a *fleck* is a piece of light, colour, substance etc. looking as though shaped or produced by such touches. *Flake* is a broad and decided *fleck*, a thin plate of something, the tone above it. Their connection is more clearly seen in the applications of the words to natural objects than in explanations. It would seem that *fillip* generally pronounced *flip* is a variation of *flick*, which however seems connected with *fly*, *flee*, *flit*, meaning to make fly off. Key to meaning of *flick*, *fleck* and *flake* is that of striking or cutting off the surface of a thing; in *flick* (as to flick off a fly) something little or light from the surface, while *flake* is a thin scale of surface. *Flay* is therefore connected, perhaps *flitch*.

1863

The sky minted into golden sequins.
Stars like gold tufts.
— —golden bees.
— —golden rowels.
Sky peak'd with tiny flames.
Stars like tiny-spoked wheels of fire.
Lantern of night pierced in eyelets, (or eye lets, which avoids ambiguity.)
Altogether peak is a good word. For sunlight through shutter, locks of hair, rays in brass knobs etc. Meadows peaked with flowers.

His gilded rowels
Now stars of blood.

1864

Tuncks is a good name.
Gerard Manley Tuncks. Poor Tuncks.

1864

Drops of rain hanging on rails etc seen with only the lower rim lighted like nails (of fingers). Screws of brooks and twines. Soft chalky look with more shadowy middles of the globes of cloud on a night with a moon faint or concealed. Mealy clouds with a not brilliant moon. Blunt buds of the ash. Pencil buds of the beech. Lobes of the trees. Cups of the eyes, Gathering back the lightly hinged eyelids. Bows of the eyelids. Pencil of eyelashes. Juices of the eyeball. Eyelids like leaves, petals, caps, tufted hats, handkerchiefs, sleeves, gloves. Also of the bones sleeved in flesh. Juices of the sunrise. Joints and veins of the same. Vermilion look of the hand held against a candle with the darker parts as the middles of the fingers and especially the knuckles covered with ash.

1866

Pigeons and Cuckoo-Song

I looked at the pigeons down in the kitchen yard and so on. They look like little gay jugs by shape when they walk, strutting and jod-jodding with their heads. The two young ones are all white and the pins of the folded wings, quill pleated over quill, are like crisp and shapely cuttleshells found on the shore. The others are dull thundercolour or black-grape-colour except in the white pieings, the quills and tail, and in the shot of the neck. I saw one up on the eaves of the roof: as it moved its head a crush of satin green came and went, a wet or soft flaming of the light.

Sometimes I hear the cuckoo with wonderful clear and plump and fluty notes: it is when the hollow of a rising ground conceives them and palms them up and throws them out, like blowing into a big humming ewer—for instance under Saddle Hill one beautiful day and another time from Hodder wood when we walked on the other side of the river . . .

Journal, 1873

Degrees of Beauty

I think then no one can admire beauty of the body more than I do, and it is of course a comfort to find beauty in a friend or a friend in beauty. But this kind of beauty is dangerous. Then comes the beauty of the mind, such as genius, and this is greater than the beauty of the body and not to call dangerous. And more beautiful than the beauty of the mind is beauty of character, the 'handsome heart'. Now every beauty is not a wit or genius nor has every wit or genius character. For though even bodily beauty, even the beauty of blooming health, is from the soul, in the sense, as we Aristotelian Catholics say, that the soul is the form of the body, yet the soul may have no other beauty, so to speak, than that which it expresses in the symmetry of the body—barring those blurs in the cast which wd. not be found in the die or the mould. This needs no illustration, as all know it. But what is more to be remarked is that in like manner the soul may have no further beauty than that which is seen in the mind, that there may be genius uninformed by character.

letter to Robert Bridges, 1879

Selfbeing

We may learn that all things are created by consideration of the world without or of ourselves the world within. The former is the consideration commonly dwelt on, but the latter takes on the mind more hold. I find myself both as man and as myself something most determined and distinctive, at pitch, more distinctive and higher pitched than anything else I see; I find myself with my pleasures and pains, my powers and my experiences, my deserts and guilt, my shame and sense of beauty, my dangers, hopes, fears, and all my fate, more important to myself than anything I see. And when I ask where does all this throng and stack of being, so rich, so distinctive, so important, come from / nothing I see can answer me. And this whether I speak of human nature or of my individuality, my selfbeing. For human nature, being more highly pitched, selved, and distinctive than anything in the world, can have been developed, evolved, condensed, from the vastness of the world not anyhow or by the working of common powers but only by one of finer or higher pitch and determination than itself and certainly than any that elsewhere we see, for this power had to force forward the starting or stubborn elements to the one pitch required. And this is much more true when we consider the mind; when I consider my selfbeing, my consciousness and feeling of myself, that taste of myself, of *I* and *me* above and in all things, which is more distinctive than the taste of ale or alum, more distinctive than the smell of walnutleaf or camphor, and is incommunicable by any means to another man (as when I was a child I used to ask myself: What must it be to be someone else?). Nothing else in nature comes near this unspeakable stress of pitch, distinctiveness, and selving, this selfbeing of my own. Nothing explains it or resembles it, except so far as this, that other men to themselves have the same feeling. But this only multiplies the phenomena to be explained so far as the cases are like and do resemble. But to me there is no resemblance: searching nature I taste *self* but at one tankard, that of my own being. The development, refinement, condensation of nothing shews any sign of being able to match this to me or give me another taste of it, a taste even resembling it.

Notes on Spiritual Exercises, 1880

Krakatoa Sunsets

[The effects of the great volcanic eruption at Krakatoa, in the Dutch East Indies, were seen as far away as Europe]

The glow is intense, this is what strikes everyone; it has prolonged the daylight, and optically changed the season; it bathes the whole sky, it is mistaken for the reflection of a great fire; at the sundown itself and southwards from that on December 4, I took a note of it as more like inflamed flesh than the lucid reds of ordinary sunsets. On the same evening the fields facing west glowed as if overlaid with yellow wax.

But it is also lustreless. A bright sunset lines the clouds so that their brims look like gold, brass, bronze, or steel. It fetches out those dazzling flecks and spangles which people call fish-scales. It gives to a mackerel or dappled cloudrack the appearance of quilted crimson silk, or a ploughed field glazed with crimson ice. These effects may have been seen in the late sunsets, but they are not the specific after-glow; that is, without gloss or lustre.

The two things together, that is intensity of light and want of lustre, give to objects on the earth a peculiar illumination which may be seen in studios and other well-like rooms, and which itself affects the practice of painters and may be seen in their works, notably Rembrandt's, disguising or feebly showing the outlines and distinctions of things, but fetching out white surfaces and coloured stuffs with a rich and inward and seemingly self-luminous glow.

letter to the periodical *Nature*, 1883

GEORGE WASHINGTON CABLE
1844–1925

An Altercation in New Orleans

'I tell you,' Doctor Keene used to say, 'that old woman's a thinker.' His allusion was to Clemence, the *marchande des calas*. Her mental activity was evinced not more in the cunning aptness of her songs than in the droll wisdom of her sayings. Not the melody only, but the often audacious, epigrammatic philosophy of her tongue as well, sold her *calas* and ginger-cakes . . .

Doctor Keene, in the old days of his health, used to enjoy an occasional skirmish with her. Once, in the course of chaffering over the price of *calas*, he enounced an old current conviction which is not without holders even to this day; for we may still hear it said by those who will not be decoyed down from the mountain fastnesses of the old Southern doctrines, that their slaves were 'the happiest people under the sun.' Clemence had made bold to deny this with argumentative indignation, and was courteously informed in retort that she had promulgated a falsehood of magnitude.

'W'y, Mawse Chawlie,' she replied, 'does you s'pose one po' nigga kin tell a big lie? No, sah! But w'en de whole people tell w'at ain' so—if dey know it, aw if dey don' know it—den dat *is* a big lie!' And she laughed to contortion.

'What is that you say?' he demanded, with mock ferocity. 'You charge white people with lying?'

'Oh, sakes, Mawse Chawlie, no! De people don't mek up dat ah; de debble pass it on 'em. Don' you know de debble ah de grett cyount'feiteh?

Ev'y piece o' money he mek he tek an' put some debblemen' on de under side, an' one o' his pootiess lies on top; an' 'e gilt dat lie, and 'e rub dat lie on 'is elbow, an' 'e shine dat lie, an' 'e put 'is bess licks on dat lie; entel ev'ybody say: "Oh, how pooty!" An' dey tek it fo' good money, yass—and pass it! Dey b'lieb it!'

'Oh,' said some one at Doctor Keene's side, disposed to quiz, 'you niggers don't know when you are happy.'

'Dass so, Mawse—*c'est vrai, oui*!' she answered quickly: 'we donno no mo'n white folks!'

The laugh was against him.

'Mawse Chawlie,' she said again, 'w'a's dis I yeh 'bout dat Eu'ope country? 's dat true de niggas is all free in Eu'ope?'

Doctor Keene replied that something like that was true.

'Well, now, Mawse Chawlie, I gwan t' ass you a riddle. If dat is *so*, den fo' w'y I yeh folks bragg'n 'bout de "stayt o' s'iety in Eu'ope"?'

The mincing drollery with which she used this fine phrase brought another peal of laughter. Nobody tried to guess.

'I gwan tell you,' said the *marchande*; ''tis becyaze dey got a "fixed wuckin' class."' She sputtered and giggled with the general ha, ha. 'Oh, ole Clemence kin talk proctah, yass!'

She made a gesture for attention.

'D'y' ebber yeh w'at de cya'ge-hoss say w'en 'e see de cyahthoss tu'n losse in de sem pawstu'e wid he, an' knowed dat some'ow de cyaht gotteh be haul'? W'y 'e jiz snawt an' kick up 'is heel''—she suited the action to the word—'an' tah' roun' de fiel' an' prance up to de fence an' say: "Whoopy! shoo! shoo! dis yeh country gittin' *too* free!"

'Oh,' she resumed, as soon as she could be heard, 'white folks is werry kine. Dey wants us to b'lieb we happy—dey *wants to b'lieb* we is. W'y, you know, dey 'bleeged to b'lieb it—fo' dey own cyumfut. 'Tis de sem weh wid de preache's; dey buil' we ow own sep'ate meet'n-houses; dey b'leebs us lak it de bess, an' dey *knows* dey lak it de bess.'

The laugh at this was mostly her own. It is not a laughable sight to see the comfortable fractions of Christian communities everywhere striving, with sincere, pious, well-meant, criminal benevolence, to make their poor brethren contented with the ditch. Nor does it become so to see these efforts meet, or seem to meet, some degree of success. Happily man cannot so place his brother that his misery will continue unmitigated. You may dwarf a man to the mere stump of what he ought to be, and yet he will put out green leaves. 'Free from care,' we benignly observe of the dwarfed classes of society; but we forget, or have never thought, what a crime we commit when we rob men and women of their cares.

The Grandissimes, 1880

GEORGE SAINTSBURY
1845–1933

Robert Southey Reviews His Friends

No doubt Southey's review of the *Lyrical Ballads* is very far from being one of his claims to respect. Taken without regard to the circumstances it proves him not a good critic at that moment; taken with regard to them it proves him not a good friend. One cannot indeed go as far as a person of distinction who once vehemently laid it down to the present writer that it was the duty of a critic to praise his friends' work. But Wordsworth, on this very occasion, was quite right in saying that if Southey could not praise he should have held his tongue. The absolutely golden rule, the counsel of perfection in reviewing is, no doubt, 'Never review a friend's book that you cannot praise, *or an un-friend's that you feel obliged to blame*', and the reviewer who has observed that need not be much afraid of his colleague Minos when he stands before him. But, short of this, Wordsworth's position is a sound one; and the only argument that is sometimes brought, indeed that has ever been brought against it—the 'sacred duty of speaking out the truth', etc.—is all bosh.

The fact is that Southey's worst good qualities, his vicious virtues, of righteousness-overmuch, and almost Miltonic self-confidence, most likely *did* make him think it his duty to express what was, however wrongly, honestly his opinion. One has known long ago that to expect justice to Southey, especially from professed Wordsworthians or Coleridgians, is vain. It serves him right enough in a way, perhaps, because of the vice-virtues just admitted; but it is a pity.

written 1907; *George Saintsbury: The Memorial Volume*, 1945

F. H. BRADLEY
1846–1924

A Weakness of the Flesh

It may come from a failure in my metaphysics, or from a weakness of the flesh which continues to blind me, but the notion that existence could be the same as understanding strikes as cold and ghost-like as the dreariest materialism. That the glory of this world in the end is appearance leaves the world more glorious, if we feel it is a show of some fuller splendour; but the sensuous curtain is a deception and a cheat, if it hides some colourless movement of atoms, some spectral woof of impalpable abstractions, or unearthly ballet of bloodless categories. Though dragged to such conclusions, we cannot embrace them. Our principles may be true, but they are not reality. They no more *make* that Whole which commands our devotion than some shredded dissection of human tatters *is* that warm and breathing beauty of flesh which our hearts found delightful.

The Principles of Logic, 1883

The Metaphysical Impulse

All of us, I presume, more or less, are led beyond the region of ordinary facts. Some in one way and some in others, we seem to touch and have communion with what is beyond the visible world. In various manners we find something higher, which both supports and humbles, both chastens and transports us. And, with certain persons, the intellectual effort to understand the universe is a principal way of thus experiencing the Deity. No one, probably, who has not felt this, however differently he might describe it, has ever cared much for metaphysics. And, where-ever it has been felt strongly, it has been its own justification. The man whose nature is such that by one path alone his chief desire will reach consummation, will try to find it on that path, whatever it may be, and whatever the world thinks of it; and, if he does not, he is contemptible. Self-sacrifice is too often the 'great sacrifice' of trade, the giving cheap what is worth nothing. To know what one wants, and to scruple at no means that will get it, may be a harder self-surrender. And this appears to be another reason for some persons pursuing the study of ultimate truth.

Appearance and Reality, 1893

RICHARD JEFFERIES
1848–1887

A Wiltshire Gamekeeper

In personal appearance he would be a tall man were it not that he has contracted a slight stoop in the passage of the years, not from weakness or decay of nature, but because men who walk much lean forward somewhat, which has a tendency to round the shoulders. The weight of the gun, and often of a heavy game-bag dragging downwards, has increased this defect of his figure, and, as is usual after a certain age, even with those who lead a temperate life, he begins to show signs of corpulency. But these shortcomings only slightly detract from the manliness of his appearance, and in youth it is easy to see that he must have been an athlete. There is still plenty of power in the long sinewy arms, brown hands, and bull-neck, and intense vital energy in the bright blue eye. He is an ash-tree man, as a certain famous writer would say; hard, tough, unconquerable by wind or weather, fearless of his fellows, yielding but by slow and imperceptible degrees to the work of time. His neck has become the colour of mahogany; sun and tempest have left their indelible marks upon his face; and he speaks from the depths of his broad chest, as men do who talk much in the open air, shouting across the fields and through the copses. There is a solidity in his very footstep, and he stands like an oak. He meets your eye full and unshirkingly, yet without insolence; not as the labourers do, who either stare with sullen ill-will or look on the earth. In brief, freedom and constant contact with nature have made him every inch a man; and here in this nineteenth century of civilized effeminacy may be seen some relic of what men were in the old feudal days when they dwelt practically in the woods. The shoulder of his coat is worn a little where the gun rubs, and so is his sleeve; otherwise he is fairly well dressed.

Perfectly civil to every one, and with a willing manner towards his master and his master's guests, he has a wonderful knack of getting his own way. Whatever the great house may propose in the shooting line, the keeper is pretty certain to dispose of in the end as he pleases; for he has a voluble 'silver' tongue, and is full of objections, reasons, excuses, suggestions, all delivered with a deprecatory air of superior knowledge which he hardly likes to intrude upon his betters, much as he would regret to see them go wrong. So he really takes the lead, and in nine cases in ten the result proves he is right, as minute local knowledge naturally must be when intelligently applied.

The Gamekeeper at Home, 1878

Crows

But upon the crow the full vials of the keeper's wrath are poured, and not without reason. The crow among birds is like the local professional among human poachers: he haunts the place and clears everything—it would be hard to say what comes amiss to him. He is the impersonation of murder. His long, stout, pointed beak is a weapon of deadly power, wielded with surprising force by the sinewy neck. From a tiny callow fledgling, fallen out of the thrush's nest, to the partridge or a toothsome young rabbit, it is all one to him. Even the swift leveret is said sometimes to fall a prey, being so buffeted by the sooty wings of the assassin and so blinded by the sharp beak striking at his eyes as to be presently overcome. For the crow has a terrible penchant for the morsel afforded by another's eyes: I have seen the skull of a miserable thrush, from which a crow rose and slowly sailed away, literally split as if by a chisel—doubtless by the blow that destroyed its sight. Birds that are at all diseased or weakly, as whole broods sometimes are in wet unkindly seasons, rabbits touched by the dread parasite that causes the fatal 'rot', the young pheasant straying from the coop, even the chicken at the lone farmstead, where the bailiff only lives and is in the fields all day—these are the victims of the crow.

Crows work almost always in pairs—it is remarkable that hawks, jays, magpies, crows, nearly all birds of prey, seem to remain in pairs the entire year—and when they have once tasted a member of a brood, be it pheasant, partridge, or chicken, they stay till they have cleared off the lot. Slow of flight and somewhat lazy of habit, they will perch for hours on a low tree, croaking and pruning their feathers; they peer into every nook and corner of the woodlands, not like the swift hawk, who circles over and is gone and in a few minutes is a mile away. So that neither the mouse in the furrow nor the timid partridge cowering in the hedge can escape their leering eyes.

Therefore the keeper smites them hip and thigh whenever he finds them; and if he comes across the nest, placed on the broad top of a pollard-tree—not in the branches, but on the trunk—sends his shot through it to smash the eggs. For if the young birds come to maturity they will remain in that immediate locality for months, working every hedge and copse and ditch with cruel pertinacity. In consequence of this unceasing destruction the crow has become much rarer of late, and its nest is hardly to be found in many woods. They breed in the scattered trees of the meadows and fields, especially where no regular game preservation is attempted, and where no keeper goes his rounds. Even to this day a lingering superstition associates this bird with coming evil; and I have heard the women working in the fields remark that such and such a farmer then lying ill would not recover, for a crow had been seen to fly over his house but just above the roof-tree.

The Gamekeeper at Home

The Farm Sale Poster

A large white poster, fresh and glaring, is pasted on the wall of a barn that stands beside a narrow country lane. So plain an advertisement, without any colour or attempt at 'display', would be passed unnoticed among the endless devices on a town hoarding. There nothing can be hoped to be looked at unless novel and strange, or even incomprehensible. But here the oblong piece of black and white contrasts sufficiently in itself with red brick and dull brown wooden framing, with tall shadowy elms, and the glint of sunshine on the streamlet that flows with a ceaseless murmur across the hollow of the lane. Every man that comes along stays to read it.

The dealer in his trap—his name painted in white letters on the shaft—pulls up his quick pony, and sits askew on his seat to read. He has probably seen it before in the bar of the wayside inn, roughly hung on a nail, and swaying to and fro with the draught along the passage. He may have seen it, too, on the handing-post at the lonely cross-roads, stuck on in such a manner that, in order to peruse it, it is necessary to walk round the post. The same formal announcement appears also in the local weekly papers—there are at least two now in the smallest place—and he has read it there. Yet he pauses to glance at it again, for the country mind requires reiteration before it can thoroughly grasp and realize the simplest fact. The poster must be read and re-read, and the printer's name observed and commented on, or, if handled, the thickness felt between thumb and finger. After a month or two of this process people at last begin to accept it as a reality, like cattle or trees—something substantial, and not mere words.

The carter, with his wagon, if he be an elderly man, cries 'Whoa!' and, standing close to the wall, points to each letter with the top of his whip—where it bends—and so spells out 'Sale by Auction'. If he be a young man he looks up at it as the heavy wagon rumbles by, turns his back, and goes on with utter indifference.

The old men, working so many years on a single farm, and whose minds were formed in days when a change of tenancy happened once in half a century, have so identified themselves with the order of things in the parish that it seems to personally affect them when a farmer leaves his place. But young Hodge cares nothing about his master, or his fellow's master. Whether they go or stay, prosperous or decaying, it matters nothing to him. He takes good wages, and can jingle some small silver in his pocket when he comes to the tavern a mile or so ahead; so 'gee-up' and let us get there as rapidly as possible.

An hour later a farmer passes on horseback; his horse all too broad for his short legs that stick out at the side and show some inches of stocking between the bottom of his trousers and his boots. A sturdy, thick-set man, with a wide face, brickdust colour, fringed with close-cut red whiskers, and chest so broad—he seems compelled to wear his coat unbuttoned. He pulls off his hat and wipes his partly bald head with a coloured handkerchief, stares at the poster a few minutes, and walks his horse away, evidently in deep thought. Two boys—cottagers' children—come home from school; they look round to see that no one observes, and then throw flints at the paper till the sound of footsteps alarms them.

Towards the evening a gentleman and lady, the first middle-aged, the latter very young—father and daughter—approach, their horses seeming to linger as they walk through the shallow stream, and the cool water splashes above their fetlocks. The shooting season is near at hand, Parliament has risen, and the landlords have returned home. Instead of the Row, papa must take his darling a ride through the lanes, a little dusty as the autumn comes on, and pauses to read the notice on the wall. It is his neighbour's tenant, not his, but it comes home to him here. It is the real thing—the fact—not the mere seeing it in the papers, or the warning hints in the letters of his own steward. 'Papa' is rather quiet for the rest of the ride. Ever since he was a lad—how many years ago is that?—he has shot with his neighbour's party over this farm, and recollects the tenant well, and with that friendly feeling that grows up towards what we see year after year. In a day or two the clergyman drives by with his low four-wheel and fat pony, notes the poster as the pony slackens at the descent to the water, and tells himself to remember and get the tithe. Some few Sundays, and Farmer Smith will appear in church no more.

Hodge and His Masters, 1880

ALICE JAMES
1848–1892

A Penny Bun

We were quite grateful for the Englishry of this: K. saw the other day a very smart lady in a victoria driving in the crowd at the canonical hour, down Piccadilly to the Park, and so far carrying out to perfection the lesson of the day, but with that homely burst of nature to which the most encrusted here are subject, she was satisfying the cravings of the stomach by eating, with the utmost complacency, in the eye of man, a huge, stodgy penny bun. The perfection in all her appointments in the way of carriage, etc—with the absence of subtlety in her palate as shown by the placid consumption of the bun, and complete indifference, at this very visible moment, at exhibiting her features distorted by the ugly process of masticating such an adhesive substance, had an incongruity very characteristic of the soil. They seem in matters of taste to have no sense of gradations. H. [her brother Henry] is always saying this, but it jumped at my eye from the first, and is therefore an original if not unique utterance. H., by the way, has embedded in his pages many pearls fallen from my lips, which he steals in the most unblushing way, saying, simply, that he knew they had been said by the family, so it did not matter.

Diary, 1891

SIR EDMUND GOSSE
1849–1928

Swinburne and 'Three Blind Mice'

Outside poetry, and, in lesser measure, his family life, Swinburne's interests were curiously limited. He had no 'small talk,' and during the discussion of the common topics of the day his attention at once flagged and fell off, the glazed eye betraying that the mind was far away. For science he had no taste whatever, and his lack of musical ear was a byword among his acquaintances. I once witnessed a practical joke played upon him, which made me indignant at the time, but which now seems innocent enough, and not without interest. A lady, having taken the rest of the company into her confidence, told Swinburne that she would render on the piano a very ancient Florentine ritornello which had just been discovered. She then played 'Three Blind Mice,' and Swinburne was enchanted. He found that it reflected to perfection the cruel beauty of the Medicis—which perhaps it does. But this exemplifies the fact that all impressions with him were intellectual, and that an appeal to his imagination would gild the most common object with romance.

Portraits and Sketches, 1912

Philip James Bailey, the Author of Festus

Mr Bailey, of whose appearance my recollections go back at least thirty years, always during that time looked robustly aged, a sort of prophet or bard, with a cloud of voluminous white hair and curled silver beard. As the years went by his head seemed merely to grow more handsome, almost absurdly, almost irritatingly so, like a picture of Connal, 'first of mortal men,' in some illustrated edition of Ossian. The extraordinary suspension of his gaze, his gentle, dazzling aspect of uninterrupted meditation, combined with a curious downward arching of the lips, seen through the white rivers of his beard, to give a distinctly vatic impression. He had an attitude of arrested inspiration, as if waiting for the heavenly spark to fall again, as it had descended from 1836 to 1839, and as it seemed never inclined to descend again.

Portraits and Sketches

SARAH ORNE JEWETT
1849–1909

Joanna's Grave

'I was talking o' poor Joanna the other day. I hadn't thought of her for a great while,' said Mrs Fosdick abruptly. 'Mis' Brayton an' I recalled her as we sat together sewing. She was one o' your peculiar persons, wa'n't she? Speaking of such persons,' she turned to explain to me, 'there was a sort of a nun or hermit person lived out there for years all alone on Shell-heap Island. Miss Joanna Todd, her name was—a cousin o' Almiry's late husband.'

I expressed my interest, but as I glanced at Mrs Todd I saw that she was confused by sudden affectionate feeling and unmistakable desire for reticence.

'I never want to hear Joanna laughed about,' she said anxiously.

'Nor I,' answered Mrs Fosdick reassuringly. 'She was crossed in love,—that was all the matter to begin with; but as I look back, I can see that Joanna was one doomed from the first to fall into a melancholy. She retired from the world for good an' all, though she was a well-off woman. All she wanted was to get away from folks; she thought she wasn't fit to live with anybody, and wanted to be free. Shell-heap Island come to her from her father, and first thing folks knew she'd gone off out there to live, and left word she didn't want no company. 'T was a bad place to get to, unless the wind an' tide were just right; 't was hard work to make a landing.' . . .

*

I stood watching while Captain Bowden cleverly found his way back to deeper water. 'You needn't make no haste,' he called to me; 'I'll keep within call. Joanna lays right up there in the far corner o' the field. There used to be a path led to the place. I always knew her well. I was out here to the funeral.'

I found the path; it was touching to discover that this lonely spot was not without its pilgrims. Later generations will know less and less of Joanna herself, but there are paths trodden to the shrines of solitude the world over,—the world cannot forget them, try as it may; the feet of the young find them out because of curiosity and dim foreboding, while the old bring hearts full of remembrance. This plain anchorite had been one of those whom sorrow made too lonely to brave the sight of men, too timid to front the simple world she knew, yet valiant enough to live alone with her poor insistent human nature and the calms and passions of the sea and sky.

The birds were flying all about the field; they fluttered up out of the grass at my feet as I walked along, so tame that I liked to think they kept some happy tradition from summer to summer of the safety of nests and good fellowship of mankind. Poor Joanna's house was gone except the stones of its foundations, and there was little trace of her flower garden except a single faded sprig of much-enduring French pinks, which a great bee and a yellow butterfly were befriending together. I drank at the spring, and thought that now and then some would follow me from the busy, hard-worked, and simple-thoughted countryside of the mainland, which lay dim and dreamlike in the August haze, as Joanna must have watched it many a day. There was the world, and here was she with eternity well begun. In the life of each of us, I said to myself, there is a place remote and islanded, and given to endless regret or secret happiness; we are each the uncompanioned hermit and recluse of an hour or a day; we understand our fellows of the cell to whatever age of history they may belong.

But as I stood alone on the island, in the sea-breeze, suddenly there came a sound of distant voices; gay voices and laughter from a pleasure-boat that was going seaward full of boys and girls. I knew, as if she had told me, that poor Joanna must have heard the like on many and many a summer afternoon, and must have welcomed the good cheer in spite of hopelessness and winter weather, and all the sorrow and disappointment in the world.

The Country of the Pointed Firs, 1896

ROBERT LOUIS STEVENSON
1850–1894

At the Admiral Benbow Inn

I remember him as if it were yesterday, as he came plodding to the inn door, his sea-chest following behind him in a hand-barrow; a tall, strong, heavy, nut-brown man; his tarry pigtail falling over the shoulders of his soiled blue coat; his hands ragged and scarred, with black, broken nails; and the sabre cut across one cheek, a dirty, livid white. I remember him looking round the cove and whistling to himself as he did so, and then breaking out in that old sea-song that he sang so often afterwards:—

'Fifteen men on the dead man's chest—
Yo-ho-ho, and a bottle of rum!'

in the high old tottering voice that seemed to have been tuned and broken at the capstan bars. Then he rapped on the door with a bit of stick like a handspike that he carried, and when my father appeared, called roughly for a glass of rum. This, when it was brought to him, he drank slowly, like a connoisseur, lingering on the taste, and still looking about him at the cliffs and up at our signboard.

'This is a handy cove,' says he, at length; 'and a pleasant sittyated grog-shop. Much company, mate?'

My father told him no, very little company, the more was the pity.

'Well, then,' said he, 'this is the berth for me. Here you, matey,' he cried to the man who trundled the barrow; 'bring up alongside and help up my chest. I'll stay here a bit,' he continued. 'I'm a plain man; rum and bacon and eggs is what I want, and that head up there for to watch ships off. What you mought call me? You mought call me captain. Oh, I see what you're at—there'; and he threw down three or four gold pieces on the threshold. 'You can tell me when I've worked through that,' says he, looking as fierce as a commander.

And, indeed, bad as his clothes were, and coarsely as he spoke, he had none of the appearance of a man who sailed before the mast; but seemed like a mate or skipper, accustomed to be obeyed or to strike. The man who came with the barrow told us the mail had set him down the morning before at the 'Royal George'; that he had inquired what inns there were along the coast, and hearing ours well spoken of, I suppose, and described as lonely, had chosen it from the others for his place of residence. And that was all we could learn of our guest.

Treasure Island, 1882

A South Seas Trader

In the back room was old Captain Randall, squatting on the floor native fashion, fat and pale, naked to the waist, gray as a badger and his eyes set with drink. His body was covered with gray hair and crawled over by flies; one was in the corner of his eye—he never heeded; and the mosquitoes hummed about the man like bees. Any clean-minded man would have had the creature out at once and buried him; and to see him, and think he was seventy, and remember he had once commanded a ship, and come ashore in his smart togs, and talked big in bars and consulates, and sat in club verandahs, turned me sick and sober.

He tried to get up when I came in, but that was hopeless; so he reached me a hand instead and stumbled out some salutation.

'Papa's pretty full this morning,' observed Case. 'We've had an epidemic here; and Captain Randall takes gin for a prophylactic—don't you, papa?'

'Never took such thing my life!' cried the captain, indignantly. 'Take gin for my health's sake, Mr Wha's-ever-your-name. 'S a precaution'ry measure.'

'That's all right, papa,' said Case. 'But you'll have to brace up. There's going to be a marriage, Mr Wiltshire here is going to get spliced.'

The old man asked to whom.

'To Uma,' said Case.

'Uma?' cried the captain. 'Wha's he want Uma for? 'S he come here for his health, anyway? Wha' 'n hell's he want Uma for?'

'Dry up papa,' said Case. ''Tain't you that's to marry her. I guess you're not her godfather and godmother; I guess Mr Wiltshire's going to please himself.'

With that he made an excuse to me that he must move about the marriage, and left me alone with the poor wretch that was his partner and (to speak truth) his gull. Trade and station belonged both to Randall; Case and the negro were parasites; they crawled and fed upon him like the flies, he none the wiser. Indeed I have no harm to say of Billy Randall, beyond the fact that my gorge rose at him, and the time I now passed in his company was like a nightmare.

The room was stifling hot and full of flies; for the house was dirty and low and small, and stood in a bad place, behind the village, in the borders of the bush, and sheltered from the trade. The three men's beds were on the floor, and a litter of pans and dishes. There was no standing furniture, Randall, when he was violent, tearing it to laths. There I sat, and had a meal which was served us by Case's wife; and there I was entertained all day by that remains of man, his tongue stumbling among low old jokes and long old stories, and his own wheezy laughter always ready, so that he had no sense of my depression. He was nipping gin all the while; sometimes he fell asleep and awoke again whimpering and shivering; and every now and again he would ask me why in Hell I wanted to marry Uma. 'My friend,' I was telling myself all day, 'you must not be an old gentleman like this.'

The Beach at Falesá, 1892

A Judge and His Son

The lamp was shaded, the fire trimmed to a nicety, the table covered deep with orderly documents, the backs of law books made a frame upon all sides that was only broken by the window and the doors.

For a moment Hermiston warmed his hands at the fire, presenting his back to Archie; then suddenly disclosed on him the terrors of the Hanging Face.

'What's this I hear of ye?' he asked.

There was no answer possible to Archie.

'I'll have to tell ye, then,' pursued Hermiston. 'It seems ye've been skirling against the father that begot ye, and one of his Maijesty's Judges in this land; and that in the public street, and while an order of the Court was being executit. Forbye which, it would appear that ye've been airing your opeenions in a Coallege Debatin' Society'; he paused a moment: and then, with extraordinary bitterness, added: 'Ye damned eediot.'

'I had meant to tell you,' stammered Archie. 'I see you are well informed.'

'Muckle obleeged to ye,' said his lordship, and took his usual seat. 'And so you disapprove of Caapital Punishment?' he added.

'I am sorry, sir, I do,' said Archie.

'I am sorry, too,' said his lordship. 'And now, if you please, we shall approach this business with a little more parteecularity. I hear that at the hanging of Duncan Jopp—and, man! ye had a fine client there—in the middle of all the riffraff of the ceety, ye thought fit to cry out, "This is a damned murder, and my gorge rises at the man that haangit him."'

'No, sir, these were not my words,' cried Archie.

'What were yer words, then?' asked the Judge.

'I believe I said, "I denounce it as a murder!"' said the son. 'I beg your pardon—a God-defying murder. I have no wish to conceal the truth,' he added, and looked his father for a moment in the face.

'God, it would only need that of it next!' cried Hermiston. 'There was nothing about your gorge rising, then?'

'That was afterwards, my lord, as I was leaving the Speculative. I said I had been to see the miserable creature hanged, and my gorge rose at it.'

'Did ye, though?' said Hermiston. 'And I suppose ye knew who haangit him?'

'I was present at the trial, I ought to tell you that, I ought to explain. I ask your pardon beforehand for any expression that may seem undutiful. The position in which I stand is wretched,' said the unhappy hero, now fairly face to face with the business he had chosen. 'I have been reading some of your cases. I was present while Jopp was tried. It was a hideous business. Father, it was a hideous thing! Grant he was vile, why should you hunt him with a vileness equal to his own? It was done with glee—that is the word—you did it with glee; and I looked on, God help me! with horror.'

Weir of Hermiston, 1896

F. W. MAITLAND
1850–1906

The Reformation and Scotland

Suddenly all farsighted eyes had turned to a backward country. Eyes at Rome and eyes at Geneva were fixed on Scotland, and, the further they could peer into the future, the more eager must have been their gaze. And still we look intently at that wonderful scene, the Scotland of Mary Stewart and John Knox: not merely because it is such glorious tragedy, but also because it is such modern history. The fate of the Protestant Reformation was being decided, and the creed of unborn millions in undiscovered lands was being determined. This we see—all too plainly perhaps—if we read the books that year by year men still are writing of Queen Mary and her surroundings. The patient analysis of those love letters in the casket may yet be perturbed by thoughts about religion. Nor is the religious the only interest. A new nation, a British nation, was in the making.

We offer no excuse for having as yet said little of Scotland. Called upon to play for some years a foremost part in the great drama, her entry upon the stage of modern history is late and sudden. In such phrases there must indeed be some untruth, for history is not drama. The annals of Scotland may be so written that the story will be continuous enough. We may see the explosion of 1559 as the effect of causes that had long been at work. We might chronicle the remote beginnings of heresy and the first glimmers of the New Learning. All those signs of the times that we have seen elsewhere in capital letters we might see here in minuscule. Also, it would not escape us that, though in the days of Luther and Calvin resistance to the English and their obstinately impolitic claim of suzerainty still seemed the vital thread of Scottish national existence, inherited enmity was being enfeebled, partly by the multiplying perfidies of venal nobles and the increasing wealth of their paymasters, and partly also by the accumulating proofs that in the new age a Scotland which lived only to help France and hamper England would herself be a poor little Power among the nations: doomed, not only to occasional Floddens and Pinkies, but to continuous misery, anarchy, and obscurity.

All this deserves, and finds, full treatment at the hands of the historians of Scotland. They will also sufficiently warn us that the events of 1560 leave a great deal unchanged. Faith may be changed; works are much what they were, especially the works of the magnates. The blood-feud is no less a blood-feud because one family calls itself Catholic and another calls itself Protestant. The 'band' is no less a 'band' because it is styled a 'Covenant' and makes free with holy names. A king shall be kidnapped, and a king shall be murdered, as of old: it is the custom of the country. What is new is that farsighted men all Europe over, not only at London and at Paris, but at Rome and at Geneva, should take interest in these barbarous deeds, this customary turmoil.

'The Anglican Settlement and the Scottish Reformation', *Cambridge Modern History*, 1903

KATE CHOPIN
1850–1904

An Escape from Love

Despondency had come upon her there in the wakeful night, and had never lifted. There was no one thing in the world that she desired. There was no human being whom she wanted near her except Robert; and she even realized that the day would come when he, too, and the thought of him would melt out of her existence, leaving her alone. The children appeared before her like antagonists who had overcome her; who had overpowered and sought to drag her into the soul's slavery for the rest of her days. But she knew a way to elude them. She was not thinking of these things when she walked down to the beach.

The water of the Gulf stretched out before her, gleaming with the million lights of the sun. The voice of the sea is seductive, never ceasing, whispering, clamoring, murmuring, inviting the soul to wander in abysses of solitude. All along the white beach, up and down, there was no living thing in sight. A bird with a broken wing was beating the air above, reeling, fluttering, circling disabled down, down to the water.

Edna had found her old bathing suit still hanging, faded, upon its accustomed peg.

She put it on, leaving her clothing in the bath-house. But when she was there beside the sea, absolutely alone, she cast the unpleasant, pricking garments from her, and for the first time in her life she stood naked in the open air, at the mercy of the sun, the breeze that beat upon her, and the waves that invited her.

How strange and awful it seemed to stand naked under the sky! how delicious! She felt like some new-born creature, opening its eyes in a familiar world that it had never known.

The foamy wavelets curled up to her white feet, and coiled like serpents about her ankles. She walked out. The water was chill, but she walked on. The water was deep, but she lifted her white body and reached out with a long, sweeping stroke. The touch of the sea is sensuous, enfolding the body in its soft, close embrace.

She went on and on. She remembered the night she swam far out, and recalled the terror that seized her at the fear of being unable to regain the shore. She did not look back now, but went on and on, thinking of the blue-grass meadow that she had traversed when a little child, believing that it had no beginning and no end.

Her arms and legs were growing tired.

She thought of Léonce and the children. They were a part of her life. But they need not have thought that they could possess her, body and soul.

How Mademoiselle Reisz would have laughed, perhaps sneered, if she knew! 'And you call yourself an artist! What pretensions, Madame! The artist must possess the courageous soul that dares and defies.'

Exhaustion was pressing upon and overpowering her.

'Good-by—because I love you.' He did not know; he did not understand. He would never understand. Perhaps Doctor Mandelet would have understood if she had seen him—but it was too late; the shore was far behind her, and her strength was gone.

She looked into the distance, and the old terror flamed up for an instant, then sank again. Edna heard her father's voice and her sister Margaret's. She heard the barking of an old dog that was chained to the sycamore tree. The spurs of the cavalry officer clanged as he walked across the porch. There was the hum of bees, and the musky odor of pinks filled the air.

The Awakening, 1899

GEORGE MOORE
1852–1933

In the Maternity Hospital

On the second landing a door was thrown open, and she found herself in a room full of people, eight or nine young men and women.

'What! in there? and all those people?' said Esther.

'Of course; those are the midwives and the students.'

The screams she had heard in the passage came from a bed on the left-hand side. A woman lay there huddled up, and Esther was taken behind a screen by the sister who brought her upstairs, undressed, and clothed in a chemise a great deal too big for her, she heard the sister say so at the time; and as she walked across the room to her bed she noticed the steel instruments on the round table and the basins on the floor.

The students and the nurses were behind her. She knew they were eating sweets, for she heard a young man ask the young women if they would have any more fondants. A moment after her pains began again, and she saw the young man whom she had seen handing the sweets approaching her bedside.

'Oh, no, not him, not him!' she cried to the nurse. 'Not him, not him! he is too young! Don't let him come near me!'

They laughed loudly, and she buried her head in the pillow, overcome with pain and shame; and when she felt him by her she tried to rise from the bed.

'Let me go! take me away! Oh, you are all beasts!'

'Come come, no nonsense!' said the nurse; 'you can't have what you like; they are here to learn;' and when he had tried the pains she heard the midwife say that it wasn't necessary to send for the doctor. Another said that it would be all over in about three hours' time. 'An easy confinement, I should say. The other will be more interesting.' And then they talked of the plays they had seen, and those they wished to see. She was soon listening to a discussion regarding the merits of a shilling novel which everyone was reading, and then Esther heard a stampede of nurses, midwives, and students in the direction of the window. A German band had come into the street.

'Is that the way to leave your patient, sister?' said the student who sat by Esther's bed, and Esther looked into his clear blue, girl-like eyes, wondered, and turned away for shame.

The sister stopped her imitation of a popular comedian, and said, 'Oh, she's all right; if they were all like her there'd be very little use our coming here.'

'Unfortunately, that's just what they are,' said another student, a stout fellow with a pointed red beard, the ends of which caught the light. Her eyes often went to those stubble ends, and she hated him for his loud voice and jocularity. One of the midwives, a woman with a long nose and small grey eyes, seemed to mock her, and she hoped that this woman would not come near her, for there was something sinister in her face, and Esther was glad when her favourite, a little blonde woman with wavy flaxen hair, came by and asked her if she felt better. She looked a little like the young student who still sat by her bedside, and Esther wondered if they were brother and sister, and then she thought that they were sweethearts.

Soon after a bell rang, and the students went down to supper, the nurse in charge promising to warn them if any change should take place. The last pains had so thoroughly exhausted her that she had fallen into a doze. But she could hear the chatter of the nurses so clearly that she did not believe herself asleep. And in this film of sleep reality was distorted, and the unsuccessful operation which the nurses were discussing Esther understood to be a conspiracy against her life. She awoke, listened, and gradually sense of the truth returned to her. She was in the hospital, and the nurses were talking of someone who had died last week. The woman in the other bed seemed to suffer dreadfully. Would she live through it? Would she herself live to see the morning? How long the time, how fearful the place! If the nurses would only stop talking. It did not matter. The pains would soon begin again. It was awful to lie listening, waiting.

The windows were open, and the mocking gaiety of the street was borne in on the night wind. Then there came a trampling of feet and sound of voices in the passage—the students and nurses were coming up from supper; and at the same moment the pains began to creep up from her knees. One of the young men said that her time had not come. The woman, with the sinister look that Esther dreaded, held a contrary opinion. The point was argued, and, interested in the question, the crowd came from the window and collected round the disputants. The young men expounded much medical and anatomical knowledge; the nurses listened with the usual deference of women.

Suddenly, the discussion was interrupted by a scream from Esther; it seemed to her that she was being torn asunder, that life was going from her. The nurse ran to her side, a look of triumph came upon her face, and she said, 'Now, we shall see who's right,' and forthwith went for the doctor. He came running up the stairs; silence and scientific collectedness gathered round Esther, and after a brief examination he said, in a low whisper:

'I'm afraid this will not be as easy a case as one might have imagined. I shall administer chloroform.'

He placed a small wire case over her mouth and nose. The sickly odour which she breathed from the cotton wool filled her brain with nausea; it seemed to choke her; life faded a little, and at every inhalation she expected to lose sight of the circle of faces.

And then the darkness began to lighten; night passed into dawn; she could hear voices, and when her eyes opened the doctors and the nurses were still standing round her, but there was no longer any expression of eager interest on their faces. She wondered at this change, and then out of the silence there came a tiny cry.

Esther Waters, 1894

An Irish Literary Dinner

'Speech time has come,' I said.

Gill read a letter from W. E. H. Lecky, who regretted that he was prevented from being present at the dinner, and then went on to say that the other letter was from a gentleman whose absence he was sure was greatly regretted. He alluded to his friend, Mr Horace Plunkett, who was, if he might be allowed to say so, one of the truest and noblest sons that Ireland had ever begotten.

'I've noticed,' I said to my young friend, 'even within the few days I have been in Ireland, that Ireland is spoken of, not as a geographical, but a sort of human entity. You are all working for Ireland, and I hear now that Ireland begets you; a sort of Wotan who goes about——'

Somebody looked in our direction, somebody said 'Hush!' And Gill continued, saying they had had an exciting week in Ireland, one that would be memorable in the history of the country. For the first time Ireland had been profoundly stirred upon the intellectual question. He said he regarded the controversy which Yeats' play had aroused as one of the best signs of the times. It showed that they had reached at last the end of the intellectual stagnation of Ireland, and that, so to speak, the grey matter of Ireland's brain was at last becoming active.

'Ireland's brain! Just now it was the loins of Ireland.'

Gill flowed along in platitudes and stereotyped sentences that evidently had a depressing effect upon Yeats, who seemed to sink further and further into himself, and was at last no longer able to raise his head. Gill talked on all the same. He for one had always regarded Yeats, broadly, as one who held the sword of spirit in his hand, and waged war upon the gross host of materialism, and as an Irishman of genius who had devoted a noble enthusiasm to honouring his country by the production of beautiful work. . . . What should he say of Mr Martyn? There was no controversy about him. Their minds were not occupied by controversy, but with that which must be gratifying to Mr Martyn and to all of them—the knowledge that he had produced a great and original play, and that Ireland had discovered in him a dramatist fitted to take rank among the first in Europe.

I think everybody present thought this eulogy a little exaggerated, for I noticed that everybody hung down his head and looked into his plate, everybody except Edward, who stared down the room unabashed, which, indeed, was the only thing for him to do, for it is better when a writer is praised that he should accept the praise loftily than that he should attempt to excuse himself, a mistake that I fell into at the St James's Theatre.

Gill continued in the same high key. This gathering of Irishmen, which he thought he might say was representative of the intellect of Dublin, and included men of the utmost differences of opinion on every question which now divided Irishmen, was, to his mind, a symbol of what they were moving towards in this country. He thought they had now reached the stage at which they had begun to recognize the profundity of the saying:

> The mills of God grind slowly,
> Yet they grind exceeding small.

They all felt, instinctively now, that the time for the reconstruction of Ireland had begun. They stood among the débris of old society and felt that out of the ruins they were called upon to build a new Ireland. No matter what their different opinions on various questions might be, they all felt within them a throb of enthusiasm for their new life, their own country, and a determination that, irrespective of the different views, they would give their country an intellectual and a political future worthy of all the sufferings that every class and creed of the country had gone through in the past.

'You're disappointed,' my young friend said, 'but if you stay here much longer you'll get used to hearing people talk about working for Ireland, helping Ireland, selling boots for Ireland, and bullocks too. You'll find if you read the papers that Gill's speech will be very much liked—much more than Yeats'. The comment will be: "We want more of that kind of thing in Ireland."'

My young friend's cynicism now began to get upon my nerves, and turning upon him rudely, I said:

'Then you don't believe in the language movement?'

His reply not being satisfactory, and his accent not convincing of his Celtic origin, I grew suddenly hostile, and resolved not to speak to him again during dinner; and to show how entirely I disapproved of his attitude towards Ireland, I affected a deep interest in the rest of Gill's speech, which, needless to say, was all about working for Ireland. Amid the applause which followed I heard a voice at the end of the table saying, 'We want more of that in Ireland.'

Hail and Farewell, 1911–14

A Reunion with Walter Sickert

He has kept in middle age a great deal of his youth, and during dinner I had noticed that not a streak of grey showed in the thick rippling shock of yellow-brown hair. The golden moustache has been shaved away, and the long mouth and closely-set lips give him a distinct clerical look. 'There was always something of the cleric and the actor in him,' I thought, as I overlooked his new appearance, drawing conclusions from the special bowler-hat of French shape that he wore. He had just come over from Dieppe, and his trousers were French corduroy, amazingly peg-top, and the wide braid on the coat recalled 1860. He was, at this time, addicted to 1860, living in a hotel in the Tottenham Court Road in which all the steads were four-posted and all the beds feather, and he was full of contempt for Steer's collection of Chelsea china, and in favour of wax fruit and rep curtains, and advocated heavy mahogany sideboards.

He was as Pro-Boer as myself, with less indignation and more wit, and Tonks and I yielded that night, as we always do, to the charm of his whimsical imagination, and we laughed when he said:

'Our latest casualties are the capture of four hundred Piccadilly dandies who had been foolish enough to go out to fight the veterans of the veldt. They were stripped of their clothes, patted on their backs, and sent home to camp in silk fleshings and embroidered braces.... Hope Bros., Regent Street.'

Sickert's wide, shaven lip laughed, and he looked so like himself in his overcoat and his French bowler-hat that we walked for some yards delighting in his personality—Tonks a little hurt, but pleased all the same, myself treasuring up each contemptuous word for further use, and considering at which of my friends' houses the repetition of Sickert's wit would give most offence.

Hail and Farewell

OSCAR WILDE
1854–1900

Wagnerian

Thanks for your congratulations. Yes, come tomorrow. The baby is wonderful: it has a bridge to its nose! which the nurse says is a proof of genius! It also has a superb voice, which it freely exercises: its style is essentially Wagnerian.

letter to Norman Forbes-Robertson, 1885

The Worst Hundred Books

Books, I fancy, may be conveniently divided into three classes:

1. Books to read, such as Cicero's *Letters*, Suetonius, Vasari's *Lives of the Painters*, the *Autobiography of Benvenuto Cellini*, Sir John Mandeville, Marco Polo, St Simon's *Memoirs*, Mommsen, and (till we get a better one) Grote's *History of Greece*.

2. Books to re-read, such as Plato and Keats: in the sphere of poetry, the masters not the minstrels; in the sphere of philosophy, the seers not the *savants*.

3. Books not to read at all, such as Thomson's *Seasons*, Rogers's *Italy*, Paley's *Evidences*, all the Fathers except St Augustine, all John Stuart Mill except the *Essay on Liberty*, all Voltaire's plays without any exception, Butler's *Analogy*, Grant's *Aristotle*, Hume's *England*, Lewes's *History of Philosophy*, all argumentative books and all books that try to prove anything.

The third class is by far the most important. To tell people what to read is, as a rule, either useless or harmful; for the appreciation of literature is a question of temperament not of teaching; to Parnassus there is no primer and nothing that one can learn is ever worth learning. But to tell people what not to read is a very different matter, and I venture to recommend it as a mission to the University Extension Scheme.

Indeed, it is one that is eminently needed in this age of ours, an age that reads so much that it has no time to admire, and writes so much that it has no time to think. Whoever will select out of the chaos of our modern curricula 'The Worst Hundred Books,' and publish a list of them, will confer on the rising generation a real and lasting benefit.

letter to the *Pall Mall Gazette*, 1886

Letter to an Income-Tax Inspector

Sir, It was arranged last year that I should send in my income-tax return from Chelsea where I reside, as I am resigning my position here and will not be with Messrs Cassell after August. I think it would be better to continue that arrangement. I wish your notices were not so agitating and did not hold out such dreadful threats. A penalty of fifty pounds sounds like a relic of mediaeval torture. Your obedient servant OSCAR WILDE

1889

The Modern Church of England

As for the Church, I cannot conceive anything better for the culture of a country than the presence in it of a body of men whose duty it is to believe in the supernatural, to perform daily miracles, and to keep alive that mythopœic faculty which is so essential for the imagination. But in the English Church a man succeeds, not through his capacity for belief, but through his capacity for disbelief. Ours is the only Church where the sceptic stands at the altar, and where St Thomas is regarded as the ideal apostle. Many a worthy clergyman, who passes his life in admirable works of kindly charity, lives and dies unnoticed and unknown; but it is sufficient for some shallow uneducated passman out of either University to get up in his pulpit and express his doubts about Noah's ark, or Balaam's ass, or Jonah and the whale, for half of London to flock to hear him, and to sit open-mouthed in rapt admiration at his superb intellect. The growth of common sense in the English Church is a thing very much to be regretted. It is really a degrading concession to a low form of realism. It is silly, too. It springs from an entire ignorance of psychology. Man can believe the impossible, but man can never believe the improbable.

'The Decay of Lying', *Intentions*, 1891

Criticism and Fair-Mindedness

Ernest. Well, I should say that a critic should above all things be fair.

Gilbert. Ah! not fair. A critic cannot be fair in the ordinary sense of the word. It is only about things that do not interest one that one can give a really unbiassed opinion, which is no doubt the reason why an unbiassed opinion is always absolutely valueless. The man who sees both sides of a question, is a man who sees absolutely nothing at all. Art is a passion, and, in matters of art, Thought is inevitably coloured by emotion, and so is fluid rather than fixed, and, depending upon fine moods and exquisite moments, cannot be narrowed into the rigidity of a scientific formula or a theological dogma. It is to the soul that Art speaks, and the soul may be made the prisoner of the mind as well as of the body. One should, of course, have no prejudices; but, as a great Frenchman remarked a hundred years ago, it is one's business in such matters to have preferences, and when one has preferences one ceases to be fair. It is only an auctioneer who can equally and impartially admire all schools of Art. No; fairness is not one of the qualities of the true critic. It is not even a condition of criticism. Each form of Art with which we come in contact dominates us for the moment to the exclusion of every other form. We must surrender ourselves absolutely to the work in question, whatever it may be, if we wish to gain its secret.

'The Critic as Artist', *Intentions*

A School Timetable

Babbacombe School

Headmaster—Mr Oscar Wilde
Second Master—Mr Campbell Dodgson
Boys—Lord Alfred Douglas

Rules.

Tea for masters and boys at 9.30 a.m.
Breakfast at 10.30.
Work. 11.30–12.30.
At 12.30 Sherry and biscuits for headmaster and boys (the second master objects to this).
12.40–1.30. Work.
1.30. Lunch.
2.30–4.30. Compulsory hide-and-seek for headmaster.
5. Tea for headmaster and second master, brandy and sodas (not to exceed seven) for boys.
6–7. Work.
7.30. Dinner, with compulsory champagne.
8.30–12. Écarté, limited to five-guinea points.
12–1.30. Compulsory reading in bed. Any boy found disobeying this rule will be immediately woken up.

letter to Campbell Dodgson, 1893

Cruelty with Good Intentions

People nowadays do not understand what cruelty is. They regard it as a sort of terrible mediaeval passion, and connect it with the race of men like Eccelino da Romano, and others, to whom the deliberate infliction of pain gave a real madness of pleasure. But men of the stamp of Eccelino are merely abnormal types of perverted individualism. Ordinary cruelty is simply stupidity. It is the entire want of imagination. It is the result in our days of stereotyped systems of hard-and-fast rules, and of stupidity. Wherever there is centralisation there is stupidity. What is inhuman in modern life is officialism. Authority is as destructive to those who exercise it as it is to those on whom it is exercised. It is the Prison Board, and the system that it carries out, that is the primary source of the cruelty that is exercised on a child in prison. The people who uphold the system have excellent intentions. Those who carry it out are humane in intention also. Responsibility is shifted on to the disciplinary regulations. It is supposed that because a thing is the rule it is right.

letter to the *Daily Chronicle*, 1897

SIR JAMES FRAZER
1854–1941

A Debt of Gratitude

Thus to students of the past the life of the old kings and priests teems with instruction. In it was summed up all that passed for wisdom when the world was young. It was the perfect pattern after which every man strove to shape his life; a faultless model constructed with rigorous accuracy upon the lines laid down by a barbarous philosophy. Crude and false as that philosophy may seem to us, it would be unjust to deny it the merit of logical consistency. Starting from a conception of the vital principle as a tiny being or soul existing in, but distinct and separable from, the living being, it deduces for the practical guidance of life a system of rules which in general hangs well together and forms a fairly complete and harmonious whole. The flaw—and it is a fatal one—of the system lies not in its reasoning, but in its premises; in its conception of the nature of life, not in any irrelevancy of the conclusions which it draws from that conception. But to stigmatise these premises as ridiculous because we can easily detect their falseness, would be ungrateful as well as unphilosophical. We stand upon the foundation reared by the generations that have gone before, and we can but dimly realise the painful and prolonged efforts which it has cost humanity to struggle up to the point, no very exalted one after all, which we have reached. Our gratitude is due to the nameless and forgotten toilers, whose patient thought and active exertions have largely made us what we are. The amount of new knowledge which one age, certainly which one man, can add to the common store is small, and it argues stupidity or dishonesty, besides ingratitude, to ignore the heap while vaunting the few grains which it may have been our privilege to add to it. There is indeed little danger at present of undervaluing the contributions which modern times and even classical antiquity have made to the general advancement of our race. But when we pass these limits, the case is different. Contempt and ridicule or abhorrence and denunciation are too often the only recognition vouchsafed to the savage and his ways. Yet of the benefactors whom we are bound thankfully to commemorate, many, perhaps most, were savages. For when all is said and done our resemblances to the savage are still far more numerous than our differences from him; and what we have in common with him, and deliberately retain as true and useful, we owe to our savage forefathers who slowly acquired by experience and transmitted to us by inheritance those seemingly fundamental ideas which we are apt to regard as original and intuitive. We are like heirs to a fortune which has been handed down for so many ages that the memory of those who built it up is lost, and its possessors for the time being regard it as having been an original and unalterable possession of their race since the beginning of the world. But reflection and enquiry should satisfy us that to our predecessors we are indebted for much of what we thought most our own, and that their errors were not wilful extravagances or the ravings of insanity, but simply hypotheses, justifiable as such at the time when they were propounded, but which a fuller experience has proved to be inadequate. It is only by the successive testing of hypotheses and rejection of the false that truth is at last elicited. After all, what we call truth is only the hypothesis which is found to work best. Therefore in reviewing the opinions and practices of ruder ages and races we shall do well to look with leniency upon their errors as inevitable slips made in the search for truth, and to give them the benefit of that indulgence which we ourselves may one day stand in need of . . .

The Golden Bough, 1890

OLIVE SCHREINER
1855–1920

Preaching the Word in Cape Colony

In the front room of the farm-house sat Tant' Sannie in her elbow-chair. In her hand was her great brass-clasped hymn-book, round her neck was a clean white handkerchief, under her feet was a wooden stove. There, too, sat Em and Lyndall, in clean pinafores and new shoes. There, too, was the spruce Hottentot in a starched white 'kappje,' and her husband on the other side of the door, with his wool oiled and very much combed out, and staring at his new leather boots. The Kaffir servants were not there, because Tant' Sannie held they were descended from apes, and needed no salvation. But the rest were gathered for the Sunday service, and waited the officiator.

Meanwhile Bonaparte and the German approached arm-in-arm—Bonaparte resplendent in the black cloth clothes, a spotless shirt, and a spotless collar; the German in the old salt-and-pepper, casting shy glances of admiration at his companion.

At the front door Bonaparte removed his hat with much dignity, raised his shirt-collar, and entered. To the centre table he walked, put his hat solemnly down by the big Bible, and bowed his head over it in silent prayer.

The Boer-woman looked at the Hottentot, and the Hottentot looked at the Boer-woman.

There was one thing on earth for which Tant' Sannie had a profound reverence, which exercised a subduing influence over her, which made her for the time a better woman—that thing was new, shining black cloth. It made her think of the 'predikant'; it made her think of the elders, who sat in the top pew of the church on Sundays, with the hair so nicely oiled, so holy and respectable, with their little swallow-tailed coats; it made her think of heaven, where everything was so holy and respectable, and nobody wore tan-cord, and the littlest angel had a black tail-coat. She wished she hadn't called him a thief and a Roman Catholic. She hoped the German hadn't told him. She wondered where those clothes were when he came in rags to her door. There was no doubt, he was a very respectable man, a gentleman.

The German began to read a hymn. At the end of each line Bonaparte groaned, and twice at the end of every verse.

The Boer-woman had often heard of persons groaning during prayers, to add a certain poignancy and finish to them; old Jan Vanderlinde, her mother's brother, always did it after he was converted; and she would have looked upon it as no especial sign of grace in anyone; but to groan at hymn-time! She was startled. She wondered if he remembered that she shook her fist in his face. This was a man of God. They knelt down to pray. The Boer-woman weighed two hundred and fifty pounds, and could not kneel. She sat in her chair, and peeped between her crossed fingers at the stranger's back. She could not understand what he said; but he was in earnest. He shook the chair by the back rail till it made quite a little dust on the mud floor.

When they rose from their knees Bonaparte solemnly seated himself in the chair and opened the Bible. He blew his nose, pulled up his shirt-collar, smoothed the leaves, stroked down his capacious waistcoat, blew his nose again, looked solemnly round the room, then began:

'All liars shall have their part in the lake which burneth with fire and brimstone, which is the second death.'

Having read this portion of Scripture, Bonaparte paused impressively, and looked all round the room.

'I shall not, my dear friends,' he said, 'long detain you. Much of our precious time has already fled blissfully from us in the voice of thanksgiving and the tongue of praise. A few, a very few words are all I shall address to you, and may they be as a rod of iron dividing the bones from the marrow, and the marrow from the bones.

'In the first place: What is a liar?'

The question was put so pointedly and followed by a pause so profound, that even the Hottentot man left off looking at his boots and opened his eyes, though he understood not a word.

'I repeat,' said Bonaparte, 'what is a liar?'

The sensation was intense; the attention of the audience was riveted.

'Have you, any of you, ever seen a liar, my dear friends?' There was a still longer pause. 'I hope not; I truly hope not. But I will tell you what a liar is. I knew a liar once—a little boy who lived in Cape Town, in Short Market Street. His mother and I sat together one day, discoursing about our souls.

'"Here, Sampson," said his mother, "go and buy sixpence of 'meiboss' from the Malay round the corner."

'When he came back she said, "How much have you got?"

'"Five," he said.

'He was afraid if he said six and a half she'd ask for some. And, my friends, that was a *lie*. The half of a "meiboss" stuck in his throat, and he died, and was buried. And where did the soul of that little liar go to, my friends? It went to the lake of fire and brimstone. This brings me to the second point of my discourse . . .'

The Story of an African Farm, 1883

GEORGE BERNARD SHAW
1856–1950

The Finality of Mozart

The Mozart Centenary has made a good deal of literary and musical business this week. Part of this is easy enough, especially for the illustrated papers. Likenesses of Mozart at all ages; view of Salzburg; portrait of Marie Antoinette (described in the text as 'the ill-fated'), to whom he proposed marriage at an early age; picture of the young composer, two and a half feet high, crushing the Pompadour with his 'Who is this woman that refuses to kiss me? The Queen kissed me! (Sensation)'; facsimile of the original MS of the first four bars of *Là ci darem*, and the like. These, with copious paraphrases of the English translation of Otto Jahn's great biography, will pull the journalists proper through the Centenary with credit. The critic's task is not quite so easy.

The word is, of course, Admire, admire, admire; but unless you frankly trade on the ignorance of the public, and cite as illustrations of his unique genius feats that come easily to dozens of organists and choirboys who never wrote, and never will write, a bar of original music in their lives; or pay his symphonies and operas empty compliments that might be transferred word for word, without the least incongruity, to the symphonies of Spohr and the operas of Offenbach; or represent him as composing as spontaneously as a bird sings, on the strength of his habit of perfecting his greater compositions in his mind before he wrote them down—unless you try these well-worn dodges, you will find nothing to admire that is peculiar to Mozart: the fact being that he, like Praxiteles, Raphael, Molière, or Shakespear, was no leader of a new departure or founder of a school.

He came at the end of a development, not at the beginning of one; and although there are operas and symphonies, and even pianoforte sonatas and pages of instrumental scoring of his, on which you can put your finger and say 'Here is final perfection in this manner; and nobody, whatever his genius may be, will ever get a step further on these lines,' you cannot say 'Here is an entirely new vein of musical art, of which nobody ever dreamt before Mozart.' Haydn, who made the mould for Mozart's symphonies, was proud of Mozart's genius because he felt his own part in it: he would have written the E flat symphony if he could, and, though he could not, was at least able to feel that the man who had reached that pre-eminence was standing on his old shoulders. Now, Haydn would have recoiled from the idea of composing—or perpetrating, as he would have put it—the first movement of Beethoven's Eroica, and would have repudiated all part in leading music to such a pass.

The more farsighted Gluck not only carried Mozart in his arms to within sight of the goal of his career as an opera composer, but even cleared a little of the new path into which Mozart's finality drove all those successors of his who were too gifted to waste their lives in making weak dilutions of Mozart's scores, and serving them up as 'classics.' Many Mozart worshipers cannot bear to be told that their hero was not the founder of a dynasty. But in art the highest success is to be the last of your race, not the first. Anybody, almost, can make a beginning: the difficulty is to make an end—to do what cannot be bettered.

written 1891; *Music in London*, 1890–4

Music Critics and Theatre Critics

I suppose no one will deny the right of the fully accomplished musical critic to look down upon the mere dramatic critic as something between an unskilled laborer and a journeyman. I have often taken a turn at dramatic work for a night merely to amuse myself and oblige a friend, wheras if I were to ask a dramatic critic to take my place, I should be regarded as no less obviously mad than a surgeon who should ask his stockbroker to cut off a leg or two for him, so as to leave him free for a trip up the river. Clearly, I may without arrogance consider my dramatic colleagues—I call them colleagues more out of politeness than from any genuine sense that they are my equals—as at best specialists in a sub-department of my art. They are men who have failed to make themselves musical critics—creatures with half-developed senses, who will listen to any sort of stage diction and look at any sort of stage picture without more artistic feeling than is involved in the daily act of listening to the accent and scrutinizing the hat of a new acquaintance in order to estimate his income and social standing.

written 1892; *Music in London*, 1890–4

Shakespear

But I am bound to add that I pity the man who cannot enjoy Shakespear. He has outlasted thousands of abler thinkers, and will outlast a thousand more. His gift of telling a story (provided some one else told it to him first); his enormous power over language, as conspicuous in his senseless and silly abuse of it as in his miracles of expression; his humor; his sense of idiosyncratic character; and his prodigious fund of that vital energy which is, it seems, the true differentiating property behind the faculties, good, bad or indifferent, of the man of genius, enable him to entertain us so effectively that the imaginary scenes and people he has created become more real to us than our actual life—at least, until our knowledge and grip of actual life begins to deepen and glow beyond the common. When I was twenty I knew everybody in Shakespear, from Hamlet to Abhorson, much more intimately than I knew my living contemporaries; and to this day, if the name of Pistol or Polonius catches my eye in a newspaper, I turn to the passage with more curiosity than if the name were that of—but perhaps I had better not mention any one in particular.

'Blaming the Bard', 1896, *Our Theatre in the Nineties*

The Secret of Style

Effectiveness of assertion is the Alpha and Omega of style. He who has nothing to assert has no style and can have none: he who has something to assert will go as far in power of style as its momentousness and his conviction will carry him.

'Epistle Dedicatory' to *Man and Superman*, 1903

Money

Money is the most important thing in the world. It represents health, strength, honor, generosity and beauty as conspicuously and undeniably as the want of it represents illness, weakness, disgrace, meanness and ugliness. Not the least of its virtues is that it destroys base people as certainly as it fortifies and dignifies noble people. It is only when it is cheapened to worthlessness for some, and made impossibly dear to others, that it becomes a curse. In short, it is a curse only in such foolish social conditions that life itself is a curse. For the two things are inseparable: money is the counter that enables life to be distributed socially: it *is* life as truly as sovereigns and bank notes are money. The first duty of every citizen is to insist on having money on reasonable terms; and this demand is not complied with by giving four men three shillings each for ten or twelve hours' drudgery and one man a thousand pounds for nothing. The crying need of the nation is not for better morals, cheaper bread, temperance, liberty, culture, redemption of fallen sisters and erring brothers, nor the grace, love and fellowship of the Trinity, but simply for enough money. And the evil to be attacked is not sin, suffering, greed, priestcraft, kingcraft, demagogy, monopoly, ignorance, drink, war, pestilence, nor any of the scapegoats which reformers sacrifice, but simply poverty.

Preface to *Major Barbara*, 1905

A Question of Moderation

Dickens's moderation in drinking must be interpreted according to the old standard for mail coach travellers. In the Staplehurst railway accident, a few years before his death, he congratulated himself on having a bottle and a half of brandy with him: and he killed several of the survivors by administering hatfulls of it as first aid. I invite you to consider the effect on the public mind if, in a railway accident today, Mr Gilbert Chesterton were reported as having been in the train with a bottle and a half of brandy on his person as normal refreshment.

letter to G. K. Chesterton, 1906

A Public Disgrace

We may be as idle as we please if only we have money in our pockets; and the more we look as if we had never done a day's work in our lives and never intend to, the more we are respected by every official we come in contact with, and the more we are envied, courted, and deferred to by everybody. If we enter a village school the children all rise and stand respectfully to receive us, whereas the entrance of a plumber or carpenter leaves them unmoved. The mother who secures a rich idler as a husband for her daughter is proud of it: the father who makes a million uses it to make rich idlers of his children. That work is a curse is part of our religion: that it is a disgrace is the first article in our social code. To carry a parcel through the streets is not only a trouble, but a derogation from one's rank. Where there are blacks to carry them, as in South Africa, it is virtually impossible for a white to be seen doing such a thing. In London we condemn these colonial extremes of snobbery; but how many ladies could we persuade to carry a jug of milk down Bond Street on a May afternoon, even for a bet?

The Intelligent Woman's Guide to Socialism and Capitalism, 1928

Men of Their Own Time

Had Marx and Engels been contemporaries of Shakespear they could not have written the Communist Manifesto, and would probably have taken a hand, as Shakespear did, in the enclosure of common lands as a step forward in civilization.

Preface to *Geneva*, 1938

The Clerk Who Got Away

What changes a man into a clerk, in Dublin or elsewhere? You cannot make a Bedouin a clerk. But you can make an Englishman a clerk quite easily. All you have to do is to drop him into a middle-class family, with a father who cannot afford to keep him nor afford to give him capital to start with, nor to carry his education beyond reading, writing, and ciphering, but who would feel disgraced if his son became a mechanic. Given these circumstances, what can the poor wretch do but become a clerk?

I became a clerk myself. An uncle who, as a high official in a Government department, had exceptional opportunities of obliging people, not to mention obstructing them if he disliked them, easily obtained for me a stool in a very genteel office; and I should have been there still if I had not broken loose in defiance of all prudence, and become a professional man of genius. I am not one of those successful men who can say 'Why dont you do as I do?'

I sometimes dream that I am back in that office again, bothered by a consciousness that a long period has elapsed during which I have neglected my most important duties. I have drawn no money at the bank in the mornings, nor lodged any in the afternoons. I have paid no insurance premiums, nor head-rents, nor mortgage interests. Whole estates must have been sold up, widows and orphans left to starve, mortgages foreclosed, and the landed gentry of Ireland abandoned to general ruin, confusion, and anarchy, all through my unaccountable omission of my daily duties for years and years, during which, equally unaccountably, neither I nor anyone else in the office has aged by a single day. I generally wake in the act of asking my principals, with the authority which belongs to my later years, whether they realize what has happened, and whether they propose to leave so disgracefully untrustworthy a person as myself in a position of such responsibility.

Sixteen Self Sketches, 1949

GEORGE GISSING
1857–1903

A Literary Man

Shortly after, Alfred Yule entered the house. It was no uncommon thing for him to come home in a mood of silent moroseness, and this evening the first glimpse of his face was sufficient warning. He entered the dining-room and stood on the hearthrug reading an evening paper. His wife made a pretence of straightening things upon the table.

'Well?' he exclaimed irritably. 'It's after five; why isn't dinner served?'

'It's just coming, Alfred.'

Even the average man of a certain age is an alarming creature when dinner delays itself; the literary man in such a moment goes beyond all parallel. If there be added the fact that he has just returned from a very unsatisfactory interview with a publisher, wife and daughter may indeed regard the situation as appalling. Marian came in, and at once observed her mother's frightened face.

'Father,' she said, hoping to make a diversion, 'Mr Hinks has sent you his new book, and wishes——'

'Then take Mr Hinks's new book back to him, and tell him that I have quite enough to do without reading tedious trash. He needn't expect that I'm going to write a notice of it. The simpleton pesters me beyond endurance. I wish to know, if you please,' he added with savage calm, 'when dinner will be ready. If there's time to write a few letters, just tell me at once, that I mayn't waste half an hour.'

Marian resented this unreasonable anger, but she durst not reply. At that moment the servant appeared with a smoking joint, and Mrs Yule followed carrying dishes of vegetables. The man of letters seated himself and carved angrily. He began his meal by drinking half a glass of ale; then he ate a few mouthfuls in a quick, hungry way, his head bent closely over the plate. It happened commonly enough that dinner passed without a word of conversation, and that seemed likely to be the case this evening. To his wife Yule seldom addressed anything but a curt inquiry or caustic comment; if he spoke humanly at table it was to Marian.

Ten minutes passed; then Marian resolved to try any means of clearing the atmosphere.

'Mr Quarmby gave me a message for you,' she said. 'A friend of his, Nathaniel Walker, has told him that Mr Rackett will very likely offer you the editorship of *The Study*.'

Yule stopped in the act of mastication. He fixed his eyes intently on the sirloin for half a minute; then, by way of the beer-jug and the salt-cellar, turned them upon Marian's face.

'Walker told him that? Pooh!'

'It was a great secret. I wasn't to breathe a word to anyone but you.'

'Walker's a fool and Quarmby's an ass,' remarked her father.

But there was a tremulousness in his bushy eyebrows; his forehead half unwreathed itself; he continued to eat more slowly, and as if with appreciation of the viands.

'What did he say? Repeat it to me in his words.'

Marian did so, as nearly as possible. He listened with a scoffing expression, but still his features relaxed.

'I don't credit Rackett with enough good sense for such a proposal,' he said deliberately. 'And I'm not very sure that I should accept it if it were made. That fellow Fadge has all but ruined the paper. It will amuse me to see how long it takes him to make Culpepper's new magazine a distinct failure.'

A silence of five minutes ensued; then Yule said of a sudden:

'Where is Hinks's book?'

Marian reached it from a side table; under this roof, literature was regarded almost as a necessary part of table garnishing.

'I thought it would be bigger than this,' Yule muttered, as he opened the volume in a way peculiar to bookish men.

A page was turned down, as if to draw attention to some passage. Yule put on his eye-glasses, and soon made a discovery which had the effect of completing the transformation of his visage. His eyes glinted, his chin worked in pleasurable emotion. In a moment he handed the book to Marian, indicating the small type of a foot-note; it embodied an effusive eulogy—introduced *à propos* of some literary discussion—of 'Mr Alfred Yule's critical acumen, scholarly research, lucid style,' and sundry other distinguished merits.

'That is kind of him,' said Marian.

'Good old Hinks! I suppose I must try to get him half a dozen readers.'

'May I see?' asked Mrs Yule, under her breath, bending to Marian.

Her daughter passed on the volume, and Mrs Yule read the foot-note with that look of slow apprehension which is so pathetic when it signifies the heart's good-will thwarted by the mind's defect.

'That'll be good for you, Alfred, won't it?' she said, glancing at her husband.

'Certainly,' he replied, with a smile of contemptuous irony. 'If Hinks goes on, he'll establish my reputation.'

And he took a draught of ale, like one who is reinvigorated for the battle of life. Marian, regarding him askance, mused on what seemed to her a strange anomaly in his character; it had often surprised her that a man of his temperament and powers should be so dependent upon the praise and blame of people whom he justly deemed his inferiors.

Yule was glancing over the pages of the work.

'A pity the man can't write English. What a vocabulary! *Obstruent—reliable—particularization—fabulosity—different to—averse to*—did one ever come across such a mixture of antique pedantry and modern vulgarism! Surely he has his name from the German *hinken*—eh, Marian?'

With a laugh he tossed the book away again. His mood was wholly changed. He gave various evidences of enjoying the meal, and began to talk freely with his daughter.

'Finished the authoresses?'

'Not quite.'

'No hurry. When you have time I want you to read Ditchley's new book, and jot down a selection of his worst sentences. I'll use them for an article on contemporary style; it occurred to me this afternoon.'

He smiled grimly. Mrs Yule's face exhibited much contentment, which became radiant joy when her husband remarked casually that the custard was very well made to-day. Dinner over, he rose without ceremony and went off to his study.

The man had suffered much and toiled stupendously. It was not inexplicable that dyspepsia, and many another ill that literary flesh is heir to, racked him sore.

New Grub Street, 1891

An Advertising Man

'Ah, those were happy days that I spent at Whitsand! Tell me what you have been doing. Is there any hope of the pier yet?'

'Why, it's as good as built!' cried the other. 'Didn't you see the advertisements, when we floated the company a month ago? I suppose you don't read that kind of thing. We shall begin at the works in early spring.—Look here!'

He unrolled a large design, a coloured picture of Whitsand pier as it already existed in his imagination. Not content with having the mere structure exhibited, Crewe had persuaded the draughtsman to add embellishments of a kind which, in days to come, would be his own peculiar care; from end to end, the pier glowed with the placards of advertisers. Below, on the sands, appeared bathing-machines, and these also were covered with manifold advertisements. Nay, the very pleasure-boats on the sunny waves declared the glory of somebody's soap, of somebody's purgatives.

'I'll make that place one of the biggest advertising stations in England—see if I don't! You remember the caves? I'm going to have them lighted with electricity, and painted all round with advertisements of the most artistic kind.'

'What a brilliant idea!'

'There's something else you might like to hear of. It struck me I would write a Guide to Advertising, and here it is.' He handed a copy of the book. 'It advertises *me*, and brings a little grist to the mill on its own account. Three weeks since I got it out, and we've sold three thousand of it. Costs nothing to print; the advertisements more than pay for that. Price, one shilling.'

'But how you do work, Mr Crewe! It's marvellous. And yet you look so well,—you have really a seaside colour!'

'I never ailed much since I can remember. The harder I work, the better I feel.'

In the Year of Jubilee, 1894

JOSEPH CONRAD
1857–1924

The Anger of the Sea

Only once in all that time he had again a glimpse of the earnestness in the anger of the sea. That truth is not so often made apparent as people might think. There are many shades in the danger of adventures and gales, and it is only now and then that there appears on the face of facts a sinister violence of intention—that indefinable something which forces it upon the mind and the heart of a man, that this complication of accidents or these elemental furies are coming at him with a purpose of malice, with a strength beyond control, with an unbridled cruelty that means to tear out of him his hope and his fear, the pain of his fatigue and his longing for rest: which means to smash, to destroy, to annihilate all he has seen, known, loved, enjoyed, or hated; all that is priceless and necessary—the sunshine, the memories, the future—which means to sweep the whole precious world utterly away from his sight by the simple and appalling act of taking his life.

Lord Jim, 1900

A Voice in the Storm

The *Nan-Shan* was being looted by the storm with a senseless, destructive fury: trysails torn out of the extra gaskets, double-lashed awnings blown away, bridge swept clean, weather-cloths burst, rails twisted, light-screens smashed—and two of the boats had gone already. They had gone unheard and unseen, melting, as it were, in the shock and smother of the wave. It was only later, when upon the white flash of another high sea hurling itself amidships, Jukes had a vision of two pairs of davits leaping black and empty out of the solid blackness, with one overhauled fall flying and an iron-bound block capering in the air, that he became aware of what had happened within about three yards of his back.

He poked his head forward, groping for the ear of his commander. His lips touched it—big, fleshy, very wet. He cried in an agitated tone, 'Our boats are going now, sir.'

And again he heard that voice, forced and ringing feebly, but with a penetrating effect of quietness in the enormous discord of noises, as if sent out from some remote spot of peace beyond the black wastes of the gale; again he heard a man's voice—the frail and indomitable sound that can be made to carry an infinity of thought, resolution and purpose, that shall be pronouncing confident words on the last day, when heavens fall, and justice is done—again he heard it, and it was crying to him, as if from very, very far—'All right.'

He thought he had not managed to make himself understood. 'Our boats—I say boats—the boats, sir! Two gone!'

The same voice, within a foot of him and yet so remote, yelled sensibly, 'Can't be helped.'

Captain MacWhirr had never turned his face, but Jukes caught some more words on the wind.

'What can—expect—when hammering through—such—— Bound to leave—something behind—stands to reason.'

Watchfully Jukes listened for more. No more came. This was all Captain MacWhirr had to say; and Jukes could picture to himself rather than see the broad squat back before him. An impenetrable obscurity pressed down upon the ghostly glimmers of the sea. A dull conviction seized upon Jukes that there was nothing to be done.

Typhoon, 1903

An Imperial Democrat

At about that time, in the Intendencia of Sulaco, Charles Gould was assuring Pedrito Montero, who had sent a request for his presence there, that he would never let the mine pass out of his hands for the profit of a Government who had robbed him of it. The Gould Concession could not be resumed. His father had not desired it. The son would never surrender it. He would never surrender it alive. And once dead, where was the power capable of resuscitating such an enterprise in all its vigour and wealth out of the ashes and ruin of destruction? There was no such power in the country. And where was the skill and capital abroad that would condescend to touch such an ill-omened corpse? Charles Gould talked in the impassive tone which had for many years served to conceal his anger and contempt. He suffered. He was disgusted with what he had to say. It was too much like heroics. In him the strictly practical instinct was in profound discord with the almost mystic view he took of his right. The Gould Concession was symbolic of abstract justice. Let the heavens fall. But since the San Tomé mine had developed its world-wide fame his threat had enough force and effectiveness to reach the rudimentary intelligence of Pedro Montero, wrapped up as it was in the futilities of historical anecdotes. The Gould Concession was a serious asset in the country's finance, and, what was more, in the private budgets of many officials as well. It was traditional. It was known. It was said. It was credible. Every Minister of Interior drew a salary from the San Tomé mine. It was natural. And Pedrito intended to be Minister of the Interior and President of the Council in his brother's Government. The Duc de Morny had occupied those high posts during the Second French Empire with conspicuous advantage to himself.

A table, a chair, a wooden bedstead had been procured for His Excellency, who, after a short siesta, rendered absolutely necessary by the labours and the pomps of his entry into Sulaco, had been getting hold of the administrative machine by making appointments, giving orders, and signing proclamations. Alone with Charles Gould in the audience room, His Excellency managed with his well-known skill to conceal his annoyance and consternation. He had begun at first to talk loftily of confiscation, but the want of all proper feeling and mobility in the Señor Administrador's features ended by affecting adversely his power of masterful expression. Charles Gould had repeated: 'The Government can certainly bring about the destruction of the San Tomé mine if it likes;

but without me it can do nothing else.' It was an alarming pronouncement, and well calculated to hurt the sensibilities of a politician whose mind is bent upon the spoils of victory. And Charles Gould said also that the destruction of the San Tomé mine would cause the ruin of other undertakings, the withdrawal of European capital, the withholding, most probably, of the last instalment of the foreign loan. That stony fiend of a man said all these things (which were accessible to His Excellency's intelligence) in a cold-blooded manner which made one shudder.

A long course of reading historical works, light and gossipy in tone, carried out in garrets of Parisian hotels, sprawling on an untidy bed, to the neglect of his duties, menial or otherwise, had affected the manners of Pedro Montero. Had he seen around him the splendour of the old Intendencia, the magnificent hangings, the gilt furniture ranged along the walls; had he stood upon a daïs on a noble square of red carpet, he would have probably been very dangerous from a sense of success and elevation. But in this sacked and devastated residence, with the three pieces of common furniture huddled up in the middle of the vast apartment, Pedrito's imagination was subdued by a feeling of insecurity and impermanence. That feeling and the firm attitude of Charles Gould who had not once, so far, pronounced the word 'Excellency', diminished him in his own eyes. He assumed the tone of an enlightened man of the world, and begged Charles Gould to dismiss from his mind every cause for alarm. He was now conversing, he reminded him, with the brother of the master of the country, charged with a reorganizing mission. The trusted brother of the master of the country, he repeated. Nothing was farther from the thoughts of that wise and patriotic hero than ideas of destruction. 'I entreat you, Don Carlos, not to give way to your anti-democratic prejudices,' he cried, in a burst of condescending effusion.

Pedrito Montero surprised one at first sight by the vast development of his bald forehead, a shiny yellow expanse between the crinkly coal-black tufts of hair without any lustre, the engaging form of his mouth, and an unexpectedly cultivated voice. But his eyes, very glistening as if freshly painted on each side of his hooked nose, had a round, hopeless, birdlike stare when opened fully. Now, however, he narrowed them agreeably, throwing his square chin up and speaking with closed teeth slightly through the nose, with what he imagined to be the manner of a *grand seigneur*.

In that attitude, he declared suddenly that the highest expression of democracy was Caesarism: the imperial rule based upon the direct popular vote. Caesarism was conservative. It was strong. It recognized the legitimate needs of democracy which requires orders, titles, and distinctions. They would be showered upon deserving men. Caesarism was peace. It was progressive. It secured the prosperity of a country. Pedrito Montero was carried away. Look at what the Second Empire had done for France. It was a régime which delighted to honour men of Don Carlos's stamp. The Second Empire fell, but that was because its chief was devoid of that military genius which had raised General Montero to the pinnacle of fame and glory. Pedrito elevated his hand jerkily to help the idea of pinnacle, of fame. 'We shall have many talks yet. We shall understand each other thoroughly, Don Carlos!' he cried in a tone of fellowship. Republicanism had done its work. Imperial democracy was the power of the future. Pedrito, the *guerrillero*, showing his hand, lowered his voice forcibly. A man singled out by his fellow-citizens for the honourable nickname of El Rey de Sulaco could not but receive a full recognition from an imperial democracy as a great captain of industry and a person of weighty counsel, whose popular designation would be soon replaced by a more solid title. 'Eh, Don Carlos? No! What do you say? Conde de Sulaco—Eh?—or marquis . . .'

He ceased. The air was cool on the Plaza, where a patrol of cavalry rode round and round without penetrating into the streets, which resounded with shouts and the strumming of guitars issuing from the open doors of *pulperías*. The orders were not to interfere with the enjoyments of the people. And above the roofs, next to the perpendicular lines of the cathedral towers, the snowy curve of Higuerota blocked a large space of darkening blue sky before the windows of the Intendencia. After a time Pedrito Montero, thrusting his hand in the bosom of his coat, bowed his head with slow dignity. The audience was over.

Nostromo, 1904

After the Bomb-Blast

'You used a shovel,' he remarked, observing a sprinkling of small gravel, tiny brown bits of bark, and particles of splintered wood as fine as needles.

'Had to in one place,' said the stolid constable. 'I sent a keeper to fetch a spade. When he heard me scraping the ground with it he leaned his forehead against a tree, and was as sick as a dog.'

The Chief Inspector, stooping guardedly over the table, fought down the unpleasant sensation in his throat. The shattering violence of destruction which had made of that body a heap of nameless fragments affected his feelings with a sense of ruthless cruelty, though his reason told him the effect must have been as swift as a flash of lightning. The man, whoever he was, had died instantaneously; and yet it seemed impossible to believe that a human body could have reached that state of disintegration without passing through the pangs of inconceivable agony. No physiologist, and still less of a metaphysician, Chief Inspector Heat rose by the force of sympathy, which is a form of fear, above the vulgar conception of time. Instantaneous! He remembered all he had ever read in popular publications of long and terrifying dreams dreamed in the instant of waking; of the whole past life lived with frightful intensity by a drowning man as his doomed head bobs up, streaming, for the last time. The inexplicable mysteries of conscious existence beset Chief Inspector Heat till he evolved a horrible notion that ages of atrocious pain and mental torture could be contained between two successive winks of an eye. And meantime the Chief Inspector went on peering at the table with a calm face and the slightly anxious attention of an indigent customer bending over what may be called the by-products of a butcher's shop with a view to an inexpensive Sunday dinner.

The Secret Agent, 1907

The Fate of a Revolution

In a real revolution—not a simple dynastic change or a mere reform of institutions—in a real revolution the best characters do not come to the front. A violent revolution falls into the hands of narrow-minded fanatics and of tyrannical hypocrites at first. Afterwards comes the turn of all the pretentious intellectual failures of the time. Such are the chiefs and the leaders. You will notice that I have left out the mere rogues. The scrupulous and the just, the noble, humane and devoted natures; the unselfish and the intelligent may begin a movement—but it passes away from them. They are not the leaders of a revolution. They are its victims: the victims of disgust, of disenchantment—often of remorse. Hopes grotesquely betrayed, ideals caricatured—that is the definition of revolutionary success. There have been in every revolution hearts broken by such successes.

Under Western Eyes, 1911

Released

We know how he arrived on board. For my part I know so little of prisons that I haven't the faintest notion how one leaves them. It seems as abominable an operation as the other, the shutting up with its mental suggestions of bang, snap, crash and the empty silence outside—where an instant before you were—you *were*—and now no longer are. Perfectly devilish. And the release! I don't know which is worse. How do they do it? Pull the string, door flies open, man flies through: Out you go! *Adios*! And in the space where a second before you were not, in the silent space there is a figure going away, limping. Why limping? I don't know. That's how I see it. One has a notion of a maiming, crippling process; of the individual coming back damaged in some subtle way. I admit it is a fantastic hallucination, but I can't help it. Of course I know that the proceedings of the best machine-made humanity are employed with judicious care and so on. I am absurd, no doubt, but still . . . Oh yes it's idiotic. When I pass one of these places . . . did you notice that there is something infernal about the aspect of every individual stone or brick of them, something malicious as if matter were enjoying its revenge on the contemptuous spirit of man. Did you notice? You didn't? Eh? Well I am perhaps a little mad on that point. When I pass one of these places I must avert my eyes . . .

Chance, 1913

A Legacy of Disillusion

For fifteen years Heyst had wandered, invariably courteous and unapproachable, and in return was generally considered a 'queer chap.' He had started off on these travels of his after the death of his father, an expatriated Swede who died in London, dissatisfied with his country and angry with all the world, which had instinctively rejected his wisdom.

Thinker, stylist, and man of the world in his time, the elder Heyst had begun by coveting all the joys, those of the great and those of the humble, those of the fools and those of the sages. For more than sixty years he had dragged on this painful earth of ours the most weary, the most uneasy soul that civilisation had ever fashioned to its ends of disillusion and regret. One could not refuse him a measure of greatness, for he was unhappy in a way unknown to mediocre souls. His mother Heyst had never known, but he kept his father's pale, distinguished face in affectionate memory. He remembered him mainly in an ample blue dressing-gown in a large house of a quiet London suburb. For three years, after leaving school at the age of eighteen, he had lived with the elder Heyst, who was then writing his last book. In this work, at the end of his life, he claimed for mankind that right to absolute moral and intellectual liberty of which he no longer believed them worthy.

Three years of such companionship at that plastic and impressionable age were bound to leave in the boy a profound mistrust of life. The young man learned to reflect, which is a destructive process, a reckoning of the cost. It is not the clear-sighted who lead the world. Great achievements are accomplished in a blessed, warm mental fog, which the pitiless cold blasts of the father's analysis had blown away from the son.

'I'll drift,' Heyst had said to himself deliberately.

He did not mean intellectually or sentimentally or morally. He meant to drift altogether and literally, body and soul, like a detached leaf drifting in the wind-currents under the immovable trees of a forest glade; to drift without ever catching on to anything.

'This shall be my defence against life,' he had said to himself with a sort of inward consciousness that for the son of his father there was no other worthy alternative.

Victory, 1915

SIR CHARLES SHERRINGTON
1857–1952

The Wisdom of the Cell

Each cell, we remember, is blind; senses it has none. It knows not 'up' from 'down'; it works in the dark. Yet the nerve-cell, for instance, 'finds' even to the fingertips the nerve-cell with which it should touch fingers. It is as if an immanent principle inspired each cell with knowledge for the carrying out of a design. And this picture which the microscope supplies to us, conveying this impression of prescience and intention, supplies us after all, because it is but a picture, with only the static form. That is but the outward and visible sign of a dynamic activity, which is a harmony in time as well as space. 'Never the time and the place and the loved one all together.' Here all three and always, save for disease.

Man on his Nature, 1940

Is Life a Sacred Thing?

Life taken in general can be no sacred thing. It has enslaved and brutalized the globe. True, life is the supreme blessing of the planet; none the less it is also the planet's crowning curse. If the planet would secure for its community a living welfare on its surface, in that aim it finds itself thwarted and tortured by unstemmable fecundity of lives teeming in backwaters of blind 'urge-to-live'. The planet has to be rescued from such 'life'.

We see that if we ask Nature the question, clearly she says, 'life is no sacred thing'. But we are doubtful whether in our sense she has 'values'. Addressing then the question to some neighbour he well may tell us:—this much is clear; where life has mind, life can suffer; it is suffering which counts. Where life ranks highest, there it can suffer most. Human life has among its privileges that of pre-eminence of pain. The civilizations have not rarely ruled that among lives one life at least is sacred, namely man's.

We think back with repugnance to that ancient biological pre-human scene whence, so we have learned, we came; there *no* life was a sacred thing. There millions of years of pain went by without one moment of pity, not to speak of mercy. Its life innately gifted with 'zest-to-live' was yet so conditioned that much of it must kill or die.

For man, partly emancipated from those conditions, the situation has changed. The rule and scene are there, and are the same, apart from himself. The change is in himself. Where have his 'values' come from? The infra-human life he escaped from knew them not. The great predaceous forms, shark, hawk, panther, wolf, are not blind; the huge past record of the rocks; they mean and meant the things they do and did; they have been given mind. But not with values. 'Wrong' is and was impossible to them. More hopeless still, equally impossible is 'right'. Those other creatures than himself, even the likest to himself, would seem without the 'values', or it may be at most some 'value' *ad hoc* for a given situation. Nothing of values as concepts such as are man's, contantly vouchsafing him counsel in situations widely circumstanced. Whence has he got them? Inventions of his own? How far can be trust them? Can *a priori* principles suffice to base them? Are they heritable? They are under test. They are in the making, man-made law has still to buttress them.

Man on his Nature

E. Œ. SOMERVILLE (1858–1949)
and
MARTIN ROSS (Violet Martin, 1862–1915)

Charlotte in Love

The movements of Charlotte's character, for it cannot be said to possess the power of development, were akin to those of some amphibious thing, whose strong, darting course under the water is only marked by a bubble or two, and it required almost an animal instinct to note them. Every bubble betrayed the creature below, as well as the limitations of its power of hiding itself, but people never thought of looking out for these indications in Charlotte, or even suspected that she had anything to conceal. There was an almost blatant simplicity about her, a humorous rough and readiness which, joined with her literary culture, proved business capacity, and dreaded temper, seemed to leave no room for any further aspect, least of all of a romantic kind.

Having opened the window for a minute to scream abusive directions to the men who were spreading gravel, she went back to the table, and, gathering her account-books together, she locked them up in her davenport. The room that, in Julia Duffy's time, had been devoted to the storage of potatoes, was now beginning life again, dressed in the faded attire of the Tally Ho dining-room. Charlotte's books lined one of its newly-papered walls; the fox-hunting prints that dated from old Mr Butler's reign at Tally Ho hung above the chimney-piece, and the maroon rep curtains were those at which Francie had stared during her last and most terrific encounter with their owner. The air of occupation was completed by a basket on the rug in front of the fire with four squeaking kittens in it, and by the Bible and the grey manual of devotion out of which Charlotte read daily prayers to Louisa the orphan and the cats. It was an ugly room, and nothing could ever make it anything else, but with the aid of the brass-mounted grate, a few bits of Mrs Mullen's silver on the sideboard, and the deep-set windows, it had an air of respectability and even dignity that appealed very strongly to Charlotte. She enjoyed every detail of her new possessions, and, unlike Norry and the cats, felt no regret for the urban charms and old associations of Tally Ho. Indeed, since her aunt's death, she had never liked Tally Ho. There was a strain of superstition in her that, like her love of land, showed how strongly the blood of the Irish peasant ran in her veins: since she had turned Francie out of the house she had not liked to think of the empty room facing her own, in which Mrs Mullen's feeble voice had laid upon her the charge that she had not kept: her dealings with table-turning and spirit-writing had expanded for her the boundaries of the possible, and made her the more accessible to terror of the supernatural. Here, at Gurthnamuckla, there was nothing to harbour these suggestions; no brooding evergreens rustling outside her bedroom window, no rooms alive with the little incidents of a past life, no doors whose opening and shutting were like familiar voices reminding her of the footsteps that they had once heralded. This new house was peopled only by the pleasant phantoms of a future that she had fashioned for herself out of the slightest and vulgarest materials, and her wakeful nights were spent in schemings in which the romantic and the practical were logically blended.

The Real Charlotte, 1894

JOHN MEADE FALKNER
1858–1932

A Single Low Note

In a minute he had made up his mind to go to the minster. As resident architect he possessed a master key which opened all the doors; he would walk round, and see if he could find anything of the missing organist before going to bed. He strode quickly through the deserted streets. The lamps were all put out, for Cullerne economized gas at times of full-moon. There was nothing moving, his footsteps rang on the pavement, and echoed from wall to wall. He took the short-cut by the wharves, and in a few minutes came to the old Bonding-house.

The shadows hung like black velvet in the spaces between the brick buttresses that shored up the wall towards the quay. He smiled to himself as he thought of the organist's nervousness, of those strange fancies as to someone lurking in the black hiding-holes, and as to buildings being in some way connected with man's fate. Yet he knew that his smile was assumed, for he felt all the while the oppression of the loneliness, of the sadness of a half-ruined building, of the gurgling mutter of the river, and instinctively quickened his pace. He was glad when he had passed the spot, and again that night, as he looked back, he saw the strange effect of light and darkness which produced the impression of someone standing in the shadow of the last buttress space. The illusion was so perfect that he thought he could make out the figure of a man, in a long loose cape that flapped in the wind.

He had passed the wrought-iron gates now—he was in the churchyard, and it was then that he first became aware of a soft, low, droning sound which seemed to fill the air all about him. He stopped for a moment to listen; what was it? Where was the noise? It grew more distinct as he passed along the flagged stone path which led to the north door. Yes, it certainly came from inside the church. What could it be? What could anyone be doing in the church at this hour of night?

He was in the north porch now, and then he knew what it was. It was a low note of the organ—a pedal-note; he was almost sure it was that very pedal-point which the organist had explained to him with such pride. The sound reassured him nothing had happened to Mr Sharnall—he was practising in the church; it was only some mad freak of his to be playing so late; he was practising that service 'Sharnall in D flat.'

He took out his key to unlock the wicket, and was surprised to find it already open, because he knew that it was the organist's habit to lock himself in. He passed into the great church. It was strange, there was no sound of music; there was no one playing; there was only the intolerably monotonous booming of a single pedal-note, with an occasional muffled thud when the water-engine turned spasmodically to replenish the emptying bellows.

'Sharnall!' he shouted—'Sharnall, what are you doing? Don't you know how late it is?'

He paused and thought at first that someone was answering him—he thought that he heard people muttering in the choir; but it was only the echo of his own voice, his own voice tossed from pillar to pillar and arch to arch, till it faded into a wail of 'Sharnall, Sharnall!' in the lantern.

It was the first time that he had been in the church at night, and he stood for a moment overcome with the mystery of the place, while he gazed at the columns of the nave standing white in the moonlight like a row of vast shrouded figures. He called again to Mr Sharnall, and again received no answer, and then he made his way up the nave to the little doorway that leads to the organ-loft stairs.

The Nebuly Coat, 1903

A. E. HOUSMAN
1859–1936

The Desire of Knowledge

It is the glory of God, says Solomon, to conceal a thing: but the honour of kings is to search out a matter. Kings have long abdicated that province; and we students are come into their inheritance: it is our honour to search out the things which God has concealed. In Germany at Easter time they hide coloured eggs about the house and the garden that the children may amuse themselves in hunting after them and finding them. It is to some such game of hide-and-seek that we are invited by that power which planted in us the desire to find out what is concealed, and stored the universe with hidden things that we might delight ourselves in discovering them. And the pleasure of discovery differs from other pleasures in this, that it is shadowed by no fear of satiety on the one hand or of frustration on the other. Other desires perish in their gratification, but the desire of knowledge never: the eye is not satisfied with seeing nor the ear filled with hearing. Other desires become the occasion of pain through dearth of the material to gratify them, but not the desire of knowledge: the sum of things to be known is inexhaustible, and however long we read we shall never come to the end of our story-book. So long as the mind of man is what it is, it will continue to exult in advancing on the unknown throughout the infinite field of the universe; and the tree of knowledge will remain for ever, as it was in the beginning, a tree to be desired to make one wise.

Introductory Lecture, University College London, 1892

Matthew Arnold

On the last day of October 1891 a bust of Matthew Arnold was unveiled in Westminster Abbey by his friend and contemporary Lord Coleridge. Lord Coleridge on that occasion delivered an address in which, by way of conveying to his audience a clear conception of what Matthew Arnold was, he explained to them with great particularity what Matthew Arnold was not. 'Thackeray' said he 'may have written more pungent social satire, Tennyson may be a greater poet, John Morley may be a greater critical biographer, Cardinal Newman may have a more splendid style, Lightfoot or Ellicott or Jowett may be greater ecclesiastical scholars and have done more for the interpretation of St Paul.' Here the list ends: I cannot imagine why; for it appears to me that if I were once started I could go on like that for ever. Mr Chevalier may be a more accomplished vocalist, Mr Gladstone may be an older Parliamentary hand, Mr Stoddart may have made higher scores against the Australians, the Lord Chief Justice may have sentenced a greater number of criminals to penal servitude—where is one to stop? all those personages have as much business here as that great biographer Mr John Morley. And as for the superb constellation of divines,—Lightfoot and Ellicott and Jowett,—what I want to know is, where is Archdeacon Farrar? But if, after all, Lord Coleridge's account of what Arnold was not, leaves it still a trifle vague what Arnold was, let me take you to the *Daily Chronicle* of April 17, 1888. I copied down its remarks that same day; and ever since, I carry them about with me wherever I go as a sort of intellectual sal-volatile. Whenever I am in any ways afflicted or distressed in mind, body or estate, I take out this extract and read it; and then, like the poet Longfellow when he gazed on the planet Mars, I am strong again. The following are the salient characteristics of Matthew Arnold's poetry—'His muse mounted upward with bright thoughts, as the skylark shakes dewdrops from its wing as it carols at "Heaven's Gate," or like a mountain brooklet carrying many a wildflower on its wavelets, his melody flowed cheerily on. Sometimes too his music rises like that of the mysterious ocean casting up pearls as it rolls.'

Now at last I hope you have a clear conception of the real Matthew Arnold: now you will be able to recognise his poetry when you come across it; and no doubt you will easily distinguish between his three poetical manners,—that in which he shakes the dewdrops from his wing, that in which he carries wildflowers on his wavelets, and that in which he casts up pearls as he rolls. I declare, I can liken such writing to nothing but the orgies in which the evil genii may be supposed to have indulged when they heard of the death of Solomon. The great critic of our land and time is dead, and the uncritical spirit of the English nation proceeds to execute this dance of freedom over his grave. He spent a lifetime trying to teach his countrymen how to use their minds, and the breath is hardly out of his body before the sow that was washed returns with majestic determination to her wallowing in the mire.

I can find no better words in which to speak of the loss of Arnold than those which were used by Gerard Hamilton at the death of Johnson. 'He has made a chasm which not only nothing can fill up, but which nothing has a tendency to fill up. Johnson is dead. Let us go to the next best: there is nobody; no man can be said to put you in mind of Johnson.' I will not compare Arnold with the mob of gentlemen who produce criticism ('quales ego vel Chorinus'), such woful stuff as I or Lord Coleridge write: I will compare him with the best. He leaves men behind him to whom we cannot refuse the name of critic; but then we need to find some other name for him and to call him more than a critic, as John the Baptist was called more than a prophet. I go to Mr Leslie Stephen, and I am always instructed, though I may not be charmed. I go to Mr Walter Pater, and I am always charmed, though I may not be instructed. But Arnold was not merely instructive or charming nor both together: he was what it seems to me no one else is: he was illuminating.

Lecture, 1890s

Scholarship and the Show of Feeling

Why is it that the scholar is the only man of science of whom it is ever demanded that he should display taste and feeling? Literature, the subject of his science, is surely not alone among the subjects of science in possessing aesthetic qualities and in making appeal to the emotions. The botanist and the astronomer have for their provinces two worlds of beauty and magnificence not inferior in their way to literature; but no one expects the botanist to throw up his hands and say 'how beautiful,' nor the astronomer to fall down flat and say 'how magnificent:' no one would praise their taste if they did perform these ceremonies, and no one calls them unappreciative pedants because they do not. Why should the scholar alone indulge in public ecstasy? why from him rather than from them is aesthetic comment to be demanded? why may not he stick to his last as well as they? To be sure, we are all told in our childhood a story of Linnaeus—how, coming suddenly on a heath covered with gorse in blossom, he fell upon his knees and gave thanks to the creator. But when Linnaeus behaved in that way, he was out for a holiday: during office hours he attended to business. If Linnaeus had spent his life in genuflexions before flowering shrubs, the classification of the vegetable kingdom would have been carried out by someone else, and neither Linnaeus himself nor this popular and edifying anecdote would ever have been heard of.

'The Application of Thought to Textual Criticism', 1922

SIR ARTHUR CONAN DOYLE

1859–1930

A Distinguished Visitor

I was living in my own rooms in Queen Anne Street at the time, but I was round at Baker Street before the time named. Sharp to the half-hour, Colonel Sir James Damery was announced. It is hardly necessary to describe him, for many will remember that large, bluff, honest personality, that broad, clean-shaven face, above all, that pleasant, mellow voice.

Frankness shone from his grey Irish eyes, and good humour played round his mobile, smiling lips. His lucent top-hat, his dark frock-coat, indeed, every detail, from the pearl pin in the black satin cravat to the lavender spats over the varnished shoes, spoke of the meticulous care in dress for which he was famous. The big, masterful aristocrat dominated the little room.

'Of course, I was prepared to find Dr Watson,' he remarked, with a courteous bow. 'His collaboration may be very necessary, for we are dealing on this occasion, Mr Holmes, with a man to whom violence is familiar and who will, literally, stick at nothing. I should say that there is no more dangerous man in Europe.'

'I have had several opponents to whom that flattering term has been applied,' said Holmes, with a smile. 'Don't you smoke? Then you will excuse me if I light my pipe. If your man is more dangerous than the late Professor Moriarty, or than the living Colonel Sebastian Moran, then he is indeed worth meeting. May I ask his name?'

'Have you ever heard of Baron Gruner?'

'You mean the Austrian murderer?'

Colonel Damery threw up his kid-gloved hands with a laugh. 'There is no getting past you, Mr Holmes! Wonderful! So you have already sized him up as a murderer?'

'It is my business to follow the details of Continental crime. Who could possibly have read what happened at Prague and have any doubts as to the man's guilt! It was a purely technical legal point and the suspicious death of a witness that saved him! I am as sure that he killed his wife when the so-called "accident" happened in the Splügen Pass as if I had seen him do it. I knew, also, that he had come to England, and had a presentiment that sooner or later he would find me some work to do. Well, what has Baron Gruner been up to? I presume it is not this old tragedy which has come up again?'

'No, it is more serious than that. To revenge crime is important, but to prevent it is more so. It is a terrible thing, Mr Holmes, to see a dreadful event, an atrocious situation, preparing itself before your eyes, to clearly understand whither it will lead, and yet to be utterly unable to avert it. Can a human being be placed in a more trying position?'

'Perhaps not.'

'Then you will sympathize with the client in whose interests I am acting.'

'I did not understand that you were merely an intermediary. Who is the principal?'

'Mr Holmes, I must beg you not to press that question. It is important that I should be able to assure him that his honoured name has been in no way dragged into the matter. His motives are, to the last degree, honourable and chivalrous, but he prefers to remain unknown. I need not say that your fees will be assured and that you will be given a perfectly free hand. Surely the actual name of your client is immaterial?'

'I am sorry,' said Holmes. 'I am accustomed to have mystery at one end of my cases, but to have it at both ends is too confusing. I fear, Sir James, that I must decline to act.'

'The Illustrious Client', *The Case-Book of Sherlock Holmes*, 1927

FREDERICK ROLFE
('Baron Corvo')
1860–1913

A Dying Man in Venice

No fruit came from his sowing. Nothing was left in him, or of him, but an unconquerable capacity for endurance till sweet white Death should have leave to touch him, with an insuperable determination to keep his crisis from the hideous eyes of all men. Terrible as was his bodily emaciation, languid as was his mind, aching and stiff and feeble as were his weary weary limbs, he contrived to preserve his leisured imperscrutable carriage, and to present to the world a face offensive, disdainful, slightly sardonic, utterly unapproachable. The short pipe, which he always sported, was long empty but not (as he believed) noticeably empty; and it added that tinge of casual insolence which freed him from suspicion of dying fast of privation and exposure.

He went, every evening, to the sermon and benediction at the church of the Gesuati on the Zattere: first, to pay the prodigious debt of the present to the past—the duty of love and piety to the dead; and, second, for the sake of an hour in quiet sheltered obscurity. The grand palladian temple, prepared for the Month of the Dead, draped in silver and black, with its forest of slim soaring tapers crowned with primrose stars in mid-air half-way up the vault, and the huge glittering constellation aloft in the apse where God in His Sacrament was enthroned, replenished his beauty-worshipping soul with peace and bliss. The patter of the preacher passed him unheard. His wordless prayer, for eternal rest in the meanest crevice of purgatory, poured forth unceasingly with the prayers of the dark crowd kneeling with him in the dimness below.

On the Day of All Saints he strolled carelessly (one would have said)—he successfully accomplished the giddy feat of not staggering (if one must speak accurately)—across the long wooden bridge of barks to the cemetery on the islet of Sammichele. It was a last pious pilgrimage, with the holy and wholesome thought of praying for the dead, that they (in turn) might pray for him who had none living to spit him a suffrage. The place was a garden. On all sides thronged the quick, to deck the graves of their dead with tapers and lamps and flowers. The place was a garden, hallowed by prayer, hallowed by human love. In the place where God deigned to mount upon The Cross, and to be crucified for love, also, there was a garden.

He slowly paced along cypress-avenues, between the graves of little children with blue or white standards and the graves of adults marked by more sombre memorials. All around him were patricians bringing sheaves of painted candles and gorgeous garlands of orchids and everlastings, or plebeians on their knees grubbing up weeks and tracing pathetic designs with cheap chrysanthemums and farthing night-lights. Here, were a baker's boy and a telegraph-messenger, repainting their father's grave-post with a tin of black and a bottle of gold. There, were half a dozen ribald venal dishonest licentious young gondolieri, quiet and alone on their wicked knees round the grave of a comrade. And there went Zildo, creeping swiftly somewhere, with an armful of dark red roses hiding his face. Nicholas turned away to the open gates of private chapels, revealing byzantine interiors, with gold-winged suns in turquoise vaults, over altars of porphyry and violet marble and alabaster inlaid with mother-o'-pearl in dull silver, and triptycks of hammered silver set with lapis lazuli and ivory, blazing with slender tapers, starred with lanthorns of beaten bronze, carpeted with dewy-fresh flowers. Even the loculi, the tombs in the cemetery-walls, each had its bordure of brilliant bloom with tapers to burn on the pavement before it. All the morning, masses were offered in the church of Saint Michael and in the chapel of Saint Christopher. From time to time a minor friar, in surplice and stole, went, with some black-robed family, to bless the new memorial on a recent grave.

He found himself in the field where Venice buries strangers, and looked for the grave of the engineer who died at the Universal Infirmary nine months before. He remembered its site, but it was unmarked, totally neglected, unrecognizable. Evidently the grave had not been bought in perpetuity; and the bones had gone (or would go) to the common ossuary, with none to care or make memorial. He went on, praying, and entered the columbarium. Here was the plain marble urn of an English baby, Lawrence, burned and forgotten. Here was the plain marble urn of that other Englishman who died at the Universal Infirmary in March: one had remembered him, then, with red roses and a card of love: but flowers fade, and love—Love can move the sun and the other stars. O loyal love! Zildo had not forgotten his father.

The Desire and Pursuit of the Whole, mainly written 1909; first published 1934

WALTER SICKERT
1860–1942

Painters and Critics

Of painters and critics my imagination has sometimes vaguely called up a vision. I seemed to see a lumbering, inarticulate, and good-natured tribe of elephants going about their business or their pleasures, with the deliberation we know. On their heavy heads and narrow backs are seated a voluble tribe of marmosets; I see these dressed in a sort of fancy Zouave costume (probably a reminiscence of a circus I saw in Munich in the early 60's), with little purple caps braided with gold. Some of these little beasts seem clever and alert, while others are either cross or indifferent. But all are voluble, and all are making gestures, which show that they conceive themselves to be directing the movements of the elephants, sometimes with threatening, but more often with gestures of grieved reproach. At a given moment one of the elephants draws the attention of his companions to the existence of their little stowaways. With a heavy gesture each elephant, without stopping in his course, swings his trunk aloft, and picking each little dead-head gently up by the ample seat of his baggy breeches, deposits him, ever so gently, on the ground, and, trumpeting loudly, gallops away. It has always been with me, as the Germans say, a long-in-silence-cherished wish to be that elephant.

There was a delicious fellow in the music halls some years ago, whose mature and sympathetic figure was tightly encased in the classic uniform of the page-boy in buttons. He was wont to complain to the audience of the stinginess and cruelty of his mistress. 'One of these days, I shall cheek her, I know I shall! I shall say . . . I shall say . . . Oh! is it indeed, mum?!' He would go on to relate how she would send him round the cab-stands to pick up oats for her chickens. 'Let her do her own oating!' he would rap out, in a terrified aside.

Réflexion faite, why should not we all do our own oating? I have in the press at present a work, which will shortly appear, on the lines of 'Every man his own Lawyer', to be entitled 'Every man his own Berenson.'

written 1910; reprinted in *A Free House!*, 1947

La Peinture

The story of the angry Delacroix enthusiast is a chestnut, but a French chestnut. It cannot too often be told. In the *Entry*, I think, some *Entry*, one of his numerous and generally prancing *Entries* of either Sardanapalus, or the plague, or Caracalla, or Severus, or Commodus, or Incommodus, there is an old man at the side, I can see him now, around whose haggard and bistred trunk has raged, and will ever rage, to the end of time, what is called a controversy. Some maintain that the pest-stricken, triumphant, conquered, converted or convicted (as the case may be) old man shows to the spectators his back, and some his front. The battle raged, of shoulder blades versus pectorals, until they called in one of those epileptic and uncompromising enthusiasts, to whom the head of Charles I is not only meat and drink, but board and lodging and reach-me-down in one. 'Which is it, you who are the greatest and most faithful of the master's admirers; back or front?' To which the enthusiast: '*Monsieur, ce n'est ni l'un ni l'autre. C'est de la PEINTURE!*'

written 1922; reprinted in Robert Emmons, *The Life and Opinions of Walter Sickert*, 1941

Frith's Derby Day

Surprises lurk in the *Derby Day* like Easter eggs. Turn for a moment from the familiar foreground figures, the languid swell with the (alas!) extinct green veil on his still, thank God, current topper, from the little acrobat, from the footman and the lobsters, from the ruined little gent, from the flurried bobby, and look at the left centre of the middle distance, at the profile of the lady under a green parasol, superb and enigmatic in the barouche, who is addressed by the *beau brun* on foot, the veritable *homme fatal*, and note how they are both silhouetted against a blaze of light. What a passage of learned chiaroscuro in colour! What a reputation a 'Modern' would have made with that passage alone! What a bobbery at the Tate!

written 1922; reprinted in *A Free House!*

CHARLOTTE PERKINS GILMAN
1860–1935

A Rest Cure

I get unreasonably angry with John sometimes. I'm sure I never used to be so sensitive. I think it is due to this nervous condition.

But John says if I feel so, I shall neglect proper self-control; so I take pains to control myself—before him, at least, and that makes me very tired.

I don't like our room a bit. I wanted one downstairs that opened on the piazza and had roses all over the window, and such pretty old-fashioned chintz hangings! but John would not hear of it.

He said there was only one window and not room for two beds, and no near room for him if he took another.

He is very careful and loving, and hardly lets me stir without special direction.

I have a schedule prescription for each hour in the day; he takes all care from me, and so I feel basely ungrateful not to value it more.

He said we came here solely on my account, that I was to have perfect rest and all the air I could get. 'Your exercise depends on your strength, my dear,' said he, 'and your food somewhat on your appetite; but air you can absorb all the time.' So we took the nursery at the top of the house.

It is a big, airy room, the whole floor nearly, with windows that look all ways, and air and sunshine galore. It was nursery first and then playroom and gymnasium, I should judge; for the windows are barred for little children, and there are rings and things in the walls.

The paint and paper look as if a boys' school had used it. It is stripped off—the paper—in great patches all around the head of my bed, about as far as I can reach, and in a great place on the other side of the room low down. I never saw a worse paper in my life.

One of those sprawling flamboyant patterns committing every artistic sin.

It is dull enough to confuse the eye in following, pronounced enough to constantly irritate and provoke study, and when you follow the lame uncertain curves for a little distance they suddenly commit suicide—plunge off at outrageous angles, destroy themselves in unheard of contradictions.

The color is repellant, almost revolting; a smouldering unclean yellow, strangely faded by the slow-turning sunlight.

It is a dull yet lurid orange in some places, a sickly sulphur tint in others.

No wonder the children hated it! I should hate it myself if I had to live in this room long.

There comes John, and I must put this away,—he hates to have me write a word.

The Yellow Wall-Paper, 1890

JAMES GIBBONS HUNEKER

1860–1921

New York by Night

In New York 'the night hath a thousand eyes.' That is why all cats are not grey by night. The Great White Way, pleasure-ground of the world, is the incandescent oven of the metropolis, and under its fierce glare all felines appear alike. But grey, never.

The sad-coloured procession that slowly moves through Piccadilly, the merry crush of the Friedrichstrasse, and the gayer swirl on the Grand Boulevard are not so cosmopolitan as Broadway on a summer's night. Every nationality swells the stream of petticoats; 'As the rill that runs from Bulicamé to be portioned out among the sinful women,' sang Dante, and one exclaims: Lo! this is the city of Dis, when in the maelstrom of faces; faces blanched by regret, sunned by crime, beaming with sin; faces rusted by vain virtue, wan, weary faces, and the triumphant regard of them that are loved. You think of Bill Sykes and his cry of terror: 'The eyes, the eyes!'

The city has begun its nocturnal carnival, and like all organised orgies the spectacle is of a consuming melancholy. No need to moralise; cause and effect speak with an appalling clarity. Through this tohubohu of noise a sinister medley of farce and flame, the Will-to-Enjoy, winds like a stream of red-hot resistless lava. In describing it your pen makes melodramatic twists or else hops deliriously.

The day birds have gone to bed, the night fowl are afield. The owl is a denizen of the dark and Minerva's counsel, for all that wisdom is not in the air. Even veritable cats as they slink or race across the highway are bathed in the blaze of a New York night with its thousands of eyes. No, all cats are not grey by night in Gotham.

But from the heights, what a different picture! Then the magic of the city begins to operate; that missing soul of New York shyly peeps forth in the nocturnal transfiguration. Not, however, in Broadway, with its thousand lies and lights, not in opera-houses, theatres, restaurants, or roof-gardens, but on some perch of vantage from which the scene in all its mysterious beauty may be studied. You see a cluster of lights on the West Side Circle, a ladder of fire the pivot. Farther down, theatreland dazzles with its tongues of flame. Across in the cool shadows are the level lines of twinkling points of the bridges. There is always the sense of waters not afar.

All the hotels, from the Majestic to the Plaza, from the Biltmore to the Vanderbilt, are tier upon tier starry with illumination. Beyond the coppery gleam of the great erect synagogue in Fifth Avenue is the placid toy lake in the park. Fifth and Madison Avenues are long shafts of bluish-white electric globes. The monoliths burn to a fire-god, votive offerings. The park, as if liquefied, flows in plastic rhythms, a lake of velvety foliage, a mezzotint of dark green dividing the east from the west. The dim, scattered plains of granite housetops are like a cemetery of titans. At night New York loses its New World aspect. Sudden furnace fires from tall chimneys leap from the Brooklyn or New Jersey shores; they are of purely commercial origin, yet you look for Whistler's rockets. Battery Park and the bay are positively operatic, the setting for some thrilling fairy spectacle. A lyric moonlight paves a path of tremulous silver along the water. From

Morningside Drive you gaze across a sunken country of myriad lamps; on Riverside the panorama exalts. We are in a city exotic, semibarbaric, the fantasy of an Eastern sorcerer mad enough to evoke from immemorial seas a lost Atlantis.

New Cosmopolis, 1915

MARY KINGSLEY
1862–1900

On Board Ship to West Africa

A government official who had been out before, would kindly turn to a colleague out for the first time, and say,

'Brought any dress clothes with you?'

The unfortunate newcomer, scenting an allusion to a more cheerful phase of Coast life, gladly answered in the affirmative.

'That's right,' says the interlocutor, 'you want them to wear at funerals. Do you know,' he remarks, turning to another old Coaster, 'my dress trousers did not get mouldy once during last wet season.'

'Get along,' says his friend, 'you can't hang a thing up for twenty-four hours without its being fit to graze a cow on.'

'Do you get anything else but fever down there?' asks a newcomer nervously.

'Haven't time as a general rule, but I have known some fellows get kraw kraw.'

'And the Portuguese itch, abscesses, ulcers, the Guinea worm and the small-pox,' observe the chorus calmly.

'Well,' says the first, kindly but regretfully, as if it pained him to admit this wealth of disease was denied his particular locality; 'they are mostly on the South West Coast.'

Travels in West Africa, 1897

Gorillas

I saw before me, some thirty yards off, busily employed in pulling down plantains, and other depredations, five gorillas: one old male, one young male, and three females. One of these had clinging to her a young fellow, with beautiful wavy black hair with just a kink in it. The big male was crouching on his haunches, with his long arms hanging down on either side, with the backs of his hands on the ground, the palms upwards. The elder lady was tearing to pieces and eating a pineapple, while the others were at the plantains destroying more than they ate.

They kept up a sort of whinnying, chattering noise, quite different from the sound I had heard gorillas give when enraged, or from the one you can hear them giving when they are what the natives call 'dancing' at night. I noticed that their reach of arm was immense and that when they went from one tree to another, they squattered across the open ground in a most inelegant style, dragging their long arms with the palms upwards. I should think the big male and female were over six feet each. The others would be from four to five. I put out my hand and laid it on Wiki's gun to prevent him from firing, and he, thinking I was going to fire, gripped my wrist.

I watched the gorillas with interest for a few seconds, until I heard Wiki make a peculiar small sound, and looking at him saw his face was working in an awful way as he clutched his throat with his hand violently.

Heavens! think I, this gentleman's going to have a fit; it's lost we are entirely this time. He rolled his head to and fro, and then buried his face into a heap of dried rubbish at the foot of a plantain stem, clasped his hands over it, and gave an explosive sneeze. The gorillas let go all, raised themselves up for a second, gave a quaint sound between a bark and a howl, and then the ladies and the young gentleman started home. The old male rose to his full height (it struck me at the time that this was ten feet at least, but for scientific purposes allowance must be made for a lady's emotions) and looked straight towards us, or rather towards where that sound came from. Wiki went off into a paroxysm of falsetto sneezes the like of which I have never heard; nor evidently had the gorilla, who doubtless thinking, as one of his black co-relatives would have thought, that the phenomenon savoured of the supernatural, went off after his family with a celerity that was amazing the moment that he touched the forest, and disappeared as they had, swinging himself along through it from bough to bough, in a way that convinced me that, given the necessity of getting about in tropical forests, man had made a mistake in getting his arms shortened. I have seen many wild animals in their native wilds but never have I seen anything to equal gorillas going through bush; it is graceful, powerful, superbly perfect hand-trapeze performance.

After this sporting adventure, we returned, as I usually return from a sporting adventure, without measurements or the body.

Travels in West Africa

EDITH WHARTON
1862–1937

A Brief Bath of Oblivion

But this was the verge of delirium . . . she had never hung so near the dizzy brink of the unreal. Sleep was what she wanted—she remembered that she had not closed her eyes for two nights. The little bottle was at her bedside, waiting to lay its spell upon her. She rose and undressed hastily, hungering now for the touch of her pillow. She felt so profoundly tired that she thought she must fall asleep at once; but as soon as she had lain down every nerve started once more into separate wakefulness. It was as though a great blaze of electric light had been turned on in her head, and her poor little anguished self shrank and cowered in it, without knowing where to take refuge.

She had not imagined that such a multiplication of wakefulness was possible: her whole past was reënacting itself at a hundred different points of consciousness. Where was the drug that could still this legion of insurgent nerves? The sense of exhaustion would have been sweet compared to this shrill beat of activities; but weariness had dropped from her as though some cruel stimulant had been forced into her veins.

She could bear it—yes, she could bear it; but what strength would be left her the next day? Perspective had disappeared—the next day pressed close upon her, and on its heels came the days that were to follow—they swarmed about her like a shrieking mob. She must shut them out for a few hours; she must take a brief bath of oblivion. She put out her hand, and measured the soothing drops into a glass; but as she did so, she knew they would be powerless against the supernatural lucidity of her brain. She had long since raised the dose to its highest limit, but tonight she felt she must increase it. She knew she took a slight risk in doing so—she remembered the chemist's warning. If sleep came at all, it might be a sleep without waking. But after all that was but one chance in a hundred: the action of the drug was incalculable, and the addition of a few drops to the regular dose would probably do no more than procure for her the rest she so desperately needed. . . .

She did not, in truth, consider the question very closely—the physical craving for sleep was her only sustained sensation. Her mind shrank from the glare of thought as instinctively as eyes contract in a blaze of light—darkness, darkness was what she must have at any cost. She raised herself in bed and swallowed the contents of the glass; then she blew out her candle and lay down.

She lay very still, waiting with a sensuous pleasure for the first effects of the soporific. She knew in advance what form they would take—the gradual cessation of the inner throb, the soft approach of passiveness, as though an invisible hand made magic passes over her in the darkness. The very slowness and hesitancy of the effect increased its fascination: it was delicious to lean over and look down into the dim abysses of unconsciousness. Tonight the drug seemed to work more slowly than usual: each passionate pulse had to be stilled in turn, and it was long before she felt them dropping into abeyance, like sentinels falling asleep at their posts. But gradually the sense of complete subjugation came over her, and she wondered languidly what had made her feel so uneasy and excited. She saw now that there was nothing to be excited about—she had returned to her normal view of life. Tomorrow would not be so difficult after all: she felt sure that she would have the strength to meet it. She did not quite remember what it was that she had been afraid to meet, but the uncertainty no longer troubled her. She had been unhappy, and now she was happy—she had felt herself alone, and now the sense of loneliness had vanished.

The House of Mirth, 1905

A Small Boy in a Big House

The trees were budding symmetrically along the avenue below; and Paul, looking down, saw, between windows and tree-tops, a pair of tall iron gates with gilt ornaments, the marble curb of a semi-circular drive, and bands of spring flowers set in turf. He was now a big boy of nearly nine, who went to a fashionable private school, and he had come home that day for the Easter holidays. He had not been back since Christmas, and it was the first time he had seen the new *hôtel* which his step-father had bought, and in which Mr and Mrs Moffatt had hastily established themselves, a few weeks earlier, on their return from a flying trip to America. They were always coming and going; during the two years since their marriage they had been perpetually dashing over to New York and back, or rushing down to Rome or up to the Engadine: Paul never knew where they were except when a telegram announced that they were going somewhere else. He did not even know that there was any method of communication between mothers and sons less laconic than that of the electric wire; and once, when a boy at school asked him if his mother often wrote, he had answered in all sincerity: 'Oh yes—I got a telegram last week.'

He had been almost sure—as sure as he ever was of anything—that he should find her at home when he arrived; but a message (for she hadn't had time to telegraph) apprised him that she and Mr Moffatt had run down to Deauville to look at a house they thought of hiring for the summer; they were taking an early train back, and would be at home for dinner—were in fact having a lot of people to dine.

It was just what he ought to have expected, and had been used to ever since he could remember; and generally he didn't mind much, especially since his mother had become Mrs Moffatt, and the father he had been most used to, and liked best, had abruptly disappeared from his life. But the new *hôtel* was big and strange, and his own room, in which there was not a toy or a book, or one of his dear battered relics (none of the new servants—they were always new—could find his things, or think where they had been put), seemed the loneliest spot in the whole house. He had gone up there after his solitary luncheon, served in the immense marble dining-room by a footman on the same scale, and had tried to occupy himself with pasting post-cards into his album; but the newness and sumptuousness of the room embarrassed him—the white fur rugs and brocade chairs seemed maliciously on the watch for smears and ink-spots—and after a while he pushed the album aside and began to roam through the house.

He went to all the rooms in turn: his mother's first, the wonderful lacy bedroom, all pale silks and velvets, artful mirrors and veiled lamps, and the boudoir as big as a drawing-room, with pictures he would have liked to know about, and tables and cabinets holding things he was afraid to touch. Mr Moffatt's rooms came next. They were soberer and darker, but as big and splendid; and in the bedroom, on the brown wall, hung a single picture—the portrait of a boy in grey velvet—that interested Paul most of all. The boy's hand rested on the head of a big dog, and he looked infinitely noble and charming, and yet (in spite of the dog) so sad and lonely that he too might have come home that very day to a strange house in which none of his old things could be found.

From these rooms Paul wandered downstairs again. The library attracted him most: there were rows and rows of books, bound in dim browns and golds, and old faded reds as rich as velvet: they all looked as if they might have had stories in them as splendid as their bindings. But the bookcases were closed with gilt trellising, and when Paul reached up to open one, a servant told him that Mr Moffatt's secretary kept them locked because the books were too valuable to be taken down. This seemed to make the library as strange as the rest of the house, and he passed on to the ballroom at the back. Through its closed doors he heard a sound of hammering, and when he tried the door-handle a servant passing with a tray-full of glasses told him that 'they' hadn't finished, and wouldn't let anybody in.

The mysterious pronoun somehow increased Paul's sense of isolation, and he went on to the drawing-rooms, steering his way prudently between the gold arm-chairs and shining tables, and wondering whether the wigged and corseleted heroes on the walls represented Mr Moffatt's ancestors, and why, if they did, he looked so little like them. The dining-room beyond was more amusing, because busy servants were already laying the long table. It was too early for the florist, and the centre of the table was empty, but down the sides were gold baskets heaped with pulpy summer fruits—figs, strawberries and big blushing nectarines. Between them stood crystal decanters with red and yellow wine, and little dishes full of sweets; and against the walls were sideboards with great pieces of gold and silver, ewers and urns and branching candelabra, which sprinkled the green marble walls with starlike reflections.

After a while he grew tired of watching the coming and going of white-sleeved footmen, and of listening to the butler's vociferated orders, and strayed back into the library. The habit of solitude had given him a passion for the printed page, and if he could have found a book anywhere—any kind of a book—he would have forgotten the long hours and the empty house. But the tables in the library held only massive unused inkstands and immense immaculate blotters: not a single volume had slipped its golden prison.

The Custom of the Country, 1913

The Longed-For Face

His wife's dark blue brougham (with the wedding varnish still on it) met Archer at the ferry, and conveyed him luxuriously to the Pennsylvania terminus in Jersey City.

It was a sombre snowy afternoon, and the gas-lamps were lit in the big reverberating station. As he paced the platform, waiting for the Washington express, he remembered that there were people who thought there would one day be a tunnel under the Hudson through which the trains of the Pennsylvania railway would run straight into New York. They were of the brotherhood of visionaries who likewise predicted the building of ships that would cross the Atlantic in five days, the invention of a flying machine, lighting by electricity, telephonic communication without wires, and other Arabian Night marvels.

'I don't care which of their visions comes true,' Archer mused, 'as long as the tunnel isn't built yet.' In his senseless school-boy happiness he pictured Madame Olenska's descent from the train, his discovery of her a long way off, among the throngs of meaningless faces, her clinging to his arm as he guided her to the carriage, their slow approach to the wharf among slipping horses, laden carts, vociferating teamsters, and then the startling quiet of the ferry-boat, where they would sit side by side under the snow, in the motionless carriage, while the earth seemed to glide away under them, rolling to the other side of the sun. It was incredible, the number of things he had to say to her, and in what eloquent order they were forming themselves on his lips . . .

The clanging and groaning of the train came nearer, and it staggered slowly into the station like a prey-laden monster into its lair. Archer pushed forward, elbowing through the crowd, and staring blindly into window after window of the high-hung carriages. And then, suddenly, he saw Madame Olenska's pale and surprised face close at hand, and had again the mortified sensation of having forgotten what she looked like.

The Age of Innocence, 1920

JOHN JAY CHAPMAN
1862–1933

World upon World

There is a world in each of Shakespeare's plays,—*the* world, I should say,—so felt and so seen as the world never was seen before nor could be felt and seen again, even by Shakespeare. Each play is a little local universe. His stage devices he repeats, but the atmosphere of a play is never repeated. *Twelfth Night*, *As You Like It*, and *The Merchant of Venice* are very unlike one another. The unity that is in each of them results from unimaginable depths of internal harmony in each. The group of persons in any play (I am speaking of the good plays) forms the unity; for the characters are psychologically interlocked with one another. Prospero implies Caliban; Toby Belch implies Malvolio; Shylock, Antonio. The effects of all imaginative art result from subtle implications and adjustments. The public recognizes these things as beauty, but cannot analyse them. To the artist, however, they have been the bricks and mortar out of which the work was builded. We feel, for instance, in the *Midsummer Night's Dream*, that the fairies are somehow correlative to the artisans. They are made out of a complementary chemical. On the other hand, Theseus and Demetrius and Hipployta, in the same play, are lay figures which set off as with a foil both the fairies and the artisans. Theseus, Hippolyta, and Demetrius are marionettes which give intellect and importance to Bottom and Flute, and lend body and life to the tiny fairies. All this miraculous subtlety of understanding on Shakespeare's part is unconscious. He has had no recipe, no *métier*.

The colouring of each play, its humour, its mood, is Shakespeare's mood as he wrote the play. The mood of desperate philosophic questioning in which he wrote *Hamlet* gives to the play its only unity. So *Macbeth* and *King Lear* are each beclouded by its own kind of passionate speculation. The story is, in each case, a mere thread to catch the crystals from an overcharged atmosphere of feeling. The tragedy of *Lear* is loftier, more abstract in thought, and at the same time more hotly human in feeling than

Macbeth. It is in these worlds of mood that we must seek Shakespeare, and we must remain somewhat moody and dreamy ourselves during the search. If we take a pair of tongs to catch him, he will elude us.

Greek Genius and Other Essays, 1915

ARTHUR MORRISON
1863–1945

Warfare in an East London Slum

That night fighting was sporadic and desultory in the Jago. Bob the Bender was reported to have a smashed nose, and Sam Cash had his head bandaged at the hospital. At the Bag of Nails in Edge Lane, Snob Spicer was knocked out of knowledge with a quart pot, and Cocko Harnwell's Missis had a piece bitten off of one ear. As the night wore on, taunts and defiances were bandied from window to door, and from door to window, between those who intended to begin fighting tomorrow; and shouts from divers corners gave notice of isolated scuffles. Once a succession of piercing screams seemed to betoken that Sally Green had begun. There was a note in the screams of Sally Green's opposites which the Jago had learned to recognise. Sally Green, though of the weaker faction, was the female champion of the Old Jago: an eminence won and kept by fighting tactics peculiar to herself. For it was her way, reserving teeth and nails, to wrestle closely with her antagonist, throw her by a dexterous twist on her face, and fall on her, instantly seizing the victim's nape in her teeth, gnawing and worrying. The sufferer's screams were audible afar, and beyond their invariable eccentricity of quality—a quality vaguely suggestive of dire surprise—they had mechanical persistence, a pump-like regularity, that distinguished them, in the accustomed ear, from other screams.

A Child of the Jago, 1896

GEORGE SANTAYANA
1863–1952

Accommodations

There are a myriad conflicts in practice and in thought, conflicts between rival possibilities, knocking inopportunely and in vain at the door of existence. Owing to the initial disorganization of things, some demands continually prove to be incompatible with others arising no less naturally.

Reason in such cases imposes real and irreparable sacrifices, but it brings a stable consolation if its discipline is accepted. Decay, for instance, is a moral and aesthetic evil; but being a natural necessity it can become the basis for pathetic and magnificent harmonies, when once imagination is adjusted to it. The hatred of change and death is ineradicable while life lasts, since it expresses that self-sustaining organization in a creature which we call its soul; yet this hatred of change and death is not so deeply seated in the nature of things as are death and change themselves, for the flux is deeper than the ideal. Discipline may attune our higher and more adaptable part to the harsh conditions of existence, and the resulting sentiment, being the only one which can be maintained successfully, will express the greatest satisfactions which can be reached, though not the greatest that might be conceived or desired. To be interested in the changing seasons is, in this middling zone, a happier state of mind than to be hopelessly in love with spring. Wisdom discovers these possible accommodations, as circumstances impose them; and education ought to prepare men to accept them.

The Life of Reason, 1905

The Fear of Death

Dying is something ghastly, as being born is something ridiculous; and, even if no pain were involved in quitting or entering this world, we might still say what Dante's Francesca says of it: *Il modo ancor m' offende*,—'I shudder at the way of it.' If the fear of death were merely the fear of dying, it would be better dealt with by medicine than by argument. There is, or there might be, an art of dying well, of dying painlessly, willingly, and in season,—as in those noble partings which Attic gravestones depict,—especially if we were allowed to choose our own time.

But the radical fear of death, I venture to think, is something quite different. It is the love of life. This love is not something rational, or founded on experience of life. It is something antecedent and spontaneous. It teaches every animal to seek its food and its mate, and to protect its offspring; as also to resist or fly from all injury to the body, and most of all from threatened death. It is the original impulse by which good is discriminated from evil, and hope from fear.

Nothing could be more futile, therefore, than to marshal arguments against that fear of death which is merely another name for the energy of life, or the tendency to self-preservation. What is most dreaded is not the agony of dying, nor yet the strange impossibility that when we do not exist we should suffer for not existing. What is dreaded is the defeat of a present will directed upon life and its various undertakings.

Such a present will cannot be argued away, but it may be weakened by contradictions arising within it, by the irony of experience, or by ascetic discipline. To introduce ascetic discipline, to bring out the irony of experience, to expose the self-contradictions of the will, would be the true means of mitigating the love of life; and if the love of life were extinguished, the fear of death, like smoke rising from that fire, would have vanished also.

Three Philosophical Poets, 1910

A Young Nation

The American is wonderfully alive; and his vitality, not having often found a suitable outlet, makes him appear agitated on the surface; he is always letting off an unnecessarily loud blast of incidental steam. Yet his vitality is not superficial; it is inwardly prompted, and as sensitive and quick as a magnetic needle. He is inquisitive, and ready with an answer to any question that he may put to himself of his own accord; but if you try to pour instruction into him, on matters that do not touch his own spontaneous life, he shows the most extraordinary powers of resistance and oblivescence; so that he often is remarkably expert in some directions and surprisingly obtuse in others. He seems to bear lightly the sorrowful burden of human knowledge. In a word, he is young.

What sense is there in this feeling, which we all have, that the American is young? His country is blessed with as many elderly people as any other, and his descent from Adam, or from the Darwinian rival of Adam, cannot be shorter than that of his European cousins. Nor are his ideas always very fresh. Trite and rigid bits of morality and religion, with much seemly and antique political lore, remain axiomatic in him, as in the mind of a child; he may carry all this about with an unquestioning familiarity which does not comport understanding. To keep traditional sentiments in this way insulated and uncriticised is itself a sign of youth. A good young man is naturally conservative and loyal on all those subjects which his experience has not brought to a test; advanced opinions on politics, marriage, or literature are comparatively rare in America; they are left for the ladies to discuss, and usually to condemn, while the men get on with their work. In spite of what is old-fashioned in his more general ideas, the American is unmistakably young; and this, I should say, for two reasons: one, that he is chiefly occupied with his immediate environment, and the other, that his reactions upon it are inwardly prompted, spontaneous, and full of vivacity and self-trust. His views are not yet lengthened; his will is not yet broken or transformed. The present moment, however, in this, as in other things, may mark a great change in him; he is perhaps now reaching his majority, and all I say may hardly apply to-day, and may not apply at all to-morrow. I speak of him as I have known him; and whatever moral strength may accrue to him later, I am not sorry to have known him in his youth.

Character and Opinion in the United States, 1920

A Note on T. S. Eliot

The thought of T. S. Eliot is subterranean without being profound. He does not describe the obvious—why should he? Nor does he trace the great lines of the hidden skeleton and vital organs of anything historical: he traces rather some part of the fine network of veins and nerves beneath the surface, necessarily picking his way in that labyrinth somewhat arbitrarily, according to his prejudices and caprice. (E.g., hanging his essay on Dante on the alleged fact that he is easy to read.) This peep-and-run intuition appears in his leading ideas, as well as in the detail of his appreciations. It appears even in his Anglo-Catholicism: he likes this in Christianity and he dislikes that, and feels a general dismay at the natural course of the world. He dreads and does not understand the radical forces at work in the world and in the church; but he is beautifully sensitive to the cross-lights that traverse the middle distance; and he hopes to set up barriers of custom and barriers of taste, to keep mankind from touching bottom or from quite seeing the light.

written mid-1930s; printed in John McCormick, *George Santayana*, 1987

SIR ARTHUR QUILLER-COUCH
1863–1944

Shuffling through the Fog

But let us close our *florilegium* and attempt to illustrate Jargon by the converse method of taking a famous piece of English (say Hamlet's soliloquy) and remoulding a few lines of it in this fashion:

To be, or the contrary? Whether the former or the latter be preferable would seem to admit of some difference of opinion; the answer in the present case being of an affirmative or of a negative character according as to whether one elects on the one hand to mentally suffer the disfavour of fortune, albeit in an extreme degree, or on the other to boldly envisage adverse conditions in the prospect of eventually bringing them to a conclusion. The condition of sleep is similar to, if not indistinguishable from, that of death; and with the addition of finality the former might be considered identical with the latter: so that in this connection it might be argued with regard to sleep that, could the addition be affected, a termination would be put to the endurance of a multiplicity of inconveniences, not to mention a number of downright evils incidental to our fallen humanity, and thus a consummation achieved of a most gratifying nature.

That is Jargon: and to write Jargon is to be perpetually shuffling around in the fog and cotton-wool of abstract terms; to be for ever hearkening, like Ibsen's Peer Gynt, to the voice of the Boyg exhorting you to circumvent the difficulty, to beat the air because it is easier than to flesh your sword in the thing. The first virtue, the touchstone of a masculine style, is its use of the active verb and the concrete noun. When you write in the active voice, 'They gave him a silver teapot,' you write as a man. When you write 'He was made the recipient of a silver teapot,' you write Jargon. But at the beginning set even higher store on the concrete noun. Somebody—I think it was FitzGerald—once posited the question 'What would have become of Christianity if Jeremy Bentham had had the writing of the Parables?' Without pursuing that dreadful inquiry I ask you to note how carefully the Parables—those exquisite short stories—speak only of 'things which you can touch and see'—'A sower went forth to sow,' 'The kingdom of heaven is like unto leaven, which a woman took'—and not the Parables only, but the Sermon on the Mount and almost every verse of the Gospel. The Gospel does not, like my young essayist, fear to repeat a word, if the word be good. The Gospel says, 'Render unto Caesar the things that are Caesar's'—not 'Render unto Caesar the things that appertain to that potentate.' The Gospel does not say 'Consider the growth of the lilies,' or even 'Consider how the lilies grow.' It says, 'Consider the lilies, how they grow.'

'Jargon', 1913

W. W. JACOBS
1863–1943

A Domestic Dialogue

Mr Chalk, with his mind full of the story he had just heard, walked homewards like a man in a dream. The air was fragrant with spring, and the scent of lilac revived memories almost forgotten. It took him back forty years, and showed him a small boy treading the same road, passing the same houses. Nothing had changed so much as the small boy himself; nothing had been so unlike the life he had pictured as the life he had led. Even the blamelessness of the latter yielded no comfort; it savoured of a lack of spirit.

His mind was still busy with the past when he reached home. Mrs Chalk, a woman of imposing appearance, who was sitting by the window at needlework, looked up sharply at his entrance. Before she spoke he had a dim idea that she was excited about something.

'I've got her,' she said triumphantly.

'Oh!' said Mr Chalk.

'She didn't want to come at first,' said Mrs Chalk; 'she'd half promised to go to Mrs Morris. Mrs Morris had heard of her through Harris, the grocer, and he only knew she was out of a place by accident. He——'

Her words fell on deaf ears. Mr Chalk, gazing through the window, heard without comprehending a long account of the capture of a new housemaid, which, slightly altered as to name and place, would have passed muster as an exciting contest between a skilful angler and a particularly sulky salmon. Mrs Chalk, noticing his inattention at last, pulled up sharply.

'You're not listening!' she cried.

'Yes, I am; go on, my dear,' said Mr Chalk.

'What did I say she left her last place for, then?' demanded the lady.

Mr Chalk started. He had been conscious of his wife's voice, and that was all. 'You said you were not surprised at her leaving,' he replied, slowly; 'the only wonder to you was that a decent girl should have stayed there so long.'

Mrs Chalk started and bit her lip. 'Yes,' she said, slowly. 'Ye-es. Go on; anything else?'

'You said the house wanted cleaning from top to bottom,' said the painstaking Mr Chalk.

'Go on,' said his wife, in a smothered voice. 'What else did I say?'

'Said you pitied the husband,' continued Mr Chalk, thoughtfully.

Mrs Chalk rose suddenly and stood over him. Mr Chalk tried desperately to collect his faculties.

'How dare you?' she gasped. 'I've never said such things in my life. Never. And I said that she left because Mr Wilson, her master, was dead and the family had gone to London. I've never been near the house; so how could I say such things?'

Mr Chalk remained silent.

'What made you *think* of such things?' persisted Mrs Chalk.

Mr Chalk shook his head: no satisfactory reply was possible . . .

Dialstone Lane, 1904

RUDYARD KIPLING
1865–1936

The Cold Lairs

In the Cold Lairs the Monkey-People were not thinking of Mowgli's friends at all. They had brought the boy to the Lost City, and were very pleased with themselves for the time. Mowgli had never seen an Indian city before, and though this was almost a heap of ruins it seemed very wonderful and splendid. Some king had built it long ago on a little hill. You could still trace the stone cause-ways that led up to the ruined gates where the last splinters of wood hung to the worn, rusted hinges. Trees had grown into and out of the walls; the battlements were tumbled down and decayed, and wild creepers hung out of the windows of the towers on the walls in bushy hanging clumps.

A great roofless palace crowned the hill, and the marble of the court-yards and the fountains was split, and stained with red and green, and the very cobble-stones in the courtyard where the king's elephants used to live had been thrust up and apart by grasses and young trees. From the palace you could see the rows and rows of roofless houses that made up the city looking like empty honeycombs filled with blackness; the shapeless block of stone that had been an idol, in the square where four roads met; the pits and dimples at street-corners where the public wells once stood, and the shattered domes of temples with wild figs sprouting on their sides. The monkeys called the place their city, and pretended to despise the Jungle-People because they lived in the forest. And yet they never knew what the buildings were made for nor how to use them. They would sit in circles on the hall of the king's council chamber, and scratch for fleas and pretend to be men; or they would run in and out of the roofless houses and collect pieces of plaster and old bricks in a corner, and forget where they had hidden them, and fight and cry in scuffling crowds, and then break off to play up and down the terraces of the king's garden, where they would shake the rose trees and the oranges in sport to see the fruit and flowers fall. They explored all the passages and dark tunnels in the palace and the hundreds of little dark rooms, but they never remembered what they had seen and what they had not; and so drifted about in ones and twos or crowds telling each other that they were doing as men did. They drank at the tanks and made the water all muddy, and then they fought over it, and then they would all rush together in mobs and shout: 'There is no one in the jungle so wise and good and clever and strong and gentle as the *Bandar-log*.' Then all would begin again till they grew tired of the city and went back to the tree-tops, hoping the Jungle-People would notice them.

The Jungle Book, 1894

The Grand Trunk Road

'Now let us walk,' muttered the lama, and to the click of his rosary they walked in silence mile upon mile. The lama, as usual, was deep in medi-tation, but Kim's bright eyes were open wide. This broad, smiling river of life, he considered, was a vast improvement on the cramped and crowded Lahore streets. There were new people and new sights at every stride—castes he knew and castes that were altogether out of his experience.

They met a troop of long-haired, strong-scented Sansis with baskets of lizards and other unclean food on their backs, the lean dogs sniffing at their heels. These people kept their own side of the road, moving at a quick, furtive jog-trot, and all other castes gave them ample room; for the Sansi is deep pollution. Behind them, walking wide and stiffly across the strong shadows, the memory of his leg-irons still on him, strode one newly released from the jail; his full stomach and shiny skin to prove that the Government fed its prisoners better than most honest men could feed themselves. Kim knew that walk well, and made broad jest of it as they passed. Then an Akali, a wild-eyed, wild-haired Sikh devotee in the blue-checked clothes of his faith, with polished-steel quoits glistening on the cone of his tall blue turban, stalked past, returning from a visit to one of the independent Sikh States, where he had been singing the ancient glories of the Khalsa to College-trained princelings in top-boots and white-cord breeches. Kim was careful not to irritate that man; for the Akali's temper is short and his arm quick. Here and there they met or were overtaken by the gaily dressed crowds of whole villages turning out to some local fair; the women, with their babes on their hips, walking behind the men, the older boys prancing on sticks of sugar-cane, dragging rude brass models of locomotives such as they sell for a halfpenny, or flashing the sun into the eyes of their betters from cheap toy mirrors. One could see at a glance what each had bought; and if there were any doubt it needed only to watch the wives comparing, brown arm against brown arm, the newly purchased dull glass bracelets that come from the North-West. These merry-makers stepped slowly, calling one to the other and stopping to haggle with sweet-meat-sellers, or to make a prayer before one of the wayside shrines—sometimes Hindu, sometimes Mussalman—which the low caste of both creeds share with beautiful impartiality. A solid line of blue, rising and falling like the back of a caterpillar in haste, would swing up through the quivering dust and trot past to a chorus of quick cackling. That was a gang of *changars*—the women who have taken all the embankments of all the Northern railways under their charge—a flat-footed, big-bosomed, strong-limbed, blue-petticoated clan of earth-carriers, hurrying north on news of a job, and wasting no time by the road. They belong to the caste whose men do not count, and they walked with squared elbows, swinging hips, and heads on high, as suits women who carry heavy weights. A little later a marriage procession would strike into the Grand Trunk with music and shoutings, and a smell of marigold and jasmine stronger even than the reek of the dust. One could see the bride's litter, a blur of red and tinsel, staggering through the haze, while the bridegroom's bewreathed pony turned aside to snatch a mouthful from a passing fodder-cart. Then Kim would join the Kentish-fire of good wishes and bad jokes, wishing the couple a hundred sons and no daughters, as the saying is. Still more interesting and more to be shouted over it was when a strolling juggler with some half-trained monkeys, or a panting, feeble bear, or a woman who tied goats' horns to her feet, and with these danced on a slack-rope, set the horses to shying and the women to shrill, long-drawn quavers of amazement.

The lama never raised his eyes. He did not note the money-lender on his goose-rumped pony, hastening alone to collect the cruel interest; or the long-shouting, deep-voiced little mob—still in military formation—of native soldiers on leave, rejoicing to be rid of their breeches and puttees, and saying the most outrageous things to the most respectable women in sight. Even the seller of Ganges-water he did not see, and Kim expected that he would at least buy a bottle of that precious stuff. He looked steadily at the ground, and strode as steadily hour after hour, his soul busied elsewhere. But Kim was in the seventh heaven of joy. The Grand Trunk at this point was built on an embankment to guard against winter floods from the foothills, so that one walked, as it were, a little above the country, along a stately corridor, seeing all India spread out to left and right. It was beautiful to behold the many-yoked grain and cotton waggons crawling over the country roads: one could hear their axles, complaining a mile away, coming nearer, till with shouts and yells and bad words they climbed up the steep incline and plunged on to the hard main road, carter reviling carter. It was equally beautiful to watch the people, little clumps of red and blue and pink and white and saffron, turning aside to go to their own villages, dispersing and growing small by twos and threes across the level plain. Kim felt these things, though he could not give tongue to his feelings, and so contented himself with buying peeled sugarcane and spitting the pith generously about his path. From time to time the lama took snuff, and at last Kim could endure the silence no longer.

'This is a good land—the land of the South!' said he. 'The air is good; the water is good. Eh?'

'And they are all bound upon the Wheel,' said the lama. 'Bound from life after life. To none of these has the Way been shown.' He shook himself back to this world.

Kim, 1901

A Downward Plunge

He showed me my room, saying cheerfully: 'You may be a little tired. One often is without knowing it after a run through traffic. Don't come down till you feel quite restored. We shall all be in the garden.'

My room was rather close, and smelt of perfumed soap. I threw up the window at once, but it opened so close to the floor and worked so clumsily that I came within an ace of pitching out, where I should certainly have ruined a rather lop-sided laburnum below. As I set about washing off the journey's dust, I began to feel a little tired. But, I reflected, I had not come down here in this weather and among these new surroundings to be depressed, so I began to whistle.

And it was just then that I was aware of a little grey shadow, as it might have been a snowflake seen against the light, floating at an immense distance in the background of my brain. It annoyed me, and I shook my head to get rid of it. Then my brain telegraphed that it was the forerunner of a swift-striding gloom which there was yet time to escape if I would force my thoughts away from it, as a man leaping for life forces his body forward and away from the fall of a wall. But the gloom overtook me before I could take in the meaning of the message. I moved toward the bed, every nerve already aching with the foreknowledge of the pain that was to be dealt it, and sat down, while my amazed and angry soul dropped, gulf by gulf, into that horror of great darkness which is spoken of in the Bible, and which, as auctioneers say, must be experienced to be appreciated.

Despair upon despair, misery upon misery, fear after fear, each causing their distinct and separate woe, packed in upon me for an unrecorded length of time, until at last they blurred together, and I heard a click in my brain like the click in the ear when one descends in a diving bell, and I knew that the pressures were equalised within and without, and that, for the moment, the worst was at an end. But I knew also that at any moment the darkness might come down anew; and while I dwelt on this speculation precisely as a man torments a raging tooth with his tongue, it ebbed away into the little grey shadow on the brain of its first coming, and once more I heard my brain, which knew what would recur, telegraph to every quarter for help, release, or diversion.

'The House Surgeon', 1909

In a Military Cemetery

A man knelt behind a line of headstones—evidently a gardener, for he was firming a young plant in the soft earth. She went towards him, her paper in her hand. He rose at her approach and without prelude or salutation asked: 'Who are you looking for?'

'Lieutenant Michael Turrell—my nephew,' said Helen slowly and word for word, as she had many thousands of times in her life.

The man lifted his eyes and looked at her with infinite compassion before he turned from the fresh-sown grass toward the naked black crosses.

'Come with me,' he said, 'and I will show you where your son lies.'

When Helen left the Cemetery she turned for a last look. In the distance she saw the man bending over his young plants; and she went away, supposing him to be the gardener.

'The Gardener', 1926

W. B. YEATS
1865–1939

Closed Minds and Empty Souls

All empty souls tend to extreme opinion. It is only in those who have built up a rich world of memories and habits of thought that extreme opinions affront the sense of probability. Propositions, for instance, which set all the truth upon one side can only enter rich minds to dislocate and strain, if they can enter at all, and sooner or later the mind expels them by instinct.

Estrangement, written 1909; published 1936

A Recommendation to Read George Eliot

Once after breakfast Dowden read us some chapters of the unpublished *Life of Shelley*, and I who had made the *Prometheus Unbound* my sacred book was delighted with all he read. I was chilled, however, when he explained that he had lost his liking for Shelley and would not have written it but for an old promise to the Shelley family. When it was published, Matthew Arnold made sport of certain conventionalities and extravagances that were, my father and I had come to see, the violence or clumsiness of a conscientious man hiding from himself a lack of sympathy.

Though my faith was shaken, it was only when he urged me to read George Eliot that I became angry and disillusioned and worked myself into a quarrel or half-quarrel. I had read all Victor Hugo's romances and a couple of Balzac's and was in no mind to like her. She seemed to have a distrust or a distaste for all in life that gives one a springing foot. Then, too, she knew so well how to enforce her distaste by the authority of her mid-Victorian science or by some habit of mind of its breeding, that I, who had not escaped the fascination of what I loathed, doubted while the book lay open whatsoever my instinct knew of splendour. She disturbed me and alarmed me, but when I spoke of her to my father, he threw her aside with a phrase, 'O, she was an ugly woman who hated handsome men and handsome women'; and he began to praise *Wuthering Heights*.

Reveries over Childhood and Youth, 1915

Oscar Wilde

He told me once that he had been offered a safe seat in Parliament and, had he accepted, he might have had a career like that of Beaconsfield, whose early style resembles his, being meant for crowds, for excitement, for hurried decisions, for immediate triumphs. Such men get their sincerity, if at all, from the contact of events; the dinner-table was Wilde's event and made him the greatest talker of his time, and his plays and dialogues have what merit they possess from being now an imitation, now a record, of his talk.

The Trembling of the Veil, 1922

Bernard Shaw

I listened to *Arms and the Man* with admiration and hatred. It seemed to me inorganic, logical straightness and not the crooked road of life, yet I stood aghast before its energy as to-day before that of the *Stone Drill* by Mr Epstein or of some design by Mr Wyndham Lewis. Shaw was right to claim Samuel Butler for his master, for Butler was the first Englishman to make the discovery that it is possible to write with great effect without music, without style, either good or bad, to eliminate from the mind all emotional implication and to prefer plain water to every vintage, so much metropolitan lead and solder to any tendril of the vine. Presently I had a nightmare that I was haunted by a sewing-machine, that clicked and shone, but the incredible thing was that the machine smiled, smiled perpetually. Yet I delighted in Shaw, the formidable man. He could hit my enemies and the enemies of all I loved, as I could never hit, as no living author that was dear to me could ever hit.

The Trembling of the Veil

W. E. Henley

Henley's troubles and infirmities were growing upon him. He, too, an ambitious, formidable man, who showed alike in his practice and in his theory—in his lack of sympathy for Rossetti and Landor, for instance—that he never understood how small a fragment of our own nature can be brought to perfect expression, nor that even but with great toil, in a much divided civilization; though, doubtless, if our own Phase be right, a fragment may be an image of the whole, the moon's still scarce-crumbled image, as it were, in a glass of wine. He would be, and have all poets be, a true epitome of the whole mass, a Herrick and Dr Johnson in the same body, and because this—not so difficult before the Mermaid closed its door—is no longer possible, his work lacks music, is abstract, as even an actor's movement can be when the thought of doing is plainer to his mind than the doing itself: the straight line from cup to lip, let us say, more plain than the hand's own sensation weighed down by that heavy spillable cup. I think he was content when he had called before our eyes—before the too understanding eyes of his chosen crowd—the violent burly man that he had dreamed, content with the mere suggestion, and so did not work long enough at his verses.

The Trembling of the Veil

H. G. WELLS
1866–1946

A Visit to a Dying World

I looked about me to see if any traces of animal life remained. A certain indefinable apprehension still kept me in the saddle of the machine. But I saw nothing moving, in earth or sky or sea. The green slime on the rocks alone testified that life was not extinct. A shallow sand-bank had appeared in the sea and the water had receded from the beach. I fancied I saw some black object flopping about upon this bank, but it became motionless as I looked at it, and I judged that my eye had been deceived, and that the black object was merely a rock. The stars in the sky were intensely bright and seemed to me to twinkle very little.

Suddenly I noticed that the circular westward outline of the sun had changed; that a concavity, a bay, had appeared in the curve. I saw this grow larger. For a minute perhaps I stared aghast at this blackness that was creeping over the day, and then I realized that an eclipse was beginning. Either the moon or the planet Mercury was passing across the sun's disk. Naturally, at first I took it to be the moon, but there is much to incline me to believe that what I really saw was the transit of an inner planet passing very near to the earth.

The darkness grew apace; a cold wind began to blow in freshening gusts from the east, and the showering white flakes in the air increased in number. From the edge of the sea came a ripple and whisper. Beyond these lifeless sounds the world was silent. Silent? It would be hard to convey the stillness of it. All the sounds of man, the bleating of sheep, the cries of birds, the hum of insects, the stir that makes the background of our lives—all that was over. As the darkness thickened, the eddying flakes grew more abundant, dancing before my eyes; and the cold of the air more intense. At last, one by one, swiftly, one after the other, the white peaks of the distant hills vanished into blackness. The breeze rose to a moaning wind. I saw the black central shadow of the eclipse sweeping towards me. In another moment the pale stars alone were visible. All else was rayless obscurity. The sky was absolutely black.

A horror of this great darkness came on me. The cold, that smote to my marrow, and the pain I felt in breathing, overcame me. I shivered, and a deadly nausea seized me. Then like a red-hot bow in the sky appeared the edge of the sun. I got off the machine to recover myself. I felt giddy and incapable of facing the return journey. As I stood sick and confused I saw again the moving thing upon the shoal—there was no mistake now that it was a moving thing—against the red water of the sea. It was a round thing, the size of a football perhaps, or, it may be, bigger, and tentacles trailed down from it; it seemed black against the weltering blood-red water, and it was hopping fitfully about. Then I felt I was fainting. But a terrible dread of lying helpless in that remote and awful twilight sustained me while I clambered upon the saddle.

The Time Machine, 1895

The Vegetation of the Moon

One after another all down the sunlit slope these miraculous little brown bodies burst and gaped apart, like seed-pods, like the husks of fruits; opened eager mouths that drank in the heat and light pouring in a cascade from the newly-risen sun.

Every moment more of these seed coats ruptured, and even as they did so the swelling pioneers overflowed their rent distended seed-cases and passed into the second stage of growth. With a steady assurance, a swift deliberation, these amazing seeds thrust a rootlet downward to the earth and a queer bundle-like bud into the air. In a little while the slope was dotted with minute plantlets standing at attention in the blaze of the sun.

They did not stand for long. The bundle-like buds swelled and strained and opened with a jerk, thrusting out a coronet of little sharp tips, spreading a whorl of tiny, spiky, brownish leaves, that lengthened rapidly, lengthened visibly even as we watched. The movement was slower than any animal's, swifter than any plant's I have ever seen before. How can I suggest it to you—the way that growth went on? The leaf tips grew so that they moved onward even while we looked at them. The brown seed-case shrivelled and was absorbed with an equal rapidity. Have you ever on a cold day taken a thermometer into your warm hand and watched the little thread of mercury creep up the tube? These moon-plants grew like that.

The First Men in the Moon, 1901

Uncle Ponderevo Builds His Palace

There he stands in my memory, the symbol of this age for me, the man of luck and advertisement, the current master of the world. There he stands upon the great outward sweep of the terrace before the huge main entrance, a little figure, ridiculously disproportionate to that forty-foot arch, with the granite ball behind him—the astronomical ball, brass coopered, that represented the world, with a little adjustable tube of lenses on a gun-metal arm that focussed the sun upon just that point of the earth on which it chanced to be shining vertically. There he stands, Napoleonically grouped with his retinue, men in tweeds and golfing-suits, a little solicitor, whose name I forget, in grey trousers and a black jacket, and Westminster [his architect] in Jaeger underclothing, a floriferous tie, and a peculiar brown cloth of his own. The downland breeze flutters my uncle's coat-tails, disarranges his stiff hair, and insists on the evidence of undisciplined appetites in face and form, as he points out this or that feature in the prospect to his attentive collaborator.

Below are hundreds of feet of wheeling-planks, ditches, excavations, heaps of earth, piles of garden stone from the Wealden ridges. On either hand the walls of his irrelevant unmeaning palace rise. At one time he had working in that place—disturbing the economic balance of the whole countryside by their presence—upwards of three thousand men. . . .

So he poses for my picture amidst the raw beginnings that were never to be completed. He did the strangest things about that place, things more and more detached from any conception of financial scale, things more and more apart from sober humanity. He seemed to think himself at last, released from any such limitations. He moved a quite considerable hill, and nearly sixty mature trees were moved with it to open his prospect eastward, moved it about two hundred feet to the south. At another time he caught a suggestion from some city restaurant and made a billiard-room roofed with plate glass beneath the waters of his ornamental lake. He furnished one wing while its roof still awaited completion. He had a swimming bath thirty feet square next to his bedroom upstairs, and to crown it all he commenced a great wall to hold all his dominions together, free from the invasion of common men. It was a ten-foot wall, glass surmounted, and had it been completed as he intended it, it would have had a total length of nearly eleven miles. Some of it towards the last was so dishonestly built that it collapsed within a year upon its foundations, but some miles of it still stand. I never think of it now but what I think of the hundreds of eager little investors who followed his 'star,' whose hopes and lives, whose wives' security and children's prospects are all mixed up beyond redemption with that flaking mortar. . . .

Tono-Bungay, 1909

Heaven lies about us . . .

There had been a time when two people had thought Mr Polly the most wonderful and adorable thing in the world, and kissed his toe-nails, saying 'myum, myum!' and marvelled at the exquisite softness and delicacy of his hair, had called to one another to remark the peculiar distinction with which he bubbled, had disputed whether the sound he had made was just da, da, or truly and intentionally dadda, had washed him in the utmost detail, and wrapped him up in soft warm blankets, and smothered him with kisses. A regal time that was, and four-and-thirty years ago; and a merciful forgetfulness barred Mr Polly from ever bringing its careless luxury, its autocratic demands and instant obedience, into contrast with his present condition of life. These two people had worshipped him from the crown of his head to the soles of his exquisite feet. And also they had fed him rather unwisely, for no one had ever troubled to teach his mother anything about the mysteries of a child's upbringing—though, of course, the monthly nurse and the charwoman gave some valuable hints—and by his fifth birthday the perfect rhythms of his nice new interior were already darkened with perplexity. . . .

The History of Mr Polly, 1910

Contentment

Mr Polly sat beside the fat woman at one of the little green tables at the back of the Potwell Inn, and struggled with the mystery of life. It was one of those evenings serenely luminous, amply and atmospherically still, when the river bend was at its best. A swan floated against the dark green masses of the further bank, the stream flowed broad and shining to its destiny, with scarce a ripple—except where the reeds came out from the headland, and the three poplars rose clear and harmonious against the sky of green and yellow. It was as if everything lay securely within a great, warm, friendly globe of crystal sky. It was as safe and enclosed and fearless as a child that has still to be born. It was an evening full of quality of tranquil, unqualified assurance. Mr Polly's mind was filled with the persuasion that indeed all things whatsoever must need be satisfying and complete. It was incredible that life had ever done more than seemed to jar, that there could be any shadow in life save such velvet softnesses as made the setting for that silent swan, or any murmur but the ripple of the water as it swirled round the chained and gently swaying punt.

The History of Mr Polly

Altogether Mysterious

It may be that we exist and cease to exist in alternations, like the minute dots in some forms of toned printing or the succession of pictures on a cinema film. It may be that consciousness is an illusion of movement in an eternal, static, multidimensional universe. We may be only a story written on a ground of inconceivable realities, the pattern of a carpet beneath the feet of the incomprehensible. We may be, as Sir James Jeans seems to suggest, part of a vast idea in the meditation of a divine circumambient mathematician. It is wonderful exercise for the mind to peer at such possibilities. It brings us to the realization of the entirely limited nature of our intelligence, such as it is, and of existence as we know it. It leads plainly towards the belief that with minds such as ours the ultimate truth of things is forever inconceivable and unknowable. . . .

It is impossible to dismiss mystery from life. Being is altogether mysterious. Mystery is all about us and in us, the Inconceivable permeates us, it is 'closer than breathing and nearer than hands and feet.' For all we know, that which we are may rise at death from living, as an intent player wakes up from his absorption when a game comes to an end, or as a spectator turns his eyes from the stage as the curtain falls, to look at the auditorium he has for a time forgotten. These are pretty metaphors, that have nothing to do with the game or the drama of space and time. Ultimately the mystery may be the only thing that matters, but *within the rules and limits of the game of life*, when you are catching trains or paying bills or earning a living, the mystery does not matter at all.

The Work, Wealth and Happiness of Mankind, 1931

JOHN GALSWORTHY
1867–1933

A Long Rich Period

The Queen was dead, and the air of the greatest city upon earth grey with unshed tears. Fur-coated and top-hatted, with Annette beside him in dark furs, Soames crossed Park Lane on the morning of the funeral procession, to the rails of Hyde Park. Little moved though he ever was by public matters, this event, supremely symbolical, this summing-up of a long rich period, impressed his fancy. In '37, when she came to the throne, 'Superior Dosset' was still building houses to make London hideous; and James, a stripling of twenty-six, just laying the foundations of his practice in the Law. Coaches still ran; men wore stocks, shaved their upper lips, ate oysters out of barrels; 'tigers' swung behind cabriolets; women said, 'La!' and owned no property; there were manners in the land, and pigsties for the poor; unhappy devils were hanged for little crimes, and Dickens had but just begun to write. Well-nigh two generations had slipped by—of steamboats, railways, telegraphs, bicycles, electric light, telephones, and now these motor-cars—of such accumulated wealth that eight percent had become three, and Forsytes were numbered by the thousand! Morals had changed, manners had changed, men had become monkeys twice-removed, God had become Mammon—Mammon so respectable as to deceive himself. Sixty-four years that favoured property, and had made the upper middle class; buttressed, chiselled, polished it, till it was almost indistinguishable in manners, morals, speech, appearance, habit, and soul from the nobility. An epoch which had gilded individual liberty so that if a man had money, he was free in law and fact, and if he had not money he was free in law and not in fact. An era which had canonised hypocrisy, so that to seem to be respectable was to be. A great Age, whose transmuting influence nothing had escaped save the nature of man and the nature of the Universe.

In Chancery, 1920

ARNOLD BENNETT
1867–1931

Sister Writes to Sister

Constance's handwriting had changed; it was, however, easily recognizable as a development of the neat caligraphy of the girl who could print window-tickets. The 'S' of Sophia was formed in the same way as she had formed it in the last letter which she had received from her at Axe!

'My Darling Sophia,

'I cannot tell you how overjoyed I was to learn that after all these years you are alive and well, and doing so well too. I long to see you, my dear sister. It was Mr Peel-Swynnerton who told me. He is a friend of Cyril's. Cyril is the name of my son. I married Samuel in 1867. Cyril was born in 1874 at Christmas. He is now twenty-two, and doing very well in London as a student of sculpture, though so young. He won a National Scholarship. There were only eight, of which he won one, in all England. Samuel died in 1888. If you read the papers you must have seen about the Povey affair. I mean of course Mr Daniel Povey, Confectioner. It was that that killed poor Samuel. Poor mother died in 1875. It doesn't seem so long. Aunt Harriet and Aunt Maria are both dead. Old Dr Harrop is dead, and his son has practically retired. He has a partner, a Scotchman. Mr Critchlow has married Miss Insull. Did you ever hear of such a thing? They have taken over the shop, and I live in the house part, the other being bricked up. Business in the Square is not what it used to be. The steam trams take all the custom to Hanbridge, and they are talking of electric trams, but I dare say it is only talk. I have a fairly good servant. She has been with me a long time, but servants are not what they were. I keep pretty well, except for my sciatica and palpitation. Since Cyril went to London I have been very lonely. But I try to cheer up and count my blessings. I am sure I have a great deal to be thankful for. And now this news of you! Please write to me a long letter, and tell me all about yourself. It is a long way to Paris. But surely now you know I am still here, you will come and pay me a visit—at least. Everybody would be *most* glad to see you. And I should be so proud and glad. As I say, I am all alone. Mr Critchlow says I am to say there is a deal of money waiting for you. You know he is the trustee. There is the half-share of mother's and also of Aunt Harriet's, and it has been accumulating. By the way, they are getting up a subscription for Miss Chetwynd, poor old thing. Her sister is dead, and she is in poverty. I have put myself down for £20. Now, my dear sister, please do write to me at once. You see it is still the old address. I remain, my darling Sophia, with much love, your affectionate sister,

'CONSTANCE POVEY

'P. S.—I should have written yesterday, but I was not fit. Every time I sat down to write, I cried.'

'Of course,' said Sophia to Fossette, 'she expects me to go to her, instead of her coming to me! And yet who's the busiest?'

But this observation was not serious. It was merely a trifle of affectionate malicious embroidery that Sophia put on the edge of her deep satisfaction. The very spirit of simple love seemed to emanate from the paper on which Constance had written. And this spirit woke suddenly and completely Sophia's love for Constance. Constance! At that moment there was assuredly for Sophia no creature in the world like Constance. Constance personified for her the qualities of the Baines family. Constance's letter was a great letter, a perfect letter, perfect in its artlessness; the natural expression of the Baines character at its best. Not an awkward reference in the whole of it! No clumsy expression of surprise at anything that she, Sophia, had done, or failed to do! No mention of Gerald! Just a sublime acceptance of the situation as it was, and the assurance of undiminished love! Tact? No; it was something finer than tact! Tact was conscious, skilful. Sophia was certain that the notion of tactfulness had not entered Constance's head. Constance had simply written out of her heart. And that was what made the letter so splendid. Sophia was convinced that no one but a Baines could have written such a letter.

She felt that she must rise to the height of that letter, that she too must show her Baines blood. And she went primly to her desk, and began to write (on private notepaper) in that imperious large hand of hers that was so different from Constance's. She began a little stiffly, but after a few lines her generous and passionate soul was responding freely to the appeal of Constance. She asked that Mr Critchlow should pay £20 for her to the Miss Chetwynd fund. She spoke of her Pension and of Paris, and of her pleasure in Constance's letter. But she said nothing as to Gerald, nor as to the possibility of a visit to the Five Towns. She finished the letter in a blaze of love, and passed from it as from a dream to the sterile banality of the daily life of the Pension Frensham, feeling that, compared to Constance's affection, nothing else had any worth.

The Old Wives' Tale, 1908

A Broken Chain

Ten o'clock. The news was abroad in the house. Alicia had gone to spread it. Maggie had startled everybody by deciding to go down and tell Clara herself, though Albert was bound to call. The nurse had laid out the corpse. Auntie Hamps and Edwin were again in the drawing-room together; the ageing lady was making up her mind to go. Edwin, in search of an occupation, prepared to write letters to one or two distant relatives of his mother. Then he remembered his promise to Big James, and decided to write that letter first.

'What a mercy he passed away peacefully!' Auntie Hamps exclaimed, not for the first time.

Edwin, at a rickety fancy desk, began to write: 'Dear James, my father passed peacefully away at——' Then, with an abrupt movement, he tore the sheet in two and threw it in the fire, and began again: 'Dear James, my father died quietly at eight o'clock to-night.'

Soon afterwards, when Mrs Hamps had departed with her genuine but too spectacular grief, Edwin heard an immense commotion coming down the road from Hanbridge: cheers, shouts, squeals, penny whistles, and trumpets. He opened the gate.

'Who's in?' he asked a stout, shabby man, who was gesticulating in glee with a little Tory flag on the edge of the crowd.

'Who do *you* think, mister?' replied the man drunkenly.

'What majority?'

'Four hundred and thirty-nine.'

The integrity of the empire was assured, and the paid agitator had received a proper rebuff.

'Miserable idiots!' Edwin murmured, with the most extraordinary violence of scorn, as he re-entered the house, and the blare of triumph receded. He was very much surprised. He had firmly expected his own side to win, though he was reconciled to a considerable reduction of the old majority. His lips curled.

It was in his resentment, in the hard setting of his teeth as he confirmed himself in the rightness of his own opinions, that he first began to realize an individual freedom. 'I don't care if we're beaten forty times,' his thoughts ran. 'I'll be a more out-and-out Radical than ever! I don't care, and I don't care!' And he felt sturdily that he was free. The chain was at last broken that had bound together those two beings so dissimilar, antagonistic, and ill-matched—Edwin Clayhanger and his father.

Clayhanger, 1910

HENRY LAWSON
1867–1922

"*Past Carin'*"

One day—I was on my way home with the team that day—Annie Spicer came running up the creek in terrible trouble.

'Oh, Mrs Wilson! something terrible's happened at home. A trooper' (mounted policeman—they called them 'mounted troopers' out there), 'a trooper's come and took Billy!' Billy was the eldest son at home.

'What?'

'It's true, Mrs Wilson.'

'What for? What did the policeman say?'

'He—he—he said, "I—I'm very sorry, Mrs Spicer; but—I—I want William."'

It turned out that William was wanted on account of a horse missed from Wall's station and sold down-country.

'An' mother took on awful,' sobbed Annie; 'an' now she'll only sit stock-still an' stare in front of her, and won't take no notice of any of us. Oh! it's awful, Mrs Wilson. The policeman said he'd tell Aunt Emma' (Mrs Spicer's sister at Cobborah), 'and send her out. But I had to come to you, an' I've run all the way.'

James put the horse to the cart and drove Mary down.

Mary told me all about it when I came home.

'I found her just as Annie said; but she broke down and cried in my arms. Oh, Joe! it was awful. She didn't cry like a woman. I heard a man at Haviland cry at his brother's funeral, and it was just like that. She came round a bit after a while. Her sister's with her now. . . . Oh, Joe! you must take me away from the bush.'

Later on Mary said:

'How the oaks are sighing tonight, Joe!'

Next morning I rode across to Wall's station and tackled the old man; but he was a hard man, and wouldn't listen to me—in fact, he ordered me off his station. I was a selector and that was enough for him. But young Billy Wall rode after me.

'Look here, Joe!' he said, 'it's a blanky shame. All for the sake of a horse! As if that poor devil of a woman hasn't got enough to put up with already! I wouldn't do it for twenty horses. *I'll* tackle the boss, and if he won't listen to me, I'll walk off the run for the last time, if I have to carry my swag.'

Billy Wall managed it. The charge was withdrawn, and we got young Billy Spicer off up-country.

But poor Mrs Spicer was never the same after that. She seldom came up to our place unless Mary dragged her, so to speak; and then she would talk of nothing but her last trouble, till her visits were painful to look forward to.

'If it only could have been kep' quiet—for the sake of the other children; they are all I think of now. I tried to bring 'em all up decent, but I s'pose it was my fault, somehow. It's the disgrace that's killin' me—I can't bear it.'

I was at home one Sunday with Mary, and a jolly bush-girl named Maggie Charlsworth, who rode over sometimes from Wall's station (I must tell you about her some other time; James was shook after her), and we got talkin' about Mrs Spicer. Maggie was very warm about old Wall.

'I expected Mrs Spicer up today.' said Mary. 'She seems better lately.'

'Why!' cried Maggie Charlsworth, 'if that ain't Annie coming running up along the creek. Something's the matter!'

We all jumped up and ran out.

'What is it, Annie?' cried Mary.

'Oh, Mrs Wilson! Mother's asleep, and we can't wake her!'

'What?'

'It's—it's the truth, Mrs Wilson.'

'How long has she been asleep?'

'Since lars' night.'

'My God!' cried Mary, '*since last night*?'

'No, Mrs Wilson, not all the time; she woke wonst, about daylight this mornin'. She called me and said she didn't feel well, and I'd have to manage the milkin'.'

'Was that all she said?'

'No. She said not to go for you; and she said to feed the pigs and calves; and she said to be sure and water them geraniums.'

Mary wanted to go, but I wouldn't let her. James and I saddled our horses and rode down the creek.

Mrs Spicer looked very little different from what she did when I last saw her alive. It was some time before we could believe that she was dead. But she was 'past carin'' right enough.

'Water Them Geraniums', *Joe Wilson and His Mates*, 1902

NORMAN DOUGLAS
1868–1952

The Song of the Sirens

It was the Emperor Tiberius who startled his grammarians with the question, what songs the Sirens sang? I suspect he knew more about the matter than they did, for he was a Siren-worshipper all his life, though fate did not allow him to indulge his genius till those last few years which he spent among them on the rock-islet of Capri. The grammarians, if they were prudent, doubtless referred him to Homer, who has preserved a portion of their lay.

Whether Sirens of this true kind are in existence at the present day is rather questionable, for the waste places of earth have been reclaimed, and the sea's untrampled floor is examined and officially reported upon. Not so long ago some such creatures were still found. Jacobus Noierus relates that in 1403 a Siren was captured in the Zuider Zee. She was brought to Haarlem and, being naked, allowed herself to be clothed; she learned to eat like a Dutchman; she could spin thread and take pleasure in other maidenly occupations; she was gentle and lived to a great age. But she never spoke. The honest burghers had no knowledge of the language of the sea-folk to enable them to teach her their own tongue, so she remained mute to the end of her days—a circumstance to be regretted, since, excepting in the Arab tale of 'Julnar the Sea-born', little information has been handed down to us regarding the conversational and domestic habits of mediaeval Sirens.

Siren Land, 1911

A Victim of Gossip

It was not true to say of Mr Eames that he lived on Nepenthe because he was wanted by the London police for something that happened in Richmond Park, that his real name was not Eames at all but Daniels—the notorious Hodgson Daniels, you know, who was mixed up in the Lotus Club scandal, that he was the local representative of an international gang of white-slave traffickers who had affiliated offices in every part of the world, that he was not a man at all but an old boarding-house keeper who had very good reasons for assuming the male disguise, that he was a morphinomaniac, a disfrocked Baptist Minister, a pawnbroker out of work, a fire-worshipper, a Transylvanian, a bank clerk who had had a fall, a decayed jockey who disgraced himself at a subsequent period in connection with some East End mission for reforming the boys of Bermondsey and then, after pawning his mother's jewellery, writing anonymous threatening letters to society ladies about their husbands and vice-versa, trying to blackmail three Cabinet Ministers and tricking poor servant-girls out of their hard-earned wages by the sale of sham Bibles, was luckily run to earth in Piccadilly Circus, after an exciting chase, with a forty-pound salmon under his arm which he had been seen to lift from the window of a Bond Street fishmonger.

All these things, and a good many more, had been said. Eames knew it. Kind friends had seen to that.

To contrive such stories was a certain lady's method of asserting her personality on the island. She seldom went into society owing to some physical defect in her structure; she could only sit at home, like Penelope, weaving these and other bright tapestries—odds and ends of servants' gossip, patched together by the virulent industry of her own disordered imagination. It consoled Mr Eames slightly to reflect that he was not the only resident singled out for such aspersions; that the more harmless a man's life, the more fearsome the legends. He suffered, none the less.

South Wind, 1917

STEPHEN LEACOCK
1869–1944

Plutoria Avenue

The Mausoleum Club stands on the quietest corner of the best residential street in the city. It is a Grecian building of white stone. About it are great elm-trees with birds—the most expensive kind of birds—singing in the branches.

The street in the softer hours of the morning has an almost reverential quiet. Great motors move drowsily along it, with solitary chauffeurs returning at 10.30 after conveying the earlier of the millionaires to their down-town offices. The sunlight flickers through the elm-trees, illuminating expensive nursemaids wheeling valuable children in little perambulators. Some of the children are worth millions and millions. In Europe, no doubt, you may see in the Unter den Linden avenue or the Champs Elysées a little prince or princess go past with a clattering military guard to do honour. But that is nothing. It is not half so impressive, in the real sense, as what you may observe every morning on Plutoria Avenue beside the Mausoleum Club in the quietest part of the city. Here you may see a little toddling princess in a rabbit suit who owns fifty distilleries in her own right. There, in a lacquered perambulator, sails past a little hooded head that controls from its cradle an entire New Jersey corporation. The United States attorney-general is suing her as she sits, in a vain attempt to make her dissolve herself into constituent companies. Near by is a child of four, in a khaki suit, who represents the merger of two trunk line railways. You may meet in the flickered sunlight any number of little princes and princesses far more real than the poor survivals of Europe. Incalculable infants wave their fifty-dollar ivory rattles in an inarticulate greeting to one another. A million dollars of preferred stock laughs merrily in recognition of a majority control going past in a go-cart drawn by an imported nurse. And through it all the sunlight falls through the elm-trees, and the birds sing and the motors hum, so that the whole world as seen from the boulevard of Plutoria Avenue is the very pleasantest place imaginable.

Just below Plutoria Avenue, and parallel with it, the trees die out and the brick and stone of the city begins in earnest. Even from the avenue you see the tops of the sky-scraping buildings in the big commercial streets, and can hear or almost hear the roar of the elevated railway, earning dividends. And beyond that again the city sinks lower, and is choked and crowded with the tangled streets and little houses of the slums.

In fact, if you were to mount to the roof of the Mausoleum Club itself on Plutoria Avenue you could almost see the slums from there. But why should you? And on the other hand, if you never went up on the roof, but only dined inside among the palm-trees, you would never know that the slums existed—which is much better.

Arcadian Adventures with the Idle Rich, 1914

GEORGE DOUGLAS BROWN
1869–1902

A Small Town and its Tyrant

Even if Gourlay had been a placable and inoffensive man, then, the malignants of the petty burgh (it was scarce bigger than a village) would have fastened on his character, simply because he was above them. No man has a keener eye for behaviour than the Scot (especially when spite wings his intuition), and Gourlay's thickness of wit, and pride of place, would in any case have drawn their sneers. So, too, on lower grounds, would his wife's sluttishness. But his repressiveness added a hundred-fold to their hate of him. That was the particular cause, which acting on their general tendency to belittle a too-successful rival, made their spite almost monstrous against him. Not a man among them but had felt the weight of his tongue—for edge it had none. He walked among them like the dirt below his feet. There was no give and take in the man; he could be verra jocose with the lairds, to be sure, but he never dropped in to the Red Lion for a crack and a dram with the town-folk; he just glowered as if he could devour them! And who was he, I should like to know? His grandfather had been noathing but a common carrier!

Hate was the greater on both sides because it was often impotent. Gourlay frequently suspected offence, and seethed because he had no idea how to meet it—except by driving slowly down the brae in his new gig and never letting on when the Provost called to him. That was a wipe in the eye for the Provost! The 'bodies,' on their part, could rarely get near enough Gourlay to pierce his armour; he kept them off him by his brutal dourness. For it was not only pride and arrogance, but a consciousness, also, that he was no match for them at their own game, that kept Gourlay away from their society. They were adepts at the under stroke and they would have given him many a dig if he had only come amongst them. But, oh, no; not he; he was the big man; he never gave a body a chance! Or if you did venture a bit jibe when you met him, he glowered you off the face of the earth with thae black e'en of his. Oh, how they longed to get at him! It was not the least of the evils caused by Gourlay's black pride that it perverted a dozen characters. The 'bodies' of Barbie may have been decent enough men in their own way, but against him their malevolence was monstrous. It shewed itself in an insane desire to seize on every scrap of gossip they might twist against him. That was why the Provost lowered municipal dignity to gossip in the street with a discharged servant. As the baker said afterwards, it was absurd for a man in his 'poseetion.' But it was done with the sole desire of hearing something that might tell against Gourlay. Even Countesses, we are told, gossip with malicious maids, about other Countesses. Spite is a great leveller.

The House with the Green Shutters, 1902

SAKI

(Hector Hugh Munro)

1870–1916

Dun Cows and Walnut Trees

Theophil Eshley was an artist by profession, a cattle painter by force of environment. It is not to be supposed that he lived on a ranch or a dairy farm, in an atmosphere pervaded with horn and hoof, milking-stool, and branding-iron. His home was in a park-like, villa-dotted district that only just escaped the reproach of being suburban. On one side of his garden there abutted a small, picturesque meadow, in which an enterprising neighbour pastured some small picturesque cows of the Channel Island persuasion. At noonday in summertime the cows stood knee-deep in tall meadow-grass under the shade of a group of walnut trees, with the sunlight falling in dappled patches on their mouse-sleek coats. Eshley had conceived and executed a dainty picture of two reposeful milch-cows in a setting of walnut tree and meadow-grass and filtered sunbeam, and the Royal Academy had duly exposed the same on the walls of its Summer Exhibition. The Royal Academy encourages orderly, methodical habits in its children. Eshley had painted a successful and acceptable picture of cattle drowsing picturesquely under walnut trees, and as he had begun, so, of necessity, he went on. His 'Noontide Peace,' a study of two dun cows under a walnut tree, was followed by 'A Mid-day Sanctuary,' a study of a walnut tree, with two dun cows under it. In due succession there came 'Where the Gad-Flies Cease from Troubling,' 'The Haven of the Herd,' and 'A Dream in Dairyland,' studies of walnut trees and dun cows. His two attempts to break away from his own tradition were signal failures: 'Turtle Doves Alarmed by Sparrow-hawk' and 'Wolves on the Roman Campagna' came back to his studio in the guise of abominable heresies, and Eshley climbed back into grace and the public gaze with 'A Shaded Nook Where Drowsy Milkers Dream.'

'The Stalled Ox', *Beasts and Super-Beasts*, 1914

HILAIRE BELLOC
1870–1953

Indifference

I looked at the Carnarvonshire coast there close at hand, the sinking lines of the mountains as they fell into the sea, and I discovered myself to be for the first time in my life entirely indifferent to my fate. It was a very odd sensation indeed, like the sensation I fancy a man must have to find he is paralysed. Once, under the influence of a drug during an illness some such indifference had pervaded me, but here it was in the broad daylight and the sun well up above the mountains, with a clear sky, in the grip of a tremendous gale and of an angry countering sea, ravening like a pack of hounds. Yet I could only look with indifference on the sea and at the land. The sensation was about as much like courage as lying in a hammock is like a hundred yards race. It had no relation to courage, nor, oddly enough, had it any relation to religion, or to a right depreciation of this detestable little world which can be so beautiful when it likes.

Such as it was, there it was. I had always particularly disliked the idea of death by drowning, and I had never believed a word of the stories which say that at the end it is a pleasant death. Indeed, as a boy I was caught under the steps of a swimming bath and held there a little too long before

I could get myself out, and pleasant it was not at all. But here in Bardsey Sound, I was indifferent, even to death by drowning. All I was really interested in was to watch what way we lost and what chance we had of getting through.

Indeed, the whole question of fear is beyond analysis, and there is only one rule, which is, that a man must try to be so much the master of himself that he shall be able to compel himself to do whatever is needful, fear or no fear. Whether there be merit or not in the absence of fear, which sentiment we commonly call courage when it is allied to action, may be, and has been, discussed without conclusion since men were men. The absence of fear makes an admirable show, and excites our respect in any man; but it is not dependent upon the will. Here was I in very great peril indeed off Bardsey, and utterly careless whether the boat should sink or swim; yet was I the same man who, in a little freshness of breeze that arose off the Owers a year or two ago, was as frightened as could well be—and with no cause. And if this be true of change of mood in one man, it must be true of the differences of mood in different men.

The Cruise of the 'Nona', 1925

The Very Best Prose

I had almost written that there is no such thing as 'great' prose, in the sense in which there is 'great' rhetoric or 'great' verse. The very best prose may be dull if the subject expressed is dull to the reader. You will get no better prose, for instance, than Newman's *Arians of the Fourth Century*. It is not dull to me, because I happen to be interested in that bit of history, but it would be fiercely dull to any reader who was not. Nevertheless it is first-rate prose. Newman having to write about a particular thing upon which he had made himself immensely learned; having to tell a certain number of facts, and to express a certain number of ideas, does so with the best choice of words in the best order—and that is prose.

The Cruise of the 'Nona'

FRANK NORRIS

1870–1902

A Couple in Decline

In these first months of their misfortunes the routine of the McTeagues was as follows: They rose at seven and breakfasted in their room, Trina cooking the very meagre meal on an oil stove. Immediately after breakfast

Trina sat down to her work of whittling the Noah's ark animals, and McTeague took himself off to walk down town. He had by the greatest good luck secured a position with a manufacturer of surgical instruments, where his manual dexterity in the making of excavators, pluggers, and other dental contrivances stood him in fairly good stead. He lunched at a sailor's boarding-house near the water front, and in the afternoon worked till six. He was home at six-thirty, and he and Trina had supper together in the 'ladies' dining parlor,' an adjunct of the car conductors' coffee-joint. Trina, meanwhile, had worked at her whittling all day long, with but half an hour's interval for lunch, which she herself prepared upon the oil stove. In the evening they were both so tired that they were in no mood for conversation, and went to bed early, worn out, harried, nervous, and cross.

Trina was not quite so scrupulously tidy now as in the old days. At one time while whittling the Noah's ark animals she had worn gloves. She never wore them now. She still took pride in neatly combing and coiling her wonderful black hair, but as the days passed she found it more and more comfortable to work in her blue flannel wrapper. Whittlings and chips accumulated under the window where she did her work, and she was at no great pains to clear the air of the room vitiated by the fumes of the oil stove and heavy with the smell of cooking. It was not gay, that life. The room itself was not gay. The huge double bed sprawled over nearly a fourth of the available space; the angles of Trina's trunk and the washstand projected into the room from the walls, and barked shins and scraped elbows. Streaks and spots of the 'non-poisonous' paint that Trina used were upon the walls and woodwork. However, in one corner of the room, next the window, monstrous, distorted, brilliant, shining with a light of its own, stood the dentist's sign, the enormous golden tooth, the tooth of a Brobdingnag.

McTeague, 1899

HENRY HANDEL RICHARDSON
(Ethel Florence Richardson)
1870–1946

A Novel-Reader

Mrs Cayhill was a handsome woman, who led a comfortable, vegetable existence, and found it a task to rise from the plump sofa-cushion. Her pleasant features were slack, and in those moments of life which called for a sudden decision, they wore the helpless bewilderment of a woman who has never been required to think for herself. Her grasp on practical matters was rendered the more lax, too, by her being an immoderate reader, who fed on novels from morning till night, and slept with a page turned down beside her bed. She was for ever lost in the joys or sorrows of some fictitious person, and, in consequence, remained for the most part completely ignorant of what was going on around her. When she did happen to become conscious of her surroundings, she was callous, or merely indifferent, to them; for, compared with romance, life was dull and diffuse; it lacked the wilful simplicity, the exaggerative omissions, and forcible perspectives, which make up art: in other words, life demanded that unceasing work of selection and rejection, which it is the story-teller's duty to perform for his readers. All novels were fish to Mrs Cayhill's net; she lived in a world of intrigue and excitement, and, seated in her easy-chair by the sitting-room window, was generally as remote from her family as though she were in Timbuctoo.

Maurice Guest, 1908

August in Leipzig

With the beginning of August, the heat grew oppressive; all day long, the sun beat, fierce and unremittent, on this city of the plains, and the baked pavements were warm to the feet. Business slackened, and the midday rest in shops and offices was extended beyond its usual limit. Conservatorium and Gewandhaus, at first given over to relays of charwomen, their brooms and buckets, soon lay dead and deserted, too; and if, in the evening, Maurice passed the former building, he would see the janitor sitting at leisure in the middle of the pavement, smoking his long black cigar. The old trees in the *Promenade*, and the young striplings that followed the river in the *Lampestrasse*, drooped their brown leaves thick with dust; the familiar smell of roasting coffee, which haunted most house- and stair-ways, was intensified; and out of drains and rivers rose nauseous and penetrating odours, from which there was no escape. Every three or four days, when the atmosphere of the town had reached a pitch of unsavouriness which it seemed impossible to surpass, sudden storms swept up, tropical in their violence: blasts of thunder cracked like splitting beams; lightning darted along the narrow streets; rain fell in white, sizzling sheets. But the morning after, it was as hot as ever.

Maurice Guest

STEPHEN CRANE
1871–1900

Advancing on the Enemy

The youth stared at the land in front of him. Its foliages now seemed to veil powers and horrors. He was aware of the machinery of orders that started the charge, although from the corners of his eyes he saw an officer, who looked like a boy a-horseback, come galloping, waving his hat. Suddenly he felt a straining and heaving among the men. The line fell slowly forward like a toppling wall, and, with a convulsive gasp that was intended for a cheer, the regiment began its journey. The youth was pushed and jostled for a moment before he understood the movement at all, but directly he lunged ahead and began to run.

He fixed his eye upon a distant and prominent clump of trees where he had concluded the enemy were to be met, and he ran toward it as toward a goal. He had believed throughout that it was a mere question of getting over an unpleasant matter as quickly as possible, and he ran desperately, as if pursued for a murder. His face was drawn hard and tight with the stress of his endeavour. His eyes were fixed in a lurid glare. And with his soiled and disordered dress, his red and inflamed features surmounted by the dingy rag with its spot of blood, his wildly swinging rifle and banging accoutrements, he looked to be an insane soldier.

As the regiment swung from its position out into a cleared space the woods and thickets before it awakened. Yellow flames leaped toward it from many directions. The forest made a tremendous objection.

The line lurched straight for a moment. Then the right wing sprung forward; it in turn was surpassed by the left. Afterward the centre careered to the front until the regiment was a wedge-shaped mass, but an instant later the opposition of the bushes, trees, and uneven places on the ground split the command and scattered it into detached clusters.

The youth, light-footed, was unconsciously in advance. His eyes still kept note of the clump of trees. From all places near it the clannish yell of the enemy could be heard. The little flames of rifles leaped from it. The song of the bullets was in the air and shells snarled among the tree-tops. One tumbled directly into the middle of a hurrying group and exploded in crimson fury. There was an instant's spectacle of a man, almost over it, throwing up his hands to shield his eyes.

Other men, punched by bullets, fell in grotesque agonies. The regiment left a coherent trail of bodies.

They had passed into a clearer atmosphere. There was an effect like a revelation in the new appearance of the landscape. Some men working madly at a battery were plain to them, and the opposing infantry's lines were defined by the grey walls and fringes of smoke.

It seemed to the youth that he saw everything. Each blade of the green grass was bold and clear. He thought that he was aware of every change in the thin, transparent vapour that floated idly in sheets. The brown or grey trunks of the trees showed each roughness of their surfaces. And the men of the regiment, with their starting eyes and sweating faces, running madly, or falling, as if thrown headlong, to queer, heaped-up corpses—all were comprehended. His mind took a mechanical but firm impression, so that afterwards everything was pictured and explained to him, save why he himself was there.

But there was a frenzy made from this furious rush. The men, pitching forward insanely, had burst into cheerings, moblike and barbaric, but tuned in strange keys that can arouse the dullard and the stoic. It made a mad enthusiasm that, it seemed, would be incapable of checking itself before granite and brass. There was the delirium that encounters despair and death, and is heedless and blind to the odds. It is a temporary but sublime absence of selfishness. And because it was of this order was the reason, perhaps, why the youth wondered, afterward, what reasons he could have had for being there.

Presently the straining pace ate up the energies of the men. As if by agreement, the leaders began to slacken their speed. The volleys directed against them had had a seeming windlike effect. The regiment snorted and blew. Among some stolid trees it began to falter and hesitate. The men, staring intently, began to wait for some of the distant walls of smoke to move and disclose to them the scene. Since much of their strength and their breath had vanished, they returned to caution. They were become men again.

The Red Badge of Courage, 1895

Capsized

Seaward the crest of a roller suddenly fell with a thunderous crash, and the long white comber came roaring down upon the boat.

'Steady now,' said the captain. The men were silent. They turned their eyes from the shore to the comber and waited. The boat slid up the incline, leaped at the furious top, bounced over it, and swung down the long back of the wave. Some water had been shipped, and the cook bailed it out.

But the next crest crashed also. The tumbling, boiling flood of white water caught the boat and whirled it almost perpendicular. Water swarmed in from all sides. The correspondent had his hands on the gunwale at this time, and when the water entered at the place he swiftly withdrew his fingers, as if he objected to wetting them.

The little boat, drunken with this weight of water, reeled and snuggled deeper into the sea.

'Bail her out, cook! Bail her out!' said the captain.

'All right, Captain,' said the cook.

'Now, boys, the next one will do for us sure,' said the oiler. 'Mind to jump clear of the boat.'

The third wave moved forward, huge, furious, implacable. It fairly swallowed the dinghy, and almost simultaneously the men tumbled into the sea. A piece of life-belt had lain in the bottom of the boat, and as the correspondent went overboard he held this to his chest with his left hand.

The January water was icy, and he reflected immediately that it was colder than he had expected to find it off the coast of Florida. This appeared to his dazed mind as a fact important enough to be noted at the time. The coldness of the water was sad; it was tragic. This fact was somehow mixed and confused with his opinion of his own situation, so that it seemed almost a proper reason for tears. The water was cold.

When he came to the surface he was conscious of little but the noisy water. Afterward he saw his companions in the sea. The oiler was ahead in the race. He was swimming strongly and rapidly. Off to the correspondent's left, the cook's great white and corked back bulged out of the water; and in the rear the captain was hanging with his one good hand to the keel of the overturned dinghy.

There is a certain immovable quality to a shore, and the correspondent wondered at it amid the confusion of the sea.

It seemed also very attractive; but the correspondent knew that it was a long journey, and he paddled leisurely. The piece of life-preserver lay under him, and sometimes he whirled down the incline of a wave as if he were on a hand-sled.

But finally he arrived at a place in the sea where travel was beset with difficulty. He did not pause swimming to inquire what manner of current had caught him, but there his progress ceased. The shore was set before him like a bit of scenery on a stage, and he looked at it and understood with his eyes each detail of it.

As the cook passed, much farther to the left, the captain was calling to him, 'Turn over on your back, cook! Turn over on your back and use the oar.'

'All right, sir.' The cook turned on his back, and, paddling with an oar, went ahead as if he were a canoe.

Presently the boat also passed to the left of the correspondent, with the captain clinging with one hand to the keel. He would have appeared like a man raising himself to look over a board fence if it were not for the extraordinary gymnastics of the boat. The correspondent marvelled that the captain could still hold to it.

They passed on nearer to shore—the oiler, the cook, the captain—and following them went the water-jar, bouncing gaily over the seas.

The correspondent remained in the grip of this strange new enemy—a current. The shore, with its white slope of sand and its green bluff topped with little silent cottages, was spread like a picture before him. It was very near to him then, but he was impressed as one who, in a gallery, looks at a scene from Brittany or Algiers.

He thought: 'I am going to drown? Can it be possible? Can it be possible? Can it be possible?' Perhaps an individual must consider his own death to be the final phenomenon of nature.

But later a wave perhaps whirled him out of this small deadly current, for he found suddenly that he could again make progress toward the shore. Later still he was aware that the captain, clinging with one hand to the keel of the dinghy, had his face turned away from the shore and toward him, and was calling his name. 'Come to the boat! Come to the boat!'

The Open Boat, 1897

THEODORE DREISER
1871–1945

The Kingdom of Greatness

Whatever a man like Hurstwood could be in Chicago, it is very evident that he would be but an inconspicuous drop in an ocean like New York. In Chicago, whose population still ranged about 500,000, millionaires were not numerous. The rich had not become so conspicuously rich as to drown all moderate incomes in obscurity. The attention of the inhabitants was not so distracted by local celebrities in the dramatic, artistic, social, and religious fields as to shut the well-positioned man from view. In Chicago the two roads to distinction were politics and trade. In New York the roads were any one of a half-hundred, and each had been diligently pursued by hundreds, so that celebrities were numerous. The sea was already full of whales. A common fish must needs disappear wholly from view—remain unseen. In other words, Hurstwood was nothing.

There is a more subtle result of such a situation as this, which, though not always taken into account, produces the tragedies of the world. The great create an atmosphere which reacts badly upon the small. This atmosphere is easily and quickly felt. Walk among the magnificent residences, the splendid equipages, the gilded shops, restaurants, resorts of all kinds; scent the flowers, the silks, the wines; drink of the laughter springing from the soul of luxurious content, of the glances which gleam like light from defiant spears; feel the quality of the smiles which cut like glistening swords and of strides born of place, and you shall know of what is the atmosphere of the high and mighty. Little use to argue that of such is not the kingdom of greatness, but so long as the world is attracted by this and the human heart views this as the one desirable realm which it must attain, so long, to that heart, will this remain the realm of greatness. So long, also, will the atmosphere of this realm work its desperate results in the soul of man. It is like a chemical reagent. One day of it, like one drop of the other, will so affect and discolour the views, the aims, the desire of the mind, that it will thereafter remain forever dyed. A day of it to the untried mind is like opium to the untried body. A craving is set up which, if gratified, shall eternally result in dreams and death. Aye! dreams unfulfilled—gnawing, luring, idle phantoms which beckon and lead, beckon and lead, until death and dissolution dissolve their power and restore us blind to nature's heart.

Sister Carrie, 1902

Stage-Managing a Scandal

At once the question was raised as to who was really guilty, the city treasurer or the broker, or both. How much money had actually been lost? Where had it gone? Who was Frank Algernon Cowperwood, anyway? Why was he not arrested? How did he come to be identified so closely with the financial administration of the city? And though the day of what later was termed 'yellow journalism' had not arrived, and the local papers were not given to such vital personal comment as followed later, it was not possible, even bound as they were, hand and foot, by the local political and social magnates, to avoid comment of some sort. Editorials had to be written. Some solemn, conservative references to the shame and disgrace which one single individual could bring to a great city and a noble political party had to be ventured upon.

That desperate scheme to cast the blame on Cowperwood temporarily, which had been concocted by Mollenhauer, Butler, and Simpson, to get the odium of the crime outside the party lines for the time being, was now lugged forth and put in operation. It was interesting and strange to note how quickly the newspapers, and even the Citizen's Municipal Reform Association, adopted the argument that Cowperwood was largely, if not solely, to blame. Stener had loaned him the money, it is true—had put bond issues in his hands for sale, it is true, but somehow every one seemed to gain the impression that Cowperwood had desperately misused the treasurer. The fact that he had taken a sixty-thousand-dollar cheque for certificates which were not in the sinking-fund was hinted at, though until they could actually confirm this for themselves both the newspapers and the committee were too fearful of the State libel laws to say so.

In due time there were brought forth several noble municipal letters, purporting to be a stern call on the part of the mayor, Mr Jacob Borchardt, on Mr George W. Stener for an immediate explanation of his conduct, and the latter's reply, which were at once given to the newspapers and the Citizen's Municipal Reform Association. These letters were enough to show, so the politicians figured, that the Republican party was anxious to purge itself of any miscreant within its ranks, and they also helped to pass the time until after election . . .

And did Mr Jacob Borchardt write the letters to which his name was attached? He did not. Mr Abner Sengstack wrote them in Mr Mollenhauer's office, and Mr Mollenhauer's comment when he saw them was that he thought they would do—that they were very good, in fact. And did Mr George W. Stener, city treasurer of Philadelphia, write that very politic reply? He did not. Mr Stener was in a state of complete collapse, even crying at one time at home in his bathtub. Mr Abner Sengstack wrote that also, and had Mr Stener sign it. And Mr Mollenhauer's comment on that, before it was sent, was that he thought it was 'all right.' It was a time when all the little rats and mice were scurrying to cover because of the presence of a great, fiery-eyed public cat somewhere in the dark, and only the older and wiser rats were able to act.

The Financier, 1912

A Terrible Item

But now once more in Lycurgus and back in his room after just explaining to Roberta, as he had, he once more encountered on his writing desk, the identical paper containing the item concerning the tragedy at Pass Lake. And in spite of himself, his eye once more followed nervously and yet unwaveringly to the last word all the suggestive and provocative details. The uncomplicated and apparently easy way in which the lost couple had first arrived at the boathouse; the commonplace and entirely unsuspicious way in which they had hired a boat and set forth for a row; the manner in which they had disappeared to the north end; and then the upturned boat, the floating oars and hats near the shore. He stood reading in the still strong evening light. Outside the windows were the dark boughs of the fir tree of which he had thought the preceding day and which now suggested all those firs and pines about the shores of Big Bittern.

But, good God! What was he thinking of anyhow? He, Clyde Griffiths! The nephew of Samuel Griffiths! What was 'getting into' him? Murder! That's what it was. This terrible item—this devil's accident or machination that was constantly putting it before him! A most horrible crime, and one for which they electrocuted people if they were caught. Besides, he could not murder anybody—not Roberta, anyhow. Oh, no! Surely not after all that had been between them. And yet—this other world!—

Sondra—which he was certain to lose now unless he acted in some way——

His hands shook, his eyelids twitched—then his hair at the roots tingled and over his body ran chill nervous titillations in waves. Murder! Or upsetting a boat at any rate in deep water, which of course might happen anywhere, and by accident, as at Pass Lake. And Roberta could not swim. He knew that. But she might save herself at that—scream—cling to the boat—and then—if there were any to hear—and she told afterwards! An icy perspiration now sprang to his forehead; his lips trembled and suddenly his throat felt parched and dry. To prevent a thing like that he would have to—to—but no—he was not like that. He could not do a thing like that—hit any one—a girl—Roberta—and when drowning or struggling. Oh, no, no—no such thing as that! Impossible.

He took his straw hat and went out, almost before any one heard him *think*, as he would have phrased it to himself, such horrible, terrible thoughts. He could not and would not think them from now on. He was no such person. And yet—and yet—these thoughts. The solution—if he wanted one. The way to stay here—not leave—marry Sondra—be rid of Roberta and all—all—for the price of a little courage or daring. But no!

He walked and walked—away from Lycurgus—out on a road to the southeast which passed through a poor and decidedly unfrequented rural section, and so left him alone to think—or, as he felt, not to be heard in his thinking.

Day was fading into dark. Lamps were beginning to glow in the cottages here and there. Trees in groups in fields or along the road were beginning to blur or smokily blend. And although it was warm—the air lifeless and lethargic—he walked fast, thinking, and perspiring as he did so, as though he were seeking to outwalk and outthink or divert some inner self that preferred to be still and think.

That gloomy, lonely lake up there!

That island to the south!

Who would see?

Who could hear?

That station at Gun Lodge with a bus running to it at this season of the year. (Ah, he remembered that, did he? The deuce!) A terrible thing, to remember a thing like that in connection with such a thought as this! But if he were going to think of such a thing as this at all, he had better think well—he could tell himself that—or stop thinking about it now—once and forever—forever. But Sondra! Roberta! If ever he were caught—electrocuted! And yet the actual misery of his present state. The difficulty! The danger of losing Sondra. And yet, murder—

An American Tragedy, 1925

JAMES WELDON JOHNSON
1871–1938

A Visit to Salt Lake City

Just before spring in 1905, Bob and Rosamond started again over the Orpheum Circuit; I made the trip with them. Some other performers who were playing the same circuit and who left Denver for San Francisco on the same train with us had planned to stop off for a day at Salt Lake City to visit the Mormon Tabernacle and see the town. They persuaded us to do likewise. We had our tickets adjusted for a stop-over until the next day and got off the train at Salt Lake City. We took a carriage, and directed the driver, a jovial Irishman, to take us to a good hotel. He took us to the best. Porters carried our luggage into the lobby, and I went to the desk, turned the register round and registered for three. The clerk was busy at the key-rack. He glanced at us furtively, but kept himself occupied. It grew obvious that he was protracting the time. Finally, he could delay no longer and came to the desk. As he came his expression revealed the lie he was to speak. He turned the register round, examined our names, and while his face flushed a bit said, "I'm sorry, but we haven't got a vacant room". This statement, which I knew almost absolutely to be false, set a number of emotions in action: humiliation, chagrin, indignation, resentment, anger; but in the midst of them all I could detect a sense of pity for the man who had to make it, for he was, to all appearances, an honest, decent person. It was then about eleven o'clock, and I sought the eyes of the clerk and asked if he expected any rooms to be vacated at noon. He stammered that he did not. I then said to him that we would check our bags and take the first room available by night. Pressure from me seemed to stiffen him, and he told us that we could not; that we had better try some other hotel. Our bags were taken out and a cab called, and we found ourselves in the same vehicle that had brought us to the hotel. Our driver voluntarily assumed a part of our mortification, and he attempted to console us by relating how ten or twelve years before he had taken Peter Jackson (the famous Negro pugilist) to that same hotel and how royally he had been entertained there. We tried two other hotels, where our experiences were similar but briefer. We did not dismiss our cabman, for we were being fast driven to the conclusion that he was probably the only compassionate soul we should meet in the whole city of the Latter-Day Saints.

We had become very hungry; we felt that it was necessary for us to eat in order to maintain both our morale and our endurance. Our cabman took us to a restaurant. When we entered it was rather crowded, but we managed to find a table and sat down. There followed that hiatus, of which every Negro in the United States knows the meaning. At length, a man in charge came over and told us without any pretense of palliation that we could not be served. We were forced to come out under the stare of a crowd that was conscious of what had taken place. Our cabman was now actually touched by our plight; and he gave vent to his feelings in explosive oaths. He suggested another restaurant to try, where we might have 'better luck'; but we were no longer up to the possible facing of another such experience. We asked the cabby if he knew of a colored family in town who might furnish us with a meal; he did not, but he had an idea; he drove along and stopped in front of a saloon and chophouse; he darted inside, leaving us in the carriage; after a few moments he emerged beaming good news. We went in and were seated at a wholly inconspicuous table, but were served with food and drink that quickly renewed our strength and revived our spirits.

However, we were almost immediately confronted with the necessity of getting a place to sleep. Our cabby had another idea; he drove us to a woman he knew who kept a lodging house for laborers. It was a pretty shabby place; nevertheless the woman demurred for quite a while. Finally, she agreed to let us stay, if we got out before her regular lodgers got up. In the foul room to which she showed us, we hesitated until the extreme moment of weariness before we could bring ourselves to bear the touch of the soiled bedclothes. We smoked and talked over the situation we were in, the situation of being outcasts and pariahs in a city of our own and native land. Our talk went beyond our individual situation and took in the common lot of Negroes in well-nigh every part of the country, a lot which lays on high and low the constant struggle to renerve their hearts and wills against the unremitting pressure of unfairness, injustice, wrong, cruelty, contempt, and hate. If what we felt had been epitomized and expressed in but six words, they would have been: A hell of a 'my country.'

We welcomed daybreak. For numerous reasons we were glad to get out of the beds of our unwilling hostess. We boarded our train with feelings of unbounded relief; I with a vow never to set foot again in Salt Lake City. Twenty-three years later, I passed through Salt Lake City, as one of a large delegation on the way to a conference of the National Association for the Advancement of Colored People held in Los Angeles. Our train had a wait of a couple of hours, and the delegation went out to see the town, the Tabernacle, and the lake. I spent the time alone at the railroad station.

Along This Way, 1933

BERTRAND RUSSELL
1872–1970

Achilles and the Tortoise and Tristram Shandy

We can now understand why Zeno believed that Achilles cannot overtake the tortoise and why as a matter of fact he can overtake it. We shall see that all the people who disagreed with Zeno had no right to do so, because they all accepted premises from which his conclusion followed. The argument is this: Let Achilles and the tortoise start along a road at the same time, the tortoise (as is only fair) being allowed a handicap. Let Achilles go twice as fast as the tortoise, or ten times or a hundred times as fast. Then he will never reach the tortoise. For at every moment the tortoise is somewhere and Achilles is somewhere; and neither is ever twice in the same place while the race is going on. Thus the tortoise goes to just as many places as Achilles does, because each is in one place at one moment, and in another at any other moment. But if Achilles were to catch up with the tortoise, the places where the tortoise would have been would be only part of the places where Achilles would have been. Here, we must suppose, Zeno appealed to the maxim that the whole has more terms than the part. Thus if Achilles were to overtake the tortoise, he would have been in more places than the tortoise; but we saw that he must, in any period, be in exactly as many places as the tortoise. Hence we infer that he can never catch the tortoise. This argument is strictly correct, if we allow the axiom that the whole has more terms than the part. As the conclusion is absurd, the axiom must be rejected, and then all goes well. But there is no good word to be said for the philosophers of the past two thousand years and more, who have all allowed the axiom and denied the conclusion.

The retention of this axiom leads to absolute contradictions, while its rejection leads only to oddities. Some of these oddities, it must be confessed, are very odd. One of them, which I call the paradox of Tristram Shandy, is the converse of the Achilles, and shows that the tortoise, if you give him time, will go just as far as Achilles. Tristram Shandy, as we know, employed two years in chronicling the first two days of his life, and lamented that, at this rate, material would accumulate faster than he could deal with it, so that, as years went by, he would be farther and farther from the end of his history. Now I maintain that, if he had lived for ever, and had not wearied of his task, then, even if his life had continued as eventfully as it began, no part of his biography would have remained unwritten. For consider: the hundredth day will be described in the hundredth year, the thousandth in the thousandth year, and so on. Whatever day we may choose as so far on that he cannot hope to reach it, that day will be described in the corresponding year. Thus any day that may be mentioned will be written up sooner or later, and therefore no part of the biography will remain permanently unwritten. This paradoxical but perfectly true proposition depends upon the fact that the number of days in all time is no greater than the number of years.

'Mathematics and the Metaphysicians', 1901

A Dream

Another time, when I lived in a cottage where there were no servants at night time, I dreamt that I heard a knock on the front door in the very early morning. I went down to the front door in my night shirt—this was before the days of pyjamas—and, when I opened the door, I found God on the doorstep. I recognized Him at once from His portraits. Now, a little before this, my brother-in-law Logan Pearsall Smith had said that he thought of God as rather like the Duke of Cambridge—that is to say, still august, but conscious of being out of date. And, remembering this, I thought, well, I must be kind to Him and show that, although of course He is perhaps a little out of date, still I quite know how one should behave to a guest. So I hit Him on the back and said, 'Come in, old fellow'. He was very much pleased at being treated so kindly by one whom He realized to be not quite of His congregation. After we had talked for some time, He said, 'Now, is there anything I could do for you?' And I thought, 'Well, He is omnipotent. I suppose there are things He could do for me'. I said, 'I should like you to give me Noah's Ark', and I thought I should put it somewhere in the suburbs and charge sixpence admission, and I should make a huge fortune. But His face fell, and He said: 'I am very sorry, I can't do that for you because I have already given it to an American friend of mine.' And that was the end of my conversation with Him.

Fact and Fiction, 1961

AUBREY BEARDSLEY
1872–1898

A Ballet Danced by the Servants of Venus

Scarcely had the stage been empty for a moment, when Sporion entered, followed by a brilliant rout of dandies and smart women. Sporion was a tall, slim, depraved young man with a slight stoop, a troubled walk, an oval impassable face, with its olive skin drawn tightly over the bone, strong scarlet lips, long Japanese eyes, and a great gilt toupet. Round his shoulders hung a high-collared satin cape of salmon pink, with long black ribands untied and floating about his body. His coat of sea-green spotted muslin was caught in at the waist by a scarlet sash with scalloped edges, and frilled out over the hips for about six inches. His trousers, loose and wrinkled, reached to the end of the calf, and were brocaded down the sides, and ruched magnificently at the ankles. The stockings were of white kid, with stalls for the toes, and had delicate red sandals strapped over them. But his little hands, peeping out from their frills, seemed quite the most insinuating things, such supple fingers tapering to the point, with tiny nails stained pink, such unquenchable palms, lined and mounted like Lord Fanny's in 'Love at all Hazards,' and such blue-veined, hairless backs! In his left hand he carried a small lace handkerchief broidered with a coronet.

As for his friends and followers they made the most superb and insolent crowd imaginable, but to catalogue the clothes they had on would require a chapter as long as the famous tenth in Pénillière's history of underlinen. On the whole they looked a very distinguished chorus.

Sporion stepped forward and explained with swift and various gesture that he and his friends were tired of the amusements, wearied with the poor pleasures offered by the civil world, and had invaded the Arcadian valley hoping to experience a new *frisson* in the destruction of some shepherd's or some satyr's naïveté, and the infusion of their venom among the dwellers of the woods.

The chorus assented with languid but expressive movements.

Curious, and not a little frightened, at the arrival of the worldly company, the sylvans began to peep nervously at those subtle souls through the branches of the trees, and one or two fauns and a shepherd or so crept out warily. Sporion and all the ladies and gentlemen made enticing sounds and invited the rustic creatures with all the grace in the world to come and join them. By little batches they came, lured by the strange looks, by the scents and the doings, and by the brilliant clothes, and some ventured quite near, timorously fingering the delicious textures of the stuffs. Then Sporion and each of his friends took a satyr or a shepherd or something by the hand, and made the preliminary steps of a courtly measure, for which the most admirable combination had been invented, and the most charming music written.

The pastoral folk were entirely bewildered when they saw such restrained and graceful movements, and made the most grotesque and futile efforts to imitate them.

Dio mio, a pretty sight! A charming effect too was obtained by the intermixture of stockinged calf and hairy leg, of rich brocaded bodice and plain blouse, of tortured headdress and loose untutored locks.

When the dance was ended, the servants of Sporion brought on champagne, and, with many pirouettes, poured it magnificently into slender glasses, and tripped about plying those Arcadian mouths that had never before tasted such a royal drink.

* * * * * * *

Then the curtain fell with a pudic rapidity.

Venus and Tannhäuser, written 1894; privately printed 1907

SIR MAX BEERBOHM
1872–1956

I Commit to the Flames . . .

'Has a profound knowledge of human character, and an essentially sane outlook' said one of the critics quoted at the end of the book that I had chosen. The wind and the rain in the chimney had not abated, but the fire was bearing up bravely. So would I. I would read cheerfully and without prejudice. I poked the fire and, pushing my chair slightly back, lest the heat should warp the book's covers, began Chapter I. A woman sat writing in a summer-house at the end of a small garden that overlooked a great valley in Surrey. The description of her was calculated to make her very admirable—a thorough *woman*, not strictly beautiful, but likely to be thought beautiful by those who knew her well; not dressed as though she gave much heed to her clothes, but dressed in a fashion that exactly harmonised with her special type. Her pen 'travelled' rapidly across the foolscap, and while it did so she was described in more and more detail. But at length she came to a 'knotty point' in what she was writing. She paused, she pushed back the hair from her temples, she looked forth at the valley; and now the landscape was described, but not at all exhaustively, it, for the writer soon overcame her difficulty, and her pen travelled faster than ever, till suddenly there was a cry of 'Mammy!' and in rushed a seven-year-old child, in conjunction with whom she was more than ever admirable; after which the narrative skipped back across eight years, and the woman became a girl giving as yet no token of future eminence in literature, but—I had an impulse which I obeyed almost before I was conscious of it.

Nobody could have been more surprised than I was at what I had done—done so neatly, so quietly and gently. The book stood closed, upright, with its back to me, just as on a book-shelf, behind the bars of the grate. There it was. And it gave forth, as the flames crept up the blue cloth sides of it, a pleasant though acrid smell. My astonishment had passed, giving place to an exquisite satisfaction. How pottering and fumbling a thing was even the best kind of written criticism! I understood the contempt felt by the man of action for the man of words. But what pleased me most was that at last, actually, I, at my age, I of all people, had committed a crime—was guilty of a crime. I had power to revoke it. I might write to my bookseller for an unburnt copy, and place it on the shelf where this one had stood—this gloriously glowing one. I would do nothing of the sort. What I had done I had done. I would wear forever on my conscience the white rose of theft and the red rose of arson. If hereafter the owner of this cottage happened to miss that volume—let him! If he were fool enough to write to me about it, would I share my grand secret with him? No. Gently, with his poker, I prodded that volume further among the coals. The all-but-consumed binding shot forth little tongues of bright colour—flamelets of sapphire, amethyst, emerald. Charming! Could even the author herself not admire them? Perhaps. Poor woman!—I had scored now, scored so perfectly that I felt myself to be almost a brute while I poked off the loosened black outer pages and led the fire on to pages that were but pale brown.

These were quickly devoured. But it seemed to me that whenever I left the fire to forage for itself it made little headway. I pushed the book over on its side. The flames closed on it, but presently, licking their lips, fell back, as though they had had enough. I took the tongs and put the book upright again, and raked it fore and aft. It seemed almost as thick as ever. With poker and tongs I carved it into two, three sections—the inner pages flashing white as when they were sent to the binders. Strange! Aforetime, a book was burnt now and again in the market-place by the common hangman. Was he, I wondered, paid by the hour? I had always supposed the thing quite easy for him—a bright little, brisk little conflagration, and so home. Perhaps other books were less resistant than this one? I began to feel that the critics were more right than they knew. Here was a book that had indeed an intense vitality, and an immense vitality. It was a book that would live—do what one might. I vowed it should not. I subdivided it, spread it, redistributed it. Ever and anon my eye would be caught by some sentence or fragment of a sentence in the midst of a charred page before the flames crept over it, 'lways loathed you, bu', I remember; and 'ning. Tolstoi was right.' Who had always loathed whom? And what, what, had Tolstoi been right about? I had an absurd but genuine desire to know. Too late! Confound the woman!—she was scoring again. I furiously drove her pages into the yawning crimson jaws of the coals. Those jaws had lately been golden. Soon, to my horror, they seemed to be growing grey. They seemed to be closing—on nothing. Flakes of black paper, full-sized layers of paper brown and white, began to hide them from me altogether. I sprinkled a boxful of wax matches. I resumed the bellows. I lunged with the poker. I held a newspaper over the whole grate. I did all that inspiration could suggest, or skill accomplish. Vainly. The fire went out—darkly, dismally, gradually, quite out.

How she had scored again! But she did not know it. I felt no bitterness against her as I lay back in my chair, inert, listening to the storm that was still raging. I blamed only myself. I had done wrong. The small room became very cold. Whose fault was that but my own? I had done wrong hastily, but had done it and been glad of it. I had not remembered the words a wise king wrote long ago, that the lamp of the wicked shall be put out, and that the way of trangressors is hard.

'The Crime', *And Even Now*, 1921

FORD MADOX FORD
1873–1939

The Backbone of England

This, Tietjens thought, is England! A man and a maid walk through Kentish grass-fields: the grass ripe for the scythe. The man honourable, clean, upright; the maid virtuous, clean, vigorous: he of good birth; she of birth quite as good; each filled with a too good breakfast that each could yet capably digest. Each come just from an admirably appointed establishment: a table surrounded by the best people: their promenade sanctioned, as it were by the Church—two clergy—the State: two Government officials; by mothers, friends, old maids. . . . Each knew the names of birds that piped and grasses that bowed: chaffinch, greenfinch, yellow-ammer (*not*, my dear, hammer! *amonrer* from the Middle High German for 'finch'), garden warbler, Dartford warbler, pied-wagtail, known as 'dish-washer.' (These *charming* local dialect names.) Marguerites over the grass, stretching in an infinite white blaze: grasses purple in a haze to the far distant hedgerow: coltsfoot, wild white clover, sainfoin, Italian rye grass (all technical names that the best people must know: the best grass mixture for permanent pasture on the Wealden loam). In the hedge: our lady's bedstraw: dead-nettle: bachelor's button (but in *Sussex* they call it ragged robin, my dear): so interesting! Cowslip (paigle, you know from the old French *pasque*, meaning Easter); burr, burdock (farmer that thy wife may thrive, but not burr and burdock wive!); violet leaves, the flowers of course over; black bryony; wild clematis, later it's old man's beard; purple loose-strife. (That our young maids long purples call and liberal shepherds give a grosser name. *So* racy of the soil!) . . . Walk, then, through the field, gallant youth and fair maid, minds cluttered up with all these useless anodynes for thought, quotation, imbecile epithets! Dead silent: unable to talk: from too good breakfast to probably extremely bad lunch. The young woman, so the young man is duly warned, to prepare it: pink india-rubber, half-cooked cold beef, no doubt: tepid potatoes, water in the bottom of willow-pattern dish. (*No! Not* genuine willow-pattern, of *course*, Mr Tietjens.) Overgrown lettuce with wood-vinegar to make the mouth scream with pain; pickles, also preserved in wood-vinegar; two bottles of public-house beer that, on opening, squirts to the wall. A glass of invalid port. . . . for the *gentleman*! . . . and the jaws hardly able to open after the too enormous breakfast at 10.15. Midday now!

'God's England!' Tietjens exclaimed to himself in high good humour. 'Land of Hope and Glory!—F natural descending to tonic C major: chord of 6–4, suspension over dominant seventh to common chord of C major. . . . All absolutely correct! Double basses, cellos, all violins: all wood wind: all brass. Full grand organ: all stops: special *vox humana* and key-bugle effect. . . . Across the counties came the sound of bugles that his father knew. . . . Pipe exactly right. It must be: pipe of Englishman of good birth: ditto tobacco. Attractive young woman's back. English midday midsummer. Best climate in the world! No day on which man may not go abroad!' Tietjens paused and aimed with his hazel stick an immense blow at a tall spike of yellow mullein with its undecided, furry, glaucous leaves and its undecided, buttony, unripe lemon-coloured flowers. The structure collapsed, gracefully, like a woman killed among crinolines!

'Now I'm a bloody murderer!' Tietjens said. 'Not gory! Green-stained with vital fluid of innocent plant. . . . And by God! Not a woman in the country who won't let you rape her after an hour's acquaintance!' He slew two more mulleins and a sow-thistle! A shadow, but not from the sun, a gloom, lay across the sixty acres of purple grass bloom and marguerites, white: like petticoats of lace over the grass!

'By God,' he said, 'Church! State! Army! HM Ministry: HM Opposition: HM City Man. . . . All the governing class! All rotten! Thank God we've got a navy! . . . But perhaps that's rotten too! Who knows! Britannia needs no bulwarks. . . . Then thank God for the upright young man and the virtuous maiden in the summer fields: he Tory of the Tories as he should be: she suffragette of the militants: militant here on earth . . . as she should be! As she should be! In the early decades of the twentieth century however else can a woman keep clean and wholesome! Ranting from platforms, splendid for the lungs: bashing in policemen's helmets. . . . No! It's I do that: my part, I think, miss! . . . Carrying heavy banners in twenty-mile processions through streets of Sodom. All splendid! I bet she's virtuous. But you can tell it in the eye. Nice eyes! Attractive back. Virginal cockiness. . . . Yes, better occupation for mothers or empire than attending on lewd husbands year in year out till you're as hysterical as a female cat on heat. . . . You could see it in her: that woman: you can see it in most of 'em! Thank God then for the Tory, upright young married man and the suffragette kid . . . Backbone of England! . . .'

He killed another flower.

Some Do Not, 1924

The Wrath of Joseph Conrad

The Conrad of those days was Romance. He was dark, black bearded, passionate in the extreme and at every minute; rather small but very broad shouldered and long in the arm. Speaking English he had so strong a French accent that few who did not know him well could understand him at first. His gestures were profuse and continuous, his politenesses Oriental and at times almost servile. Like James he would address a Society lady, if he ever met one, or an old woman in the lane, or his own servants, or the ostler at an inn, or myself who was for many years little more than his cook, slut and butler in literary matters, or Sir Sidney Colvin, or Sir Edmund Gosse, all with the same profusion of endearing adjectives. On the other hand his furies would be sudden, violent, blasting and incomprehensible to his victim. At one of my afternoon parties in London he objurgated the unfortunate Charles Lewis Hind—a thin, slightly stuttering nervous, dark fellow who was noted as a critic, mostly of paintings. Hind in a perfectly sincere mood had congratulated him because his name was on all the hoardings in London. Conrad's *Nostromo* was then being serialised in a journal that gave the fact unusual prominence in its advertisements.

Conrad on the other hand despised the journal, and himself more for letting his work appear in it. His hatred of the publicity was as real as if it were an outrage on the honour of his family. From the windows of my house his name was visible on a hoarding that some house-breakers had erected—visible in letters three feet long. This had driven him nearly mad and he had really taken the congratulations of Mr Hind as gloatings over his bitter poverty. Mr Hind had a sardonic manner and spoke with a rictus; bitter and dreadfully harassing poverty alone had driven Conrad, mercilessly, to consent to that degradation of his art.

In the event, next day Conrad was very ill with mortification and I had to write the part of the serial that remained to make up the weekly instalment. Our life was like that.

Return to Yesterday, 1931

WALTER DE LA MARE

1873–1956

An Introduction to an Aunt

We arrived at noon, and entered the gates out of the hot dust beneath the glitter of the dark-curtained windows. Seaton led me at once through the little garden-gate to show me his tadpole pond, swarming with what (being myself not in the least interested in low life) seemed to me the most horrible creatures—of all shapes, consistencies, and sizes, but with which Seaton was obviously on the most intimate of terms. I can see his absorbed face now as, squatting on his heels he fished the slimy things out in his sallow palms. Wearying at last of these pets, we loitered about awhile in an aimless fashion. Seaton seemed to be listening, or at any rate waiting, for something to happen or for someone to come. But nothing did happen and no one came.

That was just like Seaton. Anyhow, the first view I got of his aunt was when, at the summons of a distant gong, we turned from the garden, very hungry and thirsty, to go into luncheon. We were approaching the house, when Seaton suddenly came to a standstill. Indeed, I have always had the impression that he plucked at my sleeve. Something, at least, seemed to catch me back, as it were, as he cried, 'Look out, there she is!'

She was standing at an upper window which opened wide on a hinge, and at first sight she looked an excessively tall and overwhelming figure. This, however, was mainly because the window reached all but to the floor of her bedroom. She was in reality rather an undersized woman, in spite of her long face and big head. She must have stood, I think, unusually still, with eyes fixed on us, though this impression may be due to Seaton's sudden warning and to my consciousness of the cautious and subdued air that had fallen on him at sight of her. I know that without the least reason in the world I felt a kind of guiltiness, as if I had been 'caught'. There was a silvery star pattern sprinkled on her black silk dress, and even from the ground I could see the immense coils of her hair and the rings on her left hand which was held fingering the small jet buttons of her bodice. She watched our united advance without stirring, until, imperceptibly, her eyes raised and lost themselves in the distance, so that it was out of an assumed reverie that she appeared suddenly to awaken to our presence beneath her when we drew close to the house.

'So this is your friend, Mr Smithers, I suppose?' she said, bobbing to me.

'Withers, aunt,' said Seaton.

'It's much the same,' she said, with eyes fixed on me. 'Come in, Mr Withers, and bring him along with you.'

'Seaton's Aunt', *The Riddle*, 1923

In the Waiting-Room

When murky winter dusk begins to settle over the railway station at Crewe its first-class waiting-room grows steadily more stagnant. Particularly if one is alone in it. The long grimed windows do little more than sift the failing light that slopes in on them from the glass roof outside and is too feeble to penetrate into the recesses beyond. And the grained massive black-leathered furniture becomes less and less inviting. It appears to have been made for a scene of extreme and diabolical violence that one may hope will never occur. One can hardly at any rate imagine it to have been designed by a really *good* man!

'Crewe', *On the Edge*, 1930

SIR WINSTON CHURCHILL
1873–1965

Bernard Shaw and Lady Astor Visit Russia

It must have been with some trepidation that the chiefs of the Union of Socialist Soviet Republics awaited the arrival in their grim domains of a merry harlequinade. The Russians have always been fond of circuses and travelling shows. Since they had imprisoned, shot or starved most of their best comedians, their visitors might fill for a space a noticeable void. And here was the World's most famous intellectual Clown and Pantaloon in one, and the charming Columbine of the capitalist pantomime. So the crowds were marshalled. Multitudes of well-drilled demonstrators were served out with their red scarves and flags. The massed-bands blared. Loud cheers from sturdy proletarians rent the welkin. The nationalised railways produced their best accommodation. Commissar Lunacharsky delivered a flowery harangue. Commissar Litvinoff, unmindful of the food queues in the back-streets, prepared a sumptuous banquet; and Arch Commissar Stalin, 'the man of steel,' flung open the closely-guarded sanctuaries of the Kremlin, and pushing aside his morning's budget of death warrants, and *lettres de cachet*, received his guests with smiles of overflowing comradeship.

Ah! but we must not forget that the object of the visit was educational and investigatory. How important for our public figures to probe for themselves the truth about Russia: to find out by personal test how the Five Year Plan was working. How necessary to know whether Communism is really better than Capitalism, and how the broad masses of the Russian people fare in 'life, liberty and the pursuit of happiness' under the new régime. Who can grudge a few days devoted to these arduous tasks? To the aged Jester, with his frosty smile and safely-invested capital, it was a brilliant opportunity of dropping a series of disconcerting bricks upon the corns of his ardent hosts. And to Lady Astor, whose husband, according to the newspapers, had the week before been awarded three millions sterling returned taxation by the American Courts, all these communal fraternisings and sororisings must have been a pageant of delight. But it is the brightest hours that flash away the fastest.

Great Contemporaries, 1937

10 May 1940

During these last crowded days of the political crisis my pulse had not quickened at any moment. I took it all as it came. But I cannot conceal from the reader of this truthful account that as I went to bed at about 3 a.m., I was conscious of a profound sense of relief. At last I had the authority to give directions over the whole scene. I felt as if I were walking with destiny, and all my past life had been but a preparation for this hour and for this trial. Eleven years in the political wilderness had freed me from ordinary Party antagonisms. My warnings over the last six years had been so numerous, so detailed, and were now so terribly vindicated, that no one could gainsay me. I could not be reproached either for making the war or with want of preparation for it. I thought I knew a good deal about it all, and I was sure I should not fail. Therefore, although impatient for the morning, I slept soundly and had no need for cheering dreams. Facts are better than dreams.

The Second World War, vol. i, 1948

G. K. CHESTERTON
1874–1936

Grey Skies and Mean Landscapes

This is the true light in which to regard Browning as an artist. He had determined to leave no spot of the cosmos unadorned by his poetry which he could find it possible to adorn. An admirable example can be found in that splendid poem 'Childe Roland to the Dark Tower came.' It is the hint of an entirely new and curious type of poetry, the poetry of the shabby and hungry aspect of the earth itself. Daring poets who wished to escape from conventional gardens and orchards had long been in the habit of celebrating the poetry of rugged and gloomy landscapes, but Browning is not content with this. He insists upon celebrating the poetry of mean landscapes. That sense of scrubbiness in nature, as of a man unshaved, had never been conveyed with this enthusiasm and primeval gusto before.

If there pushed any ragged thistle-stalk
  Above its mates, the head was chopped; the bents
  Were jealous else. What made those holes and rents
In the dock's harsh swarth leaves, bruised as to baulk
All hope of greenness? 'tis a brute must walk
  Pashing their life out, with a brute's intents.

This is a perfect realisation of that eerie sentiment which comes upon us, not so often among mountains and water-falls, as it does on some half-starved common at twilight, or in walking down some grey mean street. It is the song of the beauty of refuse; and Browning was the first to sing it. Oddly enough it has been one of the poems about which most of those pedantic and trivial questions have been asked, which are asked invariably by those who treat Browning as a science instead of a poet, 'What does the poem of "Childe Roland" mean?' The only genuine answer to this is, 'What does anything mean?' Does the earth mean nothing? Do grey skies and wastes covered with thistles mean nothing? Does an old horse turned out to graze mean nothing? If it does, there is but one further truth to be added—that everything means nothing.

Robert Browning, 1902

On Going Back to First Principles

Suppose that a great commotion arises in the street about something, let us say a lamp-post, which many influential persons desire to pull down. A grey-clad monk, who is the spirit of the Middle Ages, is approached upon the matter, and begins to say, in the arid manner of the Schoolmen, 'Let us first of all consider, my brethren, the value of Light. If Light be in itself good——' At this point he is somewhat excusably knocked down. All the people make a rush for the lamp-post, the lamp-post is down in ten minutes, and they go about congratulating each other on their unmediaeval practicality. But as things go on they do not work out so easily. Some people have pulled the lamp-post down because they wanted the electric light; some because they wanted old iron; some because they wanted darkness, because their deeds were evil. Some thought it not enough of a lamp-post, some too much; some acted because they wanted to smash municipal machinery; some because they wanted to smash something. And there is war in the night, no man knowing whom he strikes. So, gradually and inevitably, to-day, to-morrow, or the next day, there comes back the conviction that the monk was right after all, and that all depends on what is the philosophy of Light. Only what we might have discussed under the gas-lamp, we now must discuss in the dark.

Heretics, 1906

Dickens and Greatness of Character

If we are to look for lessons, here at least is the last and deepest lesson of Dickens. It is in our own daily life that we are to look for the portents and the prodigies. This is the truth, not merely of the fixed figures of our life; the wife, the husband, the fool that fills the sky. It is true of the whole stream and substance of our daily experience; every instant we reject a great fool merely because he is foolish. Every day we neglect Tootses and Swivellers, Guppys and Joblings, Simmerys and Flashers. Every day we lose the last sight of Jobling and Chuckster, the Analytical Chemist, or the Marchioness. Every day we are missing a monster whom we might easily love, and an imbecile whom we should certainly admire. This is the real gospel of Dickens; the inexhaustible opportunities offered by the liberty and the variety of man. Compared with this life, all public life, all fame, all wisdom, is by its nature cramped and cold and small. For on that defined and lighted public stage men are of necessity forced to profess one set of accomplishments, to rise to one rigid standard. It is the utterly unknown people, who can grow in all directions like an exuberant tree. It is in our interior lives that we find that people are too much themselves. It is in our private life that we find them swelling into the enormous contours, and taking on the colours of caricature. Many of us live publicly with featureless public puppets, images of the small public abstractions. It is when we pass our own private gate, and open our own secret door, that we step into the land of the giants.

Charles Dickens, 1906

The House of Reason

They paused for a few minutes only to stuff down coffee and coarse thick sandwiches at a coffee stall, and then made their way across the river, which under the grey and growing light looked as desolate as Acheron. They reached the bottom of the huge block of buildings which they had seen from across the river, and began in silence to mount the naked and numberless stone steps, only pausing now and then to make short remarks on the rail of the banisters. At about every other flight they passed a window; each window showed them a pale and tragic dawn lifting itself laboriously over London. From each the innumerable roofs of slate looked like the leaden surges of a grey, troubled sea after rain. Syme was increasingly conscious that his new adventure had somehow a quality of cold sanity worse than the wild adventures of the past. Last night, for instance, the tall tenements had seemed to him like a tower in a dream. As he now went up the weary and perpetual steps, he was daunted and bewildered by their almost infinite series. But it was not the hot horror of a dream or of anything that might be exaggeration or delusion. Their infinity was more like the empty infinity of arithmetic, something unthinkable, yet necessary to thought. Or it was like the stunning statements of astronomy about the distance of the fixed stars. He was ascending the house of reason, a thing more hideous than unreason itself.

The Man Who Was Thursday, 1908

A Duel with a Difference

The Marquis put up his hand with a curious air of ghastly patience.

'Please let me speak,' he said. 'It is rather important. Mr Syme,' he continued, turning to his opponent, 'we are fighting to-day, if I remember right, because you expressed a wish (which I thought irrational) to pull my nose. Would you oblige me by pulling my nose now as quickly as possible? I have to catch a train.'

'I protest that this is most irregular,' said Dr Bull indignantly . . .

'Will you or will you not pull my nose?' said the Marquis in exasperation. 'Come, come, Mr Syme! You wanted to do it, do it! You can have no conception of how important it is to me. Don't be so selfish! Pull my nose at once, when I ask you!' and he bent slightly forward with a fascinating smile. The Paris train, panting and groaning, had grated into a little station behind the neighbouring hill.

Syme had the feeling he had more than once had in these adventures—the sense that a horrible and sublime wave lifted to heaven was just toppling over. Walking in a world he half understood, he took two paces forward and seized the Roman nose of this remarkable nobleman. He pulled it hard, and it came off in his hand.

The Man Who Was Thursday

Evolution and Morality

Darwinism can be used to back up two mad moralities, but it cannot be used to back up a single sane one. The kinship and competition of all living creatures can be used as a reason for being insanely cruel or insanely sentimental; but not for a healthy love of animals. On the evolutionary basis you may be inhumane, or you may be absurdly humane; but you cannot be human. That you and a tiger are one may be a reason for being tender to a tiger. Or it may be a reason for being as cruel as the tiger. It is one way to train the tiger to imitate you, it is a shorter way to imitate the tiger. But in neither case does evolution tell you how to treat a tiger reasonably, that is, to admire his stripes while avoiding his claws.

If you want to treat a tiger reasonably, you must go back to the garden of Eden. For the obstinate reminder continues to recur: only the supernaturalist has taken a sane view of Nature. The essence of all pantheism, evolutionism, and modern cosmic religion is really in this proposition: that Nature is our mother. Unfortunately, if you regard Nature as a mother, you discover that she is a step-mother. The main point of Christianity was this: that Nature is not our mother: Nature is our sister. We can be proud of her beauty, since we have the same father; but she has no authority over us; we have to admire, but not to imitate.

Orthodoxy, 1908

A Trek through North London

The yellow omnibus crawled up the northern roads for what seemed like hours on end; the great detective would not explain further, and perhaps his assistants felt a silent and growing doubt of his errand. Perhaps, also, they felt a silent and growing desire for lunch, for the hours crept long past the normal luncheon hour, and the long roads of the North London suburbs seemed to shoot out into length after length like an infernal telescope. It was one of those journeys on which a man perpetually feels that now at last he must have come to the end of the universe, and then finds he has only come to the beginning of Tufnell Park.

'The Blue Cross', *The Innocence of Father Brown*, 1911

ELLEN GLASGOW
1874–1945

A Perfect Wife

After thirty years of married happiness, he could still remind himself that Victoria was endowed with every charm except the thrilling touch of human frailty. Though her perfection discouraged pleasures, especially the pleasures of love, he had learned in time to feel the pride of a husband in her natural frigidity. For he still clung, amid the decay of moral platitudes, to the discredited ideal of chivalry. In his youth the world was suffused with the after-glow of the long Victorian age, and a graceful feminine style had softened the manners, if not the natures, of men. At the end of that interesting epoch, when womanhood was exalted from a biological fact into a miraculous power, Virginius Littlepage, the younger son of an old and affluent family, had married Victoria Brooke, the grand-daughter of a tobacco planter, who had made a satisfactory fortune by forsaking his plantation and converting tobacco into cigarettes. While Virginius had been trained by stern tradition to respect every woman who had not stooped to folly, the virtue peculiar to her sex was among the least of his reasons for admiring Victoria. She was not only modest, which was usual in the 'nineties, but she was beautiful, which is unusual in any decade. In the beginning of their acquaintance he had gone even further and ascribed intellect to her; but a few months of marriage had shown this to be merely one of the many delusions created by perfect features and a noble expression. Everything about her had been smooth and definite, even the tones of her voice and the way her light brown hair, which she wore à la Pompadour, was rolled stiffly back from her forehead and coiled in a burnished rope on the top of her head. A serious young man, ambitious to attain a place in the world more brilliant than the secluded seat of his ancestors, he had been impressed at their first meeting by the compactness and precision of Victoria's orderly mind. For in that earnest period the minds, as well as the emotions, of lovers were orderly. It was an age when eager young men flocked to church on Sunday morning, and eloquent divines discoursed upon the Victorian poets in the middle of the week. He could afford to smile now when he recalled the solemn Browning class in which he had first lost his heart. How passionately he had admired Victoria's virginal features! How fervently he had envied her competent but caressing way with the poet! Incredible as it seemed to him now, he had fallen in love with her while she recited from the more ponderous passages in *The Ring and the Book*. He had fallen in love with her then, though he had never really enjoyed Browning, and it had been a relief to him when the Unseen, in company with its illustrious poet, had at last gone out of fashion. Yet, since he was disposed to admire all the qualities he did not possess, he had never ceased to respect the firmness with which Victoria continued to deal in other forms with the Absolute. As the placid years passed, and she came to rely less upon her virginal features, it seemed to him that the ripe opinions of her youth began to shrink and flatten as fruit does that has hung too long on the tree. She had never changed, he realized, since he had first known her; she had become merely riper, softer, and sweeter in nature. Her advantage rested where advantage never fails to rest, in moral fervour. To be invariably right was her single wifely failing. For his wife, he sighed, with the vague unrest of a husband whose infidelities are imaginary, was a genuinely good woman. She was as far removed from pretence as she was from the posturing virtues that flourish in the credulous world of the drama. The pity of it was that even the least exacting husband should so often desire something more piquant than goodness.

They Stooped to Folly, 1929

W. SOMERSET MAUGHAM
1874–1965

The Out-Patients' Department

On the whole the impression was neither of tragedy nor of comedy. There was no describing it. It was manifold and various; there were tears and laughter, happiness and woe; it was tedious and interesting and indifferent; it was as you saw it; it was tumultuous and passionate; it was grave; it was sad and comic; it was trivial; it was simple and complex; joy was there and despair; the love of mothers for their children, and of men for women;

lust trailed itself through the rooms with leaden feet, punishing the guilty and the innocent, helpless wives and wretched children; drink seized men and women and cost its inevitable price; death sighed in these rooms; and the beginning of life, filling some poor girl with terror and shame, was diagnosed there. There was neither good nor bad there. There were just facts. It was life.

Of Human Bondage, 1915

A Disarming Novelist

And what, after all, can it be other than modesty that makes him even now write to the reviewers of his books, thanking them for their praise, and ask them to luncheon? Nay, more: when someone has written a stinging criticism and Roy, especially since his reputation became so great, has had to put up with some very virulent abuse, he does not, like most of us, shrug his shoulders, fling a mental insult at the ruffian who does not like our work, and then forget about it; he writes a long letter to his critic, telling him that he is very sorry he thought his book bad, but his review was so interesting in itself, and if he might venture to say so, showed so much critical sense and so much feeling for words, that he felt bound to write to him. No one is more anxious to improve himself than he, and he hopes he is still capable of learning. He does not want to be a bore, but if the critic has nothing to do on Wednesday or Friday will he come and lunch at the Savoy and tell him why exactly he thought his book so bad? No one can order a lunch better than Roy, and generally by the time the critic has eaten half a dozen oysters and a cut from a saddle of baby lamb, he has eaten his words too. It is only poetic justice that when Roy's next novel comes out the critic should see in the new work a very great advance.

Cakes and Ale, 1930

GERTRUDE STEIN
1874–1946

'The Trail of the Lonesome Pine'

Among the other young men who came to the house at the time when they came in such numbers was Bravig Imbs. We liked Bravig, even though as Gertrude Stein said, his aim was to please. It was he who brought Elliot Paul to the house and Elliot Paul brought transition.

We had liked Bravig Imbs but we liked Elliot Paul more. He was very interesting. Elliot Paul was a new englander but he was a saracen, a saracen such as you sometimes see in the villages of France where the strain from some Crusading ancestor's dependents still survives. Elliot Paul was such a one. He had an element not of mystery but of evanescence, actually little by little he appeared and then as slowly he disappeared, and Eugene Jolas and Maria Jolas appeared. These once having appeared, stayed in their appearance.

Elliot Paul was at that time working on the Paris Chicago Tribune and he was there writing a series of articles on the work of Gertrude Stein, the first seriously popular estimation of her work. At the same time he was turning the young journalists and proof-readers into writers. He started Bravig Imbs on his first book, The Professor's Wife, by stopping him suddenly in his talk and saying, you begin there. He did the same thing for others. He played the accordion as nobody else not native to the accordion could play it and he learned and played for Gertrude Stein accompanied on the violin by Bravig Imbs, Gertrude Stein's favourite ditty, The Trail of the Lonesome Pine, My name is June and very very soon.

The Trail of the Lonesome Pine as a song made a lasting appeal to Gertrude Stein. Mildred Aldrich had it among her records and when we spent the afternoon with her at Huiry, Gertrude Stein inevitably would start the Trail of the Lonesome Pine on the phonograph and play it and play it. She liked it in itself and she had been fascinated during the war with the magic of The Trail of the Lonesome Pine as a book for the doughboy. How often when a doughboy in hospital had become particularly fond of her, he would say, I once read a great book, do you know it, it is called The Trail of the Lonesome Pine. They finally got a copy of it in the camp at Nimes and it stayed by the bedside of every sick soldier. They did not read much of it, as far as she could make out sometimes only a paragraph, in the course of several days, but their voices were husky when they spoke of it, and when they were particularly devoted to her they would offer to lend her this very dirty and tattered copy.

She reads anything and naturally she read this and she was puzzled. It had practically no story to it and it was not exciting, or adventurous, and it was very well written and was mostly description of mountain scenery. Later on she came across some reminiscences of a southern woman who told how the mountaineers in the southern army during the civil war used to wait in turn to read Victor Hugo's Les Miserables, an equally astonishing thing for again there is not much of a story and a great deal of description. However Gertrude Stein admits that she loves the song of The Trail of the Lonesome Pine in the same way that the doughboy loved the book and Elliot Paul played it for her on the accordion.

The Autobiography of Alice B. Toklas, 1933

CLARENCE DAY

1874–1935

A Respectable Faith

My father's ideas of religion seemed straightforward and simple. He had noticed when he was a boy that there were buildings called churches; he had accepted them as a natural part of the surroundings in which he had been born. He would never have invented such things himself. Nevertheless they were here. As he grew up he regarded them as unquestioningly as he did banks. They were substantial old structures, they were respectable, decent, and venerable. They were frequented by the right sort of people. Well, that was enough.

On the other hand he never allowed churches—or banks—to dictate to him. He gave each the respect that was due to it from his point of view; but he also expected from each of them the respect he felt due to him.

As to creeds, he knew nothing about them, and cared nothing either; yet he seemed to know which sect he belonged with. It had to be a sect with the minimum of nonsense about it; no total immersion, no exhorters, no holy confession. He would have been a Unitarian, naturally, if he'd lived in Boston. Since he was a respectable New Yorker, he belonged in the Episcopal Church.

As to living a spiritual life, he never tackled that problem. Some men who accept spiritual beliefs try to live up to them daily: other men, who reject such beliefs, try sometimes to smash them. My father would have disagreed with both kinds entirely. He took a more distant attitude. It disgusted him when atheists attacked religion: he thought they were vulgar. But he also objected to have religion make demands upon him—he felt that religion too was vulgar, when it tried to stir up men's feelings. It had its own proper field of activity, and it was all right there, of course; but there was one place religion should let alone, and that was a man's soul. He especially loathed any talk of walking hand in hand with his Saviour. And if he had ever found the Holy Ghost trying to soften his heart, he would have regarded Its behavior as distinctly uncalled for; even ungentlemanly.

God and My Father, 1932

FORREST REID
1875–1947

A Small Boy's First Books

What seems to me really astonishing is that I cannot remember being taught to read; though I can remember quite well when I couldn't read; for I have a clear recollection of lying on my stomach on the parlour floor, a book open in front of me, along whose printed and meaningless lines I drew my finger, turning page after page till the last was reached. It seems now a singularly dull pastime, but it was at least better than being read to by my father, who chose only stories with a moral in them—edifying histories of 'ministering children' whom I loathed. The last of these sanctimonious tales I listened to was called *Cassy*. I particularly disliked *Cassy*—not because the heroine was more pious than the other small heroes and heroines I was accustomed to—but because of a scene in which she entered an empty house at night and discovered a corpse there. This gruesome adventure had an effect on my mind that for several days made me extremely reluctant to go upstairs after dark by myself. But *Jessica's First Prayer*, *Vinegar Hill*, *The Golden Ladder*, though not terrifying, were equally depressing. Every Sunday after dinner my father would take down some such volume from the shelf, open it, and put on his spectacles. Holding the book at a long distance from his eyes, he would read aloud in an unanimated voice, while I sat listening, in a mood of sullen antipathy; for on Sundays this was my only relaxation—I was not allowed to play the most innocent game, or even go for a walk. These lachrymose stories were full of the conversions of priggish children—of harrowing scenes in gin-palaces and squalid city dens. Some of them were written to inculcate temperance, some were written round the Ten Commandments, some to illustrate the petitions in the Lord's Prayer. They contained not the faintest glimmer of life or imagination; from cover to cover they were ugly, dull, stupid—filled with sickness, poverty and calamity. On the afternoon when *Cassy's* successor was produced I rebelled, and in a sudden passion snatched the book out of my father's hands and flung it on the fire. I was whipped and sent to bed, but anything was better than *Vinegar Hill*, and next Sunday also I refused to listen. This time I was not beaten, only locked up in my bedroom: and really I had triumphed, for when the fateful day came round once more the bookcase was not opened, and I had never again to listen to one of those dismal stories.

Fairy stories and animal stories were what I liked best. *The Comical Doings of a Conger Eel* I read over to myself till I knew it nearly by heart, and some of the old nursery rhymes had a mysterious fascination.

How many miles to Babylon?
Three score and ten.
Can I get there by candlelight?—
Yes, and back again.

And I did get there. Was it something in the word 'candlelight' that evoked a definite picture of an old fantastic city of towers and turrets, lit by waving candle-flames, and with the windows all ablaze in dark tall houses?

Many of these rhymes had this property of picture-making:

Hey, diddle diddle,
The cat and the fiddle,
The cow jumped over the moon;
The little dog laughed
To see such sport,
When the dish ran away with the spoon.

Pure nonsense—yet the magic was there. Before and after the cow made her amazing leap the stuff was a mere jingle: it was the word 'moon' that brought up the picture; and I saw the white docile beast abruptly transformed, pricked by some sting of midsummer madness, with lowered head and long curling horns, pawing the ground restlessly, while a round glowing harvest moon hung like a Chinese lantern in the sky.

Peter Waring, 1937 (revised version of *Following Darkness*, 1912)

JACK LONDON
1876–1916

An Old Song

It seemed the ordained order of things that dogs should work. All day they swung up and down the main street in long teams, and in the night their jingling bells still went by. They hauled cabin logs and firewood, freighted up to the mines, and did all manner of work that horses did in the Santa Clara Valley. Here and there Buck met Southland dogs, but in the main they were the wild wolf husky breed. Every night, regularly, at nine, at twelve, at three, they lifted a nocturnal song, a weird and eerie chant, in which it was Buck's delight to join.

With the aurora borealis flaming coldly overhead, or the stars leaping in the frost dance, and the land numb and frozen under its pall of snow, this song of the huskies might have been the defiance of life, only it was pitched in minor key, with long-drawn wailings and half-sobs, and was more the pleading of life, the articulate travail of existence. It was an old song, old as the breed itself—one of the first songs of the younger world in a day when songs were sad. It was invested with the woe of unnumbered generations, this plaint by which Buck was so strangely stirred. When he moaned and sobbed, it was with the pain of living that was of old the pain of his wild fathers, and the fear and mystery of the cold and dark that was to them fear and mystery. And that he should be stirred by it marked the completeness with which he harked back through the ages of fire and roof to the raw beginnings of life in the howling ages.

The Call of the Wild, 1903

G. M. TREVELYAN
1876–1962

The Laws of Historical Science

To bring the matter to the test, what are the 'laws' which historical 'science' has discovered in the last forty years, since it cleared the laboratory of those wretched 'literary historians'? Medea has successfully put the old man into the pot, but I fail to see the fine youth whom she promised us.

'Clio, A Muse', 1913

A Famous Victory

As one who ardently desires the abolition of war, I regret that the well-meaning poet who sang long ago of 'old Kaspar' was not historically better informed. To choose Blenheim as an example of a useless waste of blood and treasure was unfortunate, for it was one of the few battles thoroughly worth fighting. 'What they killed each other for'! Why, to save us all from belonging to the French king, who had at that moment got Spain, Italy, Belgium and half Germany in his pocket. To prevent Western Europe from sinking under a Czardom inspired by the Jesuits. To make the 'Sun King's' system of despotism and religious persecution look so weak and silly beside English freedom that all the philosophers and wits of the new century would make mock of it. Who would have listened to Voltaire and Rousseau, or even to Montesquieu, if Blenheim had gone the other way, and the Grand Monarch had been gathered in glory to the grave? We are always telling ourselves 'how England saved Europe' from Napoleon—truly enough, though incidentally we handed her over to taskmasters scarcely less abominable. But we hear very little of 'how England saved Europe' from Louis XIV. How many Englishmen have ever visited Blenheim? It is as good a field as Waterloo, though a little farther off in time and space, and it still lies undisfigured by monuments, its villages and fields still as old Kaspar knew them, between the wooded hills above and the reedy islands of slow-moving Danube, into which Tallard's Horse were driven headlong on that day of deliverance to mankind.

'Clio, A Muse'

SHERWOOD ANDERSON

1876–1941

A Passionate Restlessness

During the early fall of her twenty-seventh year a passionate restlessness took possession of Alice. She could not bear to be in the company of the drug clerk, and when, in the evening, he came to walk with her she sent him away. Her mind became intensely active and when, weary from the long hours of standing behind the counter in the store, she went home and crawled into bed, she could not sleep. With staring eyes she looked into the darkness. Her imagination, like a child awakened from long sleep, played about the room. Deep within her there was something that would not be cheated by phantasies and that demanded some definite answer from life.

Alice took a pillow into her arms and held it tightly against her breasts. Getting out of bed, she arranged a blanket so that in the darkness it looked like a form lying between the sheets and, kneeling beside the bed, she caressed it, whispering words over and over, like a refrain. 'Why doesn't something happen? Why am I left here alone?' she muttered. Although she sometimes thought of Ned Currie, she no longer depended on him. Her desire had grown vague. She did not want Ned Currie or any other man. She wanted to be loved, to have something answer the call that was growing louder and louder within her.

And then one night when it rained Alice had an adventure. It frightened and confused her. She had come home from the store at nine and found the house empty. Bush Milton had gone off to town and her mother to the house of a neighbor. Alice went upstairs to her room and undressed in the darkness. For a moment she stood by the window hearing the rain beat against the glass and then a strange desire took possession of her. Without stopping to think of what she intended to do, she ran downstairs through the dark house and out into the rain. As she stood on the little grass plot before the house and felt the cold rain on her body a mad desire to run naked through the streets took possession of her.

She thought that the rain would have some creative and wonderful effect on her body. Not for years had she felt so full of youth and courage. She wanted to leap and run, to cry out, to find some other lonely human and embrace him. On the brick sidewalk before the house a man stumbled homeward. 'Alice started to run. A wild, desperate mood took possession of her. 'What do I care who it is. He is alone, and I will go to him,' she thought; and then without stopping to consider the possible result of her madness, called softly. 'Wait!' she cried. 'Don't go away. Whoever you are, you must wait.'

The man on the sidewalk stopped and stood listening. He was an old man and somewhat deaf. Putting his hand to his mouth, he shouted: 'What? What say?' he called.

Alice dropped to the ground and lay trembling. She was so frightened at the thought of what she had done that when the man had gone on his way she did not dare get to her feet, but crawled on hands and knees through the grass to the house. When she got to her own room she bolted the door and drew her dressing table across the doorway. Her body shook as with a chill and her hands trembled so that she had difficulty getting into her nightdress. When she got into bed she buried her face in the pillow and wept broken-heartedly. 'What is the matter with me? I will do something dreadful if I am not careful,' she thought, and turning her face to the wall, began trying to force herself to face bravely the fact that many people must live and die alone, even in Winesburg.

Winesburg, Ohio, 1919

WILLA CATHER
1876–1947

A Small Town in Nebraska

If I loitered on the playground after school, or went to the post-office for the mail and lingered to hear the gossip about the cigar-stand, it would be growing dark by the time I came home. The sun was gone; the frozen streets stretched long and blue before me; the lights were shining pale in kitchen windows, and I could smell the suppers cooking as I passed. Few people were abroad, and each one of them was hurrying toward a fire. The glowing stoves in the houses were like magnets. When one passed an old man, one could see nothing of his face but a red nose sticking out between a frosted beard and a long plush cap. The young men capered along with their hands in their pockets, and sometimes tried a slide on the icy sidewalk. The children, in their bright hoods and comforters, never walked, but always ran from the moment they left their door, beating their mittens against their sides. When I got as far as the Methodist Church, I was about halfway home. I can remember how glad I was when there happened to be a light in the church, and the painted glass window shone out at us as we came along the frozen street. In the winter bleakness a hunger for colour came over people, like the Laplander's craving for fats and sugar. Without knowing why, we used to linger on the sidewalk outside the church when the lamps were lighted early for choir practice or prayer-meeting, shivering and talking until our feet were like lumps of ice. The crude reds and greens and blues of that coloured glass held us there.

My Ántonia, 1918

The End of the Old West

'Hullo, Niel. Thought I couldn't be mistaken.'

Niel looked up and saw the red, bee-stung face, with its two permanent dimples, smiling down at him in contemptuous jocularity.

'Hello, Ivy. I couldn't be mistaken in you, either.'

'Coming home to go into business?'

Niel replied that he was coming only for the summer vacation.

'Oh, you're not through school yet? I suppose it takes longer to make an architect than it does to make a shyster. Just as well; there's not much building going on in Sweet Water these days. You'll find a good many changes.'

'Won't you sit down?' Niel indicated the neighbouring chair. 'You are practising law?'

'Yes, along with a few other things. Have to keep more than one iron in the fire to make a living with us. I farm a little on the side. I rent that meadow-land on the Forrester place. I've drained the old marsh and put it into wheat. My brother John does the work, and I boss the job. It's quite profitable. I pay them a good rent, and they need it. I doubt if they could get along without. Their influential friends don't seem to help them out much. Remember all those chesty old boys the Captain used to drive about in his democrat wagon, and ship in barrels of Bourbon for? Good deal of bluff about all those old-timers. The panic put them out of the game. The Forresters have come down in the world like the rest. You remember how the old man used to put it over us kids and not let us carry a gun in there? I'm just mean enough to like to shoot along that creek a little better than anywhere else, now. There wasn't any harm in the old Captain, but he had the delusion of grandeur. He's happier now that he's like the rest of us and don't have to change his shirt every day.' Ivy's unblinking greenish eyes rested upon Niel's haberdashery.

Niel, however, did not notice this. He knew that Ivy wanted him to show disappointment, and he was determined not to do so. He enquired about the Captain's health, pointedly keeping Mrs Forrester's name out of the conversation.

'He's only about half there . . . seems contented enough. . . . She takes good care of him, I'll say that for her. . . . She seeks consolation, always did, you know . . . too much French brandy . . . but she never neglects him. I don't blame her. Real work comes hard on her.'

Niel heard these remarks dully, through the buzz of an idea. He felt that Ivy had drained the marsh quite as much to spite him and Mrs Forrester as to reclaim the land. Moreover, he seemed to know that until this moment Ivy himself had not realized how much that consideration weighed with him. He and Ivy had disliked each other from childhood, blindly, instinctively, recognizing each other through antipathy, as hostile insects do. By draining the marsh Ivy had obliterated a few acres of something he hated, though he could not name it, and had asserted his power over the people who had loved those unproductive meadows for their idleness and silvery beauty.

After Ivy had gone on into the smoker, Niel sat looking out at the windings of the Sweet Water and playing with his idea. The Old West had been settled by dreamers, great-hearted adventurers who were unpractical to the point of magnificence; a courteous brotherhood, strong in attack but weak in defence, who could conquer but could not hold. Now all the vast territory they had won was to be at the mercy of men like Ivy Peters, who had never dared anything, never risked anything. They would drink up the mirage, dispel the morning freshness, root out the great brooding spirit of freedom, the generous, easy life of the great land-holders. The space, the colour, the princely carelessness of the pioneer they would destroy and cut up into profitable bits, as the match factory splinters the primeval forest. All the way from the Missouri to the mountains this generation of shrewd young men, trained to petty economies by hard times, would do exactly what Ivy Peters had done when he drained the Forrester marsh.

A Lost Lady, 1923

JAMES AGATE
1877–1947

A Music-Hall Sketch

The first of Mr Carney's two 'song-scenas' is a study of grandeur and decadence, of magnificence on its last legs, dandyism in the gutter, pride surviving its fall; in plain English, a tale of that wreckage of the Embankment which was once a gentleman. He wears a morning coat which, in spite of irremediable tatters, has obviously known the sunshine of Piccadilly, has yet some hang of nobility. The torn trousers still wear their plaid with an air. *Enfin*, the fellow was at one time gloved and booted. There is something authentic, something inherited, something ghostly about this seedy figure. Trailing clouds of glory he haunts the Embankment. The ebony cane, the eyeglass with the watered ribbon, the grey topper of the wide and curling brim—all these fond accoutrements of fashion bring back the delightful 'nineties, so closely are they the presentment, the counterfeit presentment, of the swell of those days. 'Bancroft to the life!' we mutter. And our mind goes back to that bygone London of violet nights and softly-jingling hansom cabs, discreet lacquer and harness of cheerful brass—nocturnes, if ever such things were, in black and gold—the London of yellow asters and green carnations; of a long-gloved *diseuse*, and, in the photographer's window, a delicious Mrs Patrick Campbell eating something awesomely expensive off the same plate as Mr George Alexander; of a hard-working Max with one volume of stern achievement and all Time before him; of a Café Royal where poets and not yet bookmakers foregathered; of a score of music-halls which were not for the young person . . . But I am getting away from Mr Carney.

Immoment Toys, 1945

EDWARD THOMAS
1878–1918

A Welsh Interior

Having passed the ruined abbey and the orchard, I came to a long, low farmhouse kitchen, smelling of bacon and herbs and burning sycamore and ash. A gun, a blunderbuss, a pair of silver spurs, and a golden spray of last year's corn hung over the high mantelpiece and its many brass candlesticks; and beneath was an open fireplace and a perpetual red fire, and two teapots warming, for they had tea for breakfast, tea for dinner, tea for tea, tea for supper, and tea between. The floor was of sanded slate flags, and on them a long many-legged table, an oak settle, a table piano, and some Chippendale chairs. There were also two tall clocks; and they were the most human clocks I ever met, for they ticked with effort and uneasiness: they seemed to think and sorrow over time, as if they caused it, and did not go on thoughtlessly or impudently like most clocks, which are insufferable; they found the hours troublesome and did not twitter mechanically over them; and at midnight the twelve strokes always nearly ruined them, so great was the effort. On the wall were a large portrait of Spurgeon, several sets of verses printed and framed in memory of dead members of the family, an allegorical tree watered by the devil, and photographs of a bard and of Mr Lloyd George. There were about fifty well-used books near the fire, and two or three men smoking, and one man reading some serious book aloud, by the only lamp; and a white girl was carrying out the week's baking, of large loaves, flat fruit tarts of blackberry, apple, and whinberry, plain golden cakes, soft currant biscuits, and curled oat cakes. And outside, the noises of a west wind and a flooded stream, the whimper of an otter, and the long, slow laugh of an owl; and always silent, but never forgotten, the restless, towering outline of a mountain.

Beautiful Wales, 1905

A Misty Day

The ridges of trees high in the mist are very grim. The isolated trees stand cloaked in conspiracies here and there about the fields. The houses, even whole villages, are translated into terms of unreality as if they were carved in air and could not be touched; they are empty and mournful as skulls or churches. There is no life visible; for the ploughman and the cattle are figures of light dream. All is soft and grey. The land has drunken the opiate mist and is passing slowly and unreluctantly into perpetual sleep. Trees and houses are drowsed beyond awakening or farewell. The mind also is infected, and gains a sort of ease from the thought that an eternal and universal rest is at hand without any cry or any pain.

The South Country, 1909

E. M. FORSTER
1879–1970

Inexplicable City

Certainly London fascinates. One visualises it as a tract of quivering grey, intelligent without purpose, and excitable without love; as a spirit that has altered before it can be chronicled; as a heart that certainly beats, but with no pulsation of humanity. It lies beyond everything: Nature, with all her cruelty, comes nearer to us than do these crowds of men. A friend explains himself: the earth is explicable—from her we came, and we must return to her. But who can explain Westminster Bridge Road or Liverpool Street in the morning—the city inhaling—or the same thoroughfares in the evening—the city exhaling her exhausted air? We reach in desperation beyond the fog, beyond the very stars, the voids of the universe are ransacked to justify the monster, and stamped with a human face. London is religion's opportunity—not the decorous religion of theologians, but anthropomorphic, crude. Yes, the continuous flow would be tolerable if a man of our own sort—not anyone pompous or tearful—were caring for us up in the sky.

The Londoner seldom understands his city until it sweeps him, too, away from his moorings, and Margaret's eyes were not opened until the lease of Wickham Place expired. She had always known that it must expire, but the knowledge only became vivid about nine months before the event. Then the house was suddenly ringed with pathos. It had seen so much happiness. Why had it to be swept away? In the streets of the city she noted for the first time the architecture of hurry, and heard the language of hurry on the mouths of its inhabitants—clipped words, formless sentences, potted expressions of approval or disgust. Month by month things were stepping livelier, but to what goal? The population still rose, but what was the quality of the men born? The particular millionaire who owned the freehold of Wickham Place, and desired to erect Babylonian flats upon it—what right had he to stir so large a portion of the quivering jelly? He was not a fool—she had heard him expose Socialism—but true insight began just where his intelligence ended, and one gathered that this was the case with most millionaires. What right had such men—— But Margaret checked herself. That way lies madness. Thank goodness she, too, had some money, and could purchase a new home.

Howards End, 1910

Ou-boum

Professor Godbole had never mentioned an echo; it never impressed him, perhaps. There are some exquisite echoes in India; there is the whisper round the dome at Bijapur; there are the long, solid sentences that voyage through the air at Mandu, and return unbroken to their creator. The echo in a Marabar cave is not like these, it is entirely devoid of distinction. Whatever is said, the same monotonous noise replies, and quivers up and down the walls until it is absorbed into the roof. 'Boum' is the sound as far as the human alphabet can express it, or 'bou-oum,' or 'ou-boum,'—utterly dull. Hope, politeness, the blowing of a nose, the squeak of a boot, all produce 'boum.' Even the striking of a match starts a little worm coiling, which is too small to complete a circle, but is eternally watchful. And if several people talk at once, an overlapping howling noise begins, echoes generate echoes, and the cave is stuffed with a snake composed of small snakes, which writhe independently.

After Mrs Moore all the others poured out. She had given the signal for the reflux. Aziz and Adela both emerged smiling and she did not want him to think his treat was a failure, so smiled too. As each person emerged she looked for a villain, but none was there, and she realized that she had been among the mildest individuals, whose only desire was to honour her, and that the naked pad was a poor little baby, astride its mother's hip. Nothing evil had been in the cave, but she had not enjoyed herself; no, she had not enjoyed herself, and she decided not to visit a second one.

'Did you see the reflection of his match—rather pretty?' asked Adela.

'I forget . . .'

'But he says this isn't a good cave, the best are on the Kawa Dol.'

'I don't think I shall go on to there. I dislike climbing.'

'Very well, let's sit down again in the shade until breakfast's ready.'

'Ah, but that'll disappoint him so; he has taken such trouble. You should go on; you don't mind.'

'Perhaps I ought to,' said the girl, indifferent to what she did, but desirous of being amiable.

The servants, etc., were scrambling back to the camp, pursued by grave censures from Mohammed Latif. Aziz came to help the guests over the rocks. He was at the summit of his powers, vigorous and humble, too sure of himself to resent criticism, and he was sincerely pleased when he heard they were altering his plans. 'Certainly, Miss Quested, so you and I will go together, and leave Mrs Moore here, and we will not be long, yet we will not hurry, because we know that will be her wish.'

'Quite right. I'm sorry not to come too, but I'm a poor walker.'

'Dear Mrs Moore, what does anything matter so long as you are my guests? I am very glad you are *not* coming, which sounds strange, but you are treating me with true frankness, as a friend.'

'Yes, I am your friend,' she said, laying her hand on his sleeve, and thinking, despite her fatigue, how very charming, how very good, he was, and how deeply she desired his happiness. 'So may I make another suggestion? Don't let so many people come with you this time. I think you may find it more convenient.'

'Exactly, exactly,' he cried, and, rushing to the other extreme, forbade all except one guide to accompany Miss Quested and him to the Kawa Dol. 'Is that all right?' he enquired.

'Quite right, now enjoy yourselves, and when you come back tell me all about it.' And she sank into the deck-chair.

If they reached the big pocket of caves, they would be away nearly an hour. She took out her writing-pad, and began, 'Dear Stella, Dear Ralph,' then stopped, and looked at the queer valley and their feeble invasion of it. Even the elephant had become a nobody. Her eye rose from it to the entrance tunnel. No, she did not wish to repeat that experience. The more she thought over it, the more disagreeable and frightening it became. She minded it much more now than at the time. The crush and the smells she could forget, but the echo began in some indescribable way to undermine her hold on life. Coming at a moment when she chanced to be fatigued, it had managed to murmur, 'Pathos, piety, courage—they exist, but are identical, and so is filth. Everything exists, nothing has value.' If one had spoken vileness in that place, or quoted lofty poetry, the comment would have been the same—'ou-boum.' If one had spoken with the tongues of angels and pleaded for all the unhappiness and misunderstanding in the world, past, present, and to come, for all the misery men must undergo whatever their opinion and position, and however much they dodge or bluff—it would amount to the same, the serpent would descend and return to the ceiling. Devils are of the North, and poems can be written about them, but no one could romanticize the Marabar because it robbed infinity and eternity of their vastness, the only quality that accommodates them to mankind.

She tried to go on with her letter, reminding herself that she was only an elderly woman who had got up too early in the morning and journeyed too far, that the despair creeping over her was merely her despair, her personal weakness, and that even if she got a sunstroke and went mad the rest of the world would go on. But suddenly, at the edge of her mind, Religion appeared, poor little talkative Christianity, and she knew that all its divine words from 'Let there be Light' to 'It is finished' only amounted to 'boum.' Then she was terrified over an area larger than usual; the universe, never comprehensible to her intellect, offered no repose to her soul, the mood of the last two months took definite form at last, and she realized that she didn't want to write to her children, didn't want to communicate with anyone, not even with God. She sat motionless with horror, and, when old Mohammed Latif came up to her, thought he would notice a difference. For a time she thought, 'I am going to be ill,' to comfort herself, then she surrendered to the vision. She lost all interest, even in Aziz, and the affectionate and sincere words that she had spoken to him seemed no longer hers but the air's.

A Passage to India, 1924

Intimidating the Generals

It is pleasant to be transferred from an office where one is afraid of a sergeant-major into an office where one can intimidate generals, and perhaps this is why History is so attractive to the more timid amongst us. We can recover self-confidence by snubbing the dead. The captains and the kings depart at our slightest censure, while as for the 'hosts of minor officials' who cumber court and camp, we heed them not, although in actual life they entirely block our social horizon. We cannot visit either the great or the rich when they are our contemporaries, but by a fortunate arrangement the palaces of Ujjain and the warehouses of Ormus are open for ever, and we can even behave outrageously in them without being expelled. The King of Ujjain, we announce, is extravagant, the merchants of Ormus unspeakably licentious . . . and sure enough Ormus is a desert now and Ujjain a jungle. Difficult to realize that the past was once the present, and that, transferred to it, one would be just the same little worm as to-day, unimportant, parasitic, nervous, occupied with trifles, unable to go anywhere or alter anything, friendly only with the obscure, and only at ease with the dead; while up on the heights the figures and forces who make History would contend in their habitual fashion, with incomprehensible noises or in ominous quiet. 'There is money in my house . . . there is no money . . . no house.' That is all that our sort can ever know about doom. The extravagant king, the licentious merchants—they escape, knowing the ropes.

'The Consolations of History', *Abinger Harvest*, 1936

JAMES BRANCH CABELL
1879–1958

Romance

Indeed, when I consider the race to which I have the honor to belong, I am filled with respectful wonder. . . . All about us flows and gyrates unceasingly the material universe,—an endless inconceivable jumble of rotatory blazing gas and frozen spheres and detonating comets, wherethrough spins Earth like a frail midge. And to this blown molecule adhere what millions and millions and millions of parasites just such as I am, begetting and dreaming and slaying and abnegating and toiling and making mirth, just as did aforetime those countless generations of our forebears, every one of whom was likewise a creature just such as I am! Were the human beings that have been subjected to confinement in flesh each numbered, as is customary in other penal institutes, with what interminable row of digits might one set forth your number, say, or mine?

Nor is this everything. For my reason, such as it is, perceives this race, in its entirety, in the whole outcome of its achievement, to be beyond all wording petty and ineffectual: and no more than thought can estimate the relative proportion to the material universe of our poor Earth, can thought conceive with what quintillionths to express that fractional part which I, as an individual parasite, add to Earth's negligible fretting by ephemerae.

And still—behold the miracle!—still I believe life to be a personal transaction between myself and Omnipotence; I believe that what I do is somehow of importance; and I believe that I am on a journey toward some very public triumph not unlike that of the third prince in the fairy-tale. . . . Even today I believe in this dynamic illusion. For that creed was the first great inspiration of the demiurge,—man's big romantic idea of Chivalry, of himself as his Father's representative in an alien country;—and it is a notion at which mere fact and reason yelp denial unavailingly. For every one of us is so constituted that he knows the romance to be true, and corporal fact and human reason in this matter, as in divers others, to be the suborned and perjured witnesses of 'realism.'

Beyond Life, 1919

LYTTON STRACHEY
1880–1932

Queen Victoria and Mr Gladstone

Unacceptable as Mr Gladstone's policy was, there was something else about him which was even more displeasing to Victoria. She disliked his personal demeanour towards herself. It was not that Mr Gladstone, in his intercourse with her, was in any degree lacking in courtesy or respect. On the contrary, an extraordinary reverence permeated his manner, both in his conversation and his correspondence with the Sovereign. Indeed, with that deep and passionate conservatism which, to the very end of his incredible career, gave such an unexpected colouring to his inexplicable character, Mr Gladstone viewed Victoria through a haze of awe which was almost religious—as a sacrosanct embodiment of venerable traditions—a vital element in the British Constitution—a Queen by Act of Parliament. But unfortunately the lady did not appreciate the compliment. The well-known complaint—'He speaks to me as if I were a public meeting'—whether authentic or no—and the turn of the sentence is surely a little too epigrammatic to be genuinely Victorian—undoubtedly expresses the essential element of her antipathy. She had no objection to being considered as an institution; she was one, and she knew it. But she was a woman too, and to be considered *only* as an institution—that was unbearable. And thus all Mr Gladstone's zeal and devotion, his ceremonious phrases, his low bows, his punctilious correctitudes, were utterly wasted; and when, in the excess of his loyalty, he went further, and imputed to the object of his veneration, with obsequious blindness, the subtlety of intellect, the wide reading, the grave enthusiasm, which he himself possessed, the misunderstanding became complete. The discordance between the actual Victoria and this strange Divinity made in Mr Gladstone's image produced disastrous results. Her discomfort and dislike turned at last into positive animosity, and, though her manners continued to be perfect, she never for a moment unbent; while he on his side was overcome with disappointment, perplexity, and mortification.

Yet his fidelity remained unshaken. When the Cabinet met, the Prime Minister, filled with his beatific vision, would open the proceedings by reading aloud the letters which he had received from the Queen upon the questions of the hour. The assembly sat in absolute silence while, one after another, the royal missives, with their emphases, their ejaculations, and their grammatical peculiarities, boomed forth in all the deep solemnity of Mr Gladstone's utterance. Not a single comment, of any kind, was ever hazarded; and, after a fitting pause, the Cabinet proceeded with the business of the day.

Queen Victoria, 1921

H. L. MENCKEN
1880–1956

The Metaphysician

A metaphysician is one who, when you remark that twice two makes four, demands to know what you mean by twice, what by two, what by makes, and what by four. For asking such questions metaphysicians are supported in oriental luxury in the universities, and respected as educated and intelligent men.

n.d.; first published, *A Mencken Chrestomathy*, 1949

Romantic Interlude

It is the close of a busy and vexatious day—say half past five or six o'clock of a Winter afternoon. I have had a cocktail or two, and am stretched out on a divan in front of a fire, smoking. At the edge of the divan, close enough for me to reach her with my hands, sits a woman not too young, but still good-looking and well-dressed—above all, a woman with a soft, low-pitched, agreeable voice. As I snooze she talks—of anything, everything, all the things that women talk of: books, music, dress, men, other women. No politics. No business. No theology. No metaphysics. Nothing challenging and vexatious—but remember, she is intelligent; what she says is clearly expressed, and often picturesquely. I observe the fine sheen of her hair, the pretty cut of her frock, the glint of her white teeth, the arch of her eyebrow, the graceful curve of her arm. I listen to the exquisite murmur of her voice. Gradually I fall asleep—but only for an instant. At once, observing it, she raises her voice ever so little, and I am awake. Then to sleep again—slowly and charmingly down that slippery hill of dreams. And then awake again, and then asleep again, and so on.

I ask you seriously: could anything be more unutterably beautiful? The sensation of falling asleep is to me the most delightful in the world. I relish it so much that I even look forward to death itself with a sneaking wonder and desire. Well, here is sleep poetized and made doubly sweet. Here is sleep set to the finest music in the world. I match this situation against any that you can think of. It is not only enchanting; it is also, in a very true sense, ennobling. In the end, when the lady grows prettily miffed and throws me out, I return to my sorrows somehow purged and glorified. I am a better man in my own sight. I have grazed upon the fields of asphodel. I have been genuinely, completely and unregrettably happy.

In Defense of Women, 1918

The Declaration of Independence in American

When things get so balled up that the people of a country got to cut loose from some other country, and go it on their own hook, without asking no permission from nobody, excepting maybe God Almighty, then they ought to let everybody know why they done it, so that everybody can see they are not trying to put nothing over on nobody.

All we got to say on this proposition is this: first, me and you is as good as anybody else, and maybe a damn sight better; second, nobody ain't got no right to take away none of our rights; third, every man has got a right to live, to come and go as he pleases, and to have a good time whichever way he likes, so long as he don't interfere with nobody else. That any government that don't give a man them rights ain't worth a damn; also, people ought to choose the kind of government they want themselves, and nobody else ought to have no say in the matter. That whenever any government don't do this, then the people have got a right to give it the bum's rush and put in one that will take care of their interests. Of course, that don't mean having a revolution every day like them South American yellow-bellies, or every time some jobholder goes to work and does something he ain't got no business to do. It is better to stand a little graft, etc., than to have revolutions all the time, like them coons, and any man that wasn't a anarchist or one of them IWW's would say the same. But when things get so bad that a man ain't hardly got no rights at all no more, but you might almost call him a slave, then everybody ought to get together and throw the grafters out, and put in new ones who won't carry on so high and steal so much, and then watch them. This is the proposition the people of these Colonies is up against, and they have got tired of it, and won't stand it no more.

The American Language (second edition, 1921)

Calvin Coolidge

The editorial writers who had the job of concocting mortuary tributes to the late Calvin Coolidge, LL D, made heavy weather of it, and no wonder. Ordinarily, an American public man dies by inches, and there is thus plenty of time to think up beautiful nonsense about him. More often than not, indeed, he threatens to die three or four times before he actually does so, and each threat gives the elegists a chance to mellow and adorn their effusions. But Dr Coolidge slipped out of life almost as quietly and as unexpectedly as he had originally slipped into public notice, and in consequence the brethren were caught napping and had to do their poetical embalming under desperate pressure. The common legend is that such pressure inflames and inspires a true journalist, and maketh him to sweat masterpieces, but it is not so in fact. Like any other literary man, he functions best when he is at leisure, and can turn from his tablets now and then to run down a quotation, to eat a plate of ham and eggs, or to look out of the window.

The general burden of the Coolidge memoirs was that the right hon. gentleman was a typical American, and some hinted that he was the most typical since Lincoln. As the English say, I find myself quite unable to associate myself with that thesis. He was, in truth, almost as unlike the average of his countrymen as if he had been born green. The Americano is an expansive fellow, a back-slapper, full of amiability; Coolidge was reserved and even muriatic. The Americano has a stupendous capacity for believing, and especially for believing in what is palpably not true; Coolidge was, in his fundamental metaphysics, an agnostic. The Americano dreams vast dreams, and is hag-ridden by a demon; Coolidge was not mount but rider, and his steed was a mechanical horse. The Americano, in his normal incarnation, challenges fate at every step and his whole life is a struggle; Coolidge took things as they came.

Some of the more romantic of the funeral bards tried to convert the farmhouse at Plymouth into a log-cabin, but the attempt was as vain as their effort to make a Lincoln of good Cal. His early days, in fact, were anything but pinched. His father was a man of substance, and he was well fed and well schooled. He went to a good college, had the clothes to cut a figure there, and made useful friends. There is no record that he was brilliant, but he took his degree with a respectable mark, proceeded to the law, and entered a prosperous law firm on the day of his admission to the bar. Almost at once he got into politics, and by the time he was twenty-seven he was already on the public payroll. There he remained without a break for exactly thirty years, always moving up. Not once in all those years did he lose an election. When he retired in the end, it was at his own motion, and with three or four hundred thousand dollars of tax money in his tight jeans.

In brief, a darling of the gods. No other American has ever been so fortunate, or even half so fortunate. His career first amazed observers, and then dazzled them. Well do I remember the hot Saturday in Chicago when he was nominated for the Vice-Presidency on the ticket with Harding. Half a dozen other statesmen had to commit political suicide in order to make way for him, but all of them stepped up docilely and bumped themselves off. The business completed, I left the press-stand and went to the crypt below to hunt a drink. There I found a group of colleagues listening to a Boston brother who knew Coolidge well, and had followed him from the start of his career.

To my astonishment I found that this gentleman was offering to lay a bet that Harding, if elected, would be assassinated before he had served half his term. There were murmurs, and someone protested uneasily that such talk was injudicious, for A. Mitchell Palmer was still Attorney-General and his spies were all about. But the speaker stuck to his wager.

'I am simply telling you,' he roared, 'what I *know*. I know Cal Coolidge inside and out. He is the luckiest goddam ——— ——— in the whole world.'

It seemed plausible then, and it is certain now. No other President ever slipped into the White House so easily, and none other ever had a softer time of it while there. When, at Rapid City, S.D., on August 2, 1927, he loosed the occult words, 'I do not choose to run in 1928,' was it prescience or only luck? For one, I am inclined to put it down to luck. Surely there was no prescience in his utterances and maneuvers otherwise. He showed not the slightest sign that he smelt black clouds ahead; on the contrary, he talked and lived only sunshine. There was a volcano boiling under him, but he did not know it, and was not singed. When it burst forth at last, it was Hoover who got its blast, and was fried, boiled, roasted and fricasseed. How Dr Coolidge must have chuckled in his retirement, for he was not without humor of a sad, necrotic kind. He knew Hoover well, and could fathom the full depths of the joke.

The American Mercury, 1933

ROSE MACAULAY

1881–1958

London, 1946

The maze of little streets threading through the wilderness, the broken walls, the great pits with their dense forests of bracken and bramble, golden ragwort and coltsfoot, fennel and foxglove and vetch, all the wild rambling shrubs that spring from ruin, the vaults and cellars and deep caves, the wrecked guild halls that had belonged to saddlers, merchant tailors, haberdashers, waxchandlers, barbers, brewers, coopers and coachmakers, all the ancient city fraternities, the broken office stairways that spiralled steeply past empty doorways and rubbled closets into the sky, empty shells of churches with their towers still strangely spiring above the wilderness, their empty window arches where green boughs pushed in, their broken pavement floors—St Vedast's, St Alban's, St Anne's and St Agnes', St Giles Cripplegate, its tower high above the rest, the ghosts of churches burnt in an earlier fire, St Olave's and St John Zachary's, haunting the green-flowered churchyards that bore their names, the ghosts of taverns where merchants and clerks had drunk, of restaurants where they had eaten—all this scarred and haunted green and stone and brambled wilderness lying under the August sun, a-hum with insects and astir with secret, darting, burrowing life, received the returned traveller into its dwellings with a wrecked, indifferent calm. Here, its cliffs and chasms and caves seemed to say, is your home; here you belong; you cannot get away, you do not wish to get away, for this is the maquis that lies about the margins of the wrecked world, and here your feet are set; here you find the irremediable barbarism that comes up from the depth of the earth, and that you have known elsewhere. 'Where are the roots that clutch, what branches grow, out of this stony rubbish? Son of man, you cannot say, or guess. . . .' But you can say, you can guess, that it is you yourself, your own roots, that clutch the stony rubbish, the branches of your own being that grow from it and from nowhere else.

The World My Wilderness, 1947

P. G. WODEHOUSE

1881–1975

Worlds in Collision

If Muriel had hoped that a mutual esteem would spring up between her father and her betrothed during this week-end visit, she was doomed to disappointment. The thing was a failure from the start. Sacheverell's host did him extremely well, giving him the star guest-room, the Blue Suite, and bringing out the oldest port for his benefit, but it was plain that he thought little of the young man. The colonel's subjects were sheep (in sickness and in health), manure, wheat, mangold-wurzels, huntin', shootin', and fishin': while Sacheverell was at his best on Proust, the Russian Ballet, Japanese prints, and the Influence of James Joyce on the younger Bloomsbury novelists. There was no fusion between these men's souls. Colonel

Branksome did not actually bite Sacheverell in the leg, but when you had said that you had said everything.

'The Voice of the Past', *Mulliner Nights*, 1933

Land of Contrasts

In my experience, there are two kinds of elderly American. One, the stout and horn-rimmed, is matiness itself. He greets you as if you were a favourite son, starts agitating the cocktail shaker before you know where you are, slips a couple into you with a merry laugh, tells you a dialect story about two Irishmen named Pat and Mike, and, in a word, makes life one grand sweet song.

The other, which runs a good deal to the cold, grey stare and the square jaw, seems to view the English cousin with concern. It is not Elfin. It broods. It says little. And every now and again you catch its eye, and it is like colliding with a raw oyster.

Of this latter class or species J. Washburn Stoker had always been the perpetual vice-president.

Thank You, Jeeves, 1934

VIRGINIA WOOLF

1882–1941

Maynard Keynes by Lamplight

Went to Charleston for the night; & had a vivid sight of Maynard by lamplight—like a gorged seal, double chin, ledge of red lip, little eyes, sensual, brutal, unimaginative: one of those visions that come from a chance attitude, lost so soon as he turned his head. I suppose though it illustrates something I feel about him. Then he's read neither of my books—In spite of this I enjoyed myself: L. came over next day & found me neither suicidal nor homicidal.

Diary, September 1920

A Sore Point

We have dined twice at the Cock, repairing afterwards to Hussey's—no Hussey has married the dullest man in England—to Niemeyer's room; the gas fire is broken. We balance on hard chairs. But the atmosphere is easy & pleasant . . . Pale, marmoreal Eliot was there last week, like a chapped office boy on a high stool, with a cold in his head, until he warms a little, which he did. We walked back along the Strand. 'The critics say I am learned & cold' he said. 'The truth is I am neither.' As he said this, I think coldness at least must be a sore point with him.

Diary, February 1921

Father and Son

The rush of the water ceased; the world became full of little creaking and squeaking sounds. One heard the waves breaking and flapping against the side of the boat as if they were anchored in harbour. Everything became very close to one. For the sail, upon which James had his eyes fixed until it had become to him like a person whom he knew, sagged entirely; there they came to a stop, flapping about waiting for a breeze, in the hot sun, miles from shore, miles from the Lighthouse. Everything in the whole world seemed to stand still. The Lighthouse became immovable, and the line of the distant shore became fixed. The sun grew hotter and everybody seemed to come very close together and to feel each other's presence, which they had almost forgotten. Macalister's fishing line went plumb down into the sea. But Mr Ramsay went on reading with his legs curled under him.

He was reading a little shiny book with covers mottled like a plover's egg. Now and again, as they hung about in that horrid calm, he turned a page. And James felt that each page was turned with a peculiar gesture aimed at him: now assertively, now commandingly; now with the intention of making people pity him; and all the time, as his father read and turned one after another of those little pages, James kept dreading the moment when he would look up and speak sharply to him about something or other. Why were they lagging about here? he would demand, or something quite unreasonable like that. And if he does, James thought, then I shall take a knife and strike him to the heart.

He had always kept this old symbol of taking a knife and striking his father to the heart. Only now, as he grew older, and sat staring at his father in an impotent rage, it was not him, that old man reading, whom he wanted to kill, but it was the thing that descended on him—without his knowing it perhaps: that fierce sudden black-winged harpy, with its talons and its beak all cold and hard, that struck and struck at you (he could feel the beak on his bare legs, where it had struck when he was a child) and then made off, and there he was again, an old man, very sad, reading his book. That he would kill, that he would strike to the heart. Whatever he did—(and he might do anything, he felt, looking at the Lighthouse and the distant shore) whether he was in a business, in a bank, a barrister, a man at the head of some enterprise, that he would fight, that he would track down and stamp out—tyranny, despotism, he called it—making people do what they did not want to do, cutting off their right to speak.

How could any of them say, But I won't, when he said, Come to the Lighthouse. Do this. Fetch me that. The black wings spread, and the hard beak tore. And then next moment, there he sat reading his book; and he might look up—one never knew—quite reasonably. He might talk to the Macalisters. He might be pressing a sovereign into some frozen old woman's hand in the street, James thought; he might be shouting out at some fisherman's sports; he might be waving his arms in the air with excitement. Or he might sit at the head of the table dead silent from one end of dinner to the other. Yes, thought James, while the boat slapped and dawdled there in the hot sun; there was a waste of snow and rock very lonely and austere; and there he had come to feel, quite often lately, when his father said something which surprised the others, were two pairs of footprints only; his own and his father's. They alone knew each other. What then was this terror, this hatred?

To the Lighthouse, 1927

A Magic Looking-Glass

Life for both sexes—and I looked at them, shouldering their way along the pavement—is arduous, difficult, a perpetual struggle. It calls for gigantic courage and strength. More than anything, perhaps, creatures of illusion as we are, it calls for confidence in oneself. Without self-confidence we are as babes in the cradle. And how can we generate this imponderable quality, which is yet so invaluable, most quickly? By thinking that other people are inferior to oneself. By feeling that one has some innate superiority—it may be wealth, or rank, a straight nose, or the portrait of a grandfather by Romney—for there is no end to the pathetic devices of the human imagination—over other people. Hence the enormous importance to a patriarch who has to conquer, who has to rule, of feeling that great numbers of people, half the human race indeed, are by nature inferior to himself. It must indeed be one of the chief sources of his power. But let me turn the light of this observation on to real life, I thought. Does it help to explain some of those psychological puzzles that one notes in the margin of daily life? Does it explain my astonishment of the other day when Z, most humane, most modest of men, taking up some book by Rebecca West and reading a passage in it, exclaimed, 'The arrant feminist! She says that men are snobs!' The exclamation, to me so surprising—for why was Miss West an arrant feminist for making a possibly true if uncomplimentary statement about the other sex?—was not merely the cry of wounded vanity; it was a protest against some infringement of his power to believe in himself. Women have served all these centuries as looking-glasses possessing the magic and delicious power of reflecting the figure of man at twice its natural size. Without that power probably the earth would still be swamp and jungle. The glories of all our wars would be unknown. We should still be scratching the outlines of deer on the remains of mutton bones and bartering flints for sheep skins or whatever simple ornament took our unsophisticated taste. Supermen and Fingers of Destiny would never have existed. The Czar and the Kaiser would never have worn crowns or lost them. Whatever may be their use in civilized societies, mirrors are essential to all violent and heroic action. That is why Napoleon and Mussolini both insist so emphatically upon the inferiority of women, for if they were not inferior, they would cease to enlarge. That serves to explain in part the necessity that women so often are to men. And it serves to explain how restless they are under her criticism; how impossible it is for her to say to them this book is bad, this picture is feeble, or whatever it may be, without giving far more pain and rousing far more anger than a man would do who gave the same criticism. For if she begins to tell the truth, the figure in the looking-glass shrinks; his fitness for life is diminished. How is he to go on giving judgement, civilizing natives, making laws, writing books, dressing up and speechifying at banquets, unless he can see himself at breakfast and at dinner at least twice the size he really is?

A Room of One's Own, 1929

A Long Strip of Life

My life, she said to herself. That was odd, it was the second time that evening that somebody had talked about her life. And I haven't got one, she thought, Oughtn't a life to be something you could handle and produce?—a life of seventy odd years. But I've only the present moment, she thought. Here she was alive, now, listening to the fox-trot. Then she looked round. There was Morris; Rose; Edward with his head thrown back talking to a man she did not know. I'm the only person here, she thought, who remembers how he sat on the edge of my bed that night, crying—the night Kitty's engagement was announced. Yes, things came back to her. A long strip of life lay behind her. Edward crying, Mrs Levy talking; snow falling; a sunflower with a crack in it; the yellow omnibus trotting along the Bayswater Road. And I thought to myself, I'm the youngest person in this omnibus; now I'm the oldest. . . . Millions of things came back to her. Atoms danced apart and massed themselves. But how did they compose what people called a life? She clenched her hands and felt the hard little coins she was holding. Perhaps there's 'I' at the middle of it, she thought; a knot; a centre; and again she saw herself sitting at her table drawing on the blotting paper, digging little holes from which spokes radiated. Out and out they went; thing followed thing, scene obliterated scene. And then they say, she thought, 'We've been talking about you!'

The Years, 1938

Hitler on the Radio

Duty did not call me to listen to Mr Bradfield last night. Instead we listened to the ravings, the strangled hysterical sobbing swearing ranting of Hitler at the Beer Hall. The offer of mediation—Holland & Belgium—is the fat on the fire. Today they say there was an explosion after he'd left. Is it true? Theres no getting at truth now all the loud speakers are contradicting each other. Its a crosseyed squint, like the beams that make a tent over the church at night—the searchlights meet there.

Diary, November 1939

Husband and Wife

The old people had gone up to bed. Giles crumpled the newspaper and turned out the light. Left alone together for the first time that day, they were silent. Alone, enmity was bared; also love. Before they slept, they must fight; after they had fought, they would embrace. From that embrace another life might be born. But first they must fight, as the dog fox fights with the vixen, in the heart of darkness, in the fields of night.

Isa let her sewing drop. The great hooded chairs had become enormous. And Giles too. And Isa too against the window. The window was all sky without colour. The house had lost its shelter. It was night before roads were made, or houses. It was the night that dwellers in caves had watched from some high place among rocks.

Then the curtain rose. They spoke.

Between the Acts, 1941

JAMES STEPHENS

1882–1950

Philosophy with Interruptions

When the Philosopher came home late that night the Thin Woman was waiting up for him.

'Woman,' said the Philosopher. 'you ought to be in bed.'

'Ought I indeed?' said the Thin Woman. 'I'd have you know that I'll go to bed when I like and get up when I like without asking your or any one else's permission.'

'That is not true,' said the Philosopher. 'You get sleepy whether you like it or not, and you awaken again without your permission being asked. Like many other customs such as singing, dancing, music, and acting, sleep has crept into popular favour as part of a religious ceremonial. Nowhere can one go to sleep more easily than in a church.'

'Do you know,' said the Thin Woman, 'that a Leprecaun came here to-day?'

'I do not,' said the Philosopher, 'and notwithstanding the innumerable centuries which have elapsed since that first sleeper (probably with extreme difficulty) sank into his religious trance, we can to-day sleep through a religious ceremony with an ease which would have been a source of wealth and fame to that prehistoric worshipper and his acolytes.'

'Are you going to listen to what I am telling you about the Leprecaun?' said the Thin Woman.

'I am not,' said the Philosopher. 'It has been suggested that we go to sleep at night because it is then too dark to do anything else; but owls, who are a venerably sagacious folk, do not sleep in the night-time. Bats, also, are a very clear-minded race; they sleep in the broadest day, and they do it in a charming manner. They clutch the branch of a tree with their toes and hang head downwards—a position which I consider singularly happy, for the rush of blood to the head consequent on this inverted position should engender a drowsiness and a certain imbecility of mind which must either sleep or explode.'

'Will you never be done talking?' shouted the Thin Woman passionately.

'I will not,' said the Philosopher. 'In certain ways sleep is useful. It is an excellent way of listening to an opera or seeing pictures on a bioscope. As a medium for day-dreams I know of nothing that can equal it. As an accomplishment it is graceful, but as a means of spending a night it is intolerably ridiculous. If you were going to say anything, my love, please say it now, but you should always remember to think before you speak. A woman should be seen seldom but never heard. Quietness is the beginning of virtue. To be silent is to be beautiful. Stars do not make a noise. Children should always be in bed. These are serious truths, which cannot be controverted; therefore, silence is fitting as regards them.'

'Your stirabout is on the hob,' said the Thin Woman. 'You can get it for yourself. I would not move the breadth of my nail if you were dying of hunger. I hope there's lumps in it. A Leprecaun from Gort na Cloca Mora was here to-day. They'll give it to you for robbing their pot of gold. You old thief, you! you lob-eared, crock-kneed fat-eye!'

The Thin Woman whizzed suddenly from where she stood and leaped into bed. From beneath the blanket she turned a vivid, furious eye on her husband. She was trying to give him rheumatism and toothache and lockjaw all at once. If she had been satisfied to concentrate her attention on one only of these torments she might have succeeded in afflicting her husband according to her wish, but she was not able to do that.

'Finality is death. Perfection is finality. Nothing is perfect. There are lumps in it,' said the Philosopher.

The Crock of Gold, 1912

The Fearsome Hound

Now if the sheep were venomous, this dog was more venomous still, for it was fearful to look at. In body it was not large, but its head was of a great size, and the mouth that was shaped in that head was able to open like the lid of a pot. It was not teeth which were in that head, but hooks and fangs and prongs. Dreadful was that mouth to look at, terrible to look into, woeful to think about; and from it, or from the broad, loose nose that waggled above it, there came a sound which no word of man could describe, for it was not a snarl, nor was it a howl, although it was both of these. It was neither a growl nor a grunt, although it was both of these; it was not a yowl nor a groan, although it was both of these; for it was one sound made up of these sounds, and there was in it, too, a whine and a yelp, and a long-drawn snoring noise, and a deep purring noise, and a noise that was like the squeal of a rusty hinge, and there were other noises in it also. . . . 'There is nothing to frighten sheep like a dog,' said Mananán, 'and there is nothing to frighten these sheep like this dog.'

'Mongan's Frenzy', *Irish Fairy Tales*, 1920

JAMES JOYCE
1882–1941

Paralysis

There was no hope for him this time: it was the third stroke. Night after night I had passed the house (it was vacation time) and studied the lighted square of window: and night after night I had found it lighted in the same way, faintly and evenly. If he was dead, I thought, I would see the reflection of candles on the darkened blind, for I knew that two candles must be set at the head of a corpse. He had often said to me: 'I am not long for this world,' and I had thought his words idle. Now I knew they were true. Every night as I gazed up at the window I said softly to myself the word paralysis. It had always sounded strangely in my ears, like the word gnomon in the Euclid and the word simony in the Catechism. But now it sounded to me like the name of some maleficent and sinful being. It filled me with fear, and yet I longed to be nearer to it and to look upon its deadly work.

'The Sisters', *Dubliners*, 1914

The New King and the Old Chief

'And what about the address to the King?' said Mr Lyons, after drinking and smacking his lips.

'Listen to me,' said Mr Henchy. 'What we want in this country, as I said to old Ward, is capital. The King's coming here will mean an influx of money into this country. The citizens of Dublin will benefit by it. Look at all the factories down by the quays there, idle! Look at all the money there is in the country if we only worked the old industries, the mills, the ship-building yards and factories. It's capital we want.'

'But look here, John,' said Mr O'Connor. 'Why should we welcome the King of England? Didn't Parnell himself . . .'

'Parnell,' said Mr Henchy, 'is dead. Now, here's the way I look at it. Here's this chap come to the throne after his old mother keeping him out of it till the man was grey. He's a man of the world, and he means well by us. He's a jolly fine, decent fellow, if you ask me, and no damn nonsense about him. He just says to himself: 'The old one never went to see these wild Irish. By Christ, I'll go myself and see what they're like.' And are we going to insult the man when he comes over here on a friendly visit? Eh? Isn't that right, Crofton?'

Mr Crofton nodded his head.

'But after all now,' said Mr Lyons argumentatively, 'King Edward's life, you know, is not the very . . .'

'Let bygones be bygones,' said Mr Henchy. 'I admire the man personally. He's just an ordinary knockabout like you and me. He's fond of his glass of grog and he's a bit of a rake, perhaps, and he's a good sportsman. Damn it, can't we Irish play fair?'

'That's all very fine,' said Mr Lyons. 'But look at the case of Parnell now.'

'In the name of God,' said Mr Henchy, 'where's the analogy between the two cases?'

'What I mean,' said Mr Lyons, 'is we have our ideals. Why, now, would we welcome a man like that? Do you think now after what he did Parnell was a fit man to lead us? And why, then, would we do it for Edward the Seventh?'

'This is Parnell's anniversary,' said Mr O'Connor, 'and don't let us stir up any bad blood. We all respect him now that he's dead and gone—even the Conservatives,' he added, turning to Mr Crofton.

Pok! The tardy cork flew out of Mr Crofton's bottle. Mr Crofton got up from his box and went to the fire. As he returned with his capture he said in a deep voice:

'Our side of the house respects him, because he was a gentleman.'

'Right you are, Crofton!' said Mr Henchy fiercely. 'He was the only man that could keep that bag of cats in order. "Down, ye dogs! Lie down, ye curs!" That's the way he treated them. Come in, Joe! Come in!' he called out, catching sight of Mr Hynes in the doorway.

'Ivy Day in the Committee Room', *Dubliners*

A Beating

—Lazy idle little loafer! cried the prefect of studies. Broke my glasses! An old schoolboy trick! Out with your hand this moment!

Stephen closed his eyes and held out in the air his trembling hand with the palm upwards. He felt the prefect of studies touch it for a moment at the fingers to straighten it and then the swish of the sleeve of the soutane as the pandybat was lifted to strike. A hot burning stinging tingling blow like the loud crack of a broken stick made his trembling hand crumple together like a leaf in the fire: and at the sound and the pain scalding tears were driven into his eyes. His whole body was shaking with fright, his arm was shaking and his crumpled burning livid hand shook like a loose leaf in the air. A cry sprang to his lips, a prayer to be let off. But though the tears scalded his eyes and his limbs quivered with pain and fright he held back the hot tears and the cry that scalded his throat.

—Other hand! shouted the prefect of studies.

A Portrait of the Artist as a Young Man, 1916

Colour and Rhythm

—A day of dappled seaborne clouds.

The phrase and the day and the scene harmonized in a chord. Words. Was it their colours? He allowed them to glow and fade, hue after hue: sunrise gold, the russet and green of apple orchards, azure of waves, the grey-fringed fleece of clouds. No, it was not their colours: it was the poise and balance of the period itself. Did he then love the rhythmic rise and fall of words better than their associations of legend and colour? Or was it that, being as weak of sight as he was shy of mind, he drew less pleasure from the reflection of the glowing sensible world through the prism of a language many-coloured and richly storied than from the contemplation of an inner world of individual emotions mirrored perfectly in a lucid supple periodic prose?

A Portrait of the Artist as a Young Man

The Meaning of History

He raised his forefinger and beat the air oldly before his voice spoke.

—Mark my words, Mr Dedalus, he said. England is in the hands of the jews. In all the highest places: her finance, her press. And they are the signs of a nation's decay. Wherever they gather they eat up the nation's vital strength. I have seen it coming these years. As sure as we are standing here the jew merchants are already at their work of destruction. Old England is dying.

He stepped swiftly off, his eyes coming to blue life as they passed a broad sunbeam. He faced about and back again.

—Dying, he said, if not dead by now.

The harlot's cry from street to street
Shall weave old England's winding sheet.

His eyes open wide in vision stared sternly across the sunbeam in which he halted.

—A merchant, Stephen said, is one who buys cheap and sells dear, jew or gentile, is he not?

—They sinned against the light, Mr Deasy said gravely. And you can see the darkness in their eyes. And that is why they are wanderers on the earth to this day.

On the steps of the Paris Stock Exchange the gold-skinned men quoting prices on their gemmed fingers. Gabbles of geese. They swarmed loud, uncouth about the temple, their heads thickplotting under maladroit silk hats. Not theirs: these clothes, this speech, these gestures. Their full slow eyes belied the words, the gestures eager and unoffending, but knew the rancours massed about them and knew their zeal was vain. Vain patience to heap and hoard. Time surely would scatter all. A hoard heaped by the roadside: plundered and passing on. Their eyes knew the years of wandering and, patient, knew the dishonours of their flesh.

—Who has not? Stephen said.

—What do you mean? Mr Deasy asked.

He came forward a pace and stood by the table. His underjaw fell sideways open uncertainly. Is this old wisdom? He waits to hear from me.

—History, Stephen said, is a nightmare from which I am trying to awake.

From the playfield the boys raised a shout. A whirring whistle: goal. What if that nightmare gave you a back kick?

—The ways of the Creator are not our ways, Mr Deasy said. All history moves towards one great goal, the manifestation of God.

Stephen jerked his thumb towards the window, saying:

—That is God.

Hooray! Ay! Whrrwhee!

—What? Mr Deasy asked.

—A shout in the street, Stephen answered, shrugging his shoulders.

Mr Deasy looked down and held for a while the wings of his nose tweaked between his fingers. Looking up again he set them free.

Ulysses, 1922

On the Way to the Funeral

The carriage climbed more slowly the hill of Rutland square. Rattle his bones. Over the stones. Only a pauper. Nobody owns.

—In the midst of life, Martin Cunningham said.

—But the worst of all, Mr Power said, is the man who takes his own life.

Martin Cunningham drew out his watch briskly, coughed and put it back.

—The greatest disgrace to have in the family, Mr Power added.

—Temporary insanity, of course, Martin Cunningham said decisively. We must take a charitable view of it.

—They say a man who does it is a coward, Mr Dedalus said.

—It is not for us to judge, Martin Cunningham said.

Mr Bloom, about to speak, closed his lips again. Martin Cunningham's large eyes. Looking away now. Sympathetic human man he is. Intelligent. Like Shakespeare's face. Always a good word to say. They have no mercy on that here or infanticide. Refuse christian burial. They used to drive a stake of wood through his heart in the grave. As if it wasn't broken already. Yet sometimes they repent too late. Found in the riverbed clutching rushes. He looked at me. And that awful drunkard of a wife of his. Setting up house for her time after time and then pawning the furniture on him every Saturday almost. Leading him the life of the damned. Wear the heart out of a stone, that. Monday morning start afresh. Shoulder to the wheel. Lord, she must have looked a sight that night, Dedalus told me he was in there. Drunk about the place and capering with Martin's umbrella:

And they call me the jewel of Asia,
Of Asia,
The geisha.

He looked away from me. He knows. Rattle his bones.

That afternoon of the inquest. The redlabelled bottle on the table. The room in the hotel with hunting pictures. Stuffy it was. Sunlight through the slats of the Venetian blinds. The coroner's ears, big and hairy. Boots giving evidence. Thought he was asleep first. Then saw like yellow streaks on his face. Had slipped down to the foot of the bed. Verdict: overdose. Death by misadventure. The letter. For my son Leopold.

No more pain. Wake no more. Nobody owns.
The carriage rattled swiftly along Blessington street. Over the stones.

Ulysses

Nightfall

Ba. What is that flying about? Swallow? Bat probably. Thinks I'm a tree, so blind. Have birds no smell? Metempsychosis. They believed you could be changed into a tree from grief. Weeping willow. Ba. There he goes. Funny little beggar. Wonder where he lives. Belfry up there. Very likely. Hanging by his heels in the odour of sanctity. Bell scared him out, I suppose. Mass seems to be over. Could hear them all at it. Pray for us. And pray for us. And pray for us. Good idea the repetition. Same thing with ads. Buy from us. And buy from us. Yes, there's the light in the priest's house. Their frugal meal. Remember about the mistake in the valuation when I was in Thom's. Twentyeight it is. Two houses they have. Gabriel Conroy's brother is curate. Ba. Again. Wonder why they come out at night like mice. They're a mixed breed. Birds are like hopping mice. What frightens them, light or noise? Better sit still. All instinct like the bird in drouth got water out of the end of a jar by throwing in pebbles. Like a little man in a cloak he is with tiny hands. Weeny bones. Almost see them shimmering, kind of a bluey white. Colours depend on the light you see. Stare the sun for example like the eagle then look at a shoe see a blotch blob yellowish. Wants to stamp his trademark on everything. Instance, that cat this morning on the staircase. Colour of brown turf. Say you never see them with three colours. Not true. That half tabbywhite tortoiseshell in the *City Arms* with the letter em on her forehead. Body fifty different colours. Howth a while ago amethyst. Glass flashing. That's how that wise man what's his name with the burning glass. Then the heather goes on fire. It can't be tourists' matches. What? Perhaps the sticks dry rub together in the wind and light. Or broken bottles in the furze act as a burning glass in the sun. Archimedes. I have it! My memory's not so bad.

Ulysses

A Lament for a Hero

Shize? I should shee! Macool, Macool, orra whyi deed ye diie? of a trying thirstay mournin? Sobs they sighdid at Fillagain's chrissormiss wake, all the hoolivans of the nation, prostrated in their consternation and their duodisimally profusive plethora of ululation. There was plumbs and grumes and cheriffs and citherers and raiders and cinemen too. And the all gianed in with the shout-most shoviality. Agog and magog and the round of them agrog. To the continuation of that celebration until

Hanandhunigan's extermination! Some in kinkin corass, more, kankan keening. Belling him up and filling him down. He's stiff but he's steady is Priam Olim! 'Twas he was the dacent gaylabouring youth. Sharpen his pillowscone, tap up his bier! E'erawhere in this whorl would ye hear sich a din again? With their deepbrow fundigs and the dusty fidelios. They laid him brawdawn alanglast bed. With a bockalips of finisky fore his feet. And a barrowload of guenesis hoer his head. Tee the tootal of the fluid hang the twoddle of the fuddled, O!

Finnegans Wake, 1939

Anna Livia's Farewell

And can it be it's nnow fforvell? Illas! I wisht I had better glances to peer to you through this baylight's growing. But you're changing, acoolsha, you're changing from me, I can feel. Or is it me is? I'm getting mixed. Brightening up and tightening down. Yes, you're changing, sonhusband, and you're turning, I can feel you, for a daughterwife from the hills again. Imlamaya. And she is coming. Swimming in my hindmoist. Diveltaking on me tail. Just a whisk brisk sly spry spink spank sprint of a thing theresomere, saultering. Saltarella come to her own. I pity your oldself I was used to. Now a younger's there. Try not to part! Be happy, dear ones! May I be wrong! For she'll be sweet for you as I was sweet when I came down out of me mother. My great blue bedroom, the air so quiet, scarce a cloud. In peace and silence. I could have stayed up there for always only. It's something fails us. First we feel. Then we fall. And let her rain now if she likes. Gently or strongly as she likes. Anyway let her rain for my time is come. I done me best when I was let. Thinking always if I go all goes. A hundred cares, a tithe of troubles and is there one who understands me? One in a thousand of years of the nights? All me life I have been lived among them but now they are becoming lothed to me. And I am lothing their little warm tricks. And lothing their mean cosy turns. And all the greedy gushes out through their small souls. And all the lazy leaks down over their brash bodies. How small it's all! And me letting on to meself always. And lilting on all the time. I thought you were all glittering with the noblest of carriage. You're only a bumpkin. I thought you the great in all things, in guilt and in glory. You're but a puny. Home! My people were not their sort out beyond there so far as I can. For all the bold and bad and bleary they are blamed, the seahags. No! Nor for all our wild dances in all their wild din. I can seen meself among them, allaniuvia pulchrabelled. How she was handsome, the wild Amazia, when she would seize to my other breast! And what is she weird, haughty Niluna, that she will snatch from my ownest hair! For 'tis they are the stormies. Ho hang! Hang ho! And the clash of our cries till we spring to be free. Auravoles, they says, never heed of your name! But I'm loothing them that's here and all I lothe. Loonely in me loneness. For all their faults. I am passing out. O bitter ending! I'll slip away before they're up. They'll never see. Nor know. Nor miss me. And it's old and old it's sad and old it's sad and weary I go back to you, my cold father, my cold mad father, my cold mad feary father, till the near sight of the mere size of him, the moyles and moyles of it, moananoaning, makes me seasilt saltsick and I rush, my only, into your arms. I see them rising! Save me from those therrble prongs! Two more. Onetwo moremens more. So. Avelaval. My leaves have drifted from me. All. But one clings still. I'll bear it on me. To remind me of. Lff! So soft this morning, ours. Yes. Carry me along, taddy, like you done through the toy fair! If I seen him bearing down on me now under whitespread wings like he'd come from Arkangels, I sink I'd die down over his feet, humbly dumbly, only to washup. Yes, tid. There's where. First. We pass through grass behush the bush to. Whish! A gull. Gulls. Far calls. Coming, far! End here. Us then. Finn, again! Take. Bussoftlhee, mememormee! Till thousendsthee. Lps. The keys to. Given! A way a lone a last a loved a long the

Finnegans Wake

JOHN MAYNARD KEYNES
1883–1946

Clemenceau at Versailles

Clemenceau was by far the most eminent member of the Council of Four, and he had taken the measure of his colleagues. He alone both had an idea and had considered it in all its consequences. His age, his character, his wit, and his appearance joined to give him objectivity and a defined outline in an environment of confusion. One could not despise Clemenceau or dislike him, but only take a different view as to the nature of civilised man, or indulge, at least, a different hope.

The figure and bearing of Clemenceau are universally familiar. At the Council of Four he wore a square-tailed coat of a very good, thick black broadcloth, and on his hands, which were never uncovered, grey suede gloves; his boots were of thick black leather, very good, but of a country style, and sometimes fastened in front, curiously, by a buckle instead of laces. His seat in the room in the President's house, where the regular meetings of the Council of Four were held (as distinguished from their private and unattended conferences in a smaller chamber below), was on a square brocaded chair in the middle of the semicircle facing the fire-place, with

Signor Orlando on his left, the President next by the fire-place, and the Prime Minister opposite on the other side of the fire-place on his right. He carried no papers and no portfolio, and was unattended by any personal secretary, though several French ministers and officials appropriate to the particular matter in hand would be present round him. His walk, his hand, and his voice were not lacking in vigour, but he bore nevertheless, especially after the attempt upon him, the aspect of a very old man conserving his strength for important occasions. He spoke seldom, leaving the initial statement of the French case to his ministers or officials; he closed his eyes often and sat back in his chair with an impassive face of parchment, his grey-gloved hands clasped in front of him. A short sentence, decisive or cynical, was generally sufficient, a question, an unqualified abandonment of his ministers, whose face would not be saved, or a display of obstinacy reinforced by a few words in a piquantly delivered English. But speech and passion were not lacking when they were wanted, and the sudden outburst of words, often followed by a fit of deep coughing from the chest, produced their impression rather by force and surprise than by persuasion. . . .

He felt about France what Pericles felt of Athens—unique value in her, nothing else mattering; but his theory of politics was Bismarck's. He had one illusion—France; and one disillusion—mankind, including Frenchmen, and his colleagues not least. His principles for the peace can be expressed simply. In the first place, he was a foremost believer in the view of German psychology that the German understands and can understand nothing but intimidation, that he is without generosity or remorse in negotiation, that there is no advantage he will not take of you, and no extent to which he will not demean himself for profit, that he is without honour, pride, or mercy. Therefore you must never negotiate with a German or conciliate him; you must dictate to him. On no other terms will he respect you, or will you prevent him from cheating you. But it is doubtful how far he thought these characteristics peculiar to Germany, or whether his candid view of some other nations was fundamentally different. His philosophy had, therefore, no place for 'sentimentality' in international relations. Nations are real things, of whom you love one and feel for the rest indifference—or hatred. The glory of the nation you love is a desirable end—but generally to be obtained at your neighbour's expense. The politics of power are inevitable, and there is nothing very new to learn about this war or the end it was fought for; England had destroyed, as in each preceding century, a trade rival; a mighty chapter had been closed in the secular struggle between the glories of Germany and of France. Prudence required some measure of lip service to the 'ideals' of foolish Americans and hypocritical Englishmen; but it would be stupid to believe that there is much room in the world, as it really is, for such affairs as the League of Nations, or any sense in the principle of self-determination except as an ingenious formula for rearranging the balance of power in one's own interests.

The Economic Consequences of the Peace, 1919

Edwin Montagu

Mr Lloyd George was, of course, the undoing of his political career—as, indeed, Montagu always said that he would be. He could not keep away from that bright candle. But he knew, poor moth, that he would burn his wings. It was from his tongue that I, and many others, have heard the most brilliant, true, and witty descriptions of that (in his prime) undescribable. But whilst, behind the scenes, Montagu's tongue was master, his weaknesses made him, in action, the natural tool and victim; for, of all men, he was one of the easiest to use and throw on one side. It used to be alleged that a certain very Noble Lord had two footmen, of whom one was lame and the other swift of foot, so that letters of resignation carried by the one could be intercepted by the other before their fatal delivery at No. 10. Edwin Montagu's letters were not intercepted; but the subtle intelligencer of human weakness, who opened them, knew that by then the hot fit was over and the cold was blowing strong. They could be ignored or used against the writer—at choice.

Essays in Biography, 1933

G. M. YOUNG
1883–1959

Flashing Eyes and Curling Lips

Much of accident goes to the making of history, even the history of thought, which might seem to be most exempt from contingencies. The Victorian record would have been very different if Canning had lived to the years of Palmerston, if the new writers had grown up under the shadow of Byron, Keats, and Shelley. But the old men lived and the young men died. A strange pause followed their departure, and the great Victorian lights rose into a sky which, but for the rapid blaze of Bulwer Lytton, was vacant. Tennyson and Macaulay, Carlyle and Newman, Gladstone and Disraeli, Arnold and Dickens appear above the horizon together. In Sydney Smith's stately compliments to the Graduate of Oxford, the eighteenth century bows itself off the stage and introduces its successor. With the appearance of *Vanity Fair* in 1847, the constellation is complete and the stars are named. It was part of the felicity of the fifties to possess a literature which was at once topical, contemporary, and classic; to meet the Immortals in the streets, and to read them with added zest for the encounter.

Anchored to its twofold faith in goodness and progress, the early Victorian mind swung wide to the alternating currents of sentiment and party spite, but the virulence of the Press, and the gush of the popular novel were play on the surface of a deep assurance. There are whimperings, sometimes bellowings, of self-pity, but defiance was no longer the mode. The greater and better part of English society accepted the social structure and moral objective of the nation, as a community of families, all rising, or to be raised, to a higher respectability. To those postulates their criticism of life was not directed: they were satisfied, not indeed with the world as it was, for they were all, in their way, reformers, but as it would become by the application of those reasoned and tested principles which made up the scheme of progress and salvation.

Poised and convinced, they could indulge, too, in a licence of feeling impossible to a generation bred in doubt, and they could take their ease in an innocent vulgarity which to a later age would have been a hard-worked and calculated Bohemianism. They could swagger and they could be maudlin. In public they could be reserved, for they were a slow and wary race, and reserve is at once the defence of the wise and the refuge of the stupid. But cynicism and superciliousness, the stigmata of a beaten age and a waning class, were alien to the hopeful, if anxious, generation which had taken the future into its hands. In their exuberance and facility, the earlier Victorians, with their flowing and scented hair, gleaming jewellery and resplendent waistcoats, were nearer to the later Elizabethans; they were not ashamed; and, like the Elizabethans, their sense of the worthwhileness of everything—themselves, their age, and their country: what the Evangelicals called seriousness; the Arnoldians, earnestness; Bagehot, most happily, eagerness—overflowed in sentiment and invective, loud laughter, and sudden reproof. Once at Bowood, when Tom Moore was singing, one by one the audience slipped away in sobs; finally, the poet himself broke down and bolted, and the old Marquis was left alone. We are in an age when, if brides sometimes swooned at the altar, Ministers sometimes wept at the Table; when the sight of an infant school could reduce a civil servant to a passion of tears; and one undergraduate has to prepare another undergraduate for the news that a third undergraduate has doubts about the Blessed Trinity—an age of flashing eyes and curling lips, more easily touched, more easily shocked, more ready to spurn, to flaunt, to admire, and, above all, to preach.

Victorian England: Portrait of an Age, 1934

DAMON RUNYON

1884–1946

Liaison Dangereuse

Only a rank sucker will think of taking two peeks at Dave the Dude's doll, because while Dave may stand for the first peek, figuring it is a mistake, it is a sure thing he will get sored up at the second peek, and Dave the Dude is certainly not a man to have sored up at you.

But this Waldo Winchester is one hundred per cent sucker, which is why he takes quite a number of peeks at Dave's doll. And what is more, she takes quite a number of peeks right back at him. And there you are. When a guy and a doll get to taking peeks back and forth at each other, why, there you are indeed.

This Waldo Winchester is a nice-looking young guy who writes pieces about Broadway for the *Morning Item*. He writes about the goings-on in night clubs, such as fights, and one thing and another, and also about who is running around with who, including guys and dolls.

Sometimes this is very embarrassing to people who may be married and are running around with people who are not married, but of course Waldo Winchester cannot be expected to ask one and all for their marriage certificates before he writes his pieces for the paper.

The chances are if Waldo Winchester knows Miss Billy Perry is Dave the Dude's doll, he will never take more than his first peek at her, but nobody tips him off until his second or third peek, and by this time Miss Billy Perry is taking her peeks back at him and Waldo Winchester is hooked.

In fact, he is plumb gone, and being a sucker, like I tell you, he does not care whose doll she is. Personally, I do not blame him much, for Miss Billy Perry is worth a few peeks, especially when she is out on the floor of Miss Missouri Martin's Sixteen Hundred Club doing her tap dance. Still, I do not think the best tap-dancer that ever lives can make me take two peeks at her if I know she is Dave the Dude's doll, for Dave somehow thinks more than somewhat of his dolls.

He especially thinks plenty of Miss Billy Perry, and sends her fur coats, and diamond rings, and one thing and another, which she sends back to him at once, because it seems she does not take presents from guys. This is considered most surprising all along Broadway, but people figure the chances are she has some other angle.

Anyway, this does not keep Dave the Dude from liking her just the same, and so she is considered his doll by one and all, and is respected accordingly until this Waldo Winchester comes along.

It happens that he comes along while Dave the Dude is off in the Modoc on a little run down to the Bahamas to get some goods for his business, such as Scotch and champagne, and by the time Dave gets back Miss Billy Perry and Waldo Winchester are at the stage where they sit in corners between her numbers and hold hands.

Of course nobody tells Dave the Dude about this, because they do not wish to get him excited. Not even Miss Missouri Martin tells him, which is most unusual because Miss Missouri Martin, who is sometimes called 'Mizzoo' for short, tells everything she knows as soon as she knows it, which is very often before it happens.

You see, the idea is when Dave the Dude is excited he may blow somebody's brains out, and the chances are it will be nobody's brains but Waldo Winchester's, although some claim that Waldo Winchester has no brains or he will not be hanging around Dave the Dude's doll.

'Romance in the Roaring Forties', *More than Somewhat*, 1927

WYNDHAM LEWIS
1884–1957

A Young English Painter

But for Hobson's outfit Tarr had the most elaborate contempt. This was Alan Hobson's outfit: a Cambridge cut disfigured his originally manly and melodramatic form. His father was said to be a wealthy merchant somewhere in Egypt. Very athletic, his dark and cavernous features had been constructed by nature as a lurking-place for villainies and passions: but Hobson had double-crossed his rascally sinuous body. He slouched and ambled along, neglecting his muscles: and his full-blooded blackguard's countenance attempted to portray delicacies of common sense and gossamer-like backslidings into the inane that would have puzzled any analyst unacquainted with his peculiar training. Occasionally he would exploit his criminal appearance and blacksmith's muscles for a short time, however: and his strong piercing laugh threw ABC waitresses into confusion. The art-touch, the Bloomsbury technique, was very noticeable. Hobson's Harris tweeds were shabby, from beneath his dejected jacket emerged a pendant seat, his massive shoes were hooded by superfluous inches of his trousers: a hat suggesting that his ancestors had been Plainsmen or some rough sunny folk shaded unnecessarily his countenance, already far from open.

Tarr, 1918 (revised edition 1928)

Lord Osmund Finnian-Shaw

In colour Lord Osmund was a pale coral, with flaxen hair brushed tightly back, his blond pencilled pap rising straight from his sloping forehead: galb-like wings to his nostrils—the goat-like profile of Edward the Peacemaker. The lips were curved. They were thickly profiled as though belonging to a moslem portrait of a stark-lipped sultan. His eyes, vacillating and easily discomfited, slanted down to the heavy curved nose. Eyes, nose and lips contributed to one effect, so that they seemed one feature. It was the effect of the jouissant animal—the licking, eating, sniffing, fat-muzzled machine—dedicated to Wine, Womanry, and Free Verse-cum-soda-water.

The Apes of God, 1930

Ronald Firbank

Firbank is buried in Rome next to the grave of John Keats. I shouldn't like to have a grave next to his. If there's one place where one may, I suppose, expect a little rest, it is in the grave. And Firbank in his winding-sheet upon a moonlit night would be a problem for the least fussy of corpses in the same part of the cemetery. 'Thou still unravished bride of quietness!' I can imagine him hissing at Keats, 'come forth and let us seek out the tomb of Heliogabalus together shall us!' If there were only a Keats Society, I'd get up an agitation to have his grave moved.

From this you must not gather that I objected to Firbank. On the contrary, he seemed to me a pretty good clown—of the 'impersonator' type. Facially, he closely resembled Nellie Wallace. He seemed to like me—I had such relations with him as one might have had with a talking gazelle, afflicted with some nervous disorder.

In Stulik's one night I had dinner with him and a young American 'college-boy' who was stopping at the Eiffel Tower Hotel. The presence of the fawning and attentive Firbank put the little American out of countenance. He called the waiter.

'I guess I'll have something t'eat!' he announced aggressively.

'What will you have, sir?' asked the waiter.

'I guess I'll have—oh—a *rump-steak*.'

He pored over the menu: it was evident he felt that a rumpsteak would disinfect the atmosphere.

'Yessur.'

'Carrots,' he rasped out defiantly.

'Yessir. Carrots, sir.'

'Boiled pertaters.'

'Yessir.'

'What? Oh and er . . .'

But with gushing insinuation Firbank burst excitedly in at this point.

'Oh and *vi-o-lets*!' he frothed obsequiously.

Reacting darkly to the smiles of the onlookers the college-boy exclaimed, but without looking at his cringing 'fan'—

'There seems to be a lot of *fairies* round here!'

And he sniffed the air as if he could detect the impalpable aroma of an elf.

Blasting and Bombardiering, 1937

On His Blindness

The failure of sight which is already so advanced, will of course become worse from week to week until in the end I shall only be able to see the external world through little patches in the midst of a blacked out tissue. On the other hand, instead of little patches, the last stage may be the absolute black-out. Pushed into an unlighted room, the door banged and locked for ever, I shall then have to light a lamp of aggressive voltage in my mind to keep at bay the night.

New as I am to the land of blind-man's-buff I can only register the novel sensations, and not deny myself the enjoyment of this curious experience. It amuses me to collide with a walking belly; I quite enjoy being treated as a lay-figure, seized by the elbows and heaved up in the air as I approach a kerb, or flung into a car. I relish the absurdity of gossiping with somebody the other side of the partition. And everyone is at the other side of the partition. I am not allowed to see them. I am like a prisoner condemned to invisibility, although permitted an unrestricted number of visitors. Or I have been condemned to be a blind-folded delinquent, but not otherwise interfered with. And meanwhile I gaze backward over the centuries at my fellow condamnés. Homer heads the list, but there are surprisingly few. I see John Milton sitting with his three daughters (the origin of this image, is to my shame, it seems to me, a Royal Academy picture), the fearful blow at his still youthful pride distorting his face with its frustrations. He is beginning his great incantation: 'Of Man's first Disobedience and the Fruit of that Forbidden Tree', while one of the women sits, her quill-pen poised ready to transcribe the poetry. Well, Milton had his daughters, I have my dictaphone.

'The Sea-Mists of the Winter', 1951

A Conflagration in Canada

The noise, the glare, the clouds of smoke, the roaring and crackling of the flames, this great traditional spectacle only appealed to him for a moment. But he could not help being amazed at the spectral monster which had been there for so long, and what it was turning into. It was a flaming spectre, a fiery iceberg. Its sides, where there were no flames, were now a solid mass of ice. The water of the hoses had turned to ice as it ran down the walls, and had created an icy armour many feet in thickness. This enormous cocoon of ice did not descend vertically, but swept outwards for perhaps fifty yards, stopped by the wall of the house of the *Friseur*, half submerging the Beverage Room in its outward progress. The flames rising into the sky seemed somehow cold and conventional as if it had been their duty to go on aspiring, but they were doing it because they must, not because they had any lust for destruction. These were the flames that still reached up above the skyline of the façade. But a new generation of fiery monsters, a half-hour younger, appeared behind them, a darker red and full of muscular leaps, charged with the authentic will to devour and to consume. And there were dense volumes of black smoke too, where fresh areas were being brought into the holocaust.

Self Condemned, 1954

IVY COMPTON-BURNETT
1884–1969

A Headmistress and Her Staff

'I hope they none of them presume upon their friendship?'

'I trust that they deal with me fully as a friend. I hardly understand that phrase, "presume upon friendship".'

'I quite understand it. Shall we have a gossip about your staff?'

'No!' said Josephine. 'When you have known me a little longer, you will know that my mistresses, in their presence and in their absence are safe with me. I hope I could say that about all my friends.'

'I hoped you could not. But it is interesting that they would not be safe if we had the gossip. They must have treated you fully as a friend. I almost feel we have had it.'

More Women than Men, 1933

On Learning of a Calamity

'Will things go on in the same way?' said Audrey.

'Yes, people will eat and drink as usual. And, what is worse, we shall do the same. And, worse still, they will know that we do. And, worst of all, they will soon say we are quite ourselves again. Well, we can say they are quite *them*selves.'

A Father and His Fate, 1957

A Conversation with a Butler

'I think he is afraid of his mother.'

'Well, sir, that might be said of many of us.'

'Were you afraid of yours?'

'I would never open my mouth against her, sir.'

'Do you feel that she can hear you?'

'There are things beyond us, sir.'

'I suppose she is dead?'

'You are right that she has passed on, sir.'

'Do you expect to be reunited?'

'Well, sir, I would not be definite, united perhaps being hardly the word in the first place. But anything derogatory applies only to myself.'

'Do you wish you had been a better son?'

'Well, there are things in all our hearts, sir. Not that I ever forgot that she was a woman. It was only that I was confronted with her being other things.'

'Will you think of it on your deathbed?'

'That will be rather late in the day, sir.'

'It might be thought to be the right moment.'

'Well, in that case, sir, it may be put into my mind. But I shall not go to seek it. Making my peace at the last moment is hardly in my line. And my mother would have condemned it. That was hardly her tendency, sir. Indeed the whole thing was that her standard was too high. In one sense I could not have had a "better" mother.' Bullivant ended with a smile and turned towards the kitchen.

Manservant and Maidservant, 1947

D. H. LAWRENCE

1885–1930

A Miner's Breakfast

He always made his own breakfast. Being a man who rose early and had plenty of time he did not, as some miners do, drag his wife out of bed at six o'clock. At five, sometimes earlier, he woke, got straight out of bed, and went downstairs. When she could not sleep, his wife lay waiting for this time as for a period of peace. The only real rest seemed to be when he was out of the house.

He went downstairs in his shirt and then struggled into his pit-trousers, which were left on the hearth to warm all night. There was always a fire, because Mrs Morel raked. And the first sound in the house was the bang, bang of the poker against the raker, as Morel smashed the remainder of the coal to make the kettle, which was filled and left on the hob, finally boil. His cup and knife and fork, all he wanted except just the food, was laid ready on the table on a newspaper. Then he got his breakfast, made the tea, packed the bottom of the doors with rugs to shut out the draught, piled a big fire, and sat down to an hour of joy. He toasted his bacon on a fork and caught the drops of fat on his bread; then he put the rasher on his thick slice of bread, and cut off chunks with a clasp-knife, poured his tea into his saucer, and was happy. With his family about, meals were never so pleasant. He loathed a fork; it is a modern introduction which has still scarcely reached common people. What Morel preferred was a clasp-knife. Then, in solitude, he ate and drank, often sitting, in cold weather, on a little stool with his back to the warm chimney-piece, his food on the fender, his cup on the hearth. And then he read the last night's newspaper—what of it he could—spelling it over laboriously. He preferred to keep the blinds down and the candle lit even when it was daylight; it was the habit of the mine.

At a quarter to six he rose, cut two thick slices of bread-and-butter, and put them in the white calico snap-bag. He filled his tin bottle with tea. Cold tea without milk or sugar was the drink he preferred for the pit. Then he pulled off his shirt, and put on his pit-singlet, a vest of thick flannel cut low round the neck, and with short sleeves like a chemise.

Then he went upstairs to his wife with a cup of tea because she was ill, and because it occurred to him.

Sons and Lovers, 1913

Mother and Son

She went over the sheep-bridge and across a corner of the meadow to the cricket-ground. The meadows seemed one space of ripe, evening light, whispering with the distant mill-race. She sat on a seat under the alders in the cricket-ground, and fronted the evening. Before her, level and solid, spread the big green cricket-field, like the bed of a sea of light. Children played in the bluish shadow of the pavilion. Many rooks, high up, came cawing home across the softly-woven sky. They stooped in a long curve down into the golden glow, concentrating, cawing, wheeling, like black flakes on a slow vortex, over a tree-clump that made a dark boss among the pasture.

A few gentlemen were practising, and Mrs Morel could hear the chock of the ball, and the voices of the men suddenly roused; could see the white forms of men shifting silently over the green, upon which already the under shadows were smouldering. Away at the grange, one side of the haystacks was lit up, the other sides blue-grey. A wagon of sheaves rocked small across the melting yellow light.

The sun was going down. Every open evening, the hills of Derbyshire were blazed over with red sunset. Mrs Morel watched the sun sink from the glistening sky, leaving a soft flower-blue overhead, while the western space went red, as if all the fire had swum down there, leaving the bell cast flawless blue. The mountain-ash berries across the field stood fierily out from the dark leaves, for a moment. A few shocks of corn in a corner of the fallow stood up as if alive; she imagined them bowing; perhaps her son would be a Joseph. In the east, a mirrored sunset floated pink opposite the west's scarlet. The big haystacks on the hillside, that butted into the glare, went cold.

With Mrs Morel it was one of those still moments when the small frets vanish, and the beauty of things stands out, and she had the peace and the strength to see herself. Now and again, a swallow cut close to her. Now and again, Annie came up with a handful of alder-currants. The baby was restless on his mother's knee, clambering with his hands at the light.

Sons and Lovers

Father and Child

One evening, suddenly, he saw the tiny living thing rolling naked in the mother's lap, and he was sick, it was so utterly helpless and vulnerable and extraneous; in a world of hard surfaces and varying altitudes, it lay vulnerable and naked at every point. Yet it was quite blithe. And yet, in its blind, awful crying was there not the blind, far-off terror of its own nakedness, the terror of being so utterly delivered over, helpless at every point. He could not bear to hear it crying. His heart strained and stood on guard against the whole universe.

But he waited for the dread of these days to pass; he saw the joy coming. He saw the lovely, creamy, cool little ear of the baby, a bit of dark hair rubbed to a bronze floss, like bronze-dust. And he waited, for the child to become his, to look at him and answer him.

It had a separate being, but it was his own child. His flesh and blood vibrated to it. He caught the baby to his breast with his passionate, clapping laugh. And the infant knew him.

As the newly-opened, newly-dawned eyes looked at him, he wanted them to perceive him, to recognize him. Then he was verified. The child knew him, a queer contortion of laughter came on its face for him. He caught it to his breast, clapping with a triumphant laugh.

The Rainbow, 1915

Moony

He stood staring at the water. Then he stooped and picked up a stone, which he threw sharply at the pond. Ursula was aware of the bright moon leaping and swaying, all distorted, in her eyes. It seemed to shoot out arms of fire like a cuttle-fish, like a luminous polyp, palpitating strongly before her.

And his shadow on the border of the pond, was watching for a few moments, then he stooped and groped on the ground. Then again there was a burst of sound, and a burst of brilliant light, the moon had exploded on the water, and was flying asunder in flakes of white and dangerous fire. Rapidly, like white birds, the fires all broken rose across the pond, fleeing in clamorous confusion, battling with the flock of dark waves that were forcing their way in. The furthest waves of light, fleeing out, seemed to be clamouring against the shore for escape, the waves of darkness came in heavily, running under towards the centre. But at the centre, the heart of all, was still a vivid, incandescent quivering of a white moon not quite destroyed, a white body of fire writhing and striving and not even now broken open, not yet violated. It seemed to be drawing itself together with strange, violent pangs, in blind effort. It was getting stronger, it was re-asserting itself, the inviolable moon. And the rays were hastening in thin lines of light, to return to the strengthened moon, that shook upon the water in triumphant reassumption.

Birkin stood and watched, motionless, till the pond was almost calm, the moon was almost serene. Then, satisfied of so much, he looked for more stones. She felt his invisible tenacity. And in a moment again, the broken lights scattered in explosion over her face, dazzling her; and then, almost immediately, came the second shot. The moon leapt up white and burst through the air. Darts of bright light shot asunder, darkness swept over the centre. There was no moon, only a battlefield of broken lights and shadows, running close together. Shadows, dark and heavy, struck again and again across the place where the heart of the moon had been, obliterating it altogether. The white fragments pulsed up and down, and could not find where to go, apart and brilliant on the water like the petals of a rose that a wind has blown far and wide.

Yet again, they were flickering their way to the centre, finding the path blindly, enviously. And again, all was still, as Birkin and Ursula watched. The waters were loud on the shore. He saw the moon regathering itself insidiously, saw the heart of the rose intertwining vigorously and blindly, calling back the scattered fragments, winning home the fragments, in a pulse and an effort of return.

And he was not satisfied. Like a madness, he must go on. He got large stones, and threw them, one after the other, at the white-burning centre of the moon, till there was nothing but a rocking of hollow noise, and a pond surged up, no moon any more, only a few broken flakes tangled and glittering broadcast in the darkness, without aim or meaning, a darkened confusion, like a black and white kaleidoscope tossed at random. The hollow night was rocking and crashing with noise, and from the sluice came sharp, regular flashes of sound. Flakes of light appeared here and there, glittering tormented among the shadows, far off, in strange places, among the dripping shadow of the willow on the island. Birkin stood and listened, and was satisfied.

Ursula was dazed, her mind was all gone. She felt she had fallen to the ground and was spilled out, like water on the earth. Motionless and spent, she remained in the gloom. Though even now she was aware, unseeing, that in the darkness was a little tumult of ebbing flakes of light, a cluster dancing secretly in a round, twining and coming stealthily together. They were gathering a heart again, they were coming once more into being. Gradually the fragments caught together, re-united, heaving, rocking, dancing, falling back as in panic, but working their way home again persistently, making semblance of fleeing away when they had advanced, but always flickering nearer, a little closer to the mark, the cluster growing mysteriously larger and brighter, as gleam after gleam fell in with the whole, until a ragged rose, a distorted, frayed moon was shaking upon the waters again, re-asserted, renewed, trying to recover from its convulsion, to get over the disfigurement and the agitation, to be whole and composed, at peace.

Women in Love, 1920

Cagliari

Slowly, slowly we creep along the formless shore. An hour passes. We see a little fort ahead, done in enormous black-and-white checks, like a fragment of a gigantic chessboard. It stands at the end of a long spit of land—a long, barish peninsula that has no houses and looks as if it might be golf links. But it is not golf links.

And suddenly there is Cagliari: a naked town rising steep, steep, golden-looking, piled naked to the sky from the plain at the head of the formless hollow bay. It is strange and rather wonderful, not a bit like Italy. The city piles up lofty and almost miniature, and makes me think of Jerusalem: without trees, without cover, rising rather bare and proud, remote as if back in history, like a town in a monkish, illuminated missal. One wonders how it ever got there. And it seems like Spain—or Malta: not Italy. It is a steep and lonely city, treeless, as in some old illumination. Yet withal rather jewel-like: like a sudden rose-cut amber jewel naked at the depth of the vast indenture. The air is cold, blowing bleak and bitter, the sky is all curd. And that is Cagliari. It has that curious look, as if it could be seen but not entered. It is like some vision, some memory, something that has passed away. Impossible that one can actually *walk* in that city: set foot there and eat and laugh there. Ah, no! Yet the ships drift nearer, nearer, and we are looking for the actual harbour.

Sea and Sardinia, 1921

A Suburb of Sydney

Murdoch Street was an old sort of suburb, little squat bungalows with corrugated iron roofs, painted red. Each little bungalow was set in its own hand-breadth of ground, surrounded by a little wooden palisade fence. And there went the long street, like a child's drawing, the little square bungalows dot-dot-dot, close together and yet apart, like modern democracy, each one fenced round with a square rail fence. The street was wide, and strips of worn grass took the place of kerb-stones. The stretch of macadam in the middle seemed as forsaken as a desert, as the hansom clock-clocked along it.

Fifty-one had its name painted by the door. Somers had been watching these names. He had passed 'Elite,' and 'Très Bon' and 'The Angels Roost' and 'The Better 'Ole.' He rather hoped for one of the Australian names, Wallamby or Wagga-Wagga. When he had looked at the house and agreed to take it for three months, it had been dusk, and he had not noticed the name. He hoped it would not be U-and-Me, or even Stella Maris.

Kangaroo, 1923

A Bob-Cat

She took a saucepan and went down the stones to the water. It was very still and mysterious, and of a deep green colour, yet pure, transparent as glass. How cold the place was! How mysterious and fearful.

She crouched in her dark cloak by the water, rinsing the saucepan, feeling the cold heavy above her, the shadow like a vast weight upon her, bowing her down. The sun was leaving the mountain tops, departing, leaving her under profound shadow. Soon it would crush her down completely.

Sparks?—or eyes looking at her across the water? She gazed, hypnotised. And with her sharp eyes she made out in the dusk the pale form of a bob-cat crouching by the water's edge, pale as the stones among which it crouched, opposite. And it was watching her with cold, electric eyes of strange intentness, a sort of cold, icy wonder and fearlessness. She saw its *museau* pushed forward, its tufted ears pricking intensely up. It was watching her with cold, animal curiosity, something demonish and conscienceless.

She made a swift movement, spilling her water. And in a flash the creature was gone, leaping like a cat that is escaping; but strange and soft in its motion, with its little bob-tail. Rather fascinating. Yet that cold, intent, demonish watching! She shivered with cold and fear. She knew well enough the dread and repulsiveness of the wild.

St Mawr, 1925

A Mining Village in the Twenties

The car ploughed uphill through the long squalid straggle of Tevershall, the blackened brick dwellings, the black slate roofs glistening their sharp edges, the mud black with coal-dust, the pavements wet and black. It was as if dismalness had soaked through and through everything. The utter negation of natural beauty, the utter negation of the gladness of life, the utter absence of the instinct for shapely beauty which every bird and beast has, the utter death of the human intuitive faculty was appalling. The stacks of soap in the grocers' shops, the rhubarb and lemons in the greengrocers'! the awful hats in the milliners'! all went by ugly, ugly, ugly, followed by the plaster-and-gilt horror of the cinema with its wet picture announcements, 'A Woman's Love!', and the new big Primitive chapel, primitive enough in its stark brick and big panes of greenish and raspberry glass in the windows. The Wesleyan chapel, higher up, was of blackened brick and stood behind iron railings and blackened shrubs. The Congregational chapel, which thought itself superior, was built of rusticated sandstone and had a steeple, but not a very high one. Just beyond were the new school buildings, expensive pink brick, and gravelled playground inside iron railings, all very imposing, and mixing the suggestion of a chapel and a prison. Standard Five girls were having a singing lesson, just finishing the la-me-do-la exercises and beginning a 'sweet children's song.' Anything more unlike song, spontaneous song, would be impossible to imagine: a strange bawling yell that followed the outlines of a tune. It was not like savages: savages have subtle rhythms. It was not like animals: animals *mean* something when they yell. It was like nothing on earth, and it was called singing. Connie sat and listened with her heart in her boots, as Field was filling petrol. What could possibly become of such a people, a people in whom the living intuitive faculty was dead as nails, and only queer mechanical yells and uncanny will-power remained?

Lady Chatterley's Lover, privately printed 1928

The Supreme Triumph

For man, the vast marvel is to be alive. For man, as for flower and beast and bird, the supreme triumph is to be most vividly, most perfectly alive. Whatever the unborn and the dead may know, they cannot know the beauty, the marvel of being alive in the flesh. The dead may look after the afterwards. But the magnificent here and now of life in the flesh is ours, and ours alone, and ours only for a time. We ought to dance with rapture that we should be alive and in the flesh, and part of the living, incarnate cosmos. I am part of the sun as my eye is part of me. That I am part of the earth my feet know perfectly, and my blood is part of the sea. My soul knows that I am part of the human race, my soul is an organic part of the great human soul, as my spirit is part of my nation. In my own very self, I am part of my family. There is nothing of me that is alone and absolute except my mind, and we shall find that the mind has no existence by itself, it is only the glitter of the sun on the surface of the waters.

Apocalypse, 1931

SINCLAIR LEWIS
1885–1951

Gopher Prairie Conquers the World

Doubtless all small towns, in all countries, in all ages, Carol admitted, have a tendency to be not only dull but mean, bitter, infested with curiosity. In France or Tibet quite as much as in Wyoming or Indiana these timidities are inherent in isolation.

But a village in a country which is taking pains to become altogether standardized and pure, which aspires to succeed Victorian England as the chief mediocrity of the world, is no longer merely provincial, no longer downy and restful in its leaf-shadowed ignorance. It is a force seeking to dominate the earth, to drain the hills and sea of color, to set Dante at boosting Gopher Prairie, and to dress the high gods in Klassy Kollege Klothes. Sure of itself, it bullies other civilizations, as a traveling salesman in a brown derby conquers the wisdom of China and tacks advertisements of cigarettes over arches for centuries dedicate to the sayings of Confucius.

Such a society functions admirably in the large production of cheap automobiles, dollar watches, and safety razors. But it is not satisfied until the entire world also admits that the end and joyous purpose of living is to ride in flivvers, to make advertising-pictures of dollar watches, and in the twilight to sit talking not of love and courage but of the convenience of safety razors.

And such a society, such a nation, is determined by the Gopher Prairies. The greatest manufacturer is but a busier Sam Clark, and all the rotund senators and presidents are village lawyers and bankers grown nine feet tall.

Main Street, 1920

Hustle

As he approached the office he walked faster and faster, muttering, 'Guess better hustle.' All about him the city was hustling, for hustling's sake. Men in motors were hustling to pass one another in the hustling traffic. Men were hustling to catch trains, with another train a minute behind, and to leap from the trains, to gallop across the pavement, to hurl themselves into buildings, into hustling express elevators. Men in dairy lunches were hustling to gulp down the food which cooks had hustled to fry. Men in barber shops were snapping, 'Jus' shave me once over. Gotta hustle.' Men were feverishly getting rid of visitors in offices adorned with the signs, 'This Is My Busy Day' and 'The Lord Created the World in Six Days—You Can Spiel All You Got to Say in Six Minutes.' Men who had made five thousand, the year before last, and ten thousand last year, were urging on nerve-yelping bodies and parched brains so that they might make twenty thousand this year; and the men who had broken down immediately after making their twenty thousand dollars were hustling to catch trains, to hustle through the vacations which the hustling doctors had ordered.

Among them Babbitt hustled back to his office, to sit down with nothing much to do except see that the staff looked as though they were hustling.

Babbitt, 1922

RING LARDNER
1885–1933

After Fifty Years

Mother says that when I start talking I never know when to stop. But I tell her the only time I get a chance is when she ain't around, so I have to make the most of it. I guess the fact is neither one of us would be welcome in a Quaker meeting, but as I tell Mother, what did God give us tongues for if He didn't want we should use them? Only she says He didn't give them to us to say the same thing over and over again, like I do, and repeat myself. But I say:

'Well, Mother,' I say, 'when people is like you and I and been married fifty years, do you expect everything I say will be something you ain't heard me say before? But it may be new to others, as they ain't nobody else lived with me as long as you have.'

So she says:

'You can bet they ain't, as they couldn't nobody else stand you that long.'

'Well,' I tell her, 'you look pretty healthy.'

'Maybe I do,' she will say, 'but I looked even healthier before I married you.'

You can't get ahead of Mother.

Yes, sir, we was married just fifty years ago the seventeenth day of last December and my daughter and son-in-law was over from Trenton to help us celebrate the Golden Wedding. My son-in-law is John H. Kramer, the real estate man. He made $12,000 one year and is pretty well thought of around Trenton; a good, steady, hard worker. The Rotarians was after him a long time to join, but he kept telling them his home was his club. But Edie finally made him join. That's my daughter.

Well, anyway, they come over to help us celebrate the Golden Wedding and it was pretty crimpy weather and the furnace don't seem to heat up no more like it used to and Mother made the remark that she hoped this winter wouldn't be as cold as the last, referring to the winter previous. So Edie said if she was us, and nothing to keep us home, she certainly wouldn't spend no more winters up here and why didn't we just shut off the water and close up the house and go down to Tampa, Florida? You know we was there four winters ago and staid five weeks, but it cost us over three hundred and fifty dollars for hotel bill alone. So Mother said we wasn't going no place to be robbed. So my son-in-law spoke up and said that Tampa wasn't the only place in the South, and besides we didn't have to stop at no high price hotel but could rent us a couple rooms and board out somewheres, and he had heard that St Petersburg, Florida, was *the* spot and if we said the word he would write down there and make inquiries.

Well, to make a long story short, we decided to do it and Edie said it would be our Golden Honeymoon and for a present my son-in-law paid the difference between a section and a compartment so as we could have a compartment and have more privatecy. In a compartment you have an upper and lower berth just like the regular sleeper, but it is a shut in room by itself and got a wash bowl. The car we went in was all compartments and no regular berths at all. It was all compartments.

We went to Trenton the night before and staid at my daughter and son-in-law and we left Trenton the next afternoon at 3.23 P.M.

This was the twelfth day of January. Mother set facing the front of the train, as it makes her giddy to ride backwards. I set facing her, which does not affect me. We reached North Philadelphia at 4.03 P.M. and we reached

West Philadelphia at 4.14, but did not go into Broad Street. We reached Baltimore at 6.30 and Washington, D.C., at 7.25. Our train laid over in Washington two hours till another train come along to pick us up and I got out and strolled up the platform and into the Union Station. When I come back, our car had been switched on to another track, but I remembered the name of it, the La Belle, as I had once visited my aunt out in Oconomowoc, Wisconsin, where there was a lake of that name, so I had no difficulty in getting located. But Mother had nearly fretted herself sick for fear I would be left.

'Well,' I said, 'I would of followed you on the next train.'

'You could of,' said Mother, and she pointed out that she had the money.

'Well,' I said, 'we are in Washington and I could of borrowed from the United States Treasury. I would of pretended I was an Englishman.'

Mother caught the point and laughed heartily.

'The Golden Honeymoon', *How to Tell Short Stories*, 1924

RONALD FIRBANK
1886–1926

Earthquake in Cuna-Cuna

Sauntering by the dusty benches along the pavement-side, where white-robed negresses sat communing in twos and threes, he attained the Avenue Messalina with its spreading palms, whose fronds hung nerveless in the windless air.

Tinkling mandolins from restaurant gardens, light laughter, and shifting lights.

Passing before the Café de Cuna, and a people's 'Dancing,' he roamed leisurely along. Incipient Cyprians, led by vigilant, blanched-faced queens, youths of a certain life, known as bwam-wam bwam-wams, gaunt pariah dogs with questing eyes, all equally were on the prowl. Beneath the Pharaohic pilasters of the Theatre Maxine Bush a street crowd had formed before a notice described 'Important,' which informed the Public that, owing to a 'temporary hoarseness,' the rôle of Miss Maxine Bush would be taken, on that occasion, by Miss Pauline Collier.

The Marcella Gardens lay towards the end of the Avenue, in the animated vicinity of the Opera. Pursuing the glittering thoroughfare, it was interesting to observe the pleasure announcements of the various theatres, picked out in signs of fire: *Aïda: The Jewels of the Madonna: Clara Novotny and Lily Lima's Season.*

Vending bags of roasted peanuts, or sapodillas and avocado pears, insistent small boys were importuning the throng.

'Go away; I can't be bodder,' Charlie was saying, when he seemed to slip; it was as though the pavement were a carpet snatched from under him, and, looking round, he was surprised to see, in a confectioner's window, a couple of marble-topped tables start merrily waltzing together.

Driven onward by those behind, he began stumblingly to run towards the Park. It was the general goal. Footing it a little ahead, two loose women and a gay young man (pursued by a waiter with a napkin and a bill), together with the horrified, half-crazed crowd; all, helter-skelter, were intent upon the Park.

Above the Calabash-trees, bronze, demoniac, the moon gleamed sourly from a starless sky, and although not a breath of air was stirring, the crests of the loftiest palms were set arustling by the vibration at their roots.

'Oh, will nobody *stop* it?' a terror-struck lady implored.

Feeling quite white and clasping a fetish, Charlie sank all panting to the ground.

Safe from falling chimney-pots and sign-boards (that for 'Pure Vaseline,' for instance, had all but caught him), he had much to be thankful for.

'Sh'o nuff, dat was a close shave,' he gasped, gazing dazed about him.

Clustered back to back near by upon the grass, three stolid matrons, matrons of hoary England, evidently not without previous earthquake experience, were ignoring resolutely the repeated shocks.

'I always follow the Fashions, dear, at a distance!' one was saying: 'this little gingham gown I'm wearing I had made for me after a design I found in a newspaper at my hotel.'

'It must have been a pretty old one, dear—I mean the paper, of course.'

'New things are only those you know that have been forgotten.'

'Mary . . . there's a sharp pin, sweet, at the back of your . . . *Oh!*'

Venturing upon his legs, Charlie turned away.

By the Park palings a few 'Salvationists' were holding forth, while, in the sweep before the bandstand, the artists from the Opera, in their costumes of Aïda, were causing almost a greater panic among the ignorant than the earthquake itself. A crowd, promiscuous rather than representative, composed variously of chauffeurs (making a wretched pretence, poor chaps, of seeking out their masters), Cyprians, patricians (these in opera cloaks and sparkling diamonds), tourists, for whom the Hodeidah girls would *not* dance that night, and bwam-wam bwam-wams, whose equivocal behaviour, indeed, was perhaps more shocking even than the shocks, set the pent Park ahum. Yet, notwithstanding the upheavals of Nature, certain persons there were bravely making new plans.

'How I wish I could, dear! But I shall be having a houseful of women over Sunday—that's to say.'

'Then come the week after.'

'Thanks, then, I *will*.'

Prancing Nigger, 1925

HAROLD NICOLSON
1886–1968

The Head Boy

How fortuitous and yet how formative are the admirations which our school life thrusts upon us! With no man have I had less in common than with J. D. Marstock, and yet for years he exercised upon me an influence which, though negative, was intense. How clean he was, how straight, how manly! How proud we were of him, how modest he was about himself! And then those eyes—those frank and honest eyes! 'One can see,' my tutor said, 'that Marstock has never had a mean or nasty thought.' It took me six years to realise that Marstock, although stuffed with opinions, had never had a thought at all.

I can visualise him best as he appeared when head of the school, when captain of football. A tall figure, he seemed, in his black and orange jersey striped as a wasp. Upon his carefully oiled hair was stuck a little velvet cap with a gold tassel: he would walk away from the field, his large red hands pendant, a little mud upon his large red knees. He would pause for a moment and speak to a group of lower boys. 'Yes, Marstock,—no, Marstock,' they would answer, and then he would smile democratically, and walk on—a slight lilt in his gait betraying that he was not unconscious of how much he was observed. Those wide open eyes that looked life straight, if unseeingly, in the face were fixed in front of him upon that distant clump of Wellingtonias, upon the two red towers of the college emerging behind. His cheeks, a little purple in the cold, showed traces of that eczema which so often accompanies adolescent youth. But it was not an ugly face. A large and slightly fleshy nose: a thin mouth: a well-formed chin: a younger and a plumper Viscount Grey.

Under the great gate he went and across the quadrangle. He must first look in upon the Sixth Form room, a room reserved apparently for prefects who were seldom in the Sixth. He sank into a deck chair by the fire. The other prefects spoke to him about conditions in the Blucher dormitory and the date of the pancake run. Yes, he would have to tell the Master about the Blucher, and there was no reason why they should not have the run on Tuesday. And then out under the great gate again and across through pine trees to Mr Kempthorne's house. There on the floor would be his basin ready for him and a can of hot water beside it. And he had ordered that seed-cake. The smell of cocoa met him as he entered the passage. Seed-cake, and cocoa, and Pears soap, and the soft hum of a kettle on the gas: then work for two hours and then prayers. He would read the roll-call himself that evening. Oh yes! and afterwards there was a boy to be caned. The basket work of his armchair creaked as he leant forward for the towel.

Some People, 1927

SIEGFRIED SASSOON
1886–1967

The Shell-Shock Hospital

It would be an exaggeration if I were to describe Slateford as a depressing place by daylight. The doctors did everything possible to counteract gloom, and the wrecked faces were outnumbered by those who were emerging from their nervous disorders. But the War Office had wasted no money on interior decoration; consequently the place had the melancholy atmosphere of a decayed hydro, redeemed only by its healthy situation and pleasant view of the Pentland Hills. By daylight the doctors dealt successfully with these disadvantages, and Slateford, so to speak, 'made cheerful conversation'.

But by night they lost control and the hospital became sepulchral and oppressive with saturations of war experience. One lay awake and listened to feet padding along passages which smelt of stale cigarette-smoke; for the nurses couldn't prevent insomnia-ridden officers from smoking half the night in their bedrooms, though the locks had been removed from all doors. One became conscious that the place was full of men whose slumbers were morbid and terrifying—men muttering uneasily or suddenly crying out in their sleep. Around me was that underworld of dreams haunted by submerged memories of warfare and its intolerable shocks and self-lacerating failures to achieve the impossible. By daylight each mind was a sort of aquarium for the psychopath to study. In the day-time, sitting in a sunny room, a man could discuss his psycho-neurotic symptoms with his doctor, who could diagnose phobias and conflicts and formulate them in scientific terminology. Significant dreams could be noted down, and Rivers could try to remove repressions. But by night each man was back in his doomed sector of a horror-stricken front line where the panic and stampede of some ghastly experience was re-enacted among the livid faces of the dead. No doctor could save him then, when he became the lonely victim of his dream disasters and delusions.

Shell-shock. How many a brief bombardment had its long-delayed after-effect in the minds of these survivors, many of whom had looked at their companions and laughed while inferno did its best to destroy them.

Not then was their evil hour, but now; now, in the sweating suffocation of nightmare, in paralysis of limbs, in the stammering of dislocated speech. Worst of all, in the disintegration of those qualities through which they had been so gallant and selfless and uncomplaining—this, in the finer types of men, was the unspeakable tragedy of shell-shock; it was in this that their humanity had been outraged by those explosives which were sanctioned and glorified by the Churches; it was thus that their self-sacrifice was mocked and maltreated—they, who in the name of righteousness had been sent out to maim and slaughter their fellow-men. In the name of civilization these soldiers had been martyred, and it remained for civilization to prove that their martyrdom wasn't a dirty swindle.

Sherston's Progress, 1936

EDWIN MUIR
1887–1959

A Small Boy in Orkney

That summer my father took me one evening to the Haa with him. The farmer of the Haa had bought a cow and had just let it into the field where his other cows were grazing. He and his sons were standing at the gate of the field to watch how the herd would welcome the new cow. For a while the cows paid no attention; then they all began to look in the same direction and drew together as if for protection or consultation, staring at the strange cow, which had retreated into a corner of the field. Suddenly they charged in a pack, yet as if they were frightened, not angry. The farmer and his sons rushed into the field, calling on their dog, and managed to head off the herd. The new cow, trembling, was led back to the byre. My father and the farmer philosophically discussed the incident as two anthropologists might discuss the customs of strange tribes. It seemed that this treatment of new members of the herd was quite common. It frightened me, yet it did not shake my belief in the harmlessness of our own cows, but merely made me despise them a little for being subject to foolish impulses, for as they charged across the field they looked more foolish than dangerous.

The distance of my eyes from the ground influenced my image of my father and mother too. I have a vivid impression of my father's cream-coloured moleskin breeches, which resisted elastically when I flung myself against them, and of my mother's skirt, which yielded, softly enveloping me. But I cannot bring back my mental impression of them, for it is overlaid by later memories in which I saw them as a man and a woman, like, or almost like, other men and women. I am certain that I did not see them like this at first; I never thought that they were like other men and women; to me they were fixed allegorical figures in a timeless landscape. Their allegorical changelessness made them more, not less, solid, as if they were condensed into something more real than humanity; as if the image 'mother' meant more than 'woman,' and the image 'father' more than 'man.'

The Story and the Fable, 1940 (revised as *An Autobiography*, 1954)

T. E. LAWRENCE
1888–1935

Torture and Torment

They led me into a guard-room, mostly taken up by large wooden cribs, on which lay or sat a dozen men in untidy uniforms. They took away my belt, and my knife, made me wash myself carefully, and fed me. I passed the long day there. They would not let me go on any terms, but tried to reassure me. A soldier's life was not all bad. To-morrow, perhaps, leave would be permitted, if I fulfilled the Bey's pleasure this evening. The Bey seemed to be Nahi, the Governor. If he was angry, they said, I would be drafted for infantry training to the depot in Baalbek. I tried to look as though, to my mind, there was nothing worse in the world than that.

Soon after dark three men came for me. It had seemed a chance to get away, but one held me all the time. I cursed my littleness. Our march crossed the railway, where were six tracks, besides the sidings of the engine-shop. We went through a side gate, down a street, past a square, to a detached, two-storied house. There was a sentry outside, and a glimpse of others lolling in the dark entry. They took me upstairs to the Bey's room; or to his bedroom, rather. He was another bulky man, a Circassian himself, perhaps, and sat on the bed in a night-gown, trembling and sweating as though with fever. When I was pushed in he kept his head down, and waved the guard out. In a breathless voice he told me to sit on the floor in front of him, and after that was dumb; while I gazed at the top of his great head, on which the bristling hair stood up, no longer than the dark stubble on his cheeks and chin. At last he looked me over, and told me to stand up: then to turn round. I obeyed; he flung himself back on the bed, and dragged me down with him in his arms. When I saw what he wanted I twisted round and up again, glad to find myself equal to him, at any rate in wrestling.

He began to fawn on me, saying how white and fresh I was, how fine my hands and feet, and how he would let me off drills and duties, make me his orderly, even pay me wages, if I would love him.

I was obdurate, so he changed his tone, and sharply ordered me to take off my drawers. When I hesitated, he snatched at me; and I pushed him back. He clapped his hands for the sentry, who hurried in and pinioned me. The Bey cursed me with horrible threats: and made the man holding me tear my clothes away, bit by bit. His eyes rounded at the half-healed places where the bullets had flicked through my skin a little while ago. Finally he lumbered to his feet, with a glitter in his look, and began to paw me over. I bore it for a little, till he got too beastly; and then jerked my knee into him.

He staggered to his bed, squeezing himself together and groaning with pain, while the soldier shouted for the corporal and the other three men to grip me hand and foot. As soon as I was helpless the Governor regained courage, and spat at me, swearing he would make me ask pardon. He took off his slipper, and hit me repeatedly with it in the face, while the corporal braced my head back by the hair to receive the blows. He leaned forward, fixed his teeth in my neck and bit till the blood came. Then he kissed me. Afterwards he drew one of the men's bayonets. I thought he was going to kill me, and was sorry: but he only pulled up a fold of the flesh over my ribs, worked the point through, after considerable trouble, and gave the blade a half-turn. This hurt, and I winced, while the blood wavered down my side, and dripped to the front of my thigh. He looked pleased and dabbled it over my stomach with his finger-tips.

In my despair I spoke. His face changed and he stood still, then controlled his voice with an effort, to say significantly, 'You must understand that I know: and it will be easier if you do as I wish.' I was dumbfounded, and we stared silently at one another, while the men who felt an inner meaning beyond their experience, shifted uncomfortably. But it was evidently a chance shot, by which he himself did not, or would not, mean what I feared. I could not again trust my twitching mouth, which faltered always in emergencies, so at last threw up my chin, which was the sign for 'No' in the East; then he sat down, and half-whispered to the corporal to take me out and teach me everything.

They kicked me to the head of the stairs, and stretched me over a guard-bench, pommelling me. Two knelt on my ankles, bearing down on the back of my knees, while two more twisted my wrists till they cracked, and then crushed them and my neck against the wood. The corporal had run downstairs; and now came back with a whip of the Circassian sort, a thong of supple black hide, rounded, and tapering from the thickness of a thumb at the grip (which was wrapped in silver) down to a hard point finer than a pencil.

He saw me shivering, partly I think, with cold, and made it whistle over my ear, taunting me that before his tenth cut I would howl for mercy, and at the twentieth beg for the caresses of the Bey; and then he began to lash me madly across and across with all his might, while I locked my teeth to endure this thing which lapped itself like flaming wire about my body.

To keep my mind in control I numbered the blows, but after twenty lost count, and could feel only the shapeless weight of pain, not tearing claws, for which I had prepared, but a gradual cracking apart of my whole being by some too-great force whose waves rolled up my spine till they were pent within my brain, to clash terribly together. Somewhere in the place a cheap clock ticked loudly, and it distressed me that their beating was not in its time. I writhed and twisted, but was held so tightly that my struggles were useless. After the corporal ceased, the men took up, very deliberately, giving me so many, and then an interval, during which they would squabble for the next turn, ease themselves, and play unspeakably with me. This was repeated often, for what may have been no more than ten minutes. Always for the first of every new series, my head would be pulled round, to see how a hard white ridge, like a railway, darkening slowly into crimson, leaped over my skin at the instant of each stroke, with a bead of blood where two ridges crossed. As the punishment proceeded the whip fell more and more upon existing weals, biting blacker or more wet, till my flesh quivered with accumulated pain, and with terror of the next blow coming. They soon conquered my determination not to cry, but while my will ruled my lips I used only Arabic, and before the end a merciful sickness choked my utterance.

At last when I was completely broken they seemed satisfied. Somehow I found myself off the bench, lying on my back on the dirty floor, where I snuggled down, dazed, panting for breath, but vaguely comfortable. I had strung myself to learn all pain until I died, and no longer actor, but spectator, thought not to care how my body jerked and squealed. Yet I knew or imagined what passed about me.

Seven Pillars of Wisdom, 1926

T. S. ELIOT

1888–1965

Imagery and Memory

Only a part of an author's imagery comes from his reading. It comes from the whole of his sensitive life since early childhood. Why, for all of us, out of all that we have heard, seen, felt, in a lifetime, do certain images recur, charged with emotion, rather than others? The song of one bird, the leap of one fish, at a particular place and time, the scent of one flower, an old woman on a German mountain path, six ruffians seen through an open window playing cards at night at a small French railway junction where there was a water-mill: such memories may have symbolic value, but of what we cannot tell, for they come to represent the depths of feeling into which we cannot peer. We might just as well ask why, when we try to recall visually some period in the past, we find in our memory just the few meagre arbitrarily chosen set of snapshots that we do find there, the faded poor souvenirs of passionate moments.

The Use of Poetry and the Use of Criticism, 1933

Tennyson

Tennyson lived in a time which was already acutely time-conscious: a great many things seemed to be happening, railways were being built, discoveries were being made, the face of the world was changing. That was a time busy in keeping up to date. It had, for the most part, no hold on permanent things, on permanent truths about man and god and life and death. The surface of Tennyson stirred about with his time; and he had nothing to which to hold fast except his unique and unerring feeling for the sounds of words. But in this he had something that no one else had. Tennyson's surface, his technical accomplishment, is intimate with his depths: what we most quickly see about Tennyson is that which moves between the surface and the depths, that which is of slight importance. By looking innocently at the surface we are most likely to come to the depths, to the abyss of sorrow. Tennyson is not only a minor Virgil, he is also with Virgil as Dante saw him, a Virgil among the Shades, the saddest of all English poets, among the Great in Limbo, the most instinctive rebel against the society in which he was the most perfect conformist.

'*In Memoriam*', 1936

KATHERINE MANSFIELD
1888–1923

A Week Since Father Died

But at that moment in the street below a barrel-organ struck up. Josephine and Constantia sprang to their feet together.

'Run, Con,' said Josephine. 'Run quickly. There's sixpence on the——'

Then they remembered. It didn't matter. They would never have to stop the organ-grinder again. Never again would she and Constantia be told to make that monkey take his noise somewhere else. Never would sound that loud, strange bellow when father thought they were not hurrying enough. The organ-grinder might play there all day and the stick would not thump.

It never will thump again,
It never will thump again,

played the barrel-organ.

What was Constantia thinking? She had such a strange smile; she looked different. She couldn't be going to cry.

'Jug, Jug,' said Constantia softly, pressing her hands together. 'Do you know what day it is? It's Saturday. It's a week to-day, a whole week.'

A week since father died,
A week since father died,

cried the barrel-organ. And Josephine, too, forgot to be practical and sensible; she smiled faintly, strangely. On the Indian carpet there fell a square of sunlight, pale red; it came and went and came—and stayed, deepened—until it shone almost golden.

'The sun's out,' said Josephine, as though it really mattered.

A perfect fountain of bubbling notes shook from the barrel-organ, round, bright notes, carelessly scattered.

Constantia lifted her big, cold hands as if to catch them, and then her hands fell again. She walked over to the mantelpiece to her favourite Buddha. And the stone and gilt image, whose smile always gave her such a queer feeling, almost a pain and yet a pleasant pain, seemed to-day to be more than smiling. He knew something; he had a secret. 'I know something that you don't know,' said her Buddha. Oh, what was it, what could it be? And yet she had always felt there was . . . something.

The sunlight pressed through the windows, thieved its way in, flashed its light over the furniture and the photographs. Josephine watched it. When it came to mother's photograph, the enlargement over the piano, it lingered as though puzzled to find so little remained of mother, except the ear-rings shaped like tiny pagodas and a black feather boa. Why did the photographs of dead people always fade so? wondered Josephine. As soon as a person was dead their photograph died too. But, of course, this one of mother was very old. It was thirty-five years old. Josephine remembered standing on a chair and pointing out that feather boa to Constantia and telling her that it was a snake that had killed their mother in Ceylon. . . . Would everything have been different if mother hadn't died? She didn't see why. Aunt Florence had lived with them until they had left school, and they had moved three times and had their yearly holiday and . . . and there'd been changes of servants, of course.

Some little sparrows, young sparrows they sounded, chirped on the window-ledge. *Yeep—eyeep—yeep.* But Josephine felt they were not sparrows, not on the window-ledge. It was inside her, that queer little crying noise. *Yeep—eyeep—yeep.* Ah, what was it crying, so weak and forlorn?

If mother had lived, might they have married? But there had been nobody for them to marry. There had been father's Anglo-Indian friends before he quarrelled with them. But after that she and Constantia never met a single man except clergymen. How did one meet men? Or even if they'd met them, how could they have got to know men well enough to be more than strangers? One read of people having adventures, being followed, and so on. But nobody had ever followed Constantia and her. Oh yes, there had been one year at Eastbourne a mysterious man at their boarding-house who had put a note on the jug of hot water outside their bedroom door! But by the time Connie had found it the steam had made the writing too faint to read; they couldn't even make out to which of them it was addressed. And he had left next day. And that was all. The rest had been looking after father, and at the same time keeping out of father's way. But now? But now? The thieving sun touched Josephine gently. She lifted her face. She was drawn over to the window by gentle beams. . . .

'The Daughters of the Late Colonel', *The Garden Party*, 1922

RAYMOND CHANDLER
1888–1959

The Road to Stillwood Heights

The car was a dark blue seven-passenger sedan, a Packard of the latest model, custom-built. It was the kind of car you wear your rope pearls in. It was parked by a fire-hydrant and a dark foreign-looking chauffeur with a face of carved wood was behind the wheel. The interior was upholstered in quilted grey chenille. The Indian put me in the back. Sitting there alone I felt like a high-class corpse, laid out by an undertaker with a lot of good taste.

The Indian got in beside the chauffeur and the car turned in the middle of the block and a cop across the street said: 'Hey,' weakly, as if he didn't mean it, and then bent down quickly to tie his shoe.

We went west, dropped over to Sunset and slid fast and noiseless along that. The Indian sat motionless beside the chauffeur. An occasional whiff of his personality drifted back to me. The driver looked as if he was half asleep but he passed the fast boys in the convertible sedans as though they were being towed. They turned on all the green lights for him. Some drivers are like that. He never missed one.

We curved through the bright mile or two of the Strip, past the antique shops with famous screen names on them, past the windows full of point lace and ancient pewter, past the gleaming new night clubs with famous chefs and equally famous gambling rooms, run by polished graduates of the Purple Gang, past the Georgian-Colonial vogue, now old hat, past the handsome modernistic buildings in which the Hollywood flesh-peddlers never stop talking money, past a drive-in lunch which somehow didn't belong, even though the girls wore white silk blouses and drum majorettes' shakos and nothing below the hips but glazed kid Hessian boots. Past all this and down a wide smooth curve to the bridle path of Beverly Hills and lights to the south, all colours of the spectrum and crystal clear in an evening without fog, past the shadowed mansions up on the hills to the north, past Beverly Hills altogether and up into the twisting foothill boulevard and the sudden cool dusk and the drift of wind from the sea.

It had been a warm afternoon, but the heat was gone. We whipped past a distant cluster of lighted buildings and an endless series of lighted mansions, not too close to the road. We dipped down to skirt a huge green polo field with another equally huge practice field beside it, soared again to the top of a hill and swung mountainward up a steep hill road of clean concrete that passed orange groves, some rich man's pet because this is not orange country, and then little by little the lighted windows of the millionaires' homes were gone and the road narrowed and this was Stillwood Heights.

The smell of sage drifted up from a canyon and made me think of a dead man and a moonless sky. Straggly stucco houses were moulded flat to the side of the hill, like bas-reliefs. Then there were no more houses, just the still dark foothills with an early star or two above them, and the concrete ribbon of road and a sheer drop on one side into a tangle of scrub oak and manzanita where sometimes you can hear the call of the quails if you stop and keep still and wait. On the other side of the road was a raw clay bank at the edge of which a few unbeatable wild flowers hung on like naughty children that won't go to bed.

Then the road twisted into a hairpin turn and the big tyres scratched over loose stones, and the car tore less soundlessly up a long driveway lined with the wild geraniums. At the top of this, faintly lighted, lonely as a lighthouse, stood an eyrie, an eagle's nest, an angular building of stucco and glass brick, raw and modernistic and yet not ugly and altogether a swell place for a psychic consultant to hang out his shingle. Nobody would be able to hear any screams.

Farewell, My Lovely, 1940

Never the time and place . . .

'Out. I don't know you. I don't want to know you. And if I did, this wouldn't be either the day or the hour.'

'Never the time and place and the loved one all together,' I said.

'What's that?' She tried to throw me out with the point of her chin, but even she wasn't that good.

'Browning. The poet, not the automatic. I feel sure you'd prefer the automatic.'

The Little Sister, 1949

JOYCE CARY
1888–1957

A White Storekeeper in West Africa

Sergeant Gollup is a little man with a pale, lumpy face, a black moustache waxed at the points and round blue eyes. He is an old soldier. He parts his black hair down the middle, shaves carefully, and wears every day clean clothes, but not always in orthodox form. For instance, he will inspect his store and compounds in cotton drawers, a spotless singlet, a white linen coat, pale blue socks with green suspenders and white canvas shoes. He will go to bed in drawers and take an afternoon stroll in purple and green pyjamas, or he appears on the wharf in nothing but a pair of beautiful white trousers, carefully creased.

His store and compounds are kept as spotless as himself. Each path in the station is outlined with whitewashed stones and no stone is allowed out of place. But Gollup, like many old soldiers of the British Army, is not at all rigid in his ideas. He likes order, but it is his own order. He is a first-class trader, but he conducts trade by his own methods. For instance, when he gives presents in a village with which he seeks business, he does not give a big one to the chief, but many little ones to the people. He declares that he has doubled his turnover on a few bags of strong peppermint.

Gollup has built a fine store and a good trade. He struts about like a little king and when sometimes he looks round from his back stoop at the swept earth, the bright alleys, the new thatched roofs, all glittering in the sun, he purses up his lips in what is too dignified to be a grin of satisfaction. At such a moment the two points of his moustache rise as if presenting arms, and when he steps off on the left foot, he hollows his back like a guardee.

Gollup has an easy condescension to all the world, and just as, from the height of his military rank and native genius, he despises ordinary trader's and tailor's conventions, so also he refuses to condescend with the African sun. He scorns all topees, terais and sun hats and wears always, if he doesn't go bareheaded, a soft pearl-grey hat with a curled brim, which always looks new. 'Damn your old sun 'ats,' he says. 'Lot of stuff they talk. A real old coaster don't give a damn for the sun—and they're not the ones that fill the 'ospitals.'

Gollup, in fact, has had only three sunstrokes, and none of them has quite killed him. He is only inclined to lose his temper suddenly and violently, and to run a high temperature upon the least touch of fever. He is precise and polite in all his dealings with clerks, labourers and servants; but impatient with slow ones. Stupidity causes him to lose his temper and then he is ready to use his fists or his feet, or any weapon to hand. Johnson, on his first day, is surprised to see the gentlemanly Ajali receive a tremendous kick in the backside for failing to understand that 'Over there on the right, you silly bawstard' really means 'On the left, four shelves from the bottom.'

He does not see any more kicks, because Gollup, having given this one with an unexpected power and dexterity which moves Ajali visibly into the air and causes him to utter a loud squeal, turns suddenly to Johnson and says, 'You didn't see anything, did you?'

'What, sah?'

'You didn't see anything 'appen just then—to Ajali's trousers? Because if you did, you better not. See. Unless you want something to 'appen to your trousers, only more so.'

'Oh, yes, sah. I see, sah.'

'No, you silly baboon—you didn't see. See?'

'No, I didn't see, Mister Gollup.'

'That's it. You don't see and you take bleeding good care not to see, neither. I know the law as well as you do, Mr Monkeybrand.'

'Oh, yes, sah—I see, sah.'

Gollup turns upon him sharply and bawls, 'Oh, you do, do you? All right.' He swings up his fist.

'Oh, no, sah. I don't see.'

'Oh, you do see now—see—you see that you don't see. So that's all right.'

Gollup, pleased with the last joke, smiles, strokes his moustache and opening his mouth to show, unexpectedly, broken and blackened teeth utters a short laugh, 'Hawhaw.'

Johnson, seeing the joke, laughs heartily and both laugh together. Gollup then claps Johnson on the shoulder and says, 'I can see one thing—you got your 'ead screwed on—you and me's going to 'gree for each other. And all the better for you, see? I'm a good massa to the right uns. You stand by me and I'll stand by you.'

Mister Johnson, 1939

NEVILLE CARDUS
1889–1975

A Great Australian Batsman

To change the old saying about the strawberry, God no doubt could create a better batsman than Victor Trumper if He wished, but so far He hasn't. Ranjitsinhji is the only cricketer that might be instanced as Trumper's like in genius. But even 'Ranji' was not so great a match-winner on all wickets. Even 'Ranji' never smashed the best attack of his day with the sudden vehemence of Trumper. 'Ranji' did not rout his bowlers; he lured them onwards to ruin by the dark, stealthy magic of his play; the poor men were enchanted into futility. Trumper put them to the sword. . . . Yet it was a knightly sword. There never lived a more chivalrous cricketer than Trumper. I see his bat now, in my mind's eye, a banner in the air, streaming its brave runs over the field. He was ready always to take up the challenge of a good ball; Trumper never fell into the miserable philosophy of 'Safety first—wait for the bad ball.'

And what of the man's style? He had, as C. B. Fry put it, no style, yet he was all style. 'His whole bent is aggressive,' wrote Fry, 'and he plays a defensive stroke only as a very last resort.' Imagine Spooner's cover drive, Hirst's pull, MacLaren's hook, J. T. Tyldesley's square cut, Macartney's late cut through the slips—imagine a mingling of all these attributes of five great and wholly different batsmen, and perhaps some notion of Trumper will emerge in your mind. The grand manner of MacLaren, the lyrical grace of Spooner, the lion energy of Jessop, the swift opportunist spirit of Tyldesley—all these excellences were compounded proportionately in Trumper. Do I exaggerate youthful impressions of the man? Then let me give here a tribute to Trumper uttered to me by an English cricketer whose name stands for all that is masterful and majestic in our batsmanship: 'In comparison with an innings by Victor at his best my best was shoddy—hackwork!'

The Summer Game, 1929

KATHERINE ANNE PORTER
1890–1980

Berlin, 1931

Two days later he was still tramping the snowy streets, ringing doorbells and crawling back to the little hotel in the evenings pretty well dead on his feet. On the morning of the third day, when his search brought him finally to the third floor of a solid-looking apartment house in Bambergerstrasse, he took pains to observe very attentively the face of the woman who opened the door. In such a short time he had learned a wholesome terror of landladies in that city. They were smiling foxes, famished wolves, slovenly house cats, mere tigers, hyenas, furies, harpies: and sometimes, worst of all, they were sodden melancholy human beings who carried the history of their disasters in their faces, who all but wept when they saw him escape, as if he carried their last hope with him. Except for four winters in a minor southern university, Charles had lived at home. He had never looked for a lodging before, and he felt guilty, as if he had been peeping through cracks and keyholes, spying upon human inadequacy, its kitchen smells and airless bedrooms, the staleness of its poverty and the stuffiness of its prosperity. He had been shown spare cubbyholes back of kitchens where the baby's wash was drying on a string while the desolate room waited for a tenant. He had been ushered into regions of gilded carving and worn plush, full of the smell of yesterday's cabbage. He had ventured into bare expanses of glass brick and chrome-steel sparsely set out with white leather couches and mirror-topped tables, where, it always turned out, he would be expected to stay for a year at least, at frightening expense. He peered into a sodden little den fit, he felt, only for the scene of a murder; and into another where a sullen young woman was packing up, and the whole room reeked of some nasty perfume from her underwear piled upon the bed. She had given him a deliberately dirty smile, and the landlady had said something in a very brutal tone to her. But mostly, there was a stuffy tidiness, a depressing air of constant and unremitting housewifery, a kind of repellent gentility in room after room after room, varying only in the depth of feather bed and lavishness of draperies, and out of them all in turn he fled back to the street and the comparative freedom of the air.

The woman who opened the door presently, he saw, was a fairly agreeable-looking person of perhaps fifty years or more—above a certain age they all looked alike to Charles—with a pinkish face, white hair and very lively, light blue eyes. She gave the impression of being dressed up, she had a little high-falutin manner which seemed harmless, and she was evidently very pleased to see him. He noticed that the hall was almost empty but highly polished, perhaps here was the perfect compromise between overstuffed plush and a rat trap.

The Leaning Tower, 1944

JEAN RHYS
1890–1979

An Unwelcome Return

She walked in—pale as a ghost. She went straight up to Mr Mackenzie's table, and sat down opposite to him. He opened his mouth to speak, but no words came. So he shut it again. He was thinking, 'O God, oh Lord, she's come here to make a scene. . . . Oh God, oh Lord, she's come here to make a scene.'

He looked to the right and the left of him with a helpless expression. He felt a sensation of great relief when he saw that Monsieur Albert was standing near his table and looking at him with significance.

'That's the first time I've ever seen that chap look straight at anybody,' Mr Mackenzie thought.

Monsieur Albert was a small, fair man, an Alsatian. His eyes telegraphed, 'I understand; I remember this woman. Do you want to have her put out?'

Mr Mackenzie's face instinctively assumed a haughty expression, as if to say, 'What the devil do you mean?' He raised his eyebrows a little, just to put the fellow in his place.

Monsieur Albert moved away. When he had gone a little distance, he turned. This time Mr Mackenzie tried to telegraph back, 'Not yet, anyhow. But stand by.'

Then he looked at Julia for the first time. She said, 'Well, you didn't expect to see me here, did you?'

She coughed and cleared her throat.

Mr Mackenzie's nervousness left him. When she had walked in silent and ghost-like, he had been really afraid of her. Now he only felt that he disliked her intensely. He said in rather a high-pitched voice, 'I'd forgotten that I had invited you, certainly. However, as you are here, won't you have something to eat?.'

Julia shook her head.

There was a second place laid on the table. She took up the carafe of wine and poured out a glass. Mr Mackenzie watched her with a sardonic expression. He wondered why the first sight of her had frightened him so much. He was now sure that she could not make much of a scene. He knew her; the effort of walking into the restaurant and seating herself at his table would have left her in a state of collapse.

'But why do it?' thought Mr Mackenzie. 'Why in the name of common sense do a thing like that?'

Then he felt a sudden wish to justify himself, to let her know that he had not been lying when he had told her that he was going away.

He said, 'I only got back a couple of weeks ago.'

Julia said, 'Tell me, do you really like life? Do you think it's fair? Honestly now, do you?'

He did not answer this question. What a question, anyway! He took up his knife and fork and began to eat. He wanted to establish a sane and normal atmosphere.

As he put small pieces of veal and vegetable into his mouth, he was telling himself that he might just let her talk on, finish his meal, pay the bill, and walk out. Or he might accompany her out of the restaurant at once, under pretext of finding a quieter place to discuss things. Or he might hint that if she did not go he would ask Monsieur Albert to put her out. Though, of course, it was rather late to do that now.

At the same time he was thinking, 'No. Of course life isn't fair. It's damned unfair, really. Everybody knows that, but what does she expect me to do about it? I'm not God Almighty.'

After Leaving Mr Mackenzie, 1930

ZORA NEALE HURSTON
1891–1960

A True Believer

One day Tea Cake met Turner and his son on the street. He was a vanishing-looking kind of a man as if there used to be parts about him that stuck out individually but now he hadn't a thing about him that wasn't dwindled and blurred. Just like he had been sand-papered down to a long oval mass. Tea Cake felt sorry for him without knowing why. So he didn't blurt out the insults he had intended. But he couldn't hold in everything. They talked about the prospects for the coming season for a moment, then Tea Cake said, 'Yo' wife don't seem tuh have nothin' much tuh do, so she kin visit uh lot. Mine got too much tuh do tuh go visitin' and too much tuh spend time talkin' tuh folks dat visit her.'

'Mah wife takes time fuh whatever she wants tuh do. Real strong headed dat way. Yes indeed.' He laughed a high lungless laugh. 'De chillun don't keep her in no mo' so she visits when she chooses.'

'De chillun?' Tea Cake asked him in surprise. 'You got any smaller than him?' He indicated the son who seemed around twenty or so. 'Ah ain't seen yo' others.'

'Ah reckon you ain't 'cause dey all passed on befo' dis one wuz born. We ain't had no luck atall wid our chillun. We lucky to raise him. He's de last stroke of exhausted nature.'

He gave his powerless laugh again and Tea Cake and the boy joined in with him. Then Tea Cake walked on off and went home to Janie.

'Her husband can't do nothin' wid dat butt-headed woman. All you can do is treat her cold whenever she come round here.'

Janie tried that, but short of telling Mrs Turner bluntly, there was nothing she could do to discourage her completely. She felt honored by Janie's acquaintance and she quickly forgave and forgot snubs in order to keep it. Anyone who looked more white folkish than herself was better than she was in her criteria, therefore it was right that they should be cruel to her at times, just as she was cruel to those more negroid than herself in direct ratio to their negroness. Like the pecking-order in a chicken yard. Insensate cruelty to those you can whip, and grovelling submission to those you can't. Once having set up her idols and built altars to them it was inevitable that she would worship there. It was inevitable that she should accept any inconsistency and cruelty from her deity as all good worshippers do from theirs. All gods who receive homage are cruel. All gods dispense suffering without reason. Otherwise they would not be worshipped. Through indiscriminate suffering men know fear and fear is the most divine emotion. It is the stones for altars and the beginning of wisdom. Half gods are worshipped in wine and flowers. Real gods require blood.

Mrs Turner, like all other believers had built an altar to the unattainable—Caucasian characteristics for all. Her god would smite her, would hurl her from pinnacles and lose her in deserts. But she would not forsake his altars. Behind her crude words was a belief that somehow she and others through worship could attain her paradise—a heaven of straight-haired, thin-lipped, high-nose boned white seraphs. The physical impossibilities in no way injured faith. That was the mystery and mysteries are the chores of gods. Beyond her faith was a fanaticism to defend the altars of her god. It was distressing to emerge from her inner temple and find these black desecrators howling with laughter before the door. Oh, for an army, terrible with banners *and swords*!

So she didn't cling to Janie Woods the woman. She paid homage to Janie's Caucasian characteristics as such. And when she was with Janie she had a feeling of transmutation, as if she herself had become whiter and with straighter hair and she hated Tea Cake first for his defilement of divinity and next for his telling mockery of her. If she only knew something she could do about it! But she didn't.

Their Eyes Were Watching God, 1937

J. B. S. HALDANE
1892–1964

Bacillus Prodigiosus

Now, the dogma of transubstantiation, which needed such strange intellectual props, was not merely based, like many theological dogmas, on traditions of past events which had been brooded over by successive generations of the pious. It was grounded on a series of very well-attested miracles. Not only had individual ecstatics seen visions of Jesus in the host, but large numbers of people had seen hosts bleeding. The first of such events which is known to me occurred in England about AD 900, in the presence of Archbishop Odo. Among the most famous is the miracle of Bolsena (also known as the miracle of the Bloody Corporal), which is portrayed in Raphael's well-known picture, and converted a priest who doubted transubstantiation. Allowing for a certain amount of exaggeration for the glory of God, I see no reason to disbelieve in these miracles. Their nature becomes very probable from the way in which they tended to occur in series, especially in Belgium. A 'bleeding host' appeared in a certain church. The faithful went to adore it, and fairly soon others appeared in the vicinity. There is very strong reason to suppose that we have to deal with an outbreak of infection of bread by *Bacillus prodigiosus* (the miraculous bacillus), which would naturally be spread by human contacts. Their organism grows readily on bread, and produces red patches, which the eye of faith might well take for blood.

The miracle of Bolsena appears to have finally converted Pope Urban IV to the views, not only of St Thomas, but of his contemporary, St Juliana of Liège, one of the two women who have initiated important changes in Catholic practice, the other being St Marie Marguerite Alacocque, the initiator of the cult of the Sacred Heart. St Juliana had a vision of the moon with a black spot on it, and was told that the moon signified the Church, the spot being the absence of a special cult of Christ's body. As a result of this vision the Bishop of Liège instituted the feast of Corpus Christi, and in 1264 Pope Urban IV, who had been Archdeacon of Liège, made its celebration compulsory throughout Western Europe. The office for the feast was written by St Thomas Aquinas. In honour of Christ's body a college was founded at Cambridge within the next century, though the corresponding establishment at Oxford dates back only to shortly before the Reformation. There is no record of what St Juliana said to the angel who told her about the activities of the poet Kit Marlowe, student of Corpus Christi College, Cambridge. For it appears from the record of his 'damnable opinion' that he was a remarkably militant rationalist, while a spy stated that he was 'able to shewe more sound reasons for Atheisme than any devine in Englande is able to geve to prove devinitie'. Perhaps, however, such things are kept from the ears of the blessed.

Unfortunately, *Bacillus prodigiosus* did not confine its efforts to inspiring queer metaphysics and founding colleges. If a bleeding host was God's body, any bit of bread which appeared to bleed was a host, presumably stolen and desecrated. Throughout the ages of faith the same incidents reoccurred. A piece of bread in a house started to 'bleed'. An informer, generally a servant, went to the authorities. The family were tortured, and finally confessed to having stolen or bought a consecrated wafer and run daggers through it. They were then generally burned alive. Such an incident was often a signal for a massacre of Jews, as in the pogrom of 1370, commemorated in the disgusting stained-glass windows of the cathedral of Ste Gudule at Brussels, and in the French outbreaks of 1290 and 1433. Sometimes the victims were gentiles, as in the case recorded by Paolo Uccello in a series of panels which were on view at the London exhibition of Italian painting in 1930. Doubtless among them were a few fools who were genuinely celebrating black masses; but the emphasis laid on the blood in contemporary accounts seems to incriminate *Bacillus prodigiosus*. In England the belief in transubstantiation ceased abruptly in the sixteenth century to be part of the law of the land. 'Hoc est corpus' became *hocus pocus*. But in France the attempt to make injuries to consecrated wafers a capital offence, as deicide, was one of the causes of the revolution of 1830.

'God-Makers', *The Inequality of Man*, 1932

REBECCA WEST
1892–1983

William Joyce ('Lord Haw-Haw') in the Dock

The strong light was merciless to William Joyce, whose appearance was a shock to all of us who knew him only over the air. His voice had suggested a large and flashy handsomeness, but he was a tiny little creature and not handsome at all. His hair was mouse-coloured and sparse, particularly above his ears, and his pinched and misshapen nose was joined to his face at an odd angle. His eyes were hard and shiny, and above them his thick eyebrows were pale and irregular. His neck was long, his shoulders narrow and sloping, his arms very short and thick. His body looked flimsy and coarse. There was nothing individual about him except a deep scar running across his right cheek from his ear to the corner of his mouth. But this did not create the savage and marred distinction that it might suggest, for it gave a mincing immobility to his small mouth. He was dressed with a dandyish preciosity which gave no impression of well-being, only of nervousness. He was like an ugly version of Scott Fitzgerald, but more nervous. He moved with a jerky formality and, when he bowed to the judge, his bow seemed sincerely respectful but entirely inappropriate to the occasion, and it was difficult to think of any occasion to which it would have been appropriate.

He had been defying us all. Yet there was nobody in the court who did not look superior to him. The men and women in the jury box were all middle-aged, since the armies had not yet come home, and, like everybody else in England at that date, they were puffy and haggard. But they were all more pleasant to look at and more obviously trustworthy than the homely and eccentric little man in the dock; and compared with the judicial bench which he faced he was, of course, at an immense disadvantage, as we all should be, for its dignity is authentic. The judge sat in a high-backed chair, the sword of justice in its jewelled scabbard affixed to the oak panel behind him, splendid in his scarlet robe, with its neckband of fine white linen and its deep cuffs and sash of purplish-black taffeta. Beside him, their chairs set farther back as a sign of their inferiority to him, sat the Lord Mayor of London and two aldermen, wearing antique robes of black silk with flowing white cravats and gold chains with pendant badges of office worked in precious metals and enamel. It sometimes happens, and it happened then, that these pompous trappings are given real significance by the faces of men who wear them. Judges are chosen for intellect and character, and city honours must be won by intellect combined with competence at the least, and men in both positions must have the patience to carry out tedious routines over decades, and the story is often written on their features.

Looking from the bench to the dock, it could be seen that not in any sane community would William Joyce have had the ghost of a chance of holding such offices as these. This was tragic, as appeared when he was asked to plead and he said, 'Not guilty.' Those two words were the most impressive uttered during the trial. The famous voice was let loose. For a fraction of a second we heard its familiar quality. It was as it had sounded for six years, reverberating with the desire for power. Never was there a more perfect voice for a demagogue, for its reverberations were certain to awake echoes in every heart tumid with the same desire. Given this passionate ambition to exercise authority, which as this scene showed could not be gratified, what could he ever have done but use his trick of gathering together other poor fellows luckless in the same way, so that they might overturn the sane community that was bound to reject them, and substitute a mad one that would regard them kindly?

The Meaning of Treason, 1949

HERBERT READ

1893–1968

Childhood Shrines

On the south side of the Green were two familiar shrines, each with its sacred fire. The first was the saddle-room, with its pungent clean smell of saddle-soap. It was a small white-washed room, hung with bright bits and stirrups and long loops of leather reins; the saddles were in a loft above, reached by a ladder and trap-door. In the middle was a small cylindrical stove, kept burning through the Winter, and making a warm friendly shelter where we could play undisturbed. Our chief joy was to make lead shot, or bullets as we called them; and for this purpose there existed a long-handled crucible and a mould. At what now seems to me an incredibly early age we melted down the strips of lead we found in the window-sill, and poured the sullen liquid into the small aperture of the mould, which was in the form of a pair of pincers—closed whilst the pouring was in progress. When opened, the gleaming silver bullets, about the size of a pea, fell out of the matrix and rolled away to cool on the stone floor. We used the bullets in our catapults, but the joy was in the making of them, and in the sight of their shining beauty.

The blacksmith's shop was a still more magical shrine. The blacksmith came for a day periodically, to shoe or reshoe the horses, to repair waggons and make simple implements. In his dusky cave the bellows roared, the fire was blown to a white intensity, and then suddenly the bellows-shaft was released and the soft glowing iron drawn from the heart of the fire. Then clang, clang, clang on the anvil, the heavenly shower of ruby and golden sparks, and our precipitate flight to a place of safety. All around us, in dark cobwebbed corners, were heaps of old iron, discarded horseshoes, hoops and pipes. Under the window was a tank of water for slaking and tempering the hot iron, and this water possessed the miraculous property of curing warts.

In these two shrines I first experienced the joy of making things. Everywhere around me the earth was stirring with growth and the beasts were propagating their kind. But these wonders passed unobserved by my childish mind, unrecorded in memory. They depended on forces beyond our control, beyond my conception. But fire was real, and so was the skill with which we shaped hard metals to our design and desire.

The Innocent Eye, 1933

E. E. CUMMINGS
1894–1962

In the Internment Camp

Lena's confinement in the cabinot—which dungeon I have already attempted to describe but to whose filth and slime no words can begin to do justice—was in this case solitary. Once a day, of an afternoon and always at the time when all the men were upstairs after the second promenade (which gave the writer of this history an exquisite chance to see an atrocity at first-hand), Lena was taken out of the cabinot by three plantons and permitted a half-hour promenade just outside the door of the building, or in the same locality—delimited by barbed-wire on one side and the washing-shed on another—made famous by the scene of inebriety above described. Punctually at the expiration of thirty minutes she was shoved back into the cabinot by the plantons. Every day for sixteen days I saw her; noted the indestructible bravado of her gait and carriage, the unchanging timbre of her terrible laughter in response to the salutation of an inhabitant of The Enormous Room (for there were at least six men who spoke to her daily, and took their pain sec and their cabinot in punishment therefor with the pride of a soldier who takes the médaille militaire in recompense for his valour); noted the increasing pallor of her flesh; watched the skin gradually assume a distinct greenish tint (a greenishness which I cannot describe save that it suggested putrefaction); heard the coughing to which she had been always subject grow thicker and deeper till it doubled her up every few minutes, creasing her body as you crease a piece of paper with your thumb-nail, preparatory to tearing it in two—and I realized fully and irrevocably and for perhaps the first time the meaning of civilization. And I realized that it was true—as I had previously only suspected it to be true—that in finding us unworthy of helping to carry forward the banner of progress, alias the tricolour, the inimitable and excellent French Government was conferring upon B and myself—albeit with other intent—the ultimate compliment.

The Enormous Room, 1922

ALDOUS HUXLEY
1894–1963

Horoscopes in a Country House

Priscilla Wimbush was lying on the sofa. A blotting-pad rested on her knees and she was thoughtfully sucking the end of a silver pencil.

'Hullo,' she said, looking up. 'I'd forgotten you were coming.'

'Well, here I am, I'm afraid,' said Denis deprecatingly. 'I'm awfully sorry.'

Mrs Wimbush laughed. Her voice, her laughter, were deep and masculine. Everything about her was manly. She had a large, square, middle-aged face, with a massive projecting nose and little greenish eyes, the whole surmounted by a lofty and elaborate coiffure of a curiously improbable shade of orange. Looking at her, Denis always thought of Wilkie Bard as the cantatrice.

> 'That's why I'm going to
> Sing in op'ra, sing in op'ra,
> Sing in op-pop-pop-pop-popera.'

To-day she was wearing a purple silk dress with a high collar and a row of pearls. The costume, so richly dowagerish, so suggestive of the Royal Family, made her look more than ever like something on the Halls.

'What have you been doing all this time?' she asked.

'Well,' said Denis, and he hesitated, almost voluptuously. He had a tremendously amusing account of London and its doings all ripe and ready in his mind. It would be a pleasure to give it utterance. 'To begin with,' he said . . .

But he was too late. Mrs Wimbush's question had been what the grammarians call rhetorical; it asked for no answer. It was a little conversational flourish, a gambit in the polite game.

'You find me busy at my horoscopes,' she said, without even being aware that she had interrupted him.

A little pained, Denis decided to reserve his story for more receptive ears. He contented himself, by way of revenge, with saying 'Oh?' rather icily.

'Did I tell you how I won four hundred on the Grand National this year?'

'Yes,' he replied, still frigid and monosyllabic. She must have told him at least six times.

'Wonderful, isn't it? Everything is in the Stars. In the Old Days, before I had the Stars to help me, I used to lose thousands. Now'—she paused an instant—'well, look at that four hundred on the Grand National. That's the Stars.'

Denis would have liked to hear more about the Old Days. But he was too discreet and, still more, too shy to ask. There had been something of a bust up; that was all he knew. Old Priscilla—not so old then, of course, and sprightlier—had lost a great deal of money, dropped it in handfuls and hatfuls on every race-course in the country. She had gambled too. The number of thousands varied in the different legends, but all put it high. Henry Wimbush was forced to sell some of his Primitives—a Taddeo da Poggibonsi, an Amico di Taddeo, and four or five nameless Sienese—to the Americans. There was a crisis. For the first time in his life Henry asserted himself, and with good effect, it seemed.

Priscilla's gay and gadding existence had come to an abrupt end. Nowadays she spent almost all her time at Crome, cultivating a rather ill-defined malady. For consolation she dallied with New Thought and the Occult. Her passion for racing still possessed her, and Henry, who was a kind-hearted fellow at bottom, allowed her forty pounds a month betting money. Most of Priscilla's days were spent in casting the horoscopes of horses, and she invested her money scientifically, as the stars dictated. She betted on football too, and had a large notebook in which she registered the horoscopes of all the players in all the teams of the League. The process of balancing the horoscopes of two elevens one against the other was a very delicate and difficult one. A match between the Spurs and the Villa entailed a conflict in the heavens so vast and so complicated that it was not to be wondered at if she sometimes made a mistake about the outcome.

Crome Yellow, 1921

ROBERT GRAVES
1895–1985

Shell-Fire and Rifle-Fire

The roadside cottages were now showing more and more signs of dilapidation. A German shell came over and then whoo—oo—ooo-oooOOO—bump—CRASH! landed twenty yards short of us. We threw ourselves flat on our faces. Presently we heard a curious singing noise in the air, and then flop! flop! little pieces of shell-casing came buzzing down all around. 'They calls them the musical instruments,' said the sergeant. 'Damn them,' said my friend Frank Jones-Bateman, cut across the hand by a jagged little piece, 'the devils have started on me early.' 'Aye, they'll have a lot of fun with you before they're done, sir,' grinned the sergeant. Another shell came over. Everyone threw himself down again, but it burst two hundred yards behind us. Only Sergeant Jones had remained on his feet. 'You're wasting your strength, lads,' he said to the draft. 'Listen by the noise they make where they're going to burst.'

At Cambrin village, about a mile from the front trenches, we were taken into a ruined chemist's shop with its coloured glass jars still in the window: the billet of the four Welsh company-quartermaster-sergeants. Here they gave us respirators and field-dressings. This, the first respirator issued in France, was a gauze-pad filled with chemically treated cotton waste, for tying across the mouth and nose. Reputedly it could not keep out the German gas, which had been used at Ypres against the Canadian Division; but we never put it to the test. A week or two later came the 'smoke-helmet', a greasy grey-felt bag with a talc window to look through, and no mouth-piece, certainly ineffective against gas. The talc was always cracking, and visible leaks showed at the stitches joining it to the helmet.

Those were early days of trench warfare, the days of the jam-tin bomb and the gas-pipe trench-mortar: still innocent of Lewis or Stokes guns, steel helmets, telescopic rifle-sights, gas-shells, pill-boxes, tanks, well-organized trench-raids, or any of the later refinements of trench warfare.

After a meal of bread, bacon, rum, and bitter stewed tea sickly with sugar, we went through the broken trees to the east of the village and up a long trench to battalion headquarters. The wet and slippery trench ran through dull red clay. I had a torch with me, and saw that hundreds of field mice and frogs had fallen into the trench but found no way out. The light dazzled them, and because I could not help treading on them, I put the torch back in my pocket. We had no mental picture of what the trenches would be like, and were almost as ignorant as a young soldier who joined us a week or two later. He called out excitedly to old Burford, who was cooking up a bit of stew in a dixie, apart from the others: 'Hi, mate, where's the battle? I want to do my bit.'

The guide gave us hoarse directions all the time. 'Hole right.' 'Wire high.' 'Wire low.' 'Deep place here, sir.' 'Wire low.' The field-telephone wires had been fastened by staples to the side of the trench, and when it rained the staples were constantly falling out and the wire falling down and tripping people up. If it sagged too much, one stretched it across the trench to the other side to correct the sag, but then it would catch one's head. The holes were sump-pits used for draining the trenches.

We now came under rifle-fire, which I found more trying than shell-fire. The gunner, I knew, fired not at people but at map-references—crossroads, likely artillery positions, houses that suggested billets for troops, and so on. Even when an observation officer in an aeroplane or captive balloon, or on a church spire directed the guns, it seemed random, somehow. But a rifle-bullet, even when fired blindly, always seemed purposely aimed. And whereas we could usually hear a shell approaching, and take some sort of cover, the rifle-bullet gave no warning. So, though we learned not to duck a rifle-bullet because, once heard, it must have missed, it gave us a worse feeling of danger. Rifle-bullets in the open went hissing into the grass without much noise, but when we were in a trench, the bullets made a tremendous crack as they went over the hollow. Bullets often struck the barbed wire in front of the trenches, which sent them spinning with a head-over-heels motion—ping! rockety-ockety-ockety-ockety into the woods behind.

Goodbye to All That, 1929 (revised edition 1957)

DAVID JONES
1895–1974

Night in the Trenches

You can hear the silence of it:
you can hear the rat of no-man's-land
rut-out intricacies,
weasel-out his patient workings,
scrut, scrut, sscrut,
harrow-out earthly, trowel his cunning paw;
redeem the time of our uncharity, to sap his own amphibious paradise.
You can hear his carrying-parties rustle our corruptions through the night-weeds—contest the choicest morsels in his tiny conduits, bead-eyed feast on us; by a rule of his nature, at night-feast on the broken of us.
Those broad-pinioned;
blue-burnished, or brinded-back;
whose proud eyes watched
the broken emblems
droop and drag dust,
suffer with us this metamorphosis.
These too have shed their fine feathers; these too have slimed their dark-bright coats; these too have condescended to dig in.
The white-tailed eagle at the battle ebb,
where the sea wars against the river
the speckled kite of Maldon
and the crow
have naturally selected to be un-winged;
to go on the belly, to
sap sap sap
with festered spines, arched under the moon; furrit with
whiskered snouts the secret parts of us.
When it's all quiet you can hear them:
scrut scrut scrut
when it's as quiet as this is.
It's so very still.
Your body fits the crevice of the bay in the most comfortable fashion imaginable.
It's cushy enough.

The relief elbows him on the fire-step: All quiet china?—bugger all to report?—kipping mate?—christ, mate—you'll 'ave 'em all over.

In Parenthesis, 1937

EDMUND WILSON
1895–1972

New York by Day

In Brooklyn, in the neighborhood of Henry Street, the pleasant red and pink brick houses still worthily represent the generation of Henry Ward Beecher; but an eternal Sunday is on them now; they seem sunk in a final silence. In the streets one may catch a glimpse of a solitary well-dressed old gentleman moving slowly a long way off; but in general the respectable have disappeared and only the vulgar survive. The empty quiet is broken by the shouts of shrill Italian children and by incessant mechanical pianos in dingy apartment houses, accompanied by human voices that seem almost as mechanical as they. At night, along unlighted streets, one gives a wide berth to drunkards that sprawl out across the pavement from the shadow of darkened doors; and I have known a dead horse to be left in the road—two blocks from the principal post office and not much more from the Borough Hall—with no effort made to remove it, for nearly three weeks. In the summer, warm sickening fumes from a factory that makes cheap chocolate give a stagnancy of swamps to the heavy air. In the evening, an old woman steals through the streets, softly calling to cats, which she poisons and which die slowly of gripes in the areas of decorous houses from which the families have moved away.

So much for the dead and the dying; in the newer part of town, the East Forties, looking down from a high upper window, one takes account of the monstrous carcass of the Grand Central Station and Palace, with its myriad skylights and its zinc-livid roofs, stretched out like a segmented seaworm that is almost unrecognizable as a form of life. Beyond it rise the upright rectangles of drab or raw yellow brick—yellows devoid of brilliance, browns that are never rich—perforated, as if by a perforating machine, with rows of rectangular windows; the stiff black fingers of factories: blunt truncated meaningless towers; a broken scrambling of flat roofs and sharp angles which is yet a compact fitting-in; and then the lead-silver river strung across with its skeletal bridge. In the middle distance, the sky itself seems to be overdisplaced—like a pool in which a large safe has been dropped—by a disagreeably colored hotel, brownish yellow like a bronchial trochee and so immense that its cubic acres seem to weigh down the very island, almost to make it sag. A flock of pigeons that fly below have the look, in the dull light, of wastepaper blown by the wind.

Sitting indoors in New York by day, one becomes aware of mysterious noises: the drilling of granite teeth, the cackling of mechanical birds, the thudding of Cyclopean iron doors; accelerating avalanches of brick, the collapse of deserted warehouses; explosives that cause no excitement, pistol shots that are quite without consequence. Nor does one care to find out what these noises are. One goes on with whatever one is doing, incurious and wholly indifferent.

written 1925; *The American Earthquake*, 1958

Proust

Imaginatively and intellectually, Proust is prodigiously strong; and if we feel an element of decadence in his work, it may be primarily due to the decay of the society in which he lived and with which his novel exclusively deals—the society of the dispossessed nobility and the fashionable and cultivated bourgeoisie, with their physicians and their artists, their servants and their parasites. We are always feeling with Proust as if we were reading about the end of something—this seems, in fact, to be what he means us to feel: witness the implications of the bombardment of Paris during the War when Charlus is in the last stages of his disintegration. Not only do his hero and most of his other characters pass into mortal declines, but their world itself seems to be coming to an end. And it may be that Proust's strange poetry and brilliance are the last fires of a setting sun—the last flare of the æsthetic idealism of the educated classes of the nineteenth century. If Proust is more dramatic, more complete and more intense than Thackeray or Chekov or Edith Wharton or Anatole France, it may be because he comes at the close of an era and sums up the whole situation. Surely the lament over the impossibility of ideal romantic love which Proust is always chanting on a note which wavers between the tragic and the maudlin announces by its very falling into absurdity the break-up of a whole emotional idealism and its ultimate analysis and readjustment along lines which Proust's own researches, running curiously close to Freud, have been among the first to suggest. 'A la Recherche du Temps Perdu' subsumes, in this respect, 'The Great Gatsby,' 'The Sun Also Rises,' 'The Bridge of San Luis Rey,' the sketches of Dorothy Parker, and how many contemporary European novels! Proust is perhaps the last great historian of the loves, the society, the intelligence, the diplomacy, the literature and the art of the Heartbreak House of capitalist culture; and the little man with the sad appealing voice, the metaphysician's mind, the Saracen's beak, the ill-fitting dress-shirt and the great eyes that seem to see all about him like the many-faceted eyes of a fly, dominates the scene and plays host in the mansion where he is not long to be master.

Axel's Castle, 1931

EDMUND BLUNDEN
1896–1974

Ypres, 1917

One morning, dark and liquid and wild, Colonel Harrison and a number of us went off in a lorry to reconnoitre in Ypres proper, and to visit the trenches we were to hold. The sad Salient lay under a heavy silence, broken here and there by the ponderous muffled thump of trench mortar shells round the line. We passed big houses, one or two glimmering whitely, life in death; we found light come by the time that we passed the famous Asylum, a red ruin with some gildings and ornaments still surviving over its doorway, and an ambulance pulling up outside. There was in the town itself the same strange silence, and the staring pallor of the streets in that daybreak was unlike anything that I had known. The Middle Ages had here contrived to lurk, and this was their torture at last. We all felt this, as the tattered picture swung by like accidents of vision; and when we got out of the lorry by the Menin Gate (that unlovely hiatus) we scarcely seemed awake and aware. The Ramparts defended the town on the east and seemed to concentrate whatever of life and actuality dared to be in it. After the distant and alien secrecy of the Grand Place, the sound of dripping water-taps put in here by British soldiers, and the sight of dispatch-riders going in and out, had an effect of reanimation. Here we entered headquarters, or waited at the entrances among the tins of soapy water and the wet rubber boots. We went into the naked eastward area, studied the trenches and their bleak-faced sentries, shivered in the wind. Then, later in the day, we heard for the first time the bursting of shells in Ypres. Their shattering impact sent out a different noise to any before heard by me—a flat and battering, locked-in concussion. Then silence and solitude recaptured the wilderness of looped and windowed walls, unless the wind roused old voices in flues and wrenched vanes. More and more shells leapt down with the same dull and weary smashing. Our motor moved out without further delay.

I had longed to see Ypres, under the old faith that things are always described in blacker colours than they deserve; but this first view was a tribute to the soldier's philosophy. The bleakness of events had found its proper theatre. The sun could surely never shine on such a simulacrum of divine aberration.

Undertones of War, 1928

JOHN DOS PASSOS
1896–1960

Camera Eye

walk the streets and walk the streets inquiring of Coca-Cola signs Lucky Strike ads pricetags in storewindows scraps of overheard conversations stray tatters of newsprint yesterday's headlines sticking out of ashcans

for a set of figures a formula of action an address you don't quite know you've forgotten the number the street may be in Brooklyn a train leaving for somewhere a steamboat whistle stabbing your ears a job chalked up in front of an agency

to do to make there are more lives than walking desperate the streets hurry underdog do make

a speech urging action in the crowded hall after handclapping the pats and smiles of others on the platform the scrape of chairs the expectant hush the few coughs during the first stuttering attempt to talk straight tough going the snatch for a slogan they are listening and then the easy climb slogan by slogan to applause (if somebody in your head didn't say liar to you and on Union Square

that time you leant from a soapbox over faces avid young opinionated old the middleaged numb with overwork eyes bleared with newspaper-reading trying to tell them the straight dope make them laugh tell them what they want to hear wave a flag whispers the internal agitator crazy to succeed)

you suddenly falter ashamed flush red break out in sweat why not tell these men stamping in the wind that we stand on a quicksand? that doubt is the whetstone of understanding is too hard hurts instead of urging picket John D. Rockefeller and if the cops knock your blocks off it's all for the advancement of the human race while I go home after a drink and a hot meal and read (with some difficulty in the Loeb Library trot) the epigrams of Martial and ponder the course of history and what leverage might pry the owners loose from power and bring back (I too Walt Whitman) our storybook democracy

and all the time in my pocket that letter from that college-boy asking me to explain why being right which he admits the radicals are in their private lives such bastards.

lie abed underdog (peeling the onion of doubt) with the book unread in your hand and swing on the seesaw maybe after all maybe topdog make

money you understood what he meant the old party with the white beard beside the crystal inkpot at the cleared varnished desk in the walnut office in whose voice boomed all the clergymen of childhood and shrilled the hosannahs of the offkey female choirs All you say is very true but there's such a thing as sales and I have daughters I'm sure you too will end by thinking differently make

money in New York (lipstick kissed off the lips of a girl fashionably-dressed fragrant at five o'clock in a taxicab careening down Park Avenue when at the end of each crosstown street the west is flaming with gold and white smoke billows from the smokestacks of steamboats leaving port and the sky is lined with greenbacks

the riveters are quiet the trucks of the producers are shoved off on to the marginal avenues

winnings sing from every streetcorner

crackle in the ignitions of the cars swish smooth in ballbearings sparkle in the lights going on in the showwindows croak in the klaxons tootle in the horns of imported millionaire shining towncars

dollars are silky in her hair soft in her dress sprout in the elaborately contrived rosepetals that you kiss become pungent and crunchy in the speakeasy dinner sting shrill in the drinks

make loud the girlandmusic show set off the laughing jag in the cabaret swing in the shufflingshuffling orchestra click sharp in the hatcheck girl's goodnight)

if not why not? walking the streets rolling on your bed eyes sting from peeling the speculative onion of doubt if somebody in your head topdog? underdog? didn't (and on Union Square) say liar to you

U.S.A.: The Big Money, 1936

Newsreel

THRONGS IN STREETS

LUNATIC BLOWS UP PITTSBURGH BANK

Krishnamurti Here Says His Message Is
World Happiness

Close the doors
They are coming
Through the windows

AMERICAN MARINES LAND IN NICARAGUA TO
PROTECT ALIENS

PANGALOS CAUGHT; PRISONER IN ATHENS

Close the windows
They are coming through the doors

Saw Pigwoman The Other Says But Neither Can Identify
Accused

FUNDS ACCUMULATE IN NEW YORK

the desire for profits and more profits kept on increasing and the quest for easy money became well nigh universal. All of this meant an attempt to appropriate the belongings of others without rendering a corresponding service

'Physician' Who Took Prominent Part in Valentino
Funeral Exposed as Former Convict

NEVER SAW HIM SAYS MANAGER

Close the doors they are coming through the windows
My God they're coming through the floor

U.S.A.: The Big Money

WILLIAM FAULKNER
1897–1962

A Visiting Preacher

The church had been decorated, with sparse flowers from kitchen gardens and hedgerows, and with streamers of colored crepe paper. Above the pulpit hung a battered Christmas bell, the accordion sort that collapses. The pulpit was empty, though the choir was already in place, fanning themselves although it was not warm.

Most of the women were gathered on one side of the room. They were talking. Then the bell struck one time and they dispersed to their seats and the congregation sat for an instant, expectant. The bell struck again one time. The choir rose and began to sing and the congregation turned its head as one, as six small children—four girls with tight pigtails bound with small scraps of cloth like butterflies, and two boys with close-napped heads—entered and marched up the aisle, strung together in a harness of white ribbons and flowers, and followed by two men in single file. The second man was huge, of a light coffee color, imposing in a frock coat and white tie. His head was magisterial and profound, his neck rolled above his collar in rich folds. But he was familiar to them, and so the heads were still reverted when he had passed, and it was not until the choir ceased singing that they realized that the visiting clergyman had already entered, and when they saw the man who had preceded their minister enter the pulpit still ahead of him an indescribable sound went up, a sigh, a sound of astonishment and disappointment.

The visitor was undersized, in a shabby alpaca coat. He had a wizened, black face like a small, aged monkey. And all the while that the choir sang again and while the six children rose and sang in thin, frightened, tuneless whispers, they watched the insignificant-looking man sitting dwarfed and countrified by the minister's imposing bulk, with something like consternation. They were still looking at him with consternation and unbelief when the minister rose and introduced him in rich, rolling tones whose very unction served to increase the visitor's insignificance.

'En dey brung dat all de way fum Saint Looey,' Frony whispered.

'I've knowed de Lawd to use cuiser tools dan dat,' Dilsey said. 'Hush, now,' she said to Ben. 'Dey fixin' to sing again in a minute.'

When the visitor rose to speak he sounded like a white man. His voice was level and cold. It sounded too big to have come from him and they listened at first through curiosity, as they would have to a monkey talking. They began to watch him as they would a man on a tightrope. They even forgot his insignificant appearance in the virtuosity with which he ran and poised and swooped upon the cold inflectionless wire of his voice, so that at last, when with a sort of swooping glide he came to rest again beside the reading desk with one arm resting upon it at shoulder height and his monkey body as reft of all motion as a mummy or an emptied vessel, the congregation sighed as if it waked from a collective dream and moved a little in its seats. Behind the pulpit the choir fanned steadily. Dilsey whispered, 'Hush, now. Dey fixin' to sing in a minute.'

Then a voice said, 'Brethren.'

The preacher had not moved. His arm lay yet across the desk, and he still held that pose while the voice died in sonorous echoes between the walls. It was as different as day and dark from his former tone, with a sad, timbrous quality like an alto horn, sinking into their hearts and speaking there again when it had ceased in fading and cumulate echoes.

'Brethren and sisteren,' it said again. The preacher removed his arm and he began to walk back and forth before the desk, his hands clasped behind him, a meagre figure, hunched over upon itself like that of one long immured in striving with the implacable earth, 'I got the recollection and the blood of the Lamb!' He tramped steadily back and forth beneath the twisted paper and the Christmas bell, hunched, his hands clasped behind him. He was like a worn, small rock whelmed by the successive waves of his voice. With his body he seemed to feed the voice that, succubus like, had fleshed its teeth in him. And the congregation seemed to watch with its own eyes while the voice consumed him, until he was nothing and they were nothing and there was not even a voice, but instead their hearts were speaking to one another in chanting measures beyond the need for words, so that when he came to rest against the reading desk, his monkey face lifted and his whole attitude that of a serene, tortured crucifix that transcended its shabbiness and insignificance and made it of no moment, a long, moaning expulsion of breath rose from them, and a woman's single soprano: 'Yes, Jesus!'

As the scudding day passed overhead the dingy windows glowed and faded in ghostly retrograde. A car passed along the road outside, laboring in the sand, died away. Dilsey sat bolt upright, her hand on Ben's knee. Two tears slid down her fallen cheeks, in and out of the myriad coruscations of immolation and abnegation and time.

'Brethren,' the minister said in a harsh whisper, without moving.

'Yes, Jesus!' the woman's voice said, hushed yet.

'Breddren en sistuhn!' His voice rang again, with the horns. He removed his arm and stood erect and raised his hands. 'I got de ricklickshun en de blood of de Lamb!' They did not mark just when his intonation, his pronunciation, became Negroid, they just sat swaying a little in their seats as the voice took them into itself.

'When de long, cold—Oh, I tells you, breddren, when de long, cold—I sees de light en I sees de word, po' sinner! Dey passed away in Egypt, de swingin' chariots; de generations passed away. Wus a rich man: whar he now, O breddren? Wus a po' man: whar he now, O sistuhn? Oh I tells you, ef you ain't got de milk en de dew of de old salvation when de long, cold years rolls away!'

'Yes, Jesus!'

'I tells you, breddren, en I tells you, sistuhn, dey'll come a time. Po' sinner saying Let me lay down wid de Lawd, lemme lay down my load. Den whut Jesus gwine say, O breddren? O sistuhn? Is you got de ricklickshun en de blood of de Lamb? Case I ain't gwine load down heaven!'

He fumbled in his coat and took out a handkerchief and mopped his face. A low, concerted sound rose from the congregation: Mmmmmmmmmmmmm! The woman's voice said, 'Yes, Jesus! Jesus!'

'Breddren! Look at dem little chillen settin dar. Jesus wus like dat once. He mammy suffered de glory en de pangs. Sometime maybe she helt him at de nightfall, whilst de angels singin' him to sleep; maybe she look out de do' en see de Roman po-lice passin'.' He tramped back and forth, mopping his face. 'Listen breddren! I sees de day. Ma'y settin in de do' wid Jesus on her lap, de little Jesus. Like dem chillen dar, de little Jesus. I hears de angels singin' de peaceful songs en de glory; I sees de closin' eyes; sees Mary jump up, sees de sojer face: We gwine to kill! We gwine to kill! We gwine to kill yo little Jesus! I hears de weepin' en de lamentation of de po' mammy widout de salvation en de word of God!'

'Mmmmmmmmmmmmmmmm! Jesus! Little Jesus!' and another voice, rising:

'I sees, O Jesus! Oh I sees!' and still another, without words, like bubbles rising in water.

'I sees hit, breddren! I sees hit! Sees de blastin', blindin' sight! I sees Calvary, wid de sacred trees, sees de thief en de murderer en de least of dese; I hears de boastin' en de braggin': Ef you be Jesus, lif up yo' tree en walk! I hears de wailin' of women en de evenin' lamentations; I hears de weepin' en de cryin' en de turnt-away face of God: dey done kilt Jesus; dey done kilt my Son!'

'Mmmmmmmmmmmmm. Jesus! I sees, O Jesus!'

'O blind sinner! Breddren, I tells you; sistuhn, I says to you, when de Lawd did turn His mighty face, say, Ain't gwine overload heaven! I can see de widowed God shet His do'; I sees de whelmin' flood roll between; I sees de darkness en de death everlastin' upon de generations. Den, lo! Breddren! Yes, breddren! Whut I see? Whut I see, O sinner? I sees de resurrection en de light; sees de meek Jesus sayin' Dey kilt Me dat ye shall live again; I died dat dem whut sees en believes shall never die. Breddren, O breddren! I sees de doom crack en hears de golden horns shoutin' down de glory, en de arisen dead whut got de blood en de ricklickshun of de Lamb!'

In the midst of the voices and the hands Ben sat, rapt in his sweet blue gaze. Dilsey sat bolt upright beside, crying rigidly and quietly in the annealment and the blood of the remembered Lamb.

As they walked through the bright noon, up the sandy road with the dispersing congregation talking, easily again, group to group, she continued to weep, unmindful of the talk.

'He sho a preacher, mon! He didn't look like much at first, but hush!'

'He seed de power en de glory.'

'Yes, suh. He seed hit. Face to face he seed hit.'

Dilsey made no sound, her face did not quiver as the tears took their sunken and devious courses, walking with her head up, making no effort to dry them away even.

'Whyn't you quit dat, mammy?' Frony said. 'Wid all dese people lookin'. We be passin' white folks soon.'

'I've seed de first en de last,' Dilsey said. 'Never you mind me.'

'First en last whut?' Frony said.

'Never you mind,' Dilsey said. 'I seed de beginnin', en now I sees de endin'.'

The Sound and the Fury, 1929

LIAM O'FLAHERTY

1897–1984

The Coming of the Blight

Another violent storm came on the last day of the month. They did not trouble greatly about this one, since the first had done no damage. Even so, a rumour got abroad that the blight had struck in the County Cork. Would it come this far? Every day, they anxiously inspected the crop. But the days passed without any sign of the evil. The potatoes that were dug for food still remained wholesome. It promised to be a miraculous crop. Even Mary began to take courage. And then, on the fifteenth of July, the bolt fell from the heavens.

When old Kilmartin came into his yard shortly after dawn on that day, he looked up the Valley and saw a white cloud standing above the Black Lake. It was like a great mound of snow, hanging by an invisible chain, above the mountain peaks. It was dazzling white in the glare of the rising sun.

'Merciful God!' he said. 'What can that be?'

The rest of the sky was as clear as crystal. The old man stared at it in awe for some time. Then he ran into the house and called out the family to look at it. Mary and Thomsy came out. They were as startled as the old man.

'Did you ever see anything like that?' the old man said.

'Never in my natural,' said Thomsy. 'It's like a . . .'

'Snow,' Mary said. 'It's like a big heap of snow.'

'How could it be snow?' said the old man. 'And this the middle of summer? It's a miracle.'

'Or would it be a bad sign, God between us and harm?' said Thomsy.

Other people came from their cabins and stared at the cloud. There was a peculiar silence in the Valley. The air was as heavy as a drug. There was not a breath of wind. The birds did not sing. And then, as the people watched, the cloud began to move lazily down upon the Valley. It spread out on either side, lost its form and polluted the atmosphere, which became full of a whitish vapour, through which the sun's rays glistened; so that it seemed that a fine rain of tiny whitish particles of dust was gently falling from the sky. Gradually a sulphurous stench affected the senses of those who watched. It was like the smell of foul water in a sewer. Yet, there was no moisture and the stench left an arid feeling in the nostrils. Even the animals were affected by it. Dogs sat up on their haunches and howled. Not a bird was to be seen, although there had been flocks of crows and of starlings about on the previous day. Then, indeed, terror seized the people and a loud wailing broke out from the cabins, as the cloud overspread the whole Valley, shutting out the sun completely.

Famine, 1937

DAWN POWELL
1897–1965

A Wood Violet

Darcy was a wood violet, not as diminutive as she appeared at first glance, but small-boned, small-nosed, small-faced, and given to tiny gestures and a tiny baby voice. She seemed womanly and practical too, and you thought

Darcy must be like those small iron pioneer women in the Conestoga wagons, whipping men and children across the prairies, sewing, building, plowing, cooking, nursing, saving her menfolks from their natural folly and improvidence. The fact was that Darcy had never darned a sock, seldom made her own bed, thought coffee was born in delicatessen containers and all food grew in frozen packages. Her practicality exhibited itself in tender little cries of, 'But you'll be sick, honey, if you don't eat something after all that bourbon! You must eat! Here, eat this pretzel.' In other crises she could figure out efficiently in her head that four people sharing a taxi wouldn't be much more than four subway fares, and that way they could carry their drinks along. She was very firm too in insisting that a man coming out of a week-end binge still reeking of stale smoke and rye should keep away from his job Monday unless he shaved and changed his shirt.

Darcy was delicate in color, almost fading into background, but strong and gamy like those tiny weed-flowers whose roots push up boulders. A man felt that here was a real woman, an old-fashioned girl with her little footsies firmly on the ground, someone to count on, someone always behind you. Darcy's pretty feet were more likely to be on the wall or tangled up in sheets than on the ground, and as for being behind her man, he found out sooner or later she was really on his back. Alas, little women are as hard to throw out as Amazons, especially a confiding little creature like Darcy who had no place to go until there was another back to jump on. Between backs Darcy had no existence, like a hermit crab caught in a shuttle from one stolen shell to another.

The Golden Spur, 1962

SACHEVERELL SITWELL
1897–1988

Fantasia on a Victorian Song Cover

The Bond Street Beau stands before us in the summer afternoon and occupies, in every sense, the centre of the stage. This pavement is his beat. It is the west side of the street; the right side as you walk down towards Piccadilly. Of course, if you look at his portrait through the back of the page, you will see him facing in another direction, but, nevertheless, he is for ever coming down Bond Street towards the Piccadilly end. We are to infer that he appears, always, before this painted scene, with the same row of shops opposite, across the street. But for our benefit, this afternoon, we behold him in real life against the living background of his song.

He has come a step nearer. He is within a few feet of us, as though we are in the front row of the stalls. And, indeed, when our eyes look up at him, they are on a level with his waist. Yet we are on the pavement. We are not sitting in the music hall. Perhaps, on occasion, he comes on without any scene at all to sing his song. We shall discover, later, how the artist varies in his treatment according to mood and inspiration; sometimes giving the actor in a setting of real life; upon the stage of the theatre against the slanting boards; or in a symposium of words and actions from the song. It is sufficient if we note, for the moment, that the artist must have studied him many dozens of times in order to present him to us, exactly, as he came on to sing his song.

He is so near to us, now, that he could not come another step forward without knocking into us. And he has no need to. He is at the edge of the footlights. He is posing for his portrait at the moment when the music stops; and this instant we shall hear him speak, and his music will strike up again. But, all the time, he is a living person and it is our imagination that is at fault for thinking of him in the theatre. He is in the blazing sunlight. We see the shadow of his tasselled walking stick. It is a line of shadow that attaches to the ferrule of his walking stick as that touches on the pavement, and that will move with it if he so much as lifts his hand. His stick casts its own shadow, and it would be difficult to exaggerate the importance of that tasselled wand. In the company he keeps, that is to say his audience, it is a piece of impertinence to come on with a walking stick. They have never seen such a fop or beau in real life, except in Bond Street or in Rotten Row. In his other hand he holds a half-smoked cigar. And he is wearing gloves. A pair of well-made, tight-fitting chamois leather gloves—or are they grey kid?—for we cannot be quite certain, but we can see the lines of black braid, like the black keys of a keyboard, upon the backs of his knuckles, and disappearing into his cuffs.

The Bond Street Beau wears a top hat, worn at a rakish angle, an eyeglass in his right eye, and cuts so extravagant and withal immaculate a figure that we cannot but examine him from head to foot. We are not alone in our intention. Behind him, two women, who cannot be ladies, or they would not be walking down Bond Street at this hour of the afternoon, still less pausing in conversation on the kerbstone, are discussing this paragon who has passed them by, going over him from point to point, as impressed as we are ourselves, but, perhaps, a little suspicious of him. They have heard the talk and tittle-tattle. They know him by his reputation.

Morning, Noon and Night in London, 1948

NIRAD C. CHAUDHURI
1897–

A Village Ritual

Another outstanding experience of the cold season was a folk-ritual which was performed every day for one whole month from the middle of January to the middle of February. It was a ritual for little girls, but it was very elaborate and if one was to draw the fullest benefit out of it it had to be performed for twelve years in succession. Therefore the girls began quite early in life, even at the age of three or four, so that they might see a substantial portion through before they were married off. But of course one could not speak of standards of performance before they had done it for some six or seven years, because the designs which had to be executed required skill in drawing. About twelve feet square or even more of the inner courtyard had to be covered with figures of the sun and the moon, floral decorations of various sorts, and big circles which had to be truly drawn. The palette was similar to that used by the Cromagnon man—dull red, black, and white, with only a greater preponderance of white. The actual colouring material used was, however, simpler than those at the disposal of later palaeolithic society, namely, brick dust instead of red peroxide of iron, charcoal dust instead of pyrolusite, and rice powder for white. The girls took the powders in handfuls, closed their fist, and released the colours through the hole formed by the curled little finger, regulating the flow by tightening or loosening their grip. It was wonderful to see how quickly they filled up the space. The sun was a staring face about two feet in diameter, the moon slightly smaller. The first was laid out mainly in red and black, producing a fiery effect, while the moon was for the most part in rice powder which very successfully brought out its blanched appearance. The floral decorations were of course *motifs* on which Bengali women had practised no one knows for how many generations, and they came out as quickly and neatly as if they were being done from stencils.

Two girls of the house next to ours, whose parents we called uncle and aunt following Bengali custom, performed this ritual. At dawn they had their plunge in the cold river and came back singing and shivering. We, the boys, quickly collected twigs, dry leaves, bamboo scrapings, even a log or two, and made a fire for them. After they had got a little warm the girls set to work and it went on till about ten o'clock. The girls chanted hymns to the sun and the moon which could be called a crude and rudimentary version of the canticles of St Francis. We could not go near or touch them because, being unbathed, we were unclean, but we did our best to make ourselves serviceable in every possible way.

The Autobiography of an Unknown Indian, 1951

C. S. LEWIS
1899–1963

The Creature that Could Talk

There was no sound of pursuit. Ransom dropped down on his stomach and drank, cursing a world where *cold* water appeared to be unobtainable. Then he lay still to listen and recover his breath. His eyes were upon the blue water. It was agitated. Circles shuddered and bubbles danced ten yards away from his face. Suddenly the water heaved and a round, shining, black thing like a cannonball came into sight. Then he saw eyes and mouth—a puffing mouth bearded with bubbles. More of the thing came up out of the water. It was gleaming black. Finally it splashed and wallowed to the shore and rose, steaming, on its hind legs—six or seven feet high and too thin for its height, like everything in Malacandra. It had a coat of thick black hair, lucid as sealskin, very short legs with webbed feet, a broad beaver-like or fish-like tail, strong fore-limbs with webbed claws or fingers, and some complication halfway up the belly which Ransom took to be its genitals. It was something like a penguin, something like an otter, something like a seal; the slenderness and flexibility of the body suggested a giant stoat. The great round head, heavily whiskered, was mainly responsible for the suggestion of seal; but it was higher in the forehead than a seal's and the mouth was smaller.

There comes a point at which the actions of fear and precaution are purely conventional, no longer felt as terror or hope by the fugitive. Ransom lay perfectly still, pressing his body as well down into the weed as he could, in obedience to a wholly theoretical idea that he might thus pass unobserved. He felt little emotion. He noted in a dry, objective way that this was apparently to be the end of his story—caught between a *sorn* from the land and a big, black animal from the water. He had, it is true, a vague notion that the jaws and mouth of the beast were not those of a carnivore; but he knew that he was too ignorant of zoology to do more than guess.

Then something happened which completely altered his state of mind. The creature, which was still steaming and shaking itself on the bank and had obviously not seen him, opened its mouth and began to make noises. This in itself was not remarkable; but a lifetime of linguistic study assured Ransom almost at once that these were articulate noises. The creature was *talking*. It had language. If you are not yourself a philologist, I am afraid you must take on trust the prodigious emotional consequences of this realisation in Ransom's mind. A new world he had already seen—but a new, an extra-terrestrial, a non-human language was a different matter. Somehow he had not thought of this in connection with the *sorns*; now, it flashed upon him like a revelation. The love of knowledge is a kind of madness. In the fraction of a second which it took Ransom to decide that the creature was really talking, and while he still knew that he might be facing instant death, his imagination had leaped over every fear and hope and probability of his situation to follow the dazzling project of making a Malacandrian grammar. *An Introduction to the Malacandrian Language—The Lunar Verb—A Concise Martian-English Dictionary*—the titles flitted through his mind. And what might one not discover from the speech of a non-human race? The very form of language itself, the principle behind all possible languages, might fall into his hands. Unconsciously he raised himself on his elbow and stared at the black beast. It became silent. The huge bullet head swung round and lustrous amber eyes fixed him. There was no wind on the lake or in the wood. Minute after minute in utter silence the representatives of two so far-divided species stared each into the other's face.

Out of the Silent Planet, 1938

Mammon and Moloch

What, then, was I attacking? I was saying, like St James and Professor Haldane, that to be a friend of 'the World' is to be an enemy of God. The difference between us is that the Professor sees the 'World' purely in terms of those threats and those allurements which depend on money. I do not. The most 'worldly' society I have ever lived in is that of schoolboys: most worldly in the cruelty and arrogance of the strong, the toadyism and mutual treachery of the weak, and the unqualified snobbery of both. Nothing was so base that most members of the school proletariat would not do it, or suffer it, to win the favour of the school aristocracy: hardly any injustice too bad for the aristocracy to practise. But the class system did not in the least depend on the amount of pocket money. Who needs to care about money if most of the things he wants will be offered by cringing servility and the remainder can be taken by force? This lesson has remained with me all my life. That is one of the reasons why I cannot share Professor Haldane's exaltation at the banishment of Mammon from 'a sixth of our planet's surface'. I have already lived in a world from which Mammon was banished: it was the most wicked and miserable I have yet known. If Mammon were the only devil, it would be another matter. But where Mammon vacates the throne, how if Moloch takes his place? As Aristotle said, 'Men do not become tyrants in order to keep warm.' All men, of course, desire pleasure and safety. But all men also desire power and all men desire the mere sense of being 'in the know' or the 'inner ring', of not being 'outsiders': a passion insufficiently studied and the chief theme of my story. When the state of society is such that money is the passport to all these prizes, then of course money will be the prime temptation. But when the passport changes, the desires will remain. And there are many other possible passports: position in an official hierarchy, for instance. Even now, the ambitious and worldly man would not inevitably choose the post with the higher salary. The pleasure of being 'high up and far within' may be worth the sacrifice of some income.

'A Reply to Professor Haldane' (1946), *Of This and Other Worlds*, 1982

ELIZABETH BOWEN
1899–1973

Approaching Cork City by Ship

On the left shore, a steeple pricked up out of a knoll of trees, above a snuggle of gothic villas; then there was the sad stare of what looked like an orphanage. A holy bell rang and a girl at a corner mounted her bicycle and rode out of sight. The river kept washing salt off the ship's prow. Then, to the right, the tree-dark hill of Tivoli began to go up, steep, with pallid stucco houses appearing to balance on the tops of trees. Palladian columns, gazebos, glass-houses, terraces showed on the background misted with spring green, at the tops of shafts or on toppling brackets of rock, all stuck to the hill, all slipping past the ship. . . .

The river still narrowing, townish terraces of tall pink houses under a cliff drew in. In one fanlight stood a white plaster horse; clothes were spread out to dry on a briar bush. Someone watching the ship twitched back a curtain; a woman leaned out signalling with a mirror: several travellers must be expected home. A car with handkerchiefs fluttering drove alongside the ship. On the city side, a tree-planted promenade gave place to boxy warehouses; a smoky built-over hill appeared beyond Tivoli. But Cork consumes its own sound: the haze remained quite silent.

The House in Paris, 1935

The Middle of a War

That autumn of 1940 was to appear, by two autumns later, apocryphal, more far away than peace. No planetary round was to bring again that particular conjunction of life and death; that particular psychic London was to be gone for ever; more bombs would fall, but not on the same city. War moved from the horizon to the map. And it was now, when you no longer saw, heard, smelled war, that a deadening acclimatization to it began to set in. The first generation of ruins, cleaned up, shored up, began to weather—in daylight they took their places as a norm of the scene; the dangerless nights of September two years later blotted them out. It was from this new insidious echoless propriety of ruins that you breathed in all that was most malarial. Reverses, losses, deadlocks now almost unnoticed bred one another; every day the news hammered one more nail into a consciousness which no longer resounded. Everywhere hung the heaviness of the even worse you could not be told and could not desire to hear. This was the lightless middle of the tunnel.

The Heat of the Day, 1949

A Descent to a Bar or Grill

She came to a stop; he pushed against a door showing a dimmed sign, OPEN. Inside, light came up stone stairs which he took her down; at the foot he held open another door and she walked ahead of him into a bar or grill which had no air of having existed before tonight. She stared first at a row of backviews of eaters perched, packed elbow-to-elbow, along a counter. A zip fastener all the way down one back made one woman seem to have a tin spine. A dye-green lettuce leaf had fallen on to the mottled rubber floor; a man in a pin-stripe suit was enough in profile to show a smudge of face powder on one shoulder. A dog sitting scratching itself under one bar stool slowly, with each methodical convulsion, worked its collar round so that the brass studs which had been under its ear vanished one by one, being replaced in view by a brass nameplate she could just not read. Wherever she turned her eyes detail took on an uncanny salience—she marked the taut grimace with which a man carrying two full glasses to a table kept a cigarette down to its last inch between his lips. Not a person did not betray, by one or another glaring peculiarity, the fact of being human: her intimidating sensation of being crowded must have been due to this, for there were not so very many people here. The phenomenon was the lighting, more powerful even than could be accounted for by the bald white globes screwed aching to the low white ceiling—there survived in here not one shadow: every one had been ferreted out and killed.

The Heat of the Day

VLADIMIR NABOKOV
1899–1977

Professor Pnin Prepares to Lecture

Some people—and I am one of them—hate happy ends. We feel cheated. Harm is the norm. Doom should not jam. The avalanche stopping in its tracks a few feet above the cowering village behaves not only unnaturally but unethically. Had I been reading about this mild old man, instead of writing about him, I would have preferred him to discover, upon his arrival to Cremona, that his lecture was not this Friday but the next. Actually, however, he not only arrived safely but was in time for dinner—a fruit cocktail, to begin with, mint jelly with the anonymous meat course, chocolate syrup with the vanilla ice cream. And soon afterwards, surfeited with sweets, wearing his black suit, and juggling three papers, all of which he had stuffed into his coat so as to have the one he wanted among the rest (thus thwarting mischance by mathematical necessity), he sat on a chair near the lectern, while, at the lectern, Judith Clyde, an ageless blonde in aqua rayon, with large, flat cheeks stained a beautiful candy pink and two bright eyes basking in blue lunacy behind a rimless pince-nez, presented the speaker:

'Tonight,' she said, 'the speaker of the evening——This, by the way, is our third Friday night; last time, as you all remember, we all enjoyed hearing what Professor Moore had to say about agriculture in China. Tonight we have here, I am proud to say, the Russian-born, and citizen of this country, Professor—now comes a difficult one, I am afraid—Professor Pun-neen. I hope I have it right. He hardly needs any introduction, of course, and we are all happy to have him. We have a long evening before us, a long and rewarding evening, and I am sure you would all like to have time to ask him questions afterwards. Incidentally, I am told his father was Dostoevski's family doctor, and he has traveled quite a bit on both sides of the Iron Curtain. Therefore I will not take up your precious time any longer and will only add a few words about our next Friday lecture in this program. I am sure you will all be delighted to know that there is a grand surprise in store for all of us. Our next lecturer is the distinguished poet and prose writer, Miss Linda Lacefield. We all know she has written poetry, prose, and some short stories. Miss Lacefield was born in New York. Her ancestors on both sides fought on both sides in the Revolutionary War. She wrote her first poem before graduation. Many of her poems—three of them, at least—have been published in *Response, A Hundred Love Lyrics by American Women*. In 1922 she received the cash prize offered by——'

But Pnin was not listening. A faint ripple stemming from his recent seizure was holding his fascinated attention. It lasted only a few heartbeats, with an additional systole here and there—last, harmless echoes—and was resolved in demure reality as his distinguished hostess invited him to the lectern; but while it lasted, how limpid the vision was! In the middle of the front row of seats he saw one of his Baltic aunts, wearing the pearls and the lace and the blond wig she had worn at all the performances given by the great ham actor Khodotov, whom she had adored from afar before drifting into insanity. Next to her, shyly smiling, sleek dark head inclined, gentle brown gaze shining up at Pnin from under velvet eyebrows, sat a dead sweetheart of his, fanning herself with a program. Murdered, forgotten, unrevenged, incorrupt, immortal, many old friends were scattered throughout the dim hall among more recent people, such as Miss Clyde, who had modestly regained a front seat. Vanya Bednyashkin, shot by the Reds in 1919 in Odessa because his father had been a Liberal, was gaily signaling to his former schoolmate from the back of the hall. And in an inconspicuous situation Dr Pavel Pnin and his anxious wife, both a little blurred but on the whole wonderfully recovered from their obscure dissolution, looked at their son with the same life-consuming passion and pride that they had looked at him with that night in 1912 when, at a school festival, commemorating Napoleon's defeat, he had recited (a bespectacled lad all alone on the stage) a poem by Pushkin.

The brief vision was gone. Old Miss Herring, retired Professor of History, author of *Russia Awakes* (1922), was bending across one or two intermediate members of the audience to compliment Miss Clyde on her speech, while from behind that lady another twinkling old party was thrusting into her field of vision a pair of withered, soundlessly clapping hands.

Pnin, 1957

At the Enchanted Hunters Hotel

There is nothing louder than an American hotel; and, mind you, this was supposed to be a quiet, cozy, old-fashioned, homey place—'gracious living' and all that stuff. The clatter of the elevator's gate—some twenty yards northeast of my head but as clearly perceived as if it were inside my left temple—alternated with the banging and booming of the machine's various evolutions and lasted well beyond midnight. Every now and then, immediately east of my left ear (always assuming I lay on my back, not daring to direct my viler side toward the nebulous haunch of my bedmate), the corridor would brim with cheerful, resonant and inept exclamations ending in a volley of good-nights. When *that* stopped, a toilet immediately north of my cerebellum took over. It was a manly, energetic, deep-throated toilet, and it was used many times. Its gurgle and gush and long afterflow shook the wall behind me. Then someone in a southern direction was extravagantly sick, almost coughing out his life with his liquor, and his toilet descended like a veritable Niagara, immediately beyond our bathroom. And when finally all the waterfalls had stopped, and the enchanted hunters were sound asleep, the avenue under the window of my insomnia, to the west of my wake—a staid, eminently residential, dignified alley of huge trees—degenerated into the despicable haunt of gigantic trucks roaring through the wet and windy night.

And less than six inches from me and my burning life, was nebulous Lolita! After a long stirless vigil, my tentacles moved towards her again, and this time the creak of the mattress did not awake her. I managed to bring my ravenous bulk so close to her that I felt the aura of her bare shoulder like a warm breath upon my cheek. And then, she sat up, gasped, muttered with insane rapidity something about boats, tugged at the sheets and lapsed back into her rich, dark, young unconsciousness. As she tossed, within that abundant flow of sleep, recently auburn, at present lunar, her arm struck me across the face. For a second I held her. She freed herself from the shadow of my embrace—doing this not consciously, not violently, not with any personal distaste, but with the neutral plaintive murmur of a child demanding its natural rest. And again the situation remained the same: Lolita with her curved spine to Humbert, Humbert resting his head on his hand and burning with desire and dyspepsia.

Lolita, 1958

Golden Syrup and Grammar Books

The kind of Russian family to which I belonged—a kind now extinct—had, among other virtues, a traditional leaning toward the comfortable products of Anglo-Saxon civilization. Pears' Soap, tar-black when dry, topaz-like when held to the light between wet fingers, took care of one's morning bath. Pleasant was the decreasing weight of the English collapsible tub when it was made to protrude a rubber underlip and disgorge its frothy contents into the slop pail. 'We could not improve the cream, so we improved the tube,' said the English toothpaste. At breakfast, Golden Syrup imported from London would entwist with its glowing coils the revolving spoon from which enough of it had slithered onto a piece of Russian bread and butter. All sorts of snug, mellow things came in a steady procession from the English Shop on Nevski Avenue: fruitcakes, smelling salts, playing cards, picture puzzles, striped blazers, talcum-white tennis balls.

I learned to read English before I could read Russian. My first English friends were four simple souls in my grammar—Ben, Dan, Sam and Ned.

There used to be a great deal of fuss about their identities and whereabouts—'Who is Ben?' 'He is Dan,' 'Sam is in bed,' and so on. Although it all remained rather stiff and patchy (the compiler was handicapped by having to employ—for the initial lessons, at least—words of not more than three letters), my imagination somehow managed to obtain the necessary data. Wan-faced, big-limbed, silent nitwits, proud in the possession of certain tools ('Ben has an axe'), they now drift with a slow-motioned slouch across the remotest backdrop of memory; and, akin to the mad alphabet of an optician's chart, the grammar-book lettering looms again before me.

The schoolroom was drenched with sunlight. In a sweating glass jar, several spiny caterpillars were feeding on nettle leaves (and ejecting interesting, barrel-shaped pellets of olive-green frass). The oilcloth that covered the round table smelled of glue. Miss Clayton smelled of Miss Clayton. Fantastically, gloriously, the blood-colored alcohol of the outside thermometer had risen to 24° Réaumur (86° Fahrenheit) in the shade. Through the window one could see kerchiefed peasant girls weeding a garden path on their hands and knees or gently raking the sun-mottled sand. (The happy days when they would be cleaning streets and digging canals for the State were still beyond the horizon.) Golden orioles in the greenery emitted their four brilliant notes: dee-del-dee-O!

Ned lumbered past the window in a fair impersonation of the gardener's mate Ivan (who was to become in 1918 a member of the local Soviet). On later pages longer words appeared; and at the very end of the brown, inkstained volume, a real, sensible story unfolded its adult sentences ('One day Ted said to Ann: Let us—'), the little reader's ultimate triumph and reward. I was thrilled by the thought that some day I might attain such proficiency. The magic has endured, and whenever a grammar-book comes my way, I instantly turn to the last page to enjoy a forbidden glimpse of the laborious student's future, of that promised land where, at last, words are meant to mean what they mean.

'My English Education' (1948), *Speak, Memory*, 1967

RICHARD HUGHES

1900–1976

Emily and the Alligator

'What do you want?' said Emily forbiddingly.

'Harold has brought his alligator,' said Rachel.

Harold stepped forward, and laid the little creature on Emily's coverlet. It was very small: only about six inches long: a yearling: but an exact miniature of its adult self, with the snub nose and round Socratic forehead that distinguish it from the crocodile. It moved jerkily, like a clockwork toy. Harold picked it up by the tail: it spread its paws in the air, and jerked from side to side, more like clockwork than ever. Then he set it down again, and it stood there, its tongueless mouth wide open and its harmless teeth looking like grains of sand-paper, alternately barking and hissing. Harold let it snap at his finger—it was plainly hungry in the warmth down there. It darted its head so fast you could hardly see it move: but its bite was still so weak as to be painless, even to a child.

Emily drew a deep breath, fascinated.

'May I have him for the night?' she asked.

'All right,' said Harold: and he and Rachel were summoned away by some one without.

Emily was translated into Heaven. So this was an alligator! She was actually going to sleep with an alligator! She had thought that to any one who had once been in an earthquake nothing really exciting could happen again: but then, she had not thought of this.

There was once a girl called Emily, who slept with an alligator . . .

In search of greater warmth, the creature highstepped warily up the bed towards her face. About six inches away it paused, and they looked each other in the eye, those two children.

The eye of an alligator is large, protruding, and of a brilliant yellow, with a slit pupil like a cat's. A cat's eye, to the casual observer, is expressionless: though with attention one can distinguish in it many changes of emotion. But the eye of an alligator is infinitely more stony and brilliant—reptilian.

What possible meaning could Emily find in such an eye? Yet she lay there, and stared, and stared: and the alligator stared too. If there had been an observer it might have given him a shiver to see them so—well, eye to eye like that.

Presently the beast opened his mouth and hissed again gently. Emily lifted a finger and began to rub the corner of his jaw. The hiss changed to a sound almost like a purr. A thin, filmy lid first covered his eye from the front backwards, then the outer lid closed up from below.

Suddenly he opened his eyes again, and snapped on her finger: then turned and wormed his way into the neck of her night-gown, and crawled down inside, cool and rough against her skin, till he found a place to rest. It is surprising that she could stand it as she did, without flinching.

Alligators are utterly untamable.

A High Wind in Jamaica, 1929

V. S. PRITCHETT
1900–1997

Dostoevsky

Dostoevski was a spiritual sensationalist, a man of God somewhat stained with the printing ink of the late night final. He lives at first in the upper air as he plans his novels, and gradually comes down to earth, still undetermined until he is pulled up—by what? 'Ordinary' life? No, a newspaper cutting. What a passion he has for the newspapers! What significance things had once they were in headlines! The report of the Nechaev affair clinches *The Possessed*, a *cause célèbre* sets the idea of *The Idiot* in motion. These court cases pinned down his restless mind. Early in *The Possessed* Liza asks Shatov to help her compile an annual collection of newspaper cuttings of all the court cases, trials, speeches, incidents and so on, the child-beatings, thefts, accidents, will-suits, etc., which would serve to give a real picture of the Russian situation year by year. Dostoevski must often have longed for a book like that on his desk. For ordinary people were lost in an anonymity which thwarted the romantic temperament. In the *faits divers* they were transformed; give him the evidence and the process of mystification could begin. The *faits divers* could become the *faits universels.*

In My Good Books, 1942

The Gem *and the* Magnet *and Wordsworth*

My mother's tales about her childhood made the world seem like a novel to me and with her I looked back and rather feared or despised the present. The present was a chaos and a dissipation and it was humiliating to see that the boys who lived for the minute and for the latest craze or adventure, were the most intelligent and clear-headed. Their families were not claustrophobic, the sons were not prigs, as I was. There was a boy with a Japanese look to him—he had eyes like apple pips—who had introduced me to Wells's *Time Machine.* He went a step further and offered me his greatest treasures: dozens of tattered numbers of those famous stories of school life, *The Gem* and *The Magnet.* The crude illustrations, the dirty condition of the papers, indicated that they were pulp and sin. One page and I was entranced. I gobbled these stories as if I were eating pie or stuffing. To hell with poor self-pitying fellows like Oliver Twist; here were the cheerful rich. I craved for Greyfriars, that absurd Public School, as I craved for pudding. There the boys wore top-hats and tail-coats—Arthur

Augustus D'Arcy, the toff, wore a monocle—they had feasts in their 'studies'; they sent a pie containing a boot to the bounder of the Remove; they rioted; they never did a stroke of work. They 'strolled' round 'the Quad' and rich uncles tipped them a 'fivah' which they spent on more food. Sometimes a shady foreign-language master was seen to be in touch with a German spy. Very rarely did a girl appear in these tales.

The Japanese-looking boy was called Nott. He had a friend called Howard, the son of a compositor. *The Gem* and *The Magnet* united us. We called ourselves by Greyfriars' names and jumped about shouting words like 'Garoo'. We punned on our names. When anything went wrong we said, in chorus: 'How-'ard! Is it Nott?' And doubled with laughter dozens of times a day and as we 'strolled' arm in arm on the way home from school.

I knew this reading was sin and I counteracted it by reading a short life of the poet Wordsworth. There was a rustic summer-house at the end of our back garden. It had stained-glass windows. Driving my brothers and sisters out, I claimed it as my retreat and cell. When they kicked up too much noise I sat up on the thatched roof of the house where, when life at Grasmere bored me, I had a good view of what other boys were doing in their gardens. I forgot about prose and said I was going to be a poet and 'Dirty Poet' became the family name for me. Sedbergh is not far from the Lake Country: destiny pointed to my connection with Wordsworth. We had a common experience of Lakes and Fells. His lyrical poems seemed too simple and girlish to me: I saw myself writing a new *Prelude* or *Excursion*. Also the line 'Getting and spending we lay waste our powers' struck home at our family. I read that Wordsworth had been Poet-Laureate: this was the ideal. To my usual nightly prayers that the house should not catch fire and that no burglar should break in, I added a line urging God to make me Poet-Laureate 'before I am twenty-one'. This prayer lasted until I was sixteen.

A Cab at the Door, 1968

SEAN O'FAOLAIN
1900–1991

A Political Journalist

There are two types of Irishman I cannot stand. The first is always trying to behave the way he thinks the English behave. The second is always trying to behave the way he thinks the Irish behave. That sort is a roaring bore. Ike Dignam is like that. He believes that the Irish are witty, so he is forever making laborious jokes. He has a notion that the Irish have a gift for fantasy, so he is constantly talking fey. He also has a notion that the Irish have a magnificent gift for malice, mixed up with another idea of the Irish as great realists, so he loves to abuse everybody for not having more common sense. But as he also believes that the Irish are the most kind and charitable people in the world he ends up every tirade with, 'Ah, sure, God help us, maybe the poor fellow is good at heart.' The result is that you do not know, from one moment to the next, whom you are talking to—Ike the fey or Ike the realist, Ike the malicious or Ike the kind.

I am sure he has no clear idea of himself. He is a political journalist. I have seen him tear the vitals out of a man, and then, over a beer, say, with a shocked guffaw:

'I'm after doin' a terrible thing. Do you know what I said in my column this morning about Harry Lombard? I said, "There is no subject under the sun on which the eloquence does not pour from his lips with the thin fluidity of ass's milk." Honest to God, we're a terrible race. Of course, the man will never talk to me again.'

All as if right hand had no responsibility for left hand. But the exasperating thing is that his victims do talk to him again, and in the most friendly way, though why they do it I do not know considering some of the things he says and writes about them. He is the man who said of a certain woman who is in the habit of writing letters to the press in defence of the Department of Roads and Railways, 'Ah, sure, she wrote that with the minister's tongue in her cheek.' Yet the Minister for Roads and Railways is one of his best friends, and he says, 'Ike Dignam? Ah, sure! He's all right. The poor divil is good at heart.' And the cursed thing is that Ike *is* good at heart. I have long since given up trying to understand what this means. Something vaguely connected with hope, and consolation, and despair, and the endless mercy of God.

Ike naturally has as many enemies as friends, and this is something that *he* cannot understand. Somebody may say:

'But you're forgetting, Ike, what you said about him last year. You said every time he sings "Galway Bay" he turns it into a street puddle.'

Ike will laugh delightedly.

'That was only a bit o' fun. Who'd mind that?'

'How would you like to have things like that said about yourself?'

He will reply, valiantly:

'I wouldn't mind one bit. Not one bit in the world. I'd know 'twas all part of the game. I'd know the poor fellow was really good at heart.'

'Persecution Mania', *The Stories of Sean O'Faolain*, 1958

RHYS DAVIES
1901–1978

The Lady and the Sluggard

Though Catti found that Dan the Carrier fitted her nature like a key fits its lock, in the end she chose Selwyn who was the fishmonger in the little market-town six miles away. She decided (though in a temper) that her trim body, her smooth calves, her cowslip yellow hair, and her mouthful of glittering teeth deserved something better than Dan's half-a-crown cottage slunk down at the edge of a lonely wood and smelling of mice and winter mildew. The evening she made up her mind she went down to the cottage where Dan had lived alone since his parents' death, and from the patch of garden shouted at him through the open window:

'Come on out of there, you old sluggard, and listen to a lady.'

When the great hook of his nose came out of the door, she went on:

'Give me back the broidered spread I broidered last winter. No wedding for you and me, you snail. Month after next I'm marrying Selwyn the Fish, so there!' And she snapped her fingers at him, still in a temper.

Dan, swarthy of hair and skin as a gipsy, bared his yellow eyes. Just by the front door was the butt that caught the thatch drippings. In a flash he scooped a pan of water and sprung it over her as, too late, she jumped back.

'Go and marry the dirty mackerel!' he shouted in fury. 'Be off!' He scooped another panful.

She picked out a stone from the black loam and threw it at him, hitting his chest. She dodged the second lot of water but did not leave the garden. He remained on the doorstep, his muscled belly heaving up out of his loose-strapped corduroys. But he threw no more water; as the month had been dry, a pity to waste it on this baggage of a turncoat.

'The banns going to be read next Sunday,' she screeched. 'A tidy wedding I'm having. So there! Good riddance of a courter that got no more ambition than a rabbit!' Her yellow hair sprang about like wheat in wind: his yellow eyes danced in answering rage.

'Go and marry a shifty townee,' he roared. 'A couple of bad eggs, the both of you.'

'Jealous!' she sang in vengeful delight. 'Give me back my broidered spread. For wife, one-legged old Mari is proper value for you.'

Six yards between them, and approaching no nearer, they continued in abuse. But he had no intention of yielding up the spread of blue cloth, embroidered with jays, red lilies, and flying swans, which she had given him not long ago, saying it was for their wedding bed. One day it might fetch a good price in the market.

At last, with final jeers at the stick-in-the-mud blockhead, his poverty, and his paltry cottage, she went skipping into the road. Dan's pony, from the paddock beside the cottage, watched her speculatively as she climbed the short height to the village. The evening was darkening. Dan slammed his door, lit a candle, and with an oath stamped his foot on a cockroach.

'The Nature of Man', *A Finger in Every Pie*, 1942

C. L. R. JAMES
1901–1989

W. G. Grace

What manner of man was he? The answer can be given in a single sentence. He was in every respect that mattered a typical representative of the pre-Victorian Age.

The evidence for it abounds. His was a Gloucestershire country father who made a good wicket in the orchard and the whole family rose at dawn to get in a few hours of cricket. Their dogs were trained to act as retrievers. They organized clubs and played matches all over their part of the country. W.G. was taking part from the time he was nine. It is 1857, but one is continually reminded of Tom Brown's childhood thirty years before. The back-swording, running and wrestling have been replaced by a game which provides all that these gave in a more organized manner befitting a new age. But the surroundings are the same, the zest, the concentration, the desire to excel, are the same. The Grace family make their own ground at home. I am only surprised that they did not make their own bats, there must have been much splicing and binding. If they try to play according to established principles, well, the father is a trained man of science. Four sons will become doctors. The wicket the father makes is a good one. The boys are taught to play straight. With characteristically sturdy independence, one brother hits across and keeps on hitting across. They let him alone while W.G. and G.F. are encouraged to stick to first principles. Such live and let live was not the Victorian method with youth . . .

In his attitude to book-learning he belonged entirely to the school of the pre-Arnold Browns. He rebuked a fellow player who was always reading in the dressing-rooms: 'How do you expect to score if you are always reading?' Then follows this priceless piece of ingenuous self-revelation: 'I am never caught that way.' It would be idle to discount the reputation he gained for trying to diddle umpires, and even on occasions disputing with them. He is credited with inducing a batsman to look up at the sun to see a fictitious flight of birds and then calling on the bowler to send down a fast one while the victim's eyes were still hazy. Yet I think there is evidence to show that his face would have become grave and he would have pulled at his beard if a wicket turned out to be prepared in a way that was unfair to his opponents. Everyone knows such men, whom you can trust with your life, your fortune and your sacred honour, but will peep at your cards when playing bridge at a penny a hundred. His humours, his combativeness, his unashamed wish to have it his own way on the field of play, his manoeuvres to encompass this, his delight when he did, his complaints when he didn't, are the rubs and knots of an oak that was sound through and through. Once only was he known to be flustered, and that was when he approached the last few runs of his hundredth century. All who played with him testify that he had a heart of gold, loyal, generous to the end of his life, ready to place his knowledge, his experience and his time at the disposal of young players, even opponents. He is all of one piece, of the same family as the Browns with whom Thomas Hughes begins his book.

W.G. was a pre-Victorian. Yet a man of his stature does not fit easily into any one mould. When we look at the family again we see that there was a Victorian in it. The mother was one of those modern women who being born before their time did what was expected of them in the sphere to which they had been called, but made of it a field for the exercise of qualities that would otherwise have been suppressed. The prototype of them all is Florence Nightingale. Mrs Grace's place was in the home, which included the orchard. She mastered the game of cricket, was firm, not to say severe, with W.G. for not catching on quickly enough to her instructions as to how to play a certain stroke. She kept books, the scores of the family in their early matches. She wrote to the captain of the All England XI recommending her son E.M. for a place in his side. She took the opportunity to say a word for W.G., who, she said, would be the best of the Graces—his back-play showed it. The boy, it seems, was *taught* to play forward and back. Until she died the boys wired match scores and their personal scores to her at the end of each day's play. There was much of his mother in W.G.

Beyond a Boundary, 1963

JOHN STEINBECK
1902–1968

Home Improvements

In April, 1932, the boiler at the Hediondo Cannery blew a tube for the third time in two weeks and the board of directors, consisting of Mr Randolph and a stenographer, decided that it would be cheaper to buy a new boiler than to have to shut down so often. In time the new boiler arrived and the old one was moved into the vacant lot between Lee Chong's and the Bear Flag Restaurant, where it was set on blocks to await an inspiration on Mr Randolph's part on how to make some money out of it. Gradually, the plant engineer removed the tubing to use to patch other outworn equipment at the Hediondo. The boiler looked like an old-fashioned locomotive without wheels. It had a big door in the centre of its nose and a low fire door. Gradually, it became red and soft with rust and gradually the mallow weeds grew up around it and the flaking rust fed the weeds. Flowering myrtle crept up its sides and the wild anise perfumed the air about it. Then someone threw out a datura root and the thick fleshy tree grew up and the great white bells hung down over the boiler door and at night the flowers smelled of love and excitement, an incredibly sweet and moving odour.

In 1935 Mr and Mrs Sam Malloy moved into the boiler. The tubing was all gone now and it was a roomy, dry and safe apartment. True, if you came in through the fire door you had to get down on your hands and knees, but once in there was head room in the middle and you couldn't want a dryer, warmer place to stay. They shagged a mattress through the fire door and settled down. Mr Malloy was happy and contented there and for quite a long time so was Mrs Malloy.

Below the boiler on the hill there were numbers of large pipes also abandoned by the Hediondo. Toward the end of 1937 there was a great catch of fish and the canneries were working full time and a housing shortage occurred. Then it was that Mr Malloy took to renting the larger pipes as sleeping-quarters for single men at a very nominal fee. With a piece of tar paper over one end and a square of carpet over the other, they made comfortable bedrooms, although men used to sleeping curled up had to change their habits or move out. There were those too who claimed that their snores echoing back from the pipes woke them up. But on the whole Mr Malloy did a steady small business and was happy.

Mrs Malloy had been contented until her husband became a landlord and then she began to change. First it was a rug, then a wash-tub, then a lamp with a coloured silk shade. Finally, she came into the boiler on her hands and knees one day and she stood up and said a little breathlessly: 'Holman's are having a sale of curtains. Real lace curtains and edges of blue and pink—$1.98 a set with curtain rods thrown in.'

Mr Malloy set up on the mattress. 'Curtains?' he demanded. 'What in God's name do you want curtains for?'

'I like things nice,' said Mrs Malloy. 'I always did like to have things nice for you,' and her lower lip began to tremble.

'But, darling,' Sam Malloy cried. 'I got nothing against curtains. I like curtains.'

'Only $1.98,' Mrs Malloy quavered, 'and you begrutch me $1.98,' and she sniffled and her chest heaved.

'I don't begrutch you,' said Mr Malloy. 'But, darling—for Christ's sake what are we going to do with curtains? We got no windows.'

Mrs Malloy cried and cried and Sam held her in his arms and comforted her.

'Men just don't understand how a woman feels,' she sobbed. 'Men just never try to put themselves in a woman's place.'

And Sam lay beside her and rubbed her back for a long time before she went to sleep.

Cannery Row, 1945

CHRISTINA STEAD
1902–1983

A Wedding in Sydney

Malfi's husband stooped and picked up the long veil, running behind her like a woman catching chicks. By the time they reached the festal door, he had gathered up the gauze and had it frothing on his arm. Malfi was delicate, small and thin.

In the entrance, and climbing the tall wooden stairs, it was a constant hello'ing and calling out of names, rapid introductions lost in a confusion of smiles and crackling new suits and dresses, a *phew*ing and *ouf*ing over the heat, jokes about the champagne, words and phrases, family words known to them and strange jokes in the family jargon of the Bedloes and of other strangers drifted into their harbour, floating through the air like confetti, startlingly clever, with a hundred sights of old faces refurbished and new faces varnished. The girls felt happy. They allowed themselves to drift upstairs through the carnival, surreptitiously, in the crush, picking their dresses from their wet breasts and streaming thighs. 'How about a nice shower! We ought to have brought our bathers! I'm sorry for the men with their collars', rang on every side. Every word was a joke, every joke successful. They were breathless in the hall, breathless on the threshold of the hall, which was to rent for 'banquets, receptions, smoke concerts, etc.' The church, with its wilted flowers and tangled ribbons, had been disappointing but here there was a large if shabby splendour. From the roof hung the red and green streamers of a past fête. A few white ribands hung from the walls and a white bell with silver tinsel was suspended over the centrepiece of the long banqueting table. Trestle tables covered with white cloths ran round three sides of a large square. The room was spacious, with a dais for a small orchestra, a balustrade, a piano, music-stands. To everyone's surprise, a few musicians in black were actually there, a violinist with a cloth in his hand, a pianist, a cellist, all looking very off-hand. What expense! Trust Aunt Eliza and Uncle Don for the real thing, at the wedding of their only and beloved child. And then, why not?

For Love Alone, 1945

GEORGE ORWELL

1903–1950

An Execution in Burma

We set out for the gallows. Two warders marched on either side of the prisoner, with their rifles at the slope; two others marched close against him, gripping him by arm and shoulder, as though at once pushing and supporting him. The rest of us, magistrates and the like followed behind. Suddenly, when we had gone ten yards, the procession stopped short without any order or warning. A dreadful thing had happened—a dog, come goodness knows whence, had appeared in the yard. It came bounding among us with a loud volley of barks, and leapt round us wagging its whole body, wild with glee at finding so many human beings together. It was a large woolly dog, half Airedale, half pariah. For a moment it pranced round us, and then, before anyone could stop it, it had made a dash for the prisoner, and jumping up tried to lick his face. Everyone stood aghast, too taken aback even to grab at the dog.

'Who let that bloody brute in here?' said the superintendent angrily. 'Catch it, someone!'

A warder detached from the escort, charged clumsily after the dog, but it danced and gambolled just out of his reach, taking everything as part of the game. A young Eurasian jailer picked up a handful of gravel and tried to stone the dog away, but it dodged the stones and came after us again. Its yaps echoed from the jail walls. The prisoner, in the grasp of the two warders, looked on incuriously, as though this was another formality of the hanging. It was several minutes before someone managed to catch the dog. Then we put my handkerchief through its collar and moved off once more, with the dog still straining and whimpering.

It was about forty yards to the gallows. I watched the bare brown back of the prisoner marching in front of me. He walked clumsily with his bound arms, but quite steadily, with that bobbing gait of the Indian who never straightens his knees. At each step his muscles slid neatly into place, the lock of hair on his scalp danced up and down, his feet printed themselves on the wet gravel. And once, in spite of the men who gripped him by each shoulder, he stepped slightly aside to avoid a puddle on the path.

It is curious, but till that moment I had never realized what it means to destroy a healthy, conscious man. When I saw the prisoner step aside to avoid the puddle I saw the mystery, the unspeakable wrongness, of cutting a life short when it is in full tide. This man was not dying, he was alive just as we are alive. All the organs of his body were working—bowels digesting food, skin renewing itself, nails growing, tissues forming—all toiling away in solemn foolery. His nails would still be growing when he stood on the drop, when he was falling through the air with a tenth-of-a-second to live. His eyes saw the yellow gravel and the grey walls, and his brain still remembered, foresaw, reasoned—reasoned even about puddles. He and we were a party of men walking together, seeing, hearing, feeling, understanding the same world; and in two minutes, with a sudden snap, one of us would be gone—one mind less, one world less.

'A Hanging', 1931, *Collected Essays*

Returning Home from the Spanish Civil War

And then England—southern England, probably the sleekest landscape in the world. It is difficult when you pass that way, especially when you are peacefully recovering from sea-sickness with the plush cushions of a boat-train carriage under your bum, to believe that anything is really happening anywhere. Earthquakes in Japan, famines in China, revolutions in Mexico? Don't worry, the milk will be on the doorstep to-morrow morning, the *New Statesman* will come out on Friday. The industrial towns were far away, a smudge of smoke and misery hidden by the curve of the earth's surface. Down here it was still the England I had known in my childhood: the railway-cuttings smothered in wild flowers, the deep meadows where the great shining horses browse and meditate, the slow-moving streams bordered by willows, the green bosoms of the elms, the larkspurs in the cottage gardens; and then the huge peaceful wilderness of outer London, the barges on the miry river, the familiar streets, the posters telling of cricket matches and Royal weddings, the men in bowler hats, the pigeons in Trafalgar Square, the red buses, the blue policemen—all sleeping the deep, deep sleep of England, from which I sometimes fear that we shall never wake till we are jerked out of it by the roar of bombs.

Homage to Catalonia, 1938

The Sancho Panza View of Life

The Don Quixote-Sancho Panza combination, which of course is simply the ancient dualism of body and soul in fiction form, recurs more frequently in the literature of the last four hundred years than can be explained by mere imitation. It comes up again and again, in endless variations, Bouvard and Pécuchet, Jeeves and Wooster, Bloom and Dedalus, Holmes and Watson (the Holmes-Watson variant is an exceptionally subtle one, because the usual physical characteristics of two partners have been transposed). Evidently it corresponds to something enduring in our civilisation, not in the sense that either character is to be found in a 'pure' state in real life, but in the sense that the two principles, noble folly and base wisdom, exist side by side in nearly every human being. If you look into your own mind, which are you, Don Quixote or Sancho Panza? Almost certainly you are both. There is one part of you that wishes to be a hero or a saint, but another part of you is a little fat man who sees very clearly the advantages of staying alive with a whole skin. He is your unofficial self, the voice of the belly protesting against the soul. His tastes lie towards safety, soft beds, no work, pots of beer and women with 'voluptuous' figures. He it is who punctures your fine attitudes and urges you to look after Number One, to be unfaithful to your wife, to bilk your debts, and so on and so forth. Whether you allow yourself to be influenced by him is a different question. But it is simply a lie to say that he is not part of you, just as it is a lie to say that Don Quixote is not part of you either, though most of what is said and written consists of one lie or the other, usually the first.

But though in varying forms he is one of the stock figures of literature, in real life, especially in the way society is ordered, his point of view never gets a fair hearing. There is a constant world-wide conspiracy to pretend that he is not there, or at least that he doesn't matter. Codes of law and morals, or religious systems, never have much room in them for a humorous view of life. Whatever is funny is subversive, every joke is ultimately a custard pie, and the reason why so large a proportion of jokes centre round obscenity is simply that all societies, as the price of survival, have to insist on a fairly high standard of sexual morality. A dirty joke is not, of course, a serious attack upon morality, but it is a sort of mental rebellion, a momentary wish that things were otherwise. So also with all other jokes, which always centre round cowardice, laziness, dishonesty or some other quality which society cannot afford to encourage. Society has always to demand a little more from human beings than it will get in practice. It has to demand faultless discipline and self-sacrifice, it must expect its subjects to work hard, pay their taxes, and be faithful to their wives, it must assume that men think it glorious to die on the battlefield and women want to wear themselves out with child-bearing. The whole of what one may call official literature is founded on such assumptions. I never read the proclamations of generals before battle, the speeches of fuehrers and prime ministers, the solidarity songs of public schools and left-wing political parties, national anthems, Temperance tracts, papal encyclicals and sermons against gambling and contraception, without seeming to hear in the background a chorus of raspberries from all the millions of common men to whom these high sentiments make no appeal. Nevertheless the high sentiments always win in the end, leaders who offer blood, toil, tears and sweat always get more out of their followers than those who offer safety and a good time. When it comes to the pinch, human beings are heroic. Women face childbed and the scrubbing brush, revolutionaries keep their mouths shut in the torture chamber, battleships go down with their guns still firing when their decks are awash. It is only that the other element in man, the lazy, cowardly, debt-bilking adulterer who is inside all of us, can never be suppressed altogether and needs a hearing occasionally.

'The Art of Donald McGill', 1941, *Collected Essays*

Newspeak and Duckspeak

In Newspeak, euphony outweighed every consideration other than exactitude of meaning. Regularity of grammar was always sacrificed to it when it seemed necessary. And rightly so, since what was required, above all for political purposes, was short clipped words of unmistakable meaning which could be uttered rapidly and which roused the minimum of echoes in the speaker's mind. The words of the B vocabulary even gained in force from the fact that nearly all of them were very much alike. Almost invariably these words—*goodthink, Minipax, prolefeed, sexcrime, joycamp, Ingsoc, bellyfeel, thinkpol* and countless others—were words of two or three syllables, with the stress distributed equally between the first syllable and the last. The use of them encouraged a gabbling style of speech, at once staccato and monotonous. And this was exactly what was aimed at. The intention was to make speech, and especially speech on any subject not ideologically neutral, as nearly as possible independent of consciousness. For the purposes of everyday life it was no doubt necessary, or sometimes necessary, to reflect before speaking, but a Party member called upon to make a political or ethical judgment should be able to spray forth the correct opinions as automatically as a machine gun spraying forth bullets. His training fitted him to do this, the language gave him an almost foolproof instrument, and the texture of the words, with their harsh sound and a certain wilful ugliness which was in accord with the spirit of Ingsoc, assisted the process still further.

So did the fact of having very few words to choose from. Relative to our own, the Newspeak vocabulary was tiny, and new ways of reducing it were constantly being devised. Newspeak, indeed, differed from most all other languages in that its vocabulary grew smaller instead of larger every year. Each reduction was a gain, since the smaller the area of choice, the smaller the temptation to take thought. Ultimately it was hoped to make articulate speech issue from the larynx without involving the higher brain centres at all. This aim was frankly admitted in the Newspeak word *duckspeak*, meaning 'to quack like a duck'. Like various other words in the B vocabulary, *duckspeak* was ambivalent in meaning. Provided that the opinions which were quacked out were orthodox ones, it implied nothing but praise, and when the *Times* referred to one of the orators of the Party as a *doubleplusgood duckspeaker* it was paying a warm and valued compliment.

Nineteen Eighty-Four, 1949

EVELYN WAUGH
1903–1966

A Night Out

'Nina,' said Adam, 'let's get married soon, don't you think?'

'Yes, it's a bore not being married.'

The young woman who felt ill passed by them, walking shakily, to try and find her coat and her young man to take her home.

'. . . I don't know if it sounds absurd,' said Adam. 'but I do feel that a marriage ought to *go on*—for quite a long time, I mean. D'you feel that too, at all?'

'Yes, it's one of the things about a marriage!'

'I'm glad you feel that. I didn't quite know if you did. Otherwise it's all rather bogus, isn't it?'

'I think you ought to go and see papa again,' said Nina. 'It's never any good writing. Go and tell him that you've got a job and are terribly rich and that we're going to be married before Christmas!'

'All right. I'll do that.'

'. . . D'you remember last month we arranged for you to go and see him the first time? . . . just like this . . . it was at Archie Schwert's party . . .'

'Oh, Nina, *what a lot of parties*.'

(. . . Masked parties, Savage parties, Victorian parties, Greek parties, Wild West parties, Russian parties, Circus parties, parties where one had to dress as somebody else, almost naked parties in St John's Wood, parties in flats and studios and houses and ships and hotels and night clubs, in windmills and swimming baths, tea parties at school where one ate muffins and meringues and tinned crab, parties at Oxford where one drank brown sherry and smoked Turkish cigarettes, dull dances in London and comic dances in Scotland and disgusting dances in Paris—all that succession and repetition of massed humanity. . . . Those vile bodies . . .)

He leant his forehead, to cool it, on Nina's arm and kissed her in the hollow of her forearm.

'I *know*, darling,' she said, and put her hand on his hair.

Ginger came strutting jauntily by, his hands clasped under his coat-tails.

'Hullo, you two,' he said. 'Pretty good show this, what.'

'Are you enjoying yourself, Ginger?'

'*Rather*. I say, I've met an awful good chap called Miles. Regular topper. You know, *pally*. That's what I like about a really decent party—you meet such topping fellows. I mean some chaps it takes absolutely years to know, but a chap like Miles I feel is a pal straight away.'

Presently cars began to drive away again. Miss Runcible said that she had heard of a divine night club near Leicester Square somewhere where you could get a drink at any hour of the night. It was called the St Christopher's Social Club.

So they all went there in Ginger's car.

On the way Ginger said, 'That cove Miles, you know, he's awfully *queer*...'

St Christopher's Social Club took some time to find.

It was a little door at the side of a shop, and the man who opened it held his foot against it and peeped round.

They paid ten shillings each and signed false names in the visitors' book. Then they went downstairs to a very hot room full of cigarette smoke; there were unsteady tables with bamboo legs round the walls and there were some people in shirt sleeves dancing on a shiny linoleum floor.

There was a woman in a yellow beaded frock playing a piano and another in red playing the fiddle.

They ordered some whisky. The waiter said he was sorry, but he couldn't oblige, not that night he couldn't. The police had just rung up to say that they were going to make a raid any minute. If they liked they could have some nice kippers.

Miss Runcible said that kippers were not very drunk-making and that the whole club seemed bogus to her.

Ginger said well anyway they had better have some kippers now they were there. Then he asked Nina to dance and she said no. Then he asked Miss Runcible and she said no, too.

Then they ate kippers.

Presently one of the men in shirt sleeves (who had clearly had a lot to drink before the St Christopher Social Club knew about the police) came up to their table and said to Adam:

'You don't know me. I'm Gilmour. I don't want to start a row in front of ladies, but when I see a howling cad I like to tell him so.'

Adam said, 'Why do you spit when you talk?'

Gilmour said, 'That is a very unfortunate physical disability, and it shows what a howling cad you are that you mention it.'

Then Ginger said, 'Same to you, old boy, with nobs on.'

Then Gilmour said, 'Hullo, Ginger, old scout.'

And Ginger said, 'Why, it's Bill. You musn't mind Bill. Awfully stout chap. Met him on the boat.'

Gilmour said, 'Any pal of Ginger's is a pal of mine.'

So Adam and Gilmour shook hands.

Gilmour said, 'This is a pretty low joint, anyhow. You chaps come round to my place and have a drink.'

So they went to Gilmour's place.

Gilmour's place was a bed-sitting room in Ryder Street.

So they sat on the bed in Gilmour's place and drank whisky while Gilmour was sick next door.

And Ginger said, 'There's nowhere like London really you know.'

Vile Bodies, 1930

A Haunted Author

'. . . No,' the Norwegian was saying, 'I did not sign anything. It is a British matter. All I know is that he is a fascist. I have heard him speak ill of democracy. We had a few such men in the time of Quisling. We knew what to do with them. But I will not mix in these British affairs.'

'I've got a photograph of him in a black shirt taken at one of those Albert Hall meetings before the war.'

'That might be useful.'

'He was up to his eyes in it. He'd have been locked up under 18B but he escaped by joining the army.'

'He did pretty badly there, I suppose?'

'*Very* badly. There was a scandal in Cairo that had to be hushed up when his brigade-major shot himself.'

'Blackmail?'

'The next best thing.'

'I see he's wearing the Guards tie.'

'He wears any kind of tie—old Etonian usually.'

'*Was* he ever at Eton?'

'He says he was,' said Glover.

'Don't you believe it. Board-school through and through.'

'Or at Oxford?'

'No, no. His whole account of his early life is a lie. No one had ever heard of him until a year or two ago. He's one of a lot of nasty people who crept into prominence during the war . . .'

'. . . I don't say he's an actual card-carrying member of the communist party, but he's certainly mixed up with them.'

'Most Jews are.'

'Exactly. And those "missing diplomats". They were friends of his.'

'He doesn't know enough to make it worth the Russians' while to take him to Moscow.'

'Even the Russians wouldn't want Pinfold.'

The most curious encounter of that morning was with Mrs Cockson and Mrs Benson. They were sitting as usual on the verandah of the deck-bar, each with her glass, and they were talking French with what seemed to Mr Pinfold, who spoke the language clumsily, pure accent and idiom. Mrs Cockson said: 'Ce Monsieur Pinfold essaye toujours de pénétrer chez moi, et il a essayé de se faire présenter à moi par plusieurs de mes amis. Naturellement j'ai refusé.'

'Connaissez-vous un seul de ses amis? Il me semble qu'il a des relations très ordinaires.'

'On peut toujours se tromper dans le premier temps sur une relation étrangère. On a fini par s'apercevoir à Paris qu'il n'est pas de notre société . . .'

It was a put-up job, Mr Pinfold decided. People did not normally behave in this way.

When Mr Pinfold first joined Bellamy's there was an old earl who sat alone all day and every day in the corner of the stairs wearing an odd, hard hat and talking loudly to himself. He had one theme, the passing procession of his fellow members. Sometimes he dozed, but in his long waking hours he maintained a running commentary—'That fellow's chin is too big; dreadful-looking fellow. Never saw him before. Who let him in? . . . Pick your feet up, you. Wearing the carpets out . . . Dreadfully fat young Crambo's getting. Don't eat, don't drink, it's just he's hard up. Nothing fattens a man like getting hard up . . . Poor old Nailsworth, his mother was a whore, so's his wife. They say his daughter's going the same way' . . . and so on.

In the broad tolerance of Bellamy's this eccentric had been accepted quite fondly. He was dead many years now. It was not conceivable, Mr Pinfold thought, that all the passengers in the *Caliban* should suddenly have become similarly afflicted. This chatter was designed to be overheard. It was a put-up job. It was in fact the generals' subtle plan, substituted for the adolescent violence of their young.

Twenty-five years ago or more Mr Pinfold, who was in love with one of them, used to frequent a house full of bright, cruel girls who spoke their own thieves' slang and played their own games. One of these games was a trick from the schoolroom polished for drawing-room use. When a stranger came among them, they would all—if the mood took them—put out their tongues at him or her; all, that is to say, except those in his immediate line of sight. As he turned his head, one group of tongues popped in, another popped out. Those girls were adept in dialogue. They had rigid self-control. They never giggled. Those who spoke to the stranger assumed an unnatural sweetness. The aim was to make him catch another with her tongue out. It was a comic performance—the turning head, the flickering, crimson stabs, the tender smiles turning to sudden grimaces, the artificiality of the conversation which soon engendered an unidentifiable discomfort in the most insensitive visitor, made him feel that somehow he was making a fool of himself, made him look at his trouser buttons, at his face in the glass to see whether there was something ridiculous in his appearance.

Some sort of game as this, enormously coarsened, must, Mr Pinfold supposed, have been devised by the passengers in the *Caliban* for their amusement and his discomfort. Well, he was not going to give them the satisfaction of taking notice of it. He no longer glanced to see who was speaking.

'. . . His mother sold her few little pieces of jewellery, you know, to pay his debts . . .'

'. . . Were his books ever any good?'

'Never *good*. His earlier ones weren't quite as bad as his latest. He's written out.'

'He's tried every literary trick. He's finished now and he knows it.'

'I suppose he's made a lot of money?'

'Not as much as he pretends. And he's spent every penny. His debts are enormous.'

'And of course they'll catch him for income-tax soon.'

'Oh, yes. He's been putting in false returns for years. They're investigating him now. They don't hurry. They always get their man in the end.'

'They'll get Pinfold.'

'He'll have to sell Lychpole.'

'His children will go to the board-school.'

'Just as he did himself.'

'No more champagne for Pinfold.'

'No more cigars.'

'I suppose his wife will leave him?'

'Naturally. No home for her. Her family will take her in.'

'But not Pinfold.'

'No. Not Pinfold . . .'

The Ordeal of Gilbert Pinfold, 1957

ERSKINE CALDWELL
1903–1987

Poor Whites

'Ellie May's straining for Lov, ain't she?' Dude said, nudging Jeeter with his foot. 'She's liable to bust a gut if she don't look out.'

The inner-tube Jeeter was attempting to patch again was on the verge of falling into pieces. The tyres themselves were in a condition even more rotten. And the Ford car, fourteen years old that year, appeared as if it would never stand together long enough for Jeeter to put the tyre back on the wheel, much less last until it could be loaded with blackjack for a trip to Augusta. The touring-car's top had been missing for seven or eight years, and the one remaining wing was linked to the body with a piece of rusty baling wire. All the springs and horsehair had disappeared from the upholstery; the children had taken the seats apart to find out what was on the inside, and nobody had made an attempt to put them together again.

The appearance of the automobile had not been improved by the dropping off of the radiator in the road somewhere several years before, and a rusty lard-can with a hole punched in the bottom was wired to the water pipe on top of the engine in its place. The lard-can failed to fill the need for a radiator, but it was much better than nothing. When Jeeter got ready to go somewhere, he filled the lard pail to overflowing, jumped in, and drove until the water splashed out and the engine locked up with heat. He would get out then and look for a creek so he could fill the pail again. The whole car was like that. Chickens had roosted on it, when there were chickens at the Lesters' to roost, and it was speckled like a guinea-hen. Now that there were no chickens on the place, no one had ever taken the trouble to wash it off. Jeeter had never thought of doing such a thing, and neither had any of the others.

Ellie May had dragged herself from one end of the yard to the opposite side. She was now within reach of Lov where he sat by his sack of turnips. She was bolder, too, than she had ever been before, and she had Lov looking at her and undisturbed by the sight of her harelip. Ellie May's upper lip had an opening a quarter of an inch wide that divided one side of her mouth into unequal parts; the slit came to an abrupt end almost under her left nostril. The upper gum was low, and because her gums were always fiery red, opening her lip made her look as if her mouth were bleeding profusely. Jeeter had been saying for fifteen years that he was going to have Ellie May's lip sewed together, but he had not yet got around to doing it.

Tobacco Road, 1932

KENNETH CLARK
1903–1983

The Venus de Milo

Within a few years of her discovery in 1820, the *Aphrodite of Melos* had taken the central, impregnable position formerly occupied by the *Medici Venus*, and even now that she has lost favour with connoisseurs and archeologists, she has held her place in popular imagery as a symbol, or trademark, of beauty. There must be hundreds of products, from lead pencils to face tissues, from beauty parlours to motorcars, that use an image of the *Aphrodite of Melos* in their advertisements, implying thereby a standard of ideal perfection. Vast popular renown of song, novel, and poem is always hard to explain and in a piece of sculpture is more mysterious still. Coincidence, merit, and momentum are imponderably combined. The *Aphrodite of Melos* gained some of her celebrity from an accident: until 1893, when Furtwängler subjected her to a stricter analysis, she was believed to be an original of the fifth century and the only free-standing figure of a woman that had come down from the great period with the advantage of a head. She thus profited by the years of devoted partisanship that had established the supremacy of the Elgin marbles. They had been praised for their heroic naturalness, their lack of affectation and self-conscious art, and the same terms could be used in contrasting the *Aphrodite of Melos* with the frigid favourites of classicism. It remains true that she is fruitful and robust beyond the other nude Aphrodites of antiquity. If the *Medici Venus* reminds us of a conservatory, the *Aphrodite of Melos* makes us think of an elm tree in a field of corn. Yet there is a certain irony in this justification through naturalness, for, in fact, she is of all works of antiquity one of the most complex and the most artful. Her author has not only used the inventions of his own time, but has consciously attempted to give the effect of a fifth-century work. Her proportions alone demonstrate this. Whereas in the *Venus of Arles* and the *Venus of Capua* the distance between the breasts is considerably less than from breast to navel, in the *Aphrodite of Melos* the old equality is restored. The planes of her body are so large and calm that at first we do not realize the number of angles through which they pass. In architectural terms, she is a baroque composition with classic effect, which is perhaps exactly why the nineteenth century placed her in the same category of excellence as Handel's *Messiah* and Leonardo da Vinci's *Last Supper*. Even now, when we realize that she is not a work of the heroic age of Pheidias, and is perhaps somewhat lacking in the modern merit of 'sensibility,' she remains one of the most splendid physical ideals of humanity, and the noblest refutation of contemporary critical cant that a work of art must 'express its own epoch.'

The Nude, 1956

WILLIAM PLOMER
1903–1973

The Zulu Girl

The third time I went out I came face to face with Nhliziyombi on a narrow path in the bush. It was in the morning. It was the first time I had been alone with her. She was walking along in a leisurely way, playing an instrument called *makwelane*, made of a gourd with wires stretched over its mouth from the ends of a long bow of wood. You tap it with a reed, and it gives out a plaintive noise. There are only two or three notes. She was playing this thing, and singing a melancholy milking-song in a low metallic voice. She did not seem surprised at meeting me (as I was confused at meeting her) but stood aside in the foliage that I might pass.

'Greeting,' she said.

'Greeting,' I answered. "Where are you going?'

'I am just going.'

These words were a formula, but my heart was in torment, and I could hardly keep my hands and lips from hers.

On a sudden impulse I took a gold pin that I wore in my tie, and pinned it to her clothing, where it gleamed in the sun.

'There you are,' I said. 'There's a present for you.'

'Are you giving it?' she asked incredulously.

'It is yours.'

She was alarmed at being favoured by a man she had come to know as Chastity, and exclaimed softly:

'O, white men!'

Then she ran down the path, checkered with shadows. Nor did she look back.

She is curiously innocent, I thought, frank, delicate. Is it truly because I am afraid of myself that I am afraid of loving her? Is it not perhaps that I am afraid of her? How could I touch, perhaps to injure, that frail divine humanity, or human divinity? I could not give myself reasons, but suspected that I was cheating myself. They were disarming, those wide Egyptian eyes. No, I said to myself, I dare not touch her.

Turbott Wolfe, 1925

CYRIL CONNOLLY
1903–1974

Christian de Clavering at Oxford

Most of my Eton friends had also come up to the House, and, as my father had taken a flat in Bicester, 'ponies' and 'monkeys' came rolling in. I spent them on clothes and parties, on entertaining and on looking entertaining. Parties! 'Are you going to de Clavering's to-night?' and woe betide the wretch who had to say no. Nothing much happened at the time, but he soon felt he was living on an icefloe, drifting farther and farther from land, and every moment watching it melt away. De Clavering's to-night! The candles burn in their sconces. The incense glows. Yquem and Avocado pears—a simple meal—but lots and lots of both, with whisky for the hearties and champagne for the dons. 'Have a brick of caviare, Alvanley? More birds' nest, Gleneagles? There's nothing coming, I'm afraid, only Avocado pear and hot-pot.' 'Hot-pot!' 'Christian, you're magnificent!' 'Caviare and hot-pot—Prendy will be blue with envy!' And then dancing, while canons go home across the quad, and David stomps at the piano. I took care at these parties to have a word and piece of advice for everyone.

There was an alert young man in a corner, looking rather shy. 'I know—don't tell me,' I said to him, 'It's your first party.' 'Yes.' I pinched his cheek. 'Si jeunesse savait!' I laughed. It was Evelyn Waugh.

Another merry little fellow asked me if I could suggest a hobby. 'Architecture,' I gave in a flash. 'Thank you.' It was John Betjeman.

'And for me?'

'Afghanistan.'

It was Robert Byron.

'And me?'

'Byron,' I laughed back—it was Peter Quennell.[1]

And Alvanley, Gleneagles, Prince Harmatviz, Graf Slivovitz, the Ballygalley of Ballygalley, Sarsaparilla, the Duc de Dingy, the Conde de Coca y Cola—for them, my peers, I kept my serious warnings.

'These bedroom slippers, Dingy? I flew them over from my *bottier*.'

'You ought to look a little more like a public school prefect, Alvanley. The front cover of *The Captain*, it's rather more your *genre*. There! Wash out the "honey and flowers," and try a fringe effect. I want to see a pillar of the second eleven.'

'Good jazz, Gleneagles, is meant to be played just a little bit too slow.'

'Graf Slivovitz, this isn't the *Herrenclub* in Carpathian Ruthenia, you must take off your hat. Yes—that green growth with the feudal feathers.'

'Sarsaparilla, only the King rouges his knees when he wears a kilt, and then only at a Court ball.'

'Harmatviz, I can smell that Harris a mile away. What on earth is that terrifying harpoon in the lapel?'

'That, de Clavering, is a *Fogas* fly.'[2]

'More Yquem, Ballygalley?'

'What's that?'

'That—if you mean the thing under your elbow—is how I look to Brancusi; the other is a kind of wine. Stand him up, will you, Ava?'

'Before the war we heard very little of the Sarsaparillas—he would not dare wear that tartan in Madrid.'

'Before the war I hadn't heard of you, Coca y Cola, either; Count, this is a democratic country.'

'I am democrats, we are all democrats. *Vive le roi.*'

'Thank you, Dingy, you must have been reading *Some People.* Now I want all the Guinnesses and Astors to go into the next room and get a charade ready. Alvanley, Gleneagles, Harmatviz, and Slivovitz—you will drive quickly over with me for a few minutes to Bicester to say good-night to father.'

'No I don't think.'—'My price is ten guineas.'—'Jolly well not unless we go halves.'—'Where is my hat and gotha?'—and madcap youth was served.

[1] All of whom, I am told (autumn 1937), still keep afloat.
[2] An amusing fish from the Balaton.

'Where Engels Fears to Tread', *The Condemned Playground*, 1945

FRANK O'CONNOR
1903–1966

An Unsuitable Suitor

Charlie Cashman was a great friend of Nora's father and a regular visitor to her home. He had been her father's Commandant during the Troubles. He owned the big hardware store in town and this he owed entirely to his good national record. He and his mother had never got on, for she hated the Volunteers as she hated the books he read; she looked on him as a flighty fellow and had determined early in his life that the shop would go to her second son, John Joe. As Mrs Cashman was a woman who had never known what it was not to have her own way, Charlie had resigned himself to this, and after the Troubles, cleared out and worked as a shop assistant in Asragh. But then old John Cashman died, having never in his lifetime contradicted his wife, and his will was found to be nothing but a contradiction. It seemed that he had always been a violent nationalist and admired culture and hated John Joe, and Charlie, as in the novels, got every damn thing, even his mother being left in the house only on sufferance.

Charlie was a good catch and there was no doubt of his liking for Nora, but somehow Nora couldn't bear him. He was an airy, excitable man with a plump, sallow, wrinkled face that always looked as if it needed shaving, a pair of keen grey eyes in slits under bushy brows; hair on his cheekbones, hair in his ears, hair even in his nose. He wore a dirty old tweed suit and a cap. Nora couldn't stand him—even with his clothes on. She told herself that it was the cleft in his chin, which someone had once told her betokened a sensual nature, but it was really the thought of all the hair. It made him look so animal!

Besides, there was something sly and double-meaning about him. He was, by town standards, a very well-read man. Once he found Nora reading St Francis de Sales and asked her if she'd ever read *Romeo and Juliet* with such a knowing air that he roused her dislike even further. She gave him a cold and penetrating look which should have crushed him but didn't—he was so thick.

'As a matter of fact I have,' she said steadily, just to show him that true piety did not exclude a study of the grosser aspects of life.

'What did you think of it?' he asked.

'I thought it contained a striking moral lesson,' said Nora.

'Go on!' Charlie exclaimed with a grin. 'What was that, Nora?'

'It showed where unrestrained passion can carry people,' she said.

'Ah, I wouldn't notice that,' said Charlie. 'Your father and myself were a bit wild too, in our time.'

Her father, a big, pop-eyed, open-gobbed man, looked at them both and said nothing, but he knew from their tone that they were sparring across him and he wanted to know more about it. That night after Charlie had gone he looked at Nora with a terrible air.

'What's that book Charlie Cashman was talking about?' he asked. 'Did I read that?'

'*Romeo and Juliet*?' she said with a start. 'It's there on the shelf behind you. In the big Shakespeare.'

Jerry took down the book and looked even more astonished.

'That's a funny way to write a book,' he said. 'What is it about?'

She told him the story as well as she could, with a slight tendency to make Friar Laurence the hero, and her father looked more pop-eyed than ever. He had a proper respect for culture.

'But they were married all right?' he asked at last.

'They were,' said Nora. 'Why?'

'Ah, that was a funny way to take him up so,' her father said cantankerously. ''Tisn't as if there was anything wrong in it.' He went to the foot of the stairs with his hands in his trouser pockets while Nora watched him with a hypnotised air. She knew what he was thinking of. 'Mind,' he said, 'I'm not trying to force him on you, but there's plenty of girls in this town would be glad of your chance.'

That was all he said but Nora wanted no chances. She would have preferred to die in the arena like a Christian martyr sooner than marry a man with so much hair.

'The Holy Door', *The Common Chord*, 1947

FRANK SARGESON
1903–1982

Miss Briggs

There's a woman who lives in my street. Her name is Miss Briggs.

There must be thousands of such women. Such streets too. If you take the whole world, hundreds of thousands.

Miss Briggs rents a room from an old woman who rents an old house from an old man. The old man doesn't rent anything from anybody. Unless you can call taking a taxi renting anything. Or buying a grandstand ticket to see the Springboks.

The house is a very old house. Once it was a grocer's shop with rooms to live in upstairs. But the grocer went bankrupt and the old man couldn't get another shopkeeper to take it. So he had the verandah roof pulled down, and the front altered a bit, and a few rooms added on the back. Then he got the old woman as a tenant, and she got a signwriter to paint up the words, GUEST HOUSE.

But the old woman won't take you as a boarder. You have to rent a room. Though she'll always sell you a pig's trotter. I don't know how big a trade she does in pigs' trotters, but she's always got a window full of them, marked 2d each.

Whether or not Miss Briggs eats pigs' trotters I can't say. I shouldn't think so.

I've never spoken to Miss Briggs, although I see her nearly every day. Except on Sundays she's always carrying two suitcases. They're heavy by the way they drag down her shoulders. She's a mere sprig of a woman.

The queer thing is I don't know what Miss Briggs sells.

She's never tried to sell me anything. I wonder why. Perhaps she deals in ladies' requisites.

If it's anything masculine why has she never called at my place? Pooh, she needn't think I'm all that hard-up. If I wasn't frightened of frightening her I'd stop her in the street and ask her what she means by it.

Now, would anyone whose line was ladies' requisites be likely to eat pigs' trotters?

Miss Briggs is a goer anyhow. You want to see her on a wet day.

The ladies along at the croquet green have to brave out the wet days too.

They have to talk and eat all day without taking any time off to play croquet.

I think I'll write to Mr Ezra Pound about the ladies along at the croquet green. He might like to put them in his next Canto.

On a wet day Miss Briggs gets wet. Well, when you've got rent to pay what can you expect? Even the doctors can't put off their calls just because it's raining.

You know those patent windscreen wipers that doctors have on their cars. Miss Briggs would get on much better if she had the same sort of patent for her glasses.

Miss Briggs never smiles. I've never seen her talking to anyone, and who her customers are I don't know. You'd think she'd go to church but she doesn't go, although one night she went past my place singing Abide With Me.

Love?

Who can say? Could a person go through life without loving somebody?

Sometimes I think Miss Briggs is something I'm always dreaming. But if that is so why don't I dream her coming out of the Guest House eating a pig's trotter?

Miss Briggs?

My goodness yes, Miss Briggs.

'Miss Briggs', *Collected Stories*, 1964

NATHANAEL WEST
1904–1940

A Riot in Los Angeles

New groups, whole families, kept arriving. He could see a change come over them as soon as they had become part of the crowd. Until they reached the line, they looked diffident, almost furtive, but the moment they had become part of it, they turned arrogant and pugnacious. It was a mistake to think them harmless curiosity seekers. They were savage and bitter, especially the middle-aged and the old, and had been made so by boredom and disappointment.

All their lives they had slaved at some kind of dull, heavy labor, behind desks and counters, in the fields and at tedious machines of all sorts, saving their pennies and dreaming of the leisure that would be theirs when they had enough. Finally that day came. They could draw a weekly income of ten or fifteen dollars. Where else should they go but California, the land of sunshine and oranges?

Once there, they discover that sunshine isn't enough. They get tired of oranges, even of avocado pears and passion fruit. Nothing happens. They don't know what to do with their time. They haven't the mental equipment for leisure, the money nor the physical equipment for pleasure. Did they slave so long just to go to an occasional Iowa picnic? What else is there? They watch the waves come in at Venice. There wasn't any ocean where most of them came from, but after you've seen one wave, you've seen them all. The same is true of the airplanes at Glendale. If only a plane would crash once in a while so that they could watch the passengers being consumed in a 'holocaust of flame,' as the newspapers put it. But the planes never crash.

Their boredom becomes more and more terrible. They realize that they've been tricked and burn with resentment. Every day of their lives they read the newspapers and went to the movies. Both fed them on lynchings, murder, sex crimes, explosions, wrecks, love nests, fires, miracles, revolutions, wars. This daily diet made sophisticates of them. The sun is a joke. Oranges can't titillate their jaded palates. Nothing can ever be violent enough to make taut their slack minds and bodies. They have been cheated and betrayed. They have slaved and saved for nothing.

The Day of the Locust, 1939

CHRISTOPHER ISHERWOOD
1904–1986

At the Troika

On New Year's Eve I had supper at home with my landlady and the other lodgers. I must have been already drunk when I arrived at the Troika, because I remember getting a shock when I looked into the cloakroom mirror and found that I was wearing a false nose. The place was crammed. It was difficult to say who was dancing and who was merely standing up. After hunting about for some time, I came upon Arthur in a corner. He was sitting at a table with another, rather younger gentleman who wore an eyeglass and had sleek dark hair.

'Ah, here you are, William. We were beginning to fear that you'd deserted us. May I introduce two of my most valued friends to each other? Mr Bradshaw—Baron von Pregnitz.'

The Baron, who was fishy and suave, inclined his head. Leaning towards me, like a cod swimming up through water, he asked:

'Excuse me. Do you know Naples?'

'No. I've never been there.'

'Forgive me. I'm sorry. I had the feeling that we'd met each other before.'

'Perhaps so,' I said politely, wondering how he could smile without dropping his eyeglass. It was rimless and ribbonless and looked as though it had been screwed into his pink well-shaved face by means of some horrible surgical operation.

'Perhaps you were at Juan-les-Pins last year?'

'No, I'm afraid I wasn't.'

'Yes, I see.' He smiled in polite regret. 'In that case I must beg your pardon.'

'Don't mention it,' I said. We both laughed very heartily. Arthur, evidently pleased that I was making a good impression on the Baron, laughed too. I drank a glass of champagne off at a gulp. A three-man band was playing: *Gruss' mir mein Hawai, ich bleib' Dir treu, ich hab' Dich gerne.* The dancers, locked frigidly together, swayed in partial-paralytic rhythms under a huge sunshade suspended from the ceiling and oscillating gently through cigarette smoke and hot rising air.

'Don't you find it a trifle stuffy in here?' Arthur asked anxiously.

In the windows were bottles filled with coloured liquids brilliantly illuminated from beneath, magenta, emerald, vermilion. They seemed to be lighting up the whole room. The cigarette smoke made my eyes smart until the tears ran down my face. The music kept dying away, then surging up fearfully loud. I passed my hand down the shiny black oil-cloth curtains in the alcove behind my chair. Oddly enough, they were quite cold. The lamps were like alpine cowbells. And there was a fluffy white monkey perched above the bar. In another moment, when I had drunk exactly the right amount of champagne, I should have a vision. I took a sip. And now, with extreme clarity, without passion or malice, I saw what Life really is. It had something, I remember, to do with the revolving sunshade. Yes, I murmured to myself, let them dance. They are dancing. I am glad.

'You know, I like this place. Extraordinarily,' I told the Baron with enthusiasm. He did not seem surprised.

Arthur was solemnly stifling a belch.

'Dear Arthur, don't look so sad. Are you tired?'

'No, not tired, William. Only a little contemplative, perhaps. Such an occasion as this is not without its solemn aspect. You young people are quite right to enjoy yourselves. I don't blame you for a moment. One has one's memories.'

'Memories are the most precious things we have,' said the Baron with approval. As intoxication proceeded, his face seemed slowly to disintegrate. A rigid area of paralysis formed round the monocle. The monocle was holding his face together. He gripped it desperately with his facial muscles, cocking his disengaged eyebrow, his mouth sagging slightly at the corners, minute beads of perspiration appearing along the parting of his thin, satin-smooth dark hair. Catching my eye, he swam up towards me, to the surface of the element which seemed to separate us.

'Excuse me, please. May I ask you something?'

'By all means.'

'Have you read *Winnie the Pooh*, by A. A. Milne?'

'Yes, I have.'

'And tell me, please, how did you like it?'

'Very much indeed.

'Then I am very glad. Yes, so did I. Very much.'

And now we were all standing up. What had happened? It was midnight. Our glasses touched.

'Cheerio,' said the Baron, with the air of one who makes a particularly felicitous quotation.

'Allow me,' said Arthur, 'to wish you both every success and happiness in nineteen thirty-one. Every success . . .' His voice trailed off uneasily into silence. Nervously he fingered his heavy fringe of hair. A tremendous crash exploded from the band. Like a car which has slowly, laboriously reached the summit of the mountain railway, we plunged headlong downwards into the New Year.

Mr Norris Changes Trains, 1935

GRAHAM GREENE

1904–1991

A Fine Day for the Races

It was a fine day for the races. People poured into Brighton by the first train. It was like Bank Holiday all over again, except that these people didn't spend their money; they harboured it. They stood packed deep on the tops of the trams rocking down to the Aquarium, they surged like some natural and irrational migration of insects up and down the front. By eleven o'clock it was impossible to get a seat on the buses going out to the course. A negro wearing a bright striped tie sat on a bench in the Pavilion garden and smoked a cigar. Some children played touch wood from seat to seat, and he called out to them hilariously, holding his cigar at arm's length with an air of pride and caution, his great teeth gleaming like an advertisement. They stopped playing and stared at him, backing slowly. He called out to them again in their own tongue, the words hollow and unformed and childish like theirs, and they eyed him uneasily and backed farther away. He put his cigar patiently back between the cushiony lips and went on smoking. A band came up the pavement through Old Steyne, a blind band playing drums and trumpets, walking in the gutter, feeling the kerb with the edge of their shoes, in Indian file. You heard the music a long way off, persisting through the rumble of the crowd, the shots of exhaust pipes, and the grinding of the buses starting uphill for the racecourse. It rang out with spirit, marched like a regiment, and you raised your eyes in expectation of the tiger skin and the twirling drumsticks and saw the pale blind eyes, like those of pit ponies, going by along the gutter.

In the public school grounds above the sea the girls trooped solemnly out to hockey: stout goal-keepers padded like armadillos; captains discussing tactics with their lieutenants; junior girls running amok in the bright day. Beyond the aristocratic turf, through the wrought-iron main gates they could see the plebeian procession, those whom the buses wouldn't hold, plodding up the down, kicking up the dust, eating buns out of paper bags. The buses took the long way round through Kemp Town, but up the steep hill came the crammed taxicabs—a seat for anyone at ninepence a time—a Packard for the members' enclosure, old Morrises, strange high cars with family parties, keeping the road after twenty years. It was as if the whole road moved upwards like an Underground staircase in the dusty sunlight, a creaking, shouting, jostling crowd of cars moving with it. The junior girls took to their heels like ponies racing on the turf, feeling the excitement going on outside, as if this were a day on which life for many people reached a kind of climax. The odds on Black Boy had shortened, nothing could ever make life quite the same after that rash bet of a fiver on Merry Monarch. A scarlet racing model, a tiny rakish car which carried about it the atmosphere of innumerable roadhouses, of totsies gathered round swimming pools, of furtive encounters in by-lanes off the Great North Road, wormed through the traffic with incredible dexterity. The sun caught it: it winked as far as the dining-hall windows of the girls' school. It was crammed tight: a woman sat on a man's knee, and another man clung on the running board as it swayed and hooted and cut in and out uphill towards the downs. The woman was singing, her voice faint and disjointed through the horns, something traditional about brides and bouquets, something which went with Guinness and oysters and the old Leicester Lounge, something out of place in the little bright racing car. Upon the top of the down the words blew back along the dusty road to meet an ancient Morris rocking and receding in their wake at forty miles an hour, with flapping hood, bent fender and discoloured windscreen.

Brighton Rock, 1938

Childhood's End

In childhood we live under the brightness of immortality—heaven is as near and actual as the seaside. Behind the complicated details of the world stand the simplicities: God is good, the grown-up man or woman knows the answer to every question, there is such a thing as truth, and justice is as measured and faultless as a clock. Our heroes are simple: they are brave, they tell the truth, they are good swordsmen and they are never in the long run really defeated. That is why no later books satisfy us like those which were read to us in childhood—for those promised a world of great simplicity of which we knew the rules, but the later books are complicated and contradictory with experience: they are formed out of our own disappointing memories—of the VC in the police-court dock, of the faked income tax return, the sins in corners, and the hollow voice of the man we despise talking to us of courage and purity. The little duke is dead and betrayed and forgotten: we cannot recognise the villain and we suspect the hero and the world is a small cramped place. That is what people are saying all the time everywhere: the two great popular statements of faith are 'What a small place the world is' and 'I'm a stranger here myself.'

The Ministry of Fear, 1943

A. J. LIEBLING
1904–1963

An Interview with De Gaulle

I always maintained the thesis, against Frenchmen who deprecated de Gaulle and Britons who complained of his crankiness, that since he was the only horse they had entered in the race they had better try hard with him. I thought him valuable as a trade-mark and as a person. For stubbornness and a lack of objectivity, in the leader of a forlorn hope, are rather qualities than defects. And I would quote Reynaud, with the addition of a softening *peut-être*, 'He has perhaps the character of a stubborn pig—but he *has* character.' It is, believe it or not, a great asset.

The consequence of this over-elaborate discussion of every facet of de Gaulle's character was that by the time I interviewed him I was completely insulated against fresh impressions. I was in the frame of mind of a soldier entering a house that he has reason to believe booby-trapped, The General, suspicious by nature, had been made more so by numerous and probably conflicting reports on me, and my first innocent question, designed to stimulate conversation was a disaster. 'When are you coming to America, my general?' I asked him. He immediately had to decide whether I was a scout for the Foreign Office or whether Anthony J. Drexel Biddle, Jr., whom he knew I knew, had sent me over to feel him out with a view to a later official bid from the State Department. 'I have not yet been invited,' he said after a pause of a couple of minutes, and settled back in his chair as I have seen witnesses in a murder trial momentarily relax after turning a tough question from a cross-examiner.

De Gaulle is decidedly less imposing sitting down than standing up, because the part of him showing above a desk does not suggest a man of extraordinary stature. He is small-boned, with fine, slender hands and no great depth of chest or breadth of shoulder. His height folds up under his desk with his legs. He is consistently pale rather than sallow. It is as difficult to carry on a sequential conversation with de Gaulle as with de Valera. He reacts, but does not respond, to a question by delivering a speech on a tangential subject.

The General said that he was convinced the little people of France, the sailors, the peasants, the factory hands, the barbers, were for him and the rich were for Vichy and against him. I noticed, perhaps frivolously, that he did not say the little were against the rich or the rich against the little, but that he made of the breach between classes a question of reaction to de Gaulle. After the war, he said, a government with 'bold ideas,' '*des idées hardies*,' would be necessary in France. He said that the people of France must determine their own future form of government, under a plebiscite to be called after the reconquest.

I left him without any idea that in the spring of 1942 he was to be canonized alive by the stay-at-home seers of the American press. It is nice to learn, however late, that one has talked with an angel.

The Road Back to Paris, 1944

HENRY GREEN

(Henry Vincent Yorke)

1905–1973

In the Fogbound Terminus

So crowded together they were beginning to be pressed against each other, so close that every breath had been inside another past that lipstick or those cracked lips, those even teeth, loose dentures, down into other lungs, so weary, so desolate and cold it silenced them.

Then one section had begun to chant 'we want our train' over and over again and at first everyone had laughed and joined in and then had failed, there were no trains. And so, having tried everything, desolation overtook them.

They were like ruins in the wet, places that is where life has been, palaces, abbeys, cathedrals, throne rooms, pantries, cast aside and tumbled down with no immediate life and with what used to be in them lost rather than hidden now the roof has fallen in. Ruins that is not of their suburban homes for they had hearts, and feelings to dream, and hearts to make up what they did not like into other things. But ruins, for life in such circumstances was only possible because it would not last, only endurable because it had broken down and as it lasted and became more desolate and wet so, as it seemed more likely to be permanent, at least for an evening, they grew restive.

Party Going, 1939

ROBERT PENN WARREN
1905–1989

A Leader in the Making

He was a lawyer now. He could hang the overalls on a nail and let them stiffen with the last sweat he had sweated into them. He could rent himself a room over the dry-goods store in Mason City and call it his office, and wait for somebody to come up the stairs where it was so dark you had to feel your way and where it smelled like the inside of an old trunk that's been in the attic twenty years. He was a lawyer now and it had taken him a long time. It had taken him a long time because he had had to be a lawyer on his terms and in his own way. But that was over. But maybe it had taken him too long. If something takes too long, something happens to you. You become all and only the thing you want and nothing else, for you have paid too much for it, too much in wanting and too much in waiting and too much in getting. In the end they just ask you those crappy little questions.

But the wanting and the waiting were over now, and Willie had a haircut and a new hat and a new brief case with the copy of his speech in it (which he had written out in longhand and had said to Lucy with gestures, as though he were getting ready for the high-school oratorical contest) and a lot of new friends, with drooping blue jowls or sharp pale noses, who slapped him on the back, and a campaign manager, Tiny Duffy, who would introduce him to you and say with a tin-glittering heartiness, 'Meet Willie Stark, the next Governor of this state!' And Willie would put out his hand to you with the gravity of a bishop. For he never tumbled to a thing.

I used to wonder how he got that way. If he had been running for something back in Mason County he never in God's world would have been that way. He would have taken a perfectly realistic view of things and counted up his chances. Or if he had got into the gubernatorial primary on his own hook, he would have taken a realistic view. But this was different. He had been called. He had been touched. He had been summoned. And he was a little bit awestruck by the fact. It seems incredible that he hadn't taken one look at Tiny Duffy and his friends and realized that things might not be absolutely on the level. But actually, as I figured it, it wasn't incredible. For the voice of Tiny Duffy summoning him was nothing but the echo of a certainty and a blind compulsion within him, the thing that had made him sit up in his room, night after night, rubbing the sleep out of his eyes, to write the fine phrases and the fine ideas in the big ledger or to bend with a violent, almost physical intensity over the yellow page of an old law book. For him to deny the voice of Tiny Duffy would have been as difficult as for a saint to deny the voice that calls in the night.

He wasn't really in touch with the world. He was not only bemused by the voice he had heard. He was bemused by the very grandeur of the position to which he aspired. The blaze of light hitting him in the eyes blinded him. After all, he had just come out of the dark, the period when he grubbed on the farm all day and didn't see anybody but the family (and day after day he must have moved by them as though they weren't half-real) and sat at night in his room with the books and hurt inside with the effort and the groping and the wanting. So it isn't much wonder that the blaze of light blinded him.

He knew something about human nature, all right. He'd sat around the county courthouse long enough to find out something. (True, he had got himself thrown out of the courthouse. But that wasn't ignorance of human nature. It was, perhaps, a knowledge not of human nature in general but of his own nature in particular, something deeper than the mere question of right and wrong. He became a martyr, not through ignorance, not only for the right but also for some knowledge of himself deeper than right or wrong.) He knew something about human nature, but something now came between him and that knowledge. In a way, he flattered human nature. He assumed that other people were as bemused by the grandeur and as blinded by the light of the post to which he aspired, and that they would only listen to argument and language that was grand and bright. So his speeches were cut to that measure. It was a weird mixture of facts and figures on one hand (his tax program, his road program) and of fine sentiments on the other hand (a faint echo, somewhat dulled by time, of the quotations copied out in the ragged, boyish hand in the big ledger).

All the King's Men, 1946

JOHN O'HARA

1905–1970

A Doctor in Mining Country

In the afternoon Dr Myers decided he would like to go to one of the patches where the practice of medicine was wholesale, so I suggested Kelly's. Kelly's was the only saloon in a patch of about one hundred families, mostly Irish, and all except one family were Catholics. In the spring they have processions in honour of the Blessed Virgin at Kelly's patch, and a priest carries the Blessed Sacrament the length of the patch, in the open air, to the public school grounds, where they hold Benediction. The houses are older and stauncher than in most patches, and they look like pictures of Ireland, except that there are no thatched roofs. Most patches were simply unbroken rows of company houses, made of slatty wood, but Kelly's had more ground between the houses and grass for the goats and cows to feed on, and the houses had plastered walls. Kelly's saloon was frequented by the whole patch because it was the post office substation, and it had a good reputation. For many years it had the only telephone in the patch.

Mr Kelly was standing on the stoop in front of the saloon when I swung the Ford around. He took his pipe out of his mouth when he recognized the Ford, and then frowned slightly when he saw that my father was not with me. He came to my side of the car. 'Where's the dad? Does he be down wid it now himself?'

'No,' I said. 'He's just all tired out and is getting some sleep. This is Dr Myers that's taking his place till he gets better.'

Mr Kelly spat some tobacco juice on the ground and took a wad of tobacco out of his mouth. He was a white-haired, sickly man of middle age. 'I'm glad to make your acquaintance,' he said.

'How do you do, sir?' said Dr Myers.

'I guess James here told you what to be expecting?'

'Well, more or less,' said Dr Myers. 'Nice country out here. This is the nicest I've seen.'

'Yes, all right I guess, but there does be a lot of sickness now. I guess you better wait a minute here till I have a few words with them inside there. I have to keep them orderly, y'understand.'

He went in and we could hear his loud voice: '. . . young Malloy said his dad is seriously ill . . . great expense out of his own pocket secured a famous young specialist from Philadelphee so as to not have the people of the patch without a medical man. . . . And any lug of a lunkhead that don't stay in line will have me to answer to. . . .' Mr Kelly then made the people line up and he came to the door and asked Dr Myers to step in.

There were about thirty women in the saloon as Mr Kelly guided Dr Myers to an oilcloth-covered table. One Irishman took a contemptuous look at Dr Myers and said: 'Jesus, Mary and Joseph,' and walked out, sneering at me before he closed the door. The others probably doubted that the doctor was a famous specialist, but they had not had a doctor in two or three days. Two others left quietly but the rest remained. 'I guess we're ready, Mr Kelly,' said Dr Myers.

Most of the people were Irish, but there were a few Hunkies in the patch, although not enough to warrant Mr Kelly's learning any of their languages as the Irish had had to do in certain other patches. It was easy enough to deal with the Irish: a woman would come to the table and describe for Dr Myers the symptoms of her sick man and kids in language that was painfully polite. My father had trained them to use terms like 'bowel movement' instead of those that came more quickly to mind. After a few such encounters and wasting a lot of time, Dr Myers more or less got the swing of prescribing for absent patients . . .

'The Doctor's Son', *The Doctor's Son and Other Stories*, 1935

LIONEL TRILLING

1905–1975

A Career in Public Housing

Laskell had come to his profession rather late and perhaps for that reason was the more attached to it. Until he was twenty-four he had planned a literary career. He wrote quite well and he had been in revolt against the culture of his affectionate and comfortable Larchmont family. He had wanted what young men of spirit usually want, freedom and experience, and literature was the way to get them. Literature was the means by which one became sentient and free. But the literary career somehow did not develop. Perhaps it was a kind of modesty that kept Laskell from writing, a diffidence about imposing himself or about looking into himself. From literature to the study of philosophy had been an easy step, scarcely looking like a retreat. But the change did not settle him, and it might have seemed that having an income was going to mean that he would fritter away what talent he had.

But when Laskell was twenty-four a chance encounter resolved his uncertainties. He was visiting one of his liberal, well-to-do friends, and among the company there was a man who insisted on talking about public housing. Between this man and John Laskell there flared an immediate hostility. It was one of those antagonisms that give great moral satisfaction to both parties. Laskell was willing to have the man talk about anything that could be contradicted. And contradict he did, with a kind of cool persistence that surprised him, for he had never been a contentious person. He did not know where he got the ideas he used for his arguments. No doubt they came from his opponent's own laboriously acquired store, needing only to be turned upside down. He was pleased when the man became abusive and denounced not only Laskell, but what he called Laskell's 'whole school of thought.' Suddenly there he was, a member of a school of thought in a profession he had never before considered. It was, the man said, a brilliant but unsound school. The ideas that Laskell had produced only to be contrary seemed to him to be suddenly right and important.

The chance debate made up Laskell's mind. Through his years of study in America and Europe, the interest so fortuitously aroused that evening never flagged. Laskell discovered in himself gifts for practicality and detail which, in his dream of literature, he had never suspected. He could deal, he found, not only with social theories, but also, as was necessary, with rents and rules and washing machines.

The Middle of the Journey, 1947

The Buzz of Implication

Somewhere below all the explicit statements that a people makes through its art, religion, architecture, legislation, there is a dim mental region of intention of which it is very difficult to become aware. We now and then get a strong sense of its existence when we deal with the past, not by reason of its presence in the past but by reason of its absence. As we read the great formulated monuments of the past, we notice that we are reading them without the accompaniment of something that always goes along with the formulated monuments of the present. The voice of multifarious intention and activity is stilled, all the buzz of implication which always surrounds us in the present, coming to us from what never gets fully stated, coming in the tone of greetings and the tone of quarrels, in slang and humor and popular songs, in the way children play, in the gesture the waiter makes when he puts down the plate, in the nature of the very food we prefer.

Some of the charm of the past consists of the quiet—the great distracting buzz of implication has stopped and we are left only with what has been fully phrased and precisely stated. And part of the melancholy of the past comes from our knowledge that the huge, unrecorded hum of implication was once there and left no trace—we feel that because it is evanescent it is especially human. We feel, too, that the truth of the great preserved monuments of the past does not fully appear without it. From letters and diaries, from the remote, unconscious corners of the great works themselves, we try to guess what the sound of the multifarious implication was and what it meant.

Or when we read the conclusions that are drawn about our own culture by some gifted foreign critic—or by some stupid native one—who is equipped only with a knowledge of our books, when we try in vain to say what is wrong, when in despair we say that he has read the books 'out of context,' then we are aware of the matter I have been asked to speak about tonight.

What I understand by manners, then, is a culture's hum and buzz of implication. I mean the whole evanescent context in which its explicit statements are made. It is that part of a culture which is made up of half-uttered or unuttered or unutterable expressions of value. They are hinted at by small actions, sometimes by the arts of dress or decoration, sometimes by tone, gesture, emphasis, or rhythm, sometimes by the words that are used with a special frequency or a special meaning. They are the things that for good or bad draw the people of a culture together and that separate them from the people of another culture. They make the part of a culture which is not art, or religion, or morals, or politics, and yet it relates to all these highly formulated departments of culture. It is modified by them; it modifies them; it is generated by them; it generates them. In this part of culture assumption rules, which is often so much stronger than reason.

'Manners, Morals and the Novel', *The Liberal Imagination*, 1950

MULK RAJ ANAND

1905–

Caste

A small, thin man, naked except for a loin-cloth, stood outside with a small brass jug in his left hand, a round white cotton skull-cap on his head, a pair of wooden sandals on his feet, and the apron of his loin-cloth lifted to his nose.

It was Havildar Charat Singh, the famous hockey player of the 38th Dogras regiment, as celebrated for his humour as for the fact, which with characteristic Indian openness he acknowledged, that he suffered from chronic piles.

'Why aren't the latrines clean, you rogue of a Bakhe! There is not one fit to go near! I have walked all round! Do you know you are responsible for my piles! I caught the contagion sitting on one of those unclean latrines!'

'All right, Havildar ji, I will get one ready for you at once,' Bakha said cautiously as he proceeded to pick up his brush and basket from the place where these tools decorated the front wall of the house.

He worked away earnestly, quickly, without loss of effort. Brisk, yet steady, his capacity for active application to the task he had in hand seemed to flow like constant water from a natural spring. Each muscle of his body, hard as a rock when it came into play, seemed to shine forth like glass. He must have had immense pent-up resources lying deep, deep in his body, for as he rushed along with considerable skill and alacrity from one doorless latrine to another, cleaning, brushing, pouring phenoil, he seemed as easy as a wave sailing away on a deep-bedded river. 'What a dexterous workman!' the onlooker would have said. And though his job was dirty he remained comparatively clean. He didn't even soil his sleeves, handling the commodes, sweeping and scrubbing them. 'A bit superior to his job,' one would have said, 'not the kind of man who ought to be doing this.' For he looked intelligent, even sensitive, with a sort of dignity that does not belong to the ordinary scavenger, who is as a rule uncouth and unclean. It was perhaps his absorption in his task that gave him the look of distinction, or his exotic dress however loose and ill-fitting, that removed him above his odorous world. Havildar Charat Singh, who had the Hindu instinct for immaculate cleanliness, was puzzled when he emerged from his painful half an hour in the latrines and caught sight of Bakha. Here was a low-caste man who seemed clean! He became rather self-conscious, the prejudice of the 'twice born' high-caste Hindu against stink, even though he saw not the slightest suspicion of it in Bakha, rising into his mind. He smiled complacently. Then, however, he forgot his high caste and the ironic smile on his face became a childlike laugh.

'You are becoming a gentreman, Ohe Bakhya! Where did you get that uniform?'

Bakha was shy, knowing he had no right to indulge in such luxuries as apeing the high-caste people. He humbly mumbled:

'Huzoor (Sir), it is all your blessing.'

Charat Singh was feeling kind, he did not relax the grin which symbolised six thousand years of racial and class superiority. To express his goodwill, however, he said:

'Come this afternoon, Bakhe. I shall give you a hockey stick.' He knew the boy played that game very well.

Bakha stretched himself up; he was astonished yet grateful at Charat Singh's offer. It was a godsend to him, this spontaneous gesture on the part of one of the best hockey players of the regiment. 'A hockey stick! I wonder if it will be a new one!' he thought to himself, and he stood smiling with a queer humility, overcome with gratitude. Charat Singh's generous promise had called forth that trait of servility in Bakha which he had inherited from his forefathers, the weakness of the down-trodden, the helplessness of the poor and the indigent, suddenly receiving help, the passive contentment of the bottom dog suddenly illuminated by the prospect of fulfilment of a secret and long-cherished desire. He saluted his benefactor and bent down to his work again.

A soft smile lingered on his lips, the smile of a slave overjoyed at the condescension of his master, more akin to pride than to happiness. And he slowly slipped into a song. The steady heave of his body from one latrine to another made the whispered refrain a fairly audible note. And he went forward, with eager step, from job to job, a marvel of movement dancing through his work.

Untouchable, 1935

ANTHONY POWELL

1905–

Love-Making

Gwen said: 'Well, I must be going now. I'm rather late as it is.' She said to Atwater: 'Good-bye.'

'Good-bye,' said Atwater. He said: 'I expect we'll meet again soon.' Gwen went away, slamming slightly the door behind her.

'Come and sit on this,' said Lola. 'Isn't Gwen sweet?'

'Isn't she?'

'She's a darling,' said Lola.

She looked more than ever like a very knowing child. Atwater said:

'Are you going to show me some of your posters?'

'Not now. Let's sit here.'

Atwater took her hand.

'When did you first notice me at that party?' she said.

'Oh, as soon as you came in.'

'I think sometimes people do just feel that at once, don't you?'

'I'm sure they do.'

'Are you always falling for people?'

'Yes, always.'

'You brute.'

'I'm sure everybody falls for you,' he said.

'No, they don't.'

'I'm sure they do.'

In her serious voice she said: 'Don't you think sexual selection is awfully important?'

'Of course.'

'Don't,' she said. 'You're hurting. You mustn't do that.'

'Where are we going to dine tonight?'

'Anywhere you like.'

'Where do you think?'

'Don't,' she said. 'You're not allowed to do that.'

'Why not?'

'Because you're not.'

'I shall.'

She said: 'I'm glad we met. But you must behave.'

Slowly, but very deliberately, the brooding edifice of seduction, creaking and incongruous, came into being, a vast Heath Robinson mechanism, dually controlled by them and lumbering gloomily down vistas of triteness. With a sort of heavy-fisted dexterity the mutually adapted emotions of each of them became synchronised, until the unavoidable anti-climax was at hand. Later they dined at a restaurant quite near the flat.

Afternoon Men, 1931

The Maclinticks

We took a bus to Victoria, then passed on foot into a vast, desolate region of stucco streets and squares upon which a doom seemed to have fallen. The gloom was cosmic. We traversed these pavements for some distance, proceeding from haunts of seedy, grudging gentility into an area of indeterminate, but on the whole increasingly unsavoury, complexion.

'Maclintick is devoted to this part of London,' Moreland said. 'I am not sure that I agree with him. He says his mood is for ever Pimlico. I grant that a sympathetic atmosphere is an important point in choosing a residence. It helps one's work. All the same, tastes differ. Maclintick is always to be found in this neighbourhood, though never for long in the same place.'

'He never seems very cheerful when I meet him.'

I had run across Maclintick only a few times with Moreland since our first meeting in the Mortimer.

'He is a very melancholy man,' Moreland agreed. 'Maclintick is very melancholy. He is disappointed, of course.'

'About himself as a musician?'

'That—and other things. He is always hard up. Then he has an aptitude for quarrelling with anyone who might be of use to him professionally. He is writing a great tome on musical theory which never seems to get finished.'

'What is his wife like?'

'Like a wife.'

'Is that how you feel about marriage?'

'Well, not exactly,' said Moreland laughing. 'But you know one does begin to understand all the music-hall jokes and comic-strips about matrimony after you have tried a spell of it yourself. Don't you agree?'

'And Mrs Maclintick is a good example?'

'You will see what I mean.'

'What is Maclintick's form about women? I can never quite make out.'

'I think he hates them really—only likes whores.'

'Ah.'

'At least that is what Gossage used to say.'

'That's a known type.'

'All the same, Maclintick is also full of deeply romantic, hidden away sentiments about *Wein, Weib und Gesang*. That is his passionate, carefully concealed side. The gruffness is intended to cover all that. Maclintick is terrified of being thought sentimental. I suppose all his bottled-up feelings came to the surface when he met Audrey.'

'And the prostitutes?'

'He told Gossage he found them easier to converse with than respectable ladies. Of course, Gossage—you can imagine how he jumped about telling me this—was speaking of a period before Maclintick's marriage. No reason to suppose that sort of thing takes place now.'

'But if he hates women, why do you say he is so passionate?'

'It just seems to have worked out that way. Audrey is one of the answers, I suppose.'

The house, when we reached it, turned out to be a small, infinitely decayed two-storey dwelling that had seen better days; now threatened by a row of mean shops advancing from one end of the street and a fearful slum crowding up from the other. Moreland's loyalty to his friends—in a quiet way considerable—prevented me from being fully prepared for Mrs Maclintick. That she should have come as a surprise was largely my own fault. Knowing Moreland, I ought to have gathered more from his disjointed, though on the whole decidedly cautionary, account of the Maclintick household. Besides, from the first time of meeting Maclintick—when he had gone to the telephone in the Mortimer—the matrimonial rows of the Maclintick had been an accepted legend. However much one hears about individuals, the picture formed in the mind rarely approximates to the reality. So it was with Mrs Maclintick. I was not prepared for her in the flesh. When she opened the door to us, her formidable discontent with life swept across the threshold in scorching, blasting waves. She was a small dark woman with a touch of gipsy about her, this last possibility suggested by sallow skin and bright black eyes. Her black hair was worn in a fringe. Some men might have found her attractive. I was not among them, although at the same time not blind to the fact that she might be capable of causing trouble where men were concerned. Mrs Maclintick said nothing at the sight of us, only shrugging her shoulders. Then, standing starkly aside, as if resigned to our entry in spite of an overpowering distaste she felt for the two of us, she held the door open wide. We passed within the Maclintick threshold.

'It's Moreland—and another man.'

Mrs Maclintick shouted, almost shrieked these words, while at the same time she twisted her head sideways and upwards towards a flight of stairs leading to a floor above, where Maclintick might be presumed to sit at work. We followed her into a sitting-room in which a purposeful banality of style had been observed; only a glass-fronted bookcase full of composers' biographies and works of musical reference giving some indication of Maclintick's profession.

'Find somewhere to sit,' said Mrs Maclintick, speaking as if the day, bad enough before, had been finally ruined by our arrival. '*He* will be down soon.'

Casanova's Chinese Restaurant, 1960; *A Dance to the Music of Time*

SAMUEL BECKETT
1906–1989

A Quick Death

His aunt was in the garden, tending whatever flowers die at that time of year. She embraced him and together they went down into the bowels of the earth, into the kitchen in the basement. She took the parcel and undid it and abruptly the lobster was on the table, on the oilcloth, discovered.

'They assured me it was fresh' said Belacqua.

Suddenly he saw the creature move, this neuter creature. Definitely it changed its position. His hand flew to his mouth.

'Christ!' he said 'it's alive.'

His aunt looked at the lobster. It moved again. It made a faint nervous act of life on the oilcloth. They stood above it, looking down on it, exposed cruciform on the oilcloth. It shuddered again. Belacqua felt he would be sick.

'My God' he whined 'it's alive, what'll we do?'

The aunt simply had to laugh. She bustled off to the pantry to fetch her smart apron, leaving him goggling down at the lobster, and came back with it on and her sleeves rolled up, all business.

'Well' she said 'it is to be hoped so, indeed.'

'All this time' muttered Belacqua. Then, suddenly aware of her hideous equipment: 'What are you going to do?' he cried.

'Boil the beast' she said, 'what else?'

'But it's not dead' protested Belacqua 'you can't boil it like that.'

She looked at him in astonishment. Had he taken leave of his senses?

'Have sense' she said sharply, 'lobsters are always boiled alive. They must be.' She caught up the lobster and laid it on its back. It trembled. 'They feel nothing' she said.

In the depths of the sea it had crept into the cruel pot. For hours, in the midst of its enemies, it had breathed secretly. It had survived the Frenchwoman's cat and his witless clutch. Now it was going alive into scalding water. It had to. Take into the air my quiet breath.

Belacqua looked at the old parchment of her face, grey in the dim kitchen.

'You make a fuss' she said angrily 'and upset me and then lash into it for your dinner.'

She lifted the lobster clear of the table. It had about thirty seconds to live.

Well, thought Belacqua, it's a quick death, God help us all.

It is not.

'Dante and the Lobster', *More Pricks than Kicks*, 1934

Murphy's Ashes

The furnace would not draw, it was past five o'clock before Cooper got away from the Mercyseat with the parcel of ash under his arm. It must have weighed well on four pounds. Various ways of getting rid of it suggested themselves to him on the way to the station. Finally he decided that the most convenient and inconspicuous was to drop it in the first considerable receptacle for refuse that he came to. In Dublin he need only have sat down on the nearest bench and waited. Soon one of the gloomy dustmen would have come, wheeling his cart marked, 'Post your litter here.' But London was less conscious of her garbage, she had not given her scavenging to aliens.

He was turning into the station, without having met any considerable receptacle for refuse, when a burst of music made him halt and turn. It was the pub across the way, opening for the evening session. The lights sprang up in the saloon, the doors burst open, the radio struck up. He crossed the street and stood on the threshold. The floor was palest ochre, the pin-tables shone like silver, the quoits board had a net, the stools the high rungs that he loved, the whiskey was in glass tanks, a slow cascando of pellucid yellows. A man brushed past him into the saloon, one of the millions that had been wanting a drink for the past two hours. Cooper followed slowly and sat down at the bar, for the first time in more than twenty years.

'What are you taking, friend?' said the man.

'The first is mine,' said Cooper, his voice trembling.

Some hours later Cooper took the packet of ash from his pocket, where earlier in the evening he had put it for greater security, and threw it angrily at a man who had given him great offence. It bounced, burst, off the wall on to the floor, where at once it became the object of much dribbling, passing, trapping, shooting, punching, heading and even some recognition from the gentleman's code. By closing time the body, mind and soul of Murphy were freely distributed over the floor of the saloon; and before another dayspring greyened the earth had been swept away with the sand, the beer, the butts, the glass, the matches, the spits, the vomit.

Murphy, 1938

Holding On and Letting Go

My body does not yet make up its mind. But I fancy it weighs heavier on the bed, flattens and spreads. My breath, when it comes back, fills the room with its din, though my chest moves no more than a sleeping child's. I open my eyes and gaze unblinkingly and long at the night sky. So a tiny tot I gaped, first at the novelties, then at the antiquities. Between it and me the pane, misted and smeared with the filth of years. I should like to breathe on it, but it is too far away. It is such a night as Kaspar David Friedrich loved, tempestuous and bright. That name that comes back to me, those names. The clouds scud, tattered by the wind, across a limpid ground. If I had the patience to wait I would see the moon. But I have not. Now that I have looked I hear the wind. I close my eyes and it mingles with my breath. Words and images run riot in my head, pursuing, flying, clashing, merging, endlessly. But beyond this tumult there is a great calm, and a great indifference, never really to be troubled by anything again. I turn a little on my side, press my mouth against the pillow, and my nose, crush against the pillow my old hairs now no doubt as white as snow, pull the blanket over my head. I feel, deep down in my trunk, I cannot be more explicit, pains that seem new to me. I think they are chiefly in my back. They have a kind of rhythm, they even have a kind of little tune. They are bluish. How bearable all that is, my God. My head is almost facing the wrong way, like a bird's. I part my lips, now I have the pillow in my mouth. I have, I have. I suck. The search for myself is ended. I am buried in the world, I knew I would find my place there one day, the old world cloisters me, victorious. I am happy, I knew I would be happy one day. But I am not wise. For the wise thing now would be to let go, at this instant of happiness. And what do I do? I go back again to the light, to the fields I so longed to love, to the sky all astir with little white clouds as white and light as snowflakes, to the life I could never manage, through my own fault perhaps, through pride, or pettiness, but I don't think so. The beasts are at pasture, the sun warms the rocks and makes them glitter. Yes, I leave my happiness and go back to the race of men too, they come and go, often with burdens. Perhaps I have judged them ill, but I don't think so, I have not judged them at all. All I want now is to make a last effort to understand, to begin to understand, how such creatures are possible. No, it is not a question of understanding. Of what then? I don't know. Here I go none the less, mistakenly. Night, storm and sorrow, and the catalepsies of the soul, this time I shall see that they are good. The last word is not yet said between me and—yes, the last word is said. Perhaps I simply want to hear it said again. Just once again. No, I want nothing.

Malone Dies, 1956, translated from *Malone meurt* (1951) by the author

WILLIAM EMPSON
1906–1984

The Realism of Dryden

The *trumpet's* loud clangour
  Invites us to arms
With shrill notes of anger
  And mortal alarms.
The double double double beat
  Of the thundering *drum*
  Cries, heark the Foes come;
Charge, charge, 'tis too late to retreat.
(*Song for St Cecilia's Day*)

It is curious on the face of it that one should represent, in a mood of such heroic simplicity, a reckless excitement, a feverish and exalted eagerness for battle, by saying (in the most prominent part of the stanza from the point of view of final effect) that we can't get out of the battle now and must go through with it as best we can. Yet that is what has happened, and it is not a cynical by-blow on the part of Dryden; the last line is entirely rousing and single-hearted. Evidently the thought that it is no good running away is an important ingredient of military enthusiasm; at any rate in the form of consciousness of unity with comrades, who ought to be encouraged not to retreat (even if they are not going to, they cannot have not thought of it, so that this encouragement is a sort of recognition of their merits), and of consciousness of the terror one should be exciting in the foe; so that all elements of the affair, including terror, must be part of the judgment of the most normally heroic mind, and that, since it is too late for *him* to retreat, the Lord has delivered him into your hands. Horses, in a way very like this, display mettle by a continual expression of timidity.

This extremely refreshing way of understanding the elements of a situation, and putting them down flatly to act as a measure of excitement, is a characteristic of Dryden; and a much more universal characteristic of good poetry, by the way, than most we have considered so far. It is not, for instance, due to the habits of the English language; and Dryden's use of it is connected with the Restoration wish to tidy the language up, make it more rational, and produce something transferable which would be respected on the Continent. Dryden is not interested in the echoes and recesses of words; he uses them flatly; he is interested in the echoes and recesses of human judgment. (One must remember in saying this the critics who have said he was interested in rhetoric but not in character; the two things are compatible.) He is doing the same thing in the grand patriotic close of *King Arthur*, when on a public occasion, after magicians and spirits from machines have explained the glories of England that shall come after, the king replies, as from the throne:

> Wisely you have, whate'er will please, reveal'd,
> What wou'd displease, as wisely have conceal'd.

The remark is sharp but not damping; is quite different from the generous depression of Johnson which is a development from it; shows a power of understanding a situation while still feeling excited; and is not the sort of thing any one would have the courage to say on such an occasion nowadays.

Seven Types of Ambiguity, 1930

A. J. P. TAYLOR
1906–1990

Continuity and Change in the House of Commons

Historical reputations go up and down just like the length of women's skirts. We used to think that the Great Reform Bill marked the triumph of the capitalistic middle class, launched parliamentary democracy, and so on. Now we are told that it changed nothing in British politics. I suppose that is right so far as the composition of the House of Commons goes. The electors still thought mainly of local considerations. The members came from the same class as before and acted from the same motives—family connexions or trading interests, private ambitions or idealistic quirks. All very true, very instructive; but those who regard it as decisive fall into the error of imagining that the House of Commons is the sum of its parts. They suppose that if we describe every member of parliament, then we shall have described the House of that day. The same outlook underlies the *History of Parliament*, on which some of my most admired colleagues are working. When I heard of the project, I couldn't help reflecting that a History of Parliament existed already, at least for more modern times. We call it *Hansard*, or—more grandly—*Parliamentary Debates*. No doubt the accumulated biographies of members will be of much interest to the social historian—and perhaps even explain some intrigues for office. But the history of parliament is to be found in what members heard and said, in what they felt, not in what they were.

Like other collective bodies, the House of Commons has its own rules of behaviour. Its character may change even though its individual members remain the same. The 'bought' House of 1841 emerged from the most corrupt of all general elections; yet it rose five years later to a height of unselfish wisdom when it repealed the Corn Laws. Or consider the House elected in 1935 with a large majority behind Baldwin. Who could have supposed that it would sustain Winston Churchill through the greatest of our wars? The members of parliament after the Reform Bill were no doubt exactly what they had been before. Yet the House, and with it the whole political world, was entirely different. Only after the general election of 1906 was there something of the same atmosphere: the feeling that the old order had perished, a new day dawned—the feeling which Hilaire Belloc recorded so well:

> The accursed power which stands on Privilege
> (And goes with Women, and Champagne, and Bridge)
> Broke—and Democracy resumed her reign;

The last line I will here omit.

The Trouble Makers, 1957

Britain in 1945

In the second World war the British people came of age. This was a people's war. Not only were their needs considered. They themselves wanted to win. Future historians may see the war as a last struggle for the European balance of power or for the maintenance of Empire. This was not how it appeared to those who lived through it. The British people had set out to destroy Hitler and National Socialism—'Victory at all costs'. They succeeded. No English soldier who rode with the tanks into liberated Belgium or saw the German murder camps at Dachau or Buchenwald could doubt that the war had been a noble crusade. The British were the only people who went through both world wars from beginning to end.[1] Yet they remained a peaceful and civilized people, tolerant, patient, and generous. Traditional values lost much of their force. Other values took their place. Imperial greatness was on the way out; the welfare state was on the way in. The British empire declined; the condition of the people improved. Few now sang 'Land of Hope and Glory'. Few even sang 'England Arise'. England had risen all the same.

[1] 'British' here means, perhaps for the last time, the peoples of the Dominions and of the Empire as well as of the United Kingdom.

English History 1914–1945, 1965

DWIGHT MACDONALD
1906–1982

The New English Bible

I expected that the Jacobean grand style would be taken down more than a few pegs—that 'hearken to my words' would become 'give me a hearing'; that Jesus would say to the woman taken in adultery not 'Go and sin no more' but 'You may go; do not sin again' (even more 'timely' would have been, 'Don't let it happen again'); that the subtle rhythm of 'I cannot dig; to beg I am ashamed' would be hamstrung into: 'I am not strong enough to dig, and too proud to beg.' I knew all the great passages would be bull-dozed flat, but still it was a shock to go from: 'When I was a child, I spake as a child, I understood as a child, I thought as a child. But when I became a man, I put away childish things. For now we see through a glass darkly . . .' to: 'When I was a child, my speech, my outlook, and my thoughts were all childish. When I grew up, I had finished with childish things. Now we see only puzzling reflections in a mirror.' Like finding a parking lot where a great church once stood.

But what I was not prepared for was the opposite—the inflation of simple Anglo-Saxon into academese. 'In doing our work,' the translators state in their preface, 'we have constantly striven . . . to render the Greek into the English of the present day . . . the natural vocabulary, constructions, and rhythms of contemporary speech.' On the contrary, despite a panel of literary advisers, they have taken the New Testament farther away from natural speech than it was in 1611. They are addicted to officialese: 'this proposal proved acceptable,' 'these facts are beyond dispute.' 'A just man' is inflated into a 'man of principle,' 'in all goodness and honesty' into 'in full observance of religion and the highest standards of morality,' 'the proud' into 'the arrogant of heart and mind,' 'blameless' into 'of unimpeachable character.' They write that they 'have sought to avoid jargon' but I wonder whether 'his heart sank' is less jargonish than K.J.V.'s 'sorrowful,' or 'we are placing the law on a firmer footing' than 'we establish the law,' or 'rescued me from Herod's clutches' than 'delivered me out of the hand of Herod.' I also wonder whether this allegedly simpler version is not actually longer than K.J.V. And where those literary advisers were when 'stomach' was substituted for 'belly'—nice girls have stomachs—or when Jesus' 'O fools!' was stepped down into a Noel Coward line: 'How dull you are [my dear Cedric]!' True, they did preserve 'Jesus wept.' But I'm sure there was strong support for 'Jesus burst into tears.'

Against the American Grain, 1962

JOHN BETJEMAN
1906–1984

Little Posts for Lawyers

Few things are more delightful than peculiar public positions. The City Remembrancer, for instance—what does he have to remember? I rang him up to ask. He was founded by Queen Elizabeth because he was able to write and remind the Queen (from his notes, I suppose) of what she was to do. He is a lawyer and has free access to all the lobbies in Parliament and a special seat behind the Serjeant-at-Arms in the House. He is Advocate for the City of London in Parliament and Whitehall. But he tells me his position is schizophrenic as he also has to be Master of Ceremonies at City functions. I wish I had read law and passed the examinations. There are many little posts open to lawyers which I covet. The Recorder of London, Sir Gerald Dodson (author of 'The Fishermen of England' and other lyrics from the light opera *The Rebel Maid*), is also High Steward of Southwark, a post, Whitaker tells me, bringing in £79 7*s.* a year, the price of a really slap-up television set. And what about Captain C. Bettesworth Sanders, who is Secondary and High Bailiff of Southwark? What does he do? He doesn't sound like a lawyer, but his job is worth a dozen times as much as the High Steward's, though it is only secondary. Then why does the Apparitor-General for the Convocation of Canterbury, Sir John Hanham, a lawyer baronet, live far away in Dorset? Would that I were the Dean of Arches and could tell you.

The Spectator, 1955

R. K. NARAYAN
1906–

A Summons from the Professor

As he came near the Professor's room, Chandran felt very nervous. He adjusted his coat and buttoned it up. He hesitated for a moment before the door. He suddenly pulled himself up. Why this cowardice? Why should he be afraid of Ragavachar or anybody? Human being to human being. Remove those spectacles, the turban, and the long coat, and let Ragavachar appear only in a loin-cloth, and Mr Ragavachar would lose three-quarters of his appearance. Where was the sense in feeling nervous before a pair of spectacles, a turban, and a black long coat?

'Good-evening, sir,' said Chandran, stepping in.

Ragavachar looked up from a bulky red book that he was reading. He took time to switch his mind off his studies and comprehend the present.

'Well?' he said, looking at Chandran.

'You asked me to see you at four-thirty, sir.'

'Yes, yes. Sit down.'

Chandran lowered himself to the edge of a chair. Ragavachar leaned back and spent some time looking at the ceiling. Chandran felt a slight thirsty sensation, but he recollected his vision of Ragavachar in a loin-cloth, and regained his self-confidence.

'My purpose in calling you now is to ascertain your views on the question of starting an Historical Association in the college.'

Saved! Chandran sat revelling in the sense of relief he now felt.

'What do you think of it?'

'I think it is a good plan, sir,' and he wondered why he was chosen for this consultation.

'What I want you to do,' went on the commanding voice, 'is to arrange for an inaugural meeting on the fifteenth instant. We shall decide the programme afterwards.'

'Very well, sir,' said Chandran.

'You will be the Secretary of the Association. I shall be its President. The meeting must be held on the fifteenth.'

'Don't you think, sir . . .' Chandran began.

'What don't I think?' asked the Professor.

'Nothing, sir.'

'I hate these sneaky half-syllables,' the Professor said. 'You were about to say something. I won't proceed till I know what you were saying.'

Chandran cleared his throat and said, 'Nothing, sir. I was only going to say that some one else might do better as a secretary.'

'I suppose you can leave that to my judgment.'

'Yes, sir.'

'I hope you don't question the need for starting the association.'

'Certainly not, sir.'

'Very good. I for one feel that the amount of ignorance on historical matters is appalling. The only way in which we can combat it is to start an association and hold meetings and read papers.'

'I quite understand, sir.'

'Yet you ask me why we should have this association!'

'No, I did not doubt it.'

'H'm. You talk the matter over with one or two of your friends, and see me again with some definite programme for the Inaugural Meeting.'

Chandran rose.

'You seem to be in a hurry to go,' growled the tiger.

'No, sir,' said Chandran, and sat down again.

'If you are in a hurry to go, I can't stop you because it is past four-thirty, and you are free to leave the college premises. On the other hand, if you are not in a hurry, I have some more details to discuss with you.'

'Yes, sir.'

'There is no use repeating 'Yes, sir; yes, sir.' You don't come forward with any constructive suggestion.'

'I will talk it over with some friends and come later, sir.'

'Good-evening. You may go now.'

The Bachelor of Arts, 1937

W. H. AUDEN

1907–1973

After the Play: Caliban Addresses the Audience

We should not be sitting here now, washed, warm, well-fed, in seats we have paid for, unless there were others who are not here; our liveliness and good-humour, such as they are, are those of survivors, conscious that there are others who have not been so fortunate, others who did not succeed in navigating the narrow passage or to whom the natives were not friendly, others whose streets were chosen by the explosion or through whose country the famine turned aside from ours to go, others who failed to repel the invasion of bacteria or to crush the insurrection of their bowels, others who lost their suit against their parents or were ruined by wishes they could not adjust or murdered by resentments they could not control; aware of some who were better and bigger but from whom, only the other day, Fortune withdrew her hand in sudden disgust, now nervously playing chess with drunken sea-captains in sordid cafés on the equator or the Arctic Circle, or lying, only a few blocks away, strapped and screaming on iron beds or dropping to naked pieces in damp graves. And shouldn't you too, dear master, reflect—forgive us for mentioning it—that we might very well not have been attending a production of yours this evening, had not some other and maybe—who can tell?—brighter talent married a barmaid or turned religious and shy or gone down in a liner with all his manuscripts, the loss recorded only in the corner of some country newspaper below A Poultry Lover's Jottings?

The Sea and the Mirror, 1945

LOREN EISELEY
1907–1977

An Invisible Island

Islands can be regarded as something thrust up into recent time out of a primordial past. In a sense, they belong to different times: a crab time or a turtle time, or even a lemur time, as on Madagascar. It is possible to conceive an island that could contain a future time—something not quite in simultaneous relationship with the rest of the world. Perhaps in some obscure way everything living is on a different time plane. As for man, he is the most curious of all; he fits no plane, no visible island. He is bounded by no shore, except a shore of shadows. He has emerged almost as soundlessly as a mushroom in the night.

Islands are also places of extremes. They frequently produce opposites. On them may exist dwarf creations induced by lack of space or food. On the other hand, an open ecological niche, a lack of enemies, and some equally unopposed genetic drift may as readily produce giantism. The celebrated example of the monster Galápagos turtles comes immediately to mind. Man constitutes an even more unique spectacle for, beginning dwarfed and helpless within nature, he has become a Brocken specter as vast, murk-filled, and threatening as that described in old Germanic folk tales. Thomas De Quincey used to maintain that if one crossed oneself, this looming apparition of light and mist would do the same, but with reluctance and, sometimes, with an air of evasion. One may account this as natural in the case of an illusion moving against a cloud bank, but there is, in its delayed, uncertain gesture, a hint of ambiguity and terror projected from the original human climber on the mountain. To the discerning eye there is, thus, about both this creature and his reflection, something partaking of both microscopic and gigantic dimensions.

In some such way man arose upon an island—not on a visible oceanic island but in some hidden forest meadow. Man's selfhood, his future reality, was produced within the invisible island of his brain—the island clouded in a mist of sound. In this way the net of life was once more wrenched aside so that an impalpable shadow quickly wriggled through its strands into a new, unheard-of dimension of existence. Following this incredible event the natural world subsided once more into its place.

There was, of course, somewhere in the depths of time, a physical location where this episode took place. Unlike the sea barriers that Darwin had found constricting his island novelties, there had now appeared a single island whose shores seemed potentially limitless. This island, no matter where it had physically arisen, had been created by sound vibrating with meaning in the empty air. The island was based on man's most tremendous tool—the word. By degrees, the word would separate past from present, project the unseen future, contain the absent along with the real, and define them to human advantage. Man was no longer confined, like the animal, to what lay before his eyes or his own immediate attention. He could juxtapose, divide, and rearrange his world mentally. Upon the wilderness of the real, men came to project a phantom domain, the world of culture. In the end, their cities would lie congregated and gleaming like the nerve ganglions of an expanding brain.

Words would eventually raise specters so vast that man cowered and whimpered, where, as an animal, he had seen nothing either to reverence or to fear. Words expressed in substance would widen his powers; words, because he used them ill, would occasionally torture and imprison him. They would also lift him into regions of great light. Even the barbarian north, far from the white cities of the Mediterranean, would come to speak in wonder of the skald who could unlock the 'word hoard.' In our day this phantom island has embraced the planet, a world from which man has begun to eye the farther stars.

The Unexpected Universe, 1970

RICHARD WRIGHT
1908–1960

Dangerous Questions

One day I went to the optical counter of a department store to deliver a pair of eyeglasses. The counter was empty of customers and a tall, florid-faced white man looked at me curiously. He was unmistakably a Yankee, for his physical build differed sharply from that of the lanky Southerner.

'Will you please sign for this, sir?' I asked, presenting the account book and the eyeglasses.

He picked up the book and the glasses, but his eyes were still upon me.

'Say, boy, I'm from the North,' he said quietly.

I held very still. Was this a trap? He had mentioned a tabooed subject and I wanted to wait until I knew what he meant. Among the topics that southern white men did not like to discuss with Negroes were the following: American white women; the Ku Klux Klan; France, and how Negro soldiers fared while there; Frenchwomen; Jack Johnson; the entire northern part of the United States; the Civil War; Abraham Lincoln; U. S. Grant; General Sherman; Catholics; the Pope; Jews; the Republican party; slavery;

social equality; Communism; Socialism; the 13th, 14th, and 15th Amendments to the Constitution; or any topic calling for positive knowledge or manly self-assertion on the part of the Negro. The most accepted topics were sex and religion. I did not look at the man or answer. With one sentence he had lifted out of the silent dark the race question and I stood on the edge of a precipice.

'Don't be afraid of me,' he went on. 'I just want to ask you one question.'

'Yes, sir,' I said in a waiting, neutral tone.

'Tell me, boy, are you hungry?' he asked seriously.

I stared at him. He had spoken one word that touched the very soul of me, but I could not talk to him, could not let him know that I was starving myself to save money to go North. I did not trust him. But my face did not change its expression.

'Oh, no, sir,' I said, managing a smile.

I was hungry and he knew it; but he was a white man and I felt that if I told him I was hungry I would have been revealing something shameful.

'Boy, I can see hunger in your face and eyes,' he said.

'I get enough to eat,' I lied.

'Then why do you keep so thin?' he asked me.

'Well, I suppose I'm just that way, naturally,' I lied.

'You're just scared, boy,' he said.

'Oh, no, sir,' I lied again.

I could not look at him. I wanted to leave the counter, yet he was a white man and I had learned not to walk abruptly away from a white man when he was talking to me. I stood, my eyes looking away. He ran his hand into his pocket and pulled out a dollar bill.

'Here, take this dollar and buy yourself some food,' he said.

'No, sir,' I said.

'Don't be a fool,' he said. 'You're ashamed to take it. God, boy, don't let a thing like that stop you from taking a dollar and eating.'

The more he talked the more it became impossible for me to take the dollar. I wanted it, but I could not look at it. I wanted to speak, but I could not move my tongue. I wanted him to leave me alone. He frightened me.

'Say something,' he said.

All about us in the store were piles of goods; white men and women went from counter to counter. It was summer and from a high ceiling was suspended a huge electric fan that whirred. I stood waiting for the white man to give me the signal that would let me go.

'I don't understand it,' he said through his teeth. 'How far did you go in school?'

'Through the ninth grade, but it was really the eighth,' I told him, 'You see, our studies in the ninth grade were more or less a review of what we had in the eighth grade.'

Silence. He had not asked me for this long explanation, but I had spoken at length to fill up the yawning, shameful gap that loomed between us; I had spoken to try to drag the unreal nature of the conversation back to safe and sound southern ground. Of course, the conversation was real; it dealt with my welfare, but it had brought to the surface of day all the dark fears I had known all my life. The Yankee white man did not know how dangerous his words were.

(There are some elusive, profound, recondite things that men find hard to say to other men; but with the Negro it is the little things of life that become hard to say, for these tiny items shape his destiny. A man will seek to express his relation to the stars; but when a man's consciousness has been riveted upon obtaining a loaf of bread, that loaf of bread is as important as the stars.)

Another white man walked up to the counter and I sighed with relief.

'Do you want the dollar?' the man asked.

'No, sir,' I whispered.

'All right,' he said. 'Just forget it.'

He signed the account book and took the eyeglasses. I stuffed the book into my bag and turned from the counter and walked down the aisle, feeling a physical tingling along my spine, knowing that the white man knew I was really hungry. I avoided him after that. Whenever I saw him I felt in a queer way that he was my enemy, for he knew how I felt and the safety of my life in the South depended upon how well I concealed from all whites what I felt.

Black Boy, 1945

JOCELYN BROOKE
1908–1966

Soldiering and Botanizing

The Military Orchid might have eluded me once again. But Cyrenaica had its compensations. The North African flora is not unlike that of Southern Europe; and very much more 'European', of course, than that of South Africa. Botanizing round Cape Town, on the way out, I found the flora entirely bewildering: it was difficult to assign a particular plant to any Natural Order, much less to a species. But in Cyrenaica, the flowers were at least half-familiar; one could usually spot at a glance which Natural Order they belonged to. And in many cases they were plants which, in England, are exceedingly rare. Such as, for example, the wild Gladiolus, which in March grew in great drifts in the cornfields; or the Starry Clover, the commonest weed of the wayside banks. In the cornfields, too, there were the two *Adonises*—the scarlet one, an English rarity, and the yellow species, unknown in Britain. And everywhere grew the big, yellow Ranunculus, as large as a poppy, which, earlier in the year, had covered the desert round Tobruk. And in mid-winter, the meadows near the hospital had been starred with a small lily, bluish-purple and cold as Sirius, flickering like a weak spirit-flame among the drenched grasses.

After Alamein, the chase across the desert, the fall of Tripoli, the landings in Algeria, it began to seem that the War might one day be over: the 'end-of-term' was in sight, one would be going home for the holidays.

In Tripoli we had six weeks in transit, with nothing to do; if one could avoid the vigilance of the Staff-sergeant after breakfast, one could hitch-hike down to the beach and bathe. I spent a week-end, unofficially, with a friend of mine, a masseur at a Convalescent Depôt along the coast, on the way to Homs. He was a musician and a Catholic convert; in the afternoon he played the Ravel *Sonatine* on the piano in the Garrison Theatre, and in the evening, sitting on the sand beneath the tamarisks on the edge of the desert, he chanted the *Veni Sancte Spiritus* from the Sarum Gradual.

All this was, naturally, too good to last; the General Hospital to which we were attached 'borrowed' us for ward-duties. Casualties were streaming in from the Sicily landings; I was put on a Surgical-ward. I knew nothing about surgical cases. One of the Sisters, very upper-class and Miniverish, told me I was 'futile', which was probably quite true. Our patients were mostly head-injuries; they were nearly all unconscious, and wet their beds every half-hour or so. They muttered to themselves perpetually; but scarcely ever violently and obscenely as one might have expected. Mostly they murmured 'Oh dear, oh dear,' quite quietly, over and over again.

One of the patients was an enormous Basuto. He sat up in bed, supported in Fowler's position, helpless and silent, looking very sad, staring in front of him. Occasionally he smiled, but I never heard him utter a word. One afternoon an orderly came to take his temperature; he was sitting up, as always, silent and expressionless.

'Not got much to say for yourself, George, have you?' the orderly said, feeling for the patient's pulse. The black hand fell back heavily from his own as he lifted it. 'George' had been dead for some time.

The Military Orchid, 1948

J. K. GALBRAITH
1908–

Big Men and the Twenties Boom

As the boom developed, the big men became more and more omnipotent in the popular or at least in the speculative view. In March, according to this view, the big men decided to put the market up, and even some serious scholars have been inclined to think that a concerted move catalysed this upsurge. If so, the important figure was John J. Raskob. Raskob had impressive associations. He was a director of General Motors, an ally of the Du Ponts and soon to be Chairman of the Democratic National Committee by choice of Al Smith. A contemporary student of the market, Professor Charles Amos Dice of the Ohio State University, thought this latter appointment a particular indication of the new prestige of Wall Street and the esteem in which it was held by the American people. 'Today,' he observed, 'the shrewd, worldly-wise candidate of one of the great political parties chooses one of the outstanding operators in the stock market . . . as a goodwill creator and popular vote getter.'

On March 23, 1928, on taking ship for Europe, Raskob spoke favourably of prospects for automobile sales for the rest of the year and of the share in the business that General Motors would have. He may also have suggested—the evidence is not entirely clear—that G.M. stock should be selling at not less than twelve times earnings. This would have meant a price of 225 as compared with a current quotation of about 187. Such, as the *Times* put it, was 'the magic of his name' that Mr Raskob's 'temperate bit of optimism' sent the market into a boiling fury. On March 24, a Saturday, General Motors gained nearly 5 points, and the Monday following it went to 199. The surge in General Motors, meanwhile, set off a great burst of trading elsewhere in the list.

Among the others who were assumed to have put their strength behind the market that spring was William Crapo Durant. Durant was the organizer of General Motors, whom Raskob and the Du Ponts had thrown out of the company in 1920. After a further adventure in the auto business, he had turned to full-time speculation in the stock market. The seven Fisher brothers were also believed to be influential. They too were General Motors alumni and had come to Wall Street with the great fortune they had realized from the sale of the Fisher-body plants. Still another was Arthur W. Cutten, the Canadian-born grain speculator who had recently shifted his market operations to Wall Street from the Chicago Board of Trade. As a market operator, Cutten surmounted substantial personal handicaps. He was very hard of hearing, and some years later, before a congressional committee, even his own counsel conceded that his memory was very defective.

Observing this group as a whole Professor Dice was especially struck by their 'vision for the future and boundless hope and optimism'. He noted that 'they did not come into the market hampered by the heavy armour of tradition'. In recounting their effect on the market, Professor Dice obviously found the English language verging on inadequacy. 'Led by these mighty knights of the automobile industry, the steel industry, the radio industry . . .' he said, 'and finally joined, in despair, by many professional traders who, after much sack-cloth and ashes, had caught the vision of progress, the Coolidge market had gone forward like the phalanxes of Cyrus, parasang upon parasang and again parasang upon parasang . . .'

The Great Crash, 1955

JOSEPH MITCHELL
1908–1996

Moving Up the Street

It makes me lonesome to walk past the old yellow-brick building, just south of Washington Market, once occupied by Dick's Bar and Grill. The windows are so dusty and rain-streaked and plastered with 'For Rent' stickers that you can't see inside, and there is a padlock growing rusty on the door. Dick's prospered as a speakeasy throughout prohibition; after repeal, as a licensed establishment, it was just about as lawless as ever. A year or so ago, however, when Dick moved up the street, things changed. In his new place he commenced obeying the New York State Liquor Authority's regulations: he refused to let his customers shake Indian dice on the bar for rounds of drinks; he refused to put drinks on the tab; he refused to sell liquor by the bottle late at night after the liquor stores had closed. In the old days Dick was an independent man. He was delighted when he got an opportunity to tell a customer to go to hell. He and his bartenders, in fact, usually acted as if they loathed their customers and the customers liked this because it made them feel at home; most of them were men who were made ill at ease by solicitude or service. When Dick started abiding by the liquor laws, however, a hunted look appeared on his fat, sad-eyed, Neapolitan face. He began to cringe and bow and shake hands with the customers, and he would even help them on with their coats. When they finished eating, he would go over, smile with effort, and ask, 'Was the pot roast O.K.?' In the old days he never acted that way. If someone complained about a gristly steak or a baked potato raw in the middle, he would grunt and say, 'If you don't like my grub, you don't have to eat in here. I'd just as soon I never saw you again.'

The change in Dick reflects the innovations in his new saloon, which is six blocks away from the old one—a big, classy place with a chromium and glass-brick front, a neon sign in four colors, a mahogany bar, a row of chromium bar stools with red-leather seats like those in the uptown cocktail lounges, a kitchen full of gleaming copper pots, a moody chef who once worked in Moneta's, a printed menu with French all over it, and seven new brands of Scotch. He told the bartenders they would have to shave every morning and made them put on starched white coats. For several days thereafter they looked clean and aloof, like people when they first get out of the hospital. The place was so stylish that Dick did not, for good luck, frame the first dollar bill passed across the bar; he framed the first five-dollar bill.

Dick's regular customers had always been clannish—hanging together two and three deep at the end of the bar near the greasy swinging door to the kitchen—and some of them began to congregate at the fancy bar in Dick's new place. Here they resented everything. They snickered at the French on the menu, they sneered at the bartenders in their starched white coasts. One of them waved a menu in Dick's face. 'What the hell does this mean,' he demanded, 'this here "Country Sausage Gastronome"?' The question made Dick uncomfortable. 'It means meat sauce,' he said.

Before the night of the grand opening was half over, one of the customers, an amateur evangelist who used to deliver burlesque sermons regularly in the old place, climbed up on the shiny new bar and began to preach. He had given out his text for the evening and was shouting 'Brothers and sisters! You full of sin! You full of gin! You and the Devil are real close kin! Are you ready for the Judgment Day? Where will you spend eternity? Ain't it awful?' when Dick came out of the kitchen and caught sight of him. 'Oh, my God!' Dick screamed. 'Do you want to ruin me? I can't have such monkey business in here. I got a big investment in here.' The was so much genuine agony in his voice that the amateur evangelist jumped down from his pulpit and apologized. Thereupon the old customers felt sorry for Dick. Sitting behind his bar on a busy night in the old joint, Dick used to have the aplomb of a sow on her belly in a bog, but in the new place he soon became apprehensive and haggard. One night the kitchen door swung open and the old customers saw Dick bent over a big ledger, struggling with his cost accounting. From the look on his face they knew he was quite sick of the chromium stools and the French menu. 'He don't like this joint, either,' one of them said. From then on they would tone down anyone who started to holler and throw glasses when Dick insisted on obeying the letter and the spirit of one of the alcohol laws. 'After all,' they would say, 'he's got a big investment in here. He don't want to lose his license.' However, no matter how big the investment, I never felt the same about the new Dick's.

'Obituary of a Gin Mill', *McSorley's Wonderful Saloon*, 1943

MALCOLM LOWRY

1909–1957

Looping the Loop

The Consul walked on a little further, still unsteadily; he thought he had his bearings again, then stopped:

¡BRAVA ATRACCIÓN!
10 c MÁQUINA INFERNAL

he read, half struck by some coincidence in this. Wild attraction. The huge looping-the-loop machine, empty, but going full blast over his head in this dead section of the fair, suggested some huge evil spirit, screaming in its lonely hell, its limbs writhing, smiting the air like flails of paddle-wheels. Obscured by a tree, he hadn't seen it before. The machine stopped also . . .

'—Mistair. Money money money.' 'Mistair! Where har you go?'

The wretched children had spotted him again; and his penalty for avoiding them was to be drawn inexorably, though with as much dignity as possible, into boarding the monster. And now, his ten centavos paid to a Chinese hunchback in a retiform visored tennis cap, he was alone, irrevocably and ridiculously alone, in a little confession box. After a while, with violent bewildering convulsions, the thing started to go. The confession boxes, perched at the end of menacing steel cranks, zoomed upwards and heavily fell. The Consul's own cage hurled up again with a powerful thrusting, hung for a moment upside down at the top, while the other cage, which, significantly, was empty, was at the bottom, then, before this situation had been grasped, crashed down, paused a moment at the other extremity, only to be lifted upwards again cruelly to the highest point where for an interminable, intolerable period of suspension, it remained motionless.—The Consul, like that poor fool who was bringing light to the world, was hung upside down over it, with only a scrap of woven wire between himself and death. There, above him, poised the world, with its people stretching out down to him, about to fall off the road onto his head, or into the sky. 999. The people hadn't been there before. Doubtless, following the children, they had assembled to watch him. Obliquely he was aware that he was without physical fear of death, as he would have been without fear at this moment of anything else that might sober him up; perhaps this had been his main idea. But he did not like it. This was not amusing. It was doubtless another example of Jacques'—Jacques?—unnecessary suffering. And it was scarcely a dignified position for an ex-representative of His Majesty's government to find himself in, though it was symbolic, of what he could not conceive, but it was undoubtedly symbolic. Jesus. All at once, terribly, the confession boxes had begun to go in reverse: Oh, the Consul said, oh; for the sensation of falling was now as if terribly behind him, unlike anything, beyond experience; certainly this recessive unwinding was not like looping-the-loop in a plane, where the movement was quickly over, the only strange feeling one of increased weight; as a sailor he disapproved of that feeling too, but this—ah, my God! Everything was falling out of his pockets, was being wrested from him, torn away, a fresh article at each whirling, sickening, plunging, retreating, unspeakable circuit, his notecase, pipe, keys, his dark glasses he had taken off, his small change he did not have time to imagine being pounced on by the children after all, he was being emptied out, returned empty, his stick, his passport—had that been his passport? He didn't know if he'd brought it with him. Then he remembered he had brought it. Or hadn't brought it. It could be difficult even for a Consul to be without a passport in Mexico. Ex-consul. What did it matter? Let it go! There was a kind of fierce delight in this final acceptance. Let everything go! Everything particularly that provided means of ingress or egress, went bond for, gave meaning or character, or purpose or identity to that frightful bloody nightmare he was forced to carry around with him everywhere upon his back, that went by the name of Geoffrey Firmin, late of His Majesty's Navy, later still of His Majesty's Consular Service, later still of—Suddenly it struck him that the Chinaman was asleep, that the children, the people had gone, that this would go on forever; no one could stop the machine . . . It was over.

And yet not over. On terra firma the world continued to spin madly round; houses, whirligigs, hotels, cathedrals, cantinas, volcanoes: it was difficult to stand up at all. He was conscious of people laughing at him but, what was more surprising, of his possessions being restored to him, one by one. The child who had his notecase withdrew it from him playfully before returning it. No: she still had something in her other hand, a crumpled paper. The Consul thanked her for it firmly. Some telegram of Hugh's. His stick, his glasses, his pipe, unbroken; yet not his favorite pipe; and no passport. Well, definitely he could not have brought it. Putting his other things back in his pockets he turned a corner, very unsteadily, and slumped down on a bench. He replaced his dark glasses, set his pipe in his mouth, crossed his legs, and, as the world gradually slowed down, assumed the bored expression of an English tourist sitting in the Luxembourg Gardens.

Children, he thought, how charming they were at heart. The very same kids who had besieged him for money, had now brought him back even the smallest of his small change and then, touched by his embarrassment, had scurried away without waiting for a reward. Now he wished he had given them something. The little girl had gone also. Perhaps this was her exercise book open on the bench. He wished he had not been so brusque with her, that she would come back, so that he could give her the book. Yvonne and he should have had children, would have had children, could have had children, should have . . .

In the exercise book he made out with difficulty:

Escruch is an old man. He lives in London. He lives alone in a large house. Scrooge is a rich man but he never gives to the poor. He is a miser. No one loves Scrooge and Scrooge loves no one. He has no friends. He is alone in the world. The man (el hombre): the house (la casa): the poor (los pobres): he lives (el vive): he gives (el da): he has no friends (el no tiene amigos): he loves (el ama): old (viejo): large (grande): no one (nadie): rich (rico): Who is Scrooge? Where does he live? Is Scrooge rich or poor? Has he friends? How does he live? Alone. World. On.

At last the earth had stopped spinning with the motion of the Infernal Machine. The last house was still, the last tree rooted again. It was seven minutes past two by his watch. And he was cold stone sober. How horrible was the feeling. The Consul closed the exercise book: bloody old Scrooge; how queer to meet him here!

Under the Volcano, 1947

ISAIAH BERLIN

1909–1997

Herzen and Turgenev

At the heart of Herzen's outlook (and of Turgenev's too) is the notion of the complexity and insolubility of the central problems, and, therefore, of the absurdity of trying to solve them by means of political or sociological instruments. But the difference between Herzen and Turgenev is this. Turgenev is, in his innermost being, not indeed heartless but a cool, detached, at times slightly mocking observer who looks upon the tragedies of life from a comparatively remote point of view; oscillating between one vantage point and another, between the claims of society and of the individual, the claims of love and of daily life; between heroic virtue and realistic skepticism, the morality of Hamlet and the morality of Don Quixote, the necessity for efficient political organisation and the necessity for individual self-expression; remaining suspended in a state of agreeable indecision, sympathetic melancholy, ironical, free from cynicism and sentimentality, perceptive, scrupulously truthful and uncommitted. Turgenev neither quite believed nor quite disbelieved in a deity, personal or impersonal; religion is for him a normal ingredient of life, like love, or egoism, or the sense of pleasure. He enjoyed remaining in an intermediate position, he enjoyed almost too much his lack of will to believe, and because he stood aside, because he contemplated in tranquillity, he was able to produce great literary masterpieces of a finished kind, rounded stories told in peaceful retrospect, with well-constructed beginnings, middles and ends. He detached his art from himself; he did not, as a human being, deeply care about solutions; he saw life with a peculiar chilliness, which infuriated both Tolstoy and Dostoevsky, and he achieved the exquisite perspective of an artist who treats his material from a certain distance. There is a chasm between him and his material, within which alone his particular kind of poetical creation is possible.

Herzen, on the contrary, cared far too violently. He was looking for solutions for himself, for his own personal life. His novels were certainly failures. He obtrudes himself too vehemently into them, himself and his agonised point of view. On the other hand, his autobiographical sketches, when he writes openly about himself and about his friends, when he speaks about his own life in Italy, in France, in Switzerland, in England, have a kind of palpitating directness, a sense of first-handness and reality, which no other writer in the nineteenth century begins to convey. His reminiscences are a work of critical and descriptive genius with the power of absolute self-revelation that only an astonishingly imaginative, impressionable, perpetually reacting personality, with an exceptional sense both of the noble and the ludicrous, and a rare freedom from vanity and doctrine, could have attained. As a writer of memoirs he is unequalled. His sketches of England, or rather of himself in England, are better than Heine's or Taine's. To demonstrate this one need only read his wonderful account of English political trials, of how judges, for example, looked to him when they sat in court trying foreign conspirators for having fought a fatal duel in Windsor Park. He gives a vivid and entertaining description of bombastic French demagogues and gloomy French fanatics, and of the impassable gulf which divides this agitated and slightly grotesque émigré society from the dull, frigid, and dignified institutions of mid-Victorian England, typified by the figure of the presiding judge at the Old Bailey, who looks like the wolf in *Red Riding Hood*, in his white wig, his long skirts, with his sharp little wolf-like face, thin lips, sharp teeth, and harsh little words that come with an air of specious benevolence from the face encased in disarming feminine curls—giving the impression of a sweet, grandmotherly old lady, belied by the small gleaming eyes and the dry, acrid, malicious judicial humour.

'A Marvellous Decade', 1955, *Russian Thinkers*

EUDORA WELTY

1909–

At the Patient's Bedside

'What do you think of his prospects now?' Laurel asked Dr Courtland, following him out into the corridor. 'It's three weeks.'

'Three weeks! Lord, how they fly,' he said. He believed he hid the quick impatience of his mind, and moving and speaking with deliberation he did hide it—then showed it all in his smile. 'He's doing all right. Lungs clear, heart strong, blood pressure not a bit worse than it was before. And that eye's clearing. I think he's got some vision coming, just a little bit around the edge, you know, Laurel, but if the cataract catches up with him, I want him seeing enough to find his way around the garden. A little longer. Let's play safe.'

Going down on the elevator with him, another time, she asked, 'Is it the drugs he has to take that make him seem such a distance away?'

He pinched a frown into his freckled forehead. 'Well, no two people react in just the same way to anything.' They held the elevator for him to say, 'People are different, Laurel.'

'Mother was different,' she said.

Laurel felt reluctant to leave her father now in the afternoons. She stayed and read. *Nicholas Nickleby* had seemed as endless to her as time must seem to him, and it had now been arranged between them, without words, that she was to sit there beside him and read—but silently, to herself. He too was completely silent while she read. Without being able to see her as she sat by his side, he seemed to know when she turned each page, as though he kept up, through the succession of pages, with time, checking off moment after moment; and she felt it would be heartless to close her book until she'd read him to sleep.

One day, Fay came in and caught Laurel sitting up asleep herself, in her spectacles.

'Putting your eyes out, too? I told him if he hadn't spent so many years of his life poring over dusty old books, his eyes would have more strength saved up for now,' Fay told her. She sidled closer to the bed. 'About ready to get up, hon?' she cried. 'Listen, they're holding parades out yonder right now. Look what they threw me off the float!'

Shadows from the long green eardrops she'd come in wearing made soft little sideburns down her small, intent face as she pointed to them, scolding him. 'What's the good of a Carnival if we don't get to go, hon?'

It was still incredible to Laurel that her father, at nearly seventy, should have let anyone new, a beginner, walk in on his life, that he had even agreed to pardon such a thing.

'Father, where did you meet her?' Laurel had asked when, a year and a half ago, she had flown down to Mount Salus to see them married.

'Southern Bar Association.' With both arms he had made an expansive gesture that she correctly read as the old Gulf Coast Hotel. Fay had had a part-time job there; she was in the typist pool. A month after the convention, he brought her home to Mount Salus, and they were married in the Courthouse.

Perhaps she was forty, and so younger than Laurel. There was little even of forty in her looks except the line of her neck and the backs of her little square, idle hands. She was bony and blue-veined; as a child she had very possibly gone undernourished. Her hair was still a childish tow. It had the tow texture, as if, well rubbed between the fingers, those curls might have gone to powder. She had round, country-blue eyes and a little feisty jaw.

When Laurel flew down from Chicago to be present at the ceremony, Fay's response to her kiss had been to say, 'It wasn't any use in you bothering to come so far.' She'd smiled as though she meant her scolding to flatter. What Fay told Laurel now, nearly every afternoon at the changeover, was almost the same thing. Her flattery and her disparagement sounded just alike.

It was strange, though, how Fay never called anyone by name. Only she had said 'Becky': Laurel's mother, who had been dead ten years by the time Fay could have first heard of her, when she had married Laurel's father.

'What on earth made Becky give you a name like that?' she'd asked Laurel, on that first occasion.

'It's the state flower of West Virginia,' Laurel told her, smiling. 'Where my mother came from.'

Fay hadn't smiled back. She'd given her a wary look.

One later night, at the Hibiscus, Laurel tapped at Fay's door.

'What do you want?' Fay asked as she opened it.

She thought the time had come to know Fay a little better. She sat down on one of the hard chairs in the narrow room and asked her about her family.

'My family?' said Fay. 'None of 'em living. That's why I ever left Texas and came to Mississippi. We may not have had much, out in Texas, but we were always so close. Never had any secrets from each other, like some families. Sis was just like my twin. My brothers were all so unselfish! After Papa died, we all gave up everything for Mama, of course. Now that she's gone, I'm glad we did. Oh, I wouldn't have run off and left anybody that needed me. Just to call myself an artist and make a lot of money.'

Laurel did not try again, and Fay never at any time knocked at her door.

Now Fay walked around Judge McKelva's bed and cried, 'Look! Look what I got to match my eardrops! How do you like 'em, hon? Don't you want to let's go dancing?' She stood on one foot and held a shoe in the air above his face. It was green, with a stilletto heel. Had the shoe been a written page, some brief she'd concocted on her own, he looked at it in her hands there for long enough to read it through. But he didn't speak.

'But just let me try slipping *out* a minute in 'em, would he ever let me hear about it!' Fay said. She gave him a smile, to show her remark was meant for him to hear. He offered no reply.

The Optimist's Daughter, 1972

G. V. DESANI

1909–

A Conversation with a Dog

Yonder, in the horizon, was a mother-of-pearl opal splash, tinged with a rim of flame-red, testifying as to the defunct evening-sun.

I had been sitting on a chalk-hill, reflecting . . .

'Damme, Jenkins,' I asked the dog, concluding my thoughts, 'what do you think of the clinical *Presumption*, which implies, that, IN THE AFFAIRS OF MAN, GODS AND SUCH-LIKE FOREIGN-FACTORS INTERVENE? IS THERE ANY TRUTH IN THE NOTION THAT PARANORMAL INTERFERENCE IS GOING ON IN THE UNIVERSE? IS A HUMAN FELLER A FREE AGENT? IS FUTURE TENSE A MYTH-JOKE?'

And the chap whimpered!

Damme, that's a dog for you!

How many times had he bolted away like hell, his tail half mast, frightened off by a rat? And whimpering like the dickens, this feller, Jenkins, had the nerve to come to me for consolation; every time, giving me a hell of an unashamed straight look in the eye!

Certain timid bodies are known to be able to bravely cope with moral emergencies. But this feller was an out and out coward. He couldn't stand a physical emergency, nor would he face a problem pointing at a medico-philosophical *Presumption.*

'Damme, cur,' I said to the chap, not sparing his feelings, 'maybe, I am talking to a lamp-post! What the hell is the matter with you, Jenkins? I had you for company. You are having that from me, and more! You are having yourself waited on, hand and foot, getting a fine deal out of me, consolation, sympathy, company, watching, and, your keep. In return, you whimper at me!'

He gave me no option.

If ever a feller was a ripe enough case for a psychiater to treat, this canine was it. The chap suffered from extreme mental malady, *i.e.*, he oscillated between blue funk, and more!

Any little cackling from the hens could make him eat his heart out!

'They have made that noise again! Master, they have done that to me again! That mouse nearly got me! I have been chased by a rat, oh!'

All that, considering the dog's hobbledehoy temperament, I understood: as plain a glycero-phosphate as any. But, what I resented was, this feller running up to me every now and then for sympathy!

And his dam' unashamed straight looks!

'Do gods really interfere in a feller's life?' I asked myself, ignoring Jenkins.

'For instance,' I continued, now sub-vocal, and self-discoursing, 'Banerrji mentioned an Indian classic writer feller. The chap's stated that love breeds anger! He says, as natural a thing as could be!

'Damme, two lovers, hearts full to the brim with the fondest regards, actually manage to find the reasons to quarrel! They couldn't wish a billingsgate. Yet! What is the medico-dynamics? Is it the doing of some supernatural agent, '*kismet*', fate, man's inherited and imposed instincts and no escaping 'em, or what the hell?

'Are there Powers about? What Power propels the cheese-mite, and man's will to live and act as he does? His will and doing entirely, or some 'un nose-poking?'

I was perplexed over the *Presumption* that evening, and, to-day, after years, I am perplexed still!

All about H. Hatterr, 1949

PAUL BOWLES

1910–

At a Brothel in the Sahara

In front of the musicians in the middle of the floor a girl was dancing, if indeed the motions she made could properly be called a dance. She held a cane in her two hands, behind her head, and her movements were confined to her agile neck and shoulders. The motions, graceful and of an impudence verging on the comic, were a perfect translation into visual terms of the strident and wily sounds of the music. What moved him, however, was not the dance itself so much as the strangely detached, somnambulistic expression of the girl. Her smile was fixed, and, one might have added, her mind as well, as if upon some object so remote that only she knew of its existence. There was a supremely impersonal disdain in the unseeing eyes and the curve of the placid lips. The longer he watched, the more fascinating the face became; it was a mask of perfect proportions, whose beauty accrued less from the configuration of features than from the meaning that was implicit in their expression—meaning, or the withholding of it. For what emotion lay behind the face it was impossible to tell. It was as if she were saying: 'A dance is being done. I do not dance because I am not here. But it is my dance.' When the piece drew to its conclusion and the music had stopped, she stood still for a moment, then slowly lowered the cane from behind her head, and tapping vaguely on the floor a few times, turned and spoke to one of the musicians. Her remarkable expression had not changed in any respect. The musician rose and made room for her on the floor beside him. The way he helped her to sit down struck Port as peculiar, and all at once the realization came to him that the girl was blind. The knowledge hit him like an electric shock; he felt his heart leap ahead and his head grow suddenly hot.

The Sheltering Sky, 1949

MERVYN PEAKE
1911–1968

In the Castle of Gormenghast

One summer morning of bland air, the huge, corroding bell-like heart of Gormenghast was half asleep and there appeared to be no reverberation from its muffled thudding. In a hall of plaster walls the silence yawned.

Nailed above a doorway of this hall a helmet or casque, red with rust, gave forth into the stillness a sandy and fluttering sound, and a moment later the beak of a jackdaw was thrust through an eye-slit and withdrawn. The plaster walls arose on every side into a dusky and apparently ceilingless gloom, lit only by a high, solitary window. The warm light that found its way through the web-choked glass of this window gave hint of galleries yet further above but no suggestion of doors beyond, nor any indication of how these galleries could be reached. From this high window a few rays of sunlight, like copper wires, were strung steeply and diagonally across the hall, each one terminating in its amber pool of dust on the floorboards. A spider lowered itself, fathom by fathom, on a perilous length of thread and was suddenly transfixed in the path of a sunbeam and, for an instant, was a thing of radiant gold.

There was no sound, and then—as though timed to break the tension, the high window was swung open and the sunbeams were blotted out, for a hand was thrust through and a bell was shaken. Almost at once there was a sound of footsteps, and moment later a dozen doors were opening and shutting, and the hall was thronged with the criss-crossing of figures.

The bell ceased clanging. The hand was withdrawn and the figures were gone. There was no sign that any living thing had ever moved or breathed between the plaster walls, or that the many doors had ever opened, save that a small whitish flower lay in the dust beneath the rusting helmet, and that a door was swinging gently to and fro.

Gormenghast, 1950

FLANN O'BRIEN
(Brian O'Nolan)
1911–1966

Some Varieties of Madness

But which of us can hope to probe with questioning finger the dim thoughts that flit in a fool's head? One man will think he has a glass bottom and will fear to sit in case of breakage. In other respects he will be a man of great intellectual force and will accompany one in a mental ramble throughout the labyrinths of mathematics or philosophy so long as he is allowed to remain standing throughout the disputations. Another man will be perfectly polite and well-conducted except that he will in no circumstances turn otherwise than to the right and indeed will own a bicycle so constructed that it cannot turn otherwise than to that point. Others will be subject to colours and will attach undue merit to articles that are red or green or white merely because they bear that hue. Some will be exercised and influenced by the texture of a cloth or by the roundness or angularity of an object. Numbers, however, will account for a great proportion of unbalanced and suffering humanity. One man will rove the streets seeking motor-cars with numbers that are divisible by seven. Well-known, alas, is the case of the poor German who was very fond of three and who made each aspect of his life a thing of triads. He went home one evening and drank three cups of tea with three lumps of sugar in each cup, cut his jugular with a razor three times and scrawled with a dying hand on a picture of his wife good-bye, good-bye, good-bye.

At Swim-Two-Birds, 1939

J. L. AUSTIN
1911–1960

Reality

If you ask me, 'How do you know it's a real stick?' 'How do you know it's really bent?' ('Are you sure he's really angry?'), then you are querying my credentials or my facts (it's often uncertain which) in a certain special way. In various *special, recognized* ways, depending essentially upon the nature of the matter which I have announced myself to know, either my current experiencing or the item currently under consideration (or uncertain which) may be abnormal, *phoney*. Either I myself may be dreaming, or in delirium, or under the influence of mescal, &c.: or else the item may be stuffed, painted, dummy, artificial, trick, freak, toy, assumed, feigned, &c.: or else again there's an uncertainty (it's left open) whether *I* am to blame or *it* is—mirages, mirror images, odd lighting effects, &c.

These doubts are all to be allayed by means of recognized procedures (more or less roughly recognized, of course), appropriate to the particular type of case. There are recognized ways of distinguishing between dreaming and waking (how otherwise should we know how to use and to contrast the words?), and of deciding whether a thing is stuffed or live, and so forth. The doubt or question 'But is it a *real* one?' has always (*must* have) a special basis, there must be some 'reason for suggesting' that it isn't real in the sense of some specific way, or limited number of specific ways, in which it is suggested that this experience or item may be phoney. Sometimes (usually) the context makes it clear what the suggestion is: the goldfinch might be stuffed but there's no suggestion that it's a mirage, the oasis might be a mirage but there's no suggestion it might be stuffed. If the context doesn't make it clear, then I am entitled to ask 'How do you mean? Do you mean it may be stuffed or what? *What are you suggesting*?' The wile of the metaphysician consists in asking 'Is it a real table?' (a kind of object which has no obvious way of being phoney) and not specifying or limiting what may be wrong with it, so that I feel at a loss 'how to prove' it *is* a real one. It is the use of the word 'real' in this manner that leads us on to the supposition that 'real' has a single meaning ('the real world' 'material objects'), and that a highly profound and puzzling one. Instead, we should insist always on specifying with what 'real' is being contrasted—'not what' I shall have to show it is, in order to show it is 'real': and then usually we shall find some specific, less fatal, word, appropriate to the particular case, to substitute for 'real'.

'Other Minds', 1946, *Philosophical Papers*

WILLIAM GOLDING

1911–1993

Neanderthals and New Men

Lok's ears spoke to Lok.

'?'

So concerned was he with the island that he paid no attention to his ears for a time. He clung swaying gently in the tree-top while the fall grumbled at him and the space on the island remained empty. Then he heard. There were people coming, not on the other side of the water but on this side, far off. They were coming down from the overhang, their steps careless on the stones. He could hear their speech and it made him laugh. The sounds made a picture in his head of interlacing shapes, thin, and complex, voluble and silly, not like the long curve of a hawk's cry, but tangled like line weed on the beach after a storm, muddled as water. This laugh-sound advanced through the trees towards the river. The same sort of laugh-sound began to rise on the island, so that it flitted back and forth across the water. Lok half-fell, half-scrambled down the tree and was on the trail. He ran along it through the ancient smell of the people. The laugh-sound was close by the river bank. Lok reached the place where the log had lain across water. He had to climb a tree, swing and drop down before he was on the trail again. Then among the laugh-sound on this side of the river Liku began to scream. She was not screaming in anger or in fear or in pain, but screaming with that mindless and dreadful panic she might have shown at the slow advance of a snake. Lok spurted, his hair bristling. Need to get at that screaming threw him off the trail and he floundered. The screaming tore him inside. It was not like the screaming of Fa when she was bearing the baby that died, or the mourning of Nil when Mal was buried; it was like the noise the horse makes when the cat sinks its curved teeth into the neck and hangs there, sucking blood. Lok was screaming himself without knowing it and fighting with thorns. And his senses told him through the screaming that Liku was doing what no man and no woman could do. She was moving away across the river.

Lok was still fighting with bushes when the screaming stopped. Now he could hear the laugh-noise again and the new one mewing. He burst the bushes and was out in the open by the dead tree. The clearing round the trunk stank of other and Liku and fear. Across the water there was a great bowing and ducking and swishing of green sprays. He caught a glimpse of Liku's red head and the new one on a dark, hairy shoulder. He jumped up and down and shouted.

'Liku! Liku!'

The green drifts twitched together and the people on the island disappeared. Lok ran up and down along the river-bank under the dead tree with its nest of ivy. He was so close to the water that he thrust chunks of earth out that went splash into the current.

'Liku! Liku!'

The bushes twitched again. Lok steadied by the tree and gazed. A head and a chest faced him, half-hidden. There were white bone things behind the leaves and hair. The man had white bone things above his eyes and under the mouth so that his face was longer than a face should be. The man turned sideways in the bushes and looked at Lok along his shoulder. A stick rose upright and there was a lump of bone in the middle. Lok peered at the stick and the lump of bone and the small eyes in the bone things over the face. Suddenly Lok understood that the man was holding the stick out to him but neither he nor Lok could reach across the river. He would have laughed if it were not for the echo of the screaming in his head. The stick began to grow shorter at both ends. Then it shot out to full length again.

The dead tree by Lok's ear acquired a voice.

'Clop!'

His ears twitched and he turned to the tree. By his face there had grown a twig: a twig that smelt of other, and of goose, and of the bitter berries that Lok's stomach told him he must not eat. This twig had a white bone at the end. There were hooks in the bone and sticky brown stuff hung in the crooks. His nose examined this stuff and did not like it. He smelled along the shaft of the twig. The leaves on the twig were red feathers and reminded him of goose. He was lost in a generalized astonishment and excitement. He shouted at the green drifts across the glittering water and heard Liku crying out in answer but could not catch the words, They were cut off suddenly as though someone had clapped a hand over her mouth. He rushed to the edge of the water and came back. On either side of the open bank the bushes grew thickly in the flood; they waded out until at their farthest some of the leaves were opening under water; and these bushes leaned over.

The echo of Liku's voice in his head sent him trembling at this perilous way of bushes towards the island. He dashed at them where normally they would have been rooted on dry land and his feet splashed. He threw himself forward and grabbed at the branches with hands and feet. He shouted:

'I am coming!'

The Inheritors, 1955

WILLIAM SANSOM
1912–1976

An Encounter in the Zoo

Doole passed slowly along by the netted bird-runs, mildly thankful for the company of their cackling, piping inmates. Sometimes he stopped and read with interest a little white card describing the bird's astounding Latin name and its place of origin. Uganda, Brazil, New Zealand—and soon these places ceased to mean anything, life's variety proved too immense, anything might come from anywhere. A thick-trousered bird with a large pink lump on its head croaked at Doole, then swung its head back to bury its whole face in feathers, nibbling furiously with closed eyes. In the adjoining cage everything looked deserted, broken pods and old dried droppings lay scattered, the water bowl was almost dry—and then he spied a grey bird tucked up in a corner, lizard lids half-closed, sleeping or resting or simply tired of it all. Doole felt distress for this bird, it looked so lonely and grieved, he would far rather be croaked at. He passed on, and came to the peacocks: the flaming blue dazzled him and the little heads jerked so busily that he smiled again, and turned contentedly back to the path—when the smile was washed abruptly from his face. He stood frozen with terror in the warm sunshine.

The broad gravel path, walled in on the one side by dahlias, on the other by cages, stretched yellow with sunlight. A moment before it had been quite empty. Now, exactly in the centre and only some thirty feet away, stood a full-maned male lion.

It stared straight at Doole.

Doole stood absolutely still, as still as a man can possibly stand, but in that first short second, like an immensely efficient and complicated machine, his eyes and other senses flashed every detail of the surrounding scene into his consciousness—he knew instantly that on the right there were high wire cages, he estimated whether he could pull himself up by his fingers in the net, he felt the stub ends of his shoes pawing helplessly beneath; he saw the bright dahlia balls on the left, he saw behind them a high green hedge, probably privet, with underbush too thick to penetrate—it was a ten-foot hedge rising high against the sky, could one leap and plunge halfway through, like a clown through a circus hoop? And if so, who would follow? And behind the lion, cutting across the path like a wall, a further hedge—it hardly mattered what was behind the lion, though it gave in fact a further sense of impasse. And behind himself? The path stretched back past all those cages by which he had strolled at such leisure such a very little time ago—the fractional thought of it started tears of pity in his eyes—and it was far, far to run to the little thatched hut that said

Bath Chairs for Hire, he felt that if only he could get among those big old safe chairs with their blankets and pillows he would be safe. But he knew it was too far. Long before he got there those hammer-strong paws would be on him, his clothes torn and his own red meat staining the yellow gravel.

At the same time as his animal reflexes took all this in, some other instinct made him stand still, and as still as a rock, instead of running. Was this too, an animal sense? Was he, Doole, in his brown suit, like an ostrich that imagines it has fooled its enemy by burying its head in the ground? Or was it rather an educated sense—how many times had he been told that savages and animals can smell fear, one must stand one's ground and face them? In any case, he did this—he stood his ground and stared straight into the large, deep eyes of the lion, and as he stared there came over him the awful sense: *This has happened, this is happening to ME.* He had felt it in nightmares, and as a child before going up for a beating—a dreadfully condemned sense, the sense of *no way out*, never, never and *now*. It was absolute. The present moment roared loud and intense as all time put together.

'Among The Dahlias', *Among the Dahlias*, 1957

JOHN CHEEVER
1912–1982

Obsolescence

Oh world, world, world, wondrous and bewildering, when did my troubles begin? This is being written in my house in Bullet Park. The time is 10 A.M. The day is Tuesday. You might well ask what I am doing in Bullet Park on a weekday morning. The only other men around are three clergymen, two invalids, and an old codger on Turner Street who has lost his marbles. The neighborhood has the serenity, the stillness of a terrain where all sexual tensions have been suspended—excluding mine, of course, and those of the three clergymen. What is my business? What do I do? Why didn't I catch the train? I am forty-six years old, hale, well dressed, and have a more thorough knowledge of the manufacture and merchandising of Dynaflex than any other man in the entire field. One of my difficulties is my youthful looks. I have a thirty-inch waistline and jet-black hair, and when I tell people that I used to be vice-president in charge of merchandising and executive assistant to the president of Dynaflex—when I tell this to strangers in bars and on trains—they never believe me, because I look so young.

Mr Estabrook, the president of Dynaflex and in some ways my

protector, was an enthusiastic gardener. While admiring his flowers one afternoon, he was stung by a bumblebee, and he died before they could get him to the hospital. I could have had the presidency, but I wanted to stay in merchandising and manufacture. Then the directors—including myself, of course—voted a merger with Milltonium Ltd., putting Eric Penumbra, Milltonium's chief, at the helm. I voted for the merger with some misgivings, but I concealed these and did the most important part of the groundwork for this change. It was my job to bring in the approval of conservative and reluctant stockholders, and one by one I brought them around. The fact that I had worked for Dynaflex since I had left college, that I had never worked for anyone else, inspired their trust. A few days after the merger was a fact, Penumbra called me into his office. 'Well,' he said, 'you've had it.'

'Yes, I have,' I said. I thought he was complimenting me on having brought in the approvals. I had traveled all over the United States and made two trips to Europe. No one else could have done it.

'You've had it,' Penumbra said harshly. 'How long will it take you to get out of here?'

'I don't understand,' I said.

'How the hell long will it take you to get out of here!' he shouted. 'You're obsolete. We can't afford people like you in the shop. I'm asking how long it will take you to get out of here.'

'It will take about an hour,' I said.

'Well, I'll give you to the end of the week,' he said. 'If you want to send your secretary up, I'll fire her. You're really lucky. With your pension, severance pay, and the stock you own, you'll have damned near as much money as I take home, without having to lift a finger.' Then he left his desk and came to where I stood. He put an arm around my shoulders. He gave me a hug. 'Don't worry,' Penumbra said. 'Obsolescence is something we all have to face. I hope I'll be as calm about it as you when my time comes.'

'I certainly hope you will,' I said, and I left the office.

'The Ocean', *The Brigadier and the Golf Widow*, 1965

PATRICK WHITE

1912–1990

An Explorer and His Dog

Next morning the expedition rose, and proceeded along the southerly bank of the rejuvenated river, that wound in general direction westward. Green disguised the treacherous nature of the ground, and in places, where heavier rain had fallen, there was the constant danger of pack animals becoming bogged, which did occur at intervals. Then the German's hatred of mules became ungovernable. He would ride a hundred yards off his course in order to arm himself with a branch from a tree. At such times, the animals would smell danger from a distance, and would be sweating and trembling against his return; there were even some mules that would snatch at him with their long teeth as he passed, and jangle their bits, and roll their china eyes.

Of dogs, however, Voss showed every sign of approbation, and would suffer for them, when their pads split, when their sides were torn open in battle with kangaroos, or when, in the course of the journey, they simply died off. He would watch most jealously the attempts of other men to win the affection of his dogs. Until he could bear it no longer. Then he would walk away, and had been known to throw stones at a faithless animal. In general, however, the dogs ignored the advances of anyone else. They were devoted to this one man. They could have eaten him up. So it was very satisfactory. Voss was morbidly grateful for the attentions of their hot tongues, although he would not have allowed himself to be caught returning their affection.

By this stage of the journey the number of dogs had been reduced to two, a kind of rough terrier, and Gyp, the big mongrel-Newfoundland that had given good service as a sheep-dog in the days of sheep.

'Gyp is in fine condition, sir,' Judd remarked to Voss one day as they rode along.

He knew the leader's fondness for the dog, and thought secretly to humour him in this way.

The black bitch had, indeed, flourished since the sheep had been abandoned and the ground had softened. She led a life of pleasure, and would trot back and forth on spongy feet, her long tongue lolling in pink health, her coat flashing with points of jet.

'She has never looked better,' Judd ventured to add.

'Certainly,' Voss replied.

He had ridden back for company, and now sensed that he had done wrong; he must suffer for it.

'Yes,' he said, raising his voice. 'She is eating her head off, and I have been considering for several days what must be done for the common good.'

Both men were silent for a little, watching with cold fascination the activities of the fussy dog, who was passing and re-passing, and once laughed up at them.

'I have thought to destroy her,' said the fascinated Voss, 'since we have no longer sheep, hence, no longer any earthly use for Gyp.'

Judd did not answer; but Harry Robarts, who was riding close by, at the heels of the cattle, looked up, and did protest:

'Ah, no, sir! Kill Gyp?'

He was already dry of throat and hot of eye.

Others were similarly affected when they heard of the decision. Even Turner suggested:

'We will all share a bit of grub with Gyp whenever she don't catch. She will be fed out of our ration, sir, so there will be no drain on the provisions.'

Voss was grinning painfully.

'I would like very much to be in a position to enjoy the luxury of sentiment,' he said.

Accordingly, when they made the midday halt, the German called to his dog, and she followed him a short way. When he had spoken a few words to her, and was looking into the eyes of love, he pulled the trigger. He was cold with sweat. He could have shot off his own jaw. Yet, he had done right, he convinced himself through his pain, and would do better to subject himself to further drastic discipline.

Then the man scraped a hole in which to bury his dog. As the grave was rather shallow, he placed a few stones on top, and some branches from a ragged she-oak, which he found growing there beside the river.

From a distance the members of his party could have been watching him.

'What does it matter?' said Turner at last, who had been amongst the most vociferous in Gyp's defence. 'It is only a dog, is it not? And might have become a nuisance. It could be that he has done right to kill it. Only, in these here circumstances, we are all, every one of us, dogs.'

After going about for several days like one dead, Voss was virtually consoled. Burying other motives with the dog, he decided that his act could but have been for the common good. If he had mystified his men, mystery was his personal prerogative. If Laura did not accept, it was because Laura herself was dog-eyed love.

As they rode along he explained to that loving companion who lived and breathed inside him: he had only to hold the muzzle to his own head, to win a victory over her. At night, though, his body was sick with the spasms of the dying dog. Until the continuous lovers felt for each other's hand, to hear the rings chatter together. Truly, they were married. But I cannot, he said, stirring in his sleep, both kill and have. He was tormented by the soft coat of love. So he at once left it, and walked away. He was his former skeleton, wiry and obsessed.

Voss, 1957

ANGUS WILSON

1913–1991

A Mother's Solicitude

Just before they went to bed, Kay whispered to John and Robin, 'Mother's going to have a *Grossmutter* tomorrow.' It was their childhood way of describing the moods of moralizing and intrigue that descended upon their mother when she felt frustrated and neglected. Her manner, at such times, became sweeter, more intimate as her fear of isolation became more desperate. Her children had decided that she inherited such reactions from their Bavarian grandmother with her *Gemütlichkeit* and her sense of persecution; this attribution to heredity at once exculpated her from all blame and made more excusable their own acquiescence in her demands. They had learned such acquiescence in childhood; their mother had been a great believer in such character-training. And, as nobody, except Inge, could remember their grandmother, it was not an explanation that could be contradicted.

As the day wore on, Mrs Middleton took her children aside one by one, and tried to reassure herself that no one and nothing came before herself in their feelings.

'Now little Kay,' she said, 'I am going to show you how to make a real old-fashioned turkey soup. There is no need, you know, to have poor food because one is living on the little, tiny income that my poor Kay has.' She led her daughter into the vast kitchen, which, like everything else in her house, was equipped with the greatest modern simplicity at the greatest possible expense. It was the simplicity only that Mrs Middleton saw, she constantly exclaimed at the frittering and waste of more old-fashioned homes where large capital outlay had been less possible. 'And all that old-fashioned way of living is so unhygienic too,' she would say.

She dispersed the maids from their current tasks. 'Later!' she said. 'Now I am going to give Mrs Consett a cookery lesson. You see, Kay,' she continued, putting herbs into a little muslin bag, 'first the bouquet, so simple and so wholesome. But you are tired, my darling,' she said. 'Tired and sad. That is wrong. A young mother should look so happy. When you were all little babies, I used to sing and dance all day. The English neighbours would say 'That young Mrs Middleton's quite mad', and look down their noses—so! And then I would dance and sing all the more. It is not right that you should have to worry and save so.'

'But, darling,' said Kay, 'really we're not paupers. I get £980 a year from my shares in the firm and then there's what Donald earns with his articles.'

'Now Kay,' said Ingeborg, 'that *really* makes me sad. It is bad when you feel ashamed and have to tell lies to your mother. I don't mind that Donald does not make any money. It is not always the fine people who make money. I am only sad for him. To have no work is bad for people, and for a little orphan boy . . .' She left the horrible possibilities of this situation in the air.

'I don't think,' said Kay, laughing, 'that Donald feels unloved, if that's what you mean.'

'Oh, no!' cried her mother, 'you give him so much. But now there is baby.' She paused and went on with her soup-making lesson, then she said, 'Donald is a little shy with baby, I think. Perhaps he is a little frightened of this new stranger who has come to share his Kay with him.'

'He's just awkward,' said Kay.

'Oh, my dear, you need not tell me such things,' her mother laughed, 'I remember Gerald with little Johnnie. But Donald will be happier now that he has this work to do for Robin. I am *so* glad that I found this job for him. It will make him feel more a part of the family.'

'Mummy,' said Kay, 'you realize he will only do this lecturing for Robin until a university post comes along, He's not going to give up his academic career.'

'No, of course not,' said Mrs Middleton, 'but since your father did nothing for him in the university world, it was time that your silly old mother thought of something.'

'Oh! I think Daddy did his best, but it's not his subject and Donald's very bad at interviews.'

But Ingeborg had had enough, and, in addition, she had really become interested in the soup-making. She patted her daughter's cheek. 'Always so loyal to your father,' she said.

Anglo-Saxon Attitudes, 1956

BARBARA PYM
1913–1980

Offprints

'They are coming in,' she said. 'Have the committee decided yet when they will hold the interviews?'

Professor Mainwaring tweaked at his beard with an almost pizzicato gesture. 'Ah, *that*! I have a new plan this year and one which I think Fairfax and Vere should approve. I will reveal it to you in due course.'

'It seems difficult to introduce any novelty into the ways of selecting holders for the grants. Are the young people to be made to sing for their supper, or entertain the board in some unacademic way?' suggested Miss Clovis, hoping to draw out some details.

But the Professor would not give anything away, and soon afterwards he left her, brooding among her collection of offprints which she was sorting out.

These single articles, detached from the learned journals in which they have appeared, have a peculiar significance in the academic world. Indeed, the giving and receiving of an offprint can often bring about a special relationship between the parties concerned in the transaction. The young author, bewildered and delighted at being presented with perhaps twenty-five copies of his article, may at first waste them on his aunts and girl friends, but when he is older and wiser he realizes that a more carefully planned distribution may bring him definite advantages. It was thought by many to be 'good policy' to send an offprint to Esther Clovis, though it was not always known exactly why this should be. In most cases she had done nothing more than express a polite interest in the author's work, but in others the gift was prompted by a sort of undefined fear, as a primitive tribesman might leave propitiatory gifts of food before a deity or ancestral shrine in the hope of receiving some benefit.

Most of the offprints bore inscriptions of some kind—'with best wishes', 'grateful thanks', 'cordial greetings', 'warmest regards'—every degree of respect and esteem short of the highest emotion was represented. Love itself had not been inspired; perhaps it was hardly likely that it would have been or that the author would have thought it fitting to express it even if it had. Some of the inscriptions were in foreign languages and one even had a photograph of its African author pinned to it.

Each article, and some were now yellowed with age, had its memories, and Esther turned the pages thoughtfully, sometimes half smiling at the persons and incidents they recalled. *Mit bestem Grüssen*, Hermann Obst . . . This offprint, in heavy German script, was one of the first she had ever received and its author was dead. Poor Dr Obst . . . once, many years ago, at some learned conference abroad, they had been walking together one evening after dinner and he had taken hold of her in a most suggestive way. Not to put too fine a point on it, he had made a pass at her. Miss Clovis smiled; she was older and more tolerant now, and wondered if she need have slapped his face with quite such outraged dignity. Why had she done it? Had she been thinking of her rights as a woman, the equal of man and not to be treated as his plaything, or had it been because she had not found Dr Obst particularly attractive? Would she have slapped Felix Mainwaring's face if it had been he who had made the pass? The question hung in the air, unanswered. Her German was rusty now, but she could make out the title—*Blutfreundschaft*, Blood brotherhood—and perhaps it was pathetically appropriate. She was back in the warm velvety darkness, hearing the soft splash of fountains and seeing dimly the broad sword-shaped leaves of some exotic plant with huge red flowers—'It is canna, I sink', in Dr Obst's gentle foreign voice—and then the 'incident'. Madrid, 1928 or 1929, she couldn't remember the exact year. Such a thing had not happened to her since and it would not again. She put the offprint back into its folder and turned to the next one.

Less than Angels, 1955

Reminders of Mortality

So often now Letty came upon reminders of her own mortality or, regarded less poetically, the different stages towards death. Less obvious than the obituaries in *The Times* and the *Telegraph* were what she thought of as 'upsetting' sights. This morning, for instance, a woman, slumped on a seat on the Underground platform while the rush hour crowds hurried past her, reminded her so much of a school contemporary that she forced herself to look back, to make quite sure that it was *not* Janet Belling. It appeared not to be, yet it could have been, and even if it wasn't it was still somebody, some woman driven to the point where she could find herself in this situation. Ought one to *do* anything? While Letty hesitated, a young woman, wearing a long dusty black skirt and shabby boots, bent over the slumped figure with a softly spoken enquiry At once the figure reared itself up and shouted in a loud, dangerously uncontrolled voice, 'Fuck off!' Then it couldn't be Janet Belling, Letty thought, her first feeling one of relief; Janet would never have used such an expression But fifty years ago nobody did—things were different now, so that was nothing to go by. In the meantime, the girl moved away with dignity. She had been braver than Letty.

Quartet in Autumn, 1977

ROBERTSON DAVIES
1913–1995

A Poor Show

Ellerman's funeral was a sad affair, which is not as silly as it sounds, because I have known funerals of well-loved or brave people which were buoyant. But this was a funeral without personal quality or grace. Funeral 'homes' are places that exist for convenience; to excuse families from straining small houses with a ceremony they cannot contain, and to excuse churches from burying people who had no inclination toward churches and did nothing whatever to sustain them. People are said to be drifting away from religion, but few of them drift so far that when they die there is not a call for some kind of religious ceremony. Is it because mankind is naturally religious, or simply because mankind is naturally cautious? For whatever reason, we don't like to part with a friend without some sort of show, and too often it is a poor show.

A parson of one of the sects which an advertising man would call a Smooth Blend read scriptural passages and prayers, and suggested that Ellerman had been a good fellow. Amen to that.

He had been a man who liked a touch of style, and he had been hospitable. This affair would have dismayed him; he would have wanted things done better. But how do you do better when nobody believes anything very firmly, and when the Canadian ineptitude for every kind of ceremony reduces the obsequies to mediocrity?

What would I have done if I had been in charge? I would have had Ellerman's war medals, which were numerous and honourable, on display, and I would have draped his doctor's red gown and his hood over the coffin. These, as reminders of what he had been, of where his strengths had lain. But—*Naked came I out of my mother's womb, and naked shall I return thither*—so at the grave I would have stripped away these evidences of a life, and on the bare coffin I would have thrown earth, instead of the rose-leaves modern funeral directors think symbolic of the words *Earth to earth, ashes to ashes, dust to dust*; there is something honest about hearing the clods rattling on the coffin lid. Ellerman had taught English Literature, and he was an expert on Browning; might not somebody have read some passages from *A Grammarian's Funeral*? But such thoughts are idle; you are asking for theatricalism, Darcourt; grief must be meagre, and mean, and cheap—not in money, of course, but in expression and invention. Death, be not proud; neither the grinning skull nor the panoply of ceremonial, nor the heart-catching splendour of faith is welcome at a modern, middle-class city funeral; grief must be huddled away, as the Lowest Common Denominator of permissible emotion.

The Rebel Angels, 1982

DYLAN THOMAS

1914–1953

A Cub Reporter

Saturday was my free afternoon. It was one o'clock and time to leave, but I stayed on; Mr Farr said nothing. I pretended to be busy scribbling words and caricaturing with no likeness Mr Solomon's toucan profile and the snub copy-boy who whistled out of tune behind the windows of the telephone box. I wrote my name, 'Reporters' Room, *Tawe News*, Tawe, South Wales, England, Europe, The Earth.' And a list of books I had not written: 'Land of My Fathers, a Study of the Welsh Character in all its aspects'; 'Eighteen, a Provincial Autobiography'; 'The Merciless Ladies, a Novel.' Still Mr Farr did not look up. I wrote 'Hamlet.' Surely Mr Farr, stubbornly transcribing his council notes, had not forgotten. I heard Mr Solomon mutter, leaning over his shoulder: 'To aitch with Alderman Daniels.' Half-past one. Ted was in a dream. I spent a long time putting on my overcoat, tied my Old Grammarian's scarf one way and then another.

'Some people are too lazy to take their half-days off,' said Mr Farr suddenly. 'Six o'clock in the "Lamps" back bar.' He did not turn round or stop writing.

'Going for a nice walk?' asked my mother.

'Yes, on the common. Don't keep tea waiting.'

I went to the Plaza. 'Press,' I said to the girl with the Tyrolean hat and skirt.

'There's been two reporters this week.'

'Special notice.'

She showed me to a seat. During the educational film, with the rude seeds hugging and sprouting in front of my eyes and plants like arms and legs, I thought of the bob women and the pansy sailors in the dives. There might be a quarrel with razors, and once Ted Williams found a lip outside the Mission to Seamen. It had a small moustache. The sinuous plants danced on the screen. If only Tawe were a larger sea-town, there would be curtained rooms underground with blue films. The potato's life came to an end. Then I entered an American college and danced with the president's daughter. The hero, called Lincoln, tall and dark with good teeth, I displaced quickly, and the girl spoke my name as she held his shadow, the singing college chorus in sailors' hats and bathing dresses called me big boy and king, Jack Oakie and I sped up the field, and on the shoulders of the crowd the president's daughter and I brought across the shifting-coloured curtain with a kiss that left me giddy and bright-eyed as I walked out of the cinema into the strong lamplight and the new rain.

A whole wet hour to waste in the crowds. I watched the queue outside the Empire and studied the posters of *Nuit de Paris*, and thought of the long legs and startling faces of the chorus girls I had seen walking arm in arm, earlier that week, up and down the streets in the winter sunshine, their mouths, I remembered remarking and treasuring for the first page of 'The Merciless Ladies' that was never begun, like crimson scars, their hair raven-black or silver; their scent and paint reminded me of the hot and chocolate-coloured East, their eyes were pools. Lola de Kenway, Babs Courcey, Ramona Day would be with me all my life. Until I died, of a wasting, painless disease, and spoke my prepared last words, they would always walk with me, recalling me to my dead youth in the vanished High

Street nights when the shop windows were blazing, and singing came out of the pubs, and sirens from the Hafod sat in the steaming chip shops with their handbags on their knees and their ear-rings rattling. I stopped to look at the window of Dirty Black's, the Fancy Man, but it was innocent; there were only itching and sneezing powders, stink bombs, rubber pens, and Charlie masks; all the novelties were inside, but I dared not go in for fear a woman should serve me, Mrs Dirty Black with a moustache and knowing eyes, or a thin, dog-faced girl I saw there once, who winked and smelt of seaweed. In the market I bought pink cachous. You never knew.

A Portrait of the Artist as a Young Dog, 1940

H. R. TREVOR-ROPER

1914–

A Royal Martyr

An aesthete need not be an intellectual. Charles I had perfect taste, but he was not interested in thought, and in literature as in life he sought not meaning but sensuous beauty and theatrical effect. In religion he sought not a rule of conduct but a graceful liturgy. Above all literature he preferred the drama and the masque. Oxford was his spiritual home; at Cambridge they thought too much, but in Oxford Laud had corrected that. Oxford was 'the only city of England that he could say was entirely to his devotion'. Thither he went in his prosperity to see plays and yet more plays, on new stages where the genius of Inigo Jones had contrived mechanical billows and shifting scenes; thither he went in adversity, as to a refuge, to be received 'with that joy and affection as Apollo should be by the Muses'. There he sadly forecast his fate from a prophecy in Virgil and at the news of the poet Cartwright's death, 'it is not to be forgot that His Sacred Majesty dropt a tear'.

To the end he retained his love of masques and pictures, poetry and plays. A prisoner at Hampton Court, he commissioned a portrait from the newly-found Dutch painter Lely; and immured 'in his doleful restraint in Carisbrooke Castle' he consoled himself with Tasso and Ariosto, George Herbert and Edmund Spenser and a book of plays. Driven from comedy to more melancholy thoughts, he turned to religion. In the days of Laud he had been somewhat inattentive, for the archbishop had made Anglicanism, like himself, practical and boring. Even his plays at Oxford had been made tedious by politics and morality. Now, with bishops abolished and church-lands for sale, it was too late to be practical. The busy, complacent, persecuting Church of Laud had gone, and religion had become consolatory and devotional, the gentle ministrations of Juxon and the consecrated phrases of the Book of Prayer. Charles's taste for religion, his taste for drama, and his refusal to compromise all combined at the end. He managed his last act with flawless taste; Inigo Jones could not have designed more perfectly that final *mise-en-scène.*

When mythology is sustained by art, history strives in vain. The regicides, when they cut off King Charles's head, sealed their own historical doom. If the King's faults were personal, his death logically ended them; they could not invalidate the claims of the monarchy. By destroying him the rebels had destroyed his liabilities, which were their own assets and sole justification, and had to fight against the myth which they had enabled him to create. They sought to liquidate the monarchy and the Church. They sold their lands and property, but they could not dispose of their intangible assets. They sold King Charles's pictures, and kings and cardinals and bankers sent their agents to so memorable a sale. They nearly sold all the English cathedrals for scrap. And they protested, ever more shrilly, the virtues of republics, the justice of the deed, and the clarity of their consciences. But it was no good; they convinced no one. 'They were an oligarchy, detested by all men,' was the reply of a real republican. And meanwhile Dr John Gauden, a prudent clergyman who contrived to write an Anglican best-seller while drawing the salary of a Presbyterian minister, was plying his indefatigable pen. Within a few days of the execution his *Eikon Basiliké, the Pourtraicture of His Sacred Majestie in His Solitudes and Sufferings* appeared as the genuine work of the royal martyr. Conquered and frustrated people hunger for a myth, and provided they have a symbolical figure and a dramatic immolation they are seldom fastidious about the literal truth or authenticity of the gospel. *Eikon Basiliké* supplied the need; it ran through edition after edition. The function of a myth is to compensate for the loss of reality; and when the royal Government and Church returned, shorn of their old powers, and the happy author was blackmailing his way from bishopric to bishopric, doubtless there were many who found in his skilful mythology balm for their final defeat.

'The Myth of Charles I', *Historical Essays*, 1957

RANDALL JARRELL
1914–1965

The Critic Among the Peaks

Critics can easily infect their readers (though usually less by precept than example) with the contempt or fretful tolerance which they feel for 'minor' works of art. If you work away, with sober, methodical, and industrious complication, at the masterpieces of a few great or fashionable writers, you after a while begin to identify yourself with these men; your manner takes on the authority your subject matter has unwittingly delegated to you, and when—returned from the peaks you have spent your life among, picking a reluctant way over those Parnassian or Castalian foothills along whose slopes herdboys sit playing combs—you are required to judge the competitions of such artists, you do so with a certain reluctance. Everybody has observed this in scholars, who feel that live authors, as such, are self-evidently inferior to dead ones; though a broadminded scholar will look like an X-ray machine at such a writer as Thomas Mann, and feel, relenting: 'He's as good as dead.' This sort of thing helps to make serious criticism as attractive as it is to critics: they live among the great, and some of the greatness comes off on them. No wonder poor poets become poor critics, and count themselves blest in their bargain; no wonder young intellectuals become critics before, and not after, they have failed as artists. And sometimes—who knows?—they might not have failed; besides, to have failed as an artist may be a respectable and valuable thing.

'The Age of Criticism', *Poetry and the Age*, 1953

BERNARD MALAMUD
1914–1986

A Jewbird

The window was open so the skinny bird flew in. Flappity-flap with its frazzled black wings. That's how it goes. It's open, you're in. Closed, you're out and that's your fate. The bird wearily flapped through the open kitchen window of Harry Cohen's top-floor apartment on First Avenue near the lower East River. On a rod on the wall hung an escaped canary cage, its door wide open, but this black-type long-beaked bird—its ruffled head and small dull eyes, crossed a little, making it look like a dissipated crow—landed if not smack on Cohen's thick lamb chop, at least on the table, close by. The frozen foods salesman was sitting at supper with his wife and young son on a hot August evening a year ago. Cohen, a heavy man with hairy chest and beefy shorts; Edie, in skinny yellow shorts and red halter; and their ten-year-old Morris (after her father)—Maurie, they called him, a nice kid though not overly bright—were all in the city after two weeks out, because Cohen's mother was dying. They had been enjoying Kingston, New York, but drove back when Mama got sick in her flat in the Bronx.

'Right on the table,' said Cohen, putting down his beer glass and swatting at the bird. 'Son of a bitch.'

'Harry, take care with your language,' Edie said, looking at Maurie, who watched every move.

The bird cawed hoarsely and with a flap of its bedraggled wings—feathers tufted this way and that—rose heavily to the top of the open kitchen door, where it perched staring down.

'Gevalt, a pogrom!'

'It's a talking bird,' said Edie in astonishment.

'In Jewish,' said Maurie.

'Wise guy,' muttered Cohen. He gnawed on his chop, then put down the bone. 'So if you can talk, say what's your business. What do you want here?'

'If you can't spare a lamb chop,' said the bird, 'I'll settle for a piece of herring with a crust of bread. You can't live on your nerve for ever.'

'This ain't a restaurant,' Cohen replied. 'All I'm asking is what brings you to this address?'

'The window was open,' the bird sighed; adding after a moment, 'I'm running. I'm flying but I'm also running.'

'From whom?' asked Edie with interest.

'Anti-Semeets.'

'Anti-Semites?' they all said.

'That's from whom.'

'What kind of anti-Semites bother a bird?' Edie asked.

'Any kind,' said the bird, 'also including eagles, vultures, and hawks. And once in a while some crows will take your eyes out.'

'But aren't you a crow?'

'Me? I'm a Jewbird.'

'The Jewbird', *Idiots First*, 1964

RALPH ELLISON
1914–1994

A Deathbed Injunction

It goes a long way back, some twenty years. All my life I had been looking for something, and everywhere I turned someone tried to tell me what it was. I accepted their answers too, though they were often in contradiction and even self-contradictory. I was naïve. I was looking for myself and asking everyone except myself questions which I, and only I, could answer. It took me a long time and much painful boomeranging of my expectations to achieve a realization everyone else appears to have been born with: That I am nobody but myself. But first I had to discover that I am an invisible man!

And yet I am no freak of nature, nor of history. I was in the cards, other things having been equal (or unequal) eighty-five years ago. I am not ashamed of my grandparents for having been slaves. I am only ashamed of myself for having at one time been ashamed. About eighty-five years ago they were told that they were free, united with others of our country in everything pertaining to the common good, and, in everything social, separate like the fingers of the hand. And they believed it. They exulted in it. They stayed in their place, worked hard, and brought up my father to do the same. But my grandfather is the one. He was an odd old guy, my grandfather, and I am told I take after him. It was he who caused the trouble. On his death-bed he called my father to him and said, 'Son, after I'm gone I want you to keep up the good fight. I never told you, but our life is a war and I have been a traitor all my born days, a spy in the enemy's country ever since I give up my gun back in the Reconstruction. Live with your head in the lion's mouth. I want you to overcome 'em with yeses, undermine 'em with grins, agree 'em to death and destruction, let 'em swoller you till they vomit or bust wide open.' They thought the old man had gone out of his mind. He had been the meekest of men. The younger children were rushed from the room, the shades drawn and the flame of the lamp turned so low that it sputtered on the wick like the old man's breathing. 'Learn it to the younguns,' he whispered fiercely; then he died.

But my folks were more alarmed over his last words than over his dying. It was as though he had not died at all, his words caused so much anxiety. I was warned emphatically to forget what he had said and, indeed, this is the first time it has been mentioned outside the family circle. It had a tremendous effect upon me, however, I could never be sure of what he meant. Grandfather had been a quiet old man who never made any trouble, yet on his deathbed he had called himself a traitor and a spy, and he had spoken of his meekness as a dangerous activity. It became a constant puzzle which lay unanswered in the back of my mind. And whenever things went well for me I remembered my grandfather and felt guilty and uncomfortable. It was as though I was carrying out his advice in spite of myself. And to make it worse, everyone loved me for it: I was praised by the most lily-white men of the town. I was considered an example of desirable conduct—just as my grandfather had been. And what puzzled me was that the old man had defined it as *treachery*. When I was praised for my conduct I felt a guilt that in some way I was doing something that was really against the wishes of the white folks, that if they had understood they would have desired me to act just the opposite, that I should have been sulky and mean, and that that really would have been what they wanted, even though they were fooled and thought they wanted me to act as I did. It made me afraid that some day they would look upon me as a traitor and I would be lost. Still I was more afraid to act any other way because they didn't like that at all. The old man's words were like a curse.

Invisible Man, 1952

PETER MEDAWAR
1915–1987

Improving upon Nature

It is a profound truth—realized in the nineteenth century by only a handful of astute biologists and by philosophers hardly at all (indeed, most of those who held any views on the matter held a contrary opinion)—a profound truth that Nature does *not* know best; that genetical evolution, if we choose to look at it liverishly instead of with fatuous good humour, is a story of waste, makeshift, compromise, and blunder . . .

We can, then, improve upon nature; but the possibility of our doing so depends, very obviously, upon our continuing to explore into nature and to enlarge our knowledge and understanding of what is going on. If I were to argue the scientists' case, the case that exploration is a wise and sensible thing to do, I should try to convince you of it by particular reasoning and particular examples, each one of which could be discussed and weighed up; some, perhaps, to be found faulty. I should not say: Man is driven onwards by an exploratory instinct, and can only fulfil himself and his destiny by the ceaseless quest for Truth. As a matter of fact, animals do have what might be loosely called an inquisitiveness, an exploratory instinct; but even if it were highly developed and extremely powerful, it would still not be binding upon us. We should not be *driven* to explore.

Contrariwise, if someone were to plead the virtues of an intellectually pastoral existence, not merely quiet but acquiescent, and with no more than a pensive regret for not understanding what could have been understood; then I believe I could listen to his arguments and, if they were good ones, might even be convinced. But if he were to say that this course of action or inaction was the life that was authorized by Nature; that this was the life Nature provided for and intended us to lead; then I should tell him that he had no proper conception of Nature. People who brandish naturalistic principles at us are usually up to mischief. Think only of what we have suffered from a belief in the existence and overriding authority of a fighting instinct; from the doctrines of racial superiority and the metaphysics of blood and soil; from the belief that warfare between men or classes of men or nations represents a fulfilment of historical laws. These are all excuses of one kind or another, and pretty thin excuses. The inference we can draw from an analytical study of the differences between ourselves and other animals is surely this: that the bells which toll for mankind are—most of them, anyway—like the bells on Alpine cattle; they are attached to our own necks, and it must be *our* fault if they do not make a cheerful and harmonious sound.

The Future of Man, 1960

SAUL BELLOW
1915–

Mintouchian

I see before me next a fellow named Mintouchian, who is an Armenian, of course. We are sitting together in a Turkish bath having a conversation, except that Mintouchian is doing most of the talking, explaining various facts of existence to me, by allegory mostly. The time is a week before Stella and I were married and I shipped out.

This Mintouchian was a monument of a person, with his head very abrupt at the back, as Armenian heads tend sometimes to be, but lionlike in front, with red cheekbones. He had legs on him like that statue of Clemenceau on the Champs Elysées where Clemenceau is striding against a wind and is thinking of bread and war, and the misery and grandeur, going on with last strength in his longjohns and gaiters.

Sitting together in this little white-tile room, Mintouchian and I were quite pals in spite of differences of age and income—Mintouchian was supposed to be loaded. He looked overpowering, and he had tones in his voice like the dumping of coal. This must have done him good in court, as he was a lawyer. He was a friend of a friend of Stella whose name was Agnes Kuttner. Agnes lived in big style in an apartment off Fifth Avenue near one of the Latin-American embassies, furnished in Empire, with tremendous mirrors and chandeliers, Chinese screens, alabaster birds of night, thick drapes, and all luxuries like that. She went around to auction rooms and bought up treasures of the Romanoffs and Hapsburgs; she herself came from Vienna. Mintouchian had set up a trust fund for her, so she wasn't at all in the business of antiques, and her apartment was his home away from home, as hotels sometimes falsely speak of themselves. His other home was also in New York, but his wife was an invalid. Every evening he went and had dinner with her, served by her nurse in the bedroom. But before this he had visited Agnes. Usually his chauffeur was driving him across Central Park at 7:45 for the meal with his wife.

The reason why I was with him in the bath this particular afternoon was that Stella had gone shopping with Agnes for the wedding. These two,

Agnes and Mintouchian, were the only people we ever saw when I got liberty from the base on weekends. He enjoyed taking us to Toots Shor's or the Diamond Horseshoe, I think, and other scarlet-and-gold-door places. The one time I tried to pick up the tab he pushed me away. I would have had to borrow from Stella to pay it. But Mintouchian was very open-handed, a grand good-time Charlie. Almost always in evening clothes of Rembrandt blackness, with his red-edged eyes and craggy head and ears, and as if smelling the sands and savannahs with his flat nose, but a smile of spin-on-the-music, spend-the-money; his teeth were long, and he was ever so slightly feline-whiskered to go with his corrupt, intelligent wrinkles and expanding mouth. Amid the ladies he didn't let go with this smile, but now when he sat like a village headman of the south of Asia in his carnival-colors towel, he did; and while conversing more man to man he was pinching himself under the eyes to make the bags disappear—his yellow toenails were lacquered with clear polish, except the small toes grievously buried in the lifeworn foot with its skinful of vessels. I wondered if he was really one of those hot-to-the-touch and perilous guys like Zaharoff or Juan March, or the Swedish Match King or Jake the Barber or Three-Finger Brown. Stella said he had money he hadn't even folded yet. He certainly was laying out plenty for Agnes, whom he had met in Cuba; he paid her husband a remittance to stay there. However, even though I found out that Mintouchian wasn't strictly honest, he was never a rogue's-gallery character. To get his legal education, as a matter of fact, he had played the organ in silent movies. But he was a crack lawyer now and had global business interests, and, moreover, he was a lettered person and reader. It was one of his curiosities to figure out historical happenings like the building of the Berlin-Baghdad Railway or the Battle of Tannenberg, and he furthermore knew a lot about the lives of Martyrs. He was another of those persons who persistently arise before me with life counsels and illumination throughout my entire earthly pilgrimage.

The Adventures of Augie March, 1953

The Octopus

I looked in at an octopus, and the creature seemed also to look at me and press its soft head to the glass, flat, the flesh becoming pale and granular—blanched, speckled. The eyes spoke to me coldly. But even more speaking, even more cold, was the soft head with its speckles, a cosmic coldness in which I felt I was dying. The tentacles throbbed and motioned through the glass, the bubbles sped upward, and I thought, 'This is my last day. Death is giving me notice.'

Henderson the Rain King, 1959

A Moment of Happiness

In the mild end of the afternoon, later, at the waterside in Woods Hole, waiting for the ferry, he looked through the green darkness at the net of bright reflections on the bottom. He loved to think about the power of the sun, about light, about the ocean. The purity of the air moved him. There was no stain in the water, where schools of minnows swam. Herzog sighed and said to himself, 'Praise God—praise God.' His breathing had become freer. His heart was greatly stirred by the open horizon; the deep colors; the faint iodine pungency of the Atlantic rising from weeds and mollusks; the white, fine, heavy sand; but principally by the green transparency as he looked down to the stony bottom webbed with golden lines. Never still. If his soul could cast a reflection so brilliant, and so intensely sweet, he might beg God to make such use of him. But that would be too simple. But that would be too childish. The actual sphere is not clear like this, but turbulent, angry. A vast human action is going on. Death watches. So if you have some happiness, conceal it. And when your heart is full, keep your mouth shut also.

Herzog, 1964

Acting Their Parts

What one sees on Broadway while bound for the bus. All human types reproduced, the barbarian, redskin, or Fiji, the dandy, the buffalo hunter, the desperado, the queer, the sexual fantasist, the squaw; bluestocking, princess, poet, painter, prospector, troubadour, guerrilla, Che Guevara, the new Thomas à Becket. Not imitated are the businessman, the soldier, the priest, and the square. The standard is aesthetic. As Mr Sammler saw the thing, human beings, when they have room, when they have liberty and are supplied also with ideas, mythologize themselves. They legendize. They expand by imagination and try to rise above the limitations of the ordinary forms of common life. And what is 'common' about 'the common life'? What if some genius were to do with 'common life' what Einstein did with 'matter'? Finding its energetics, uncovering its radiance. But at the present level of crude vision, agitated spirits fled from the oppressiveness of 'the common life,' separating themselves from the rest of their species, from the life of their species, hoping perhaps to get away (in some peculiar sense) from the death of their species. To perform higher actions, to serve the imagination with special distinction, it seems essential to be histrionic. This, too, is a brand of madness. Madness has always been a favorite choice of the civilized man who prepares himself for a noble achievement. It is often the simplest state of availability to ideals. Most of us are satisfied with that: signifying by a kind of madness devotion to, availability for, higher purposes. Higher purposes do not necessarily appear.

If we are about to conclude our earth business—or at least the first great phase of it—we had better sum these things up. But briefly. As briefly as possible.

Short views, for God's sake!

Then: a crazy species? Yes, perhaps. Though madness is also a masquerade, the project of a deeper reason, a result of the despair we feel before infinities and eternities. Madness is a diagnosis or verdict of some of our greatest doctors and geniuses, and of their man-disappointed minds. Oh, man stunned by the rebound of man's powers. And what to do? In the matter of histrionics, see, for instance, what that furious world-boiler Marx had done, insisting that revolutions were made in historical costume, the Cromwellians as Old Testament prophets, the French in 1789 dressed in Roman outfits. But the proletariat, he said, he declared, he affirmed, would make the first non-imitative revolution. It would not need the drug of historical recollection. From sheer ignorance, knowing no models, it would simply do the thing pure. He was as giddy as the rest about originality. And only the working class was original. Thus history would get away from mere poetry. Then the life of humankind would clear itself of copying. It would be free from Art. Oh, no. No, no, not so, thought Sammler. Instead, Art increased, and a sort of chaos. More possibility, more actors, apes, copycats, more invention, more fiction, illusion, more fantasy, more despair. Life looting Art of its wealth, destroying Art as well by its desire to become the thing itself. Pressing itself into pictures. Reality forcing itself into all these shapes. Just look (Sammler looked) at this imitative anarchy of the streets—these Chinese revolutionary tunics, these babes in unisex toyland, these surrealist warchiefs, Western stagecoach drivers—Ph.D.s in philosophy, some of them (Sammler had met such, talked matters over with them). They sought originality. They were obviously derivative. And of what—of Paiutes, of Fidel Castro? No, of Hollywood extras. Acting mythic. Casting themselves into chaos, hoping to adhere to higher consciousness, to be washed up on the shores of truth. Better, thought Sammler, to accept the inevitability of imitation and then to imitate good things. The ancients had this right. Greatness without models? Inconceivable. One could not be the thing itself—Reality. One must be satisfied with the symbols. Make it the object of imitation to reach and release the high qualities. Make peace therefore with intermediacy and representation. But choose higher representations. Otherwise the individual must be the failure he now sees and knows himself to be. Mr Sammler, sorry for all, and sore at heart.

Mr Sammler's Planet, 1970

PATRICK LEIGH FERMOR

1915–

Through the German Winter

[The journey described took place in 1933–4]

Of the village in the snowy dark outside, nothing has stuck. But unlike the three overnight halts that follow—Riedering, Söllhuben and Röttau, that is to say—it is at least marked on maps.

Each of these little unmarked hamlets seems smaller in retrospect than the other two, and remoter, and more deeply embedded in hills and snow and dialect. They have left an impression of women scattering grain in their yards to a rush of poultry, and of hooded children returning from school with hairy satchels and muffled ears: homing goblins, slapping along lanes on skis as short and wide as barrel-staves and propelling themselves with sticks of unringed hazel. When we passed each other, they would squeak '*Grüss Gott*!' in a polite shrill chorus. One or two were half gagged by cheekfuls bitten from long slices of black bread and butter.

All was frozen. There was a particular delight in treading across the hard puddles. The grey discs and pods of ice creaked under hobnails and clogs with a mysterious sigh of captive air: then they split into stars and whitened as the spiders-web fissures expanded. Outside the villages the telegraph wire was a single cable of flakes interrupted by birds alighting and I would follow the path below and break through the new and sparkling crust to sink in powdery depths. I travelled on footpaths and over stiles and across fields and along country roads that ran through dark woods and out again into the white ploughland and pasture. The valleys were dotted with villages that huddled round the shingle roofs of churches, and all the belfries tapered and then swelled again into black ribbed cupolas. These onion-domes had a fleetingly Russian look. Otherwise, especially when the bare hardwoods were replaced by conifers, the décor belonged to Grimms' Fairy Tales. 'Once upon a time, on the edge of a dark forest, there lived an old woodman, with a single beautiful daughter', it was that sort of a region. Cottages that looked as innocent as cuckoo-clocks turned into witches' ginger-bread after dark. Deep and crusted loads of snow weighed the conifer-branches to the ground. When I touched them with the tip of my new walking stick, up they sprang in sparkling explosions. Crows, rooks and magpies were the only birds about and the arrows of their footprints were sometimes crossed by the deeper slots of hares' pads. Now and again I came on a hare, seated alone in a field and looking enormous; hindered by the snow it would lope awkwardly away to cover, for the snow slowed everything up, especially when the rails and the posts beside the path were buried. The only people I saw outside the villages were woodcutters. They were indicated, long before they appeared, by the wide twin grooves of their sledges, with cart-horses' crescent-shaped tracks stamped deep between. Then they would come into view on a clearing or the edge of a distant spinney and the sound of axes and the rasp of two-handed saws would reach my ears a second after my eye had caught the vertical fall or the horizontal slide of the blades. If, by the time I reached them, a tall tree was about to come down, I found it impossible to move on. The sledge-horses, with icicled fetlocks and muzzles deep in their nosebags, were rugged up in sacking and I stamped to keep warm as I watched. Armed with beetles, rustic bruisers at work in a ring of chips and sawdust and trodden snow banged the wedges home. They were rough and friendly men, and one of them, on the pretext of a strange presence and with a collusive wink, was sure to pull out a bottle of schnapps. Swigs, followed by gasps of fiery bliss, sent prongs of vapour into the frosty air. I took a turn with the saw once or twice, clumsily till I got the hang of it, unable to tear myself away till at last the tree came crashing down.

A Time of Gifts, 1977

CARSON McCULLERS
1917–1967

A Girl Apart

It was the year when Frankie thought about the world. And she did not see it as a round school globe, with the countries neat and different-colored. She thought of the world as huge and cracked and loose and turning a thousand miles an hour. The geography book at school was out of date; the countries of the world had changed. Frankie read the war news in the paper, but there were so many foreign places, and the war was happening so fast, that sometimes she did not understand. It was the summer when Patton was chasing the Germans across France. And they were fighting, too, in Russia and Saipan. She saw the battles, and the soldiers. But there were too many different battles, and she could not see in her mind the millions and millions of soldiers all at once. She saw one Russian soldier, dark and frozen with a frozen gun, in Russian snow. The single Japs with slanted eyes on a jungle island gliding among green vines. Europe and the people hung in trees and the battleships on the blue oceans. Four-motor planes and burning cities and a soldier in a steel war helmet, laughing. Sometimes these pictures of the war, the world, whirled in her mind and she was dizzy. A long time ago she had predicted that it would take two months to win the whole war, but now she did not know. She wanted to be a boy and go to the war as a Marine. She thought about flying aeroplanes and winning gold medals for bravery. But she could not join the war, and this made her sometimes feel restless and blue. She decided to donate blood to the Red Cross: she wanted to donate a quart a week and her blood would be in the veins of Australians and Fighting French and Chinese, all over the whole world, and it would be as though she were close kin to all of these people. She could hear the army doctors saying that the blood of Frankie Addams was the reddest and the strongest blood that they had ever known. And she could picture ahead, in the years after the war, meeting the soldiers who had her blood, and they would say that they owed their life to her; and they would not call her Frankie—they would call her Addams. But this plan for donating her blood to the war did not come true. The Red Cross would not take her blood. She was too young. Frankie felt mad with the Red Cross, and left out of everything. The war and the world were too fast and big and strange. To think about the world for very long made her afraid. She was not afraid of Germans or bombs or Japanese. She was afraid because in the war they would not include her, and because the world seemed somehow separate from herself.

So she knew she ought to leave the town and go to some place far away. For the late spring, that year, was lazy and too sweet. The long afternoons flowered and lasted and the green sweetness sickened her. The town began to hurt Frankie. Sad and terrible happenings had never made Frankie cry, but this season many things made Frankie suddenly wish to cry. Very early in the morning she would sometimes go out into the yard and stand for a long time looking at the sunrise sky. And it was as though a question came into her heart, and the sky did not answer. Things she had never noticed much before began to hurt her: home lights watched from the evening sidewalks, an unknown voice from an alley. She would stare at the lights and listen to the voice, and something inside her stiffened and waited. But the lights would darken, the voice fall silent, and though she waited, that was all. She was afraid of these things that made her suddenly wonder who she was, and what she was going to be in the world, and why she was standing at that minute, seeing a light, or listening, or staring up into the sky: alone. She was afraid, and there was a queer tightness in her chest.

The Member of the Wedding, 1946

ANTHONY BURGESS

1917–1993

A Poetry Prize

While Enderby was breakfasting off reheated hare stew with pickled walnuts and stepmother's tea, the postman came with a fateful letter. The envelope was thick, rich, creamy; richly black the typed address, as though a new ribbon had been put in just for that holy name. The note-paper was embossed with the arms of a famous firm of chain booksellers. The letter congratulated Enderby on his last year's volume—*Revolutionary Sonnets*—and was overjoyed to announce that he had been awarded the firm's annual Poetry Prize of a gold medal and fifty guineas. Enderby was cordially invited to a special luncheon to be held in the banqueting-room of an intimidating London hotel, there to receive his prizes amid the plaudits of the literary world. Enderby let his hare stew go cold. The third Tuesday in January. Please reply. He was dazed. And, again, congratulations. London. The very name evoked the same responses as *lung cancer*, *overdrawn*, *stepmother* . . .

*

He decided, wiping the dishes, that he would, after all, go to London. After all, it wasn't very far—only an hour by electric train—and there would be no need to spend the night in a hotel. It was an honour really, he supposed. He would have to borrow a suit from somebody. Arry, he was sure, had one. They were much of a size.

Enderby, sighing, went to the bathroom to start work. He gazed doubtfully at the bathtub, which was full of notes, drafts, fair copies not yet filed for their eventual volume, books, ink-bottles, cigarette-packets, the remains of odd snacks taken while writing. There were also a few mice that lived beneath the detritus, encouraged in their busy scavenging by Enderby. Occasionally one would surface and perch on the bath's edge to watch the poet watching the ceiling, pen in hand. With him they were neither cowering nor timorous (he had forgotten the meaning of 'sleekit'). Enderby recognized that the coming occasion called for a bath. Lustration before the sacramental meal. He had once read in some women's magazine a grim apothegm he had never forgotten: 'Bath twice a day to be really clean, once a day to be passably clean, once a week to avoid being a public menace.' On the other hand, Frederick the Great had never bathed in his life; his corpse had been a rich mahogany colour. Enderby's view of bathing was neither obsessive nor insouciant. ('Sans Souci', Frederick's palace, was it not?) He was an empiricist in such matters. Though he recognized that a bath would, in a week or two, seem necessary, he recoiled from the prospect of preparing the bathtub and evicting the mice. He would compromise. He would wash very nearly all over in the basin. More, he would shave with exceptional care and trim his hair with nail-scissors.

Gloomily, Enderby reflected that most modern poets were not merely sufficiently clean but positively natty. T. S. Eliot, with his Lloyd's Bank nonsense, had started all that, a real treason of clerks. Before him, Enderby liked to believe, cleanliness and neatness had been only for writers of journalistic ballades and triolets. Still, he would show them when he went for his gold medal; he would beat them at their own game. Enderby sighed again as, with bare legs, he took his poetic seat. His first job was to compose a letter of gratitude and acceptance. Prose was not his *métier*.

After several pompous drafts which he crumpled into the waste-basket on which he sat, Enderby dashed off a letter in *In Memoriam* quatrains, disguised as prose. 'The gratitude for this award, though sent in all humility, should not, however, come from me, but from my Muse, and from the Lord . . .' He paused as a bizarre analogue swam up from memory. In a London restaurant during the days of fierce post-war food shortage he had ordered rabbit pie. The pie, when it had arrived, had contained nothing but breast of chicken. A mystery never to be solved. He shrugged it away and went on disguising the chicken-breast of verse as rabbit-prose. A mouse, forepaws retracted like those of a kangaroo, came up to watch.

Inside Mr Enderby, 1966

RICHARD COBB
1917–1996

Memories of the Métro

One could never associate the *métro* with threat, not then anyhow, it represented the map, just below the surface, sometimes high above the rooftops, of journeys regularly undertaken, in the knowledge of a welcome at the far end, then of the return, among a few sleepy passengers, to the comfort and safety of bed. As one emerged below the aggressive and posturing statue of Danton—*de l'audace, encore de l'audace*, and all that—it was indeed the sense of returning home, to base. Danton was like a familiar lighthouse, a symbol of peace, the promise of sleep. How often would I emerge there, just before the *métro* closed for the night, in the late 1940s and the early 1950s, having travelled back from Mme Thomas's, changing at CONCORDE! There would be other regular destinations, on the outward journey: *PORTE DE CHARENTON*, *PORTE DE VERSAILLES*, *BALARD*, *PORTE D'ORLEANS*, indeed most places save *PIGALLE* or *BLANCHE*. The poesy of the *métro* draws heavily both on its familiarity and its banality, its *ordinariness*: it is hard to take *FILLES DU CALVAIRE* seriously, *SEVRES-BABYLONE* poses no threat, *SOLFERINO*, *CHAMBRE DES DEPUTES*, as seen from below ground, are entirely unprestigious. *LOURMEL*, despite its vague promise of aristocratic distinction, is seen only in passing; it is somewhere I have never got out at. *MALESHERBES*, on the other hand, offers the prospect of comfortable wealth, slow-moving, roomy lifts and carpeted stairs, of medical reassurance (especially during my hepatic period of the early 1950s when I used to consult a liver specialist there: he was much more interested in Marat, a doctor of sorts, than in my liver) and of very good china tea with a retired cavalry General, who was also a historian and an antique-dealer, and who lived in a flat crammed with medieval ecclesiastical statues, reredoses and pictures, rue Jacques-Bingen, opposite the Soviet Trade Mission.

STRASBOURG-SAINT-DENIS represents the promise of the end of the month Friday girls, indeed, of one particular girl, nicknamed *Gaby la Landaise* (like Monsieur Alexandre, she seems to have gone through life, in her case, brief, without the benefit of a surname), the object of my evening visits on the last Friday of the month, when I had been paid: *Hôtel du Centre*, on the corner of the Porte Saint-Denis and the rue d'Aboukir. I liked Gaby, a good-looking girl with high cheek-bones and a delicate bone structure, well-spoken, intelligent, and amusing; and I was always prepared to wait till she was free, *l'affaire d'un instant*, the *patronne* would assure me. I did not have to tell whom I was waiting for. I called on Gaby I suppose something like twelve or thirteen Fridays, anyhow, just over a year. Then, one Friday, I asked the *patronne* if I would have long to wait; she said that I would indeed. Gaby was no longer there, nor anywhere. The week before, she had shot herself, placing a revolver in her mouth, in one of the sparse bedrooms on the fifth floor, No 78. There had been trouble with her man. She seemed genuinely upset, commenting that Gaby had been a well-educated girl, more than her *certificat d'études primaires*, perhaps even a *bachelière*, that she came from a very good home, and that her parents had a large shop—a grocery—in Dax. Gaby was only twenty-seven when she shot herself. Over the last forty years, she has often been in my thoughts, and I can still recall the unusual, rather striking lines of her face. She was amusing and observant and always seemed good-humoured. I think I most liked talking to her, we would start up much at the point at which we had left off, a month before. It seemed such a brutally short life. That was the end of *STRASBOURG-SAINT-DENIS* as far as my monthly Friday visits were concerned. After that, I moved further west, to *RUE-MONMARTRE* or *RICHELIEU-DROUOT* (*VAVIN* or the appropriately named GAITE might offer similar services, there was something to be said for varying the Banks).

So, on the whole, the *carte du métro* represents, or used to represent, an ever-reliable map of reassurance, familiarity, and often, as in the case of GAITE, appropriateness: GLACIERE really is what it says it is, NATIONALE, as one would expect of that adjective, is scruffy, run-down and dreary, even if the old, sculpted, filigreed carriages of the *Nord-Sud* (so much in that name, too, a monument to Paris—1900) have been replaced, and ORLEANS-CLIGNANCOURT has become *inodore*, and the little *Dubo, Dubon, Dubonnet* man, in his bowler, raising his glass and emptying it *d'un seul trait*, has long since disappeared from the tunnels. How suitable that the evocation of the *métro* should have played such a large part in the literature of exile, during the Occupation years, in the pages of the London monthly, *La France Libre*! How appropriate, too, that, in his recollections of a very deprived childhood in the XIIIme *arrondissement*, the populist writer and *argotier*, Alphonse Boudard, should have associated the *métro* with his generally unsuccessful pursuit, as a pimply sixteen-year-old, of girls encountered in the favourable conditions, below ground, of the evening rush-hour: ('She got out at PLACE D'ITALIE, unfortunately she took the corridor DIRECTION ETOILE, and I was heading NATION'), the surest enthronement in individual memory.

Something to Hold Onto, 1988

MURIEL SPARK
1918–

A Daughter Burned to Death

The tape-recording had been erased for economy reasons, so that the tape could be used again. That is how things were in 1945. Nicholas was angry in excess of the occasion. He had wanted to play back Joanna's voice to her father who had come up after her funeral to fill in forms as to the effects of the dead. Nicholas had written to him, partly with an urge to impart his last impressions of Joanna, partly from curiosity, partly, too, from a desire to stage a dramatic play-back of Joanna doing *The Wreck of the Deutschland.* He had mentioned the tape-recording in his letter.

But it was gone. It must have been wiped out by someone at his office.

Thou hast bound bones and veins in me, fastened me flesh,
And after it almost unmade, what with dread,
Thy doing: and dost thou touch me afresh?

Nicholas said to the rector, 'It's infuriating. She was at her best in *The Wreck of the Deutschland.* I'm terribly sorry.'

Joanna's father sat, pink-faced and white-haired. He said, 'Oh, please don't worry.'

'I wish you could have heard it.'

As if to console Nicholas in his loss, the rector murmured with a nostalgic smile:

It was the schooner Hesperus
That sailed the wintry sea,

'No, no, the *Deutschland. The Wreck of the Deutschland.*'

'Oh, the *Deutschland.*' With a gesture characteristic of the English aquiline nose, his seemed to smell the air for enlightenment.

Nicholas was moved by this to a last effort to regain the lost recording. It was a Sunday, but he managed to get one of his colleagues on the telephone at home.

'Do you happen to know if anyone removed a tape from that box I borrowed from the office? Like a fool I left it in my room at the office. Someone's removed an important tape. Something private.'

'No, I don't think . . . just a minute . . . yes, in fact, they've wiped out the stuff. It was poetry. Sorry, but the economy regulations, you know . . . What do you think of the news? Takes your breath away, doesn't it?'

Nicholas said to Joanna's father, 'Yes, it really has been wiped out.'

'Never mind. I remember Joanna as she was in the rectory. Joanna was a great help in the parish. Her coming to London was a mistake, poor girl.'

Nicholas refilled the man's glass with whisky and started to add water. The clergyman signed irritably with his hand to convey the moment when the drink was to his taste. He had the mannerisms of a widower of long years, or of one unaccustomed to being in the company of critical women. Nicholas perceived that the man had never seen the reality of his daughter. Nicholas was consoled for the blighting of his show; the man might not have recognised Joanna in the *Deutschland.*

The frown of his face
Before me, the hurtle of hell
Behind, where, where was a, where was a place?

'I dislike London. I never come up unless I've got to,' the clergyman said, 'for convocation or something like that. If only Joanna could have settled down at the rectory . . . She was restless, poor girl.' He gulped his whisky like a gargle, tossing back his head.

Nicholas said, 'She was reciting some sort of office just before she went down. The other girls were with her, they were listening in a way. Some psalms.'

'Really? No one else has mentioned it.' The old man looked embarrassed.

He swirled his drink and swallowed it down, as if Nicholas might be going on to tell him that his daughter had gone over to Rome at the last, or somehow died in bad taste.

Nicholas said violently, 'Joanna had religious strength.'

'I know that, my boy,' said the father, surprisingly.

'She had a sense of Hell. She told a friend of hers that she was afraid of Hell.'

'Really? I didn't know that. I've never heard her speak morbidly. It must have been the influence of London. I never come here, myself, unless I've got to. I had a curacy once, in Balham, in my young days. But since then I've had country parishes. I prefer country parishes. One finds better, more devout, and indeed in some cases, quite holy souls in the country parishes.'

Nicholas was reminded of an American acquaintance of his, a psychoanalyst who had written to say he intended to practise in England after the war, 'away from all these neurotics and this hustling scene of anxiety.'

'Christianity is all in the country parishes these days,' said this shepherd of the best prime mutton. He put down his glass as if to seal his decision on the matter, his grief for the loss of Joanna turning back, at every sequence, on her departure from the rectory.

He said, 'I must go and see the spot where she died.'

Nicholas had already promised to take him to the demolished house in Kensington Road. The father had reminded Nicholas of this several times as if afraid he might inattentively leave London with his duty unfulfilled.

'I'll walk along with you.'

'Well, if it's not out of your way I'll be much obliged. What do you make of this new bomb? Do you think it's only propaganda stuff?'

'I don't know, sir,' said Nicholas.

'It leaves one breathless with horror. They'll have to make an armistice if it's true.' He looked around him as they walked towards Kensington. 'These bomb-sites look tragic. I never come up if I can help it, you know.'

Nicholas said, presently, 'Have you seen any of the girls who were trapped in the house with Joanna, or any of the other members of the club?'

The rector said, 'Yes, quite a few. Lady Julia was kind enough to have a few to tea to meet me yesterday afternoon. Of course, those poor girls have been through an ordeal, even the on-lookers among them. Lady Julia suggested we didn't discuss the actual incident. You know, I think that was wise.'

'Yes. Do you recall the girls' names at all?'

'There was Lady Julia's niece, Dorothy, and a Miss Baberton who escaped, I believe, through a window. Several others.'

'A Miss Redwood? Selina Redwood?'

'Well, you know, I'm rather bad at names.'

'A very tall, very slender girl, very beautiful. I want to find her. Dark hair.'

'They were all charming, my dear boy. All young people are charming. Joanna was, to me, the most charming of all, but there I'm partial.'

'She was charming,' said Nicholas, and held his peace.

The Girls of Slender Means, 1963

CHRISTOPHER BURNEY
1919–1980

At Buchenwald

The sub-executive power in the camp lay in the hands of the Lagerschutz, or Camp Police. Until 1943 all the police work in the camp had been done by the SS themselves, but with the disciplinary stabilisation which followed the access to power of the Communists, they authorised the formation of a force composed entirely of prisoners. This Lagerschutz consisted originally only of German Communists, was later supplemented by a few Luxemburgers, and was finally increased to a strength of about 120 by the addition of prisoners of nearly all nationalities except British and Spanish, and almost all of whom were elected at the proposal of their respective Communist committees. They were almost without exception men of the roughest type, and little good can be said of them.

The job of the Lagerschutz was to keep two kinds of discipline: the one the discipline of the SS and the other that of the governing body. In many things the second included the first.

In the late autumn of 1944 a transport of Jews was returned from the synthetic petrol works at Zeitz as being no longer capable of working. Many died in Buchenwald, but it was decided to send the remainder to Auschwitz for gassing. They were all in barracks in the Little Camp, and on the morning of their departure a squad of Lagerschutz was detailed to divide them into groups and march them to the station. Although nothing official had been given out about their destination, the wretches knew, as the rest of the camp knew, that it was beyond all doubt, and one would have expected that their fellow-prisoners would have taken the opportunity afforded to them by the SS to make at least their departure as easy as possible. The contrary was the case.

Imagine a thousand walking skeletons, out of their wits, driven by starvation, brutality and overwork beyond the memory of things human, beyond all reaction save only the recognition of the imminence of death, and so dazed by this that they could neither act of their own accord nor understand an order. Their despair was more vocal than dumb, and the morning was filled with a low moaning, interrupted from time to time by a scream of frenzy, as they set about gathering up their few filthy belongings.

Then the Lagerschutz came. They were led by their chief, a little cocky man, who swaggered like a sparrow sergeant and shouted like an angry frog and who loved no man but hated Englishmen the most. His men were armed with short rubber truncheons to make them feel brave among this crippled wreckage, and when they went in to the Little Camp we could hear the moaning rise as they sought to hasten the wandering Jews on to their last parade.

There were a few prisoners standing along the road to watch them go. They came out by groups of a hundred, columns of five, hardly able to walk and shuffling along with arms linked so that none should fall. There was a Lagerschutz at the head and tail of each group.

As they passed the first group of onlookers, one of them finished rolling a sort of cigarette made with a piece of newspaper and some dust scrabbled out of his pocket, and he limped out of the ranks towards the side looking from one to the other and murmuring: 'Bitte, feuer.'

It was a Belgian Lagerschutz who was leading the group, who saw him, who came up behind him and struck him with his fist in the face so that he fell and lay moaning until some of his companions picked him up and took him into their rank.

Such men were the Lagerschutz: cowards aping their coward masters.

The Dungeon Democracy, 1945

IRIS MURDOCH

1919–

The Miming Theatre

I found myself on a broad landing, with a carved wooden balustrade behind me and several doors in front of me. Everything seemed neat and nicely appointed. The carpets were thick, and the woodwork as clean as an apple. I looked about me. It didn't occur to me to doubt that Anna was somewhere near, any more than it occurred to me to call her name or utter any other sound. I moved to the nearest door and opened it wide. Then I got a shock that stiffened me from head to toe.

I was looking straight into seven or eight pairs of staring eyes, which seemed to be located a few feet from my face. I stepped back hastily, and the door swung to again with a faint click which was the first sound I had heard since I entered the house. I stood still for a moment in utter incomprehension, my scalp prickling. Then I seized the handle firmly and opened the door again, stepping as I did so into the doorway. The faces had moved, but were still turned towards me; and then in an instant I understood. I was in the gallery of a tiny theatre. The gallery, sloping and foreshortened, seemed to give immediately onto the stage; and on the stage were a number of actors, moving silently to and fro, and wearing masks which they kept turned toward the auditorium. These masks were a little larger than life, and this fact accounted for the extraordinary impression of closeness which I had received when I first opened the door. My perceptual field now adjusted itself, and I looked with fascinated interest and surprise upon the strange scene.

The masks were not attached to the face, but mounted upon a rod which the actor held in his right hand and skilfully maintained in parallel to the footlights, so that no hint of the actor's real features could be seen. Most of the masks were made full face, but two of them, which were worn by the only two women on the scene, were made in profile. The mask features were grotesque and stylized, but with a certain queer beauty. I noticed particularly the two female masks, one of them sensual and serene, and the other nervous, watchful, hypocritical. These two masks had the eyes filled in, but the male masks had empty eyes through which the eyes of the actors gleamed oddly. All were dressed in white, the men in white peasant shirts and breeches, and the women in plain ankle-length white robes caught in at the waist . . .

The actors meanwhile were continuing to execute their movements in the extraordinary silence which seemed to keep the whole house spellbound. I saw that they were wearing soft close-fitting slippers and that the stage was carpeted. They moved about the stage with gliding or slouching movements, turning their masked heads from side to side, and I observed something of that queer expressiveness of neck and shoulder in which Indian dancers excel. Their left hands performed a variety of simple conventional gestures. I had never seen mime quite like this before. The effect was hypnotic. What was going on was not clear to me, but it seemed that a huge burly central figure, wearing a mask which expressed a sort of humble yearning stupidity, was being mocked by the other players. I examined the two women carefully, wondering if either of them was Anna; but I was certain that neither was. I should have known her at once. Then my attention was caught by the burly simpleton. For some time I stared at the mask, with its grotesque immobility and the flash of eyes behind it. A sort of force seemed to radiate from those eyes which entered into me with a gentle shock. I stared and stared. There was something about that hulking form that seemed vaguely familiar.

At that moment, with one of the movements, the stage creaked, and the backcloth shivered slightly. This sound brought me to myself, and brought with it the sudden alarming realization that the actors could see me. On tiptoe I moved back onto the landing and closed the door. The silence was over me like a great bell, but the whole place throbbed with a soundless vibration which it took me a moment to recognize as the beating of my own heart.

Under the Net, 1954

DORIS LESSING

1919–

At a Communist Publisher's

I read magazines and periodicals published in English in the communist countries: Russia, China, East Germany, etc. etc., and if there is a story or an article or a novel 'suitable for British conditions,' I draw Jack's, and therefore John Butte's, attention to it. Very little is 'suitable for British conditions;' an occasional article or a short story. Yet I read all this material avidly, as Jack does, and for the same reasons: we read between and behind lines, to spot trends and tendencies.

But—as I became aware recently—there is more to it than that. The reason for my fascinated absorption is something else. Most of this writing is flat, tame, optimistic, and on a curiously jolly note, even when dealing with war and suffering. It all comes out of the myth. But this bad, dead, banal writing is the other side of my coin. I am ashamed of the psychological impulse that created *Frontiers of War*. I have decided never to write again, if that is the emotion which must feed my writing.

During the last year, reading these stories, these novels, in which there might be an occasional paragraph, a sentence, a phrase, of truth; I've been forced to acknowledge that the flashes of genuine art are all out of deep, suddenly stark, undisguisable private emotion. Even in translation there is no mistaking these lightning flashes of genuine personal feeling. And I read this dead stuff praying that just once there may be a short story, a novel, even an article, written wholly from genuine personal feeling.

And so this is the paradox: I, Anna, reject my own 'unhealthy' art; but reject 'healthy' art when I see it.

The point is that this writing is essentially impersonal. Its banality is that of impersonality. It is as if there were a new Twentieth Century Anon at work.

Since I have been in the Party, my 'party work' has consisted mostly of giving lectures on art to small groups. I say something like this: 'Art during the Middle Ages was communal, unindividual; it came out of a group consciousness. It was without the driving painful individuality of the art of the bourgeois era. And one day, we will leave behind the driving egotism of individual art. We will return to an art which will express not man's self-divisions and separateness from his fellows but his responsibility for his fellows and his brotherhood. Art from the West . . .' to use the useful catchphrase '—becomes more and more a shriek of torment from souls recording pain. Pain is becoming our deepest reality . . .' I've been saying something like this. About three months ago, in the middle of this lecture, I began to stammer and couldn't finish. I have not given any more lectures. I know what that stammer means.

It occurred to me that the reason I came to work for Jack, without knowing why, was that I wanted to have my deep private preoccupations about art, about literature (and therefore about life), about my refusal to write again, put into a sharp focus, where I must look at it, day after day.

I have been discussing this with Jack. He listens and understands. (He always understands.) And he says: 'Anna, communism isn't four decades old yet. So far, most of the art it has produced is bad. But what makes you think these aren't the first steps of a child learning to walk? And in a century's time . . .' 'Or in five centuries,' I say, teasing him—'In a century's time the new art may be born. Why not?' And I say: 'I don't know what to think. But I'm beginning to be afraid that I've been talking nonsense. Do you realise that all the arguments we ever have are about the same thing—the individual conscience, the individual sensibility?' And he teases me saying: 'And is the individual conscience going to produce your joyful communal unselfish art?' 'Why not? Perhaps the individual conscience is also a child learning how to walk?' And he nods; and the nod means: Yes, this is all very interesting, but let's get on with our work.

The Golden Notebook, 1962

BENEDICT KIELY

1919–

An Escapade

On a warm but not sunny June afternoon on a crowded Dublin street, by no means one of the city's most elegant streets, a small hotel, a sort of bed-and-breakfast place, went on fire. There was pandemonium at first, more panic than curiosity in the crowd. It was a street of decayed Georgian houses, high and narrow, with steep wooden staircases, and cluttered small shops on the ground floors: all great nourishment for flames. The fire, though, didn't turn out to be serious. The brigade easily contained and controlled it. The panic passed, gave way to curiosity, then to indignation and finally, alas, to laughter about the odd thing that had happened when the alarm was at its worst.

This was it.

From a window on the top-most floor a woman, scantily-clad, puts her head out and waves a patchwork bed coverlet, and screams for help. The stairway, she cries, is thick with smoke, herself and her husband are afraid to face it. On what would seem to be prompting from inside the room, she calls down that they are a honeymoon couple up from the country. That would account fairly enough for their still being abed on a warm June afternoon.

The customary ullagone and ullalu goes up from the crowd. The fire-engine ladder is aimed up to the window. A fireman begins to run up the ladder. Then suddenly the groom appears in shirt and trousers, and bare-footed. For, to the horror of the beholders, he makes his bare feet visible by pushing the bride back into the room, clambering first out of the window, down the ladder like a monkey although he is a fairly corpulent man; with monkey-like agility dodging round the ascending fireman, then disappearing through the crowd. The people, indignant enough to trounce him, are still too concerned with the plight of the bride, and too astounded to seize him. The fireman ascends to the nuptial casement, helps the lady through the window and down the ladder, gallantly offering his jacket which covers some of her. Then when they are halfways down, the fireman, to the amazement of all, is seen to be laughing right merrily, the bride vituperating. But before they reach the ground she also is laughing. She is brunette, tall, but almost Japanese in appearance, and very handsome. A voice says: If she's a bride I can see no confetti in her hair.

She has fine legs which the fireman's jacket does nothing to conceal and which she takes pride, clearly, in displaying. She is a young woman of questionable virginity and well known to the firemen. She is the toast of a certain section of the town to whom she is affectionately known as Madame Butterfly, although unlike her more famous namesake she has never been married, nor cursed by an uncle bonze for violating the laws of the gods of her ancestors. She has another, registered, name: her mother's name. What she is her mother was before her, and proud of it.

The bare-footed fugitive was not, of course, a bridegroom, but a long-established married man with his wife and family and a prosperous business in Longford, the meanest town in Ireland. For the fun of it the firemen made certain that the news of his escapade in the June afternoon got back to Longford. They were fond of, even proud of, Butterfly as were many other men who had nothing at all to do with the quenching of fire.

'A Ball of Malt and Madame Butterfly', *A Ball of Malt and Madame Butterfly*, 1973

AMOS TUTUOLA

1920–1997

A Consuming Thirst

I was a palm-wine drinkard since I was a boy of ten years of age. I had no other work more than to drink palm-wine in my life. In those days we did not know other money, except COWRIES, so that everything was very cheap, and my father was the richest man in our town.

My father got eight children and I was the eldest among them, all of the rest were hard workers, but I myself was an expert palm-wine drinkard. I was drinking palm-wine from morning till night and from night till morning. By that time I could not drink ordinary water at all except palm-wine.

But when my father noticed that I could not do any work more than to drink, he engaged an expert palm-wine tapster for me; he had no other work more than to tap palm-wine every day.

So my father gave me a palm-tree farm which was nine miles square and it contained 560,000 palm-trees, and this palm-wine tapster was tapping one hundred and fifty kegs of palm-wine every morning, but before 2 o'clock p.m., I would have drunk all of it; after that he would go and tap another 75 kegs in the evening which I would be drinking till morning. So my friends were uncountable by that time and they were drinking palm-wine with me from morning till a late hour in the night. But when my palm-wine tapster completed the period of 15 years that he was tapping the palm-wine for me, then my father died suddenly, and when it was the 6th month after my father had died, the tapster went to the palm-tree farm on a Sunday evening to tap palm-wine for me. When he reached the farm, he climbed one of the tallest palm-trees in the farm to tap palm-wine but as he was tapping on, he fell down unexpectedly and died at the foot of the palm-tree as a result of injuries. As I was waiting for him to bring the palm-wine, when I saw that he did not return in time, because he was not keeping me long like that before, then I called two of my friends to accompany me to the farm. When we reached the farm, we began to look at every palm-tree, after a while we found him under the palm-tree, where he fell down and died.

But what I did first when we saw him dead there, was that I climbed another palm-tree which was near the spot, after that I tapped palm-wine and drank it to my satisfaction before I came back to the spot. Then both my friends who accompanied me to the farm and I dug a pit under the palm-tree that he fell down as a grave and buried him there, after that we came back to the town.

When it was early in the morning of the next day, I had no palm-wine to drink at all, and throughout that day I felt not so happy as before; I was seriously sat down in my parlour, but when it was the third day that I had no palm-wine at all, all my friends did not come to my house again, they left me there alone, because there was no palm-wine for them to drink.

But when I completed a week in my house without palm-wine, then I went out and, I saw one of them in the town, so I saluted him, he answered but he did not approach me at all, he hastily went away.

Then I started to find out another expert palm-wine tapster, but I could not get me one who could tap the palm-wine to my requirement. When there was no palm-wine for me to drink I started to drink ordinary water which I was unable to taste before, but I did not satisfy with it as palm-wine.

The Palm-Wine Drinkard, 1952

D. J. ENRIGHT

1920–

Hiroshima, 1954

The new makeshift houses were already drab and decrepit, the Atomic Bomb Souvenir Shop was a modern ruin, the Peace Park was largely mud during my visit, and the various other commemorative objects sited about the centre of the explosion appeared rather to have fallen under the bomb than to have been raised in its memory. No doubt by now this whole area has been trimmed into the properly and safely historical, but at that date it was all too contemporaneous, as if the survivors had only had time and strength to shift some of the debris around to make an impromptu cairn. No doubt the present Atomic Bomb Museum is a museum in the accepted sense of the word, a clean and sober structure housing a smart and orderly collection of exhibits in glass cases, labelled accurately and grammatically in a number of languages, and furnished with benches for visitors whose feet are beginning to pain them. No doubt it is more instructive than the original little museum, and a good deal less horrifying, and much less admonitory. Pointing backwards, not forwards.

The museum as I saw it was a smallish building of mean and makeshift appearance, and its interior was at first reminiscent of those haphazard and dusty aquariums so commonly to be found in small towns in Japan, perhaps marking the strong maritime strand in the national character, perhaps in deference to the passionate Japanese appetite for information of any kind. An aquarium? No, rather a junk shop. Tiles melted out of shape and a few fried shoes dumped on a trestle table. Some second-hand tombstones in poor condition, several oddly grained blocks of granite, a bicycle which had apparently been left out in the sun too long and had melted and reset in a different shape. Some humorous photographs, not too well defined, of atomic tricks, of the shadow of a spiral staircase imprinted by the atomic flash on the side of a gas tank and of the upper slab of a tomb which had been lifted by the blast and fell back to trap a flying stone; some less amusing photographs of the shadows left behind by pedestrians crossing a bridge and by somebody sitting on the steps of a bank when the bomb exploded, and a photograph of the pattern of a dress left on the wearer's back; also some unfunny but happily indistinct photographs of scorched and corrugated flesh. And hanging on the wall, a shabby pair of the baggy trousers worn by women workers, with an explanation scrawled underneath: 'The lady who weared this *mompei* was working 1,300 meters away from the center of the explosion.' The seat of the trousers was badly burnt.

On the way out, passing over the little badges decorated with a stodgy dove and the letters 'H.P.S.' for Hiroshima Peace Society, I purchased a souvenir brochure packed with statistics and mathematical calculations, which among other things described with no trace of irony how the location of the epicentre and hypocentre of the explosion was determined by examining the exfoliation or surface mutation on tombstones situated in different sections of the city and then backtracking the heat rays. As I left, I realized that the tank filled with ashes at the door was not a refuse bin but a model of Hiroshima as it looked directly after the bomb had fallen.

Memoirs of a Mendicant Professor, 1969

BRIAN MOORE

1921–

An Emissary from Rome

As they went down the path—'The man with that creel is Father Manus, a very good soul. He is the priest who said the Mass that Sunday when the television fellows came. The other monks make fun of him, now. The reporters tried to interview him on the television but he wouldn't speak.' The Abbot kicked a stone clear of the path. 'He will speak to you, never fear. He's dying to get a chance at you, I warn you. Still, that's what you're here for, I suppose. Explanations, wasn't that what Father General called them?'

'Yes.'

'Maaaaa-nus! Did you get a fish?'

Shouting, his voice lifted and lost in the wind. Implacable, the loud sea on grey-green rocks. The man in oilskins heard, held up his creel.

'We have our fish,' the Abbot said.

'Good.'

'When Manus catches a salmon he puts it in an ocean pool and the next day, when the boat goes over, we sell on the mainland. Salmon gets a big price. So tonight is a special treat. Eating salmon ourselves. It's things like that—' the Abbot turned on the path and looked back up, his fisher hawk's eyes searching Kinsella's face—'it's the little things that keep us going, here. like the jam I was talking about. Do you follow me? That is the jam in our lives.'

Then turned and went on down, a heavy old man in black oilskins, his head hidden by the sou'wester hat.

While the needs of your particular congregation might seem to be served by retention of the Latin Mass, nevertheless, as Father Kinsella will explain to you, your actions in continuing to employ the older form are, at this time, particularly susceptible to misinterpretation elsewhere as a deliberate contravention of the spirit of aggiornamento. *Such an interpretation can and will be made, not only within the councils of the Church itself, but within the larger councils of the ecumenical movement. This is particularly distressful to us at this time, in view of the* apertura, *possibly the most significant historical event of our century, when interpenetration between Christian and Buddhist faiths is on the verge of reality.*

For all of these reasons, in conclusion, I will only say that, while Father Kinsella is with you to hear explanations, be it understood his decision is mine and, as such, is irrevocable.

English was not, of course, Father General's first language. *Explanations* was an unfortunate choice of word. Kinsella watched the Abbot jump from rock to shore, landing heavily but surely, striding across the rain-damp sand to meet the other monk whose habit hung down soaking beneath his black oilskin coat. I would be angered by the tone of that last paragraph. And this is an Abbot who ignored his own Provincial for a dozen years. What if he ignores me? In Brazil, when the Bishop of Manáos denounced Hartmann as a false priest he was banished from the city and, up river, the villagers refused him food. But he stayed, eating wild roots, waiting in the rain forest until he had sapped the bishop's power. What could *I* do in this godforsaken spot?

'Hey!'

The other monk, grinning, held open his creel as the Abbot drew close. Three large salmon, silver-scaled, on a bed of green moss. Grinning, arrested as though in some long-ago school snapshot, the old monk seemed, somehow, to have retained the awkward, boyish grace of his adolescent days.

'Well, Father Abbot, and how will these suit you?' he said, then turned to nod and grin at Kinsella, as though inviting him to share an enormous and obvious joke.

'They will do,' the Abbot said, playing his part with great deliberation as he held the creel up. 'Yes, I will say they will do nicely, Manus. And this is Father Kinsella, all the way from Rome. Father Manus, our champion fisherman.'

'Hello, there,' Kinsella said.

'From Rome? So you're the man from Rome. I'd never have thought it.'

'What were you expecting?'

'Well, somebody older. A real sergeant-major. And most likely an Italian, or something on that order. You're American, are you?'

'I am.'

'Anyway, I'm delighted to see you. Oh, God forgive me, I'm not delighted at all. Sure we're all in fear and trembling of what you're going to do here.'

'Manus!' The Abbot, amused, hit Father Manus a thump between the shoulderblades. 'Hold your tongue, man. Aren't you the alpha and the omega. When Manus was a little boy they told him it was a sin to tell a lie. I do believe he has not committed that sin since.'

'Ah, but seriously, Father Kinsella,' Father Manus said. 'I have to talk to you. I mean it is an astonishing thing that's happened here. I go over to the mainland every Sunday. And you should just see the way the people react.'

'It's beginning to rain,' the Abbot warned. 'If you want to talk to Father Kinsella, I'd suggest we do it inside. Come along, now.'

Catholics, 1972

KINGSLEY AMIS

1922–1995

Dear Mr Jhons

Dear Mr Jhons, Dixon wrote, gripping his pencil like a breadknife. *This is just to let you no that I no what you are up to with yuong Marleen Richards, yuong Marleen is a desent girl and has got no tim for your sort, I no your sort. She is a desent girl and I wo'nt have you filing her head with a lot of art and music, she is to good for that, and I am going to mary her which is more than your sort ever do. So just you keep of her, Mr Jhons this will be your olny warning. This is just a freindly letter and I am not threatenning you, but you just do as I say else me and some of my palls from the Works will be up your way and we sha'nt be coming along just to say How do you can bet. So just you wach out and lay of yuong Marleen if you no whats good for you. Yours fathfully, Joe Higgins.*

He read it through, thinking how admirably consistent were the style and orthography. Both derived, in large part, from the essays of some of his less proficient pupils. He could hardly hope, even so, to deceive Johns for long, especially since Johns had almost certainly got no further with Marlene Richards, a typist in his office, than staring palely at her across it. But the letter would at any rate give him a turn and his dig-mates a few moments' amusement when it was opened, according to his habit, at the breakfast-table and read over cornflakes. Dixon wrote *To:—Mr Jhons* and the address of the digs on a cheap envelope not specially bought for the purpose, sealed the letter up in it and then, griming his finger on the floor, drew a heavy smudge across the flap. Finally he stuck a stamp on, slobbering on it for further verisimilitude. He'd post the letter on his way down to the pub for a lunch-time drink, but before that he must write up some of his notes for the Merrie England lecture. Before that in turn he must review his financial position, see if he could somehow restore it from complete impossibility to its usual level of merely imminent disaster . . .

Lucky Jim, 1954

A Twinge of Melancholy

As Patrick parked the 110 outside the College and got out, a thin rain was falling. The sight of clouds of it swirling softly under a street lamp, with the vague glimpse beyond this of the High Street traffic and the rounded hill above, where chains of lights stretched upward until they were lost in the woods, made a picture sugary enough to remind him of how appealing the town had looked when it was new to him, how certain to offer up someone he would fall authentically in love with. The most that could rationally be said for the dump now was that it was not the London suburb where his mother ran her dress-shop. And yet, well, there was something about the look of the train beginning to move out of the station above the canal bend, the way a line of young trees in a nearby front garden caught the light from the uncurtained windows, the sound of the church clock striking the half-hour through the noise of vehicles, something which made it not impossible to believe that even here and any time now that simple and final encounter might take place—to believe it for a moment, before the image was blurred and fouled by the inevitable debris of obligation and deceit and money and boredom and jobs and egotism and disappointment and habit and parents and inconvenience and homes and custom and fatigue: the whole gigantic moral and social flux which would wash away in the first few minutes any conceivable actualisation of that image. Was it really he who had spent a whole string of autumn evenings fifteen or sixteen years ago in the front room just off the London–Croydon road, playing his Debussy and Delius records by the open windows, in the hope that the girl who lived at the end of the street, and whom he had never dared speak to, would pass by, hear the music, look in and see him? Well, it was a good thing, and impressive too, that he could still feel a twinge of that uncomplicated and ignorant melancholy.

Take a Girl Like You, 1960

RONALD BLYTHE

1922–

A Village Gravedigger

'Tender' Russ is a widower and lives by himself in a severe brick cottage called Malyons. The cottage is built endways to the road and into a bank so high that blackberries can hang away from their roots and trail on the slates. The garden is planted but rank. Rows of sprouts have rotted until they have become yellow pustulate sticks; potatoes have reached up as far as they could go and fallen back into faded tangles. Tender sows but apparently doesn't reap. He has retreated to one room in the cottage and closed all the others up. It is a Charles Spencelayghe room, a jackdaw's nest of saved matchsticks, preserved newspapers, clung-to coronation mugs and every kind of clutter. In a corner a bakelite radio gives every news bulletin there ever was. Tender's two budgies, Boy and Girl, drown announcements of famine, war, murder and sport with an incessant chatter. He is short but strongly built. Vivid blue eyes strain and flash to add meaning and explanation to what he feels are inadequate words.

Tender is a monopolist and a pluralist. He amalgamates graveyards and pounces on cemeteries. Although there has been little or no competition for this great accumulation of burial grounds, Tender has a right to feel unique and powerful, privileged and indispensable. He has buried 608 people in thirty different churchyards since 1961 and keeps his own records of 'where they lie and *how* they lie'. And this is only the work of his maturity. Before this mortuary climax there were decades of interrings. Tender has never had a day's holiday, never missed a church service on a Sunday and also never missed an opportunity to carry on his rancorous love-hate debate with his God, the clergy and the quick. The dead are exempt from his fury and he is on their side against the living. He has all their names in an address book contrived out of shelf-paper and a bulldog-clip. The young and the old, the rich and the poor are listed in violent pencil at first, and in biro later.

He works incredibly hard and with great independence, travelling from village to village on a moped to the carrier of which is tied a gleaming spade and fork. He drives well out towards the centre of the road and the Anglo-American traffic has to swerve and swear to avoid him. Quite a lot of people recognize him, however, for he is a famous person, and give him a wide berth. They know they are seeing Time's winged chariot with a two-stroke.

When people need Tender they need him badly, and will make much of him because of this. The need over, they avoid him. Or is it that he avoids them? His eloquence is enormous and violent, and seems to be only indirectly aimed at God and man. He is arguing with the mindless knife-bearing wind which carries the ice of the sea to the vulnerable flesh and fields of the inhabited places. He is a religious man who is listening for God in a hurricane. There used to be certainties but now the parsons say they aren't so certain after all. The Bible itself has whirled past him—a mocking paper-chase of discarded views. Almost every day he hears about the 'resurrection of the body' as he waits tactfully behind a tree, filling-in spade covered with a sack. Most days he is left alone with the new dead. The pity of it all! The muddle of it all! Automatic bird-scarers go off in the pea-fields like minute guns. Something has gone wrong—very wrong.

'Why "Tender"?'

'Oh, that's not *his* name,' said the woman at the pub. 'He inherited it from his father. We call him Tender because of his father, but that's not his name.'

Akenfield, 1969

NORMAN MAILER

1923–

A Path through the Jungle

The river seemed deep in its middle, but along the banks a band of shallow water, perhaps fifteen yards wide, pebbled and rippled over the stones. The platoon set out in a single column of fourteen men. Overhead the jungle soon met in an archway, and by the time they passed the first bend in the stream it had become a tunnel whose walls were composed of foliage and whose roadbed was covered with slime. The sunlight filtered through a vast intricate web of leaves and fronds and vines and trees, until it absorbed the color of the jungle and became at last a green shimmering wash of velvet. The light eddied and shifted as though refracting through the intricate vaults of a cathedral; all about they were surrounded by the jungle, dark and murmurous. They were engulfed in sounds and smells, absorbed in the fatty compacted marrows of the jungle. The moist ferny odors, the rot and ordure, the wet pungent smell of growing things, filled their senses and loosed a stifled horror, close to nausea. 'Goddam, it stinks,' Red muttered. They had lived in the jungle for so long that they had forgotten its odor, but in the night, on the water, their nostrils had cleared; they had forgotten the oppression, the intense clammy weight of the air.

'Smells like a nigger woman,' Wilson announced.

Brown guffawed nervously. 'When the hell'd you ever have a nigger?' But he was troubled for a moment; the acute stench of fertility and decay loosed a fragile expectation.

The stream wound its burrow into the jungle. Already they had forgotten how the mouth appeared in sunlight. Their ears were filled with the quick frenetic rustling of insects and animals, the thin screeching rage of mosquitoes and the raucous babbling of monkeys and parakeets. They sweated terribly; although they had marched only a few hundred yards, the languid air gave them no nourishment, and black stains of moisture spread on their uniforms wherever the pack straps made contact. In the early morning, the jungle was exuding its fog-drip; about their legs the waist-high mists skittered apart for the passage of their bodies, and closed again sluggishly, leisurely, like a slug revolving in its cell. For the men at the point of the column every step demanded an inordinate effort of will. They shivered with revulsion, halted often to catch their breath. The jungle dripped wetly about them everywhere; the groves of bamboo trees grew down to the river edge, their lacy delicate foliage lost in the welter of vines and trees. The brush mounted on the tree trunks grew over their heads; the black river silt embedded itself in the roots of the bushes and between the pebbles under their feet. The water trickled over the stream bank tinkling pleasantly, but it was lost in the harsh uprooted cries of the jungle birds, the thrumming of the insects.

Slowly, inevitably, the men felt the water soak through the greased waterproofing of their shoes, slosh up to their knees whenever they had to wade through a deeper portion of the stream. Their packs became heavy, their arms grew numb and their backs began to ache. Most of the men were carrying thirty pounds of rations and bedding, and with their two canteens of water, their ten clips of ammunition, their two or three grenades, their rifles and machetes, each of them had distributed almost sixty pounds of equipment over his body, the weight of a very heavy suitcase. Most of them became tired in walking the first few hundred yards; by the time they had gone perhaps half a mile they were weary and their breath was short; the weaker ones were beginning to have the sour flat taste of fatigue. The density of the jungle, the miasmal mists, the liquid rustlings, the badgering of the insects lost their first revulsion and terror. They were no longer so conscious of the foreboding wilderness before them; the vague unnamed stimulations and terrors of exploring this tunnel through the jungle became weaker, sank at last into the monotonous grinding demands of the march. Despite Croft's lecture, they began to walk with their heads down, looking at their feet.

The river narrowed, and the ribbon of shallow water contracted to a strip along the bank, no wider than a footpath. They were beginning to climb. Already the stream had dropped from a few minor waterfalls, had churned over a short stretch of tumbled rocks. The pebbles underfoot slowly were replaced by river sand and then by mud. The men marched closer to the bank, and at last the foliage began to whip at them, obstructing their way. They proceeded much more slowly now.

Around a turn they halted and surveyed the stretch ahead. The foliage grew into the water at this point, and Croft, after considering the problem, waded out to the center of the stream. Five yards from the shore he halted. The water was close to his waist, swirling powerfully about him. 'We're gonna have to hold to the bank, Lootenant,' he decided. He began to fight his way along the edge of the stream, holding to the foliage, the water covering his thighs. Laboriously the men followed him, strung out along the bank. They proceeded for the next few hundred yards by grasping the nearest bushes, yanking and tugging themselves up the stream against the current. Their rifles kept slipping off their shoulders, almost dipping into the water, and their feet sunk loathsomely in the river mud. Their shirts, from perspiration, became as wet as their trousers. Besides their fatigue and the dank moist air, they were sweating from anxiety. The stream had a force and a persistence which seemed alive; they felt something of the frenzy they would have known if an animal had been snarling at their feet. Their hands began to bleed from the thorns and the paper-edged leaves, and their packs hung heavy.

They moved like this until the stream widened again, became shallower. Here the current was not so rapid, and they made better progress sloughing through the knee-deep water. After a few more turns, they came upon a broad flat rock about which the river curved, and Hearn called a break.

The Naked and the Dead, 1948

BRENDAN BEHAN

1923–1964

Christmas-Time in Walton Jail

It was dark in the cell, and after I washed up, I sat at the table and listened to what few noises there were going on. The fellows had not got up to the windows yet, because a screw was going round the RC's cells and seeing if they wanted to go to Confession.

I'd have liked to have gone on account of Christmas-time, even apart from the walk with the other blokes to the chapel, but being excommunicated I could not.

Nearly all the others went, and the screw came round to all the cells with red cards, and when he came to mine he looked in and said, 'Going to Confession?' but then he recognized me and muttered something and went off to the next cell with a red card at it.

That fat bastard of a priest. I chewed my lips to myself when I heard the others all going down the stairs like free men.

Then the blokes got up to the windows.

It was too dark to read and anyway, I wanted to save all the reading I could for these four days, and there was a bit of white light in the sky and the snow coming, and I decided the screws might be a bit easy on us even if they caught us, it being the day before Christmas Eve, so I pulled over my table and got up.

And as well that I did.

Our Chief Officer, the stocky cruel-faced turkey-toed bastard, walks out with his glare and his strut, looking round and down at the snow, and up at the windows, five tiers of them in a square round the yard, in dead silence, and he knowing we were looking at him, and he glaring up at the barred windows, and some near me, though they must have known he could not have seen them at that distance, got down in fear. But I did not, thank God that I did not, and those that got down must have been cutting their throats a minute later, for the next thing is, the Chief Officer, with his red-faced glare and his strut, walks clean off the steps and into six foot of snow.

He floundered and was lost in it, there was even hope he'd smother in it, and oh, Jesus, what a shout went up from all the windows. What delight, what joy, and as a bonus on it, didn't the old bastard, when he struggled up a step, shake his fists in anger and fall down again, and the boys roared from the windows so that the screws came rushing out, thinking we'd all broken loose, and they shouted at us to get down from the windows, even as they helped the Chief up, covered in snow, and brushing himself while we roared, till the screws came rushing into the wings and round the landings, and we jumped down double-quick before they'd look in our spy-holes and catch us.

I sat down again at my table, and was thankful to God and His Blessed Mother for this.

If I had gone to Confession, I'd have missed it, and I was consoled. God never closes one door but He opens another, and if He takes away with His right hand, He gives it back with His left, and more besides.

Borstal Boy, 1958

KAMALA MARKANDAYA
1923–

Borne Away on the Thames

In her last weeks it was his name she called most frequently, her eyes very bright and clear, high spots of color purplish under her yellowed skin. Srinivas heard her cries, night after night, lying on the narrow camp cot rigged up next to the double bed, and was wracked. For there were no ready-made comforts to hand. Their faith offered no anodynes, no cheery resurrections and ascensions and meetings-up with cherished ones in heaven: only a formidable purification through rebirth, and the final ineffable bliss of divine union.

Toward the end, however, peace returned to Vasantha. She was very calm, very lucid, putting her affairs in order insofar as she could, though with a certain detachment, as if the concerns and liaisons of the world had fallen into place, if not insignificance. Yet they were close: closer perhaps than many couples, since there had been no alternative vines and supports to which each might have attached.

'It has been,' said Vasantha, hoarsely, the breath from her ruined lungs coming up rough, 'a happy marriage.'

Srinivas could not speak. He clutched at her hand, whitening her bones with the strength of his grip, and rebelled at her going.

Outside the crematorium chapel a green-coated attendant handed Srinivas the casket. It was very light. Five pounds, or so, of ash. The finest human ash, for they had raked through the embers and taken out unsightly gobbets and unconsumed bits of bone and sieved out the rest.

'It's all done up, guv',' he said. 'Sealed, so you won't have no trouble with spillage.' He paused, considering, then came out with it. 'Now don't you fret yourself,' he said kindly. 'I mean it comes to us all in the end. If you take my advice you'll scatter the ashes. It don't do any good brooding over them like.'

'I shall take your advice,' promised Srinivas, and got on a bus with the casket. It was a difficult thing to do, for besides the casket he was carrying Vasantha's sandalwood box which she had filled with earth from India and brought with her, and her hair-oil bottle half full of Ganges water. Laxman should have carried these, but Laxman was in bed with influenza. So he managed, somehow, on his own.

At London Bridge he alighted. There was a catwalk, and steps leading down to the river. The tide was in, there was not far to go: five or six steps, and the sluggish Thames was slopping over his toe-caps. Srinivas put down the box and bottle while he broke the seals on the casket. Then he opened it gently, and leaning out as far as he could so that they should not be washed back, he tipped the ashes into the river. Afterwards there remained only the small service she had asked of him and this he performed, sprinkling earth and Ganges water onto the ashes being borne away on the Thames.

He was, at that period of his life, beginning to lose the fetters which tied him to any one country. He was a human being, and as such felt he belonged to a wider citizenship. Yet, in this moment, he could not help feeling with Vasantha, who in her breath and bones had remained wholly Indian. She would have liked her remains committed to the currents of an Indian river, though she had scrupulously refrained from such onerous impositions; and now, watching her ashes drift away downstream, he wished he could have found some way to avoid consigning them to these alien waters. A sauntering policeman, pausing to lean over the parapet, observed the proceedings. He waited for Srinivas to come up and said reprovingly, 'You are not allowed to tip your household rubbish into the river.'

'I would not dream of doing so,' said Srinivas.

'I'm sorry, sir, but you did,' accused the policeman. 'I saw you. If everyone carried on the same the river would soon be polluted.' Here it occurred to him that it already was: a very fine array of floating debris was being shunted gently along by the tide. The constable averted his eyes. 'Well, just see you don't do it again,' he said, and prepared to move on. 'The river's not the place for rubbish.'

'It was not rubbish,' said Srinivas, and found to his dismay that his throat was working painfully. 'It was my wife.'

Joker, eh, thought the policeman tersely; but the sharp words died on his lips as he whipped around smartly, because he could see that the middle-aged Indian before him was weeping. Or was as close to it as any man could be, in the presence of another. The constable reddened, being young, and decent as the young often are; then he touched his helmet, awkwardly, to the stricken man, and walked on.

The Nowhere Man, 1972

SAM SELVON

1923–1994

A West Indian in London

The summer night descend with stars, they walking hand in hand, and Galahad feeling hearts.

'It was a lovely evening—' Daisy began.

'Come and go in the yard,' Galahad say.

'What?' Daisy say.

'The yard. Where I living.'

All this time he was stalling, because he feeling sort of shame to bring the girl in that old basement room, but if the date end in fiasco he know the boys would never finish giving him tone for spending all that money and not eating.

Daisy start to hesitate but he make haste and catch a number twelve, telling she that it all on the way home. When they hop off by the Water she was still getting on prim, but Galahad know was only grandcharge, and besides the old blood getting hot, so he walk Daisy brisk down the road, and she quiet as a mouse. They went down the basement steps and Galahad fumble for the key, and when he open the door a whiff of stale food and old clothes and dampness and dirt come out the door and he only waiting to hear what Daisy would say.

But she ain't saying nothing, and he walk through the passage and open the door and put the light on.

Daisy sit down on the bed and Galahad say: 'You want a cup of char?' And without waiting for any answer he full the pot in the tap and put it on the ring and turn the gas on. He feel so excited that he had to light a cigarette, and he keep saying Take it easy to himself.

'Is this your room?' Daisy say, looking around and shifting about as if she restless.

'Yes,' Galahad say. 'You like it?'

'Yes,' Daisy say.

Galahad throw a copy of *Ebony* to her and she begin to turn the pages.

With all the excitement Galahad taking off the good clothes carefully and slowly, putting the jacket and trousers on the hanger right away, and folding up the shirt and putting it in the drawer.

When the water was boiling he went to the cupboard and take out a packet of tea, and he shake some down in the pot.

Daisy look at him as if he mad.

'Is that how you make tea?' she ask.

'Yes,' Galahad say. 'No foolishness about it. Tea is tea—you just drop some in the kettle. If you want it strong, you drop plenty. If you want it weak, you drop little bit. And so you make a lovely cuppa.'

He take the kettle off and rest it on a sheet of *Daily Express* on the ground. He bring two cups, a spoon, a bottle of milk and a packet of sugar.

'Fix up,' he say, handing Daisy a cup.

They sit down there sipping the tea and talking.

'You get that raise the foreman was promising you?' Galahad ask, for something to say.

'What did you say? You know it will take me some time to understand everything you say. The way you West Indians speak!'

'What wrong with it?' Galahad ask. 'Is English we speaking.'

And so he coasting a little oldtalk until the tea finish, and afterwards he start to make one set of love to Daisy.

'It was battle royal in that basement, man,' he tell Moses afterwards, and he went on to give a lot of detail, though all of that is nothing to a old veteran like Moses, is only to Galahad is new because is the first time with a white number. Moses smile a knowing smile, a tired smile, and 'Take it easy,' he tell Sir Galahad.

The Lonely Londoners, 1956

NADINE GORDIMER

1923–

A South African Township

Thousands of pieces of paper take to the air and are plastered against the location fence when the August winds come. The assortment of covering worn by the children and old people who scavenge the rubbish dump is moulded against their bodies or bloated away from them. Sometimes the wind is strong enough to cart-wheel sheets of board and send boxes slamming over and over until they slither across the road and meet the obstacle of the fence, or are flattened like the bodies of cats or dogs under the wheels of the traffic. The newspaper, ash, bones and smashed bottles come from the location; the boxes and board and straw come from the factories and warehouses not far across the veld where many of the location people work. People waiting at the roadside for buses cover their mouths with woollen scarves against the red dust; so do the women who sit at their pitches selling oranges or yellow mealies roasting on braziers. The scavengers are patient—leisurely or feeble, it's difficult, in passing, to judge—and their bare feet and legs and the hands with which they pick over the dirt are coated grey with ash. Two of the older children from the farm go to school in the location. They could return as they come, across the veld and through the gap cut in the fence by gangs who bring stolen goods in that way, but they lengthen the long walk home by going to have a look at what people are seeking, on the dump. They do not know what it is they would hope to find; they learn that what experienced ones seek is whatever they happen to find. They have seen an ash-covered forefinger the size of their own dipping into a sardine-tin under whose curled-back top some oil still shone. When the oil was licked up there was still the key to be unravelled from the tin. There have been odd shoes, casts of bunions and misshapen toes in sweat and dirt and worn leather; a broken hat. The old tyres are hardest to get because people make sandals out of them. From hoardings along the railway line, which also runs through the industries, providing sidings, black men with strong muscles and big grins look down, brushing their teeth, drinking canned beer or putting money in a savings bank. Industries and factories announce themselves—gas welding, artistic garden pots, luxury posture-corrective mattresses, THIS IS THE HOME OF FIAT.

The location is like the dump; the children do not know what there is to find there, either. It is not at all like the farm, where what you will find is birds' eggs, wire, or something (a coin, a pocket comb, cigar stumps) white people have dropped or thrown away. A ring was lost; the children were told to look for a shiny stone in the grass. Once there was a tortoise, and the parents ate it and the shell is still in Jacobus's house.

They roamed the streets of the location seeing in to houses that had furniture, like the white farmer's house, and peach trees fenced in, with dogs like the India's barking, and they passed other kinds of houses, long rows of rooms marked off into separate dwellings by the pink and blue paint used on the exterior, where a lot of men from the factories lived and made mounds of beer cartons on the waste ground around. Outside a hall as big as a church they saw the huge coloured pictures of white men shooting each other or riding horses but they had never paid to go inside. They went into little shops like the India's and bought five cents' hot chips wetted with vinegar, and hung about against the glass walls of the biggest store in the location with thousands of different coloured bottles of liquor behind its fancy steel burglar grilles. They saw men in clothes better than anything Izak had, white caps and sunglasses, wonderful watches and rings on hands resting on coloured fur-covered steering wheels of cars. There were women wearing the straight hair of white people and hospital nurses in uniforms clean and stiff as paper. There was an abundance of the rarities carefully saved, on the farm: everybody here had boxes and carriers and bottles and plastic cans in their hands or on their heads. A child had a little three-wheeled bicycle; a shopkeeper chased a screaming girl who had taken a pineapple. They played in the streets with some children who suddenly snatched their chips off them and disappeared; a balloon was handed to them from a van with a voice like Izak's radio, telling people to buy medicine for their blood. Looking on at boys their own age gambling they saw one pull a knife and thrust it into the back of the other's hand. They ran. But they went back; always they went back . . .

The Conservationist, 1974

JAMES PURDY

1923–

A Consultation

Sweat poured down from Cabot's armpits as he walked into Dr Bigelow-Martin's office for his first treatment. He had never felt so apprehensive since he reported to the induction centre for the army.

'We are beginning a new life,' Dr Bigelow-Martin intoned, putting his hand on Cabot's knee. 'You are about to study yourself, see what you yourself do to yourself. You have been tense and tired, tired and tense, puffing and straining, expending far too much energy and getting oh so little back in return. Your case is not exceptional, Mr Cabot Wright. Indeed it's not. Put it out of your mind that you are different. Your case is, in fact, my young man, the rule. Americans are tired. America is tired. What is the root? We do not know. Is it world-wide? Perhaps, perhaps. Lie down, please,' and the doctor suppressed a yawn.

Cabot Wright was already nude except for his shorts.

The doctor, bending over the day-bed where Cabot lay, suddenly with a remarkable show of strength picked him up bodily and put him over a kind of padded hook which had come out of the wall, and hung his patient on it, much as one would a side of beef.

'Do not move,' Bigelow-Martin admonished. 'No matter how much you may wish to change your position, resist it, simply give in to your fatigue, let go, let go, Cabot, let go.'

Struggling on the immense mattress-padded hook which had come out of the wall, Cabot felt very much like a fish—caught but not pulled in. The blood rushed violently to his head. His shorts, which he had laundered many times, snapped, and fell down about his legs. Visions of gauchos riding on the pampas came to him, together with memories of bull-fights he had seen on TV. His forehead was swimming with sweat, he felt his intestines give, spittle flowed freely from his mouth, and his navel suddenly contracting violently seemed to explode and vanish, as will the top crust of a pie in the oven when the proper slits have not been made in it. Cabot felt he was saying *adios* from a boat rapidly advancing from the shore on which stood his adopted father and mother in their Florida clothes, and his recent bride, Mrs Cabot Wright Junior in her Vogue pattern dress.

When Cabot Wright regained consciousness. Dr Bigelow-Martin was bathing his forehead with some drugstore witch hazel.

'How did we do?' the doctor was saying.

When Cabot did not reply, Bigelow-Martin waited a bit, then said: 'I'll tell you, sir. We did fine.'

'Did I pass out, doctor?' Cabot wondered.

'You went to sleep,' was the reply. 'You relaxed. Probably for the first time in your life.'

The vision of the gauchos came back to Cabot.

'Can I tell people about this?' Cabot inquired.

The doctor appeared to be studying his question.

'At least I can tell my wife?' he appealed to Bigelow-Martin in an almost wistful voice.

'Just as you wish,' the doctor was grudgingly acquiescent, and he turned away from his patient, humming a tune.

There were certain obvious warnings in what the doctor did not say, and Cabot understood that secrecy and indirection were characteristic of the profession. Yet, as Cabot asked himself, who would want to tell on himself and reveal what he had undergone in Bigelow-Martin's office? Who would believe it?

'My God, you look different,' Cynthia said when he came into the apartment. 'You look like *you'd* been to Florida.'

But Cabot was already unbuttoning his wife's blouse.

Cabot Wright Begins, 1964

JAMES BALDWIN
1924–1987

A Boyhood Task—and a Face in the Mirror

'John,' said his mother, 'you sweep the front room for me like a good boy, and dust the furniture. I'm going to clean up in here.'

'Yes'm,' he said, and rose. She *had* forgotten about his birthday. He swore he would not mention it. He would not think about it any more.

To sweep the front room meant, principally, to sweep the heavy red and green and purple Oriental-style carpet that had once been that room's glory, but was now so faded that it was all one swimming colour, and so frayed in places that it tangled with the broom. John hated sweeping this carpet, for dust rose, clogging his nose and sticking to his sweaty skin, and he felt that should he sweep it for ever, the clouds of dust would not diminish, the rug would not be clean. It became in his imagination his impossible, lifelong task, his hard trial, like that of a man he had read about somewhere, whose curse it was to push a boulder up a steep hill, only to have the giant who guarded the hill roll the boulder down again—and so on, for ever, throughout eternity; he was still out there, that hapless man, somewhere at the other end of the earth, pushing his boulder up the hill. He had John's entire sympathy, for the longest and hardest part of his Saturday mornings was his voyage with the broom across this endless rug; and, coming to the French doors that ended the living-room and stopped the rug, he felt like an indescribably weary traveller who sees his home at last. Yet for each dustpan he so laboriously filled at the door-sill demons added to the rug twenty more; he saw in the expanse behind him the dust that he had raised settling again into the carpet; and he gritted his teeth, already on edge because of the dust that filled his mouth, and nearly wept to think that so much labour brought so little reward.

Nor was this the end of John's labour; for, having put away the broom and the dustpan, he took from the small bucket under the sink the dust rag and the furniture oil and a damp cloth, and returned to the living-room to excavate, as it were, from the dust that threatened to bury them, his family's goods and gear. Thinking bitterly of his birthday, he attacked the mirror with the cloth, watching his face appear as out of a cloud. With a shock he saw that his face had not changed, that the hand of Satan was as yet invisible. His father had always said that his face was the face of Satan—and was there not something—in the lift of the eyebrow, in the way his rough hair formed a V on his brow—that bore witness to his father's words? In the eye there was a light that was not the light of Heaven, and the mouth trembled, lustful and lewd, to drink deep of the wines of Hell. He stared at his face as though it were, as indeed it soon appeared to be, the face of a stranger, a stranger who held secrets that John could never know. And, having thought of it as the face of a stranger, he tried to look at it as a stranger might, and tried to discover what other people saw. But he saw only details: two great eyes, and a broad, low forehead, and the triangle of his nose, and his enormous mouth, and the barely perceptible cleft in his chin, which was, his father said, the mark of the devil's little finger. These details did not help him, for the principle of their unity was undiscoverable, and he could not tell what he most passionately desired to know: whether his face was ugly or not.

Go Tell It on the Mountain, 1953

TRUMAN CAPOTE
1924–1984

Two Killers Arrive at the County Jail

Among Garden City's animals are two grey tomcats who are always together—thin, dirty strays with strange and clever habits. The chief ceremony of their day is performed at twilight. First they trot the length of Main Street, stopping to scrutinize the engine grilles of parked automobiles, particularly those stationed in front of the two hotels, the Windsor and Warren, for these cars, usually the property of travellers from afar, often yield what the bony, methodical creatures are hunting: slaughtered birds—crows, chickadees, and sparrows foolhardy enough to have flown into the path of oncoming motorists. Using their paws as though they are surgical instruments, the cats extract from the grilles every feathery particle. Having cruised Main Street, they invariably turn the corner at Main and Grant, then lope along towards Courthouse Square, another of their hunting grounds—and a highly promising one on the afternoon of Wednesday, January 6, for the area swarmed with Finney County vehicles that had brought to town part of the crowd populating the square.

The crowd started forming at four o'clock, the hour that the county attorney had given as the probable arrival time of Hickock and Smith. Since the announcement of Hickock's confession on Sunday evening, newsmen of every style had assembled in Garden City: representatives of the major wire services, photographers, newsreel and television cameramen, reporters from Missouri, Nebraska, Oklahoma, Texas, and, of course, all the principal Kansas papers—twenty or twenty-five men altogether. Many of them had been waiting three days without much to do except interview the service-station attendant James Spor, who, after seeing published photographs of the accused killers, had identified them as customers to whom he'd sold three dollars and six cents' worth of gas the night of the Holcomb tragedy.

It was the return of Hickock and Smith that these professional spectators were on hand to record, and Captain Gerald Murray, of the Highway Patrol, had reserved for them ample space on the sidewalk fronting the courthouse steps—the steps the prisoners must mount on their way to the county jail, an institution that occupies the top floor of the four-story limestone structure. One reporter, Richard Parr, of the Kansas City *Star*, had obtained a copy of Monday's Las Vegas *Sun*. The paper's headline raised rounds of laughter: FEAR LYNCH MOB AWAITING RETURN OF KILLER SUSPECTS. Captain Murray remarked, 'Don't look much like a necktie party to me.'

Indeed, the congregation in the square might have been expecting a parade, or attending a political rally. High-school students, among them former classmates of Nancy and Kenyon Clutter, chanted cheerleader rhymes, bubbled bubble gum, gobbled hot dogs and soda pop. Mothers soothed wailing babies. Men strode about with young children perched on their shoulders. The Boy Scouts were present—an entire troop. And the middle-aged membership of a women's bridge club arrived *en masse*. Mr J. P. (Jap) Adams, head of the local Veterans Commission office, appeared, attired in a tweed garment so oddly tailored that a friend yelled, 'Hey, Jap! What ya doin' wearin' ladies' clothes?'—for Mr Adams, in his haste to reach the scene, had unwittingly donned his secretary's coat. A roving radio reporter interviewed sundry other townsfolk, asking them what, in their opinion, the proper retribution would be for 'the doers of such a dastardly deed', and while most of his subjects said gosh or gee whiz, one student replied, 'I think they ought to be locked in the same cell for the rest of their lives. Never allowed any visitors. Just sit there staring at each other till the day they die.' And a tough, strutty little man said, 'I believe in capital punishment. It's like the Bible says—an eye for an eye. And even so we're two pair short!'

In Cold Blood, 1966

FLANNERY O'CONNOR
1925–1964

A Soldier and His Soul

The only things from Eastrod he took into the army with him were a black Bible and a pair of silver-rimmed spectacles that had belonged to his mother. He had gone to a country school where he had learned to read and write but that it was wiser not to; the Bible was the only book he read. He didn't read it often but when he did he wore his mother's glasses. They tired his eyes so that after a short time he was always obliged to stop. He meant to tell anyone in the army who invited him to sin that he was from Eastrod, Tennessee, and that he meant to get back there and stay back there, that he was going to be a preacher of the gospel and that he wasn't going to have his soul damned by the government or by any foreign place it sent him to.

After a few weeks in the camp, when he had some friends—they were not actually friends but he had to live with them—he was offered the chance he had been waiting for; the invitation. He took his mother's glasses out of his pocket and put them on. Then he told them he wouldn't go with them for a million dollars and a feather bed to lie on; he said he was from Eastrod, Tennessee, and that he was not going to have his soul damned by the government or any foreign place they . . . but his voice cracked and he didn't finish. He only stared at them, trying to steel his face. His friends told him that nobody was interested in his goddam soul unless it was the priest and he managed to answer that no priest taking orders from no pope was going to tamper with his soul. They told him he didn't have any soul and left for their brothel.

He took a long time to believe them because he wanted to believe them. All he wanted was to believe them and get rid of it once and for all, and he saw the opportunity here to get rid of it without corruption, to be converted to nothing instead of to evil. The army sent him halfway around the world and forgot him. He was wounded and they remembered him long enough to take the shrapnel out of his chest—they said they took it out but they never showed it to him and he felt it still in there, rusted, and poisoning him—and then they sent him to another desert and forgot him again. He had all the time he could want to study his soul in and assure himself that it was not there. When he was thoroughly convinced, he saw that this was something that he had always known. The misery he had was a longing for home; it had nothing to do with Jesus. When the army finally let him go, he was pleased to think that he was still uncorrupted. All he wanted was to get back to Eastrod, Tennessee. The black Bible and his mother's glasses were still in the bottom of his duffel bag. He didn't read any book now but he kept the Bible because it had come from home. He kept the glasses in case his vision should ever become dim.

Wise Blood, 1952

GORE VIDAL
1925–

In the Gilded Age

My piece on the Centennial Exhibition is finally finished and set in type. It was not easy to do for Bryant is still very much the stern editor of my youth. Exhausting arguments over words, grammar, wit; the last is a quality he does not enjoy even on those occasions when he recognizes it.

'But surely, Schuyler, Cleopatra is *not* the most beautiful of all the exhibits. Everyone else says that the work is in bad taste.'

I had written an apostrophe to the astonishing lifesize waxen Cleopatra in the Annex. This popular exhibit shows the famous lady reclining on her barge, one waxy wrist supporting a stuffed parrot whose wings at regular intervals open and shut. The Serpent of the Nile is accompanied by pink wax Cupids whose heads turn from left to right while their mistress's eyes blink in a manner suggestive not so much of lust as of the early stages of glaucoma.

Bryant forced me to jettison a number of telling adverbs, and all irony. On the other hand he found most interesting my account of the receptions for Grant, Bristow, Blaine. He listened attentively, sitting very straight at his desk: the Moses-head seemed all afire from a convenient sunset just behind him.

'We shall be meeting at your hotel tomorrow,' he said, tickling one ear with the tip of his feather pen. 'A number of—virtuous liberal Republicans. We are trying to find a way of salvaging our poor country's reputation.'

'This might be done by voting for the other party.'

Bryant sighed. Then: 'I was at Albany right after Governor Tilden was inaugurated. He was kind enough to present me to the legislators, a truly generous act. You know, he is one of my oldest and dearest friends.'

'But you cannot vote for him.'

The magnificent head shook angrily. 'That is not the point! I mistrust his party. And would like to revive the Republican party.'

'With Bristow?'

'I know that many of our group prefer him to the other candidates. But Bristow will only accept the Republican nomination. He'll never run on a separate ticket, the way Greeley did. Bristow is from Kentucky, he keeps telling us, and so a party regular.'

'Except that he is honest.'

'What a terrible thing it is, Schuyler! Imagine demanding nothing more of a president than that he not steal money.'

'How have things managed to go so very wrong with us?' I was genuinely curious to hear what Bryant would say.

'The war.' The answer was quick, and already thought out. 'So much money had to be raised and spent in order to put down the rebellion. And whenever there is a lot of money being spent, there will be a lot of corruption. The railroads have also made their contribution. The scramble for government grants, for rights of way, for the votes of individual congressmen. Well, it would take a strong man to say no forever to temptation.'

'As you said "no" to Tweed.' I cannot think why I was so tactless, even cruel. Could it be resentment at what he had done to my Cleopatra?

'I had no dealings with Mr Tweed.' The answer was smooth and oblique. But Bryant has been a famous public man for more than half a century and he cannot be taken by surprise. 'At one time I believe the *Post* took some money from City Hall. But when your friend Nordhoff attacked the Tweed Ring in our columns, I was in no way disturbed. But then you saw his statement of April 21.'

'Yes. He showed it to me before it was published.'

'Then you know that he has said, categorically, that I did not let him go because of his attacks on the Tweed Ring.'

'But *why* was he let go?'

'Other reasons entirely. But he is a splendid journalist and I compliment the two of you for what you have done in the way of illuminating Mr Blaine. In fact. . . .' And so on.

1876, 1976

ALISON LURIE

1926–

Great Old Bear

I am even getting a new line on Oswald McBane, the head of the English Department and patent Great Old Man of Convers. Or Great Old Bear; he is far more bear than man. Think of him as that big grey grizzly up on his hind legs in the habitat group at the Natural History Museum, the one Jane liked so much. McBane has just that profuse, dead-looking grey fur, heavy paws hanging down, fiercely quizzical expression. The first time we met, as you recall, he did nothing at all but grunt.

Yet it is McB who counts in this department—the rest are nothing. The two other full professors, Knight and Baker, I have christened collectively Tweedledumdee. Trite, I admit, and if you could see them you would say it was inappropriate too. Knight is tall, lean, dark, with a thin, elegant, stupid wife; Baker is short, plump, fair, with a fat, dowdy, clever wife. But they weren't smart enough for me. I soon found out that they are really twins in disguise. My first clue was that they have each other's centuries: Knight, so melancholy-metaphysical, specializes in the Victorian novel, while Baker, who looks like Thackeray, is 'in' the Elizabethan period.

This afternoon I was invited to sit in on a meeting of the big course that McBane runs, and what I discovered is that he absolutely detests Billy the Boy Dean; quite a feat, really. We were all sitting about before the meeting began and someone came out with the information that the college stood to lose money from the Fenn fire because Lumkin hadn't taken out enough insurance. 'You don't say?' McBear grunted, and positively roared with laughter for three minutes. All the other members of the course, who are nothing but instructors, dutifully laughed too, except for Julian, who merely smiled, and a little man from Wisconsin who actually frowned. McBane saw him, stopped laughing, and growled: 'Would you kindly get up and close the window, Mr Green, and contribute something to this course?' 'Yes, sir,' said Mr Green. The merest slap from McBear's forepaw can knock the little animals off their perches.

Love and Friendship, 1962

KENNETH TYNAN
1927–1980

Pausing on the Stairs

Would you know the shortest way to bad playwriting? I will tell you. It is to begin with a great theme, a Grand Purpose, in the hope that it will throw forth, of its own essential energy, such desirable by-products as character and dialogue. Woe to him who so far misunderstands the nature of drama as to suppose that abstractions can breed human beings! The diary of such a man might read: 'Really must decide on Theme tomorrow. Torn between Problems of Power, Loneliness, Colour, H-Bomb Threat, and Revolutionary Spirit in Eastern Europe. All major, surely? At least they can't say I'm ignoring the crisis of our time. Have worked out just what I feel about all five Themes, so the big creative effort is over. All that remains is the donkey-work of filling in dialogue and characters. But which Theme to choose? Went out for walk to clear head. Strange encounter with landlady on stairs: she said I looked like George III and tittered. Silly woman.'

Useless, of course, to point out that the genesis of good plays is hardly ever abstract; that it tends, on the contrary, to be something as concrete and casual as a glance intercepted, a remark overheard, or an insignificant news item buried at the bottom of page three. Yet it is by trivialities like these that the true playwright's blood is fired. They spur him to story-telling; they bring on the narrative fit that is his glory and his only credential. Show me a congenital eavesdropper with the instincts of a peeping Tom, and I will show you the makings of a dramatist. Only the makings, of course: curiosity about people is merely the beginning of the road to the masterpiece: but if that curiosity is sustained you will find, when the rules have been mastered and the end has been reached, that a miracle has happened. Implicit in the play, surging between and beneath the lines, will be exactly what the author feels about the Major Issues of his Time.

To take off from a generality is an infertile exercise, as if a man should carry about with him the plan of some mighty edifice, hoping that if he stares at it long enough the human beings needed to build it will spring full-grown from the parchment. Vain hope, for the secret of life is not there. It hides where it has always hidden, in the most obvious and unguarded place. It lies somewhere within that staircase eccentric, my diarist's landlady, who likened him to George III and tittered. Study her, or your wife, or the grocer; probe them patiently; and you will find, to your resounding amazement, that you have written a play about power, loneliness, colour, bomb-fright, and revolution to boot. Would you know the shortest way to good playwriting? Pause on the stairs.

Curtains, 1961

ALAN SILLITOE

1928–

Cunning is What Counts

As soon as I got to Borstal they made me a long-distance cross-country runner. I suppose they thought I was just the build for it because I was long and skinny for my age (and still am) and in any case I didn't mind it much, to tell you the truth, because running had always been made much of in our family, especially running away from the police. I've always been a good runner, quick and with a big stride as well, the only trouble being that no matter how fast I run, and I did a very fair lick even though I do say so myself, it didn't stop me getting caught by the cops after that bakery job.

You might think it a bit rare, having long-distance cross-country runners in Borstal, thinking that the first thing a long-distance cross-country runner would do when they set him loose at them fields and woods would be to run as far away from the place as he could get on a bellyful of Borstal slumgullion—but you're wrong, and I'll tell you why. The first thing is that them bastards over us aren't as daft as they most of the time look, and for another thing I'm not so daft as I would look if I tried to make a break for it on my long-distance running, because to abscond and then get caught is nothing but a mug's game, and I'm not falling for it. Cunning is what counts in this life, and even that you've got to use in the slyest way you can; I'm telling you straight: they're cunning, and I'm cunning. If only 'them' and 'us' had the same ideas we'd get on like a house on fire, but they don't see eye to eye with us and we don't see eye to eye with them, so that's how it stands and how it will always stand. The one fact is that all of us are cunning, and because of this there's no love lost between us. So the thing is that they know I won't try to get away from them: they sit there like spiders in that crumbly manor house, perched like jumped-up jackdaws on the roof, watching out over the drives and fields like German generals from the tops of tanks. And even when I jog-trot on behind a wood and they can't see me anymore they know my sweeping-brush head will bob along that hedge-top in an hour's time and that I'll report to the bloke on the gate.

The Loneliness of the Long-Distance Runner, 1959

DAN JACOBSON

1929–

Business Partners

Fink, poor fellow, was a widower, and each of his daughters had said that she would rather be dead than live in a dump like Lyndhurst, so he had to live all by himself in the Diamond Hotel, near the office, on the other side of the Market Square. The food at the Diamond, Fink said, was giving him an ulcer in the stomach, so he ate his lunch with Gottlieb, at the Gottliebs' house. Carefully they drove to Gottlieb's house for lunch—one day in Gottlieb's car and the next day in Fink's—and ate the lunch that Sylvia and Mrs Gottlieb served them both. Then Gottlieb retired to his bedroom with the newspaper and had a little sleep until two o'clock, and Fink did the same in the lounge, with his shoes off and his stockinged feet pointing to the ceiling from the end of the sofa.

'It's no life for a man without a wife,' Mrs Gottlieb reported to her husband. 'He had holes in his socks today.'

'Holes in his socks! A fine advertisement for his soft-goods!'

Mrs Gottlieb was not amused. 'It's a shame. I'd offer to darn them, but he'd be offended. You know what he's like.'

'Very well,' Gottlieb nodded. 'Poor fellow.'

'He'd be hurt that I saw the holes in his socks. He has such terrible pride.'

'Fink's pride is a terrible thing. It is eating him away.'

Sometimes Riva cast about in her mind for a suitable widow for Fink. 'It's what he needs,' she said. 'Then he'll be happy again.'

Gottlieb was more cautious. 'Perhaps he would be a little happier, and not so proud.'

At other times Gottlieb reminded her that the man had *three* daughters, not one of whom had made it her business to stay in Lyndhurst and look after her father. Instead each one of them, as she had reached maturity of a sort, and eligibility without doubt for marriage, had deliberately gone off to Johannesburg in search of the professional man that each had succeeded in marrying. 'A girl has to get married,' Gottlieb admitted to his wife, 'but is it impossible to manage it in Lyndhurst?'

And when he wanted to goad Fink, Gottlieb always inquired after Fink's daughters. 'What has happened to Althea?' he would ask. 'She married the lawyer?'

Fink would know what was coming. 'Yes.'

'He's doing well?'

'He's making a living.'

Gottlieb would think this over for a moment or two.

'And Lynda? She married the doctor?'

'Yes.'

'And how is his practice?'

'Very good. An excellent practice in a good suburb.'

'And Claire, her husband is also making a living?'

'A first-class living.'

'That's a good thing to hear. Three daughters, all married to good men, all making a living.' Gottlieb would nod, Gottlieb would suck at his tea, absently Gottlieb would deliver his blow.

'I haven't seen them for a long time. I'd like to see them again. Are they coming down to Lyndhurst soon?'

'Yes.'

'Oh—so?'

'Yes.'

Gottlieb would smile, Gottlieb would know he was on top. 'When?'

'I don't know,' Fink would shout. 'I don't know their plans.'

But if Fink had been really angered by Gottlieb's inquiries, he would tell Gottlieb, 'They're coming down when your Irvine comes down. On exactly the same train, that's when they're coming down.'

'My Irvine?' Gottlieb could see no connection between his Irvine and the questions he had been asking. Haughtily he asked, 'My Irvine? He's very well. He's learning hard to be a specialist.'

'And when he's finished he's coming to practice in Lyndhurst?'

'Perhaps,' Gottlieb would lie uneasily; and Fink would reply with a pitying shrug of his shoulders:

'Perhaps is as good as a feast.'

The Price of Diamonds, 1957

J. G. BALLARD

1930–

A Journey into Deep Time

Deep Time: 1,000,000 mega-years. I saw the Milky Way, a wheeling carousel of fire, and Earth's remote descendants, countless races inhabiting every stellar system in the galaxy. The dark intervals between the stars were a continuously flickering field of light, a gigantic phosphorescent ocean, filled with the vibrating pulses of electromagnetic communication pathways.

To cross the enormous voids between the stars they have progressively slowed their physiological time, first ten, then a hundred-fold, so accelerating stellar and galactic time. Space has become alive with transient swarms of comets and meteors, the constellations have begun to dislocate and shift, the slow majestic rotation of the universe itself is at last visible.

Deep Time: 10,000,000 mega-years. Now they have left the Milky Way, which has started to fragment and dissolve. To reach the island galaxies they have further slowed their time schemes by a factor of 10,000, and can thus communicate with each other across vast inter-galactic distances in a subjective period of only a few years. Continuously expanding into deep space, they have extended their physiological dependence upon electronic memory banks which store the atomic and molecular patterns within their bodies, transmit them outward at the speed of light, and later re-assemble them.

Deep Time: 100,000,000 mega-years. They have spread now to all the neighbouring galaxies, swallowing thousands of nebulae. Their time schemes have decelerated a million-fold, they have become the only permanent forms in an ever-changing world. In a single instant of their lives a star emerges and dies, a sub-universe is born, a score of planetary life-systems evolve and vanish. Around them the universe sparkles and flickers with myriad points of light, as untold numbers of constellations appear and fade.

Now, too, they have finally shed their organic forms and are composed of radiating electromagnetic fields, the primary energy substratum of the universe, complex networks of multiple dimensions, alive with the constant tremor of the sentient messages they carry, bearing the life-ways of the race.

To power these fields, they have harnessed entire galaxies riding the wave-fronts of the stellar explosions out toward the terminal helixes of the universe.

Deep Time: 1,000,000,000 mega-years. They are beginning to dictate the form and dimensions of the universe. To girdle the distances which circumscribe the cosmos they have reduced their time period to 0.00000001 of its previous phase. The great galaxies and spiral nebulae which once seemed to live for eternity are now of such brief duration that they are no longer visible. The universe is now almost filled by the great vibrating mantle of ideation, a vast shimmering harp which has completely translated itself into pure wave form, independent of any generating source.

As the universe pulses slowly, its own energy vortices flexing and dilating, so the force-fields of the ideation mantle flex and dilate in sympathy, growing like an embryo within the womb of the cosmos, a child which will soon fill and consume its parent.

Deep Time: 10,000,000,000 mega-years. The ideation-field has now swallowed the cosmos, substituted its own dynamic, its own spatial and temporal dimensions. All primary time and energy fields have been engulfed. Seeking the final extension of itself within its own bounds the mantle has reduced its time period to an almost infinitesimal 0.00000000 . . . *n* of its previous interval. Time has virtually ceased to exist, the ideation-field is nearly stationary, infinitely slow eddies of sentience undulating outward across its mantles.

Ultimately it achieves the final predicates of time and space, eternity and infinity, and slows to absolute zero. Then with a cataclysmic eruption it disintegrates, no longer able to contain itself. Its vast energy patterns begin to collapse, the whole system twists and thrashes in its mortal agony, thrusting outwards huge cataracts of fragmenting energy. In parallel, time emerges.

Out of this debris the first proto-galactic fields are formed, coalescing to give the galaxies and nebulae, the stars encircled by their planetary bodies. Among these, from the elemental seas, based on the carbon atom, emerge the first living forms.

So the cycle renews itself . . .

'The Waiting Grounds', *The Day of Forever*, 1967

WAGUIH GHALI
1930?–1969

An Egyptian Jimmy Porter

I left and went to Groppi's. I drank whisky and ate peanuts, watching the sophisticated crowd and feeling happy that my aunt had refused to give me the money. I had asked simply because my conscience was nagging. It was something I vaguely had to do but had kept putting off. Soon Omar and Jameel came in, then Yehia, Fawzi and Ismail. Groppi's is perhaps one of the most beautiful places to drink whisky in. The bar is under a large tree in the garden and there is a handsome black barman who speaks seven languages. We drank a bottle of whisky between us and I watched them fight to pay for it. Yehia paid, then we all left together. They each possess a car.

I am always a bit bored in the mornings because they are all either at the university or working. Sometimes I go and play snooker with Jameel at the billiards' club. You can find him there anytime—in fact he owns it. I would go there more often if it weren't for Font. Whenever I reproach myself for drinking too much, I tell myself it's Font who is driving me to drink. 'Font,' I told him once, 'just tell me what you want me to do?'

'Run away, you scum,' he answered. So I went to Groppi's and drank more whisky. There you are, although, of course, I still read *The New Statesman* and *The Guardian* and mine is perhaps the only copy of *Tribune* which comes to Egypt.

'Font,' I said another time, when I was nicely oiled and in a good mood, 'Font,' I said, 'you're about the only angry young man in Egypt.' And I laughed. It struck me as very funny.

'Go,' he replied. 'Go and sponge some more on these parasites.'

It was I who made Font work in the snooker club. Jameel thought I was joking when I told him it was the only thing would keep Font off the streets. In fact I had to show him Font with his barrow in Sharia-el-Sakia. Jameel was shocked to see one of his old school-friends on the street. It was all I could do to stop him from offering Font enough money to live on for the rest of his life. Font would have spat on him and probably hit me.

There he was then. Selling cucumbers. Cucumbers of all things. Of course I understood. He was Jimmy Porter. We had seen the play together in London and there he was, a degree in his pocket and selling cucumbers. There were other barrows too; lettuce, onions, sunflower seeds, beans. We stopped the car in front of Font and looked at him.

'Get going,' he said.

I said I wanted to buy cucumbers but that I didn't trust his weights.

'Scram,' he shouted. 'I'll break your rotten face if you don't scram.' (This is typical Font. He'll be sarcastic to the other boys but when it's me, he's infuriated.) Jameel told him he needed someone to look after the snooker place for him.

'He's too much of a snob,' I said. 'He wouldn't like to be seen working where his old school-friends might come in.'

'Do you think I give a damn about you idiots,' Font screamed. Jameel is a quiet fellow and told him he really needed someone. Font might have accepted if I had not been there, so he looked at me with his 'you dirty traitor' expression instead.

'Font,' I asked in English, 'what do the other barrow boys think of Virginia Woolf?'

He fell into the trap and answered in English.

'You making fun of them? They never had a chance to go to school, you scum. Has that parasite beside you ever read a book in his life? With all his money he's nothing but a fat, ignorant pig.'

Jameel is so docile he doesn't mind being called a fat, ignorant pig at all. However, by then the other barrow boys were approaching. Font, dressed in Arab clothes, looking after a barrow and speaking in English, awoke their curiosity. 'What's that? What's that?' they asked.

'He's a spy,' I told them and they immediately became threatening. 'We'll deal with that son of a dog,' they shouted. Font became incoherent with rage. We pulled him into the car and drove away quickly.

I had to leave the car soon afterwards to escape Font's wrath, but a week later he was brushing the snooker tables with the *Literary Supplement.*

Beer in the Snooker Club, 1964

CHINUA ACHEBE

1930–

Poisoned Coffee

My host did not waste time. At about five o'clock that afternoon he told me to get ready and go with him to see the Hon. Simon Koko, Minister for Overseas Training. Earlier that day one of those unseasonal December rains which invariably brought on the cold harmattan had fallen. It had been quite heavy and windy and the streets were now littered with dry leaves, and sometimes half-blocked by broken-off tree branches; and one had to mind fallen telegraph and high-voltage electric wires.

Chief Koko, a fat jovial man wearing an enormous home-knitted red-and-yellow sweater was about to have coffee. He asked if we would join him or have some alcohol.

'I no follow you black white-men for drink tea and coffee in the hot afternoon,' said Chief Nanga. 'Whisky and soda for me and for Mr Samalu.'

Chief Koko explained that nothing warmed the belly like hot coffee and proceeded to take a loud and long sip followed by a satisfied Ahh! Then he practically dropped the cup and saucer on the drinks-table by his chair and jumped up as though a scorpion had stung him.

'They have killed me,' he wailed, wringing his hands, breathing hard and loud and rolling his eyes. Chief Nanga and I sprang up in alarm and asked together what had happened. But our host kept crying that *they* had killed him and they could now go and celebrate.

'What is it, S.I.?' asked Chief Nanga, putting an arm around the other's neck.

'They have poisoned my coffee,' he said, and broke down completely. Meanwhile the steward, hearing his master's cry, had rushed in.

'Who poisoned my coffee?' he asked.

'Not me-o!'

'Call the cook!' thundered the Minister. 'Call him here. I will kill him before I die. Go and bring him.'

The steward dashed out again and soon returned to say the cook had gone out. The Minister slumped into his chair and began to groan and hold his stomach. Then his bodyguard whom we had seen dressed like a cowboy hurried in from the front gate, and hearing what had happened dashed out at full speed to try and catch the cook.

'Let's go and call a doctor,' I said.

'That's right,' said Chief Nanga with relief and, leaving his friend, rushed towards the telephone. I hadn't thought about the telephone.

'What is the use of a doctor?' moaned our poisoned host. 'Do they know about African poison? They have killed me. What have I done to them? Did I owe them anything? Oh! Oh! Oh! What have I done?'

Meanwhile Chief Nanga had been trying to phone a doctor and was not apparently getting anywhere. He was now shouting threats of immediate sacking at some invisible enemy.

'This is Chief the Honourable Nanga speaking,' he was saying. 'I will see that you are dealt with. Idiot. That is the trouble with this country. Don't worry, you will see. Bloody fool. . . .'

At this point the cowboy bodyguard came in dragging the cook by his shirt collar. The Minister sprang at him with an agility which completely belied his size and condition.

'Wait, Master,' pleaded the cook.

'Wait your head!' screamed his employer, going for him. 'Why you put poison for my coffee?' His huge body was quivering like jelly.

'Me? Put poison for master? Nevertheless!' said the cook, side-stepping to avoid a heavy blow from the Minister. Then with surprising presence of mind he saved himself. (Obviously the cowboy had already told him of his crime.) He made for the cup of coffee quickly, grabbed it and drank every drop. There was immediate silence. We exchanged surprised glances.

'Why I go kill my master?' he asked of a now considerably sobered audience. 'Abi my head no correct? And even if to say I de craze why I no go go jump for inside lagoon instead to kill my master?' His words carried conviction. He proceeded to explain the mystery of the coffee. The Minister's usual Nescafé had run out at breakfast and he had not had time to get a new tin. So he had brewed some of his own locally processed coffee which he maintained he had bought from OHMS.

There was an ironic twist to this incident which neither of the ministers seemed to notice. OHMS—Our Home Made Stuff—was the popular name of the gigantic campaign which the Government had mounted all over the country to promote the consumption of locally made products. Newspapers, radio and television urged every patriot to support this great national effort which, they said, held the key to economic emancipation without which our hard-won political freedom was a mirage. Cars equipped with loudspeakers poured out new jingles up and down the land as they sold their products in town and country. In the language of the ordinary people these cars, and not the wares they advertised, became known as OHMS. It was apparently from one of them the cook had bought the coffee that had nearly cost him his life.

A Man of the People, 1966

IAN NAIRN
1930–1983

Piccadilly Circus

This really is the centre of London. But why? What makes it the focus of everyone's night out; why, when you stand under Eros, with the traffic swirling endlessly round, does it suddenly feel as though the whole enormous city is in the palm of your hand? What happens, I think, is a mixture of Nash and accident. Every important line of force in the West End goes through here: not only Nash's axis of Regent Street dividing Mayfair and Soho, which now leads directly to the Victoria Tower of the Houses of Parliament in one of London's great views. Piccadilly comes in, looking utterly respectable and club-like. Coventry Street slips in short and lewd from Leicester Square. Shaftesbury Avenue creeps out as though it knew that it led nowhere. And behind the bland façades on the north side, a dozen alleys slip away into Soho and sin. Long may they stay sinful. Every scale and temperament of London is represented somewhere, nowhere more than in the contrast between east and west sides of the Circus. Swan & Edgar's has all the circumstance that Norman Shaw could give it, and also pomp rather than pomposity, which is quite a rare thing. The buildings opposite on the east side are small, cramped, and covered with illuminated signs which are one of the best, least self-conscious displays of popular art anywhere in London. (The rooms behind them are quite windowless.) And all this fits together. Piccadilly Circus is not one or another, but the mixture. The east side will be rebuilt soon, and the architects of Britain will find themselves stretched not to put the dreary finger of good taste on it. This is a bit of real life, not an academic design problem, and if the circus is reconstructed the traffic must stay visible and circulating, for it is an essential part of the hub-of-the-world feeling. At the very centre, the hub of the hub, is Eros. Pellucid and innocent, quite free of Alfred Gilbert's neurotic manoeuvres, and utterly right. This is T. S. Eliot's 'voice . . . in the stillness between two waves of the sea'. And it all depends on traffic.

Nairn's London, 1966

Highgate Cemetery

There are better reasons for going here than to look at the grave of Karl Marx. This is the creepiest place in London; no Dickensian stretch of the river can match this calculated exercise in stucco horror, now itself decomposing. The entrance is well downhill in Swains Lane, and at first the landscape is ordinary. But as you wind up the hill it becomes more and more overgrown, choked in winter by dead fronds with an unnerving resemblance to spanish moss. The landscape looks less and less like London, more and more like Louisiana. Then, with a shock like a blood-curdling scream, the Egyptian entrance shows up. Beyond it, the Catacombs, a sunken rotunda lined with stucco-faced vaults, gently deliquescent, crumbling away. Inside them, coffins on ledges. A familiar name like Carl Rosa on one of the vaults seems to accentuate the terror. Nothing seems real but death at its greyest and clammiest. The cemetery closes well before dark, and a good job too.

Nairn's London

MORDECAI RICHLER

1931–

Back Home Again in Montreal

Sitting with the Hershes, day and night, a bottle of Remy Martin parked between his feet, such was Jake's astonishment, commingled with pleasure, in their responses, that he could not properly mourn for his father. He felt cradled, not deprived. He also felt like Rip Van Winkle returned to an innocent and ordered world he had mistakenly believed long extinct. Where God watched over all, doing His sums. Where everything fit. Even the holocaust which, after all, had yielded the state of Israel. Where to say, 'Gentlemen, the Queen,' was to offer the obligatory toast to Elizabeth II at an affair, not to begin a discussion on Andy Warhol. Where smack was not habit-forming, but what a disrespectful child deserved; pot was what you simmered the chicken soup in; and camp was where you sent the boys for the summer. It was astounding, Jake was incredulous, that after so many years and fevers, after Dachau, after Hiroshima, revolution, rockets in space, DNA, bestiality in the streets, assassinations in and out of season, there were still brides with shining faces who were married in white gowns, posing for the *Star* social pages with their prizes, pear-shaped boys in evening clothes. There were aunts who sold raffles and uncles who swore by the *Reader's Digest*. French Canadians, like overflying airplanes distorting the TV picture, were only tolerated. DO NOT ADJUST YOUR SET, THE

TROUBLE IS TEMPORARY. Aunts still phoned each other every morning to say what sort of cake they were baking. Who had passed this exam, who had survived that operation. A scandal was when a first cousin was invited to the bar mitzvah *kiddush*, but not the dinner. Eloquence was the rabbi's sermon. They were ignorant of the arts, they were overdressed, they were overstuffed, and their taste was appallingly bad. But within their self-contained world, there was order. It worked.

As nobody bothered to honor them, they very sensibly celebrated each other at fund-raising synagogue dinners, taking turns at being Man-of-the-Year, awarding each other ornate plaques to hang over the bar in the rumpus room. Furthermore, God was interested in the fate of the Hershes, with time and consideration for each one. To pray was to be heard. There was not even death, only an interlude below ground. For one day, as Rabbi Polsky assured them, the Messiah would blow his horn, they would rise as one and return to Zion. Buried with twigs in their coffins, as Baruch had once said, to dig their way to him before the neighbors.

St Urbain's Horseman, 1971

TOM WOLFE

1931–

Glassy Brilliance

The Bavardages' dining-room walls had been painted with so many coats of burnt-apricot lacquer, fourteen in all, they had the glassy brilliance of a pond reflecting a campfire at night. The room was a triumph of nocturnal reflections, one of many such victories by Ronald Vine, whose forte was the creation of glitter without the use of mirrors. Mirror Indigestion was now regarded as one of the gross sins of the 1970s. So in the early 1980s, from Park Avenue to Fifth, from Sixty-second Street to Ninety-sixth, there had arisen the hideous cracking sound of acres of hellishly expensive plate-glass mirror being pried off the walls of the great apartments. No, in the Bavardages' dining room one's eyes fluttered in a cosmos of glints, twinkles, sparkles, highlights, sheens, shimmering pools, and fiery glows that had been achieved in subtler ways, by using lacquer, glazed tiles in a narrow band just under the ceiling cornices, gilded English Regency furniture, silver candelabra, crystal bowls, School of Tiffany vases, and sculpted silverware that was so heavy the knives weighed on your fingers like saber handles.

The two dozen diners were seated at a pair of round Regency tables. The banquet table, the sort of Sheraton landing field that could seat twenty-four if you inserted all the leaves, had disappeared from the smarter dining rooms. One shouldn't be so formal, so grand. Two small tables were much better. So what if these two small tables were surrounded and bedecked by a buildup of *objets*, fabrics, and *bibelots* so lush it would have made the Sun King blink? Hostesses such as Inez Bavardage prided themselves on their gift for the informal and intimate.

To underscore the informality of the occasion there had been placed, in the middle of each table, deep within the forest of crystal and silver, a basket woven from hardened vines in a highly rustic Appalachian Handicrafts manner. Wrapped around the vines, on the outside of the basket, was a profusion of wildflowers. In the centre of the basket were massed three or four dozen poppies. This *faux-naïf* centerpiece was the trademark of Huck Thigg, the young florist, who would present the Bavardages with a bill for $3,300 for this one dinner party.

Sherman stared at the plaited vines. They looked like something dropped by Gretel or little Heidi of Switzerland at a feast of Lucullus. He sighed. All . . . too much.

The Bonfire of the Vanities, 1987

ANITA BROOKNER

Key Questions

On my last visit to America, where I gave my talk on Sleeping Beauty and other related topics to two women's colleges, I was interested to note the variety of female responses. The older members of the faculty regarded it politely as a feminist entertainment, while the younger ones debated it fervently. I found to my surprise that I was more impressed by the former than by the latter. These placid dignified women, mostly in their fifties, mostly long divorced or else widowed, pursued a life of study in an all female atmosphere as if they were nuns in a mediaeval abbey. All had children or stepchildren, all taught a full syllabus, all had made their homes in the charming small towns and suburbs of Massachusetts and New Hampshire. They were all extremely gracious, in the American fashion, and manifested none of the recklessness, the combative vivacity of their younger counterparts.

Walking with one of these older women through the idyllic streets surrounding the campus I was not questioned on whether I had endured much sexual harassment in England but was shown the garden, invited to admire the dogwood, or indeed 'Janet's copper beech. I confess to a little envy: I haven't one of my own. But I can always look at hers. We have tea together at her house, when it's at its best, in October. Have you noticed that when the leaves fall they turn a dark ox-blood red? I dare say you have a fine garden at home.'

In the face of such magnificence I hardly care to tell her that I live in a small flat and that when I look out of the window all I see is the dirty river and the distant dull green of the park, no longer familiar to me. These days my walks no longer take me to the park, but only along streets increasingly choked with traffic. For this reason I am always glad, when I am on campus, to accept an invitation to walk round the lake from one of the younger women, perhaps a full professor at the age of thirty-two. They are so convivial that it would be churlish to refuse. But I find them exhausting, these women of goodwill, with their agenda of wrongs to be righted, of injustices to be eliminated. I want to stand still in the dusk and contemplate the lake, seeing only mist, hearing only a brief ripple where the wing of a bird disturbs the surface of the water, but I must respond intelligently, employ a certain kind of feminised argument, feel myself to be the victim of a monstrous wrong which has been passed down to me from generation to generation.

I am invited to share my experience in the workplace, and, remembering ABC Enterprises, reply truthfully that I was never happier. This seems to disappoint them, until I tell them that my colleagues were all women, when their faces clear. Then in all conscience I describe to them the later months, when the business was run by James Hemmings and his friends, and they become alert again. Any discrimination? I am demanded. Only being taken out to dinner by the boss, I reply, by which time I am regarded with the purest suspicion.

I am then questioned much more closely, and almost as a hostile witness, on my views on the position of women today. This is a key question, the answer to which will furnish material for seminar after seminar of feminist studies. These young women are painfully preoccupied with questions of gender. Yet most of them are married or in a relationship with some man. I have been introduced to one or two of the husbands and partners. They seemed nice enough, perhaps a little too conscious of sharing, as they put it. And yet their small children, where they exist, seem oddly anxious, as if this sharing were an alien concept, fit only for emancipated adults, who could discuss the matter until late into the night.

What the children want is not clear: perhaps they want a formal or even a traditional childhood, the kind they no longer read about in their politically correct story-books or encounter at their politically correct playgroups. Their parents reason with them, and the children know instinctively that they have not yet reached the age of reason. Besides, the reason they are being offered exists somewhere in the region of exasperation, and this they reject absolutely. And are right to do so.

As I stand on the edge of the lake, in the evening mist, urgent words are being poured into my ears to which I must respond. Although I am still young I want to assure my interlocutor that she will not be sexually harassed in perpetuity, that when her hair becomes less abundant and her skin loses its colour and its firmness she will be able to pursue a peaceful career studying something non-sexist like physics, or better still agronomy. I do not do this because I want to remain a polite guest, and also because I do not want to fall into my old position of class enemy. 'What is that bird?' I ask, in an effort to divert this so well-meaning young woman. 'Look! The new moon!' These observations are regarded as frivolous, for there is work to be done, there are categories to be redefined, laws to be changed. And underneath it all I sense a bewilderment which I in fact share. Will we be loved, will we be saved? And if so, by what or by whom?

A Family Romance, 1993

JOHN UPDIKE

1932–

Searching for a Way Out

The land refuses to change. The more he drives the more the region resembles the country around Mt Judge. The same scruff on the embankments, the same weathered billboards for the same insane products. At the upper edge of his headlight beams the naked tree-twigs make the same net. Indeed the net seems thicker now.

The animal in him swells its protest that he is going west. His mind stubbornly resists. The only way to get somewhere is to decide where you're going and go. His plan calls for him to bear left 28 miles after Frederick and that 28 miles is used up now and, though his instincts cry out against it, when a broad road leads off to the left, though it's unmarked, he takes it. It is unlikely that the road *would* be marked, from its thickness on the map. But it is a shortcut, he knows . . .

The road is broad and confident for miles, but there is a sudden patched stretch, and after that it climbs and narrows. Narrows not so much by plan as naturally, the edges crumbling in and the woods on either side crowding down. The road twists more and more wildly in its struggle to gain height and then without warning sheds its skin of asphalt and worms on in dirt. By now Rabbit knows this is not the road but he is afraid to stop the car to turn it around. He has left the last light of a house miles behind. When he strays from straddling the mane of weeds, brambles rake his painted sides. Tree-trunks and low limbs are all his headlights pick up; the scrabbling shadows spider backward through the web of wilderness into a black core where he fears his probe of light will stir some beast or ghost.

He supports speed with prayer, praying that the road not stop, remembering how on Mt. Judge even the shaggiest most forgotten logging lane eventually sloped to the valley. His ears itch; his height presses on them.

The prayer's answer is blinding. The trees at a far bend leap like flame and a car comes around and flies at him with its beams tilted high. Rabbit slithers over into the ditch and, faceless as death, the bright car rips by at a speed twice his own. For more than a minute Rabbit drives through this bastard's insulting dust. Yet the good news makes him meek, the news that this road goes two ways. And shortly he seems to be in a park. His lights pick up green little barrels stenciled PLEASE and the trees are thinned on both sides and in among them picnic tables and pavilions and outhouses show their straight edges. The curves of cars show too, and a few are parked close to the road, their passengers down out of sight. So the road of horror is a lovers' lane. In a hundred yards it ends.

It meets at right angles a smooth broad highway overhung by the dark cloud of a mountain ridge. One car zips north. Another zips south. There are no signs. Rabbit puts the shift in neutral and pulls out the emergency brake and turns on the roof light and studies his map. His hands and shins are trembling. His brain flutters with fatigue behind sandy eyelids; the time must be 12:30 or later. The highway in front of him is empty. He has forgotten the numbers of the routes he has taken and the names of the towns he has passed through. He remembers Frederick but can't find it and in time realizes he is searching in a section due west of Washington where he has never been. There are so many red lines and blue lines, long names, little towns, squares and circles and stars. He moves his eyes north but the only line he recognizes is the straight dotted line of the Pennsylvania–Maryland border. The Mason–Dixon Line. The schoolroom in which he learned this recurs to him, the rooted desk rows, the scarred varnish, the milky black of the blackboard, the sweet pieces of ass all up and down the aisles in alphabetical order. His eyes blankly founder. Rabbit hears a clock in his head beat, monstrously slow, the soft ticks as far apart as the sound of waves on the shore he had wanted to reach. He burns his attention through the film fogging his eyes down into the map again. At once 'Frederick' pops into sight, but in trying to steady its position he loses it, and fury makes the bridge of his nose ache. The names melt away and he sees the map whole, a net, all those red lines and blue lines and stars, a net he is somewhere caught in.

Rabbit, Run, 1960

From the Annals of Popular Music

The popular music of the late Forties and early Fifties, falling between the fading of the big bands and the beginning of rock, is generally forgotten:

no jazzomaniacs or rock addicts or show-tune nuts visit its files, and Golden Oldie disc jockeys rarely touch it. But it has preëmpted millions of my neurons with half-remembered titles and lyrics. Girls' names: 'Peg o My Heart' and 'Amy' and 'Laura' and 'Linda' ('when I go to sleep, I never count sheep. I count all the charms about Linda'). Strange little men: 'The Old Lamplighter' and 'Nature Boy' and that old master painter from the faraway hills whom we teen-agers so inevitably recast as the old masturbator. Who could get moony over 'Golden Earrings' or 'Tree in the Meadow'? We could, that's who. In 1948 James C. Petrillo called every orthodox musician out on strike and left us to dream along with ununionized sweet potatoes, banjos, bones, whistling choruses ('Heartaches'), and musical saws; we dreamed on anyhow. 'So Tired,' made great in Russ Morgan's arrangement, was, with 'Star Dust,' the epitome of violet-spotlight chic, the draggy end of the high-school dance, the fag end of our sophisticated smoky days—'so tired, so tired of living' and all of seventeen.

Then came college and, for me, a kind of pop silence. There was no music in the libraries then, and little in the dorms—it was believed to interfere with thought processes, rather than (as now) to be essential to them. I do seem to recall, from those four lost years, incredulously auditing in a humble Cambridge eatery Johnny Ray's 'The Little White Cloud That Cried.' I knew it was the end of something, but I didn't know of how very much. Rock 'n' roll began to shake the Eisenhower chapel; Elvis Presley suddenly achieved divinity—but all out of my earshot. The first song I remember distinctly getting to me, post-grad, was 'Blueberry Hill', where Fats Domino claimed to have found his thrill. Was finding your thrill anything like kiddley-diveying? No matter: I knew in my hormones what he meant, and just why Chubby Checker wanted to twist again like we did last summer. We had become suburbanites and wage-earners and parents, but our glands were less quiescent than they should have been: the sounds of revolution (Baez and Dylan; Peter, Paul, and Mary; Sonny and Cher) trickled through the Marimekko curtains, and our children taught us to frug. Oh, those glorious piping sugar-harmonied Supremes records before Diana Ross became a law unto herself! And of course the Beatles, who were intellectually ambitious even, and kept going deeper, just like Beethoven. I suppose my heartfelt farewell to popular music came in England, at the end of the Sixties, crooning and thumping and blinking back tears through the endless chorus of 'Hey Jude,' in which the Beatles could be heard dissolving. Take a sad song and make it better.

But you never really say goodbye; popular music is always there, flavoring our American lives, keeping our mortal beat, a murmuring subconscious sneaking up out of the car radio with some abrupt sliding phrase that hooks us into jubilation, into aspiration. I like it when, say, Madonna's 'True Blue' comes on: catchy. Long ago, driving to school with my father on cold winter mornings, I would lean into the feeble glow of the radio dial as if into warmth: this was me, this yearniness canned in New York and beamed from Philadelphia, beamed through the air to guide me, somehow, toward a wonderful life.

'Popular Music', *Odd Jobs*, 1992

V. S. NAIPAUL

1932–

Encountering Indian Poverty

India is the poorest country in the world. Therefore, to see its poverty is to make an observation of no value; a thousand newcomers to the country before you have seen and said as you. And not only newcomers. Our own sons and daughters, when they return from Europe and America, have spoken in your very words. Do not think your anger and contempt are marks of your sensitivity. You might have seen more: the smiles on the faces of the begging children, that domestic group among the pavement sleepers waking in the cool Bombay morning, father, mother and baby in a trinity of love, so self-contained that they are as private as if walls had separated them from you: it is your gaze that violates them, your sense of outrage that outrages them. . . . But wait. Stay six months. The winter will bring fresh visitors. Their talk will also be of poverty; they too will show their anger. You will agree; but deep down there will be annoyance; it will seem to you then, too, that they are seeing only the obvious; and it will not please you to find your sensibility so accurately parodied.

Ten months later I was to revisit Bombay and to wonder at my hysteria. It was cooler, and in the crowded courtyards of Colaba there were Christmas decorations, illuminated stars hanging out of windows against the black sky. It was my eye that had changed.

An Area of Darkness, 1964

A Politician in Exile

I know that return to my island and to my political life is impossible. The pace of colonial events is quick, the turnover of leaders rapid. I have already been forgotten; and I know that the people who supplanted me are themselves about to be supplanted. My career is by no means unusual. It falls into the pattern. The career of the colonial politician is short and ends brutally. We lack order. Above all, we lack power, and we do not understand that we lack power. We mistake words and the acclamation of words for power; as soon as our bluff is called we are lost. Politics for us are a do-or-die, once-for-all charge. Once we are committed we fight more than political battles; we often fight quite literally for our lives. Our transitional or makeshift societies do not cushion us. There are no universities or City houses to refresh us and absorb us after the heat of battle. For those who lose, and nearly everyone in the end loses, there is only one course: flight. Flight to the greater disorder, the final emptiness: London and the home counties.

There are many of us around living modestly and without recognition in small semi-detached suburban houses. We go out on a Saturday morning to do the shopping at Sainsbury's and jostle with the crowd. We have known grandeur beyond the football-pool dreams of our neighbours; but in the lower-middle-class surroundings to which we are condemned we pass for immigrants. The pacific society has its cruelties. Once a man is stripped of his dignities he is required, not to die or to run away, but to find his level. Occasionally I read a letter in *The Times*, a communication on a great topic from a mean address; I recognize a name and see with enormous sympathy the stirring of some chained and desperate spirit. Just the other day I was in the West End, in the basement of one of those department stores where the assistants carry their names on little plastic badges. I was among the unpainted kitchen furniture. I required a folding wooden clothes-airer, which I thought I might introduce at nights into the bathroom of the hotel where I now live. An assistant had her back to me. I went up to her. She turned. Her face was familiar, and a quick glance at the name pinned to her blouse left no room for doubt. We had last met at a conference of non-aligned nations; her husband had been one of the firebrands. We had seen one another in a glittering blur of parties and dinners. Then she had worn her 'national costume'. It had given her a seductive appearance, and the colours of her silks had set off her own rich Asiatic complexion. Now the regulation skirt and blouse of the department store converted her breasts and hips into untidy bundles. I remembered how, when we were saying our good-byes at the airport, the third secretary of her embassy, breaking the precise arrangements of protocol, had run up at the last moment with a bunch of flowers, which he offered to her, the personal gift of a man desperate to keep his job in the diplomatic service, fearful of being recalled to the drabness of his own background. Now she stood among the unpainted kitchen furniture. I couldn't face her. I left the purchase unmade, hoping that she would not recognize me, and turned away.

Later, sitting in the train, going past the backs of tall sooty houses, tumbledown sheds, Victorian working-class tenements whose gardens, long abandoned, had for stretches been turned into Caribbean backyards, I wondered about the firebrand. Was he pining away tamely in some office job? Or was he, too broken to take up employment, idling on a meagre income in a suburban terrace? Many of us, it must be said, are poor. The tale is there in the occasional small paragraph on the financial page which tells of the collapse of some little-known Swiss bank. Too much shouldn't be made of this, however. Most of us were too timid to make a fortune, or too ignorant; we measured both our opportunities and our needs by the dreams of our previous nonentity.

The Mimic Men, 1967

EDWARD HOAGLAND

1932–

Stuttering and Smiling

Somerset Maugham described his bitter discovery when he was a boy that prayer was no help: he woke up next morning still clamped to his adamant stutter. I was more of a pantheist; I kept trusting to the efficacy of sleep itself, or to the lilting lift that caused birds to fly. Also I went to a bunch of speech therapists. At the Ethical Culture School in New York, for example, a woman taught me to stick my right hand in my pocket and, with that hidden hand, to write down over and over the first letter of the word I was stuttering on. This was intended to distract me from stuttering, and it did for a week or two. The trouble was that watching me play pocket pool that way was more unsettling to other people than the ailment it was meant to cure. At a camp in northern Michigan I was trained by a team from the university to speak so slowly that in effect I wasn't speaking at all; I talked with the gradualism of a flower growing—so absurdly tardy a process that my mind unhinged itself from what was going on. In Cambridge, Massachusetts, a young fellow from the University of Iowa—and oh, how *he* stuttered—took the most direct approach. He got me to deliberately imitate myself, which was hard on me since I was already terribly tired of stuttering, and to stare, as well, at the people whom I was talking to in order to find out what their reactions were. I found out, for one thing, that some of my friends and about a fifth of the strangers I met smiled when the difficulty occurred, though they generally turned their heads to the side or wiped their mouths with one hand to hide the smile. Thereafter, life seemed simpler if I avoided looking at anybody, whoever he was, when I was stuttering badly, and I wasn't so edgily on the alert to see if I'd spit inadvertently.

Not that I lacked understanding for the smilers, though, because for many years I too had had the strange impulse, hardly controllable, to smile if somebody bumped his head on a low door lintel or received sad news. The phenomenologists say this is a form of defense. It goes with childhood especially, and I stopped indulging in it one night in Boston when I was in a police patrol wagon. A friend and I had been out for a walk, he was hit by a car, and as he woke from unconsciousness during the ride to the hospital and asked what had happened, I found myself grinning down at him while I answered. A few weeks later I was walking past an apartment building just as a rescue squad carried out a would-be suicide. He was alive, on a stretcher. When our eyes touched he smiled impenetrably, but I didn't smile back.

'The Threshold and the Jolt of Pain', *Heart's Desire*, 1988

MALCOLM BRADBURY

1932–

Howard Kirk Takes a Class

The seminar room where Howard meets this weekly class, Socsci 4.17, is an interior room without windows, lit by artificial light. The room is a small one; on three of its walls are pinned large charts, illustrating global poverty, while the fourth wall is occupied by a large green chalkboard, on which someone has written, as people are always writing, 'Workers unite'. The room contains a number of tables with gunmetal legs and bright yellow tops; these have been pushed together in the centre to form one large table, where some previous tutor has been holding a formal class. In the room stand three students, positioned somewhere indeterminate between the tables and the walls; it does not do, at Watermouth, to take it for granted that a room arrangement that suits one teacher will ever suit another. Classes at Watermouth are not simply occasions for the one-directional transmission of knowledge; no, they are events, moments of communal interaction, or, like Howard's party, happenings. There are students from Waternouth who, visiting some other university, where traditional teaching prevails, stare in amazement, as if confronted by some remarkable and exciting innovation; their classes are not like that. For Watermouth does not only educate its students; it teaches its teachers. Teams of educational specialists, psychologists, experts in group dynamics, haunt the place; they film seminars, and discuss them, and, unimpressed by anything as thin as a manifestation of pure intellectual distinction, demonstrate how student C has got through the class without speaking, or student F is expressing boredom by picking his nose, or student H has never, during an hour-long class, had eye-contact with the teacher once. They have sample classes, where the faculty teach each other, sessions in which permanent enmities are founded, and clothes get torn, and elderly professors of international reputation burst into tears. So Howard comes into the room, and he looks around it, and he inspects the arrangement of the tables. 'I'm afraid this is what Goffman would call a bad eye-to-eye ecological huddle,' he says. 'We don't want these tables here like this, do we?'

The History Man, 1975

PHILIP ROTH

1933–

The Men

On Sunday mornings, when the weather is warm enough, twenty of the neighborhood men (this in the days of short center field) play a round of seven-inning softball games, starting at nine in the morning and ending about one in the afternoon, the stakes for each game a dollar a head. The umpire is our dentist, old Dr Wolfenberg, the neighborhood college graduate—night school on High Street, but as good as Oxford to us. Among the players is our butcher, his twin brother our plumber, the grocer, the owner of the service station where my father buys his gasoline—all of them ranging in age from thirty to fifty, though I think of them not in terms of their years, but only as 'the men.' In the on-deck circle, even at the plate, they roll their jaws on the stumps of soggy cigars. Not boys, you see, but men. Belly! Muscle! Forearms black with hair! Bald domes! And then the voices they have on them—cannons you can hear go off from as far as our front stoop a block away. I imagine vocal cords inside them thick as clotheslines! lungs the size of zeppelins! Nobody has to tell them to stop mumbling and speak up, never! And the outrageous things they say! The chatter in the infield isn't chatter, it's kibbitzing, and (to this small boy, just beginning to learn the art of ridicule) hilarious, particularly the insults that emanate from the man my father has labeled 'The Mad Russian,' Biderman, owner of the corner candy store (and bookie joint) who has a 'hesitation' side-arm delivery, not only very funny but very effective. 'Abracadabra,' he says, and pitches his backbreaking drop. And he is always giving it to Dr Wolfenberg: 'A blind ump, okay, but a blind dentist?' The idea causes him to smite his forehead with his glove. 'Play ball, comedian,' calls Dr Wolfenberg, very Connie Mack in his perforated two-tone shoes and Panama hat, 'start up the game, Biderman, unless you want to get thrown out of here for insults—!' 'But how do they teach you in that dental school, Doc, by Braille?'

Meanwhile, all the way from the outfield comes the badinage of one who in appearance is more cement-mixer than Homo sapiens, the prince of the produce market, Allie Sokolow. The *pisk* he opens on him! (as my mother would put it). For half an inning the invective flows in toward home plate from his position in deep center field, and then when his team comes to bat, he stations himself in the first-base coaching box and the invective flows uninterruptedly out in the opposite direction—and none of it has anything to do with any contretemps that may actually be taking place on the field. Quite the opposite. My father, when he is not out working on Sunday mornings, comes by to sit and watch a few innings with me; he knows Allie Sokolow (as he knows many of the players), since they were all boys together in the Central Ward, before he met my mother and moved to Jersey City. He says that Allie has always been like this, 'a real showman.' When Allie charges in toward second base, screaming his gibberish and double-talk in the direction of home plate (where there isn't even a batter as yet—where Dr Wolfenberg is merely dusting the plate with the whisk broom he brings to the game), the people in the stands couldn't be more delighted: they laugh, they clap, they call out, 'You tell him, Allie! You give it to him, Sokolow!' And invariably Dr Wolfenberg, who takes himself a little more seriously than your ordinary nonprofessional person (and is a German Jew to boot), holds up his palm, halting an already Sokolow-stopped game, and says to Biderman, 'Will you please get that *meshuggener* back in the out-field?'

I tell you, they are an endearing lot! I sit in the wooden stands alongside first base, inhaling that sour springtime bouquet in the pocket of my fielder's mitt—sweat, leather, vaseline—and laughing my head off. I cannot imagine myself living out my life any other place but here. Why leave, why go, when there is everything here that I will ever want? The ridiculing, the joking, the acting-up, the pretending—anything for a laugh! I love it! And yet underneath it all, *they mean it, they are in dead earnest.* You should see them at the end of the seven innings when that dollar has to change hands. Don't tell *me* they don't mean it! Losing and winning is not a joke . . . and yet it is! And that's what charms me most of all. Fierce as the competition is, they cannot resist clowning and kibbitzing around. Putting on a show! How I am going to love growing up to be a Jewish man! Living forever in the Weequahic section, and playing softball on Chancellor Avenue from nine to one on Sundays, a perfect joining of clown and competitor, kibbitzing wiseguy and dangerous long-ball hitter.

Portnoy's Complaint, 1969

OLIVER SACKS

1933–

Becoming a Patient

As I was taken in the ambulance from London airport, to the great hospital where I was to be operated the next day, my good humour and sanity began to leave me, and in their place came a most terrible dread. I cannot call it the dread of death, though doubtless that was contained in it. It was rather a dread of something dark and nameless and secret—a nightmarish feeling, uncanny and ominous, such as I had not experienced on the Mountain at all. Then, on the whole, I had faced what reality had in store, but now I felt distortion rising, taking over. I saw it, I felt it, and I felt powerless to combat it. It would not go away, and the most I could do was to sit tight and hold fast, murmuring a litany of reassurance and commonsense to myself. That journey in the ambulance was a bad trip, in all ways—and behind the dread (which I could not vanquish as its creator), I felt delirium rocking my mind—such a delirium as I had used to know, all too well, as a child, whenever I was feverish or had one of my migraines. My brother, who was riding with me, observed some of this, and said:

'Easy now, Ollie, it won't be so bad. But you *do* look dead white, and clammy and ill. I think you've a fever, and you look toxic and shocked. Try and rest. Keep calm. Nothing terrible will happen.'

Yes, indeed I had a fever. I felt myself burning and freezing. Obsessive fears gnawed at my mind. My perceptions were unstable. Things seemed to change—to lose their reality and become, in Rilke's phrase, 'things made of fear'. The hospital, a prosaic Victorian building, looked for a moment like the Tower of London. The wheeled stretcher I was placed on made me think of a tumbril, and the tiny room I was given, with its window blocked out (it had been improvised at the last minute, all the wards and side-wards being taken), put me in mind of the notorious torture chamber, 'Little Ease', in the Tower. Later, I was to become very fond of my tiny womb-like room, and because it was windowless, I christened it 'The Monad'. But on that ghastly, ominous evening of the 25th, seized by fever and fantastical neurosis, shaking with secret dread, I perceived everything amiss and could do nothing about it.

'Execution tomorrow,' said the clerk in Admissions.

I knew it must have been '*Operation* tomorrow', but the feeling of execution overwhelmed what he said. And if my room was 'Little Ease', it was also the Condemned Cell. I could see in my mind, with hallucinatory vividness, the famous engraving of Fagin in his cell. My gallows-humour consoled me and undid me and got me through the other grotesqueries of admission. (It was only up on the ward that humanity broke in). And to these grotesque fantasies were added the realities of admission, the systematic depersonalisation which goes with becoming-a-patient. One's own clothes are replaced by an anonymous white nightgown, one's wrist is clasped by an identification bracelet with a number. One becomes subject to institutional rules and regulations. One is no longer a free agent; one no longer has rights; one is no longer in the world-at-large. It is strictly analogous to becoming a prisoner, and humiliatingly reminiscent of one's first day at school. One is no longer a person—one is now an inmate. One understands that this is protective, but it is quite dreadful too. And I was seized, overwhelmed, by this dread, this elemental sense and dread of degradation, throughout the dragged-out formalities of admission, until—suddenly, wonderfully—humanity broke in, in the first lovely moment I was addressed as myself, and not merely as an 'admission' or *thing*.

Suddenly into my condemned cell a nice jolly Staff-Nurse, with a Lancashire accent, burst in, a person, a woman, sympathetic—and comic. She was 'tickled pink', as she put it, when she unpacked my rucksack and found fifty books and a virtual absence of clothes.

'Oh, Dr Sacks, you're potty!' she said, and burst into jolly laughter.

And then I laughed too. And in that healthy laughter the tension broke and the devils disappeared.

A Leg to Stand On, 1984

MICHAEL FRAYN

1933–

A Journalist Looks Back

Raindrops trembled on the office windows, coalesced, and ran down, leaving paths like silver snail tracks against the lightness of the sky. Dyson watched them absently, grimacing as he bit each of the finger-nails on his right hand trim in turn. Bob sat sucking toffees, and watching Dyson from behind his hand. Old Eddy Moulton, who was awake and in an unusually forthcoming mood, looked at Dyson and Bob alternately as he talked.

'I knew Stanford Roberts,' he said. 'But then I knew most of them. Walter Belling, Stanley Furle, Sir Redvers Tilley—you name them, I knew them. Stanley Furle carried a cane with a solid gold knob—never went anywhere without it. The knob unscrewed and the inside of the cane was hollow. Stanley used to keep it filled with Scotch—three solid feet of Johnnie Walker. One night he was at the old Blackfriars Ring. At the end of every round off came the gold knob and up went the stick. He was with a man called Naylor—not Freddie Naylor of the *Mail*, but Allington Naylor, who later worked for A. W. Simpson on the *Morning Post*. A. W. Simpson was one of the great ones. So was Allington Naylor. So was Stanford Roberts, for that matter. Real journalists. Real professionals. Stanford could turn you out an impeccable paragraph on any subject you liked to name at the drop of a hat. He'd have done a par about the lead in his pencil if you'd asked him—a stick and a half—a column—whatever you needed; and all of it full of wit and erudition.'

Dyson went on staring at the raindrops, saying nothing.

'Honestly, John,' said Bob, 'you were great. I don't know what you're worrying about.'

Dyson gave no sign that he had heard.

'Anyway,' said old Eddy Moulton, 'when Stanley Furle came out of the Ring at the end of the evening, he fell down the stairs and blacked his eye on the knob of his cane! I was in the Kings and Keys the night J. D. Maconochie told Bentham Miller that O. M. Pargetter's Tibetan Terror story was a hoax. Oswald hadn't been nearer Tibet than the end of Folkestone pier! I was in the Feathers the night Sandy MacAllister punched Laurence Uden on the nose for saying that Stanford Roberts had been drunk at poor old Sidney Cunningham's funeral.'

'Come on, John,' said Bob. 'Cheer up.'

'In fact,' said old Eddy Moulton, 'Stanford *was* drunk at Sidney Cunningham's funeral. I met R. D. Case afterwards—he was on the *Westminster Gazette* at that time—and he told me that Stanford was so drunk that he'd almost fallen into the grave! Apparently he'd just been caught in time by George Watson-Forbes, who later wrote a remarkable series of articles in the *Daily News* on the Home Rule question.'

Dyson stirred himself, and sighed.

'Would somebody ring Morley, Bob?' he said, scarcely opening his mouth to let the words out, 'and ask him where his copy is? I can't face talking to him to-day.'

'Now don't be silly, John,' said Bob. 'Jannie and I both thought you were tremendously good.'

'The last job I went on with Sidney Cunningham,' said old Eddy Moulton, 'was an explosion in a gas-main at Newark, which killed thirteen people. I travelled up from King's Cross with Sidney, Daryl Bligh of the *Graphic*, K. B. D. Clarke of *The Times*, "Tibby" Tisdale of the *News*, Stanford Roberts, of course, and I think we had Norton Malley with us, who would at that time I suppose have been on the *Morning Post*, though he later went back to the *Irish Times*. Anyway, the day after we all arrived in Newark, Tibby announced that it was his birthday, and Stanford had the idea of hiring a private dining-room at the Ram . . .'

Dyson suddenly turned on old Eddy Moulton, silencing him with the sourness of his expression.

'You never went on a gas-main explosion in Newark, Eddy,' he said irritably. 'You're getting mixed up with one of your "In Years Gone By" columns.'

Old Eddy Moulton stared at Dyson, his mouth slightly open.

'You did a fifty-years-ago about a gas-main explosion in Newark the week before last,' said Dyson. 'Don't you remember?'

'I went to Newark on the story, too,' said old Eddy Moulton.

'You're getting mixed up, Eddy.'

'That was my own story I put in the column,' said old Eddy Moulton stubbornly.

'Oh, for God's sake, Eddy!' snapped Dyson. He jumped to his feet and walked quickly out of the room, slamming the door behind him. Old Eddy Moulton looked at Bob, who looked away.

'I was only trying to cheer him up,' said old Eddy Moulton.

Towards the End of the Morning, 1967

WOLE SOYINKA

1934–

A Nigerian Childhood and the Coming of Radio

Now the workmen were threading the walls again, we wondered what the new magic would produce. This time there was no bulb, no extra switches on the wall. Instead, a large wooden box was brought into the house and installed at the very top of the tallboy, displacing the old gramophone which now had to be content with one of the lower shelves on the same furniture. The face of the box appeared to be made of thick plaited silk.

But the functions continued to be the same. True, there was no need to put on a black disc, no need to crank a handle or change a needle, it only required that the knob be turned for sounds to come on. Unlike the gramophone however, the box could not be made to speak or sing at any time of the day. It began its monologue early in the morning, first playing 'God save The King'. The box went silent some time in the afternoon, resumed late afternoon, then, around ten or eleven in the evening, sang 'God Save the King' once more and went to sleep . . .

At certain set hours, the box delivered THE NEWS. The News soon became an object of worship to Essay and a number of his friends. When the hour approached, something happened to this club. It did not matter what they were doing, they rushed to our house to hear the Oracle. It was enough to watch Essay's face to know that the skin would be peeled off the back of any child who spoke when he was listening to The News. When his friends were present, the parlour with its normal gloom resembled a shrine, rapt faces listened intently, hardly breathing. When The Voice fell silent all faces turned instinctively to the priest himself. Essay reflected for a moment, made a brief or long comment and a babble of excited voices followed.

The gramophone fell into disuse. The voices of Denge, Ayinde Bakare, Ambrose Campbell; a voice which was so deep that I believed it could only have been produced by a special trick of His Master's Voice, but which father assured me belonged to a black man called Paul Robeson—they all were relegated to the cocoon of dust which gathered in the gramophone section. Christmas carols, the songs of Marian Anderson; oddities, such as a record in which a man did nothing but laugh throughout, and the one concession to a massed choir of European voices—the Hallelujah Chorus—all were permanently interned in the same cupboard. Now voices sang, unasked, from the new box. Once that old friend the Hallelujah Chorus burst through the webbed face of the box and we had to concede that it sounded richer and fuller than the old gramophone had ever succeeded in rendering it. Most curious of all the fare provided by the radio however were the wranglings of a family group which were relayed every morning, to the amusement of a crowd, whose laughter shook the box. We tried to imagine where this took place. Did this family go into the streets to carry on their interminable bickering or did the idle crowd simply hang around their home, peeping through the windows and cheering them on? We tried to imagine any of the Aké families we knew exposing themselves this way—the idea was unthinkable. It was some time, and only by listening intently before I began to wonder if this daily affair was that dissimilar from the short plays which we sometimes acted in school on prize-giving day. And I began also to respond to the outlandish idiom of their humour.

Hitler monopolized the box. He had his own special programme and somehow, far off as this war of his whim appeared to be, we were drawn more and more into the expanding arena of menace. Hitler came nearer home every day. Before long the greeting, Win-The-War replaced some of the boisterous exchanges which took place between Essay and his friends. The local barbers invented a new style which joined the repertory of Bentigo, Girls-Follow-Me, Oju-Aba, Missionary Cut and others. The women also added Win-de-woh to their hair-plaits, and those of them who presided over the local foodstalls used it as a standard response to complaints of a shortage in the quantity they served. Essay and his correspondents vied with one another to see how many times the same envelope could be used between them. Windows were blacked over, leaving just tiny spots to peep through, perhaps in order to obtain an early warning when Hitler came marching up the path. Household heads were dragged to court and fined for showing a naked light to the night. To reinforce the charged atmosphere of expectations, the first aeroplane flew over Abeokuta; it had a heavy drone which spoke of Armageddon and sent Christians fleeing into churches to pray and stay the wrath of God. Others simply locked their doors and windows and waited for the end of the world. Only those who had heard about these things, and flocks of children watched in fascination, ran about the fields and the streets, following the flying miracle as far as they could, shouting greetings, waving to it long after it had gone and returning home to await its next advent.

Aké, 1981

ALASDAIR GRAY

1934–

Dragonhide

With no will to see anyone or do anything he immersed himself in sleep as much as possible, only waking to stare at the wall until sleep returned. It was a sullen pleasure to remember that the disease spread fastest in sleep. Let it spread! he thought. What else can I cultivate? But when the dragonhide had covered the arm and hand it spread no further, though the length of the limb as a whole increased by six inches. The fingers grew stouter, with a slight web between them, and the nails got longer and more curving. A red point like a rose-thorn formed on each knuckle. A similar point, an inch and a half long, grew on the elbow and kept catching the sheets, so he slept with his right arm hanging outside the cover onto the floor. This was no hardship as there was no feeling in it, though it did all he wanted with perfect promptness and sometimes obeyed wishes before he consciously formed them. He would find it holding a glass of water to his lips and only then notice he was thirsty, and on three occasions it hammered the floor until he waked up and Mrs Fleck came running with a cup of tea. He felt embarrassed and told her to ignore it. She said, 'No, no, Lanark, my husband had that before he disappeared. You must never ignore it.'

He thanked her. She rubbed her hands on her apron as if drying them and said abruptly, 'Do you mind if I ask you something?'

'No.'

'Why don't you get up, Lanark, and look for work? I've lost a husband by that'—she nodded to the arm—'and a couple of lodgers, and all of them, before the end, just lay in bed, and all of them were decent quiet fellows like yourself.'

'Why should I get up?'

'I don't like talking about it, but I've an illness of my own—not what you have, a different one—and it's never spread very far because I've had work to do. First it was a husband, then lodgers, now it's these bloody weans. I'm sure if you get up and work your arm will improve.'

'What work can I get?'

'The Forge over the road is wanting men.'

Lanark laughed harshly and said, 'You want me to make components for the Q39.'

'I know nothing about factory work, but if a man gets pay and exercise by it I don't see why he should complain.'

'How can I go for work with an arm like this?'

'I'll tell you how. My husband had the same trouble on exactly the same arm. So I knitted him a thick woollen glove and lined it with wash leather. He never used it. But if you wear it along with your jacket nobody will notice, and if they do, why bother? There are plenty of men with crabby hands.'

Lanark said, 'I'll think about it.'

He was prevented from saying more by the hand's raising the teacup to his lips and holding it there.

Lanark, 1981

DAVID MALOUF

1934–

The Last Survivor

He has already been pointed out to me: a flabby, thickset man of fifty-five or sixty, very black, working alongside the others and in no way different from them—or so it seems. When they work he swings his pick with the same rhythm. When they pause he squats and rolls a cigarette, running his tongue along the edge of the paper while his eyes, under the stained hat, observe the straight line of the horizon; then he sets it between his lips, cups flame, draws in, and blows out smoke like all the rest.

Wears moleskins looped low under his belly and a flannel vest. Sits at smoko on one heel and sips tea from an enamel mug. Spits, and his spit hisses on stone. Then rises, spits in his palm and takes up the pick. They are digging holes for fencing-posts at the edge of the plain. When called he answers immediately, 'Here, boss,' and then, when he has approached, 'Yes boss, you wanna see me?' I am presented and he seems amused, as if I were some queer northern bird he had heard about but never till now believed in, a sort of crane perhaps, with my grey frock-coat and legs too spindly in their yellow trousers; an odd, angular fellow with yellow-grey side-whiskers, half spectacles and a cold-sore on his lip. So we stand face to face.

He is, they tell me, the one surviving speaker of his tongue. Half a century back, when he was a boy, the last of his people were massacred. The language, one of hundreds (why make a fuss?) died with them. Only not quite. For all his lifetime this man has spoken it, if only to himself. The words, the great system of sound and silence (for all languages, even the simplest, are a great and complex system) are locked up now in his heavy skull, behind the folds of the black brow (hence my scholarly interest), in the mouth with its stained teeth and fat, rather pink tongue. It is alive still in the man's silence, a whole alternative universe, since the world as we know it is in the last resort the words through which we imagine and name it; and when he narrows his eyes, and grins and says 'Yes, boss, you wanna see me?', it is not breathed out.

I am (you may know my name) a lexicographer. I come to these shores from far off, out of curiosity, a mere tourist, but in my own land I too am the keeper of something: of the great book of words of my tongue. No, not mine, my people's, which they have made over centuries, up there in our part of the world, and in which, if you have an ear for these things and a nose for the particular fragrance of a landscape, you may glimpse forests, lakes, great snow-peaks that hang over our land like the wings of birds. It is all there in our mouths. In the odd names of our villages, in the pet-names we give to pigs or cows, and to our children too when they are young, Little Bean, Pretty Cowslip; in the nonsense rhymes in which so much simple wisdom is contained (not by accident, the language itself discovers these truths), or in the way, when two consonants catch up a repeated sound, a new thought goes flashing from one side to another of your head.

All this is mystery. It is a mystery of the deep past, but also of now. We recapture on our tongue, when we first grasp the sound and make it, the same word in the mouths of our long dead fathers, whose blood we move in and whose blood still moves in us. Language *is* that blood. It is the sun taken up where it shares out heat and light to the surface of each thing and made whole, hot, round again. *Solen*, we say, and the sun stamps once on the plain and pushes up in its great hot body, trailing streams of breath.

O holiest of all holy things!—it is a stooped blond crane that tells you this, with yellow side-whiskers and the grey frockcoat and trousers of his century—since we touch here on beginnings, go deep down under Now to the remotest dark, far back in each ordinary moment of our speaking, even in gossip and the rigmarole of love words and children's games, into the lives of our fathers, to share with them the single instant of all our seeing and making, all our long history of doing and being. When I think of my tongue being no longer alive in the mouths of men a chill goes over me that is deeper than my own death, since it is the gathered death of all my kind. It is black night descending once and forever on all that world of forests, lakes, snow peaks, great birds' wings; on little fishing sloops, on foxes nosing their way into a coop, on the piles of logs that make bonfires, and the heels of the young girls leaping over them, on sewing-needles, milk pails, axes, on gingerbread moulds made out of good birchwood, on fiddles, school slates, spinning-tops—my breath catches, my heart jumps. O the holy dread of it! Of having under your tongue the first and last words of all those generations down there in your blood, down there in the earth, for whom these syllables were the magic once for calling the whole of creation to come striding, swaying, singing towards them. I look at this old fellow and my heart stops, I do not know what to say to him.

'The Only Speaker of His Tongue', *Antipodes*, 1985

DAVID LODGE
1935–

A Master of Theory

In Chicago it is midnight; yesterday hesitates for a second before turning into today. A cold wind blows off the lake, sends litter bowling across the pavement like tumbleweed, chills the bums and whores and drug addicts who huddle for shelter beneath the arches of the elevated railway. Inside the city's newest and most luxurious hotel, however, it is almost tropically warm. The distinctive feature of this building is that everything you would expect to find outside it is inside, and vice versa, except for the weather. The rooms are stacked around a central enclosed space, and their balconies project inwards, into a warm, air-conditioned atmosphere, overlooking a fountain and a lily pond filled with multi-coloured fish. There are palm-trees growing in here, and flowering vines that climb up the walls and cling to the balconies. Outside, transparent elevators like tiny glass bubbles creep up and down the sheer curtain walling of the building, giving the occupants vertigo. It is the architecture of inside-out.

In a penthouse suite from whose exterior windows the bums and whores and drug addicts are quite invisible, and even the biggest automobiles on the Loop look like crawling bugs, a man lies, naked, on his back, at the centre of a large circular bed. His arms and legs are stretched out in the form of an X, so that he resembles a famous drawing by Leonardo, except that his body is thin and scraggy, an old man's body, tanned but blotchy, the chest hair grizzled, the legs bony and slightly bowed, the feet calloused and horny. The man's head, however, is still handsome: long and narrow, with a hooked nose and a mane of white hair. The eyes, if they were open, would be seen to be dark brown, almost black. On the bedside table is a pile of magazines, academic quarterlies, some of which have fallen, or been thrown, to the floor. They have titles like *Diacritics, Critical Inquiry, New Literary History, Poetics and Theory of Literature, Metacriticism.* They are packed with articles set in close lines of small print, with many footnotes in even smaller print, and long lists of references. They contain no pictures. But who needs pictures when he has a living breathing centrefold all his own?

Kneeling on the bed beside the man, in the space between his left arm and his left leg, is a shapely young Oriental woman, with long, straight, shining black hair falling down over her golden-hued body. Her only garment is a tiny *cache-sexe* of black silk. She is massaging the man's scrawny limbs and torso with a lightly perfumed mineral oil, paying particular attention to his long, thin, circumcised penis. It does not respond to this treatment, flopping about in the young woman's nimble fingers like an uncooked chippolata.

This is Arthur Kingfisher, doyen of the international community of literary theorists, Emeritus Professor of Columbia and Zürich Universities, the only man in academic history to have occupied two chairs simultaneously in different continents (commuting by jet twice a week to spend Mondays to Wednesdays in Switzerland and Thursdays to Sundays in New York), now retired but still active in the world of scholarship, as attender of conferences, advisory editor to academic journals, consultant to university presses. A man whose life is a concise history of modern criticism: born (as Arthur Klingelfischer) into the intellectual ferment of Vienna at the turn of the century, he studied with Shklovsky in Moscow in the Revolutionary period, and with I. A. Richards in Cambridge in the late twenties, collaborated with Jakobson in Prague in the thirties, and emigrated to the United States in 1939 to become a leading figure in the New Criticism in the forties and fifties, then had his early work translated from the German by the Parisian critics of the sixties, and was hailed as a pioneer of structuralism. A man who has received more honorary degrees than he can remember, and who has at home, at his house on Long Island, a whole room full of the (largely unread) books and offprints sent to him by disciples and admirers in the world of scholarship. And this is Song-mi Lee, who came ten years ago from Korea on a Ford Foundation fellowship to sit at Arthur Kingfisher's feet as a research student, and stayed to become his secretary, companion, amanuensis, masseuse and bedfellow, her life wholly dedicated to protecting the great man against the importunities of the academic world and soothing his despair at no longer being able to achieve an erection or an original thought. Most men of his age would have resigned themselves to at least the first of these impotencies, but Arthur Kingfisher had always led a very active sex life and regarded it as vitally connected, in some deep and mysterious way, with his intellectual creativity.

The telephone beside the bed emits a discreet electronic cheep. Song-mi Lee wipes her oily fingers on a tissue and stretches across the prone body of Arthur Kingfisher, her rosy nipples just grazing his grizzled chest, to pick up the receiver. She squats back on her heels, listens, and says into the instrument, 'One moment please, I will see if he is available.' Then, holding her hand over the mouthpiece, she says to Arthur Kingfisher: 'A call from Berlin—will you take it?'

'Why not? It's not as though it's interrupting anything,' says Arthur Kingfisher gloomily. 'Who do I know in Berlin?'

Small World, 1984

JOYCE CAROL OATES
1938–

A Slight Paternal Interest

Came to Yewville, as I recall, to put my life in order. To experiment with solitude. *Via* negative. Asceticism. Alternative to suicide. Brought along my treasures, left the other books behind, filled this apartment with books I have dragged everywhere with me in the past fifteen years; and now I can't read them. Can't concentrate. On my best days, out of bed early and a half-hour of exercises, heaving and puffing, poor Kasch forty years old and twenty years out of condition, and then at the table by the window here, eager, expectant as a student, buoyed up by a sense of tremulous hope, as if God were about to speak, about to open one of the books to *the* page: but even then, on my best days, I read for only an hour at the most, and then the thoughts intrude, her image rushes in, I am miserable with desire, miserable with affection that cannot be discharged. . . . *Childwold*, murmur the voices, *Childwold Childwold.*

God speaks. In these voices. Haunting, tender, maddening. . . . But there is no God, there are no voices. These are phantasms in my brain, mere projections, shards of old desires, split-off fragments of my soul that yearn to coalesce, to be born. There is no God. I am not filled with God. I am pure consciousness trapped in time, in a body, I am unenlightened, I am dragged in a circle, I am helpless to fight free, I am licking the feet, the dirty feet, of the devils who dance about me, mocking me, I am prostrate before them, I am weeping onto their dirty toes, I would suck their toes, I would grovel in the dirt before them, I would do anything they bid me in order to be free. But there is no God, there are no voices. The girl is no one. I feel a slight paternal interest in her. I pity her. What she has told me of her family makes me shudder, with revulsion as much as pity; I don't want to meet them. I don't care about them. The sister, Nancy—the baby she carried on her hip: no. Hillbillies, nearly. White trash. My mother hated them, though she tried to disguise her hatred by being so generous, so broad-minded. I hate them too. I really do. I hate Laney's smoke-stinking clothes, her premature cynicism, her slight, almost dwarfish figure. I hate her fate—her doom. I am not involved with it or with her. The Kasches made their fortune in lumber, in pine and oak, they deforested many a mountain in the Chautauquas, they were neither good nor evil, they were selfish like everyone, less selfish perhaps than the other lumber barons in the state, less megalomaniac, less driven; I am not one of them, it is only an accident that I was born one of them, I might have been born anywhere at all, to any parents at all, and so I am not tainted with ancestral guilt: but even if I were, I would not be as guilty as others who have exploited the farmers in the Valley. I would not be as guilty as the corporate farms that are buying up their land so greedily. I am not involved with them, so God tells me. I know. There is no God. The voice is a delusion. I am not connected except by a stray, vagrant desire, an altogether contemptible lust. . . . Still her face presses against mine, something brushes near, I imagine someone is hurrying up the stairs as she did the other week, I sit alert, waiting, painfully expectant; the book before me lies forgotten.

The works of Meister Eckhart, of Pascal, of Shakespeare, of Boehme, of Saint Augustine, of Thoreau, of Kierkegaard, of Rilke, and Nietzsche and Santayana; the Upanishads, the Bible, the Tibetan Book of the Dead. . . . Can't read, can't concentrate. I hear her tell me that her mother knows about us, someone telephoned, I hear her raspish indifferent voice saying she likes me, she *does* like me, but . . . but what do I want with her, what is the point of it? . . . Just friendship, I tell her. And laugh. And make jokes. And run my hand lightly through her hair, a fatherly gesture she cannot misinterpret.

Childwold, 1976

MARGARET ATWOOD

1939–

In Love with Raymond Chandler

An affair with Raymond Chandler, what a joy! Not because of the mangled bodies and the marinated cops and hints of eccentric sex, but because of his interest in furniture. He knew that furniture could breathe, could feel, not as we do but in a way more muffled, like the word *upholstery*, with its overtones of mustiness and dust, its bouquet of sunlight on ageing cloth or of scuffed leather on the backs and seats of sleazy office chairs. I think of his sofas, stuffed to roundness, satin-covered, pale-blue like the eyes of his cold blonde unbodied murderous women, beating very slowly, like the hearts of hibernating crocodiles; of his chaises longues, with their malicious pillows. He knew about front lawns too, and greenhouses, and the interiors of cars.

This is how our love affair would go. We would meet at a hotel, or a motel, whether expensive or cheap it wouldn't matter. We would enter the room, lock the door, and begin to explore the furniture, fingering the curtains, running our hands along the spurious gilt frames of the pictures, over the real marble or the chipped enamel of the luxurious or tacky washroom sink, inhaling the odour of the carpets, old cigarette smoke and spilled gin and fast meaningless sex or else the rich abstract scent of the oval transparent soaps imported from England, it wouldn't matter to us; what would matter would be our response to the furniture, and the furniture's response to us. Only after we had sniffed, fingered, rubbed, rolled on and absorbed the furniture of the room would we fall into each other's arms, and onto the bed (king-sized? peach-coloured? creaky? narrow? four-posted? pioneer-quilted? lime-green chenille-covered?), ready at last to do the same things to each other.

Good Bones, 1992

CLIVE JAMES

1939–

Lollies

When you got to the Odeon the first thing you did was stock up with lollies. Lollies was the word for what the English call sweets and the Americans call candy. Some of the more privileged children had upwards of five shillings each to dispose of, but in fact two bob was enough to buy you as much as you could eat. Everyone, without exception, bought at least one Hoadley's Violet Crumble Bar. It was a slab of dense, dry honeycomb coated with chocolate. So frangible was the honeycomb that it would shatter when bitten, scattering bright yellow shrapnel. It was like trying to eat a Ming vase. The honeycomb would go soft only after a day's exposure to direct sunlight. The chocolate surrounding it, however, would liquefy after only ten minutes in a dark cinema.

Fantails came in a weird, blue, rhomboidal packet shaped like an isosceles triangle with one corner missing. Each individual Fantail was wrapped in a piece of paper detailing a film star's biography—hence the pun, fan tales. The Fantail itself was a chocolate-coated toffee so glutinous that it could induce lockjaw in a mule. People had to have their mouths chipped open with a cold chisel. One packet of Fantails would last an average human being for ever. A group of six small boys could go through a packet during the course of a single afternoon at the pictures, but it took hard work and involved a lot of strangled crying in the dark. Any fillings you had in your second teeth would be removed instantly, while children who still had any first teeth left didn't keep them long.

The star lolly, outstripping even the Violet Crumble Bar and the Fantail in popularity, was undoubtedly the Jaffa. A packet of Jaffas was loaded like a cluster bomb with about fifty globular lollies the size of ordinary marbles. The Jaffa had a dark chocolate core and a brittle orange candy coat: in cross section it looked rather like the planet Earth. It presented two alternative ways of being eaten, each with its allure. You could fondle the Jaffa on the tongue until your saliva ate its way through the casing, whereupon the taste of chocolate would invade your mouth with a sublime, majestic inevitability. Or you could bite straight through and submit the interior of your head to a stunning explosion of flavour. Sucking and biting your way through forty or so Jaffas while Jungle Jim wrestled with the crocodiles, you nearly always had a few left over after the stomach could take no more. The spare Jaffas made ideal ammunition. Flying through the dark, they would bounce off an infantile skull with the noise of bullets hitting a bell. They showered on the stage when the manager came out to announce the lucky ticket. The Jaffa is a part of Australia's theatrical heritage. There was a famous occasion, during the Borovansky Ballet production of *Giselle* at the Tivoli in Sydney, when Albrecht was forced to abandon the performance. It was a special afternoon presentation of the ballet before an audience of schoolchildren. Lying in a swoon while awaiting the reappearance of Giselle, Albrecht aroused much comment because of his protuberant codpiece. After being hit square on the power-bulge by a speeding Jaffa, he woke up with a rush and hopped off the stage in the stork position.

Unreliable Memoirs, 1980

MARGARET DRABBLE

1939–

Disappointments

She had been completely perverted, poor Julie, somewhere, by someone, given desires that could never be assuaged, given the knowledge to know what she was missing, the sensitivity to suffer at the loss. Like talentless artists or writers, whose lack of talent in no way kindly diminishes their insatiable craving to succeed, she was doomed to disappointment. He was too moved by her to betray her. A stronger man than himself would not, in the first place, have married her, as he had done, but at least he had the strength to stick it out.

Her looks had not deteriorated as much as her temper, however. She still looked quite presentable. He thought of her, as a girl, in that white jacket, her reddish hair all bouncy round her face. Now, as a woman, shiny with good health and lipstick, driving along in her big fat car. Julie on the telephone, giggling like a schoolgirl to her so-called friends: Julie betrayed by those same friends, furious about the betrayal, abusing them as wantonly as she had praised them, resorting to the gross terms of childhood—'Stinking bitch,' she would say, violently, 'Great fat old cow—' referring to some smart young woman who had withdrawn her attendance or stood her up at some lunch date in favour of a more profitable, wealthier, more sophisticated host. And the childish crudity of these terms would horrify him: they reminded him of his own grandfather, if of anything, and of his mother's pained wincing and refined agonies beneath such abuse—abuse directed not at her, because his grandfather was afraid of his mother, as who would not be, but at all the undistinguished world around. There was in Julie a coarseness and a lack of discrimination that must have attracted him to her, as one is attracted, compelled, to approach one's own doom, to live out one's own hereditary destiny: coarseness she had from his grandfather, coldness from his mother, and their good qualities she lacked. She must have good qualities of her own, he would tell himself, but he was too deeply entrenched in her, in his own past, to perceive them. He grieved for her: her disappointments and childish enthusiasms grieved him: but what could one do about them? She lacked all judgement, all reserve: her emotions swung violently, creaking and screeching like a weather vane in uncertain weather.

The Needle's Eye, 1972

BRUCE CHATWIN
1940–1989

Tierra del Fuego

The Strait of Magellan is another case of Nature imitating Art. A Nuremberg cartographer, Martin Beheim, drew the South-West Passage for Magellan to discover. His premise was entirely reasonable. South America, however peculiar, was normal compared to the Unknown Antarctic Continent, the Antichthon of the Pythagoreans, marked FOGS on mediaeval maps. In this Upside-down-land, snow fell upwards, trees grew downwards, the sun shone black, and sixteen-fingered Antipodeans danced themselves into ecstasy. WE CANNOT GO TO THEM, it was said, THEY

CANNOT COME TO US. Obviously a strip of water had to divide this chimerical country from the rest of Creation.

On October 21st 1520, the Feast of St Ursula and her Eleven Thousand (shipwrecked) Virgins, the fleet rounded a headland which the Captain called Cabo Vírgenes. Yawning before them was a bay, apparently landlocked. In the night a gale blew from the north-east and swept the *Concepcíon* and the *San Antonio* through the First Narrows, through the Second Narrows, and into a broad reach bearing south-west. When they saw the tidal rips, they guessed it led to the further ocean. They returned to the flagship with the news. Cheers, cannonades and pennons flying.

On the north shore a landing party found a stranded whale and a charnel-place of two hundred corpses raised on stilts. On the southern shore they did not land.

Tierra del Fuego—The Land of Fire. The fires were the camp-fires of the Fuegian Indians. In one version Magellan saw smoke only and called it Tierra del Humo, the Land of Smoke, but Charles V said there was no smoke without fire and changed the name.

The Fuegians are dead and all the fires snuffed out. Only the flares of oil rigs cast a pall over the night sky.

Until in 1619 the Dutch fleet of Schouten and LeMaire rounded the Horn—and named it, not for its shape, but after Hoorn on the Zuyder Zee, cartographers drew Tierra del Fuego as the northern cape of the Antichthon and filled it with suitable monstrosities: gorgons, mermaids and the Roc, that outsize condor which carried elephants.

Dante placed his Hill of Purgatory at the centre of the Antichthon. In Canto 26 of *The Inferno*, Ulysses, swept on his mad track south, sights the island-mountain looming from the sea as the waves close over his ship—*infin che 'l mar fu sopra noi richiuso*—destroyed by his passion to exceed the boundaries set for man.

Fireland then is Satan's land, where flames flicker as fireflies on a summer night, and, in the narrowing circles of Hell, ice holds the shades of traitors as straws in glass.

This perhaps is why they did not land.

In Patagonia, 1977

ANNE TYLER

1941–

A Perky Young Girl, a Blind Old Woman

He opened a maroon velvet album, each of its pulpy gray pages grown bright yellow as urine around the edges. None of the photos here was properly glued down. A sepia portrait of a bearded man was jammed into the binding alongside a Kodachrome of a pink baby in a flashy vinyl wading pool, with SEPT '63 stamped on the border. His mother poked her face out, expectant. He said, 'Here's a man with a beard. I think it's your father.'

'Possibly,' she said, without interest.

He turned the page. 'Here's a group of ladies underneath a tree.'

'Ladies?'

'None of them look familiar.'

'What are they wearing?'

'Long, baggy dresses,' he told her. 'Everything seems to be sagging at the waist.'

'That would be nineteen-ten or so. Maybe Iola's engagement party.'

'Who was Iola?'

'Look for me in a navy stripe,' she told him.

'There's no stripes here.'

'Pass on.'

She had never been the type to gaze backward, had not filled his childhood with 'When I was your age,' as so many mothers did. And even now, she didn't use these photos as an excuse for reminiscing. She hardly discussed them at all, in fact—even those in which she appeared. Instead, she listened, alert, to any details he could give her about her past self. Was it that she wanted an outsider's view of her? Or did she hope to solve some mystery? 'Am I smiling, or am I frowning? Would you say that I seemed happy?'

When Ezra tried to ask *her* any questions, she grew bored. 'What was your mother like?' he would ask.

'Oh, that was a long time ago,' she told him.

She hadn't had much of a life, it seemed to him. He wondered what, in all her history, she would enjoy returning to. Her courtship, even knowing how it would end? Childbirth? Young motherhood? She did speak often and wistfully of the years when her children were little. But most of the photos in this drawer dated from long before then, from back in the early part of the century, and it was those she searched most diligently. 'The Baker family reunion, that would be. Nineteen-o-eight. Beulah's sweet sixteen party. Lucy and Harold's silver anniversary.' The events she catalogued were other people's; she just hung around the fringes, watching. 'Katherine Rose, the summer she looked so beautiful and met her future husband.'

He peered at Katherine Rose. 'She doesn't look so beautiful to *me*,' he said.

'It faded soon enough.'

Katherine Rose, whoever she was, wore a severe and complicated dress of a type not seen in sixty years or more. He was judging her rabbity face as if she were a contemporary, some girl he'd glimpsed in a bar, but she had probably been dead for decades. He felt he was being tugged back through layers of generations.

He flipped open tiny diaries, several no bigger than a lady's compact, and read his mother's cramped entries aloud. '*December eighth, nineteen-twelve. Paid call on Edwina Barrett. Spilled half-pint of top cream in the buggy coming home and had a nice job cleaning it off the cushions I can assure you . . .*' '*April fourth, nineteen-o-eight. Went into town with Alice and weighed on the new weighing machine in Mr Salter's store. Alice is one hundred thirteen pounds, I am one hundred ten and a half.*' His mother listened, tensed and still, as if expecting something momentous, but all he found was *purchased ten yards heliotrope brilliantine*, and *made chocolate blanc-mange for the Girls' Culture Circle*, and *weighed again at Mr Salter's store.* During the summer of 1908—her fourteenth summer, as near as he could figure—she had weighed herself about every two days, hitching up her pony Prince and riding clear downtown to do so. '*August seventh,*' he read. '*Had my measurements taken at the dressmaker's and she gave me a copy to keep. I have developed in every possible sense.*' He laughed, but his mother made an impatient little movement with one hand. '*September ninth,*' he read, and then all at once had the feeling that the ground had rushed away beneath his feet. Why, that perky young girl was this old woman! This blind old woman sitting next to him! She had once been a whole different person, had a whole different life separate from his, had spent her time *swinging clubs with the Junior Amazons* and *cutting up with the Neal boys something dreadful* and *taking first prize at the Autumn Recital Contest. (I hoped that poor Nadine would win,* she wrote in a chubby, innocent script, *but of course it was nice to get it myself.)* His mother sat silent, absently stroking the dead corsage. 'Never mind,' she told him.

'Shall I stop?'

'It wasn't what I wanted after all.'

Dinner at the Homesick Restaurant, 1982

SALMAN RUSHDIE

1947–

The Hour of Birth Draws Near

August 13th, 1947: discontent in the heavens. Jupiter, Saturn and Venus are in quarrelsome vein; moreover, the three crossed stars are moving into the most ill-favoured house of all. Benarsi astrologers name it fearfully: 'Karamstan! They enter Karamstan!'

While astrologers make frantic representations to Congress Party bosses, my mother lies down for her afternoon nap. While Earl Mountbatten deplores the lack of trained occultists on his General Staff, the slowly turning shadows of a ceiling fan caress Amina into sleep. While M. A. Jinnah, secure in the knowledge that his Pakistan will be born in just eleven hours, a full day before independent India, for which there are still thirty-five hours to go, is scoffing at the protestations of horoscope-mongers, shaking his head in amusement, Amina's head, too, is moving from side to side.

But she is asleep. And in these days of her boulder-like pregnancy, an enigmatic dream of flypaper has been plaguing her sleeping hours . . . in which she wanders now, as before, in a crystal sphere filled with dangling strips of the sticky brown material, which adhere to her clothing and rip it off as she stumbles through the impenetrable papery forest; and now she struggles, tears at paper, but it grabs at her, until she is naked, with the baby kicking inside her, and long tendrils of flypaper stream out to seize her by her undulating womb, paper glues itself to her hair nose teeth breasts thighs, and as she opens her mouth to shout a brown adhesive gag falls across her parting lips . . .

'Amina Begum!' Musa is saying. 'Wake up! Bad dream, Begum Sahiba!'

Incidents of those last few hours—the last dregs of my inheritance: when there were thirty-five hours to go, my mother dreamed of being glued to brown paper like a fly. And at the cocktail hour (thirty hours to go) William Methwold visited my father in the garden of Buckingham Villa. Centre-parting strolling beside and above big toe, Mr Methwold reminisced. Tales of the first Methwold, who had dreamed the city into existence, filled the evening air in that penultimate sunset. And my father—apeing Oxford drawl, anxious to impress the departing Englishman—responded with, 'Actually, old chap, ours is a pretty distinguished family, too.' Methwold listening: head cocked, red rose in cream lapel, wide-brimmed hat concealing parted hair, a veiled hint of amusement in his eyes . . . Ahmed Sinai, lubricated by whisky, driven on by self-importance, warms to his theme. 'Mughal blood, as a matter of fact.' To which Methwold, 'No! Really? You're pulling my leg.' And Ahmed, beyond the point of no return, is obliged to press on. 'Wrong side of the blanket, of course; but Mughal, certainly.'

That was how, thirty hours before my birth, my father demonstrated that he, too, longed for fictional ancestors . . . how he came to invent a family pedigree that, in later years, when whisky had blurred the edges of his memory and djinn-bottles came to confuse him, would obliterate all traces of reality . . . and how, to hammer his point home, he introduced into our lives the idea of the family curse.

'Oh yes,' my father said as Methwold cocked a grave unsmiling head, 'many old families possessed such curses. In our line, it is handed down from eldest son to eldest son—in writing only, because merely to speak it is to unleash its power, you know.' Now Methwold: 'Amazing! And you know the words?' My father nods, lip jutting, toe still as he taps his forehead for emphasis. 'All in here; all memorized. Hasn't been used since an ancestor quarrelled with the Emperor Babar and put the curse on his son Humayun . . . terrible story, that—every schoolboy knows.'

And the time would come when my father, in the throes of his utter retreat from reality, would lock himself in a blue room and try to remember a curse which he had dreamed up one evening in the gardens of his house while he stood tapping his temple beside the descendant of William Methwold.

Saddled now with flypaper-dreams and imaginary ancestors, I am still over a day away from being born . . . but now the remorseless ticktock reasserts itself: twenty-nine hours to go, twenty-eight, twenty-seven . . .

Midnight's Children, 1981

MARTIN AMIS

1949–

My Head is a City

My head is a city, and various pains have now taken up residence in various parts of my face. A gum-and-bone ache has launched a cooperative on my upper west side. Across the park, neuralgia has rented a duplex in my fashionable east seventies. Downtown, my chin throbs with lofts of jaw-loss. As for my brain, my hundreds, it's Harlem up there, expanding in the summer fires. It boils and swells. One day soon it is going to burst.

Memory's a funny thing, isn't it. You don't agree? I don't agree either. Memory has never amused me much, and I find its tricks more and more wearisome as I grow older. Perhaps memory simply stays the same but has less work to do as the days fill out. My memory's in good shape, I think. It's just that my life is getting less memorable all the time. Can you remember where you left those keys? Why should you? Lying in the tub some slow afternoon, can you remember if you've washed your toes? (Taking a leak is boring, isn't it, after the first few thousand times? Whew, isn't *that* a drag?) I can't remember half the stuff I do any more. But then I don't want to much.

Waking now at noon, for example, I have a strong sense that I spoke to Selina in the night. It would be just like her to haunt me during the black hours, when I am weak and scared. Selina knows something that everyone ought to know by now. She knows that people are easy to frighten and haunt. People are easy to terrify. Me too, and I'm braver than most. Or drunker, anyway. I got into a fight last night. Put it this way: I'm a lovely boy when I'm asleep. It began in the bar and ended on the street. I started the fight. I finished it too, fortunately—but only just. The guy was much better at fighting than he looked . . . No, Selina didn't call, it didn't happen. I would have remembered. I have this heart condition and it hurts all the time anyway, but this is a new pain, a new squeeze right in the ticker. I didn't know Selina had such power of pain over me. It is that feeling of helplessness, far from home. I've heard it said that absence makes the heart grow fonder. It's true, I think. I certainly miss being promiscuous. I keep trying to remember my last words to her, or hers to me, the night before I left. They can't have been that interesting, that memorable. And when I woke the next day to ready myself for travel, she was gone.

Money, 1984

PETER ACKROYD

1949–

A Vagrant

And the years have passed before he wakes now, after a night in the same warehouse beside the Thames—although, during the night, he had returned to Bristol and watched himself as a child. The years have passed and he has remained in the city, so that now he has become tired and grey; and when he roamed through its streets, he was bent forward as if searching the dust for lost objects. He knew the city's forgotten areas and the shadows which they cast: the cellars of ruined buildings, the small patches of grass or rough ground which are to be found between two large thoroughfares, the alleys in which Ned sought silence, and even the building sites where he might for one night creep into the foundations out of the rain and wind. Sometimes dogs would follow him: they liked his smell, which was of lost or forgotten things, and when he slept in a corner they licked his face or burrowed their noses into his ragged clothes; he no longer beat them off, as once he had, but accepted their presence as natural. For the dogs' city was very like his own: he was close to it always, following its smells, sometimes pressing his face against its buildings to feel their warmth, sometimes angrily chipping or cutting into its brick and stone surfaces.

There were some places, and streets, where he did not venture since he had learnt that others had claims there greater than his own—not the gangs of meths drinkers who lived in no place and no time, nor the growing number of the young who moved on restlessly across the face of the city, but vagrants like himself who, despite the name which the world has given them, had ceased to wander and now associated themselves with one territory or 'province' rather than another. All of them led solitary lives, hardly moving from their own warren of streets and buildings: it is not known whether they chose the area, or whether the area itself had callen them and taken them in, but they had become the guardian spirits (as it were) of each place. Ned now knew some of their names: Watercress Joe, who haunted the streets by St Mary Woolnoth, Black Sam who lived and slept beside the Commercial Road between Whitechapel and Limehouse, Harry the Goblin who was seen only by Spitalfields and Artillery Lane, Mad Frank who walked continually through the streets of Bloomsbury, Italian Audrey who was always to be found in the dockside area of Wapping (it was she who had visited Ned in his shelter many years before), and 'Alligator' who never moved from Greenwich.

But, like Ned, they inhabited a world which only they could see: he sometimes sat on the same spot for hours at a time, until its contours and shadows were more real to him than the people who passed by. He knew the places where the unhappy came, and there was one street corner at a meeting of three roads where he had seen the figure of despair many times—the man with his feet and arms splayed out in front of him, the woman embracing his neck and weeping. He knew the places which had always been used for sex, and afterwards he could smell it on the stones; and he knew the places which death visited, for the stones carried that mark also. Those who passed in front of him scarcely noticed that he was there, although some might murmur to each other 'Poor man!' or 'Such a pity!' before hurrying forward. And yet there was once a time, as he walked by the side of London Wall, when a man appeared in front of him and smiled.

'Is it still hard for you?' he asked Ned.

'Hard? Now there you're asking.'

'Yes, I am asking. Is it still bad?'

'Well, I'll tell you, it's not so bad.'

'Not so bad?'

'I've known worse, after all this time.'

'What time was it, Ned, that we met before?' And the man moved closer to him so that Ned could see the dark weave of his coat (for he would not look into his face).

'What time is it now, Sir?'

'Now, now *you're* asking.' The man laughed, and Ned looked down at the cracks in the pavement.

'Well,' he said to this half-recognised stranger, 'I'll just be on my way now.'

'Don't be long, Ned, don't be long.'

And Ned walked away without looking back, and without remembering.

Hawksmoor, 1985

MATTHEW PARRIS

1949–

The Fall of Mrs Thatcher

There will be people who will portray what has passed in recent days as an embarrassing lapse. Such people speak of chaos and confusion, of panic and self-destructive anger. Soon they will be referring to these past few weeks as an awkward wobble, when the Tory party temporarily took leave of its senses, then recovered its nerve.

Nothing could be further from the truth. As in some tribal folk-mystery, the Conservative party has suffered a great internal convulsion, triggered as much by the collective unconscious of the tribe as by any conscious plan to contrive its survival. They have not, as individual men and women, known what they were doing, but the tribe has known what it was doing, and has done it with ruthless efficiency. The instinct to survive has triumphed.

Not that they were aware of that. All they knew was that they were heading for disaster. Each had his own opinion as to why. What they concurred upon was the imminence of danger; and when they concurred on that, the convulsion began.

At their conference in Bournemouth, a strange, flat despair gripped the occasion. We all noticed it, but none of us knew how to interpret it. Then they began to fight. They lashed out at the media, they lashed out at Europe, they lashed out at the Opposition, and they lashed out at each other. The tribe was in turmoil.

Michael Heseltine—as much, by now, a totem of dissent as a person—found members of the tribe dancing around him and chanting. He responded. The media took up the chant. Michael Heseltine started a teasing dance: was it a war dance? Nobody knew. He did not know himself.

At this point their leader took on the dervish character. Saddam Hussein said she was 'possessed'. In a series of sustained rants she stunned the Chamber, alienated half her party and scared hell out of most of us.

There followed a short silence, and then the murmurs began. They grew until an extraordinary thing happened. One of the elders of the tribe, Sir Geoffrey Howe, began to speak. He spoke almost in tongues: he spoke as he had never spoken. He poured down imprecations upon the head of the leader.

Around Mr Heseltine the dance now reached a pitch of excitement that demanded answer. He rose, took the dagger and stabbed her.

What happened next is folklore. With the leader now wounded, but still alive, her own senior tribesmen drew back with one accord and left her. Suddenly alone, she hesitated a moment, then staggered from the stage.

The tribe mourned her departure. Not falsely or without feeling, they wept. Then, last night, the final twist occurred. The tribe fell upon her assailant, Michael Heseltine, and slew him, too—with many shouts of anger. Real anger.

All drew back, and the new leader, already blessed by the old leader, clean, apart, and uninvolved, stepped forward. With cries of adoration, the tribe gathered around him.

It could have been done as a ballet. It had all the elements of a classical drama. Like Chinese opera or Greek tragedy, the rules required that certain human types be represented; certain ambitions be portrayed; certain actions punished. Every convention was obeyed: every actor played out his role. The dramatic unities of time, place and action were fulfilled. It started in autumn 1990, and ended in the same season; it started in Committee Room 12 at Westminster, and ended there.

It started with an old leader, who was assassinated as she deserved; then her assassin was assassinated, as he deserved. Then the new leader stepped forward; and here the ballet ended.

And the tribe danced. As I write, they are dancing still.

written 1990; *I Couldn't Possibly Comment . . .*, 1997

TIMOTHY MO

1950–

A Visit from the Tax Man

The tax man spread the assortment of papers on the counter in an intimidating silence. He had already asserted himself by refusing to allow customers in, not one, and making Mui turn the TV off. Otherwise they would have to come to the tax office with him, way up in another part of the country.

That would have been terrible; they preferred to confront authority on home ground. For some reason this seemed to have won them favour with this official. This good start was quickly lost. The tax man, who had been given Lily's stool, held a gas bottle's creased tag by its string with the same distaste as one might convey a dead rat to the dust bin by the tip of its scaly tail (always assuming the necessity). He poked the pile of papers—a heap of rubbish, the gesture implied—with the butt of his Bic biro.

'Are you seriously telling me that this is all you have to show the Inland Revenue?'

Lily nodded. She and Husband were on the customer side of the counter. How humiliating! Would their business be taken away from them? At least Husband had never sunk to drawing unemployment benefit, a disgraceful surrender which instantly and forever disqualified you from running a business of your own.

The tax man had not taken off his fawn trenchcoat nor had he accepted a cup of rapidly cooling tea (Lily's little litmus test of his amenability) but now he took off his wire-framed spectacles and wiped his bald head with a handkerchief. He sighed. 'Do you realise you have a legal obligation to keep a record for Sales Tax and Purchase Tax? You do? Where is your till roll then? A cash book, a day book, your invoices in order? Would it be impertinent of me to enquire why you bother with a cash till at all when you have no record of your business?'

Lily smiled serenely but was inwardly frightened and, forgetting herself, nervously depressed one of the keys of the said till (which *all* lucky and well-run businesses had to have). She wished to assert her right to it in case this brigand in a raincoat tried to confiscate it. By an unfortunate coincidence the ringing of the bell was the signal she had agreed on with Mui. The drawer slid out with a *ting!* and, on cue, Mui entered with a small apparition. Not content with the beggar's fancy-dress contrived by Lily, Mui had also smeared her nephew's face and hands with soot.

This is going too far, Lily thought.

But incredulity was not among the things registered on the tax man's surprisingly expressive currant-bun of a face. He watched Man Kee run in his peculiar way over to his father before putting on his spectacles again.

'How many children do you have, Mrs . . ., Mrs Chen?'

'This son only.'

'Well, you can claim child allowance for him.'

'Hah?'

Mui came over. She said to Lily: 'Because you have children you pay less tax.'

'Ah!'

'Any aged dependents?'

Chen shook his head vigorously and the girls, puzzled but quick-thinking as well as obedient, kept blank faces.

The tax man produced a form from his tattered black plastic briefcase. 'This is a tax return, like the ones we sent you. Do you know how to fill it in? No.' He took his spectacles off again. His eyes looked tired to Mui. 'All right. Now listen closely.'

Mui crossed to the owner's side of the counter, while Lily took Man Kee away from Chen.

'You must put a roll in your till and keep it. You must also keep receipts for purchases. Do you have a wholesaler?'

'Buy from Co-op.'

'Well, it's not for me to tell you but you would get a much more advantageous price from a wholesaler. Never mind. Just keep all your bills in order in a file, or even a box would do. No bank account? No. Now let me explain about a cash book, you won't need a day book. . . .'

Mui's earlier suspicion about the simplicity of the procedures was officially confirmed. She felt she had a natural, untutored flair for these things. Finally, the tax man said: 'The inspector of taxes will have to make an assessment on what I recommend, which you will pay in two parts in the next twelve months. We can make some estimate from similar businesses in your area. It may be higher than if you had kept a record but that will be your own fault.'

'You do our tax from Kebab House tax?' Lily asked hopefully, remembering how empty that establishment always was.

'I can't speak for the inspector, I'm afraid.'

Mui saw him personally to the door. It was a pity he was too upright to reward for his kindness, though his probity made her feel warm. A real mother and father official. She felt she had proved a point to Lily. Mui explained the situation to her. Lily was jubilant, and Mui was aghast when she shouted: 'Husband! We can cheat almost all the tax!' She passed on Mui's good news and her own analysis of it: tips need not be declared, ice-cream and drinks were invisible earnings, they could keep a separate box for, say, a quarter of the earnings and not put it on the till roll. And the cost of heating and provisions could actually be deducted from the tax liability! Idiots!

Chen was not at all interested, although he had suffered one worrying moment. He was sponging Man Kee's face and hands in the kitchen. The boy was filthy. The girls really ought to look after him better. That kind of thing wasn't his responsibility at all.

Sour Sweet, 1982

A. N. WILSON

1950–

A Publisher

Everyone who knew about Madge made jokes about her. Like Fenella or Day Muckley, she was one of those people who had decided to become a caricature of themselves. Perhaps it is wrong to say that they decided on it. One naively wondered whether there was ever a time when they were less 'themselves,' when the persona so garishly thrust at the world had been rather less violently Technicolored. This is a question which I still have not resolved in my mind about those who set out to be 'characters' and end as the prisoners of their own act. Madge was a by-word, not just among publishers but in London generally, for being a 'battle-axe.' Bawling out secretaries, throwing books around the office, spitting insults at literary agents down the telephone: these, legend had it, were her favourite games. If you wanted to appear discerning, it was usual to add, after some account of Boadicea-like office ferocity, that Madge had extraordinary literary discernment, a wonderful eye for a book. If my own case was anything to go by, she was not one of the world's great editors. I had spent an afternoon in her office while she chain-smoked Gauloises over my poor little quarto-leaved typescript, turning each page with rapidity and with no sign whatsoever of any enjoyment. It felt like taking work up to teacher's desk. The only things for which she seemed to be on the lookout were errors of spelling or punctuation.

Until that afternoon, I had sincerely believed that it was impossible to read my account of Uncle Roy (Uncle Hector in the book) getting tangled up in Tinker's (Smudge's) lead without laughter. Indeed, any normal person would, I considered, be in hysterics over this passage, as over the invented scene of Aunt Dolly (Deirdre) holding a meeting of the Mother's Union at the rectory and the Lady Novelist, loosely based on Deborah Maddock, who used to live in our village, introducing a frank discussion of sexual morals.

Madge read through these superb pieces of burlesque without the smallest flicker of amusement on her face. Her only comment on the Mother's Union scene was to squiggle her pen twice through the word *ciotus* and add the symbol TRS. in the margin.

'You've made that mistake twice, Mr Ramsay.'

'I thought it was funnier if Mrs Sidebotham believed it was pronounced like that. It's a sort of malapropism.'

'But it isn't the right spelling. *Coitus* is what you meant.' She showed real impatience as she explained this to me.

'I did mean to spell it like that.'

'Well, it was wrong.'

She read on for some time, making innumerable tiny adjustments to the page with her blue pencil. At length she sighed and said, 'Mr Ramsay, where did you go to school?'

I told her.

'And did they teach you nothing about punctuation?'

'I think they did.'

'One day you and I must have a word about commas.'

A Bottle in the Smoke, 1990

VIKRAM SETH

1952–

Rose Aylmer

When they got to the Park Street Cemetery, Amit and Lata got out of the car. Dipankar decided he'd wait in the car with Tapan, since they were only going to be a few minutes and, besides, there were only two umbrellas.

They walked through a wrought-iron gate. The cemetery was laid out in a grid with narrow avenues between clusters of tombs. A few soggy palm trees stood here and there in clumps, and the cawing of crows interspersed with thunder and the noise of rain. It was a melancholy place. Founded in 1767, it had filled up quickly with European dead. Young and old alike—mostly victims of the feverish climate—lay buried here, compacted under great slabs and pyramids, mausolea and cenotaphs, urns and columns, all decayed and greyed now by ten generations of Calcutta heat and rain. So densely packed were the tombs that it was in places difficult to walk between them. Rich, rain-fed grass grew between the graves, and the rain poured down ceaselessly over it all. Compared to Brahmpur or Banaras, Allahabad or Agra, Lucknow or Delhi, Calcutta could hardly be considered to have a history, but the climate had bestowed on its comparative recency a desolate and unromantic sense of slow ruin.

'Why have you brought me here?' asked Lata.

'Do you know Landor?'

'Landor? No.'

'You've never heard of Walter Savage Landor?' asked Amit, disappointed.

'Oh yes. Walter Savage Landor. Of course. "Rose Aylmer, whom these watchful eyes."'

'Wakeful. Well, she lies buried here. As does Thackeray's father and one of Dickens' sons, and the original for Byron's *Don Juan*,' said Amit, with a proper Calcuttan pride.

'Really?' said Lata. 'Here? Here in Calcutta?' It was as if she had suddenly heard that Hamlet was the Prince of Delhi. 'Ah, what avails the sceptred race!'

'Ah, what the form divine!' continued Amit.

'What every virtue, every grace!' cried Lata with sudden enthusiasm.

'Rose Aylmer, all were thine.'

A roll of thunder punctuated the two stanzas.

'Rose Aylmer, whom these watchful eyes—' continued Lata.

'Wakeful.'

'Sorry, wakeful. Rose Aylmer, whom these wakeful eyes—'

'May weep, but never see,' said Amit, brandishing his umbrella.

'A night of memories and sighs,'

'I consecrate to thee.'

Amit paused. 'Ah, lovely poem, lovely poem,' he said, looking delightedly at Lata. He paused again, then said: 'Actually, it's "A night of memories and of sighs".'

'Isn't that what I said?' asked Lata, thinking of nights—or parts of nights—that she herself had recently spent in a similar fashion.

'No. You left out the second "of".'

'A night of memories and sighs. Of memories and of sighs. I see what you mean. But does it make such a difference?'

'Yes, it makes a difference. Not all the difference in the world but, well, a difference. A mere "of"; conventionally permitted to rhyme with "love". But she is in her grave, and oh, the difference to him.'

They walked on. Walking two abreast was not possible, and their umbrellas complicated matters among the cluttered monuments. Not that her tomb was so far away—it was at the first intersection—but Amit had chosen a circuitous route. It was a small tomb capped by a conical pillar with swirling lines; Landor's poem was inscribed on a plaque on one side beneath her name and age and a few lines of pedestrian pentameter:

> What was her fate? Long, long before her hour,
> Death called her tender soul by break of bliss
> From the first blossoms, from the buds of joy;
> Those few our noxious fate unblasted leaves
> In this inclement clime of human life.

Lata looked at the tomb and then at Amit, who appeared to be deep in thought. She thought to herself: he has a comfortable sort of face.

'So she was twenty when she died?' said Lata.

'Yes. Just about your age. They met in the Swansea Circulating Library. And then her parents took her out to India. Poor Landor. Noble Savage. Go, lovely Rose.'

'What did she die of? The sorrow of parting?'

'A surfeit of pineapples.'

Lata looked shocked.

'I can see you don't believe me, but oh, 'tis true, 'tis true,' said Amit. 'We'd better go back,' he continued. 'They will not wait for us—and who can wonder? You're drenched.'

'And so are you.'

'Her tomb,' continued Amit, 'looks like an upside-down ice-cream cone.'

Lata said nothing. She was rather annoyed with Amit.

A Suitable Boy, 1993

HILARY MANTEL

1952–

A Student in the Seventies

When I returned to my desk after dinner, these evenings at Tonbridge Hall, my foot would ruck up the cotton rug on the polished floor, and I would imagine sliding lightly on my back across the room and through the wall, floating out, weightless, over Bloomsbury. Some evenings I took a spoonful or two of soup, made my apologies, pulled on my coat and sped out again into the autumn evening, and I see myself now as if—FLASH—an inner camera has caught me forever, hand flung up before a white face. *Carmel McBain, on her way to a meeting of the student Labour Club.*

In Drury Lane, in the Aldwych, the theatres were opening their doors; in Houghton Street, a hot little café steamed its fumes over the pavement. I would run up the steps, into my place of work, my palace of wonders; the half-deserted building came with its echo, its ever-burning strip lights, its tar-smell of typewriter ribbons and smoke; in the mazes and catacombs you could sniff out your meeting, guided by your nose towards the dusty scent of composite resolutions, sub-sections and sub-clauses, stacking chairs, tobacco: the reek of Afghan coats and flying jackets, the vaporous traces left in the air they inhabit by weak heads and fainter hearts.

I do not remember that political philosophy was ever discussed, or political issues: only organization, personalities, how the Labour student movement should be run. In Paris, the ashes of the *événements* were hardly cool. Here in London, we discussed whether to go by coach (collectively) or to set out (individually) to some all-day-Saturday students' meeting in some seedy provincial hall; and how much the coach would cost per seat. Whether there should be a joint social evening with the Women's Liberation Group: would that be profitable to both, or end in some ideological and financial disaster?

It was men who spoke; not young and fresh ones, but crease-browed and leather-jacketed elders, men with bad teeth from obscure post-graduate specialities. They would shuffle or lurch to their feet; then would come nose-rubbing, throat-clearing; then their voices would rumble just audibly, like spent thunder in a distant valley. Some would speak slumped in their seats, eyes fixed on the ceiling, ash dripping from a cigarette. Their manner was weary, as if they knew everything and had seen everything, and they paused often, perhaps in the middle of a phrase, to blow their noses or make a snickering sound that must have been laughter. Their remarks reached no conclusion; at a certain point, they would become slower, more sporadic, and finally peter out. Then another would draw attention to himself, with the bare flutter of an agenda in the stale air: and grunting, shrugging, turning down his mouth, begin in the middle of a sentence . . . Dave and Mike and Phil were their names, Phil and Dave and Mike. Young women carried them drinks from the vending-machine, black coffee's frail white shell hardly dented by their light fingertips.

I would put my head in my hands, sometimes, for even I must yawn; I would with delicacy track my fingertips back through my inch of hair, and say to myself, am I, can I be, she who so lately at the Holy Redeemer wore an air of purpose and expectation, and a prefect's deep blue gown? So many years of preparation, for what was called adult life: was it for this? Were these meetings as aimless as they appeared, or was I too untutored to see the importance of what was going on, or was I, in some deeper way, missing the point? Yes: that must be it.

As the clock ticked away, a fantasy would creep up and possess me: that if you could stay on and on—if you could stay at the meeting till midnight or the hour beyond—then the masks would slip, the falsity be laid aside, the real business would begin. For it seemed to me that my fellow socialists were talking in code, a code designed perhaps to freeze out strangers and weed out the dilettante. Only the pure of heart were welcome here. They must submit to a new version of the medieval ordeal: instead of poison, water, fire, a Trial by Pointlessness. Once you had passed it—once you had endured the full rigours of a full debate on a revitalized constitution for a revitalized Labour students' movement—then, in the hour after midnight, the chatter would cease—glances be exchanged—the talk begin, hesitant at first, half-smiling, people near-apologetic about their passions and their expertise, quoting Engels, Nye Bevan, Daniel Cohn-Bendit; we would exchange our intuitions and half-perceptions, pass on our visions and dreams, each vision and each dream justified by some reference, recondite or popular. Comrades would say, 'This is what makes me a socialist . . .' and speak from the heart; perhaps someone would mention Lenin, and wages councils, and coal-miners, and the withering away of the state. Dawn would break: gentle humming of the Red Flag.

But in real life, nothing like this occurred at all. By ten-thirty the men would be looking at their watches, drifting and grumbling towards the union bar. I would hover a little, in the corners of rooms, on the edges of groups, hoping that someone would turn to me and begin a real conversation, one I could join in. Stacking chairs squeaked on a dirty floor, the women of the socialists stooped to haul up their fringed and scruffy shoulder bags; in the bar the women stood in a huddle, excluded by the ramparts of turned shoulders, with tepid glasses of pineapple juice clenched in bony white hands. Their eyes avoided mine; they smoked, and muttered to each other in code.

Disillusioned, I would trail back up Drury Lane. The theatres would have turned out already, and the stage doors would be barred. An empty Malteser box bowling towards the Thames would bear witness to the evening passed. My eyes would be heavy and stinging with cigarette smoke and lack of sleep. Behind my ribs was a weight of disappointment. Still the lines ran through my head, distressing, irrelevant: Is this the hill? Is this the kirk?/Is this mine own countree? The irresponsive silence of the land,/The irresponsive sounding of the sea.

An Experiment in Love, 1995

KAZUO ISHIGURO

1954–

The Rehearsal Room

I entered a long narrow room with a grey stone floor. The walls were covered to the ceiling with white tiles. I had the impression there was a row of sinks to my left, but I was by this point so anxious to get to the piano I paid little attention to such details. My gaze, in any case, had been immediately drawn to the wooden cubicles on my right. There were three of these, painted an unpleasant frog-green colour, standing side by side. The doors to the two outer cubicles were closed, but the central cubicle—which looked to have slightly broader dimensions—had its door ajar and I could see inside it a piano, the lid left open to display the keys. Without further ado I attempted to make my way inside, only to find this a frustratingly difficult task. The door—which swung inwards into the cubicle—was prevented from opening fully by the piano itself, and in order to get inside and close the door again I was obliged to squeeze myself tightly into a corner and to tug the edge of the door slowly past my chest. Eventually I succeeded in closing and locking the door, then managed—again with some difficulty in the cramped conditions—to pull the stool out from under the piano. Once I had seated myself, however, I felt reasonably comfortable, and when I ran my fingers up and down the keys I discovered that for all its discoloured notes and scratched outer body, the piano possessed a mellow sensitive tone and had been perfectly tuned. The acoustics within the cubicle, moreover, were not nearly as claustrophobic as one might have supposed.

A great sense of relief swept over me at this discovery and I suddenly realised how tense I had been over the past hour. I took several slow deep breaths and set about preparing myself for this most important of practice sessions. It was then I remembered I had still not resolved the question of which piece to perform this evening. My mother, I knew, would find particularly moving the central movement of Yamanaka's

Globestructures: Option II. But my father would certainly prefer Mullery's *Asbestos and Fibre.* In fact it was even possible he would not approve much of the Yamanaka. I sat gazing at the keys for a few more moments before deciding firmly in favour of the Mullery.

The decision made me feel all the better and I was just preparing to embark on those explosive opening chords when I felt something hard tap against the back of my shoulder. Turning, I saw with dismay that the door of the cubicle had somehow come unlocked and was hanging open.

I clambered to a standing position and pushed the door closed. I then noticed the latch mechanism was dangling upside down on the door frame. After further examination, and with a little ingenuity, I managed to fix the latch back in place, but even as I locked the door once more I could see I had effected only the most temporary of solutions. The latch was liable to slip down again at any moment. I could be in the middle of *Asbestos and Fibre*—in the midst, say, of one of the highly intense passages in the third movement—and the door could easily swing open again exposing me to whoever happened by then to be wandering about outside my cubicle. And certainly, if some obtuse person, not realising I was inside, were to attempt to gain entry, the lock would not offer even nominal resistance.

All these thoughts ran through my mind as I seated myself back on the stool. But after a little while, I came to the conclusion that if I did not make full use of this opportunity to practise, I might never get another. And if the conditions were less than ideal, the piano itself was perfectly adequate. With some determination, I willed myself to stop worrying about the faulty door behind me and to prepare myself once more for the opening bars of the Mullery.

Then, just as my fingers were poised over the keys, I heard a noise—a small creaking sound such as might be made by a shoe or some piece of clothing—somewhere alarmingly close by. I spun round on my stool. Only then did I notice that although the door had stayed closed, the whole of its upper section was missing, so that it more or less resembled a stable door. I had been so preoccupied with the faulty latch I had somehow completely failed to register this glaring fact. I now saw how the door ended at a rough edge just above waist height. Whether the upper section had been torn off as a result of wanton vandalism or because some renovation was taking place I could not be sure. In any case, even from my seated position I could, by craning my neck slightly, gain a clear view of the white tiles and sinks outside.

I could not believe Hoffman had had the effrontery to offer me such conditions. To be sure, no one else had come into the room so far, but it was perfectly conceivable a group of six or seven hotel staff could come in at any moment and begin using the sinks. The situation seemed to me untenable and I was about to abandon the cubicle angrily when I caught sight of a rag hanging from a nail on the door post close to the upper hinge.

I stared at this for a second, and then spotted another nail on the other door post at exactly the same height. Immediately guessing the purpose of the rag and the nails, I rose to my feet again to examine them further. The rag turned out to be an old bath towel. When I opened it out and hung it across the two nails, I found it formed a perfectly good curtain over the missing section of the door.

I sat down again feeling much better and prepared myself once more for the opening bars. Then, just as I was about to start playing, I was yet again stopped by the creaking noise. Then I heard it once more, and I realised it was coming from the cubicle on my left. It now dawned on me not only that someone had been in the next cubicle the whole time, but that the sound insulation between the cubicles was virtually non-existent, and that I had remained unaware of the person until this point only because—for whatever reason—he had remained very still.

Furious, I rose again and pulled at the door, causing the latch to come loose again and the towel to fall to the ground. As I squeezed my way out, the man in the next cubicle, perhaps seeing no further reason to restrain himself, cleared his throat noisily. I hurried out of the room feeling thoroughly disgusted.

The Unconsoled, 1995

Acknowledgements

Extracts from the *Authorized Version of the Bible* (*The King James Bible*), the rights in which are vested in the Crown, are reproduced by permission of the Crown's Patentee, Cambridge University Press.

Extracts from *New English Bible*, © Oxford University Press and Cambridge University Press 1961, 1970, by permission of Cambridge University Press.

Chinua Achebe: from *A Man of the People* (1966), by permission of the author.

Peter Ackroyd: from *Hawksmoor* (Hamish Hamilton, 1985), copyright © Peter Ackroyd 1985, by permission of Sheil Land Associates and Penguin Books Ltd.

James Agate: from *Immoment Toys* (Jonathan Cape, 1945), by permission of the Peters Fraser & Dunlop Group Ltd.

Kingsley Amis: from *Take a Girl Like You* (1960), copyright © 1960 Kingsley Amis, by permission of the publishers, Victor Gollancz Ltd, and of Jonathan Clowes Ltd, London, on behalf of the Literary Estate of Sir Kingsley Amis; and from *Lucky Jim* (1954), copyright © 1954 by Kingsley Amis, by permission of the publishers, Victor Gollancz Ltd, and Doubleday, a division of Bantam Doubleday Dell Publishing Group.

Martin Amis: from *Money* (Jonathan Cape 1984), copyright © Martin Amis 1984, by permission of the Peters Fraser & Dunlop Group Ltd.

Mulk Raj Anand: from *Untouchable* (1935).

Margaret Atwood: from 'In Love with Raymond Chandler' in *Good Bones and Simple Murders* by Margaret Atwood (a Nan A. Talese book), copyright © 1983, 1992, 1994 by O. W. Toad Ltd, by permission of Doubleday, a division of Bantam Doubleday Dell Publishing Group, Inc.; and in *Good Bones* by Margaret Atwood (1992), by permission of the publishers Bloomsbury Publishing plc on behalf of the author, and McLelland & Stewart, Inc., the Canadian publishers.

W. H. Auden: from 'III, Caliban to the Audience' in *The Sea and the Mirror* (1945), by permission of the publishers, Faber & Faber Ltd.

J. L. Austin: from 'Other Minds' in *Philosophical Papers* edited by J. O. Urmson and G. J. Warnock (3rd edn. 1979), by permission of Oxford University Press.

James Baldwin: from *Go Tell it on the Mountain* (Penguin, 1952), copyright © 1952, 1953 by James Baldwin, copyright renewed, by permission of Doubleday, a division of Bantam Doubleday Dell Publishing Group, Inc. and by arrangement with the James Baldwin Estate.

J. G. Ballard: from 'The Waiting Grounds' in *The Day of Forever*, © 1967 J. G. Ballard, by permission of the author, c/o Margaret Hanbury, 27 Walcot Square, London SE11 4UB. All rights reserved.

Samuel Beckett: from 'Dante and the Lobster' in *More Pricks Than Kicks* (1934), from *Murphy* (1938), and from *Malone Dies* (1956), by permission of Calder Publications Ltd, and Grove/Atlantic, Inc.

Max Beerbohm: from 'The Crime' in *And Even Now*, by permission of Sir Rupert Hart-Davis on behalf of Mrs Eva Reichman.

Brendan Behan: from *Borstal Boy* (1958), by permission of the Tessa Sayle Agency on behalf of the Estate of Brendan Behan.

Hilaire Belloc: from *The Cruise of the 'Nona'* (Random House UK), copyright © Hilaire Belloc 1925, 1955, by permission of the Peters Fraser & Dunlop Group Ltd on behalf of the Estate of Hilaire Belloc.

Saul Bellow: from *The Adventures of Augi March* (1953), *Henderson, the Rain King* (1959), *Herzog* (1964), and *Mr Sammler's Planet* (1970), by permission of the Wylie Agency.

Isaiah Berlin: from 'A Marvellous Decade' in *Russian Thinkers* edited by Henry Hardy and Aileen Kelly, Copyright 1948, 1951, 1953, © 1955, 1956, 1960, 1961, 1972, 1978 by Isaiah Berlin, copyright © 1978 by Henry Hardy, copyright © The Berlin Literary Trust, by permission of Curtis Brown Ltd, London, and Viking Penguin, a division of Penguin Books USA, Inc.

John Betjeman: from 'Little Posts for Lawyers' from *The Spectator* (1955), by permission of *The Spectator*.

Edmund Blunden: from *Undertones of War* (1928), copyright © Edmund Blunden 1964, by permission of the Peters Fraser & Dunlop Group Ltd.

Ronald Blythe: from *Akenfield* (1969), by permission of David Higham Associates.

Elizabeth Bowen: from *The Heat of the Day* (Jonathan Cape/Knopf, 1949), and from *The House in Paris* (Jonathan Cape/Knopf 1935), by permission of Random House UK Ltd on behalf of Elizabeth Bowen.

Paul Bowles: from *The Sheltering Sky* (1949), copyright holder not traced.

Malcolm Bradbury: from *The History Man* (Martin Secker & Warburg, 1975), by permission of Random House UK Ltd, and Curtis Brown Ltd, London, on behalf of Malcolm Bradbury.

Jocelyn Brooke: from *The Military Orchid*, copyright © the Estate of Jocelyn Brooke, by permission of A. M. Heath & Co. Ltd on behalf of Dr John Urmston and the Estate of Jocelyn Brooke.

Anita Brookner: from *A Family Romance* (Jonathan Cape, 1993), published in the USA and Canada as *Dolly*, copyright © Anita Brookner 1993, 1994, by permission of Random House UK Ltd on behalf of the author and of Random House, Inc. and Random House of Canada Ltd.

Anthony Burgess: from *Inside Mr Enderby* (1963), copyright © Estate of Anthony Burgess, by permission of Artellus Ltd.

Christopher Burney: from *The Dungeon Democracy* (William Heinemann, 1945), by permission of Random House UK Ltd.

Erskine Caldwell: from *Tobacco Road*, copyright © 1932 by Erskine Caldwell, by permission of Laurence Pollinger Ltd and the Estate of Erskine Caldwell, and of McIntosh and Otis, Inc.

Truman Capote: from *In Cold Blood: A True Account of a Multiple Murder and its Consequences* (Hamish Hamilton, 1966), copyright © 1965, 1966 and renewed 1993 by Alan U. Schwartz, by permission of Penguin Books Ltd and Random House Inc. Originally published in *The New Yorker* in slightly different form.

Neville Cardus: from *The Summer Game*, copyright holder not traced.

Joyce Cary: from *Mr Johnson* (Michael Joseph, 1939), by permission of the Andrew Lownie Literary Agency on behalf of the Estate of Joyce Cary.

Raymond Chandler: from *Farewell, My Lovely* (Hamish Hamilton, 1940), copyright © 1940 by Raymond Chandler and renewed 1968 by the Executrix of the author, Mrs Helga Greene; and from *The Little Sister* (Hamish Hamilton, 1988), copyright © Raymond Chandler 1949, both by permission of Alfred A. Knopf Inc. and Penguin Books Ltd.

Bruce Chatwin: from *In Patagonia* (Jonathan Cape, 1977), copyright © 1977 Bruce Chatwin by permission of Random House UK Ltd on behalf of the author and of Aitken & Stone Ltd.

Nirad C. Chaudhuri: from *The Autobiography of an Unknown Indian* (first published by Chatto & Windus in 1951, to be reissued by Picador in 1999), by permission of the publishers and the author.

John Cheever: from 'The Ocean' in *The Brigadier and the Golf Widow* (1965), (Alfred A. Knopf, Inc.).

Winston Churchill: from *Great Contemporaries* and from *The Second World War*, volume 1, both copyright Winston S. Churchill, by permission of Curtis Brown Ltd, London, on behalf of the Estate of Sir Winston S. Churchill.

Kenneth Clark: from *The Nude* (1956), by permission of John Murray (Publishers) Ltd.

Richard Cobb: from *Something to Hold Onto* (1988), by permission of John Murray (Publishers) Ltd.

Ivy Compton-Burnett: from *More Women Than Men* (1933), copyright © the Estate of Ivy Compton-Burnett 1933; from *Manservant and Maidservant* (1947), and from *A Father and His Fate* (1957), all by permission of the Peters Fraser & Dunlop Group Ltd on behalf of the Estate of Ivy Compton-Burnett.

Cyril Connolly: from 'Where Engels Fears to Tread' in *The Condemned Playground* (Routledge, 1945), copyright © the Estate of Cyril Connolly 1945, by permission of the Estate of Cyril Connolly, c/o Rogers, Coleridge, & White Ltd, 20 Powis Mews, London W11 1JN.

E. E. Cummings: from *The Enormous Room*, copyright © 1922, 1950, 1978, 1991 by the Trustees for the E. E. Cummings Trust and George James Firmage, by permission of W. W. Norton & Co.

Robertson Davies: from *The Rebel Angels* (Allen Lane, 1982), copyright © 1981, 1982 by Robertson Davies, by permission of Penguin Books Ltd and Viking Penguin, a division of Penguin Putnam, Inc.

Rhys Davies: from 'The Nature of Man' in *A Finger in Every Pie* (1942), copyright holder not traced.

Clarence Day: from *God and My Father* (1932), copyright holder not traced.

G. V. Desani: from *All About H. Hatterr* (The Bodley Head, 1949), by permission of Random House UK Ltd on behalf of the author.

Emily Dickinson: letters no. 260 (April 1862) and no. 268 (July 1862) from *The Letters of Emily Dickinson* edited by Thomas H. Johnson (Cambridge, Mass.: The Belknap Press of Harvard University Press), copyright © 1958, 1986 by the President and Fellows of Harvard College, by permission of the publishers.

John Dos Passos: from *U.S.A.*, *The Big Money* (Constable, 1936), copyright holder not traced.

Norman Douglas: from *Siren Land* (1911), and from *South Wind* (1917), by permission of The Society of Authors as the Literary Representative of the Estate of Norman Douglas.

Margaret Drabble: from *The Needle's Eye* (1972), copyright © Margaret Drabble 1972, by permission of the Peters Fraser & Dunlop Group Ltd.

Theodore Dreiser: from *An American Tragedy* (1925), by permission of the publishers, Addison Wesley Longman Ltd.

Loren Eiseley: from 'An Invisible Island' in *The Unexpected Universe*, copyright © 1969 by Loren Eiseley, by permission of the publishers, Victor Gollancz Ltd and Harcourt Brace & Co.

T. S. Eliot: from 'In Memoriam' (1936), by permission of Faber & Faber Ltd; from *The Use of Poetry and the Use of Criticism* (1933), by permission of Faber & Faber Ltd and Harvard University Press.

Ralph Ellison: from *Invisible Man* (Random House Inc., 1952), copyright © 1947, 1948, 1952 by Ralph Ellison, by permission of Laurence Pollinger Ltd, and Random House, Inc.

William Empson: from *Seven Types of Ambiguity* (Chatto & Windus, 1930), copyright © 1930 by William Empson, by permission of Random House UK Ltd on behalf of the author, and of New Directions Publishing Corp.

D. J. Enright: from *Memoirs of a Mendicant Professor* (1969), by permission of the publishers, Carcanet Press Ltd.

John Evelyn: from John Evelyn: *Diary*, by permission of the publishers, Boydell & Brewer Ltd.

William Faulkner: from *The Sound and the Fury* (1929), by permission of The American Play Company.

Patrick Leigh Fermor: from *A Time of Gifts* (1977), by permission of John Murray (Publishers) Ltd.

Ronald Firbank: from *Prancing Nigger* (1925) in *Five Novels*, copyright © 1961 by Ronald Firbank, by permission of New Directions Publishing Corp.

Ford Madox Ford: from *Some Do Not* (1924) and from *Return to Yesterday* (1931), by permission of David Higham Associates.

E. M. Forster: from *Howards End* (1910), copyright 1921 by E. M. Forster, by permission of Alfred A. Knopf Inc.; from 'The Consolations of History' in *Abinger Harvest* (1936), copyright 1936 and renewed 1964 by Edward M. Forster, by permission of Harcourt Brace & Co.; both also by permission of King's College, Cambridge, and The Society of Authors as the Literary Representative of the E. M. Forster Estate; and from *A Passage to India* (1924), by permission of King's College, Cambridge, and The Society of Authors as the Literary Representative of the E. M. Forster Estate.

Michael Frayn: from *Towards the End of Morning* (HarperCollins, 1967), copyright © 1967 by Michael Frayn by permission of Greene & Heaton Ltd and HarperCollins Publishers Ltd.

John Kenneth Galbraith: from *The Great Crash, 1929* (Hamish Hamilton, 1965, revised edition 1975), copyright © 1954, 1955, 1961, 1972, 1979, 1988 by John Kenneth Galbraith, by permission of Houghton Mifflin Co., and Penguin Books Ltd. All rights reserved.

Waguih Ghali: from *Beer in the Snooker Club* by permission of the publishers, Andre Deutsch Ltd.

Ellen Glasgow: from *They Stooped to Folly* (William Heinemann, 1929), copyright holder not traced.

William Golding: from *The Inheritors*, copyright © 1955 by William Golding, by permission of the publishers, Faber & Faber Ltd and Harcourt Brace & Co.

Nadine Gordimer: from *The Conservationist* (Jonathan Cape), copyright © 1972, 1973, 1974 by Nadine Gordimer, by permission of Viking Penguin, a division of Penguin Books USA, Inc. and Random House UK Ltd on behalf of the author.

Robert Graves: from *Goodbye to All That* (first published in 1929), by permission of the publishers of the Collected Works of Robert Graves, Carcanet Press Ltd.

Alasdair Gray: from *Lanark* (1981) by permission of the publishers, Canongate Books Ltd, 14 High Street, Edinburgh EH1 1TE.

Henry Green: from *Party Going* (first published in Great Britain by The Hogarth Press, 1939 and by Harvill Press, 1996), © Henry Green 1939, by permission of Random House UK Ltd on behalf of the author, and The Harvill Press.

Grahame Greene: from *Brighton Rock* (Heinemann, 1938), and from *The Ministry of Fear* (Heinemann, 1943), by permission of David Higham Associates.

J. B. S. Haldane: from 'God-Makers' in *The Inequality of Man* (Chatto & Windus, 1932), copyright holder not traced.

Edward Hoagland: from 'The Threshold and the Jolt of Pain' in *Heart's Desire* (Summit Books, 1988), copyright holder not traced.

Richard Hughes: from *A High Wind in Jamaica* (Chatto & Windus, 1929), by permission of David Higham Associates.

Zora Neale Hurston: from *Their Eyes Were Watching God*, copyright 1937 by Harper & Row, Publishers, Inc., renewed 1965 by John C. Hurston and Joel Hurston, by permission of Virago Press and HarperCollins Publishers, Inc.

Aldous Huxley: from *Crome Yellow* (Chatto & Windus, 1921), by permission of Mrs Laura Huxley and of Random House UK Ltd on behalf of the Estate of Aldous Huxley.

Christopher Isherwood: from *Mr Norris Changes Trains* (1935), copyright Christopher Isherwood, by permission of Curtis Brown Ltd, London on behalf of the Estate of Christopher Isherwood.

Kazuo Ishiguro: from *The Unconsoled* (Faber, 1995), copyright © 1995 by Kazuo Ishiguro, by permission of the author, c/o Rogers, Coleridge, & White Ltd, 20 Powis Mews, London W11 1JN.

Dan Jacobson: from *The Price of Diamonds*, copyright © 1987 by Dan Jacobson, by permission of A. M. Heath & Co. Ltd on behalf of the author.

C. L. R. James: from *Beyond a Boundary* (Stanley Paul, 1963), by permission of Random House UK Ltd on behalf of the author.

Clive James: from *Unreliable Memoirs* (Jonathan Cape, 1980), copyright © Clive James 1980, by permission of the Peters Fraser & Dunlop Group Ltd.

Randall Jarrell: from 'The Age of Criticism' in *Poetry and the Age* (1953) (Alfred A. Knopf, Inc.).

James Weldon Johnson: from *Along This Way*, copyright 1933 by James Weldon Johnson, renewed © 1961 by Grace Nail Johnson, by permission of Viking Penguin, a division of Penguin Putnam, Inc.

David Jones: from *In Parenthesis* (1937), by permission of the publishers, Faber & Faber Ltd.

James Joyce: from *Finnegans Wake* (1939), by permission of the Wylie Agency.

John Maynard Keynes: from 'The Economic Consequences of Peace', and 'Essays in Biography' in *The Collected Writings of John Maynard Keynes*, copyright © The Royal Economic Society, by permission of Macmillan Ltd.

Benedict Kiely: from *A Ball of Malt and Madame Butterfly* (1973), by permission of A. P. Watt Ltd on behalf of the author.

Ring Lardner: from 'The Golden Honeymoon' in *How to Write Short Stories* (Scholarly Press, 1971).

D. H. Lawrence: from *St Mawr*, *Lady Chatterley's Lover*, and *Apocalypse* (Alfred A. Knopf, Inc.).

T. E. Lawrence: from *Seven Pillars of Wisdom*, copyright 1926, 1935 by Doubleday, a division of Bantam Doubleday Dell Publishing Group, Inc.

Doris Lessing: from *The Golden Notebook* (Michael Joseph, 1962), copyright © 1962 by Doris Lessing, by permission of Penguin Books Ltd.

C. S. Lewis: from 'A Reply to Professor Haldane' in *Of This and Other Worlds, Essays and Stories* (1982), copyright © 1966 by the Executors of the Estate of C. S. Lewis and renewed 1994 by C. S. Lewis Pte Ltd, by permission of HarperCollins Publishers Ltd and Harcourt Brace & Co.; and from *Out of the Silent Planet* (The Bodley Head, 1938), by permission of Random House UK Ltd on behalf of the author.

Sinclair Lewis: from *Main Street: The Story of Carol Kennicott*, copyright 1920 by Harcourt Brace & Co. and renewed 1948 by Sinclair Lewis, and from *Babbitt* (1922), both by permission of the publisher.

Wyndham Lewis: from *Tarr* (1918, revised 1928), from *The Apes of God* (1930), from *Blasting and Bombardiering* (1937), from *Sea Mists of the Winter* (1951), and from *Self Condemned* (1954), all by permission of the Peters Fraser & Dunlop Group Ltd.

A. J. Liebling: from *The Road Back to Paris* (1944), copyright holder not traced.

David Lodge: from *Small World* (Secker & Warburg, 1984), copyright © David Lodge 1984, by permission of Curtis Brown, London, on behalf of David Lodge.

Malcolm Lowry: from *Under the Volcano* (Jonathan Cape/Random House, 1947), copyright © 1947 by Malcolm Lowry, copyright renewed 1975, by permission of Random House UK Ltd and Sterling Lord Literistic, Inc.

Alison Lurie: from *Love and Friendship* (William Heinemann 1962), copyright © 1962 by Alison Lurie, by permission of Random House UK Ltd and Melanie Jackson Agency, LLC.

Rose Macaulay: from *The World My Wilderness* (1947), by permission of Virago Press.

Carson McCullers: from *The Member of the Wedding* (Hutchinson, 1946). Copyright holder not traced.

Dwight MacDonald: from *Against the American Grain* (Da Capo Press, 1990), copyright holder not traced.

Norman Mailer: from *The Naked and the Dead*, copyright 1948, 1976 by Norman Mailer, by permission of Curtis Brown Ltd, London and of Henry Holt & Co., Inc.

Bernard Malamud: from 'The Jewbird' in *Idiots First* (Methuen), copyright © 1963, 1964 by Bernard Malamud, copyright renewed © 1991 by Anne Malamud, by permission of Anne Malamud, A. M. Heath, & Co. Ltd on behalf of the Estate of Bernard Malamud, and of Farrar, Straus, & Giroux, Inc.

David Malouf: from 'The Only Speaker of His Tongue' in *Antipodes* (Chatto & Windus, 1985), copyright © David Malouf 1985, by permission of the author, c/o Rogers, Coleridge, & White Ltd, 20 Powis Mews, London W11 1JN and of Random House UK Ltd.

Hilary Mantel: from *An Experiment in Love* (Viking 1995), copyright © 1995 by Hilary Mantel, by permission of Penguin Books Ltd, Henry Holt & Co., Inc.

Kamala Markandaya: from *The Nowhere Man* (1972), by permission of Vanessa Holt Ltd.

W. Somerset Maugham: from *Of Human Bondage* (William Heinemann, 1915) and from *Cakes and Ale* (William Heinemann, 1930), by permission of Random House UK Ltd on behalf of the author and by permission of A. P. Watt Ltd on behalf of The Royal Literary Fund.

Peter Medawar: from *The Future of Man* (Methuen, 1960), by permission of Routledge.

H. L. Mencken: from *A Mencken Chrestomathy* (1949) and from *The American Mercury* (1933) (Alfred A. Knopf, Inc.).

Joseph Mitchell: from 'Obituary of a Gin Mill' in *McSorley's Wonderful Saloon* (1943), republished in *Up in the Old Hotel*, copyright © 1992 by Joseph Mitchell, by permission of Pantheon Books, a division of Random House, Inc. and the Henry Dunnow Literary Agency on behalf of the Estate of Joseph Mitchell.

Timothy Mo: from *Sour Sweet* (1982), by permission of Hodder & Stoughton Educational.

Brian Moore: from *Catholics* (Holt, Rinehart, & Winston, 1972), copyright © 1972 by Brian Moore, by permission of Curtis Brown Ltd, New York.

Edwin Muir: from *The Story and the Fable* (1940), revised as *An Autobiography* (Chatto & Windus, 1954), by permission of Random House UK Ltd on behalf of the author.

Iris Murdoch: from *Under the Net* (Chatto & Windus, 1954), copyright 1954, renewed © 1982 by Iris Murdoch, by permission of Random House UK Ltd on behalf of the author and of Viking Penguin, a division of Penguin Books USA, Inc.

Vladimir Nabokov: from *Pnin* (1957), *Lolita* (1958), and 'My English Education' in *Speak, Memory* (1967) (Alfred A. Knopf, Inc.).

V. S. Naipaul: from *An Area of Darkness* (Penguin, 1964), copyright © V. S. Naipaul 1964, and from *The Mimic Men* (Penguin, 1967), copyright © V. S. Naipaul 1967, by permission of Penguin Books Ltd and Aitken & Stone Ltd.

Ian Nairn: from *Nairn's London*, revisited by Peter Gasson (Penguin Books, 1966, revised edition 1988), copyright © Ian Nairn 1966, additional material copyright © Peter Gasson 1988, by permission of Penguin Books Ltd.

R. K. Narayan: from *The Bachelor of Arts* (William Heinemann, 1937), by permission of Random House UK Ltd on behalf of the author and of The University of Chicago Press.

Harold Nicolson: from *Some People*, by permission of the publishers, Constable & Co. Ltd.

Joyce Carol Oates: from *Childwold* (Vanguard Press/Victor Gollancz, 1976), copyright © 1976 by Joyce Carol Oates, by permission of John Hawkins & Associates, Inc., and David Higham Associates.

Flann O'Brien: from *At Swim-Two-Birds*, copyright © Brian O'Nolan 1939, by permission of HarperCollins Publishers, the Estate of the late Brian O'Nolan, and A. M. Heath & Co. Ltd.

Flannery O'Connor: from *Wise Blood* (1952), by permission of the publishers, Faber & Faber Ltd and the Peters Fraser & Dunlop Group Ltd.

Frank O'Connor: from 'The Holy Door' in *The Common Chord* (1947), and reprinted in *The Short Stories of Frank O'Connor* (Penguin), copyright © Frank O'Connor 1953, by permission of the Peters Fraser & Dunlop Group Ltd on behalf of the Estate of Frank O'Connor.

Sean O'Faolain: from 'Persecution Mania' in *The Stories of Sean O'Faolain* (1958), copyright © 1958 Sean O'Faolain, by permission of the Estate of Sean O'Faolain, c/o Rogers, Coleridge, & White Ltd, 20 Powis Mews, London W11 1JN.

Liam O'Flaherty: from *Famine* (Jonathan Cape, 1937), copyright © Liam O'Flaherty 1979, by permission of the Peters Fraser & Dunlop Group Ltd on behalf of the Estate of Liam O'Flaherty.

John O'Hara: from 'The Doctor's Son' in *The Doctor's Son and Other Stories* (The Cresset Press, 1935), copyright holder not traced.

George Orwell: from 'The Art of Donald McGill' in *Dickens, Dali & Others: Studies in Popular Culture*, copyright 1946 by George Orwell and renewed 1974 by Sonia Brownell Orwell, and from 'A Hanging' in *Shooting an Elephant and Other Essays* by George Orwell, copyright 1950 by Sonia Brownell Orwell and renewed 1978 by Sonia Pitt-Rivers [both these essays also from *Collected Essays*]; from *Nineteen Eighty-Four*, copyright 1949 by Harcourt Brace & Co. and renewed 1977 by Sonia Brownell Orwell; and from *Homage to Catalonia*, copyright 1952 and renewed 1980 by Sonia Brownell Orwell; all also copyright © Mark Hamilton as the Literary Executor of the Estate of the late Sonia Brownell Orwell and Martin Secker & Warburg Ltd; all by permission of A. M. Heath & Co. Ltd on behalf of the Estate of George Orwell and of Harcourt Brace & Co.

Mathew Parris: from *I Couldn't Possibly Comment . . .* (Robson, 1997), by permission of Robson Books Ltd.

Mervyn Peake: from *Gormenghast* (Penguin, 1950), by permission of David Higham Associates.

Samuel Pepys: from *Samuel Pepys' Diary*, edited by Robert Latham and L. E. Matthews (HarperCollins), copyright © The Master, Fellows, and Scholars of Magdalene College, Cambridge, Robert Latham and the Executors of William Matthews, 1983, by permission of the Peters Fraser & Dunlop Group Ltd.

William Plomer: from *Turbott Wolfe* by permission of Sir Rupert Hart-Davis, as Literary Executor.

Katherine Anne Porter: from 'The Leaning Tower' in *The Leaning Tower and Other Stories* (Jonathan Cape/Harcourt Brace), copyright 1941 and renewed 1969 by Katherine Anne Porter, by permission of Random House UK Ltd on behalf of the author and of Harcourt Brace & Co.

Anthony Powell: from *Afternoon Men* (Heinemann, 1931) and from *A Dance to the Music of Time: Casanova's Chinese Restaurant* (Heinemann, 1960), by permission of David Higham Associates.

Dawn Powell: from *The Golden Spur* (1962), copyright © 1997, 1962 by the Estate of Dawn Powell, by permission of Melanie Jackson Agency, LLC and Virago Press.

V. S. Pritchett: from *In My Good Books* (1942), copyright © V. S. Pritchett 1942, and from *A Cab at the Door* (1968), copyright © V. S. Pritchett 1968, by permission of the Peters Fraser & Dunlop Group Ltd.

James Purdy: from *Cabot Wright Begins* (Secker & Warburg/Farrar, Straus, & Giroux, 1964), by permission of the author.

Barbara Pym: from *Less Than Angels* (Jonathan Cape, 1955), by permission of Random House UK Ltd on behalf of the author, and from *Quartet in Autumn* (Macmillan, 1977), by permission of Macmillan General Books.

Herbert Read: from *The Innocent Eye* (1933), by permission of David Higham Associates.

Forrest Reid: from *Peter Waring* (1937), by permission of John Johnson (Author's Agent) Ltd.

Jean Rhys: from *After Leaving Mr Mackenzie* (Jonathan Cape, 1930), copyright © Jean Rhys 1930, by permission of Sheil Land Associates.

Henry Handel Richardson: from *Maurice Guest* (William Heinemann, 1908), by permission of Random House UK Ltd.

Mordecai Richler: from *St Urbain's Horseman* (Alfred A. Knopf, 1971), copyright © Mordecai Richler 1966, 1967, 1971 by permission of the author c/o Rogers, Coleridge, & White Ltd, 20 Powis Mews, London W11 1JN.

Philip Roth: from *Portnoy's Complaint* (Jonathan Cape, 1969), copyright © 1969 by Philip Roth, by permission of Random House, Inc. and of Random House UK Ltd on behalf of the author.

Damon Runyon: from 'Romance in the Roaring Forties' in *More Than Somewhat* by Damon Runyon, by permission of the publishers Constable & Co. Ltd, and of The American Play Company.

Salman Rushdie: from *Midnight's Children* (Jonathan Cape, 1981), by permission of Random House UK Ltd on behalf of the author.

Bertrand Russell: from 'Mathematics and the Metaphysicians' (1901) in *Mysticism and Logic*, and from *Fact and Fiction* (1961), by permission of the publishers, Routledge and of the Bertrand Russell Peace Foundation.

Oliver Sacks: from *A Leg to Stand On* (Duckworth, 1984), copyright © 1984 by Oliver Sacks, by permission of the Wylie Agency, Inc.

William Sansom: from *Among the Dahlias* (The Hogarth Press, 1957), copyright © 1957 by William Sansom, by permission of Greene & Heaton Ltd.

George Santayana: from *Character and Opinion in the United States* (Scribners, 1920), by permission of the copyright holders, The MIT Press; from 'A Note on T. S. Eliot' in John McCormick: *George Santayana: A Biography* (Alfred A. Knopf, 1987) by permission of the publisher; from *The Life of Reason* (1905), and from *Three Philosophical Poets* (H. Milford 1910), copyright holder not traced.

Frank Sargeson: from 'Miss Briggs' in *Collected Stories* (1964), copyright holder not traced.

Siegfried Sassoon: from *Sherston's Progress* (1936), by permission of George Sassoon.

Samuel Selvon: from *The Lonely Londoners* (1956), by permission of Mrs Althea Selvon.

Vikram Seth: from *A Suitable Boy* (Orion Books, 1993), copyright © Vikram Seth 1993, by permission of Sheil Land Associates.

Bernard Shaw: from *Music in London 1890–94*; from 'Blaming the Bard' and from 'Lorenzaccio' from *Our Theatre in the Nineties*; from 'Epistle Dedicatory' to *Man and Superman*; from Preface to *Major Barbara*; from *An Intelligent Woman's Guide to Socialism and Capitalism*; from Preface to *Geneva*; from *Sixteen Self Sketches*; and from letter to G. K. Chesterton, 1906; all by permission of The Society of Authors, on behalf of the Bernard Shaw Estate.

Charles Sherrington: from *Man on His Nature*, by permission of Miss U. M. Sherrington and of the publishers, Cambridge University Press.

Alan Sillitoe: from *The Loneliness of the Long-Distance Runner* (W. H. Allen, 1959), copyright © Alan Sillitoe 1959, by permission of Sheil Land Associates.

Sacheverell Sitwell: from *Morning Noon and Night in London* (1948), by permission of David Higham Associates.

Edith Somerville: from *The Real Charlotte*, copyright E. Œ. Somerville and Martin Ross, by permission of Curtis Brown, London.

Wole Soyinka: from *Aké* (1981), copyright holder not traced.

Muriel Spark: from *The Girls of Slender Means* (Penguin, 1963), by permission of David Higham Associates.

Christine Stead: from *For Love Alone* (1945) by permission of the present publishers, ETT Imprint, Sydney.

Gertrude Stein: from *The Autobiography of Alice B. Toklas* (1933), by permission of David Higham Associates.

John Steinbeck: from *Cannery Row* (William Heinemann), copyright 1945 by John Steinbeck, renewed © 1973 by Elaine Steinbeck, John Steinbeck IV, and Thom Steinbeck, by permission of Viking Penguin, a division of Penguin Books USA, Inc. and of Random House UK Ltd on behalf of the author.

James Stephens: from *The Crock of Gold* (1912) and from 'Mongan's Frenzy' in *Irish Fairy Tales* (1920), by permission of The Society of Authors as the Literary Representative of the Estate of James Stephens.

A. J. P. Taylor: from *The Trouble Makers* (Hamish Hamilton, 1957), by permission of David Higham Associates, and from *English History 1914–1945* (OUP, 1965), by permission of Oxford University Press.

Dylan Thomas: from *A Portrait of the Artist as a Young Dog* (J. M. Dent, 1940), by permission of David Higham Associates.

G. M. Trevelyan: from *Clio, a Muse* (1913), by permission of George Trevelyan.

Hugh Trevor-Roper: from 'The Myth of Charles I' in *Historical Essays* (1957), by permission of the Peters Fraser & Dunlop Group Ltd.

Lionel Trilling: from *The Middle of the Journey* (Secker & Warburg, 1947) and from 'Manners, Morals and the Novel' in *The Liberal Imagination* (Secker & Warburg, 1950), copyright © 1950 and 1975, by permission of Laurence Pollinger Ltd and the Wylie Agency.

Amos Tutuola: from *The Palm-Wine Drunkard* (1952), by permission of the publishers, Faber & Faber Ltd and Grove/Atlantic, Inc.

Anne Tyler: from *Dinner at the Homesick Restaurant* (Chatto & Windus/Alfred Knopf, 1982), copyright © 1982 by Anne Tyler Modarressi, by permission of Random House UK Ltd and of Alfred A. Knopf Inc.

Kenneth Tynan: from *Curtains* (1961), by permission of Roxana Tynan.

John Updike: from *Rabbit, Run* (Viking/Deutsch, 1961), copyright © John Updike 1960, 1964, and renewed 1988 by John Updike; and from 'Popular Music' in *Odd Jobs: Essays and Criticism* (Penguin, 1992), copyright © John Updike 1991, both by permission of Penguin Books Ltd and Alfred A. Knopf, Inc.

Gore Vidal: from *1876* (1976) by permission of Curtis Brown Ltd, London, on behalf of Gore Vidal.

Robert Penn Warren: from *All the King's Men*, copyright 1946 and renewed 1974 by Robert Penn Warren, by permission of Harcourt Brace & Co.

Evelyn Waugh: from *Vile Bodies* (1930), copyright © Evelyn Waugh 1930, and from *The Ordeal of Gilbert Penfold* (1957), copyright © Mrs Laura Waugh 1957, by permission of the Peters Fraser & Dunlop Group Ltd.

H. G. Wells: from *The Time Machine* (1895); from *The First Men on the Moon* (1901); from *Tono Bungay* (1909); from *The History of Mr Polly* (1910); and from *The Work, Wealth and Happiness of Mankind* (1931); all by permission of A. P. Watt Ltd on behalf of the Literary Executors of the Estate of H. G. Wells.

Eudora Welty: from *The Optimist's Daughter*, copyright © 1969, 1972 by Eudora Welty, by permission of the publishers, Virago Press and Random House, Inc.

Nathanael West: from *Miss Lonelyhearts and The Day of the Locust*, copyright © 1939 by the Estate of Nathanael West, by permission of New Directions Publishing Corp.

Rebecca West: from *The Meaning of Treason* (1949), copyright © Rebecca West 1949, 1965, by permission of the Peters Fraser & Dunlop Group Ltd.

Patrick White: from *Voss* (Jonathan Cape), copyright © 1957, renewed 1985 by Patrick White, by permission of Viking Penguin, a division of Penguin Books USA, Inc., and of Random House UK Ltd.

A. N. Wilson: from *A Bottle in the Smoke* (1990), by permission of the author.

Angus Wilson: from *Anglo-Saxon Attitudes* (1956) by permission of Curtis Brown, London, on behalf of the author.

Edmund Wilson: from *The American Earthquake*, copyright © 1958 by Edmund Wilson, copyright renewed © 1986 by Helen Miranda Wilson; and from *Axel's Castle* (Penguin Books, 1993), copyright © 1931 by Charles Scribner's Sons, copyright renewed © 1959 by Edmund Wilson, both by permission of Farrar, Straus, & Giroux, Inc.; extract from *Axel's Castle* also by permission of Penguin Books Ltd.

P. G. Wodehouse: from 'The Voice of the Past' in *Mulliner Nights* (1933), and from *Thank You Jeeves* (1934), by permission of A. P. Watt Ltd on behalf of the Trustees of the Wodehouse Estate, and of Random House UK Ltd.

Tom Wolfe: from *The Bonfire of the Vanities* (Jonathan Cape, 1987), copyright © 1987, 1988 by Tom Wolfe, by permission of Random House UK Ltd on behalf of the author and Farrar, Straus, & Giroux, Inc.

Virginia Woolf: from *The Diary of Virginia Woolf*, 1920, 1921 (The Hogarth Press), by permission of Random House UK Ltd on behalf of the Executors of the Estate of Virginia Woolf.

Richard Wright: from *Black Boy*, copyright 1937, 1942, 1944, 1945 by Richard Wright, copyright renewed 1973 by Ellen Wright, by permission of HarperCollins Publishers, Inc. and Random House UK Ltd, on behalf of the author.

W. B. Yeats: from *The Autobiography of William Butler Yeats*, copyright 1935 by

Macmillan Publishing Co., copyright renewed © 1963 by Bertha Georgie Yeats, by permission of A. P. Watt Ltd on behalf of Michael Yeats, and Scribner, a Division of Simon & Schuster.

G. M. Young: from *Victorian England: Portrait of an Age* (OUP, 1934), by permission of Oxford University Press.

Every effort has been made to trace and contact copyright holders prior to publication. If notified, the publisher undertakes to rectify any errors or omissions at the earliest opportunity.

Index of Authors

The authors listed below are British except where indicated. The names of other authors are followed by their nationality or, where they settled elsewhere, by their country of origin and subsequent residence.